Steven Erikson is an archaeologist and anthropologist and a graduate of the Iowa Writers' Workshop. The first five novels in his *Malazan Book of the Fallen* sequence – *Gardens of the Moon, Deadhouse Gates, Memories of Ice, House of Chains* and *Midnight Tides* – have met with widespread international acclaim and established him as a major voice in the world of fantasy fiction. He lives in Canada.

The Bonehunters

Steven Erikson

BANTAM PRESS

LONDON · TORONTO · SYDNEY · AUCKLAND · JOHANNESBURG

TRANSWORLD PUBLISHERS
61–63 Uxbridge Road, London W5 5SA
a division of The Random House Group Ltd

RANDOM HOUSE AUSTRALIA (PTY) LTD
20 Alfred Street, Milsons Point, Sydney,
New South Wales 2061, Australia

RANDOM HOUSE NEW ZEALAND LTD
18 Poland Road, Glenfield, Auckland 10, New Zealand

RANDOM HOUSE SOUTH AFRICA (PTY) LTD
Isle of Houghton, Corner of Boundary and Carse O'Gowrie Roads,
Houghton 2198, South Africa

Published 2006 by Bantam Press
a division of Transworld Publishers

A catalogue record for this book is available from the British Library.
ISBNs 0593046293 (cased)
(from Jan 07) 9780593046293 (cased)
0593046307 (tpb)
(from Jan 07) 9780593046307 (tpb)

Typeset in 10½/12 Sabon
by Falcon Oast Graphic Art Ltd.

Printed and bound in Great Britain
by Clays Ltd, St Ives plc

5 7 9 10 8 6 4

Papers used by Transworld Publishers are natural, recyclable products
made from wood grown in sustainable forests. The manufacturing
processes conform to the environmental regulations of the country
of origin.

To Courtney Welch. Keep the music coming, friend.

Acknowledgements

Thanks to the usual suspects, including my early-draft readers Chris, Mark, Rick, Courtney, and Bill Hunter who has proved invaluable on the mechanics and full listing of variants of the Deck of Dragons – but listen, Bill, no more walking miles through the rain, right? Cam Esslemont for a most diligent read-through – I'm glad at least one of us has got the timeline right. Clare and Bowen, as always. To the staff at Bar Italia for seeing me through another one – three novellas and four novels and twenty-two thousand lattes, that was quite a run, wasn't it? Steve, Perry and Ross Donaldson, for the friendship. Simon Taylor, Patrick Walsh and Howard Morhaim, for the good work done each and every time.

Contents

SEVEN CITIES

The Malazan Empire

ca. 1160 Burn's Sleep

BANDIKO SEA

KARAKARANG

Galladi

SEA of GALLADA

TALGAI SEA

Kuhl Jella

OTATARAL DESERT

BANDIKO DESERT

SKRA BRAE

OLENBRAE

OTATARAL SEA

ARATH FOREST

Kansu

EHRLITAN

Ahol Tapur

'Dosin Pali

SAHUL SEA

DOJAL HADING SEA

YATHENDRU SEEP

SEA of KALTEPE KADESH

Canhasan

Korokitch

Kalibort

G'danisban

Belbasi

MAADIL SEA

Ghulora

Noh

Fur

Longshan

EHRLITAN SEA

Alrit

Pan'potsun

Gelamisban

PADDHAPUR

PAN'POTSUN ODHAN

 ODHAN

SIALK

Caron Tepasi

Sialk

Asmar

CARON MTNS.

Bilan

Ehrlitan

Teppes

Jandat

Ranga

Taxila

Asoki

A'karonys

 G'ladan

Y'Ghatan

THALAS MTNS.

N'apan Sotka

Inja

E'starb

RARAKU

Lato Revae

KARASHIMESH

Mersin

N'KARA

UGARAT ODHAN

UBARYD ODHAN

Omari

Halaf

Bylan

Geleen

Tarxian

Sarsa

AREN

To Quon Tali

KOKARAL SEA

ARATH

LOTHAL

G'ELBARA ALBEN

Y'Ghatan

Lothal

Sotka

Kayhum

UGARAT ODHAN

NATHAR FOREST

JHENA

G'HAN ODHAN

Nahal

Sarpachiya

Dobre

CLATAR SEA

MORKAN

Sepik

MORN

SEPIK SEA

OLPHARA MOUNTAINS

OLPHARA FOREST

JHAG ODHAN

DRYJHNA OCEAN

PERISH

NEMILL

N

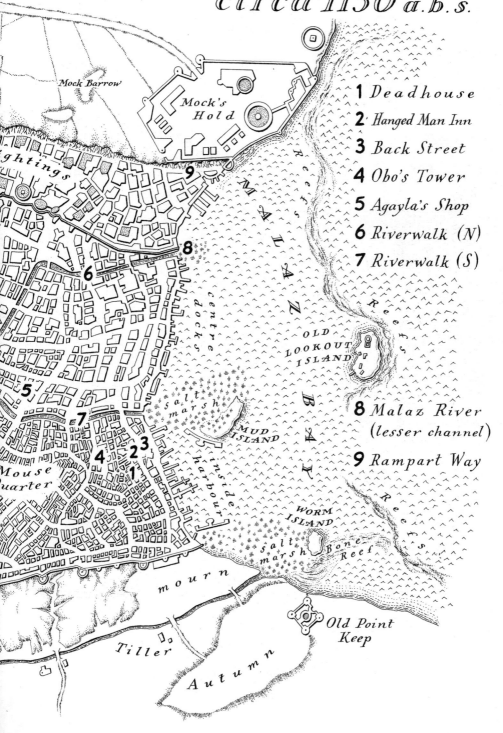

MALAZ CITY
circa 1150 a.b.s.

1 Deadhouse
2 Hanged Man Inn
3 Back Street
4 Obo's Tower
5 Agayla's Shop
6 Riverwalk (N)
7 Riverwalk (S)

8 Malaz River (lesser channel)
9 Rampart Way

Mock Barrow

Mock's Hold

ghtings

MALAZ BAY

Reefs

OLD LOOKOUT ISLAND

Reefs

centre docks

salt marsh

MUD ISLAND

inside harbour

Mouse Quarter

WORM ISLAND

salt marsh

Bone Reef

Reefs

mourn

Old Point Keep

Tiller

Autumn

DRAMATIS PERSONAE

THE MALAZANS

Empress Lazeen, ruler of the Malazan Empire
Adjunct Tavore, commander of the Fourteenth Army
Fist Keneb, division commander
Fist Blistig, division commander
Fist Tene Baralta, division commander
Fist Temul, division commander
Nil, a Wickan warlock
Nether, a Wickan witch
T'amber, Tavore's aide
Lostara Yil, aide to Pearl
Pearl, a Claw
Nok, Admiral of the Imperial Fleet

Banaschar, an ex-priest of D'rek
Hellian, a sergeant in the city guard of Kartool
Urb, a city guard in Kartool
Brethless, a city guard in Kartool
Touchy, a city guard in Kartool

Quick Ben, High Mage in the Fourteenth Army
Kalam Mekhar, an assassin
Grub, a foundling

SELECTED SOLDIERS IN THE FOURTEENTH ARMY

Captain Kindly, Ashok Regiment
Lieutenant Pores, Ashok Regiment
Captain Faradan Sort
Sergeant Fiddler/Strings
Corporal Tarr
Cuttle
Bottle
Koryk
Smiles
Sergeant Gesler
Corporal Stormy
Master Sergeant Braven Tooth
Maybe
Lutes
Ebron
Sinn
Crump
Sergeant Balm
Corporal Deadsmell
Throatslitter
Masan Gilani

OTHERS

Barathol Mekhar, a blacksmith
Kulat, a villager
Nulliss, a villager
Hayrith, a villager
Chaur, a villager

Noto Boil, company cutter (healer) in Onearm's Host
Hurlochel, an outrider in Onearm's Host
Captain Sweetcreek, an officer in Onearm's Host
Corporal Futhgar, an officer in Onearm's Host
Fist Rythe Bude, an officer in Onearm's Host
Ormulogun, artist
Gumble, his critic

Apsalar, an assassin
Telorast, a spirit
Curdle, a spirit

Samar Dev, a witch of Ugarat
Karsa Orlong, a Teblor warrior
Ganath, a Jaghut
Spite, a Soletaken and sister to Lady Envy

Corabb Bhilan Thenu'alas
Leoman of the Flails, last leader of the rebellion
Captain Dunsparrow, Y'Ghatan city guard

Karpolan Demesand, Trygalle Trade Guild
Torahaval Delat, a priestess of Poliel

Cutter, once Crokus of Daurjhistan
Heboric Ghost Hands, Destraint of Treach
Scillara, refugee from Raraku
Felisin the Younger, refugee from Raraku
Greyfrog, a demon

Mappo Runt, a Trell
Icarium, a Jhag
Iskaral Pust, a priest of Shadow
Mogora, a D'ivers

Taralack Veed, a Gral and agent of the Nameless Ones
Dejim Nebrahl, a D'ivers T'rolbarahl of the First Empire

Trull Sengar, a Tiste Edur
Onrack the Broken, an unbound T'lan Imass

Ibra Gholan, a T'lan Imass
Monok Ochem, a T'lan Imass Bonecaster
Minala, commander of the Company of Shadow

Tomad Sengar, a Tiste Edur
Feather Witch, a Letherii slave

Atri-Preda Yan Tovis (Twilight), commander of Letherii forces
Captain Varat Taun, officer under Twilight's Command
Taxilian, an interpreter
Ahlrada Ahn, a Tiste Andii spy among the Tiste Edur
Sathbaro Rangar, Arapay warlock

For all that is made real
In this age descending
Where heroes leave naught
But the iron ring of their names
From bardic throats
I stand in this silent heart
Yearning the fading beat
Of lives fallen to dust
And the sifting whisper
Proclaims glory's passing
As the songs fail
In dwindling echoes
For all that is made real
The chambers and halls
Yawn empty to my cries –
For someone must
Give answer
Give answer
To all of this
Someone

The Age Descending
Torbora Fethena

PROLOGUE

1164 Burn's Sleep
Istral'fennidahn, the season of D'rek, Worm of Autumn
Twenty-four days since the Execution of Sha'ik in Raraku

THE WEBS BETWEEN THE TOWERS WERE VISIBLE IN GLISTENING SHEETS far overhead, and the faint wind coming in from the sea shivered the vast threads so that a mist of rain descended on Kartool City, as it did every morning in the Clear Season.

Most things a person could get used to, eventually, and since the yellow-banded paralt spiders had been the first to occupy the once infamous towers following the Malazan conquest of the island, and that was decades past now, there had been plenty of time to become inured to such details. Even the sight of gulls and pigeons suspended motionless between the score of towers every morning, before the fist-sized spiders emerged from their upper-floor dens to retrieve their prey, yielded little more than faint revulsion among the citizens of Kartool City.

Sergeant Hellian of the Septarch District city guard, alas, was an exception to this. There were gods, she suspected, convulsed in perpetual hilarity at her wretched fate, for which they were no doubt responsible. Born in the city, cursed with a fear of all manner of spiders, she had lived the entirety of her nineteen years in unrelieved terror.

Why not just leave? A question asked by comrades and acquaintances more times than she cared to count. But it wasn't that simple. It was impossible, in fact. The murky waters of the harbour were fouled with moult-skins and web-fragments and sodden, feather-tufted carcasses bobbing here and there. Inland, things got even worse. The young paralt, upon escaping their elders in the city, struggled to maturity among the limestone cliffs ringing Kartool. And though young, they were no less aggressive or virulent. While traders and

1

farmers told her that one could walk the trails and roads all day without encountering a single one, Hellian didn't care. She knew the gods were waiting. Just like the spiders.

When sober, the sergeant noticed things, in a proper and diligent manner suited to a city guard. And while she was not consistently drunk, cold sobriety was an invitation to hysteria, so Hellian endeavoured to proceed steadily on the wobbly rope of not-quite-drunk. Accordingly, she had not known of the odd ship now moored in the Free Docks, that had arrived before sunrise, its pennons indicating that it had come from Malaz Island.

Ships hailing from Malaz Island were not of themselves unusual or noteworthy; however, autumn had arrived, and the prevailing winds of the Clear Season made virtually all lanes to the south impossible to navigate for at least the next two months.

Were things less bleary, she might also have noticed – had she taken the time to head down to the docks, which perhaps could have been managed at sword-point – that the ship was not the usual barque or trader, nor a military dromon, but a sleek, gracile thing, styled in a manner not employed in the past fifty years by any shipbuilders of the empire. Arcane carvings adorned the blade-like prow, minuscule shapes detailing serpents and worms, the panels sweeping back along the gunnels almost halfway down the length of the ship. The stern was squared and strangely high, with a side-mounted steering oar. The crew numbered about a dozen, quiet for sailors, and disinclined to leave the ship as it lolled alongside the dock. A lone figure had disembarked as soon as the gangplank had settled, shortly before dawn.

For Hellian, these details came later. The runner that found her was a local brat who, when he wasn't breaking laws, loitered around the docks in the hopes of being hired as a guide for visitors. The fragment of parchment he handed her was, she could feel, of some quality. On it was written a terse message, the contents of which made her scowl.

'All right, lad, describe the man gave this to you.'

'I can't.'

Hellian glanced back at the four guards standing behind her on the street corner. One of them stepped behind the boy and picked him up, one-handed, gripping the back of the ratty tunic. A quick shake.

'Loosed your memory some?' Hellian asked. 'I hope so, because I ain't paying coin.'

'I can't remember! I looked right into his face, Sergeant! Only . . . I can't remember what it looked like!'

She studied the boy for a moment, then grunted and turned away.

The guard set the lad down but did not release his grip.

'Let him go, Urb.'

The lad scampered away.

With a vague gesture for her guards to follow, she set off.

The Septarch District was the city's most peaceful area, not through any particular diligence on Hellian's part, however. There were few commercial buildings, and those residences that existed served to house acolytes and support staff of the dozen temples commanding the district's main avenue. Thieves who wanted to stay alive did not steal from temples.

She led her squad onto the avenue, noting once again how decrepit many of the temples had become. The paralt spiders liked the ornate architecture and the domes and lesser towers, and it seemed the priests were losing the battle. Chitinous rubbish crackled and crunched underfoot as they walked.

Years ago, the first night of Istral'fennidahn, just past, would have been marked with an island-wide fete, filled with sacrifices and propitiations to Kartool's patron goddess, D'rek, the Worm of Autumn, and the archpriest of the Grand Temple, the Demidrek, would lead a procession through the city on a carpet of fecund rubbish, his bared feet sweeping through maggot- and worm-ridden refuse. Children would chase lame dogs down the alleys, and those they cornered they would stone to death whilst shrieking their goddess's name. Convicted criminals sentenced to execution would have their skins publicly flailed, their long-bones broken, then the hapless victims would be flung into pits aswarm with carrion beetles and red fireworms, that would devour them over the course of four or five days.

All of this was before the Malazan conquest, of course. The Emperor's principal target had been the cult of D'rek. He'd well understood that the heart of Kartool's power was the Grand Temple, and the island's master sorcerors were the priests and priestesses of D'rek, ruled over by the Demidrek. Further, it was no accident that the night of slaughter that preceded the naval battle and the subsequent invasion, a night led by the infamous Dancer and Surly, Mistress of the Claw, had so thoroughly obliterated the cult's sorcerors, including the Demidrek. For the archpriest of the Grand Temple had only recently gained his eminence via an internal coup, and the ousted rival had been none other than Tayschrenn, the Emperor's new – at the time – High Mage.

Hellian had but heard tales of the celebrations, since they had been outlawed as soon as the Malazan occupiers settled the imperial mantle upon the island, but she had been told often enough about those glorious days of long ago, when Kartool Island had been at the pinnacle of civilization.

The present sordid condition was the fault of the Malazans, everyone agreed. Autumn had in truth arrived upon the island and its morose inhabitants. More than the cult of D'rek had been crushed, after all. Slavery was abolished, the execution pits had been scoured clean and permanently sealed. There was even a building hosting a score misguided altruists who adopted lame dogs.

They passed the modest temple of the Queen of Dreams and, squatting on the opposite side, the much-hated Temple of Shadows. There had once been but seven religions permitted upon Kartool, six subservient to D'rek – hence the district's name. Soliel, Poliel, Beru, Burn, Hood and Fener. Since the conquest, more had arrived – the two aforementioned, along with Dessembrae, Togg and Oponn. And the Grand Temple of D'rek, still the largest of all the structures in the city, was in a pathetic state of disrepair.

The figure standing before the broad-stepped entrance wore the garb of a Malazan sailor, faded waterproofed leathers, a worn shirt of thin, ragged linen. His dark hair was in a queue, hanging down between his shoulders and otherwise unadorned. As he turned at their approach, the sergeant saw a middle-aged face with even, benign features, although there was something odd about the man's eyes, something vaguely fevered.

Hellian drew a deep breath to help clear her sodden thoughts, then raised the parchment between them. 'This is yours, I presume?'

The man nodded. 'You are the guard commander in this district?'

She smiled. 'Sergeant Hellian. The captain died last year of a septic foot. We're still waiting for a replacement.'

Brows rose with irony. 'Not a promotion, Sergeant? One presumes, therefore, that sobriety would be a decisive virtue for a captain.'

'Your note said there's trouble at the Grand Temple,' Hellian said, ignoring the man's rudeness and turning to study the massive edifice. The double doors, she noted with a frown, were closed. On this day of all days, this was unprecedented.

'I think so, Sergeant,' the man said.

'Had you come to pay your respects to D'rek?' Hellian asked him, as faint unease struggled through the alcoholic haze. 'Are the doors locked? What's your name and where are you from?'

'I am named Banaschar, from Malaz Island. We arrived this morning.'

A grunt from one of the guards behind her, and Hellian thought about it. Then she shot Banaschar a more careful look. 'By ship? At this time of year?'

'We made what haste we could. Sergeant, I believe we need to break into the Grand Temple.'

'Why not just knock?'

'I have tried,' Banaschar replied. 'No-one comes.'

Hellian hesitated. *Break into the Grand Temple? The Fist will have my tits on a fry pan for this.*

'There are dead spiders on the steps,' Urb said suddenly.

They turned.

'Hood's blessing,' Hellian muttered, 'lots of them.' Curious now, she walked closer. Banaschar followed, and after a moment the squad fell in.

'They look . . .' She shook her head.

'Decayed,' Banaschar said. 'Rotting. Sergeant, the doors, please.'

Still she hesitated. A thought occurred to her and she glared at the man. 'You said you made all haste to get here. Why? Are you an acolyte of D'rek? – You don't look it. What brought you here, Banaschar?'

'A presentiment, Sergeant. I was . . . many years past . . . a priest of D'rek, in the Jakatakan temple on Malaz Island.'

'A presentiment brought you all the way to Kartool? Do you take me for a fool?'

Anger flashed in the man's eyes. 'Clearly you're too drunk to smell what I can smell.' He eyed the guards. 'Do you share your sergeant's failings, or am I alone in this matter?'

Urb was frowning, then he said, 'Sergeant, we should kick in these doors, I think.'

'So do it then, damn you!'

She watched as her guards battered away at the door. The noise attracted a crowd, and Hellian saw, threading to the forefront, a tall, robed woman who was clearly a priestess from one of the other temples. *Oh, now what?*

But the woman's eyes were fixed on Banaschar, who had in turn noted her approach and stared steadily back, his expression setting hard.

'What are *you* doing here?' the woman demanded.

'Have you sensed nothing, High Priestess? Complacency is a disease fast spreading, it seems.'

The woman's gaze shifted to the guards kicking at the doors. 'What has happened?'

The door on the right splintered, then was knocked back by a final kick.

Hellian gestured for Urb to enter then followed, Banaschar behind her.

The stench was overwhelming, and in the gloom was visible great splashes of blood on the walls, fragments of meat scattered on the polished tiles, and pools of bile, blood and faeces, as well as scraps of clothing and clumps of hair.

Urb had taken no more than two steps and now stood, staring down

5

at what he was standing in. Hellian edged past him, her hand of its own accord reaching for the flask tucked in her belt. Banaschar's hand stayed her. 'Not in here,' he said.

She roughly shook him off. 'Go to Hood,' she growled, pulling the flask loose and tugging free the stopper. She drank three quick mouthfuls. 'Corporal, go find Commander Charl. We'll need a detachment to secure the area. Have word sent to the Fist, I want some mages down here.'

'Sergeant,' said Banaschar, 'this is a matter for priests.'

'Don't be an idiot.' She waved at her remaining guards. 'Conduct a search. See if there's any survivors—'

'There are none,' Banaschar pronounced. 'The High Priestess of the Queen of Dreams has already left, Sergeant. Accordingly, all of the temples will be informed. Investigations will begin.'

'What sort of investigations?' Hellian demanded.

He grimaced. 'Priestly sorts.'

'And what of you?'

'I have seen enough,' he said.

'Don't even think of going anywhere, Banaschar,' she said, scanning the scene of slaughter. 'First night of the Clear Season in the Grand Temple, that used to involve an orgy. Looks like it got out of hand.' Two more quick swallows from the flask, and blessed numbness beckoned. 'You've a lot of questions you need to answer—'

Urb's voice cut in, 'He's gone, Sergeant.'

Hellian swung about. 'Damn! Weren't you keeping an eye on the bastard, Urb?'

The big man spread his hands. 'You was talking away to 'im, Sergeant. I was eyeing the crowd out front. He didn't get past me, that's for sure.'

'Get a description out. I want him found.'

Urb frowned. 'Uh, I can't remember what he looked like.'

'Damn you, neither can I.' Hellian walked over to where Banaschar had been standing. Squinted down at his footprints in the blood. They didn't lead anywhere.

Sorcery. She hated sorcery. 'You know what I'm hearing right now, Urb?'

'No.'

'I'm hearing the Fist. Whistling. You know why he's whistling?'

'No. Listen, Sergeant—'

'It's the fry pan, Urb. It's that nice, sweet sizzle that makes him so happy.'

'Sergeant—'

'Where will he send us, do you think? Korel? That one's a real mess.

6

Maybe Genabackis, though that's quieted down some. Seven Cities, maybe.' She drained the last of the pear brandy in the flask. 'One thing's for sure, we'd better set stones to our swords, Urb.'

The tramp of heavy boots sounded in the street beyond. A half dozen squads at the very least.

'Don't get many spiders on ships, right, Urb?' She glanced over, fought the bleariness and studied the miserable expression on his face. 'That's right, isn't it? Tell me I'm right, damn you.'

A hundred or so years ago, lightning had struck the huge guldindha tree, the white fire driving like a spear down its heartwood and splitting wide the ancient trunk. The blackened scorch-marks had long since bleached away as the desert sun burned its unceasing light upon the worm-riven wood. Swaths of bark had peeled back and now lay heaped over the bared roots that were wrapped about the hill's summit like a vast net.

The mound, misshapen where once it had been circular, commanded the entire basin. It stood alone, an island profoundly deliberate in the midst of a haphazard, random landscape. Beneath the jumbled boulders, sandy earth and snaking dead roots, the capstone that had once protected a slab-walled burial chamber had cracked, collapsing to swallow the space beneath, and in so doing settling an immense weight upon the body interred within.

The tremor of footfalls reaching down to that body were a rare enough occurrence – perhaps a handful of times over the past countless millennia – that the long-slumbering soul was stirred into wakefulness, then intense awareness, upon the sensation of not one set of feet, but a dozen, ascending the steep, rough slopes and assembling at last around the shattered tree.

The skein of wards embracing the creature was twisted and tangled, yet persistent in its multi-layered power. The one who had imprisoned it had been thorough, fashioning rituals of determined permanence, blood-traced and chaos-fed. They were intended to last for ever.

Such intentions were a conceit, asserted in the flawed belief that mortals would one day be without malice, or desperation. That the future was a safer place than the brutal present, and that all that was once past would never again be revisited. The twelve lean figures, bodies swathed in ragged, stained linen, their heads hooded and faces hidden behind grey veils, well understood the risks entailed when driven to precipitous acts. Alas, they also understood desperation.

All were destined to speak at this gathering, the order specified by the corresponding position of various stars, planets and constellations, all unseen behind blue sky yet the locations known nonetheless. Upon taking their positions, a long moment of stillness passed, then the first of the Nameless Ones spoke.

'We stand once more before necessity. These are the patterns long ago foreseen, revealing all our struggles to have been for naught. In the name of the Warren of Mockra, I invoke the ritual of release.'

At these words, the creature within the barrow felt a sudden snap, and the awakened awareness all at once found its own identity. Its name was Dejim Nebrahl. Born on the eve of the death of the First Empire, when the streets of the city beyond burned and screams announced unrelieved slaughter. For the T'lan Imass had come.

Dejim Nebrahl, born into fullest knowledge, a child with seven souls, climbing blood-smeared and trembling from his mother's cooling body. A child. An abomination.

T'rolbarahl, demonic creations by the hand of Dessimbelackis himself, long before the Dark Hounds took shape in the Emperor's mind. T'rolbarahl, misshapen errors in judgement, had been expunged, exterminated at the Emperor's own command. Blood-drinkers, eaters of human flesh, yet possessing depths of cunning even Dessimbelackis could not have imagined. And so, seven T'rolbarahl had managed to elude their hunters for a time, sufficient to impart something of their souls to a mortal woman, widowed by the Trell Wars and without family, a woman whom none would notice, whose mind could be broken, whose body could be made into a feeding vessel, a M'ena Mahybe, for the seven-faced D'ivers T'rolbarahl child swiftly growing within her.

Born into a night of terror. The T'lan Imass, had they found Dejim, would have acted without hesitation: dragging forth those seven demonic souls, binding them into an eternity of pain, their power bled out, slowly and incrementally, to feed the T'lan bonecasters in their unceasing wars against the Jaghut.

But Dejim Nebrahl had escaped. His power growing as he fed, night after night through the ruins of the First Empire. Always hidden, even from those few Soletaken and D'ivers that had survived the Great Slaughter, for even they would not abide Dejim's existence. He fed on some of them as well, for he was smarter than they, and quicker, and had not the Deragoth stumbled onto his trail . . .

The Dark Hounds had a master in those days, a clever master, who excelled in ensnaring sorceries and, once decided upon a task, he would not relent.

A single mistake, and Dejim's freedom was ended. Binding upon binding, taking away his self-awareness, and with it all sense of having once been . . . otherwise.

Yet now . . . *awake once more.*

The second Nameless One, a woman, spoke: 'There stands a plain west and south of Raraku, vast and level for leagues in all directions. When the sands blow away, the shards of a million broken pots are exposed, and to cross the plain barefooted is to leave a trail of blood. In this scene are found unmitigated truths. On the trail out of savagery ... some vessels must needs break. And for the sojourner, a toll in blood must be paid. By the power of the Warren of Telas, I invoke the ritual of release.'

Within the barrow, Dejim Nebrahl became aware of his body. Battered flesh, straining bone, sharp gravel, sifting sands, the immense weight lying upon him. *Agony.*

'As we fashioned this dilemma,' the third priest said, 'so we must initiate its resolution. Chaos pursues this world, and every world beyond this one. In the seas of reality can be found a multitude of layers, one existence flowing upon another. Chaos threatens with storms and tides and wayward currents, sending all into dread tumult. We have chosen one current, a terrible, unchained force – chosen to guide it, to shape its course unseen and unchallenged. We intend to drive one force upon another, and so effect mutual annihilation. We assume a terrible responsibility in this, yet the only hope of success lies with us, with what we do here on this day. In the name of the Warren of Denul, I invoke the ritual of release.'

Pain faded from Dejim's body. Still trapped and unable to move, the D'ivers T'rolbarahl felt his flesh heal.

The fourth Nameless One said, 'We must acknowledge grief for the impending demise of an honourable servant. It must, alas, be a short-lived grief, and so unequal to the measure of the unfortunate victim. This, of course, is not the only grief demanded of us. Of the other, I trust we have all made our peace, else we would not be here. In the name of the Warren of D'riss, I invoke the ritual of release.'

Dejim Nebrahl's seven souls became distinct from one another. D'ivers, yet far more so, not seven who are one – although that could be said to be true – but seven separate in identity, independent yet together.

'We do not yet understand every facet of this trail,' the fifth, a priestess, said, 'and to this our absent kin must not relent in their pursuit. Shadowthrone cannot – must not – be underestimated. He possesses too much knowledge. Of the Azath. Perhaps, too, of us. He is not yet our enemy, but that alone does not make him our ally. He ... perturbs. And I would we negate his existence at the earliest opportunity, although I recognize that my view is in the minority within our cult. Yet, who else is more aware than I, of the Realm of Shadow and its new master? In the name of the Warren of Meanas, I invoke the ritual of release.'

9

And so Dejim came to comprehend the power of his shadows, seven spawned deceivers, his ambushers in the necessary hunt that sustained him, that gave him so much pleasure, far beyond that of a filled belly and fresh, warm blood in his veins. The hunt delivered . . . domination, and domination was exquisite.

The sixth Nameless One spoke, her accent strange, otherworldly: 'All that unfolds in the mortal realm gives shape to the ground upon which the gods walk. Thus, they are never certain of their stride. It falls to us to prepare the footfalls, to dig the deep, deadly pits, the traps and snares that shall be shaped by the Nameless Ones, for we are the hands of the Azath, we are the shapers of the will of the Azath. It is our task to hold all in place, to heal what is torn asunder, to lead our enemies into annihilation or eternal imprisonment. We shall not fail. I call upon the power of the Shattered Warren, Kurald Emurlahn, and invoke the ritual of release.'

There were favoured paths through the world, fragment paths, and Dejim had used them well. He would do so again. Soon.

'Barghast, Trell, Tartheno Toblakai,' said the seventh priest, his voice a rumble, 'these are the surviving threads of Imass blood, no matter their claims to purity. Such claims are inventions, yet inventions have purpose. They assert distinction, they redirect the path walked before, and the path to come. They shape the emblems upon the standards in every war, and so give justification to slaughter. Their purpose, therefore, is to assert convenient lies. By the Warren of Tellann, I invoke the ritual of release.'

Fire in the heart, a sudden drumming of life. Cold flesh grew warm.

'Frozen worlds hide in darkness,' came the rasping words of the eighth Nameless One, 'and so hold the secret of death. The secret is singular. Death arrives as knowledge. Recognition, comprehension, acceptance. It is this and nothing more and nothing less. There shall come a time, perhaps not too far off, when death discovers its own visage, in a multitude of facets, and something new will be born. In the name of Hood's Warren, I invoke the ritual of release.'

Death. It had been stolen from him by the master of the Dark Hounds. It was, perhaps, something to be longed for. But not yet.

The ninth priest began with a soft, lilting laugh, then said, 'Where all began, so it will return in the end. In the name of the Warren of Kurald Galain, of True Darkness, I invoke the ritual of release.'

'And by the power of Rashan,' the tenth Nameless One hissed with impatience, 'I invoke the ritual of release!'

The ninth priest laughed again.

'The stars are wheeling,' the eleventh Nameless One said, 'and so the tension burgeons. There is justice in all that we do. In the name of the Warren of Thyrllan, I invoke the ritual of release.'

They waited. For the twelfth Nameless One to speak. Yet she said nothing, instead reaching out a slim, rust-red, scaled hand that was anything but human.

And Dejim Nebrahl sensed a presence. An intelligence, cold and brutal, seeping down from above, and the D'ivers was suddenly afraid.

'Can you hear me, T'rolbarahl?'

Yes.

'We would free you, but you must pay us for that release. Refuse to pay us, and we shall send you once more into mindless oblivion.'

Fear became terror. *What is this payment you demand of me?*

'Do you accept?'

I do.

She explained to him, then, what was required. It seemed a simple thing. A minor task, easily achieved. Dejim Nebrahl was relieved. It would not take long, the victims were close by, after all, and once it was done the D'ivers would be freed of all obligation, and could do as he pleased.

The twelfth and last Nameless One, who had once been known as Sister Spite, lowered her hand. She knew that, of the twelve gathered here, she alone would survive the emergence of this fell demon. For Dejim Nebrahl would be hungry. Unfortunate, and unfortunate too the shock and dismay of her comrades upon witnessing her escape – in the brief moment before the T'rolbarahl attacked. She had her reasons, of course. First and foremost being the simple desire to stay among the living, for a while longer, anyway. As for the other reasons, they belonged to her and her alone.

She said, 'In the name of the Warren of Starvald Demelain, I invoke the ritual of release.' And from her words descended, through dead tree root, through stone and sand, dissolving ward after ward, a force of entropy, known to the world as otataral.

And Dejim Nebrahl rose into the world of the living.

Eleven Nameless Ones began invoking their final prayers. Most of them never finished.

Some distance away, seated cross-legged before a small fire, a tattooed warrior cocked his head at the sound of distant screams. He looked southward and saw a dragon rising heavily from the hills lining the horizon, mottled scales glimmering in the sun's dying light. Watching it climb ever higher, the warrior scowled.

'Bitch,' he muttered. 'I should've guessed.'

He settled back down, even as the screams faded in the distance. The lengthening shadows among the rock outcrop surrounding his camp were suddenly unpleasant, thick and smeared.

Taralack Veed, a Gral warrior and the last survivor of the Eroth bloodline, gathered a mouthful of phlegm and spat it onto the palm of his left hand. He brought both hands together to spread the mucus evenly, which he then used to flatten down his swept-back black hair in an elaborate gesture that startled the mass of flies crawling through it, momentarily, before they settled once again.

After a time, he sensed that the creature had finished feeding, and was on the move. Taralack straightened. He pissed on the fire to douse it, then collected his weapons and set off to find the demon's trail.

There were eighteen residents living in the scatter of hovels at the cross-roads. The track running parallel to the coast was Tapur Road, and three days' trek north was the city of Ahol Tapur. The other road, little more than a rutted trail, crossed the Path'Apur Mountains far inland, then stretched eastward, past this hamlet, for another two days of travel, where it finally reached the coast road alongside the Otataral Sea.

Four centuries ago a village had thrived in this place. The ridge to the south had been clothed in hardwood trees with a distinctive, feathery foliage, trees now extinct on the subcontinent of Seven Cities. Appropriately, the wood from these trees had been used to carve sarcophagi, and the village had become renowned in cities as far away as Hissar to the south, Karashimesh to the west, and Ehrlitan to the northwest. The industry died with the last tree. Low-growth vanished into the gullets of goats, the topsoil blew away and the village shrank within a single generation to its present decrepit state.

The eighteen residents who remained now provided services growing ever less in demand, supplying water to passing caravans, repairing tack and such. A Malazan official had been through once, two years back, muttering something about a new raised road, and a garrisoned out-post, but this had been motivated by the illegal trade in raw otataral, which, through other imperial efforts, had since dried up.

The recent rebellion had barely brushed the collective awareness of the residents, apart from the occasional rumour arriving with a messenger or outlaw riding through, but even they no longer came to the hamlet. In any case, rebellions were for other people.

Thus it was that the appearance of five figures, standing on the nearest rise of the inland track, shortly after midday, was quickly noticed, and word soon reached the nominal head of the community, the blacksmith, whose name was Barathol Mekhar, and who was the only resident who had not been born there. Of his past in the world beyond, little was known except what was self-evident – his deep, almost onyx black skin marked him as from a tribe of the southwestern

12

corner of the subcontinent, hundreds, perhaps thousands of leagues distant. And the curled scarification on his cheeks looked martial, as did the skein of blade-cuts puckering his hands and forearms. He was known as a man of few words and virtually no opinions – at least none he cared to share – and so was well-suited as the hamlet's unofficial leader.

Trailed by a half-dozen adults who still professed to curiosity, Barathol Mekhar walked up the only street until he came to the hamlet's edge. The buildings to either side were ruined, long abandoned, their roofs caved in and walls crumbling and sand-heaped. Sixty or so paces away stood the five figures, motionless, barring the ripple of the ragged strips of their fur cloaks. Two held spears, the other three carrying long two-handed swords slung across their backs. Some of them appeared to be missing limbs.

Barathol's eyes were not as sharp as they once had been. Even so . . . 'Jhelim, Filiad, go to the smithy. Walk, don't run. There's a trunk behind the hide bolts. It's got a lock – break it. Take out the axe and shield, and the gauntlets, and the helm – never mind the chain – there's no time for that. Now, go.'

In the eleven years that Barathol had lived among them, he had never spoken so many words in a row to anyone. Jhelim and Filiad both stared in shock at the blacksmith's broad back, then, sudden fear filling their guts, they turned about and walked, stiffly, with awkward, over-long strides, back down the street.

'Bandits,' whispered Kulat, the herder who'd butchered his last goat in exchange for a bottle of liquor from a caravan passing through seven years ago, and had done nothing since. 'Maybe they just want water – we ain't got nothing else.' The small round pebbles he kept in his mouth clicked as he spoke.

'They don't want water,' Barathol said. 'The rest of you, go find weapons – anything – no, never mind that. Just go to your homes. Stay there.'

'What are they waiting for?' Kulat asked, as the others scattered.

'I don't know,' the blacksmith admitted.

'Well, they look to be from a tribe I ain't never seen before.' He sucked on the stones for a moment, then said, 'Those furs – ain't it kind of hot for furs? And those bone helmets—'

'They're bone? Your eyes are better than mine, Kulat.'

'Only things still working, Barathol. Squat bunch, eh? You recognize the tribe, maybe?'

The blacksmith nodded. From the village behind them, he could now hear Jhelim and Filiad, their breaths loud as they hurried forward. 'I think so,' Barathol said in answer to Kulat's question.

'They going to be trouble?'

Jhelim stepped into his view, struggling beneath the weight of the double-bladed axe, the haft encased in strips of iron, a looping chain at the weighted pommel, the Aren steel of the honed edges gleaming silver. A three-pronged punch-spike jutted from the top of the weapon, edged like a crossbow quarrel-head. The young man was staring down at it as if it were the old Emperor's sceptre.

Beside Jhelim was Filiad, carrying the iron-scaled gauntlets, a round-shield and the camailed, grille-faced helm.

Barathol collected the gauntlets and tugged them on. The rippling scales reached up his forearms to a hinged elbow-cup, and the gauntlets were strapped in place just above the joint. The underside of the sleeves held a single bar, the iron black and notched, reaching from wrist to cup. He then took the helm, and scowled. 'You forgot the quilted under-padding.' He handed it back. 'Give me the shield – strap it on my arm, damn you, Filiad. Tighter. Good.'

The blacksmith then reached out for the axe. Jhelim needed both arms and all his strength to raise the weapon high enough for Barathol's right hand to slip through the chain loop, twisting twice before closing about the haft, and lifting it seemingly effortlessly from Jhelim's grasp. To the two men, he said, 'Get out of here.'

Kulat remained. 'They're coming forward now, Barathol.'

The blacksmith had not pulled his gaze from the figures. 'I'm not that blind, old man.'

'You must be, to stay standing here. You say you know the tribe – have they come for you, maybe? Some old vendetta?'

'It's possible,' Barathol conceded. 'If so, then the rest of you should be all right. Once they're done with me, they'll leave.'

'What makes you so sure?'

'I'm not.' Barathol lifted the axe into readiness. 'With T'lan Imass, there's no way to tell.'

BOOK ONE

THE THOUSAND-FINGERED GOD

I walked the winding path down into the valley,
Where low stone walls divided the farms and holds
And each measured plot had its place in the scheme
That all who lived there well understood,
To guide their travels and hails in the day
And lend a familiar hand in the darkest night
Back to home's door and the dancing dogs.
I walked until called up short by an old man
Who straightened from work in challenge,
And smiling to fend his calculation and judgement,
I asked him to tell me all he knew
Of the lands to the west, beyond the vale,
And he was relieved to answer that there were cities,
Vast and teeming with all sorts of strangeness,
And a king and feuding priesthoods and once,
He told me, he saw a cloud of dust flung up
By the passing of an army, off to battle
Somewhere, he was certain, in the chilly south,
And so I gleaned all that he knew, and it was not much,
Beyond the vale he had never been, from birth
Until now, he had never known and had,
Truth to tell, never been for thus it is
That the scheme transpires for the low kind
In all places in all times and curiosity lies unhoned
And pitted, although he gave breath enough to ask
Who I was and how had I come here and where
My destination, leaving me to answer with fading smile,
That I was bound for the teeming cities yet must needs
Pass first through here and had he yet noticed
That his dogs were lying still on the ground,
For I had leave to answer, you see, that I am come,
Mistress of Plague and this, alas, was proof
Of a far grander scheme.

Poliel's Leave
Fisher kel Tath

CHAPTER ONE

The streets are crowded with lies these days.

High Mage Tayschrenn, Empress Laseen's Coronation
Recorded by Imperial Historian Duiker

1164 Burn's Sleep
Fifty-eight days after the Execution of Sha'ik

WAYWARD WINDS HAD STIRRED THE DUST INTO THE AIR EARLIER that day, and all who came into Ehrlitan's eastern inland gate were coated, clothes and skin, with the colour of the red sandstone hills. Merchants, pilgrims, drovers and travellers appeared before the guards as if conjured, one after another, from the swirling haze, heads bent as they trudged into the gate's lee, eyes slitted behind folds of stained linen. Rust-sheathed goats stumbled after the drovers, horses and oxen arrived with drooped heads and rings of gritty crust around their nostrils and eyes, wagons hissed as sand sifted down between weathered boards in the beds. The guards watched on, thinking only of the end of their watch, and the baths, meals and warm bodies that would follow as proper reward for duties upheld.

The woman who came in on foot was noted, but for all the wrong reasons. Sheathed in tight silks, head wrapped and face hidden beneath a scarf, she was nonetheless worth a second glance, if only for the grace of her stride and the sway of her hips. The guards, being men and slavish to their imaginations, provided the rest.

She noted their momentary attention and understood it well enough to be unconcerned. More problematic had one or both of the guards been female. They might well have wondered that she was entering the city by this particular gate, having come down, on foot, this particular road, which wound league upon league through parched, virtually

17

lifeless hills, then ran parallel to a mostly uninhabited scrub forest for yet more leagues. An arrival, then, made still more unusual since she was carrying no supplies, and the supple leather of her moccasins was barely worn. Had the guards been female, they would have accosted her, and she would have faced some hard questions, none of which she was prepared to answer truthfully.

Fortunate for the guards, then, that they had been male. Fortunate, too, the delicious lure of a man's imagination as those gazes followed her into the street, empty of suspicion yet feverishly disrobing her curved form with every swing of her hips, a motion she only marginally exaggerated.

Coming to an intersection she turned left and moments later was past their lines of sight. The wind was blunted here in the city, although fine dust continued to drift down to coat all in a monochrome powder. The woman continued through the crowds, her route a gradual, inward spiral towards the Jen'rahb, Ehrlitan's central tel, the vast multi-layered ruin inhabited by little more than vermin, of both the four-legged and two-legged kind. Arriving at last within sight of the collapsed buildings, she found a nearby inn, modest in presentation and without ambition to be other than a local establishment housing a few whores in the second-floor rooms and a dozen or so regulars in the ground-floor tavern.

Beside the tavern's entrance was an arched passage leading into a small garden. The woman stepped into that passage to brush the dust from her clothing, then walked on to the shallow basin of silty water beneath a desultorily trickling fountain, where she unwound the scarf and splashed her face, sufficient to take the sting from her eyes.

Returning through the passage, the woman then entered the tavern.

Gloomy, the smoke from fires, oil lanterns, durhang, itralbe and rustleaf drifting beneath the low plaster ceiling, three-quarters full and all of the tables occupied. A youth had preceded her by a few moments, and was now breathlessly expounding on some adventure barely survived. Noting this as she walked past the young man and his listeners, the woman allowed herself a faint smile that was, perhaps, sadder than she had intended.

She found a place at the bar and beckoned the tender over. He stopped opposite and studied her intently while she ordered, in un-accented Ehrlii, a bottle of rice wine.

At her request he reached under the counter and she heard the clink of bottles as he said, in Malazan, 'Hope you're not expecting anything worth the name, lass.' He straightened, brushing dust from a clay bottle then peering at the stopper. 'This one's at least still sealed.'

'That will do,' she said, still speaking the local dialect, laying out on the bar-top three silver crescents.

'Plan on drinking all of it?'

'I'd need a room upstairs to crawl into,' she replied, tugging the stopper free as the barman set down a tin goblet. 'One with a lock,' she added.

'Then Oponn's smiling on you,' he said. 'One's just become available.'

'Good.'

'You attached to Dujek's army?' the man asked.

She poured out a full draught of the amber, somewhat cloudy wine. 'No. Why, is it here?'

'Tail ends,' he replied. 'The main body marched out six days ago. Left a garrison, of course. That's why I was wondering—'

'I belong to no army.'

Her tone, strangely cold and flat, silenced him. Moments later, he drifted away to attend to another customer.

She drank. Steadily working through the bottle as the light faded outside, and the tavern grew yet more crowded, voices getting louder, elbows and shoulders jostling against her more often than was entirely necessary. She ignored the casual groping, eyes on the liquid in the goblet before her.

At last she was done, and so she turned about and threaded her way, unsteadily, through the press of bodies to arrive finally at the stairs. She made her ascent cautiously, one hand on the flimsy railing, vaguely aware that someone was, unsurprisingly, following her.

At the landing she set her back against a wall.

The stranger arrived, still wearing a stupid grin – that froze on his face as the point of a knife pressed the skin beneath his left eye.

'Go back downstairs,' the woman said.

A tear of blood trickled down the man's cheek, gathered thick along the ridge of his jaw. He was trembling, wincing as the point slipped in ever deeper. 'Please,' he whispered.

She reeled slightly, inadvertently slicing open the man's cheek, fortunately downward rather than up into his eye. He cried out and staggered back, hands up in an effort to stop the flow of blood, then stumbled his way down the stairs.

Shouts from below, then a harsh laugh.

The woman studied the knife in her hand, wondering where it had come from, and whose blood now gleamed from it.

No matter.

She went in search of her room, and, eventually, found it.

The vast dust storm was natural, born out on the Jhag Odhan and cycling widdershins into the heart of the Seven Cities subcontinent. The

19

winds swept northward along the east side of the hills, crags and old mountains ringing the Holy Desert of Raraku – a desert that was now a sea – and were drawn into a war of lightning along the ridge's breadth, visible from the cities of Pan'potsun and G'danisban. Wheeling westward, the storm spun out writhing arms, one of these striking Ehrlitan before blowing out above the Ehrlitan Sea, another reaching to the city of Pur Atrii. As the main body of the storm curled back inland, it gathered energy once more, battering the north side of the Thalas Mountains, engulfing the cities of Hatra and Y'Ghatan before turning southward one last time. A natural storm, one final gift, perhaps, from the old spirits of Raraku.

The fleeing army of Leoman of the Flails had embraced that gift, riding into that relentless wind for days on end, the days stretching into weeks, the world beyond reduced to a wall of suspended sand all the more bitter for what it reminded the survivors of – their beloved Whirlwind, the hammer of Sha'ik and Dryjhna the Apocalyptic. Yet, even in bitterness, there was life, there was salvation.

Tavore's Malazan army still pursued, not in haste, not with the reckless stupidity shown immediately following the death of Sha'ik and the shattering of the rebellion. Now, the hunt was a measured thing, a tactical stalking of the last organized force opposed to the empire. A force believed to be in possession of the Holy Book of Dryjhna, the lone artifact of hope for the embattled rebels of Seven Cities.

Though he possessed it not, Leoman of the Flails cursed that book daily. With almost religious zeal and appalling imagination, he growled out his curses, the rasping wind thankfully stripping the words away so that only Corabb Bhilan Thenu'alas, riding close alongside his commander, could hear. When tiring of that tirade, Leoman would concoct elaborate schemes to destroy the tome once it came into his hands. Fire, horse piss, bile, Moranth incendiaries, the belly of a dragon . . . until Corabb, exhausted, pulled away to ride in the more reasonable company of his fellow rebels.

Who would then ply him with fearful questions, casting uneasy glances Leoman's way. What was he saying?

Prayers, Corabb would answer. Our commander prays to Dryjhna all day. Leoman of the Flails, he told them, is a pious man.

About as pious as could be expected. The rebellion was collapsing, whipped away on the winds. Cities had capitulated, one after another, upon the appearance of imperial armies and ships. Citizens turned on neighbours in their zeal to present criminals to answer for the multitude of atrocities committed during the uprising. Once-heroes and petty tyrants alike were paraded before the reoccupiers, and blood-lust was high. Such grim news reached them from caravans they intercepted as they fled ever onward. And with each tatter of news, Leoman's expression darkened yet further, as if it was all he could do to bind taut the rage within him.

It was disappointment, Corabb told himself, punctuating the thought each time with a long sigh. The people of Seven Cities so quickly relinquished the freedom won at the cost of so many lives, and this was indeed a bitter truth, a most sordid comment on human nature. Had it all been for nothing, then? How could a pious warrior not experience soul-burning disappointment? How many tens of thousands of people had died? *For what?*

And so Corabb told himself he understood his commander. Understood that Leoman could not let go, not yet, perhaps never. Holding fast to the dream gave meaning to all that had gone before.

Complicated thoughts. It had taken Corabb many hours of frowning regard to reach them, to make that extraordinary leap into the mind of another man, to see through his eyes, if only for a moment, before reeling back in humble confusion. He had caught a glimpse, then, of what made great leaders, in battle, in matters of state. The facility of their intelligence in shifting perspectives, in seeing things from all sides. When, for Corabb, it was all he could manage, truth be told, to cling to a single vision – his own – in the midst of so much discord as the world was wont to rear up before him.

If not for his commander, Corabb well knew, he would be lost.

A gloved hand, gesturing, and Corabb kicked his mount forward until he was at Leoman's side.

The hooded, cloth-wrapped face swung close, leather-clad fingers tugging the stained silk away from the mouth, and words shouted so that Corabb could hear them: 'Where in Hood's name are we?'

Corabb stared, squinted, then sighed.

Her finger provided the drama, ploughing a traumatic furrow across the well-worn path. The ants scurried in confusion, and Samar Dev watched them scrabbling fierce with the insult, the soldiers with their heads lifted and mandibles opened wide as if they would challenge the gods. Or, in this case, a woman slowly dying of thirst.

She was lying on her side in the shade of the wagon. It was just past midday, and the air was still. The heat had stolen all strength from her limbs. It was unlikely she could continue her assault on the ants, and the realization gave her a moment of regret. The deliverance of discord into otherwise predictable, truncated and sordid lives seemed a worthwhile thing. Well, perhaps not worthwhile, but certainly interesting. God-like thoughts, then, to mark her last day among the living.

Motion caught her attention. The dust of the road, shivering, and

21

now she could hear a growing thunder, reverberating like earthen drums. The track she was on was not a well-traversed one here on the Ugarat Odhan. It belonged to an age long past, when the caravans plied the scores of routes between the dozen or more great cities of which ancient Ugarat was the hub, and all those cities, barring Kayhum on the banks of the river and Ugarat itself, were dead a thousand years or more.

Still, a lone rider could as easily be one too many as her salvation, for she was a woman with ample womanly charms, and she was alone. Sometimes, it was said, bandits and raiders used these mostly forgotten tracks as they made their way between caravan routes. Bandits were notoriously ungenerous.

The hoofs approached, ever louder, then the creature slowed, and a moment later a sultry cloud of dust rolled over Samar Dev. The horse snorted, a strangely vicious sound, and there was a softer thud as the rider slipped down. Faint footfalls drew nearer.

What was this? A child? A woman?

A shadow slid into view beyond that cast by the wagon, and Samar Dev rolled her head, watching as the figure strode round the wagon and looked down on her.

No, neither child nor woman. Perhaps, she considered, not even a man. An apparition, tattered white fur riding the impossibly broad shoulders. A sword of flaked flint strapped to his back, the grip wrapped in hide. She blinked hard, seeking more details, but the bright sky behind him defeated her. A giant of a man who walked quiet as a desert cat, a nightmare vision, a hallucination.

And then he spoke, but not, it was clear, to her. 'You shall have to wait for your meal, Havok. This one still lives.'

'Havok eats dead women?' Samar asked, her voice ragged. 'Who do you ride with?'

'Not with,' the giant replied. 'On.' He moved closer and crouched down beside her. There was something in his hands – a waterskin – but she found she could not pull her gaze from his face. Even, hard-edged features, broken and crazed by a tattoo of shattered glass, the mark of an escaped slave. 'I see your wagon,' he said, speaking the language of the desert tribes yet oddly accented, 'but where is the beast that pulled it?'

'In the bed,' she replied.

He set the skin at her side and straightened, walked over and leaned in for a look. 'There's a dead man in there.'

'Yes, that's him. He's broken down.'

'He was pulling this wagon? No wonder he's dead.'

She reached over and managed to close both hands around the waterskin's neck. Tugged the stopper free and tilted it over her mouth.

Warm, delicious water. 'Do you see those double levers beside him?' she asked. 'Work those and the wagon moves. It's my own invention.'

'Is it hard work? Then why hire an old man to do it?'

'He was a potential investor. Wanted to see how it would work for himself.'

The giant grunted, and she saw him studying her. 'We were doing fine,' she said. 'At first. But then it broke. The linkage. We were only planning half a day, but he'd taken us too far out before dropping dead. I thought to walk, but then I broke my foot—'

'How?'

'Kicking the wheel. Anyway, I can't walk.'

He continued staring down at her, like a wolf eyeing a lame hare. She sipped more water. 'Are you planning on being unpleasant?' she asked.

'It is blood-oil that drives a Teblor warrior to rape. I have none. I have not taken a woman by force in years. You are from Ugarat?'

'Yes.'

'I must enter that city for supplies. I want no trouble.'

'I can help with that.'

'I want to remain beneath notice.'

'I'm not sure that's possible,' she said.

'Make it possible and I will take you with me.'

'Well, that's not fair. You are half again taller than a normal man. You are tattooed. You have a horse that eats people – assuming it is a horse and not an enkar'al. And you seem to be wearing the skin of a white-furred bear.'

He turned away from the wagon.

'All right!' she said hastily. 'I'll think of something.'

He came close again, collected the waterskin, slung it over a shoulder, and then picked her up by the belt, one-handed. Pain ripped through her right leg as the broken foot dangled. 'Seven Hounds!' she hissed. 'How undignified do you have to make this?'

Saying nothing, the warrior carried her over to his waiting horse. Not an enkar'al, she saw, but not quite a horse either. Tall, lean and pallid, silver mane and tail, with eyes red as blood. A single rein, no saddle or stirrups. 'Stand on your good leg,' he said, lifting her straight. Then he picked up a loop of rope and vaulted onto the horse.

Gasping, leaning against the horse, Samar Dev tracked the double strands of the rope the man held, and saw that he had been dragging something while he rode. Two huge rotted heads. Dogs or bears, as oversized as the man himself.

The warrior reached down and unceremoniously pulled her up until she was settled behind him. More waves of pain, darkness threatening.

'Beneath notice,' he said again.

Samar Dev glanced back at those two severed heads. 'That goes without saying,' she said.

Musty darkness in the small room, the air stale and sweaty. Two slitted, rectangular holes in the wall just beneath the low ceiling allowed the cool night air to slip inside in fitful gusts, like sighs from a waiting world. For the woman huddled on the floor beside the narrow bed, that world would have to wait a little longer. Arms closed about her drawn-up knees, head lowered, sheathed in black hair that hung in oily strands, she wept. And to weep was to be inside oneself, entirely, an inner place far more unrelenting and unforgiving than anything that could be found outside.

She wept for the man she had abandoned, fleeing the pain she had seen in his eyes, as his love for her kept him stumbling in her wake, matching each footfall yet unable to come any closer. For that she could not allow. The intricate patterns on a hooded snake held mesmerizing charms, but the bite was no less deadly for that. She was the same. There was nothing in her – nothing that she could see – worth the overwhelming gift of love. Nothing in her worthy of him.

He had blinded himself to that truth, and that was his flaw, the flaw he had always possessed. A willingness, perhaps a need, to believe in the good, where no good could be found. Well, this was a love she could not abide, and she would not take him down her path.

Cotillion had understood. The god had seen clearly into the depths of this mortal darkness, as clearly as had Apsalar. And so there had been nothing veiled in the words and silences exchanged between her and the patron god of assassins. A mutual recognition. The tasks he set before her were of a nature suited to his aspect, and to her particular talents. When condemnation had already been pronounced, one could not be indignant over the sentence. But she was no god, so far removed from humanity as to find amorality a thing of comfort, a refuge from one's own deeds. Everything was getting . . . harder, harder to manage.

He would not miss her for long. His eyes would slowly open. To other possibilities. He travelled now with two other women, after all – Cotillion had told her that much. So. He would heal, and would not be alone for long, she was certain of that.

More than sufficient fuel to feed her self-pity.

Even so, she had tasks set before her, and it would not do to wallow overlong in this unwelcome self-indulgence. Apsalar slowly raised her head, studied the meagre, grainy details of the room. Trying to recall how she had come to be here. Her head ached, her throat was parched. Wiping the tears from her cheeks, she slowly stood. Pounding pain behind her eyes.

From somewhere below she could hear tavern sounds, a score of voices, drunken laughter. Apsalar found her silk-lined cloak, reversed it and slipped the garment over her shoulders, then she walked over to the door, unlocked it, and stepped out into the corridor beyond. Two wavering oil-lamps set in niches along the wall, a railing and stairs at the far end. From the room opposite hers came the muffled noise of love-making, the woman's cries too melodramatic to be genuine. Apsalar listened a moment longer, wondering what it was about the sounds that disturbed her so, then she moved through the flicker of shadows, reaching the steps, and made her way down.

It was late, probably well after the twelfth bell. Twenty or so patrons occupied the tavern, half of them in the livery of caravan guards. They were not regulars, given the unease with which they were regarded by the remaining denizens, and she noted, as she approached the counter, that three were Gral, whilst another pair, both women, were Pardu. Both rather unpleasant tribes, or so Cotillion's memories informed her in a subtle rustle of disquiet. Typically raucous and overbearing, their eyes finding and tracking her progress to the bar; she elected caution and so kept her gaze averted.

The barman walked over as she arrived. 'Was beginning to think you'd died,' he said, as he lifted a bottle of rice wine into view and set it before her. 'Before you dip into this, lass, I'd like to see some coin.'

'How much do I owe you so far?'

'Two silver crescents.'

She frowned. 'I thought I'd paid already.'

'For the wine, aye. But then you spent a night and a day and an evening in the room – and I have to charge you for tonight as well, since it's too late to try renting it out now. Finally,' he gestured, 'there's this bottle here.'

'I didn't say I wanted it,' she replied. 'But if you've any food left . . .'

'I've some.'

She drew out her coin pouch and found two crescents. 'Here. Assuming this is for tonight's room as well.'

He nodded. 'You don't want the wine, then?'

'No. Sawr'ak beer, if you please.'

He collected the bottle and headed off.

A figure pushed in on either side of her. The Pardu women. 'See those Gral?' one asked, nodding to a nearby table. 'They want you to dance for them.'

'No they don't,' Apsalar replied.

'No,' the other woman said, 'they do. They'll even pay. You walk like a dancer. We could all see that. You don't want to upset them—'

'Precisely. Which is why I won't dance for them.'

The two Pardu were clearly confused by that. In the interval the barman arrived with a tankard of beer and a tin bowl of goat soup, the layer of fat on the surface sporting white hairs to give proof of its origin. He added a hunk of dark bread. 'Good enough?'

She nodded. 'Thank you.' Then turned to the woman who had first spoken. 'I am a Shadow Dancer. Tell them that, Pardu.'

Both women backed off suddenly, and Apsalar leaned on the counter, listening to the hiss of words spreading out through the tavern. All at once she found she had some space around her. *Good enough.*

The bartender was regarding her warily. 'You're full of surprises,' he said. 'That dance is forbidden.'

'Yes, it is.'

'You're from Quon Tali,' he said in a quieter voice. 'Itko Kan, I'd guess, by the tilt of your eyes and that black hair. Never heard of a Shadow Dancer out of Itko Kan.' He leaned close. 'I was born just outside Gris, you see. Was regular infantry in Dassem's army, took a spear in the back my first battle and that was it for me. I missed Y'Ghatan, for which I daily give thanks to Oponn. You understand. Didn't see Dassem die and glad for it.'

'But you still have stories aplenty,' Apsalar said.

'That I have,' he said with an emphatic nod. Then his gaze sharpened on her. After a moment he grunted and moved away.

She ate, sipped ale, and her headache slowly faded.

Some time later, she gestured to the barman and he approached. 'I am going out,' she said, 'but I wish to keep the room so do not rent it out to anyone else.'

He shrugged. 'You've paid for it. I lock up at fourth bell.'

She straightened and made her way towards the door. The caravan guards tracked her progress, but none made move to follow – at least not immediately.

She hoped they would heed the implicit warning she'd given them. She already intended to kill a man this night, and one was enough, as far as she was concerned.

Stepping outside, Apsalar paused for a moment. The wind had died. The stars were visible as blurry motes behind the veil of fine dust still settling in the storm's wake. The air was cool and still. Drawing her cloak about her and slipping her silk scarf over the lower half of her face, Apsalar swung left down the street. At the juncture of a narrow alley, thick with shadows, she slipped suddenly into the gloom and was gone.

A few moments later the two Pardu women padded towards the alley. They paused at its mouth, looking down the twisted track, seeing no-one.

'She spoke true,' one hissed, making a warding sign. 'She walks the shadows.'

The other nodded. 'We must inform our new master.'

They headed off.

Standing within the warren of Shadow, the two Pardu looking ghostly, seeming to shiver into and out of existence as they strode up the street, Apsalar watched them for another dozen heartbeats. She was curious as to who their master might be, but that was a trail she would follow some other night. Turning away, she studied the shadow-wrought world she found herself in. On all sides, a lifeless city. Nothing like Ehrlitan, the architecture primitive and robust, with gated lintel-stone entrances to narrow passageways that ran straight and high-walled. No-one walked those cobbled paths. The buildings to either side of the passageways were all two storeys or less, flat-roofed, and no windows were visible. High narrow doorways gaped black in the grainy gloom.

Even Cotillion's memories held no recognition of this manifestation in the Shadow Realm, but this was not unusual. There seemed to be uncounted layers, and the fragments of the shattered warren were far more extensive than one might expect. The realm was ever in motion, bound to some wayward force of migration, scudding ceaseless across the mortal world. Overhead, the sky was slate grey – what passed for night in Shadow, and the air was turgid and warm.

One of the passageways led in the direction of Ehrlitan's central flat-topped hill, the Jen'rahb, once the site of the Falah'd Crown, now a mass of rubble. She set off down it, eyes on the looming, near-transparent wreckage of tumbled stone. The path opened out onto a square, each of the four walls lined with shackles. Two sets still held bodies. Desiccated, slumped in the dust, skin-wrapped skulls sunk low, resting on gracile-boned chests; one was at the end opposite her, the other at the back of the left-hand wall. A portal broke the line of the far wall near the right-side corner.

Curious, Apsalar approached the nearer figure. She could not be certain, but it appeared to be Tiste, either Andii or Edur. The corpse's long straight hair was colourless, bleached by antiquity. Its accoutrements had rotted away, leaving only a few withered strips and corroded bits of metal. As she crouched before it, there was a swirl of dust beside the body, and her brows lifted as a shade slowly rose into view. Translucent flesh, the bones strangely luminescent, a skeletal face with black-pitted eyes.

'The body's mine,' it whispered, bony fingers clutching the air. 'You can't have it.'

The language was Tiste Andii, and Apsalar was vaguely surprised that she understood it. Cotillion's memories and the knowledge hidden within them could still startle her on occasion. 'What would I do with the body?' she asked. 'I have my own, after all.'

'Not here. I see naught but a ghost.'

'As do I.'

It seemed startled. 'Are you certain?'

'You died long ago,' she said. 'Assuming the body in chains is your own.'

'My own? No. At least, I don't think so. It might be. Why not? Yes, it was me, once, long ago. I recognize it. You are the ghost, not me. I've never felt better, in fact. Whereas you look . . . unwell.'

'Nonetheless,' Apsalar said, 'I have no interest in stealing a corpse.'

The shade reached out and brushed the corpse's lank, pale hair. 'I was lovely, you know. Much admired, much pursued by the young warriors of the enclave. Perhaps I still am, and it is only my spirit that has grown so . . . tattered. Which is more visible to the mortal eye? Vigour and beauty moulding flesh, or the miserable wretch hiding beneath it?'

Apsalar winced, looked away. 'Depends, I think, on how closely you look.'

'And how clear your vision. Yes, I agree. And beauty, it passes so quickly, doesn't it just? But misery, ah, misery abides.'

A new voice hissed from where the other corpse hung in its chains. 'Don't listen to her! Treacherous bitch, look where we ended up! My fault? Oh no, I was the honest one. Everyone knew that – and prettier besides, don't let her tell you otherwise! Come over here, dear ghost, and hear the truth!'

Apsalar straightened. 'I am not the ghost here—'

'Dissembler! No wonder you prefer her to me!'

She could see the other shade now, a twin to the first one, hovering over its own corpse, or at least the body it claimed as its own. 'How did you two come to be here?' she asked.

The second shade pointed at the first. 'She's a thief!'

'So are you!' the first one retorted.

'I was only following you, Telorast! "Oh, let's break into Shadowkeep! There's no-one there, after all! We could make off with uncounted riches!" Why did I believe you? I was a fool—'

'Well,' cut in the other, 'that's something we can agree on, at least.'

'There is no purpose,' Apsalar said, 'to the two of you remaining here. Your corpses are rotting away, but those shackles will never release them.'

'You serve the new master of Shadow!' The second shade seemed most agitated with its own accusation. 'That miserable, slimy, wretched—'

'Quiet!' hissed the first shade, Telorast. 'He'll come back to taunt us some more! I, for one, have no desire ever to see him again. Nor those damned Hounds.' The ghost edged closer to Apsalar. 'Most kind servant of the wondrous new master, to answer your question, we would indeed love to leave this place. Alas, where would we go?' It gestured with one filmy, bony hand. 'Beyond the city, there are terrible creatures. Deceitful, hungry, numerous! Now,' it added in a purr, 'had we an escort . . .'

'Oh yes,' cried the second shade, 'an escort, to one of the gates – a modest, momentary responsibility, yet we would be most thankful.'

Apsalar studied the two creatures. 'Who imprisoned you? And speak the truth, else you'll receive no help from me.'

Telorast bowed deeply, then seemed to settle even lower, and it was a moment before Apsalar realized it was grovelling. 'Truth to tell. We would not lie as to this. No clearer recollection and no purer integrity in relating said recollection will you hear in any realm. 'Twas a demon lord—'

'With seven heads!' the other interjected, bobbing up and down in some ill-contained excitement.

Telorast cringed. 'Seven heads? Were there seven? There might well have been. Why not? Yes, seven heads!'

'And which head,' Apsalar asked, 'claimed to be the lord?'

'The sixth!'

'The second!'

The two shades regarded each other balefully, then Telorast raised a skeletal finger. 'Precisely! Sixth from the right, second from the left!'

'Oh, very good,' crooned the other.

Apsalar faced the shade. 'Your companion's name is Telorast – what is yours?'

It flinched, bobbed, then began its own grovelling, raising minute clouds of dust. 'Prince – King Cruel, the Slayer of All Foes. The Feared. The Worshipped.' It hesitated, then, 'Princess Demure? Beloved of a thousand heroes, bulging, stern-faced men one and all!' A twitch, low muttering, a brief clawing at its own face. 'A warlord, no, a twenty-two-headed dragon, with nine wings and eleven thousand fangs. Given the chance . . .'

Apsalar crossed her arms. 'Your name.'

'Curdle.'

'Curdle.'

'I do not last long.'

'Which is what brought us to this sorry demise in the first place,' Telorast said. 'You were supposed to watch the path – I specifically told you to watch the path—'

'I did watch it!'

'But failed to see the Hound Baran—'

'I saw Baran, but I was watching the path.'

'All right,' Apsalar said, sighing, 'why should I provide you two with an escort? Give me a reason, please. Any reason at all.'

'We are loyal companions,' Telorast said. 'We will stand by you no matter what horrible end you come to.'

'We'll guard your torn-up body for eternity,' Curdle added, 'or at least until someone else comes along—'

'Unless it's Edgewalker.'

'Well, that goes without saying, Telorast,' Curdle said. 'We don't like him.'

'Or the Hounds.'

'Of course—'

'Or Shadowthrone, or Cotillion, or an Aptorian, or one of those—'

'All right!' Curdle shrieked.

'I will escort you,' Apsalar said, 'to a gate. Whereupon you may leave this realm, since that seems to be your desire. In all probability, you will then find yourselves walking through Hood's Gate, which would be a mercy to everyone, except perhaps Hood himself.'

'She doesn't like us,' Curdle moaned.

'Don't say it out loud,' Telorast snapped, 'or she'll actually realize it. Right now she's not sure, and that's good for us, Curdle.'

'Not sure? Are you deaf? She just insulted us!'

'That doesn't mean she doesn't like us. Not necessarily. Irritated with us, maybe, but then, we irritate everyone. Or, rather, you irritate everyone, Curdle. Because you're so unreliable.'

'I'm not always unreliable, Telorast.'

'Come along,' Apsalar said, walking towards the far portal. 'I have things to do this night.'

'But what about these bodies?' Curdle demanded.

'They stay here, obviously.' She turned and faced the two shades. 'Either follow me, or don't. It's up to you.'

'But we liked those bodies—'

'It's all right, Curdle,' Telorast said in a soothing tone. 'We'll find others.'

Apsalar shot Telorast a glance, bemused by the comment, then she set off, striding into the narrow passageway.

The two ghosts scurried and flitted after her.

The basin's level floor was a crazed latticework of cracks, the clay silts of the old lake dried by decades of sun and heat. Wind and sands had polished the surface so that it gleamed in the moonlight, like tiles of silver. A deep-sunk well, encircled by a low wall of bricks, marked the centre of the lake-bed.

Outriders from Leoman's column had already reached the well, dismounting to inspect it, while the main body of the horse-warriors filed down onto the basin. The storm was past, and stars glistened overhead. Exhausted horses and exhausted rebels made a slow procession over the broken, webbed ground. Capemoths flitted over the heads of the riders, weaving and spinning to escape the hunting rhizan lizards that wheeled in their midst like miniature dragons. An incessant war overhead, punctuated by the crunch of carapaced armour and the thin, metallic death-cries of the capemoths.

Corabb Bhilan Thenu'alas leaned forward on his saddle, the hinged horn squealing, and spat to his left. Defiance, a curse to these clamouring echoes of battle. And to get the taste of grit from his mouth. He glanced over at Leoman, who rode in silence. They had been leaving a trail of dead horses, and almost everyone was on their second or third mount. A dozen warriors had surrendered to the pace this past day, older men who had dreamed of a last battle against the hated Malazans, beneath the blessed gaze of Sha'ik, only to see that opportunity torn away by treachery. There were more than a few broken spirits in this tattered regiment, Corabb knew. It was easy to understand how one could lose hope during this pathetic journey.

If not for Leoman of the Flails, Corabb himself might have given up long ago, slipping off into the blowing sands to seek his own destiny, discarding the trappings of a rebel soldier, and settling down in some remote city with memories of despair haunting his shadow until the Hoarder of Souls came to claim him. If not for Leoman of the Flails.

The riders reached the well, spreading out to create a circle encampment around its life-giving water. Corabb drew rein a moment after Leoman had done so, and both dismounted, boots crunching on a carpet of bones and scales from long-dead fish.

'Corabb,' Leoman said, 'walk with me.'

They set off in a northerly direction until they were fifty paces past the outlying pickets, standing alone on the cracked pan. Corabb noted a depression nearby in which sat half-buried lumps of clay. Drawing his dagger, he walked over and crouched down to retrieve one of the lumps. Breaking it open to reveal the toad curled up within it, he dug the creature out and returned to his commander's side. 'An unexpected treat,' he said, pulling off a withered leg and tearing at the tough but sweet flesh.

Leoman stared at him in the moonlight. 'You will have strange dreams, Corabb, eating those.'

'Spirit dreams, yes. They do not frighten me, Commander. Except for all the feathers.'

Making no comment on that, Leoman unstrapped his helm and pulled it off. He stared up at the stars, then said, 'What do my soldiers want of me? Am I to lead us to an impossible victory?'

'You are destined to carry the Book,' Corabb said around a mouthful of meat.

'And the goddess is dead.'

'Dryjhna is more than that goddess, Commander. The Apocalyptic is as much a time as it is anything else.'

Leoman glanced over. 'You do manage to surprise me still, Corabb Bhilan Thenu'alas, after all these years.'

Pleased by this compliment, or what he took for a compliment, Corabb smiled, then spat out a bone and said, 'I have had time to think, Commander. While we rode. I have thought long and those thoughts have walked strange paths. We are the Apocalypse. This last army of the rebellion. And I believe we are destined to show the world the truth of that.'

'Why do you believe that?'

'Because you lead us, Leoman of the Flails, and you are not one to slink away like some creeping meer-rat. We journey towards something – I know, many here see this as a flight, but I do not. Not all the time, anyway.'

'A meer-rat,' Leoman mused. 'That is the name for those lizard-eating rats in the Jen'rahb, in Ehrlitan.'

Corabb nodded. 'The long-bodied ones, with the scaly heads, yes.'

'A meer-rat,' Leoman said again, oddly thoughtful. 'Almost impossible to hunt down. They can slip through cracks a snake would have trouble with. Hinged skulls . . .'

'Bones like green twigs, yes,' Corabb said, sucking at the skull of the toad, then flinging it away. Watching as it sprouted wings and flew off into the night. He glanced over at his commander's feather-clad features. 'They make terrible pets. When startled, they dive for the first hole in sight, no matter how small. A woman died with a meer-rat halfway up her nose, or so I heard. When they get stuck, they start chewing. Feathers everywhere.'

'I take it no-one keeps them as pets any more,' Leoman said, studying the stars once again. 'We ride towards our Apocalypse, do we? Yes, well.'

'We could leave the horses,' Corabb said. 'And just fly away. It'd be much quicker.'

'That would be unkind, wouldn't it?'

'True. Honourable beasts, horses. You shall lead us, Winged One, and we shall prevail.'

'An impossible victory.'

'Many impossible victories, Commander.'

'One would suffice.'

'Very well,' Corabb said. 'One, then.'

'I don't want this, Corabb. I don't want any of this. I'm of a mind to disperse this army.'

'That will not work, Commander. We are returning to our birthplace. It is the season for that. To build nests on the rooftops.'

'I think,' Leoman said, 'it is time you went to sleep.'

'Yes, you are right. I will sleep now.'

'Go on. I will remain here for a time.'

'You are Leoman of the Feathers, and it shall be as you say.' Corabb saluted, then strode back towards the encampment and its host of over-sized vultures. It was not so bad a thing, he mused. Vultures survived because other things did not, after all.

Now alone, Leoman continued studying the night sky. Would that Toblakai rode with him now. The giant warrior was blind to uncertainty. *Alas, also somewhat lacking in subtlety.* The bludgeon of Karsa Orlong's reasoning would permit no disguising of unpleasant truths.

A meer-rat. He would have to think on that.

'You can't come in here with those!'

The giant warrior looked back at the trailing heads, then he lifted Samar Dev clear of the horse, set her down, and slipped off the beast himself. He brushed dust from his furs, walked over to the gate guard. Picked him up and threw him into a nearby cart.

Someone screamed – quickly cut short as the warrior swung round.

Twenty paces up the street, as dusk gathered the second guard was in full flight, heading, Samar suspected, for the blockhouse to round up twenty or so of his fellows. She sighed. 'This hasn't started well, Karsa Orlong.'

The first guard, lying amidst the shattered cart, was not moving.

Karsa eyed Samar Dev, then said, 'Everything is fine, woman. I am hungry. Find me an inn, one with a stable.'

'We shall have to move quickly, and I for one am unable to do that.'

'You are proving a liability,' Karsa Orlong said.

Alarm bells began ringing a few streets away. 'Put me back on your horse,' Samar said, 'and I will give you directions, for all the good that will do.'

He approached her.

'Careful, please – this leg can't stand much more jostling.'

He made a disgusted expression. 'You are soft, like all children.' Yet he was less haphazard when he lifted her back onto the horse.

'Down this side track,' she said. 'Away from the bells. There's an inn on Trosfalhadan Street, it's not far.' Glancing to her right, she saw a squad of guards appear further down the main street. 'Quickly, warrior, if you don't want to spend this night in a gaol cell.'

Citizens had gathered to watch them. Two had walked over to the dead or unconscious guard, crouching to examine the unfortunate man. Another stood nearby, complaining about his shattered cart and pointing at Karsa – although only when the huge warrior wasn't looking.

They made their way down the avenue running parallel to the ancient wall. Samar scowled at the various bystanders who had elected to follow them. 'I am Samar Dev,' she said loudly. 'Will you risk a curse from me? Any of you?' People shrank back, then quickly turned away.

Karsa glanced back at her. 'You are a witch?'

'You have no idea.'

'And had I left you on the trail, you would have cursed me?'

'Most certainly.'

He grunted, said nothing for the next ten paces, then turned once again. 'Why did you not call upon spirits to heal yourself?'

'I had nothing with which to bargain,' she replied. 'The spirits one finds in the wastelands are hungry things, Karsa Orlong. Covetous and not to be trusted.'

'You cannot be much of a witch, then, if you need to bargain. Why not just bind them and demand that they heal your leg?'

'One who binds risks getting bound in return. I will not walk that path.'

He made no reply to that.

'Here is Trosfalhadan Street. Up one avenue, there, see that big building with the walled compound beside it? Inn of the Wood, it's called. Hurry, before the guards reach this corner.'

'They will find us nonetheless,' Karsa said. 'You have failed in your task.'

'I wasn't the one who threw that guard into a cart!'

'He spoke rudely. You should have warned him.'

They reached the double gates at the compound.

From the corner behind them came shouts. Samar twisted round on the horse and watched the guards rush towards them. Karsa strode past her, drawing free the huge flint sword. 'Wait!' she cried. 'Let me speak with them first, warrior, else you find yourself fighting a whole city's worth of guards.'

He paused. 'They are deserving of mercy?'

She studied him a moment, then nodded. 'If not them, then their families.'

'You are under arrest!' The shout came from the rapidly closing guards.

Karsa's tattooed face darkened.

Samar edged down from the horse and hobbled to place herself between the giant and the guards, all of whom had drawn scimitars and were fanning out on the street. Beyond, a crowd of onlookers was gathering. She held up her hands. 'There has been a misunderstanding.'

'Samar Dev,' one man said in a growl. 'Best you step aside – this is no affair of yours—'

'But it is, Captain Inashan. This warrior has saved my life. My wagon broke down out in the wastes, and I broke my leg – look at me. I was dying. And so I called upon a spirit of the wild-lands.'

The captain's eyes widened as he regarded Karsa Orlong. 'This is a spirit?'

'Most assuredly,' Samar replied. 'One who is of course ignorant of our customs. That gate guard acted in what this spirit perceived as a hostile manner. Does he still live?'

The captain nodded. 'Knocked senseless, that is all.' The man then pointed towards the severed heads. 'What are those?'

'Trophies,' she answered. 'Demons. They had escaped their own realm and were approaching Ugarat. Had not this spirit killed them, they would have descended upon us with great slaughter. And with not a single worthy mage left in Ugarat, we would have fared poorly indeed.'

Captain Inashan narrowed his gaze on Karsa. 'Can you understand my words?'

'They have been simple enough thus far,' the warrior replied.

The captain scowled. 'Does she speak the truth?'

'More than she realizes, yet even so, there are untruths in her tale. I am not a spirit. I am Toblakai, once bodyguard to Sha'ik. Yet this woman bargained with me as she would a spirit. More, she knew nothing of where I came from or who I was, and so she might well have imagined I was a spirit of the wild-lands.'

Voices rose among both guards and citizens at the name *Sha'ik*, and Samar saw a dawning recognition in the captain's expression. 'Toblakai, companion to Leoman of the Flails. Tales of you have reached us.' He pointed with his scimitar at the fur riding Karsa's shoulders. 'Slayer of a Soletaken, a white bear. Executioner of Sha'ik's betrayers in Raraku. It is said you slew demons the night before Sha'ik was killed,' he added, eyes on the rotted, flailed heads. 'And, when she had been slain by the Adjunct, you rode out to face the Malazan army – and they would not fight you.'

'There is some truth in what you have spoken,' Karsa said, 'barring the words I exchanged with the Malazans—'

'One of Sha'ik's own,' Samar quickly said, sensing the warrior was

35

about to say something unwise, 'how could we of Ugarat not welcome you? The Malazan garrison has been driven from this city and is even now starving in Moraval Keep on the other side of the river, besieged with no hope of succour.'

'You are wrong in that,' Karsa said.

She wanted to kick him. Then again, look how that had turned out the last time? *All right, you ox, go and hang yourself.*

'What do you mean?' Captain Inashan asked.

'The rebellion is broken, the Malazans have retaken cities by the score. They will come here, too, eventually. I suggest you make peace with the garrison.'

'Would that not put you at risk?' Samar asked.

The warrior bared his teeth. 'My war is done. If they cannot accept that, I will kill them all.'

An outrageous claim, yet no-one laughed. Captain Inashan hesitated, then he sheathed his scimitar, his soldiers following suit. 'We have heard of the rebellion's failure,' he said. 'For the Malazans in the keep, alas, it might well be too late. They have been trapped in there for months. And no-one has been seen on the walls for some time—'

'I will go there,' Karsa said. 'Gestures of peace must be made.'

'It is said,' Inashan muttered, 'that Leoman still lives. That he leads the last army and has vowed to fight on.'

'Leoman rides his own path. I would place no faith in it, were I you.'

The advice was not well received. Arguments rose, until Inashan turned on his guards and silenced them with an upraised hand. 'These matters must be brought to the Falah'd.' He faced Karsa again. 'You will stay this night at the Inn of the Wood?'

'I shall, although it is not made of wood, and so it should be called Inn of the Brick.'

Samar laughed. 'You can bring that up with the owner, Toblakai. Captain, are we done here?'

Inashan nodded. 'I will send a healer to mend your leg, Samar Dev.'

'In return, I bless you and your kin, Captain.'

'You are too generous,' he replied with a bow.

The squad headed off. Samar turned to regard the giant warrior. 'Toblakai, how have you survived this long in Seven Cities?'

He looked down at her, then slung the stone sword once more over his shoulder. 'There is no armour made that can withstand the truth . . .'

'When backed by that sword?'

'Yes, Samar Dev. I find it does not take long for children to understand that. Even here in Seven Cities.' He pushed open the gates.

36

'Havok will require a stable away from other beasts . . . at least until his hunger is appeased.'

'I don't like the looks of that,' Telorast muttered, nervously shifting about.

'It is a gate,' Apsalar said.

'But where does it lead?' Curdle asked, indistinct head bobbing.

'It leads out,' she replied. 'Onto the Jen'rahb, in the city of Ehrlitan. It is where I am going.'

'Then that is where we are going,' Telorast announced. 'Are there bodies there? I hope so. Fleshy, healthy bodies.'

She regarded the two ghosts. 'You intend to steal bodies to house your spirits? I am not sure that I can permit that.'

'Oh, we wouldn't do that,' Curdle said. 'That would be possession, and that's difficult, very difficult. Memories seep back and forth, yielding confusion and inconsistency.'

'True,' Telorast said. 'And we are most consistent, are we not? No, my dear, we just happen to like bodies. In proximity. They . . . comfort us. You, for example. You are a great comfort to us, though we know not your name.'

'Apsalar.'

'She's dead!' Curdle shrieked. To Apsalar: 'I knew you were a ghost!'

'I am named after the Mistress of Thieves. I am not her in the flesh.'

'She must be speaking the truth,' Telorast said to Curdle. 'If you recall, Apsalar looked nothing like this one. The real Apsalar was Imass, or very nearly Imass. And she wasn't very friendly—'

'Because you stole from her temple coffers,' Curdle said, squirming about in small dust-clouds.

'Even before then. Decidedly unfriendly, where this Apsalar, this one here, she's kind. Her heart is bursting with warmth and generosity—'

'Enough of that,' Apsalar said, turning to the gate once more. 'As I mentioned earlier, this gate leads to the Jen'rahb . . . for me. For the two of you, of course, it might well lead into Hood's Realm. I am not responsible for that, should you find yourselves before Death's Gate.'

'Hood's Realm? Death's Gate?' Telorast began moving from side to side, a strange motion that Apsalar belatedly realized was pacing, although the ghost had sunk part-way into the ground, making it look more like wading. 'There is no fear of that. We are too powerful. Too wise. Too cunning.'

'We were great mages, once,' Curdle said. 'Necromancers, Spiritwalkers, Conjurers, Wielders of Fell Holds, Masters of the Thousand Warrens—'

'Mistresses, Curdle. Mistresses of the Thousand Warrens.'

'Yes, Telorast. Mistresses indeed. What was I thinking? Beauteous mistresses, curvaceous, languid, sultry, occasionally simpering—'

Apsalar walked through the gate.

She stepped onto broken rubble alongside the foundations of a collapsed wall. The night air was chill, stars sharp overhead.

'—and even Kallor quailed before us, isn't that right, Telorast?'

'Oh yes, he quailed.'

Apsalar looked down to find herself flanked by the two ghosts. She sighed. 'You evaded Hood's Realm, I see.'

'Clumsy grasping hands,' Curdle sniffed. 'We were too quick.'

'As we knew we'd be,' Telorast added. 'What place is this? It's all broken—'

Curdle clambered atop the foundation wall. 'No, you are wrong, Telorast, as usual. I see buildings beyond. Lit windows. The very air reeks of life.'

'This is the Jen'rahb,' Apsalar said. 'The ancient centre of the city, which collapsed long ago beneath its own weight.'

'As all cities must, eventually,' Telorast observed, trying to pick up a brick fragment. But its hand slipped ineffectually through the object. 'Oh, we are most useless in this realm.'

Curdle glanced down at its companion. 'We need bodies—'

'I told you before—'

'Fear not, Apsalar,' Curdle replied in a crooning tone, 'we will not unduly offend you. The bodies need not be sentient, after all.'

'Are there the equivalent of Hounds here?' Telorast asked.

Curdle snorted. 'The Hounds are sentient, you fool!'

'Only stupidly so!'

'Not so stupid as to fall for our tricks, though, were they?'

'Are there imbrules here? Stantars? Luthuras – are there luthuras here? Scaly, long grasping tails, eyes like the eyes of purlith bats—'

'No,' Apsalar said. 'None of those creatures.' She frowned. 'Those you have mentioned are of Starvald Demelain.'

A momentary silence from the two ghosts, then Curdle snaked along the top of the wall until its eerie face was opposite Apsalar. 'Really? Now, that's a peculiar coincidence—'

'Yet you speak the language of the Tiste Andii.'

'We do? Why, that's even stranger.'

'Baffling,' Telorast agreed. 'We, uh, we assumed it was the language you spoke. Your native language, that is.'

'Why? I am not Tiste Andii.'

'No, of course not. Well, thank the Abyss that's been cleared up. Where shall we go from here?'

'I suggest,' Apsalar said after a moment's thought, 'that you two remain here. I have tasks to complete this night, and they are not suited to company.'

'You desire stealth,' Telorast whispered, crouching low. 'We could tell, you know. There's something of the thief about you. Kindred spirits, the three of us, I think. A thief, yes, and perhaps something darker.'

'Well of course darker,' Curdle said from the wall. 'A servant of Shadowthrone, or the Patron of Assassins. There will be blood spilled this night, and our mortal companion will do the spilling. She's an assassin, and we should know, having met countless assassins in our day. Look at her, Telorast, she has deadly blades secreted about her person—'

'And she smells of stale wine.'

'Stay here,' Apsalar said. 'Both of you.'

'And if we don't?' Telorast asked.

'Then I shall inform Cotillion that you have escaped, and he will send the Hounds on your trail.'

'You bind us to servitude! Trap us with threats! Curdle, we have been deceived!'

'Let's kill her and steal her body!'

'Let's not, Curdle. Something about her frightens me. All right, Apsalar who is not Apsalar, we shall stay here . . . for a time. Until we can be certain you are dead or worse, that's how long we'll stay here.'

'Or until you return,' Curdle added.

Telorast hissed in a strangely reptilian manner, then said, 'Yes, idiot, that would be the other option.'

'Then why didn't you say so?'

'Because it's obvious, of course. Why should I waste breath mentioning what's obvious? The point is, we're waiting here. That's the point.'

'Maybe it's your point,' Curdle drawled, 'but it's not necessarily mine, not that I'll waste my breath explaining anything to you, Telorast.'

'You always were too obvious, Curdle.'

'Both of you,' Apsalar said. 'Be quiet and wait here until I return.'

Telorast slumped down against the wall's foundation stones and crossed its arms. 'Yes, yes. Go on. We don't care.'

Apsalar quickly made her way across the tumbled stone wreckage, intending to put as much distance between herself and the two ghosts as possible, before seeking out the hidden trail that would, if all went well, lead her to her victim. She cursed the sentimentality that left her so weakened of resolve that she now found herself shackled with two insane ghosts. It would not do, she well knew, to abandon them. Left to their own devices, they would likely unleash mayhem upon Ehrlitan.

They worked too hard to convince her of their harmlessness, and, after all, they had been chained in the Shadow Realm for a reason – a warren rife with eternally imprisoned creatures, few of whom could truly claim injustice.

There was no distinct Azath House in the warren of Shadow, and so, accordingly, more mundane methods had been employed in the negation of threats. Or so it seemed to Apsalar. Virtually every permanent feature in Shadow was threaded through with unbreakable chains, and bodies lay buried in the dust, shackled to those chains. Both she and Cotillion had come across menhirs, tumuli, ancient trees, stone walls and boulders, all home to nameless prisoners – demons, ascendants, revenants and wraiths. In the midst of one stone circle, three dragons were chained, to all outward appearances dead, yet their flesh did not wither or rot, and dust sheathed eyes that remained open. That dread place had been visited by Cotillion, and some faint residue of disquiet clung to the memory – there had been more to that encounter, she suspected, but not all of Cotillion's life remained within the grasp of her recollection.

She wondered who had been responsible for all those chainings. What unknown entity possessed such power as to overwhelm three dragons? So much of the Shadow Realm defied her understanding. As it did Cotillion's, she suspected.

Curdle and Telorast spoke the language of the Tiste Andii. Yet betrayed intimate knowledge of the draconean realm of Starvald Demelain. They had met the Mistress of Thieves, who had vanished from the pantheon long ago, although, if the legends of Darujhistan held any truth, she had reappeared briefly less than a century past, only to vanish a second time.

She sought to steal the moon. One of the first stories Crokus had told her, following Cotillion's sudden departure from her mind. A tale with local flavour to bolster the cult in the region, perhaps. She admitted to some curiosity. The goddess was her namesake, after all. *An Imass? There are no iconic representations of the Mistress – which is odd enough, possibly a prohibition enforced by the temples. What are her symbols? Oh, yes. Footprints. And a veil.* She resolved to question the ghosts more on this subject.

In any case, she was fairly certain that Cotillion would not be pleased that she had freed those ghosts. Shadowthrone would be furious. All of which might have spurred her motivation. *I was possessed once, but no longer. I still serve, but as it suits me, not them.*

Bold claims, but they were all that remained that she might hold on to. A god uses, then casts away. The tool is abandoned, forgotten. True, it appeared that Cotillion was not as indifferent as most gods in this matter, but how much of that could she trust?

Beneath moonlight, Apsalar found the secret trail winding through the ruins. She made her way along it, silent, using every available shadow, into the heart of the Jen'rahb. Enough of the wandering thoughts. She must needs concentrate, lest she become this night's victim.

Betrayals had to be answered. This task was more for Shadowthrone than Cotillion, or so the Patron of Assassins had explained. An old score to settle. The schemes were crowded and confused enough as it was, and that situation was getting worse, if Shadowthrone's agitation of late was any indication. Something of that unease had rubbed off on Cotillion. There had been mutterings of another convergence of powers. Vaster than any that had occurred before, and in some way Shadowthrone was at the centre of it. *All of it.*

She came within sight of the sunken temple dome, the only nearly complete structure this far into the Jen'rahb. Crouching behind a massive block whose surfaces were crowded with arcane glyphs, she settled back and studied the approach. There were potential lines of sight from countless directions. It would be quite a challenge if watchers had been positioned to guard the hidden entrance to that temple. She had to assume those watchers were there, secreted in cracks and fissures on all sides.

As she watched, she caught movement, coming out from the temple and moving furtively away to her left. Too distant to make out any details. In any case, one thing was clear. The spider was at the heart of its nest, receiving and sending out agents. Ideal. With luck, the hidden sentinels would assume she was one of those agents, unless, of course, there were particular paths one must use, a pattern altered each night.

Another option existed. Apsalar drew out the long, thin scarf known as the telab, and wrapped it about her head until only her eyes were left exposed. She unsheathed her knives, spent twenty heartbeats studying the route she would take, then bolted forward. A swift passage held the element of the unexpected, and made her a more difficult target besides. As she raced across the rubble, she waited for the heavy snap of a cross-bow, the whine of the quarrel as it cut through the air. But none came. Reaching the temple, she saw the fissured crack that served as the entrance and made for it.

She slipped into the darkness, then paused.

The passageway stank of blood.

Waiting for her eyes to adjust, she held her breath and listened. Nothing. She could now make out the sloping corridor ahead. Apsalar edged forward, halted at the edge of a larger chamber. A body was lying on the dusty floor, amidst a spreading pool of blood. At the chamber's opposite end was a curtain, drawn across a doorway. Apart from the body, a few pieces of modest furniture were visible in the room. A brazier cast fitful, orange light. The air was bitter with death and smoke.

She approached the body, eyes on the curtained doorway. Her senses told her there was no-one behind it, but if she was in error then the mistake could prove fatal. Reaching the crumpled figure, she sheathed one knife, then reached out with her hand and pulled the body onto its back. Enough to see its face.

Mebra. It seemed that someone had done her work for her.

A flit of movement in the air behind her. Apsalar ducked and rolled to her left as a throwing star flashed over her, punching a hole through the curtain. Regaining her feet in a crouch, she faced the outside passage.

Where a figure swathed in tight grey clothing stepped into the chamber. Its gloved left hand held another iron star, the multiple edges glittering with poison. In its right hand was a kethra knife, hooked and broad-bladed. A telab hid the assassin's features, but around its dark eyes was a mass of white-etched tattoos against black skin.

The killer stepped clear of the doorway, eyes fixed on Apsalar. 'Stupid woman,' hissed a man's voice, in accented Ehrlii.

'South Clan of the Semk,' Apsalar said. 'You are far from home.'

'There were to be no witnesses.' His left hand flashed.

Apsalar twisted. The iron star whipped past to strike the wall behind her.

The Semk rushed in behind the throw. He chopped down and crossways with his left hand to bat aside her knife-arm, then thrust with the kethra, seeking her abdomen, whereupon he would tear the blade across in a disembowelling slash. None of which succeeded.

Even as he swung down with his left arm, Apsalar stepped to her right. The heel of his hand cracked hard against her hip. Her movement away from the kethra forced the Semk to attempt to follow with the weapon. Long before he could reach her, she had driven her knife between ribs, the point piercing the back of his heart.

With a strangled groan, the Semk sagged, slid off the knife-blade, and pitched to the floor. He sighed out his last breath, then was still.

Apsalar cleaned her weapon across the man's thigh, then began cutting away his clothing. The tattoos continued, covering every part of him. A common enough trait among warriors of the South Clan, yet the style was not Semk. Arcane script wound across the assassin's brawny limbs, similar to the carving she had seen in the ruins outside the temple.

The language of the First Empire.

42

With growing suspicion, she rolled the body over to reveal the back. And saw a darkened patch, roughly rectangular, over the Semk's right shoulder-blade. Where the man's name had once been, before it had been ritually obscured.

This man had been a priest of the Nameless Ones.

Oh, Cotillion, you won't like this at all.

'Well?'

Telorast glanced up. 'Well what?'

'She is a pretty one.'

'We're prettier.'

Curdle snorted. 'At the moment, I'd have to disagree.'

'All right. If you like the dark, deadly type.'

'What I was asking, Telorast, is whether we stay with her.'

'If we don't, Edgewalker will be very unhappy with us, Curdle. You don't want that, do you? He's been unhappy with us before, or have you forgotten?'

'Fine! You didn't have to bring that up, did you? So it's decided. We stay with her.'

'Yes,' Telorast said. 'Until we can find a way to get out of this mess.'

'You mean, cheat them all?'

'Of course.'

'Good,' Curdle said, stretching out along the ruined wall and staring up at the strange stars. 'Because I want my throne back.'

'So do I.'

Curdle sniffed. 'Dead people. Fresh.'

'Yes. But not her.'

'No, not her.' The ghost was silent a moment, then added, 'Not just pretty, then.'

'No,' Telorast glumly agreed, 'not just pretty.'

CHAPTER TWO

It must be taken as given that a man who happens to
be the world's most powerful, most terrible, most
deadly sorceror, must have a woman at his side.
But it does not follow, my children, that a woman
of similar proportions requires a man at hers.
Now then, who wants to be a tyrant?

Mistress Wu
Malaz City School of Waifs and Urchins
1152 Burn's Sleep

INSUBSTANTIAL, FADING IN AND OUT OF SIGHT, SMOKY AND WISP-threaded, Ammanas fidgeted on the ancient Throne of Shadow. Eyes like polished haematite were fixed on the scrawny figure standing before it. A figure whose head was hairless except for a wild curly grey and black tangle over the ears and round the back of the subtly misshapen skull. And twin eyebrows that rivalled the fringe in chaotic waywardness, beetling and knotting to match the baffling and disquieting mêlée of emotions on the wrinkled face beneath them.

The subject was muttering, not quite under his breath, 'He's not so frightening, is he? In and out, off and on, here and elsewhere, a wavering apparition of wavering intent and perhaps wavering intellect – best not let him read my thoughts – look stern, no, attentive, no, pleased! No, wait. Cowed. Terrified. No, in awe. Yes, in awe. But not for long, that's tiring. Look bored. Gods, what am I thinking? Anything but bored, no matter how boring this might be, what with him looking down on me and me looking up at him and Cotillion over there with his arms crossed, leaning against that wall and smirking – what kind of audience is he? The worst kind, I say. What was I thinking? Well, at least I was thinking. I *am* thinking, in fact, and one might presume that

Shadowthrone is doing the same, assuming of course that his brain hasn't leaked away, since he's nothing but shadows so what holds it in? The point is, I am well advised to remind myself, as I am now doing, the point is, he summoned me. And so here I am. Rightful servant. Loyal. Well, more or less loyal. Trustworthy. Most of the time. Modest and respectful, always. To all outward appearances, and what is outward in appearance is all that matters in this and every other world. Isn't it? Smile! Grimace. Look helpful. Hopeful. Harried, hirsute, happenstance. Wait, how does one look happenstance? What kind of expression must that one be? I must think on that. But not now, because this isn't happenstance, it's circumstance—'

'Silence.'

'My lord? I said nothing. Oh, best glance away now, and think on this. I said nothing. Silence. Perhaps he's making an observation? Yes, that must be it. Look back, now, deferentially, and say aloud: Indeed, my lord. Silence. There. How does he react? Is that growing apoplexy? How can one tell, with all those shadows? Now, if I sat on that throne—'

'Iskaral Pust!'

'Yes, my lord?'

'I have decided.'

'Yes, my lord? Well, if he's decided something, why doesn't he just say it?'

'I have decided, Iskaral Pust—'

'He's doing some more! Yes, my lord?'

'That you . . .' Shadowthrone paused and seemed to pass a hand over his eyes. 'Oh my . . .' he added in a murmur, then straightened. 'I have decided that you will have to do.'

'My lord? Flick eyes away! This god is insane. I serve an insane god! What kind of expression does that warrant?'

'Go! Get out of here!'

Iskaral Pust bowed. 'Of course, my lord. Immediately!' Then he stood, waiting. Looking around, one pleading glance to Cotillion. 'I was summoned! I can't leave until this foaming idiot on the throne releases me! Cotillion understands – that might be amusement in those horribly cold eyes – oh, why doesn't he say something? Why doesn't he remind this blathering smudge on this throne—'

A snarl from Ammanas, and the High Priest of Shadow, Iskaral Pust, vanished.

Shadowthrone then sat motionless for a time, before slowly turning his head to regard Cotillion. 'What are you looking at?' he demanded.

'Not much,' Cotillion replied. 'You have become rather insubstantial of late.'

'I like it this way.' They studied each other for a moment. 'All right,

I'm a little stretched!' The shriek echoed away, and the god subsided. 'Do you think he'll get there in time?'

'No.'

'Do you think, if he does, he'll be sufficient?'

'No.'

'Who asked you!?'

Cotillion watched as Ammanas seethed, fidgeted and squirmed on the throne. Then the Lord of Shadow fell still, and slowly raised a single, spindly finger. 'I have an idea.'

'And I shall leave you to it,' Cotillion said, pushing himself from the wall. 'I am going for a walk.'

Shadowthrone did not reply.

Glancing over, Cotillion saw that he had vanished. 'Oh,' he murmured, 'that *was* a good idea.'

Emerging from Shadowkeep, he paused to study the landscape beyond. It was in the habit of changing at a moment's notice, although not when one was actually looking, which, he supposed, was a saving grace. A line of forested hills to the right, gullies and ravines directly ahead, and a ghostly lake to the left, on which rode a half-dozen grey-sailed ships in the distance. Artorallah demons, off to raid the Aptorian coastal villages, he suspected. It was rare to find the lake region appearing so close to the keep, and Cotillion felt a moment of unease. The demons of this realm seemed to do little more than bide their time, paying scant attention to Shadowthrone, and more or less doing as they pleased. Which generally involved feuds, lightning attacks on neighbours and pillaging.

Ammanas could well command them, if he so chose. But he hardly ever did, perhaps not wanting to test the limits of their loyalty. Or perhaps just preoccupied with some other concern. With his schemes.

Things were not well. *A little stretched, are you, Ammanas? I am not surprised.* Cotillion could sympathize, and almost did. Momentarily, before reminding himself that Ammanas had invited most of the risks upon himself. *And, by extension, upon me as well.*

The paths ahead were narrow, twisted and treacherous. Requiring utmost caution with every measured step.

So be it. After all, we have done this before. And succeeded. Of course, far more was at stake this time. Too much, perhaps.

Cotillion set off for the broken grounds opposite him. Two thousand paces, and before him was a trail leading into a gully. Shadows roiled between the rough rock walls. Reluctant to part as he walked the track, they slid like seaweed in shallows around his legs.

So much in this realm had lost its rightful ... place. Confusion triggered a seething tumult in pockets where shadows gathered. Faint cries whispered against his ears, as if from a great distance, the voice of multitudes drowning. Sweat beaded Cotillion's brow, and he quickened his pace until he was past the sinkhole.

The path sloped upward and eventually opened out onto a broad plateau. As he strode into the clear, eyes fixed on a distant ring of standing stones, he felt a presence at his side, and turned to see a tall, skeletal creature, bedecked in rags, walking to match his pace. Not close enough to reach out and touch, but too close for Cotillion's comfort nonetheless. 'Edgewalker. It has been some time since I last saw you.'

'I cannot say the same of you, Cotillion. I walk—'

'Yes, I know,' Cotillion cut in, 'you walk paths unseen.'

'By you. The Hounds do not share your failing.'

Cotillion frowned at the creature, then glanced back, to see Baran thirty paces back, keeping its distance. Massive head low to the ground, eyes glowing bruised crimson. 'You are being stalked.'

'It amuses them, I imagine,' Edgewalker said.

They continued on for a time, then Cotillion sighed. 'You have sought me out?' he asked. 'What do you want?'

'From you? Nothing. But I see your destination, and so would witness.'

'Witness what?'

'Your impending conversation.'

Cotillion scowled. 'And if I'd rather you did not witness?'

The skeletal face held a permanent grin, but in some way it seemed to broaden slightly. 'There is no privacy in Shadow, Usurper.'

Usurper. I'd have long since killed this bastard if he wasn't already dead. Long since.

'I am not your enemy,' Edgewalker said, as if guessing Cotillion's thoughts. 'Not yet.'

'We have more than enough enemies as it is. Accordingly,' Cotillion continued, 'we have no wish for more. Unfortunately, since we have no knowledge as to your purpose, or your motivations, we cannot predict what might offend you. So, in the interests of peace between us, enlighten me.'

'That I cannot do.'

'Cannot, or will not?'

'The failing is yours, Cotillion, not mine. Yours, and Shadowthrone's.'

'Well, that is convenient.'

Edgewalker seemed to consider Cotillion's sardonic observation for a moment, then he nodded. 'Yes, it is.'

Long since . . .

They approached the standing stones. Not a single lintel left to bridge

47

the ring, just rubble scattered about down the slopes, as if some ancient detonation at the heart of the circle had blasted the massive structure – even the upright stones were all tilted outward, like the petals of a flower.

'This is an unpleasant place,' Edgewalker said as they swung right to take the formal approach, an avenue lined with low, rotted trees, each standing upended with the remnant roots clutching the air.

Cotillion shrugged. 'About as unpleasant as virtually anywhere else in this realm.'

'You might believe that, given you have none of the memories I possess. Terrible events, long, long ago, yet the echoes remain.'

'There is little residual power left here,' Cotillion said as they neared the two largest stones, and walked between them.

'That is true. Of course, that is not the case on the surface.'

'The surface? What do you mean?'

'Standing stones are always half-buried, Cotillion. And the makers were rarely ignorant of the significance of that. Overworld and underworld.'

Cotillion halted and glanced back, studying the upended trees lining the avenue. 'And this manifestation we see here is given to the underworld?'

'In a manner of speaking.'

'Is the overworld manifestation to be found in some other realm? Where one might see an inward-tilting ring of stones, and right-side-up trees?'

'Assuming they are not entirely buried or eroded to nothing by now. This circle is very old.'

Cotillion swung round again and observed the three dragons opposite them, each at the base of a standing stone, although their massive chains reached down into the rough soil, rather than into the weathered rock. Shackled at the neck and at the four limbs, with another chain wrapped taut behind the shoulders and wings of each dragon. Every chain drawn so tight as to prevent any movement, not even a lifting of the head. 'This,' Cotillion said in a murmur, 'is as you said, Edgewalker. An unpleasant place. I'd forgotten.'

'You forget every time,' Edgewalker said. 'Overcome by your fascination. Such is the residual power in this circle.'

Cotillion shot him a quick look. 'I am ensorcelled?'

The gaunt creature shrugged in a faint clatter of bones. 'It is a magic without purpose beyond what it achieves. Fascination ... and forgetfulness.'

'I have trouble accepting that. All sorcery has a desired goal.'

Another shrug. 'They are hungry, yet unable to feed.'

After a moment, Cotillion nodded. 'The sorcery belongs to the dragons, then. Well, I can accept that. Yet, what of the circle itself? Has its power died? If so, why are these dragons still bound?'

'Not dead, simply not acting in any manner upon you, Cotillion. You are not its intent.'

'Well enough.' He turned as Baran padded into view, swinging wide to avoid Edgewalker's reach, then fixing its attention on the dragons. Cotillion saw its hackles stiffen. 'Can you answer me this,' he said to Edgewalker, 'why will they not speak with me?'

'Perhaps you have yet to say anything worth a reply.'

'Possibly. What do you think the response will be, then, if I speak of freedom?'

'I am here,' said Edgewalker, 'to discover that for myself.'

'You can read my thoughts?' Cotillion asked in a low voice.

Baran's huge head slowly swung round to regard Edgewalker. The Hound took a single step closer to the creature.

'I possess no such omniscience,' Edgewalker calmly replied, seeming to take no notice of Baran's attention. 'Although to one such as you, it might appear so. But I have existed ages beyond your reckoning, Cotillion. All patterns are known to me, for they have been played out countless times before. Given what approaches us all, it was not hard to predict. Especially given your uncanny prescience.' The dead pits that were Edgewalker's eyes seemed to study Cotillion. 'You suspect, do you not, that dragons are at the heart of all that will come?'

Cotillion gestured at the chains. 'They reach through to the over-world presumably? And that warren is what?'

'What do you think?' Edgewalker countered.

'Try reading my mind.'

'I cannot.'

'So, you are here because you are desperate to know what I know, or even what I suspect.'

Edgewalker's silence was answer enough to that question. Cotillion smiled. 'I think I will make no effort to communicate with these dragons after all.'

'But you will, eventually,' Edgewalker replied. 'And when you do, I will be here. Thus, what does it avail you to remain silent now?'

'Well, in order to irritate you, I suppose.'

'I have existed ages beyond your—'

'So you have been irritated before, yes, I know. And will be again, without question.'

'Make your effort, Cotillion. Soon if not now. If you wish to survive what is to come.'

'All right. Provided you tell me the names of these dragons.'

A clearly grudging reply: 'As you wish—'

'And why they have been imprisoned here, and by whom.'

'That I cannot do.'

They studied each other, then Edgewalker cocked its head, and observed, 'It seems we are at an impasse, Cotillion. What is your decision?'

'Very well. I will take what I can get.'

Edgewalker faced the three dragons. 'These are of the pure blood. Eleint. Ampelas, Kalse and Eloth. Their crime was . . . ambition. It is a common enough crime.' The creature turned back to Cotillion. 'Perhaps endemic.'

In answer to that veiled judgement, Cotillion shrugged. He walked closer to the imprisoned beasts. 'I shall assume you can hear me,' he said in a low voice. 'A war is coming. Only a few years away. And it will, I suspect, draw into its fray virtually every ascendant from all the realms. I need to know, should you be freed, upon which side shall you fight.'

There was silence for a half-dozen heartbeats, then a voice rasped in Cotillion's mind. '*You come here, Usurper, in a quest for allies.*'

A second voice cut through, this one distinctly female, '*Bound by gratitude for freeing us. Were I to bargain from your position, I would be foolish to hope for loyalty, for trust.*'

'I agree,' said Cotillion, 'that that is a problem. Presumably, you will suggest I free you before we bargain.'

'*It is only fair,*' the first voice said.

'Alas, I am not that interested in being fair.'

'*You fear we will devour you?*'

'In the interest of brevity,' Cotillion said, 'and I understand that your kind delight in brevity.'

The third dragon spoke then, a heavy, deep voice: '*Freeing us first would indeed spare us the effort of then negotiating. Besides, we are hungry.*'

'What brought you to this realm?' Cotillion asked.

There was no reply.

Cotillion sighed. 'I shall be more inclined to free you – assuming I am able – if I have reason to believe your imprisonment was unjust.'

The female dragon asked, '*And you presume to make that decision?*'

'This hardly seems the right moment to be cantankerous,' he replied in exasperation. 'The last person who made that judgement clearly did not find in favour of you, and was able to do something about it. I would have thought that all these centuries in chains might have led you three to re-evaluate your motivations. But it seems your only regret is that you were unequal to the last entity that presumed to judge you.'

'Yes,' she said, '*that is a regret. But it is not our only one.*'

'All right. Let's hear some of the others.'

'*That the Tiste Andii who invaded this realm were so thorough in their destruction,*' the third dragon said, '*and so absolute in their insistence that the throne remain unclaimed.*'

Cotillion drew a slow, long breath. He glanced back at Edgewalker, but the apparition said nothing. 'And what,' he asked the dragons, 'so spurred their zeal?'

'*Vengeance, of course. And Anomandaris.*'

'Ah, I think I can now assume I know who imprisoned the three of you.'

'*He very nearly killed us,*' said the female dragon. '*An over-reaction on his part. After all, better Eleint on the Throne of Shadow than another Tiste Edur, or worse, a usurper.*'

'And how would Eleint *not* be usurpers?'

'*Your pedantry does not impress us.*'

'Was all this before or after the Sundering of the Realm?'

'*Such distinctions are meaningless. The Sundering continues to this day, and as for the forces that conspired to trigger the dread event, those were many and varied. Like a pack of enkar'al closing on a wounded drypthara. What is vulnerable attracts . . . feeders.*'

'Thus,' said Cotillion, 'if freed, you would once again seek the Shadow Throne. Only this time, someone occupies that throne.'

'*The veracity of that claim is subject to debate,*' the female dragon said.

'*A matter,*' added the first dragon, '*of semantics. Shadows cast by shadows.*'

'You believe that Ammanas is sitting on the wrong Shadow Throne.'

'*The true throne is not even in this fragment of Emurlahn.*'

Cotillion crossed his arms and smiled. 'And is Ammanas?'

The dragons said nothing, and he sensed, with great satisfaction, their sudden disquiet.

'That, Cotillion,' said Edgewalker behind him, 'is a curious distinction. Or are you simply being disingenuous?'

'That I cannot tell you,' Cotillion said, with a faint smile.

The female dragon spoke, '*I am Eloth, Mistress of Illusions – Meanas to you – and Mockra and Thyr. A Shaper of the Blood. All that K'rul asked of me, I have done. And now you presume to question my loyalty?*'

'Ah,' Cotillion said, nodding, 'then I take it you are aware of the impending war. Are you also aware of the rumours of K'rul's return?'

'*His blood is growing sickly,*' said the third dragon. '*I am Ampelas, who shaped the Blood in the paths of Emurlahn. The sorcery wielded by the Tiste Edur was born of my will – do you now understand, Usurper?'*

'That dragons are prone to grandiose claims and sententiousness? Yes, I do indeed understand, Ampelas. And I should now presume that for each of the warrens, Elder and new, there is a corresponding dragon? You are the *flavours* of K'rul's blood? What of the Soletaken dragons, such as Anomandaris and, more relevantly, Scabandari Bloodeye?'

'*We are surprised,*' said the first dragon after a moment, '*that you know that name.*'

'Because you killed him so long ago?'

'*A poor guess, Usurper, poorer for that you have revealed the extent of your ignorance. No, we did not kill him. In any case, his soul remains alive, although tormented. The one whose fist shattered his skull and so destroyed his body holds no allegiance to us, nor, we suspect, to anyone but herself.*'

'You are Kalse, then,' Cotillion said. 'And what path do you claim?'

'*I leave the grandiose claims to my kin. I have no need to impress you, Usurper. Furthermore, I delight in discovering how little you comprehend.*'

Cotillion shrugged. 'I was asking about the Soletaken. Scabandari, Anomandaris, Osserc, Olar Ethil, Draconus—'

Edgewalker spoke behind him: 'Cotillion, surely you have surmised by now that these three dragons sought the Shadow Throne for honourable reasons?'

'To heal Emurlahn, yes, Edgewalker, I understand that.'

'And is that not what you seek as well?'

Cotillion turned to regard the creature. 'Is it?'

Edgewalker seemed taken aback for a moment, then, head cocking slightly, it said, 'It is not the healing that concerns you, it is who will be sitting on the Throne afterwards.'

'As I understand things,' Cotillion replied, 'once these dragons did what K'rul asked of them, they were compelled to return to Starvald Demelain. As the sources of sorcery, they could not be permitted to interfere or remain active across the realms, lest sorcery cease to be predictable, which in turn would feed Chaos – the eternal enemy in this grand scheme. But the Soletaken proved a problem. They possessed the blood of Tiam, and with it the vast power of the Eleint. Yet, they could travel as they pleased. They could interfere, and they did. For obvious reasons. Scabandari was originally Edur, and so he became their champion—'

'*After murdering the royal line of the Edur!*' Eloth said in a hiss. '*After spilling draconean blood in the heart of Kurald Emurlahn! After*

52

opening the first, fatal wound upon that warren! What did he think gates were?'

'The Tiste Andii for Anomandaris,' Cotillion continued. 'Tiste Liosan for Osserc. The T'lan Imass for Olar Ethil. These connections and the loyalties born of them are obvious. Draconus is more of a mystery, of course, since he has been gone a long time—'

'The most reviled of them all!' Eloth shrieked, the voice filling Cotillion's skull so that he winced.

Stepping back, he raised a hand. 'Spare me, please. I am not really interested in all that, to be honest. Apart from discovering if there was enmity between Eleint and Soletaken. It seems there is, with the possible exception of Silanah—'

'Seduced by Anomandaris's charms,' snapped Eloth. *'And Olar Ethil's endless pleadings . . .'*

'To bring fire to the world of the Imass,' Cotillion said. 'For that is her aspect, is it not? Thyr?'

Ampelas observed, *'He is not so uncomprehending as you believed, Kalse.'*

'Then again,' Cotillion continued, 'you too claim Thyr, Eloth. Ah, that was clever of K'rul, forcing you to share power.'

'Unlike Tiam,' Ampelas said, *'when we're killed we stay dead.'*

'Which brings me to what I truly need to understand. The Elder Gods. They are not simply of one world, are they?'

'Of course not.'

'And how long have they been around?'

'Even when Darkness ruled alone,' Ampelas replied, *'there were elemental forces. Moving unseen until the coming of Light. Bound only to their own laws. It is the nature of Darkness that it but rules itself.'*

'And is the Crippled God an Elder?'

Silence.

Cotillion found he was holding his breath. He had taken a twisted path to this question, and had made discoveries along the way – so much to think about, in fact, that his mind was numb, besieged by all that he had learned. 'I need to know,' he said in a slow release of his breath.

'Why?' Edgewalker asked.

'If he is,' Cotillion said, 'then another question follows. How does one kill an elemental force?'

'You would shatter the balance?'

'It's already been shattered, Edgewalker! That god was brought down to the surface of a world. And chained. His power torn apart and secreted in minuscule, virtually lifeless warrens, but all of them linked to the world I came from—'

'*Too bad for that world,*' Ampelas said.

The smug disregard in that reply stung Cotillion. He breathed deep and remained silent, until the anger passed. Then he faced the dragons again. 'And from that world, Ampelas, he is poisoning the warrens. Every warren. Are you capable of fighting that?'

'*Were we freed—*'

'Were you freed,' Cotillion said, with a hard smile, 'you would resume your original purpose, and there would be more draconean blood spilled in the Realm of Shadow.'

'*And you and your fellow usurper believe you are capable of that?*'

'You as much as admitted it,' Cotillion said. 'You can be killed, and when you have been killed, you stay dead. It is no wonder Anomandaris chained the three of you. In obstinate stupidity you have no equals—'

'*A sundered realm is the weakest realm of all! Why do you think the Crippled God is working through it?*'

'Thank you,' said Cotillion to Ampelas in a quiet tone. 'That is what I needed to know.' He turned away and began walking back down the approach.

'*Wait!*'

'We will speak again, Ampelas,' he said over a shoulder, 'before it all goes to the Abyss.'

Edgewalker followed.

As soon as they were clear of the ring of stones, the creature spoke: 'I must chide myself. I have underestimated you, Cotillion.'

'It's a common enough mistake.'

'What will you do now?'

'Why should I tell you?'

Edgewalker did not immediately reply. They continued down the slope, strode out onto the plain. 'You should tell me,' the apparition finally said, 'because I might be inclined to give you assistance.'

'That would mean more to me if I knew who – what – you are.'

'You may consider me . . . an elemental force.'

A dull chill seeped through Cotillion. 'I see. All right, Edgewalker. It appears that the Crippled God has launched an offensive on multiple fronts. The First Throne of the T'lan Imass and the Throne of Shadow are the ones that concern us the most, for obvious reasons. In these two, we feel we are fighting alone – we cannot even rely upon the Hounds, given the mastery the Tiste Edur seem to hold over them. We need allies, Edgewalker, and we need them now.'

'You have just walked away from three such allies—'

'Allies who won't rip our heads off once the threat's been negated.'

'Ah, there is that. Very well, Cotillion, I will give the matter some consideration.'

'Take your time.'

'That seems a contrary notion.'

'If one is lacking a grasp of sarcasm, I imagine it does at that.'

'You do interest me, Cotillion. And that is a rare thing.'

'I know. You have existed longer . . .' Cotillion's words died away. *An elemental force. I guess he has at that. Dammit.*

There were so many ways of seeing this dreadful need, the vast conspiracy of motivations from which all shades and casts of morality could be culled, that Mappo Runt was left feeling overwhelmed, from which only sorrow streamed down, pure and chilled, into his thoughts. Beneath the coarse skin of his hands, he could feel the night's memory slowly fading from the stone, and soon this rock would know the assault of the sun's heat – this pitted, root-tracked underbelly that had not faced the sun in countless millennia.

He had been turning over stones. Six since dawn. Roughly chiselled dolomite slabs, and beneath each one he had found a scatter of broken bones. Small bones, fossilized, and though in countless pieces after the interminable crushing weight of the stone, the skeletons were, as far as Mappo could determine, complete.

There were, had been, and would always be, all manner of wars. He knew that, in all the seared, scar-hardened places in his soul, so there was no shock in his discovery of these long-dead Jaghut children. And horror had run a mercifully swift passage through his thoughts, leaving at the last his old friend, sorrow.

Streaming down, pure and chilled.

Wars in which soldier fought soldier, sorceror clashed with sorceror. Assassins squared off, knife-blades flickering in the night. Wars in which the lawful battled the wilfully unlawful; in which the sane stood against the sociopath. He had seen crystals growing up in a single night from the desert floor, facet after facet revealed like the petals of an opening flower, and it seemed to him that brutality behaved in a like manner. One incident leading to another, until a conflagration burgeoned, swallowing everyone in its path.

Mappo lifted his hands from the slab's exposed underside and slowly straightened. To look over at his companion, still wading the warm shallows of the Raraku Sea. Like a child unfolding to a new, unexpected pleasure. Splashing about, running his hands through the reeds that had appeared as if remembered into existence by the sea itself.

Icarium.

My crystal.

When the conflagration consumed children, then the distinction between the sane and the sociopath ceased to exist. It was his flaw, he well knew, to yearn to seek the truth of every side, to comprehend the myriad justifications for committing the most brutal crimes. Imass had been enslaved by deceitful Jaghut tyrants, led down paths of false worship, made to do unspeakable things. Until they had uncovered the deceivers. Unleashing vengeance, first against the tyrants, then against all Jaghut. And so the crystal grew, facet after facet . . .

Until this . . . He glanced down once more upon the child's bones. Pinned beneath dolomite slabs. Not limestone, for dolomite provided a good surface for carving glyphs, and though soft, it absorbed power, making it slower to erode than raw limestone, and so it held those glyphs, faded and soft-edged after all these thousands of years to be sure, but discernible still.

The power of those wards persisted, long after the creature imprisoned by them had died.

Dolomite was said to hold memories. A belief among Mappo's own people, at least, who in their wanderings had encountered such Imass edifices, the impromptu tombs, the sacred circles, the sight-stones on hill summits – encountered, and then studiously avoided. For the hauntings in these places was a palpable thing.

Or so we managed to convince ourselves.

He sat here, on the edge of Raraku Sea, in the place of an ancient crime, and beyond what his own thoughts conjured, there was nothing. The stone he had set his hands upon seemed possessed of the shortest of memories. The cold of darkness, the heat of the sun. That, and nothing more.

The shortest of memories.

Splashing, and Icarium was striding up onto the shoreline, his eyes bright with pleasure. 'Such a worthy boon, yes, Mappo? I am enlivened by these waters. Oh, why will you not swim and so be blessed by Raraku's gift?'

Mappo smiled. 'Said blessing would quickly wash off this old hide, my friend. I fear the gift would be wasted, and so will not risk disappointing the awakened spirits.'

'I feel,' Icarium said, 'as if the quest begins anew. I will finally discover the truth. Who I am. All that I have done. I will discover, too,' he added as he approached, 'the reason for your friendship – that you should always be found at my side, though I lose myself again and again. Ah, I fear I have offended you – no, please, do not look so glum. It is only that I cannot understand why you have sacrificed yourself so. As far as friendships go, this must be a most frustrating one for you.'

'No, Icarium, there is no sacrifice involved. Nor frustration. This is what we are, and this is what we do. That is all.'

Icarium sighed and turned to look out over the new sea. 'If only I could be as restful of thought as you, Mappo . . .'

'Children have died here.'

The Jhag swung round, his green eyes studying the ground behind the Trell. 'I saw you pitching rocks. Yes, I see them. Who were they?'

Some nightmare the night before had scoured away Icarium's memories. This had been happening more often of late. Troubling. And . . . crushing. 'Jaghut. From the wars with the T'lan Imass.'

'A terrible thing to have done,' Icarium said. The sun was fast drying the water beaded on his hairless, green-grey skin. 'How is it that mortals can be so cavalier with life? Look at this freshwater sea, Mappo. The new shoreline burgeons with sudden life. Birds, and insects, and all the new plants, there is so much joy revealed, my friend, that my heart feels moments from bursting.'

'Infinite wars,' Mappo said. 'Life's struggles, each trying to push the other aside, and so win out.'

'You are grim company this morning, Mappo.'

'Aye, I am at that. I am sorry, Icarium.'

'Shall we remain here for a time?'

Mappo studied his friend. Bereft of his upper garments, he looked more savage, more barbaric than usual. The dye with which he had disguised the colour of his skin had mostly faded away. 'As you like. This journey is yours, after all.'

'Knowledge is returning,' Icarium said, eyes still on the sea. 'Raraku's gift. We were witness to the rise of the waters, here on this west shore. Further west, then, there will be a river, and many cities—'

Mappo's gaze narrowed. 'Only one, now, to speak of,' he said.

'Only one?'

'The others died thousands of years ago, Icarium.'

'N'karaphal? Trebur? Inath'an Merusin? Gone?'

'Inath'an Merusin is now called Mersin. It is the last of the great cities lining the river.'

'But there were so many, Mappo. I recall all their names. Vinith, Hedori Kwil, Tramara . . .'

'All practising intensive irrigation, drawing the river's waters out onto the plains. All clearing forests to build their ships. Those cities are dead now, my friend. And the river, its waters once so clear and sweet, is now heavy with silts and much diminished. The plains have lost their topsoil, becoming the Lato Odhan to the east of the Mersin River, and Ugarat Odhan to the west.'

Icarium slowly raised his hands, set them against his temples, and closed his eyes. 'That long, Mappo?' he asked in a frail whisper.

'Perhaps the sea has triggered such memories. For it was indeed a sea

57

back then, freshwater for the most part, although there was seepage through the limestone escarpment from Longshan Bay – that vast barrier was rotting through, as it will do again, I imagine, assuming this sea reaches as far north as it once did.'

'The First Empire?'

'It was falling even then. There was no recovery.' Mappo hesitated, seeing how his words had wounded his friend. 'But the people returned to this land, Icarium. Seven Cities – yes, the name derives from old remembrances. New cities have grown from the ancient rubble. We are only forty leagues from one right now. Lato Revae. It is on the coast—'

Icarium turned away suddenly. 'No,' he said. 'I am not yet ready to leave, to cross any oceans. This land holds secrets – my secrets, Mappo. Perhaps the antiquity of my memories will prove advantageous. The lands of my mindscape are the lands of my own past, after all, and they might well yield truths. We shall walk those ancient roads.'

The Trell nodded. 'I will break camp, then.'

'Trebur.'

Mappo turned, waited with growing dread.

Icarium's eyes were fixed on him now, the vertical pupils narrowed to black slivers by the bright sunlight. 'I have memories of Trebur. I spent time there, in the City of Domes. I did something. An important thing.' He frowned. 'I did . . . something.'

'It is an arduous journey ahead of us, then,' Mappo said. 'Three, maybe four days to the edge of the Thalas Mountains. Ten more at the least to reach the Mersin River's Wend. The channel has moved from the site of ancient Trebur. A day's travel west of the river, then, and we will find those ruins.'

'Will there be villages and such on our route?'

Mappo shook his head. 'These Odhans are virtually lifeless now, Icarium. Occasionally, Vedanik tribes venture down from the Thalas Mountains, but not at this time of year. Keep your bow at the ready – there are antelope and hares and drolig.'

'Waterholes, then?'

'I know them,' Mappo said.

Icarium walked over to his gear. 'We have done this before, haven't we?'

Yes. 'Not for a long while, my friend.' *Almost eighty years, in fact. But the last time, we stumbled onto it – you remembered nothing. This time, I fear, it will be different.*

Icarium paused, the horn-rimmed bow in his hands, and looked over at Mappo. 'You are so patient with me,' he said, with a faint, sad smile, 'whilst I wander, ever lost.'

Mappo shrugged. 'It is what we do.'

The Path'Apur Mountains rimmed the far horizon to the south. It had been almost a week since they had left the city of Pan'potsun, and with each day the number of villages they passed through had dwindled, whilst the distance between them lengthened. Their pace was torturously slow, but that was to be expected, travelling on foot as they did, and with a man in their company who had seemingly lost his mind.

Sun-darkened skin almost olive beneath the dust, the demon Greyfrog clambered onto the boulder and squatted at Cutter's side.

'*Declaration. It is said that the wasps of the desert guard gems and such. Query. Has Cutter heard such tales? Anticipatory pause.*'

'Sounds more like someone's bad idea of a joke,' Cutter replied. Below them was a flat clearing surrounded by massive rock out-croppings. It was the place of their camp. Scillara and Felisin Younger sat in view, tending the makeshift hearth. The madman was nowhere to be seen. Off wandering again, Cutter surmised. Holding conversations with ghosts, or, perhaps more likely, the voices in his head. Oh, Heboric carried curses, the barbs of a tiger on his skin, the benediction of a god of war, and those voices in his head might well be real. Even so, break a man's spirit enough times . . .

'*Belated observation. Grubs, there in the dark reaches of the nest. Nest? Bemused. Hive? Nest.*'

Frowning, Cutter glanced over at the demon. Its flat, hairless head and broad, four-eyed face were lumpy and swollen with wasp stings. 'You didn't. You did.'

'*Irate is their common state, I now believe. Breaking open their cave made them more so. We clashed in buzzing disagreement. I fared the worse, I think.*'

'Black wasps?'

'*Tilt head, query. Black? Dreaded reply, why yes, they were. Black. Rhetorical, was that significant?*'

'Be glad you're a demon,' Cutter said. 'Two or three stings from those will kill a grown man. Ten will kill a horse.'

'*A horse – we had those – you had them. I was forced to run. Horse. Large four-legged animal. Succulent meat.*'

'People tend to ride them,' Cutter said. 'Until they drop. Then we eat them.'

'*Multiple uses, excellent and unwasteful. Did we eat yours? Where can we find more such creatures?*'

'We have not the money to purchase them, Greyfrog. And we sold ours for food and supplies in Pan'potsun.'

'*Obstinate reasonableness. No money. Then we should take, my*' *young friend. And so hasten this journey to its much-awaited conclusion. Latter tone indicating mild despair.'*

'Still no word from L'oric?'

'Worriedly. No. My brother is silent.'

Neither spoke for a time. The demon was picking the serrated edges of its lips, where, Cutter saw upon a closer look, grey flecks and crushed wasps were snagged. Greyfrog had eaten the wasp nest. No wonder the wasps had been irate. Cutter rubbed at his face. He needed a shave. And a bath. And clean, new clothes.

And a purpose in life. Once, long ago, when he had been Crokus Younghand of Darujhistan, his uncle had begun preparing the way for a reformed Crokus. A youth of the noble courts, a figure of promise, a figure inviting to the young, wealthy, pampered women of the city. A short-lived ambition, in every way. His uncle dead, and dead, too, Crokus Younghand. No heap of ashes left to stir.

What I was is not what I am. Two men, identical faces, but different eyes. In what they have seen, in what they reflect upon the world.

'Bitter taste,' Greyfrog said in his mind, long tongue slithering out to collect the last fragments. A heavy, gusty sigh. *'Yet oh so filling. Query. Can one burst from what one has inside?'*

I hope not. 'We'd best find Heboric, if we are to make use of this day.'

'Noted earlier. Ghost Hands was exploring the rocks above. The scent of a trail led him onward and upward.'

'A trail?'

'Water. He sought the source of the spring we see pooling below near the fleshy women who, said jealously, so adore you.'

Cutter straightened. 'They don't seem so fleshy to me, Greyfrog.'

'Curious. Mounds of flesh, water storage vessels, there on the hips and behind. On the chest—'

'All right. That kind of fleshy. You are too much the carnivore, demon.'

'Yes. Fullest delicious agreement. Shall I go find Ghost Hands?'

'No, I will. I think those riders who passed us yesterday on the track are not as far away as they should be, and I would be relieved to know you are guarding Scillara and Felisin.'

'None shall take them away,' Greyfrog said.

Cutter looked down at the squatting demon. 'Scillara and Felisin are not horses.'

Greyfrog's large eyes blinked slowly, first the two side-by-side, then the pair above and below. Tongue darted. *'Blithe. Of course not. Insufficient number of legs, worthily observed.'*

Cutter edged to the back of the boulder, then leapt across to another one tucked deeper into the talus-heaped cliff-side. He grasped a ledge and pulled himself up. Little different from climbing a balcony, or an estate wall. *Adore me, do they?* He had trouble believing that. Easier to rest eyes upon, he imagined, than an old man and a demon, but that was not adoration. He could make no sense of those two women. Bickering like sisters, competing over everything in sight, and over things Cutter couldn't see or comprehend. At other times, unaccountably close, as if sharing a secret. Both fussed over Heboric Ghost Hands, Destriant of Treach.

Maybe war needs nurturers. Maybe the god is happy with this. The priest needs acolytes, after all. That might have been expected with Scillara, since Heboric had drawn her out of a nightmarish existence, and indeed had healed her in some as-yet unspecified way – if Cutter had surmised correctly from the meagre comments overheard now and then. Scillara had a lot to be grateful for. And for Felisin, there had been something about revenge, delivered to her satisfaction against someone who had done her a terrible wrong. It was complicated. *So, a moment's thought, and it's obvious they do possess secrets. Too many of them. Oh, what do I care? Women are nothing but a mass of contradictions surrounded by deadly pitfalls. Approach at your own risk. Better yet, approach not at all.*

He reached a chimney in the cliff-side and began working his way up it. Water trickled down vertical cracks in the rock. Flies and other winged insects swarmed him; the corners of the chimney were thickly webbed by opportunistic spiders. By the time he climbed free of it, he had been thoroughly bitten and was covered in thick, dusty strands. He paused to brush himself off, then looked around. A rough trail continued upward, winding between collapsed shelves of stone. He headed up the path.

At their meandering, desultory pace, they were months from the coast, as far as he could determine. Once there, they would have to find a boat to take them across to Otataral Island. A forbidden journey, and Malazan ships patrolled those waters diligently – or at least they did before the uprising. It might be that they were yet to fully reorganize such things.

They would begin the passage at night, in any case.

Heboric had to return something. Something found on the island. It was all very vague. And for some reason Cotillion had wanted Cutter to accompany the Destriant. Or, rather, to protect Felisin Younger. *A path to take, when before there had been none.* Even so, it was not the best of motivations. A flight from despair was pathetic, especially since it could not succeed.

Adore me, do they? What is here to adore?

A voice ahead: 'All that is mysterious is as a lure to the curious. I hear your steps, Cutter. Come, see this spider.'

Cutter stepped round an outcrop and saw Heboric, kneeling beside a stunted scrub oak.

'And where there is pain and vulnerability bound into the lure, it becomes all the more attractive. See this spider? Below this branch, yes? Trembling on its web, one leg dismembered, thrashing about as if in pain. Its quarry, you see, is not flies, or moths. Oh no, what she hunts is fellow spiders.'

'Who care nothing for pain or mystery, Heboric,' Cutter said, crouching down to study the creature. The size of a child's hand. 'That's not one of its legs. It's a prop.'

'You are assuming other spiders can count. She knows better.'

'All very interesting,' Cutter said, straightening, 'but we must get going.'

'We're all watching this play out,' Heboric said, leaning back and studying the strangely pulsing, taloned hands that flitted in and out of existence at the ends of his wrists.

We? Oh, yes, you and your invisible friends. 'I wouldn't think there'd be many ghosts in these hills.'

'Then you would be wrong. Hill tribes. Endless warfare – it's those who fall in battle that I see, only those who fall in battle.' The hands flexed. 'The mouth of the spring is just ahead. They fought over control of it.' His toad-like features twisted. 'There's always a reason, or reasons. Always.'

Cutter sighed, studied the sky. 'I know, Heboric.'

'Knowing means nothing.'

'I know that, too.'

Heboric rose. 'Treach's greatest comfort, understanding that there are infinite reasons for waging war.'

'And are you comforted by that, too?'

The Destriant smiled. 'Come. That demon who speaks in our heads is obsessing about flesh at the moment, with watering mouth.'

They made their way down the trail. 'He won't eat them.'

'I am not convinced that is the nature of his appetite.'

Cutter snorted. 'Heboric, Greyfrog is a four-handed, four-eyed, over-sized toad.'

'With a surprisingly boundless imagination. Tell me, how much do you know of him?'

'Less than you.'

'It has not occurred to me, until now,' Heboric said, as he led Cutter onto a path offering a less precarious climb – but more roundabout – than the one the Daru had used, 'that we know virtually nothing

62

of who Greyfrog was, and what he did, back in his home realm.'

This was proving an unusually long lucid episode for Heboric. Cutter wondered if something had changed – he hoped it would stay this way. 'Then we could ask him.'

'I shall.'

In the camp, Scillara kicked sand over the few remaining coals of the cookfire. She walked over to her pack and sat down, settling her back against it as she pushed more rustleaf into her pipe and drew hard until smoke streamed from it. Across from her, Greyfrog squatted in front of Felisin, making strange whimpering sounds.

She had seen so little for so long. Drugged insensate by durhang, filled with infantile thoughts by her old master, Bidithal. And now she was free, and still wide-eyed with the complexities of the world. The demon lusted after Felisin, she believed. Either to mate with or to devour – it was hard to tell. While Felisin regarded Greyfrog as if it was a dog better to stroke than kick. Which might in turn be giving the demon the wrong notions.

It spoke with the others in their minds, but had yet to do so with Scillara. Out of courtesy to her, the ones the demon addressed replied out loud, although of course they did not have to – and perhaps didn't more often than not. There was no way for Scillara to tell. She wondered why she had been set apart – what did Greyfrog see within her that so affected its apparent loquaciousness?

Well, poisons do linger. I may be . . . unpalatable. In her old life, she might have felt some resentment, or suspicion, assuming she felt any-thing at all. But now, it appeared to her that she didn't much care. Something had taken shape within her, and it was self-contained and, oddly enough, self-assured.

Perhaps that came with being pregnant. Just beginning to show, and that would only get worse. And this time there would be no alchemies to scour the seed out of her. Although other means were possible, of course. She was undecided on whether to keep the child, whose father was probably Korbolo Dom but could have been one of his officers, or someone else. Not that that mattered, since whoever he had been he was probably dead now, a thought that pleased her.

The constant nausea was wearying, although the rustleaf helped. There was the ache in her breasts, and the weight of them made her back ache, and that was unpleasant. Her appetite had burgeoned, and she was getting heavier, especially on the hips. The others had simply assumed that such changes were coming with her returning health – she hadn't coughed in over a week, and all this walking had strengthened her legs – and she did not disabuse them of their assumptions.

A child. What would she do with it? What would it expect of her? What was it mothers did anyway? *Sell their babies, mostly. To temples, to slavers, to the harem merchants if it's a girl. Or keep it and teach it to beg. Steal. Sell its body.* This, born of sketchy observations and the stories told by the waifs of Sha'ik's encampment. Meaning, a child was an investment of sorts, which made sense. A return on nine months of misery and discomfort.

She supposed she could do something like that. Sell it. Assuming she let it live that long.

It was a dilemma indeed, but she had plenty of time to think on it. To make her decision.

Greyfrog's head twisted round, looking past Scillara's position. She turned to see four men emerge and halt at the edge of the clearing. The fourth one was leading horses. The riders who had passed them yesterday. One was carrying a loaded crossbow, the weapon trained on the demon.

'Be sure,' the man said in a growl to Felisin, 'that you keep that damned thing away from us.'

The man on his right laughed. 'A four-eyed dog. Yes, woman, get a leash on it . . . now. We don't want any blood spilled. Well,' he added, 'not much.'

'Where are the two men you were with?' the man with the crossbow asked.

Scillara set down her pipe. 'Not here,' she said, rising and tugging at her tunic. 'Just do what you've come here to do and then leave.'

'Now that's accommodating. You, with the dog, are you going to be as nice as your friend here?'

Felisin said nothing. She had gone white.

'Never mind her,' Scillara said. 'I'm enough for all of you.'

'But maybe you ain't enough, as far as we're concerned,' the man said, smiling.

It wasn't even an ugly smile, she decided. She could do this. 'I plan on surprising you, then.'

The man handed the crossbow over to one of his comrades and unclasped the belt of his telaba. 'We'll see about that. Guthrim, if that dog-thing moves, kill it.'

'It's a lot bigger than most dogs I've seen,' Guthrim replied.

'Quarrel's poisoned, remember? Black wasp.'

'Maybe I should just kill it now.'

The other man hesitated, then nodded. 'Go ahead.'

The crossbow thudded.

Greyfrog's right hand intercepted the quarrel, plucking it out of the air, then the demon studied it, and slithered out its tongue to lick the poison.

'The Seven take me!' Guthrim whispered in disbelief.

'Oh,' Scillara said to Greyfrog, 'don't make a mess of this. There's no problem here—'

'He disagrees,' Felisin said, her voice thin with fear.

'Well, convince him otherwise.' *I can do this. Just like it was before. Doesn't matter, they're just men.*

'I can't, Scillara.'

Guthrim was reloading the crossbow, whilst the first man and the one not holding the reins of the horses both drew scimitars.

Greyfrog bounded forward, appallingly fast, and leapt upward, mouth opening wide. That mouth clamped onto Guthrim's head. The demon's lower jaw slipped out from its hinges and the man's head disappeared. Greyfrog's momentum and weight toppled him. Horrific crunching sounds, Guthrim's body spasming, spraying fluids, then sagging limp.

Greyfrog's jaws closed with a scraping, then snapping sound, then the demon clambered away, leaving behind a headless corpse.

The remaining three men had stared in shock during this demonstration. But now they acted. The first one cried out, a strangled, terror-filled sound, and rushed forward, raising his scimitar.

Spitting out a mangled, crushed mess of hair and bone, Greyfrog jumped to meet him. One hand caught the man's sword-arm, twisted hard until the elbow popped, flesh tore, and blood spurted. Another hand closed on his throat and squeezed, crushing cartilage. The man's scream never reached the air. Eyes bulging, face rushing to a shade of dark grey, tongue jutting like some macabre creature trying to climb free, he collapsed beneath the demon. A third hand held the other arm. Greyfrog used the fourth one to reach back and scratch itself.

The remaining swordsman fled to where the fourth man was already scrabbling onto his horse.

Greyfrog leapt again. A fist cracked against the back of the swordsman's head, punching the bone inward. He sprawled, weapon flying. The demon's charge caught the last man with one leg in the stirrup.

The horse shied away with a squeal, and Greyfrog dragged the man down, then bit his face.

A moment later this man's head vanished into the demon's maw as had the first one. More crunching sounds, more twitching kicks, grasping hands. Then, merciful death.

The demon spat out shattered bone still held in place by the scalp. It fell in such a way that Scillara found herself looking at the man's face

– no flesh, no eyes, just the skin, puckered and bruised. She stared at it a moment longer, then forced herself to look away.

At Felisin, who had backed up as far as she could against the stone wall, knees drawn up, hands covering her eyes.

'It's done,' Scillara said. 'Felisin, it's over.'

The hands lowered, revealing an expression of terror and revulsion.

Greyfrog was dragging bodies away, round behind a mass of boulders, moving with haste. Ignoring the demon for the moment, Scillara walked over to crouch in front of Felisin. 'It would have been easier my way,' she said. 'At least a lot less messy.'

Felisin stared at her. 'He sucked out their brains.'

'I could see that.'

'Delicious, he said.'

'He's a demon, Felisin. Not a dog, not a pet. A demon.'

'Yes.' The word was whispered.

'And now we know what he can do.'

A mute nod.

'So,' Scillara said quietly, 'don't get too friendly.' She straightened, and saw Cutter and Heboric clambering down from the ridge.

'Triumph and pride! We have horses!'

Cutter slowed. 'We heard a scream—'

'Horses,' Heboric said as he walked towards the skittish animals. 'That's a bit of luck.'

'Innocent. Scream? No, friend Cutter. Was Greyfrog . . . breaking wind.'

'Really. And did these horses just wander up to you?'

'Bold. Yes! Most curious!'

Cutter headed over to study some odd stains in the scuffled dust. Greyfrog's palm-prints were evident in the effort to clean up the mess. 'Some blood here . . .'

'Shock, dismay . . . remorse.'

'Remorse. At what happened here, or at being found out?'

'Sly. Why, the former, of course, friend Cutter.'

Grimacing, Cutter glanced over at Scillara and Felisin, studied their expressions. 'I think,' he said slowly, 'that I am glad I was not here to see what you two saw.'

'Yes,' Scillara replied. 'You should be.'

'Best keep your distance from these beasts, Greyfrog,' Heboric called out. 'They may not like me, much, but they *really* don't like you.'

'Confident. They just don't know me yet.'

*

'I wouldn't feed this to a rat,' Smiles said, picking desultorily at the fragments of meat on the tin plate resting in her lap. 'Look, even the flies are avoiding it.'

'It's not the food they're avoiding,' Koryk said. 'It's you.'

She sneered across at him. 'That's called respect. A foreign word to you, I know. Seti are just failed Wickans. Everybody knows that. And you, you're a failed Seti.' She took her plate and sent it skidding across the sand towards Koryk. 'Here, stick it in your half-blood ears and save it for later.'

'She's so sweet after a day's hard riding,' Koryk said to Tarr, with a broad, white smile.

'Keep baiting her,' the corporal replied, 'and you'll probably regret it.' He too was eyeing what passed for supper on his plate, his normally placid expression wrinkling into a slight scowl. 'It's horse, I'm sure of it.'

'Dug up from some horse cemetery,' Smiles said, stretching out her legs. 'I'd kill for some grease-fish, baked in clay over coals down on the beach. Yellow-spiced, weed-wrapped. A jug of Meskeri wine and some worthy lad from the inland village. A farm-boy, big—'

'Hood's litany, enough!' Koryk leaned forward and spat into the fire. 'You rounding up some pig-swiller with fluff on his chin is the only story you know, that much is obvious. Dammit, Smiles, we've heard it all a thousand times. You crawling out of Father's estate at night to get your hands and knees wet down on the beach. Where was all this again? Oh, right, little-girl dream-land, I'd forgotten—'

A knife thudded into Koryk's right calf. Bellowing, he scrambled back, then sank down to clutch at his leg.

Soldiers from nearby squads looked over, squinting through the dust that suffused the entire camp. A moment's curiosity, quickly fading.

As Koryk loosed a stream of indignant curses, both hands trying to stem the bleeding, Bottle sighed and rose from where he sat. 'See what happens when the old men leave us to play on our own? Hold still, Koryk,' he said as he approached. 'I'll get you mended – won't take long—'

'Make it soon,' the half-blood Seti said in a growl, 'so I can slit that bitch's throat.'

Bottle glanced over at the woman, then leaned in close to Koryk. 'Easy. She's looking a little pale. A bad throw—'

'Oh, and what *was* she aiming at?'

Corporal Tarr climbed to his feet. 'Strings won't be happy with you, Smiles,' he said, shaking his head.

'He moved his leg—'

'And you threw a knife at him.'

'It was that little-girl thing. I was provoked.'

'Never mind how it started. You might try apologizing – maybe Koryk will leave it at that—'

'Sure,' Koryk said. 'The day Hood climbs into his own grave.'

'Bottle, you stopped the bleeding yet?'

'Pretty much, Corporal.' Bottle tossed the knife over towards Smiles. It landed at her feet, the blade slick.

'Thanks, Bottle,' Koryk said. 'Now she can try again.'

The knife thudded into the ground between the half-blood's boots.

All eyes snapped to stare at Smiles.

Bottle licked his lips. That damned thing had come all too close to his left hand.

'That's where I was aiming,' Smiles said.

'What did I tell you?' Koryk asked, his voice strangely high.

Bottle drew a deep breath to slow his pounding heart.

Tarr walked over and pulled the knife from the ground. 'I'll keep this for a while, I think.'

'I don't care,' Smiles said. 'I got plenty more.'

'And you will keep them sheathed.'

'Aye, Corporal. So long as no-one provokes me.'

'She's insane,' Koryk muttered.

'She's not insane,' Bottle replied. 'Just lonely for . . .'

'Some farm-boy from the inland village,' Koryk finished, grinning.

'Probably a cousin,' Bottle added, low so that only Koryk heard.

The man laughed.

There. Bottle sighed. Another hairy moment on this endless march passed by, with only a little blood spilled. The Fourteenth Army was tired. Miserable. It didn't like itself, much. Deprived of delivering fullest vengeance upon Sha'ik and the murderers, rapists and cut-throats who followed her, and now in slow pursuit of the last remnant of that rebel army, along crumbling, dusty roads in a parched land, through sand-storms and worse, the Fourteenth still waited for a resolution. It wanted blood, but so far most of the blood spilled had been its own, as altercations turned into feuds and things got ugly.

The Fists were doing their best to keep things under control, but they were as worn down as everyone else. It didn't help that there were very few captains worthy of the rank in the companies.

And we don't have one at all, now that Keneb got moved. There was the rumour of a new contingent of recruits and officers disembarking at Lato Revae and now somewhere behind them, hurrying to catch up, but that rumour had begun ten days ago. The fools should have caught them by now.

Messengers had been coming and going in the last two days, pelting along the track from their wake, then back again. Dujek Onearm and the Adjunct were doing a lot of talking, that much was clear. What wasn't was what they were talking about. Bottle had thought about eavesdropping on the command tent and its occupants, as he had done many times before, between Aren and Raraku, but the presence of Quick Ben made him nervous. A High Mage. If Quick turned over a rock and found Bottle under it, there'd be Hood to pay.

The damned bastards fleeing ahead of them could run for ever, and probably would if their commander had any brains. He could have chosen a last stand at any time. Heroic and inspiring in its pointlessness. But it seemed he was too clever for that. Westward, ever westward, out into the wastes.

Bottle returned to where he had been sitting, collecting handfuls of sand to scrub Koryk's blood from his fingers and palms. *We're just getting on each other's nerves. That's all.* His grandmother would know what to do about this situation, but she was long dead and her spirit was anchored to the old farm outside Jakata, a thousand leagues from here. He could almost see her, shaking her head and squinting in that half-crazed genius way she'd had. Wise in the ways of mortals, seeing through to every weakness, every flaw, reading unconscious gestures and momentary expressions, cutting through the confused surface to lay bare the bones of truth. Nothing was hidden from her.

He could not talk with her, however.

But there's another woman . . . isn't there? Despite the heat, Bottle shivered. She still haunted his dreams, that Eres'al witch. Still showed him the ancient hand-axes spread out over this land like the stone leaves of a world-encompassing tree, scattered by the winds of countless passing ages. He knew, in fact, that fifty or so paces south of this track, there was a basin cluttered with the damned things. Out there, a short walk, waiting for him.

I see them, but I do not yet understand their significance. That's the problem. I'm not equal to this.

His eyes caught movement down by his boots and he saw a locust, swollen with eggs and crawling slowly. Bottle leaned forward and picked it up by pinching together its folded wings. With his other hand he reached into his pack, and removed a small black wooden box, its lid and sides pierced through with small holes. He flicked open the clasp and lifted the lid.

Joyful Union, their prized Birdshit scorpion. In the sudden light, the creature's tail lifted as it backed into a corner.

Bottle tossed the locust into the box.

The scorpion had known what was coming, and it darted forward, and moments later was feeding on the still-kicking insect.

69

'Simple for you, isn't it?' Bottle said under his breath.

Something thumped into the sand beside him – a karybral fruit, round and dusty-lime-coloured. Bottle looked up to find Cuttle standing over him.

The sapper had an armful of the fruit. 'A treat,' he said.

Grimacing, Bottle closed the lid on Joyful Union. 'Thanks. Where did you get them?'

'Went for a walk.' Cuttle nodded southward. 'A basin, karybral vines everywhere.' He started tossing them to the others in the squad.

A basin. 'Plenty of hand-axes, too, right?'

Cuttle squinted. 'Didn't notice. Is that dried blood on your hands?'

'That would be mine,' Koryk said in a growl, already husking the fruit.

The sapper paused, studied the rough circle of soldiers around him, finishing on Corporal Tarr, who shrugged. This seemed sufficient, as Cuttle flung the last karybral globe over to Smiles.

Who caught it on a knife.

The others, Cuttle included, watched as she proceeded to slice the skin away with deft strokes.

The sapper sighed. 'Think I'll go find the sergeant.'

'Good idea,' Bottle said.

'You should let Joyful out for the occasional walk,' Cuttle said. 'Stretch the old legs. Maybe and Lutes have found a new scorpion – never seen its like before. They're talking re-match.'

'Scorpions can't stretch their legs,' Bottle replied.

'A figure of speech.'

'Oh.'

'Anyway,' Cuttle said, then ambled off.

Smiles had managed to remove the entire husk in one strip, which she lobbed in Koryk's direction. He had been looking down, and he jumped at the motion in the edge of his vision.

She snorted. 'There you go. Add it to your collection of charms.'

The half-Seti set down his karybral and slowly stood, then winced and threw Bottle a glare. 'I thought you healed this damned thing.'

'I did. It's still going to be sore, though.'

'Sore? I can barely stand.'

'It'll get better.'

'She's liable to run,' Tarr observed. 'It should be amusing, Koryk, seeing you hobbling after her.'

The big man subsided. 'I'm patient enough,' he said, sitting back down.

'Ooh,' Smiles said, 'I'm all in a sweat.'

Bottle climbed to his feet. 'I'm going for a walk,' he said. 'Nobody kill anybody until I get back.'

'If someone gets killed,' Tarr pointed out, 'your healing skills won't be much help.'

'I wasn't thinking about healing, just watching.'

They had ridden north, out of sight of the encamped column, over a low ridge and onto a flat, dusty plain. Three guldindha trees rose from a low knoll two hundred paces distant, and they had reined in beneath the shade of the leathery, broad leaves, unpacking food and a jug of Gredfalan ale Fiddler had procured from somewhere, and there they awaited the High Mage's arrival.

Something of Fiddler's old spirit had been dampened, Kalam could see. More grey in the russet beard, a certain far-off look in his pale blue eyes. True, the Fourteenth was an army filled with resentful, bitter soldiers, the glory of an empire's vengeance stolen from them the very night before battle; and this march wasn't helping. These things alone could suffice to explain Fiddler's condition, but Kalam knew better.

Tanno song or no, Hedge and the others were dead. Ghosts on the other side. Then again, Quick Ben had explained that the official reports were slightly inaccurate. Mallet, Picker, Antsy, Blend, Spindle, Bluepearl ... there were survivors, retired and living soft in Darujhistan. Along with Captain Ganoes Paran. So, some good news, and it had helped. A little.

Fiddler and Hedge had been as close as brothers. When together, they had been mayhem. A conjoined mindset more dangerous than amusing most of the time. As legendary as the Bridgeburners themselves. It had been a fateful decision back there on the shoreline of Lake Azur, their parting. *Fateful for all of us, it turns out.*

Kalam could make little sense of the ascendancy. This Spiritwalker's blessing on a company of soldiers, the parting of the fabric at Raraku. He was both comforted and uneasy with the notion of unseen guardians – Fiddler's life had been saved by Hedge's ghost ... but where was Whiskeyjack? Had he been there as well?

That night in the camp of Sha'ik had been nightmarish. Too many knives to count had been unsheathed in those dark hours. And he had seen some of those ghosts with his own eyes. Bridgeburners long dead, come back grim as a hangover and as ugly as they had been in life. If he ever met that Tanno Spiritwalker Fid had talked to ...

The sapper was pacing in the shade of the trees.

Crouching, Kalam Mekhar studied his old friend. 'All right, Fid, out with it.'

'Bad things,' the sapper muttered. 'Too many to count. Like storm-clouds, gathering on every horizon.'

'No wonder you've been miserable company.'

Fiddler squinted over at him. 'You ain't been much better.'

The assassin grimaced. 'Pearl. He's keeping out of my sight, but he's hovering nonetheless. You'd think that Pardu woman – what's her name?'

'Lostara Yil.'

'Her. You'd think she'd have unhorsed him by now.'

'The game those two play is all their own,' Fiddler said, 'and they're welcome to it. Anyway, it's clear he's still here because the Empress wants someone close to Tavore.'

'That was always her problem,' Kalam said, sighing.

'Trust.'

Kalam regarded the sapper. 'You've marched with Tavore since Aren. Any sense of her? Any at all?'

'I'm a sergeant, Kalam.'

'Exactly.' The assassin waited.

Fiddler scratched his beard, tugged at the strap of his battered helm, then unclasped it and tossed it to one side. He continued pacing, kicking at the leaves and nutshells in the sand. He waved at an errant bloodfly hovering in front of his face. 'She's cold iron, Kalam. But it's untested. Can she think in battle? Can she command on the run? Hood knows, her favoured Fist, that old man Gamet, he couldn't. Which doesn't bode well for her judgement.'

'She knew him from before, didn't she?'

'Someone she trusted, aye, there's that. He was worn out, that's all. I ain't as generous as I used to be.'

Kalam grinned, looking away. 'Oh yes, generous, that's Fid all right.' He gestured at the finger bones hanging from the sapper's belt. 'What about those?'

'She walked straight with that, it's true. Oponn's shove, maybe.'

'Or maybe not.'

Fiddler shrugged. His hand snapped out and closed on the bloodfly. He smeared it to death between his palms with evident satisfaction.

Looking older, true enough, but fast and mean as ever. A wash of gritty, dead air sent the leaves scrabbling over the sand, the air audibly splitting a few paces away, and Quick Ben emerged from a warren. Coughing.

Kalam collected the jug of ale and walked over. 'Here.'

The wizard drank, coughed once more, then spat. 'Gods below, that imperial warren is awful.' He swallowed another mouthful.

'Send me in there,' Fiddler said, striding over, 'then I can drink some of that, too.'

'Glad to see your mood's improved,' Quick Ben said, handing the jug over. 'We will be having some company in a short while . . . after we eat, that is,' he added, spying the wrapped foodstuffs and heading over. 'I'm so hungry I could eat bloodflies.'

'Lick my palm,' Fiddler said.

The wizard halted, looked over. 'You've lost your mind. I'd sooner lick the hand of a camel-dung hawker.' He began unwrapping the leaves protecting the food.

'How was your meeting with Tavore?' Kalam asked, joining him.

'Your guess is as good as mine,' Quick Ben replied. 'I've seen people under siege before, but she's raised walls so thick and so high I doubt a dozen irate dragons would get through . . . and not an enemy in sight, either.'

'You might be wrong there,' the assassin said. 'Was Pearl around?'

'Well, one curtain moved a bit.'

Fiddler snorted. 'He ain't that obvious. Was probably T'amber.'

'I wasn't being literal, Fid. Somebody in a warren, close and watchful.'

'Tavore wasn't wearing her sword, then,' Kalam said.

'No, she never does when talking with me, thank the gods.'

'Ah, considerate, then!'

The wizard shot a dark glare at Kalam. 'Doesn't want to suck everything out of her High Mage, you mean.'

'Stop,' Fiddler said. 'I don't like the images popping into my head. Hand me a chunk of that sepah bread – no, not the one you've taken a bite out of, Quick, thanks anyway. There – oh, never mind.' He reached across.

'Hey, you're raining sand on my food!'

Kalam settled back on his haunches. Fiddler was looking younger by the minute. Especially with that scowl. This break away from the army and all that went with it was long overdue.

'What?' Fiddler demanded. 'Worried you'll wear your teeth down? Better stop chewing on that bread, then.'

'It's not that hard,' the wizard replied in a mouth-full muffle.

'No, but it's full of grit, Quick Ben. From the millstones. Anyway, I'm always raining sand these days. I got sand in places you wouldn't imagine—'

'Stop, images popping into my head and all that.'

'After this,' Fiddler continued remorselessly, 'a year's worth of sitting sweet in Darujhistan and I'll still be shitting gritty bricks—'

'Stop, I said!'

Kalam's eyes narrowed on the sapper. 'Darujhistan? Planning on joining the others, then?'

The sapper's gaze shied away. 'Some day . . .'

'Some day soon?'

'I ain't planning on running, Kalam.'

The assassin met Quick Ben's eyes, just a flicker of contact, and Kalam cleared his throat. 'Well . . . maybe you should, Fid. If I was giving advice—'

'If you're giving advice then I know we're all doomed. Thanks for ruining my day. Here, Quick, some more of that ale, please, I'm parched.'

Kalam subsided. *All right, at least that's cleared up.*

Quick Ben brushed crumbs from his long-fingered hands and sat back. 'She has ideas about you, Kalam . . .'

'I've got one wife too many as it is.'

'Maybe she wants you to put together a squad of assassins?'

'A what? From this lot?'

'Hey,' Fiddler growled, 'I know this lot.'

'And?'

'And you're right, is all. They're a mess.'

'Even so,' the wizard said, shrugging. 'And she probably wants you to do it on the sly—'

'With Pearl listening in on your conversation, right.'

'No, that was later. The second half of our meetings is for our audience. The first half, before Pearl and whoever else arrives, is when we talk privately. She makes these meetings as impromptu as possible. Uses Grub as a messenger.' The wizard made a warding gesture.

'Just a foundling,' Fiddler said.

But Quick Ben simply shook his head.

'So she wants her own cadre of assassins,' Kalam said. 'Unknown to the Claw. Oh, I don't like where this is going, Quick.'

'Whoever is hiding behind those walls might be scared, Kal, but stupid it ain't.'

'This whole thing is stupid,' Fiddler pronounced. 'She crushed the rebellion – what more does Laseen want?'

'Strong, when it comes to dealing with our enemies,' Kalam said. 'And weak when it comes to popularity.'

'Tavore ain't the popular sort of person, so what's the problem?'

'She might get popular. A few more successes – ones where it's clear it's not dumb luck. Come on, Fid, you know how fast an army can turn round.'

'Not this army,' the sapper said. 'It barely got up off the ground to start with. We're a damned shaky bunch – Quick Ben, does she have any idea of that?'

The wizard considered for a time, then he nodded. 'I think so. But she doesn't know what to do about it, beyond catching Leoman of the Flails and obliterating him and his army. Thoroughly.'

Fiddler grunted. 'That's what Cuttle is afraid of. He's convinced we're all going to end up wearing Ranal before this is done.'

'Ranal? Oh, right.'

'He's being a right pain about it, too,' Fiddler went on. 'Keeps talking about the cusser he's holding back, the one he'll sit on when the doom descends on us all. You should see the look on the recruits' faces when he goes on like that.'

'Sounds like Cuttle needs a talking to.'

'He needs a fist in the face, Kal. Believe me, I've been tempted . . .'

'But sappers don't do that to each other.'

'I'm a sergeant, too.'

'But you need him still on your side.'

Glumly, 'Aye.'

'All right,' Kalam said, 'I'll put him right.'

'Careful, he might toss a sharper at your feet. He don't like assassins.'

'Who does?' Quick Ben commented.

Kalam frowned. 'And here I thought I was popular . . . at least with my friends.'

'We're only playing it safe, Kalam.'

'Thanks, Quick, I'll remember that.'

The wizard rose suddenly. 'Our guests are about to arrive . . .'

Fiddler and Kalam stood as well, turning to see the imperial warren open once more. Four figures strode out.

The assassin recognized two of them, and felt both tension and pleasure rising within him; the sudden hackles for High Mage Tayschrenn, and the genuine pleasure at seeing Dujek Onearm. Flanking Tayschrenn were two bodyguards, one an aged Seti with a waxed moustache – vaguely familiar in some distant way, as if Kalam had perhaps seen him once before, long ago. The other was a woman somewhere between twenty-five and thirty-five, lithe and athletic beneath tight silks. The eyes were soft and dark brown, watchful; her hair was cut short in the imperial fashion around her heart-shaped face.

'Relax,' Quick Ben murmured low beside Kalam. 'Like I said before, Tayschrenn's role in . . . things past . . . was misunderstood.'

'So you say.'

'And he did try to protect Whiskeyjack.'

'But was too late.'

'Kalam . . .'

'All right, I'll be civil. Is that Seti his old bodyguard – from the days of the Emperor?'

'Aye.'

'Miserable bastard? Never said anything?'

'That's him.'

'Looks like he's mellowed some.'

Quick Ben snorted.

'Something amusing you, High Mage?' Dujek asked as the group approached.

'Welcome, High Fist,' Quick Ben said, straightening, adding a slightly deferential bow to Tayschrenn. 'Colleague . . .'

Tayschrenn's thin, almost hairless brows rose. 'A field promotion, wasn't it? Well, perhaps long overdue. Nonetheless, I do not believe the Empress has sanctioned that title as yet.'

Quick Ben offered him a broad, white smile. 'Do you recall, High Mage, a certain other High Mage, sent by the Emperor, early on in the Blackdog Campaign? Kribalah Rule?'

'Rule the Rude? Yes, he died after a month or so—'

'In a horrible conflagration, aye. Well, that was me. Thus, I've been a High Mage before, colleague . . .'

Tayschrenn was frowning, clearly thinking back, then the frown became a scowl. 'And the Emperor knew this? He must have, having sent you – unless, of course, he didn't send you at all.'

'Well, granted, there were some improprieties involved, and had one set out on that particular trail they might well have been noted. But you did not feel the need to do so, evidently, since, although briefly, I more than held my own – pulling you out of trouble once, I seem to recall . . . something about Tiste Andii assassin-mages—'

'When I lost a certain object containing a demon lord . . .'

'You did? Sorry to hear that.'

'The same demon that later died by Rake's sword in Darujhistan.'

'Oh, how unfortunate.'

Kalam leaned close to Quick Ben. 'I thought,' he said in a whisper, 'you told *me* to relax.'

'Long ago and far away,' Dujek Onearm said gruffly, 'and I'd slap my hands together if I had more than one. Tayschrenn, rein in that Seti before he does something stupid. We have things to discuss here. Let's get on with it.'

Kalam glanced across at Fiddler and winked. *Just like old times . . .*

Lying flat at the crest of the ridge, Pearl grunted. 'That's Dujek Onearm out there,' he said. 'He's supposed to be in G'danisban right now.'

Beside him, Lostara Yil hissed and began slapping about her body. 'Chigger fleas, damn you. They're swarming this ridge. I hate chigger fleas—'

'Why not jump up and dance about, Captain?' Pearl asked. 'Just to make certain they know we're here.'

'Spying is stupid. I hate this, and I am rediscovering my hatred for you, too, Claw.'

'You say the sweetest things. Anyway, the bald one's Tayschrenn, with Hattar and Kiska this time, meaning he's serious about the risks. Oh, why did they have to do this, now?'

'Do what now?'

'Whatever it is they're doing, of course.'

'So run back to Laseen like the eager puppy you are, Pearl, and tell her all about it.'

He edged back down the side of the ridge, twisted round and sat up. 'No need for haste. I have to think.'

Lostara clambered down the slope until she could stand. She began scratching under her armour. 'Well, I'm not waiting around for that. I need a milk bath, with escura leaves, and I need it now.'

He watched her stalk away, back towards the encampment. A nice walk, apart from the sudden twitches.

A simple cantrip, keeping the fleas away from his body. Perhaps he should have extended the courtesy to her.

No. This is much better.

Gods, we're made for each other.

CHAPTER THREE

Yareth Ghanatan, the city stands still
First and last and where the old causeway
Curves in its half-circle there are towers
Of sand seething with empires and
Marching armies, broken wing banners
And the dismembered lining the walkways
Are soon the bones of the edifices, warriors
And builders both, the city ever stands
To house insect hordes, oh those towers
Rear so proud, rising as dreams on the
Heated breath of the sun, Yareth Ghanatan.
The city is the empress, wife and lover,
Crone and child of the First Empire,
And I yet remain, with all my kin,
The bones in the walls, the bones
Beneath the floor, the bones that cast
Down this gentle shade – first and last,
I see what comes, all that has gone,
And the clay of my flesh has felt your hands
The old warmth of life, for the city,
My city, it stands still, and it stands,
Stands ever still.

Bones in the Walls
(stela fragment, *circa* First Empire)
Author unknown

'I CAN BE THIS URN.'
    'You don't want to be *that* urn.'
    'It's got legs.'
'Stubby ones, and I don't think they move. They're just for show.

78

I remember things like that.'

'But it's pretty.'

'And she pees in it.'

'Pees? Are you sure? Have you seen her pee in it?'

'Take a look, Curdle. That's her pee in it. You don't want to be that urn. You want something alive. Really alive, with legs that work. Or wings . . .'

They were still whispering when Apsalar removed the last bar in the window and set it down. She climbed onto the sill, twisting sideways to reach up to the nearest roof-post.

'Where are you going?' Telorast demanded.

'To the roof.'

'Shall we join you?'

'No.'

Apsalar pulled herself upward and moments later was crouched on the sun-baked clay, the stars glistening overhead. Dawn was not far off, and the city below was silent and motionless like a thing dead in the night. Ehrlitan. The first city they had come to in this land, the city where this particular journey had begun, a group fated to break apart beneath a host of burdens. Kalam Mekhar, Fiddler, Crokus and herself. Oh, Crokus had been so angry to discover that their companions had come with hidden motives – not just escorting her home, not just righting an old wrong. He had been so naïve.

She wondered how he was faring, thought to ask Cotillion the next time the god visited, then decided she would not do so. It would not do to let herself continue to care about him; even to think on him, achieving little more than loosing the flood-gates of yearning, desire and regret.

Other, more immediate issues demanded her thought. Mebra. The old spy was dead, which was what Shadowthrone had wanted, although the why of it escaped Apsalar. Granted, Mebra had been working all sides, serving the Malazan Empire at one moment, Sha'ik's cause the next. And . . . someone else. That someone else's identity was important, and, she suspected, it was the true reason for Shadowthrone's decision.

The Nameless Ones? Had the Semk assassin been sent to cover a trail? Possible, and it made sense. *No witnesses*, the man had said. To what? What service could Mebra have provided the Nameless Ones? *Hold off pursuing an answer to that. Who else?*

Adherents to the old cult of Shadow in Seven Cities no doubt remained, survivors of the purges that had accompanied the conquest. Another possible employer of Mebra's many skills, and more likely to have caught Shadowthrone's attention, as well as his ire.

She had been told to kill Mebra. She had not been told why, nor had she been told to initiate any investigations on her own. Suggesting Shadowthrone felt he knew enough. The same for Cotillion. Or, conversely, they were both woefully ignorant, and Mebra had simply switched sides once too often.

There were more targets on her list, a random collection of names, all of which could be found in Cotillion's memories. She was expected simply to proceed from one to the next, with the final target the most challenging of all . . . but that one was in all likelihood months away, and she would need to do some deft manoeuvring to get close enough to strike, a slow, careful stalking of a very dangerous individual. For whom she felt no enmity.

This is what an assassin does. And Cotillion's possession has made me an assassin. That and nothing else. I have killed and will continue to kill. I need think of nothing else. It is simple. It should be simple.

And so she would make it so.

Still, what made a god decide to kill some lowly mortal? The minor irritation of a stone in a moccasin. The slap of a branch on a wooded trail. Who thinks twice plucking that stone out and tossing it away? Or reaching out and snapping that branch? *It seems I do, for I am that god's hand in this.*

Enough. No more of this weakness . . . this . . . uncertainty. Complete the tasks, then walk away. Vanish. Find a new life.

Only . . . how does one do that?

There was someone she could ask – he was not far off, she knew, having culled his identity from Cotillion's memories.

She had moved to sit with her legs dangling on the roof's edge. Someone now sat at her side.

'Well?' Cotillion asked.

'A Semk assassin of the Nameless Ones completed my mission for me.'

'This very night?'

'I met him, but was unable to question him.'

The god slowly nodded. 'The Nameless Ones again. This is unexpected. And unwelcome.'

'So they were not the reason for killing Mebra.'

'No. Some stirrings of the old cult. Mebra was positioning himself to become a High Priest. The best candidate – we're not worried about the others.'

'Cleaning house.'

'Necessary, Apsalar. We're in for a scrap. A bad one.'

'I see.'

They were silent for a time, then Cotillion cleared his throat. 'I have not yet had time to check on him, but I know he is hale, although understandably dispirited.'

'All right.'

He must have sensed she wanted it left at that, for, after a pause, he then said, 'You freed two ghosts . . .'

She shrugged.

Sighing, Cotillion ran a hand through his dark hair. 'Do you know what they once were?'

'Thieves, I think.'

'Yes, that.'

'Tiste Andii?'

'No, but they lingered long over those two bodies and so . . . absorbed certain essences.'

'Ah.'

'They are now agents of Edgewalker. I am curious to see what they will do.'

'For the moment they seem content to accompany me.'

'Yes. I think Edgewalker's interests include you, Apsalar, because of our past . . . relationship.'

'Through me, to you.'

'I seem to warrant his curiosity.'

'Edgewalker. That apparition seems a rather passive sort,' she observed.

'We first met him,' Cotillion said slowly, 'the night we ascended. The night we made passage into the realm of Shadow. He made my spine crawl right then, and it's been crawling ever since.'

She glanced over at him. 'You are so unsuited to be a god, Cotillion, did you know that?'

'Thank you for the vote of confidence.'

She reached up with one hand and brushed the line of his jaw, the gesture close to a caress. She caught the sudden intake of his breath, the slight widening of his eyes, but he would not look at her. Apsalar lowered her hand. 'I'm sorry. Another mistake. It's all I seem to make these days.'

'It's all right,' he replied. 'I understand.'

'You do? Oh, of course you do.'

'Complete your mission, and all that is asked of you will end. You will face no more demands from me. Or Shadowthrone.'

There was something in his tone that gave her a slight shiver. Something like . . . remorse. 'I see. That is good. I'm tired. Of who I am, Cotillion.'

'I know.'

'I was thinking of a detour. Before my next task.'

'Oh?'

'The coastal road, east. Just a few days by Shadow.'

He looked across at her, and she saw his faint smile and was un-accountably pleased by it. 'Ah, Apsalar . . . that should be fun. Send him my greetings.'

'Really?'

'Absolutely. He needs a little shaking up.' He straightened. 'I must leave. It's almost dawn. Be careful, and do not trust those ghosts.'

'They are bad liars.'

'Well, I know a High Priest who employs a similar tactic to confound others.'

Iskaral Pust. Now it was Apsalar who smiled, but she said nothing, for Cotillion was gone.

The east horizon was in flames with the rising of the sun.

'Where did the darkness go?' Curdle demanded.

Apsalar stood near the bed, running through her assortment of con-cealed weapons. She would need to sleep soon – perhaps this afternoon – but first she would make use of the daylight. There was something important hidden within the killing of Mebra by the Semk. Cotillion had been shaken by that detail. Although he had not asked her to pursue it, she would nonetheless, for a day or two at least. 'The sun has risen, Curdle.'

'The sun? By the Abyss, there's a sun in this world? Have they gone mad?'

Apsalar glanced over at the cowering ghost. It was dissolving in the grainy light. Huddled in a shadow nearby, Telorast looked on, mute with terror. 'Has who gone mad?' Apsalar asked Curdle.

'Well, them! The ones who created this place!'

'We're fading!' Telorast hissed. 'What does it mean? Will we cease to exist?'

'I don't know,' Apsalar replied. 'Probably you will lose some substance, assuming you have any, but it will be temporary. Best you two remain here, and be silent. I will be back before dusk.'

'Dusk! Yes, excellent, we will wait here for dusk. Then night and all that darkness, and the shadows, and things to possess. Yes, fearful woman, we shall wait here.'

She headed down, paid for another night, then emerged onto the dusty street. The market-bound citizens were already on the move, hawkers dragging burdened mules, carts crowded with caged songbirds or slabs of salted meat or casks of oil or honey. Old men laboured beneath bundles of firewood, baskets of clay. Down the centre of the street strode two Red Blades – feared sentinels of order and law once again now that the empire's presence had been emphatically reasserted. They were headed in the same direction as Apsalar – and indeed as most of the people – towards the vast sprawl of caravan camps beyond the city wall just south of the harbour.

The Red Blades were provided a wide berth, and the swagger of their stride, their gauntleted hands resting on the grips of their sheathed but not peace-strapped tulwars, made of their arrogance a deliberate, provocative affront. Yet they passed unchallenged.

Moments before she caught up with them, Apsalar swung left down a side passage. There was more than one route to the caravan camps.

A merchant employing Pardu and Gral guards, and appearing to display unusual interest in the presence of a Shadow Dancer in the city, made him or herself in turn the subject of interest. It might simply be that the merchant was a buyer and seller of information, but even that could prove useful to Apsalar – not that she was prepared to pay for any information she gleaned. The tribal guards suggested extensive overland travel, between distant cities and the rarely frequented tracks linking them. That merchant would know things.

And so, indeed, might those guards.

She arrived at the outskirts of the first camp. If seen from the sky, the caravan city would look pockmarked, as merchants came and went in a steady stream of wagons, horse-warriors, herd dogs and camels. The outer edges were home to lesser merchants, their positions fixed according to some obscure hierarchy, whilst the high-status caravans occupied the centre.

Entering the main thoroughfare from a side path between tents, Apsalar began the long search.

At midday she found a tapu-hawker and sat at one of the small tables beneath an awning eating the skewered pieces of fruit and meat, the grease running hot tracks down her hands. She had noted a renewed energy among the merchant camps she had visited so far. Insurrection and strife were bad for business, obviously. The return of Malazan rule was a blessing on trade in all its normal avaricious glory, and she had seen the exultation on all sides. Coins were flowing in a thousand streams.

Three figures caught her eye. Standing before the entrance to a large tent and arguing, it seemed, over a cage of puppies. The two Pardu women and one of the Gral tribesmen she had seen at the tavern. They were too preoccupied to have spied her, she hoped. Wiping her hands on her thighs, Apsalar rose and walked, keeping to the shadier areas, out from under the awning and away from the guards and the merchant's tent.

It was enough to have found them, for now. Before she would

endeavour to interrogate the merchant, or the guards, another task awaited her.

The long walk back to the inn was uneventful, and she climbed the stairs and made her way to her room. It was mid-afternoon, and her mind was filled with thoughts of sleep.

'She's back!'

The voice, Curdle's, came from under the wood-framed cot.

'Is it her?' asked Telorast from the same place.

'I recognize the moccasins, see the sewn-in ridges of iron? Not like the other one.'

Apsalar paused her removing of her leather gloves. 'What other one?'

'The one who was here earlier, a bell ago—'

'A bell?' Telorast wondered. 'Oh, those bells, now I understand. They measure the passing of time. Yes, Not-Apsalar, a bell ago. We said nothing. We were silent. That one never knew we were here.'

'The innkeeper?'

'Boots, stirrup-worn and threaded with bronze scales, they went here and there – and crouched to look under here, but saw naught of us, of course, and naught of anything else, since you have no gear for him to rifle through—'

'It was a man, then.'

'Didn't we say earlier? Didn't we, Curdle?'

'We must have. A man, with boots on, yes.'

'How long did he stay?' Apsalar asked, looking around the room. There was nothing there for the thief to steal, assuming he had been a thief.

'A hundred of his heartbeats.'

'Hundred and six, Telorast.'

'Hundred and six, yes.'

'He came and went by the door?'

'No, the window – you removed the bars, remember? Down from the roof, isn't that right, Telorast?'

'Or up from the alley.'

'Or maybe from one of the other rooms, thus from the side, right or left.'

Apsalar frowned and crossed her arms. 'Did he come in by the window at all?'

'No.'

'By warren, then.'

'Yes.'

'And he wasn't a man,' Curdle added. 'He was a demon. Big, black, hairy, with fangs and claws.'

'Wearing boots,' Telorast said.

'Exactly. Boots.'

Apsalar pulled off her gloves and slapped them down on the bedstand. She sprawled on the cot. 'Wake me if he returns.'

'Of course, Not-Apsalar. You can depend upon us.'

When she awoke it was dark. Cursing, Apsalar rose from the cot. 'How late is it?'

'She's awake!' The shade of Telorast hovered nearby, a smeared body-shape in the gloom, its eyes dully glowing.

'Finally!' Curdle whispered from the window sill, where it crouched like a gargoyle, head twisted round to regard Apsalar still seated on the cot. 'It's two bells after the death of the sun! We want to explore!'

'Fine,' she said, standing. 'Follow me, then.'

'Where to?'

'Back to the Jen'rahb.'

'Oh, that miserable place.'

'I won't be there long.'

'Good.'

She collected her gloves, checked her weapons once more – a score of aches from knife pommels and scabbards attested that they remained strapped about her person – and headed for the window.

'Shall we use the causeway?'

Apsalar stopped, studied Curdle. 'What causeway?'

The ghost moved to hug one edge of the window and pointed outward. 'That one.'

A shadow manifestation, something like an aqueduct, stretched from the base of the window out over the alley and the building beyond, then curving – towards the heart of the Jen'rahb. It had the texture of stone, and she could see pebbles and pieces of crumbled mortar along the path. 'What is this?'

'We don't know.'

'It is from the Shadow Realm, isn't it? It has to be. Otherwise I would be unable to see it.'

'Oh yes. We think. Don't we, Telorast?'

'Absolutely. Or not.'

'How long,' Apsalar asked, 'has it been here?'

'Fifty-three of your heartbeats. You were stirring to wakefulness, right, Curdle? She was stirring.'

'And moaning. Well, one moan. Soft. A half-moan.'

'No,' Telorast said, 'that was me.'

Apsalar clambered up onto the sill, then, still gripping the edges of the wall, she stepped out onto the causeway. Solid beneath her feet. 'All right,' she muttered, more than a little shaken as she released her hold on the building behind her. 'We might as well make use of it.'

'We agree.'

They set out, over the alley, the tenement, a street and then the rubble of the ruins. In the distance rose ghostly towers. A city of shadow, but this one thoroughly unlike the one of the night before. Vague structures lay over the wreckage below – canals, the glimmer of something like water. Lower bridges spanned these canals. A few thousand paces distant, to the southeast, rose a massive domed palace, and beyond it what might have been a lake, or a wide river. Ships plied those waters, square-sailed and sleek, the wood midnight black. She saw tall figures crossing a bridge fifty paces away.

Telorast hissed. 'I recognize them!'

Apsalar crouched low, suddenly feeling terribly vulnerable here on this high walkway.

'Tiste Edur!'

'Yes,' she half-breathed.

'Oh, can they see us?'

I don't know. At least none walked the causeway they were on . . . not yet. 'Come on, it's not far. I want us away from this place.'

'Agreed, oh yes, agreed.'

Curdle hesitated. 'Then again . . .'

'No,' Apsalar said. 'Attempt nothing, ghost.'

'Oh all right. It's just that there's a body in the canal below.'

Damn this. She edged to the low wall and looked down. 'That's not Tiste Edur.'

'No,' Curdle confirmed. 'It most certainly isn't, Not-Apsalar. It is like you, yes, like you. Only more bloated, not long dead – we want it—'

'Don't expect help if trying for it attracts attention.'

'Oh, she has a point, Curdle. Come on, she's moving away from us! Wait! Don't leave us here!'

Reaching a steep staircase, Apsalar quickly descended. As soon as she stepped onto the pale dusty ground, the ghostly city vanished. In her wake the two shades appeared, sinking towards her.

'A most dreadful place,' Telorast said.

'But there was a throne,' Curdle cried. 'I sensed it! A most delicious throne!'

Telorast snorted. 'Delicious? You have lost your mind. Naught but pain. Suffering. Affliction—'

'Quiet,' Apsalar commanded. 'You will tell me more about this throne you two sensed, but later. Guard this entrance.'

'We can do that. We're very skilled guards. Someone died down there, yes? Can we have the body?'

'No. Stay here.' Apsalar entered the half-buried temple.

The chamber within was not as she had left it. The Semk's corpse was gone. Mebra's body had been stripped of its clothing, the clothing itself cut apart. What little furnishings occupied the room had been methodically dismantled. Cursing under her breath, Apsalar walked to the doorway leading to the inner chamber – the curtain that had covered it had been torn away. In the small room beyond – Mebra's living quarters – the searcher or searchers had been equally thorough. Indifferent to the absence of light, she scanned the detritus. Someone had been looking for something, or deliberately obscuring a trail.

She thought about the Semk assassin's appearance last night. She had assumed he'd somehow seen her sprint across the rubble and so was compelled to return. But now she wondered. Perhaps he'd been sent back, his task only half-completed. In either case, he had not been working alone that night. She had been careless, thinking otherwise.

From the outer chamber came a wavering whisper, 'Where are you?'

Apsalar stepped back through the doorway. 'What are you doing here, Curdle? I told you to—'

'Two people are coming. Women, like you. Like us, too. I forgot. Yes, we're all women here—'

'Find a shadow and hide,' Apsalar cut in. 'Same for Telorast.'

'You don't want us to kill them?'

'Can you?'

'No.'

'Hide yourselves.'

'A good thing we decided to guard the door, isn't it?'

Ignoring the ghost, Apsalar positioned herself beside the outer entrance. She drew her knives, set her back against the sloping stone, and waited.

She heard their quick steps, the scuffing as they halted just outside, their breathing. Then the first one stepped through, in her hands a shuttered lantern. She strode in further as she flipped back one of the hinged shutters, sending a shaft of light against the far wall. Behind her entered the second woman, a scimitar unsheathed and held out.

The Pardu caravan guards.

Apsalar stepped close and drove the point of one dagger into the woman's elbow joint on the sword-arm, then swung the other weapon, pommel-forward, into the woman's temple.

She dropped, as did her weapon.

The other spun round.

A high swinging kick caught her above the jaw. She reeled, lantern flying to crack against the wall.

Sheathing her knives, Apsalar closed in on the stunned guard. A punch to the solar plexus doubled her over. The guard dropped to her knees, then fell onto one side, curling up around the pain.

'This is convenient,' Apsalar said, 'since I was intending to question you anyway.'

She walked back to the first woman and checked on her condition. Unconscious, and likely would remain so for some time. Even so, she kicked the scimitar into a corner, then stripped her of the knives she found hidden under her arms. Walking back to the other Pardu, she looked down on the groaning, motionless woman for a moment, then crouched and dragged her to her feet.

She grasped the woman's right arm, the one she used to hold a weapon, and, with a sharp twist, dislocated it at the elbow.

The woman cried out.

Apsalar closed a hand on her throat and slammed her against the wall, the head cracking hard. Vomit spilled onto the assassin's glove and wrist. She held the Pardu there. 'Now you will answer my questions.'

'Please!'

'No pleading. Pleading only makes me cruel. Answer me to my satisfaction and I might let you and your friend live. Do you understand?'

The Pardu nodded, her face smeared with blood and an elongated bump swelling below her right eye where the iron-embedded moccasin had struck.

Sensing the arrival of the two ghosts, Apsalar glanced over her shoulder. They were hovering over the body of the other Pardu.

'One of us might take her,' Telorast whispered.

'Easy,' agreed Curdle. 'Her mind is addled.'

'Absent.'

'Lost in the Abyss.'

Apsalar hesitated, then said, 'Go ahead.'

'Me!' hissed Curdle.

'No, me!' snarled Telorast.

'Me!'

'I got to her first!'

'You did not!'

'I choose,' said Apsalar. 'Acceptable?'

'Yes.'

'Oh yes, you choose, dearest Mistress—'

'You're grovelling again!'

'Am not!'

'Curdle,' Apsalar said. 'Possess her.'

'I knew you'd pick her!'

'Patience, Telorast. This night's not yet done.'

The Pardu woman before her was blinking, a wild look in her eyes.

'Who are you talking to? What language is that? Who's out there – I can't see—'

'Your lantern's out. Never mind. Tell me about your master.'

'Gods below, it hurts—'

Apsalar reached down and twisted the dislocated arm again.

The woman shrieked, then sagged, unconscious.

Apsalar let her slide down the wall until the woman was roughly in a sitting position. Then she drew out a flask and splashed water into the Pardu's face.

The eyes opened, comprehension returned, and with it, terror.

'I don't want to hear about what hurts,' Apsalar said. 'I want to hear about the merchant. Your employer. Now, shall we try again?'

The other Pardu was sitting up near the entrance, making grunting noises, then coughing, until she spat out bloody phlegm. 'Ah!' Curdle cried. 'Better! Oh, everything aches, oh, the arm!'

'Be quiet,' Apsalar commanded, then fixed her attention once more on the woman in front of her. 'I am not a patient person.'

'Trygalle Trade Guild,' the woman said in a gasp.

Apsalar slowly leaned back on her haunches. A most unexpected answer. 'Curdle, get out of that body.'

'What?'

'Now.'

'Just as well, she was all broken. Ah, free of pain again! This is better – I was a fool!'

Telorast's laughter was a rasp. 'And you still are, Curdle. I could have told you, you know. She wasn't right for you.'

'No more talking,' Apsalar said. She needed to think on this. The Trygalle Trade Guild's centre of operations was Darujhistan. It had been a long time since they'd visited the fragment of the Shadow Realm with munitions for Fiddler, assuming it was the same caravan – and she suspected it was. As purveyors of items and information, it now seemed obvious that more than one mission had brought them to Seven Cities. On the other hand, perhaps they were doing little more than recovering here in the city – given their harrowing routes through the warrens – and the merchant-mage had instructed his guards to deliver any and all unusual information. Even so, she needed to be certain. 'The Trygalle merchant – what brought him or her here to Ehrlitan?'

The swelling was closing the Pardu's right eye. 'Him.'

'His name?'

'Karpolan Demesand.'

At that, Apsalar allowed herself a faint nod.

'We, uh, we were making a delivery – us guards, we're shareholders—'

'I know how the Trygalle Trade Guild works. A delivery, you said.'

'Yes, to Coltaine. During the Chain of Dogs.'

'That was some time ago.'

'Yes. I'm sorry, the pain, it hurts to talk.'

'It'll hurt more if you don't.'

The Pardu grimaced, and it was a moment before Apsalar realized it had been a smile. 'I do not doubt you, Shadow Dancer. Yes, there was more. Altar stones.'

'What?'

'Cut stones, to line a holy pool . . .'

'Here in Ehrlitan?'

The woman shook her head, winced, then said, 'No. Y'Ghatan.'

'Are you on your way there, or returning?'

'Returning. Outward journeys are through warrens. We're . . . uh . . . resting.'

'So Karpolan Demesand's interest in a Shadow Dancer is just passing.'

'He likes to know . . . everything. Information buys us advantages. No-one likes rearguard on the Ride.'

'The Ride.'

'Through the warrens. It's . . . hairy.'

I imagine it would be. 'Tell your master,' Apsalar said, 'that this Shadow Dancer does not appreciate the attention.'

The Pardu nodded.

Apsalar straightened. 'I am done with you.'

The woman flinched back, up against the wall, her left forearm rising to cover her face.

The assassin looked down on the guard, wondering what had set her off.

'We understand that language now,' Telorast said. 'She thinks you are going to kill her, and you are, aren't you?'

'No. That should be obvious, if she's to deliver a message to her master.'

'She's not thinking straight,' Curdle said. 'Besides, what better way to deliver your message than with two corpses?'

Apsalar sighed, said to the Pardu, 'What brought you to this place? To Mebra's?'

Muffled from behind the forearm, the woman replied, 'Purchasing information . . . but he's dead.'

'What information?'

'Any. All. Comings and goings. Whatever he was selling. But you've killed Mebra—'

'No, I did not. By way of peace between me and your master, I will tell you this. An assassin of the Nameless Ones murdered Mebra. There was no torture involved. A simple assassination. The Nameless Ones weren't looking for information.'

The Pardu's lone visible eye, now above the guarding wrist, was fixed on her. 'The Nameless Ones? Seven Holies protect us!'

'Now,' Apsalar said, drawing her knife, 'I need some time.' With that she struck the woman with the pommel of her knife, hard against the temple, and watched the Pardu's eye roll up, the body slump over.

'Will she live?' Telorast demanded, slinking closer.

'Leave her alone.'

'She may wake up not remembering anything you told her.'

'It doesn't matter,' Apsalar replied, sheathing her knife. 'Her master will glean all he needs to know anyway.'

'A sorceror. Ah, they travel the warrens, they said. Risky. This Karpolan Demesand must be a formidable wielder of magic – you have made a dangerous enemy.'

'I doubt he will pursue this, Telorast. I let his shareholders live, and I have provided him with information.'

'And what of the tablets?' Curdle asked.

Apsalar turned. 'What tablets?'

'The ones hidden under the floor.'

'Show me.'

The shade drifted towards Mebra's naked corpse. 'Under him. A secret cache, beneath this pavestone. Hard clay, endless lists, they probably mean nothing.'

Apsalar rolled the body over. The stone was easily pried loose, and she wondered at the carelessness of the searchers. Then again, perhaps Mebra had had some control over where he would die. He had been lying directly over it. A rough pit had been excavated, and it was crowded with clay tablets. In one corner sat a damp burlap sack filled with soft clay, and a half-dozen bone scribers bound in twine.

She rose and retrieved the lantern. When it had struck the wall, the shutter had closed – the flame within remained. She pulled the top ring to draw up the hinged shutters part-way. Returning to the secret cache, she collected the topmost dozen tablets then sat cross-legged beside the pit within the small circle of light, and began reading.

Attending the Grand Meeting of the Cult of Rashan was Bridthok of G'danisban, Septhune Anabhin of Omari, Sradal Purthu of Y'Ghatan, and Torahaval Delat of Karashimesh. Fools and charlatans one and all, although it must be said, Sradal is a dangerous fool. Torahaval is a bitch, with nothing of the humour of her cousin, nor his deadliness. She plays at this and nothing more, but she will make a fine head-piece, a High Priestess with seductive charms and so the acolytes shall flock. Of Septhune and Bridthok, the latter is my nearest rival, leaning heavily on his bloodline to that madman Bidithal, but I know well his weaknesses now and soon he shall be eliminated from the final vote by misfortune. Septhune is a follower and no more need be said of him.

Two of these cultists numbered among Apsalar's targets for assassination. She memorized the other names, in case the opportunity arose.

The second, third and fourth tablets contained lists of contacts made in the past week, with notes and observations that made it plain that Mebra had been busy weaving his usual web of extortion among a host of dimwitted victims. Merchants, soldiers, amorous wives, thieves and thugs.

The fifth tablet proved interesting.

Sribin, my most trusted agent, has confirmed it. The outlawed Gral, Taralack Veed, was in Ehrlitan one month past. Truly a man to be feared, the most secret dagger of the Nameless Ones. This only reinforces my suspicion that they have done something, an unleashing of some ancient, terrible demon. Even as the Khundryl wanderer said, and so it was no lie, that harrowing tale of the barrow and the fleeing dragon. A hunt has begun. Yet, who is the prey? And what role has Taralack Veed in all this? Oh, the name alone, scribed here in damp clay, fills my bones with ice. Dessimbelackis curse the Nameless Ones. They never play fair.

'How much longer are you going to do that?' Curdle demanded beside her.

Ignoring the shade, Apsalar continued working her way through the tablets, now seeking the name of Taralack Veed. The ghosts wandered about, sniffing every now and then at the two unconscious Pardu, slipping outside occasionally then returning, muttering in some unknown language.

There were thirty-three tablets in the pit, and as she removed the last one, she noted something odd about the pit's base. She brought the lantern closer. Shattered pieces of dried clay. Fragments of writing in Mebra's hand. 'He destroys them,' she said under her breath. 'Periodically.' She studied the last tablet in her hand. It was dustier by far than all the others, the script more faded by wear. 'But he saved this one.' Another list. Only, in this one she recognized names. Apsalar began reading aloud: 'Duiker has finally freed Heboric Light Touch. Plan ruined by the rebellion, and Heboric lost. Coltaine marches with his refugees, yet there are vipers among the Malazans. Kalam Mehkar sent to Sha'ik, the Red Blades following. Kalam will deliver the Book into Sha'ik's hands. The Red Blades will kill the bitch. I am well pleased.' The next few lines had been carved into the clay after it had hardened, the script looking ragged and hurried. 'Heboric is with Sha'ik. Known now as Ghost Hands, and in those hands is the power to destroy us all. This entire world. And none can stop him.'

Written in terror and panic. Yet . . . Apsalar glanced over at the other tablets. Something must have happened to have eased his mind. Was Heboric now dead? She did not know. Had someone else stumbled on the man's trail, someone aware of the threat? And how in Hood's name had Heboric – a minor historian of Unta – ended up in Sha'ik's company?

Clearly the Red Blades had failed in their assassination attempt. After all, the Adjunct Tavore had killed the woman, hadn't she? In front of ten thousand witnesses.

'This woman is waking up.'

She looked over at Telorast. The shade was hovering over the Pardu guard lying near the entrance. 'All right,' Apsalar said, pushing the heap of tablets back into the pit and replacing the stone. 'We're leaving.'

'Finally! It's almost light outside!'

'No causeway?'

'Nothing but ruin, Not-Apsalar. Oh, this place looks too much like home.'

Curdle hissed. 'Quiet, Telorast, you idiot! We don't talk about that, remember?'

'Sorry.'

'When we reach my room,' Apsalar said, 'I want you two to tell me about that throne.'

'She remembered.'

'I don't,' Curdle said.

'Me neither,' Telorast said. 'Throne? What throne?'

Apsalar studied the two ghosts, the faintly luminous eyes peering up at her. 'Oh, never mind.'

The Falah'd was a head shorter than Samar Dev – and she was of barely average height – and he likely weighed less than would one of her legs cut clean away at the hip. An unpleasant image, she allowed, but one frighteningly close to reality. A fierce infection had set in the broken bones and it had taken four witches to draw the malign presence out. That had been the night before and she still felt weak and light-headed, and standing here in this blistering sun wasn't helping.

However short and slight the Falah'd was, he worked hard at

presenting a noble, imposing figure, perched there atop his long-legged white mare. Alas, the beast was trembling beneath him, flinching every time Karsa Orlong's Jhag stallion tossed its head and rolled its eyes menacingly in the mare's direction. The Falah'd gripped the saddle horn with both hands, his thin dark lips pinched and a certain timidity in his eyes. His ornate, jewel-studded telaba was dishevelled, and the round, silken and padded hat on his head was askew as he looked on the one known to all as Toblakai, once-champion of Sha'ik. Who, standing beside his horse, was still able, had he so chosen, to look down on the ruler of Ugarat.

Fifty palace guards accompanied the Falah'd, none of them – nor their mounts – at ease.

Toblakai was studying the massive edifice known as Moraval Keep. An entire flat-topped mesa had been carved hollow, the rock walls shaped into imposing fortifications. A deep, steep-walled moat surrounded the keep. Moranth munitions or sorcery had destroyed the stone bridge spanning it, and the doors beyond, battered and scorched, were of solid iron. A few scattered windows were visible, high up and unadorned, each sealed by iron doors barbed with angled arrow-slits.

The besieging encampment was squalid, a few hundred soldiers sitting or standing near cookfires and looking on with vaguely jaded interest. Off to one side, just north of the narrow road, sprawled a rough cemetery of a hundred or so makeshift, shin-high wooden platforms, each holding a cloth-wrapped corpse.

Toblakai finally turned to the Falah'd. 'When last was a Malazan seen at the battlements?'

The young ruler started, then scowled. 'I am to be addressed,' he said in his piping voice, 'in a manner due my authority as Holy Falah'd of Ugarat—'

'When?' Toblakai demanded, his expression darkening.

'Well, uh, well – Captain Inashan, answer this barbarian!'

With a quick salute, the captain walked over to the soldiers in the encampment. Samar watched him speaking with a half-dozen besiegers, saw the various shrugs in answer to his question, saw Inashan's back straighten and heard his voice get louder. The soldiers started arguing amongst themselves.

Toblakai made a grunting sound. He pointed at his horse. 'Stay here, Havok. Kill nothing.' Then the warrior strode to the edge of the moat.

Samar Dev hesitated, then followed.

He glanced at her when she stopped at his side. 'I will assault this keep alone, witch.'

'You certainly will,' she replied. 'I'm just here for a closer look.'

'I doubt there will be much to see.'

'What are you planning, Toblakai?'

'I am Karsa Orlong, of the Teblor. You know my name and you will use it. To Sha'ik I was Toblakai. She is dead. To Leoman of the Flails, I was Toblakai, and he is as good as dead. To the rebels I was—'

'All right, I understand. Only dead or nearly dead people called you Toblakai, but you should know, it is only that name that has kept you from rotting out the rest of your life in the palace pits.'

'That pup on the white horse is a fool. I could break him under one arm—'

'Yes, that likely would break him. And his army?'

'More fools. I am done speaking, witch. Witness.'

And so she did.

Karsa clambered down into the moat. Rubble, broken weapons, siege-stones and withered bodies. Lizards scampered on the rocks, capemoths rising like pale leaves caught in an updraught. He made his way to a point directly beneath the two massive iron doors. Even with his height he could barely reach the narrow ledge at their base. He scanned the wreckage of the bridge around him, then began piling stones, choosing the larger fragments and fashioning rough steps.

Some time later he was satisfied. Drawing his sword, he climbed the steps, and found himself at the same level as the broad, riveted locking mechanism. Raising his stone sword in both hands, he set the point in the join, in front of where he judged the lock to be. He waited a moment, until the position of his arms and the angle of the blade was set in his mind, then he lifted the sword away, edged back as far as he could on the makeshift platform of rubble, drew the weapon back, and swung.

The blow was true, the unbreakable chalcedony edge driving into the join between the doors. Momentum ceased with a snapping sound as the blade jammed in an unseen, solid iron bar, the reverberations pounding through Karsa's arms and into his shoulders.

He grunted, waited until the pain ebbed, then tugged the weapon free in a screech of metal. And took aim once again.

He both felt and heard the crack of the bar.

Karsa pulled the sword loose then threw his shoulder against the doors.

Something fell with a loud clang, and the door on the right swung back.

On the other side of the moat, Samar Dev stared. She had just witnessed something . . . extraordinary.

Captain Inashan came up alongside her. 'The Seven Holies protect us,' he whispered. 'He just cut through an iron door.'

'Yes, he did.'

'We need . . .'

She glanced over. 'We need what, Captain?'

'We need to get him out of Ugarat. Away, as soon as possible.'

Darkness in the funnel within – angled walls, chutes and arrow-slits. Some mechanism had lowered the arched ceiling and narrowed the walls – he could see that they were suspended, perhaps a finger's width from contact with each other and with the paved floor. Twenty murderous paces to an inner gate, and that gate was ajar.

Karsa listened but heard nothing. The air smelled rank, bitter. He squinted at the arrow-slits. They were dark, the hidden chambers to either side unlit.

Readying the sword in his hands, Karsa Orlong entered the keep.

No hot sand from the chutes, no arrows darting out from the slits, no boiling oil. He reached the gate. A courtyard beyond, one third sharply bathed in white sunlight. He strode forward until he was past the gate and then looked up. The rock had been hollowed out indeed – above was a rectangle of blue sky, the fiery sun filling one corner. The walls on all four sides were tiered with fortified landings and balconies, countless windows. He could make out doorways on those balconies, some yawning black, others closed. Karsa counted twenty-two levels on the wall opposite him, eighteen on the one to his left, seventeen to the right, and behind him – the outer wall – twelve in the centre flanked by projections each holding six more. The keep was a veritable city.

And, it seemed, lifeless.

A gaping pit, hidden in the shadow in one corner of the courtyard, caught his attention. Pavestones lifted clear and piled to the sides, an excavated shaft of some sort, reaching down into the foundations. He walked over.

The excavators had cleared the heavy pavestones to reach what looked to be bedrock but had proved to be little more than a cap of stone, perhaps half an arm's length thick, covering a hollowed-out subterranean chamber. That stank.

A wooden ladder led down into the vault.

A makeshift cesspit, he suspected, since the besiegers had likely blocked the out-drains into the moat, in the hopes of fostering plague or some such thing. The stench certainly suggested that it had been used as a latrine. Then again, why the ladder? 'These Malazans have odd interests,' he muttered. In his hands he could feel a tension building in the stone sword – the bound spirits of Bairoth Gild and Delum Thord were suddenly restive. 'Or a chance discovery,' he added. 'Is this what you warn me of, kindred spirits?'

He eyed the ladder. 'Well, as you say, brothers, I have climbed into worse.' Karsa sheathed his sword and began his descent.

Excrement smeared the walls, but not, fortunately, the rungs of the ladder. He made his way past the broken shell of stone, and what little clean air drifted down from above was overwhelmed by a thick, pungent reek. There was more to it than human waste, however. Something else . . .

Reaching the floor of the chamber, Karsa waited, ankle-deep in shit and pools of piss, for his eyes to adjust to the gloom. Eventually, he could make out the walls, rounded, the stones bearing horizontal undulations but otherwise unadorned. A beehive tomb, then, but not in a style Karsa had seen before. Too large, for one thing, and there was no evidence of platforms or sarcophagi. No grave-goods, no inscriptions.

He could see no formal entranceway or door revealed on any of the walls. Sloshing through the sewage for a closer look at the stonework, Karsa almost stumbled as he stepped off an unseen ledge – he had been standing on a slightly raised dais, extending almost out to the base of the walls. Back-stepping, he edged carefully along its circumference. In the process he discovered six submerged iron spikes, driven deep into the stone in two sets of three. The spikes were massive, thicker across than Karsa's wrists.

He made his way back to the centre, stood near the base of the ladder. Were he to lie down with the middle spike of either set under his head, he could not have reached the outer ones with arms outstretched. Half again as tall and he might manage it. Thus, if something had been pinned here by these spikes, it had been huge.

And, unfortunately, it looked as if the spikes had failed—

A slight motion through the heavy, turgid air, a shadowing of the faint light leaking down. Karsa reached for his sword.

An enormous hand closed on his back, a talon lancing into each shoulder, two beneath his ribs, one larger one stabbing down and around, just under his left clavicle. The fingers clenched and he was being hauled straight up, the ladder passing in a blur. The sword was pinned against his back. Karsa reached up with both hands and they closed about a scaled wrist thicker than his upper arm.

He cleared the hole in the capstone, and the tugs and tearing in his muscles told him the beast was clambering up the side of the pit, nimble as a bhok'aral. Something heavy and scaled slithered across his arms.

Then into bright sunlight.

The beast flung the Teblor across the courtyard. He landed hard, skidding until he crashed up against the keep's outer wall.

Spitting blood, every bone in his back feeling out of place, Karsa Orlong pushed himself to his feet, reeled until he could lean against the sun-heated stone.

Standing beside the pit was a reptilian monstrosity, two-legged, the hanging arms oversized and overlong, talons scraping the pavestones. It was tailed, but that tail was stunted and thick. The broad-snouted jaws were crowded with interlocking rows of dagger-long fangs, above them flaring cheekbones and brow-ridges protecting deep-set eyes that glistened like wet stones on a strand. A serrated crest bisected the flat, elongated skull, pale yellow above the dun green hide. The beast reared half again as tall as the Toblakai.

Motionless as a statue, it studied him, blood dripping from the talons of its left hand.

Karsa took a deep breath, then drew his sword and flung it aside.

The creature's head twitched, a strange sideways tilt, then it charged, leaning far over as the massive legs propelled it forward.

And Karsa launched himself straight at it.

Clearly, an unanticipated response, as he found himself inside those raking hands and beneath the snapping jaws. He flung his head straight up, cracking hard against the underside of the beast's jaw, then ducked back down, sliding his right arm between the legs, wrapping it about the creature's right one. Shoulder pounding into its belly, his hands closing tight on the other side of the captured leg. Then lifting, a bellow escaping him as he heaved the beast up until it tottered on one leg.

The taloned hands hammered down on his back, slicing through the bear fur, ravaging his flesh in a frenzy.

Karsa planted his right leg behind the beast's left one, then pushed hard in that direction.

It crashed down and he heard bones snap.

The short tail whipped round, struck him in his midsection. Air exploded from Karsa's four lungs, and once more he was spinning through the air, striking the pavestones and leaving most of the skin of his right shoulder and hip on the hard stone as he skidded another four paces—

Over the edge of the pit. Down, cracking hard against one edge of the capstone, breaking it further, then landing face first in the pool of sewage in the tomb, rubble splashing on all sides.

He lifted himself, twisting into a half-seated position, spitting out foul fluids even as he tried to draw air into his lungs. Coughing, choking, he crawled towards one side of the tomb, away from the hole in the ceiling.

Moments later he managed to restore his breathing. Shaking the muck from his head, he peered at the shaft of sunlight reaching down around the ladder. The beast had not come after him . . . or had not seen him fall.

He rose and made his way to the ladder. Looked straight up, and saw nothing but sunlight.

Karsa climbed. As he drew level with the pit's edge, he slowed, then lifted himself until he could just see the courtyard. The creature was nowhere in sight. He clambered quickly onto the pavestones. Spitting again, he shook himself, then made his way towards the keep's inner entrance. Hearing no screams from beyond the moat, he assumed that the beast had not gone in that direction. Which left the keep itself.

The double doors were ajar. He entered a broad chamber, its floor tiled, the walls bearing the ghosts of long-faded murals.

Pieces of mangled armour and bits of blood-crusted clothing lay scattered about. Nearby stood a boot, twin bones jutting from it.

Directly opposite, twenty paces away, was another doorway, both doors battered down and smashed. Karsa padded towards it, then froze upon hearing the scrape of claws on tile in the gloom beyond. From his left, close by the entrance. He backed up ten paces, then sprinted forward. Through the doorway. Hands slashed down in his wake, and he heard a frustrated hiss – even as he collided with a low divan, propelling him forward, down onto a low table. The wooden legs exploded beneath his weight. He rolled onward, sending a high-backed chair cartwheeling, then sliding on a rug, the thump and click of the creature's clawed feet grew louder as it lunged in pursuit.

Karsa got his feet under him and he dove sideways, once more evading the descending claws. Up against another chair, this one massive. Grasping the legs, Karsa heaved it into the path of the creature – it had launched itself into the air. The chair caught both its outstretched legs, snapped them out to the side.

The beast crashed down, cracking its head, broken tiles flying.

Karsa kicked it in the throat.

The beast kicked him in the chest, and he was pitched backward once more, landing on a discarded helmet that rolled, momentarily, sending him back further, up against a wall.

Pain thundering in his chest, the Toblakai climbed to his feet.

The beast was doing the same, slowly, wagging its head from side to side, its breath coming in rough wheezes punctuated by sharp, barking coughs.

Karsa flung himself at it. His hands closed on its right wrist and he ducked under, twisting the arm as he went, then spun round yet again, turning the arm until it popped at the shoulder.

The creature squealed.

Karsa clambered onto its back, his fists hammering on the dome of its skull. Each blow shook the beast's bones. Teeth snapped, the head driven down at each blow, springing back up in time to meet the next one. Staggering beneath him, the right arm hanging limp, the left one attempting to reach up to scrape him off, the creature careened across the room.

Karsa continued swinging, his own hands numbed by the impacts.

Finally, he heard the skull crack.

A rattling gasp of breath – from him or the beast, he wasn't sure which – then the creature dropped and rolled.

Most of its immense weight settled for a brief moment between Karsa's thighs, and a roar burst from his throat as he clenched the muscles of his legs to keep that ridged spine away from his crotch. Then the reptile pitched sideways, pinning his left leg. He reached up to wrap an arm around its thrashing neck.

Rolling further, it freed its own left arm, scythed it up and around. Talons sank into Karsa's left shoulder. A surge of overpowering strength dragged the Toblakai off, sending him tumbling into the wreckage of the collapsed table.

Karsa's grasping hand found one of the table legs. He scrambled up and swung it hard against the beast's outstretched arm.

The leg shattered, and the arm was snatched back with a squeal.

The beast reared upright once more.

Karsa charged again.

Was met by a kick, high on his chest.

Sudden blackness.

His eyes opened. Gloom. Silence. The stink of faeces and blood and settling dust. Groaning, he sat up.

A distant crash. From somewhere above.

He studied his surroundings, until he spied the side doorway. He rose, limped towards it. A wide hallway beyond, leading to a staircase.

'Was that a scream, Captain?'

'I am not sure, Falah'd.'

Samar Dev squinted in the bright light at the soldier beside her. He had been muttering under his breath since Toblakai's breach of the iron doors. Stone swords, iron and locks seemed to have been the focus of his private monologue, periodically spiced with some choice curses. That, and the need to get the giant barbarian as far away from Ugarat as possible.

She wiped sweat from her brow, returned her attention to the keep's entrance. Still nothing.

100

'They're negotiating,' the Falah'd said, restless on the saddle as servants stood to either side, alternately sweeping the large papyrus fans to cool Ugarat's beloved ruler.

'It did sound like a scream, Holy One,' Captain Inashan said after a moment.

'Then it is a belligerent negotiation, Captain. What else can be taking so long? Were they all starved and dead, that barbarian would have returned. Unless, of course, there's loot. Hah, am I wrong in that? I think not! He's a savage, after all. Cut loose from Sha'ik's leash, yes? Why did he not die protecting her?'

'If the tales are true,' Inashan said uncomfortably, 'Sha'ik sought a personal duel with the Adjunct, Falah'd.'

'Too much convenience in that tale. Told by the survivors, the ones who abandoned her. I am unconvinced by this Toblakai. He is too rude.'

'Yes, Falah'd,' Inashan said, 'he is that.'

Samar Dev cleared her throat. 'Holy One, there is no loot to be found in Moraval Keep.'

'Oh, witch? And how can you be so certain?'

'It is an ancient structure, older even than Ugarat itself. True, alterations have been made every now and then – all the old mechanisms were beyond our understanding, Falah'd, even to this day, and all we have now from them is a handful of pieces. I have made long study of those few fragments, and have learned much—'

'You bore me, now, witch. You have still not explained why there is no loot.'

'I am sorry, Falah'd. To answer you, the keep has been explored countless times, and nothing of value has ever been found, barring those dismantled mechanisms—'

'Worthless junk. Very well, the barbarian is not looting. He is negotiating with the squalid, vile Malazans – whom we shall have to kneel before once again. I am betrayed into humiliation by the cowardly rebels of Raraku. Oh, one can count on no-one these days.'

'It would seem not, Falah'd,' Samar Dev murmured.

Inashan shot her a look.

Samar wiped another sheath of sweat from her brow.

'Oh!' the Falah'd cried suddenly. 'I am melting!'

'Wait!' Inashan said. 'Was that a bellow of some sort?'

'He's probably raping someone!'

He found the creature hobbling down a corridor, its head wagging from side to side, pitching into one wall then the other. Karsa ran after it.

It must have heard him, for it wheeled round, jaws opening in a hiss, moments before he closed. Battering a raking hand aside, the Toblakai kneed the beast in the belly. The reptile doubled over, chest-ridge cracking down onto Karsa's right shoulder. He drove his thumb up under its left arm, where it found doeskin-soft tissue. Puncturing it, the thumb plunging into meat, curling round ligaments. Closing his hand, Karsa yanked on those ligaments.

Dagger-sharp teeth raked the side of his head, slicing a flap of skin away. Blood gushed into Karsa's right eye. He pulled harder, throwing himself back.

The beast plunged with him. Twisting to one side, Karsa narrowly escaped the crashing weight, and was close enough to see the unnatural splaying of its ribs at the impact.

It struggled to rise, but Karsa was faster. Straddling it once more. Fists hammering down on its skull. With each blow the lower jaws cracked against the floor, and he could feel a sagging give in the plates of the skull's bones beneath his fists. He kept pounding.

A dozen wild heartbeats later and he slowed, realizing the beast was no longer moving beneath him, the head flat on the floor, getting wider and flatter with each impact of his battered fists. Fluids were leaking out. Karsa stopped swinging. He drew in a ragged, agony-filled breath, held it against the sudden waves of darkness thundering through his brain, then released it steady and long. Another mouthful of bloody phlegm to spit out, onto the dead beast's shattered skull.

Lifting his head, Karsa glared about. A doorway on his right. In the room beyond, a long table and chairs. Groaning, he slowly rose, stumbled into the chamber.

A jug of wine sat on the table. Cups were lined up in even rows down both sides, each one opposite a chair. Karsa swept them from the table, collected the jug, then lay down on the stained wood surface. He stared up at the ceiling, where someone had painted a pantheon of unknown gods, all looking down.

Mocking expressions one and all.

Karsa pushed the flap of loose skin back against his temple, then sneered at the faces on the ceiling, before lifting the jug to his lips.

Blessed cool wind, now that the sun was so close to the horizon. Silence for a while now, too, since that last bellow. A number of soldiers, standing for bell after bell all afternoon, had passed out and were being tended to by the lone slave the Falah'd had relinquished from his entourage.

Captain Inashan had been assembling a squad to lead into the keep for some time now.

The Falah'd was having his feet massaged and bathed in mint-leaves chewed in mouthfuls of oil by the slaves. 'You are taking too long, Captain!' he said. 'Look at that demonic horse, the way it eyes us! It will be dark by the time you storm the keep!'

'Torches are being brought along, Falah'd,' Inashan said. 'We're almost ready.'

His reluctance was almost comical, and Samar Dev dared not meet his eye again, not after the expression her wink earlier had elicited.

A shout from the besiegers' encampment.

Toblakai had appeared, climbing down from the ledge, back onto the makeshift steps. Samar Dev and Inashan made their way to the moat, arriving in time to see him emerge. The bear fur was in ribbons, dark with blood. He had tied a strip of cloth about his head, holding the skin in place over one temple. Most of his upper clothing had been torn away, revealing countless gouges and puncture wounds.

And he was covered in shit.

From the Falah'd twenty paces behind them came a querulous enquiry: 'Toblakai! The negotiations went well?'

In a low voice, Inashan said, 'No Malazans left, I take it?'

Karsa Orlong scowled. 'Didn't see any.' He strode past them.

Turning, Samar Dev flinched at the horror of the warrior's ravaged back. 'What happened in there?' she demanded.

A shrug that jostled the slung stone sword. 'Nothing important, witch.'

Not slowing, not turning, he continued on.

A smudge of light far to the south, like a cluster of dying stars on the horizon, marked the city of Kayhum. The dust of the storm a week past had settled and the night sky was bright with the twin sweeps of the Roads of the Abyss. There were scholars, Corabb Bhilan Thenu'alas had heard, who asserted that those broad roads were nothing more than stars, crowded in multitudes beyond counting, but Corabb knew that was folly. They could be naught but celestial roads, the paths walked by the dragons of the deep, and Elder Gods and the blacksmiths with suns for eyes who hammered stars into life; and the worlds spinning round those stars were simply dross, cast-offs from the forges, pale and smudged, on which crawled creatures preening with conceit.

Preening with conceit. An old seer had told him that once, and for some reason the phrase lodged in Corabb's mind, allowing him to pull it free every now and then to play with, his inner eye bright with shining wonder. People did that, yes. He had seen them, again and again. Like birds. Obsessed with self-importance, thinking themselves tall, as tall as the night sky. That seer had been a genius, to have seen so clearly, and to manage so much in three simple words. Not that conceit was a simple thing, and Corabb recalled having to ask an old woman what the word meant, and she had cackled and reached under his tunic to tug on his penis, which had been unexpected and, instinctive response notwithstanding, unwelcome. A faint wave of embarrassment accompanied the recollection, and he spat into the fire flickering before him.

Leoman of the Flails sat opposite him, a hookah filled with wine-soaked durhang at the man's side, at his thin lips the mouthpiece of hard wood carved into the semblance of a woman's nipple and stained magenta to add to the likeness. His leader's eyes glistened dark red in the fire's light, the lids low, the gaze seemingly fixed on the licking flames.

Corabb had found a piece of wood the length of his arm, light as a woman's breath – telling him that a birit slug dwelt within – and he had just dug it out with the point of his knife. The creature squirmed on the blade's tip, and it had been the sight of this that had, alas, reminded him of the debacle with his penis. Feeling morose, he bit the slug in half and began chewing, juices spurting down into his beard. 'Ah,' he said around the mouthful, 'she has roe. Delicious.'

Leoman looked over, then he drew once more on the mouthpiece. 'We're running out of horses,' he said.

Corabb swallowed. The other half of the slug was writhing on the knife tip, threads of pink eggs dangling like tiny pearls. 'We'll make it, Commander,' he said, then poked out his tongue to lap up the roe, following up by inserting the rest of the slug into his mouth. He chewed, then swallowed. 'Four, five days, I would judge.'

Leoman's eyes glittered. 'You know, then.'

'Where we're going? Yes.'

'Do you know why?'

Corabb tossed the piece of wood onto the fire. 'Y'Ghatan. The First Holy City. Where Dassem Ultor, curse his name, died in betrayal. Y'Ghatan, the oldest city in the world. Built atop the forge of a black-smith of the Abyss, built on his very bones. Seven Y'Ghatans, seven great cities to mark the ages we have seen, the one we see now crouched on the bones of the other six. City of the Olive Groves, city of the sweet oils—' Corabb paused, frowned. 'What was your question, Commander?'

'Why.'

'Oh, yes. Do I know why you have chosen Y'Ghatan? Because we invite a siege. It is a difficult city to conquer. The fool Malazans will bleed themselves to death attempting to storm its walls. We shall add their bones to all the others, to Dassem Ultor's very own—'

'He didn't die there, Corabb.'

'What? But there were witnesses—'

'To his wounding, yes. To the assassination . . . attempt. But no, my friend, the First Sword did not die, and he lives still.'

'Then where is he?'

'Where doesn't matter. You should ask: *Who is he?* Ask that, Corabb Bhilan Thenu'alas, and I will give you answer.'

Corabb thought about that. Even swimming in the fumes of durhang, Leoman of the Flails was too smart for him. Clever, able to see all that Corabb could not. He was the greatest commander Seven Cities had ever produced. He would have defeated Coltaine. Honourably. And, had he been left to it, he would have crushed Adjunct Tavore, and then Dujek Onearm. There would have been true liberation, for all Seven Cities, and from here the rebellion against the damned empire would have rippled outward, until the yoke was thrown off by all. This was the tragedy, the true tragedy. 'Blessed Dessembrae hounds our heels . . .'

Leoman coughed a cloud of smoke. He doubled over, still coughing.

Corabb reached for a skin of water and thrust it into his leader's hands. The man finally drew breath, then drank deep. He leaned back with a gusty sigh, and then grinned. 'You are a wonder, Corabb Bhilan Thenu'alas! To answer you, I certainly hope not!'

Corabb felt sad. He said, 'You mock me, Commander.'

'Not at all, you Oponn-blessed madman – my only friend left breathing – not at all. It is the cult, you see. The Lord of Tragedy. Dessembrae. That is Dassem Ultor. I don't doubt you understood that, but consider this – for there to be a cult, a religion, with priests and such, there must be a god. A living god.'

'Dassem Ultor is ascended?'

'I believe so, although he is a reluctant god. A denier, like Anomander Rake of the Tiste Andii. And so he wanders, in eternal flight, and in, perhaps, eternal hunt as well.'

'For what?'

Leoman shook his head. Then said, 'Y'Ghatan. Yes, my friend. There, we will make our stand, and the name shall be a curse among the Malazans, for all time, a curse, bitter on their tongues.' His eyes hardened suddenly on Corabb. 'Are you with me? No matter what I command, no matter the madness that will seem to afflict me?'

Something in his leader's gaze frightened Corabb, but he nodded. 'I am with you, Leoman of the Flails. Do not doubt that.'

A wry smile. 'I shall not hold you to that. But I thank you for your words nonetheless.'

'Why would you doubt them?'

'Because only I know what I intend to do.'

'Tell me.'

'No, my friend. This burden is mine.'

'You lead us, Leoman of the Flails. We shall follow. As you say, you carry all of us. We are the weight of history, of liberty, and yet you are not bowed—'

'Ah, Corabb . . .'

'I only say what is known but has never before been said aloud, Commander.'

'There is mercy in silence, my friend. But no mind. It is done, you have indeed spoken.'

'I have assailed you further. I am sorry, Leoman of the Flails.'

Leoman drank again from the waterskin, then spat into the fire. 'We need say no more of it. Y'Ghatan. This shall be our city. Four, five days. It is just past crushing season, yes?'

'The olives? Yes, we shall arrive when the grovers have gathered. A thousand merchants will be there, and workers out on the road leading to the coast, setting new stones. And potters, and barrel-makers, and wagoners and caravans. The air shall be gold with dust and dusted with gold—'

'You are a poet indeed, Corabb. Merchants, and their hired guards. Tell me, will they bow to my authority, do you think?'

'They must.'

'Who is the city's Falah'd?'

'Vedor.'

'Which one?'

'The ferret-faced one, Leoman. His fish-faced brother was found dead in his lover's bed, the whore nowhere to be found, but likely rich and in hiding or in a shallow grave. It's the old story among the Fala'dhan.'

'And we are certain Vedor continues to deny the Malazans?'

'No fleet or army could have reached them yet. You know this, Leoman of the Flails.'

The man slowly nodded, eyes once more on the flames.

Corabb looked up at the night sky. 'One day,' he said, 'we shall walk the Roads to the Abyss. And so witness all the wonders of the universe.'

Leoman squinted upward. 'Where the stars are thick as veins?'

'They are roads, Leoman. Surely you do not believe those insane scholars?'

'All scholars are insane, yes. They say nothing worth believing. The roads, then. The trail of fire.'

'Of course,' Corabb continued, 'that shall be many years from now . . .'

'As you say, friend. Now, best get some sleep.'

Corabb rose, bones cracking. 'May you dream of glory this night, Commander.'

'Glory? Oh, yes, my friend. Our trail of fire . . .'

'Aai, that slug has given me indigestion. It was the roe.'

'The bastard's heading for Y'Ghatan.'

Sergeant Strings glanced over at Bottle. 'You've been thinking, haven't you? That's not good, soldier. Not good at all.'

'Can't help it.'

'That's even worse. Now I have to keep an eye on you.'

Koryk was on his hands and knees, head lowered as he sought to breathe life back into the bed of coals from the night just past. He suddenly coughed as he inhaled a cloud of ashes and ducked away, blinking and hacking.

Smiles laughed. 'The wise plainsman does it again. You were asleep, Koryk, but I should tell you, Tarr pissed that fire out last night.'

'What!?'

'She's lying,' Tarr said from where he crouched beside his pack, repairing a strap. 'Even so, it was a good one. You should have seen your expression, Koryk.'

'How can anyone, with that white mask he's wearing? Shouldn't you be painting death lines through that ash, Koryk? Isn't that what Seti do?'

'Only when going into battle, Smiles,' the sergeant said. 'Now, leave off, woman. You're as bad as that damned Hengese lapdog. It bit a Khundryl's ankle last night and wouldn't let go.'

'Hope they skewered it,' Smiles said.

'Not a chance. Bent was standing guard. Anyway, they had to get Temul to pry the thing off. My point is, Smiles, you ain't got a Wickan cattle-dog to guard your back, so the less you snipe the safer you'll be.'

No-one mentioned the knife Koryk had taken in the leg a week past.

Cuttle came wandering into the camp. He'd found a squad that had already brewed some foul-smelling tea and was sipping from his tin cup. 'They're here,' he said.

'Who?' Smiles demanded.

Bottle watched as their sergeant settled back down, leaning against his pack. 'All right,' Strings said, sighing. 'March will be delayed. Someone help Koryk get the fire going – we're going to have a real breakfast. Cuttle the cook.'

'Me? All right, just don't blame me.'

'For what?' Strings asked with an innocent smile.

Cuttle walked over to the hearth, reaching into a pouch. 'Got some sealed Flamer dust—'

Everyone scattered, Strings included. Suddenly, Cuttle was alone, looking round bemusedly at his fellow soldiers, now one and all at least

107

fifteen paces distant. He scowled. 'A grain or two, nothing more. Damn, do you think I'm mad?'

Everyone looked to Strings, who shrugged. 'Instinctive reaction, Cuttle. Surprised you ain't used to it by now.'

'Yeah? And how come you were the first belting out of here, Fid?'

'Who'd know better than me?'

Cuttle crouched down beside the hearth. 'Well,' he muttered, 'I'm absolutely crushed.' He withdrew a small clay disk from the pouch. It was a playing piece for the board-game called Troughs, the game being Cuttle's favourite pastime. The sapper spat on it, then tossed it into the coals. And quickly backed away.

No-one else moved.

'Hey,' Koryk said, 'that wasn't a *real* Troughs piece, was it?'

Cuttle glanced over. 'Why wouldn't it be?'

'Because those things get thrown around!'

'Only when I lose,' the sapper replied.

A burst of ash, sudden flames. Cuttle walked back and began flinging pieces of dung on the fire. 'All right, somebody tend to this. I'll get what passes for food around here and figure something out.'

'Bottle has some lizards,' Smiles said.

'Forget it,' Bottle shot back. 'They're my, uh, friends.' He flinched as the other squad members turned to regard him.

'Friends?' Strings asked. He scratched his beard, studying his soldier.

'What,' Smiles said, 'the rest of us too smart for you, Bottle? All these confounding words we use? The fact we can read those squiggly etchings on clay and wax tablets and scrolls? Well, except for Koryk, of course. Anyway. Feeling insufficient, Bottle? I don't mean physically – that goes without saying. But, mentally, right? Is that the problem?'

Bottle glared at her. 'You'll regret all that, Smiles.'

'Oh, he's going to send his lizard friends after me! Help!'

'That's enough, Smiles,' Strings said in a warning growl.

She rose, ran her hands through her still-unbound hair. 'Well, I'm off to gossip with Flashwit and Uru Hela. Flash said she saw Neffarias Bredd a couple of days ago. A horse had died and he carried it back to his squad's camp. They roasted it. Nothing but bones left.'

'The squad ate an entire horse?' Koryk snorted. 'How come I've never seen this Neffarias Bredd, anyway? Has anybody here seen him?'

'I have,' Smiles replied.

'When?' Koryk demanded.

'A few days ago. I'm bored talking to you. Your fire's going out.' She walked off.

The sergeant was still tugging at his beard. 'Gods below, I need to hack this thing off,' he muttered.

'But the chicks ain't left the nest yet,' Cuttle said, settling down with an armful of foodstuffs. 'Who's been collecting snakes?' he asked, letting the various objects drop. He picked up a long, rope-like thing. 'They stink—'

'That's the vinegar,' Koryk said. 'It's an old Seti delicacy. The vinegar cooks the meat, you see, for when you ain't got the time to smoke it slow.'

'What are you doing killing snakes?' Bottle demanded. 'They're useful, you know.'

Strings rose. 'Bottle, walk with me.'

Oh damn. I've got to learn to say nothing. 'Aye, Sergeant.'

They crossed the ditch and headed onto the broken sweep of the Lato Odhan, the mostly level, dusty ground home to a scattering of shattered rock, no piece larger than a man's head. Somewhere far to the southwest was the city of Kayhum, still out of sight, whilst behind them rose the Thalas Mountains, treeless for centuries and now eroded like rotting teeth. No cloud relieved the bright morning sun, already hot.

'Where do you keep your lizards?' Strings asked.

'In my clothes, out of the sun, during the day, I mean. They wander at night.'

'And you wander with them.'

Bottle nodded.

'That's a useful talent,' the sergeant commented, then went on, 'especially for spying. Not on the enemy, of course, but on everyone else.'

'So far. I mean, we haven't been close enough to the enemy—'

'I know. And that's why you ain't told nobody yet about it. So, you've listened in on the Adjunct much? I mean, since that time you learned about the fall of the Bridgeburners.'

'Not much, to tell the truth.' Bottle hesitated, wondering how much he should say.

'Out with it, soldier.'

'It's that Claw . . .'

'Pearl.'

'Aye, and, well, uh, the High Mage.'

'Quick Ben.'

'Right, and now there's Tayschrenn, too—'

Strings grasped Bottle's arm and pulled him round. 'He left. He was only here for a few bells, and that was a week ago—'

'Aye, but that doesn't mean he can't come back, at any time, right? Anyway, all these powerful, scary mages, well, they make me nervous.'

'You're making *me* nervous, Bottle!'

'Why?'

The sergeant squinted at him, then let go of his arm and resumed walking.

'Where are we going?' Bottle demanded.

'You tell me.'

'Not that way.'

'Why?'

'Uh. Nil and Nether, just the other side of that low rise.'

Strings loosed a half-dozen dockside curses. 'Hood take us! Listen, soldier, I ain't forgotten anything, you know. I remember you playing dice with Meanas, making dolls of Hood and the Rope. Earth-magic and talking with spirits – gods below, you're so much like Quick Ben it makes my hair stand on end. Oh, right, it all comes from your grandmother – but you see, I *know* where Quick got his talents!'

Bottle frowned at the man. 'What?'

'What do you mean *what*?'

'What are you talking about, Sergeant? You've got me confused.'

'Quick's got more warrens to draw on than any mage I've ever heard about. Except,' he added in a frustrated snarl, 'except maybe *you*.'

'But I don't even like warrens!'

'No, you're closer to Nil and Nether, aren't you? Spirits and stuff. When you're not playing with Hood and Shadow, that is!'

'They're older than warrens, Sergeant.'

'Like that! What do you mean by that?'

'Well. Holds. They're holds. Or they were. Before warrens. It's old magic, that's what my grandmother taught me. Real old. Anyway, I've changed my mind about Nil and Nether. They're up to something and I want to see it.'

'But you don't want them to see us.'

Bottle shrugged. 'Too late for that, Sergeant. They know we're here.'

'Fine, lead on, then. But I want Quick Ben to meet you. And I want to know all about these holds you keep talking about.'

No you don't. 'All right.' Quick Ben. A meeting. That was bad. *Maybe I could run away. No, don't be an idiot. You can't run away, Bottle.* Besides, what were the risks of talking with the High Mage? He wasn't doing anything wrong, exactly. Not really. Not so anybody would know, anyway. *Except a sneaky bastard like Quick Ben. Abyss, what if he finds out who's walking in my shadow? Well, it's not like I asked for the company, is it?*

'Whatever you're thinking,' Strings said in a growl, 'it's got my skin crawling.'

'Not me. Nil and Nether. They've begun a ritual. I've changed my mind again – maybe we should go back.'

'No.'

110

They began ascending the gentle slope.

Bottle felt sudden sweat trickling beneath his clothes. 'You've got some natural talent, haven't you, Sergeant? Skin crawling and all that. You're sensitive to . . . stuff.'

'I had a bad upbringing.'

'Where's Gesler's squad gone?'

Strings shot him a glance. 'You're doing it again.'

'Sorry.'

'They're escorting Quick and Kalam – they've gone ahead. So, your dreaded meeting with Quick is still some time off, you'll be glad to know.'

'Gone ahead. By warren? They shouldn't be doing that, you know. Not now. Not here—'

'Why?'

'Well. Because.'

'For the first time in my career as a soldier of the Malazan Empire, I truly want to strangle a fellow soldier.'

'Sorry.'

'Stop saying that name!'

'It's not a name. It's a word.'

The sergeant's battered hands clenched into fists.

Bottle fell silent. Wondering if Strings might actually strangle him.

They reached the crest. Thirty paces beyond, the Wickan witch and warlock had arranged a circle of jagged stones and were seated within it, facing each other. 'They're travelling,' Bottle said. 'It's a kind of Spiritwalking, like the Tanno do. They're aware of us, but only vaguely.'

'I assume we don't step within that ring.'

'Not unless we need to pull them out.'

Strings looked over.

'Not unless I need to pull them out, I mean. If things go wrong. If they get in trouble.'

They drew nearer. 'What made you join the army, Bottle?'

She insisted. 'My grandmother thought it would be a good idea. She'd just died, you see, and her spirit was, um, agitated a little. About something.' *Oh, steer away from this, Bottle.* 'I was getting bored. Restless. Selling dolls to pilots and sailors on the docks—'

'Where?'

'Jakatakan.'

'What kind of dolls?'

'The kind the Stormriders seem to like. Appeasement.'

'Stormriders? Gods below, Bottle, I didn't think anything worked with them lately. Not for years.'

'The dolls didn't always work, but they sometimes did, which was better than most propitiations. Anyway, I was making good coin, but it didn't seem enough—'

'Are you feeling cold all of a sudden?'

Bottle nodded. 'It makes sense, where they've gone.'

'And where is that?'

'Through Hood's Gate. It's all right, Sergeant. I think. Really. They're pretty sneaky, and so long as they don't attract the wrong attention . . .'

'But . . . why?'

Bottle glanced over. The sergeant was looking pale. Not surprising. Those damned ghosts at Raraku had rattled him. 'They're looking for . . . people. Dead ones.'

'Sormo E'nath?'

'I guess. Wickans. Ones who died on the Chain of Dogs. They've done this before. They don't find them—' He stopped as a gust of bitter cold wind swirled up round the circle of stones. Sudden frost limned the ground. 'Oh, that's not good. I'll be right back, Sergeant.'

Bottle ran forward, then leapt into the ring.

And vanished.

Or, he assumed he had, since he was no longer on the Lato Odhan, but ankle-deep in rotting, crumbling bones, a sickly grey sky overhead. Someone was screaming. Bottle turned at the sound and saw three figures thirty paces away. Nil and Nether, and facing them, a horrific apparition, and it was this lich that was doing the screaming. The two young Wickans were flinching before the tirade.

A language Bottle did not understand. He walked closer, bone-dust puffing with each step.

The lich suddenly reached out and grasped both Wickans, lifting them into the air, then shaking them.

Bottle ran forward. *And what do I do when I get there?*

The creature snarled and flung Nil and Nether to the ground, then abruptly disappeared amidst the clouds of dust.

He reached them as they were climbing to their feet. Nether was swearing in her native tongue as she brushed dust from her tunic. She glared over at Bottle as he arrived. 'What do you want?'

'Thought you were in trouble.'

'We're fine,' Nil snapped, yet there was a sheepish expression on his adolescent face. 'You can lead us back, mage.'

'Did the Adjunct send you?' Nether demanded. 'Are we to have no peace?'

'Nobody sent me. Well, Sergeant Strings – we were just out walking—'

'Strings? You mean Fiddler.'

'We're supposed to—'

'Don't be an idiot,' Nether said. 'Everybody knows.'

'We're not idiots. It clearly hasn't occurred to either of you that maybe Fiddler wants it that way. Wants to be called Strings, now, because his old life is gone, and with the old name comes bad memories, and he's had enough of those.'

Neither Wickan replied.

After a few more strides, Bottle asked, 'So, was that a Wickan lich? One of the dead you were looking for?'

'You know too much.'

'Was it?'

Nil cursed under his breath, then said, 'Our mother.'

'Your . . .' Bottle fell silent.

'She was telling us to stop moping and grow up,' Nil added.

'She was telling you that,' Nether retorted. 'She told me to—'

'To take a husband and get pregnant.'

'That was just a suggestion.'

'Made while she was shaking you?' Bottle asked.

Nether spat at his feet. 'A suggestion. Something I should maybe think about. Besides, I don't have to listen to you, soldier. You're Malazan. A squad mage.'

'He's also the one,' pointed out Nil, 'who rides life-sparks.'

'Small ones. The way we did as children.'

Bottle smiled at her remark.

She caught it. 'What's so amusing?'

'Nothing. Sorry.'

'I thought you were going to lead us back.'

'I thought so, too,' Bottle said, halting and looking round. 'Oh, I think we've been noticed.'

'It's your fault, mage!' Nil accused.

'Probably.'

Nether hissed and pointed.

Another figure had appeared, and to either side padded dogs. Wickan cattle dogs. Nine, ten, twelve. Their eyes gleamed silver. The man in their midst was clearly Wickan, greying and squat and bow-legged. His face was savagely scarred.

'It is Bult,' Nether whispered. She stepped forward.

The dogs growled.

'Nil, Nether, I have been searching for you,' the ghost named Bult said, halting ten paces away, the dogs lining up on either side. 'Hear me. We do not belong here. Do you understand? We do not belong.' He paused and pulled at his nose in a habitual gesture. 'Think hard on my words.' He turned away, then paused and glanced back over a shoulder, 'And Nether, get married and have babies.'

The ghosts vanished.

Nether stamped her foot. Dust rose up around her. 'Why does everyone keep telling me that!?'

'Your tribe's been decimated,' Bottle said reasonably. 'It stands to reason—'

She advanced on him.

Bottle stepped back—

And reappeared within the stone circle.

A moment later gasps came from Nil and Nether, their crosslegged bodies twitching.

'I was getting worried,' Strings said behind him, standing just outside the ring.

The two Wickans were slow in getting to their feet.

Bottle hurried to his sergeant's side. 'We should get going,' he said. 'Before she comes fully round, I mean.'

'Why?'

Bottle started walking. 'She's mad at me.'

The sergeant snorted, then followed. 'And why is she mad at you, soldier? As if I need ask.'

'Just something I said.'

'Oh, I am surprised.'

'I don't want to go into it, Sergeant. Sorry.'

'I'm tempted to throw you down and pin you for her.'

They reached the crest. Behind them, Nether began shouting curses. Bottle quickened his pace. Then he halted and crouched down, reaching under his shirt, and gingerly drew out a placid lizard. 'Wake up,' he murmured, then set it down. It scampered off.

Strings watched. 'It's going to follow them, isn't it?'

'She might decide on a real curse,' Bottle explained. 'And if she does, I need to counter it.'

'Hood's breath, what did you say to her?'

'I made a terrible mistake. I agreed with her mother.'

'We should be getting out of here. Or . . .'

Kalam glanced over. 'All right, Quick.' He raised a hand to halt the soldiers flanking them and the one trailing behind, then uttered a low whistle to alert the huge, red-bearded corporal on point.

The squad members drew in to surround the assassin and the High Mage.

'We're being followed,' Sergeant Gesler said, wiping sweat from his burnished brow.

'It's worse than that,' Quick Ben said.

The soldier named Sands muttered, 'Isn't it just.'

Kalam turned and studied the track behind them. He could see nothing in the colourless swirl. 'This is still the Imperial Warren, isn't it?'

Quick Ben rubbed at his neck. 'I'm not so sure.'

'But how can that happen?' This from the corporal, Stormy, his forehead buckling and small eyes glittering as though he was about to fly into a berserk rage at any moment. He was holding his grey flint sword as if expecting some demon to come bursting into existence right in front of them.

The assassin checked his long-knives, and said to Quick Ben, 'Well?'

The wizard hesitated, then nodded. 'All right.'

'What did you two just decide?' Gesler asked. 'And would it be so hard explaining it to us?'

'Sarcastic bastard,' Quick Ben commented, then gave the sergeant a broad, white smile.

'I've punched a lot of faces in my day,' Gesler said, returning the smile, 'but never one belonging to a High Mage before.'

'You might not be here if you had, Sergeant.'

'Back to business,' Kalam said in a warning rumble. 'We're going to wait and see what's after us, Gesler. Quick doesn't know where we are, and that in itself is troubling enough.'

'And then we leave,' the wizard added. 'No heroic stands.'

'The Fourteenth's motto,' Stormy said, with a loud sigh.

'Which?' Gesler asked. '*And then we leave* or *No heroic stands?*'

'Take your pick.'

Kalam studied the squad, first Gesler, then Stormy, then the lad, Truth, and Pella and the minor mage, Sands. *What a miserable bunch.*

'Let's just go kill it,' Stormy said, shifting about. 'And then we can talk about what it was.'

'Hood knows how you've lived this long,' Quick Ben said, shaking his head.

'Because I'm a *reasonable* man, High Mage.'

Kalam grunted. *All right, they might grow on me at that.* 'How far away is it, Quick?'

'Closing. Not it. Them.'

Gesler unslung his crossbow and Pella and Truth followed suit. They loaded quarrels, then fanned out.

'Them, you said,' the sergeant muttered, glaring over at Quick Ben. 'Would that be two? Six? Fifty thousand?'

'It's not that,' Sands said in a suddenly shaky voice. 'It's where they've come from. Chaos. I'm right, ain't I, High Mage?'

'So,' Kalam said, 'the warrens really are in trouble.'

'I did tell you that, Kal.'

'You did. And you told the Adjunct the same thing. But she wanted us to get to Y'Ghatan before Leoman. And that means the warrens.'

'There!' Truth hissed, pointing.

Emerging from the grey gloom, something massive, towering, black as a storm-cloud, filling the sky. And behind it, another, and another . . .

'Time to go,' Quick Ben said.

CHAPTER FOUR

All that K'rul created, you understand, was born of the Elder God's love of possibility. Myriad paths of sorcery spun out a multitude of strands, each wild as hairs in the wind, hackled to the wandering beast. And K'rul was that beast, yet he himself was a parody of life, for blood was his nectar, the spilled gift, red tears of pain, and all that he was, was defined by that singular thirst.

For all that, thirst is something we all share, yes?

Brutho and Nullit speak on Nullit's Last Night
Brutho Parlet

THE LAND WAS VAST, BUT IT WAS NOT EMPTY. SOME ANCIENT cataclysm had torn through the scoured bedrock, splitting it with fissures in a chaotic crisscross skein over the plain. If sand had once covered this place, even filling the chasms, wind or water had swept away the very last grain. The stone looked polished and the sun's light bounced from it in a savage glare.

Squinting, Mappo Runt studied the tormented landscape in front of them. After a time, he shook his head. 'I have never seen this place before, Icarium. It seems as though something has just peeled back the skin of the world. Those cracks . . . how can they run in such random directions?'

The half-blood Jaghut standing at his side said nothing for a moment, his pallid eyes scanning the scene as if seeking a pattern. Then he crouched down and picked up a piece of broken bedrock. 'Immense pressures,' he murmured. 'And then . . . violence.' He straightened, tossing the rock aside. 'The fissures follow no fault lines – see that nearest one? It cuts directly across the seams in the stone. I am intrigued, Mappo.'

The Trell set down his burlap sack. 'Do you wish to explore?'

'I do.' Icarium glanced at him and smiled. 'None of my desires surprise you, do they? It is no exaggeration that you know my mind better than I. Would that you were a woman.'

'Were I a woman, Icarium, I would have serious concerns about your taste in women.'

'Granted,' the Jhag replied, 'you are somewhat hairy. Bristly, in fact. Given your girth, I believe you capable of wrestling a bull bhederin to the ground.'

'Assuming I had reason to . . . although none comes to mind.'

'Come, let us explore.'

Mappo followed Icarium out onto the blasted plain. The heat was vicious, desiccating. Beneath their feet, the bedrock bore twisted swirls, signs of vast, contrary pressures. No lichen clung to the stone. 'This has been long buried.'

'Yes, and only recently exposed.'

They approached the sharp edge of the nearest chasm.

The sunlight reached down part-way to reveal jagged, sheer walls, but the floor was hidden in darkness.

'I see a way down,' Icarium said.

'I was hoping you had missed it,' Mappo replied, having seen the same chute with its convenient collection of ledges, cracks for hand- and foot-holds. 'You know how I hate climbing.'

'Until you mentioned it, no. Shall we?'

'Let me retrieve my pack,' Mappo said, turning about. 'We'll likely be spending the night down there.' He made his way back towards the edge of the plain. The rewards of curiosity had diminished for Mappo, over the years since he had vowed to walk at Icarium's side. It was now a sentiment bound taut with dread. Icarium's search for answers was not a hopeless one, alas. And if truth was discovered, it would be as an avalanche, and Icarium would not, could not, withstand the revelations. About himself. And all that he had done. He would seek to take his own life, if no-one else dared grant the mercy.

That was a precipice they had both clung to not so long ago. *And I betrayed my vow.* In the name of friendship. He had been broken, and it shamed him still. Worse, to see the compassion in Icarium's eyes, that had been a sword through Mappo's heart, an unhealed wound still haunting him.

But curiosity was a fickle thing, as well. Distractions devoured time, drew Icarium from his relentless path. *Yes, time. Delays. Follow where he will lead, Mappo Runt. You can do naught else. Until . . . until what?* Until he finally failed. And then, another would come, if it was not already too late, to resume the grand deceit.

He was tired. His very soul was weary of the whole charade. Too many lies had led him onto this path, too many lies held him here to this day. *I am no friend. I broke my vow – in the name of friendship? Another lie. No. Simple, brutal self-interest, the weakness of my selfish needs.*

Whilst Icarium called him friend. Victim of a terrible curse, yet he remained, trusting, honourable, filled with the pleasure of living. *And here I am, happily leading him astray, again and again.* Oh, the word for it was indeed *shame*.

He found himself standing before his pack. How long he had stood there, unseeing, unmoving, he did not know. *Ah, now that is just, that I begin to lose myself.* Sighing, he picked it up and slung it over a shoulder. *Pray we cross no-one's path. No threat. No risk. Pray we never find a way out of the chasm.* But to whom was he praying? Mappo smiled as he made his way back. He believed in nothing, and would not presume the conceit of etching a face on oblivion. Thus, empty prayers, uttered by an empty man.

'Are you all right, my friend?' Icarium asked as he arrived.

'Lead on,' Mappo said. 'I must secure my pack first.'

A flash of something like concern in the Jhag's expression, then he nodded and walked over to where the chute debouched, slipped over the edge, and vanished from sight.

Mappo tugged a small belt-pouch free and loosened the drawstrings. He pulled another pouch from the first one and unfolded it, revealing that it was larger than the one it had been stored in. From this second pouch he withdrew another, again larger once unfolded. Mappo then, with some effort, pushed the shoulder pack into this last one. Tightened the strings. He stuffed that pouch into the next smaller and followed by forcing that one into the small belt-pouch, which he tied at his waist. Inconvenient, though temporary. He would have no quick access to his weapons should some calamity arise, at least for the duration of the descent. Not that he could fight clinging like a drunk goat to the cliff-side in any case.

He made his way to the chute and looked over the edge. Icarium was making swift progress, already fifteen or more man-heights down.

What would they find down there? *Rocks.* Or something that should have remained buried for all time.

Mappo began his descent.

Before long, the passage of the sun swept all light from the crevasse. They continued in deep gloom, the air cool and stale. There was no sound, barring the occasional scrape of Icarium's scabbard against stone from somewhere below, the only indication that the Jhag still lived, that he had not fallen, for, had he lost his grip and plummeted, Mappo knew that he would make no outcry.

The Trell's arms were getting tired, the calves of his legs aching, his fingers growing numb, but he maintained his steady pace, feeling strangely relentless, as if this was a descent with no end and he was eager to prove it, the only possible proof being to continue on. For ever. There was something telling in that desire, but he was not prepared to be mindful of it.

The air grew colder. Mappo watched the plumes of his breath frosting the stone face opposite him, sparkling in some faint, sourceless illumination. He could smell old ice, somewhere below, and a whisper of unease quickened his breathing.

A hand on the heel of his left, down-reaching foot startled him.

'We are here,' Icarium murmured.

'Abyss take us,' Mappo gasped, pushing away from the wall and landing with sagging legs on a slick, slanted floor. He flung his arms out to regain balance, then straightened. 'Are you certain? Perhaps this slope is but a ledge, and should we lose our footing—'

'We will get wet. Come, there is a lake of some sort.'

'Ah, I see it. It . . . glows . . .'

They edged down until the motionless sweep of water was before them. A vague, greenish-blue illumination, coming from below, revealed the lake's depth. They could see to the bottom, perhaps ten man-heights down, rough and studded with rotted tree stumps or broken stalagmites, pale green and limned in white.

'We descended a third of a league for this?' Mappo asked, his voice echoing, then he laughed.

'Look further in,' Icarium directed, and the Trell heard excitement in his companion's tone.

The stumps marched outward four or five paces, then stopped. Beyond, details indistinct, squatted a massive, blockish shape. Vague patterns marked its visible sides, and its top. Odd, angular projections reached out from the far side, like spider's legs. The breath hissed from Mappo. 'Does it live?' he asked.

'A mechanism of some sort,' Icarium said. 'The metal is very nearly white, do you see? No corrosion. It looks as if it had been built yesterday . . . but I believe, my friend, that it is ancient.'

Mappo hesitated, then asked, 'Is it one of yours?'

Icarium glanced at him, eyes bright. 'No. And that is the wonder of it.'

'No? Are you sure? We have found others—'

'I am certain. I do not know how, but there is no doubt in my mind. This was constructed by someone else, Mappo.'

The Trell crouched down and dipped his hand into the water, then snatched it back. 'Gods, that's cold!'

'No obstacle to me,' Icarium said, smiling, the polished lower tusks sliding into view.

'You mean to swim down and examine it? Never mind, the answer is plain. Very well, I shall seek out some level ground, and pitch our camp.'

The Jhag was tugging off his clothes.

Mappo set off along the slope. The gloom was sufficiently relieved by the glowing water that he was able to make certain of each step he took, moving up until his left hand was brushing the cold stone wall. After fifteen or so paces that hand slipped into a narrow crack, and, upon regaining contact, immediately noted a change of texture and shape in the surface under his blunt fingertips. The Trell halted and began a closer examination along its length.

This stone was basalt, ragged, bulging out until the slope beneath his feet dwindled, then disappeared. Sharp cracks emanated out across the angled floor and into the lake, the black fissures reappearing on the lake's bottom. The basalt was some kind of intrusion, he concluded. Perhaps the entire crevasse had been created by its arrival.

Mappo retreated until he had room to sit, perched with his back against the rock, eyes on the now rippled surface of the lake. He drew out a reed and began cleaning his teeth as he considered the matter. He could not imagine a natural process creating such an intrusion. Contrary as earth pressures were, far beneath the land's surface, there was no colliding escarpment shaping things in this part of the subcontinent.

No, there had been a gate, and the basalt formation had come through it. Catastrophically. From its realm . . . into solid bedrock on this world.

What was it? But he knew.

A sky keep.

Mappo rose and faced the ravaged basalt once more. *And that which Icarium now studies at the bottom of the lake . . . it came from this. So it follows, does it not, that there must be some sort of portal. A way in.* Now he was curious indeed. What secrets lay within? Among the rituals of inculcation the Nameless Ones had intoned in the course of Mappo's vow were tales of the sky keeps, the dread K'Chain Che'Malle fortresses that floated like clouds in the air. An invasion of sorts, according to the Nameless Ones, in the ages before the rise of the First Empire, when the people who would one day found it did little more than wander in small bands – not even tribes, little different, in fact, from mortal Imass. An invasion that, in this region at least, failed. The tales said little of who or what had opposed them. Jaghut, perhaps. Or Forkrul Assail, or the Elder Gods themselves.

He heard splashing and peered through the gloom to see Icarium pull himself, awkwardly, onto the strand. Mappo rose and approached.

'Dead,' Icarium gasped, and Mappo saw that his friend was racked with shivers.

'The mechanism?'

The Jhag shook his head. 'Omtose Phellack. This water . . . dead ice. Dead . . . blood.'

Mappo waited for Icarium to recover. He studied the now swirling, agitated surface of the lake, wondering when last that water had known motion, the heat of a living body. For the latter, it had clearly been thirsty.

'There is a corpse inside that thing,' the Jhag said after a time.

'K'Chain Che'Malle.'

'Yes. How did you know?'

'I have found the sky keep it emerged from. Part of it remains exposed, extruding from the wall.'

'A strange creature,' Icarium muttered. 'I have no memory of ever seeing one before, yet I knew its name.'

'As far as I know, friend, you have never encountered them in your travels. Yet you hold knowledge of them, nonetheless.'

'I need to think on this.'

'Yes.'

'Strange creature,' he said again. 'So reptilian. Desiccated, of course, as one would expect. Powerful, I would think. The hind limbs, the fore-arms. Huge jaws. Stubby tail—'

Mappo looked up. 'Stubby tail. You are certain of that?'

'Yes. The beast was reclined, and within reach were levers – it was a master of the mechanism's operation.'

'There was a porthole you could look through?'

'No. The white metal became transparent wherever I cast my gaze.'

'Revealing the mechanism's inner workings?'

'Only the area where the K'Chain Che'Malle was seated. A carriage of some sort, I believe, a means of transportation and exploration . . . yet not intended to accommodate being submerged in water; nor was it an excavating device – the jointed arms would have been insufficient for that. No, the unveiling of Omtose Phellack caught it unawares. Devoured, trapped in ice. A Jaghut arrived, Mappo, to make certain that none escaped.'

Mappo nodded. Icarium's descriptions had led him to conclude much the same sequence of events. Like the sky keep itself, the mechanism was built to fly, borne aloft by some unknown sorcery. 'If we are to find level ground,' he said, 'it shall have to be within the keep.'

The Jhag smiled. 'Is that a glimmer of anticipation in your eyes? I am beginning to see the Mappo of old, I suspect. Memory or no, you are no stranger to me, and I have been much chagrined of late, seeing you so forlorn. I understood it, of course – how could I not? I am what haunts you, friend, and for that I grieve. Come, shall we find our way inside this fell keep?'

Mappo watched Icarium stride past, and slowly turned to follow him with his eyes.

Icarium, the Builder of Mechanisms. Where did such skills come from? He feared they were about to find out.

The monastery was in the middle of parched, broken wasteland, not a village or hamlet within a dozen leagues in either direction along the faint tracks of the road. On the map Cutter had purchased in G'danisban, its presence was marked with a single wavy line of reddish-brown ink, upright, barely visible on the worn hide. The symbol of D'rek, Worm of Autumn.

A lone domed structure stood in the midst of a low-walled, rectangular compound, and the sky over it was dotted with circling vultures.

Beside him and hunched in the saddle, Heboric Ghost Hands spat, then said, 'Decay. Rot. Dissolution. When what once worked suddenly breaks. And like a moth the soul flutters away. Into the dark. Autumn awaits, and the seasons are askew, twisting to avoid all the unsheathed knives. Yet the prisoners of the jade, they are forever trapped. There, in their own arguments. Disputes, bickering, the universe beyond unseen – they care not a whit, the fools. They wear ignorance like armour and wield spite like swords. What am I to them? A curio. Less. So it's a broken world, why should I care about that? I did not ask for this, for any of this . . .'

He went on, but Cutter stopped listening. He glanced back at the two women trailing them. Listless, uncaring, brutalized by the heat. The horses beneath them walked with drooped heads; their ribs were visible beneath dusty, tattered hide. Off to one side clambered Greyfrog, looking fat and sleek as ever, circling the riders with seemingly boundless energy.

'We should visit that monastery,' Cutter said. 'Make use of the well, and if there's any foodstuffs—'

'They're all dead,' Heboric croaked.

Cutter studied the old man, then grunted. 'Explains the vultures. But we still need water.'

The Destriant of Treach gave him an unpleasant smile.

Cutter understood the meaning of that smile. He was becoming heartless, inured to the myriad horrors of this world. A monastery filled with dead priests and priestesses was as . . . nothing. And the old man could see it, could see into him. *His new god is the Tiger of Summer, Lord of War. Heboric Ghost Hands, the High Priest of strife, he sees how cold I have become. And is . . . amused.*

Cutter guided his horse up the side track leading to the monastery. The others followed. The Daru reined in in front of the gates, which were closed, and dismounted. 'Heboric, do you sense any danger to us?'

'I have that talent?'

Cutter studied him, said nothing.

The Destriant clambered down from his horse. 'Nothing lives in there. Nothing.'

'No ghosts?'

'Nothing. She took them.'

'Who?'

'The unexpected visitor, that's who.' He laughed, raised his hands. 'We play our games. We never expect . . . umbrage. Outrage. I could have told them. Warned them, but they wouldn't have listened. The conceit consumes all. A single building can become an entire world, the minds crowding and jostling, then clawing and gouging. All they need do is walk outside, but they don't. They've forgotten that outside exists. Oh, all these faces of worship, none of which is *true* worship. Never mind the diligence, it does naught but serve the demon hatreds within. The spites and fears and malice. I could have told them.'

Cutter walked to the wall, leading his horse. He climbed onto its back, perched on the saddle, then straightened until he was standing. The top of the wall was within easy reach. He pulled himself up. In the compound beyond, bodies. A dozen or so, black-skinned, mostly naked, lying here and there on the hard-packed, white ground. Cutter squinted. The bodies looked to be . . . boiling, frothing, melting. They roiled before his eyes. He pulled his gaze away from them. The domed temple's doors were yawning open. To the right was a low corral surrounding a low, long structure, the mud-bricks exposed for two thirds of the facing wall. Troughs with plaster and tools indicated a task never to be completed. Vultures crowded the flat roof, yet none ventured down to feast on the corpses.

Cutter dropped down into the compound. He walked to the gates and lifted the bar clear, then pulled the heavy doors open.

Greyfrog was waiting on the other side. '*Dispirited and distraught. So much unpleasantness, Cutter, in this fell place. Dismay. No appetite.*' He edged past, scuttled warily towards the nearest corpse. '*Ah! They seethe! Worms, aswarm with worms. The flesh is foul, foul even for Greyfrog. Revulsed. Let us be away from this place!*'

Cutter spied the well, in the corner between the outbuilding and the temple. He returned to where the others still waited outside the gate. 'Give me your waterskins. Heboric, can you check that outbuilding for feed?'

Heboric smiled. 'The livestock were never let out. It's been days. The heat killed them all. A dozen goats, two mules.'

'Just see if there's any feed.'

The Destriant headed towards the outbuilding.

Scillara dismounted, lifted clear the waterskins from Felisin Younger's saddle and, with her own thrown over a shoulder, approached Cutter. 'Here.'

He studied her. 'I wonder if this is a warning.'

Her brows lifted fractionally, 'Are we that important, Cutter?'

'Well, I don't mean us, specifically. I meant, maybe we should take it as a warning.'

'Dead priests?'

'Nothing good comes of worship.'

She gave him an odd smile, then held out the skins.

Cutter cursed himself. He rarely made sense when trying to talk with this woman. Said things a fool would say. It was the mocking look in her eyes, the expression ever anticipating a smile as soon as he opened his mouth to speak. Saying nothing more, he collected the waterskins and walked back into the compound.

Scillara watched him for a moment, then turned as Felisin slipped down from her horse. 'We need the water.'

The younger woman nodded. 'I know.' She reached up and tugged at her hair, which had grown long. 'I keep seeing those bandits. And now, more dead people. And those cemeteries the track went right through yesterday, that field of bones. I feel we've stumbled into a nightmare, and every day we go further in. It's hot, but I'm cold all the time and getting colder.'

'That's dehydration,' Scillara said, repacking her pipe.

'That thing's not left your mouth in days,' Felisin said.

'Keeps the thirst at bay.'

'Really?'

'No, but that is what I keep telling myself.'

Felisin looked away. 'We do that a lot, don't we?'

'What?'

She shrugged. 'Tell ourselves things. In the hope that it'll make them true.'

Scillara drew hard on the pipe, blew a lungful of smoke upward, watching as the wind took it away.

125

'You look so healthy,' Felisin said, eyes on her once more. 'Whilst the rest of us wither away.'

'Not Greyfrog.'

'No, not Greyfrog.'

'Does he talk with you much?'

Felisin shook her head. 'Not much. Except when I wake up at night, after my bad dreams. Then he sings to me.'

'Sings?'

'Yes, in his people's language. Songs for children. He says he needs to practise them.'

Scillara shot her a glance. 'Really? Did he say why?'

'No.'

'How old were you, Felisin, when your mother sold you off?'

Another shrug. 'I don't remember.'

That might have been a lie, but Scillara did not pursue it.

Felisin stepped closer. 'Will you take care of me, Scillara?'

'What?'

'I feel as if I am going backwards. I felt . . . older. Back in Raraku. Now, with every day, I feel more and more like a child. Smaller, ever smaller.'

Uneasy, Scillara said, 'I have never been much good at taking care of people.'

'I don't think Sha'ik was, either. She had . . . obsessions . . .'

'She did fine by you.'

'No, it was mostly Leoman. Even Toblakai. And Heboric, before Treach claimed him. She didn't take care of me, and that's why Bidithal . . .'

'Bidithal is dead. He got his own balls shoved down his scrawny throat.'

'Yes,' a whisper. 'If what Heboric says really happened. Toblakai . . .'

Scillara snorted. 'Think on that, Felisin. If Heboric had said that L'oric had done it, or Sha'ik, or even Leoman, well, you might have some reason to doubt. But Toblakai? No, you can believe it. Gods below, how can you not?'

The question forced a faint smile from Felisin and she nodded. 'You are right. Only Toblakai would have done that. Only Toblakai would have killed him . . . in that way. Tell me, Scillara, do you have a spare pipe?'

'A spare pipe? How about a dozen? Want to smoke them all at once?'

Felisin laughed. 'No, just one. So, you'll take care of me, won't you?'

'I will try.' And maybe she would. Like Greyfrog. Practice. She went looking for that pipe.

*

Cutter lifted the bucket clear and peered at the water. It looked clean, smelling of nothing in particular. Nonetheless, he hesitated.

Footsteps behind him. 'I found feed,' Heboric said. 'More than we can carry.'

'Think this water is all right? What killed those priests?'

'It's fine. I told you what killed them.'

You did? 'Should we look in the temple?'

'Greyfrog's already in there. I told him to find money, gems, food that hasn't spoiled yet. He wasn't happy about it, so I expect he'll be quick.'

'All right.' Cutter walked to a trough and dumped the water into it, then returned to the well. 'Think we can coax the horses in here?'

'I'll try.' But Heboric made no move to do so.

Cutter glanced over at him, saw the old man's strange eyes fixed on him. 'What's wrong?'

'Nothing, I think. I was noticing something. You have certain qualities, Cutter. Leadership, for one.'

The Daru scowled. 'If you want to be in charge, fine, go ahead.'

'I wasn't twisting a knife, lad. I meant what I said. You have taken command, and that's good. It's what we need. I have never been a leader. I've always followed. It's my curse. But that's not what they want to hear. Not from me. No, they want me to lead them out. Into freedom. I keep telling them, I know nothing of freedom.'

'Them? Who? Scillara and Felisin?'

'I'll get the horses,' Heboric said, turning about and walking off in his odd, toad-like gait.

Cutter refilled the bucket and poured the water into the trough. They would feed the horses here with what they couldn't take with them. Load up on water. *And, even now, loot the temple.* Well, he had been a thief once, long ago. Besides, the dead cared nothing for wealth, did they?

A splitting, tearing sound from the centre of the compound behind him. The sound of a portal opening. Cutter spun round, knives in his hands.

A rider emerged from the magical gate at full gallop. Reining in hard, hoofs skidding in clouds of dust, the dark grey horse a monstrous apparition, the hide worn away in places, exposing tendons, dried muscle and ligaments. Its eyes were empty pits, its mane long and greasy, whipping as the beast tossed its head. Seated in a high-backed saddle, the rider was, if anything, even more alarming in appearance. Black, ornate armour, patched with verdigris, a dented, gouged helm, open-faced to reveal mostly bone, a few strips of flesh hanging from the cheek ridges, tendons binding the lower jaw, and a row of blackened, filed teeth.

In the brief moment as the horse reared, dust exploding outward, Cutter saw more weapons on the rider than he could count. Swords at his back, throwing axes, sheathed handles jutting upward from the saddle, something like a boar-spitter, the bronze point as long as a short sword, gripped in the gauntleted left hand. A long bow, a short bow, knives—

'*Where is he!?*' The voice was a savage, enraged roar. Pieces of armour bounced on the ground as the figure twisted round, searching the compound. 'Damn you, Hood! *I was on the trail!*' He saw Cutter and was suddenly silent, motionless. 'She left one alive? I doubt it. You're no whelp of D'rek. Drink deep that water, mortal, it matters not. You're dead anyway. You and every damned blood-swishing living thing in this realm and every other!'

He pulled his horse around to face the temple, where Greyfrog had appeared, arms heaped with silks, boxes, foodstuffs and cooking utensils. 'A toad who likes to cook in comfort! The madness of the Grand Ending is upon us! Come any closer, demon, and I'll spit your legs and roast them over a fire – do you think I no longer eat? You are right, but I will roast you in vicious spite, drooling with irony – ah! You liked that, didn't you?' He faced Cutter once more. 'Is this what he wanted me to see? He pulled me from the trail . . . *for this?*'

Cutter sheathed his knives. Through the gates beyond came Heboric Ghost Hands, leading the horses. The old man paused upon seeing the rider, head cocking, then he continued on. 'Too late, Soldier,' he said. 'Or too early!' He laughed.

The rider lifted the spear high. 'Treach made a mistake, I see, but I must salute you nonetheless.'

Heboric halted. 'A mistake, Soldier? Yes, I agree, but there is little I can do about it. I acknowledge your reluctant salute. What brings you here?'

'Ask Hood if you want the answer to that!' He upended the spear and drove it point first into the ground, then swung down from the saddle, more fragments of the rotting armour falling away. 'I expect I must look around, as if I cannot already see all there is to see. The pantheon is riven asunder, what of it?'

Heboric pulled the nervous horses towards the trough, giving the warrior a wide berth. As he approached Cutter he shrugged. 'The Soldier of Hood, High House Death. He'll not trouble us, I think.'

'He spoke to me in Daru,' Cutter said. 'At first. And Malazan with you.'

'Yes.'

The Soldier was tall, and Cutter now saw something hanging from a knife-studded belt. An enamel mask, cracked, smudged, with a single streak of red paint along one cheek. The Daru's eyes widened. 'Beru fend,' he whispered. 'A Seguleh!'

At that the Soldier turned, then walked closer. 'Daru, you are far from home! Tell me, do the Tyrant's children still rule Darujhistan?'

Cutter shook his head.

'You look crazed, mortal, what ails you?'

'I – I'd heard, I mean – Seguleh usually say nothing – to anyone. Yet you . . .'

'The fever zeal still grips my mortal kin, does it? Idiots! The Tyrant's army still holds sway in the city, then?'

'Who? What? Darujhistan is ruled by a council. We have no army—'

'Brilliant insanity! No Seguleh in the city?'

'No! Just . . . stories. Legends, I mean.'

'So where are my masked stick-pivoting compatriots hiding?'

'An island, it's said, far to the south, off the coast, beyond Morn—'

'Morn! Now the sense of it comes to me. They are being held in readiness. Darujhistan's council – mages one and all, yes? Undying, secretive, paranoid mages! Crouching low, lest the Tyrant returns, as one day he must! Returns, looking for his army! Hah, a council!'

'That's not the council, sir,' Cutter said. 'If you are speaking of mages, that would be the T'orrud Cabal—'

'T'orrud! Yes, clever. Outrageous! Barukanal, Derudanith, Travalegrah, Mammoltenan? These names strike your soul, yes? I see it.'

'Mammot was my uncle—'

'Uncle! Hah! Absurd!' He spun round. 'I have seen enough! Hood! I am leaving! She's made her position clear as ice, hasn't she? Hood, you damned fool, you didn't need me for this! Now I must seek out his trail all over again, damn your hoary bones!' He swung back onto the undead horse.

Heboric called out from where he stood by the trough, 'Soldier! May I ask – who do you hunt?'

The sharpened teeth lifted and lowered in a silent laugh. 'Hunt? Oh yes, we all hunt, but I was closest! Piss on Hood's bony feet! Pluck out the hairs of his nose and kick his teeth in! Drive a spear up his puckered behind and set him on a windy mountain top! Oh, I'll find him a wife some day, lay coin on it! But first, I hunt!'

He collected the reins, pulled the horse round. The portal opened. 'Skinner! Hear me, you damned Avowed! Cheater of death! I am coming for you! Now!' Horse and rider plunged into the rent, vanished, and a moment later the gate disappeared as well.

The sudden silence rang like a dirge in Cutter's head. He took a ragged breath, then shook himself. 'Beru fend,' he whispered again. 'He was my uncle . . .'

'I will feed the horses, lad,' Heboric said. 'Go out to the women. They've likely been hearing shouting and don't know what's going on. Go on, Cutter.'

Nodding, the Daru began walking. *Barukanal. Mammoltenan . . .* What had the Soldier revealed? What ghastly secret hid in the apparition's words? *What do Baruk and the others have to do with the Tyrant? And the Seguleh? The Tyrant is returning?* 'Gods, I've got to get home.'

Outside the gates, Felisin and Scillara were seated on the track. Both puffing rustleaf, and although Felisin looked sickly, there was a determined, defiant look in her eyes.

'Relax,' Scillara said. 'She's not inhaling.'

'I'm not?' Felisin asked her. 'How do you do that?'

'Don't you have any questions?' Cutter demanded.

They looked at him. 'About what?' Scillara asked.

'Didn't you hear?'

'Hear what?'

They didn't hear. They weren't meant to. But we were. Why? Had the Soldier been mistaken in his assumptions? Sent by Hood, not to see the dead priests and priestesses of D'rek . . . *but to speak with us.*

The Tyrant shall return. This, to a son of Darujhistan. 'Gods,' he whispered again, 'I've got to get home.'

Greyfrog's voice shouted in his skull, *'Friend Cutter! Surprise and alarm!'*

'What now?' he asked, turning to see the demon bounding into view.

'The Soldier of Death. Wondrous. He left his spear!'

Cutter stared, with sinking heart, at the weapon clutched between the demon's teeth. 'Good thing you don't need your mouth to talk.'

'Solemn agreement, friend Cutter! Query. Do you like these silks?'

The portal into the sky keep required a short climb. Mappo and Icarium stood on the threshold, staring into a cavernous chamber. The floor was almost level. A faint light seemed to emanate from the walls of stone. 'We can camp here,' the Trell said.

'Yes,' Icarium agreed. 'But first, shall we explore?'

'Of course.'

The chamber housed three additional mechanisms, identical to the one submerged in the lake, each positioned on trestles like ships in dry-dock. The hatches yawned open, revealing the padded seats within. Icarium walked to the nearest one and began examining its interior.

Mappo untied the pouch at his belt and began removing the larger one within. A short time later he laid out the bedrolls, food and wine. Then he drew out from his pack an iron-banded mace, not his favourite one, but another, expendable since it possessed no sorcerous virtues.

Icarium returned to his side. 'They are lifeless,' he said. 'Whatever energy was originally imbued within the machinery has ebbed away, and I see no means of restoring it.'

'That is not too surprising, is it? I suspect this keep has been here a long time.'

'True enough, Mappo. But imagine, were we able to enliven one of these mechanisms! We could travel at great speed and in comfort! One for you and one for me, ah, this is tragic. But look, there is a passageway. Let us delve into the greater mystery this keep offers.'

Carrying only his mace, Mappo followed Icarium into the broad corridor.

Storage rooms lined the passage, whatever they had once held now nothing more than heaps of undisturbed dust.

Sixty paces in, they reached an intersection. An arched barrier was before them, shimmering like a vertical pool of quicksilver. Corridors went to the right and left, both appearing to curve inward in the distance.

Icarium drew out a coin from the pouch at his belt, and Mappo was amused to see that it was of a vintage five centuries old.

'You are the world's greatest miser, Icarium.'

The Jhag smiled, then shrugged. 'I seem to recall that no-one ever accepts payment from us, no matter how egregious the expense of the service provided. Is that an accurate memory, Mappo?'

'It is.'

'Well, then, how can you accuse me of being niggardly?' He tossed the coin at the silver barrier. It vanished. Ripples rolled outward, went beyond the stone frame, then returned.

'This is a passive manifestation,' Icarium said. 'Tell me, did you hear the coin strike anything beyond?'

'No, nor did it make a sound upon entering the … uh, the door.'

'I am tempted to pass through.'

'That might prove unhealthy.'

Icarium hesitated, then drew a skinning-knife and inserted the blade into the barrier. Gentler ripples. He pulled it out. The blade looked intact. None of the substance had adhered to it. Icarium ran a fingertip along the iron. 'No change in temperature,' he observed.

'Shall I try a finger I won't miss much?' Mappo asked, holding up his left hand.

'And which one would that be, friend?'

'I don't know. I expect I'd miss any of them.'

'The tip?'

'Sound caution.' Making a fist, barring the last, smallest finger, Mappo stepped close, then dipped the finger up to the first knuckle into the shimmering door. 'No pain, at least. It is, I think, very thin.' He drew his hand back and examined the digit. 'Hale.'

'With the condition of your fingers, Mappo, how can you tell?'

'Ah, I see a change. No dirt left, not even crusted under the nail.'

'To pass through is to be cleansed. Do you think?'

Mappo reached in with his whole hand. 'I feel air beyond. Cooler, damper.' He withdrew his hand and peered at it. 'Clean. Too clean. I am alarmed.'

'Why?'

'Because it makes me realize how filthy I've become, that's why.'

'I wonder, will it do the same with our clothes?'

'That would be nice, although it may possess some sort of threshold. Too filthy, and it simply annihilates the offending material. We might emerge on the other side naked.'

'Now I am alarmed, friend.'

'Yes. Well, what shall we do, Icarium?'

'Do we have any choice?' With that, the Jhag strode through the barrier.

Mappo sighed, then followed.

Only to be clutched at the shoulder and pulled back from a second step – which, he saw, would have been into empty air.

The cavern before them was vast. A bridge had once connected the ledge they stood on to an enormous, towering fortress floating in space, a hundred or more paces opposite them. Sections of that stone span remained, seemingly unsupported, but others had broken away and now floated, motionless, in the air.

Far below, dizzyingly far, the cavern was swallowed in darkness. Above them, a faintly glittering dome of black rough-hewn stone, like a night sky. Tiered buildings rose along the inner walls, rows of dark windows but no balconies. Dust and rubble clouded the air, none of it moving. Mappo said nothing, he was too stunned by the vista before them.

Icarium touched his shoulder, then pointed to something small hovering directly before them. The coin, but not motionless as it had first seemed. It was drifting away, slowly. The Jhag reached out and retrieved it, returning it to the pouch at his waist. 'A worthy return on my investment,' he murmured. 'Since there is momentum, we should be able to travel. Launch ourselves from this ledge. Over to the fortress.'

'Sound plan,' Mappo said, 'but for all the obstacles in between.'

'Ah, good point.'

'There may be an intact bridge, on the opposite side. We could take one of the side passages behind us. If such a bridge exists, likely it will be marked with a silver barrier as this one was.'

'Have you never wished you could fly, Mappo?'

'As a child, perhaps, I am sure I did.'

'Only as a child?'

'It is where dreams of flight belong, Icarium. Shall we explore one of the corridors behind us?'

'Very well, although I admit I hope we fail in finding a bridge.'

Countless rooms, passages and alcoves along the wide, arched corridor, the floors thick with dust, odd, faded symbols etched above doorways, possibly a numerical system of some sort. The air was stagnant, faintly acrid. No furnishings remained in the adjoining chambers. Nor, Mappo realized, any corpses such as the one Icarium had discovered in the mechanism resting on the lake-bed. An orderly evacuation? If so, where had the Short-Tails gone?

Eventually, they came upon another silver door. Cautiously passing through it, they found themselves standing on the threshold of a narrow bridge. Intact, leading across to the floating fortress, which hovered much closer on this, the opposite side from whence they had first seen it. The back wall of the island keep was much rougher, the windows vertical slashes positioned seemingly haphazardly on the misshapen projections, crooked insets and twisted towers.

'Extraordinary,' Icarium said in a low voice. 'What, I wonder, does this hidden face of madness reveal of the makers? These K'Chain Che'Malle?'

'A certain tension, perhaps?'

'Tension?'

'Between,' Mappo said, 'order and chaos. An inner dichotomy, conflicting impulses . . .'

'The contradictions evident in all intelligent life,' Icarium said, nodding. He stepped onto the span, then, arms wheeling, began drifting away.

Mappo reached out and just managed to grasp the Jhag's flailing foot. He pulled Icarium back down onto the threshold. 'Well,' he said, grunting, 'that was interesting. You weighed nothing, when I had you in my grip. As light as a mote of dust.'

Slowly, tentatively, the Jhag clambered upright once more. 'That was most alarming. It seems we may have to fly after all.'

'Then why build bridges?'

'I have no idea. Unless,' he added, 'whatever mechanism invokes this weightlessness is breaking down, losing its precision.'

'So the bridges should have been exempted? Possibly. In any case, see the railings, projecting not up but out to either side? Modest, but sufficient for handholds, were one to crawl.'

'Yes. Shall we?'

The sensation, Mappo decided as he reached the midway point, Icarium edging along ahead of him, was not a pleasant one. Nausea, vertigo, a strange urge to pull one's grip loose due to the momentum provided by one's own muscles. All sense of up and down had vanished, and at times Mappo was convinced they were climbing a ladder, rather than snaking more or less horizontally across the span of the bridge.

A narrow but tall entranceway gaped ahead, where the bridge made contact with the fortress. Fragments of the door it had once held floated motionless before it. Whatever had shattered it had come from within.

Icarium reached the threshold and climbed to his feet. Moments later Mappo joined him. They peered into the darkness.

'I smell . . . vast . . . death.'

Mappo nodded. He drew out his mace, looked down at the spiked ball of iron, then slipped the handle back through the leather loop at his belt.

Icarium in the lead, they entered the fortress.

The corridor was as narrow as the doorway itself, the walls uneven, black basalt, wet with condensation, the floor precarious with random knobs and projections, and depressions slick with ice that cracked and shifted underfoot. It ran more or less straight for forty paces. By the time they reached the opening at the end their eyes had adjusted to the gloom.

Another enormous chamber, as if the heart of the keep had been carved out. A massive cruciform of bound, black wood filled the cavern, and on it was impaled a dragon. Long dead, once frozen but now rotting. An iron spike as thick around as Mappo's torso had been driven into the dragon's throat, just above the breast bones. Aquamarine blood had seeped down from the wound and still dripped heavy and turgid onto the stone floor in slow, steady, fist-sized drops.

'I know this dragon,' Icarium whispered.

How? No, ask not.

'I know this dragon,' Icarium said again. 'Sorrit. Its aspect was . . . Serc. The warren of the sky.' He lifted both hands to his face. 'Dead. Sorrit has been slain . . .'

'A most delicious throne. No, not delicious. Most bitter, foul, ill-tasting, what was I thinking?'

'You don't think, Curdle. You never think. I can't remember any throne. What throne? There must be some mistake. Not-Apsalar heard wrong, that much is obvious. Completely wrong, an absolute error. Besides, someone's sitting in it.'

'Deliciously.'

'I told you, there was no throne—'

The conversation had been going on for half the night, as they travelled the strange paths of Shadow, winding across a ghostly landscape that constantly shifted between two worlds, although both were equally ravaged and desolate. Apsalar wondered at the sheer extent of this fragment of the Shadow Realm. If her recollection of Cotillion's memories was accurate, the realm wandered untethered to the world Apsalar called her own, and neither the Rope nor Shadowthrone possessed any control over its seemingly random peregrinations. Even stranger, it was clear that roads of a sort stretched out from the fragment, twisting and wending vast distances, like roots, or tentacles, and sometimes their motions proved independent of the larger fragment.

As with the one they now traversed. More or less following the eastern road leading out from Ehrlitan, skirting the thin ribbon of cedars on their left, beyond which was the sea. And as the traders' track began to curve northward to meet the coastline, the Shadow Road joined with it, narrowing until it was barely the width of the track itself.

Ignoring the ceaseless nattering from the two ghosts flitting behind her, Apsalar pushed on, fighting the lack of sleep and eager to cover as much ground as possible before the sun's rise. Her control of the Shadow Road was growing more tenuous – it vanished with every slip of her concentration. Finally, she halted.

The warren crumbled around them. The sky to the east was lightening. They stood on the traders' track at the base of a winding climb to the coastal ridge, rhizan darting through the air around them.

'The sun returns! Not again! Telorast, we need to hide! Somewhere!'

'No we don't, you idiot. We just get harder to see, that's all, unless you're not mindful. Of course, Curdle, you are incapable of being mindful, so I look forward to your wailing dissolution. Peace, at last. For a while, at least—'

'You are evil, Telorast! I've always known it, even before you went and used that knife on—'

'Be quiet! I never used that knife on anyone.'

'And you're a liar!'

'Say that again and I'll stick you!'

'You can't! I'm dissolving!'

Apsalar ran a hand across her brow. It came away glistening with sweat. 'That thread of Shadow felt . . . wrong,' she said.

'Oh yes,' Telorast replied, slipping round to crouch before her in a miasma of swirling grey. 'It's sickly. All the outer reaches are. Poisoned, rotting with chaos. We blame Shadowthrone.'

'Shadowthrone? Why?'

'Why not? We hate him.'

'And that is sufficient reason?'

'The sufficientest reason of all.'

Apsalar studied the climbing track. 'I think we're close.'

'Good. Excellent. I'm frightened. Let's stop here. Let's go back, now.'

Stepping through the ghost, Apsalar began the ascent.

'That was a vicious thing to do,' Telorast hissed behind her. 'If I possessed you I wouldn't do that to me. Not even to Curdle, I wouldn't. Well, maybe, if I was mad. You're not mad at me, are you? Please don't be mad at me. I'll do anything you ask, until you're dead. Then I'll dance on your stinking, bloated corpse, because that's what you would want me to do, isn't it? I would if I was you and you were dead and I lingered long enough to dance on you, which I would do.'

Reaching the crest, Apsalar saw that the track continued along the ridge another two hundred paces before twisting back down onto the lee side. Cool morning wind plucked the sweat from her face, sighing in from the vast, dark cape that was the sea on her left. She looked down to see a narrow strand of beach fifteen or so man-heights below, cluttered with driftwood. Along the track to her right, near the far end, a stand of stunted trees rose from a niche in the cliff-side, and in their midst stood a stone tower. White plaster covered its surface for most of its height, barring the uppermost third, where the rough-cut stones were still exposed.

She walked towards it as the first spears of sunlight shot over the horizon.

Heaps of slate filled the modest enclosure surrounding the tower. No-one was visible, and Apsalar could hear nothing from within as she strode across to halt in front of the door.

Telorast's faint whisper came to her: 'This isn't good. A stranger lives here. Must be a stranger, since we've never met. And if not a stranger then somebody I know, which would be even worse—'

'Be quiet,' Apsalar said, reaching up to pound on the door – then stopped, and stepping back, stared up at the enormous reptilian skull set in the wall above the doorway. 'Hood's breath!' She hesitated, Telorast voicing minute squeals and gasps behind her, then thumped on the weathered wood with a gloved fist.

The sounds of something falling over, then of boots crunching on grit and gravel. A bolt was tugged aside, and the door swung open in a cloud of dust.

The man standing within filled the doorway. Napan, massive

muscles, blunt face, small eyes. His scalp shaved and white with dust, through which a few streaks of sweat ran down to glisten in his thick, wiry eyebrows.

Apsalar smiled. 'Hello, Urko.'

The man grunted, then said, 'Urko drowned. They all drowned.'

'It's that lack of imagination that gave you away,' she replied.

'Who are you?'

'Apsalar—'

'No you're not. Apsalar was an Imass—'

'Not the Mistress of Thieves. It is simply the name I chose—'

'Damned arrogant of you, too.'

'Perhaps. In any case, I bring greetings from Dancer.'

The door slammed in her face.

Coughing in the dust gusting over her, Apsalar stepped back and wiped grit from her eyes.

'Hee hee,' said Telorast behind her. 'Can we go now?'

She pounded on the door again.

After a long moment, it opened once more. He was scowling. 'I once tried to drown him, you know.'

'No, yes, I recall. You were drunk.'

'You couldn't have recalled anything – you weren't there. Besides, I wasn't drunk.'

'Oh. Then . . . why?'

'Because he irritated me, that's why. Just like you're doing right now.'

'I need to talk to you.'

'What for?'

She suddenly had no answer to give him.

His eyes narrowed. 'He really thought I was drunk? What an idiot.'

'Well, I suppose the alternative was too depressing.'

'I never knew he was such a sensitive soul. Are you his daughter? Something . . . in the way you stand . . .'

'May I come in?'

He moved away from the door. Apsalar entered, then halted once more, her eyes on the enormous headless skeleton commanding the interior, reaching all the way up to the tower's ceiling. Bipedal, long-tailed, the bones a burnished brown colour. 'What is this?'

Urko said, 'Whatever it was, it could swallow a bhederin in one bite.'

'How?' Telorast asked Apsalar in a whisper. 'It has no head.'

The man heard the question, and he now scowled. 'You have company. What is it, a familiar or something? I can't see it, and that I don't like. Not at all.'

'A ghost.'

'You should banish it to Hood,' he said. 'Ghosts don't belong here, that's why they're ghosts.'

'He's an evil man!' Telorast hissed. 'What are those?'

Apsalar could just make out the shade as it drifted towards a long table to the right. On it were smaller versions of the skeletal behemoth, three of them crow-sized, although instead of beaks the creatures possessed long snouts lined with needle-like teeth. The bones had been bound together with gut and the figures were mounted so that they stood upright, like sentry meer-rats.

Urko was studying Apsalar, an odd expression on his blunt, strong-featured face. Then he seemed to start, and said, 'I have brewed some tea.'

'That would be nice, thank you.'

He walked over to the modest kitchen area and began a search for cups. 'It's not that I don't want visitors . . . well, it is. They always bring trouble. Did Dancer have anything else to say?'

'No. And he now calls himself Cotillion.'

'I knew that. I'm not surprised he's the Patron of Assassins. He was the most feared killer in the empire. More than Surly, who was just treacherous. Or Topper, who was just cruel. I suppose those two still think they won. Fools. Who now strides among the gods, eh?' He brought a clay cup over. 'Local herbs, mildly toxic but not fatal. Antidote to buther snake bites, which is a good thing, since the bastards infest the area. Turns out I built my tower near a breeding pit.'

One of the small skeletons on the tabletop fell over, then jerkily climbed back upright, the tail jutting out, the torso angling almost horizontal.

'One of my ghost companions has just possessed that creature,' Apsalar said.

A second one lurched into awkward motion.

'Gods below,' whispered Urko. 'Look how they stand! Of course! It has to be that way. Of course!' He stared up at the massive fossil skeleton. 'It's all wrong! They lean forward – for balance!'

Telorast and Curdle were quickly mastering their new bodies, jaws snapping, hopping about on the tabletop.

'I suspect they won't want to relinquish those skeletons,' Apsalar said.

'They can have them – as reward for this revelation!' He paused, looked round, then muttered, 'I'll have to knock down a wall . . .'

Apsalar sighed. 'I suppose we should be relieved one of them did not decide on the big version.'

Urko looked over at her with slightly wide eyes, then he grunted. 'Drink your tea – the toxicity gets worse as it cools.'

She sipped. And found her lips and tongue suddenly numb.

Urko smiled. 'Perfect. This way the conversation stays brief and you can be on your way all the sooner.'

'Mathard.'

'It wears off.' He found a stool and sat down facing her. 'You're Dancer's daughter. You must be, although I see no facial similarities – your mother must have been beautiful. It's in your walk, and how you stand there. You're his beget, and he was selfish enough to teach you, his own child, the ways of assassination. I can see how that troubles you. It's there in your eyes. The legacy haunts you – you're feeling trapped, caged in. There's already blood on your hands, isn't there? Is he proud of that?' He grimaced, then spat. 'I should've drowned him then and there. Had I been drunk, I would have.'

'You are wong.'

'Wong? Wrong, you mean? Am I?'

She nodded, fighting her fury at his trickery. She had come with the need to talk, and he had stolen from her the ability to shape words. 'Nnnoth th-aughther. Mmothethed.'

He frowned.

Apsalar pointed at the two reptilian skeletons now scuttling about on the stone-littered floor. 'Mmothethion.'

'Possession. He possessed you? The god possessed you? Hood pluck his balls and chew slow!' Urko heaved himself to his feet, hands clenching into fists. 'Here, hold on, lass. I have an antidote to the antidote.' He found a dusty beaker, rubbed at it until a patch of the glazed reddish earthenware was visible. 'This one, aye.' He found another cup and poured it full. 'Drink.'

Sickly sweet, the taste then turning bitter and stinging. 'Oh. That was . . . fast.'

'My apologies, Apsalar. I'm a miserable sort most of the time, I admit it. And I've talked more since you arrived than I have in years. So I'll stop now. How can I help you?'

She hesitated, then looked away. 'You can't, really. I shouldn't have come. I still have tasks to complete.'

'For him?'

She nodded.

'Why?'

'Because I gave my word.'

'You owe him nothing, except maybe a knife in his back.'

'Once I am done . . . I wish to disappear.'

He sat down once more. 'Ah. Yes, well.'

'I think an accidental drowning won't hold any longer, Urko.'

A faint grin. 'It was our joke, you see. We all made the pact . . . to drown. Nobody got it. Nobody gets it. Probably never will.'

'I did. Dancer does. Even Shadowthrone, I think.'

'Not Surly. She never had a sense of humour. Always obsessing on the details. I wonder, are people like that ever happy? Are they even capable of it? What inspires their lives, anyway? Give 'em too much and they complain. Give 'em too little and they complain some more. Do it right and half of them complain it's too much and the other half too little.'

'No wonder you gave up consorting with people, Urko.'

'Aye, I prefer bones these days. People. Too many of them by far, if you ask me.'

She looked round. 'Dancer wanted you shaken up some. Why?'

The Napan's eyes shifted away, and he did not answer.

Apsalar felt a tremor of unease. 'He knows something, doesn't he? That's what he's telling you by that simple greeting.'

'Assassin or not, I always liked Dancer. Especially the way he could keep his mouth shut.'

The two reptilian skeletons were scrabbling at the door. Apsalar studied them for a moment. 'Disappearing . . . from a god.'

'Aye, that won't be easy.'

'He said I could leave, once I'm done. And he won't come after me.'

'Believe him, Apsalar. Dancer doesn't lie, and I suspect even godhood won't change that.'

I think that is what I needed to hear. 'Thank you.' She headed towards the door.

'So soon?' Urko asked.

She glanced back at him. 'Too much or too little?'

He narrowed his gaze, then grunted a laugh. 'You're right. It's about perfect – I need to be mindful about what I'm asking for.'

'Yes,' she said. *And that is also what Dancer wanted to remind you about, isn't it?*

Urko looked away. 'Damn him, anyway.'

Smiling, Apsalar opened the door. Telorast and Curdle scurried outside. She followed a moment later.

Thick spit on the palms of the hands, a careful rubbing together, then a sweep back through the hair. The outlawed Gral straightened, kicked sand over the small cookfire, then collected his pack and slung it over his shoulders. He picked up his hunting bow and strung it, then fitted an arrow. A final glance around, and he began walking.

The trail was not hard to follow. Taralack Veed continued scanning the rough, broken scrubland. A hare, a desert grouse, a mamlak lizard, anything would do; he was tired of the sun-dried strips of bhederin and he'd eaten the last date two nights previously. No shortage of tubers, of course, but too much and he'd spend half the day squatting over a hastily dug hole.

The D'ivers demon was closing on its quarry, and it was vital that Taralack remain in near proximity, so that he could make certain of the outcome. He was being well paid for the task ahead and that was all that mattered. Gold, and with it, the clout to raise a company of mercenaries. Then back to his village, to deliver well-deserved justice upon those who had betrayed him. He would assume the mantle of warleader then, and lead the Gral to glory. His destiny lay before him, and all was well.

Dejim Nebrahl revealed no digressions, no detours in its path. The D'ivers was admirably singular, true to its geas. There would be no deviation, for it lusted for the freedom that was the reward for the task's completion. This was the proper manner in which to make bargains, and Taralack found himself admiring the Nameless Ones. No matter how dread-filled the tales he had heard of the secret cult, his own dealings with them had been clean, lucrative and straightforward.

It had survived the Malazan conquest, and that was saying something. The old Emperor had displayed uncanny skill at infiltrating the innumerable cults abounding in Seven Cities, then delivering unmitigated slaughter upon the adherents.

That, too, was worthy of admiration.

This distant Empress, however, was proving far less impressive. She made too many mistakes. Taralack could not respect such a creature, and he ritually cursed her name with every dawn and every dusk, with as much vehemence as he cursed the seventy-four other avowed enemies of Taralack Veed.

Sympathy was like water in the desert. Hoarded, reluctantly meted out in the barest of sips. And he, Taralack Veed, could walk a thousand deserts on a single drop.

Such were the world's demands. He knew himself well enough to recognize that his was a viper's charm, alluring and mesmerizing and ultimately deadly. A viper made guest in a nest-bundle of meer-rats, how could they curse him for his very nature? He had killed the husband, after all, in service to her heart, a heart that had swallowed him whole. He had never suspected that she would then cast him out, that she would have simply made use of him, that another man had been waiting in the hut's shadow to ease the tortured spirit of the grieving widow. He had not believed that she too possessed the charms of a viper.

He halted near a boulder, collected a waterskin from his pack and removed the broad fired-clay stopper. Tugging his loincloth down he squatted and peed into the waterskin. There were no rock-springs for fifteen or more leagues in the direction the D'ivers was leading him. That path would eventually converge on a traders' track, of course, but that was a week or more away. Clearly, the D'ivers Dejim Nebrahl did not suffer the depredations of thirst.

The rewards of singular will, he well knew. Worthy of emulation, as far as was physically possible. He straightened, tugged the loincloth back up. Replacing the stopper, Taralack Veed slung the skin over a shoulder and resumed his measured pursuit.

Beneath glittering stars and a pale smear in the east, Scillara knelt on the hard ground, vomiting the last of her supper and then nothing but bile as heave after heave racked through her. Finally the spasms subsided. Gasping, she crawled away a short distance, then sat with her back to a boulder.

The demon Greyfrog watched from ten paces away, slowly swaying from side to side.

Watching him invited a return of the nausea, so she looked away, pulled out her pipe and began repacking it. 'It's been days,' she muttered. 'I thought I was past this. Dammit . . .'

Greyfrog ambled closer, approached the place where she had been sick. It sniffed, then pushed heaps of sand over the offending spot.

With a practised gesture, Scillara struck a quick series of sparks down into the pipe's bowl with the flint and iron striker. The shredded sweet-grass mixed in with the rustleaf caught, and moments later she was drawing smoke. 'That's good, Toad. Cover my trail . . . it's a wonder you've not told the others. Respecting my privacy?'

Greyfrog, predictably, did not reply.

Scillara ran a hand along the swell of her belly. How could she be getting fatter and fatter when she'd been throwing back one meal in three for weeks? There was something diabolical about this whole pregnancy thing. As if she possessed her own demon, huddled there in her belly. Well, the sooner it was out the quicker she could sell it to some pimp or harem master. There to be fed and raised and to learn the trade of the supplicant.

Most women who bothered stopped at two or three, she knew, and now she understood why. Healers and witches and midwives and sucklers kept the babies healthy enough, and the world remained to teach them its ways. The misery lay in the bearing, in carrying this growing weight, in its secret demands on her reserves.

And something else was happening as well. Something that proved the child's innate evil. She'd been finding herself drifting into a dreamy, pleasant state, inviting a senseless smile that, quite simply, horrified Scillara. What was there to be happy about? The world was not pleasant. It did not whisper contentment. No, the poisonous seduction stealing through her sought delusion, blissful stupidity – and she had had enough of that already. As nefarious as durhang, this deadly lure.

Her bulging belly would soon be obvious, she knew. Unless she tried to make herself even fatter. There was something comforting about all that solid bulk – but no, that was the delusional seduction all over again, finding a new path into her brain.

Well, it seemed the nausea was fully past, now. Scillara regained her feet and made her way back to the encampment. A handful of coals in the hearth, drifting threads of smoke, and three recumbent figures wrapped in blankets. Greyfrog appeared in her wake, moving past her to squat near the hearth. It snapped a capemoth out of the air and stuffed it into its broad mouth. Its eyes were a murky green as it studied Scillara.

She refilled her pipe. Why was it just women that had babies, anyway? Surely some ascendant witch could have made some sorcerous adjustment to the inequity by now? Or was it maybe not a flaw at all, but an advantage of some sort? Not that any obvious advantages came to mind. Apart from this strange, suspicious bliss constantly stealing through her. She drew hard on the rustleaf. Bidithal had made the cutting away of pleasure the first ritual among girls in his cult. He had liked the notion of feeling nothing at all, removing the dangerous desire for sensuality. She could not recall if she had ever known such sensations.

Bidithal had inculcated religious rapture, a state of being, she now suspected, infinitely more selfish and self-serving than satisfying one's own body. Being pregnant whispered of a similar kind of rapture, and that made her uneasy.

A sudden commotion. She turned to see that Cutter had sat up.

'Something wrong?' she asked in a low voice.

He faced her, his expression indistinct in the darkness, then sighed shakily. 'No. A bad dream.'

'It's nearing dawn,' Scillara said.

'Why are you awake?'

'No particular reason.'

He shook off the blanket, rose and walked over to the hearth. Crouched, tossing a handful of tinder onto the glowing coals, waited until it flared to life, then began adding dung chips.

'Cutter, what do you think will happen on Otataral Island?'

'I'm not sure. That old Malazan's not exactly clear on the matter, is he?'

'He is Destriant to the Tiger of Summer.'

Cutter glanced across at her. 'Reluctantly.'

She added more rustleaf to her pipe. 'He doesn't want followers. And if he did, it wouldn't be us. Well, not me, nor Felisin. We're not warriors. You,' she added, 'would be a more likely candidate.'

He snorted. 'No, not me, Scillara. It seems I follow another god.'

'It seems?'

She could just make out his shrug. 'You fall into things,' he said.

A woman. Well, that explains a lot. 'As good a reason as any other,' she said behind a lungful of smoke.

'What do you mean?'

'I mean, I don't see much reason behind following any god or goddess. If you're worth their interest, they use you. I know about being used, and most of the rewards are anything but, even if they look good at the time.'

'Well,' he said after a moment, 'someone's rewarded you.'

'Is that what you call it?'

'Call what? You're looking so . . . healthy. Full of life, I mean. And you're not as skinny as before.' He paused, then hastily added, 'Which is good. Half-starved didn't suit you – doesn't suit anyone, of course. You, included. Anyway, that's all.'

She sat, smoking, watching him in the growing light. 'We are quite a burden to you, aren't we, Cutter?'

'No! Not at all! I'm to escort you, a task I happily accepted. And that hasn't changed.'

'Don't you think Greyfrog is sufficient to protect us?'

'No, I mean, yes, he probably is. Even so, he is a demon, and that complicates things – it's not as if he can just amble into a village or city, is it? Or negotiate supplies and passage or stuff like that.'

'Felisin can. So can I, in fact.'

'Well. You're saying you don't want me here?'

'I'm saying we don't need you. Which isn't the same as saying we don't want you, Cutter. Besides, you've done well leading this odd little company, although it's obvious you're not used to doing that.'

'Listen, if you want to take over, that's fine by me.'

Ah, a woman who wouldn't follow, then. 'I see no reason to change anything,' she said offhandedly.

He was staring at her as she in turn regarded him, her gaze as level and as unperturbed as she could manage. 'What is the point of all this?' he demanded.

'Point? No point. Just making conversation, Cutter. Unless . . . is there something in particular you would like to talk about?'

She watched him pull back in every way but physically, as he said, 'No, nothing.'

'You don't know me well enough, then, is that it? Well, we'll have plenty of time.'

'I know you . . . I think. I mean, oh, you're right, I don't know you at all. I don't know women, is what I really mean. And how could I? It's impossible, trying to follow your thoughts, trying to make sense out of what you say, what is hidden behind your words—'

'Would that be me, specifically, or women in general?'

He threw more dung on the fire. 'No,' he muttered, 'nothing in particular I'd like to talk about.'

'All right, but I have a few topics . . .'

He groaned.

'You were given the task,' she said. 'To escort us, correct? Who gave you that task?'

'A god.'

'But not Heboric's god.'

'No.'

'So there's at least two gods interested in us. That's not good, Cutter. Does Ghost Hands know about this? No, he wouldn't, would he? No reason to tell him—'

'It's not hard to figure out,' Cutter retorted. 'I was waiting for you. In Iskaral Pust's temple.'

'Malazan gods. Shadowthrone or Cotillion. But you're not Malazan, are you?'

'Really, Scillara,' Cutter said wearily, 'do we have to discuss this right now?'

'Unless,' she went on, 'your lover was. Malazan, that is. The original follower of those gods.'

'Oh, my head hurts,' he mumbled, hands up over his eyes, the fingers reaching into his hair, then clenching as if to begin tearing it out. 'How – no, I don't want to know. It doesn't matter. I don't care.'

'So where is she now?'

'No more.'

Scillara subsided. She pulled out a narrow-bladed knife and began cleaning her pipe.

He suddenly rose. 'I'll start on breakfast.'

A sweet boy, she decided. Like damp clay in a woman's hands. A woman who knew what she was doing, that is. *Now the question is, should I be doing this?* Felisin adored Cutter, after all. *Then again, we could always share.*

'*Smirking observation. Soft-curved, large-breasted woman wants to press flesh with Cutter.*'

Not now, Greyfrog, he replied without speaking aloud as he removed food from the pack.

'*Alarm. No, not now indeed. The others are wakening from their*

145

uneasy dreams. Awkward and dismay to follow, especially with Felisin Younger.'

Cutter paused. *What? Why – but she's barely of age! No, this can't be. Talk her out of it, Greyfrog!*

'*Greyfrog's own advances unwelcome. Despondent sulk. You, Cutter, of seed-issuing capacity, capable of effecting beget. Past revelation. Human women carry breeding pond in bellies. But one egg survives, only one. Terrible risk! You must fill pond as quickly as possible, before rival male appears to steal your destiny. Greyfrog will defend your claim. Brave self-sacrifice, such as Sentinel Circlers among own kind. Altruistic enlightenment of reciprocity and protracted slant reward once or even many times removed. Signifier of higher intelligence, acknowledgement of community interests. Greyfrog is already Sentinel Circler to soft-curved, large-breasted goddess-human.'*

Goddess? What do you mean, goddess?

'*Lustful sigh, is worthy of worship. Value signifiers in male human clouding the pond's waters in Greyfrog's mind. Too long association. Happily. Sexual desires long withheld. Unhealthy.'*

Cutter set a pot of water on the fire and tossed in a handful of herbs. *What did you say earlier about uneasy dreams, Greyfrog?*

'*Observation, skimming the mind ponds. Troubled. Approaching danger. There are warning signs.'*

What warning signs?

'*Obvious. Uneasy dreams. Sufficient unto themselves.'*

Not always, Greyfrog. Sometimes it's things from the past that haunt us. That's all.

'*Ah. Greyfrog will think on this. But first, pangs. Greyfrog is hungry.'*

The grey haze of the heat and the dust made the distant walls barely visible. Leoman of the Flails rode at the head of the ragged column, Corabb Bhilan Thenu'alas at his side, as a company of riders approached from Y'Ghatan's gates.

'There,' Corabb said, 'front rider on the right of the standard-bearer, that is Falah'd Vedor. He looks . . . unhappy.'

'He'd best begin making peace with that sentiment,' Leoman said in a growl. He raised a gloved hand and the column behind him slowed to a halt.

They watched the company close.

'Commander, shall you and I meet them halfway?' Corabb asked.

'Of course not,' Leoman snapped.

Corabb said nothing more. His leader was in a dark mood. A third of his warriors were riding double. A much-loved old healer witch had

146

died this very morning, and they'd pinned her corpse beneath a slab of stone lest some wandering spirit find her. Leoman himself had spat in the eight directions to hallow the ground, and spilled drops of his own blood from a slash he opened on his left hand onto the dusted stone, voicing the blessing in the name of the Apocalyptic. Then he had wept. In front of all his warriors, who had stood silent, awestruck by the grief and the love for his followers Leoman had revealed in that moment.

The Falah'd and his soldiers approached, then drew to a halt five paces in front of Leoman and Corabb.

Corabb studied Vedor's sallow, sunken face, murky eyes, and knew him for an addict of d'bayang poppy. His thick-veined hands trembled on the saddle horn, and, when it became evident that Leoman would not be the first to speak, he scowled and said, 'I, Falah'd Vedor of Y'Ghatan, the First Holy City, do hereby welcome you, Leoman of the Flails, refugee of Sha'ik's Fall in Raraku, and your broken followers. We have prepared secure barracks for your warriors, and the tables wait, heaped with food and wine. You, Leoman, and your remaining officers shall be the Falah'd's guests in the palace, for as long as required for you to reprovision your army and recover from your flight. Inform us of your final destination and we shall send envoys in advance to proclaim your coming to each and every village, town and city on your route.'

Corabb found he was holding his breath. He watched as Leoman nudged his horse forward, until he was positioned side by side with the Falah'd.

'We have come to Y'Ghatan,' Leoman said, in a low voice, 'and it is in Y'Ghatan that we shall stay. To await the coming of the Malazans.'

Vedor's stained mouth worked for a moment without any sound issuing forth, then he managed a hacking laugh. 'Like a knife's edge, your sense of humour, Leoman of the Flails! It is as your legend proclaims!'

'My legend? Then this, too, will not surprise you.' The kethra knife was a blinding flash, sweeping to caress Vedor's throat. Blood spurted, and the Falah'd's head rolled back, thumped on the rump of the startled horse, then down to bounce and roll in the dust of the road. Leoman reached out to steady the headless corpse still seated in the saddle, and wiped the blade on the silken robes.

From the company of city soldiers, not a sound, not a single motion. The standard-bearer, a youth of perhaps fifteen years, stared open-mouthed at the headless body beside him.

'In the name of Dryjhna the Apocalyptic,' Leoman said, 'I now rule the First Holy City of Y'Ghatan. Who is the ranking officer here?'

A woman pushed her horse forward. 'I am. Captain Dunsparrow.'

Corabb squinted at her. Solid features, sun-darkened, light grey eyes. Twenty-five years of age, perhaps. The glint of a chain vest was just visible beneath her plain telaba. 'You,' Corabb said, 'are Malazan.'

The cool eyes fixed on him. 'What of it?'

'Captain,' Leoman said, 'your troop will precede us. Clear the way to the palace for me and my warriors. The secure barracks spoken of by the late Falah'd will be used to house those soldiers in the city garrison and from the palace who might be disinclined to follow my orders. Please ensure that they are indeed secured. Once you have done these things, report to me in the palace for further orders.'

'Sir,' the woman said, 'I am of insufficient rank to do as you ask—'

'No longer. You are now my Third, behind Corabb Bhilan Thenu'alas.'

Her gaze briefly flicked back to Corabb, revealing nothing. 'As you command, Leoman of the Flails, Falah'd of Y'Ghatan.'

Dunsparrow twisted in her saddle and bellowed out to her troops, 'About face! Smartly now, you damned pig-herders! We advance the arrival of the new Falah'd!'

Vedor's horse turned along with all the others, and began trotting, the headless body pitching about in its saddle.

Corabb watched as, twenty paces along, the dead Falah'd's mount came up alongside the captain. She noted it and with a single straight-armed shove sent the corpse toppling.

Leoman grunted. 'Yes. She is perfect.'

A Malazan. 'I have misgivings, Commander.'

'Of course you have. It's why I keep you at my side.' He glanced over. 'That, and the Lady's tug. Come now, ride with me into our new city.'

They kicked their horses into motion. Behind them followed the others.

'Our new city,' Corabb said, grinning. 'We shall defend it with our lives.'

Leoman shot him an odd look, but said nothing.

Corabb thought about that. *Commander, I have more misgivings . . .*

CHAPTER FIVE

The first cracks appeared shortly after the execution of Sha'ik. None could know the mind of Adjunct Tavore. Not her closest officers, and not the common soldier under her command. But there were distant stirrings, to be sure, more easily noted in retrospect, and it would be presumptuous and indeed dismissive to claim that the Adjunct was ignorant of the growing troubles, not only in her command, but at the very heart of the Malazan Empire. Given that, the events at Y'Ghatan could have been a fatal wound. Were someone else in command, were that someone's heart any less hard, any less cold.

This, more than at any other time beforehand, gave brutal truth to the conviction that Adjunct Tavore was cold iron, thrust into the soul of a raging forge . . .

'None to Witness'
(*The Lost History of the Bonehunters*)
Duiker of Darujhistan

'PUT THAT DOWN,' SAMAR DEV SAID WEARILY FROM WHERE SHE SAT near the window.

'Thought you were asleep,' Karsa Orlong said. He returned the object to the tabletop. 'What is it?'

'Two functions. The upper beaker contains filters for the water, removing all impurities. The water gathering in the lower beaker is flanked by strips of copper, which livens the water itself through a complicated and mysterious process. A particular ethereal gas is released, thus altering the air pressure above the water, which in turn—'

'But what do you use it for?'

Samar's eyes narrowed. 'Nothing in particular.'

He moved away from the table, approached the work benches and shelves. She watched him examining the various mechanisms she had invented, and the long-term experiments, many of which showed no evident alteration of conditions. He poked. Sniffed, and even sought to taste one dish filled with gelatinous fluid. She thought to stop him, then decided to remain quiet. The warrior's wounds had healed with appalling swiftness, with no signs of infection. The thick liquid he was licking from his finger wasn't particularly healthy to ingest, but not fatal. Usually.

He made a face. 'This is terrible.'

'I am not surprised.'

'What do you use it for?'

'What do you think?'

'Rub it into saddles. Leather.'

'Saddles? Indirectly, I suppose. It is an ointment, for the suppurating wounds that sometimes arise on the lining of the anus—'

He grunted loudly, then said, 'No wonder it tasted awful,' and resumed his examination of the room's contents.

She regarded him thoughtfully. Then said, 'The Falah'd sent soldiers into the keep. They found signs of past slaughter – as you said, not one Malazan left alive. They also found a demon. Or, rather, the corpse of a demon, freshly killed. They have asked me to examine it, for I possess a little knowledge of anatomy and other, related subjects.'

He made no reply, peering into the wrong end of a spyglass.

'If you come to the window, and look through the other end, Karsa, you will see things far away drawn closer.'

He scowled at her, and set the instrument down. 'If something is far away, I simply ride closer.'

'And if it is at the top of a cliff? Or a distant enemy encampment and you want to determine the picket lines?'

He retrieved the spyglass and walked over. She moved her chair to one side to give him room. 'There is a falcon's nest on the ledge of that tower, the copper-sheathed one.'

He held up the glass. Searched until he found the nest. 'That is no falcon.'

'You are right. It's a bokh'aral that found the abandoned nest to its liking. It carries up armfuls of rotting fruit and it spends the morning dropping them on people in the streets below.'

'It appears to be snarling . . .'

'That would be laughter. It is forever driven to bouts of hilarity.'

'Ah – no, that wasn't fruit. It was a brick.'

'Oh, unfortunate. Someone will be sent to kill it, now. After all, only people are allowed to throw bricks at people.'

He lowered the spyglass and studied her. 'That is madness. What manner of laws do you possess, to permit such a thing?'

'Which thing? Stoning people or killing bokh'arala?'

'You are strange, Samar Dev. But then, you are a witch, and a maker of useless objects—'

'Is that spyglass useless?'

'No, I now understand its value. Yet it was lying on a shelf . . .'

She leaned back. 'I have invented countless things that would prove of great value to many people. And that presents me with a dilemma. I must ask myself, with each invention, what possible abuses await such an object? More often than not, I conclude that those abuses outweigh the value of the invention. I call this Dev's First Law of Invention.'

'You are obsessed with laws.'

'Perhaps. In any case, the law is simple, as all true laws must be—'

'You have a law for that, too?'

'Founding principle, rather than law. In any case, ethics are the first consideration of an inventor following a particular invention.'

'You call that simple?'

'The statement is, the consideration is not.'

'Now that sounds more like a true law.'

She closed her mouth after a moment, then rose and walked over to the scriber's desk, sat and collected a stylus and a wax tablet. 'I distrust philosophy,' she said as she wrote. 'Even so, I will not turn away from the subject . . . when it slaps me in the face. Nor am I particularly eloquent as a writer. I am better suited to manipulating objects than words. You, on the other hand, seem to possess an unexpected talent for . . . uh . . . cogent brevity.'

'You talk too much.'

'No doubt.' She finished recording her own unexpectedly profound words – profound only in that Karsa Orlong had recognized a far vaster application than she had intended. She paused, wanting to dismiss his genius as blind chance, or even the preening false wisdom of savage nobility. But something whispered to her that Karsa Orlong had been underestimated before, and she vowed not to leap into the same pit. Setting the stylus down, she rose to her feet. 'I am off to examine the demon you killed. Will you accompany me?'

'No, I had a close enough examination the first time.'

She collected the leather satchel containing her surgical instruments. 'Stay inside, please, and try not to break anything.'

'How can you call yourself an inventor if you dislike breaking things?'

At the door, she paused and glanced back at him. His head was brushing the ceiling in this, the highest chamber in her tower. There was something . . . there in his eyes. 'Try not to break any of *my* things.'

'Very well. But I am hungry. Bring more food.'

The reptilian corpse was lying on the floor of one of the torture chambers situated in the palace crypts. A retired Avower had been given the task of standing guard. Samar Dev found him asleep in one corner of the room. Leaving him to his snores, she stationed around the huge demon's body the four lit lanterns she had brought down from above, then settled onto her knees and untied the flap of her satchel, withdrawing a variety of polished surgical instruments. And, finally, her preparations complete, she swung her attention to the corpse.

Teeth, jaws, forward-facing eyes, all the makings of a superior carnivore, likely an ambush hunter. Yet, this was no simple river lizard. Behind the orbital ridges the skull swept out broad and long, with massive occipital bulges, the sheer mass of the cranial region implying intelligence. Unless, of course, the bone was absurdly thick.

She cut away the torn and bruised skin to reveal broken fragments of that skull. Not so thick, then. Indentations made it obvious that Karsa Orlong had used his fists. In which, it was clear, there was astonishing strength, and an equally astonishing will. The brain beneath, marred with broken vessels and blood leakage and pulped in places by the skull pieces, was indeed large, although arranged in a markedly different manner from a human's. There were more lobes, for one thing. Six more, in all, positioned beneath heavy ridged projections out to the sides, including two extra vessel-packed masses connected by tissue to the eyes. Suggesting these demons saw a different world, a more complete one, perhaps.

Samar extracted one mangled eye and was surprised to find two lenses, one concave, the other convex. She set those aside for later examination.

Cutting through the tough, scaled hide, she opened the neck regions, confirming the oversized veins and arteries necessary to feed an active brain, then continued on to reveal the chest region. Many of the ribs were already broken. She counted four lungs and two proto-lungs attached beneath them, these latter ones saturated with blood.

She cut through the lining of the first of three stomachs, then moved quickly back as the acids poured out. The blade of her knife sizzled and she watched as pitting etched into the iron surface. More hissing sounds, from the stone floor. Her eyes began watering.

Movement from the stomach, and Samar rose and took a step back. Worms were crawling out. A score, wriggling then dropping to the muddy stone. The colour of blued iron, segmented, each as long as an index finger. She glanced down at the crumbling knife in her hand and dropped the instrument, then collected wooden tongs from her satchel, moved to the edge of the acid pool, reached down and retrieved one of the worms.

Not a worm. Hundreds of legs, strangely finned, and, even more surprising, the creatures were mechanisms. Not living at all, the metal of their bodies somehow impervious to the acids. The thing twisted about in the grip of the tongs, then stopped moving. She shook it, but it had gone immobile, like a crooked nail. An infestation? She did not think so. No, there were many creatures that worked in concert. The pond of stomach acid had been home to these mechanisms, and they in turn worked in some fashion to the demon's benefit.

A hacking cough startled her, and she turned to see the Avower stumble to his feet. Hunched, twisted with arthritis, he shambled over. 'Samar Dev, the witch! What's that smell? Not you, I hope. You and me, we're the same sort, aren't we just?'

'We are?'

'Oh yes, Samar Dev.' He scratched at his crotch. 'We strip the layers of humanity, down to the very bones, but where does humanity end and animal begin? When does pain defeat reason? Where hides the soul and to where does it flee when all hope in the flesh is lost? Questions to ponder, for such as you and me. Oh how I have longed to meet you, to share knowledge—'

'You're a torturer.'

'Someone has to be,' he said, offended. 'In a culture that admits the need for torture, there must perforce be a torturer. A culture, Samar Dev, that values the acquisition of truths more than it does any single human life. Do you see? Oh,' he added, edging closer to frown down at the demon's corpse, 'the justifications are always the same. To save many more lives, this one must be surrendered. Sacrificed. Even the words used disguise the brutality. Why are torture chambers in the crypts? To mask the screams? True enough, but there's more. This,' he said, waving one gnarled hand, 'is the nether realm of humanity, the rotted heart of unpleasantness.'

'I am seeking answers from something already dead. It is not the same—'

'Details. We are questioners, you and I. We slice back the armour to uncover the hidden truth. Besides, I'm retired. They want me to train another, you know, now that the Malazan laws have been struck down and torture's popular once more. But, the fools they send me! Ah, what is the point? Now, Falah'd Krithasanan, now he was something – you were likely just a child, then, or younger even. My, how he liked torturing people. Not for truths – he well understood that facile rubbish for what it was – facile rubbish. No, the greater questions interested him. How far along can a soul be dragged, trapped still within its broken body, how far? How far until it can no longer crawl back? This was my challenge, and oh how he appreciated my artistry!'

Samar Dev looked down to see that the rest of the mechanisms had all ceased to function. She placed the one she had retrieved in a small leather pouch, then repacked her kit, making sure to include the eye lenses. She'd get them to burn the rest of the body – well away from the city, and upwind.

'Will you not dine with me?'

'Alas, I cannot. I have work to do.'

'If only they'd bring your guest down here. Toblakai. Oh, he would be fun, wouldn't he?'

She paused. 'I doubt I could talk him into it, Avower.'

'The Falah'd has been considering it, you know.'

'No, I didn't know. I think it would be a mistake.'

'Well, *those* things are not for us to question, are they?'

'Something tells me Toblakai would be delighted to meet you, Avower. Although it would be a short acquaintance.'

'Not if I have my way, Samar Dev!'

'Around Karsa Orlong, I suspect, only Karsa Orlong has his way.'

She returned to find the Teblor warrior poring over her collection of maps, which he'd laid out on the floor in the hallway. He had brought in a dozen votive candles, now lit and set out around him. He held one close as he perused the precious parchments. Without looking up, he said, 'This one here, witch. The lands and coast west and north . . . I was led to believe the Jhag Odhan was unbroken, that the plains ran all the way to the far-lands of Nemil and the Trell, yet here, this shows something different.'

'If you burn holes in my maps,' Samar Dev said, 'I will curse you and your bloodline for all eternity.'

'The Odhan sweeps westward, it seems, but only in the south. There are places of ice marked here. This continent looks too vast. There has been a mistake.'

'Possibly,' she conceded. 'Since that is the one direction I have not travelled, I can make no claim as to the map's accuracy. Mind you, that one was etched by Othun Dela Farat, a century ago. He was reputed to be reliable.'

'What of this region of lakes?' he asked, pointing to the northerly bulge along the coast, west of Yath Alban.

She set her equipment down, then, sighing, she crouched at his side. 'Difficult to cross. The bedrock is exposed there, badly folded, pocked with lakes and only a few, mostly impassable rivers. The forest is spruce, fir and pine, with low-lying thickets in the basins.'

'How do you know all that if you have never been there?'

She pointed. 'I am reading Dela's notes, there, along the border. He also says he found signs suggesting there were people living there, but no contact was ever made. Beyond lies the island kingdom of Sepik, now a remote subject of the Malazan Empire, although I would be surprised if the Malazans ever visited. The king was clever enough to send delegates proposing conditions of surrender, and the Emperor simply accepted.'

'The mapmaker hasn't written that much.'

'No, some of that information was mine. I have heard, now and then, certain odd stories about Sepik. There are, it seems, two distinct populations, one the subject of the other.' She shrugged at his blank look. 'Such things interest me.' Then frowned, as it became obvious that the distant expression on the giant's tattooed visage was born of something other than indifference. 'Is something wrong?'

Karsa Orlong bared his teeth. 'Tell me more of this Sepik.'

'I am afraid I have exhausted my knowledge.'

Scowling at her answer, he hunched down over the map once more. 'I shall need supplies. Tell me, is the weather the same as here?'

'You are going to Sepik?'

'Yes. Tell the Falah'd that I demand equipment, two extra horses, and five hundred crescents in silver. Dried foods, more waterskins. Three javelins and a hunting bow with thirty arrows, ten of them bird-pointed. Six extra bowstrings and a supply of fletching, a brick of wax—'

'Wait! Wait, Karsa Orlong. Why would the Falah'd simply gift you all these things?'

'Tell him, if he does not, I will stay in this city.'

'Ah, I see.' She considered for a time, then asked, 'Why are you going to Sepik?'

He began rolling up the map. 'I want this one—'

'Sorry, no. It is worth a fortune—'

'I will return it.'

'No, Karsa Orlong.' She straightened. 'If you are prepared to wait, I will copy it – on hide, which is more resilient—'

'How long will that take?'

'I don't know. A few days . . .'

'Very well, but I am getting restless, witch.' He handed her the rolled-up map and walked into the other chamber. 'And hungry.'

She stooped once more to gather in the other maps. The candles she left alone. Each one was aspected to a local, minor god, and the flames had, one and all, drawn the attention of the host of spirits. This hall-way was crowded with presences, making the air taut, bridling, since many of them counted others as enemies. Yet, she suspected, it had been more than just the flickering flames that had earned the regard of the spirits. Something about Toblakai himself . . .

There were mysteries, she believed, swirling in Karsa Orlong's history. And now, the spirits drawn close, close and . . . frightened . . .

'Ah,' she whispered, 'I see no choice in the matter. None at all . . .' She drew out a belt-knife, spat on the blade, then began waving the iron through the flame of each candle.

The spirits howled in her mind, outraged at this unexpected, brutal imprisonment. She nodded. 'Yes, we mortals are cruel . . .'

'Three leagues,' Quick Ben said under his breath.

Kalam scratched at the stubble on his chin. Some old wounds – that enkar'al at the edge of the Whirlwind's wall had torn him up pretty bad – were aching after the long forced march back towards the Fourteenth Army. After what they had seen in the warren, no-one was in the mood to complain, however. Even Stormy had ceased his endless griping. The squad was hunkered down behind the assassin and the High Mage, motionless and virtually invisible in the darkness.

'So,' Kalam mused, 'do we wait for them here, or do we keep walking?'

'We wait,' Quick Ben replied. 'I need the rest. In any case, we all more or less guessed right, and the trail isn't hard to follow. Leoman's reached Y'Ghatan and that's where he'll make his stand.'

'And us with no siege equipment to speak of.'

The wizard nodded. 'This could be a long one.'

'Well, we're used to that, aren't we?'

'I keep forgetting, you weren't at Coral.'

Kalam settled down with his back against the ridge's slope and pulled free a flask. He drank then handed it to the High Mage. 'As bad as the last day at Pale?'

Quick Ben sipped, then made a face. 'This is water.'

'Of course it is.'

'Pale . . . we weren't fighting anyone. Just collapsing earth and raining rocks.'

'So, the Bridgeburners went down fighting.'

'Most of Onearm's Host went down fighting,' Quick Ben said. 'Even Whiskeyjack,' he added. 'His leg gave out under him. Mallet won't forgive himself for that, and I can't say I'm surprised.' He shrugged in the gloom. 'It was messy. A lot went wrong, as usual. But Kallor turning on us . . . that we should have foreseen.'

'I've got a space on my blade for a notch in his name,' Kalam said, retrieving the flask.

'You're not the only one, but he's not an easy man to kill.'

Sergeant Gesler edged into view. 'Saw you two passing something.'

'Just water,' Kalam said.

'The last thing I wanted to hear. Well, don't mind me.'

'We were discussing the siege to come,' the assassin said. 'Could be a long one.'

'Even so,' Gesler said with a grunt, 'Tavore's a patient woman. We know that much about her, anyway.'

'Nothing else?' Quick Ben asked.

'You've talked with her more than any of us, High Mage. She keeps her distance. No-one really seems to know what she is, behind the title of Adjunct. Nobleborn, aye, and from Unta. From House Paran.'

Kalam and Quick Ben exchanged glances, then the assassin pulled out a second flask. 'This one ain't water,' he said, tossing it to the sergeant. 'We knew her brother. Ganoes Paran. He was attached to the Bridgeburners, rank as captain, just before we infiltrated Darujhistan.'

'He led the squads into Coral,' Quick Ben said.

'And died?' Gesler asked after pulling at the flask.

'Most everyone died,' answered the High Mage. 'At any rate, he wasn't an embarrassment as far as officers go. As for Tavore, well, I'm in the dark as much as the rest of you. She's all edges, but they're for keeping people away, not cutting them. At least from what I've seen.'

'She's going to start losing soldiers at Y'Ghatan,' Kalam said.

No-one commented on that observation. Different commanders reacted in different ways to things like that. Some just got stubborn and threw more and more lives away. Others flinched back and if nothing then happened, the spirit of the army drained away. Sieges were battles of will, for the most part, along with cunning. Leoman had shown a capacity for both in this long pursuit west of Raraku. Kalam wasn't sure what Tavore had shown at Raraku – someone else had done most of the killing for her, for the entire Fourteenth, in fact.

Ghosts. Bridgeburners . . . ascended. Gods, what a chilling thought. They were all half-mad when alive, and now . . . 'Quick,' Kalam said, 'those ghosts at Raraku . . . where are they now?'

'No idea. Not with us, though.'

'Ghosts,' Gesler said. 'So the rumours were true – it wasn't no sorcerous spell that slaughtered the Dogslayers. We had unseen allies – who were they?' He paused, then spat. 'You both know, don't you, and you're not telling. Fiddler knows, too, doesn't he? Never mind. Everybody's got secrets and don't bother asking me to share mine. So that's that.' He handed the flask back. 'Thanks for the donkey piss, Kalam.'

They listened as he crawled back to rejoin his squad.

'Donkey piss?' Quick Ben asked.

'Ground-vine wine, and he's right, it tastes awful. I found it at the Dogslayer camp. Want some?'

'Why not? Anyway, when I said the ghosts weren't with us, I think I was telling the truth. But something *is* following the army.'

'Well, that's just great.'

'I'm not—'

'Hush! I hear—'

Figures rose from behind the ridge. Gleaming, ancient armour, axes and scimitars, barbaric, painted faces – Khundryl Burned Tears. Swearing, Kalam settled back down, resheathing his long-knives. 'That was a stupid move, you damned savages—'

One spoke: 'Come with us.'

Three hundred paces up the road waited a number of riders, among them the Adjunct Tavore. Flanked by the troop of Khundryl Burned Tears, Kalam, Quick Ben and Gesler and his squad approached the group.

The misshapen moon now cast down a silvery light on the land – it was looking rougher round the edges, Kalam realized, as if the surrounding darkness was gnawing at it – he wondered that he'd not noticed before. Had it always been like that?

'Good evening, Adjunct,' Quick Ben said as they arrived.

'Why have you returned?' she demanded. 'And why are you not in the Imperial Warren?'

With Tavore were the Fists, the Wickan Temul, Blistig, Keneb and Tene Baralta, as well as Nil and Nether. They looked, one and all, to have been recently roused from sleep, barring the Adjunct herself.

Quick Ben shifted uneasily. 'The warren was being used . . . by something else. We judged it unsafe, and we concluded you should be told of that as soon as possible. Leoman is now in Y'Ghatan.'

'And you believe he will await us there?'

'Y'Ghatan,' Kalam said, 'is a bitter memory to most Malazans – those that care to remember, anyway. It is where the First—'

'I know, Kalam Mekhar. You need not remind me of that. Very well, I shall assume your assessment is correct. Sergeant Gesler, please join the Khundryl pickets.'

The marine's salute was haphazard, his expression mocking.

Kalam watched Tavore's eyes follow the sergeant and his squad as they headed off. Then she fixed her gaze on Quick Ben once more.

'High Mage.'

He nodded. 'There were . . . Moon's Spawns in the Imperial Warren. Ten, twelve came into sight before we retreated.'

'Hood take us,' Blistig muttered. 'Floating fortresses? Has that white-haired bastard found more of them?'

'I don't think so, Fist,' Quick Ben said. 'Anomander Rake has settled in Black Coral, now, and he abandoned Moon's Spawn, since it was falling to pieces. No, I believe the ones we saw in the warren have their, uh, original owners inside.'

'And who might they be?' Tavore asked.

'K'Chain Che'Malle, Adjunct. Long-Tails or Short-Tails. Or both.'

'And why would they be using the Imperial Warren?'

'I don't know,' Quick Ben admitted. 'But I have some notions.'

'Let us hear them.'

'It's an old warren, effectively dead and abandoned, although, of course, not nearly as dead or abandoned as it first seems. Now, there is no known warren attributed to the K'Chain Che'Malle, but that does not mean one never existed.'

'You believe the Imperial Warren was originally the K'Chain Che'Malle warren?'

The High Mage shrugged. 'It's possible, Adjunct.'

'What else?'

'Well, wherever the fortresses are going, they don't want to be seen.'

'Seen by whom?'

'That I don't know.'

The Adjunct studied the High Mage for a long moment, then she said, 'I want you to find out. Take Kalam and Gesler's squad. Return to the Imperial Warren.'

The assassin slowly nodded to himself, not at all surprised at this insane, absurd command. Find out? Precisely how?

'Have you any suggestions,' Quick Ben asked, his voice now strangely lilting, as it always was when he struggled against speaking his mind, 'on how we might do that?'

'As High Mage, I am certain you can think of some.'

'May I ask, why is this of particular importance to us, Adjunct?'

'The breaching of the Imperial Warren is important to all who would serve the Malazan Empire, would you not agree?'

'I would, Adjunct, but are we not engaged in a military campaign here? Against the last rebel leader in Seven Cities? Are you not about to lay siege to Y'Ghatan, wherein the presence of a High Mage, not to mention the empire's most skilled assassin, might prove pivotal to your success?'

'Quick Ben,' Tavore said coolly, 'the Fourteenth Army is quite capable of managing this siege without your assistance, or that of Kalam Mekhar.'

All right, that clinches it. She knows about our clandestine meeting with Dujek Onearm and Tayschrenn. And she does not trust us. Probably with good reason.

'Of course,' Quick Ben said, with a modest bow. 'I trust the Burned

Tears can resupply our soldiers, then. I request we be permitted to rest until dawn.'

'Acceptable.'

The High Mage turned away, his eyes momentarily meeting Kalam's own. *Aye, Quick, she wants me as far away from her back as possible.* Well, this was the Malazan Empire, after all. Laseen's empire, to be more precise. *But Tavore, it's not me you have to worry about . . .*

At that moment a figure emerged from the darkness, approaching from one side of the road. Green silks, graceful motion, a face very nearly ethereal in the moonlight. 'Ah, a midnight assignation! I trust all matters of grave import have already been addressed.'

Pearl. Kalam grinned at the man, one hand making a gesture that only another Claw would understand.

Seeing it, Pearl winked.

Soon, you bastard.

Tavore wheeled her horse round. 'We are done here.'

'Might I ride double with one of you?' Pearl asked the assembled Fists.

None replied, and moments later they were cantering up the road.

Pearl coughed delicately in the dust. 'How rude.'

'You walked out here,' Quick Ben said, 'you can walk back in, Claw.'

'It seems I have no choice.' A fluttering wave of a gloved hand. 'Who knows when we'll meet again, my friends. But until then . . . good hunting . . .' He walked off.

Now how much did he hear? Kalam took a half-step forward, but Quick Ben reached out and restrained him.

'Relax, he was just fishing. I sensed him circling closer – you had him very nervous, Kal.'

'Good.'

'Not really. It means he isn't stupid.'

'True. Too bad.'

'Anyway,' Quick Ben said, 'you and me and Gesler have to come up with a way to hitch a ride on one of those fortresses.'

Kalam turned his head. Stared at his friend. 'That wasn't a joke, was it?'

'I'm afraid not.'

Joyful Union was basking in the sun as it dined, ringed in by stones, with Bottle lying close by and studying the way it fed as the scorpion snipped apart the capemoth he had given it for breakfast, when a military issue boot crunched down on the arachnid, the heel twisting.

Bottle jerked back in dumbfounded horror, stared up at the figure standing over him, a surge of murderous intent filling his being.

Backlit by the morning light, the figure was little more than a silhouette.

'Soldier,' the voice was a woman's, the accent Korelri, 'which squad is this?'

Bottle's mouth opened and closed a few times, then he said in a low tone, 'This is the squad that will start making plans to kill you, once they find out what you've just done.'

'Allow me,' she said, 'to clarify matters for you, soldier. I am Captain Faradan Sort, and I cannot abide scorpions. Now, I want to see how well you manage a salute while lying down.'

'You want a salute, Captain? Which one? I have plenty of salutes to choose from. Any preference?'

'The salute that tells me you have just become aware of the precipice I am about to kick your ass over. After I shove the sack of bricks up it, of course.'

Oh. 'Standard salute, then. Of course, Captain.' He arched his back and managed to hold the salute for a few heartbeats . . . waiting for her to respond, which she did not. Gasping, he collapsed back down, inhaling a mouthful of dust.

'We will try that again later, soldier. Your name?'

'Uh, Smiles, sir.'

'Well, I doubt I will see many of those on your ugly face, will I?'

'No, sir.'

She then walked on.

Bottle stared down at the mashed, glittering pulp that had been Joyful Union and half a capemoth. He wanted to cry.

'Sergeant.'

Strings glanced up, noted the torc on the arm, and slowly climbed to his feet. He saluted, studying the tall, straight-backed woman standing before him. 'Sergeant Strings, Captain. Fourth Squad.'

'Good. You are mine, now. My name is Faradan Sort.'

'I was wondering when you'd show up, sir. The replacements have been here for days, after all.'

'I was busy. Do you have a problem with that, Sergeant?'

'No, sir, not one.'

'You are a veteran, I see. You might think that fact yields some relief on my part. It does not. I do not care where you have been, who you served under, or how many officers you knifed in the back. All I care about is how much you know about fighting.'

'Never knifed a single officer, sir . . . in the back. And I don't know a damned thing about fighting, except surviving it.'

'That will do. Where are the rest of my squads?'

'Well, you're missing one. Gesler's. They're on a reconnaissance mission, no idea when they'll be back. Borduke's squad is over there.' He pointed. 'With Cord's just beyond. The rest you'll find here and there.'

'You do not bivouac together?'

'As a unit? No.'

'You will from now on.'

'Yes sir.'

She cast her eyes over the soldiers still sprawled in sleep around the hearth. 'The sun is up. They should be awake, fed and equipped for the march by now.'

'Yes sir.'

'So . . . wake them.'

'Yes sir.'

She started to walk off, then turned and added, 'You have a soldier named Smiles in your squad, Sergeant Strings?'

'I have.'

'Smiles is to carry a double load today.'

'Sir?'

'You heard me.'

He watched her leave, then swung about and looked down at his soldiers. All were awake, their eyes on him.

'What did I do?' Smiles demanded.

Strings shrugged. 'She's a captain, Smiles.'

'So?'

'So, captains are insane. At least, this one is, which proves my claim. Wouldn't you agree, Cuttle?'

'Oh yes, Strings. Raving wide-eyed insane.'

'A double load!'

Bottle stumbled into the camp, in his cupped hands a mangled mess. 'She stepped on Joyful Union!'

'Well, that settles it,' Cuttle said, grunting as he sat up. 'She's dead.'

Fist Keneb strode into his tent, unstrapping his helm and pulling it free to toss it on the cot, then paused upon seeing a tousled head lift clear of the opened travel trunk at the back wall. 'Grub! What were you doing in there?'

'Sleeping. She is not stupid, no. They are coming, to await the resurrection.' He clambered out of the trunk, dressed, as ever, in ragged leathers, Wickan in style yet badly worn. The childish roundness of his cheeks had begun to thin, hinting at the man he would one day become.

'She? Do you mean the Adjunct? Who is coming? What resurrection?'

'They will try to kill her. But that is wrong. She is our last hope. Our last hope. I'm going to find something to eat, we're marching to Y'Ghatan.' He rushed past Keneb. Outside the tent, dogs barked. The Fist pulled the flap aside and stepped out to see Grub hurrying down the aisle between the tents, flanked by the Wickan cattle-dog, Bent, and the Hengese lapdog, Roach. Soldiers deferentially moved aside to let them pass.

The Fist headed back inside. A baffling child. He sat down on the cot, stared at nothing in particular.

A siege. Ideally, they needed four or five thousand more soldiers, five or six Untan catapults and four towers. Ballistae, mangonels, onagers, scorpions, wheeled rams and ladders. Perhaps a few more units of sappers, with a few wagons loaded with Moranth munitions. And High Mage Quick Ben.

Had it been just a matter of pride, sending the wizard away? The meetings with Dujek Onearm had been strained. Tavore's refusal of assistance beyond a contingent of replacements from Quon Tali made little sense. Granted, Dujek had plenty to occupy himself and his Host, reinforcing garrisons and pacifying recalcitrant towns and cities. Then again, the arrival of Admiral Nok and a third of the imperial fleet in the Maadil Sea had done much to quell rebellious tendencies among the locals. And Keneb suspected that the anarchy, the horrors, of the rebellion itself was as much a force for pacification as any military presence.

A scratch against the outer wall of his tent. 'Enter.'

Blistig ducked under the flap. 'Good, you're alone. Tene Baralta has been speaking with Warleader Gall. Look, we knew a siege was likely—'

'Blistig,' Keneb cut in, 'this isn't right. The Adjunct leads the Fourteenth Army. She was commanded to crush the rebellion, and she is doing just that. Fitting that the final spark should be snuffed out at Y'Ghatan, the mythical birthplace of the Apocalypse—'

'Aye, and we're about to feed that myth.'

'Only if we fail.'

'Malazans die at Y'Ghatan. That city burned to the ground that last siege. Dassem Ultor, the company of the First Sword. The First Army, the Ninth. Eight, ten thousand soldiers? Y'Ghatan drinks Malazan blood, and its thirst is endless.'

'Is this what you're telling your officers, Blistig?'

The man walked over to the trunk, tipped down the lid, and sat. 'Of course not. Do you think me mad? But, gods, man, can't you feel this growing dread?'

'The same as when we were marching on Raraku,' Keneb said, 'and the resolution was frustrated, and that is the problem. The only problem, Blistig. We need to blunt our swords, we need that release, that's all.'

'She should never have sent Quick Ben and Kalam away. Who gives a rhizan's squinting ass what's going on in the Imperial Warren?'

Keneb looked away, wishing he could disagree. 'She must have her reasons.'

'I'd like to hear them.'

'Why did Baralta speak with Gall?'

'We're all worried, is why, Keneb. We want to corner her, all the Fists united on this, and force some answers. Her reasons for things, some real sense of how she thinks.'

'No. Count me out. We haven't even reached Y'Ghatan yet. Wait and see what she has in mind.'

Blistig rose with a grunt. 'I'll pass your suggestions along, Keneb. Only, well, it ain't just the soldiers who are frustrated.'

'I know. Wait and see.'

After he had left, Keneb settled back on the cot. Outside, he could hear the sounds of tents being struck, equipment packed away, the distant lowing of oxen. Shouts filled the morning air as the army roused itself for another day of marching. *Burned Tears, Wickans, Seti, Malazans. What can this motley collection of soldiers do? We are facing Leoman of the Flails, dammit. Who's already bloodied our noses. Mind you, hit-and-run tactics are one thing, a city under siege is another. Maybe he's as worried as we are.*

A comforting thought. Too bad he didn't believe a word of it.

The Fourteenth had been kicked awake and was now swarming with activity. Head pounding, Sergeant Hellian sat on the side of the road. Eight days with this damned miserable army and that damned tyrant of a captain, and now she was out of rum. The three soldiers of her under-sized squad were packing up the last of their kits, none daring to address their hungover, murderously inclined sergeant.

Bitter recollections of the event that had triggered all this haunted Hellian. A temple of slaughter, the frenzy of priests, officials and investigators, and the need to send all witnesses as far away as possible, preferably into a situation they would not survive. Well, she couldn't blame them – no, wait, of course she could. The world was run by stupid people, that was the truth of it. Twenty-two followers of D'rek had been butchered in their own temple, in a district that had been her responsibility – but patrols were never permitted inside any of the temples, so she could have done nothing to prevent it in any case. But no, that wasn't good enough. Where had the killers gone, Sergeant Hellian? And why didn't you see them leave?

And what about that man who accompanied you, who then vanished?

Killers. There weren't any. Not natural ones. A demon, more likely, escaped from some secret ritual, a conjuration gone awry. The fools killed themselves, and that was the way of it. The man had been some defrocked priest from another temple, probably a sorceror. Once he figured out what had happened, he'd hightailed it out of there, leaving her with the mess.

Not fair, but what did fairness have to do with anything?

Urb lowered his massive bulk in front of her. 'We're almost ready, Sergeant.'

'You should've strangled him.'

'I wanted to. Really.'

'Did you? Truth?'

'Truth.'

'But then he slipped away,' Hellian said. 'Like a worm.'

'Captain wants us to join the rest of the squads in her company. They're up the road some. We should get going before the march begins.'

She looked over at the other two soldiers. The twins, Brethless and Touchy. Young, lost – well, maybe not young in years, but young anyway. She doubted they could fight their way out of a midwives' picnic – though, granted, she'd heard those could be rough events, especially if some fool pregnant woman wandered in. Oh, well, that was Kartool, city of spiders, city that crunched underfoot, city of webs and worse. They were a long way from any midwives' picnic.

Out here, spiders floated in the air, but at least they were tiny, easily destroyed with a medium-sized stone. 'Abyss below,' she groaned. 'Find me something to drink.'

Urb handed her a waterskin.

'Not that, idiot.'

'Maybe in the company we're joining . . .'

She looked up, squinted at him. 'Good idea. All right, help me up – no, don't help me up.' She staggered upright.

'You all right, Sergeant?'

'I will be,' she said, 'after you take my skull in your hands and crush it flat.'

He frowned. 'I'd get in trouble if I did that.'

'Not with me you wouldn't. Never mind. Touchy, take point.'

'We're on a road, Sergeant.'

'Just do it. Practice.'

'I won't be able to see anything,' the man said. 'Too many people and things in the way.'

Oh, gods crawling in the Abyss, just let me live long enough

165

to kill that man. 'You got any problem with taking point, Brethless?'

'No, Sergeant. Not me.'

'Good. Do it and let's get going.'

'Want me out on flank?' Touchy asked.

'Yeah, somewhere past the horizon, you brain-stunted cactus.'

'It's not your average scorpion,' Maybe said, peering close but not too close.

'It's damned huge,' Lutes said. 'Seen that type before, but never one so . . . huge.'

'Could be a freak, and all its brothers and sisters were tiny. Making it lonely and that's why it's so mean.'

Lutes stared across at Maybe. 'Yeah, could be it. You got a real brain in that skull. All right, now, you think it can kill Joyful Union? I mean, there's two of those . . .'

'Well, maybe we need to find another one just like this one.'

'But I thought all its brothers and sisters were tiny.'

'Oh, right. Could be it's got an uncle, or something.'

'Who's big.'

'Huge. Huger than this one.'

'We need to start looking.'

'I wouldn't bother,' Bottle said from where he sat in the shadow of a boulder, five paces away from the two soldiers of Borduke's squad.

They started, then Lutes hissed and said, 'He's been spying!'

'Not spying. Grieving.'

'What for?' Maybe demanded. 'We ain't even arrived at Y'Ghatan yet.'

'Met our new captain?'

The two looked at each other, then Lutes said, 'No. Knew one was coming, though.'

'She's here. She killed Joyful Union. Under her heel. *Crunch!*'

Both men jumped. 'That murderer!' Maybe said in a growl. He looked down at the scorpion ringed in by stones at his feet. 'Oh yes, let's see her try with Sparkle here – he'd get her ankle for sure, right through the boot leather—'

'Don't be a fool,' Bottle said. 'Anyway, Sparkle's not a boy. Sparkle's a girl.'

'Even better. Girls are meaner.'

'The smaller ones you always see are the boys. Not as many girls around, but that's just the way of it. They're coy. Anyway, you'd better let her go.'

'Why?' Lutes demanded. 'Ain't no prissy captain going to—'

'She'd be the least of your problems, Lutes. The males will pick up her distress scent. You'll have hundreds following you. Then thousands, and they'll be damned aggressive, if you get my meaning.'

Maybe smiled. 'Interesting. You sure of that, Bottle?'

'Don't get any stupid ideas.'

'Why not? We're good at stupid ideas. I mean, uh, well—'

'What Maybe means,' Lutes said, 'is we can think things through. Right through, Bottle. Don't you worry about us.'

'She killed Joyful Union. There won't be any more fights – spread the word, all those squads with new scorpions – let the little ones go.'

'All right,' Lutes said, nodding.

Bottle studied the two men. 'That includes the one you got there.'

'Sure. We'll just look at her a while longer, that's all.' Maybe smiled again.

Climbing to his feet, Bottle hesitated, then shook his head and walked off, back towards the squad's camp. The army was almost ready to resume the march. With all the desultory lack of enthusiasm one might expect of an army about to lay siege to a city.

A sky without clouds. Again. More dust, more heat, more sweat. Bloodflies and chigger fleas, and the damned vultures wheeling overhead – as they had been doing since Raraku – but this, he knew, would be the last day of that march. The old road ahead, a few more abandoned hamlets, feral goats in the denuded hills, distant riders tracking them from the ridge.

The others in the squad were on their feet and waiting when he arrived. Bottle saw that Smiles was labouring under two packs. 'What happened to you?' he asked her.

The look she turned on him was filled with abject misery. 'I don't know. The new captain ordered it. I hate her.'

'I'm not surprised,' Bottle said, collecting his own gear and shrugging into the pack's straps. 'Is that Strings's kit you got there?'

'Not all of it,' she said. 'He won't trust me with the Moranth munitions.'

Thank Oponn for that. 'The captain been by since?'

'No. The bitch. We're going to kill her, you know.'

'Really. Well, I won't shed any tears. Who is this "we" anyway?'

'Me and Cuttle. He'll distract her, I'll stick a knife in her back. Tonight.'

'Fist Keneb will have you strung up, you know.'

'We'll make it look like an accident.'

Distant horns sounded. 'All right, everyone,' Strings said from the road. 'Let's move.'

Groaning wagon wheels, clacking and thumping on the uneven cobbles, rocking in the ruts, the lowing of oxen, thousands of soldiers lurching into motion, the sounds a rising clatter and roar, the first dust swirling into the air.

Koryk fell in alongside Bottle. 'They won't do it,' he said.

'Do what? Kill the captain?'

'I got a long look at her,' he said. 'She's not just from Korelri. She's from the Stormwall.'

Bottle squinted at the burly warrior. 'How do you know that?'

'There's a silver tracing on her scabbard. She was a section commander.'

'That's ridiculous, Koryk. First, standing the Wall isn't something you can just resign from, if what I've heard is true. Besides, this woman's a captain, in the least-prepared Malazan army in the entire empire. If she'd commanded a section against the Stormriders, she'd rank as Fist at the very least.'

'Only if she told people, Bottle, but that tracing tells another story.'

Two strides ahead of them, Strings turned his head to regard them. 'So, you saw it too, Koryk.'

Bottle swung round to Smiles and Cuttle. 'You two hearing this?'

'So?' Smiles demanded.

'We heard,' Cuttle said, his expression sour. 'Maybe she just looted that scabbard from somewhere . . . but I don't think that's likely. Smiles, lass, we'd best put our plans on a pyre and strike a spark.'

'Why?' she demanded. 'What's this Stormwall mean, anyway? And how come Koryk thinks he knows so much? He doesn't know anything, except maybe the back end of a horse and that only in the dark. Look at all your faces – I'm saddled with a bunch of cowards!'

'Who plan on staying alive,' Cuttle said.

'Smiles grew up playing in the sand with farm boys,' Koryk said, shaking his head. 'Woman, listen to me. The Stormwall is leagues long, on the north coast of Korelri. It stands as the only barricade between the island continent and the Stormriders, those demonic warriors of the seas between Malaz Island and Korelri – you must have heard of them?'

'Old fishers' tales.'

'No, all too real,' Cuttle said. 'I seen them myself, plying those waters. Their horses are the waves. They wield lances of ice. We slit the throats of six goats to paint the water in appeasement.'

'And it worked?' Bottle asked, surprised.

'No, but tossing the cabin boy over the side did.'

'Anyway,' Koryk said after a moment of silence, 'only chosen warriors are given the task of standing the Wall. Fighting those eerie hordes. It's an endless war, or at least it was . . .'

'It's over?'

The Seti shrugged.

'So,' Smiles said, 'what's she doing here? Bottle's right, it doesn't make sense.'

'You could ask her,' Koryk replied, 'assuming you survive this day's march.'

'This isn't so bad,' she sniffed.

'We've gone a hundred paces, soldier,' Strings called back. 'So best save your breath.'

Bottle hesitated, then said to Smiles. 'Here, give me that – that captain ain't nowhere about, is she?'

'I never noticed nothing,' Strings said without turning round.

'I can do this—'

'We'll spell each other.'

Her eyes narrowed suspiciously, then she shrugged. 'If you like.'

He took the second pack from her.

'Thanks, Bottle. At least someone in this squad's nice to me.'

Koryk laughed. 'He just doesn't want a knife in his leg.'

'We got to stick together,' Bottle said, 'now that we got ourselves a tyrant officer over us.'

'Smart lad,' Strings said.

'Still,' Smiles said, 'thanks, Bottle.'

He smiled sweetly at her.

'They've stopped moving,' Kalam muttered. 'Now why would that be?'

'No idea,' Quick Ben said at his side.

They were lying flat on the summit of a low ridge. Eleven Moon's Spawns hovered in an even row above another rise of hills two thousand paces distant. 'So,' the assassin asked, 'what passes for night in this warren?'

'It's on its way, and it isn't much.'

Kalam twisted round and studied the squad of soldiers sprawled in the dust of the slope behind them. 'And your plan, Quick?'

'We make use of it, of course. Sneak up under one—'

'Sneak up? There's no cover, there's nothing to even throw shadows!'

'That's what makes it so brilliant, Kalam.'

The assassin reached out and cuffed Quick Ben.

'Ow. All right, so the plan stinks. You got a better one?'

'First off, we send this squad behind us back to the Fourteenth. Two people sneaking up is a lot better than eight. Besides, I've no doubt they can fight but that won't be much use with a thousand K'Chain Che'Malle charging down on us. Another thing – they're so cheery it's a struggle to keep from dancing.'

At that, Sergeant Gesler threw him a kiss.

Kalam rolled back round and glared at the stationary fortresses.

Quick Ben sighed. Scratched his smooth-shaven jaw. 'The Adjunct's orders . . .'

'Forget that. This is a tactical decision, it's in our purview.'

Gesler called up from below, 'She don't like us around either, Kalam.'

'Oh? And why's that?'

'She keeps cracking up in our company. I don't know. We was on the *Silanda*, you know. We went through walls of fire on that ship.'

'We've all led hard lives, Gesler . . .'

'Our purview?' Quick Ben asked. 'I like that. You can try it on her, later.'

'Let's send them back.'

'Gesler?'

'Fine with us. I wouldn't follow you two into a latrine, begging your sirs' pardon.'

Stormy added, 'Just hurry up about it, wizard. I'm getting grey waiting.'

'That would be the dust, Corporal.'

'So you say.'

Kalam considered, then said, 'We could take the hairy Falari with us, maybe. Care to come along, Corporal? As rearguard?'

'Rearguard? Hey, Gesler, you were right. They *are* going into a latrine. All right, assuming my sergeant here won't miss me too much.'

'Miss you?' Gesler sneered. 'Now at least I'll get women to talk to me.'

'It's the beard puts them off,' Stormy said, 'but I ain't changing for nobody.'

'It's not the beard, it's what lives in the beard.'

'Hood take us,' Kalam breathed, 'send them away, Quick Ben, please.'

Four leagues north of Ehrlitan, Apsalar stood facing the sea. The promontory on the other side of A'rath Strait was just visible, rumpling the sunset's line on the horizon. Kansu Reach, which stretched in a long, narrow arm westward to the port city of Kansu. At her feet prowled two gut-bound skeletons, pecking at grubs in the dirt and hissing in frustration as the mangled insects they attempted to swallow simply fell out beneath their jaws.

Even bone, or the physical remembrance of bone, held power, it seemed. The behaviour patterns of the lizard-birds the creatures once were had begun to infect the ghost spirits of Telorast and Curdle. They now chased snakes, leapt into the air after rhizan and capemoths, duelled each other in dominance contests, strutting, spitting and kicking sand. She believed they were losing their minds.

No great loss. They had been murderous, vile, entirely untrustworthy in their lives. And, perhaps, they had ruled a realm. As usurpers, no doubt. She would not regret their dissolution.

'Not-Apsalar! Why are we waiting here? We dislike water, we have discovered. The gut bindings will loosen. We'll fall apart.'

'We are crossing this strait, Telorast,' Apsalar said. 'Of course, you and Curdle may wish to stay behind, to leave my company.'

'Do you plan on swimming?'

'No, I intend to use the warren of Shadow.'

'Oh, that won't be wet.'

'No,' Curdle laughed, prancing around to stand before Apsalar, head bobbing. 'Not wet, oh, that's very good. We'll come along, won't we, Telorast?'

'We promised! No, we didn't. Who said that? We're just eager to stand guard over your rotting corpse, Not-Apsalar, that's what we promised. I don't understand why I get so confused. You have to die eventually. That's obvious. It's what happens to mortals, and you are mortal, aren't you? You must be, you have been bleeding for three days – we can smell it.'

'Idiot!' Curdle hissed. 'Of course she's mortal, and besides, we were women once, remember? She bleeds because that's what happens. Not all the time, but sometimes. Regularly. Or not. Except just before she lays eggs, which would mean a male found her, which would mean . . .'

'She's a snake?' Telorast asked in a droll tone.

'But she isn't. What were you thinking, Telorast?'

The sun's light was fading, the waters of the strait crimson. A lone sail from a trader's carrack was cutting a path southward into the Ehrlitan Sea. 'The warren feels strong here,' Apsalar said.

'Oh yes,' Telorast said, bony tail caressing Apsalar's left ankle. 'Fiercely manifest. This sea is new.'

'That is possible,' she replied, eyeing the jagged cliffs marking the narrows. 'Are there ruins beneath the waves?'

'How would we know? Probably. Likely, absolutely. Ruins. Vast cities. Shadow Temples.'

Apsalar frowned. 'There were no Shadow Temples in the time of the First Empire.'

Curdle's head dipped, then lifted suddenly. 'Dessimbelackis, a curse on his multitude of souls! We speak of the time of the Forests. The great forests that covered this land, long before the First Empire. Before even the T'lan Imass—'

'Shhh!' Telorast hissed. 'Forests? Madness! Not a tree in sight, and those who were frightened of shadows never existed. So why would they worship them? They didn't, because they never existed. It's a natural ferocity, this shadow power. It's a fact that the first worship was born of fear. The terrible unknown—'

'Even more terrible,' Curdle cut in, 'when it becomes known! Wouldn't you say, Telorast?'

'No I wouldn't. I don't know what you're talking about. You've been babbling too many secrets, none of which are true in any case. Look! A lizard! It's mine!'

'No, mine!'

The two skeletons scrambled along the rocky ledge. Something small and grey darted away.

A wind was picking up, sweeping rough the surface of the strait, carrying with it the sea's primal scent to flow over the cliff where she stood. Crossing stretches of water, even through a warren, was never a pleasant prospect. Any waver of control could fling her from the realm, whereupon she would find herself leagues from land in dhenrabi-infested waters. Certain death.

She could, of course, choose the overland route. South from Ehrlitan, to Pan'potsun, then skirting the new Raraku Sea westward. But she knew she was running out of time. Cotillion and Shadowthrone had wanted her to take care of a number of small players, scattered here and there inland, but something within her sensed a quickening of distant events, and with it the growing need – a desperate insistence – that she be there without delay. To cast her dagger, to affect, as best she could, a host of destinies.

She assumed Cotillion would understand all of this. That he would trust her instincts, even if she was, ultimately, unable to explain them.

She must . . . *hurry*.

A moment's concentration. And the scene before her was transformed. The cliff now a slope, crowded with collapsed trees, firs, cedars, their roots torn loose from dark earth, the boles flattened as if the entire hillside had been struck by some unimaginable wind. Beneath a leaden sky, a vast forested valley clothed in mist stretched out across what had moments before been the waters of the strait.

The two skeletons pattered up to crowd her feet, heads darting.

'I told you there'd be a forest,' Telorast said.

Apsalar gestured at the wreckage on the slope immediately before them. 'What happened here?'

'Sorcery,' Curdle said. 'Dragons.'

'Not dragons.'

'No, not dragons. Telorast is right. Not dragons.'

'Demons.'

'Yes, terrible demons whose very breath is a warren's gate, oh, don't jump down those throats!'

172

'No breath, Curdle,' Telorast said. 'Just demons. Small ones. But lots of them. Pushing trees down, one by one, because they're mean and inclined to senseless acts of destruction.'

'Like children.'

'Right, as Curdle says, like children. Children demons. But strong. Very strong. Huge, muscled arms.'

'So,' Apsalar said, 'dragons fought here.'

'Yes,' Telorast said.

'In the Shadow Realm.'

'Yes.'

'Presumably, the same dragons that are now imprisoned within the stone circle.'

'Yes.'

Apsalar nodded, then began making her way down. 'This will be hard going. I wonder if I will save much time traversing the forest.'

'Tiste Edur forest,' Curdle said, scampering ahead. 'They like their forests.'

'All those natural shadows,' Telorast added. 'Power in permanence. Blackwood, bloodwood, all sorts of terrible things. The Eres were right to fear.'

In the distance a strange darkness was sliding across the treetops. Apsalar studied it. The carrack, casting an ethereal presence into this realm. She was seeing both worlds, a common enough occurrence. Yet, even so . . . *someone is on that carrack. And that someone is important . . .*

T'rolbarahl, ancient creature of the First Empire of Dessimbelackis, Dejim Nebrahl crouched at the base of a dead tree, or, rather, flowed like a serpent round the bleached, exposed roots, seven-headed, seven-bodied and mottled with the colours of the ground, the wood and the rocks. Fresh blood, slowly losing its heat, filled the D'ivers' stomachs. There had been no shortage of victims, even in this wasteland. Herders, salt-miners, bandits, desert wolves, Dejim Nebrahl had fed continuously on this journey to the place of ambush.

The tree, thick-boled, squat, with only a few twisted branches surviving the centuries since it had died, rose from a crack in the rock between a flat stretch that marked the trail and an upthrust tower of pitted, wind-worn stone. The trail twisted at this point, skirting the edge of a cliff, the drop below ten or more man-heights to boulders and jagged rubble.

On the other side of the trail, more rocks rose, heaped, the stone cracked and shelved.

The D'ivers would strike here, from both sides, lifting free of the shadows.

Dejim Nebrahl was content. Patience easily purchased by fresh meat, the echoing screams of death, and now it need but await the coming of the victims, the ones the Nameless Ones had chosen.

Soon, then.

Plenty of room between the trees, a cathedral of shadows and heavy gloom, the flow of damp air like water against her face as Apsalar jogged onward, flanked by the darting forms of Telorast and Curdle. To her surprise, she was indeed making good time. The ground was surprisingly level and tree-falls seemed nonexistent, as if no tree in this expanse of forest ever died. She had seen no wildlife, had come upon no obvious game trail, yet there had been glades, circular sweeps of moss tightly ringed by evenly spaced cedars, or, if not cedar, then something much like it, the bark rough, shaggy, black as tar. The circles were too perfect to be natural, although no other evidence of intent or design was visible. In these places, the power of shadow was, as Telorast had said, fierce.

Tiste Edur, Kurald Emurlahn, their presence lingered, but only in the same manner as memories clung to graveyards, tombs and barrows. Old dreams snarled and fading in the grasses, in the twist of wood and the crystal latticework of stone. Lost whispers in the winds that ever wandered across such death-laden places. The Edur were gone, but their forest had not forgotten them.

A darkness ahead, something reaching down from the canopy, straight and thin. A rope, as thick round as her wrist, and, resting on the needle-strewn humus of the floor, an anchor.

Directly in her path. *Ah, so even as I sensed a presence, so it in turn sensed me. This is, I think, an invitation.*

She approached the rope, grasped it in both hands, then began climbing.

Telorast hissed below, 'What are you doing? No, dangerous intruder! Terrible, terrifying, horrible, cruel-faced stranger! Don't go up there! Oh, Curdle, look, she's going.'

'She's not listening to us!'

'We've been talking too much, that's the problem.'

'You're right. We should say something important, so she starts listening to us again.'

'Good thinking, Curdle. Think of something!'

'I'm trying!'

Their voices faded away as Apsalar continued climbing. Among thick-needled branches now, old cobwebs strung between them, small, glittering shapes scampering about. The leather of her gloves was hot against her palms and her calves were beginning to ache. She reached the first of a series of knots and, planting her feet on it, she paused to rest. Glancing down, she saw nothing but black boles vanishing into mist, like the legs of some giant beast. After a few moments, she resumed her climb. Knots, now, every ten or so arm-lengths. Someone was being considerate.

The ebon hull of the carrack loomed above, crusted with barnacles, glistening. Reaching it, she planted her boots against the dark planks and climbed the last two man-heights to where the anchor line ran into a chute in the gunnel. Clambering over the side, she found herself near the three steps leading to the aft deck. Faint smudges of mist, slightly glowing, marked where mortals stood or sat: here and there, near rigging, at the side-mounted steering oar, one perched high among the shrouds. A far more substantial, solid figure was standing before the mainmast.

Familiar. Apsalar searched her memory, her mind rushing down one false trail after another. Familiar . . . yet not.

With a faint smile on his clean-shaven, handsome face, he stepped forward and held up both hands. 'I'm not sure which name you go by now. You were little more than a child – was it only a few years ago? Hard to believe.'

Her heart was thudding hard against her chest, and she wondered at the sensation within her. *Fear?* Yes, but more than that. Guilt. Shame. She cleared her throat. 'I have named myself Apsalar.'

A quick nod. Recognition, then his expression slowly changed. 'You do not remember me, do you?'

'Yes. No, I'm not sure. I should – I know that much.'

'Difficult times, back then,' he said, lowering his hands, but slowly, as if unsure how he would be received as he said, 'Ganoes Paran.'

She drew off her gloves, driven by the need to be doing something, and ran the back of her right hand across her brow, was shocked to see it come away wet, the sweat beading, trickling, suddenly cold on her skin. 'What are you doing here?'

'I might ask you the same. I suggest we retire to my cabin. There is wine. Food.' He smiled again. 'In fact, I am sitting there right now.'

Her eyes narrowed. 'It seems you have come into some power, Ganoes Paran.'

'In a manner of speaking.'

She followed him to the cabin. As he closed the door behind her, his form faded, and she heard movement from the other side of the map-table. Turning, she saw a far less substantial Ganoes Paran. He was pouring wine, and when he spoke the words seemed to come from a vast distance. 'You had best emerge from your warren now, Apsalar.'

She did so, and for the first time felt the solid wood beneath her, the pitch and sway of a ship at sea.

'Sit,' Paran said, gesturing. 'Drink. There's bread, cheese, salted fish.'

'How did you sense my presence?' she asked, settling into the bolted-down chair nearest her. 'I was travelling through a forest—'

'A Tiste Edur forest, yes. Apsalar, I don't know where to begin. There is a Master of the Deck of Dragons, and you are sharing a bottle of wine with him. Seven months ago I was living in Darujhistan, in the Finnest House, in fact, with two eternally sleeping house-guests and a Jaghut manservant . . . although he'd likely kill me if he heard that word ascribed to him. Raest is not the most pleasant company.'

'Darujhistan,' she murmured, looking away, the glass of wine forgotten in her hand. Whatever confidence she felt she had gained since her time there was crumbling away, assailed by a swarm of disconnected, chaotic memories. Blood, blood on her hands, again and again. 'I still do not understand . . .'

'We are in a war,' Paran said. 'Oddly enough, there was something one of my sisters once said to me, when we were young, pitching toy armies against each other. To win a war you must come to know all the players. All of them. Living ones, who will face you across the field. Dead ones, whose legends are wielded like weapons, or held like eternally beating hearts. Hidden players, inanimate players – the land itself, or the sea, if you will. Forests, hills, mountains, rivers. Currents both seen and unseen – no, Tavore didn't say all that; she was far more succinct, but it's taken me a long time to fully understand. It's not "know your enemy". That's simplistic and facile. No, it's "know your enemies". There's a big difference, Apsalar, because one of your enemies could be the face in the silver mirror.'

'Yet now you call them players, rather than enemies,' she said. 'Suggesting to me a certain shift in perspective – what comes, yes, of being the Master of the Deck of Dragons?'

'Huh, I hadn't thought about that. Players. Enemies. Is there a difference?'

'The former implies . . . manipulation.'

'And you would understand that well.'

'Yes.'

'Does Cotillion haunt you still?'

'Yes, but not as . . . intimately.'

'And now you are one of his chosen servants, an agent of Shadow. An assassin, just like the assassin you once were.'

She levelled her gaze on him. 'What is your point?'

'I'm not sure. I'm just trying to find my feet, regarding you, and whatever mission you are on right now.'

'If you want details of that, best speak with Cotillion yourself.'

'I am considering it.'

'Is that why you have crossed an ocean, Ganoes Paran?'

'No. As I said, we are at war. I was not idle in Darujhistan, or in the weeks before Coral. I was discovering the players . . . and among them, true enemies.'

'Of you?'

'Of peace.'

'I trust you will kill them all.'

He seemed to wince, looked down at the wine in his glass. 'For a short time, Apsalar, you were innocent. Naïve, even.'

'Between the possession of a god and my awakening to certain memories.'

'I was wondering, who created in you such cynicism?'

'Cynicism? You speak of peace, yet twice you have told me we are at war. You have spent months learning the lie of the battle to come. But I suspect that even you do not comprehend the vastness of the coming conflict, the conflict we are in right now.'

'You are right. Which is why I wanted to speak with you.'

'It may be we are on different sides, Ganoes Paran.'

'Maybe, but I don't think so.'

She said nothing.

Paran refilled their glasses. 'The pantheon is splitting asunder. The Crippled God is finding allies.'

'Why?'

'What? Well . . . I don't really know. Compassion?'

'And is that something the Crippled God has earned?'

'I don't know that, either.'

'Months of study?' Her brows rose.

He laughed, a response that greatly relieved her.

'You are likely correct,' she said. 'We are not enemies.'

'By "we" I take it you include Shadowthrone and Cotillion.'

'As much as is possible, which isn't as much as I would like. None can fathom Shadowthrone's mind. Not even Cotillion, I suspect. Certainly not me. But he has shown . . . restraint.'

'Yes, he has. Quite surprising, if you think about it.'

'For Shadowthrone, the pondering of the field of battle has consumed years, maybe decades.'

He grunted, a sour expression on his face. 'Good point.'

'What role do you possess, Paran? What role are you seeking to play?'

'I have sanctioned the Crippled God. A place in the Deck of Dragons. A House of Chains.'

She considered for a time, then nodded. 'I can see the reason in that. All right, what has brought you to Seven Cities?'

He stared at her, then shook his head. 'A decision I chewed on for what seemed forever, and you grasp my motives in an instant. Fine. I am here to counter an enemy. To remove a threat. Only, I am afraid I will not get there in time, in which case I will clean up the mess as best I can, before moving on—'

'To Quon Tali.'

'How – how did you know that?'

She reached for the brick of cheese, produced a knife from her sleeve and sliced off a piece. 'Ganoes Paran, we are going to have a rather long conversation now. But first, where do you plan to make landfall?'

'Kansu.'

'Good, this will make my journey quicker. Two minuscule companions of mine are even now clambering onto the deck, having ascended via the trees. They will any moment begin hunting rats and other vermin, which should occupy them for some time. As for you and me, let us settle to this meal.'

He slowly leaned back in his chair. 'We will reach port in two days. Something tells me those two days will fly past like a gull in a gale.'

For me as well, Ganoes Paran.

Ancient memories whispered through Dejim Nebrahl, old stone walls lit red with reflected fire, the cascade of smoke down streets filled with the dead and the dying, the luscious flow of blood in the gutters. Oh, there was a grandness to the First Empire, that first, rough flowering of humanity. The T'rolbarahl were, in Dejim's mind, the culmination of truly human traits, blended with the strength of beasts. Savagery, the inclination towards vicious cruelty, the cunning of a predator that draws no boundaries and would sooner destroy one of its own kind than another. Feeding the spirit on the torn flesh of children. That stunning exercise of intelligence that could justify any action, no matter how abhorrent.

Mated with talons, dagger-long teeth and the D'ivers gift of becoming many from one . . . *we should have survived, we should have ruled. We were born masters and all humanity were rightly our slaves. If only Dessimbelackis had not betrayed us. His own children.*

Well, even among T'rolbarahl, Dejim Nebrahl was supreme. A creation beyond even the First Emperor's most dread nightmare. Domination, subjugation, the rise of a new empire, this is what awaited Dejim, and oh how he would feed. Bloated, sated by human blood. He would make the new, fledgling gods kneel before him.

Once his task was complete, the world awaited him. No matter its ignorance, its blind disregard. That would all change, so terribly change.

Dejim's quarry neared, drawn ever so subtly onto this deadly track. Not long now.

The seashell vest glimmered white in the morning light. Karsa Orlong had drawn it from his pack to replace the shredded remnants of the padded leather he had worn earlier. He sat on his tall, lean horse, the blood-spattered, stitched white fur cloak sweeping down from his broad shoulders. Bare-headed, with a lone, thick braid hanging down the right side of his chest, the dark hair knotted with fetishes: finger bones, strips of gold-threaded silk, bestial canines. A row of withered human ears was sewn onto his belt. The huge flint sword was strapped diagonally across his back. Two bone-handled daggers, each as long and broad-bladed as a short sword, were sheathed in the high moccasins that reached to just below his knees.

Samar Dev studied the Toblakai a moment longer, gaze lifting to fix on his tattooed face. The warrior was facing west, his expression unreadable. She turned back to check the tethers of the packhorses once more, then drew herself up and into the saddle. She settled the toes of her boots into the stirrups and gathered the reins. 'Contrivances,' she said, 'that require no food or water, that do not tire or grow lame, imagine the freedom of such a world as that would bring, Karsa Orlong.'

The eyes he set upon her were those of a barbarian, revealing suspicion and a certain animal wariness. 'People would go everywhere. What freedom in a smaller world, witch?'

Smaller? 'You do not understand—'

'The sound of this city is an offence to peace,' Karsa Orlong said. 'We leave it, now.'

She glanced back at the palace gate, closed with thirty soldiers guarding it. Hands restless near weapons. 'The Falah'd seems disinclined for a formal leavetaking. So be it.'

The Toblakai in the lead, they met few obstacles passing through the city, reaching the west gate before the morning's tenth bell. Initially discomforted by the attention they received from virtually every citizen, on the street and at windows of flanking buildings, Samar Dev had begun to see the allure of notoriety by the time they rode past the silent guards at the gate, enough to offer one of the soldiers a broad smile and a parting wave with one gloved hand.

The road they found themselves on was not one of the impressive Malazan feats of engineering linking the major cities, for the direction they had chosen led ... nowhere. West, into the Jhag Odhan, the ancient plains that defied the farmer's plough, the mythical conspiracy of land, rain and wind spirits, content only with the deep-rooted natural grasses, eager to wither every planted crop to blackened stalks, the soil blown into the sky. One could tame such land for a generation or two, but in the end the Odhan would reclaim its wild mien, fit for naught but bhederin, jackrabbits, wolves and antelope.

Westward, then, for a half-dozen or so days. Whereupon they would come to a long-dead river-bed wending northwestward, the valley sides cut and gnawed by the seasonal run-off from countless centuries past, gnarled now with sage brush and cacti and grey-oaks. Dark hills on the horizon where the sun set, a sacred place, the oldest maps noted, of some tribe so long extinct their name meant nothing.

Out onto the battered road, then, the city falling away behind them. After a time, Karsa glanced back and bared his teeth at her. 'Listen. That is better, yes?'

'I hear only the wind.'

'Better than ten thousand tireless contrivances.'

He turned back, leaving Samar to mull on his words. Inventions cast moral shadows, she well knew, better than most, in fact. But . . . could simple convenience prove so perniciously evil? The action of doing things, laborious things, repetitive things, such actions invited ritual, and with ritual came meaning that expanded beyond the accomplishment of the deed itself. From such ritual self-identity emerged, and with it self-worth. Even so, to make life easier must possess some inherent value, mustn't it?

Easier. Nothing earned, the language of recompense fading away until as lost as that ancient tribe's cherished tongue. Worth diminished, value transformed into arbitrariness, oh gods below, and I was so bold as to speak of freedom! She kicked her horse forward until she came alongside the Toblakai. 'But is that all? Karsa Orlong! I ask you, is that all?'

'Among my people,' he said after a moment, 'the day is filled, as is the night.'

'With what? Weaving baskets, trapping fish, sharpening swords, training horses, cooking, eating, sewing, fucking—'

'Telling stories, mocking fools who do and say foolish things, yes, all that. You must have visited there, then?'

'I have not.'

A faint smile, then gone. 'There are things to do. And, always, witch, ways of cheating them. But no-one truly in their lives is naïve.'

'Truly in their lives?'

'Exulting in the moment, witch, does not require wild dancing.'

'And so, without those rituals . . .'

'The young warriors go looking for war.'

'As you must have done.'

Another two hundred paces passed before he said, 'Three of us, we came to deliver death and blood. Yoked like oxen, we were, to glory. To great deeds and the heavy shackles of vows. We went hunting children, Samar Dev.'

'Children?'

He grimaced. 'Your kind. The small creatures who breed like maggots in rotting meat. We sought – no, I sought – to cleanse the world of you and your kin. You, the cutters of forests, the breakers of earth, the binders of freedom. I was a young warrior, looking for war.'

She studied the escaped slave tattoo on his face. 'You found more than you bargained for.'

'I know all about small worlds. I was born in one.'

'So, experience has now tempered your zeal,' she said, nodding. 'No longer out to cleanse the world of humanity.'

He glanced across and down at her. 'I did not say that.'

'Oh. Hard to manage, I would imagine, for a lone warrior, even a Toblakai warrior. What happened to your companions?'

'Dead. Yes, it is as you say. A lone warrior cannot slay a hundred thousand enemies, even if they are children.'

'A hundred thousand? Oh, Karsa, that's barely the population of two Holy Cities. Your enemy does not number in the hundreds of thousands, it numbers in the tens of millions.'

'That many?'

'Are you reconsidering?'

He shook his head slowly, clearly amused. 'Samar Dev, even tens of millions can die, one city at a time.'

'You will need an army.'

'I have an army. It awaits my return.'

Toblakai. An army of Toblakai, now that would be a sight to loosen the bladder of the Empress herself. 'Needless to say, Karsa Orlong, I hope you never make it home.'

'Hope as you like, Samar Dev. I shall do what needs doing in my own time. None can stop me.'

A statement, not a boast. The witch shivered in the heat.

They approached a range of cliffs marking the Turul'a Escarpment, the sheer face of the limestone pocked with countless caves. Cutter watched Heboric Ghost Hands urge his mount into a canter, drawing ahead, then reining in sharply, the reins cutting into his wrists, a flare of greenish fire blossoming at his hands.

'Now what?' the Daru asked under his breath.

Greyfrog bounded forward and halted at the old man's side.

'They sense something,' Felisin Younger said behind Cutter. 'Greyfrog says the Destriant is suddenly fevered, a return of the jade poison.'

'The what?'

'Jade poison, the demon says. I don't know.'

Cutter looked at Scillara, who rode at his side, head lowered, almost sleeping in the saddle. *She's getting fat. Gods, on the meals we cook? Incredible.*

'His madness returns,' Felisin said, her voice fearful. 'Cutter, I don't like this—'

'The road cuts through, there.' He pointed. 'You can see the notch, beside that tree. We'll camp just up ahead, at the base, and make the climb tomorrow.'

Cutter in the lead, they rode forward until they reached Heboric Ghost Hands. The Destriant was glaring at the cliff rearing before them, muttering and shaking his head. 'Heboric?'

A quick, fevered glance. 'This is the war,' he said. Green flames flickered across his barbed hands. 'The old belong to the ways of blood. The new proclaim their own justice.' The old man's toadlike face stretched into a ghastly grimace. 'These two cannot – *cannot* – be reconciled. It is so simple, do you see? So simple.'

'No,' Cutter replied, scowling. 'I do not see. What war are you talking about? The Malazans?'

'The Chained One, perhaps he was once of the old kind. Perhaps, yes, he was that. But now, now he is sanctioned. He is of the pantheon. He is *new*. But then, what are we? Are we of the blood? Or do we bow to the justice of kings, queens, emperors and empresses? Tell me, Daru, is justice written in blood?'

Scillara asked, 'Are we going to camp or not?'

Cutter looked at her, watched as she pushed rustleaf into the bowl of her pipe. Struck sparks.

'They can talk all they want,' Heboric said. 'Every god must choose. In the war to come. Blood, Daru, burns with fire, yes? Yet . . . yet, my friend, it tastes of cold iron. You must understand me. I am speaking of what cannot be reconciled. This war – so many lives, lost, all to bury the Elder Gods once and for all. That, my friends, is the heart of this war. The very heart, and all their arguing means nothing. I am done with them. Done with all of you. Treach has chosen. He has chosen. And so must you.'

'I don't like choosing,' Scillara said behind a wreath of smoke. 'As for blood, old man, that's a justice you can never put to sleep. Now, let us find a camp site. I'm hungry, tired and saddlesore.'

Heboric slipped down from his horse, gathered the reins, and made his way towards a side track. 'There's a hollow in the wall,' he said. 'People have camped there for millennia, why not us? One day,' he added as he continued on, 'the jade prison shall shatter, and the fools will stumble out, coughing in the ashes of their convictions. And on that day, they will realize that it's too late. Too late to do a damned thing.'

More sparks and Cutter glanced over to see Felisin Younger lighting her own pipe. The Daru ran a hand through his hair, squinting in the glare of the sun's light reflecting off the cliff-side. He dismounted. 'All right,' he said, leading his horse. 'Let's camp.'

Greyfrog bounded after Heboric, clambering over the rock like a bloated lizard.

'What did he mean?' Felisin asked Cutter as they made their way along the trail. 'Blood and Elder Gods – what are Elder Gods?'

'Old ones, mostly forgotten ones. There's a temple dedicated to one in Darujhistan, must have stood there a thousand years. The god was named K'rul. The worshippers vanished long ago. But maybe that doesn't matter.'

Tugging her own horse along in their wake, Scillara stopped listening to Cutter as he went on. Elder gods, new gods, blood and wars, it made little difference to her. She just wanted to rest her legs, ease the aches in her lower back, and eat everything they still had in the saddle-packs.

Heboric Ghost Hands had saved her, drawn her back into life, and that had lodged something like mercy in her heart, stifling her inclination to dismiss the mad old man outright. He was haunted in truth, and such things could drag the sanest mind into chaos. But what value could be found in trying to make sense of all that he said?

The gods, old or new, did not belong to her. Nor did she belong to them. They played their ascendancy games as if the outcome mattered, as if they could change the hue of the sun, the voice of the wind, as if they could make forests grow in deserts and mothers love their children enough to keep them. The rules of mortal flesh were all that mattered, the need to breathe, to eat, drink, to find warmth in the cold of night. And, beyond these struggles, when the last breath had been taken inside, well, she would be in no condition to care about anything, about what happened next, who died, who was born, the cries of starving children and the vicious tyrants who starved them – these were, she understood, the simple legacies of indifference, the consequences of the expedient, and this would go on in the mortal realm until the last spark winked out, gods or no gods.

And she could make peace with that. To do otherwise would be to rail at the inevitable. To do otherwise would be to do as Heboric Ghost

Hands did, and look where it took him. Into madness. The truth of futility was the hardest truth of all, and for those clear-eyed enough to see it, there was no escape.

She had been to oblivion, after all, and had returned, and so she knew there was nothing to fear in that dream-thick place.

True to Heboric's words, the rock shelter revealed the signs of countless generations of occupation. Boulder-lined hearths, red ochre paintings on the bleached walls, heaps of broken pottery and fire-split, charred bones. The clay floor of the hollow was packed hard as stone by countless passings. Nearby was the sound of trickling water, and Scillara saw Heboric crouched there, before a spring-fed pool, his glowing hands held over the placid, dark-mirror surface, as if hesitating to plunge them down into the coolness. White-winged butterflies danced in the air around him.

He journeyed with the gift of salvation. Something to do with the green glow of his hands, and the ghosts haunting him. Something to do with his past, and what he saw of the future. But he belonged to Treach now, Tiger of Summer. *No reconciliation.*

She spied a flat rock and walked over to sit, stretching out her weary legs, noting the bulge of her belly as she leaned back on her hands. Staring down upon it, cruel extrusion on what had once been a lithe form, forcing an expression of disgust on her features.

'Are you with child?'

She glanced up, studied Cutter's face, amused at his dawning revelation as it widened his eyes and filled them with alarm.

'Bad luck happens,' she said. Then, 'I blame the gods.'

CHAPTER SIX

Paint a line with blood and, standing over it, shake a nest of spiders
good and hard. They fall to this side of the divide. They fall to that
side of the divide. Thus did the gods fall, taut-legged and ready, as the
heavens trembled, and in the scattering rain of drifting web – all these
dread cut threads of scheming settling down – skirling now in the
winds that roared sudden, alive and vengeful, to pronounce in
tongues of thunder, the gods were at war.

Slayer of Magic
A history of the Host of Days
Sarathan

THROUGH SLITTED EYES, IN THE BAR OF SHADOW CAST BY THE GREAT
helm's ridged brow, Corabb Bhilan Thenu'alas studied the
woman.

Harried aides and functionaries rushed past her and Leoman of the
Flails, like leaves in a torrential flood. *And the two, standing there, like
stones. Boulders. Like things . . . rooted, yes, rooted to bedrock.*
Captain Dunsparrow, now Third Dunsparrow. A Malazan.

A woman, and Leoman . . . well, Leoman liked women.

So they stood, oh yes, discussing details, finalizing the preparations
for the siege to come. The smell of sex a heady smugness enveloping the
two like a poisonous fog. He, Corabb Bhilan Thenu'alas, who had
ridden at Leoman's side through battle after battle, who had saved
Leoman's life more than once, who had done all that had ever been
asked of him, was loyal. *But she, she is desirable.*

He told himself it made no difference. There had been other women.
He'd had a few himself from time to time, although not the same ones
as Leoman had known, of course. And, one and all, they had been
nothing before the faith, withering into insignificance in the face of

185

hard necessity. The voice of Dryjhna the Apocalyptic overwhelmed with its descending squall of destruction. This was as it should be.

Dunsparrow. Malazan, woman, distraction and possible corrupter. For Leoman of the Flails was hiding something from Corabb, and that had never before happened. Her fault. She was to blame. He would have to do something about her, but what?

He rose from the Falah'd's old throne, that Leoman had so contemptuously discarded, and walked to the wide, arched window overlooking the inner keep compound. More chaotic scurrying below, dust twisting in the sun-speared air. Beyond the palace wall, the bleached rooftops of Y'Ghatan, clothes drying in the sun, awnings rippling in the wind, domes and the cylindrical, flat-topped storage buildings called maethgara that housed in vast containers the olive oil for which the city and its outlying groves were renowned. In the very centre of the city rose the eight-sided, monstrously buttressed Temple of Scalissara, with its inner dome a mottled hump of remnant gold-leaf and green copper tiles liberally painted by bird droppings.

Scalissara, Matron Goddess of Olives, the city's own, cherished protector, now in abject disrepute. Too many conquests she could not withstand, too many gates battered down, walls pounded into rubble. While the city itself seemed capable of ever rising again from the dust of destruction, Scalissara had revealed a more finite number of possible resurrections. And, following the last conquest, she did not return to pre-eminence. Indeed, she did not return at all.

Now, the temple belonged to the Queen of Dreams.

A foreign goddess. Corabb scowled. Well, maybe not entirely foreign, but still . . .

The great statues of Scalissara that once rose from the corners of the city's outer fortifications, marble arms plump and fleshy, upraised, an uprooted olive tree in one hand, a newborn babe in the other, the umbilical cord wrapped snake-like up her forearm, then across and down, into her womb – the statues were gone. Destroyed in the last conflagration. Now, on three of the four corners, only the pedestal remained, bare feet broken clean above the ankles, and on the fourth even that was gone.

In the days of her supremacy, every foundling child was named after her if female, and, male or female, every abandoned child was taken into the temple to be fed, raised and schooled in the ways of the Cold Dream, a mysterious ritual celebrating a kind of divided spirit or something – the esoterica of cults were not among Corabb's intellectual strengths, but Leoman had been one such foundling child, and had spoken once or twice of such things, when wine and durhang loosened his tongue. Desire and necessity, the war within a mortal's spirit, this

186

was at the heart of the Cold Dream. Corabb did not understand much of that. Leoman had lived but a few years under the guidance of the temple's priestesses, before his wild indulgences saw him expelled into the streets. And from the streets, out into the Odhans, to live among the desert tribes, and so to be forged by the sun and blowing sands of Raraku into the greatest warrior Seven Cities had ever beheld. At least in Corabb's lifetime. The Fala'dhan of the Holy Cities possessed grand champions in their day, of course, but they were not leaders, they had nothing of the wiles necessary for command. Besides, Dassem Ultor and his First Sword had cut them down, every one of them, and that was that.

Leoman had sealed Y'Ghatan, imprisoning within its new walls an emperor's ransom in olive oil. The maethgara were filled to bursting and the merchants and their guilds were shrieking their outrage, although less publicly since Leoman, in a fit of irritation, had drowned seven representatives in the Grand Maeth attached to the palace. Drowned them in their very own oil. Priests and witches were now petitioning for beakers of that fell amber liquid.

Dunsparrow had been given command of the city garrison, a mob of drunken, lazy thugs. The first tour of the barracks had revealed the military base as little more than a raucous harem, thick with smoke and pool-eyed, prepubescent boys and girls staggering about in a nightmare world of sick abuse and slavery. Thirty officers were executed that first day, the most senior one by Leoman's own hand. The children had been gathered up and redistributed among the temples of the city with the orders to heal the damage and purge what was possible of their memories. The garrison soldiers had been given the task of scouring clean every brick and tile of the barracks, and Dunsparrow had then begun drilling them to counter Malazan siege tactics, with which she seemed suspiciously familiar.

Corabb did not trust her. It was as simple as that. Why would she choose to fight against her own people? Only a criminal, an outlaw, would do that, and how trustworthy was an outlaw? No, there were likely horrific murders and betrayals crowding her sordid past, and now here she was, spreading her legs beneath Falah'd Leoman of the Flails, the known world's most feared warrior. He would have to watch her carefully, hand on the grip of his new cutlass, ready at a moment's notice to cut her clean in half, head to crotch, then across, diagonally, twice – *swish swish!* – right shoulder to left hip, left shoulder to right hip, and watch her part ways. A duty-bound execution, yes. At the first hint of betrayal.

'What has so lightened your expression, Corabb Bhilan Thenu'alas?'

Stiffening, he turned, to find Dunsparrow standing at his side.

'Third,' he said in sour grunt of greeting. 'I was thinking, uh, of the blood and death to come.'

'Leoman says you are the most reasonable of the lot. I now dread closer acquaintance with his other officers.'

'You fear the siege to come?'

'Of course I do. I know what Imperial Armies are capable of. There is said to be a High Mage among them, and that is the most disturbing news of all.'

'The woman commanding them is simple-minded,' Corabb said. 'No imagination, or none that she's bothered showing.'

'And that is my point on that issue, Corabb Bhilan Thenu'alas.'

He frowned. 'What do you mean?'

'She's had no need, as yet, to display the extent of her imagination. Thus far, it's been easy for her. Little more than marching endless leagues in Leoman's dust.'

'We are her match, and better,' said Corabb, straightening, chest swelling. 'Our spears and swords have already drawn their foul Malazan blood, and shall do so again. More of it, much more.'

'That blood,' she said after a moment, 'is as red as yours, warrior.'

'Is it? Seems to me,' he continued, looking out upon the city once more, 'that betrayal is a dark taint upon it, to so easily twist one of its own into switching sides.'

'As with, for example, the Red Blades?'

'Corrupted fools!'

'Of course. Yet . . . Seven Cities born, yes?'

'They have severed their own roots and now flow on the Malazan tide.'

'Nice image, Corabb. You do stumble on those often, don't you?'

'You'd be amazed at the things I stumble on, woman. And I will tell you this, I guard Leoman's back, as I have always done. Nothing has changed that. Not you and your . . . your—'

'Charms?'

'Wiles. I have marked you, Third, and best you be mindful of that.'

'Leoman has done well to have such a loyal friend.'

'He shall lead the Apocalypse—'

'Oh, he will at that.'

'—for none but he is equal to such a thing. Y'Ghatan shall be a curse name in the Malazan Empire for all time—'

'It already is.'

'Yes, well, it shall be more so.'

'What is it about this city, I wonder, that has driven so deep a knife into the empire? Why did the Claw act here against Dassem Ultor? Why not somewhere else? Somewhere less public, less risky? Oh yes, they made it seem like a wayward accident of battle, but no-one was fooled. I admit to a fascination with this city, indeed, it is what brought me here in the first place.'

'You are an outlaw. The Empress has a price on your head.'

'She does? Or are you just guessing?'

'I am certain of it. You fight against your own people.'

'My own people. Who are they, Corabb Bhilan Thenu'alas? The Malazan Empire has devoured many peoples, just as it has done those of Seven Cities. Now that the rebellion is over, are your kin now Malazan? No, that thought is incomprehensible to you, isn't it? I was born on Quon Tali, but the Malazan Empire was born on Malaz Island. My people too were conquered, just as yours have been.'

Corabb said nothing, too confused by her words. Malazans were . . . Malazans, dammit. All of a kind, no matter the hue of their skin, the tilt of their eyes, no matter all the variations within that Hood-cursed empire. *Malazans!* 'You will get no sympathy from me, Third.'

'I did not ask for it.'

'Good.'

'Now, will you accompany us?'

Us? Corabb slowly turned. Leoman stood a few paces behind them, arms crossed, leaning against the map-table. In his eyes a sly, amused expression.

'We are going into the city,' Leoman said. 'I wish to visit a certain temple.'

Corabb bowed. 'I shall accompany you, sword at the ready, Warleader.'

Leoman's brows lifted fractionally. 'Warleader. Is there no end of titles you will bestow upon me, Corabb?'

'None, Hand of the Apocalypse.'

He flinched at that honorific, then turned away. A half-dozen officers stood waiting at one end of the long table, and to these warriors, Leoman said, 'Begin the evacuation. And no undue violence! Kill every looter you catch, of course, but quietly. Ensure the protection of families and their possessions, including livestock—'

One of the warriors started. 'But Commander, we shall need—'

'No, we shall not. We have all we need. Besides, those animals are the only wealth most of the refugees will have to take with them. I want escorts on the west road.' He glanced over at Dunsparrow. 'Have the messengers returned from Lothal?'

'Yes, with delighted greetings from the Falah'd.'

'Delighted that I am not marching on to his city, you mean.'

Dunsparrow shrugged.

'And so he is dispatching troops to manage the road?'

'He is, Leoman.'

Ah! She is already beyond titles! Corabb struggled to keep the snarl from his voice. 'He is Warleader to you, Third. Or Commander, or Falah'd—'

'Enough,' cut in Leoman. 'I am pleased enough with my own name to hear it used. From now on, friend Corabb, we shall dispense with titles when only officers are present.'

As I thought, the corruption has begun. He glared at Dunsparrow, but she was paying him no attention, her eyes settled possessively on Leoman of the Flails. Corabb's own gaze narrowed. *Leoman the Fallen.*

No track, alley or street in Y'Ghatan ran straight for more than thirty paces. Laid upon successive foundations, rising, it was likely, from the very first maze-wound fortress city built here ten thousand years or more past, the pattern resembled a termite mound with each twisting passageway exposed to the sky, although in many cases that sky was no more than a slit, less than an arm's length wide, overhead.

To look upon Y'Ghatan, and to wander its corridors, was to step into antiquity. Cities, Leoman had once told Corabb, were born not of convenience, nor lordship, nor markets and their babbling merchants. Born not even of harvest and surplus. No, said Leoman, cities were born from the need for protection. Fortresses, that and nothing more, and all that followed did just that: follow. And so, cities were always walled, and indeed, walls were often all that remained of the oldest ones.

And this was why, Leoman had explained, a city would always build upon the bones of its forebears, for this lifted its walls yet higher, and made of the place a more formidable protection. It was the marauding tribes, he had said, laughing, that forced the birth of cities, of the very cities capable of defying them and, ultimately, conquering them. Thus did civilization arise from savagery.

All very well, Corabb mused as they walked towards this city's heart, and possibly even true, but already he longed for the open lands of the Odhans, the desert's sweet whispering wind, the sultry heat that could bake a man's brain inside his helmet until he dreamed raving that he was being pursued by herds of fat aunts and leathery grandmothers who liked to pinch cheeks.

Corabb shook his head to dispel the recollection and all its attendant terrors. He walked at Leoman's left, cutlass drawn and a scowl of belligerence ready for any suspicious-looking citizen. Third Dunsparrow was to Leoman's right, the two brushing arms every now and then and exchanging soft words, probably grim with romance, that Corabb was pleased he could not overhear. That, or they were talking about ways of doing away with him.

'Oponn pull me, push her,' he said under his breath.

Leoman's head turned. 'You said something, Corabb?'

'I was cursing this damned rat path, Avenger.'

'We're almost there,' Leoman said, uncharacteristically considerate, which only deepened Corabb's foul mood. 'Dunsparrow and I were discussing what to do with the priesthood.'

'Were you now? That's nice. What do you mean, what to do with them?'

'They are resisting the notion of leaving.'

'I am not surprised.'

'Nor am I, but leave they shall.'

'It's all the wealth,' Corabb said. 'And their reliquaries and icons and wine cellars – they fear they will be set upon on the road, raped and robbed and their hair all unbunned.'

Both Leoman and Dunsparrow peered over at him with odd expressions.

'Corabb,' Leoman said, 'I think it best you remove that new great helm of yours.'

'Yes,' Dunsparrow added. 'There are streams of sweat pouring down your face.'

'I am fine,' Corabb said in growl. 'This was the Champion's helm. But Leoman would not take it. He should have. In truth, I am only carrying it for him. At the appropriate time, he will discover the need to tear it from my head and don it himself, and the world shall right itself once more, may all the yellow and blue gods be praised.'

'Corabb—'

'I am fine, although we had better do something about all those old women following us. I will spit myself on my own sword before I let them get me. Ooh what a nice little boy! Enough of that, I say.'

'Give me that helm,' Leoman said.

'It's about time you recognized your destiny, Adjunct Slayer.'

Corabb's head was pounding by the time they reached the Temple of Scalissara. Leoman had elected not to wear the great helm, even with its sodden quilted under-padding removed – without which it would have been too loose in any case. At least the old women were gone; in fact, the route they had taken was almost deserted, although they could hear the chaotic sounds of crowds in the main thoroughfares, being driven from the city, out onto the west road that led to Lothal on the coast. Panic rode the sweltering currents, yet it was clear that most of the four thousand soldiers now under Leoman's command were out in the streets, maintaining order.

Seven lesser temples, each dedicated to one of the Seven Holies, encircled the octagonal edifice now sanctified in the name of the Queen of Dreams. The formal approach was spiral, wending through these smaller domed structures. The flanking compound walls had been twice defaced, first with rededication to Malazan gods soon after the conquest; then again with the rebellion, when the temples and their new foreign priesthoods had been assailed, the sanctuaries sundered and hundreds slaughtered. Friezes and metopes, caryatids and panels were all ruined now, entire pantheons defiled and made incomprehensible.

All, that is, but the temple of the Queen of Dreams, its impressive fortifications making it virtually impregnable. There were in any case mysteries surrounding the Queen, Corabb knew, and it was generally believed that her cult had not originated in the Malazan Empire. The Goddess of Divinations cast a thousand reflections upon a thousand peoples, and no one civilization could claim her as exclusively its own. So, having battered futilely at the temple's walls for six days, the rebels had concluded that the Queen was not their enemy after all, and had thereafter left her in peace. Desire and necessity, Leoman had said, laughing, upon hearing the tale.

Nonetheless, as far as Corabb was concerned, the goddess was . . . foreign.

'What business do we have,' Corabb asked, 'visiting this temple?'

Leoman replied with a question of his own: 'Do you recall, old friend, your vow to follow me no matter what seeming madness I undertake?'

'I do, Warleader.'

'Well, Corabb Bhilan Thenu'alas, you shall find yourself sorely tested in that promise. For I intend to speak with the Queen of Dreams.'

'The High Priestess—'

'No, Corabb,' said Leoman, 'with the goddess herself.'

'It is a difficult thing, killing dragons.'

Blood the colour of false dawn continued to spread across the buckled pavestones. Mappo and Icarium remained beyond its reach, for it would not do to make contact with that dark promise. The Jhag was seated on a stone block that might have once been an altar but had been pushed up against the wall to the left of the entrance. The warrior's head was in his hands, and he had said nothing for some time.

Mappo alternated his attention between his friend and the enormous draconean corpse rearing over them. Both scenes left him distraught. There was much worthy of grieving in this cavern, in the terrible ritual murder that had taken place here, and in the fraught torrent of memories unleashed within Icarium upon its discovery.

'This leaves naught but Osserc,' Mappo said. 'And should he fall, the warren of Serc shall possess no ruler. I believe, Icarium, that I am beginning to see a pattern.'

'Desecration,' the Jhag said in a whisper, not looking up.

'The pantheon is being made vulnerable. Fener, drawn into this world, and now Osserc – the very source of his power under assault. How many other gods and goddesses are under siege, I wonder? We have been away from things too long, my friend.'

'Away, Mappo? There is no *away*.'

The Trell studied the dead dragon once more. 'Perhaps you are right. Who could have managed such a thing? Within the dragon is the heart of the warren itself, its well-fount of power. Yet . . . someone defeated Sorrit, drove her down into the earth, into this cavern within a sky keep, and spiked her to Blackwood – how long ago, do you think? Would we not have felt her death?' With no answers forthcoming from Icarium, Mappo edged closer to the blood pool and peered upward, focusing on that massive iron, rust-streaked spike. 'No,' he murmured after a moment, 'that is not rust. Otataral. She was bound by otataral. Yet, she was Elder – she should have been able to defeat that eager entropy. I do not understand this . . .'

'Old and new,' Icarium said, his tone twisting the words into a curse. He rose suddenly, his expression ravaged and eyes hard. 'Speak to me, Mappo. Tell me what you know of spilled blood.'

He turned away. 'Icarium—'

'Mappo, tell me.'

Gaze settling on the aquamarine pool, the Trell was silent as emotions warred within him. Then he sighed. 'Who first dipped their hands into this fell stream? Who drank deep and so was transformed, and what effect did that otataral spike have upon that transformation? Icarium, this blood is fouled—'

'Mappo.'

'Very well. All blood spilled, my friend, possesses power. Beasts, humans, the smallest bird, blood is the life-force, the soul's own stream. Within it is locked the time of living, from beginning to end. It is the most sacred force in existence. Murderers with their victims' blood staining their hands feed from that force, whether they choose to or not. Many are sickened, others find a new hunger within themselves, and so become slaves to the violence of slaying. The risk is this: blood and its power become tainted by such things as fear and pain. The stream, sensing its own demise, grows stressed, and the shock is as a poison.'

'What of fate?' Icarium asked in a heavy voice.

Mappo flinched, his eyes still on the pool. 'Yes,' he whispered, 'you cut to the matter's very heart. What does anyone take upon themselves when such blood is absorbed, drawn into their own soul? Must violent death be in turn delivered upon them? Is there some overarching law, seeking ever to redress the imbalance? If blood feeds us, what in turn feeds it, and is it bound by immutable rules or is it as capricious as we are? Are we creatures on this earth the only ones free to abuse our possessions?'

'The K'Chain Che'Malle did not kill Sorrit,' Icarium said. 'They knew nothing of it.'

'Yet this creature here was frozen, so it must have been encompassed in the Jaghut's ritual of Omtose Phellack – how could the K'Chain Che'Malle not have known of this? They must have, even if they themselves did not slay Sorrit.'

'No, they are innocent, Mappo. I am certain of it.'

'Then . . . how?'

'The crucifix, it is Blackwood. From the realm of the Tiste Edur. From the Shadow Realm, Mappo. In that realm, as you know, things can be in two places at once, or begin in one yet find itself eventually manifesting in another. Shadow wanders, and respects no borders.'

'Ah, then . . . this . . . was trapped here, drawn from Shadow—'

'Snared by the Jaghut's ice magic – yet the spilled blood, and perhaps the otataral, proved too fierce for Omtose Phellack, thus shattering the Jaghut's enchantment.'

'Sorrit was murdered in the Shadow Realm. Yes. Now the pattern, Icarium, grows that much clearer.'

Icarium fixed bright, fevered eyes upon the Trell. 'Is it? You would blame the Tiste Edur?'

'Who else holds such command of Shadow? Not the Malazan pretender who now sits on the throne!'

The Jhag warrior said nothing. He walked along the pool's edge, head down as if seeking signs from the battered floor. 'I know this Jaghut. I recognize her work. The carelessness in the unleashing of Omtose Phellack. She was . . . distraught. Impatient, angry, weary of the endless paths the K'Chain Che'Malle employed in their efforts to invade, to establish colonies on every continent. She cared nothing for the civil war afflicting the K'Chain Che'Malle. These Short-Tails were fleeing their kin, seeking a refuge. I doubt she bothered asking questions.'

'Do you think,' Mappo asked, 'that she knows of what has happened here?'

'No, else she would have returned. It may be that she is dead. So many are . . .'

Oh, Icarium, would that such knowledge remained lost to you.

The Jhag halted and half-turned. 'I am cursed. This is the secret you ever keep from me, isn't it? There are . . . recollections. Fragments.' He lifted a hand as if to brush his brow, then let it fall. 'I sense. . . terrible things . . .'

'Yes. But they do not belong to you, Icarium. Not to the friend standing before me now.'

Icarium's deepening frown tore at Mappo's heart, but he would not look away, would not abandon his friend at this tortured moment.

'You,' Icarium said, 'are my protector, but that protection is not as it seems. You are at my side, Mappo, to protect the world. From me.'

'It is not that simple.'

'Isn't it?'

'No. I am here to protect the friend I look upon now, from the . . . the other Icarium . . .'

'This must end, Mappo.'

'No.'

Icarium faced the dragon once more. 'Ice,' he said in murmur. 'Omtose Phellack.' He turned to Mappo. 'We shall leave here now. We travel to the Jhag Odhan. I must seek out kin of my blood. Jaghut.'

To ask for imprisonment. Eternal ice, sealing you from all life. But they will not trust that. No, they will seek to kill you. Let Hood deal with you. And this time, they will be right. For their hearts do not fear judgement, and their blood . . . their blood is as cold as ice.

Sixteen barrows had been raised half a league south of Y'Ghatan, each one a hundred paces long, thirty wide, and three man-heights high. Rough-cut limestone blocks and internal columns to hold up the curved roofs, sixteen eternally dark abodes, home to Malazan bones. Newly cut, stone-lined trenches reached out to them from the distant city, carrying Y'Ghatan's sewage in turgid flows swarming with flies. Sentiments, Fist Keneb reflected sourly, could not be made any clearer.

Ignoring the stench as best he could, Keneb guided his horse towards the central barrow, which had once been surmounted by a stone monument honouring the empire's fallen. The statue had been toppled, leaving only the broad pedestal. Standing on it now were two men and two dogs, all facing Y'Ghatan's uneven, whitewashed walls.

The Barrow of Dassem Ultor and his First Sword, which held neither Dassem nor any of his guard who had fallen outside the city all those years ago. Most soldiers knew the truth of that. The deadly, legendary fighters of the First Sword had been buried in unmarked graves, to keep them from desecration, and Dassem's own grave was believed to be somewhere outside Unta, on Quon Tali.

Probably empty.

The cattle-dog, Bent, swung its huge head to watch Keneb push his horse up the steep slope. Red-rimmed eyes, set wide in a nest of scars, a regard that chilled the Malazan, reminding him yet again that he but imagined his own familiarity with that beast. It should have died with Coltaine. The animal looked as though pieced together from disparate, unidentifiable parts, only roughly approximating a dog's shape. Humped, uneven shoulder muscles, a neck as thick round as a grown man's thigh, misshapen, muscle-knitted haunches, a chest deep as a desert lion's. Beneath the empty eyes the creature was all jaw, overwide, the snout misaligned, the three remaining canines visible even when Bent's fierce mouth was closed, for most of the skin covering them had been torn away at the Fall, and nothing had replaced it. One shorn ear, the other healed flat and out to the side.

The stub that was all that was left of Bent's tail did not wag as Keneb dismounted. Had it done so, Keneb allowed the possibility that he would have been shocked to death.

The mangy, rat-like Hengese dog, Roach, trotted up to sniff at Keneb's left boot, whereupon it squatted ladylike and urinated against the leather. Cursing, the Malazan stepped away, cocking one foot for a savage kick, then halting the motion at a deep growl from Bent.

Warleader Gall rumbled a laugh. 'Roach but claims this heap of stones, Fist. Hood knows, there's no-one below to get offended.'

'Too bad one cannot say the same for the other barrows,' Keneb said, drawing off his riding gloves.

'Ah, but that insult belongs at the feet of the citizens of Y'Ghatan.'

'Roach should have displayed more patience, then, Warleader.'

'Hood take us, man, she's a damned dog. Besides, you think she'll run out of piss any time soon?'

If I had my way, she'd run out of a lot more besides. 'Not likely, I'll grant you. That rat has more malign fluids in it than a rabid bhederin bull.'

'Poor diet.'

Keneb addressed the other man: 'Fist Temul, the Adjunct wishes to know if your Wickan scouts have ridden round the city.'

The young warrior was a child no longer. He had grown two hand's-widths since Aren. Lean, hawk-faced, with far too many losses pooled in his black eyes. The Crow clan warriors who had so resented his command at Aren were silent these days. Gaze fixed on Y'Ghatan, he gave no indication of having heard Keneb's words.

More and more like Coltaine with every passing day, Gall says. Keneb knew enough to wait.

Gall cleared his throat. 'The west road shows signs of an exodus, no more than a day or two before we arrived. A half-dozen old Crow horse-warriors demanded that they pursue and ravage the fleeing refugees.'

'And where are they now?' Keneb asked.

'Guarding the baggage train, hah!'

Temul spoke. 'Inform the Adjunct that all gates are sealed. A trench has been dug at the base of the tel, cutting through the ramped roads on all sides, to a depth of nearly a man's height. Yet, this trench is but two paces wide – clearly the enemy ran out of time.'

Out of time. Keneb wondered at that. With pressed workers, Leoman could have had a far broader barrier excavated within the span of a single day. 'Very well. Did your scouts report any large weapons mounted on the walls or on the roofs of the corner towers?'

'Malazan-built ballistae, an even dozen,' Temul replied, 'ranged about at equal intervals. No sign of concentrations.'

'Well,' Keneb said with a grunt, 'foolish to suppose that Leoman would give away his perceived weak-points. And those walls were manned?'

'Yes, crowds, all shouting taunts to my warriors.'

'And showing their naked backsides,' Gall added, turning to spit.

Roach trotted over to sniff at the gleaming phlegm, then licked it up.

Nauseous, Keneb looked away, loosening the chin-strap of his helm. 'Fist Temul, have you made judgement as to our surest approach?'

Temul glanced over, expressionless. 'I have.'

'And?'

'And what, Fist? The Adjunct cares nothing for our opinions.'

'Perhaps not, but I would like to hear your thoughts in any case.'

'Ignore the gates. Use Moranth munitions and punch right through a wall midway between tower and gate. Any side will do. Two sides would be even better.'

'And how will the sappers survive camping out at the base of a wall?'

'We attack at night.'

'That is a risky thing to do.'

Temul scowled, and said nothing.

Gall turned to regard Keneb, his tear-etched face mildly incredulous. 'We begin a siege, man, not a Hood-damned fly dance.'

'I know. But Leoman must have mages, and night will not hide sappers from them.'

'They can be countered,' Gall retorted. 'It's what *our* mages are for. But we waste our breaths with such things. The Adjunct will do as she chooses.'

Keneb faced right and studied the vast encampment of the Fourteenth Army, arrayed to fend off a sortie, should Leoman prove so foolish. The investiture would be a careful, measured exercise, conducted over two or three days. The range of the Malazan ballistae on the walls was well known, so there would be no surprises there. Even so, encirclement would stretch their lines appallingly thin. They would need advance emplacements to keep an eye on the gates, and Temul's Wickans and Seti, as well as Gall's Khundryl horse-warriors, divided into companies and positioned to respond should Leoman surprise them.

The Fist shook his head. 'This is what I do not understand. Admiral Nok's fleet is even now sailing for Lothal with five thousand marines on board, and once Dujek forces the last city to capitulate he will begin a fast march to join us. Leoman must know his position is hopeless. He cannot win, even should he maul us. We will still be able to keep this noose knotted tight round Y'Ghatan, whilst we wait for reinforcements. He is finished. So why does he continue to resist?'

'Aye,' said Gall. 'He should have carried on riding west, out into the odhan. We would never have caught him out there, and he could begin rebuilding, drawing warriors to his cause.'

Keneb glanced over. 'So, Warleader, you are as nervous about this as I am.'

'He means to bleed us, Keneb. Before he falls, he means to bleed us.' A rough gesture. 'More barrows to ring this cursed city. And he will die fighting, and so will become yet another martyr.'

'So, the killing of Malazans is sufficient cause to fight. What have we done to deserve this?'

'Wounded pride,' Temul said. 'It is one thing to suffer defeat on a field of battle, it is another to be crushed when your foe has no need even to draw a sword.'

'Humiliated in Raraku,' Gall said, nodding. 'The growing cancer in their souls. This cannot be carved out. The Malazans must be made to know pain.'

'That is ridiculous,' Keneb said. 'Was not the Chain of Dogs glory enough for the bastards?'

'The first casualty among the defeated is recalling their own list of crimes, Fist,' Temul said.

Keneb studied the young man. The foundling Grub was often in Temul's company, and among the strange lad's disordered host of peculiar observations, Grub had hinted of glory, or perhaps infamy, bound to Temul's future. *Of course, that future could be tomorrow. Besides, Grub might be no more than a brain-addled waif . . . all right, I don't believe that – he seems to know too much. If only half the things he said made any sense . . .* Well, in any case, Temul still managed to startle Keneb with statements more suited to some veteran campaigner. 'Very well, Fist Temul. What would you do, were you in Leoman's place?'

Silence, then a quick look at Keneb, something like surprise in

Temul's angular features. A moment later the expressionless mask returned, and he shrugged.

'Coltaine walks in your shadow, Temul,' Gall said, running his fingers down his own face as if to mimic the tears tattooed there. 'I see him, again and again—'

'No, Gall. I have told you before. You see naught but the ways of the Wickans; all else is but your imagination. Coltaine sent me away; it is not to me that he will return.'

He haunts you still, Temul. Coltaine sent you with Duiker to keep you alive, not to punish or shame you. Why won't you accept that?

'I have seen plenty of Wickans,' Gall said in a growl.

This had the sound of an old argument. Sighing, Keneb walked over to his horse. 'Any last words for the Adjunct? Either of you? No? Very well.' He swung up into the saddle and gathered the reins.

The cattle-dog Bent watched him with its sand-coloured, dead eyes. Nearby, Roach had found a bone and was lying sprawled on its belly, legs spread out as it gnawed with the mindless concentration unique to dogs.

Halfway down the slope, Keneb realized where that bone had likely come from. *A kick, all right, hard enough to send that rat straight through Hood's Gate.*

Corporal Deadsmell, Throatslitter and Widdershins were sitting round a game of Troughs, black stones bouncing off the rudder and rolling in the cups, as Bottle walked up.

'Where's your sergeant?' he asked.

Deadsmell glanced up, then back down. 'Mixing paint.'

'Paint? What kind of paint?'

'It's what Dal Honese do,' said Widdershins, 'death-mask paint.'

'Before a siege?'

Throatslitter hissed – what passed for laughter, Bottle supposed – and said, 'Hear that? Before a siege. That's very cute, very cute, Bottle.'

'It's a death mask, idiot,' Widdershins said to Bottle. 'He paints it on when he thinks he's about to die.'

'Great attitude for a sergeant,' Bottle said, looking around. The other two soldiers of the Ninth Squad, Galt and Lobe, were feuding over what to put in a pot of boiling water. Both held handfuls of herbs, and as each reached to toss the herbs in the other soldier pushed that hand away and sought to throw in his own. Again and again, over the boiling water. Neither spoke. 'All right, where is Balm finding his paint?'

'There's a local cemetery north of the road,' Deadsmell said. 'I'd guess maybe there.'

'If I don't find him,' Bottle said, 'the captain wants a meeting with all the sergeants in her company. Dusk.'

'Where?'

'The sheep pen back of the farm south of the road, the one with the caved-in roof.'

Over by the hearth the pot had boiled dry and Galt and Lobe were fighting over water jugs.

Bottle moved on to the next encampment. He found Sergeant Moak sprawled with his back resting on a heap of bedrolls. The Falari, copper-haired and bearded, was picking at his overlarge teeth with a fish spine. His soldiers were nowhere in sight.

'Sergeant. Captain Faradan Sort's called a meeting—'

'I heard. I ain't deaf.'

'Where's your squad?'

'Got the squats.'

'All of them?'

'I cooked last night. They got weak stomachs, that's all.' He belched, and a moment later Bottle caught a whiff of something like rotting fish guts.

'Hood take me! Where'd you find anywhere to catch fish on this trail?'

'Didn't. Brought it with me. Was a bit high, it's true, but nothing a real soldier couldn't handle. There's some scrapings in the pot – want some?'

'No.'

'No wonder the Adjunct's in trouble, what with a whole damn army of cowardly whiners.'

Bottle stepped past to move on.

'Hey,' Moak called out, 'tell Fid the wager's still on as far as I'm concerned.'

'What wager?'

'Between him and me and that's all you got to know.'

'Fine.'

He found Sergeant Mosel and his squad dismantling a broken wagon in the ditch. They had piled up the wood and Flashwit and Mayfly were prying nails, studs and fittings from the weathered planks, whilst Taffo and Uru Hela struggled with an axle under the sergeant's watchful eye.

Mosel glanced over. 'Bottle, isn't it? Fourth Squad, Fid's, right? If you're looking for Neffarias Bredd you just missed him. A giant of a man, must have Fenn blood in him.'

'No, I wasn't, Sergeant. You saw Bredd?'

'Well, not me, I've just come back, but Flashwit . . .'

At mention of her name the burly woman looked up. 'Yah. I heard he was just by here. Hey, Mayfly, who was it said he was just by?'

'Who?'

'Neffarias Bredd, you fat cow, who else would we be talking 'bout?'

'I don't know who said what. I was only half listening, anyway. I think it was Smiles, was it Smiles? Might have been. Anyway, I'd like to roll in the blankets with that man—'

'Smiles isn't a man—'

'Not her. Bredd, I mean.'

Bottle asked, 'You want to bed Bredd?'

Mosel stepped closer, eyes narrowing. 'You making fun of my soldiers, Bottle?'

'I'd never do that, Sergeant. Just came to tell there's a meeting—'

'Oh, yes, I heard.'

'From who?'

The lean man shrugged. 'Can't remember. Does it matter?'

'It does if it means I'm wasting my time.'

'You ain't got time to waste? Why, what makes you unique?'

'That axle doesn't look broken,' Bottle observed.

'Who said it was?'

'Then why are you taking the wagon apart?'

'We been eating its dust so long we just took revenge.'

'Where's the wagoner, then? The load crew?'

Flashwit laughed an ugly laugh.

Mosel shrugged again, then gestured further down the ditch. Four figures, bound and gagged, were lying motionless in the yellow grass.

The two squads of sergeants Sobelone and Tugg were gathered round a wrestling match between, Bottle saw as he pushed his way in for a better look, Saltlick and Shortnose. Coins were being flung down, puffing the dust of the road, as the two heavy infantrymen strained and heaved in a knot of arm and leg holds. Saltlick's massive, round face was visible, red, sweaty and streaked with dust, the expression fixed in its usual cow-like, uninterested incomprehensibility. He blinked slowly, and seemed to be concentrating on chewing something.

Bottle nudged Toles, the soldier on his right. 'What are they fighting over?'

Toles looked down on Bottle, his thin, pallid face twitching. 'It's very simple. Two squads, marching in step, one behind the other, then the other in front of the one that had been in front beforehand, proving the mythical camaraderie to be no more than some epic instigator of bad poetry and bawdy songs designed to appease lowbrows, in short, a lie. Culminating at the last in this disreputable display of animal instincts—'

'Saltlick bit Shortnose's ear off,' cut in Corporal Reem, standing on Bottle's left.

'Oh. Is that what he's chewing?'

'Yeah. Taking his time with it, too.'

201

'Do Tugg and Sobelone know about the captain's meeting?'

'Yeah.'

'So, Shortnose who got his nose tip cut off now has only one ear, too.'

'Yeah. He'll do anything to spite his face.'

'Is he the one who got married last week?'

'Yeah, to Hanno there. She's the one betting against him. Anyway, from what I hear, it ain't his face that she adores, if you know what I mean.'

Bottle caught sight of a low hill on the north side of the road on which stood a score of twisted, hunched guldindha trees. 'Is that the old cemetery?'

'Looks like it, why?'

Without answering, Bottle pushed his way back through the crowd and set off for the burial ground. He found Sergeant Balm in a looter's pit, face streaked with ash, making a strange monotonous nasal groaning sound as he danced in tight circles.

'Sergeant, captain wants a meeting—'

'Shut up, I'm busy.'

'Dusk, in the sheep pen—'

'Interrupt a Dal Honese death dirge and you'll know a thousand thousand lifetimes of curses, your bloodlines for ever. Hairy old women will steal your children and your children's children and chop them up and cook them with vegetables and tubers and a few precious threads of saffron—'

'I'm done, Sergeant. Orders delivered. Goodbye.'

'—and Dal Honese warlocks wearing snake girdles will lie with your woman and she'll birth venomous worms all covered in curly black hair—'

'Keep it up, Sergeant, and I'll make a doll of you—'

Balm leapt from the pit, eyes suddenly wide. 'You evil man! Get away from me! I never done nothing to you!' He spun about and ran away, gazelle-skins flapping.

Bottle turned and began the long walk back to the camp.

He found Strings assembling his crossbow, Cuttle watching with avid interest. A crate of Moranth munitions was to one side, the lid pried loose and the grenados lying like turtle eggs in nests of padding. The others of the squad were sitting some distance away, looking nervous.

The sergeant glanced up. 'Bottle, you found them all?'

'Aye.'

'Good. So, how are the other squads holding up?'

'Just fine,' Bottle replied. He regarded the others on the far side of the hearth. 'What's the point?' he asked. 'If that box goes up, it'll knock down Y'Ghatan's wall from here, and you and most of this army will be red hail.'

Sudden sheepish expressions. Grunting, Koryk rose, deliberately casual. 'I was already sitting here,' he said. 'Then Tarr and Smiles crawled over to huddle in my shadow.'

'The man lies,' Smiles said. 'Besides, Bottle, why did you volunteer to go wandering with the captain's orders?'

'Because I'm not stupid.'

'Yeah?' Tarr said. 'Well, you're back now, aren't you?'

'I thought they'd be finished by now.' He waved a fly away that had been buzzing in front of his face, then walked over to sit downwind of the hearth. 'So, Sergeant, what do you figure the captain's got to say?'

'Sappers and shields,' Cuttle said in a growl.

'Shields?'

'Aye. We scurry in hunched low and the rest of you shield us from all the arrows and rocks until we're done planting the mines, then whoever's left runs back out, as fast as they can and it won't be fast enough.'

'A one-way trip, then.'

Cuttle grinned.

'It'll be more elaborate than that,' Strings said. 'I hope.'

'She goes straight in, that's what she does.'

'Maybe, Cuttle. Maybe not. She wants most of her army still breathing when the dust's settled.'

'Minus a few hundred sappers.'

'We're getting rare enough as it is,' Strings said. 'She won't want to waste us.'

'That'd be a first for the Malazan Empire.'

The sergeant looked over at Cuttle. 'Tell you what, why don't I just kill you now and be done with it?'

'Forget it. I want to take the rest of you sorry humpers with me.'

Nearby, Sergeant Gesler and his squad had appeared and were making their camp. Corporal Stormy, Bottle noted, wasn't with them. Gesler strode over. 'Fid.'

'Kalam and Quick back, too?'

'No, they went on, with Stormy.'

'On? Where?'

Gesler crouched opposite Strings. 'Let's just say I'm actually glad to see your ugly face, Fid. Maybe they'll make it back, maybe they won't. I'll tell you about it later. Spent the morning with the Adjunct. She had lots of questions.'

'About what?'

'About the stuff I'll tell you about later. So we've got a new captain.'

'Faradan Sort.'

'Korelri?'

Strings nodded. 'Stood the Wall, we think.'

'So she can probably take a punch.'

'Then punch back, aye.'

'Well that's just great.'

'She wants all the sergeants for a meeting tonight.'

'I think I'll go back and answer a few more of the Adjunct's questions.'

'You can't avoid meeting her for ever, Gesler.'

'Oh yeah? Watch me. So, where did they move Captain Kindly to?'

Strings shrugged. 'To some company that needs pulling into shape, I'd imagine.'

'And we don't?'

'Harder terrifying us than most in this army, Gesler. I think he'd already given up on us, in any case. I'm not sorry to see the miserable bastard on his way. This meeting tonight will likely be about what we'll be doing in the siege. Either that or she just wants to waste our time with some inspiring tirade.'

'For the glory of the empire,' Gesler said, grimacing.

'For vengeance,' Koryk said from where he sat tying fetishes onto his baldric.

'Vengeance is glorious, so long as it's us delivering it, soldier.'

'No it's not,' said Strings. 'It's sordid, no matter how you look at it.'

'Ease up, Fid. I was only half serious. You're so tense you'd think we was heading into a siege or something. Anyway, why ain't there a few hands of Claw to do the dirty work? You know, infiltrate the city and the palace and stick a knife in Leoman and be done with it. Why do we have to get messed up with a real fight? What kind of empire are we, these days?'

No-one spoke for a time. Bottle watched his sergeant. Strings was testing the pull on the crossbow, but Bottle could see that he was thinking.

Cuttle said, 'Laseen's pulled 'em in. Close and tight.'

The regard Gesler fixed on the sapper was level, gauging. 'That the rumour, Cuttle?'

'One of 'em. What do I know? Maybe she caught something on the wind.'

'*You* certainly have,' Strings muttered as he examined the case of quarrels.

'Only that the few veteran companies still on Quon Tali were ordered to Unta and Malaz City.'

Strings finally looked up. 'Malaz City? Why there?'

'The rumour weren't that specific, Sergeant. Just the where, not the why. Anyway, there's something going on.'

'Where'd you catch all this?' Gesler asked.

'That new sergeant, Hellian, from Kartool.'

'The drunk one?'

'That's her.'

'Surprised she noticed anything,' Strings observed. 'What got her shipped out here?'

'That she won't talk about. In the wrong place at the wrong time, I figure, from the way her face twists all sour on the subject. Anyway, she went to Malaz City first, then joined up with the transports at Nap, then on to Unta. She never seems so drunk she can't keep her eyes open.'

'You trying to get your hand on her thigh, Cuttle?'

'A bit too young for me, Fid, but a man could do worse.'

'A bleary-eyed wife,' Smiles said with a snort. 'That's probably the best you could manage, Cuttle.'

'When I was a lad,' the sapper said, reaching out to collect a grenado – a sharper, Bottle noted with alarm as Cuttle began tossing it up in the air and catching it one-handed – 'every time I said something disrespectful of my betters, my father'd take me out back and slap me half-unconscious. Something tells me, Smiles, your da was way too indulgent when it came to his little girl.'

'You just try it, Cuttle, and I'll stick a knife in your eye.'

'If I was your da, Smiles, I'd have long ago killed myself.'

She went pale at that, although no-one else seemed to notice, since their eyes were following the grenado up and down.

'Put it away,' Strings said.

An ironic lifting of the brows, then, smiling, Cuttle returned the sharper to the crate. 'Anyway, it looks like Hellian's got a capable corporal, which tells me she'd held onto good judgement, despite drinking brandy like water.'

Bottle rose. 'Actually, I forgot about her. Where are they camped, Cuttle?'

'Near the rum wagon. But she already knows about the meeting.'

Bottle glanced over at the crate of munitions. 'Oh. Well, I'm going for a walk in the desert.'

'Don't stray too far,' the sergeant said, 'could be some of Leoman's warriors out there.'

'Right.'

A short while later he came within sight of the intended meeting place. Just beyond the collapsed building was an overgrown rubbish heap, misshapen with tufts of yellow grass sprouting from the barrow-sized mound. There was no-one in sight. Bottle made his way towards the midden, the sounds of the encampment dwindling behind him. It was late afternoon but the wind remained hot as the breath of a furnace.

Chiselled wall and foundation stones, shattered idols, lengths of splintered wood, animal bones and broken pottery. Bottle clambered up the side, noting the most recent leavings – Malazan-style pottery, black-glazed, squat, fragmented images of the most common motifs: Dassem Ultor's death outside Y'Ghatan, the Empress on her throne, the First Heroes and the Quon pantheon. The local style, Bottle had seen from the villages they had passed through, was much more elegant, elongated with cream or white glazing on the necks and rims and faded red on the body, adorned with full-toned and realistic images. Bottle paused at see-ing one such shard, a body-piece, on which had been painted the Chain of Dogs. He picked it up, wiped dust from the illustrated scene. Part of Coltaine was visible, affixed to the cross of wood, overhead a wild flurry of black crows. Beneath him, dead Wickans and Malazans, and a cattle-dog impaled on a spear. A chill whispered along his spine and he let the shard drop.

Atop the mound, he stood for a time, studying the sprawl of the Malazan army along the road and spilling out to the sides. The occasional rider wending through carrying messages and reports; carrion birds, capemoths and rhizan wheeling overhead like swarming flies.

He so disliked omens.

Drawing off his helm, Bottle wiped sweat from his brow and turned to face the odhan to the south. Once fertile, perhaps, but now a waste-land. Worth fighting for? No, but then, there wasn't much that was. The soldier at your side, maybe – he'd been told that enough times, by old veterans with nothing left but that dubious companionship. Such bonds could only be born of desperation, a closing in of the spirit, down to a manageable but pitiful area containing things and people one could care about. For the rest, pure indifference, twisting on occasion into viciousness.

Gods, what am I doing here?

Stumbling into ways of living didn't seem a worthy path to take. Barring Cuttle and the sergeant, the squad was made up of people no different from Bottle. Young, eager for a place to stand that didn't feel so isolated and lonely, or filling oneself with bravado to mask the fragile self hiding within. But all that was no surprise. Youth was head-long, even when it felt static, stagnant and stifling. It liked its emotions extreme, doused in fiery spices, enough to burn the throat and set flame to the heart. The future was not consciously rushed into – it was just the place you suddenly ended up in, battered and weary and wondering how in Hood's name you got there. Well. He could see that. He didn't need the echoes of his grandmother's ceaseless advice whispering through his thoughts.

Assuming, of course, that voice belonged to his grandmother. He had begun to suspect otherwise.

Bottle crossed the heap, moved down onto the south side. At the base here the desiccated ground was pitted, revealing much older leavings of rubbish – red-glazed sherds with faded images of chariots and stilted figures wearing ornate headdresses and wielding strange hook-bladed weapons. The massive olive-oil jars common to this region retained these old forms, clinging to a mostly forgotten antiquity as if the now lost golden age was any different from the present one.

His grandmother's observations, those ones. She'd had nothing good to say about the Malazan Empire, but even less about the Untan Confederacy, the Li Heng League and all the other despotic rulers of the pre-empire days on Quon Tali. She had been a child through all the Itko Kan–Cawn Por wars, the Seti Tide, the Wickan migrations, the Quon attempt at hegemony. *All blood and stupidity*, she used to say. *All prod and pull. The old with their ambitions and the young with their eager mindless zeal. At least the Emperor put an end to all that – a knife in the back for those grey tyrants and distant wars for the young zealots. It ain't right but nothing ever is. Ain't right, as I said, but better than worst, and I remember the worst.*

Now here he was, in the midst of one of those distant wars. Yet there had been no zeal in his motivations. No, something far more pathetic. Boredom was a poor reason to do anything. Better to hold high some raging brand of righteousness, no matter how misguided and lacking in subtlety.

Cuttle talks of vengeance. But he makes his trying to feed us something too obvious, and we're not swelling with rage like we're supposed to. He couldn't be sure of it, but this army felt lost. At its very core was an empty place, waiting to be filled, and Bottle feared it would wait for ever.

He settled down onto the ground, began a silent series of summonings. Before long, a handful of lizards scampered across the dusty earth towards him. Two rhizan settled down onto his right thigh, their wings falling still. An arch spider, big as a horse's hoof and the colour of green glass, leapt from a nearby rock and landed light as a feather on his left knee. He studied his array of companions and decided they would do. Gestures, the stroke of fingers, silent commands, and the motley servants hurried off, making one and all towards the sheep pen where the captain would address the sergeants.

It paid to know just how wide Hood's Gate was going to be come the assault.

And then something else was on its way.

Sudden sweat on Bottle's skin.

She appeared from the heat haze, moving like an animal – prey, not predator, in her every careful, watchful motion – fine-furred, deep brown, a face far more human than ape, filled with expression – or at least its potential, for the look she fixed upon him now was singular in its curiosity. As tall as Bottle, lean but heavy-breasted, belly distended. Skittish, she edged closer.

She is not real. A manifestation, a conjuration. A memory sprung from the dust of this land.

He watched her crouch to collect a handful of sand, then fling it at him, voicing a loud barking grunt. The sand fell short, a few pebbles bouncing off his boots.

Or maybe I am the conjured, not her. In her eyes the wonder of coming face to face with a god, or a demon. He looked past her, and saw the vista of a savannah, thick with grasses, stands of trees and wildlife. Nothing like it should have been, only what it once was, long ago. *Oh, spirits, why won't you leave me alone?*

She had been following. Following them all. The entire army. She could smell it, see the signs of its passing, maybe even hear the distant clack of metal and wooden wheels punching down the sides of stones in the road as they rocked along. Driven on by fear and fascination, she had followed, not understanding how the future could echo back to her world, her time. Not understanding? Well, he couldn't either. *As if all is present, as if every moment co-exists. And here we two are, face to face, both too ignorant to partition our faith, our way of seeing the world – and so we see them all, all at once, and if we're not careful it will drive us mad.*

But there was no turning back. Simply because *back* did not exist.

He remained seated and she came closer, chattering now in some strange glottal tongue filled with clicks and stops. She gestured at her own belly, ran an index figure along it as if drawing a shape on the downy, paler pelt.

Bottle nodded. *Yes, you carry a child. I understand that much. Still, what is that to me?*

She threw more sand at him, most of it striking below his chest. He waved at the cloud in front of his stinging eyes.

A lunge forward, surprisingly swift, and she gripped his wrist, drew his arm forward, settled his hand on her belly.

He met her eyes, and was shaken to his very core. This was no mindless creature. *Eres'al.* The yearning in those dark, stunningly beautiful eyes made him mentally reel.

'All right,' he whispered, and slowly sent his senses questing, into that womb, into the spirit growing within it.

For every abomination, there must emerge its answer. Its enemy, its counterbalance. Here, within this Eres'al, is such an answer. To a distant abomination, the corruption of a once-innocent spirit. Innocence must be reborn. Yet . . . I can see so little . . . not human, not even of this world, barring what the Eres'al herself brought to the union. Thus, an intruder. From another realm, a realm bereft of innocence. To make them part of this world, one of their kind must be born . . . in this way. Their blood must be drawn into this world's flow of blood.

But why an Eres'al? *Because . . . gods below . . . because she is the last innocent creature, the last innocent ancestor of our line. After her . . . the degradation of spirit begins. The shifting of perspective, the separation from all else, the carving of borders – in the ground, in the mind's way of seeing. After her, there's only . . . us.*

The realization – the *recognition* – was devastating. Bottle pulled his hand away. But it was too late. He knew too many things, now. The father . . . Tiste Edur. The child to come . . . the only pure candidate for a new Throne of Shadow – a throne commanding a *healed* realm.

And it would have so many enemies. *So many . . .*

'No,' he said to the creature, shaking his head. 'You cannot pray to me. Must not. I'm not a god. I'm only a . . .'

Yet . . . to her I must seem just that. A vision. She is spirit-questing and she barely knows it. She's stumbling, as much as we all are, but within her there's a kind of . . . certainty. Hope. Gods . . . faith.

Humbled beyond words, filling with shame, Bottle pulled away, clawing up the slope of the mound, amidst the detritus of civilization, potsherds and fragments of mortar, rusted pieces of metal. No, he didn't want this. Could not encompass this . . . this need in her. He could not be her . . . *her faith.*

She drew yet closer, hands closing round his neck, and dragged him back. Teeth bared, she shook him.

Unable to breathe, Bottle flailed in her grip.

She threw him down, straddled him, released his neck and raised two fists as if to batter him.

'You want me to be your god?' he gasped, 'Fine, then! Have it your way!' He stared up at her eyes, at the fists lifted high, framed by bright, blinding sunlight.

So, is this how a god feels?

A flash of glare, as if a sword had been drawn, an eager hiss of iron filling his head. Something like a fierce challenge—

Blinking, he found himself staring up at the empty sky, lying on the rough scree. She was gone, but he could still feel the echo of her weight on his hips, and the appalling erection her position had triggered in him.

Fist Keneb walked into the Adjunct's tent. The map-table had been assembled and on it was an imperial map of Y'Ghatan that had been delivered a week earlier by a rider from Onearm's Host. It was a scholar's rendition drawn shortly after Dassem's fall. Standing at Tavore's side was Tene Baralta, busy scrawling all over the vellum with a charcoal stick, and the Red Blade was speaking.

'. . . rebuilt here, and here, in the Malazan style of sunk columns and counter-sunk braces. The engineers found the ruins beneath the streets to be a maze of pockets, old rooms, half-buried streets, wells and inside-wall corridors. It should all have been flattened, but at least one age of construction was of a stature to rival what's possible these days. Obviously, that gave them problems, which is why they gave up on the fourth bastion.'

'I understand,' the Adjunct said, 'however, as I stated earlier, Fist Baralta, I am not interested in assailing the fourth bastion.'

Keneb could see the man's frustration, but he held his tongue, simply tossing down the charcoal stick and stepping away from the table.

Over in the corner sat Fist Blistig, legs sprawled out in a posture bordering on insubordination.

'Fist Keneb,' Tavore said, eyes still on the map, 'have you met with Temul and Warleader Gall?'

'Temul reports the city has been evacuated – an exodus of citizens on the road to Lothal. Clearly, Leoman is planning for a long siege, and is not interested in feeding anyone but soldiers and support staff.'

'He wants room to manoeuvre,' said Blistig from where he sat. 'Panic in the streets won't do. We shouldn't read too much into it, Keneb.'

'I suspect,' Tene Baralta said, 'we're not reading *enough* into it. I am nervous, Adjunct. About this whole damned situation. Leoman didn't come here to defend the last rebel city. He didn't come to protect the last believers – by the Seven Holies, he has driven them from their very homes, from their very own city! No, his need for Y'Ghatan was tactical, and that's what worries me, because I can make no sense of it.'

The Adjunct spoke: 'Did Temul have anything else to say, Keneb?'

'He had thoughts of a night attack, with sappers, taking out a section of wall. Presumably, we would then follow through in strength, into that breach, thrusting deep into Y'Ghatan's heart. Cut through far enough and we can isolate Leoman in the Falah'd's palace . . .'

'Too risky,' Tene Baralta said in a grumble. 'Darkness won't cover those sappers from their mages. They'd get slaughtered—'

'Risks cannot be avoided,' Tavore said.

Keneb's brows rose. 'Temul said much the same, Adjunct, when the danger was discussed.'

'Tene Baralta,' Tavore continued after a moment, 'you and Blistig have been directed as to the disposition of your companies. Best you begin preparations. I have spoken directly with Captain Faradan Sort on what will be required of her and her squads. We shall not waste time on this. We move tonight. Fist Keneb, remain, please. The rest of you are dismissed.'

Keneb watched Blistig and Baralta leave, reading in an array of small signs – posture, the set of their shoulders and the stiffness of their gaits – the depth of their demoralization.

'Command does not come from consensus,' the Adjunct said, her tone suddenly hard as she faced Keneb. 'I deliver the orders, and my officers are to obey them. They should be relieved that is the case, for all responsibility lies with me and me alone. No-one else shall have to answer to the Empress.'

Keneb nodded, 'As you say, Adjunct. However, your officers do feel responsible – for their soldiers—'

'Many of whom will die, sooner or later, on some field of battle. Perhaps even here in Y'Ghatan. This is a siege, and sieges are messy. I do not have the luxury of starving them out. The longer Leoman resists, the greater the risk of flare-ups all over Seven Cities. High Fist Dujek and I are fully agreed on this.'

'Then why, Adjunct, did we not accept his offer of more troops?'

She was silent for a half-dozen heartbeats, then, 'I am aware of the sentiments among the squads of this army, none of whom, it seems, are aware of the true condition of Onearm's Host.'

'The true condition?'

She stepped closer. 'There's almost nothing left, Keneb. The core – the very heart – of Onearm's Host – it's *gone*.'

'But – Adjunct, he has received replacements, has he not?'

'What was lost cannot be replaced. Recruits: Genabarii, Nathii, half the Pale Garrison, oh, count the boots and they look to be intact, up to full complement, but Keneb, know this – Dujek is *broken*. And so is the Host.'

Shaken, Keneb turned away. He unstrapped his helm and drew the battered iron from his head, then ran a hand through his matted, sweaty hair. 'Hood take us, the last great imperial army . . .'

'Is now the Fourteenth, Fist.'

He stared at her.

She began pacing. 'Of course Dujek offered, for he is, well, he is Dujek. Besides, the ranking High Fist could do no less. But he – they – have suffered enough. Their task now is to make the imperial presence felt – and we should all pray to our gods that they do not find their mettle tested, by anyone.'

'That is why you are in such a hurry.'

'Leoman must be taken down. Y'Ghatan must fall. Tonight.'

Keneb said nothing for a long moment, then he asked, 'Why, Adjunct, are you telling me this?'

'Because Gamet is dead.'

Gamet? Oh, I see.

'And T'amber is not respected by any of you. Whereas,' she glanced at him, with an odd expression, 'you are.'

'You wish for me to inform the other Fists, Adjunct?'

'Regarding Dujek? Decide that for yourself, but I advise you, Fist, to think very carefully before reaching that decision.'

'But they should be told! At least then they will understand . . .'

'Me? Understand me? Perhaps. But that is not the most important issue here.'

He did not comprehend. Not at once. Then, a growing realization. 'Their faith, beyond you, beyond the Fourteenth, lies with Dujek Onearm. So long as they believe he is there, poised behind us and ready to march to our aid, they will do as you command. You do not want to take that away from them, yet by your silence you sacrifice yourself, you sacrifice the respect they would accord you—'

'Assuming such respect would be granted, Fist, and of that I am not convinced.' She returned to the map-table. 'The decision is yours, Fist.'

He watched her studying the map, then, concluding he had been dismissed, Keneb left the tent.

He felt sick inside. The Host – broken? Was that simply her assessment? Maybe Dujek was just tired . . . yet, who might know better? Quick Ben, but he wasn't here. Nor that assassin, Kalam Mekhar. Leaving . . . well, one man. He paused outside the tent, studied the sun's position. There might be time, before Sort spoke to them all, if he hurried.

Keneb set out towards the camps of the marines.

'What do you want me to say, Fist?' The sergeant had laid out a half-dozen heavy quarrels. He had already tied sharpers to two of them and was working on a third.

Keneb stared at the clay-ball grenado in Strings's hands. 'I don't know, but make it honest.'

Strings paused and looked over at his squad, eyes narrowing. 'Adjunct's hoping for reinforcements if things go bad?' He was speaking in a low voice.

'That's just it, Sergeant. She isn't.'

'So, Fist,' Strings said, 'she thinks Dujek's finished. And so's the Host. Is that what she thinks?'

'Yes. You know Quick Ben, and the High Mage was there, after all. At Coral. He's not here for me to ask him, so I'm asking you. Is the Adjunct right?'

He resumed affixing the grenado to the quarrel head.

Keneb waited.

'Seems,' the sergeant muttered, 'I misjudged the Adjunct.'

'In what way?'

'She's better at reading signs than I thought.'

Hood's balls, I really did not want to hear that.

'You are looking well, Ganoes Paran.'

His answering smile was wry. 'My new life of ease, Apsalar.'

Shouts from the sailors on the deck as the carrack swung towards the harbour of Kansu, the sound of gulls a muted accompaniment to the creak of cordage and timber. A cool breeze rode the salty air coming through the cabin's round window portside, smelling of the shore.

Apsalar studied the man seated across from her a moment longer, then returned to her task of roughing with a pumice stone the grip of one of her in-fighting knives. Polished wood was pretty, but far too slick in a sweaty hand. Normally she used leather gloves, but it never hurt to consider less perfect circumstances. For an assassin, the ideal situation was choosing when and where to fight, but such luxuries were not guaranteed.

Paran said, 'I see that you're as methodical as ever. Although at least now, there's more animation in your face. Your eyes . . .'

'You've been at sea too long, Captain.'

'Probably. Anyway, I'm not a captain any more. My days as a soldier are done.'

'Regrets?'

He shrugged. 'Some. I was never where I wanted to be with them. Until the very end, and then,' he paused, 'well, it was too late.'

'That might have been for the better,' Apsalar said. 'Less . . . sullied.'

'Odd, how the Bridgeburners mean different things for us. Memories, and perspectives. I was treated well enough among the survivors—'

'Survivors. Yes, there's always survivors.'

'Picker, Antsy, Blend, Mallet, a few others. Proprietors of K'rul's Bar, now, in Darujhistan.'

'K'rul's Bar?'

'The old temple once sanctified to that Elder God, aye. It's haunted, of course.'

'More than you realize, Paran.'

'I doubt that. I've learned a lot, Apsalar, about a lot of things.'

A heavy thud to starboard, as the harbour patrol arrived to collect the mooring fees. The slap of lines. More voices.

'K'rul played a very active role against the Pannion Domin,' Paran went on. 'Since that time, I've grown less easy with his presence – the Elder Gods are back in the game—'

'Yes, you've already said something to that effect. They are opposing the Crippled God, and one cannot find fault in that.'

'Are they? Sometimes I'm convinced ... other times,' he shook his head. Then rose. 'We're pulling in. I need to make arrangements.'

'What kind of arrangements?'

'Horses.'

'Paran.'

'Yes?'

'Are you now ascended?'

His eyes widened. 'I don't know. Nothing feels different. I admit I'm not even sure what ascendancy means.'

'Means you're harder to kill.'

'Why?'

'You have stumbled onto power, of a personal nature, and with it, well, power draws power. Always. Not the mundane kind, but something other, a force in nature, a confluence of energies. You begin to see things differently, to think differently. And others take notice of you – that's usually bad, by the way.' She sighed, studying him, and said, 'Perhaps I don't need to warn you, but I will. Be careful, Paran; of all the lands in this world, there are two more dangerous than all others—'

'Your knowledge, or Cotillion's?'

'Cotillion's for one, mine for the other. Anyway, you're about to set foot on one of those two. Seven Cities, Paran, is not a healthy place to be, especially not for an ascendant.'

'I know. I can feel that . . . what's out there, what I have to deal with.'

'Get someone else to do your fighting for you, if possible.'

His gaze narrowed on her. 'Now that's a clear lack of faith.'

'I killed you once—'

'And you were possessed by a god, by the Patron of Assassins himself, Apsalar.'

'Who played by the rules. There are things here that do not.'

'I'll give that some consideration, Apsalar. Thank you.'

'And remember, bargain from strength or don't bargain at all.'

He gave her a strange smile, then headed topside.

A skittering sound from one corner, and Telorast and Curdle scampered into view, bony feet clattering on the wooden floor.

'He is dangerous, Not-Apsalar! Stay away, oh, you've spent too long with him!'

'Don't worry about me, Telorast.'

'Worry? Oh, we have worries, all right, don't we, Curdle?'

'Endless worries, Telorast. What am I saying? We're not worried.'

Apsalar said, 'The Master of the Deck knows all about you two, no doubt compounding those worries.'

'But he told you nothing!'

'Are you so certain of that?'

'Of course!' The bird-like skeleton bobbed and weaved in front of its companion. 'Think on it, Curdle! If she knew she'd step on us! Wouldn't she?'

'Unless she has a more devious betrayal in mind, Telorast! Have you thought of that? No, you haven't, have you? I have to do all the thinking.'

'You never think! You never have!'

Apsalar rose. 'They've dropped the gangplank. Time to leave.'

'Hide us under your cloak. You have to. There are dogs out there, in the streets!'

She sheathed the knife. 'All right, but no squirming.'

A squalid port, four of the six piers battered into treacherous hulks by Nok's fleet a month earlier, Kansu was in no way memorable, and Apsalar was relieved as they rode past the last sprawl of shanties on the inland road and saw before them a scattering of modest stone buildings, marking the herders, the pens and the demon-eyed goats gathered beneath guldindha trees. And beyond that, tharok orchards with their silvery, thread-like bark prized for rope-making, the uneven rows looking ghostly with their boles shimmering in the wind.

There had been something odd in the city behind them, the crowds smaller than was normal, the voices more muted. A number of merchant shops had been shut, and this during peak market time. The modest garrison of Malazan soldiers was present only at the gates and down at the docks, where at least four trader ships had been denied berths. And no-one seemed inclined to offer explanations to outsiders.

Paran had spoken quietly with the horse trader and Apsalar had watched as more coin than was necessary changed hands, but the ex-captain had said nothing during their ride out.

Reaching a crossroads, they drew rein.

'Paran,' Apsalar said, 'did you note anything strange about Kansu?'

He grimaced. 'I don't think we need worry,' he said. 'You've been possessed by a god, after all, and as for me, well, as I said, there's no real cause for worry.'

'What are you talking about?'

'Plague. Hardly surprising, given all the unburied corpses following this rebellion. It began a week or so ago, somewhere east of Ehrlitan. Any ships that made port or hail from there are being turned away.'

Apsalar said nothing for a time. Then she nodded. 'Poliel.'

'Aye.'

'And not enough healers left to intercede.'

'The horse trader said officials went to the Temple of D'rek, in Kansu. The foremost healers are found there, of course. They found everyone within slaughtered.'

She glanced over at him.

'I take the south track,' Paran said, fighting with his edgy gelding.

Yes, there is nothing more to be said, is there. The gods are indeed at war. 'The west for us,' Apsalar replied, already uncomfortable with the Seven Cities style of saddle. Neither she nor Cotillion had ever had much success with horses, but at least the mare beneath her seemed a docile beast. She opened her cloak and dragged out Telorast, then Curdle, tossing them both onto the ground, where they raced ahead, long tails flicking.

'All too short,' Paran said, meeting her eyes.

She nodded. 'But just as well, I think.'

Her comment was not well received. 'I am sorry to hear you say that.'

'I do not mean to offend, Ganoes Paran. It's just that, well, I was rediscovering . . . things.'

'Like comradeship?'

'Yes.'

'And that is something you feel you cannot afford.'

'Invites carelessness,' she said.

'Ah, well. For what it is worth, Apsalar, I believe we will see each other again.'

She allowed that sentiment, and nodded. 'I will look forward to that.'

'Good, then there's hope for you yet.'

She watched him ride away, his two packhorses trailing. Changes came to a man in ways few could imagine. He seemed to have let go of so much . . . she was envious of that. And already, she realized with a faint stab of regret, already she missed him. *Too close, too dangerous by far. Just as well.*

216

As for plague, well, he was probably right. Neither he nor Apsalar had much to fear. *Too bad for everyone else, though.*

The broken remnants of the road made for an agonized traverse up the limestone hillside, rocks tumbling and skittering down in clouds of dust. A flash flood had cut through the passage unknown years or decades past, revealing countless layers of sediments on the channel's steep-cut walls. Leading her horse and the pack-mules by the reins, Samar Dev studied those multi-hued layers. 'Wind and water, Karsa Orlong, without end. Time's endless dialogue with itself.'

Three paces ahead, the Toblakai warrior did not reply. He was nearing the summit, taking the down-flow path of the past flood, ragged, gnawed rock rising to either side of him. The last hamlet was days behind them now; these lands were truly wild. Reclaimed, since surely this road must have led somewhere, once, but there were no other signs of past civilization. In any case, she was less interested in what had gone before. What was to come was her fascination, the wellspring of all her inventions, her inspirations.

'Sorcery, Karsa Orlong, that is the heart of the problem.'

'What problem now, woman?'

'Magic obviates the need for invention, beyond certain basic requirements, of course. And so we remain eternally stifled—'

'To the Faces with stifled, witch. There is nothing wrong with where we are, how we are. You spit on satisfaction, leaving you always unsettled and miserable. I am a Teblor – we live simply enough, and we see the cruelty of your so-called progress. Slaves, children in chains, a thousand lies to make one person better than the next, a thousand lies telling you this is how things should be, and there's no stopping it. Madness called sanity, slavery called freedom. I am done talking now.'

'Well, I'm not. You're no different, calling ignorance wisdom, savagery noble. Without striving to make things better, we're doomed to repeat our litany of injustices—'

Karsa reached the summit and turned to face her, his expression twisting. 'Better is never what you think it is, Samar Dev.'

'What does *that* mean?'

He raised a hand, suddenly still. 'Quiet. Something's not right.' He slowly looked round, eyes narrowing. 'There's a . . . smell.'

She joined him, dragging the horse and mules onto level ground. High rocks to either side, the edge of a gorge just beyond – the hill they were on was a ridge, blade-edged, with more jagged rock beyond. A twisted ancient tree squatting on the summit. 'I don't smell anything . . .'

217

The Toblakai drew his stone sword. 'A beast has laired here, nearby, I think. A hunter, a killer. And I think it is close . . .'

Eyes widening, Samar Dev scanned the area, her heart pounding hard in her chest. 'You may be right. There are no spirits here . . .'

He grunted. 'Fled.'

Fled. Oh.

Like a mass of iron filings, the sky was slowly lowering on all sides, a heavy mist that was dry as sand. Not that that made any sense, Kalam Mekhar allowed, but this was what came of sustained terror, the wild pathetic conjurations of a beleaguered imagination. He was clinging with every part of his body that was capable of clinging to the sheer, battered underside of a sky keep, the wind or whatever it was moaning in his ears, a trembling stealing the strength from his limbs as he felt the last of Quick Ben's magic seep away.

Unanticipated, this sudden repudiation of sorcery – he could see no otataral, nothing veined through this brutal, black basalt. No obvious explanation. Leather gloves cut through, blood slicking his hands, and above, a mountain to climb, with this dry silver mist closing in around him. Somewhere far below crouched Quick Ben and Stormy, the former wondering what had gone wrong and, hopefully, trying to come up with an idea for dealing with it. The latter likely scratching his armpits and popping lice with his fingernails.

Well, there was no point in waiting for what might not come, when what was going to come was inevitable. Groaning with the effort, Kalam began pulling himself along the rock.

The last sky keep he had seen had been Moon's Spawn, and its pocked sides had been home to tens of thousands of Great Ravens. Fortunately, this did not seem to be the case here. A few more man-heights' worth of climbing and he would find himself on a side, rather than virtually upside-down as he was now. Reach there, he knew, and he would be able to rest.

Sort of.

That damned wizard. That damned Adjunct. Damned everybody, in fact, since not one of them was here, and of course they weren't, since this was madness and nobody else was this stupid. Gods, his shoulders were on fire, the insides of his thighs a solid ache edging towards numbness. *And that wouldn't be good, would it?*

Too old for this by far. Men his age didn't reach his age falling for stupid plans like this one. Was he getting soft? *Soft-brained.*

He pulled himself round a chiselled projection, scrabbled with his feet for a moment, then edged over, drew himself up and found ledges that would take his weight. A whimper escaped him, sounding pathetic even to his own ears, as he settled against the stone.

A while later, he lifted his head and began looking round, searching for a suitable outcrop or knob of rock that he could loop his rope over. *Quick Ben's rope, conjured out of nothing. Will it even work here, or will it just vanish? Hood's breath, I don't know enough about magic. Don't even know enough about Quick, and I've known the bastard for bloody ever. Why isn't he the one up here?*

Because, if the Short-Tails noticed the gnat on their hide, Quick was better backup, even down there, than Kalam could have been. A crossbow quarrel would be spent by the time it reached this high – you could just pluck it out of the air. As for Stormy – *a whole lot more expendable than me, as far as I'm concerned* – the man swore he couldn't climb, swore that as a babe he never once made it out of his crib without help.

Hard imagining that hairy-faced miserable hulk ever fitting into a crib in the first place.

Regaining control of his breathing, Kalam looked down.

To find Quick Ben and Stormy nowhere in sight. *Gods below, now what?* The modest features of the ash-laden plain beneath offered little in the way of cover, especially from this height. Yet, no matter where he scanned, he saw no-one. The tracks they had made were faintly visible, leading to where the assassin had left them, and at that location there was . . . something dark, a crack in the ground. Difficult to determine scale, but maybe . . . *maybe big enough to swallow both of the bastards.*

He resumed his search for projections for the rope. And could see none. 'All right, I guess it's time. Cotillion, consider this a sharp tug on your rope. No excuses, you damned god, I need your help here.'

He waited. The moan of the wind, the slippery chill of the mist.

'I don't like this warren.'

Kalam turned his head to find Cotillion alongside him, one hand and one foot holding the god in place. He held an apple in the other hand, from which he now took a large bite.

'You think this is funny?' Kalam demanded.

Cotillion chewed, then swallowed. 'Somewhat.'

'In case you hadn't noticed, we're clinging to a sky keep, and it's got companions, a whole damned row of them.'

'If you needed a ride,' the god said, 'you'd be better off with a wagon, or a horse.'

'It's not moving. It stopped. And I'm trying to break into this one. Quick Ben and a marine were waiting below, but they've just vanished.'

Cotillion examined the apple, then took another bite.

'My arms are getting tired.'

Chewing. Swallowing. 'I'm not surprised, Kalam. Even so, you will have to be patient, since I have some questions. I'll start with the most obvious one. Why are you trying to break into a fortress filled with K'Chain Che'Malle?'

'Filled? Are you sure?'

'Reasonably.'

'Then what are they doing here?'

'Waiting, looks like. Anyway, I'm the one asking questions.'

'Fine. Go ahead, I've got all day.'

'Actually, I think that was my only question. Oh, wait, there's one more. Would you like me to return you to solid ground, so we can resume our conversation in more comfort?'

'You're enjoying this way too much, Cotillion.'

'The opportunities for amusement grow ever rarer. Fortunately, we're in something like this keep's shadow, so our descent will be relatively easy.'

'Any time.'

Cotillion tossed the apple aside, then reached out to grasp Kalam's upper arm. 'Step away and leave the rest to me.'

'Hold on a moment. Quick Ben's spells were dispelled – that's how I ended up stuck here—'

'Probably because he's unconscious.'

'He is?'

'Or dead. We should confirm things either way, yes?'

You sanctimonious blood-lapping sweat-sucking—

'Risky,' Cotillion cut in, 'making your cursing sound like praying.' A sharp tug, and Kalam bellowed as he was snatched out from the rock-face. And was held, suspended in the air by Cotillion's grip on his arm. 'Relax, you damned ox, "easy" is a relative term.'

Thirty heartbeats later their feet touched ground. Kalam pulled his arm away and headed over to the fissure gaping in the place where Quick and Stormy had been waiting. He approached the edge carefully. Called down into the dark. 'Quick! Stormy!' No answer.

Cotillion was at his side. 'Stormy? That wouldn't be Adjutant Stormy, would it? Pig-eyed, hairy, scowling—'

'He's now a corporal,' Kalam said. 'And Gesler's a sergeant.'

A snort from the god, but no further comment.

The assassin leaned back and studied Cotillion. 'I didn't really think you'd answer my prayer.'

'I am a god virtually brimming with surprises.'

Kalam's gaze narrowed. 'You came damned fast, too. As if you were . . . close by.'

'An outrageous assumption,' Cotillion said. 'Yet, oddly enough, accurate.'

The assassin drew the coil of rope from his shoulder, then looked around, and swore.

Sighing, Cotillion held out one hand.

Kalam gave him one end of the rope. 'Brace yourself,' he said, as he tumbled the coil down over the pit's edge. He heard a distant snap.

'Don't worry about that,' Cotillion said. 'I'll make it as long as you need.'

Hood-damned gods. Kalam worked his way over the edge, then began descending through the gloom. *Too much climbing today. Either that or I'm gaining weight.* His moccasins finally settled on stone. He stepped away from the rope.

From overhead a small globule of light drifted down, illuminating the nearest wall, vertical, man-made, featuring large painted panels, the images seeming to dance in the descending light. For a moment, Kalam simply stared. No idle decoration, this, but a work of art, a master's hand exuberantly displayed in each and every detail. Heavily clothed, more or less human in form, the figures were in positions of transcendence, arms upraised in worship or exaltation, faces filled with joy. Whilst, crowding their feet, dismembered body parts had been painted, blood-splashed and buzzing with flies. The mangled flesh continued down to the chamber's floor, then on out, and Kalam saw now that the bloody scene covered the entire expanse of floor, as far as he could see in every direction.

Pieces of rubble were scattered here and there, and, less than a half-dozen paces away, two motionless bodies.

Kalam headed over.

Both men lived, he was relieved to discover, though it was difficult to determine the extent of their injuries, beyond the obvious. Stormy had broken both legs, one above the knee, the other both bones below the knee. The back of his helm was dented, but he breathed evenly, which Kalam took for a good sign. Quick Ben seemed physically intact – nothing obviously shattered, at least, nor any blood. For both of them, however, internal injuries were another matter. Kalam studied the wizard's face for a moment, then slapped it.

Quick's eyes snapped open. He blinked, looked round, coughed, then sat up. 'One half of my face is numb – what happened?'

'No idea,' Kalam said. 'You and Stormy fell through a hole. The Falari's in rough shape. But somehow you made it unscathed – how did you do that?'

'Unscathed? I think my jaw's broken.'

'No it isn't. Must have hit the floor – looks a little puffy but you wouldn't be talking if it was broke.'

'Huh, good point.' He climbed to his feet and approached Stormy. 'Oh, those legs look bad. We need to set those before I can do any healing.'

'Healing? Dammit, Quick, you never did any healing in the squad.'

'No, that was Mallet's task. I was the brains, remember?'

'Well, as I recall, that didn't take up much of your time.'

'That's what you think.' The wizard paused and looked round. 'Where are we? And where did that light come from?'

'Compliments of Cotillion, who is on the other end of that rope.'

'Oh. Well, he can do the healing, then. Get him down here.'

'Then who will hold the rope?'

'We don't need it. Hey, weren't you climbing the Moon's Spawn? Ah, that's why your god is here. Right.'

'To utter the demon's name is to call him,' Kalam said, looking up to watch Cotillion's slow, almost lazy descent.

The god settled near Stormy and Quick Ben. A brief nod to the wizard, one eyebrow lifting, then Cotillion crouched beside the marine. 'Adjutant Stormy, what has happened to you?'

'That should be obvious,' Kalam said. 'He broke his legs.'

The god rolled the marine onto his back, pulled at each leg, drawing the bones back in line, then rose. 'That will do, I think.'

'Hardly—'

'Adjutant Stormy,' Cotillion said, 'is not quite as mortal as he might seem. Annealed in the fires of Thyrllan. Or Kurald Liosan. Or Tellann. Or all three. In any case, as you can see, he's mending already. The broken ribs are completely healed, as is the failing liver and shattered hip. And the cracked skull. Alas, nothing can be done for the brain within it.'

'He's lost his mind?'

'I doubt he ever had one,' the god replied. 'He's worse than Urko. At least Urko has interests, peculiar and pointless as they are.'

A groan from Stormy.

Cotillion walked over to the nearest wall. 'Curious,' he said. 'This is a temple to an Elder God. Not sure which one. Kilmandaros, maybe. Or Grizzin Farl. Maybe even K'rul.'

'A rather bloody kind of worship,' Kalam muttered.

'The best kind,' Quick Ben said, brushing dust from his clothes.

Kalam noted Cotillion's sly regard of the wizard and wondered at it. *Ben Adaephon Delat, Cotillion knows something about you, doesn't he? Wizard, you've got too many secrets by far.* The assassin then noticed the rope, still dangling from the hole far above. 'Cotillion, what did you tie the rope to?'

The god glanced over, smiled. 'A surprise. I must be going. Gentlemen . . .' And he faded, then was gone.

'Your god makes me nervous, Kalam,' Quick Ben said as Stormy groaned again, louder this time.

And you in turn make him nervous. And now . . . He looked down at Stormy. The rips in the leggings were all that remained of the ghastly compound fractures. *Adjutant Stormy. Annealed in holy fires. Still scowling.*

High rock, the sediments stepped and ragged, surrounded their camp, an ancient tree to one side. Cutter sat near the small dung-fire they had lit, watching as Greyfrog circled the area, evincing ever more agitation. Nearby, Heboric Ghost Hands looked to be dozing, the hazy green emanations at the ends of his wrists dully pulsing. Scillara and Felisin Younger were packing their pipes for their new sharing of a post-meal ritual. Cutter's gaze returned to the demon.

Greyfrog, what's ailing you?

'Nervous. I have intimations of tragedy, swiftly approaching. Something . . . worried and uncertain. In the air, in the sands. Sudden panic. We should leave here. Turn back. Flee.'

Cutter felt sweat bead his skin. He had never heard the demon so . . . frightened. 'We should get off this ridge?'

The two women looked up at his spoken words. Felisin Younger glanced at Greyfrog, frowned, then paled. She rose. 'We're in trouble,' she said.

Scillara straightened and walked over to Heboric, nudged him with a boot. 'Wake up.'

The Destriant of Treach blinked open his eyes, then sniffed the air and rose in a single, fluid motion.

Cutter watched all this in growing alarm. *Shit.* He kicked sand over the fire. 'Collect your gear, everyone.'

Greyfrog paused in his circling and watched them. 'So imminent? Uncertain. Troubled, yes. Need for panic? Changing of mind? Foolishness? Uncertain.'

'Why take chances?' Cutter asked. 'There's enough light – we'll see if we can find a more defensible place to camp.'

'Appropriate compromise. Nerves easing their taut sensitivity. Averted? Unknown.'

'Usually,' Heboric said in a rough voice, pausing to spit. 'Usually, running from one thing throws you into the path of another.'

'Well, thanks for that, old man.'

Heboric gave Cutter an unpleasant smile. 'My pleasure.'

*

The cliff-face was pocked with caves which had, over countless centuries, seen use as places of refuge, as crypts for internment of the dead, as storage chambers, and as sheltered panels for rock-paintings. Detritus littered the narrow ledges that had been used as pathways; here and there a dark sooty stain marred overhangs and crevasses where fires had been lit, but nothing looked recent to Mappo's eye, and he recognized the funerary ceramics as belonging to the First Empire era.

They were approaching the summit of the escarpment, Icarium scrambling up towards an obvious notch cut into the edge by past rains. The lowering sun on their left was red behind a curtain of suspended dust that had been raised by the passing of a distant storm. Bloodflies buzzed the air around the two travellers, frenzied by the storm's brittle, energized breath.

Icarium's drive had become obsessive, a barely restrained ferocity. He wanted judgement, he wanted the truth of his past revealed to him, and when that judgement came, no matter how harsh, he would stand before it and raise not a single hand in his own defence.

And Mappo could think of nothing to prevent it, short of somehow incapacitating his friend, of striking him into unconsciousness. Perhaps it would come to that. But there were risks to such an attempt. Fail and Icarium's rage would burgeon into life, and all would be lost.

He watched as the Jhag reached the notch and clambered through, then out of sight. Mappo quickly followed. Reaching the summit, he paused, wiping grit from his hands. The old drainage channel had carved a channel through the next tiers of limestone, creating a narrow, twisting track flanked by steep walls. A short distance beyond, Mappo could see the edge of another drop-off, towards which Icarium was heading.

Thick shadows within the channel, insects swarming in the few shafts of sunlight spearing through a gnarled tree. Three strides from reaching Icarium's side, and the gloom seemed to explode around the Trell. He caught a momentary glimpse of something closing on Icarium from the pinnacle of stone to the Jhag's right, then figures swarmed him.

The Trell lashed out, felt his fist connect with flesh and bone to his left, the sound solid and crunching. A spatter of blood and phlegm.

A brawny arm snaked round from behind to close on his neck, twisting his head back, the glistening skin of that limb sliding as if oiled before the arm locked tight. Another figure plunged into view from the front, long-taloned hands snapping out, puncturing Mappo's belly. He bellowed in agony as the claws raked across in an eviscerating slash.

That failed, for the Trell's hide was thicker than the leather armour covering it. Even so, blood sprayed. The creature behind him tightened its stranglehold. He could feel something of its immense weight and size. Unable to draw a weapon, Mappo pivoted, then flung himself backward into a rock wall. The crunch of bone and skull behind him, a gasp from the beast that rose into a screech of pain.

The creature with its claws in Mappo's belly had been dragged closer by the Trell's backward lunge. He closed his hands round its squat, bony skull, flexed, then savagely twisted the head to one side. The neck snapped. Another scream, this time seeming to come from all sides.

Roaring, Mappo staggered forward, grasping at the forearm drawn across his neck. The beast's weight slammed into him, sent him stumbling.

He caught a glimpse of Icarium, collapsing beneath a swarm of dark, writhing creatures.

Too late he felt his leading foot pitch down over the crumbled edge of the cliff-side, down into . . . open air. The creature's weight pushed him further forward, then, as it saw the precipice they were both about to plunge over, the forearm loosened.

But Mappo held fast, twisting to drag the beast with him as he fell.

Another shriek, and he finally caught full sight of the thing. Demonic, mouth opened wide, needle-like fangs fully locked in their hinges, each as long as Mappo's thumb, glistening black eyes, the pupils vertical and the hue of fresh blood.

T'rolbarahl.

How?

He saw its rage, its horror, as they both plummeted from the cliff.

Falling.

Falling . . .

Gods, this was—

BOOK TWO

BENEATH THIS NAME

In darkness he came, this brutal slayer of kin,
discharged and unleashed, when all but ghosts
fled the wild dishevelled swagger – oh he knew pain,
twin fires of vast oblivion burning his soul—
and so the ghosts did gather, summoned by
one who would stand, mortal and feckless,
in the terrible slayer's path, would stand,
this precious fool, and gamble all in the clasping
of hand, warm to cold, and be led to the place
long vanished, and beasts long vanquished
would at his word awaken once more.

And who was there to warn him? Why, no-one,
and what found its way free was no friend to
the living. When you play horror against horror,
dear listener, leave all hope behind—
and ride a fast horse.

Master Blind
Saedevar of the Widecut Jhag

CHAPTER SEVEN

Never bargain with a man who has nothing to lose.

Sayings of the Fool
Thenys Bule

LEOMAN OF THE FLAILS STAGGERED FROM THE INNER SANCTUM, A sheen of sweat on his face. In a hoarse voice he asked, 'Is it night yet?'

Corabb rose quickly, then sat back down on the bench as blackness threatened to engulf him – he had been sitting too long, watching Dunsparrow attempt to pace a trench in the stone floor. He opened his mouth to reply, but the Malazan woman spoke first.

'No, Leoman, the sun rides the horizon.'

'Movement yet from the Malazan camps?'

'The last runner reported half a bell ago. Nothing at that time.'

There was a strange, triumphant gleam in Leoman's eyes that troubled Corabb, but he had no time to ask as the great warrior strode past. 'We must hurry. Back to the palace – some final instructions.'

The enemy was attacking this very night? How could Leoman be so certain? Corabb stood once again, more slowly this time. The High Priestess had forbidden witnesses to the ritual, and when the Queen of Dreams manifested, even the High Priestess and her acolytes had left the chamber with discomfited expressions, leaving Leoman alone with the goddess. Corabb fell in two steps behind his leader, prevented from drawing closer by that damned woman, Dunsparrow.

'Their mages will make detection difficult,' the Third was saying as they headed out of the temple.

'No matter,' Leoman snapped. 'It's not like we have any worthy of the name anyway. Even so, we need to make it look as if we're trying.'

Corabb frowned. Trying? He did not understand any of this.

'We need soldiers on the walls!' he said. 'As many as can be mustered!'

'We can't hold the walls,' Dunsparrow said over her shoulder. 'You must have realized that, Corabb Bhilan Thenu'alas.'

'Then – then, why are we here?'

The sky overhead was darkening, the bruise of dusk only moments away.

Through empty streets, the three of them rushed along. Corabb's frown deepened. The Queen of Dreams. Goddess of divination and who knew what else. He despised all gods, except, of course, for Dryjhna the Apocalyptic. Meddlers, deceivers, murderers one and all. That Leoman would seek one out . . . this was troubling indeed.

Dunsparrow's fault, he suspected. She was a woman. The Queen's priesthood was mostly women – at least, he thought it was – there'd been a High Priestess, after all, a blurry-eyed matron swimming in the fumes of durhang and likely countless other substances. Just to stand near her was to feel drunk. Too seductive by far. Nothing good was going to come of this, nothing at all.

They approached the palace and, finally, some signs of activity. Warriors moving about, weapons clanking, shouts from the fortifications. So, the outer walls would be breached – no other reason for all this preparation. Leoman expected a second siege, here at the palace itself. And soon.

'Warleader!' Corabb said, shouldering Dunsparrow aside. 'Give me command of the palace gates! We shall hold against the Malazan storm in the name of the Apocalypse!'

Leoman glanced back at him, considering, then he shook his head. 'No, friend. I need you for a far more important task.'

'What will that be, Great Warrior? I am equal to it.'

'You'd better be,' Leoman said.

Dunsparrow snorted.

'Command me, Commander.'

This time she laughed outright. Corabb scowled at her.

Leoman replied, 'Your task this night is this, my friend. Guard my back.'

'Ah, we shall be leading the fight, then, in the very frontmost ranks! Glorious, we shall deliver unto the Malazan dogs a judgement they shall never forget.'

Leoman slapped him on the shoulder. 'Aye, Corabb,' he said. 'That we shall.'

They continued on, into the palace.

Dunsparrow was still laughing.

Gods, how Corabb hated her.

*

Lostara Yil swept back the tent-flap and marched inside. She found Pearl lounging on looted silk pillows, a hookah of wine-flavoured durhang settled like a bowl in his lap. Through the smoke haze, he met her fury with a lazy, fume-laden regard, which of course made her even angrier.

'I see you've planned out the rest of this night, Pearl. Even as this damned army prepares to assault Y'Ghatan.'

He shrugged. 'The Adjunct doesn't want my help. I could have snuck into the palace by now, you know – they have no mages to speak of. I could be at this very moment sliding a knife across Leoman's throat. But no, she won't have it. What am I to do?'

'She doesn't trust you, Pearl, and to be honest, I'm not surprised.'

His brows lifted. 'Darling, I am offended. You, more than anyone else, know the sacrifices I have made to protect the Adjunct's fragile psyche. Needless to say,' he added, pausing for a lungful of the cloying smoke, 'I have of late been tempted to shatter that psyche with the truth about her sister, just out of spite.'

'Your restraint impresses me,' Lostara said. 'Of course, if you did something as cruel as that, I'd have to kill you.'

'What a relief, knowing how you endeavour to protect the purity of my soul.'

'Purity is not the issue,' she replied. 'Not yours, at least.'

He smiled. 'I was attempting to cast myself in a more favourable light, my sweet.'

'It is clear to me, Pearl, that you imagined our brief romance – if one could call it that – as indicative of genuine feelings. I find that rather pathetic. Tell me, do you plan on ever returning me to my company in the Red Blades?'

'Not quite yet, I'm afraid.'

'Has she given us another mission?'

'The Adjunct? No, but as you may recall, what we did for Tavore was a favour. We work for the Empress.'

'Fine. What does our Empress command?'

His eyes were heavy-lidded as they studied her for a moment. 'Wait and see.'

'She commands us to wait and see?'

'All right, since you insist, you are temporarily detached from me, a notion that should give you untold satisfaction. Go join the marines, or the sappers, or whoever in Hood's name is attacking tonight. And if you get a limb lopped off don't come crawling back to me – gods, I can't believe I just said that. Of course you can come crawling back to me, just be sure to bring the limb along.'

'You don't possess High Denul, Pearl, so what point in bringing back the limb?'

231

'I'd just like to see it, that's all.'

'If I do come crawling back, Pearl, it will be to stick a knife in your neck.'

'With those cheery words you can go now, dear.'

She wheeled and marched from the tent.

Fist Keneb joined Tene Baralta in the mustering area just inside the north pickets. Moths and biting flies were swarming in the crepuscular air. Heaps of rocky earth rose like modest barrows where the soldiers had dug their trenches. As yet, few squads had assembled, so as not to reveal the army's intentions too early, although Keneb suspected that Leoman and his warriors already knew all that needed to be known. Even so, the Fist noted as he stared at the distant, uneven wall, topmost among the tiers of earth and rubble, there seemed to be no activity. Y'Ghatan was deathly quiet, virtually unlit as darkness spread its cloak.

Tene Baralta was in full armour: scaled vest, chain skirt and camail, greaves and vambraces of beaten bronze rimmed with iron. He was adjusting the straps of his helm as Keneb came to his side.

'Blistig is not happy,' Keneb said.

Baralta's laugh was low. 'Tonight belongs to you and me, Keneb. He only moves in if we get in trouble. Temul was wondering . . . this plan, it matches his own. Did you advise the Adjunct?'

'I did. Inform Temul that she was pleased that his strategy matched her own in this matter.'

'Ah.'

'Have your company's mages begun?' Keneb asked.

A grunt, then, 'They say there's no-one there, no-one waiting to counter them. Nil and Nether have made the same discovery. Could Leoman have lost all his mages, do you think?'

'I don't know. Seems unlikely.'

'I trust you've heard the rumours, Keneb.'

'About what?'

'Plague. From the east. It has swept through Ehrlitan. If we fail tonight and find ourselves bogged down outside this city . . .'

Keneb nodded. 'Then we must succeed, Tene Baralta.'

A rider was galloping on the road behind and to their right, fast approaching. Both men turned as the pounding hoofs reverberated through the ground at their feet. 'An urgent message?' Keneb wondered, squinting to make out the grey-cloaked figure, face hidden by a hood. A longsword at his side, the scabbard banded in white enamel. 'I do not recog—'

The rider rode straight for them. Bellowing in anger, Tene Baralta leapt to one side. Keneb followed, then spun as the rider flew past, his white horse reaching the trenches, and launching itself over. The picket guards shouted. A crossbow discharged, the quarrel striking the stranger on the back, then caroming off into the night. Still riding at full gallop, the figure now leaning forward over the horse's neck, they sailed over the narrow inside trench, then raced for the city.

Where a gate cracked open, spilling muted lantern light.

'Hood's breath!' Tene Beralta swore, regaining his feet. 'An enemy rides right through our entire army!'

'We've no exclusive claim on bravery,' Keneb said. 'And I admit to a grudging admiration – I am glad to have witnessed it.'

'A rider to bring word to Leoman—'

'Nothing he doesn't already know, Tene Baralta. Consider this a lesson, a reminder—'

'I need none, Keneb. Look at this, my helm's full of dirt. Light grey cloak, white horse and white-banded sword. A tall bastard. I will find him, I swear it, and he will pay for his temerity.'

'We've enough concerns ahead of us this night,' Keneb said. 'If you go off hunting one man, Tene Baralta . . .'

He emptied the dirt from the helm. 'I hear you. Pray to Treach, then, that the bastard crosses my path one more time this night.'

Treach, is it? Fener . . . gone so quickly from men's minds. A message no god would dare to heed, I think.

Lieutenant Pores stood with Captain Kindly and the Korelri Faradan Sort, within sight of their respective companies. Word of a spy in the army's midst, boldly riding into Y'Ghatan, had everyone more on edge than they already were, given that at any moment would come the order to move. Sappers in the lead, of course, disguised within gloomy magic.

Magic. *It's all gloomy.* Worse than sappers, in fact. In combination, well, this night was headed straight into the Abyss, as far as Pores was concerned. He wondered where old Ebron was, and if he was participating in the rituals – he missed his old squad. Limp, Bell, and that new lass, Sinn – now there was a scary creature. Well, maybe he didn't miss them all that much. Dangerous, one and all, and mostly to each other.

Captain Kindly had been trying to take the measure of the woman standing beside him – a choice of phrase that brought a small smile to the lieutenant's mouth. *Take her measure. But ain't nobody's got that close, from what I hear.* In any case, it was frustrating being unable to get a sense of a fellow officer. Cold iron, probably – you don't stand the Wall long enough to survive without something icy, brutal and calculated wrapped round the soul – but this one was cold in every other way besides. Rarest of all, a woman of few words. He smiled again.

'Wipe that grin off your face, Lieutenant,' Kindly said, 'or I'll conclude you've lost your mind and promote you.'

'Apologies, Captain, I promise I won't do it again. Please don't promote me.'

'You two are idiots,' Faradan Sort said.

Well, that's one way to halt a conversation.

Sergeant Hellian looked on the wavering scene, comforted by an over-whelming sense of propriety, although the way everyone was swaying was making her nauseous. Corporal Urb separated himself from the squad and came up to her.

'You ready for this, Sergeant?'

'Ready for what?' she demanded. Then scowled, all sense of propriety vanishing. 'If that bastard hadn't disappeared the way he did, I wouldn't be trading my sword for a jug of that local rot, would I?' She reached down for the weapon, her hand groping as it found only air, then the empty scabbard. 'Why didn't you stop me, Urb? I mean, it was my sword, after all. What am I s'posed to use?'

He shifted nervously, then leaned closer. 'Get a new one from the armoury, Sergeant.'

'And that'll get back to the captain and we'll get shipped off some-where even worse.'

'Worse? Where is worse than this, Sergeant?'

'Korel. Theftian Penins'la. Black Coral, under the empty eyes of the Tiste Andii. The Wreckers' Coast on North Assail—'

'Ain't no Malazan forces there.'

'No, but it's worse than this.'

'One story from some addled sailor in Kartool and you're now convinced that Hood himself strides the shadows—'

'He's stridin' our shallows – shadows, I mean.'

'Listen, Sergeant, we're about to head into battle—'

'Right, where's that jug?' She looked round, found it lying on its side near somebody's bedroll. 'Hey, who in my squad ain't packed up their kit?'

'That's yours, Sergeant,' Urb said.

'Oh.' Collecting the jug, she gave it a shake and was pleased at the sloshing sounds within. She glanced over to stare at her . . . squad. There were two soldiers. Two. Some squad. Captain had said some-thing about a few newcomers on the way. 'Well, where are they?'

'Who?' Urb asked. 'Your squad? They're right in front of you.'

'Touchy and Brethless.'

'That's right.'

'Well, where are the rest? Didn't we have more?'

'Had four marching with us the last day, but they were re-assigned.'

'So my squad is a corporal and two soljers.'

'Twins, Sergeant,' Touchy said. 'But I'm older, as I'm sure you can tell.'

'And mentally underdeveloped, Sergeant,' Brethless said. 'Those last few minutes were obviously crucial, as I'm sure you can tell.'

Hellian turned away. 'They look the same to me, Urb. All right, has the word come yet? We s'posed to be mustering somewhere right now?'

'Sergeant, you might want to pass that jug around – we're about to get in a fight and I don't know about you and them two, but I joined the local city guard so's I wouldn't have to do any of this. I been to the latrines four times since supper and I'm still all squishy inside.'

At Urb's suggestion Hellian clutched the jug tight to her chest. 'Getyerown.'

'Sergeant.'

'All right, a couple mouthfuls each, then I get the rest. I see anybody take more'n two swallows and I cut 'em down where they stand.'

'With what?' Urb asked as he pulled the jug from her reluctant hands.

Hellian frowned. With what? What was he talking about? Oh, right. She thought for a moment, then smiled. 'I'll borrow your sword, of course.' There, what a pleasing solution.

Sergeant Balm squatted in the dirt, studying the array of pebbles, stone discs and clay buttons resting on the elongated Troughs board. He muttered under his breath, wondering if this was a dream, a nightmare and he was still asleep. He glanced across at Sergeant Moak, then looked back down at the game-board.

Something was wrong. He could make no sense of the pieces. He'd forgotten how to play the game. Straws, discs, buttons, pebbles – what were they all about? What did they signify? Who was winning? 'Who's playing this damned game?' he demanded.

'You and me, you Dal Honese weasel,' Moak said.

'I think you're lying. I never seen this game before in my life.' He glared round at all the faces, the soldiers all looking down to watch, all looking at him now. Strange expressions – had he ever seen any of them before? He was a sergeant, wasn't he? 'Where's my damned squad? I'm supposed to be with my damned squad. Has the call come? What am I doing here?' He shot upright, making sure one foot toppled the game-board. Pieces flew, soldiers jumping back.

'Bad omen!' one hissed, backing away.

Growling, Moak rose, reaching for the knife at his belt. 'Swamp scum, you'll pay for that. I was winning—'

'No you weren't! Those pieces were a mess! A jumble! They didn't make sense!' He reached up and scratched at his face. 'What – this is clay! My face is covered in clay! A death mask! Who did this to me?'

A familiar but musty-smelling man stepped close to Balm. 'Sergeant, your squad's right here. I'm Deadsmell—'

'I'll say.'

'Corporal Deadsmell. And that's Throatslitter, and Widdershins, Galt and Lobe—'

'All right, all right, be quiet, I ain't blind. When's the call coming? We should've heard something by now.'

Moak closed in. 'I wasn't finished with you – that was a curse, what you did, Balm, on me and my squad – since I was winning the game. You cursed us, you damned warlock—'

'I did not! It was an accident. Come on, Deadsmell, let's make our way to the pickets, I'm done waiting here.'

'You're headed the wrong way, Sergeant!'

'Lead on, then! Who designed this damned camp, anyway? None of it makes any sense!'

Behind them, Sergeant Moak made to step after them, but his corporal, Stacker, pulled him back. 'It's all right, Sergeant. I heard about this from my da. It's the Confusion. Comes to some before a battle. They lose track – of everything. It should settle down once the fighting starts – but sometimes it don't, and if that's the case with Balm, then it's his squad that's doomed, not us.'

'You sure about all that, Stacker?'

'Yeah. Remember Fist Gamet? Listen. It's all right. We should check our weapons, one last time.'

Moak sheathed his knife. 'Good idea, get them on it, then.'

Twenty paces away, Deadsmell fell in step alongside his sergeant. 'Smart, all that back there. You was losing bad. Faking the Confusion, well, Sergeant, I'm impressed.'

Balm stared at the man. Who was he again? And what was he blathering on about? What language was the fool speaking, anyway?

'I got no appetite,' Lutes said, tossing the chunk of bread away. A camp dog closed in, collected the food and scampered off. 'I feel sick,' the soldier continued.

'You ain't the only one,' Maybe said. 'I'm in there first, you know. Us sappers. Rest of you got it easy. We got to set charges, meaning we're running with cussers and crackers over rough ground, climbing rubble, probably under fire from the walls. Then, down at the foot of the wall and Hood knows what's gonna pour down on us. Boiling water, oil, hot sand, bricks, offal, barrack-buckets. So it's raining down. Set the munitions. Acid on the wax – too much and we all go up right there and then. Dozens of sappers, and any one of 'em makes a mistake, or some piece of rock drops smack onto a munition. Boom! We're as good as dead already, if you ask me. Bits of meat. Tomorrow morning the crows will come down and that's that. Send word to my family, will you? Maybe was blown to bits at Y'Ghatan, that's all. No point in going into the gory details – hey, where you going? Gods below, Lutes, do your throwing up outa my sight, will you? Hood take us, that's awful. Hey, Balgrid! Look! Our squad healer's heaving his guts out!'

Gesler, Strings, Cuttle, Truth and Pella sat around the dying coals of a hearth, drinking tea.

'They're all losing their minds with this waiting,' Gesler said.

'I get just as bad before every battle,' Strings admitted. 'Cold and loose inside, if you know what I mean. It never goes away.'

'But you settle once it's begun,' Cuttle said. 'We all do, 'cause we've done this before. We settled, and we know we settle. Most of these soldiers, they don't know nothing of the sort. They don't know how they'll be once the fighting starts. So they're all terrified they'll curl up into cringing cowards.'

'Most of them probably will,' Gesler said.

'I don't know about that, Sergeant,' Pella said. 'Saw plenty of soldiers just like these ones at Skullcup. When the rebellion hit, well, they fought and they fought well, all things considered.'

'Outnumbered.'

'Yes.'

'So they died.'

'Most of them.'

'That's the thing with war,' Gesler said. 'Ain't nearly as many surprises, when all's said and done, as you might think. Or hope. Heroic stands usually end up with not a single hero left standing. Held out longer than expected, but the end was the same anyway. The end's always the same.'

'Abyss below, Gesler,' Strings said, 'ain't you a cheery one.'

'Just being realistic, Fid. Damn, I wish Stormy was here, now it's up to me to keep an eye on my squad.'

'Yes,' Cuttle said, 'that's what sergeants do.'

'You suggesting Stormy should've been sergeant and me corporal?'

'Now why would I do that?' the sapper asked. 'You're both just as bad as each other. Now Pella here . . .'

'No thanks,' Pella said.

Strings sipped his tea. 'Just make sure everybody sticks together. Captain wants us on the tip of the spear, as fast and as far in as we can get – the rest will just have to catch up. Cuttle?'

'Once the wall's blown I'll pull our sappers together and we meet you inside the breach. Where's Borduke right now?'

'Went for a walk. Seems his squad got into some kind of sympathetic heaves. Borduke got disgusted and stormed off.'

'So long as everybody's belly is empty by the time we get the call,' Cuttle said. 'Especially Maybe.'

'Especially maybe,' Gesler said, with a low laugh. 'That's a good one. You've made my day, Cuttle.'

'Believe me, it wasn't intentional.'

Seated nearby, hidden from the others in a brush-bordered hollow, Bottle smiled. *So that's how the veterans get ready for a fight. Same as everyone else.* That did indeed comfort him. Mostly. Well, maybe not. Better had they been confident, brash and swaggering. This – what was coming – sounded all too uncertain.

He had just returned from the mage gathering. Magical probes had revealed a muted presence in Y'Ghatan, the priestly kind, for the most part, and what there was of that was confused, panicked. Or strangely quiescent. For the sappers' advance, Bottle would be drawing upon Meanas, rolling banks of mist, tumbling darkness on all sides. Easily dispelled, if a mage of any skill was on the wall, but there didn't seem to be any. Most troubling of all, Bottle would need all his concentration to work Meanas, thus preventing him from using spirit magic. Leaving him as blind as those few enemy soldiers on the wall.

He admitted to a bad run of nerves – he hadn't been nearly so shaky at Raraku. And with Leoman's ambush in the sandstorm, well, it was an ambush, wasn't it – there'd been no time for terror. In any case, he didn't like this feeling.

Rising into a crouch, he moved away, up and out of the hollow, straightening and walking casually into the squad's camp. It seemed Strings didn't mind leaving his soldiers alone for a while before things heated up, letting them chew on their own thoughts, then – hopefully – reining everyone in at the last moment.

Koryk was tying yet more fetishes onto the various rings and loops in his armour, strips of coloured cloth, bird bones and chain-links to add to the ubiquitous finger bones that now signified the Fourteenth Army. Smiles was flipping her throwing-knives, the blades slapping softly on the leather of her gloves. Tarr stood nearby, shield already strapped on his left arm, short sword in his gauntleted right hand, most of his face hidden by his helm's cheek-guards.

Turning, Bottle studied the distant city. Dark – there seemed not a single lantern glowing from that squat, squalid heap. He already hated Y'Ghatan.

A low whistle in the night. Sudden stirring. Cuttle appeared. 'Sappers, to me. It's time.'

Gods below, so it is.

Leoman stood in the Falah'd's throne room. Eleven warriors were arrayed before him, glassy-eyed, their leather armour webbed in harnesses with straps and loops dangling. Corabb Bhilan Thenu'alas studied them – familiar faces one and all, yet now barely recognizable beneath the blood and strips of skin. Deliverers of the Apocalypse, sworn now to fanaticism, sworn not to see the coming dawn, bound to death this night. The very sight of them, with their drug-soaked eyes, chilled Corabb.

'You know what is asked of you this night,' Leoman said to his chosen warriors. 'Leave now, my brothers and sisters, under the pure eyes of Dryjhna, and we shall meet again at Hood's Gate.'

They bowed and headed off.

Corabb watched until the last of them vanished beyond the great doors, then faced Leoman. 'Warleader, what is to happen? What have you planned? You spoke of Dryjhna, yet this night you have bargained with the Queen of Dreams. Speak to me, before I begin to lose faith.'

'Poor Corabb,' Dunsparrow murmured.

Leoman shot her a glare, then said, 'No time, Corabb, but I tell you this – I have had my fill of fanatics, through this lifetime and a dozen others, I have had my fill—'

Boots sounded on the floor in the hallway beyond, and they turned as a tall, cloaked warrior strode in, drawing his hood back. Corabb's eyes widened, and hope surged through him as he stepped forward. 'High Mage L'oric! Truly, Dryjhna shines bright in the sky tonight!'

The tall man was massaging one shoulder, wincing as he said, 'Would that I could have arrived within the damned city walls – too many mages stirring in the Malazan camp. Leoman, I did not know you had the power to summon – I tell you, I was headed elsewhere—'

'The Queen of Dreams, L'oric.'

'Again? What does she want?'

Leoman shrugged. 'You were part of the deal, I'm afraid.'

'What deal?'

'I will explain later. In any case, we need you this night. Come, we climb to the South Tower.'

Another surge of hope. Corabb knew he could trust Leoman. The Holy Warrior possessed a plan, a diabolical, brilliant plan. He had been a fool to doubt. He set off in the wake of Dunsparrow, High Mage L'oric and Leoman of the Flails.

L'oric. Now we can fight the Malazans on equal terms. And in such a contest, we can naught but win!

In the dark, beyond the rough ground of the pickets, Bottle crouched a few paces away from the handful of sappers he had been assigned to protect. Cuttle, Maybe, Crump, Ramp and Widdershins. Nearby was a second group being covered by Balgrid: Taffo, Able, Gupp, Jump and Bowl. People he knew from the march, now revealed as sappers or would-be sappers. *Insane. Never knew there were so many in our company.* Strings was in neither group; he would be leading the rest of the squads into the breach before the smoke and dust settled.

Y'Ghatan's walls were a mess, tiered with older efforts, the last series Malazan-built in the classic sloping style, twenty paces thick at its base. As far as anyone knew, this would be the first time the sappers would challenge the engineering of imperial fortifications – he could see the gleam in their eyes.

Someone approached from his right and Bottle squinted through the gloom as the man arrived to crouch down beside him. 'Ebron, isn't it?'

'Aye, Ashok Regiment.'

Bottle smiled. 'They don't exist no more, Ebron.'

He tapped his chest, then said, 'You got a squad-mate of mine in your group.'

'The one named Crump.'

'Aye. Just thought you should know – he's dangerous.'

'Aren't they all?'

'No, this one especially. He was tossed out of the Mott Irregulars back on Genabackis.'

'Sorry, that don't mean nothing to me, Ebron.'

'Too bad. Anyway, consider yourself warned. Might think about mentioning it to Cuttle.'

'All right, I will.'

'Oponn's pull on you this night, lad.'

'And on you, Ebron.'

The man vanished into the darkness once more.

More waiting. No lights visible along the city's wall, nor the flanking corner bastions. No movement among the battlements.

A low whistle. Bottle met Cuttle's eyes, and the sapper nodded.

Meanas, the warren of shadows, illusion and deception. He fashioned a mental image of the warren, a swirling wall before him, then began focusing his will, watched as a wound formed, lurid red at first, then a hole burning through. Power poured into him. *Enough! No*

240

more. *Gods, why is it so strong?* Faint sound, something like move-ment, a presence, there, on the other side of the warren's wall . . .

Then . . . nothing.

Of course there was no wall. That had been simply a construct, a fashioning in Bottle's mind to manifest an idea into something physical. Something that he could then breach.

Simple, really. *Just incredibly dangerous. We damned mages must be mad, to play with this, to persist in the conceit that it can be managed, shaped, twisted by will alone.*

Power is blood.

Blood is power.

And this blood, it belongs to an Elder God . . .

A hiss from Cuttle. He blinked, then nodded as he began shaping the sorcery of Meanas. Mists, shot through with inky gloom, spreading out across the rough ground, snaking among the rubble, and the sappers set out, plunged into it, and moved on, unseen.

Bottle followed a few paces behind. The soldiers hiding in that magic could see. Nothing of the illusion confounded their senses. Illusions were usually one- or at best two-sided; seen from the other sides, well, there was nothing to see. True masters, of course, could cheat light in all directions, could fashion something that looked physically real, that moved as it should, casting its own shadow, even scuffing up illusional dust. Bottle's level of skill was nowhere near that. Balgrid had managed it – barely, it was true, but still . . . impressive.

But I hate this kind of sorcery. Sure, it's fascinating. Fun to play with, on occasion, but not like tonight, not when it's suddenly life and death.

They threw wagon-planks across the narrow moat Leoman's soldiers had dug, then drew closer to the wall.

Lostara Yil came to Tene Baralta's side. They were positioned at the picket line, behind them the massed ranks of soldiery. Her former commander's face revealed surprise as he looked upon her.

'I did not think to see you again, Captain.'

She shrugged. 'I was getting fat and lazy, Commander.'

'That Claw you were with is not a popular man. The decision was made that he was better off staying in his tent – indefinitely.'

'I have no objection to that.'

Through the gloom they could see swirling clouds of deeper dark-ness, rolling ominously towards the city's wall.

'Are you prepared, Captain,' Baralta asked, 'to bloody your sword this night?'

'More than you could imagine, Commander.'

*

Waves of vertigo rippled through Sergeant Hellian, nausea threatening as she watched the magics draw ever closer to Y'Ghatan. It was Y'Ghatan, wasn't it? She turned to the sergeant standing beside her. 'What city is that? Y'Ghatan. I know about that city. It's where Malazans die. Who are you? Who's undermining the walls? Where are the siege weapons? What kind of siege is this?'

'I'm Strings, and you look to be drunk.'

'So? I hate fighting. Strip me of my command, throw me in chains, find a dungeon – only, no spiders. And find that bastard, the one who disappeared, arrest him and chain him within reach. I want to rip out his throat.'

The sergeant was staring at her. She stared back – at least he wasn't weaving back and forth. Not much, anyway.

'You hate fighting, and you want to rip out someone's throat?'

'Stop trying to confuse me, Stirrings. I'm confused 'nough as it is.'

'Where's your squad, Sergeant?'

'Somewhere.'

'Where is your corporal? What is his name?'

'Urb? I don't know.'

'Hood's breath.'

Pella sat watching his sergeant, Gesler, talking with Borduke. The sergeant of the Sixth Squad had only three soldiers left under his command – Lutes, Ibb and Corporal Hubb – the others either magicking or sapping. Of course, there were only two left to Gesler's Fifth Squad – Truth and Pella himself. The plan was to link up after the breach, and that had Pella nervous. They might have to grab anyone close by and to Hood with real squads.

Borduke was tugging at his beard as if he wanted to yank it off. Hubb stood close to his sergeant, a sickly expression on his face.

Gesler looked damn near bored.

Pella thought about his squad. *Something odd about all three of them. Gesler, Stormy and Truth. Not just that strangely gold skin, either . . .* Well, he'd stick close to Truth – that lad still seemed too wide-eyed for all of this, despite what he'd already gone through. That damned ship, *Silanda*, which had been commandeered by the Adjunct and was now likely north of them, somewhere in the Kansu Sea or west of it. Along with the transport fleet and a sizeable escort of dromons. The three had sailed it, sharing the deck with still-alive severed heads and a lot worse below-decks.

Pella checked his sword one more time. He'd tied new leather strapping round the grip's tang – not as tight as he would have liked. He hadn't soaked it yet, either, not wanting the grip still wet when he went into battle. He drew the crossbow from his shoulder, kept a quarrel in hand, ready for a quick load once the order came to advance.

Bloody marines. Should've volunteered for plain old infantry. Should've gotten a transfer. Should've never joined up at all. Skullcup was more than enough for me, dammit. Should've run, that's what I should've done.

Night wind whistling about them, Corabb, Leoman, L'oric, Dunsparrow and a guard stood on the gently swaying platform atop the palace tower. The city spread out in all directions, frighteningly dark and seeming lifeless.

'What are we here to see, Leoman?' L'oric asked.

'Wait, my friend – ah, there!' He pointed to the rooftop of a distant building near the west wall. On its flat top flickered muted lantern-light. Then . . . gone.

'And there!'

Another building, another flash of light.

'Another! More, they are all in place! Fanatics! Damned fools! Dryjhna take us, this is going to work!'

Work? Corabb frowned, then scowled. He caught Dunsparrow's gaze on him – she mouthed a kiss. Oh how he wanted to kill her.

Heaps of rubble, broken pots, a dead, bloated dog, and animal bones, there wasn't a single stretch of even ground at the base of the wall. Bottle had followed on the heels of the sappers, up the first tier, brick fragments spilling away beneath their boots, then cries of pain and cursing as someone stumbled over a wasp nest – darkness alone had saved them from what could have been a fatal few moments – the wasps were sluggish – Bottle was astonished they had come out at all, until he saw what the soldier had managed. Knocking over one rock, then thumping his entire foot down the nest's maw.

He'd momentarily relinquished Meanas, then, to slip into the swarming soul-sparks of the wasps, quelling their panic and anger. Devoid of disguising magic for the last two tiers, the sappers had scrambled like terrified beetles – the rock they had hidden under suddenly vanishing – and made the base of the wall well ahead of the others. Where they crouched, unlimbering their packs of munitions.

Bottle scampered up to crouch at Cuttle's side. 'The gloom's back,' he whispered. 'Sorry about that – good thing they weren't black wasps – Maybe'd be dead by now.'

'Not to mention yours truly,' Cuttle said. 'It was me who stepped in the damned thing.'

'How many stings?'

'Two or three, right leg's numb, but that's better than it was fifteen heartbeats ago.'

'Numb? Cuttle, that's bad. Find Lutes fast as you can once we're done here.'

'Count on it. Now, shut up, I got to concentrate.'

Bottle watched him lift out from his pack a bundle of munitions – two cussers strapped together, looking like a pair of ample breasts. Affixed to them at the base were two spike-shaped explosives – crackers. Gingerly setting the assemblage on the ground beside him, Cuttle then turned his attention to the base of the wall. He cleared bricks and rocks to make an angled hole, large and deep enough to accommodate the wall-breaker.

That was the easy part, Bottle reminded himself as he watched Cuttle place the explosive into the hole. *Now comes the acid on the wax plug.* He glanced up and down the length of wall, saw other sappers doing the very same thing Cuttle had just done. 'Don't get ahead of the rest,' Bottle said.

'I know what needs knowing, mage. Stick to your spells and leave me alone.'

Miffed, Bottle looked away again. Then his eyes widened. 'Hey, what's he doing – Cuttle, what's Crump doing?'

Cursing, the veteran glanced over. 'Gods below—'

The sapper from Sergeant Cord's squad had prepared not one wall-breaker, but three, the mass of cussers and crackers filling his entire pack. His huge teeth were gleaming, eyes glittering as he wrestled it loose and, lying on his back, head closest to the wall, settled it on his stomach and began crawling until there was the audible crunch of the back of his skull contacting the rearing stonework.

Cuttle scrambled over. '*You!*' he hissed. 'Are you mad? Take those damned things apart!'

The man's grin collapsed. 'But I made it myself!'

'Keep your voice down, idiot!'

Crump rolled and shoved the mass of munitions up against the wall. A small glittering vial appeared in his right hand. 'Wait till you see this!' he whispered, smiling once more.

'*Wait! Not yet!*'

A sizzle, threads of smoke rising—

Cuttle was on his feet, and, dragging a leg, he began running. And he began screaming. '*Everyone! Back! Run, you fools! Run!*'

Figures pelting away on all sides, Bottle among them. Crump raced past as if the mage had been standing still, the man's absurdly long legs pumping high and wild, knobby knees and huge boots scything the air. Munitions had been left against the wall but unset, others remained a

pace or more back. Sacks of sharpers, smokers and burners left behind
– *gods below, this is going to be bad*—

Shouts from atop the wall, now, voices raised in alarm. A ballista
thumped as a missile was loosed at the fleeing sappers. Bottle heard the
crack and skitter as it struck the ground.

Faster— He glanced over his shoulder, and saw Cuttle hobbling
along in his wake. *Hood take us!* Bottle skidded to a halt, turned and
ran back to the sapper's side.

'Fool!' Cuttle grunted. 'Just *go*!'

'Lean on my shoulder—'

'You've just killed yourself—'

Cuttle was no lightweight. Bottle sagged with his weight as they ran.
'Twelve!' the sapper gasped.

The mage scanned the ground ahead in growing panic. *Some cover*—
'Eleven!'

A shelf of old foundation, solid limestone, *there, ten, nine paces*—
'Ten!'

Five more paces – it was looking good – a hollow on the other side—
'Nine!'

Two paces, then down, as Cuttle screamed: 'Eight!'

The night vanished, flinging stark shadows forward as the two men
tumbled down behind the shelf of limestone, into a heap of rotting
vegetation. The ground lifted to meet them, a god's uppercut, driving
the air from Bottle's lungs.

Sound, like a collapsing mountain, then a wall of stone, smoke, fire,
and a rain filled with flames—

The concussion threw Lostara Yil from her feet moments after she'd
stared, uncomprehending, at the squads of marines arrayed beyond the
picket line – stared, as they were one and all flattened, rolling back
before an onrushing wave – multiple explosions now, rapid-fire, marching along the wall to either side – then she was hammered in the chest,
flung to the ground amidst other soldiers.

Rocks arrived in an almost-horizontal hail, fast as slingstones, cracking off armour, thudding deep into exposed flesh – bones snapping,
screams—

—the light dimmed, wavered, then contracted to a knot of flames,
filling an enormous gap in Y'Ghatan's wall, almost dead-centre, and as
Lostara – propped on one elbow, braving the hail of stones – watched,
she saw the flanks of that huge gap slowly crumble, and, beyond, two
three-storey tenements folding inward, flames shooting up like fleeing
souls—

Among the slowing rain, now, body-parts.

Atop the palace tower, Corabb and the others had been thrown down – the guard who had accompanied them cartwheeling over the platform's low wall and vanishing with a dwindling scream, barely heard as the tower swayed, as the roar settled around them like the fury of a thousand demons, as huge stones slammed into the tower's side, others ricocheting off to crash among the buildings below, and, now, a terrible cracking, popping sound that sent Corabb clawing across the pavestones towards the hatch.

'It's going down!' he screamed.

Two figures reached the hatch before him – Leoman and Dunsparrow.

Cracking, sagging, the platform starting its inexorable pitch. Clouds of choking dust. Corabb reached the hatch and pulled himself into it headfirst, joining Leoman and the Malazan woman as they slithered like snakes down the winding steps. Corabb's left heel connected with a jaw and he heard L'oric's grunt of pain, then cursing in unknown languages.

That explosion – the breach of the wall – gods below, he had never seen anything like it. How could one challenge these Malazans? With their damned Moranth munitions, their gleeful disregard of the rules of honourable war.

Tumbling, rolling, sprawling out onto a scree of rubble on the main floor of the palace – chambers to their left had vanished beneath the section of tower that had broken off. Corabb saw a leg jutting from the collapsed ceiling, strangely unmarred, free even of blood or dust.

Coughing, Corabb clambered upright, eyes stinging, countless bruises upon his body, and stared at Leoman, who was already on his feet and brushing mortar dust from his clothes. Near him, L'oric and Dunsparrow were also pulling themselves free of bricks and shards of wood.

Glancing over, Leoman of the Flails said, 'Maybe the tower wasn't such a good idea after all. Come on, we need to saddle our horses – if they still live – and ride to the Temple!'

The Temple of Scalissara? But— what— why?

The rattle of gravel, the thump of larger chunks, and gusts of smoky, dusty heat. Bottle opened his eyes. Sebar husks, hairy and leathery, crowded his vision, his nose filling with the pungent overripe scent of sebar pulp. The fruit's juice was considered a delicacy – the reek was nauseating – he knew he'd never be able to drink the stuff again. A groan from the rubbish somewhere to his left. 'Cuttle? That you?'

'The numb feeling's gone. Amazing what a shot of terror can do to a body.'

'You sure the leg's still there?'

'Reasonably.'

'You counted down to eight!'

'What?'

'You said eight! Then – boom!'

'Had to keep your hopes up, didn't I? Where in Hood's pit are we, anyway?'

Bottle began clawing his way free, amazed that he seemed uninjured – not even a scratch. 'Among the living, sapper.' His first view of the scene on the killing ground made no sense. Too much light – it had been dark, hadn't it? Then he saw soldiers amidst the rubble, some writhing in pain, others picking themselves up, covered in dust, coughing in the foul air.

The breach on Y'Ghatan's south wall ran a full third of its length, fifty paces in from the southwest bastion to well beyond the centre gate fortifications. Buildings had collapsed, whilst those that remained upright, flanking the raging flames of the gap, were themselves burning, although it seemed that most of that had come from the innumerable burners among the sapper-kits left behind. The fires danced on cracked stone as if seeking somewhere to go before the fuel vanished.

The light cast by the aftermath of the detonation was dimming, shrouded by descending dust. Cuttle appeared at his side, plucking scraps of rotted fruit from his armour. 'We can head into that gap soon – gods, when I track down Crump—'

'Get in line, Cuttle. Hey, I see Strings . . . and the squad . . .'

Horns sounded, soldiers scrambling to form up. Darkness was closing in once more, as the last of the fires dwindled in the breach. The rain of dust seemed unending as Fist Keneb moved to the rally position, his officers drawing round him and bellowing orders. He saw Tene Baralta and Captain Lostara Yil at the head of a narrow column that had already begun moving.

The sappers had messed up. That much was clear. And some of them had not made it back. *Damned fools, and they weren't even under fire.*

He saw the fires guttering out in the gap, although webs of flame clung stubbornly to the still-upright buildings to either side. 'First, second and third squads,' Keneb said to Captain Faradan Sort. 'The heavies lead the way into the breach.'

'The marines are already through, Fist.'

'I know, Captain, but I want backup close behind them if things get hairy. Get them moving.'

'Aye, Fist.'

Keneb glanced back to the higher ground on the other side of the road and saw a row of figures watching. The Adjunct, T'amber, Nil and Nether. Fist Blistig and Warleader Gall. Fist Temul was likely out with his horse-warriors, ranging round the city on the other sides. There was always a chance Leoman would leave his followers to their grisly fate and attempt to escape on his own. Such things were not unknown.

'Sergeant Cord!'

The soldier strolled up. Keneb noted the sigil of the Ashok Regiment on the man's battered leather armour, but elected to ignore it. For now. 'Lead the mediums in, seventh through twelfth squads.'

'Aye, Fist, we're dogging the heavies' heels.'

'Good. This will be street and alley fighting, Sergeant, assuming the bastards don't surrender outright.'

'I'd be surprised if they did that, Fist.'

'Me too. Get going, Sergeant.'

Finally, some motion among the troops of his company. The waiting was over. The Fourteenth was heading into battle. *Hood look away from us this night. Just look away.*

Bottle and Cuttle rejoined their squad. Sergeant Strings carried his lobber crossbow, a cusser quarrel slotted and locked.

'There's a way through the flames,' Strings said, wiping sweat from his eyes, then spitting. 'Koryk and Tarr up front. Cuttle to the rear and keep a sharper in your hand. Behind the front two, me and Smiles. You're a step behind us, Bottle.'

'You want more illusions, Sergeant?'

'No, I want your other stuff. Ride the rats and pigeons and bats and spiders and whatever in Hood's name else is in there. I need eyes you can look through into places we can't see.'

'Expecting a trap?' Bottle asked.

'There's Borduke and his squad, dammit. First into the breach. Come on, on their heels!'

They sprinted forward across the uneven, rock-littered ground. Moonlight struggled through the dust haze. Bottle quested with his senses, seeking life somewhere ahead, but what he found was in pain, dying, trickling away beneath mounds of rubble, or stunned insensate by the concussions. 'We have to get past the blast area,' he said to Strings.

'Right,' the sergeant replied over a shoulder. 'That's the idea.'

They reached the edge of the vast, sculpted crater created by Crump's munitions. Borduke and his squad were scrambling up the other side, and Bottle saw that the wall they climbed was tiered with once-buried city ruins, ceilings and floors compressed, cracked, collapsed, sections of wall that had slid out and down into the pit itself, taking with them older layers of floor tiles. He saw that both Balgrid and Maybe had survived the explosion, but wondered how many sappers and squad mages they had lost. Some gut instinct told him Crump had survived.

Borduke and his squad were having a hard time of it.

'To the right,' Strings said. 'We can skirt it and get through before them!'

Borduke heard and twisted round from where he clung to the wall, three quarters of the way up. 'Bastards! Balgrid, get that fat butt of yours moving, damn you!'

Koryk found a way round the crater, clambering over the rubble, and Bottle and the others followed. Too distracted for the moment by the effort of staying on his feet, Bottle did not attempt to sense the myriad, minuscule life beyond the blast area, in the city itself. Time for that later, he hoped.

The half-blood Seti's progress halted suddenly, and the mage looked up to see that Koryk had encountered an obstacle, a broad crack in a sharply angled, subterranean floor, a man's height below ground-level. Dust-smeared tiles revealed the painted images of yellow birds in flight, all seeming to be heading deep underground with the slanting pitch of the floor.

Koryk glanced back at Strings. 'Saw the whole slab move, Sergeant. Not sure how solid our footing will be.'

'Hood take us! All right, get the ropes out, Smiles—'

'I tossed 'em,' she said, scowling. 'On the run in here. Too damned heavy—'

'And I picked them up,' Cuttle interjected, tugging the coils from his left shoulder and flinging them forward.

Strings reached out and rapped a knuckle against Smiles's chin – her head snapped back, eyes widening in shock, then fury. 'You carry what I tell you to carry, soldier,' the sergeant said.

Koyrk collected one end of the rope, backed up a few paces, then bolted forward and leapt over the fissure. He landed clean, although with very little room to spare. There was no way Tarr or Cuttle could manage such a long jump.

Strings cursed, then said, 'Those who can do what Koryk just did, go to it. And nobody leave gear behind, either.'

Moments later both Bottle and Smiles crouched at Koryk's side, helping anchor the rope as the sergeant, twin sacks of munitions dangling from him, crossed hand over hand, the bags swinging wild but positioned so that they never collided with one another. Bottle released the rope and moved forward to help, once Strings found footing on the edge.

Cuttle followed. Then Tarr, with the rope wrapped about himself, made his way down onto the slanted floor and was dragged quickly across as it shifted then slid away beneath his weight. Armour and weapons clanking, the rest of the squad pulled the corporal onto level ground.

'Gods,' Cuttle gasped. 'The man weighs as much as a damned bhederin!'

Koryk re-coiled the rope and handed it, grinning, to Smiles.

They set off once more, up over a ridge of wreckage from some kind of stall or lean-to that had abutted the inner wall, then more rubble, beyond which was a street.

And Borduke and his squad were just entering it, spread out, cross-bows at the ready. The bearded sergeant was in the lead, Corporal Hubb on his right and two steps behind. Ibb was opposite the corporal, and two paces behind the pair were Tavos Pond and Balgrid, followed by Lutes, with the rear drawn up by the sapper Maybe. Classic marine advance formation.

The buildings to the sides were dark, silent. Something odd about them, Bottle thought, trying to work out what it might be . . . *no shutters on the windows – they're all open. So are the doors . . . every door, in fact—* 'Sergeant—'

The arrows that suddenly sped down from flanking windows, high up, were loosed at the precise moment that a score of figures rushed out from nearby buildings, screaming, spears, scimitars and shields at the ready. Those arrows had been fired without regard to the charging warriors, and two cried out as iron-barbed points tore into them.

Bottle saw Borduke spin round, saw the arrow jutting from his left eye socket, saw a second arrow transfixing his neck. Blood was spraying as he staggered, clawing and clutching at his throat and face. Behind him, Corporal Hubb curled up round an arrow in his gut, then sank to the cobbles. Ibb had taken an arrow in the left shoulder, and he was plucking at it, swearing, when a warrior rushed in on him, scimitar swinging to strike him across the side of his head. Bone and helm caved in, a gush of blood, and the soldier fell.

Strings's squad arrived, intercepting a half-dozen warriors. Bottle found himself in the midst of a vicious exchange, Koryk on his left, the half-Seti's longsword batting away a scimitar, then driving point first into the man's throat. A screaming visage seemed to lunge at Bottle, as if the warrior was seeking to tear into his neck with bared teeth, and Bottle recoiled at the madness in the man's eyes, then reached in with his mind, into the warrior's fierce maelstrom of thoughts – little more than fractured images and black rage – and found the most primitive part of his brain; a burst of power and the man's coordination vanished. He crumpled, limbs twitching.

Cold with sweat, Bottle backed away another step, wishing he had a weapon to draw, beyond the bush-knife in his right hand.

Fighting on all sides. Screams, the clash of metal, snapping of chain links, grunts and gasps.

And still arrows rained down.

One cracked into the back of Strings's helm, pitching him down to his knees. He twisted round, lifting his crossbow, glaring at the building opposite – its upper windows crowded with archers.

Bottle reached out and grasped Koryk's baldric. 'Back! Fid's cusser! *Everyone! Back!*'

The sergeant raised the crossbow to his shoulder, aimed towards an upper window—

There were heavy infantry among them now, and Bottle saw Taffo, from Mosel's squad, wading into a crowd of warriors, now ten paces from the building – from Strings's target—

—as the crossbow *thunked*, the misshapen quarrel flying out, up, into the maw of the window.

Bottle threw himself flat, arms covering his head—

The upper floor of the building exploded, huge sections of wall bulging, then crashing down into the street. The cobbles jumped beneath Bottle.

Someone rolled up against him and he felt something flop heavy and slimy onto his forearm, twitching and hot. A sudden reek of bile and faeces.

The patter of stones, piteous moans, the lick of flames. Then another massive crash, as what remained of the upper floor collapsed into the level below. The groan of the nearest wall preceded its sagging dissolution. Then, beyond the few groans, silence.

Bottle lifted his head. To find Corporal Harbyn lying beside him. The lower half of the soldier's body was gone, entrails spilled out. Beneath the helm's ridge, eyes stared sightlessly. Pulling away, Bottle leaned back on his hands and crabbed across the rock-strewn street. Where Taffo had been fighting a mob of warriors, there was now nothing but a heap of rubble and a few dust-sheathed limbs jutting from beneath it, all motionless.

Koryk moved past him, stabbing down at stunned figures with his sword. Bottle saw Smiles cross the half-Seti's path, her two knives already slick with blood.

Bodies in the street. Figures slowly rising, shaking their heads, spitting blood. Bottle twisted round onto his knees, dipped his head, and vomited onto the cobbles.

'Fiddler – you bastard!'

Coughing, but stomach quiescent for the moment, Bottle looked over to see Sergeant Mosel advancing on Strings.

'We had them! We were rushing the damned building!'

'Then rush that one!' Strings snapped, pointing at the tenement on the other side of the street. 'They just been knocked back, that's all – any moment now and another rain of arrows—'

Cursing, Mosel gestured at the three heavies left – Mayfly, Flashwit and Uru Hela – and they lumbered into the building's doorway.

Strings was fitting another quarrel into his crossbow, this one loaded with a sharper. 'Balgrid! Who's left in your squad?'

The portly mage staggered over. 'What?' he shouted. 'I can't hear you! What?'

'Tavos Pond!'

'Here, Sergeant. We got Maybe, uhm, Balgrid – but he's bleeding out from his ears. Lutes is down, but he should live – with some healing. We're out of this—'

'To Hood you are. Pull Lutes clear – there's a squad coming up – the rest of you are with me—'

'Balgrid's deaf!'

'Better he was mute – we got hand signals, remember? Now remind the bastard of that! Bottle, help Tarr out. Cuttle, take Koryk to that corner up ahead and wait there for us. Smiles, load up on quarrels – I want that weapon of yours cocked and your eyes sharp on everything from rooftops on down.'

Bottle climbed to his feet and made his way to where Tarr was struggling to clamber free of rubble – a part of the wall had fallen on him, but it seemed his armour and shield had withstood the impact. Lots of swearing, but nothing voiced in pain. 'Here,' Bottle said, 'give me your arm—'

'I'm fine,' the corporal said, grunting as he kicked his feet clear. He still gripped his shortsword, and snagged on its tip was a hairy piece of scalp, coated in dust and dripping from the underside. 'Look at that,' he said, gesturing up the street with his sword, 'even Cuttle's shut up now.'

'Fid had no choice,' Bottle said. 'Too many arrows coming down—'

'I ain't complaining, Bottle. Not one bit. See Borduke go down? And Hubb? That could've been us, if we'd reached here first.'

'Abyss take me, I hadn't thought of that.'

He glanced over as a squad of medium infantry arrived – Sergeant Cord's – Ashok Regiment and all that. 'What in Hood's name happened?'

'Ambush,' Bottle said. 'Sergeant Strings had to take a building down. Cusser.'

Cord's eyes widened. 'Bloody marines,' he muttered, then headed over to where Strings crouched. Bottle and Tarr followed.

'You formed up again?' Cord asked their sergeant. 'We're bunching up behind you—'

'We're ready, but send word back. There'll be ambushes aplenty. Leoman means us to buy every street and every building with blood. Fist Keneb might want to send the sappers ahead again, under marine cover, to drop buildings – it's the safest way to proceed.'

Cord looked round. 'Safest way? Gods below.' He turned. 'Corporal Shard, you heard Fid. Send word back to Keneb.'

'Aye, Sergeant.'

'Sinn,' Cord added, speaking to a young girl nearby, 'put that knife away – he's already dead.'

She looked up, even as her blade cut through the base of the dead warrior's right index finger. She held it up for display, then stuffed it into a belt pouch.

'Nice girl you got there,' Strings said. 'Had us one of those, once.'

'Shard! Hold back there! Send Sinn with the message, will you?'

'I don't want to go back!' Sinn shouted.

'Too bad,' Cord said. Then, to Strings: 'We'll link up with Mosel's heavies behind you.'

Strings nodded. 'All right, squad, let's try out the next street, shall we?'

Bottle swallowed back another surge of nausea, then he joined the others as they scrambled towards Koryk and Cuttle. *Gods, this is going to be brutal.*

Sergeant Gesler could smell it. Trouble in the night. Unrelieved darkness from gaping windows, yawning doorways, and on flanking streets, where other squads were moving, the sounds of pitched battle. Yet, before them, no movement, no sound – nothing at all. He raised his right hand, hooked two fingers and made a downward tugging motion. Behind him he heard boots on the cobbles, one padding off to his left, the other to his right, away, halting when the soldiers reached the flanking buildings. Truth on his left, Pella on his right, crossbows out, eyes on opposite rooftops and upper windows.

Another gesture and Sands came up from behind to crouch at his side. 'Well?' Gesler demanded, wishing for the thousandth time that Stormy was here.

'It's bad,' Sands said. 'Ambushes.'

'Right, so where's ours? Go back and call up Moak and his squad, and Tugg's – I want those heavies clearing these buildings, before it all comes down on us. What sappers we got with us?'

'Thom Tissy's squad's got some,' Sands said. 'Able, Jump and Gupp, although they just decided to become sappers tonight, a bell or so ago.'

'Great, and they got munitions?'

'Aye, Sergeant.'

'Madness. All right. Get Thom Tissy's squad up here, too. I heard one cusser go off already – might be the only way to do this.'

'Okay, Sergeant. I'll be right back.'

Under-strength squads and a night engagement in a strange, hostile city. Had the Adjunct lost her mind?

Twenty paces away, Pella crouched low, his back against a mud-brick wall. He thought he'd caught movement in a high window opposite, but he couldn't be certain – not enough to call out the alarm. Might well have been a curtain or something, plucked by the wind.

Only . . . there ain't much wind.

Eyes fixed on that particular window, he slowly raised his crossbow. Nothing. Just darkness.

Distant detonations – sharpers, he guessed, somewhere to the south. *We're supposed to be pushing in hard and fast, and here we are, bogged down barely one street in from the breach. Gesler's gotten way too cautious, I think.*

He heard the clank of weapons, armour and the thud of footfalls as more squads came up. Flicking his gaze away from the window, he watched as Sergeant Tugg led his heavies towards the building opposite. Three soldiers from Thom Tissy's squad padded up to the doorway of the building Pella was huddled against. Jump, Gupp and Able. Pella saw sharpers in their hands – and nothing else. He crouched lower, then returned his attention to the distant window, cursing under his breath, waiting for one of them to toss a grenado in through the doorway.

On the other side of the street, Tugg's squad plunged into the building – there was a shout from within, the clang of weapons, sudden screams—

Then more shrieking, this time from the building at Pella's back, as the three sappers rushed inside. Pella cringed – *no, you fools! You don't carry them inside – you throw them!*

A sharp crack, shaking dust from the wall behind Pella, grit raining down onto the back of his neck, then screams. Another concussion – ducking still lower, Pella looked back up at the opposite window—

To see, momentarily, a single flash—

—to feel the shock of surprise—

—as the arrow sped at him. A hard, splintering cracking sound. Pella's head was thrown back, helm crunching against the wall. Something, wavering, at the upper edge of his vision, but those edges were growing darker. He heard his crossbow clatter to the cobbles at his feet, then distant pain as his knees struck the stones, the jolt peeling skin away – he'd done that once, as a child, playing in the alley. Stumbling, knees skidding on gritty, filthy cobbles—

So filthy, the murk of hidden diseases, infections – his mother had been so angry, angry and frightened. They'd had to go to a healer, and that had cost money – money they had been saving for a move. To a better part of the slum. The dream . . . put away, all because he'd skinned his knees.

Just like now. And darkness closing in.

Oh Momma, I skinned my knees. I'm sorry. I'm so sorry. I skinned my knees . . .

As mayhem was exploding in the buildings to either side, Gesler crouched lower. He glanced over to his right and saw Pella. An arrow was jutting from his forehead. He was on his knees for a moment, his weapon falling, then he sank down to the side.

Sharpers going off in that building, then something worse – a burner, the flare of red flame bursting through the ground-floor windows. Shrieks – someone stumbled outside, wreathed in flames – a Malazan, running, arms waving, slapping – straight for Moak and his squad—

'Get away!' Gesler bellowed, rising and raising his crossbow.

Moak had pulled out his rain-cape – the soldiers were rushing towards the burning man – they didn't see – *the satchel – the munitions—*

Gesler fired his crossbow. The quarrel caught the sapper in the midsection, even as the munitions went off.

Flung back, punched in the chest, Gesler sprawled, rolled, then came to his feet.

Moak, Stacker, Rove. Burnt, Guano and Mud. *All gone, all pieces of meat and shattered bone.* A helm, the head still in it, struck a wall, spun wildly for a moment, then wobbled to a halt.

'Truth! To me!' Gesler waved as he ran towards the building the heavies had entered, and where the sounds of fighting had grown fiercer. 'You see Sands?' he demanded as he reloaded his crossbow.

'N-no, Sergeant. Pella—'

'Pella's dead, lad.' He saw Thom Tissy and what was left of his squad – Tulip and Ramp – heading towards the doorway after Tugg and his heavies. *Good, Thom's thinking clear—*

The building that had swallowed Able, Jump and Gupp was a mass of flames, the heat pouring out like scalding liquid. *Gods, what did they set off in there?*

He darted through the doorway, skidded to a halt. Sergeant Tugg's fighting days were over – the soldier had been speared through just below the sternum. He had thrown up a gout of bloody bile before

255

dying. At the inner doorway opposite, leading into a hall, lay Robello, his head caved in. Beyond, out of sight, the rest of the heavies were fighting.

'Hang back, Truth,' Gesler said, 'and use that crossbow to cover our backs. Tissy, let's go.'

The other sergeant nodded, gesturing towards Tulip and Ramp.

They plunged into the hallway.

Hellian stumbled after Urb, who suddenly halted – it was like hitting a wall – she bounced off, fell on her behind. 'Ow, you bloody ox!'

All at once there were soldiers around them, pulling back from the street corner, dragging fallen comrades.

'Who? What?'

A woman dropped down beside her. 'Hanno. We lost our sergeant. We lost Sobelone. And Toles. Ambush—'

One hand leaning hard on Hanno's shoulder, Hellian pulled herself upright. She shook her head. 'Right,' she said, something cold and hard straightening within her, as if her spine had turned into a sword, or a spear, *or whatever else won't bend, no, it'll bend, maybe, but not break. Gods, I feel sick.* 'Join up with my squad. Urb, what squad are we?'

'No idea, Sergeant.'

'Don't matter, then, you're with us, Hanno. Ambush? Fine, let's go get the bastards. Touchy, Brethless, pull out those grenados you stole—'

The twins faced her – innocence, indignation, both dreadful efforts, then the two pulled out munitions. 'They're smokers, Sergeant, and one cracker,' Touchy said. 'That's all—'

'Smokers? Perfect. Hanno, you're going to lead us into the building the bastards attacked from. Touchy, you throw yours ahead of her. Brethless, pick the open flank and do the same. We ain't gonna stand around – we ain't even going in slow and cautious. I want fast, you all got that? *Fast.*'

'Sergeant?'

'What is it, Urb?'

'Nothing. Only, I'm ready, I guess.'

Well that makes one of us. I knew I'd hate this city. 'Weapons out, soldiers, it's time to kill people.'

They set off.

'We done left everybody behind,' Galt said.

'Shut that whining,' Sergeant Balm snapped, wiping sweat and mud from his eyes. 'We just made it easier for the rest of 'em.' He glared at the soldiers in his squad. Breathing hard, a few cuts here and there, but nothing serious. They'd carved through that ambush quick and dirty, like he'd wanted it.

They were on a second floor, in a room filled with bolts of cloth – a fortune's worth of silks. Lobe had said they'd come from Darujhistan, of all places. A damned fortune's worth, and now most of it was soaked with blood and bits of human meat.

'Maybe we should check the top floor,' Throatslitter said, eyeing the nicks in his long-knives. 'Thought I heard some scuffing, maybe.'

'All right, take Widdershins. Deadsmell, go to the stairs—'

'Leading up? It's a ladder.'

'Fine, the Hood-damned fucking ladder, then. You're backup and mouthpiece, got it? Hear any scrapping upstairs and you join it, but not before letting us know about it. Understood?'

'Clear as piss, Sergeant.'

'Good, the three of you go. Galt, stay at the window and keep looking at what's opposite you. Lobe, do the same at that window. There's more crap waiting for us and we're gonna carve right through all of it.'

A short while later, the sound of footfalls padding back and forth from above ceased and Deadsmell called out from the hallway that Throatslitter and Widdershins were coming down the ladder. A dozen heartbeats later and all three entered the silk room. Throatslitter came close to Balm's side and crouched. 'Sergeant,' he said, his voice near a whisper.

'What?'

'We found something. Don't much like the looks of it. We think you should take a look.'

Balm sighed, then straightened. 'Galt?'

'They're there, all right, all three floors.'

'Lobe?'

'Same here, including on the roof, some guy with a hooded lantern.'

'Okay, keep watching. Lead on, Throatslitter. Deadsmell, back into the hallway. Widdershins, do some magic or something.'

He followed Throatslitter back to the ladder. The floor above was low-ceilinged, more of an attic than anything else. Plenty of rooms, the walls thick, hardened clay.

Throatslitter led him up to one such wall. At his feet stood huge urns and casks. 'Found these,' he said, reaching down behind one cask and lifting into view a funnel, made from a gourd of some sort.

'All right,' Balm said, 'what about it?'

His soldier kicked one of the casks. 'These ones are full. But the urns are empty. All of 'em.'

'Okay . . .'

'Olive oil.'

'Right, this city's famous for it. Go on.'

Throatslitter tossed the funnel aside, then drew a knife. 'See these damp spots on these walls? Here.' He pointed with the knife-tip, then dug into the patch. 'The clay's soft, recently plugged. These walls, they're hollow.'

'For Fener's sake, man, what are you going on about?'

'Just this. I think these walls – the whole building, it's filled with oil.'

'Filled? With . . . with *oil*?'

Throatslitter nodded.

Filled with oil? What, some kind of piping system to supply it down-stairs? No, for Hood's sake, Balm, don't be an idiot. 'Throatslitter, you think other buildings are rigged like this? Is that what you're thinking?'

'I think, Sergeant, that Leoman's turned Y'Ghatan into one big trap. He wants us in here, fighting in the streets, pushing in and in—'

'But what about his followers?'

'What about them?'

But . . . that would mean . . . He thought back – the faces of the enemy, the fanaticism, the gleam of drugged madness. *'Abyss take us!'*

'We got to find Fist Keneb, Sergeant. Or the captains. We got—'

'I know, I know. Let's get out of here, before that bastard with the lantern throws it!'

It had begun messy, only to get messier still. Yet, from that initial reeling back, as ambushes were unveiled one after another, mauling the advance squads of marines, Fist Keneb's and Fist Tene Baralta's companies had rallied, regrouped, then pushed inward, building by building, street by street. Somewhere ahead, Keneb knew, what was left of the marines was penetrating still further, cutting through the fanatic but poorly armed and thoroughly undisciplined warriors of Leoman's renegade army.

He had heard that those warriors were in a drug-fuelled frenzy, that they fought without regard to injury, and that none retreated, dying where they stood. What he had expected, truth be told. A last stand, a heroic, martyred defence. For that was what Y'Ghatan had been, what it was, and what it would always be.

They would take this city. The Adjunct would have her first true victory. Bloody, brutal, but a victory nonetheless.

He stood one street in from the breach, smouldering rubble behind him, watching the line of wounded and unconscious soldiers being helped back to the healers in camp, watching fresh infantry filing forward, through the secured areas, and ahead to the battle that was the closing of the Malazan fist around Leoman and his followers, around the last living vestiges of the rebellion itself.

He saw that Red Blade officer of Tene Baralta's, Lostara Yil, leading three squads towards the distant sounds of fighting. And Tene himself stood nearby, speaking with Captain Kindly.

Keneb had sent Faradan Sort ahead, to make contact with the advance squads. There was to be a second rendezvous, near the palace itself, and hopefully everyone was still following the battle plan.

Shouts, then cries of alarm – *from behind him. From outside the breach!* Fist Keneb spun round, and saw a wall of flame rising in the killing field beyond – where the narrow, deep trench had been dug by Leoman's warriors. Buried urns filled with olive oil began exploding from the trench, spraying burning liquid everywhere. Keneb saw the line of retreating wounded scatter apart near the trench, figures aflame. Shrieks, the roar of fire—

His horrified gaze caught motion to his right, up on the nearest building's rooftop, where it faced onto the rubble of the breach. A figure, lantern in one hand, flaring torch in the other – bedecked in web-slung flasks, surrounded by amphorae, at the very edge of the roof, arms outstretched, kicking over the tall clay jars – ropes affixed between them and his ankles, the weight then plunging the figure over the side.

Down into the rubble of the breach.

He struck, vanished from view, then a sudden flaring of flames, rushing out in sheets—

And Keneb saw, upon other rooftops, lining the city's walls, more figures – flinging themselves down. Down, then the glow of raging fire, rising up, encircling – from the bastions, more flames, billowing out, spreading wild like a flood unleashed.

Heat rushed upon Keneb, driving him back a step. Oil from shattered casks, beneath the wreckage of fallen wall and collapsed buildings, suddenly caught flame. The breach was closing, demonic fire lunging into sight.

Keneb looked about, horror rising within him, and saw the half-dozen signallers of his staff huddled near a fragment of rubble. Bellowing, he ran to them. 'Sound the recall! Damn you, soldiers, sound the recall!'

Northwest of Y'Ghatan, Temul and a company of Wickans rode up the slope to the Lothal road. They had seen no-one. Not a single soul fleeing the city. The Fourteenth's horse-warriors had fully encircled it. Wickans, Seti, Burned Tears. There would be no escape.

Temul had been pleased, hearing that the Adjunct's thinking had followed identical tracks with his own. A sudden strike, hard as a knife pushed into a chest, straight into the heart of this cursed rebellion. They had heard the munitions go off – loud, louder than expected, and had seen the flame-shot black clouds billowing upward, along with most of Y'Ghatan's south wall.

Reining in on the road, seeing beneath them the signs of the massive exodus that had clogged this route only days earlier.

A flaring of firelight, distant rumbling, as of thunder, and the horse-warriors turned as one to face the city. Where walls of flame rose behind the stone walls, from the bastions, and the sealed gates, then, building after building within, more flames, and more.

Temul stared, his mind battered by what he was seeing, what he now understood.

A third of the Fourteenth Army was in that city by now. A third.

And they were already as good as dead.

Fist Blistig stood beside the Adjunct on the road. He felt sick inside, the feeling rising up from a place and a time he had believed left behind him. Standing on the walls of Aren, watching the slaughter of Coltaine's army. Hopeless, helpless—

'Fist,' the Adjunct snapped, 'get more soldiers filling in that trench.'

He started, then half-turned and gestured towards one of his aides – the woman had heard the command, for she nodded and hurried off. *Douse the trench, aye. But . . . what's the point?* The breach had found a new wall, this one of flames. And more had risen all round the city, beginning just within the tiered walls, buildings bursting, voicing terrible roars as fiery oil exploded out, flinging mud-bricks that were themselves deadly, burning missiles. And now, further in, at junctures and along the wider streets, more buildings were igniting. One, just beyond the palace, had moments earlier erupted, with geysers of burning oil shooting skyward, obliterating the darkness, revealing the sky filling with tumbling black clouds.

'Nil, Nether,' the Adjunct said in a brittle voice, 'gather our mages – all of them – I want the flames smothered in the breach. I want—'

'Adjunct,' Nether cut in, 'we have not the power.'

'The old earth spirits,' Nil added in a dull tone, 'are dying, fleeing the flames, the baking agony, all dying or fleeing. Something is about to be born . . .'

Before them, the city of Y'Ghatan was brightening into day, yet a lurid, terrible day.

Coughing, staggering, wounded soldiers half-carried, half-dragged through the press – but there was nowhere to go. Keneb stared – the air burning his eyes – at the mass of his soldiers. Seven, eight hundred. Where were the others? But he knew.

Gone. Dead.

In the streets beyond, he could see naught but fire, leaping from building to building, filling the fierce, hot air, with a voice of glee, demonic, hungry and eager.

He needed to do something. Think of something, but this heat, this terrible heat – his lungs were heaving, desperate despite the searing pain that blossomed with each strained breath. Lungful after lungful, yet it was as if the air itself had died, all life sucked from it, and so could offer him nothing.

His own armour was cooking him alive. He was on his knees, now, with all the others. 'Armour!' he rasped, not knowing if anyone could hear him. 'Get it off! Armour! Weapons!' *Gods below, my chest – the pain—*

A blade-on-blade parry, holding contact, two edges rasping against each other, then, as the warrior pushed harder with his scimitar, Lostara Yil ducked low, disengaged her sword downward, slashing up and under, taking him in the throat. Blood poured out. Stepping past, she batted aside another weapon thrusting at her – a spear – hearing splinters from the shaft as she pushed it to one side. In her left hand was her kethra knife, which she punched into her foe's belly, twisting as she yanked it back out again.

Lostara staggered free of the crumpling warrior, a flood of sorrow shooting through her as she heard him call out a woman's name before he struck the cobbles.

The fight raged on all sides, her three squads now down to fewer than a dozen soldiers, whilst yet more of the berserk fanatics closed in from the flanking buildings – market shops, shuttered doors kicked down and now billowing smoke, carrying out into the street the reek of overheated oil, spitting, crackling sounds – something went *thump* and all at once there was fire—

Everywhere.

Lostara Yil cried out a warning, even as another warrior rushed her. Parrying with the knife, stop-thrusting with her sword, then kicking the impaled body from her blade, his sagging weight nearly tugging the weapon from her hand.

Terrible shrieks behind her. She whirled.

A flood of burning oil, roaring out from buildings to either side, sweeping among the fighters – their legs, then clothes – telaba, leathers, linens, the flames appearing all over them. Warrior and soldier, the fire held to no allegiance – it was devouring everyone.

She staggered away from that onrushing river of death, stumbled and fell, sprawling, onto a corpse, clambered onto it a moment before fiery

261

oil poured around her, swept past her already burning island of torn flesh—

A building exploded, the fireball expanding outward, plunging towards her. She cried out, throwing up both arms, as the searing incandescence reached out to take her—

A hand from behind, snagging her harness—

Pain – the breath torn from her lungs – then . . . nothing.

'Stay low!' Balm shouted as he led his squad down the twisting alley. After his bellowed advice, the sergeant resumed his litany of curses. They were lost. Pushed back in their efforts to return to Keneb and the breach, they were now being herded. By flames. They had seen the palace a short while earlier, through a momentary break in the smoke, and as far as Balm could determine they were still heading in that direction – but the world beyond had vanished, in fire and smoke, and pursuing in their wake was the growing conflagration. Alive, and hunting them.

'It's building, Sergeant! We got to get out of this city!'

'You think I don't know that, Widdershins? What in Hood's name do you think we're trying to do here? Now be quiet—'

'We're gonna run out of air.'

'We are already, you idiot! Now shut that mouth of yours!'

They reached an intersection and Balm halted his soldiers. Six alley-mouths beckoned, each leading into tracks as twisted and dark as the next. Smoke was tumbling from two of them, on their left. Head spinning, every breath growing more pained, less invigorating, the Dal Honese wiped hot sweat from his eyes and turned to study his soldiers. Deadsmell, Throatslitter, Widdershins, Galt and Lobe. Tough bastards one and all. This wasn't the right way to die – there were right ones, and this wasn't one of them. 'Gods,' he muttered, 'I'll never look at a hearth the same again.'

'You got that right, Sergeant,' said Throatslitter, punctuating his agreement with a hacking cough.

Balm pulled off his helm. 'Strip down, you damned fools, before we bake ourselves. Hold on to your weapons, if you can. We ain't dying here tonight. You understand me? All of you listen – do you understand me?'

'Aye, Sergeant,' Throatslitter said. 'We hear you.'

'Good. Now, Widdershins, got any magic to make us a path? Anything at all?'

The mage shook his head. 'Wish I did. Maybe soon, though.'

'What do you mean?'

'I mean a fire elemental's being born here, I think. A fire spirit, a godling. We got a firestorm on the way, and that will announce its arrival – and that's when we die if we ain't dead already. But an elemental is alive. It's got a will, a mind, damned hungry and eager to kill. But it knows fear, fear because it knows it won't last long – too fierce, too hot – days at best. And it knows other kinds of fear, too, and that's where maybe I can do something – illusions. Of water, but not just water. A water elemental.' He stared round at the others, who were all staring back, then shrugged. 'Maybe, maybe not. How smart is an elemental? Got to be smart to be fooled, you see. Dog-smart, at least, better if it was smarter. Problem is, not everybody agrees that elementals even exist. I mean, I'm convinced it's a good theory—'

Balm cracked him across the head. 'All this on a *theory*? You wasted all that air on that? Gods below, Widdershins, I'm minded to kill you right now.' He rose. 'Let's get going, while we can. To Hood with the damned palace – let's take the alley opposite and when the theoretical elemental arrives we can shake its hand and curse it to the nonexistent Abyss. Come on – and you, Widdershins, not another word, got it?'

The soldier returned, wreathed in flames. Running, running from the pain, but there was nowhere to go. Captain Faradan Sort aimed the crossbow and loosed a quarrel. Watched the poor man fall, grow still as the flames leapt all over him, blackening the skin, cracking open the flesh. She turned away. 'Last quarrel,' she said, tossing the weapon to one side.

Her new lieutenant, with the mouthful name of Madan'Tul Rada, said nothing – a characteristic Faradan was already used to, and of which she was, most of the time, appreciative.

Except now, when they were about to roast. 'All right,' she said, 'scratch that route – and I'm out of scouts. No back, no forward, and, from the looks of it, no left and no right. Any suggestions?'

Madan'Tul Rada's expression soured, jaw edging down as tongue probed a likely rotted molar, then he spat, squinted in the smoke, and unslung his round shield to study its charred face. Looked up again, slowly tracking, then: 'No.'

They could hear a wind above them, shrieking, whirling round and round over the city, drawing the flames up, spinning tails of fire that slashed like giant swords through the convulsing smoke. It was getting harder and harder to breathe.

The lieutenant's head lifted suddenly, and he faced the wall of flame up the street, then rose.

Faradan Sort followed suit, for she could now see what he had seen – a strange black stain spreading out within the flames, the tongues of fire flickering back, dying, the stain deepening, circular, and out from its heart staggered a figure shedding charred leathers, clasps and buckles falling away to bounce on the street.

Stumbling towards them, flames dancing in the full head of hair – dancing, yet not burning. Closer, and Faradan Sort saw it was a girl, a face she then recognized. 'She's from Cord's Ashok squad. That's Sinn.'

'How did she do that?' Madan'Tul Rada asked.

'I don't know, but let's hope she can do it again. Soldier! Over here!'

An upper level had simply sheared away, down, crashing in an explosion of dust and smoke onto the street. Where Bowl had been crouching. He had not even seen it coming, Hellian suspected. *Lucky bastard.* She looked back at her squad. Blistered, red as boiled lobsters. Armour shed, weapons flung away – too hot to hold. Marines and heavies. Herself the only sergeant. Two corporals – Urb and Reem – their expressions dulled. Red-eyed all of them, gasping in the dying air, damn near hairless. *Not much longer, I think. Gods, what I would do for a drink right now. Something nice. Chilled, delicate, the drunk coming on slow and sly, peaceful sleep beckoning as sweet as the last trickle down my ravaged throat. Gods, I'm a poet when it comes to drink, oh yes.* 'Okay, that way's blocked now. Let's take this damned alley—'

'Why?' Touchy demanded.

'Because I don't see flames down there, that's why. We keep moving until we can't move no more, got it?'

'Why don't we just stay right here – another building's bound to land on us sooner or later.'

'Tell you what,' Hellian snarled. 'You do just that, but me, I ain't waiting for nothing. You want to die alone, you go right ahead.'

She set off.

Everyone followed. There was nothing else to do.

Eighteen soldiers – Strings had carried them through. Three more skirmishes, bloody and without mercy, and now they crouched before the palace gates – which yawned wide, a huge mouth filled with fire. Smoke billowed above the fortification, glowing in the night. Bottle, on his knees, gasping, slowly looked round at his fellow soldiers. A few heavies, the whole of Strings's squad, and most of Sergeant Cord's, along with the few marines surviving from Borduke's squad.

They had hoped, prayed, even, to arrive and find other squads – anyone, more survivors, defying this damned conflagration . . . this far. *Just this far, that's all. It would have been enough.* But they were alone, with no sign anywhere that any other Malazans had made it.

If Leoman of the Flails was in the palace, he was naught but ashes, now.

'Crump, Maybe, Cuttle, over to me,' Strings ordered, crouching and setting down his satchel. 'Any other sappers? No? Anyone carrying munitions? All right, I just checked mine – the wax is way too soft and getting softer – it's all gonna go up, and that's the plan. All of it, except the burners – toss those – the rest goes right into the mouth of that palace—'

'What's the point?' Cord demanded. 'I mean, fine by me if you're thinking it's a better way to go.'

'I want to try and blow a hole in this growing firestorm – knock it back – and we're heading through that hole, for as long as it survives – Hood knows where it'll lead. But I don't see any fire right behind the palace, and that'll do for me. Problems with that, Cord?'

'No. I love it. It's brilliant. Genius. If only I hadn't tossed my helm away.'

A few laughs. *Good sign.*

Then hacking coughs. *Bad sign.*

Someone shrieked, and Bottle turned to see a figure lumbering out from a nearby building, flasks and bottles hanging from him, another bottle in one hand, a torch in the other – heading straight for them. And they had discarded their crossbows.

A bellowing answer from a soldier in Cord's squad, and the man, Bell, rushed forward to intercept the fanatic.

'Get back!' Cord screamed.

Sprinting, Bell flung himself at the man, colliding with him twenty paces away, and both went down.

Bottle dropped flat, rolled away, bumping up against other soldiers doing the same.

A whoosh, then more screams. Terrible screams. And a wave of heat, blistering, fierce as the breath of a forge.

Then Strings was swearing, scrambling with his collection of satchels. 'Away from the palace! Everyone!'

'Not me!' Cuttle growled. 'You need help.'

'Fine. Everyone else! Sixty, seventy paces at least! More if you can! Go!'

Bottle climbed upright, watched as Strings and Cuttle ran crab-like towards the palace gates. Then he looked round. *Sixty paces? We ain't got sixty paces* – flames were devouring buildings in every direction he could see, now.

Still, as far away as possible. He began running.

And found himself colliding with someone – who gripped his left arm and spun him round.

Gesler. And behind him Thom Tissy, then a handful of soldiers. 'What are those fools doing?' Gesler demanded.

'Blow – a hole – through the storm—'

'Puckered gods of the Abyss. Sands – you still got your munitions?'

'Aye, Sergeant—'

'Damned fool. Give 'em to me—'

'No,' said Truth, stepping in between. 'I'll take them. We've gone through fire before, right, Sergeant?' With that he snatched the satchel from Sands's hands and ran towards the palace gates—

Where Strings and Cuttle had been forced back – the heat too fierce, the flames slashing bright arms out at them.

'Damn him!' Gesler hissed. 'That was a different kind of fire—'

Bottle pulled loose from the sergeant's grip. 'We got to get going! Away!'

Moments later all were running – except Gesler, who was heading towards the sappers outside the gate. Bottle hesitated. He could not help it. He had to see—

Truth reached Cuttle and Strings, tugged their bags away, slung them over a shoulder, then shouted something and ran towards the palace gates.

Both sappers leapt to their feet, retreating, intercepting Gesler – who looked determined to follow his young recruit – Cuttle and Strings dragged the sergeant back. Gesler struggled, turning a ravaged face in Truth's direction—

But the soldier had plunged into the flames.

Bottle ran back, joined with the two sappers to help drag a shrieking Gesler away.

Away.

They had managed thirty paces down the street, heading towards a huddled mass of soldiers shying from a wall of flames, when the palace blew up behind them.

And out, huge sections of stone flung skyward.

Batted into the air, tumbling in a savage wind, Bottle rolled in the midst of bouncing rubble, limbs and bodies, faces, mouths opened wide, everyone screaming – in silence. No sound – no ... *nothing.*

Pain in his head, stabbing fierce in his ears, a pressure closing on his temples, his skull ready to implode—

The wind suddenly reversed, pulling sheets of flame after it, closing in from every street. The pressure loosed. And the flames drew back, writhing like tentacles.

Then the air was still.

Coughing, staggering upright, Bottle turned.

The palace's heart was gone, split asunder, and naught but dust and smoke filled the vast swath of rubble.

'*Now!*' Strings shrieked, his voice sounding leagues away. 'Go! Everyone! *Go!*'

The wind returned, sudden, a scream rising to a wail, pushing them onward – onto the battered road between jagged, sagging palace walls.

Dunsparrow had been first to the temple doors, shoving them wide even as explosions of fire lit up the horizon, all round the city . . . *all within the city walls.*

Gasping, heart pounding and something like a knife-blade twisting in his gut, Corabb Bhilan Thenu'alas followed Leoman and the Malazan woman into the Temple of Scalissara, L'oric two paces behind him.

No, not Scalissara – the Queen of Dreams. Scalissara the matron goddess of olive oil would not have . . . no, she would not have allowed this. Not . . . this.

And things had begun to make sense. Terrible, awful sense, like chiselled stones fitting together, raising a wall between humanity . . . and what Leoman of the Flails had become.

The warriors – who had ridden with them, lived with them since the rebellion first began, who had fought at their side against the Malazans, who even now fought like fiends in the streets – they were all going to die. Y'Ghatan, this whole city, *it's going to die.*

Hurrying down the central hallway, into the nave, from which gusted a cold, dusty wind, wind that seemed to come from nowhere and every-where at once. Reeking of mould, rot and death.

Leoman spun to L'oric. 'Open a gate, High Mage! Quickly!'

'You must not do this,' Corabb said to his commander. 'We must die, this night. Fighting in the name of Dryjhna—'

'Hood take Dryjhna!' Leoman rasped.

L'oric was staring at Leoman, as if seeing him, understanding him, for the first time. 'A moment,' he said.

'We've no time for that!'

'Leoman of the Flails,' the High Mage said, unperturbed, 'you have bargained with the Queen of Dreams. A precipitous thing to do. That goddess has no interest in what's right and what's wrong. If she once possessed a heart, she flung it away long ago. And now you have drawn me into this – you have used me, so that a goddess may make use of me in turn. I do not—'

'The gate, damn you! If you have objections, L'oric, raise them with *her*!'

'They are all to die,' Corabb said, backing away from his commander, 'so that you can live.'

'So that *we* can live, Corabb! There is no other way – do you think that the Malazans would ever leave us be? No matter where or how far we fled? I thank Hood's dusty feet the Claw hasn't struck already, but I do not intend to live the rest of my life looking over my shoulder! I was a bodyguard, damn you – it was *her* cause, not mine!'

'Your warriors – they expected you to fight at their sides—'

'They expected nothing of the sort. The fools wanted to die. In Dryjhna's name.' He bared his teeth in contempt. 'Well, let them! Let them die! And best of all, they are going to take half the Adjunct's army with them. There's your glory, Corabb!' He advanced on him, pointing towards the temple doors. 'You want to join the fools? You want to feel your lungs searing with the heat, your eyes bursting, skin cracking? You want your blood to boil in your veins?'

'An honourable death, Leoman of the Flails, compared to this.'

He voiced something like a snarl, spun back to L'oric. 'Open the way – and fear not, I made no promises to her regarding you, beyond bringing you here.'

'The fire grows into life outside this temple, Leoman,' L'oric said. 'I may not succeed.'

'Your chances diminish with each moment that passes,' Leoman said in a growl.

There was panic in the man's eyes. Corabb studied it, the way it seemed so . . . out of place. There, in the features he thought he knew so well. Knew every expression possible. Anger, cold amusement, disdain, the stupor and lidded eyes within the fumes of durhang. Every expression . . . except this one. Panic.

Everything was crumbling inside, and Corabb could feel himself drowning. Sinking ever deeper, reaching up towards a light that grew ever more distant, dimmer.

With a hissed curse, L'oric faced the altar. Its stones seemed to glow in the gloom, so new, the marble unfamiliar – from some other continent, Corabb suspected – traced through with purple veins and capillaries that seemed to pulse. There was a circular pool beyond the altar, the water steaming – it had been covered the last time they had visited; he could see the copper panels that had sealed it lying against a side-wall.

The air swirled above the altar.

She was waiting on the other side. A flicker, as if reflected from the pool of water, then the portal opened, engulfing the altar, edges spreading, curling black, then wavering fitfully. L'oric gasped, straining beneath some invisible burden. 'I cannot hold this long! I see you, Queen!'

From the portal came a languid, cool voice, 'L'oric, son of Osserc. I seek no geas from you.'

'Then what do you want?'

A moment, during which the portal wavered, then: 'Sha'ik is dead.

The Whirlwind Goddess is no more. Leoman of the Flails, a question.'
A new tone to her voice, something like irony. 'Is Y'Ghatan – what you
have done here – is this your Apocalypse?'

The desert warrior scowled, then said, 'Well, yes.' He shrugged. 'Not
as big as we'd hoped . . .'

'But, perhaps, enough. L'oric. The role of Sha'ik, the Seer of Dryjhna,
is . . . vacant. It needs to be filled—'

'Why?' L'oric demanded.

'Lest something else, something less desirable, assume the mantle.'

'And the likelihood of that?'

'Imminent.'

Corabb watched the High Mage, sensed a rush of thoughts behind
the man's eyes, as mysterious implications fell into place following the
goddess's words. Then, 'You have chosen someone.'

'Yes.'

'Someone who needs . . . protecting.'

'Yes.'

'Is that someone in danger?'

'Very much so, L'oric. Indeed, my desires have been anticipated, and
we may well have run out of time.'

'Very well. I accept.'

'Come forward, then. You, and the others. Do not delay – I too am
sorely tried maintaining this path.'

His soul nothing but ashes, Corabb watched the High Mage stride
into the portal, and vanish within the swirling, liquid stain.

Leoman faced him one more time, his voice almost pleading as he
said, 'My friend . . .'

Corabb Bhilan Thenu'alas shook his head.

'Did you not hear? Another Sha'ik – a new Sha'ik—'

'And will you find her a new army as well, Leoman? More fools to
lead to their deaths? No, I am done with you, Leoman of the Flails.
Take your Malazan wench and be gone from my sight. I choose to die
here, with my fellow warriors.'

Dunsparrow reached out and grasped Leoman's arm. 'The portal's
crumbling, Leoman.'

The warrior, last commander of Dryjhna, turned away, and, the
woman at his side, strode into the gate. Moments later it dissolved, and
there was nothing.

Nothing but the strange, swirling wind, skirling dust-devils tracking
the inlaid tile floor.

Corabb blinked, looked round. Outside the temple, it seemed the
world was ending, voicing a death-cry ever rising in timbre. *No . . . not
a death-cry. Something else . . .*

Hearing a closer sound – from a side passage – a scuffle – Corabb drew his scimitar. Approached the curtain barring the corridor. With the tip of his blade, he swung the cloth aside.

To see children. Crouching, huddled. Ten, fifteen – sixteen in all. Smudged faces, wide eyes, all looking up at him. 'Oh gods,' he murmured. 'They have forgotten you.'

They all have. Every single one of them.

He sheathed his weapon and stepped forward. 'It's all right,' he said. 'We shall find us a room, yes? And wait this out.'

Something else . . . Thunder, the death of buildings, the burgeoning wails of fire, howling winds. *This is what is outside, the world beyond, this . . . spirits below, Dryjhna—*

Outside, the birth-cries of the Apocalypse rose still higher.

'There!' Throatslitter said, pointing.

Sergeant Balm blinked, the smoke and heat like broken glass in his eyes, and could just make out a half-score figures crossing the street before them. 'Who?'

'Malazans,' Throatslitter said.

From behind Balm: 'Great, more for the clam-bake, what a night we're going to have—'

'When I said be quiet, Widdershins, I meant it. All right, let's go meet them. Maybe they ain't as lost as us.'

'Oh yeah? Look who's leading them! That drunk, what's her name? They're probably trying to find a bar!'

'I ain't lying, Widdershins! One more word and I'll skewer you!'

Urb's huge hand landed on her arm, gripping hard, turning her round, and Hellian saw a squad stumbling towards them. 'Thank the gods,' she said in a ravaged voice, 'they got to know where they're going—'

A sergeant approached in a half-crouch. Dal Honese, his face patchy with dried mud. 'I'm Balm,' he said. 'Wherever you're headed, we're with you!'

Hellian scowled. 'Fine,' she said. 'Just fall in and we'll all be rosy in no time.'

'Got us a way out?'

'Yeah, down that alley.'

'Great. What's down there?'

'The only place not yet burning, you Dal Honese monk-rat!' She waved at her troop and they continued on. Something was visible ahead. A huge, smudgy dome of some kind. They were passing temples now, the doors swinging wide, banging in the gusting, furnace-hot wind. What little clothes she was still wearing had begun smoking, thready wisps stretching out from the rough weave. She could smell her own burning hair.

A soldier came up alongside her. He was holding twin long-knives in gloved hands. 'You ain't got no cause to curse Sergeant Balm, woman. He brought us through this far.'

'What's your name?' Hellian demanded.

'Throatslitter—'

'Nice. Now go and slit your own throat. Nobody's gotten through nowhere, you damned idiot. Now, unless you got a bottle of chilled wine under that shirt, go find someone else to annoy.'

'You was nicer drunk,' he said, falling back.

Yeah, everyone's nicer drunk.

At the far edge of the collapsed palace, Limp's left leg was trapped by a sliding piece of stonework, his screams loud enough to challenge the fiery wind. Cord, Shard and a few others from the Ashok squad pulled him free, but it was clear the soldier's leg was broken.

Ahead was a plaza of some sort, once the site of a market of some kind, and beyond it rose a huge domed temple behind a high wall. Remnants of gold leaf trickled down the dome's flanks like rainwater. A heavy layer of smoke roiled across the scene, making the dome seem to float in the air, firelit and smeared. Strings gestured for everyone to close in.

'We're heading for that temple,' he said. 'It likely won't help – there's a damned firestorm coming. Never seen one myself, and I'm wishing that was still the case. Anyway,' he paused to cough, then spit, 'I can't think of anything else.'

'Sergeant,' Bottle said, frowning, 'I sense . . . something. Life. In that temple.'

'All right, maybe we'll have to fight to find a place to die. Fine. Maybe there's enough of 'em to kill us all and that ain't so bad.'

No, Sergeant. Nowhere close. But never mind.

'All right, let's try and get across this plaza.'

It looked easy, but they were running out of air, and the winds racing across the concourse were blistering hot – no cover provided by building walls. Bottle knew they might not make it. Rasping heat tore at his eyes, poured like sand into his throat with every gasping breath. Through blurred pain, he saw figures appear off to his right, racing out of the smoke. Ten, fifteen, then scores, spilling onto the concourse, some of them on fire, others with spears— 'Sergeant!'

'Gods below!'

The warriors were attacking. Here, in this square, this . . . furnace.

271

Burning figures fell away, stumbling, clawing at their faces, but the others came on.

'Form up!' Strings bellowed. 'Fighting retreat – to that temple wall!'

Bottle stared at the closing mass. Form up? Fighting retreat? *With what?*

One of Cord's soldiers appeared beside him, and the man reached out, gesturing. 'You! A mage, right?'

Bottle nodded.

'I'm Ebron – we got to take these bastards on – with magic – no other weapons left—'

'All right. Whatever you got, I'll add to it.'

Three heavy infantry, the women Flashwit, Mayfly and Uru Hela, had drawn knives and were forming up a front line. A heartbeat later, Shortnose joined them, huge hands closed into fists.

The lead score of attackers closed to within fifteen paces, and launched their spears as if they were javelins. In the momentary flash of the shafts crossing the short distance, Bottle saw that the wood had ignited, spinning wreaths of smoke.

Shouted warnings, then the solid impact of the heavy weapons. Uru Hela was spun round, a spear transfixing her left shoulder, the shaft scything into Mayfly's neck with a cracking sound. As Uru Hela stumbled to her knees, Mayfly staggered, then straightened. Sergeant Strings sprawled, a spear impaling his right leg. Swearing, he pulled at it, his other leg kicking like a thing gone mad. Tavos Pond staggered into Bottle, knocking him down as the soldier, one side of his face slashed away, the eye dangling, stumbled on, screaming.

Moments before the frenzied attackers reached them, a wave of sorcery rose in a wall of billowing, argent smoke, sweeping out to engulf the warriors. Shrieks, bodies falling, skin and flesh blackening, curling away from bones. Sudden horror.

Bottle had no idea what kind of magic Ebron was using, but he unleashed Meanas, redoubling the smoke's thickness and breadth – illusional, but panic tore into the warriors. Falling, tumbling out of the smoke, hands at their eyes, writhing, vomit gushing onto the cobbles. The attack shattered against the sorcery, and as the wind whipped the poisonous cloud away, they could see nothing but fleeing figures, already well beyond the heap of bodies.

Bodies smouldering, catching fire.

Koryk had reached Strings, who had pulled the spear from his leg, and began stuffing knots of cloth into the puncture wounds. Bottle went to them – no spurting blood from the holes, he saw. Still, lots of blood had smeared the cobbles. 'Wrap that leg!' he ordered the half-Seti. 'We've got to get off this plaza!'

Cord and Corporal Tulip were attending to Uru Hela, whilst Scant and Balgrid had chased down and tackled Tavos Pond to the ground. Bottle watched as Scant pushed the dangling eye back into its socket, then fumbled with a cloth to wrap round the soldier's head.

'Drag the wounded!' Sergeant Gesler yelled. 'Come on, you damned fools! To that wall! We need to find us a way in!'

Numbed, Bottle reached down to help Koryk lift Strings.

He saw that his fingers had turned blue. He was deafened by a roaring in his head, and everything was spinning round him.

Air. We need air.

The wall rose before them, and then they were skirting it. Seeking a way in.

Lying in heaps, dying of asphyxiation. Keneb pulled himself across shattered stone, blistered hands clawing through the rubble. Blinding smoke, searing heat, and now he could feel his mind, starving, disintegrating – wild, disjointed visions – a woman, a man, a child, striding out from the flames.

Demons, servants of Hood.

Voices, so loud, the wail endless, growing – and darkness flowed out from the three apparitions, poured over the hundreds of bodies—

Yes, his mind was dying. For he felt a sudden falling off of the vicious heat, and sweet air filled his lungs. *Dying, what else can this be? I have arrived. At Hood's Gate. Gods, such blessed relief*— Someone's hands pulled at him – spasms of agony from fingers pressing into burnt skin – and he was being rolled over.

Blinking, staring up into a smeared, blistered face. A woman. He knew her.

And she was speaking.

We're all dead, now. Friends. Gathering at Hood's Gate—

'Fist Keneb! There are hundreds here!'

Yes.

'Still alive! Sinn is keeping the fire back, but she can't hold on much longer! We're going to try and push through! Do you understand me! We need help, we need to get everyone on their feet!'

What? 'Captain,' he whispered. 'Captain Faradan Sort.'

'Yes! Now, on your feet, Fist!'

A storm of fire was building above Y'Ghatan. Blistig had never seen anything like it. Flames, twisting, spinning, slashing out long tendrils that seemed to shatter the billowing smoke. Wild winds tore into the clouds, annihilating them in flashes of red.

The heat— *Gods below, this has happened before. This Hood-damned city . . .*

A corner bastion exploded in a vast fireball, the leaping gouts writhing, climbing—

The wind that struck them from behind staggered everyone on the road. In the besiegers' camp, tents were torn from their moorings, flung into the air, then racing in wild billows towards Y'Ghatan. Horses screamed amidst curtains of sand and dust rising up, whipping like the fiercest storm.

Blistig found himself on his knees. A gloved hand closed on his cloak collar, pulled him round. He found himself staring into a face that, for a moment, he did not recognize. Dirt, sweat, tears, and an expression buckled by panic – the Adjunct. *'Pull the camp back! Everyone!'*

He could barely hear her, yet he nodded, turned into the wind and fought his way down from the road. *Something is about to be born, Nil said. Something . . .*

The Adjunct was shouting. More commands. Blistig, reaching the edge of the road, dragged himself down onto the back slope. Nil and Nether moved past him, towards where the Adjunct still stood on the road.

The initial blast of wind had eased slightly, this time a longer, steadier breath drawn in towards the city and its burgeoning conflagration.

'There are soldiers!' the Adjunct screamed. 'Beyond the breach! I want them out!'

The child Grub clambered up the slope, flanked by the dogs Bent and Roach.

And now other figures were swarming past Blistig. Khundryl. Warlocks, witches. Keening voices, jabbering undercurrents, a force building, rising from the battered earth. Fist Blistig twisted round – a ritual, magic, what were they doing? He shot a glance back at the chaos of the encampment, saw officers amidst scrambling figures – they weren't fools. They were already pulling back—

Nil's voice, loud from the road. 'We can feel her! Someone! Spirits below, *such power!*'

'Help her, damn you!'

A witch shrieked, bursting into flames on the road. Moments later, two warlocks huddled near Blistig seemed to melt before his eyes, crumbling into white ash. He stared in horror. *Help her? Help who? What is happening?* He pulled himself onto the road's edge once more.

And could see, in the heart of the breach, a darkening within the flames.

Fire flickered round another witch, then snapped out as *something* rolled over everyone on the road – cool, sweet power – *like a merciful god's breath*. Even Blistig, despiser of all things magic, could feel this emanation, this terrible, beautiful will.

Driving the flames in the breach back, opening a swirling dark tunnel.

From which figures staggered.

Nether was on her knees near the Adjunct – the only person on the road still standing – and Blistig saw the Wickan girl turn to Tavore, heard her say, 'It's Sinn. Adjunct, that child's a High Mage. And she doesn't even know it—'

The Adjunct turned, saw Blistig.

'Fist! On your feet. Squads and healers forward. Now! They're coming through – Fist Blistig, do you understand me? They need help!'

He clambered to his knees, but got no further. He stared at the woman. She was no more than a silhouette, the world behind her nothing but flames, a firestorm growing, ever growing. Something cold, riven through with terror, filled his chest.

A vision.

He could only stare.

Tavore snarled, then turned to the scrawny boy standing nearby. 'Grub! Find some officers down in our camp! We need—'

'Yes, Adjunct! Seven hundred and ninety-one, Adjunct. Fist Keneb. Fist Tene Baralta. Alive. I'm going to get help now.'

And then he was running past Blistig, down the slope, the dogs padding along in his wake.

A vision. An omen, yes. I know now, what awaits us. At the far end. At the far end of this long, long road. Oh gods . . .

She had turned about, now, her back to him. She was staring at the burning city, at the pathetic, weaving line of survivors stumbling through the tunnel. Seven hundred and ninety-one. Out of three thousand.

But she is blind. Blind to what I see.

The Adjunct Tavore. And a burning world.

The doors slammed open, pulling in an undercurrent of smoke and heat that swept across Corabb's ankles, then up and round, the smoke massing in the dome, pulled and tugged by wayward currents. The warrior stepped in front of the huddled children and drew out his scimitar.

He heard voices – Malazan – then saw figures appearing from the hallway's gloom. Soldiers, a woman in the lead. Seeing Corabb, they halted.

A man stepped past the woman. His blistered face bore the mangled traces of tattooing. 'I am Iutharal Galt,' he said in a ragged voice. 'Pardu—'

'Traitor,' Corabb snapped. 'I am Corabb Bhilan Thenu'alas, Second to Leoman of the Flails. You, Pardu, are a traitor.'

'Does that matter any more? We're all dead now, anyway.'

'Enough of this,' a midnight-skinned soldier said in badly accented Ehrlii. 'Throatslitter, go and kill the fool—'

'Wait!' the Pardu said, then ducked his head and added: 'Sergeant. Please. There ain't no point to this—'

'It was these bastards that led us into this trap, Galt,' the sergeant said.

'No,' Corabb said, drawing their attention once more. 'Leoman of the Flails has brought us to this. He and he alone. We – we were all betrayed—'

'And where's he hiding?' the one named Throatslitter asked, hefting his long-knives, a murderous look in his pale eyes.

'Fled.'

'Temul will have him, then,' Iutharal Galt said, turning to the sergeant. 'They've surrounded the city—'

'No use,' Corabb cut in. 'He did not leave that way.' He gestured behind him, towards the altar. 'A sorcerous gate. The Queen of Dreams – she took him from here. Him and High Mage L'oric and a Malazan woman named Dunsparrow—'

The doors opened once again and the Malazans whirled, then, as voices approached – cries of pain, coughing, cursing – they relaxed. More brethren, Corabb realized. More of the damned enemy. But the Pardu had been right. The only enemy now was fire. He swung back to look upon the children, flinched at their terror-filled eyes, and turned round once more, for he had nothing to say to them. Nothing worth hearing.

As he stumbled into the hallway, Bottle gasped. Cold, dusty air, rushing past him – where? how? – and then Cuttle pushed the doors shut once more, swearing as he burned his hands.

Ahead, at the threshold leading into the altar chamber, stood more Malazans. Balm and his squad. The Kartoolian drunk, Hellian. Corporal Reem and a few others from Sobelone's heavies. And, beyond them in the nave itself, a lone rebel warrior, and behind him, children.

But the air – the air . . .

Koryk and Tarr dragged Strings past him. Mayfly and Flashwit had drawn their meat-knives again, even as the rebel flung his scimitar to one side, the weapon clanging hollowly on the tiled floor. *Gods below, one of them has actually surrendered.*

Heat was radiating from the stone walls – the firestorm outside would not spare this temple for much longer. The last twenty paces round the temple corner to the front façade had nearly killed them – no wind, the air filled with the crack of exploding bricks, buckling cobblestones, the flames seeming to feed upon the very air itself, roaring down the streets, spiralling upward, flaring like huge hooded snakes above the city. And the sound – he could hear it still, beyond the walls, closing in – the sound . . . *is terrible. Terrible.*

Gesler and Cord strode over to Balm and Hellian, and Bottle moved closer to listen in on their conversation.

'Anybody here worship the Queen of Dreams?' Gesler asked.

Hellian shrugged. 'I figure it's a little late to start. Anyway, Corabb Bhilan Thenu'alas – our prisoner over there – he said Leoman's already done that deal with her. Of course, maybe she ain't into playing favourites—'

A sudden loud crack startled everyone – the altar had just shattered – and Bottle saw that Crump, the insane saboteur, had just finished pissing on it.

Hellian laughed. 'Well, scratch that idea.'

'Hood's balls,' Gesler hissed. 'Someone go kill that bastard, please.'

Crump had noticed the sudden attention. He looked round innocently. 'What?'

'Want a word or two with you,' Cuttle said, rising. ''Bout the wall—'

'It weren't my fault! I ain't never used cussers afore!'

'Crump—'

'And that ain't my name neither, Sergeant Cord. It's Jamber Bole, and I was High Marshall in the Mott Irregulars—'

'Well, you ain't in Mott any more, Crump. And you ain't Jamber Bole either. You're Crump, and you better get used to it.'

A voice from behind Bottle: 'Did he say Mott Irregulars?'

Bottle turned, nodded at Strings. 'Aye, Sergeant.'

'Gods below, who recruited *him*?'

Shrugging, Bottle studied Strings for a moment. Koryk and Tarr had carried him to just within the nave's entrance, and the sergeant was leaning against a flanking pillar, the wounded leg stretched out in front of him, his face pale. 'I better get to that—'

'No point, Bottle – the walls are going to explode – you can feel the heat, even from this damned pillar. It's amazing there's air in here . . .' His voice fell away, and Bottle saw his sergeant frown, then lay both hands palm-down on the tiles. 'Huh.'

'What is it?'

'Cool air, coming up from between the tiles.'

Crypts? Cellars? But that would be dead air down there . . . 'I'll be back in a moment, Sergeant,' he said, turning and heading towards the cracked altar. A pool of water steamed just beyond. He could feel that wind, now, the currents rising up from the floor. Halting, he settled down onto his hands and knees.

And sent his senses downward, seeking life-sparks.

Down, through layers of tight-packed rubble, then, movement in the darkness, the flicker of life. Panicked, clambering down, ever down, the rush of air sweeping past slick fur – rats. Fleeing rats.

Fleeing. Where? His senses danced out, through the rubble beneath, brushing creature after creature. Darkness, sighing streams of air. Smells, echoes, damp stone . . .

'Everyone!' Bottle shouted, rising. 'We need to break through this floor! Whatever you can find – we need to bash through!'

They looked at him as if he'd gone mad.

'We dig down! This city – it's built on ruins! We need to find a way down – through them – damn you all – that air is coming from *somewhere*!'

'And what are we?' Cord demanded. 'Ants?'

'There's rats, below – I looked through their eyes – I saw! Caverns, caves – passages!'

'You did what?' Cord advanced on him.

'Hold it, Cord!' Strings said, twisting round where he sat. 'Listen to him. Bottle – can you follow one of those rats? Can you control one?'

Bottle nodded. 'But there are foundation stones, under this temple – we need to get through—'

'How?' Cuttle demanded. 'We just got rid of all our munitions!'

Hellian cuffed one of her soldiers. 'You, Brethless! Still got that cracker?'

Every sapper in the chamber suddenly closed in on the soldier named Brethless. He stared about in panic, then pulled out a wedge-shaped copper-sheathed spike.

'Back off him!' Strings shouted. 'Everyone. Everyone but Cuttle. Cuttle, you can do this, right? No mistakes.'

'None at all,' Cuttle said, gingerly taking the spike from Brethless's hand. 'Who's still got a sword? Anything hard and big enough to break these tiles—'

'I do.' The man who spoke was the rebel warrior. 'Or, I did – it's over there.' He pointed.

The scimitar went into the hands of Tulip, who battered the tiles in a frenzy that had inset precious stones flying everywhere, until a rough angular hole had been chopped into the floor.

'Good enough, back off, Tulip. Everybody, get as close to the outer walls as you can and cover your faces, your eyes, your ears—'

'How many hands you think each of us has got?' Hellian demanded.

Laughter.

Corabb Bhilan Thenu'alas stared at them all as if they'd lost their minds.

A reverberating *crack* shuddered through the temple, and dust drifted down. Bottle looked up with all the others to see tongues of fire reaching down through a fissure in the dome, which had begun sagging. 'Cuttle—'

'I see it. Pray this cracker don't bring it all down on us.'

He set the spike. 'Bottle, which way you want it pointing?'

'Towards the altar side. There's a space, two maybe three arm-lengths down.'

'Three? Gods below. Well, we'll see.'

The outer walls were oven-hot, sharp cracking sounds filling the air as the massive temple began settling. They could hear the grate of foundation stones sliding beneath shifting pressures. The heat was building.

'Six and counting!' Cuttle shouted, scrambling away.

Five . . . four . . . three . . .

The cracker detonated in a deadly hail of stone-chips and tile shards. People cried out in pain, children screamed, dust and smoke filling the air – and then, from the floor, the sounds of rubble falling, striking things far below, bouncing, tumbling down, down . . .

'Bottle.'

At Strings's voice, he crawled forward, towards the gaping hole. He needed to find another rat. Somewhere down below. *A rat my soul can ride. A rat to lead us out.*

He said nothing to the others of what else he had sensed, flitting among life-sparks in the seeming innumerable layers of dead, buried city below – that it went down, and down, and down – the air rising up stinking of decay, the pressing darkness, the cramped, tortured routes. *Down. All those rats, fleeing, downward. None, none within my reach clambering free, into the night air. None.*

Rats will flee. Even when there's nowhere to go.

Wounded, burned soldiers were being carried past Blistig. Pain and shock, flesh cracked open and lurid red, like cooked meat – which, he realized numbly, was what it was. The white ash of hair – on limbs, where eyebrows had once been, on blistered pates. Blackened remnants of clothing, hands melted onto weapon grips – he wanted to turn away, so desperately wanted to turn away, but he could not.

He stood fifteen hundred paces away, now, from the road and its fringes of burning grass, and he could still feel the heat. Beyond, a fire god devoured the sky above Y'Ghatan – Y'Ghatan, crumbling inward, melting into slag – the city's death was as horrible to his eyes as the file of Keneb and Baralta's surviving soldiers.

How could he do this? Leoman of the Flails, you have made of your name a curse that will never die. Never.

Someone came to his side and, after a long moment, Blistig looked over. And scowled. The Claw, Pearl. The man's eyes were red – durhang, it could be nothing else, for he had remained in his tent, at the far end of the encampment, as if indifferent to this brutal night.

'Where is the Adjunct?' Pearl asked in a low, rough voice.

'Helping with the wounded.'

'Has she broken? Is she on her hands and knees in the blood-soaked mud?'

Blistig studied the man. Those eyes – had he been weeping? No. Durhang. 'Say that again, Claw, and you won't stay alive for much longer.'

The tall man shrugged. 'Look at these burned soldiers, Fist. There are worse things than dying.'

'The healers are among them. Warlocks, witches, from my company—'

'Some scars cannot be healed.'

'What are you doing here? Go back to your tent.'

'I have lost a friend this night, Fist. I will go wherever I choose.'

Blistig looked away. Lost a friend. What of over two thousand Malazan soldiers? *Keneb has lost most of his marines and among them, invaluable veterans. The Adjunct has lost her first battle – oh, the imperial records will note a great victory, the annihilation of the last vestiges of the Sha'ik rebellion. But we, we who are here this night, we will know the truth for the rest of our lives.*

And this Adjunct Tavore, she is far from finished. I have seen. 'Go back to the Empress,' Blistig said. 'Tell her the truth of this night—'

'And what would be the point of that, Fist?'

He opened his mouth, then shut it again.

Pearl said, 'Word will be sent to Dujek Onearm, and he in turn will report to the Empress. For now, however, it is more important that Dujek know. And understand, as I am sure he will.'

'Understand what?'

'That the Fourteenth Army can no longer be counted on as a fighting force on Seven Cities.'

Is that true? 'That remains to be seen,' he said. 'In any case, the rebellion is crushed—'

'Leoman escaped.'

'What?'

'He has escaped. Into the Warren of D'riss, under the protection of the Queen of Dreams – only she knows, I suppose, what use he will be to her. I admit, that part worries me – gods are by nature unfathomable, most of the time, and she is more so than most. I find this detail . . . troubling.'

'Stand here, then, and fret.' Blistig turned away, made for the hastily erected hospital tents. Hood take that damned Claw. The sooner the better. How could he know such things? Leoman . . . alive. Well, perhaps that could be made to work in their favour, perhaps his name would become a curse among the people of Seven Cities as well. The Betrayer. The commander who murdered his own army.

But it is how we are. Look at High Fist Pormqual, after all. Yet, his crime was stupidity. Leoman's was . . . pure evil. If such a thing truly exists.

The storm raged on, unleashing waves of heat that blackened the surrounding countryside. The city's walls had vanished – for no human-built wall could withstand this demon's fury. A distant, pale reflection was visible to the east. The sun, rising to meet its child.

His soul rode the back of a small, insignificant creature, fed on a tiny, racing heart, and looked through eyes that cut into the darkness. Like some remote ghost, tethered by the thinnest of chains, Bottle could feel his own body, somewhere far above, slithering through detritus, cut and scraped raw, face gone slack, eyes straining. Battered hands pulled him along – his own, he was certain – and he could hear soldiers moving behind him, the crying of children, the scrape and catch of buckles, leather straps snagging, rubble being pushed aside, clawed at, clambered over.

He had no idea how far they had gone. The rat sought out the widest, highest passages, following the howling, whistling wind. If people remained in the temple, awaiting their turn to enter this tortured tunnel, that turn would never come, for the air itself would have burst aflame by now, and soon the temple would collapse, burying their blackened corpses in melting stone.

Strings would have been among those victims, for the sergeant had insisted on going last, just behind Corabb Bhilan Thenu'alas. Bottle thought back to those frantic moments, before the dust-clouds had even cleared, as chunks of the domed ceiling rained down . . .

'*Bottle!*'

'I'm looking!' Questing down, through cracks and fissures, hunting life. Warm-blooded life. Brushing then closing in on the muted awareness of a rat, sleek, healthy – but overheating with terror. Overwhelming its meagre defences, clasping hard an iron control about its soul – that faint, flickering force, yet strong enough to reach beyond the flesh and bones that sheltered it. Cunning, strangely proud, warmed by the presence of kin, the rule of the swarm's master, but now all was in chaos, the drive of survival overpowering all else.

Racing down, following spoor, following the rich scents in the air—

And then it turned about, began climbing upwards once more, and Bottle could feel its soul in his grasp. Perfectly still, unresisting now that it had been captured. Observing, curious, calm. There was more, he had always known – so much more to creatures. And so few who understood them the way he did, so few who could reach out and grasp such souls, and so find the strange web of trust all tangled with suspicion, fear with curiosity, need with loyalty.

He was not leading this morsel of a creature to its death. He would not do that, could not, and somehow it seemed to understand, to sense, now, a greater purpose to its life, its existence.

'I have her,' Bottle heard himself saying.

'Get down there, then!'

'Not yet. She needs to find a way up – to lead us back down—'

'Gods below!'

Gesler spoke: 'Start adopting children, soldiers. I want one between everyone behind Cuttle, since Cuttle will be right behind Bottle—'

'Leave me to the last,' Strings said.

'Your leg—'

'That's exactly right, Gesler.'

'We got other injured – got someone guiding or dragging each of 'em. Fid—'

'No. I go last. Whoever's right ahead of me, we're going to need to close up this tunnel, else the fire'll follow us down—'

'There are copper doors. They covered the pool.' That was Corabb Bhilan Thenu'alas. 'I will stay with you. Together, we shall use those panels to seal our retreat.'

'Second to last?' someone snarled. 'You'll just kill Fid and—'

'And what, Malazan? No, would I be allowed, I would go last. I stood at Leoman's side—'

'I'm satisfied with that,' Strings said. 'Corabb, you and I, that will do.'

'Hold on,' said Hellian, leaning close to Bottle. 'I ain't going down there. Someone better kill me right now—'

'Sergeant—'

'No way, there's spiders down there—'

The sound of a fist cracking into a jaw, then a collapsing body.

'Urb, you just knocked out your own sergeant.'

'Aye. I known her a long time, you see. She's a good sergeant, no matter what all of you think.'

'Huh. Right.'

'It's the spiders. No way she'd go down there – now I got to gag her and tie her arms and feet – I'll drag her myself—'

'If she's a good sergeant, Urb, how do you treat bad ones?'

282

'Ain't had any other sergeant, and I mean to keep it that way.'

Below, the broad crevasse that Bottle had sensed earlier, his rat scrambling free, now seeking to follow that wide but shallow crack – too shallow? No, they could scrape through, and there, beneath it, a tilted chamber of some kind, most of the ceiling intact, and the lower half of a doorway – he sent the rat that way, and beyond the doorway . . . 'I have it! There's a street! Part of a street – not sure how far—'

'Never mind! Lead us down, damn you! I'm starting to blister everywhere! Hurry!'

All right. Why not? At the very least, it'll purchase us a few more moments. He slithered down into the pit. Behind him, voices, the scrabble of boots, the hissing of pain as flesh touched hot stone.

Faintly: 'How hot is that water in that pool? Boiling yet? No? Good, those with canteens and skins, fill 'em now—'

Into the crevasse . . . while the rat scurried down the canted, littered street, beneath a ceiling of packed rubble . . .

Bottle felt his body push through a fissure, then plunge downward, onto the low-ceilinged section of street. Rocks, mortar and potsherds under his hands, cutting, scraping as he scrabbled forward. Once walked, this avenue, in an age long past. Wagons had rattled here, horse-hoofs clumping, and there had been rich smells. Cooking from nearby homes, livestock being driven to the market squares. Kings and paupers, great mages and ambitious priests. *All gone. Gone to dust.*

The street sloped sharply, where cobbles had buckled, sagging down to fill a subterranean chamber – no, an old sewer, brick-lined, and it was into this channel his rat had crawled.

Pushing aside broken pieces of cobble, he pulled himself down into the shaft. Desiccated faeces in a thin, shallow bed beneath him, the husks of dead insects, carapaces crunching as he slithered along. A pale lizard, long as his forearm, fled in a whisper into a side crack. His forehead caught strands of spider's web, tough enough to halt him momentarily before audibly snapping. He felt something alight on his shoulder, race across his back, then leap off.

Behind him Bottle heard Cuttle coughing in the dust in his wake, as it swept over the sapper on the gusting wind. A child had been crying somewhere back there, but was now silent, only the sound of movement, gasps of effort. Just ahead, a section of the tunnel had fallen in. The rat had found a way through, so he knew the barrier was not impassable. Reaching it, he began pulling away the rubble.

Smiles nudged the child ahead of her. 'Go on,' she murmured, 'keep going. Not far now.' She could still hear the girl's sniffles – not crying, not yet, anyway, just the dust, so much dust now, with those people crawling ahead. Behind her, small hands touched her blistered feet again and again, lancing vicious stabs of pain up her legs, but she bit back on it, making no outcry. *Damned brat don't know any better, does he? And why they got such big eyes, looking up like that? Like starving puppies.* 'Keep crawling, little one. Not much farther . . .'

The child behind her, a boy, was helping Tavos Pond, whose face was wrapped in bloody bandages. Koryk was right behind them. Smiles could hear the half-Seti, going on and on with some kind of chant. Probably the only thing keeping the fool from deadly panic. He liked his open savannah, didn't he. Not cramped, twisting tunnels.

None of this bothered her. She'd known worse. Times, long ago, she'd *lived* in worse. You learned to only count on what's in reach, and so long as the way ahead stayed clear, there was still hope, still a chance.

If only this brat of a girl wouldn't keep stopping. Another nudge. 'Go on, lass. Not much more, you'll see . . .'

Gesler pulled himself along in pitch darkness, hearing Tulip's heavy grunts ahead of him, Crump's maddening singing behind him. The huge soldier whose bare feet Gesler's outstretched hands kept touching was having a hard time, and the sergeant could feel the smears of blood Tulip left behind as he squeezed and pulled himself through the narrow, twisting passage. Thick gasps, coughing – no, not coughing—

'Abyss take us, Tulip,' Gesler hissed, 'what's so funny?'

'Tickling,' the man called back. 'You. Keep. Tickling. My. Feet.'

'Just keep moving, you damned fool!'

Behind him, Crump's idiotic song continued.

> *'and I says oh I says them marsh trees*
> *got soft feet, and moss beards all the way down*
> *and they sway in the smelly breeze*
> *from that swamp water all yella'n'brown*
>
> *oh we was in the froggy toady dawn*
> *belly-down in the leeches and collectin' spawn*
> *'cause when you give those worms a squeeze*
> *the blue pinky ropes come slimin' down—*
>
> *and don't they taste sweet!*
> *and don't they taste sweet!*
> *sweet as peat, oh yes*
> *sweet as peat—'*

Gesler wanted to scream, like someone up ahead was doing. Scream, but he couldn't summon the breath – it was all too close, too fetid, the once cool sliding air rank with sweat, urine and Hood knew what else. Truth's face kept coming back to him, rising in his mind like dread accusation. Gesler and Stormy, they'd pulled the recruit through so much since the damned rebellion. Kept him alive, showed him the ways of *staying* alive in this Hood-cursed world.

And what does he do? He runs into a burning palace. With a half-dozen cussers on his back. Gods, he was right on one thing, though, the fire couldn't take him – he went way in, and that's what's saved us . . . so far. Blew that storm back. Saved us . . .

Soldiers all round him were blistered, burned. They coughed with every breath drawn into scorched lungs. *But not me.* He could sense that godling, within that firestorm. Could sense it, a child raging with the knowledge that it was going to die all too soon. *Good, you don't deserve nothing more.* Fire couldn't hurt him, but that didn't mean he had to kneel before it in prayer, did it? He didn't ask for any of this. Him and Stormy and Truth – only, Truth was dead, now. He'd never expected . . .

> *'and I says oh I says that ole bridge*
> *got feeta stone, and mortar white as bone*
> *and the badgers dangle from the ledge*
> *swingin' alla day alla way home*
>
> *oh we was pullin' vines from you know where*
> *and stuffin' our ears with sweety sweet loam*
> *jus t'get them badgers flyin' outa there*
> *inta them cook pots in the hearthy home—*
>
> *and don't they taste sweet!*
> *and don't they taste sweet!*
> *sweet as peat, oh yes*
> *sweet as peat—'*

When he got out of here, he was going to wring Crump's scrawny neck. High Marshal? Gods below—

> *'and I says oh I says that warlock's tower—'*

Corporal Tarr pulled on Balgrid's arms, ignoring the man's squeals. How the mage had managed to stay fat through that endless march was baffling. And now, all too likely to prove deadly. Mind you, fat could be squeezed, when muscled bulk couldn't. That was something, at least.

Balgrid shrieked as Tarr dragged him through the crevasse. 'You're tearing my arms off!'

'You plug up here, Balgrid,' Tarr said, 'and Urb behind you's gonna take out his knife—'

A muted voice from the huge man behind Balgrid: 'Damn right. I'll joint you like a pig, mage. I swear it.'

The darkness was the worst of all – never mind the spiders, the scorpions and centipedes, it was the darkness that clawed and chewed on Tarr's sanity. At least Bottle had a rat's eyes to look through. Rats could see in the dark, couldn't they? Then again, maybe they couldn't. Maybe they just used their noses, their whiskers, their ears. Maybe they were too stupid to go insane.

Or they're already insane. We're being led by an insane rat—

'I'm stuck again, oh gods! I can't move!'

'Stop yelling,' Tarr said, halting and twisting round yet again. Reaching out for the man's arms. 'Hear that, Balgrid?'

'What? *What?*'

'Not sure. Thought I heard Urb's knives coming outa their sheaths.'

The mage heaved himself forward, kicking, clawing.

'You stop moving again,' Balm snarled to the child in front of him, 'and the lizards will get you. Eat you alive. Eat us all alive. Those are crypt lizards, you damned whelp. You know what crypt lizards do? I'll tell you what they do. They eat human flesh. That's why they're called crypt lizards, only they don't mind if it's living flesh—'

'For Hood's sake!' Deadsmell growled behind him. 'Sergeant – that ain't the way—'

'Shut your mouth! He's still moving, ain't he? Oh yes, ain't he just. Crypt lizards, runt! Oh yes!'

'Hope you ain't nobody's uncle, Sergeant.'

'You're getting as bad as Widdershins, Corporal, with that babbling mouth of yours. I want a new squad—'

'Nobody'll have you, not after this—'

'You don't know nothing, Deadsmell.'

'I know if I was that child ahead of you, I'd shit right in your face.'

'Quiet! You give him ideas, damn you! Do it, boy, and I'll tie you up, oh yes, and leave you for the crypt lizards—'

'Listen to me, little one!' Deadsmell called out, his voice echoing. 'Them crypt lizards, they're about as long as your thumb! Balm's just being a—'

'I'm going to skewer you, Deadsmell. I swear it!'

Corabb Bhilan Thenu'alas dragged himself forward. The Malazan in his wake was gasping – the only indication that the man still followed. They had managed to drop one of the copper panels over the pit, burning their hands – bad burns, the pain wouldn't go away – Corabb's palms felt like soft wax, pushed out of shape by the stones they gripped, the ledges they grasped.

He had never felt such excruciating pain before. He was sheathed in sweat, his limbs trembling, his heart hammering like a trapped beast in his chest.

Pulling himself through a narrow space, he sank down onto what seemed to be the surface of a street, although his head scraped stone rubble above. He slithered forward, gasping, and heard the sergeant slip down after him.

Then the ground shook, dust pouring down thick as sand. Thunder, one concussion after another, pounding down from above. A rush of searing hot air swept over them from behind. Smoke, dust—

'Forward!' Strings screamed. 'Before the ceiling goes—'

Corabb reached back, groping, until he clasped one of the Malazan's hands – the man was half-buried under rubble, his breath straining beneath the settling weight. Corabb pulled, then pulled harder.

A savage grunt from the Malazan, then, amidst clattering, thumping bricks and stones, Corabb tugged the man clear.

'Come on!' he hissed. 'There's a pit ahead, a sewer – the rest went down there – grab my ankles, Sergeant—'

The wind was beating back the roiling heat.

Corabb pitched headfirst into the pit, dragging Strings with him.

The rat had reached a vertical shaft, rough-walled enough so that she could climb down. The wind howled up it, filled with rotted leaves, dust and insect fragments. The creature was still descending when Bottle pulled himself up to the ledge. The detritus bit at his eyes as he peered down.

Seeing nothing. He pulled free a piece of rubble and tossed it downward, out from the wall. His soul, riding the rat's own, sensed its passage. Rodent ears pricked forward, waiting. Four human heartbeats later there was a dull, muted crack of stone on stone, a few more, then nothing. *Oh gods . . .*

Cuttle spoke behind him. 'What's wrong?'

'A shaft, goes straight down – a long away down.'

'Can we climb it?'

'My rat can.'

'How wide is it?'

'Not very, and gets narrower.'

'We got wounded people back here, and Hellian's still unconscious.'

Bottle nodded. 'Do a roll call – I want to know how many made it. We also need straps, rope, anything and everything. Was it just me or did you hear the temple come down?'

Cuttle turned about and started the roll call and the request for straps and rope, then twisted round once more. 'Yeah, it went down all right. When the wind dropped off. Thank Hood it's back, or we'd be cooking or suffocating or both.'

Well, we're not through this yet . . .

'I know what you're thinking, Bottle.'

'You do?'

'Think there's a rat god? I hope so, and I hope you're praying good and hard.'

A rat god. Maybe. *Hard to know with creatures that don't think in words.* 'I think one of us, one of the bigger, stronger ones, could wedge himself across. And help people down.'

'If we get enough straps and stuff to climb down, aye. Tulip, maybe, or that other corporal, Urb. But there ain't room to get past anyone.'

I know. 'I'm going to try and climb down.'

'Where's the rat?'

'Down below. It's reached the bottom. It's waiting there. Anyway, here goes.' Drawing on the Thyr Warren to pierce the darkness, he moved out to the very edge. The wall opposite looked to be part of some monumental structure, the stones skilfully cut and fitted. Patches of crumbling plaster covered parts of it, as did sections of the frieze fronting that plaster. It seemed almost perfectly vertical – the narrowing of the gap was caused by the wall on his side – a much rougher facing, with projections remaining from some kind of elaborate ornamentation. A strange clash of styles, for two buildings standing so close together. Still, both walls had withstood the ravages of being buried, seemingly unaffected by the pressures of sand and rubble. 'All right,' he said to Cuttle, who had drawn up closer, 'this might not be so bad.'

'You're what, twenty years old? No wounds, thin as a spear . . .'

'Fine, you've made your point.' Bottle pushed himself further out, then drew his right leg round. Stretching it outward, he slowly edged over, onto his stomach. 'Damn, I don't think my leg's long—'

The ledge he leaned on splintered – it was, he suddenly realized, nothing but rotted wood – and he began sliding, falling.

He spun over, kicking out with both legs as he plummeted, throwing both arms out behind and to the sides. Those rough stones tore into his back, one outcrop cracking into the base of his skull and throwing his head forward. Then both feet contacted the stone of the wall opposite.

Flinging him over, headfirst—

Oh Hood—

Sudden tugs, snapping sounds, then more, pulling at him, resisting, slowing his descent.

Gods, webs—

His left shoulder was tugged back, turning him over. He kicked out again and felt the plastered wall under his foot. Reached out with his right arm, and his hand closed on a projection that seemed to sink like sponge beneath his clutching fingers. His other foot contacted the wall, and he pushed with both legs until his back was against rough stone.

And there were spiders, each as big as an outstretched hand, crawling all over him.

Bottle went perfectly still, struggling to slow his breathing.

Hairless, short-legged, pale amber – but there was no light – and he realized that the creatures were glowing, somehow lit from within, like lantern-flame behind thick, gold-tinted glass. They had swarmed him, now. From far above, he heard Cuttle calling down in desperate, frightened tones.

Bottle reached out with his mind, and immediately recoiled at the blind rage building in the spiders. And flashes of memory – the rat – their favoured prey – somehow evading all their snares, climbing down right past them, unseeing, unaware of the hundreds of eyes tracking its passing. And now . . . *this.*

Heart thundering in his chest, Bottle quested once more. A hive mind, of sorts – no, an extended family – they would mass together, exchange nutrients – when one fed, they all fed. They had never known light beyond what lived within them, and, until recently, never known wind. *Terrified . . . but not starving, thank Hood.* He sought to calm them, flinched once more as all motion ceased, all attention fixed now on him. Legs that had been scrambling over his body went still, tiny claws clasping hard in his skin.

Calm. No reason to fear. An accident, and there will be more – it cannot be helped. Best go away now, all of you. Soon, the silence will return, we will have gone past, and before long, this wind will end, and you can begin to rebuild. Peace . . . please.

They were not convinced.

The wind paused suddenly, then a gust of heat descended from above.

Flee! He fashioned images of fire in his mind, drew forth from his own memory scenes of people dying, destruction all around—

The spiders fled. Three heartbeats, and he was alone. Nothing clinging still to his skin, nothing but strands of wiry anchor lines, tattered sheets of web. And, trickling down his back, from the soles of his feet, from his arms: blood.

Damn, I'm torn up bad, I think. Pain, now, awakening . . . *everywhere. Too much* – Consciousness fled.

From far above: '*Bottle!*'

Stirring . . . blinking awake. How long had he been hanging here?

'I'm here, Cuttle! I'm climbing down – not much farther, I think!' Grimacing against the pain, he started working his feet downward – the space was narrow enough, now, that he could straddle the gap. He gasped as he pulled his back clear of the wall.

Something whipped his right shoulder, stinging, hard, and he ducked – then felt the object slide down the right side of his chest. The strap of a harness.

From above: 'I'm climbing down!'

Koryk called behind him, 'Shard, you still with us?' The man had been gibbering – they'd all discovered an unexpected horror. That of *stopping*. Moving forward had been a tether to sanity, for it had meant that, somewhere ahead, Bottle was still crawling, still finding a way through. When everyone had come to a halt, terror had slipped among them, closing like tentacles around throats, and squeezing.

Shrieks, panicked fighting against immovable, packed stone and brick, hands clawing at feet. Rising into a frenzy.

Then, voices bellowing, calling back – they'd reached a shaft of some kind – they needed rope, belts, harness straps – they were going to climb down.

There was still a way ahead.

Koryk had, through it all, muttered his chant. The Child Death Song, the Seti rite of passage from whelp into adulthood. A ritual that had, for girl and boy alike, included the grave log, the hollowed-out coffin and the night-long internment in a crypt of the bloodline. Buried alive, for the child to die, for the adult to be born. A test against the spirits of madness, the worms that lived in each person, coiled at the base of the skull, wrapped tight about the spine. Worms that were ever eager to awaken, to crawl, gnawing a path into the brain, whispering and laughing or screaming, or both.

He had survived that night. He had defeated the worms.

And that was all he needed, for this. All he needed.

He had heard those worms, eating into soldiers ahead of him, soldiers behind him. Into the children, as the worms raced out to take them as well. For an adult to break under fear – there could be no worse nightmare for the child that witnessed such a thing. For with that was torn away all hope, all faith.

Koryk could save none of them. He could not give them the chant, for they would not know what it meant, and they had never spent a night in a coffin. And he knew, had it gone on much longer, people would start dying, or the madness would devour their minds, completely, permanently, and that would kill everyone else. Everyone.

The worms had retreated, and now all he could hear was weeping – not the broken kind, but the relieved kind – weeping and gibbering. And he knew they could taste it, could taste what those worms had left behind, and they prayed: *not again. No closer, please. Never again.* 'Corporal Shard?'

'W-what, damn you?'

'Limp. How is he? I keep kicking at him, hitting what I think is an arm, but he's not moving. Can you climb ahead, can you check?'

'He's knocked out.'

'How did that happen?'

'I crawled onto him and pounded his head against the floor until he stopped screaming.'

'You sure he's alive?'

'Limp? His skull's solid rock, Koryk.'

He heard movement back there, asked, 'What now?'

'I'll prove it to you. Give this broke leg a twist—'

Limp shrieked.

'Glad you're back, soldier,' Shard said.

'Get away from me, you bastard!'

'Wasn't me who panicked. Next time you think about panicking, Limp, just remind yourself I'm here, right behind you.'

'I'm going to kill you someday, Corporal—'

'As you like. Just don't do it again.'

Koryk thought back to the babbling noises he'd heard from Shard, but said nothing.

More scuffling sounds, then a bundle of rope and leather straps – most of them charred – was pushed into Koryk's hands. He dragged it close, then shoved it out ahead to the small boy huddled behind Tavos Pond. 'Push it on, lad,' he said.

'You,' the boy said. 'I heard you. I listened.'

'And you was all right, wasn't you?'

'Yes.'

'I'll teach it to you. For the next time.'

'Yes.'

Someone had shouted back instructions, cutting through the frenzy of terror, and people had responded, stripping away whatever could be used as a rope. Chilled beneath a gritty layer of sweat, Tarr settled his forehead onto the stones under him, smelling dust mingled with the remnants of his own fear. When the bundle reached him he drew it forward, then struggled out of what was left of his own harness and added it to the pathetic collection.

Now, at least, they had a reason to wait, they weren't stopped because Bottle had run out of places to crawl. Something to hold onto. He prayed it would be enough.

Behind him, Balgrid whispered, 'I wish we was marching across the desert again. That road, all that space on both sides . . .'

'I hear you,' Tarr said. 'And I also remember how you used to curse it. The dryness, the sun—'

'Sun, hah! I'm so crisp I'll never fear the sun again. Gods, I'll kneel in prayer before it, I swear it. If freedom was a god, Tarr . . .'

If freedom was a god. Now that's an interesting thought . . .

'Thank Hood all that screaming's stopped,' Balm said, plucking at whatever was tingling against all his skin, tingling, prickling like some kind of heat rash. Heat rash, that was funny—

'Sergeant,' Deadsmell said, 'it was you doing all that screaming.'

'Quiet, you damned liar. Wasn't me, was the kid ahead of me.'

'Really? I didn't know he spoke Dal Honese—'

'I will skewer you, Corporal. Just one more word, I swear it. Gods, I'm itchy all over, like I been rolling in Fool's pollen—'

'You get that after you been panicking, Sergeant. Fear sweat, it's called. You didn't piss yourself too, did you? I'm smelling—'

'I got my knife out, Deadsmell. You know that? All I got to do is twist round and you won't be bothering me no more.'

'You tossed your knife, Sergeant. In the temple—'

'Fine! I'll kick you to death!'

'Well, if you do, can you do it before I have to crawl through your puddle?'

'The heat is winning the war,' Corabb said.

'Aye,' answered Strings behind him, his voice faint, brittle. 'Here.'

Something was pushed against Corabb's feet. He reached back, and his hand closed on a coil of rope. 'You were carrying this?'

'Was wrapped around me. I saw Smiles drop it, outside the temple – it was smouldering, so that's not a surprise . . .'

As he drew it over him, Corabb felt something wet, sticky on the rope. Blood. 'You're bleeding out, aren't you?'

'Just a trickle. I'm fine.'

Corabb crawled forward – there was some space between them and the next soldier, the one named Widdershins. Corabb could have kept

292

up had he been alone back here, but he would not leave the Malazan sergeant behind. Enemy or no, such things were not done.

He had believed them all monsters, cowards and bullies. He had heard that they ate their own dead. But no, they were just people. No different from Corabb himself. *The tyranny lies at the feet of the Empress. These – they're all just soldiers. That's all they are.* Had he gone with Leoman . . . he would have discovered none of this. He would have held onto his fierce hatred for all Malazans and all things Malazan.

But now . . . the man behind him was dying. A Falari by birth – just another place conquered by the empire. Dying, and there was no room to get to him, not here, not yet.

'Here,' he said to Widdershins. 'Pass this up.'

'Hood take us, that's real rope!'

'Aye. Move it along fast now.'

'Don't order me around, bastard. You're a prisoner. Remember that.'

Corabb crawled back.

The heat was building, devouring the thin streams of cool air sliding up from below. They couldn't lie still for much longer. *We must move on.*

From Strings: 'Did you say something, Corabb?'

'No. Nothing much.'

From above came sounds of Cuttle making his way down the makeshift rope, his breath harsh, strained. Bottle reached the rubble-filled base of the fissure. It was solidly plugged. Confused, he ran his hands along both walls. His rat? *Ah, there* – at the bottom of the sheer, vertical wall his left hand plunged into air that swept up and past. An archway. Gods, what kind of building was this? An archway, holding the weight of at least two – maybe three – storeys' worth of stonework. And neither the wall nor the arch had buckled, after all this time. *Maybe the legends are true. Maybe Y'Ghatan was once the first Holy City, the greatest city of all. And when it died, at the Great Slaughter, every building was left standing – not a stone taken. Standing, to be buried by the sands.*

He lowered himself to twist feet-first through the archway, almost immediately contacting heaps of something – rubble? – nearly filling the chamber beyond. Rubble that tipped and tilted with clunking sounds, rocked by his kicking feet.

Ahead, his rat roused itself, startled by the loud sounds as Bottle slid into the chamber. Reaching out with his will, he grasped hold of the creature's soul once more. 'All right, little one. The work begins again . . .' His voice trailed away.

He was lying on row upon row of urns, stacked so high they were an arm's reach from the chamber's ceiling. Groping with his hands, Bottle found that the tall urns were sealed, capped in iron, the edges and level tops of the metal intricately incised with swirling patterns. The ceramic beneath was smooth to the touch, finely glazed. Hearing Cuttle shouting that he'd reached the base behind him, he crawled in towards the centre of the room. The rat slipped through another archway opposite, and Bottle sensed it clambering down, alighting on a clear, level stone floor, then waddling ahead.

Grasping the rim of one urn's iron cap, he strained to pull it loose. The seal was tight, his efforts eliciting nothing. He twisted the rim to the right – nothing – then the left. A grating sound. He twisted harder. The cap slid, pulled loose from its seal. Crumbled wax fell away. Bottle pulled upward on the lid. When that failed, he resumed twisting it to the left, and quickly realized that the lid was rising, incrementally, with every full turn. Probing fingers discovered a canted, spiralling groove on the rim of the urn, crusted with wax. Two more turns and the iron lid came away.

A pungent, cloying smell arose.

I know that smell . . . honey. These things are filled with honey. For how long had they sat here, stored away by people long since dust? He reached down, and almost immediately plunged his hand into the cool, thick contents. A balm against his burns, and now, an answer to the sudden hunger awakening within him.

'Bottle?'

'Through here. I'm in a large chamber under the straight wall. Cuttle, there's urns here, hundreds of them. Filled with honey.' He drew his hands free and licked his fingers. 'Gods, it tastes fresh. When you get in here, salve your burns, Cuttle—'

'Only if you promise we're not going to crawl through an ant nest anywhere ahead.'

'No ants down here. What's the count?'

'We got everybody.'

'Strings?'

'Still with us, though the heat's working its way down.'

'Enough rope and straps, then. Good.'

'Aye. So long as they hold. Seems Urb's proposing to carry Hellian down. On his back.'

'Is the next one on their way?'

'Aye. How do these lids come off?'

'Turn them, widdershins. And keep turning them.'

Bottle listened as the man worked on one of the lids. 'Can't be very old, this stuff, to still be fresh.'

'There's glyphs on these lids, Cuttle. I can't see them, but I can feel them. My grandmother, she had a ritual blade she used in her witchery – the markings are the same, I think. If I'm right, Cuttle, this iron work is Jaghut.'

'*What?*'

'But the urns are First Empire. Feel the sides. Smooth as eggshell – if we had light I'd wager anything they're sky-blue. So, with a good enough seal . . .'

'I can still taste the flowers in this, Bottle.'

'I know.'

'You're talking thousands and thousands of years.'

'Yes.'

'Where's your favourite rat?'

'Hunting us a way through. There's another chamber opposite, but it's open, empty, I mean – we should move in there to give the others room . . .'

'What's wrong?'

Bottle shook his head. 'Nothing, just feeling a little . . . strange. Cut my back up some . . . it's gone numb—'

'Hood's breath, there was some kind of poppy in that honey, wasn't there? I'm starting to feel … gods below, my head's swimming.'

'Yeah, better warn the others.'

Though he could see nothing, Bottle felt as if the world around him was shuddering, spinning. His heart was suddenly racing. *Shit.* He crawled towards the other archway. Reached in, pulled himself forward, and was falling.

The collision with the stone floor felt remote, yet he sensed he'd plunged more than a man's height. He remembered a sharp, cracking sound, realized it had been his forehead, hitting the flagstones.

Cuttle thumped down on top of him, rolled off with a grunt.

Bottle frowned, pulling himself along the floor. The rat – where was she? *Gone. I lost her. Oh no, I lost her.*

Moments later, he lost everything else as well.

Corabb had dragged an unconscious Strings down the last stretch of tunnel. They'd reached the ledge to find the rope dangling from three sword scabbards wedged across the shaft, and vague sounds of voices far below. Heat swirled like serpents around him as he struggled to pull the Malazan up closer to the ledge.

Then he reached out and began drawing up the rope.

The last third of the line consisted of knots and straps and buckles – he checked each knot, tugged on each strand, but none seemed on the verge of breaking. Corabb bound the Malazan's arms, tight at the wrists; then the man's ankles – one of them sheathed in blood, and, checking for bandages, he discovered none remaining, just the ragged holes left by the spear – and from the rope at the ankles he made a centre knot between the sergeant's feet. With the rope end looped in one hand, Corabb worked the man's arms over his head, then down so that the bound wrists were against his sternum. He then pushed his own legs through, so that the Malazan's bound feet were against his shins. Drawing up the centre-knotted rope he looped it over his head and beneath one arm, then cinched it into a tight knot.

He worked his way into the shaft, leaning hard for the briefest of moments on the wedged scabbards, then succeeding in planting one foot against the opposite wall. The distance was a little too great – he could manage only the tips of his feet on each wall, and as the weight of Strings on his back fully settled, the tendons in his ankles felt ready to snap.

Gasping, Corabb worked his way down. Two man-heights, taken in increasing speed, control slipping away with every lurch downward, then he found a solid projection on which he could rest his right foot, and the gap had narrowed enough to let his left hand reach out and ease the burden on that leg.

Corabb rested.

The pain of deep burns, the pounding of his heart. Some time later, he resumed the descent. Easier now, the gap closing, closing.

Then he was at the bottom, and he heard something like laughter from his left, low, which then trailed away.

He searched out that side and found the archway, through which he tossed the rope, hearing it strike a body a little way below.

Everyone's asleep. No wonder. I could do with that myself.

He untied Strings, then clambered through, found his feet balancing on tight-packed, clunking jars, the sounds of snoring and breathing on all sides and a sweet, cloying smell. He pulled Strings after him, eased the man down.

Honey. Jars and jars of honey. *Good for burns, I think. Good for wounds.* Finding an opened jar, Corabb scooped out a handful, crawled over to the sergeant and pushed the honey into the puncture wounds. Salved the burns, on Strings and on himself. Then he settled back. Numbing bliss stole through him.

Oh, this honey, it's Carelbarra. The God Bringer. Oh . . .

Fist Keneb tottered into the morning light, stood, blinking, looking round at the chaotic array of tents, many of them scorched, and all the soldiers – stumbling, wandering or standing motionless, staring across the blasted landscape towards the city. Y'Ghatan, blurred by waves of rising heat, a misshapen mound melted down atop its ragged hill, fires still flickering here and there, pale orange tongues and, lower down, fierce deep red.

Ash filled the air, drifting down like snow.

It hurt to breathe. He was having trouble hearing – the roar of that firestorm still seemed to rage inside his head, as hungry as ever. How long had it been? A day? Two days? There had been healers. Witches with salves, practitioners of Denul from the army itself. A jumble of voices, chanting, whispers, some real, some imagined.

He thought of his wife. Selv was away from this accursed continent, safe in her family estate back on Quon Tali. And Kesen and Vaneb, his children. They'd survived, hadn't they? He was certain they had. A memory of that, strong enough to convince him of its truth. That assassin, Kalam, he'd had something to do with that.

Selv. They had grown apart, in the two years before the rebellion, the two years – was it two? – that they had been in Seven Cities, in the garrison settlement. The uprising had forced them both to set aside all of that, for the children, for survival itself. He suspected she did not miss him; although his children might. He suspected she would have found someone else by now, a lover, and the last thing she would want was to see him again.

Well, there could be worse things in this life. He thought back on those soldiers he'd seen with the fiercest burns – gods how they had screamed their pain.

Keneb stared at the city. And hated it with all his soul.

The dog Bent arrived to lie down beside him. A moment later Grub appeared. 'Father, do you know what will come of this? Do you?'

'Come of what, Grub?'

The boy pointed at Y'Ghatan with one bare, soot-stained arm. 'She wants us to leave. As soon as we can.' He then pointed towards the morning sun. 'It's the plague, you see, in the east. So. We're marching west. To find the ships. But I already know the answer. To find what's inside us, you got to take everything else away, you see?'

'No, Grub. I don't see.'

The Hengese lapdog, Roach, scrambled into view, sniffing the ground. Then it began digging, as if in a frenzy. Dust engulfed it.

'Something's buried,' Grub said, watching Roach.

'I imagine there is.'

'But she won't see that.' The boy looked up at Keneb. 'Neither will you.'

Grub ran off, Bent loping at his side. The lapdog kept digging, making snuffling, snorting sounds.

Keneb frowned, trying to recall what Grub had said earlier – was it the night of the breach? Before the fated order went out? Had there been a warning hidden in the lad's words? He couldn't remember – the world before the fire seemed to have burned away to nothing in his mind. It had been a struggle to conjure up the names of his wife, his children, their faces. *I don't understand. What has happened to me?*

In the command tent, the Adjunct stood facing Nil and Nether. Fist Blistig watched from near the back wall, so exhausted he could barely stand. Tavore had placed him in charge of the healing – setting up the hospitals, organizing the Denul healers, the witches and the warlocks. Two days and one or maybe one and a half nights – he was not sure he could count the short chaotic time before the sun rose on the night of the breach. Without his officers that first night, he would have been relieved of command before dawn. His soul had been drowning in the pit of the Abyss.

Blistig was not yet certain he had climbed back out.

Nil was speaking, his voice a monotone, dulled by too long in the sorcery he had grown to hate. '. . . nothing but death and heat. Those who made it out – their agony deafens me – they are driving the spirits insane. They flee, snapping their bindings. They curse us, for this vast wound upon the land, for the crimes we have committed—'

'Not our crimes,' the Adjunct cut in, turning away, her gaze finding Blistig. 'How many did we lose today, Fist?'

'Thirty-one, Adjunct, but the witches say that few will follow, now. The worst are dead, the rest will live.'

'Begin preparations for the march – have we enough wagons?'

'Provided soldiers pack their own food for a while,' Blistig said. 'Speaking of which, some stores were lost – we'll end up chewing leather unless we can arrange a resupply.'

'How long?'

'A week, if we immediately begin rationing. Adjunct, where are we going?'

Her eyes grew veiled for a moment, then she looked away. 'The plague is proving ... virulent. It is the Mistress's own, I gather, the kiss of the goddess herself. And there is a shortage of healers . . .'

'Lothal?'

Nil shook his head. 'The city has already been struck, Fist.'

'Sotka,' said the Adjunct. 'Pearl has informed me that Admiral Nok's fleet and the transports have been unable to dock in any city east of Ashok on the Maadil Peninsula, so he has been forced around it, and expects to reach Sotka in nine days, assuming he can draw in for water and food in Taxila or Rang.'

'Nine days?' asked Blistig. 'If the plague's in Lothal already . . .'

'Our enemy now is time,' the Adjunct said. 'Fist, you have orders to break camp. Do it as quickly as possible. The Rebellion is over. Our task now is to survive.' She studied Blistig for a moment. 'I want us on the road tonight.'

'Tonight? Aye, Adjunct. I had best be on my way, then.' He saluted, then headed out. Outside, he halted, momentarily blinking, then, recalling his orders, he set off.

After Blistig's footsteps had trailed away, the Adjunct turned to Nether. 'The Mistress of Plague, Nether. Why now? Why here?'

The Wickan witch snorted. 'You ask me to fathom the mind of a goddess, Adjunct? It is hopeless. She may have no reason. Plague is her aspect, after all. It is what she does.' She shook her head, said nothing more.

'Adjunct,' Nil ventured, 'you have your victory. The Empress will be satisfied – she has to be. We need to rest—'

'Pearl informs me that Leoman of the Flails is not dead.'

Neither Wickan replied, and the Adjunct faced them once more. 'You both knew that, didn't you?'

'He was taken . . . away,' Nil said. 'By a goddess.'

'Which goddess? Poliel?'

'No. The Queen of Dreams.'

'The Goddess of Divination? What possible use could she have for Leoman of the Flails?'

Nil shrugged.

Outside the tent a rider reined in and a moment later Temul, dust-sheathed and dripping blood from three parallel slashes tracking the side of his face, strode in, dragging a dishevelled child with him. 'Found her, Adjunct,' he said.

'Where?'

'Trying to get back into the ruins. She has lost her mind.'

The Adjunct studied the child, Sinn, then said, 'She had best find it again. I have need of High Mages. Sinn, look at me. Look at me.'

She gave no indication of even hearing Tavore, her head still hanging down, ropes of burnt hair hiding her face.

Sighing, the Adjunct said, 'Take her and get her cleaned up. And keep her under guard at all times – we will try this again later.'

After they had left, Nil asked, 'Adjunct, do you intend to pursue Leoman? How? There is no trail to follow – the Queen of Dreams could have spirited him to another continent by now.'

'No, we shall not pursue, but understand this, Wickan, while he yet lives there will be no victory in the eyes of the Empress. Y'Ghatan will remain as it always has been, a curse upon the empire.'

'It will not rise again,' Nil said.

Tavore studied him. 'The young know nothing of history. I am going for a walk. Both of you, get some rest.'

She left.

Nil met his sister's eyes, then smiled. 'Young? How easily she forgets.'

'They all forget, brother.'

'Where do you think Leoman has gone?'

'Where else? Into the Golden Age, Nil. The glory that was the Great Rebellion. He strides the mists of myth, now. They will say he breathed fire. They will say you could see the Apocalypse in his eyes. They will say he sailed from Y'Ghatan on a river of Malazan blood.'

'The locals believe Coltaine ascended, Nether. The new Patron of Crows—'

'Fools. Wickans do not ascend. We just . . . reiterate.'

Lieutenant Pores was awake, and he lifted his good hand to acknowledge his captain as Kindly halted at the foot of the camp cot.

'They say your hand melted together, Lieutenant.'

'Yes, sir. My left hand, as you see.'

'They say they have done all they could, taken away the pain, and maybe one day they will manage to cut each finger free once again. Find a High Denul healer and make your hand look and work like new again.'

'Yes, sir. And until then, since it's my shield hand, I should be able to—'

'Then why in Hood's name are you taking up this cot, Lieutenant?'

'Ah, well, I just need to find some clothes, then, sir, and I'll be right with you.'

Kindly looked down the row of cots. 'Half this hospital is filled with bleating lambs – you up to being a wolf, Lieutenant? We march tonight. There's not enough wagons and, even more outrageous, not enough palanquins and no howdahs to speak of – what is this army coming to, I wonder?'

'Shameful, sir. How does Fist Tene Baralta fare, sir?'

'Lost that arm, but you don't hear him whining and fussing and moaning.'

'No?'

'Of course not, he's still unconscious. Get on your feet, soldier. Wear that blanket.'

'I lost my arm torc, sir—'

'You got the burn mark where it was, though, haven't you? They see that and they'll know you for an officer. That and your ferocious comportment.'

'Yes, sir.'

'Good, now enough of wasting my time. We've work to do, Lieutenant.'

'Yes, sir.'

'Lieutenant, if you remain lying there another heartbeat, I will fold that cot up with you in it, do you understand me?'

'Yes, sir!'

She sat unmoving, limbs limp as a doll's, while an old Wickan woman washed her down and another cut away most of her hair, and did not look up as Captain Faradan Sort entered the tent.

'That will do,' she said, gesturing for the two Wickans to leave. 'Get out.'

Voicing, in tandem, strings of what the captain took to be curses, the two women left.

Faradan Sort looked down on the girl. 'Long hair just gets in the way, Sinn. You're better off without it. I don't miss mine at all. You're not talking, but I think I know what is going on. So listen. Don't say anything. Just listen to me . . .'

The dull grey, drifting ash devoured the last light of the sun, while dust-clouds from the road drifted down into the cut banks to either side. Remnant breaths of the dead city still rolled over the Fourteenth Army – all that remained of the firestorm, yet reminder enough for the mass of soldiers awaiting the horn blasts that would announce the march.

Fist Keneb lifted himself into the saddle, gathered the reins. All round him he could hear coughing, from human and beast alike, a terrible sound. Wagons, burdened with the cloth-swathed wounded, were lined up on the road like funeral carts, smoke-stained, flame-blackened and reeking of pyres. Among them, he knew, could be found Fist Tene Baralta, parts of his body burned away and his face horribly scarred – a Denul healer had managed to save his eyes, but the man's beard had caught fire, and most of his lips and nose were gone. The concern now was for his sanity, although he remained, mercifully, unconscious. And there were others, so many others . . .

He watched Temul and two riders cantering towards him. The Wickan leader reined in, shaking his head. 'Nowhere to be found, Fist. It's no surprise – but know this: we've had other desertions, and we've tracked them all down. The Adjunct has issued the command to kill the next ones on sight.'

Keneb nodded, looked away.

'From now on,' Temul continued, 'my Wickans will not accept counter-orders from Malazan officers.'

The Fist's head turned back and he stared at Temul. 'Fist, your Wickans *are* Malazans.'

The young warrior grimaced, then wheeled his horse. 'They're your problem now, Fist. Send out searchers if you like, but the Fourteenth won't wait for them.'

Even as he and his aides rode away, the horns sounded, and the army lurched into motion.

Keneb rose in his saddle and looked around. The sun was down, now. Too dark to see much of anything. And somewhere out there were Captain Faradan Sort and Sinn. Two deserters. *That damned captain. I thought she was . . . well, I didn't think she'd do something like this.*

Y'Ghatan had broken people, broken them utterly – he did not think many would recover. *Ever.*

The Fourteenth Army began its march, down the western road, towards the Sotka Fork, in its wake dust and ash, and a destroyed city.

Her head was serpentine, the slitted, vertical eyes lurid green, and Balm watched her tongue slide in and out with fixed, morbid fascination. The wavy, ropy black tendrils of her hair writhed, and upon the end of each was a tiny human head, mouth open in piteous screams.

Witch Eater, Thesorma Raadil, all bedecked in zebra skins, her four arms lifting this way and that, threatening with the four sacred weapons of the Dal Hon tribes. Bola, kout, hook-scythe and rock – he could never understand that: where were the more obvious ones? Knife? Spear? Bow? Who thought up these goddesses anyway? What mad, twisted, darkly amused mind conjured such monstrosities? *Whoever it was – is – I hate him. Or her. Probably her. It's always her. She's a witch, isn't she? No, Witch Eater. Likely a man, then, and one not mad or stupid after all. Someone has to eat all those witches.*

Yet she was advancing on him. Balm. A mediocre warlock – no, a lapsed warlock – just a soldier, now, in fact. A sergeant, but where in Hood's name was his squad? The army? What was he doing on the savannah of his homeland? *I ran from there, oh yes I did. Herd cattle? Hunt monstrous, vicious beasts and call it a fun pastime? Not for me. Oh no, not Balm. I've drunk enough bull blood to sprout horns, enough cow milk to grow udders –* 'so you, Witch Eater, get away from me!'

She laughed, the sound a predictable hiss, and said, 'I'm hungry for wayward warlocks—'

'No! You eat witches! Not warlocks!'

'Who said anything about eating?'

Balm tried to get away, scrabbling, clawing, but there were rocks, rough walls, projections that snagged him. He was trapped. *'I'm trapped!'*

'Get away from him, you rutting snake!'

A voice of thunder. Well, minute thunder. Balm lifted his head, looked round. A huge beetle stood within arm's reach – reared up on its hind legs, its wedge-shaped head would have been level with Balm's knees, could he stand. So, huge in a relative sense. *Imparala Ar, the Dung God* – 'Imparala! Save me!'

'Fear not, mortal,' the beetle said, antennae and limbs waving about. 'She'll not have you! No, *I* have need of you!'

'You do? For what?'

'To dig, my mortal friend. Through the vast dung of the world! Only your kind, human, with your clear vision, your endless appetite! You, conveyor of waste and maker of rubbish! Follow me, and we shall eat our way into the very Abyss itself!'

'Gods, you stink!'

'Never mind that, my friend – before too long you too—'

'Leave him alone, the both of you!' A third voice, shrill, descending from above and closing fast. 'It's the dead and dying who cry out the truth of things!'

Balm looked up. Brithan Troop, the eleven-headed vulture goddess. 'Oh, leave me alone! All of you!'

From every side, now, a growing clamour of voices. Gods and goddesses, the whole Dal Honese menagerie of disgusting deities.

Oh, why do we have so many of them?

It was her sister, not her. She remembered, as clearly as if it had been yesterday, the night of lies that lumbered into the Itko Kanese village when the seas had been silent, empty, for too long. When hunger, no, starvation, had arrived, and all the civil, modern beliefs – the stately, just gods – were cast off once again. In the name of Awakening, the old grisly rites had returned.

The fish had gone away. The seas were lifeless. Blood was needed, to stir the Awakening, to save them all.

They'd taken her sister. Smiles was certain of it. Yet, here were the rough, salt-gnawed hands of the elders, carrying her drugged, insensate body down onto the wet sands – the tide drawn far back and waiting patiently for this warm gift – whilst she floated above herself, looking on in horror.

All wrong. Not the way it had happened. They'd taken her twin sister – so much power in the Mirror Birth, after all, and so rare in the small village where she'd been born.

Her sister. That was why she'd fled them all. Cursing every name, every face glimpsed that night. Running and running, all the way to the great city to the north – and, had she known what awaited her there . . .

No, I'd do it again. I would. Those bastards. 'For the lives of everyone else, child, give up your own. This is the cycle, this is life and death,
and that eternal path lies in the blood. Give up your own life, for the
lives of all of us.'

Odd how those priests never volunteered themselves for that glorious
gift. How they never insisted that they be the ones tied and weighted
down to await the tide's wash, and the crabs, the ever hungry crabs.

And, if it was so damned blissful, why pour durhang oil down her
throat, until her eyes were like black pearls and she couldn't even walk,
much less think? Still less comprehend what was happening, what they
were planning to do to her?

Drifting above the body of herself, Smiles sensed the old spirits drawing close, eager and gleeful. And, somewhere in the depths beyond the
bay, waited the Eldest God. Mael himself, that feeder on misery,
the cruel taker of life and hope.

Rage rising within her, Smiles could feel her body straining at the
numbing turgid chains – she would not lie unmoving, she would not
smile up when her mother kissed her one last time. She would not blink
dreamily when the warm water stole over her, into her.

Hear me! All you cursed spirits, hear me! I defy you!

*Oh yes, flinch back! You know well enough to fear, because I swear
this – I will take you all down with me. I will take you all into the
Abyss, into the hands of the demons of chaos. It's the cycle, you see.
Order and chaos, a far older cycle than life and death, wouldn't you
agree?*

So, come closer, all of you.

In the end, it was as she had known. They'd taken her sister, and she,
well, let's not be coy now, you delivered the last kiss, dear girl. And no
durhang oil to soothe away the excuse, either.

Running away never feels as fast, never as far, as it should.

You could believe in whores. He had been born to a whore, a Seti girl
of fourteen who'd been flung away by her parents – of course, she
hadn't been a whore then, but to keep her new son fed and clothed,
well, it was the clearest course before her.

And he had learned the ways of worship among whores, all those
women knitted close to his mother, sharing fears and everything else
that came with the profession. Their touch had been kindly and sincere,
the language they knew best.

A half-blood could call on no gods. A half-blood walked the gutter
between two worlds, despised by both.

Yet he had not been alone, and in many ways it was the half-
bloods who held closest to the traditional ways of the Seti. The

full-blood tribes had gone off to wars – all the young lance warriors and the women archers – beneath the standard of the Malazan Empire. When they had returned, they were Seti no longer. They were Malazan.

And so Koryk had been immersed in the old rituals – those that could be remembered – and they had been, he had known even then, godless and empty. Serving only the living, the half-blood kin around each of them.

There was no shame in that.

There had been a time, much later, when Koryk had come upon his own language, protecting the miserable lives of the women from whom he had first learned the art of empty worship. A mindful dialect, bound to no cause but that of the living, of familiar, ageing faces, of repaying the gifts the now unwanted once-whores had given him in his youth. And then watching them one by one die. Worn out, so scarred by so many brutal hands, the indifferent usage by the men and women of the city – who proclaimed the ecstasy of god-worship when it suited them, then defiled human flesh with the cold need of carnivores straddling a kill.

Deep in the sleep of Carelbarra, the God Bringer, Koryk beheld no visitors. For him, there was naught but oblivion.

As for the fetishes, well, they were for something else. Entirely something else.

'Go on, mortal, pull it.'

Crump glowered, first at Stump Flit, the Salamander God, Highest of High Marshals, then at the vast, gloomy swamp of Mott. What was he doing here? He didn't want to be here. What if his brothers found him? 'No.'

'Go on, I know you want to. Take my tail, mortal, and watch me thrash about, a trapped god in your hands, it's what you all do anyway. All of you.'

'No. Go away. I don't want to talk to you. Go away.'

'Oh, poor Jamber Bole, all so alone, now. Unless your brothers find you, and then you'll want me on your side, yes you will. If they find you, oh my, oh my.'

'They won't. They ain't looking, neither.'

'Yes they are, my foolish young friend—'

'I ain't your friend. Go away.'

'They're after you, Jamber Bole. Because of what you did—'

'I didn't do nothing!'

'Grab my tail. Go on. Here, just reach out . . .'

Jamber Bole, now known as Crump, sighed, reached out and closed his hand on the Salamander God's tail.

It bolted, and he was left holding the end of the tail in his hand.

Stump Flit raced away, laughing and laughing.

Good thing too, Crump reflected. It was the only joke it had.

Corabb stood in the desert, and through the heat-haze someone was coming. A child. Sha'ik reborn, the seer had returned, to lead still more warriors to their deaths. He could not see her face yet – there was something wrong with his eyes. Burned, maybe. Scoured by blowing sand, he didn't know, but to see was to feel pain. To see *her* was . . . terrible.

No, Sha'ik, please. This must end, it must all end. We have had our fill of holy wars – how much blood can this sand absorb? When will your thirst end?

She came closer. And the closer she drew to where he was standing, the more his eyes failed him, and when he heard her halt before him, Corabb Bhilan Thenu'alas was blind.

Yet not deaf, as she whispered, '*Help me.*'

'Open your eyes, friend.'

But he didn't want to. Everybody demanded decisions. From him, all the time, and he didn't want to make any more. Never again. The way it was now was perfect. This slow sinking away, the whisperings that meant nothing, that weren't even words. He desired nothing more, nothing else.

'Wake up, Fiddler. One last time, so we can talk. We need to talk, friend.'

All right. He opened his eyes, blinked to clear the mists – but they didn't clear – in fact, the face looking down at him seemed to be made of those mists. 'Hedge. What do you want?'

The sapper grinned. 'I bet you think you're dead, don't you? That you're back with all your old buddies. A Bridgeburner, where the Bridgeburners never die. The deathless army – oh, we cheated Hood, didn't we just. Hah! That's what you're thinking, yeah? Okay, then, so where's Trotts? Where are all the others?'

'You tell me.'

'I will. You ain't dead. Not yet, maybe not for a while either. And that's my point. That's why I'm here. You need a kicking awake, Fid, else Hood'll find you and you won't see none of us ever again. The world's been burned through, where you are right now. Burned through, realm after realm, warren after warren. It ain't a place anybody can claim. Not for a long time. Dead, burned down straight to the Abyss.'

'You're a ghost, Hedge. What do you want with me? From me?'

'You got to keep going, Fid. You got to take us with you, right to the end—'

'What end?'

'The end and that's all I can say—'

'Why?'

''Cause it ain't happened yet, you idiot! How am I supposed to know? It's the future and I can't see no future. Gods, you're so thick, Fid. You always were.'

'Me? I didn't blow myself up, Hedge.'

'So? You're lying on a bunch of urns and bleeding out – that's better? Messing up all that sweet honey with your blood—'

'What honey? What are you talking about?'

'You better get going, you're running outa time.'

'Where are we?'

'No place, and that's the problem. Maybe Hood'll find you, maybe no-one will. The ghosts of Y'Ghatan – they all burned. Into nothing. Destroyed, all those locked memories, thousands and thousands. Thousands of years . . . gone, now. You've no idea the loss . . .'

'Be quiet. You're sounding like a ghost.'

'Time to wake up, Fid. Wake up, now. Go on . . .'

Wildfires had torn across the grasslands, and Bottle found himself lying on blackened stubble. Nearby lay a charred carcass. Some kind of four-legged grass-eater – and around it had gathered a half-dozen human-like figures, fine-furred and naked. They held sharp-edged stones and were cutting into the burnt flesh.

Two stood as sentinels, scanning the horizons. One of them was . . . *her.*

My female. Heavy with child, so heavy now. She saw him and came over. He could not look away from her eyes, from that regal serenity in her gaze.

There had been wild apes on Malaz Island once. He remembered, in Jakatakan, when he was maybe seven years old, seeing a cage in the market, the last island ape left, captured in the hardwood forests on the north coast. It had wandered down into a village, a young male seeking a mate – but there were no mates left. Half-starved and terrified, it had been cornered in a stable, clubbed unconscious, and now it crouched in a filthy bamboo cage at the dockside market in Jakatakan.

The seven-year-old boy had stood before it, his eyes level with that black-furred, heavy-browed beast's own eyes, and there had been a moment, a single moment, when their gazes locked. A single moment that broke Bottle's heart. He'd seen misery, he'd seen *awareness* – the

307

glint that knew itself, yet did not comprehend what it had done wrong, what had earned it the loss of its freedom. It could not have known, of course, that it was now alone in the world. The last of its kind. And that somehow, in some exclusively human way, that was its crime.

Just as the child could not have known that the ape, too, was aged seven.

Yet both saw, both knew in their souls – those darkly flickering shapings, not yet solidly formed – that, for this one time, they were each looking upon a brother.

Breaking his heart.

Breaking the ape's heart, too – but maybe, he'd thought since, maybe he just needed to believe that, a kind of flagellation in recompense. For being the one outside the cage, for knowing that there was blood on the hands of himself and his kind.

Bottle's soul, broken away . . . and so freed, gifted or cursed with the ability to travel, to seek those duller life-sparks and to find that, in truth, they were not dull at all, that the failure in fully seeing belonged to himself.

Compassion existed when and only when one could step outside oneself, to suddenly see the bars from inside the cage.

Years later, Bottle had tracked down the fate of that last island ape. Purchased by a scholar who lived in a solitary tower on the wild, unsettled coast of Geni, where there dwelt, in the forests inland, bands of apes little different from the one he had seen; and he liked to believe, now, that that scholar's heart had known compassion; and that those foreign apes had not rejected this strange, shy cousin. His hope: that there had been a reprieve, for that one, solitary life.

His fear was that the creature's wired skeleton stood in one of the tower's dingy rooms, a trophy of uniqueness.

Amidst the smell of ash and charred flesh, the female crouched down before him, reached out to brush hard finger pads across his forehead.

Then that hand made a fist, lifting high, then flashing down—

He flinched, eyes snapping open and seeing naught but darkness. Hard rims and shards digging into his back – *the chamber, the honey, oh gods my head aches* . . . Groaning, Bottle rolled over, the shard fragments cutting and crunching beneath him. He was in the room beyond the one containing the urns, although at least one had followed him to shatter on the cold stone floor. He groaned again. Smeared in sticky honey, aches all over him . . . but the burns, the pain – gone. He drew a deep breath, then coughed. The air was foul. He needed to get everyone going – he needed—

'Bottle? That you?'

Cuttle, lying nearby. 'Aye,' said Bottle. 'That honey—'

'Kicked hard, didn't it just. I dreamed . . . a tiger, it had died – cut to pieces, in fact, by these giant undead lizards that ran on two feet. Died, yet ascended, only it was the death part it was telling me about. The dying part – I don't understand. Treach had to die, I think, to arrive. The dying part was important – I'm sure of it, only . . . gods below, listen to me. This air's rotten – we got to get moving.'

Yes. But he'd lost the rat, he remembered that, he'd lost her. Filled with despair, Bottle sought out the creature—

—and found her. Awakened by his touch, resisting not at all as he captured her soul once more, and, seeing through her eyes, he led the rat back into the room.

'Wake the others, Cuttle. It's time.'

Shouting, getting louder, and Gesler awoke soaked in sweat. That, he decided, was a dream he would never, ever revisit. Given the choice. Fire, of course, so much fire. Shadowy figures dancing on all sides, dancing around him, in fact. Night, snapped at by flames, the drumming of feet, voices chanting in some barbaric, unknown language, and he could feel his soul responding, flaring, burgeoning as if summoned by some ritual.

At which point Gesler realized. They were dancing round a hearth. And he was looking out at them – from the very flame itself. No, he *was* the flame.

Oh Truth, you went and killed yourself. Damned fool.

Soldiers were awakening on all sides of the chamber – shouts and moans and a chorus of clunking urns.

This journey was not yet done. They would go on, and on, deeper and deeper, until the passage dead-ended, until the air ran out, until a mass of rubble shook loose and crushed them all.

Any way at all, please, except fire.

How long had they been down here? Bottle had no idea. Memories of open sky, of sunlight and the wind, were invitations to madness, so fierce was the torture of recalling all those things one took for granted. Now, the world was reduced to sharp fragments of brick, dust, cobwebs and darkness. Passages that twisted, climbed, dropped away. His hands were a battered, bloody mess from clawing through packed rubble.

And now, on a sharp down-slope, he had reached a place too small to get through. Feeling with his half-numbed hands, he tracked the edges. Some kind of cut cornerstone had sagged down at an angle from the ceiling. Its lowermost corner – barely two hand's-widths above the rutted, sandy floor – neatly bisected the passage.

Bottle settled his forehead against the gritty floor. Air still flowed past, a faint stirring now, nothing more than that. And water had run down this track, heading somewhere.

'What's wrong?' Cuttle asked behind him.

'We're blocked.'

Silence for a moment, then, 'Your rat gone ahead? Past the block?'

'Yes. It opens out again – there's an intersection of some kind ahead, a hole coming down from above, with air pulling down from it and straight into a pit in the floor. But, Cuttle – there's a big cut stone, no way to squeeze past it. I'm sorry. We have to go back—'

'To Hood we do, move aside if you can, I want to feel this for myself.'

It was not as easy as it sounded, and it was some time before the two men managed to swap positions. Bottle listened to the sapper muttering under his breath, then cursing.

'I told you—'

'Be quiet, I'm thinking. We could try and break it loose, only the whole ceiling might come down with it. No, but maybe we can dig under, into the floor here. Give me your knife.'

'I ain't got a knife any more. Lost it down a hole.'

'Then call back for one.'

'Cuttle—'

'You ain't giving up on us, Bottle. You can't. You either take us through or we're all dead.'

'Damn you,' Bottle hissed. 'Hasn't it occurred to you that maybe there's no way through? Why should there be? Rats are small – Hood, rats can *live* down here. Why should there be a tunnel big enough for us, some convenient route all the way out from under this damned city? To be honest, I'm amazed we've gotten this far. Look, we could go back, right to the temple – and dig our way out—'

'You're the one who doesn't understand, soldier. There's a mountain sitting over the hole we dropped into, a mountain that used to be the city's biggest temple. Dig out? Forget it. There's no going back, Bottle. Only forward; now get me a knife, damn you.'

Smiles drew out one of her throwing-knives and passed it up to the child ahead of her. Something told her that this was it – as far as they would go. Except maybe for the children. The call had come to send the urchins ahead. At the very least, then, they could to go on, find a way out. All this effort – *somebody had better live through it.*

Not that they'd get very far, not without Bottle. That spineless bastard – imagine, depending on *him*. The man who could see eye to eye with rats, lizards, spiders, fungi. Matching wits, and it was a tough battle, wasn't it just.

310

Still, he wasn't a bad sort – he'd taken half the load that day on the march, after that bitch of a captain revealed just how psychotic she really was. That had been generous of him. Strangely generous. But men were like that, on occasion. She never used to believe that, but now she had no choice. They could surprise you.

The child behind Smiles was climbing over her, all elbows and knees and running, drippy, smearing nose. It smelled, too. Smelled bad. Awful things, children. Needy, self-centred tyrants, the boys all teeth and fists, the girls all claws and spit. Gathering into snivelling packs and sniffing out vulnerabilities – and woe to the child not cunning enough to hide their own – the others would close in like the grubby sharks they were. Great pastime, savaging someone.

If these runts are the only ones here who survive, I will haunt them. Every one of them, for the rest of their days. 'Look,' she snarled after an elbow in the nose, 'just get your smelly slimy hide out of my face! Go on, you little ape!'

A voice from behind her: 'Easy there. You was a child once, you know—'

'You don't know nothing about me, so shut it!'

'What, you was hatched? Hah! I believe it! Along with all the other snakes!'

'Yeah, well, whoever you are, don't even think of climbing past me.'

'And get that close? Not a chance.'

She grunted. 'Glad we're understood, then.'

If there was no way through – they'd all lose their minds. No doubt of that at all. Well, at least she had a couple knives left – anybody fool enough to come for her and they'd pay.

The children were squirming through – even as Cuttle dug into the floor with the knife – and then huddling on the other side. Weeping, clinging to each other, and Bottle's heart cried out for them. They would have to find courage, but for the moment, there seemed to be no hope of that.

Cuttle's grunts and gasps, then his curse as he broke the knife's point – not very promising sounds. Ahead, the rat circled the edge of the pit, whiskers twitching at the flow of warm air coming from the shaft. She could climb round to the other side, and Bottle was willing the creature to do so – yet it seemed his control was weakening, for the rat was resisting, her head tilted over the edge of the pit, claws gripping the pocked side, the air flowing up over her . . .

Bottle frowned. From the shaft above, the air had been coming down. And from the pit, flowing *up*. Conjoining in the tunnel, then drifting towards the children.

But the rat . . . that air from below. Warm, not cool. *Warm, smelling of sunlight.*

'Cuttle!'

The sapper halted. 'What?'

'We've got to get past this! That pit – its edges, they've been cut. That shaft, Cuttle, it's been mined, cut through – someone's dug into the side of the tel – there's no other possibility!'

The children's cries had ceased with Bottle's words. He went on, 'That explains this, don't you see? We ain't the first ones to use this tunnel – people have been mining the ruins, looking for loot—'

He could hear Cuttle moving about.

'What are you doing?'

'I'm gonna kick this block out of the way—'

'No, wait! You said—'

'I can't dig through the damned floor! I'm gonna kick this bastard outa the way!'

'Cuttle, wait!'

A bellow, then a heavy thump, dust and gravel streaming from above. A second thump, then thunder shook the floor, and the ceiling was raining down. Screams of terror through the dust-clouds. Ducking, covering his head as stones and sherds descended on him, Bottle squeezed his eyes shut – the dust, so bright—

Bright.

But he couldn't breathe – he could barely move beneath the weight of rubble atop him.

Muted yells from behind, but the terrible hiss of rubble had ceased.

Bottle lifted his head, gasping, coughing.

To see a white shaft of sunlight, dust-filled, cutting its way down. Bathing Cuttle's splayed legs, the huge foundation stone between them. 'Cuttle?'

A cough, then, 'Gods below, that damned thing – it came down between my legs – just missed my . . . oh Hood take me, I feel sick—'

'Never mind that! There's light, coming down. *Sunlight!*'

'Call your rat back – I can't see . . . how far up. I think it narrows. Narrows bad, Bottle.'

The rat was clambering over the children, and he could feel its racing heart.

'I see it – your rat—'

'Take her in your hands, help her into the shaft over you. Yes, there's daylight – oh, it's too narrow – I might make it, or Smiles maybe, but most of the others . . .'

'You just dig when you're up there, make it wider, Bottle. We're too close, now.'

'Can the children get back here? Past the block?'

'Uh, I think so. Tight, but yes.'

Bottle twisted round. 'Roll call! And listen, we're almost there! Dig your way free! We're almost there!'

The rat climbed, closer and closer to that patch of daylight.

Bottle scrambled free of the gravel. 'All right,' he gasped as he moved over Cuttle.

'Watch where you step!' the sapper said. 'My face is ugly enough without a damned heel print on it.'

Bottle pulled himself into the uneven shaft, then halted. 'I got to pull stuff away, Cuttle. Move from directly below . . .'

'Aye.'

Names were being called out . . . hard to tell how many . . . maybe most of them. Bottle could not afford to think about it now. He began tugging at outcrops, bricks and rocks, widening the shaft. 'Stuff coming down!'

As each piece thumped down or bounced off the foundation stone, Cuttle collected it and passed it back.

'Bottle!'

'What?'

'One of the urchins – she fell into the pit – she ain't making any sound – I think we lost her.'

Shit. 'Pass that rope ahead – can Smiles get over to them?'

'I'm not sure. Keep going, soldier – we'll see what we can do down here.'

Bottle worked his way upward. A sudden widening, then narrowing once more – almost within reach of that tiny opening – too small, he realized, for even so much as his hand. He pulled a large chunk of stone from the wall, dragged himself as close as he could to the hole. On a slight ledge near his left shoulder crouched the rat. He wanted to kiss the damned thing.

But not yet. Things looked badly jammed up around that hole. Big stones. Panic whispered through him.

With the rock in his hand, Bottle struck at the stone. A spurt of blood from one fingertip, crushed by the impact – he barely felt it. Hammering, hammering away. Chips raining down every now and then. His arm tiring – he was running out of reserves, he didn't have the strength, the endurance for this. Yet he kept swinging.

Each impact weaker than the one before.

No, damn you! No!

He swung again.

Blood spattered his eyes.

*

313

Captain Faradan Sort reined in on the ridge, just north of the dead city. Normally, a city that had fallen to siege soon acquired its scavengers, old women and children scrambling about, picking through the ruins. But not here, not yet, anyway. Maybe not for a long time.

Like a cracked pot, the steep sides of Y'Ghatan's tel had bled out – melted lead, copper, silver and gold, veins and pools filled with accreted stone chips, dust and potsherds.

Offering an arm, Sort helped Sinn slip down from the saddle behind her – she'd been squirming, whimpering and clutching at her, growing more agitated the closer the day's end came, the light failing. The Fourteenth Army had left the night before. The captain and her charge had walked their lone horse round the tel, not once, but twice, since the sun's rise.

And the captain had begun to doubt her own reading of the child Sinn, her own sense that this half-mad, now seemingly mute creature had known something, sensed something – Sinn had tried and tried to get back into the ruins before her arrest. There had to be a reason for that.

Or, perhaps not. Perhaps nothing more than an insane grief – for her lost brother.

Scanning the rubble-strewn base below the tel's north wall one more time, she noted that one scavenger at least had arrived. A child, smeared in white dust, her hair a matted snarl, was wandering perhaps thirty paces from the rough wall.

Sinn saw her as well, then began picking her way down the slope, making strange mewling sounds.

The captain unstrapped her helm and lifted it clear to settle it on the saddle horn. She wiped grimy sweat from her brow. Desertion. Well, it wasn't the first time, now, was it? If not for Sinn's magic, the Wickans would have found them. And likely executed them. She'd take a few with her, of course, no matter what Sinn did. People learned that you had to pay to deal with her. Pay in every way. A lesson she never tired of teaching.

She watched as Sinn ran to the city's cliff-side, ignoring the scavenger, and began climbing it.

Now what?

Replacing the helm, the sodden leather inside-rim momentarily cool against her brow, the strap feeling stretched as she fixed the clasp beneath her jaw, Faradan Sort collected the reins and guided her horse into a slow descent down the scree.

The scavenger was crying, grubby hands pressed against her eyes. All that dust on her, the webs in her hair – this was the true face of war, the captain knew. That child's face would haunt her memories, joining the many other faces, for as long as she lived.

314

Sinn was clinging to the rough wall, perhaps two man-heights up, motionless.

Too much, Sort decided. The child was mad. She glanced again at the scavenger, who did not seem aware that they had arrived. Hands still pressed against eyes. Red scrapes through the dust, a trickle of blood down one shin. Had she fallen? From where?

The captain rode up to halt her horse beneath Sinn. 'Come down now,' she said. 'We need to make camp, Sinn. Come down, it's no use – the sun's almost gone. We can try again tomorrow.'

Sinn tightened her grip on the broken outcrops of stone and brick.

Grimacing, the captain side-stepped the mount closer to the wall, then reached up to pull Sinn from her perch.

Squealing, the girl lunged upward, one hand shooting into a hole—

His strength, his will, was gone. A short rest, then he could begin again. A short rest, the voices below drifting away, it didn't matter. Sleep, now, the dark, warm embrace – drawing him down, ever deeper, then a blush of sweet golden light, wind rippling yellow grasses—

—and he was free, all pain gone. This, he realized, was not sleep. It was death, the return to the most ancient memory buried in each human soul. *Grasslands, the sun and wind, the warmth and click of insects, dark herds in the distance, the lone trees with their vast canopies and the cool shade beneath, where lions dozed, tongues lolling, flies dancing round indifferent, languid eyes . . .*

Death, and this long buried seed. *We return. We return to the world . . .*

And *she* reached for him, then, her hand damp with sweat, small and soft, prying his fingers loose from the rock they gripped, blood sticking – she clutched at his hand, as if filled with fierce need, and he knew the child within her belly was calling out in its own silent language, its own needs, so demanding . . .

Nails dug into the cuts on his hand—

Bottle jolted awake, eyes blinking – daylight almost gone – and a small hand reaching through from outside, grasping and tugging at his own.

Help. 'Help – you, outside – help us—'

As she reached up yet further to tug the girl down, Sort saw Sinn's head snap around, saw something blazing in her eyes as she stared down at the captain.

'What now—' And then there came a faint voice, seemingly from the very stones. Faradan Sort's eyes widened. 'Sinn?'

The girl's hand, shoved into that crack – it was holding on to something.

Someone.

'Oh, gods below!'

Crunching sounds outside, boots digging into stone, then gloved fingers slipped round one edge beside the child's forearm, and Bottle heard: 'You, inside – who? Can you hear me?'

A woman. Accented Ehrlii . . . familiar? 'Fourteenth Army,' Bottle said. 'Malazans.' The child's grip tightened.

'Oponn's pull, soldier,' the woman said in Malazan. 'Sinn, let go of him. I need room. Make the hole bigger. Let go of him – it's all right – you were right. We're going to get them out.'

Sinn? The shouts from below were getting louder. Cuttle, calling up something about a way out. Bottle twisted to call back down. 'Cuttle! We've been found! They're going to dig us out! Let everyone know!'

Sinn's hand released his, withdrew.

The woman spoke again. 'Soldier, move away from the hole – I'm going to use my sword.'

'Captain? Is that you?'

'Aye. Now, move back and cover your eyes – what? Oh, where'd all those children come from? Is that one of Fiddler's squad with them? Get down there, Sinn. There's another way out. Help them.'

The sword-point dug into the concreted brick and stone. Chips danced down.

Cuttle was climbing up from below, grunting. 'We gotta widen this some more, Bottle. That runt who dropped down the hole. We sent Smiles after her. A tunnel, angling back up – and out. A looter's tunnel. The children're all out—'

'Good. Cuttle, it's the captain. The Adjunct, she must have waited for us – sent searchers out to find us.'

'That makes no sense—'

'You're right,' Faradan Sort cut in. 'They've marched, soldiers. It's just me, and Sinn.'

'They left you behind?'

'No, we deserted. Sinn knew – she knew you were still alive, don't ask me how.'

'Her brother's down here,' Cuttle said. 'Corporal Shard.'

'Alive?'

'We think so, Captain. How many days has it been?'

'Three. Four nights if you count the breach. Now, no more questions, and cover your eyes.'

She chopped away at the hole, tugged loose chunks of brick and stone. The dusk air swept in, cool and, despite all the dust, sweet in

Bottle's lungs. Faradan Sort began work on one large chunk, and broke her sword. A stream of Korelri curses.

'That your Stormwall sword, Captain? I'm sorry—'

'Don't be an idiot.'

'But your scabbard—'

'Aye, my scabbard. The sword it belonged to got left behind . . . in somebody. Now, let me save my breath for this.' And she began chopping away with the broken sword. 'Hood-damned piece of Falari junk—' The huge stone groaned, then slid away, taking the captain with it.

A heavy thump from the ground beyond and below, then more cursing.

Bottle clawed his way into the gap, dragged himself through, then was suddenly tumbling down, landing hard, rolling, winded, onto his stomach.

After a long moment he managed a gasp of air, and he lifted his head – to find himself staring at the captain's boots. Bottle arched, raised a hand and saluted – briefly.

'You managed that better the last time, Bottle.'

'Captain, I'm Smiles—'

'You know, soldier, it was a good thing you assumed half the load I dumped on Smiles's back. If you hadn't done that, well, you likely wouldn't have lived this long—'

He saw her turn, heard a grunted snarl, then one boot lifted, moved out slightly to the side, hovered—

—above Bottle's rat—

—then stamped down – as his hand shot out, knocked the foot aside at the last moment. The captain stumbled, then swore. 'Have you lost your mind—'

Bottle rolled closer to the rat, collected her in both hands and held her against his chest as he settled down onto his back. 'Not this time, Captain. This is *my* rat. She saved our lives.'

'Vile, disgusting creatures.'

'Not her. Not Y'Ghatan.'

Faradan Sort stared down at him. 'She is named Y'Ghatan?'

'Aye. I just decided.'

Cuttle was clambering down. 'Gods, Captain—'

'Quiet, sapper. If you've got the strength left – and you'd better – you need to help the others out.'

'Aye, Captain.' He turned about and began climbing back up.

Still lying on his back, Bottle closed his eyes. He stroked Y'Ghatan's smooth-furred back. *My darling. You're with me, now. Ah, you're hungry – we'll take care of that. Soon you'll be waddling fat again, I promise, and you and your kits will be . . . gods, there's more of you, isn't there? No problem. When it comes to your kind, there's never a shortage of food . . .*

He realized Smiles was standing over him. Staring down.

He managed a faint, embarrassed smile, wondering how much she'd heard, how much she'd just put together.

'All men are scum.'

So much for wondering.

Coughing, crying, babbling, the soldiers were lying or sitting all around Gesler, who stood, trying to make a count – the names, the faces, exhaustion blurred them all together. He saw Shard, with his sister, Sinn, wrapped all around him like a babe, fast asleep, and there was something like shock in the corporal's staring, unseeing eyes. Tulip was nearby – his body was torn, shredded everywhere, but he'd dragged himself through without complaint and now sat on a stone, silent and bleeding.

Crump crouched near the cliff-side, using rocks to pry loose a slab of melted gold and lead, a stupid grin on his ugly, overlong face. And Smiles, surrounded by children – she looked miserable with all the attention, and Gesler saw her staring up at the night sky again and again, and again, and that gesture he well understood.

Bottle had pulled them through. With his rat. *Y'Ghatan.* The sergeant shook his head. Well, why not? *We're all rat-worshippers right now. Oh, right, the roll call . . .* Sergeant Cord, with Ebron, Limp and his broken leg. Sergeant Hellian, her jaw swollen in two places, one eye closed up, and blood matting her hair, just now coming round – under the tender ministrations of her corporal, Urb. Tarr, Koryk, Smiles and Cuttle. Tavos Pond, Balgrid, Mayfly, Flashwit, Saltlick, Hanno, Shortnose and Masan Gilani. Bellig Harn, Maybe, Brethless and Touchy. Deadsmell, Galt, Sands and Lobe. The sergeants Thom Tissy and Balm. Widdershins, Uru Hela, Ramp, Scant and Reem. Throatslitter . . . Gesler's gaze swung back to Tarr, Koryk, Smiles and Cuttle.

Hood's breath.

'Captain! We've lost two!'

Every head turned.

Corporal Tarr shot to his feet, then staggered like a drunk, spinning to face the cliff-wall.

Balm hissed, 'Fiddler . . . and that prisoner! The bastard's killed him and he's hiding back in there! Waiting for us to leave!'

Corabb had dragged the dying man as far as he could, and now both he and the Malazan were done. Crammed tight in a narrowing of the tunnel, the darkness devouring them, and Corabb was not even sure he was going in the right direction. Had they been turned round? He could hear nothing . . . no-one. All that dragging, and pushing . . . they'd turned round, he was sure of it.

No matter, they weren't going anywhere.

Never again. Two skeletons buried beneath a dead city. No more fitting a barrow for a warrior of the Apocalypse and a Malazan soldier. That seemed just, poetic even. He would not complain, and when he stood at this sergeant's side at Hood's Gate, he would be proud for the company.

So much had changed inside him. He was no believer in causes, not any more. Certainty was an illusion, a lie. Fanaticism was poison in the soul, and the first victim in its inexorable, ever-growing list was compassion. Who could speak of freedom, when one's own soul was bound in chains?

He thought, now, finally, that he understood Toblakai.

And it was all too late. This grand revelation. *Thus, I die a wise man, not a fool. Is there any difference? I still die, after all.*

No, there is. I can feel it. That difference – I have cast off my chains. I have cast them off!

A low cough, then, 'Corabb?'

'I am here, Malazan.'

'Where? Where is that?'

'In our tomb, alas. I am sorry, all strength has fled. I am betrayed by my own body. I am sorry.'

Silence for a moment, then a soft laugh. 'No matter. I've been unconscious – you should have left me – where are the others?'

'I don't know. I was dragging you. We were left behind. And now, we're lost, and that's that. I am sorry—'

'Enough of that, Corabb. You dragged me? That explains all the bruises. For how long? How far?'

'I do not know. A day, maybe. There was warm air, but then it was cool – it seemed to breathe in and out, past us, but which breath was in and which was out? I do not know. And now, there is no wind.'

'A day? Are you mad? Why did you not leave me?'

'Had I done so, Malazan, your friends would have killed me.'

'Ah, there is that. But, you know, I don't believe you.'

'You are right. It is simple. I could not.'

'All right, that will do.'

Corabb closed his eyes – the effort making no difference. He was probably blind by now. He had heard that prisoners left too long without light in their dungeon cells went blind. Blind before mad, but mad, too, eventually.

And now he heard sounds, drawing nearer . . . from somewhere. He'd heard them before, a half-dozen times at least, and for a short while there had been faint shouting. Maybe that had been real. The demons of panic come to take the others, one by one. 'Sergeant, are you named Strings or Fiddler?'

'Strings for when I'm lying, Fiddler for when I'm telling the truth.'

'Ah, is that a Malazan trait, then? Strange—'

'No, not a trait. Mine, maybe.'

'And how should I name you?'

'Fiddler.'

'Very well.' *A welcome gift.* 'Fiddler. I was thinking. Here I am, trapped. And yet, it is only now, I think, that I have finally escaped my prison. Funny, isn't it?'

'Damned hilarious, Corabb Bhilan Thenu'alas. What is that sound?'

'You hear it, too?' Corabb held his breath, listened. Drawing closer—

Then something touched his forehead.

Bellowing, Corabb tried to twist away.

'Wait! Damn you, I said wait!'

Fiddler called out, 'Gesler?'

'Aye, calm down your damned friend here, will you?'

Heart pounding, Corabb settled back. 'We were lost, Malazan. I am sorry—'

'Be quiet! Listen to me. You're only about seventy paces from a tunnel, leading out – we're all out, you understand me? Bottle got us out. His rat brought us through. There was a rock fall blocking you up ahead – I've dug through—'

'You crawled back in?' Fiddler demanded. 'Gesler—'

'Believe me, it was the hardest thing I've ever done in my life. Now I know – or I think I know – what Truth went through, running into that palace. Abyss take me, I'm still shaking.'

'Lead us on, then,' Corabb said, reaching back to grasp Fiddler's harness once more.

Gesler made to move past him. 'I can do that—'

'No. I have dragged him this far.'

'Fid?'

'For Hood's sake, Gesler, I've never been in better hands.'

CHAPTER EIGHT

Sarkanos, Ivindonos and Ganath stood looking down on the heaped corpses, the strewn pieces of flesh and fragments of bone. A field of battle knows only lost dreams and the ghosts clutch futilely at the ground, remembering naught but the last place of their lives, and the air is sullen now that the clangour is past, and the last moans of the dying have dwindled into silence.

While this did not belong to them, they yet stood. Of Jaghut, one can never know their thoughts, nor even their aspirations, but they were heard to speak, then.

'All told,' said Ganath. 'This sordid tale here has ended, and there is no-one left to heave the standard high, and proclaim justice triumphant.'

'This is a dark plain,' said Ivindonos, 'and I am mindful of such things, the sorrow untold, unless witnessed.'

'Not mindful enough,' said Sarkanos.

'A bold accusation,' said Ivindonos, his tusks bared in anger. 'Tell me what I am blind to. Tell me what greater sorrow exists than what we see before us.'

And Sarkanos made reply, 'Darker plains lie beyond.'

Stela Fragment (Yath Alban)
Anonymous

THERE WERE TIMES, CAPTAIN GANOES PARAN REFLECTED, WHEN A man could believe in nothing. No path taken could alter the future, and the future remained ever unknown, even by the gods. Sensing those currents, the tumult that lay ahead, achieved little except the loss of restful sleep, and a growing suspicion that all his efforts to shape that future were naught but conceit.

He had pushed the horses hard, staying well clear of villages and hamlets where the Mistress stalked, sowing her deadly seeds, gathering to herself the power of poisoned blood and ten thousand deaths by her hand. Before long, he knew, that toll would rise tenfold. Yet for all his caution, the stench of death was inescapable, arriving again and again as if from nowhere, and no matter how great the distance between him and inhabited areas.

Whatever Poliel's need, it was vast, and Paran was fearful, for he could not understand the game she played here.

Back in Darujhistan, ensconced within the Finnest House, this land known as Seven Cities had seemed so far from the centre of things – or what he believed would soon become the centre of things. And it had been, in part, that mystery that had set him on this path, seeking to discover how what happened here would become enfolded into the greater scheme. Assuming, of course, that such a greater scheme existed.

Equally as likely, he allowed, this war among the gods would implode into a maelstrom of chaos. There had been need, he had once been told, for a Master of the Deck of Dragons. There had been need, he had been told, for *him*. Paran had begun to suspect that, even then, it was already too late. This web was growing too fast, too snarled, for any single mind to fathom.

Except maybe Kruppe, the famed Eel of Darujhistan . . . gods, I wish he was here, in my place, right now. Why wasn't he made the Master of the Deck of Dragons? Or maybe that incorrigible aplomb was naught but bravado, behind which the real Kruppe cowered in terror.

Imagine Raest's thoughts . . . Paran smiled, recollecting. It had been early morning when that little fat man knocked on the door of the Finnest House, flushed of face and beaming up at the undead Jaghut Tyrant who opened it wide and stared down upon him with pitted eyes. Then, hands fluttering and proclaiming something about a crucial meeting, Kruppe somehow slid past the Azath guardian, waddling into the main hall and sinking with a delighted sigh of contentment into the plush chair beside the fireplace.

An unexpected guest for breakfast; it seemed even Raest could do nothing about it. Or would not. The Jaghut had been typically reticent on the subject.

And so Paran had found himself seated opposite the famed Defier of Caladan Brood – this corpulent little man in his faded waistcoat who had confounded the most powerful ascendants on Genabackis – and watched him eat. And eat. While somehow, at the same time, talking nonstop.

'Kruppe knows the sad dilemma, yes indeed, of sad befuddled Master. Twice sad? Nay, thrice sad! Four times sad – ah, how usage of the dread word culminates! Cease now, Sir Kruppe, lest we find ourselves weeping without surcease!' Lifting one greasy finger. 'Ah, but Master wonders, does he not, how can one man such as Kruppe know all these things? What things, you would also ask, given the chance, said chance Kruppe hastens to intercept with suitable answer. Had Kruppe such an answer, that is. But lo! He does not, and is that not the true wonder of it all?'

'For Hood's sake,' Paran cut in – and got no further.

'Yes indeed! For Hood's sake indeed, oh, you are brilliant and so worthy of the grand title of Master of the Deck of Dragons and Kruppe's most trusted friend! Hood, at the very centre of things, oh yes, and that is why you must hasten, forthwith, to Seven Cities.'

Paran stared, dumbfounded, wondering what detail in that barrage of words he had missed. 'What?'

'The gods, dear precious friend of Kruppe's! They are at war, yes? Terrible thing, war. Terrible things, gods. The two, together, ah, most terribler!'

'Terri— what? Oh, never mind.'

'Kruppe never does.'

'Why Seven Cities?'

'Even the gods cast shadows, Master of the Deck. But what do shadows cast?'

'I don't know. Gods?'

Kruppe's expression grew pained. 'Oh my, a nonsensical reply. Kruppe's faith in dubious friend lies shaking. No, shaken. Not lies, is. See how Kruppe shakens? No, not gods. How can gods be cast? Do not answer that – such is the nature and unspoken agreement regards rhetoric. Now, where was Kruppe? Oh yes. Most terrible crimes are in the offing off in Seven Cities. Eggs have been laid and schemes have hatched! One particularly large shell is about to be broken, and will have been broken by the time you arrive, which means it is as good as broken right now so what are you waiting for? In fact, foolish man, you are already too late, or will be, by then, and if not then, then soon, in the imminent sense of the word. Soon, then, you must go, despite it being too late – I suggest you leave tomorrow morning and make use of warrens and other nefarious paths of inequity to hasten your hopeless quest to arrive. On time, and in time, and in due time you will indeed arrive, and then you must walk the singular shadow – between, dare Kruppe utter such dread words – between life and death, the wavy, blurry metaphor so callously and indifferently trespassed by things that should know better. Now, you have worn out Kruppe's ears, distended Kruppe's largesse unto bursting his trouser belt, and heretofore otherwise exhausted his vast intellect.' He rose with a grunt, then patted his tummy. 'A mostly acceptable repast, although Kruppe advises that you

323

inform your cook that the figs were veritably mummified – from the Jaghut's own store, one must assume, yes, hmm?'

There had been some sense, Paran had eventually concluded, within that quagmire of verbosity. Enough to frighten him, in any case, leading him to a more intense examination of the Deck of Dragons. Wherein the chaos was more pronounced than it ever had been before. And there, in its midst, the glimmer of a path, a way through – perhaps simply imagined, an illusion – but he would have to try, although the thought terrified him.

He was not the man for this. He was stumbling, half-blind, within a vortex of converging powers, and he found he was struggling to maintain even the illusion of control.

Seeing Apsalar again had been an unexpected gift. A girl no longer, yet, it appeared, as deadly as ever. Nonetheless, something like humanity had revealed itself, there in her eyes every now and then. He wondered what she had gone through since Cotillion had been banished from her outside Darujhistan – beyond what she had been willing to tell him, that is, and he wondered if she would complete her journey, to come out the other end, reborn one more time.

He rose in his stirrups to stretch his legs, scanning the south for the telltale shimmer that would announce his destination. Nothing but heat-haze yet, and rugged, treeless hills rising humped on the pan. Seven Cities was a hot, blasted land, and he decided that even without plague, he didn't like it much.

One of those hills suddenly vanished in a cloud of dust and flying debris, then a thundering boom drummed through the ground, startling the horses. As he struggled to calm them – especially his own mount, which had taken this opportunity to renew its efforts to unseat him, bucking and kicking – he sensed something else rolling out from the destroyed mound.

Omtose Phellack.

Settling his horse as best he could, Paran collected the reins and rode at a slow, jumpy canter towards the ruined hill.

As he neared, he could hear crashing sounds from within the barrow – for a barrow it was – and when he was thirty paces distant, part of a desiccated body was flung from the hole, skidding in a clatter through the rubble. It came to a stop, then one arm lifted tremulously, dropping back down a moment later. A bone-helmed skull flew into view, ropes of hair twisting about, to bounce and roll in the dust.

Paran reined in, watching as a tall, gaunt figure climbed free of the barrow, slowly straightening. Grey-green skin, trailing dusty cobwebs, wearing a silver-clasped harness and baldric of iron mail from which hung knives in copper scabbards – the various metals blackened or

324

green with verdigris. Whatever clothing had once covered the figure's body had since rotted away.

A Jaghut woman, her long black hair drawn into a single tail that reached down to the small of her back. Her tusks were silver-sheathed and thus black. She slowly looked round, her gaze finding and settling on him. Vertical pupils set in amber studied Paran from beneath a heavy brow. He watched her frown, then she asked, 'What manner of creature are you?'

'A well-mannered one,' Paran replied, attempting a smile. She had spoken in the Jaghut tongue and he had understood . . . somehow. One of the many gifts granted by virtue of being the Master? Or long proximity with Raest and his endless muttering? Either way, Paran surprised himself by replying in the same language.

At which her frown deepened. 'You speak my tongue as would an Imass . . . had any Imass bothered to learn it. Or a Jaghut whose tusks had been pulled.'

Paran glanced over at the partial corpse lying nearby. 'An Imass like that one?'

She drew her thin lips back in what he took to be a smile. 'A guardian left behind – it had lost its vigilance. Undead have a tendency towards boredom, and carelessness.'

'T'lan Imass.'

'If others are near, they will come now. I have little time.'

'T'lan Imass? None, Jaghut. None anywhere close.'

'You are certain?'

'I am. Reasonably. You have freed yourself . . . why?'

'Freedom needs an excuse?' She brushed dust and webs from her lean body, then faced west. 'One of my rituals has been shattered. I must needs repair it.'

Paran thought about that, then asked, 'A binding ritual? Something, or someone was imprisoned, and, like you just now, it seeks freedom?'

She looked displeased with the comparison. 'Unlike the entity I imprisoned, I have no interest in conquering the world.'

Oh. 'I am Ganoes Paran.'

'Ganath. You look pitiful, like a malnourished Imass – are you here to oppose me?'

He shook his head. 'I was but passing by, Ganath. I wish you good fortune—'

She suddenly turned, stared eastward, head cocking.

'Something?' he asked. 'T'lan Imass?'

She glanced at him. 'I am not certain. Perhaps . . . nothing. Tell me, is there a sea south of here?'

'Was there one when you were . . . not yet in your barrow?'

'Yes.'

Paran smiled. 'Ganath, there is indeed a sea just south of here, and it is where I am headed.'

'Then I shall travel with you. Why do you journey there?'

'To talk with some people. And you? I thought you were in a hurry to repair that ritual?'

'I am, yet I find a more pressing priority.'

'And that is?'

'The need for a bath.'

Too bloated to fly, the vultures scattered with outraged cries, hopping and waddling with wings crooked, leaving the once-human feast exposed in their wake. Apsalar slowed her steps, not sure whether she wanted to continue walking down this main street, although the raucous chattering and bickering of feeding vultures sounded from the side avenues as well, leading her to suspect that no alternative route was possible.

The villagers had died suffering – there was no mercy in this plague, for it had carved a long, tortured path to Hood's Gate. Swollen glands, slowly closing the throat, making it impossible to eat solid food, and narrowing the air passages, making every breath drawn agony. And, in the gut, gases distending the stomach. Blocked from any means of escape, they eventually burst the stomach lining, allowing the victim's own acids to devour them from within. These, alas, were the final stages of the disease. Before then, there was fever, so hot that brains were cooked in the skull, driving the person half-mad – a state from which, even were the disease somehow halted then and there – there was no recovery. Eyes wept mucus, ears bled, flesh grew gelatinous at the joints – this was the Mistress in all her sordid glory.

The two skeletal reptiles accompanying Apsalar had sprinted ahead, entertaining themselves by frightening the vultures and bursting through buzzing masses of flies. Now they scampered back, unmindful of the blackened, half-eaten corpses they clambered over.

'Not-Apsalar! You are too slow!'

'No, Telorast,' cried Curdle, 'not slow enough!'

'Yes, not slow enough! We like this village – we want to play!'

Leading her placid horse, Apsalar began picking her way down the street. A score of villagers had crawled out here for some unknown reason, perhaps in some last, pathetic attempt to escape what could not be escaped. They had died clawing and fighting each other. 'You are welcome to stay as long as you like,' she said to the two creatures.

'That cannot be,' Telorast said. 'We are your guardians, after all.

Your sleepless, ever-vigilant sentinels. We shall stand guard over you no matter how diseased and disgusting you become.'

'And then we'll pick out your eyes!'

'Curdle! Don't tell her that!'

'Well, we'll wait until she's sleeping, of course. Thrashing in fever.'

'Exactly. She'll want us to by then, anyway.'

'I know, but we've walked through two villages now and she still isn't sick. I don't understand. All the other mortals are dead or dying, what makes her so special?'

'Chosen by the usurpers of Shadow – that's why she can just saunter through with her nose in the air. We may have to wait before we can pick out her eyes.'

Apsalar stepped past the heap of corpses. Just ahead, the village came to an abrupt end and beyond stood the charred remnants of three out-lying buildings. A crow-haunted cemetery surmounted a nearby low hill where stood a lone guldindha tree. The black birds crowded the branches in sullen silence. A few makeshift platforms attested to some early efforts at ceremony to attend the dead, but clearly that had been short-lived. A dozen white goats stood in the tree's shade, watching Apsalar as she continued on down the road, flanked by the skeletons of Telorast and Curdle.

Something had happened, far to the north and west. No, she could be more precise than that. Y'Ghatan. There had been a battle . . . and the committing of a terrible crime. Y'Ghatan's lust for Malazan blood was legendary, and Apsalar feared that it had drunk deep once more.

In every land, there were places that saw battle again and again, an endless succession of slaughter, and more often than not such places held little strategic value in any greater scheme, or were ultimately indefensible. As if the very rocks and soil mocked every conqueror foolish enough to lay claim to them. Cotillion's thoughts, these. He had never been afraid to recognize futility, and the world's pleasure in defying human grandiosity.

She passed the last of the burned-out buildings, relieved to have left their stench behind – rotting bodies she was used to, but something of that charred reek slipped beneath her senses like a premonition. It was nearing dusk. Apsalar climbed back into the saddle and gathered up the reins.

She would attempt the warren of Shadow, even though she already knew it was too late – something had happened at Y'Ghatan; at the very least, she could look upon the wounds left behind and pick up the trail of the survivors. If any existed.

'She dreams of death,' Telorast said. 'And now she's angry.'

'With us?'

'Yes. No. Yes. No.'

'Ah, she's opened a warren! Shadow! Lifeless trail winding through lifeless hills, we shall perish from ennui! Wait, don't leave us!'

They climbed out of the pit to find a banquet awaiting them. A long table, four high-backed Untan-style chairs, a candelabra in the centre bearing four thick-stemmed beeswax candles, the golden light flickering down on silver plates heaped with Malazan delicacies. Oily santos fish from the shoals off Kartool, baked with butter and spices in clay; strips of marinated venison, smelling of almonds in the northern D'avorian style; grouse from the Seti plains stuffed with bull-berries and sage; baked gourds and fillets of snake from Dal Hon; assorted braised vegetables and four bottles of wine: a Malaz Island white from the Paran Estates, warmed rice wine from Itko Kan, a full-bodied red from Gris, and the orange-tinted belack wine from the Napan Isles.

Kalam stood staring at the bounteous apparition, as Stormy, with a grunt, walked over, boots puffing in the dust, and sat down in one of the chairs, reaching for the Grisian red.

'Well,' Quick Ben said, dusting himself off, 'this is nice. Who's the fourth chair for, you think?'

Kalam looked up at the looming bulk of the sky keep. 'I'd rather not think about that.'

Snorting sounds from Stormy as he launched into the venison strips.

'Do you suspect,' Quick Ben ventured as he sat down, 'there is some significance to the selection provided us?' He collected an alabaster goblet and poured himself a helping of the Paran white. 'Or is it the sheer decadence that he wants to rub our noses in?'

'My nose is just fine,' Stormy said, tipping his head to one side and spitting out a bone. 'Gods, I could eat all of this myself! Maybe I will at that!'

Sighing, Kalam joined them at the table. 'All right, at least this gives us time to talk about things.' He saw the wizard glance suspiciously at Stormy. 'Relax, Quick, I doubt Stormy can hear us above his own chewing.'

'Hah!' the Falari laughed, spitting fragments across the table, one landing with a plop in the wizard's goblet. 'As if I give a Hood's toenail about all your self-important preening! You two want to talk yourselves blue, go right ahead – I won't waste my time listening.'

Quick Ben found a silver meat-spear and delicately picked the piece of venison from the goblet. He took a tentative sip, made a face, and poured the wine away. As he refilled the goblet, he said, 'Well, I'm not entirely convinced Stormy here is irrelevant to our conversation.'

The red-bearded soldier looked up, small eyes narrowing with sudden unease. 'I couldn't be more irrelevant if I tried,' he said in a growl, reaching again for the bottle of red.

Kalam watched the man's throat bob as he downed mouthful after mouthful.

'It's that sword,' said Quick Ben. 'That T'lan Imass sword. How did you come by it, Stormy?'

'Huh, santos. In Falar only poor people eat those ugly fish, and the Kartoolii call it a delicacy! Idiots.' He collected one and began scooping the red, oily flesh from the clay shell. 'It was given to me,' he said, 'for safekeeping.'

'By a T'lan Imass?' Kalam asked.

'Aye.'

'So it plans on coming back for it?'

'If it can, aye.'

'Why would a T'lan Imass give you its sword? They generally use them, a lot.'

'Not where it was headed, assassin. What's this? Some kind of bird?'

'Yes,' said Quick Ben. 'Grouse. So, where was the T'lan Imass headed, then?'

'Grouse. What's that, some kind of duck? It went into a big wound in the sky, to seal it.'

The wizard leaned back. 'Don't expect it any time soon, then.'

'Well, it took the head of a Tiste Andii with it, and that head was still alive – Truth was the only one who saw that – the other T'lan Imass didn't, not even the bonecaster. Small wings – surprised the thing could fly at all. Not very well, hah, since someone caught it!' He finished the Grisian and tossed away the bottle. It thumped in the thick dust. Stormy then reached for the Napan belack. 'You know what's the problem with you two? I'll tell ya. I'll tell ya the problem. You both think too much, and you think that by thinking so much you get somewhere with all that thinking, only you don't. Look, it's simple. Something you don't like gets in your way you kill it, and once you kill it you can stop thinking about it and that's that.'

'Interesting philosophy, Stormy,' said Quick Ben. 'But what if that "something" is too big, or too many, or nastier than you?'

'Then you cut it down to size, wizard.'

'And if you can't?'

'Then you find someone else who can. Maybe they end up killing each other, and that's that.' He waved the half-empty bottle of belack. 'You think you can make all sortsa plans? Idiots. I squat down and shit on your plans!'

Kalam smiled at Quick Ben. 'Stormy's onto something there, maybe.'

The wizard scowled. 'What, squatting—'

'No, finding someone else to do the dirty work for us. We're old hands at that, Quick, aren't we?'

'Only, it gets harder.' Quick Ben gazed up at the sky keep. 'All right, let me think—'

'Oh we're in trouble now!'

'Stormy,' said Kalam, 'you're drunk.'

'I ain't drunk. Two bottlesa wine don't get me drunk. Not Stormy, they don't.'

'The question,' said the wizard, 'is this. Who or what defeated the K'Chain Che'Malle the first time round? And then, is that powerful force still alive? Once we work out the answers to those—'

'Like I said,' the Falari growled, 'you talk and talk and talk and you ain't getting a damned thing.'

Quick Ben settled back, rubbing at his eyes. 'Fine, then. Go on, Stormy, let's hear your brilliance.'

'First, you're assuming those lizard things are your enemy in the firs' place. Third, if the legends are true, those lizards defeated themselves, so what in Hood's soiled trousers are you panicking 'bout? Second, the Adjunct wanted to know all 'bout them and where they're going and all that. Well, the sky keeps ain't going nowhere, and we already know what's inside 'em, so we done our job. You idiots want to break into one – what for? You ain't got a clue what for. And five, you gonna finish that white wine, wizard? 'Cause I ain't touching that rice piss.'

Quick Ben slowly sat forward and slid the bottle towards Stormy.

No better gesture of defeat was possible, Kalam decided. 'Finish up, everyone,' he said, 'so we can get outa this damned warren and back to the Fourteenth.'

'Something else,' said Quick Ben, 'I wanted to talk about.'

'So go ahead,' Stormy said expansively, waving a grouse leg. 'Stormy's got your answers, yes he does.'

'I've heard stories . . . a Malazan escort, clashing with a fleet of strange ships off the Geni coast. From the descriptions of the foe, they sound like Tiste Edur. Stormy, that ship of yours, what was it called?'

'The *Silanda*. Dead grey-skinned folk, all cut down on the deck, and the ship's captain, speared right through, pinned to his Hood-damned chair in his cabin – gods below, the arm that threw that . . .'

'And Tiste Andii . . . heads.'

'Bodies were below, manning the sweeps.'

'Those grey-skinned folk were Tiste Edur,' Quick Ben said. 'I don't know, maybe I shouldn't put the two together, but something about them makes me nervous. Where did that Tiste Edur fleet come from?'

Kalam grunted, then said, 'It's a big world, Quick. They could've come from anywhere, blown off course by some storm, or on an exploratory mission of some kind.'

'More like raiding,' Stormy said. 'If they attacked right off like they did. Anyway, where we found the *Silanda* in the first place – there'd been a battle there, too. Against Tiste Andii. Messy.'

Quick Ben sighed and rubbed his eyes again. 'Near Coral, during the Pannion War, the body of a Tiste Edur was found. It had come up from deep water.' He shook his head. 'I've a feeling we haven't seen the last of them.'

'The Shadow Realm,' Kalam said. 'It was theirs, once, and now they want it back.'

The wizard's gaze narrowed on the assassin. 'Cotillion told you this?'

Kalam shrugged.

'It keeps coming back to Shadowthrone, doesn't it? No wonder I'm nervous. That slimy, slippery bastard—'

'Oh Hood's balls,' Stormy groaned, 'give me that rice piss, if you're gonna go on and on. Shadowthrone ain't scary. Shadowthrone's just Ammanas, and Ammanas is just Kellanved. Just like Cotillion's Dancer. Hood knows, we knew the Emperor well enough. And Dancer. They up to something? No surprise. They were always up to something, from the very start. I tell you both right now,' he paused for a swig of rice wine, made a face, then continued, 'when all the dust's settled, they'll be shining like pearls atop a dung-heap. Gods, Elder Gods, dragons, undead, spirits and the scary empty face of the Abyss itself – they won't none a them stand a chance. You want to worry about Tiste Edur, wizard? Go ahead. Maybe they ruled Shadow once, but Shadowthrone'll take 'em down. Him and Dancer.' He belched. 'An' you know why? I'll tell you why. They never fight fair. That's why.'

Kalam looked over at the empty chair, and his eyes slowly narrowed.

Stumbling, crawling, or dragging themselves along through the bed of white ash, they all came to where Bottle sat, the sky a swirl of stars overhead. Saying nothing, not one of those soldiers, but each in turn managing one gentle gesture – reaching out and with one finger, touching the head of Y'Ghatan the rat.

Tender, with great reverence – until she bit that finger, and the hand would be snatched back with a hissed curse.

One after another, Y'Ghatan bit them all.

She was hungry, Bottle explained, and pregnant. So he explained. Or tried to, but no-one was really listening. It seemed that they didn't even care, that her bite was part of the ritual, now, a price of blood, the payment of sacrifice.

He told those who would listen that she had bitten him too.

But she hadn't. Not her. Not him. Their souls were inextricably bound, now. And things like that were complicated, profound even. He studied the creature where it was settled in his lap. Profound, yes, that was the word.

He stroked her head. *My dear rat. My sweet— ow! Damn you! Bitch!*

Black, glittering eyes looked up at him, whiskered nose twitching.

Vile, disgusting creatures.

He set the creature down and it could wander over a precipice for all he cared. Instead, the rat snuggled up against his right foot and curled into sleep. Bottle looked over at the makeshift camp, at the array of dim faces he could see here and there. No-one had lit a fire. Funny, that, in a sick way.

They had come through it. Bottle still found it difficult to believe. And Gesler had gone back in, only to return a while later. Followed by Corabb Bhilan Thenu'alas, the warrior dragging Strings into view, then himself collapsing. Bottle could hear the man's snores that had been going on uninterrupted half the night.

The sergeant was alive. The honey smeared into his wounds seemed to have delivered healing to match High Denul, making it obvious that it had been anything but ordinary honey – as if the strange visions weren't proof enough of that. Still, even that was unable to replace the blood Strings had lost, and that blood loss should have killed him. Yet now the sergeant slept, too weak to manage much else, but alive.

Bottle wished he was as tired . . . in that way, at least, the kind that beckoned warm and welcoming. Instead of this spiritual exhaustion that left his nerves frayed, images returning again and again of their nightmare journey among the buried bones of Y'Ghatan. And with them, the bitter taste of those moments when all seemed lost, hopeless.

Captain Faradan Sort and Sinn had stashed away a supply of water-casks and food-packs, which they had since retrieved, but for Bottle no amount of water could wash the taste of smoke and ashes from his mouth. And there was something else that burned still within him. The Adjunct had abandoned them, forcing the captain and Sinn to desert. True enough, it was only reasonable to assume no-one had been left alive. He knew his feeling was irrational, yet it gnawed at him nonetheless.

The captain had talked about the plague, sweeping towards them from the east, and the need to keep the army well ahead of it. The Adjunct had waited as long as she could. Bottle knew all that. Still . . .

'We're dead, you know.'

He looked over at Koryk, who sat cross-legged nearby, a child sleeping beside him. 'If we're dead,' Bottle said, 'why do we feel so awful?'

'As far as the Adjunct's concerned. We're dead. We can just . . . leave.'

'And go where, Koryk? Poliel stalks Seven Cities—'

'Ain't no plague gonna kill us. Not now.'

'You think we're immortal or something?' Bottle asked. He shook his head. 'We survived this, sure, but that doesn't mean a damned thing. It sure as Hood doesn't mean that the next thing to come along won't kill us right and quick. Maybe you're feeling immune – to anything and everything the world can throw at us, now. But, believe me, we're not.'

'Better that than anything else,' Koryk muttered.

Bottle thought about the soldier's words. 'You think some god decided to use us? Pulled us out for a reason?'

'Either that, Bottle, or your rat's a genius.'

'The rat was four legs and a good nose, Koryk. Her soul was bound. By me. I was looking through her eyes, sensing everything she sensed—'

'And did she dream when you dreamed?'

'Well, I don't know—'

'Did she run away, then?'

'No, but—'

'So she waited around. For you to wake back up. So you could imprison her soul again.'

Bottle said nothing.

'Any god tries to use me,' Koryk said in a low voice, 'it'll regret it.'

'With all those fetishes you wear,' Bottle noted, 'I'd have thought you'd be delighted at the attention.'

'You're wrong. What I wear ain't for seeking blessings.'

'Then what are they?'

'Wards.'

'All of them?'

Koryk nodded. 'They make me invisible. To gods, spirits, demons . . .'

Bottle studied the soldier through the gloom. 'Well, maybe they don't work.'

'Depends,' he replied.

'On what?'

'Whether we're dead or not.'

Smiles laughed from nearby. 'Koryk's lost his mind. No surprise, it being so small, and things being so dark in there . . .'

'Not like ghosts and all that,' Koryk said in a sneering tone. 'You think like a ten-year-old, Smiles.'

Bottle winced.

Something skittered off a rock close to Koryk and the soldier started. 'What in Hood's name?'

'That was a knife,' Bottle said, having felt it whip past him. 'Amazing, she saved one for you.'

'More than one,' Smiles said. 'And Koryk, I wasn't aiming for your leg.'

'I told you you weren't immune,' Bottle said.

'I'm – never mind.'

I'm still alive, you were going to say. Then, wisely, decided not to.

Gesler crouched down in front of the captain. 'We're a hairless bunch,' he said, 'but otherwise pretty well mending. Captain, I don't know what made you believe in Sinn, enough to run from the army, but I'm damned glad you did.'

'You were all under my command,' she said. 'Then you got too far ahead of me. I did my best to find you, but the smoke, the flames – all too much.' She looked away. 'I didn't want to leave it at that.'

'How many did the legion lose?' Gesler asked.

She shrugged. 'Maybe two thousand. Soldiers were still dying. We were trapped, Fist Keneb and Baralta and about eight hundred, on the wrong side of the breach – until Sinn pushed the fire back – don't ask me how. They say she's a High Mage of some kind. There was nothing addled about her that night, Sergeant, and I didn't think she was addled when she tried getting back into the city.'

Nodding, Gesler was silent for a moment, then he rose. 'I wish I could sleep . . . and it looks like I'm not alone in that. I wonder why that is . . .'

'The stars, Sergeant,' said Faradan Sort. 'They're glittering down.'

'Aye, might be that and nothing more.'

'Nothing more? I would think, more than enough.'

'Aye.' He looked down at the small bite on his right index finger. 'All for a damned rat, too.'

'All of you fools are probably infected with plague, now.'

He started, then smiled. 'Let the bitch try.'

Balm rubbed the last crusted mud from his face, then scowled over at his corporal. 'You, Deadsmell, you think I didn't hear you praying and gibbering down there? You ain't fooled me about nothing worth fooling about.'

The man, leaning against a rock, kept his eyes closed as he replied, 'Sergeant, you keep trying, but we know. We all know.'

'You all know what?'

'Why you're talking and talking and still talking.'

'What are you talking about?'

'You're glad to be alive, Sergeant. And you're glad your squad's made

334

it through in one piece, the only one barring Fid's, and maybe Hellian's, as far as I can tell. We were charmed and that's all there was to it. Damned charmed, and you still can't believe it. Well, neither can we, all right?'

Balm spat into the dust. 'Listen to you mewling on and on. Sentimental tripe, all of it. I'm wondering who cursed me so that I'm still stuck with all of you. Fiddler I can understand. He's a Bridgeburner. And gods run when they see a Bridgeburner. But you, you ain't nobody, and that's what I don't get. In fact, if I did get it . . .'

Urb. He's as bad as the priest who disappeared. The once-priest, what was his name again? What did he look like? Nothing like Urb, that's for sure. But just as treacherous, treasonous, just as rotten and vile as whatever his name was.

He ain't my corporal no more, that's for sure. I want to kill him . . . oh gods, my head aches. My jaw . . . my teeth all loose.

Captain says she needs more sergeants. Well, she can have him, and whatever squad he ends up with has my prayers and pity. That's for sure. Said there were spiders and maybe there were and maybe I wasn't conscious so's I couldn't go crazy, which maybe I woulda done, but that don't change one truth, and that's for sure as sure can be that they crawled on me. All over me – I can still feel where their little sticky pointy legs dug into my skin. All over. Everywhere. And he just let 'em do it.

Maybe captain's got a bottle of something. Maybe if I call her over and talk real sweet, real sane and reasonable, maybe then they'd untie me. I won't kill Urb. I promise. You can have him, Captain. That's what I'll say. And she'll hesitate – I would – but then nod – the idiot – and cut these ropes. And hand me a bottle and I'll finish it. Finish it and everybody'll say, hey, it's all right, then. She's back to normal.

And that's when I'll go for his throat. With my teeth – no, they're loose, can't use 'em for that. Find a knife, that's what I have to do. Or a sword. I could trade the bottle for a sword. I did it the other way round, didn't I? Half the bottle. I'll drink the other half. Half a bottle, half a sword. A knife. Half a bottle for a knife. Which I'll stick in his throat, then trade back, for the other half of the bottle – if I'm quick that should work fine. I get the knife and the whole bottle.

But first, she should untie me. That's only fair.

I'm fine, as everyone can see. Peaceful, thoughtful—

'Sergeant?'

'What is it, Urb?'

'I think you still want to kill me.'

'What makes you say that?'

'The way you growl and gnash your teeth, I guess.'

Not me, that's for sure.

Oh, that's why my teeth still hurt so. I've made them even looser with all that gnashing. Gods, I used to dream stuff like this, my teeth all coming loose. The bastard punched me. No different from that man who disappeared, what was his name again?

Flashwit levered her bulk further down in the soft bed her weight had impressed in the sand. 'I wish,' she said.

Mayfly pursed her lips, then adjusted the nose she'd had broken more times than she could count. Moving it around made clicking sounds that she found, for some reason, vaguely satisfying. 'You wish what?'

'I wish I knew things, I guess.'

'What things?'

'Well, listen to Bottle there. And Gesler, and Deadsmell. They're smart. They talk about things and all that other stuff. That's what I wish.'

'Yeah, well, all those brains are goin' t'waste though, ain't they?'

'What do you mean?'

Mayfly snorted. 'You and me, Flashwit, we're heavy infantry, right? We plant our feet and we make the stand, and it don't matter what it's for. None a that don't matter.'

'But Bottle—'

'Waste, Flashwit. They're soldiers, for Treach's sake. *Soldiers*. So who needs brains to soldier? They just get in the way of soldierin' and it's no good things gettin' in the way. They figure things out and that gives 'em opinions and then maybe they don't want t'fight as much no more.'

'Why wouldn't they want to fight no more 'cause of 'pinions?'

'It's simple, Flashwit. Trust me. If soldiers thought too much about what they're doin', they wouldn't fight no more.'

'So how come I'm so tired, anyway, only I can't sleep?'

'That's simple, too.'

'It is?'

'Yeah, an' it ain't the stars neither. We're waitin' for the sun to come up. We all want to see that sun, because it was looking like we'd never see it no more.'

'Yeah.' A long contemplative silence, then, 'I wish.'

'Now what do you wish?'

'Only, that I was smart as you, Mayfly. You're so smart you got no 'pinions and that's pretty smart an' it makes me wonder if you ain't goin' t'waste being a heavy an' that. A soljer.'

'I ain't smart, Flashwit. Trust me on that, an' you know how I know?'

'No, how?'

''Cause . . . down there . . . you an' me, an' Saltlick an' Shortnose an' Uru Hela an' Hanno, us heavies. We didn't get scared, not one of us, and that's how I know.'

'It wasn't scary. Jus' dark, an' it seemed t'go on for ever an' waitin' for Bottle to get us through, well that got boring sometimes, you know.'

'Right, and did the fire get you scared?'

'Well, burnin' hurt, didn't it?'

'Sure did.'

'I didn't like that.'

'Me neither.'

'So, what do you think we're all gonna do now?'

'The Fourteenth? Don't know, save the world, maybe.'

'Yeah. Maybe. I'd like that.'

'Me too.'

'Hey, is that the sun comin' up?'

'Well, it's east where it's getting brighter, so I guess, yeah, it must be.'

'Great. I bin waiting for this. I think.'

Cuttle found sergeants Thom Tissy, Cord and Gesler gathered near the base of the slope leading up to the west road. It seemed they weren't much interested in the rising sun. 'You're all looking serious,' the sapper said.

'We got a walk ahead of us,' Gesler said, 'that's all.'

'The Adjunct had no choice,' Cuttle said. 'That was a firestorm – there was no way she could have known there'd be survivors – digging under it all that way.'

Gesler glanced at the other two sergeants, then nodded. 'It's all right, Cuttle. We know. We're not contemplating murder or anything.'

Cuttle turned to face the camp. 'Some of the soldiers are thinking wrong on all of this.'

'Aye,' said Cord, 'but we'll put 'em straight on it before this day's out.'

'Good. Thing is,' he hesitated, turning back to the sergeants, 'I've been thinking on that. Who in Hood's name is going to believe us? More like we did our own deal with the Queen of Dreams. After all, we got one of Leoman's officers with us. And now, with the captain and Sinn going and getting themselves outlawed, well, it could be seen we're all traitors or something.'

'We made no deal with the Queen of Dreams,' Cord said.

'Are you sure about that?'

337

All three sergeants looked at him then.

Cuttle shrugged. 'Bottle, he's a strange one. Maybe he did make some deal, with somebody. Maybe the Queen of Dreams, maybe some other god.'

'He'd have told us, wouldn't he?' Gesler asked.

'Hard to say. He's a sneaky bastard. I'm getting nervous about that damned rat biting every one of us, like it knew what it was doing and we didn't.'

'Just a wild rat,' said Thom Tissy. 'Ain't nobody's pet, so why wouldn't it bite?'

Gesler said, 'Listen, Cuttle, sounds like you're just finding new things to worry about. What's the point of doing that? What we've got ahead of us right now is a long walk, and us with no armour, no weapons and virtually no clothing – the sun's gonna bake people crisp.'

'We need to find a village,' Cord said, 'and hope to Hood plague ain't found it first.'

'There you go, Cuttle,' Gesler said, grinning. 'Now you got another thing to worry about.'

Paran began to suspect that his horse knew what was coming: nostrils flaring, tossing its head as it shied and stamped, fighting the reins all the way down the trail. The freshwater sea was choppy, silty waves in the bay rolling up to batter at sun-bleached limestone crags. Dead desert bushes poked skeletal limbs out of the muddy shallows and insects swarmed everywhere.

'This is not the ancient sea,' Ganath said as she approached the shoreline.

'No,' Paran admitted. 'Half a year ago Raraku was a desert, and had been for thousands of years. Then, there was a . . . rebirth of sorts.'

'It will not last. Nothing lasts.'

He eyed the Jaghut woman for a moment. She stood looking out on the ochre waves, motionless for a dozen heartbeats, then she made her way down into the shallows. Paran dismounted and hobbled the horses, narrowly evading an attempted bite from the gelding he had been riding. He unpacked his camp kit and set about building a hearth. Plenty of driftwood about, including entire uprooted trees, and it was not long before he had a cookfire lit.

Finished her bathing, Ganath joined him and stood nearby, water streaming down her oddly coloured, smooth skin. 'The spirits of the deep springs have awakened,' she said. 'It feels as if this place is young once again. Young, and raw. I do not understand.'

Paran nodded. 'Young, aye. And vulnerable.'

'Yes. Why are you here?'

'Ganath, it might be safer for you if you left.'

'When do you begin the ritual?'

'It's already begun.'

She glanced away. 'You are a strange god. Riding a miserable creature that dreams of killing you. Building a fire with which to cook food. Tell me, in this new world, are all gods such as you?'

'I'm not a god,' Paran said. 'In place of the ancient Tiles of the Holds – and I'll grant you I'm not sure that's what they were called – in any case, there is now the Deck of Dragons, a fatid containing the High Houses. I am the Master of that Deck—'

'A Master, in the same manner as the Errant?'

'Who?'

'The Master of the Holds in my time,' she replied.

'I suppose so, then.'

'He was an ascendant, Ganoes Paran. Worshipped as a god by enclaves of Imass, Barghast and Trell. They kept his mouth filled with blood. He never knew thirst. Nor peace. I wonder how he fell.'

'I think I'd like to know that detail myself,' Paran said, shaken by the Jaghut's words. 'No-one worships me, Ganath.'

'They will. You are newly ascended. Even in this world of yours, I am certain that there is no shortage of followers, of those who are desperate to believe. And they will hunt down others and make of them victims. They will cut them and fill bowls with their innocent blood, in your name, Ganoes Paran, and so beseech your intercession, your adherence to whatever cause they righteously fashion. The Errant thought to defeat them, as you might well seek to do, and so he became the god of change. He walked the path of neutrality, yet flavoured it with a pleasure taken in impermanence. The Errant's enemy was ennui, stagnation. This is why the Forkrul Assail sought to annihilate him. And all his mortal followers.' She paused, then added, 'Perhaps they succeeded. The Assail were never easily diverted from their chosen course.'

Paran said nothing. There were truths in her words that even he recognized, and they now weighed upon him, settling heavy and imponderable upon his spirit. Burdens were born from the loss of innocence. Naïveté. While the innocent yearned to lose their innocence, those who had already done so in turn envied the innocent, and knew grief in what they had lost. Between the two, no exchange of truths was possible. He sensed the completion of an internal journey, and Paran found he did not appreciate recognizing that fact, nor the place where he now found himself. It did not suit him that ignorance remained inextricably bound to innocence, and the loss of one meant the loss of the other.

'I have troubled your mind, Ganoes Paran.'

He glanced up, then shrugged. 'You have been . . . timely. Much to my regret, yet still,' he shrugged again, 'perhaps all for the best.'

She faced the sea again and he followed her gaze. A sudden calm upon the modest bay before them, whilst white-caps continued to chop the waters beyond. 'What is happening?' she asked.

'They're coming.'

Some distant clamour, now, rising as if from a deep cavern, and the sunset seemed to have grown sickly, its very fires slave to a chaotic tumult, as if the shades of a hundred thousand sunsets and sunrises now waged celestial war. Whilst the horizons closed in, flickering with darkness, smoke and racing storms of sand and dust.

A stirring upon the pellucid waters of the bay, silt clouds rising from beneath, and the calm was spreading outward now, south, stilling the sea's wildness.

Ganath stepped back. 'What have you done?'

Muted but growing, the scuffle and rumble, the clangour and throat-hum, the sound of marching armies, the echoing of locked shields, the tympanous beat of iron and bronze weapons upon battered rims, of wagons creaking and churning rutted roads, and now the susurration, thrumming collisions, walls of horseflesh hammering into rows of raised pikes, the animal screams filling the air, then fading, only for the collision to repeat, louder this time, closer, and there was a violent patter cutting a swath across the bay, leaving a pale, muddy red road in its wake that bled outward, edges tearing, even as it sank down into the depths. Voices, now, crying out, bellowing, piteous and enraged, a cacophony of enmeshed lives, each one seeking to separate itself, seeking to claim its own existence, unique, a thing with eyes and voice. Fraught minds clutching at memories that tore away like shredded banners, with every gush of lost blood, with every crushing failure – soldiers, dying, ever dying—

Paran and Ganath watched, as colourless, sodden standards pierced the surface of the water, the spears lifting into the air, streaming mud – standards, banners, pikes bearing grisly, rotting trophies, rising along the entire shoreline now.

Raraku Sea had given up its dead.

In answer to the call of one man.

White, like slashes of absence, bone hands gripping shafts of black wood, forearms beneath tattered leather and corroded vambraces, and then, lifting clear of the water, rotted helms and flesh-stripped faces. Human, Trell, Barghast, Imass, Jaghut. *The races, and all their race-wars. Oh, could I drag every mortal historian down here, to this shore, so that they could look upon our true roll, our progression of hatred and annihilation.*

How many would seek, desperate in whatever zealotry gripped them, to hunt reasons and justifications? Causes, crimes and justices – Paran's thoughts stuttered to a halt, as he realized that, like Ganath, he had been backing up, step by step, pushed back, in the face of revelation. *Oh, these messengers would earn so much . . . displeasure. And vilification. And these dead, oh how they'd laugh, understanding so well the defensive tactic of all-out attack. The dead mock us, mock us all, and need say nothing . . .*

All those enemies of reason – yet not reason as a force, or a god, not reason in the cold, critical sense. Reason only in its purest armour, when it strides forward into the midst of those haters of tolerance, oh gods below, I am lost, lost in all of this. You cannot fight unreason, and as these dead multitudes will tell you – are telling you even now – certitude is the enemy.

'These,' Ganath whispered, 'these dead have no blood to give you, Ganoes Paran. They will not worship. They will not follow. They will not dream of glory in your eyes. They are done with that, with all of that. What do you see, Ganoes Paran, in these staring holes that once were eyes? *What do you see?*'

'Answers,' he replied.

'Answers?' Her voice was harsh with rage. 'To what?'

Not replying, Paran forced himself forward, one step, then another.

The first ranks stood upon the shore's verge, foam swirling round their skeletal feet, behind them thousands upon thousands of kin. Clutching weapons of wood, bone, horn, flint, copper, bronze and iron. Arrayed in fragments of armour, fur, hide. Silent, now, motionless.

The sky overhead was dark, lowering and yet still, as if a storm had drawn its first breath . . . only to hold it.

Paran looked upon that ghastly rank facing him. He was not sure how to do this – he had not even known if his summoning would succeed. And now . . . *there are so many.* He cleared his throat, then began calling out names.

'Shank! Aimless! Runter! Detoran! Bucklund, Hedge, Mulch, Toes, Trotts!' And still more names, as he scoured his memory, his recollection, for every Bridgeburner he knew had died. At Coral, beneath Pale, in Blackdog Forest and Mott Wood, north of Genabaris and northeast of Nathilog – names he had once fixed in his mind as he researched – for Adjunct Lorn – the turgid, grim history of the Bridgeburners. He drew upon names of the deserters, although he knew not if they lived still or, if indeed dead, whether or not they had returned to the fold. The ones that had vanished in Blackdog's great marshes, that had disappeared after the taking of Mott City.

And when he was done, when he could remember no more names, he began his list again.

Then saw one figure in the front row dissolving, melting into sludge that pooled in the shallow water, slowly seeping away. And in its place arose a man he recognized, the fire-scorched, blasted face grinning – Paran belatedly realized that the brutal smile held no amusement, only the memory of a death-grimace. That and the terrible damage left behind by a weapon.

'Runter,' Paran whispered. 'Black Coral—'

'Captain,' cut in the dead sapper, 'what are you doing here?'

I wish people would stop asking me that. 'I need your help.'

More Bridgeburners were forming in the front ranks. Detoran. Sergeant Bucklund. Hedge, who now stepped from the water's edge. 'Captain. I always wondered why you were so hard to kill. Now I know.'

'You do?'

'Aye, you're doomed to haunt us! Hah! Hah hah!' Behind him, the others began laughing.

Hundreds of thousands of ghosts, all joined in laughter, was a sound Ganoes Paran never, ever wanted to hear again. Mercifully, it was shortlived, as if all at once the army of dead forgot the reason for their amusement.

'Now,' Hedge finally said, 'as you can see, we're busy. Hah!'

Paran shot out a hand. 'No, please, don't start again, Hedge.'

'Typical. People need to be dead to develop a real sense of humour. You know, Captain, from this side the world seems a whole lot funnier. Funny in a stupid, pointless way, I'll grant you—'

'Enough of that, Hedge. You think I don't sense the desperation here? You're all in trouble – even worse, you need us. The living, that is, and that's the part you don't want to admit—'

'I admitted it clear enough,' Hedge said. 'To Fid.'

'Fiddler?'

'Aye. He's not too far away from here, you know. With the Fourteenth.'

'He's with the Fourteenth? What, has he lost his mind?'

Hedge smirked. 'Damn near, but, thanks to me, he's all right. For now. This ain't the first time we've walked among the living, Captain. Gods below, you shoulda seen us twist Korbolo's hair – him and his damned Dogslayers – that was a night, let me tell you—'

'No, don't bother. I need your help.'

'Fine, be that way. With what?'

Paran hesitated. He'd needed to get to this point, yet now that he'd arrived, this was suddenly the last place he wanted to be. 'You, here,' he said, 'in Raraku – this sea, it's a damned gate. Between whatever nightmare world you're from, and mine. I need you, Hedge, to summon . . . something. From the other side.'

The mass of ghosts collectively recoiled, the motion snatching a tug of air seaward.

The dead Bridgeburner mage Shank asked, 'Who you got in mind, Captain, and what do you want it to do?'

Paran glanced back over a shoulder at Ganath, then back again. 'Something's escaped, Shank. Here, in Seven Cities. It needs to be hunted down. Destroyed.' He hesitated. 'I don't know, maybe there are entities out there that could do it, but there's no time to go looking for them. You see, this . . . thing . . . it feeds on blood, and the more blood it feeds on, the more powerful it gets. The First Emperor's gravest mistake, attempting to create his own version of an Elder God – you know, don't you? What – who – I am talking about. You know . . . it's out there, loose, unchained and hunting—'

'Oh it hunted all right,' Hedge said. 'They set it free, under a geas, then gave their own blood to it – the blood of six High Mages, priests and priestesses of the Nameless Ones – the fools sacrificed themselves.'

'Why? Why set Dejim Nebrahl free? What geas did they set upon it?'

'Just another path. Maybe it'll lead where they wanted it to, maybe not, but Dejim Nebrahl is now free of its geas. And now it just . . . hunts.'

Shank asked, in a tone filled with suspicion, 'So, Captain, who is it you want? To take the damned thing down?'

'I could only think of one . . . entity. The same entity that did it the first time. Shank, I need you to find the Deragoth.'

CHAPTER NINE

If thunder could be caught, trapped in stone, and all its violent
concatenation stolen from time, and tens of thousands of years were
freed to gnaw and scrape this racked visage, so would this first
witnessing unveil all its terrible meaning. Such were my thoughts,
then, and such they are now, although decades have passed in the
interval, when I last set eyes upon that tragic ruin, so fierce was its
ancient claim to greatness.

The Lost City of the Path'Apur
Prince I'farah of Bakun, 987–1032 Burn's Sleep

HE HAD WASHED MOST OF THE DRIED BLOOD AWAY AND THEN HAD
watched, as time passed, the bruises fade. Blows to the head
were, of course, more problematic, and so there had been fever,
and with fever in the mind demons were legion, the battles endless, and
there had been no rest then. Just the heat of war with the self, but,
finally, that too had passed, and shortly before noon on the second day,
he watched the eyes open.

Incomprehension should have quickly vanished, yet it did not, and
this, Taralack Veed decided, was as he had expected. He poured out
some herbal tea as Icarium slowly sat up. 'Here, my friend. You have
been gone from me a long time.'

The Jhag reached for the tin cup, drank deep, then held it out for
more.

'Yes, thirst,' the Gral outlaw said, refilling the cup. 'Not surprising.
Blood loss. Fever.'

'We fought?'

'Aye. A sudden, inexplicable attack. D'ivers. My horse was killed
and I was thrown. When I awoke, it was clear that you had driven
off our assailant, yet a blow to your head had dragged you into

unconsciousness.' He paused, then added, 'We were lucky, friend.'

'Fighting. Yes, I recall that much.' Icarium's unhuman gaze sought out Taralack Veed's eyes, searching, quizzical.

The Gral sighed. 'This has been happening often of late. You do not remember me, do you, Icarium?'

'I – I am not sure. A companion . . .'

'Yes. For many years now. Your companion. Taralack Veed, once of the Gral Tribe, yet now sworn to a much higher cause.'

'And that is?'

'To walk at your side, Icarium.'

The Jhag stared down at the cup in his hands. 'For many years now, you say,' he whispered. 'A higher cause . . . that I do not understand. I am . . . nothing. No-one. I am lost—' He looked up. 'I am lost,' he repeated. 'I know nothing of a higher cause, such that would make you abandon your people. To walk at my side, Taralack Veed. Why?'

The Gral spat on his palms, rubbed them together, then slicked his hair back. 'You are the greatest warrior this world has ever seen. Yet cursed. To be, as you say, forever lost. And that is why you must have a companion, to recall to you the great task that awaits you.'

'And what task is this?'

Taralack Veed rose. 'You will know when the time comes. This task shall be made plain, so plain to you, and so perfect, you will know that you have been fashioned – from the very start – to give answer. Would that I could be more helpful, Icarium.'

The Jhag's gaze scanned their small encampment. 'Ah, I see you have retrieved my bow and sword.'

'I have. Are you mended enough to travel?'

'Yes, I think so. Although . . . hungry.'

'I have smoked meat in my pack. The very hare you killed three days ago. We can eat as we walk.'

Icarium climbed to his feet. 'Yes. I do feel some urgency. As if, as if I have been looking for something.' He smiled at the Gral. 'Perhaps my own past . . .'

'When you discover what you seek, my friend, all knowledge of your past will return to you. So it is prophesied.'

'Ah. Well then, friend Veed, have we a direction in mind?'

Taralack gathered his gear. 'North, and west. We are seeking the wild coast, opposite the island of Sepik.'

'Do you recall why?'

'Instinct, you said. A sense that you are . . . compelled. Trust those instincts, Icarium, as you have in the past. They will guide us through, no matter who or what stands in our way.'

'Why should anyone stand in our way?' The Jhag strapped on his

345

sword, then retrieved the cup and downed the last of the herbal tea.

'You have enemies, Icarium. Even now, we are being hunted, and that is why we can delay here no longer.'

Collecting his bow, then stepping close to hand the Gral the empty tin cup, Icarium paused, then said, 'You stood guard over me, Taralack Veed. I feel . . . I feel I do not deserve such loyalty.'

'It is no great burden, Icarium. True, I miss my wife, my children. My tribe. But there can be no stepping aside from this responsibility. I do what I must. You are chosen by all the gods, Icarium, to free the world of a great evil, and I know in my heart that you will not fail.'

The Jhag warrior sighed. 'Would that I shared your faith in my abilities, Taralack Veed.'

'E'napatha N'apur – does that name stir your memories?'

Frowning, Icarium shook his head.

'A city of evil,' Taralack explained. 'Four thousand years ago – with one like me standing at your side – you drew your fearsome sword and walked towards its barred gates. Five days, Icarium. Five days. That is what it took you to slaughter the tyrant and every soldier in that city.'

A look of horror on the Jhag's face. 'I – I did what?'

'You understood the necessity, Icarium, as you always do when faced with such evil. You understood, too, that none could be permitted to carry with them the memory of that city. And why it was necessary to then slay every man, woman and child in E'napatha N'apur. To leave none breathing.'

'No. I would not have. Taralack, no, please – there is no necessity so terrible that could compel me to commit such slaughter—'

'Ah, dear companion,' said Taralack Veed, with great sorrow. 'This is the battle you must always wage, and this is why one such as myself must be at your side. To hold you to the truth of the world, the truth of your own soul. You are the Slayer, Icarium. You walk the Blood Road, but it is a straight and true road. The coldest justice, yet a pure one. So pure even you recoil from it.' He settled a hand on the Jhag's shoulder. 'Come, we can speak more of it as we travel. I have spoken these words many, many times, my friend, and each time you are the same, wishing with all your heart that you could flee from yourself, from who and what you are. Alas, you cannot, and so you must, once more, learn to harden yourself.

'The enemy is evil, Icarium. The face of the world is evil. And so, friend, your enemy is . . .'

The warrior looked away, and Taralack Veed barely heard his whispered reply, 'The world.'

'Yes. Would that I could hide such truth from you, but I could not claim to be your friend if I did such a thing.'

'No, that is true. Very well, Taralack Veed, let us as you say speak more of this whilst we journey north and west. To the coast opposite the island of Sepik. Yes, I feel . . . there is something there. Awaiting us.'

'You must needs be ready for it,' the Gral said.

Icarium nodded. 'And so I shall, my friend.'

Each time, the return journey was harder, more fraught, and far, far less certain. There were things that would have made it easier. Knowing where he had been, for one, and knowing where he must return to, for another. *Returning to . . . sanity?* Perhaps. But Heboric Ghost Hands had no firm grasp of what sanity was, what it looked like, felt like, smelled like. It might be that he had never known.

Rock was bone. Dust was flesh. Water was blood. Residues settled in multitudes, becoming layers, and upon those layers yet more, and on and on until a world was made, until all that death could hold up one's feet where one stood, and rise to meet every step one took. A solid bed to lie on. So much for the world. *Death holds us up.* And then there were the breaths that filled, that *made* the air, the heaving assertions measuring the passing of time, like notches marking the arc of a life, of every life. How many of those breaths were last ones? The final expellation of a beast, an insect, a plant, a human with film covering his or her fading eyes? And so how, how could one draw such air into the lungs? Knowing how filled with death it was, how saturated it was with failure and surrender?

Such air choked him, burned down his throat, tasting of the bitterest acid. Dissolving and devouring, until he was naught but . . . residue.

They were so young, his companions. There was no way they could understand the filth they walked on, walked in, walked through. And took into themselves, only to fling some of it back out again, now flavoured by their own sordid additions. And when they slept, each night, they were as empty things. While Heboric fought on against the knowledge that the world did not breathe, not any more. No, now, the world drowned.

And I drown with it. Here in this cursed wasteland. In the sand and heat and dust. I am drowning. Every night. Drowning.

What could Treach give him? This savage god with its overwhelming hungers, desires, needs. Its mindless ferocity, as if it could pull back and reclaim every breath it drew into its bestial lungs, and so defy the world, the ageing world and its deluge of death. He was wrongly chosen, so every ghost told him, perhaps not in words, but in their constant crowding him, rising up, overwhelming him with their silent, accusatory regard.

And there was more. The whisperings in his dreams, voices emerging from a sea of jade, beseeching. He was the stranger who had come among them; he had done what none other had done: he had reached through the green prison. And they prayed to him, begging for his return. Why? What did they want?

No, he did not want answers to such questions. He would return this cursed gift of jade, this alien power. He would cast it back into the void and be done with it.

Holding to that, clinging to that, was keeping him sane. If this torment of living could be called sane. *Drowning, I am drowning, and yet . . . these damned feline gifts, this welter of senses, so sweet, so rich, I can feel them, seeking to seduce me. Back into this momentary world.*

In the east the sun was clawing its way back into the sky, the edge of some vast iron blade, just pulled from the forge. He watched the red glow cutting the darkness, and wondered at this strange sense of imminence that so stilled the dawn air.

A groan from the bundle of blankets where Scillara slept, then: 'So much for the blissful poison.'

Heboric flinched, then drew a deep breath, released a slow sigh. 'Which blissful poison would that be, Scillara?'

Another groan, as she worked her way into a sitting position. 'I ache, old man. My back, my hips, everywhere. And I get no sleep – no position is comfortable and I have to pee all the time. This, this is awful. Gods, why do women do it? Again and again and again – are they all mad?'

'You'd know better than I,' Heboric said. 'But I tell you, men are no less inexplicable. In what they think. In what they do.'

'The sooner I get this beast out the better,' she said, hands on her swollen belly. 'Look at me, I'm sagging. Everywhere. *Sagging.*'

The others had woken, Felisin staring wide-eyed at Scillara – with the discovery that the older woman was pregnant, there had been a time of worship for young Felisin. It seemed that the disillusionment had begun. Cutter had thrown back his blankets and was already resurrecting last night's fire. The demon, Greyfrog, was nowhere to be seen. Off hunting, Heboric supposed.

'Your hands,' Scillara noted, 'are looking particularly green this morning, old man.'

He did not bother confirming this observation. He could feel that alien pressure well enough. 'Naught but ghosts,' he said, 'the ones from beyond the veil, from the very depths of the Abyss. Oh how they cry out. I was blind once. Would that I were now deaf.'

They looked at him strangely, as they often did after he'd spoken. Truths. His truths, the ones they couldn't see, nor understand. It didn't matter. He knew what he knew. 'There is a vast dead city awaiting us this day,' he said. 'Its residents were slain. All of them. By Icarium, long ago. There was a sister city to the north – when they heard what had happened, they journeyed here to see for themselves. And then, my young companions, they chose to bury E'napatha N'apur. The entire city. They buried it intact. Thousands of years have passed, and now the winds and rains have rotted away that solid face. Now, the old truths are revealed once more.'

Cutter poured water into a tin pot and set it on the hook slung beneath an iron tripod. 'Icarium,' he said. 'I travelled with him for a time. With Mappo, and Fiddler.' He then made a face. 'And Iskaral Pust, that insane little stoat of a man. Said he was a High Priest of Shadow. A High Priest! Well, if that's the best Shadowthrone can do . . .' He shook his head. 'Icarium . . . was a . . . well, he was tragic, I guess. Yet, he would not have attacked that city without a reason, I think.'

Heboric barked a laugh. 'Aye, no shortage of reasons in this world. The King barred the gates, would not permit him to enter. Too many dark tales surrounding the name of Icarium. A soldier on the battlements fired a warning arrow. It ricocheted off a rock and grazed Icarium's left leg, then sank deep into the throat of his companion – the poor bastard drowned in his own blood – and so Icarium's rage was unleashed.'

'If there were no survivors,' Scillara said, 'how do you know all this?'

'The ghosts wander the region,' Heboric replied. He gestured. 'Farms once stood here, before the desert arrived.' He smiled at the others. 'Indeed, today is market day, and the roads – which none but I can see – are crowded with push-carts, oxen, men and women. And children and dogs. On either side, drovers whistle and tap their staves to keep the sheep and goats moving. From the poor farms this close to the city, old women come out with baskets to collect the dung for their fields.'

Felisin whispered, 'You see all this?'

'Aye.'

'Right now?'

'Only fools think the past is invisible.'

'Do those ghosts,' Felisin asked, 'do they see you?'

'Perhaps. Those that do, well, they know they are dead. The others do not know, and do not see me. The realization of one's own death is a terrifying thing; they flee from it, returning to their illusion – and so I appear, then vanish, and I am naught but a mirage.' He rose. 'Soon, we will approach the city itself, and there will be soldiers, and these ghosts see me, oh yes, and call out to me. But how can I answer, when I don't understand what they want of me? They cry out, as if in recognition—'

'You are the Destriant of Treach, the Tiger of Summer,' Cutter said.

'Treach was a First Hero,' Heboric replied. 'A Soletaken who escaped the Slaughter. Like Ryllandaras and Rikkter, Tholen and Denesmet. Don't you see? These ghost soldiers – they did not worship Treach! No, their god of war belonged to the Seven, who would one day become the Holies. A single visage of Dessimbelackis – that and nothing more. I am nothing to them, Cutter, yet they will not leave me alone!'

Both Cutter and Felisin had recoiled at his outburst, but Scillara was grinning.

'You find all this amusing?' he demanded, glaring at her.

'I do. Look at you. You were a priest of Fener, and now you're a priest of Treach. Both gods of war. Heboric, how many faces do you think the god of war has? Thousands. And in ages long past? Tens of thousands? Every damned tribe, old man. All different, but all the same.' She lit her pipe, smoke wreathing her face, then said, 'Wouldn't surprise me if all the gods are just aspects of one god, and all this fighting is just proof that that one god is insane.'

'Insane?' Heboric was trembling. He could feel his heart hammering away like some ghastly demon at the door to his soul.

'Or maybe just confused. All those bickering worshippers, each one convinced their version is the right one. Imagine getting prayers from ten million believers, not one of them believing the same thing as the one kneeling beside him or her. Imagine all those Holy Books, not one of them agreeing on anything, yet all of them purporting to be the word of that one god. Imagine two armies annihilating each other, both in that god's name. Who wouldn't be driven mad by all that?'

'Well,' Cutter said into the silence that followed Scillara's diatribe, 'the tea's ready.'

Greyfrog squatted atop a flat rock, looking down on the unhappy group. The demon's belly was full, although the wild goat still kicked on occasion. *Morose. They are not getting along. Tragic list, listlessly reiterated. Child-swollen beauty is miserable with aches and discomfort. Younger beauty feels shocked, frightened and alone. Yet likely to reject soft comfort given by adoring Greyfrog. Troubled assassin beset by impatience, for what, I know not. And terrible priest. Ah, shivering haunt! So much displeasure! Dismay! Perhaps I could regurgitate the goat, and we could share said fine repast. Fine, still kicking repast. Aai, worst kind of indigestion!*

'Greyfrog!' Cutter called up. 'What are you doing up there?'

'*Friend Cutter. Discomfort. Regretting the horns.*'

*

Thus far, Samar Dev reflected, the notations on the map had proved accurate. From dry scrubland to plains, and now, finally, patches of deciduous forest, arrayed amidst marshy glades and stubborn remnants of true grassland. Two, perhaps three days of travel northward and they would reach boreal forest.

Bhederin-hunters, travelling in small bands, shared this wild, unbroken land. They had seen such bands from a distance and had come upon signs of camps, but it was clear that these nomadic savages had no interest in contacting them. Hardly surprising – the sight of Karsa Orlong was frightening enough, astride his Jhag horse, weapons bristling, bloodstained white fur riding his broad shoulders.

The bhederin herds had broken up and scattered into smaller groups upon reaching the aspen parkland. There seemed little sense, as far as Samar Dev could determine, to the migration of these huge beasts. True, the dry, hot season was nearing its end, and the nights were growing cool, sufficient to turn rust-coloured the leaves of the trees, but there was nothing fierce in a Seven Cities winter. More rain, perhaps, although that rarely reached far inland – the Jhag Odhan to the south was unchanging, after all.

'I think,' she said, 'this is some kind of ancient memory.'

Karsa grunted, then said, 'Looks like forest to me, woman.'

'No, these bhederin – those big hulking shapes beneath the trees over there. I think it's some old instinct that brings them north into these forests. From a time when winter brought snow and wind to the Odhan.'

'The rains will make the grass lush, Samar Dev,' the Teblor said. 'They come up here to get fat.'

'All right, that sounds reasonable enough. I suppose. Good for the hunters, though.' A few days earlier they had passed a place of great slaughter. Part of a herd had been separated and driven off a cliff. Four or five dozen hunters had gathered and were butchering the meat, women among them tending smoke-fires and pinning strips of meat to racks. Half-wild dogs – more wolf than dog, in truth – had challenged Samar Dev and Karsa when they rode too close, and she had seen that the beasts had no canines, likely cut off when they were young, although they presented sufficient threat that the travellers elected to draw no closer to the kill-site.

She was fascinated by these fringe tribes living out here in the wastes, suspecting that nothing had changed for them in thousands of years; oh, iron weapons and tools, evincing some form of trade with the more civilized peoples to the east, but they used no horses, which she found odd. Instead, their dogs were harnessed to travois. And mostly basketry instead of fired-clay pots, which made sense given that the bands travelled on foot.

Here and there, lone trees stood tall on the grasslands, and these seemed to be a focal point for some kind of spirit worship, given the fetishes tied to branches, and the antlers and bhederin skulls set in notches and forks, some so old that the wood had grown round them. Invariably, near such sentinel trees there would be a cemetery, signified by raised platforms housing hide-wrapped corpses, and, of course, the crows squabbling over every perch.

Karsa and Samar had avoided trespass on such sites. Though Samar suspected that the Teblor would have welcomed a succession of running battles and skirmishes, if only to ease the boredom of the journey. Yet for all his ferocity, Karsa Orlong had proved an easy man to travel with, albeit somewhat taciturn and inclined to brooding – but whatever haunted him had nothing to do with her, nor was he inclined to take it out on her – a true virtue rare among men.

'I am thinking,' he said, startling her.

'What about, Karsa Orlong?'

'The bhederin and those hunters at the base of the cliff. Two hundred dead bhederin, at least, and they were stripping them down to the bone, then boiling the bones themselves. Whilst we eat nothing but rabbits and the occasional deer. I think, Samar Dev, we should kill ourselves one of these bhederin.'

'Don't be fooled by them, Karsa Orlong. They are a lot faster than they look. And agile.'

'Yes, but they are herd animals.'

'What of it?'

'The bulls care more about protecting ten females and their calves than one female separated out from the others.'

'Probably true. So, how do you plan on separating one out? And don't forget, that female won't be a docile thing – it could knock you and your horse down given the chance. Then trample you.'

'I am not the one to worry about that. It is you who must worry, Samar Dev.'

'Why me?'

'Because you will be the bait, the lure. And so you must be sure to be quick and alert.'

'Bait? Now hold on—'

'Quick and alert. I will take care of the rest.'

'I can't say I like this idea, Karsa Orlong. I am in fact quite content with rabbits and deer.'

'Well, I'm not. And I want a hide.'

'What for? How many hides do you plan to wear?'

'Find us a small clump of the beasts – they are not frightened by your horse as much as they are by mine.'

'That's because Jhag horses will take calves on occasion. So I read . . . somewhere.'

The Teblor bared his teeth, as if he found the image amusing.

Samar Dev sighed, then said, 'There's a small herd just ahead and to the left – they moved out of this glade as we approached.'

'Good. When we reach the next clearing I want you to begin a canter towards them.'

'That will draw out the bull, Karsa – how close do you expect me to get?'

'Close enough to be chased.'

'I will not. That will achieve nothing—'

'The females will bolt, woman. And from them I shall make my kill – how far do you think the bull will chase you? He will turn about, to rejoin his harem—'

'And so become your problem.'

'Enough talk.' They were picking their way through a stand of poplar and aspen, the horses pushing through chest-high dogwood. Just beyond was another glade, this one long, the way the green grasses were clumped suggesting wet ground. On the far side, perhaps forty paces distant, a score of hulking dark shapes loomed beneath the branches of more trees.

'This is swamp,' Samar Dev noted. 'We should find another—'

'Ride, Samar Dev.'

She halted her horse. 'And if I don't?'

'Stubborn child. I shall leave you here, of course – you are slowing me down as it is.'

'Was that supposed to hurt my feelings, Karsa Orlong? You want to kill a bhederin just to prove to yourself that you can best the hunters. So, no cliff, no blinds or corrals, no pack of wolf-dogs to flank and drive the bhederin. No, you want to leap off your horse and wrestle one to the ground, then choke it to death, or maybe throw it against a tree, or maybe just lift it up and spin it round until it dies of dizziness. And you dare to call *me* a child?' She laughed. Because, as she well knew, laughter would sting.

Yet no sudden rage darkened his face, and his eyes were calm as they studied her. Then he smiled. 'Witness.'

And with that he rode out into the clearing. Inky water spraying from the Jhag horse's hoofs, the beast voicing something like a snarl as it galloped towards the herd. The bhederin scattered in a thunderous crash of bushes and snapping branches. Two shot out directly towards Karsa.

A mistake, Samar Dev realized in that moment, to assume there was but one male. One was clearly younger than the other, yet both were huge, eyes red-rimmed with rage, water exploding round them as they charged their attacker.

The Jhag horse, Havok, swerved suddenly, legs gathering beneath him, then the young stallion launched himself over the back of the larger bull. But the bhederin was quicker, twisting and heaving its massive head upward, horns seeking the horse's exposed underbelly.

That upward lunge killed the bull, for the beast's head met the point of Karsa's stone sword, which slid into the brain beneath the base of the skull, severing most of its spine in the process.

Havok landed in a splash and spray of muck on the far side of the collapsing bull, well beyond the range of the second male – which now pivoted, stunningly fast, and set off in pursuit of Karsa.

The warrior swung his horse to the left, hoofs pounding as Havok ran parallel to the edge of trees, chasing after the half-dozen females and calves that had lumbered out into the clearing. The second bull closed fast behind them.

The cows and calves scattered once more, one bolting in a direction different from the others. Havok swerved into its wake, and a heartbeat later was galloping alongside the beast. Behind them, the second male had drawn up to flank the other females – and one and all, this group then crashed back into the thicket.

Samar Dev watched Karsa Orlong lean far to one side, then slash down with his sword, taking the beast in the spine just above its hips.

The cow's back legs collapsed under the blow, sluicing through the muck as the creature struggled to drag them forward.

Wheeling round in front of the bhederin, Karsa held his sword poised until he reached the cow's left side, then he lunged down, the sword's point driving into the animal's heart.

Front legs buckled, and the cow sagged to one side, then was still.

Halting his horse, Karsa slid off and approached the dead cow. 'Make us a camp,' he said to Samar Dev.

She stared at him, then said, 'Fine, you have shown me that I am, in fact, unnecessary. As far as you're concerned. Now what? You expect me to set up camp, and then, I presume, help you butcher that thing. Shall I lie beneath you tonight just to round things out?'

He had drawn a knife and now knelt in the pooling water beside the cow. 'If you like,' he said.

Barbarian bastard . . . well, I should not have expected anything else, should I? 'All right, I have been thinking, we will need this meat – the land of rocks and lakes north of here no doubt has game, but far less plentiful and far more elusive.'

'I shall take the bull's skin,' Karsa said, slicing open the bhederin's belly. Entrails tumbled out to splash in the swampy water. Already, hundreds of insects swarmed the kill-site. 'Do you wish this cow's skin, Samar Dev?'

'Why not? If a glacier lands on us we won't freeze, and that's something.'

He glanced over at her. 'Woman, glaciers don't jump. They crawl.'

'That depends on who made them in the first place, Karsa Orlong.'

He bared his teeth. 'Legends of the Jaghut do not impress me. Ice is ever a slow-moving river.'

'If you believe that, Karsa Orlong, you know far less than you think you do.'

'Do you plan on sitting on that horse all day, woman?'

'Until I find high ground to make a camp, yes.' And she gathered the reins.

Witness, he said. He's said that before, hasn't he? Some kind of tribal thing, I suppose. Well, I witnessed all right. As did that savage hiding in the shadows at the far end of the glade. I pray the locals do not feel proprietary towards these bhederin. Or we will find excitement unending, which Karsa might well enjoy. As for me, I'll just likely end up dead.

Well, too late to worry much about that.

She then wondered how many of Karsa Orlong's past companions had had similar thoughts. In those times just before the Teblor barbarian found himself, once again, travelling alone.

The rough crags of the ridge cast a maze of shadows along the ledge just beneath, and in these shadows five sets of serpentine eyes stared down at the winding wall of dust on the plain below. A trader's caravan, seven wagons, two carriages, twenty guards on horses. And three war-dogs.

There had been six, but three had caught Dejim Nebrahl's scent and, stupid creatures that they were, had set off to hunt the T'rolbarahl down. They had succeeded in finding the D'ivers, and their blood now filled the bellies of the five remaining beasts.

The Trell had stunned Dejim Nebrahl. To snap one of his necks – not even a Tartheno could manage such a thing – and one had tried, long ago. Then, to drag the other down, over the cliff's edge, to plunge to its death among the jagged rocks below. This audacity was . . . unforgivable. Weak and wounded, Dejim Nebrahl had fled the scene of ambush, wandering half-crazed with anger and pain until stumbling upon the trail of this caravan. How many days and nights had passed, the T'rolbarahl had no idea. There was hunger, the need to heal, and these demands filled the mind of the D'ivers.

Before Dejim Nebrahl, now, waited his salvation. Enough blood to spawn replacements for those he had lost in the ambush; perhaps enough blood to fashion yet another, an eighth.

He would strike at dusk, the moment the caravan halted for the day. Slaughter the guards first, then the remaining dogs, and finally the fat weaklings riding in their puny carriages. The merchant with his harem of silent children, each one chained to the next and trailing behind the carriage. A trader in mortal flesh.

The notion sickened Dejim Nebrahl. There had been such detestable creatures in the time of the First Empire, and depravity never went extinct. When the T'rolbarahl ruled this land, a new justice would descend upon the despoilers of flesh. Dejim would feed upon them first, and then all other criminals, the murderers, the beaters of the helpless, the stone-throwers, the torturers of the spirit.

His creator had meant him and his kind to be guardians of the First Empire. Thus the conjoining of bloods, making the sense of perfection strong, god-like. Too strong, of course. The T'rolbarahl would not be ruled by an imperfect master. No, they would rule, for only then could true justice be delivered.

Justice. And ... of course ... natural hunger. Necessity carved out its own laws, and these could not be denied. When he ruled, Dejim Nebrahl would fashion a true balance between the two dominant forces in his D'ivers soul, and if the mortal fools suffered beneath the weight of his justice, then so be it. They deserved the truth of their own beliefs. Deserved the talon-sharp edges of their own vaunted virtues, for virtues were more than just words, they were weapons, and it was only right that such weapons be turned upon their wielders.

The shadows had descended the cliff-face here in the lee of the setting sun's light. Dejim Nebrahl followed those shadows downward to the plain, five sets of eyes, but one mind. The focus of all absolute and unwavering.

Delicious slaughter. Splashing red to celebrate the sun's lurid fire.

As he flowed out onto the plain, he heard the dogs begin barking.

A moment of pity for them. Stupid as they were, they knew about necessity.

Something of a struggle, but he managed to unfold himself and descend, groaning with stiffness, from the mule's broad back. And, despite the awkward effort, he spilled not a single drop from his cherished bucket. Humming beneath his breath some chant or other – he'd forgotten where in the vast tome of Holy Songs it had come from, and really, did it actually matter? – he waddled with his burden to the simpering waves of Raraku Sea, then walked out amidst the softly swirling sands and eagerly trembling reeds.

Pausing suddenly.

A desperate scan of the area, sniffing the humid, sultry, dusky air. Another scan, eyes darting, seeking out every nearby shadow, every wayward rustle of reed and straggly bush. Then he ducked lower, soaking his frayed robes as he knelt in the shallows.

Sweet, sun-warmed waters.

A final, suspicious look round, all sides – could never be too careful – then, with solemn delight, he lowered the bucket into the sea.

And watched, eyes shining, as the scores of tiny fish raced out in all directions. Well, not exactly raced, more like sat there, for a time, as if stunned by freedom. Or perhaps some temporary shock of altered temperature, or the plethora of unseen riches upon which to gorge, to grow fat, sleek and blissfully energetic.

The first fish of Raraku Sea.

Iskaral Pust left the shallows then, flinging the bucket to one side. 'Tense thy back, mule! I shall now leap astride, oh yes, and won't you be surprised, to find yourself suddenly galloping – oh believe me, mule, you know how to gallop, no more of that stupid fast trot that rattles loose my poor teeth! Oh no, we shall be as the wind! Not a fitful, gusting wind, but a steady, roaring wind, a stentorian wind that races across the entire world, the very wake of our extraordinary speed, oh, how your hoofs shall blur to all eyes!'

Reaching the mule, the High Priest of Shadow leapt into the air.

Shying in alarm, the mule sidestepped.

A squeal from Iskaral Pust, then a grunt and muted *oof* as he struck and rolled in the dust and stones, wet robes flapping heavily and spraying sand about, while the mule trotted a safe distance away then turned to regard its master, long-lashed eyes blinking.

'You disgust me, beast! And I bet you think it's mutual, too! Yet even if you thought that, why, then I'd agree with you! Out of spite! How would you like that, horrid creature?' The High Priest of Shadow picked himself up and brushed sand from his robes. 'He thinks I will hit him. Strike him, with a large stick. Foolish mule. Oh no, I am much more cunning. I will surprise him with kindness . . . until he grows calm and dispenses with all watchfulness, and then . . . ha! I shall punch him in the nose! Won't he be surprised! No mule can match wits with me. Oh yes, many have tried, and almost all have failed!'

He worked a kindly smile on to his sun-wizened face, then slowly approached the mule. 'We must ride,' he murmured, 'you and I. Fraught with haste, my friend, lest we arrive too late and too late will never do.' He came within reach of the reins where they dangled beneath the mule's head. Paused as he met the creature's eyes. 'Oh ho, sweet servant, I see malice in that so-placid gaze, yes? You want to bite

357

me. Too bad. I'm the only one who bites around here.' He snatched up the reins, narrowly avoiding the snapping teeth, then clambered onto the mule's broad, sloped back.

Twenty paces from the shoreline and the world shifted around them, a miasmic swirl of shadows closing on all sides. Iskaral Pust cocked his head, looked round, then, satisfied, settled back as the mule plodded on.

A hundred heartbeats after the High Priest of Shadow vanished into his warren, a squat, wild-haired Dal Honese woman crept out of some nearby bushes, dragging a large ale cask behind her. It held water, not ale, and the lid had been pried off.

Grunting and gasping with the effort, Mogora struggled to bring the cask down into the shallows. She tipped it to one side and – a mostly toothless grin on her wrinkled features – watched a half-dozen young freshwater sharks slide like snakes into Raraku Sea.

Then she kicked the cask over and scrambled out of the water, a cackle escaping her as, with a flurry of gestures, she opened a warren and plunged into it.

Folding one shadow upon another, Iskaral Pust swiftly traversed a score of leagues. He could half-see, half-sense the desert, buttes and chaotic folds of arroyo and canyon he passed through, but none of it interested him much, until, after almost a full day's travel, he caught sight of five sleek shapes crossing the floor of a valley ahead and to his left.

He halted the mule on the ridge and, eyes narrowing, studied the distant shapes. In the midst of attacking a caravan. 'Arrogant pups,' he muttered, then drove his heels into the mule's flanks. 'Charge, I say! Charge, you fat, waddling bastard!'

The mule trotted down the slope, braying loudly.

The five shapes caught the sound and their heads turned. As one, the T'rolbarahl shifted direction and now raced towards Iskaral Pust.

The mule's cries rose in pitch.

Spreading out, the D'ivers flowed noiselessly over the ground. Rage and hunger rushed ahead of them in an almost visible bow wave, the power crackling, coruscating between the Shadow warren and the world beyond.

The beasts to either side wheeled out to come in from a flanking position, while the three in the centre staggered their timing, intending to arrive in quick succession.

Iskaral Pust was having trouble focusing on them, so jolted and tossed about was he on the mule's back. When the T'rolbarahl had closed to within thirty paces, the mule suddenly skidded to a halt. And the High Priest of Shadow was thrown forward, lunging over the animal's head. Head ducking, somersaulting over, then thumping down hard on his back in a spray of gravel and dust.

The first creature reached him, forearms lifting, talons unsheathed as it sailed through the air, then landing on the spot where Iskaral Pust had fallen – only to find him not there. The second and third beasts experienced a moment of confusion as the quarry vanished, then they sensed a presence at their side. Their heads snapped round, but too late, as a wave of sorcery hammered into them. Shadow-wrought power cracked like lightning, and the creatures were batted into the air, leaving in their wakes misty clouds of blood. Writhing, they both struck the ground fifteen paces away, skidding then rolling.

The two flanking D'ivers attacked. And, as Iskaral Pust vanished, they collided, chests reverberating like heavy thunder, teeth and talons raking through hide. Hissing and snarling, they scrambled away from each other.

Reappearing twenty paces behind the T'rolbarahl, Iskaral Pust unleashed another wave of sorcery, watched it strike each of the five beasts in turn, watched blood spray and the bodies tumble away, kicking frenziedly as the magic wove flickering nets about them. Stones popped and exploded on the ground beneath them, sand shot upward in spear-like geysers, and everywhere there was blood, whipping out in ragged threads.

The T'rolbarahl vanished, fleeing the warren of Shadow – out into the world, where they scattered, all thoughts of the caravan gone as panic closed on their throats with invisible hands.

The High Priest of Shadow brushed dust from his clothes, then walked over to where stood the mule. 'Some help you were! We could be hunting each one down right now, but oh no, you're tired of running. Whoever thought mules deserved four legs was an idiot! You are most useless! Bah!' He paused, then, and lifted a gnarled finger to his wrinkled lips. 'But wait, what if they got *really* angry? What if they decided to make a fight to the finish? What then? Messy, oh, very messy. No, best leave them for someone else to deal with. I must not get distracted. Imagine, though! Challenging the High Priest of Shadow of all Seven Cities! Dumber than cats, that T'rolbarahl. I am entirely without sympathy.'

He climbed back onto the mule. 'Well, that was fun, wasn't it? Stupid mule. I think we'll have mule for supper tonight, what do you think of that? The ultimate sacrifice is called for, as far as you're concerned, don't you think? Well, who cares what you think? Where to now? Thank the gods at least one of us knows where we're going. That way, mule, and quickly now. Trot, damn you, trot!'

Skirting the caravan, where dogs still barked, Iskaral Pust began shifting shadows once more.

Dusk had arrived in the world beyond when he reached his destination, reining in the plodding mule at the foot of a cliff.

Vultures clambered amongst the tumbled rocks, crowding a fissure but unable or, as yet, unwilling to climb down into it. One edge of that crevasse was stained with dried blood, and among rocks to one side were the remains of a dead beast – devoured to bones and ragged strips by the scavengers, it was nonetheless easy to identify. One of the T'rolbarahl.

The vultures voiced a chorus of indignation as the High Priest of Shadow dismounted and approached. Spitting curses, he chased away the ugly, Mogora-like creatures, then eased himself down into the fissure. Deep, the close air smelling of blood and rotting meat.

The crevasse narrowed a little more than a man's height down, and into this was wedged a body. Iskaral Pust settled down beside it. He laid a hand on the figure's broad shoulder, well away from the obvious breaks in that arm. 'How many days, friend? Ah, only a Trell would survive this. First, we shall have to get you out of here, and for that I have a stalwart, loyal mule. Then, well, then, we shall see, won't we?'

Neither stalwart nor particularly loyal, the mule's disinclination towards cooperation slowed down the task of extracting Mappo Runt considerably, and it was full dark by the time the Trell was pulled from the fissure and dragged onto a flat patch of wind-blown sand.

The two compound fractures in the left arm were the least of the huge Trell's injuries. Both legs had broken, and one edge of the fissure had torn a large flap of skin and flesh from Mappo's back – the exposed meat was swarming with maggots, and the mostly hanging flap of tissue was clearly unsalvageable, grey in the centre and blackening round the edges, smelling of rot. Iskaral Pust cut that away and tossed it back into the fissure.

He then leaned close and listened to the Trell's breathing. Shallow, yet slow – another day without attention and he would have died. As it was, the possibility remained distinct. 'Herbs, my friend,' the High Priest said as he set to cleaning the visible wounds. 'And High Denul ointments, elixirs, tinctures, salves, poultices . . . have I forgotten any? No, I think not. Internal injuries, oh yes, crushed ribs, that whole side. So, much bleeding inside, yet, obviously, not enough to kill you outright. Remarkable. You are almost as stubborn as my servant here—' He looked up. 'You, beast, set up the tent and start us a fire! Do that and then maybe I'll feed you and not, hee hee, feed *on* you—'

'You are an idiot!' This cry came from the darkness off to one side, and a moment later Mogora appeared from the gloom.

The gloom, yes, that explains everything. 'What are you doing here, hag?'

'Saving Mappo, of course.'

'What? I have saved him already!'

'Saving him from you, I meant!' She scrabbled closer. 'What's that vial in your hand? That's venom of paralt! You damned idiot, you were going to kill him! After all he's been through!'

'Paralt? That's right, wife, it's paralt. You arrived, so I was about to drink it.'

'I saw you deal with that T'rolbarahl, Iskaral Pust.'

'You did?' He paused, ducked his head. 'Now her adoration is complete! How could she not adore me? It must be near worship by now. That's why she followed me all the way. She can't get enough of me. It's the same with everyone – they just can't get enough of me—'

'The most powerful High Priest of Shadow,' cut in Mogora as she removed various healing unguents from her pack, 'cannot survive without a good woman at his side. Failing that, you have me, so get used to it, warlock. Now, get out of my way so I can tend to this poor, hapless Trell.'

Iskaral Pust backed away. 'So what do I do now? You've made me useless, woman!'

'That's not hard, husband. Make us camp.'

'I already told my mule to do that.'

'It's a mule, you idiot . . .' Her words trailed away as she noted the flicker of firelight off to one side. Turning, she studied the large canvas tent, expertly erected, and the stone-ringed hearth where a pot of water already steamed beneath a tripod. Nearby stood the mule, eating from its bag of oats. Mogora frowned, then shook her head and returned to her work. 'Tend to the tea, then. Be useful.'

'I was being useful! Until you arrived and messed everything up! The most powerful High Priest in Seven Cities does *not* need a woman! In fact, that's the very last thing he needs!'

'You couldn't heal a hangnail, Iskaral Pust. This Trell has the black poison in his veins, the glittering vein-snake. We shall need more than High Denul for this—'

'Oh here we go! All your witchy rubbish. High Denul will conquer the black poison—'

'Perhaps, but the dead flesh will remain dead. He will be crippled, half-mad, his hearts will weaken.' She paused and glared over at him. 'Shadowthrone sent you to find him, didn't he? Why?'

Iskaral Pust smiled sweetly. 'Oh, she's suspicious now, isn't she? But

I won't tell her anything. Except the hint, the modest hint, of my vast knowledge. Yes indeed, I know my dear god's mind – and a twisted, chaotic, weaselly mind it is. In fact, I know so much I am speechless – hah, look at her, those beetle eyes narrowing suspiciously, as if she dares grow aware of my profound ignorance in all matters pertaining to my cherished, idiotic god. Dares, and would challenge me openly. I would crumble before that onslaught, of course.' He paused, reworked his smile, then spread his hands and said, 'Sweet Mogora, the High Priest of Shadow must have his secrets, kept even from his wife, alas. And so I beg you not to press me on this, else you suffer Shadowthrone's random wrath—'

'You are a complete fool, Iskaral Pust.'

'Let her think that,' he said, then added a chuckle. 'Now she'll wonder why I have laughed – no, not laughed, but *chuckled*, which, all things considered, is far more alarming. I mean, it sounded like a chuckle so it must have been one, though it's the first I've ever tried, or heard, for that matter. Whereas a chortle, well, that's different. I'm not fat enough to chortle, alas. Sometimes I wish—'

'Go sit by your mule's fire,' Mogora said. 'I must prepare my ritual.'

'See how that chuckle has discomfited her! Of course, my darling, you go and play with your little ritual, that's a dear. Whilst I make tea for myself and my mule.'

Warmed by the flames and his tralb tea, Iskaral Pust watched – as best as he was able in the darkness – Mogora at work. First, she assembled large chunks of stone, each one broken, cracked or otherwise rough-edged, and set them down in the sand, creating an ellipse that encompassed the Trell. She then urinated over these rocks, achieving this with an extraordinary half-crab half-chicken wide-legged waddle, straddling the stones and proceeding widdershins until returning to the place she had started. Iskaral marvelled at the superior muscle control, not to mention the sheer volume, that Mogora obviously possessed. In the last few years his own efforts at urination had met with mixed success, until even starting and stopping now seemed the highest of visceral challenges.

Satisfied with her piddle, Mogora then started pulling hairs from her head. She didn't have that many up there, and those she selected seemed so deeply rooted that Iskaral feared she would deflate her skull with every successful yank. His anticipation of seeing such a thing yielded only disappointment, as, with seven long wiry grey hairs in one hand, Mogora stepped into the ellipse, one foot planted to either side of the Trell's torso. Then, muttering some witchly thing, she flung the hairs into the inky blackness overhead.

Instinct guided Iskaral's gaze upward after those silvery threads, and he was somewhat alarmed to see that the stars had vanished overhead. Whereas, out on the horizons, they remained sharp and bright. 'Gods, woman! What have you done?'

Ignoring him, she stepped back out of the ellipse and began singing in the Woman's Language, which was, of course, unintelligible to Iskaral's ears. Just as the Man's Language – which Mogora called gibberish – was beyond her ability to understand. The reason for that, Iskaral Pust knew, was that the Man's Language *was* gibberish, designed specifically to confound women. *It's a fact that men don't need words, but women do. We have penises, after all. Who needs words when you have a penis? Whereas with women there are two breasts, which invites conversation, just as a good behind presents perfect punctuation, something every man knows.*

What's wrong with the world? You ask a man and he says, 'Don't ask.' Ask a woman and you'll be dead of old age before she's finished. Hah. Hah ha.

Strange streams of gossamer began descending through the reflected light of the fire, settling upon the Trell's body.

'What are those?' Iskaral asked. Then started as one brushed his forearm and he saw that it was a spider's silk, and there was the spider at one end, tiny as a mite. He looked skyward in alarm. 'There are *spiders* up there? What madness is this? What are they doing up there?'

'Be quiet.'

'Answer me!'

'The sky is filled with spiders, husband. They float on the winds. Now I've answered you, so close that mouth of yours lest I send a few thousand of my sisters into it.'

His teeth clacked and he edged closer to the hearth. *Burn, you horrid things. Burn!*

The strands of web covered the Trell now. Thousands, tens, hundreds of thousands – the spiders were wrapping about Mappo Runt's entire body.

'And now,' Mogora said, 'time for the moon.'

The blackness overhead vanished in a sudden bloom of silver, incandescent light. Squealing, Iskaral Pust fell onto his back, so alarming was the transformation, and he found himself staring straight up at a massive, full moon, hanging so low it seemed within reach. If he but dared. Which he did not. 'You've brought the moon down! Are you mad? It's going to crash on us!'

'Oh, stop it. It only seems that way – well, maybe I nudged it a bit – but I told you this was a serious ritual, didn't I?'

'*What have you done with the moon?*'

She crowed with manic laughter. 'It's just my little ritual, darling. How do you like it?'

'Make it go away!'

'Frightened? You should be! I'm a woman! A witch! So why don't you just drag that scrawny behind of yours into that tent and cower, dear husband. This is real power, here, *real* magic!'

'No it isn't! I mean, it's not witch magic, not Dal Honese – I don't know *what* this is—'

'You're right, you don't. Now be a good little boy and go to sleep, Iskaral Pust, while I set about saving this Trell's miserable life.'

Iskaral thought to argue, then decided against it. He crawled into the tent.

From outside, 'Is that you gibbering, Iskaral?'

Oh be quiet.

Lostara Yil opened her eyes, then slowly sat up.

A grey-cloaked figure was standing near a stone-arched portal, his back to her. Rough-hewn walls to either side, forming a circular chamber with Lostara – who had been lying on an altar – in the centre. Moonlight was flooding in from in front of the figure, yet it seemed to be sliding in visible motion. As if the moon beyond was plunging from the sky.

'What—?' she asked, then began to cough uncontrollably, sharp pain biting in her lungs. Finally recovering, she blinked tears from her eyes, looked up once again.

He was facing her now.

The Shadow Dancer. The god. Cotillion. Seemingly in answer to her initial question, he said, 'I am not sure. Some untoward sorcery is at work, somewhere in the desert. The moon's light has been . . . stolen. I admit I have never seen anything like it before.'

Even as he was speaking, Lostara's memories returned in a rush. Y'Ghatan. Flames, everywhere. Blistering heat. Savage burns – oh how her flesh screamed its pain – 'What – what happened to me?'

'Oh, that was what you meant. My apologies, Lostara Yil. Well, in short, I pulled you out of the fire. Granted, it's very rare for a god to intervene, but T'riss kicked open the door—'

'T'riss?'

'The Queen of Dreams. Set the precedent, as it were. Most of your clothes had burned – I apologize if you find the new ones not to your liking.'

She glanced down at the rough-woven shift covering her.

'A neophyte's tunic,' Cotillion said. 'You are in a Temple of Rashan, a secret one. Abandoned with the rebellion, I believe. We are a league and a half from what used to be Y'Ghatan, forty or so paces north of the Sotka Road. The temple is well concealed.' He gestured with one gloved hand at the archway. 'This is the only means of ingress and egress.'

'Why – why did you save me?'

He hesitated. 'There will come a time, Lostara Yil, when you will be faced with a choice. A dire one.'

'What kind of choice?'

He studied her for a moment, then asked, 'How deep are your feelings for Pearl?'

She started, then shrugged. 'A momentary infatuation. Thankfully passed. Besides, he's unpleasant company these days.'

'I can understand that,' Cotillion said, somewhat enigmatically. 'You will have to choose, Lostara Yil, between your loyalty to the Adjunct . . . and all that Pearl represents.'

'Between the Adjunct and the Empress? That makes no sense—'

He stayed her with a raised hand. 'You need not decide immediately, Lostara. In fact, I would counsel against it. All I ask is that you consider the question, for now.'

'What is going on? What do you know, Cotillion? Are you planning vengeance against Laseen?'

His brows lifted. 'No, nothing like that. In fact, I am not directly involved in this ... uh, matter. At the moment, anyway. Indeed, the truth is, I am but anticipating certain things, some of which may come to pass, some of which may not.' He faced the portalway again. 'There is food near the altar. Wait until dawn, then leave here. Down to the road. Where you will find . . . welcome company. Your story is this: you found a way out of the city, then, blinded by smoke, you stumbled, struck your head and lost consciousness. When you awoke, the Fourteenth was gone. Your memory is patchy, of course.'

'Yes, it is, Cotillion.'

He turned at her tone, half-smiled. 'You fear that you are now in my debt, Lostara Yil. And that I will one day return to you, demanding payment.'

'It's how gods work, isn't it?'

'Some of them, yes. But you see, Lostara Yil, what I did for you in Y'Ghatan four days ago was my repayment, of a debt that I owed you.'

'What debt?'

Shadows were gathering about Cotillion now, and she barely heard his reply, 'You forget, I once watched you dance . . .' And then he was gone.

Moonlight streamed into his wake like quicksilver. And she sat for a time, bathed in its light, considering his words.

Snoring from the tent. Mogora sat on a flat stone five paces from the dying fire. Had he been awake, Iskaral Pust would be relieved. The moon was back where it belonged, after all. Not that she'd actually moved it. That would have been very hard indeed, and would have attracted far too much attention besides. But she'd drawn away its power, somewhat, briefly, enough to effect the more thorough healing the Trell had required.

Someone stepped from the shadows. Walked a slow circle round the recumbent, motionless form of Mappo Trell, then halted and looked over at Mogora.

She scowled, then jerked a nod towards the tent. 'Iskaral Pust, he's the Magi of High House Shadow, isn't he?'

'Impressive healing, Mogora,' Cotillion observed. 'You do understand, of course, that the gift may in truth be a curse.'

'You sent Pust here to find him!'

'Shadowthrone, actually, not me. For that reason, I cannot say if mercy counted for anything in his decision.'

Mogora glanced again at the tent. 'Magi . . . that blathering idiot.'

Cotillion was gazing steadily at her, then he said, 'You're one of Ardata's, aren't you?'

She veered into a mass of spiders.

The god watched as they fled into every crack and, moments later, were gone. He sighed, took one last look round, momentarily meeting the placid eyes of the mule, then vanished in a flowing swirl of shadows.

CHAPTER TEN

When the day knew only darkness,
the wind a mute beggar stirring ashes and stars
in the discarded pools beneath the old
retaining wall, down where the white rivers
of sand slip grain by grain into the unseen,
and every foundation is but a moment
from a horizon's stagger, I found myself
among friends and so was made at ease
with my modest list of farewells.

Soldier Dying
Fisher kel Tath

T HEY EMERGED FROM THE WARREN INTO THE STENCH OF SMOKE AND ashes, and before them, in the growing light of dawn, reared a destroyed city. The three stood unmoving for a time, silent, each seeking to comprehend this vista.

Stormy was the first to speak. 'Looks like the Imperial Warren's spilled out here.'

Ash and dead air, the light seeming listless – Kalam was not surprised by the marine's observation. They had just left a place of death and desolation, only to find themselves in another. 'I still recognize it,' the assassin said. 'Y'Ghatan.'

Stormy coughed, then spat. 'Some siege.'

'The army's moved on,' Quick Ben observed, studying the tracks and rubbish where the main encampment had been. 'West.'

Stormy grunted, then said, 'Look at that gap in the wall. Moranth munitions, a whole damned wagon of 'em, I'd say.'

A viscous river had flowed out through that gap, and, motionless now, it glittered in the morning light. Fused glass and metals. There had been a firestorm, Kalam realized. Yet another one to afflict poor Y'Ghatan. Had the sappers set that off?

'Olive oil,' said Quick Ben suddenly. 'The oil harvest must have been in the city.' He paused, then added, 'Makes me wonder if it was an accident.'

Kalam glanced over at the wizard. 'Seems a little extreme, Quick. Besides, from what I've heard of Leoman, he's not the kind to throw his own life away.'

'Assuming he stayed around long enough.'

'We took losses here,' Stormy said. 'There's a grave mound there, under that ash.' He pointed. 'Scary big, unless they included rebel dead.'

'We make separate holes for them,' Kalam said, knowing that Stormy knew that as well. None of this looked good, and they were reluctant to admit that. Not out loud. 'The tracks look a few days old, at least. I suppose we should catch up with the Fourteenth.'

'Let's circle this first,' Quick Ben said, squinting at the ruined city. 'There's something . . . some residue . . . I don't know. Only . . .'

'Sound argument from the High Mage,' Stormy said. 'I'm convinced.'

Kalam glanced over at the mass burial mound, and wondered how many of his friends were lying trapped in that earth, unmoving in the eternal dark, the maggots and worms already at work to take away all that had made each of them unique. It wasn't something he enjoyed thinking about, but if he did not stand here and gift them a few more moments of thought, then who would?

Charred rubbish lay strewn on the road and in the flats to either side. Tent stakes still in place gripped burnt fragments of canvas, and in a trench beyond the road's bend as it made its way towards what used to be the city's gate, a dozen bloated horse carcasses had been dumped, legs upthrust like bony tree-stumps in a flyblown swamp. The stench of burnt things hung in the motionless air.

Apsalar reined in on the road as her slow scan of the devastation before her caught movement a hundred paces ahead and to her left. She settled back in the saddle, seeing familiarity in the gaits and demeanours of two of the three figures now walking towards what remained of Y'Ghatan. Telorast and Curdle scampered back to flank her horse.

'Terrible news, Not-Apsalar!' Telorast cried. 'Three terrible men await us, should we continue this course. If you seek to destroy them, well then, that is fine. We wish you well. Otherwise, I suggest we escape. Now.'

'I agree,' Curdle added, small skeletal head bobbing as the creature paced, grovelled, then paced again, tail spiking the air.

Her horse lifted a front hoof and the demonic skeletons scattered, having learned that near proximity to the beast was a treacherous thing.

'I know two of them,' Apsalar said. 'Besides, they have seen us.' She nudged her mount forward, walking it slowly towards the mage, his assassin companion, and the Malazan soldier, all of whom had now shifted direction and approached with a measured pace.

'They will annihilate us!' Telorast hissed. 'I can tell – oh, that mage, he's not nice, not at all—'

The two small creatures raced for cover.

Annihilation. The possibility existed, Apsalar allowed, given the history she shared with Quick Ben and Kalam Mekhar. Then again, they had known of the possession, and she had since travelled with Kalam for months, first across the Seeker's Deep, from Darujhistan all the way to Ehrlitan, during which nothing untoward had occurred. This eased her mind somewhat as she waited for them to arrive.

Kalam was the first to speak. 'Few things in the world make sense, Apsalar.'

She shrugged. 'We have each had our journeys, Kalam Mekhar. I, for one, am not particularly surprised to find our paths converging once more.'

'Now that,' said Quick Ben, 'is an alarming statement. Unless you're here to satisfy Shadowthrone's desire for vengeance, there is no possible reason at all that our paths should converge. Not here. Not now. I certainly haven't been pushed and pulled by any conniving god—'

'You have the aura of Hood about you, Quick Ben,' Apsalar said, an observation that clearly startled Kalam and the soldier. 'Such residue comes only from long conversations with the Lord of Death, and so, while you might claim freedom for yourself, perhaps your motives for what you do and where you choose to go are less purely your own than you would have others believe. Or, for that matter, than what you yourself would like to believe.' Her gaze slid across to Kalam. 'Whilst the assassin has known the presence of Cotillion, only a short while ago. And as for this Falari soldier here, his spirit is bound to a T'lan Imass, and to the Fire of Life that passes for worship among the T'lan Imass. Thus, fire, shadow and death, drawn together even as the forces and gods of such forces find alignment against a single foe. Yet, I feel I should warn you all – that foe is no longer singular and, perhaps, never was. And present alliances may not last.'

'What is it about all this,' Quick Ben said, 'that I'm not enjoying?'

Kalam rounded on the wizard. 'Maybe, Quick, you're sensing something of my desire – which I am barely restraining – to plant my fist in your face. The Lord of Death? What in the name of the Abyss *happened* at Black Coral?'

369

'Expedience,' the wizard snapped, eyes still on Apsalar. 'That's what happened. In that whole damned war against the Pannion Domin. That should have been obvious from the outset – Dujek joining forces with Caladan Brood was simply the first and most egregious breaking of the rules.'

'So now you're working for Hood?'

'Not even close, Kalam. To stretch a pun, Hood knows, he was working for *me*.'

'Was? And now?'

'And now,' he nodded towards Apsalar, 'as she says, the gods are at war.' He shrugged, but it was an uneasy shrug. 'I need to get a sense of the two sides, Kalam. I need to ask questions. I need answers.'

'And is Hood providing them?'

The glance he shot the assassin was skittish, almost diffident. 'Slowly.'

'And what is Hood getting from you?'

The wizard bridled. 'Ever try twisting a dead man's arm? It doesn't work!' His glare switched between Kalam and Apsalar. 'Listen. Remember those games Hedge and Fid played? With the Deck of Dragons? Idiots, but never mind that. The point is, they made up the rules as they went along, and that's what I'm doing, all right? Gods, even a genius like me has limits!'

A snort from the Falari soldier, and Apsalar saw him bare his teeth.

The wizard stepped towards him. 'Enough of that, Stormy! You and your damned stone sword!' He waved wildly at the city of Y'Ghatan. 'Does this smell sweet to you?'

'What would smell even sweeter is the Adjunct's High Mage all chopped up and served in a stew to Hood himself.' He reached for the Imass sword, his grin broadening. 'And I'm just the man to do—'

'Settle down, you two,' Kalam said. 'All right, Apsalar, we're all here and that's passing strange but not as strange maybe as it should be. Doesn't matter.' He made a gesture that encompassed himself, Quick Ben and Stormy. 'We're returning to the Fourteenth Army. Or, we will be, once we've circled the city and Quick's satisfied it's as dead as it looks—'

'Oh,' the wizard cut in, 'it's dead all right. Still, we're circling the ruin.' He pointed a finger at Apsalar. 'As for you, woman, you're not travelling alone, are you? Where are they hiding? And what are they? Familiars?'

'You could call them that,' she replied.

'Where are they hiding?' Quick Ben demanded again.

'Not sure. Close by, I suspect. They're . . . shy.' And she added nothing more, for now, satisfied as she was by the wizard's answering scowl.

'Where,' Kalam asked, 'are you going, Apsalar?'

Her brows rose. 'Why, with you, of course.'

She could see that this did not please them much, yet they voiced no further objections. As far as she was concerned, this was a perfect conclusion to this part of her journey. For it coincided with her most pressing task – the final target for assassination. The only one that could not be ignored.

She'd always known Cotillion for a most subtle bastard.

'All right, then,' Sergeant Hellian said, 'which one of you wants to be my new corporal?'

Touchy and Brethless exchanged glances.

'What?' Touchy asked. 'Us? But you got Balgrid and Tavos Pond, now. Or even—'

'It's my new squad and I decide these things.' She squinted over at the other soldiers. 'Balgrid's a mage. So's Tavos Pond.' She scowled at the two men. 'I don't like mages, they're always disappearing, right when you want to ask them something.' Her gaze slid across to the last two soldiers. 'Maybe's a sapper and enough said about that, and Lutes is our healer. That leaves . . .' Hellian returned her attention to the twins, 'you two.'

'Fine,' said Touchy. 'I'll be corporal.'

'Hold on,' Brethless said. 'I want to be corporal! I ain't taking no orders from him, Sergeant. Not a chance. I got the brains, you know—'

Touchy snorted. 'Then, since you didn't know what to do with them, you threw them away.'

'You're a big fat liar, Touchy—'

'Quiet!' Hellian reached for her sword. But then remembered and drew a knife instead. 'Another word either of you and I'll cut myself.'

The squad stared at her.

'I'm a woman, see, and with women, it's how we deal with men. You're all men. Give me trouble and I'll stick this knife in my arm. Or leg. Or maybe I'll slice a nipple off. And you bastards will have to live with that. For the rest of your days, you'll have to live with the fact that you were being such assholes that Hellian went and disfigured herself.'

No-one spoke.

Smiling, Hellian resheathed the knife. 'Good. Now, Touchy and Brethless, I've decided. You're both corporals. There.'

'But what if I want to order Brethless—'

'Well you can't.'

Brethless raised a finger. 'Wait, what if we give different orders to the others?'

'Don't worry 'bout that,' Maybe said, 'we ain't gonna listen to you anyways. You're both idiots, but if the sergeant wants to make you corporals, that's fine. We don't care. Idiots make good corporals.'

'All right,' Hellian said, rising, 'it's settled. Now, nobody wander off, since the captain wants us ready to march.' She walked away, up towards the ridge. Thinking.

The captain had dragged off Urb and made him a sergeant. Madness. That old rule about idiots making good corporals obviously extended to sergeants, but there wasn't anything she could do about it. Besides, she might go and kill him and then there'd be trouble. Urb was big, after all, and there wasn't much in the way of places to hide his body. Not around here, anyway, she concluded, scanning the broken rocks, bricks and potsherds strewn on the slope.

They needed to find a village. She could trade her knife – no, that wouldn't work, since it would mess up her threat and the squad might mutiny. Unless, next time, she added nails to the possible weapons – scratch her own eyes out, something like that. She glanced down at her nails – *oh, mostly gone. What a mess . . .*

'Look at her,' Maybe said. 'Tells us not to wander off then what does she do? Wanders off. Finds a ridge to do what? Why, check out her nails. Ooh, they're chipped! Gods, we've got a real woman for our Hood-damned sergeant—'

'She ain't a real woman,' Touchy said. 'You don't know her at all, sapper. Now, me and Brethless, we were two of the poor fools who came first to the temple in Kartool, where this whole nightmare started.'

'What are you talking about?' Balgrid demanded.

'Someone went and butchered all the priests in the D'rek temple, and we was the first ones on the scene. Anyway, you know how this goes. That was our quarter, right? Not that we could patrol *inside* temples, of course, so we weren't to blame. But since when does common sense count for anything in the empire? So, they had to send us away. Hopefully to get killed, so none of it gets out—'

'It just did,' Tavos Pond said, scratching beneath the rough, crusted bandages swathing one side of his face.

'What are you talking about?' Balgrid demanded again. 'And what's the sergeant doing over there?'

Maybe glared at Lutes. 'He's still deaf. Do something!'

'It'll come back,' the healer replied, shrugging. 'Mostly. It takes time, that's all.'

'Anyway,' Touchy resumed, 'she ain't a real woman. She drinks—'

'Right,' Brethless cut in, 'and why does she drink? Why, she's scared of spiders!'

372

'That don't matter,' his brother retorted. 'And now she's stuck sober and that's bad. Listen, all of you—'

'What?' Balgrid asked.

'Listen, the rest of you, we just keep her drunk and everything'll be fine—'

'Idiot,' Maybe said. 'Probably you didn't catch whoever killed all those priests because your sergeant *was* drunk. She did good in Y'Ghatan, or have you forgotten? You're alive 'cause of her.'

'That'll wear off, sapper. Just you wait. I mean, look at her – she's fussing over her nails!'

Adopting heavies into a squad was never easy, Gesler knew. They didn't think normally; in fact, the sergeant wasn't even sure they were human. Somewhere between a flesh-and-blood Imass and a Barghast, maybe. And now he had four of them. Shortnose, Flashwit, Uru Hela and Mayfly. Flashwit could probably out-pull an ox, and she was Napan besides, though those stunning green eyes came from somewhere else; and Shortnose seemed in the habit of losing body parts, and there was no telling how far that had gone beyond the missing nose and ear. Uru was a damned Korelri who'd probably been destined for the Stormwall before stowing aboard a Jakatakan merchanter, meaning she felt she didn't owe anybody anything. Mayfly was just easily confused, but clearly as tough as they came.

And Heavies came tough. He'd have to adjust his thinking on how to work the squad. *But if he ever shows up, Stormy will love these ones.*

Maybe in one way it made sense to reorganize the squads, but Gesler wasn't sure of the captain's timing. It was Fist Keneb's responsibility, anyway, and he'd likely prefer splitting up soldiers who were, one and all now, veterans. Well, that was for the damned officers to chew over. What concerned him the most at the moment, was the fact that they were mostly unarmed and unarmoured. A score of raiders or even bandits happening upon them and there'd be more Malazan bones bleaching in the sun. They needed to get moving, catch up with the damned army.

He fixed his gaze on the west road, up on the ridge. Hellian was there already, he saw. Lit up by the rising sun. Odd woman, but she must have done something right, to have led her soldiers through that mess. Gesler would not look back at Y'Ghatan. Every time he had done that before, the images returned: Truth shouldering the munitions packs, running into the smoke and flames. Fiddler and Cuttle racing back, away from what was coming. No, it wasn't worth any last looks back at that cursed city.

What could you take from it that was worth a damned thing,

anyway? Leoman had drawn them right in, made the city a web from which there was no escape – *only . . . we made it, didn't we? But, how many didn't?* The captain had told them. Upwards of two thousand, wasn't it? All to kill a few hundred fanatics who would probably have been just as satisfied killing themselves and no-one else, to make whatever mad, futile point they felt worth dying for. It was how fanatics thought, after all. Killing Malazans simply sweetened an already sweet final meal. *All to make some god's eyes shine.*

Mind you, polish anything long enough and it'll start to shine.

The sun lifted its blistered eye above the horizon, and it was almost time to begin the march.

Ten, maybe more pups, all pink, wrinkled and squirming inside an old martin's nest that had dislodged from an exploding wall. Bottle peered down at them, the nest in his hands. Their mother clung to his left shoulder, nose twitching as if she was contemplating a sudden leap – either towards her helpless brood or towards Bottle's neck.

'Relax, my dear,' he whispered. 'They're as much mine as they are yours.'

A half-choking sound nearby, then a burst of laughter.

Bottle glared over at Smiles. 'You don't understand a thing, you miserable cow.'

'I can't believe you want to take that filthy thing with you. All right, it got us out, so now leave it be. Besides, there's no way you can keep them alive – she's got to feed 'em, right, meaning she has to scrounge. When's she gonna be able to do that? We're about to march, you fool.'

'We can manage,' he replied. 'They're tribal creatures, rats. Besides, we've already scrounged enough food – it's only Y'Ghatan who needs to eat lots, for now. The pups just suckle.'

'Stop, you're making me sick. There's enough rats in the world already, Bottle. Take the big one, sure, but leave the others for the birds.'

'She'd never forgive me.'

Sitting nearby, Koryk studied the two bickering soldiers a moment longer, then he rose.

'Don't go far,' Strings said.

The half-Seti grunted a wordless reply, then headed towards the far, northern end of the flats, where broad, deep pits pockmarked the ground. He arrived at the edge of one and looked down. Long ago, these pits had yielded clay for the potters, back when there had been water close to the surface. When that had dried up, they had proved useful for the disposal of refuse, including the bodies of paupers.

The pits nearest the city's walls held only bones, bleached heaps, sun-cracked amidst tattered strips of burial cloth.

He stood above the remains for a moment longer, then descended the crumbling side.

The soldiers had lost most of the bones affixed to their armour and uniforms. It seemed only fitting, Koryk thought, that these long-dead citizens of Y'Ghatan offer up their own. *After all, we crawled through the city's own bones. And we can't even measure what we left behind.*

Knee-deep in bones, he looked round. No shortage of fetishes here. Satisfied, he began collecting.

'You look damn near naked without all that armour.'

Corporal Tarr grimaced. 'I *am* damn near naked without all my armour, Sergeant.'

Smiling, Strings looked away, searching until he found Koryk, who was in the process of climbing into the ground. At least, it looked that way from here. Strange, secretive man. Then again, if he wanted to crawl into the earth, that was his business. So long as he showed up for the call to march.

Cuttle was near the fire, pouring out the last of the tea, a brew concocted from a half-dozen local plants Bottle had identified as palatable, although he'd been a little cagey on toxicity.

After a moment surveying his squad, the sergeant returned to shaving off his beard, hacking at the foul-smelling, singed hair with his camp knife – the only weapon left to him.

One of the foundling children had attached herself to him and sat opposite, watching with wide eyes, her round face smeared with ash and two wet, dirty streaks running down from her nose. She had licked her lips raw.

Strings paused, squinted at her, then raised one eyebrow. 'You need a bath, lass. We'll have to toss you into the first stream we run across.'

She made a face.

'Can't be helped,' he went on. 'Malazan soldiers in the Fourteenth are required to maintain a certain level of cleanliness. So far, the captain's been easy about it, but trust me, that won't last . . .' He trailed off when he saw that she wasn't listening any more. Nor was she looking at him, but at something beyond his left shoulder. Strings twisted round to follow her gaze.

And saw a rider, and three figures on foot. Coming down from the road that encircled Y'Ghatan. Coming towards them.

From a short distance to the sergeant's right, he heard Gesler say, 'That's Stormy – I'd recognize that bludgeon walk anywhere. And Kalam and Quick. Don't know the woman on the horse, though . . .'

But I do. Strings rose. Walked up the slope to meet them. He heard Gesler behind him, following.

'Hood take us,' Strings said, studying first Apsalar, then Kalam and Quick Ben, 'half the old squad. All here.'

Quick Ben was squinting at Fiddler. 'You shaved,' he said. 'Reminds me just how young you are – that beard turned you into an old man.'

He paused, then added, 'Be nice to have Mallet here with us.'

'Forget it,' Strings said, 'he's getting fat in Darujhistan and the last thing he'd want to do is see our ugly faces again.' He coughed. 'And I suppose Paran's there, too, feet up and sipping chilled Saltoan wine.'

'Turned out to be a good captain,' the wizard said after a moment. 'Who'd have thought it, huh?'

Strings nodded up at the woman on the horse. 'Apsalar. So where's Crokus Younghand?'

She shrugged. 'He goes by the name of Cutter, now, Fiddler.'

Oh.

'In any case,' she continued, 'we parted ways some time ago.'

Stormy stepped closer to Gesler. 'We lost him?' he asked.

Gesler looked away, then nodded.

'What happened?'

Strings spoke in answer: 'Truth saved all our skins, Stormy. He did what we couldn't do, when it needed to be done. And not a word of complaint. Anyway, he gave up his life for us. I wish it could have been otherwise . . .' He shook his head. 'I know, it's hard when they're so young.'

There were tears now, running down the huge man's sunburnt face. Saying nothing, he walked past them all, down onto the slope towards the encamped Malazans. Gesler watched, then followed.

No-one spoke.

'I had a feeling,' Quick Ben said after a time. 'You made it out of Y'Ghatan – but the Fourteenth's marched already.'

Fiddler nodded. 'They had to. Plague's coming from the east. Besides, it must've seemed impossible – anyone trapped in the city surviving the firestorm.'

'How did you pull it off?' Kalam demanded.

'We're about to march,' Fiddler said as Faradan Sort appeared, clambering onto the road. 'I'll tell you along the way. And Quick, I've got a mage in my squad I want you to meet – he saved us all.'

'What do you want me to do?' the wizard asked. 'Shake his hand?'

'Not unless you want to get bit.' *Hah, look at his face. That was worth it.*

The bridge was made of black stones, each one roughly carved yet perfectly fitted. Wide enough to accommodate two wagons side by side, although there were no barriers flanking the span and the edges looked worn, crumbly, enough to make Paran uneasy. Especially since there was nothing beneath the bridge. Nothing at all. Grey mists in a depthless sea below. Grey mists swallowing the bridge itself twenty paces distant; grey mists refuting the sky overhead.

A realm half-born, dead in still-birth, the air was cold, clammy, smelling of tidal pools. Paran drew his cloak tighter about his shoulders. 'Well,' he muttered, 'it's pretty much how I saw it.'

The ghostly form of Hedge, standing at the very edge of the massive bridge, slowly turned. 'You've been here before, Captain?'

'Visions,' he replied. 'That's all. We need to cross this—'

'Aye,' the sapper said. 'Into a long forgotten world. Does it belong to Hood? Hard to say.' The ghost's hooded eyes seemed to shift, fixing on Ganath. 'You should've changed your mind, Jaghut.'

Paran glanced over at her. Impossible to read her expression, but there was a stiffness to her stance, a certain febrility to the hands she lifted to draw up the hood of the cape she had conjured.

'Yes,' she said. 'I should have.'

'This is older than the Holds, isn't it?' Paran asked her. 'And you recognize it, don't you, Ganath?'

'Yes, in answer to both your questions. This place belongs to the Jaghut – to our own myths. This is our vision of the underworld, Master of the Deck. Verdith'anath, the Bridge of Death. You must find another path, Ganoes Paran, to find those whom you seek.'

He shook his head. 'No, this is the one, I'm afraid.'

'It cannot be.'

'Why?'

She did not reply.

Paran hesitated, then said, 'This is the place in my visions. Where I have to begin. But . . . well, those dreams never proceeded from here – I could not see what lay ahead, on this bridge. So, I had this, what you see before us, and the knowledge that only a ghost could guide me across.' He studied the mists engulfing the stone path. 'There's two ways of seeing it, I eventually concluded.'

'Of seeing what?' Ganath asked.

'Well, the paucity of those visions, and my hunches on how to proceed. I could discard all else and attempt to appease them with precision, never once straying – for fear that it would prove disastrous. Or, I could see all those uncertainties as opportunities, and so allow my imagination fullest rein.'

Hedge made a motion something like spitting, although nothing left his mouth. 'I take it you chose the latter, Captain.'

Paran nodded, then faced the Jaghut again. 'In your myths, Ganath, who or what guards this bridge?'

She shook her head. 'This place lies beneath the ground beneath Hood's feet. He may well know of this realm, but would not presume to claim dominance over it . . . or its inhabitants. This is a primal place, Master of the Deck, as are those forces that call it home. It is a conceit to believe that death has but a single manifestation. As with all things, layer settles upon layer, and in time the deepest, darkest ones become forgotten – yet they have shaped all that lies above.' She seemed to study Paran for a moment, then said, 'You carry an otataral sword.'

'Reluctantly,' he admitted. 'Most of the time I keep it buried by the back wall of Coll's estate, in Darujhistan. I am surprised you sensed it – the scabbard is made of iron and bronze and that negates its effect.'

The Jaghut shrugged. 'The barrier is imperfect. The denizens in this realm – if the myths hold truth and they always do – prefer brute force over sorcery. The sword will be just a sword.'

'Well, I wasn't planning on using it, anyway.'

'So,' Hedge said, 'we just start on our way, across this bridge, and see what comes for us? Captain, I may be a sapper, and a dead one at that, but even I don't think that's a good idea.'

'Of course not,' Paran said. 'I have planned for something else.' He drew out from his pack a small object, spoked and circular, which he then tossed on the ground. 'Shouldn't be long,' he said. 'They were told to stay close.'

A moment later sounds came through the mists behind them, the thunder of hoofs, the heavy clatter of massive wheels. A train of horses appeared, heads tossing, froth-flecked and wild-eyed, and behind them a six-wheeled carriage. Guards were clinging to various ornate projections on the carriage's flanks, some of them strapped in place by leather harnesses. Their weapons were out, and they glared fiercely into the mists on all sides.

The driver leaned back on the reins, voicing a weird cry. Hoofs stamping, the train reared back, slewing the huge carriage round to a stone-snapping, skidding halt.

The guards unhitched themselves and swarmed off, establishing a perimeter with crossbows out and cocked. On the bench the driver set the brake, looped the reins about the handle, then pulled out a flask and downed its contents in seven successive swallows. Belched, restoppered the flask, pocketed it, then clambered down the carriage side. He unlatched the side door even as Paran caught movement through its barred window.

The man pushing his way through was huge, dressed in sodden silks, his pudgy hands and round face sheathed in sweat.

Paran spoke: 'You must be Karpolan Demesand. I am Ganoes Paran. Thank you for arriving so quickly. Knowing the reputation of the Trygalle Trade Guild, of course, I am not at all surprised.'

'Nor should you be!' the huge man replied with a broad smile that revealed gold-capped, diamond-studded teeth. The smile slowly faded as his gaze found the bridge. 'Oh dear.' He gestured to two of the nearest guards, both Pardu women, both badly scarred. 'Nisstar, Artara, to the edge of the mists on that bridge, if you please. Examine the edges carefully – without a retaining wall we face a treacherous path indeed.' The small, bright eyes fixed on Paran once more. 'Master of the Deck, forgive me, I am fraught with exhaustion! Oh, how this dread land taxes poor old Karpolan Demesand! After this, we shall hasten our return to our most cherished native continent of Genabackis! Naught but tragedy haunts Seven Cities – see how I have lost weight! The stress! The misery! The bad food!' He snapped his fingers and a servant emerged from the carriage behind him, somehow managing to balance a tray crowded with goblets and a crystal decanter in one hand while navigating his egress with the other. 'Gather, my friends! Not you, damned shareholders! Keep a watch out, fools! There are *things* out there and you know what happens when *things* arrive! Nay, I spoke to my guests! Ganoes Paran, Master of the Deck, his ghostly companion and the Jaghut sorceress – join me, fretful three, in this one peaceable toast . . . before the mayhem begins!'

'Thanks for the invitation,' Hedge said, 'but since I'm a ghost—'

'Not at all,' Karpolan Demesand cut in, 'know that in close proximity to my contrivance here, you are not cursed insubstantial – not at all! So,' he passed a goblet to the sapper, 'drink, my friend! And revel once more in the delicious sensation of taste, not to mention alcohol!'

'If you say so,' Hedge said, accepting the goblet. He swallowed a mouthful, and his hazy expression somehow brightened. 'Gods below! You've done it now, merchant! I think I'll end up haunting this carriage for all time!'

'Alas, my friend, the effect wears off, eventually. Else we face im-possible burden, as you might imagine! Now you, Jaghut, please, the significance of the myriad flavours in this wine shall not be lost on you, I'm sure.' Beaming, he handed her a goblet.

She drank, then bared her tusks in what Paran took to be a smile. 'Bik'trara – ice flowers – you must have crossed a Jaghut glacier some time in the past, to have harvested such rare plants.'

'Indeed, my dear! Jaghut glaciers, and much more besides, I assure you! To explain, the Trygalle Trade Guild travels the warrens – a claim no other merchants in this world dare make. Accordingly, we are very expensive.' He gave Paran a broad wink. 'Very, as the Master of the Deck well knows. Speaking of which, I trust you have your payment with you?'

Paran nodded.

Karpolan proffered the third goblet to Paran. 'I note you have brought your horse, Master of the Deck. Do you intend to ride along-side us, then?'

'I think so. Is that a problem?'

'Hard to say – we do not yet know what we shall encounter on this fell bridge. In any case, you must ride close, unless you mean to assert your own protection – in which case, why hire us at all?'

'No, your protection I shall need, I'm sure,' Paran said. 'And yes, that is why I contracted with your guild in Darujhistan.' He sipped at the wine, and found his head swimming. 'Although,' he added, eyeing the golden liquid, 'if I drink any more of this, I might have trouble staying in the saddle.'

'You must strap yourself tightly, Ganoes Paran. In the stirrups, and to the saddle. Trust me in this, such a journey is best managed drunk – or filled with the fumes of durhang. Or both. Now, I must begin preparations – although I have never before visited this warren, I am beginning to suspect we will be sorely tested on this dread bridge.'

'If you are amenable,' Ganath said, 'I would ride with you within.'

'Delightful, and I suggest you ready yourself to access your warren, Jaghut, should the need arise.'

Paran watched as the two climbed back into the carriage, then he turned to regard Hedge.

The sapper finished the wine in his goblet and set it back down on the tray, which was being held still by the servant – an old man with red-rimmed eyes and grey hair that looked singed at its ends. 'How many of these journeys have you made?' Hedge asked him.

'More'n I can count, sir.'

'I take it Karpolan Demesand is a High Mage.'

'That he be, sir. An' for that, us shareholders bless 'im every day.'

'No doubt,' Hedge said, then turned to Paran. 'If you ain't gonna drink that, Captain, put it down. You and me need to talk.'

Paran risked another mouthful then replaced the goblet, following as, with a gesture, Hedge set off towards the foot of the bridge.

'Something on your ghostly mind, sapper?'

'Plenty, Captain, but first things first. You know, when I tossed that cusser back in Coral, I figured that was it. Hood knows, I didn't have a choice, so I'd do the same thing if I had to do it over again. Anyway –' he paused, then said, 'for a time there was, well, just darkness. The occasional flicker of something like light, something like awareness.'

He shook his head. 'It was like, well,' he met Paran's eyes, 'like I had nowhere to go. My soul, I mean. Nowhere at all. And trust me on this, that ain't a good feeling.'

'But then you did,' Paran said. 'Have somewhere to go, I mean.'

Hedge nodded, eyes once more on the mists engulfing the way ahead. 'Heard voices, at first. Then . . . old friends, coming outa the dark. Faces I knew, and sure, like I said, friends. But some who weren't. You got to understand, Captain, before your time, a lot of Bridgeburners were plain bastards. When a soldier goes through what we went through, in Raraku, at Black Dog, you come out one of two kinds of people. Either you're damned humbled, or you start believing the Empress worships what slides outa your ass, and not just the Empress, but everyone else besides. Now, I never had time for those bastards when I was alive – now I'm looking at spending an eternity with 'em.'

Paran was silent for a moment, thoughtful, then he said, 'Go on.'

'Us Bridgeburners, we got work ahead of us, and some of us don't like it. I mean, we're dead, right? And sure, it's good helping friends who are still alive, and maybe helping all of humanity if it comes to that and I'm sorry to say, it will come to that. Still, you end up with questions, questions that can't be answered.'

'Such as?'

The sapper's expression twisted. 'Damn, sounds awful, but . . . what's in it for us? We find ourselves in an army of the dead in a damned sea where there used to be desert. We're all done with our wars, the fighting's over, and now it looks like we're having to march – and it's a long march, longer than you'd think possible. But it's our road, now, isn't it?'

'And where does it lead, Hedge?'

He shook his head again. 'What's it mean to die? What's it mean to *ascend*? It's not like we're gonna gather ten thousand worshippers among the living, is it? I mean, the only thing us dead soldiers got in common is that none of us was good enough or lucky enough to survive the fight. We're a host of failures.' He barked a laugh. 'I better remember that one for the bastards. Just to get under their skins.'

Paran glanced back at the carriage. Still no activity there, although the servant had disappeared back inside. He sighed. 'Ascendants, Hedge. Not an easy role to explain – in fact, I've yet to find a worthwhile explanation for what ascendancy is – among all the scholarly tracts I've pored through in Darujhistan's libraries and archives. So, I've had to come up with my own theory.'

'Let's hear it, Captain.'

'All right, we'll start with this. Ascendants who find worshippers become gods, and that binding goes both ways. Ascendants without worshippers are, in a sense, unchained. Unaligned, in the language of the Deck of Dragons. Now, gods who once had worshippers but don't have them any more are still ascendant, but effectively emasculated, and they remain so unless the worship is somehow renewed. For the Elder Gods, that means the spilling of blood on hallowed or once-hallowed ground. For the more primitive spirits and the like, it could be as simple as the recollection or rediscovery of their name, or some other form of awakening. Mind you, none of that matters if the ascendant in question has been well and truly annihilated.

'So, to backtrack slightly, ascendants, whether gods or not, seem to possess some form of power. Maybe sorcery, maybe personality, maybe something else. And what that seems to mean is, they possess an unusual degree of efficacy—'

'Of what?'

'They're trouble if you mess with them, is what I'm saying. A mortal man punches someone and maybe breaks the victim's nose. An ascendant punches someone and they go through a wall. Now, I don't mean that literally – although that's sometimes the case. Not necessarily physical strength, but strength of will. When an ascendant acts, ripples run through . . . everything. And that's what makes them so dangerous. For example, before Fener's expulsion, Treach was a First Hero, an old name for an ascendant, and that's all he was. Spent most of his time either battling other First Heroes, or, towards the end, wandering around in his Soletaken form. If nothing untoward had happened to Treach in that form, his ascendancy would have eventually vanished, lost in the primitive bestial mind of an oversized tiger. But something untoward did happen – actually, two things. Fener's expulsion, and Treach's unusual death. And with those two events, everything changed.'

'All right,' Hedge said, 'that's all just fine. When are you getting to your theory, Captain?'

'Every mountain has a peak, Hedge, and throughout history there have been mountains and mountains – more than we could imagine, I suspect – mountains of humanity, of Jaghut, of T'lan Imass, of Eres'al, Barghast, Trell, and so on. Not just mountains, but whole ranges. I believe ascendancy is a natural phenomenon, an inevitable law of probability. Take a mass of people, anywhere, any kind, and eventually enough pressure will build and a mountain will rise, and it will have a peak. Which is why so many ascendants become gods – after the passing of generations, the great hero's name becomes sacred, representative of some long-lost golden age, and so it goes.'

'So if I understand you, Captain – and I admit, it's not easy and it's never been easy – there's too much pressure these days and because of that there's too many ascendants, and things are getting hairy.'

Paran shrugged. 'It might feel that way. It probably always does. But these things shake themselves out, eventually. Mountains collide, peaks fall, are forgotten, crumble to dust.'

'Captain, are you planning to make a new card in the Deck of Dragons?'

Paran studied the ghost for a long time, then he said, 'In many of the Houses, the role of Soldier already exists—'

'But not unaligned soldiers, Captain. Not . . . us.'

'You say you have a long road ahead, sapper. How do you know that? Who is guiding you?'

'I got no answer to that one, Captain. That's why we figured – our payment for this bargain – that you constructing a card for us would, well, be like shaking a handful of wheat flour over an invisible web.'

'Part of the bargain? You might have mentioned that at the start, Hedge.'

'No, better when it's too late.'

'For you, yes. All right, I'll think on it. I admit, you've made me curious, especially since I don't think you and your ghostly army are being directly manipulated. I suspect that what calls to you is something far more ephemeral, more primal. A force of nature, as if some long lost law was being reasserted, and you're the ones who will deliver it. Eventually.'

'An interesting thought, Captain. I always knew you had brains, now I'm finally getting a hint of what they're good for.'

'Now let me ask you a question, Hedge.'

'If you must.'

'That long road ahead of you. Your march – it's to war, isn't it? Against whom?'

'More like what—'

Commotion behind them, the shareholders rushing back to the carriage, the snap of leather and the clunk of buckles as the dozen or so men and women began strapping themselves in place. The horses, suddenly agitated, tossed their heads and stamped, nostrils flaring. The driver had the traces in his hands once more.

'You two!' he said in a growl. 'It's time.'

'Think I'll sit beside the driver,' Hedge said. 'Captain, like the High Mage said, be sure you ride close. I knew how to get us here, but I ain't got a clue what's coming.'

Nodding, Paran headed towards his horse, whilst Hedge clambered up the side of the carriage. The two Pardu women returned from their stations on the bridge and climbed up to take flanking positions on the roof, both checking their heavy crossbows and supply of broad-headed quarrels.

Paran swung himself into the saddle.

A shutter in the side door was opened and the captain could make out Karpolan's round, shiny face. 'We travel perilously fast, Ganoes Paran. If some transformation occurs on the horse you ride, consider abandoning it.'

'And if some transformation besets me?'

'Well, we shall do our best not to abandon you.'

'That's reassuring, Karpolan Demesand.'

A brief smile, then the shutter snapped shut once more.

Another weird cry from the driver and a snap of the traces. The horses lunged forward, carriage slewing straight behind them. Rolling forward. Onto the stone bridge.

Paran rode up alongside it, opposite one of the shareholders. The man threw him a wild, half-mad grin, gloved hands gripping a massive Malazan-made crossbow.

Climbing the slope, then into the mists.

That closed like soft walls round them.

A dozen heartbeats, then chaos. Ochre-skinned creatures swarmed in from both sides, as if they had been clinging beneath the bridge. Long arms, clawed at the ends, short, ape-like legs, small heads that seemed filled with fangs. They flung themselves at the carriage, seeking to drag off the shareholders.

Screams, the thud of quarrels striking bodies, hissing pain from the creatures. Paran's horse reared, forelegs kicking at a beast scrambling beneath it. Sword out, Paran slashed the blade into the back of the creature clinging and biting fierce chunks of meat from the nearest shareholder's left thigh. He saw the flesh and muscle part, revealing ribs. Then blood sluiced out. Squealing, the beast fell away.

More had reached the carriage, and Paran saw one shareholder torn from her perch, swearing as she was dragged down onto the stones, then vanishing beneath seething, smooth-skinned bodies.

The captain swung his horse round and closed on the writhing mass.

No skill involved – it was simply lean down and hack and slash, until the last bleeding body fell away.

The woman lying on the bloody stones looked as though she had been chewed by a shark, then spat out. Yet she lived. Paran sheathed his sword, dismounted and threw the dazed, bleeding woman over a shoulder.

Heavier than she'd looked. He managed to settle her down over the back of his horse, then vaulted once more into the saddle.

The carriage already vanishing into the mists, ochre bodies tumbling from it. The back wheels both rose and thumped as they rolled over flopping corpses.

And between Paran and the carriage, half a hundred or more of the creatures, now wheeling towards him, claws raised and clicking. He drew out his sword again, and drove his heels into the horse's flanks. The animal voiced an indignant grunt, then charged forward. Legs and chest battering bodies aside, Paran slashing right and left, seeing limbs lopped off, skulls opened wide. Hands closed on the shareholder and sought to pull her off. Twisting round, Paran cut at them until they fell away.

A beast landed in his lap.

Hot breath, smelling distinctly of over-ripe peaches. Hinged fangs spreading wide – the damned thing was moments from biting off Paran's face.

He head-butted it, the rim of his helm smashing nose and teeth, blood gushing into Paran's eyes, nose and mouth.

The creature reeled back.

Paran swung his weapon from above, hammering the sword's pommel into the top of the creature's skull. Punching through with twin sprays of blood from its tiny ears. Tugging his weapon free, he shoved the dead beast to the side.

His horse was still pushing forward, squealing as talons and fangs slashed its neck and chest. Paran leant over his mount's neck, flailing with his sword in its defence.

Then they were through, the horse lunging into a canter, then a gallop. All at once, the carriage's battered, swaying and pitching back reared up before them. Free of attackers. Paran dragged on his reins until the horse slowed, and came up alongside. He gestured at the nearest shareholder. 'She's still alive – take her—'

'Is she now?' the man replied, then turned his head and spat out a gleaming red stream.

Paran now saw that blood was spurting from the ragged holes in the man's left leg, and those spurts were slowing down. 'You need a healer and fast—'

'Too late,' the man replied, leaning out to drag the unconscious woman from the back of Paran's horse. More hands reached down from above and took her weight, then pulled her upwards. The dying shareholder sagged back against the carriage, then gave Paran a red-stained smile. 'The spike,' he said. 'Doubles my worth – hope the damned wife's grateful.' As he spoke he fumbled with the harness buckle, then finally pulled it loose. With a final nod at Paran, he let go, and fell.

A tumble and a roll, then . . . nothing.

Paran looked back, stared at the motionless body on the bridge. Beasts were swarming towards it. *Gods, these people have all lost their minds.*

'Stebar's earned the spike!' someone said from the carriage roof. 'Who's got one of his chips?'

Another voice said, 'Here, down the slot – how bad is Thyrss?'

'She'll make it, poor girl, ain't gonna be pretty no more.'

'Knowing her, she'd have been happier with the spike—'

'Not a chance, got no kin, Ephras. What's the point of a spike with no kin?'

'Funny man, Yorad, and I bet you don't even know it.'

'What did I say now?'

The carriage's wild careening had slowed as more and more detritus appeared on the bridge's road. Pieces of corroding armour, broken weapons, bundles of nondescript clothing.

Looking down, Paran saw a slab of wood that looked to have once been a Troughs game-board, now splintered and gnawed down one side as if some creature had tried to eat it. *So, here in this deathly underworld, there are things that still need food. Meaning, they're alive. Meaning, I suppose, they don't belong. Intruders, like us.* He wondered at all those other visitors to this realm, those who'd fallen to the horde of ochre-hued beast-men. How had they come to be here? An accident, or, like Paran, seeking to cross this damned bridge for a reason?

'Hedge!'

The ghost, perched beside the driver, leaned forward. 'Captain?'

'This realm – how did you know of it?'

'Well, you came to us, didn't you? Figured you was the one who knew about it.'

'That makes no sense. You led, I followed, remember?'

'You wanted to go where the ancient things went, so here we are.'

'But where is here?'

Shrugging, the sapper leaned back.

It was the one bad thing about following gut-feelings, Paran reflected. Where they came from and what fed them was anybody's guess.

After perhaps a third of a league, the slope still perceptibly climbing, the road's surface cleared, and although the mists remained thick, they seemed to have lightened around them, as if some hidden sun of white fire had lifted clear of the horizon. Assuming there was such a horizon. Not every warren played by the same rules, Paran knew.

The driver cursed suddenly and sawed back on the traces, one foot pushing the brake lever. Paran reined in alongside as the train lurched to a halt.

Wreckage ahead, a single, large heap surrounded by scattered pieces.

A carriage.

Everyone was silent for a moment, then Karpolan Demesand's voice emerged from a speak-tube near the roof. 'Nisstar, Artara, if you will, examine yon barricade.'

Paran dismounted, his sword still out, and joined the two Pardu women as they crept cautiously towards the destroyed carriage.

'That's Trygalle Trade Guild,' Paran said in low tones, 'isn't it?'

'Shhh.'

They reached the scene. Paran held back as the shareholders, exchanging gestures, each went to one side, crossbows held at the ready. In moments, they moved out of his line of sight.

The carriage was lying on its side, the roof facing Paran. One back wheel was missing. The copper sheets of the roof looked battered, peeled away in places, cut and gouged in others. On two of the visible iron attachment loops, strips of leather remained.

One of the Pardu women appeared on top, perching on the frame of the side door, then crouching to look straight down, inside the carriage. A moment later, she disappeared inside. The other shareholder came from around the wreck. Paran studied her. Her nose had been shattered, not long ago, he judged, as the remnant of bruises marred the area beneath her eyes with faint crescents. The eyes above those bruises were now filled with fear.

Behind them, Karpolan Demesand emerged and, the Jaghut at his side and Hedge trailing, they slowly approached.

Paran turned, studied the pale, expressionless visage of the High Mage. 'Do you recognize this particular carriage, Karpolan?'

A nod. 'Trade Mistress Darpareth Vayd. Missing, with all her shareholders, for two years. Ganoes Paran, I must think on this, for she was my superior in the sorcerous arts. I am deeply saddened by this discovery, for she was my friend. Saddened, and alarmed.'

'Do you recall the details of her last mission?'

'Ah, a prescient question. Generally,' he paused, folding his hands on his lap, 'such details remain the property of the Trygalle Trade Guild, for as you must realize, confidentiality is a quality our clients pay for, in fullest trust that we reveal nothing. In this instance, however, two things are clear that mitigate such secrecy. One: it seems, if we continue on, we shall face what Darpareth faced. Two: in this, her last mission, she failed. And presumably, we do not wish to share her fate. Accordingly, we shall here and now pool our talents, first, to determine what destroyed her mission, and secondly, to effect a reasonable defence against the enemy responsible.'

The other Pardu clambered once more into view. Seeing Karpolan she paused, then shook her head.

'No bodies,' Paran said. 'Of course, those hungry beasts we ran into may well have cleaned up afterwards—'

'I think not,' said Ganath. 'I suspect they too fear what lies ahead, and would not venture this far along the bridge. In any case, the damage on that carriage came from something far larger, stronger. If this bridge has a true guardian, then I suspect these poor travellers met it.'

Paran frowned. 'Guardian. Why would there be a guardian? That kind of stuff belongs to fairy tales. How often does someone or something try to cross this bridge? It's got to be rare, meaning there's some guardian with a lot of spare time on its hands. Why not just wander off? Unless the thing has no brain at all, such a geas would drive it mad—'

'Mad enough to tear apart whatever shows up,' Hedge said.

'More like desperate for a scratch behind the ear,' Paran retorted. 'It doesn't make sense. Creatures need to eat, need company—'

'And if the guardian has a master?' Ganath asked.

'This isn't a Hold,' Paran said. 'It has no ruler, no master.'

Karpolan grunted, then said, 'You are sure of this, Ganoes Paran?'

'I am. More or less. This realm is buried, forgotten.'

'It may be, then,' Karpolan mused, 'that someone needs to inform the guardian that such is the case – that its task is no longer relevant. In other words, we must release it from its geas.'

'Assuming such a guardian exists,' Paran said, 'rather than some chance meeting of two forces, both heading the same way.'

The Trygalle master's small eyes narrowed. 'You know more of this, Ganoes Paran?'

'What was Darpareth Vayd's mission here?'

'Ah, we are to exchange secrets, then. Very well. As I recall, the client was from Darujhistan. Specifically, the House of Orr. The contact was a woman, niece of the late Turban Orr. Lady Sedara.'

'And the mission?'

'It seems this realm is home to numerous entities, powers long forgotten, buried in antiquity. The mission involved an assay of such creatures. Since Lady Sedara was accompanying the mission, no other details were available. Presumably, she knew what she was looking for. Now, Ganoes Paran, it is your turn.'

His frown deepening, Paran walked closer to the destroyed carriage. He studied the tears and gouges in the copper sheathing on the roof. 'I'd always wondered where they went,' he said, 'and, eventually, I realized where they were *going*.' He faced Karpolan Demesand. 'I don't think there's a guardian here. I think the travellers met on this bridge, all headed the same way, and the misfortune was with Darpareth and

Sedara Orr. This carriage was destroyed by two Hounds of Shadow.'

'You are certain?'

I am. I can smell them. My . . . kin. 'We'll need to get this moved to one side, over the edge, I suppose.'

'One question,' Karpolan Demesand said. 'What happened to the bodies?'

'Hounds are in the habit of dragging and throwing their victims. Occasionally, they feed, but for the most part they take pleasure in the killing – and they would, at that time, have been both enraged and exuberant. For they had just been freed from Dragnipur, the sword of Anomander Rake.'

'Impossible,' the High Mage snapped.

'No, just exceedingly difficult.'

'How do you know all this?' Karpolan demanded.

'Because I freed them.'

'Then . . . you are responsible for this.'

Paran faced the huge man, his now hard, dangerous eyes. 'Much to my regret. You see, they should never have been there in the first place. In Dragnipur. I shouldn't have been, either. And, at the time, I didn't know where they would escape to, or even that they would escape at all. It looked, in fact, as though I'd sent them to oblivion – to the Abyss itself. As it turned out,' he added as he faced the wreckage once more, 'I needed them to do precisely this – I needed them to blaze the trail. Of course, it would have been better if they'd met no-one on the way. It's easy to forget just how nasty they are . . .

Karpolan Demesand turned to his shareholders. 'Down, all of you! We must clear the road!'

'Captain,' Hedge muttered, 'you're really starting to make me nervous.'

The wreckage groaned, then slid over the edge, vanishing into the mists. The shareholders, gathered at the side of the bridge, all waited for a sound from below, but there was none. At a command from Karpolan, they returned to their positions on the Trygalle carriage.

It seemed the High Mage was in no mood to conduct idle conversation with Paran, and he caught the Jaghut sorceress eyeing him sidelong a moment before she climbed into the carriage. He sighed. Delivering unpleasant news usually did this – he suspected if trouble arrived there wouldn't be many helping hands reaching down for him. He climbed into the saddle once more and gathered the reins.

They resumed their journey. Eventually, they began on the downslope – the bridge was at least a league long. There was no way to tell, unless one sought to climb beneath the span, whether pillars or buttressing held up this massive edifice; or if it simply hung, suspended and un-anchored, above a vast expanse of nothing.

Ahead, something took shape in the mists, and as they drew closer, they could make out a vast gateway that marked the bridge's end, the flanking uprights thick at the base and tapering as they angled inward to take – precariously, it seemed – the weight of a huge lintel stone. The entire structure was covered with moss.

Karpolan halted the carriage in front of it and, as was his custom, sent the two Pardu shareholders through that gateway. When nothing untoward happened to them and they returned to report that the way beyond was clear – as much as they could make out, anyway – the carriage was driven through.

Only to halt just beyond, as the lead horses splashed into the silty water of a lake or sea.

Paran rode his horse down to the water's edge. Frowning, he looked right, then left, eyes tracking the shoreline.

From the carriage, Hedge spoke: 'Something wrong, Captain?'

'Yes. This lake is what's wrong.'

'Why?'

'It's not supposed to be here.'

'How do you know?'

Dismounting, Paran crouched by the water. No waves – perfect calm. He cupped his hand and dipped it into the cool, silty liquid. Raised it up, sniffed. 'Smells like rot. This is flood water—'

He was interrupted by an eerie, wailing cry, coming from somewhere downshore.

'Hood's breath!' Hedge hissed. 'The lungs that punched that out are huge.'

Straightening, Paran squinted into the vague mists where it seemed the sound had come from. Then he pulled himself into the saddle once more. 'I think I was wrong about there being no guardian,' he said.

Dull thunder, rising up from the ground beneath them. Whatever it was was on its way. 'Let's get going,' Paran said. 'Up the shoreline, and fast.'

CHAPTER ELEVEN

My faith in the gods is this: they are indifferent to my suffering.

Tomlos, Destriant of Fener
?827 Burn's Sleep

HIS HANDS REACHED INTO ANOTHER WORLD. IN, THEN OUT, IN, then out again. Taking, giving – Heboric could not tell which, if either. Perhaps nothing more than the way a tongue worried a loose tooth, the unceasing probing that triggered stabs of confirmation that things still weren't quite right. He reached in, and touched something, the impulsive gesture bitter as benediction, as if he could not help but repeat, endlessly, a mocking healer's touch.

To the souls lost in the shattered pieces of jade giants, Heboric offered only lies. Oh, his touch told them of his presence, his attention, and they in turn were reminded of the true lives they once possessed, but what sort of gift could such knowledge provide? He voiced no promises, yet they believed in him nonetheless, and this was worse than torture, for both him and them.

The dead city was two days behind them now, yet its ignorant complacency haunted him still, the ghosts and their insensate, repetitive lives measured out stride by stride again and again. Too many truths were revealed in that travail, and when it came to futility Heboric needed no reminders.

Unseasonal clouds painted silver the sky, behind which the sun slid in its rut virtually unseen. Biting insects swarmed in the cooler air, danced in the muted light on the old traders' road on which Heboric and his comrades travelled, rising up in clouds before them.

The horses snorted to clear their nostrils, rippled the skin of their necks and flanks. Scillara worked through her impressive list of curses, fending off the insects with clouds of rustleaf smoke swirling about her head. Felisin Younger did much the same, but without the blue tirade. Cutter rode ahead, and so, Heboric realized, was both responsible for stirring the hordes and blessed by quickly passing through them.

It seemed that Scillara too had noticed the same thing. 'Why isn't he back here? Then the bloodflies and chigger fleas would be chasing all of us, instead of this – this nightmare!'

Heboric said nothing. Greyfrog was bounding along on the south side of the road, keeping pace. Unbroken scrubland stretched out beyond the demon, whilst to the north ran a ridge of hills – the tail end of the ancient mountain range that held the long-dead city.

Icarium's legacy. Like a god loosed and walking the land, Icarium left bloody footprints. *Such creatures should be killed. Such creatures are an abomination.* Whereas Fener – Fener had simply disappeared. Dragged as the Boar God had been into this realm, most of its power had been stripped away. To reveal itself would be to invite annihilation. There were hunters out there. *I need to find a way, a way to send Fener back.* And if Treach didn't like it, too bad. The Boar and the Wolf could share the Throne of War. In fact, it made sense. There were always two sides in a war. *Us and them, and neither can rightly be denied their faith.* Yes, there was symmetry in such a notion. 'It's true,' he said, 'I have never believed in single answers, never believed in this . . . this divisive clash of singularity. Power may have ten thousand faces, but the look in the eyes of every one of them is the same.' He glanced over to see Scillara and Felisin staring at him. 'There's no difference,' he said, 'between speaking aloud or in one's own head – either way, no-one listens.'

'Hard to listen,' Scillara said, 'when what you say makes no sense.'

'Sense takes effort.'

'Oh, I'll tell you what makes sense, old man. Children are a woman's curse. They start with weighing you down from the inside, then they weigh you down from the outside. For how long? No, not days, not months, not even years. Decades. Babies, better they were born with tails and four legs and eager to run away and crawl into some hole in the ground. Better they could fend for themselves the moment they scuttle free. Now, that would make sense.'

'If that was the way it was,' Felisin said, 'then there'd be no need for families, for villages, for towns and cities. We'd all be living in the wilderness.'

'Instead,' Scillara said, 'we live in a prison. Us women, anyway.'

'It can't be as bad as that,' Felisin insisted.

'Nothing can be done,' Heboric said. 'We each fall into our lives and that's that. Some choices we make, but most are made for us.'

'Well,' Scillara retorted, 'you would think that, wouldn't you? But look at this stupid journey here, Heboric. True, at first we were just fleeing Raraku, that damned sea rising up out of the sands. Then it was that idiot priest of Shadow, and Cutter there, and suddenly we were following you – where? The island of Otataral. Why? Who knows, but it has something to do with those ghost hands of yours, something to do with you righting a wrong. And now I'm pregnant.'

'How does that last detail fit?' Felisin demanded, clearly exasperated.

'It just does, and no, I'm not interested in explaining. Gods below, I'm choking on these damned bugs! Cutter! Get back here, you brainless oaf!'

Heboric was amused by the stunned surprise in the young man's face as he turned round at the shout.

The Daru reined in and waited.

By the time the others arrived, he was cursing and slapping at insects.

'Now you know how we feel,' Scillara snapped.

'Then we should pick up our pace,' Cutter said. 'Is everyone all right with that? It'd be good for the horses, besides. They need some stretching out.'

I think we all need that. 'Set the pace, Cutter. I'm sure Greyfrog can keep up.'

'He jumps with his mouth open,' Scillara said.

'Maybe we should all try that,' Felisin suggested.

'Hah! I'm full up enough as it is!'

No god truly deserved its acolytes. It was an unequal relationship in every sense, Heboric told himself. Mortals could sacrifice their entire adult life in the pursuit of communion with their chosen god, and what was paid in return for such devotion? Not much at best; often, nothing at all. Was the faint touch from something, someone, far greater in power – was that enough?

When I touched Fener . . .

The Boar God would have been better served, he realized, with Heboric's indifference. The thought cut into him like a saw-bladed, blunt knife – nothing smooth, nothing precise – and, as Cutter led them into a canter down the track, Heboric could only bare his teeth in a hard grimace against the spiritual pain.

From which rose a susurration of voices, all begging him, pleading with him. For what he could not give. Was this how gods felt? Inundated with countless prayers, the seeking of blessing, the gift of redemption sought by myriad lost souls. So many that the god could only reel back, pummelled and stunned, and so answer every beseeching voice with nothing but silence.

But redemption was not a gift. Redemption had to be earned.

And so on we ride . . .

Scillara drew up alongside Cutter. She studied him until he became aware of the attention and swung his head round.

'What is it? What's wrong?'

'Who said anything was wrong?'

'Well, it's been a rather long list of complaints from you of late, Scillara.'

'No, it's been a short list. I just like repeating myself.'

She watched him sigh, then he shrugged and said, 'We're maybe a week from the coast. I'm beginning to wonder if it was a good thing to take this overland route ... through completely unpopulated areas. We're always rationing our food and we're all suffering from that, excepting maybe you and Greyfrog. And we're growing increasingly paranoid, fleeing from every dust-trail and journey-house.' He shook his head. 'Nothing's after us. We're not being hunted. Nobody gives a damn what we're up to or where we're going.'

'What if you're wrong?' Scillara asked. She looped the reins over the saddle horn and began repacking her pipe. His horse misstepped, momentarily jolting her. She winced. 'Some advice for you, Cutter. If you ever get pregnant, don't ride a horse.'

'I'll try to remember that,' he said. 'Anyway, you're right. I might be wrong. But I don't think I am. It's not like we've set a torrid pace, so if hunters were after us, they'd have caught up long ago.'

She had an obvious reply to that, but let it go. 'Have you been looking around, Cutter? As we've travelled? All these weeks in this seeming wasteland?'

'Only as much as I need to, why?'

'Heboric's chosen this path, but it's not by accident. Sure, it's a wasteland now, but it wasn't always one. I've started noticing things, and not just the obvious ones like that ruined city we passed near. We've been on old roads – roads that were once bigger, level, often raised. Roads from a civilization that's all gone now. And look at that stretch of ground over there,' she pointed southward. 'See the ripples? That's furrowing, old, almost worn away, but when the light lengthens you can start to make it out. It was all once tilled. Fertile. I've been seeing this for weeks, Cutter. Heboric's track is taking us through the bones of a dead age. Why?'

'Why don't you ask him?'

'I don't want to.'

'Well, since he's right behind us, he's probably listening right now, Scillara.'

'I don't care. I was asking you.'

'Well, I don't know why.'

'I do,' she said.

'Oh. All right, then, why?'

'Heboric likes his nightmares. That's why.'

Cutter met her eyes, then the Daru twisted in his saddle and looked back at Heboric.

Who said nothing.

'Death and dying,' Scillara continued. 'The way we suck the land dry. The way we squeeze all colour from every scene, even when that scene shows us paradise. And what we do to the land, we also do to each other. We cut each other down. Even Sha'ik's camp had its tiers, its hierarchy, keeping people in their place.'

'You don't have to tell me about that,' Cutter said. 'I lived under something similar, in Darujhistan.'

'I wasn't finished. It's why Bidithal found followers for his cult. What gave it its strength was the injustice, the unfairness, and the way bastards always seemed to win. You see, Bidithal had been one of those bastards, once. Luxuriating in his power – then the Malazans arrived, and they tore it all apart, and Bidithal found himself on the run, just one more hare fleeing the wolves. For him, well, he wanted it back, all that power, and this new cult he created was for that purpose. The problem was, either he was lucky or a genius, because the idea behind his cult – not the vicious rituals he imposed, but the *idea* – it struck a nerve. It reached the dispossessed, and that was its brilliance—'

'It wasn't his idea,' Heboric said behind them.

'Then whose was it?' Cutter asked.

'It belongs to the Crippled God. The Chained One. A broken creature, betrayed, wounded, imperfect in the way of street beggars, abandoned urchins, the physically and the morally damaged. And the promise of something better, beyond death itself – the very paradise Scillara spoke of, but one we could not deface. In other words, the dream of a place immune to our natural excesses, to our own depravity, and accordingly, to exist within it is to divest oneself of all those excesses, all those depravities. You just have to die first.'

'Do you feel fear, Heboric?' Scillara asked. 'You describe a very seductive faith.'

'Yes, to both. If, however, its heart is in fact a lie, then we must make the truth a weapon, a weapon that, in the end, must reach for the Crippled God himself. To shy from that final act would be to leave unchallenged the greatest injustice of all, the most profound unfairness, and the deepest betrayal imaginable.'

'If it's a lie,' Scillara said. 'Is it? How do you know?'

'Woman, if absolution is free, then all that we do here and now is meaningless.'

'Well, maybe it is.'

'Then it would not even be a question of justifying anything – justification itself would be irrelevant. You invite anarchy – you invite chaos itself.'

She shook her head. 'No, because there's one force more powerful than all of that.'

'Oh?' Cutter asked. 'What?'

Scillara laughed. 'What I was talking about earlier.' She gestured once more at the ancient signs of tillage. 'Look around, Cutter, look around.'

Iskaral Pust plucked at the thick strands of web covering Mappo Runt's massive chest. 'Get rid of this! Before he wakes up, you damned hag. You and your damned moon – look, it's going to rain. This is a desert – what's it doing raining? It's all your fault.' He glanced up, smiling evilly. 'She suspects nothing, the miserable cow. Oh I can't wait.' Straightening, he scurried back to the long bamboo stick he'd found – *bamboo, for god's sake* – and resumed drilling the tiny fixing holes in the base.

Twisted wire eyelets, bound at intervals with wet gut right up to the finely tapered end. A carved and polished wooden spool and half a league's worth of Mogora hair, spun together and felted or something similar, strong enough to reel in anything, including a miserable cow flopping about in the shallows. True, he'd have to wait a year or two, until the little wriggling ones grew to a decent size. Maybe he'd add a few bigger ones – there were those giant catfish he'd seen in that flooded realm, the one with all the monsters padding the shorelines. Iskaral Pust shivered at the recollection, but a true lover of fishing would understand the lengths an aficionado would go to in the hunt for worthy spawn. Even the extreme necessity of killing demons and such. Granted, that particular sojourn had been a little hairy. But he'd come back with a string of beauties.

As a child he'd wanted to learn the art of angling, but the women and elders in the tribe weren't interested in that, no, just weirs and collecting pools and nets. That was harvesting, not fishing, but young Iskaral Pust, who'd once run away with a caravan and had seen the sights of Li Heng – for a day and a half, until his great-grandmother had come to retrieve him and drag him screaming like a gutted piglet back to the tribe – well, Iskaral Pust had discovered the perfect expression of creative predation, an expression which was – as everyone knew – the ideal manly endeavour.

Soon, then, and he and his mule would have the ultimate excuse to leave the hoary temple of home. *Going fishing, dear.* Ah, how he longed to say those words.

'You are an idiot,' Mogora said.

'A clever idiot, woman, and that's a lot more cleverer than you.' He paused, eyeing her, then said, 'Now all I need to do is wait until she's asleep, so I can cut off all her hair – she won't notice, it's not like we have silver mirrors hanging about, is it? I'll mix it all up, the hair from her head, from her ears, from under her arms, from—'

'You think I don't know what you're up to?' Mogora asked, then cackled as only an old woman begotten of hyenas could. 'You are not just an idiot. You're also a fool. And deluded, and immature, and obsessive, and petty, spiteful, patronizing, condescending, defensive, aggressive, ignorant, wilful, inconsistent, contradictory, and you're ugly as well.'

'So what of it?'

She gaped at him like a toothless spider. 'You have a brain like pumice stone – throw stuff at it and it just sinks in! Disappears. Vanishes. Even when I piss on it, the piss just *poofs!* Gone! Oh how I hate you, husband. With all your obnoxious, smelly habits – gods, picking your nose for breakfast – I still get sick thinking about it – a sight I am cursed never to forget—'

'Oh be quiet. There's nutritious pollen entombed in snot, as everyone well knows—'

A heavy sigh interrupted him, and both Dal Honese looked down at Mappo. Mogora scrabbled over and began stripping away the webs from the Trell's seamed face.

Iskaral Pust leaned closer. 'What's happened to his skin? It's all lined and creased – what did you do to him, woman?'

'The mark of spiders, Magi,' she replied. 'The price for healing.'

'Every strand's left a line!'

'Well, he was no beauty to begin with.'

A groan, then Mappo half-lifted a hand. It fell back and he groaned again.

'He's now got a spider's brain, too,' Iskaral predicted. 'He'll start spitting on his food – like you do, and you dare call picking my nose disgusting.'

'No self-respecting creature does what you did this morning, Iskaral Pust. You won't get no spiders picking their noses, will you? Ha, you know I'm right.'

'No I don't. I was just picturing a spider with eight legs up its nose, and that reminded me of you. You need a haircut, Mogora, and I'm just the man to do it.'

'Come near me with intentions other than amorous and I'll stick you.'

'Amorous. What a horrible thought—'

'What if I told you I was pregnant?'

'I'd kill the mule.'

She leapt at him.

Squealing, then spitting and scratching, they rolled in the dust.

The mule watched them with placid eyes.

Crushed and scattered, the tiles that had once made the mosaic of Mappo Runt's life were little more than faint glimmers, as if dispersed at the bottom of a deep well. Disparate fragments he could only observe, his awareness of their significance remote, and for a seemingly long time they had been retreating from him, as if he was slowly, inexorably floating towards some unknown surface.

Until the silver threads arrived, descending like rain, sleeting through the thick, murky substance surrounding him. And he felt their touch, and then their weight, halting his upward progress, and, after a time of motionlessness, Mappo began sinking back down. Towards those broken pieces far below.

Where pain awaited him. Not of the flesh – there was no flesh, not yet – this was a searing of the soul, the manifold wounds of betrayal, of failure, of self-recrimination, the very fists that had shattered all that he had been . . . *before the fall.*

Yet still the threads drew the pieces together, unmindful of agony, ignoring his every screamed protest.

He found himself standing amidst tall pillars of stone that had been antler-chiselled into tapering columns. Heavy wrought-iron clouds scudded over one half of the sky, a high wind spinning strands across the other half, filling a void – as if something had punched through from the heavens and the hole was slow in healing. The pillars, Mappo saw, rose on all sides, scores of them, forming some pattern indefinable from where he stood in their midst. They cast faint shadows across the battered ground, and his gaze was drawn to those shadows, blankly at first, then with growing realization. Shadows cast in impossible directions, forming a faint array, a web, reaching out on all sides.

And, Mappo now understood, he stood at its very centre.

A young woman stepped into view from behind one of the pillars. Long hair the colours of dying flames, eyes the hue of beaten gold, dressed in flowing black silks. 'This,' she said in the language of the Trell, 'is long ago. Some memories are better left alone.'

'I have not chosen it,' Mappo said. 'I do not know this place.'

'Jacuruku, Mappo Runt. Four or five years since the Fall. Yet one more abject lesson in the dangers that come with pride.' She lifted her arms, watched as the silks slid free, revealing unblemished skin, smooth hands. 'Ah, look at me. I am young again. Extraordinary, that I once believed myself fat. Does it afflict us all, I wonder, the way one's sense of self changes over time? Or, do most people contend, wilfully or otherwise, a changeless persistence in their staid lives? When you have lived as long as I have, of course, no such delusions survive.' She looked up, met his eyes. 'But you know this, Trell, don't you? The gift of the Nameless Ones shrouds you, the longevity haunts your eyes like scratched gemstones, worn far past beauty, far past even the shimmer of conceit.'

'Who are you?' Mappo asked.

'A queen about to be driven from her throne, banished from her empire. My vanity is about to suffer an ignominious defeat.'

'Are you an Elder Goddess? I believe I know you . . .' He gestured. 'This vast web, the unseen pattern amidst seeming chaos. Shall I name you?'

'Best you did not. I have since learned the art of hiding. Nor am I inclined to grant favours. Mogora, that old witch, will rue this day. Mind you, perhaps she is not to blame. There is a whisper in the shadows about you, Mappo. Tell me, what possible interest would Shadowthrone have in you? Or in Icarium, for that matter?'

He started. *Icarium. I failed him – Abyss below, what has happened?* 'Does he yet live?'

'He does, and the Nameless Ones have gifted him with a new companion.' She half-smiled. 'You have been . . . discarded. Why, I wonder? Perhaps some failing of purpose, a faltering – you have lost the purity of your vow, haven't you?'

He looked away. 'Why have they not killed him, then?'

She shrugged. 'Presumably, they foresee a use for his talents. Ah, the notion terrifies you, doesn't it? Can it be true that you have, until this moment, retained your faith in the Nameless Ones?'

'No. I am distressed by the notion of what they will release. Icarium is not a weapon—'

'Oh you fool, of course he is. They made him, and now they will use him . . . ah, now I understand Shadowthrone. Clever bastard. Of course, I am offended that he would so blithely assume my allegiance. And even more offended to realize that, in this matter, his assumption was correct.' She paused, then sighed. 'It is time to send you back.'

'Wait – you said something – the Nameless Ones, that they *made* Icarium. I thought—'

'Forged by their own hands, and then, through the succession of guardians like you, Mappo, honed again and yet again. Was he as deadly when he first crawled from the wreckage they'd made of his young life? As deadly as he is now? I would imagine not.' She studied him. 'My words wound you. You know, I dislike Shadowthrone more and more, as my every act and every word here complies with his nefarious expectation. I wound you, then realize that he needs you wounded. How is it he knows us so well?'

'Send me back.'

'Icarium's trail grows cold.'

'Now.'

'Oh, Mappo, you incite me unto weeping. I did that, on occasion, when I was young. Although, granted, most of my tears were inspired by self-pity. And so, we are transformed. Leave now, Mappo Runt. Do what you must.'

He found himself lying on the ground, bright sun overhead. Two beasts were fighting nearby – no, he saw as he turned his head, two people. Slathered in dusty spit, dark streaks of gritty sweat, tugging handfuls of hair, kicking and gouging.

'Gods below,' Mappo breathed. 'Dal Honese.'

They ceased scrapping, looked over.

'Don't mind us,' Iskaral Pust said with a blood-smeared smile, 'we're married.'

There was no outrunning it. Scaled and bear-like, the beast massed as much as the Trygalle carriage, and its long, loping run covered more ground than the terrified horses could manage, exhausted as they now were. The red and black, ridged scales covering the animal were each the size of bucklers, and mostly impervious to missile fire, as had been proved by the countless quarrels that had skidded from its hide as it drew ever closer. It possessed a single, overlarge eye, faceted like an insect's and surrounded by a projecting ridge of protective bone. Its massive jaws held double rows of sabre teeth, each one as long as a man's forearm. Old battle-scars had marred the symmetry of the beast's wide, flat head.

The distance between the pursuer and the pursued had closed to less than two hundred paces. Paran abandoned his over-the-shoulder study of the beast and urged his horse ahead. They were pounding along a rocky shoreline. Twice they had clattered over the bones of some large creature, whale-like although many of the bones had been split and crushed. Up ahead and slightly inland, the land rose into something like a hill – as much as could be found in this realm. Paran waved towards it. 'That way!' he shouted to the driver.

'What?' the man shrieked. 'Are you mad?'

'One last push! Then halt and leave the rest to me!'

The old man shook his head, yet steered the horses up onto the slope, then drove them hard as, hoofs churning in the mud, they strained to pull the huge carriage uphill.

Paran slowed his horse once more, caught a glimpse of shareholders gathered round the back of the carriage, all staring at him as he reined in, directly in the beast's path.

One hundred paces.

Paran fought to control his panicking horse, even as he drew a wooden card from his saddlebag. On which he scored a half-dozen lines with his thumbnail. A moment to glance up – fifty paces, head lowering, jaws opening wide. *Oh, a little close—*

Two more deeper scores into the wood, then he flung the card out, into the path of the charging creature.

Four soft words under his breath—

The card did not fall, but hung, motionless.

The scaled bear reached it, voicing a bellowing roar – and vanished.

Paran's horse reared, throwing him backward, his boots leaving the stirrups as he slid onto its rump, then off, landing hard to skid in the mud. He picked himself up, rubbing at his behind.

Shareholders rushed down to gather round him.

'How'd you do that?'

'Where'd it go?'

'Hey, if you coulda done that any time what was we runnin' for?'

Paran shrugged. 'Where – who knows? And as for the "how", well, I am Master of the Deck of Dragons. Might as well make the grand title meaningful.'

Gloved hands slapped his shoulders – harder than necessary, but he noted their relieved expressions, the terror draining from their eyes.

Hedge arrived. 'Nice one, Captain. I didn't think any of you'd make it. From what I saw, though, you left things nearly too late – too close. Saw your mouth moving – some kind of spell or something? Didn't know you were a mage—'

'I'm not. I was saying "I hope this works".'

Once again, everyone stared at him.

Paran walked over to his horse.

Hedge said, 'Anyway, from that hilltop you can see our destination. The High Mage thought you should know.'

From the top of the hill, five huge black statues were visible in the distance, the intervening ground broken by small lakes and marsh grasses. Paran studied the rearing edifices for a time. Bestial hounds, seated on their haunches, perfectly rendered yet enormous in scale, carved entirely of black stone.

'About what you had expected?' Hedge asked, clambering back aboard the carriage.

'Wasn't sure,' Paran replied. 'Five . . . or seven. Well, now I know.

The two shadow hounds from Dragnipur found their . . . counterparts, and so were reunited. Then, it seems, someone freed them.'

'Something paid us a visit,' Hedge said, 'the night us ghosts annihilated the Dogslayers. Into Sha'ik's camp.'

Paran turned to regard the ghost. 'You haven't mentioned this before, sapper.'

'Well, they didn't last long anyway.'

'What in Hood's name do you mean, *they didn't last long*?'

'I mean, someone killed them.'

'Killed them? Who? Did a god visit that night? One of the First Heroes? Or some other ascendant?'

Hedge was scowling. 'This is all second-hand, mind you, but from what I gathered, it was Toblakai. One of Sha'ik's bodyguards, a friend of Leoman's. Afraid I don't know much about him, just the name, or, I suppose, title, since it's not a real name—'

'A bodyguard named Toblakai killed two Deragoth Hounds?'

The ghost shrugged, then nodded. 'Aye, that's about right, Captain.'

Paran drew off his helm and ran a hand through his hair – *gods below, do I need a bath* – then returned his attention to the distant statues and the intervening lowlands. 'Those lakes look shallow – we should have no trouble getting there.'

The carriage door opened and the Jaghut sorceress Ganath emerged. She eyed the black stone monuments. 'Dessimbelackis. One soul made seven – he believed that would make him immortal. An ascendant eager to become a god—'

'The Deragoth are far older than Dessimbelackis,' Paran said.

'Convenient vessels,' she said. 'Their kind were nearly extinct. He found the few last survivors and made use of them.'

Paran grunted, then said, 'That was a mistake. The Deragoth had their own history, their own story and it was not told in isolation.'

'Yes,' Ganath agreed, 'the Eres'al, who were led unto domestication by the Hounds that adopted them. The Eres'al, who would one day give rise to the Imass, who would one day give rise to humans.'

'As simple as that?' Hedge asked.

'No, far more complicated,' the Jaghut replied, 'but for our purposes, it will suffice.'

Paran returned to his horse. 'Almost there – I don't want any more interruptions – so let's get going, shall we?'

The water they crossed stank with decay, the lake bottom thick with black mud and, it turned out, starfish-shaped leeches. The train of horses struggled hard to drag the carriage through the sludge, although it was clear to Paran that Karpolan Demesand was using sorcery to lighten the vehicle in some way. Low mudbanks ribboning the lake afforded momentary respite, although these were home to hordes of biting insects that swarmed hungrily as the shareholders came down from the carriage to pull leeches from horse-legs. One such bank brought them close to the far shore, separated only by a narrow channel of sluggish water that they crossed without difficulty.

Before them was a long, gentle slope of mud-streaked gravel. Reaching the summit slightly ahead of the carriage, Paran reined in.

Nearest him, two huge pedestals surrounded in rubble marked where statues had once been. In the eternally damp mud around them were tracks, footprints, signs of some kind of scuffle. Immediately beyond rose the first of the intact monuments, the dull black stone appallingly lifelike in its rendition of hide and muscle. At its base stood a structure of some kind.

The carriage arrived, and Paran heard the side door open. Shareholders were leaping down to establish a defensive perimeter.

Dismounting, Paran walked towards the structure, Hedge coming up alongside him.

'Someone built a damned house,' the sapper said.

'Doesn't look lived in.'

'Not now, it don't.'

Constructed entirely from driftwood, the building was roughly rectangular, the long sides parallel to the statue's pedestal. No windows were visible, nor, from this side, any entrance. Paran studied it for a time, then headed towards one end. 'I don't think this was meant as a house,' he said. 'More like a temple.'

'Might be right – that driftwood makes no joins and there ain't no chinking or anything to fill the gaps. A mason would look at this and say it was for occasional use, which makes it sound more like a temple or a corral . . .'

They reached one end and saw a half-moon doorway. Branches had been set in rows in the loamy ground before it, creating a sort of walkway. Muddy feet had trod its length, countless sets, but none very recent.

'Wore leather moccasins,' Hedge observed, crouching close to study the nearest prints. 'Seams were topside except at the back of the heel where there's a cross-stitch pattern. If this was Genabackis, I'd say Rhivi, except for one thing.'

'What?' Paran asked.

'Well, these folk have wide feet. Really wide.'

The ghost's head slowly turned towards the building's entrance. 'Captain, someone died in there.'

Paran nodded. 'I can smell it.'

They looked over as Ganath and Karpolan Demesand – the latter flanked by the two Pardu shareholders – approached. The Trygalle merchant-mage made a face as the foul stench of rotting meat reached him. He scowled over at the open doorway. 'The ritual spilling of blood,' he said, then uncharacteristically spat. 'These Deragoth have found worshippers. Master of the Deck, will this detail prove problematic?'

'Only if they show up,' Paran said. 'After that, well, they might end up having to reconsider their faith. This could prove tragic for them . . .'

'Are you reconsidering?' Karpolan asked.

'I wish I had that luxury. Ganath, will you join me in exploring the interior of the temple?'

Her brows rose fractionally, then she nodded. 'Of course. I note that darkness rules within – do you have need for light?'

'It wouldn't hurt.'

Leaving the others, they walked side by side towards the doorway. In a low voice, Ganath said, 'You suspect as I do, Ganoes Paran.'

'Yes.'

'Karpolan Demesand is no fool. He will realize before long.'

'Yes.'

'Then we should display brevity in our examination.'

'Agreed.'

Reaching the doorway, Ganath gestured and a dull, bluish light slowly rose in the chamber beyond.

They stepped within.

A single room – no inner walls. The floor was mud, packed by traffic. A shattered, up-ended tree-stump dominated the centre, the roots reaching out almost horizontally, as if the tree had grown on flat bedrock, sending its tendrils out to all sides. In the centre of this makeshift altar the core of the bole itself had been carved into a basin shape, filled now by a pool of black, dried blood. Bound spreadeagled to outstretched roots were two corpses, both women, once bloated by decay but now rotted into gelatinous consistency as if melting, bones protruding here and there. Dead maggots lay in heaps beneath each body.

'Sedora Orr,' Paran surmised, 'and Darpareth Vayd.'

'That seems a reasonable assumption,' Ganath said. 'The Trygalle sorceress must have been injured in some way, given her stated prowess.'

'Well, that carriage was a mess.'

'Indeed. Have we seen enough, Ganoes Paran?'

'Blood ritual – an *Elder* propitiation. I would think the Deragoth have been drawn near.'

'Yes, meaning you have little time once you have effected their release.'

'I hope Karpolan is up to this.' He glanced over at the Jaghut. 'In a true emergency, Ganath, can you . . . assist?'

'Perhaps. As you know, I am not pleased with what you intend here. What would please me even less, however, is being torn apart by Hounds of Darkness.'

'I share that aversion. Good. So, if I call upon your assistance, Ganath, you will know what to do?'

'Yes.'

Paran turned about. 'It may sound unreasonable,' he said, 'but my sympathy for the likely plight of these worshippers has diminished somewhat.'

'Yes, that is unreasonable. Your kind worship from fear, after all. And what you unleash here will be the five faces of that fear. And so shall these poor people suffer.'

'If they weren't interested in the attention of their gods, Ganath, they would have avoided the spilling of blood on consecrated ground.'

'Someone among them sought that attention, and the power that might come from it. A High Priest or shaman, I suspect.'

'Well then, if the Hounds don't kill that High Priest, his followers will.'

'A harsh lesson, Ganoes Paran.'

'Tell that to these two dead women.'

The Jaghut made no reply.

They walked from the temple, the light fading behind them.

Paran noted Karpolan Demesand's fixed regard, the dread plain, undeniable, and he slowly nodded. The Trygalle master turned away and, exhausted as he had been earlier, his weariness seemed to increase tenfold.

Hedge came close. 'Could've been shareholders,' he suggested.

'No,' said Ganath. 'Two women, both expensively attired. One must presume that the shareholders met their fate elsewhere.'

Paran said to Hedge, 'Now comes your final task, sapper. Summoning the Deragoth – but consider this first – they're close, and we need time to—'

'Run like Hood's bowels, aye.' Hedge lifted a satchel into view. 'Now, before you ask me where I been hiding this, don't bother. Here in this place, details like that don't matter.' He grinned. 'Some people would like to take gold with 'em when they go. Me, I'll take Moranth munitions over gold any day. After all, you don't know what you're going to meet on the other side, right? So, it's always better holding onto the option of blowing things up.'

'Wise counsel, Hedge. And those munitions will work here?'

'Absolutely, Captain. Death once called this home, remember?'

Paran studied the nearest statue. 'You intend to shatter them.'

'Aye.'

'Timed charge.'

'Aye.'

'Only, you have five to set, and the farthest one looks two, three hundred paces away.'

'Aye. That's going to be a problem – well, let's call it a challenge. Granted, Fid's better at this finesse stuff than me. But tell me something, Captain – you're sure these Deragoth ain't just going to hang round here?'

'I'm sure. They'll return to their home realm – that's what the first two did, didn't they?'

'Aye, but they had their shadows. Might be these ones will go hunting their own first.'

Paran frowned. He'd not considered that. 'Oh, I see. Into the Realm of Shadow, then.'

'If that's where the Hounds of Shadow are at the moment, aye.'

Damn. 'All right, set your charges, Hedge, but don't start the sand grains running just yet.'

'Right.'

Paran watched the sapper head off. Then he drew out his Deck of Dragons. Paused, glancing over at Ganath, then Karpolan Demesand. Both saw what he held in his hands. The Trygalle master visibly blanched, then hurried back to his carriage. After a moment – and a long, unreadable look – the Jaghut followed suit.

Paran allowed himself a small smile. *Yes, why announce yourselves to whomever I'm about to call upon?* He squatted, setting the deck face-down on the mudstained walkway of branches. Then lifted the top card and set it down to the right. *High House Shadow – who's in charge here, damned Deck, you or me?* 'Shadowthrone,' he murmured, 'I require your attention.'

The murky image of the Shadow House remained singularly lifeless on the lacquered card.

'All right,' Paran said, 'I'll revise my wording. Shadowthrone, talk to me here and now or everything you've done and everything you're planning to do will get, quite literally, torn to pieces.'

A shimmer, further obscuring the House, then something like a vague figure, seated on a black throne. A voice hissed out at him, 'This had better be important. I'm busy and besides, even the *idea* of a Master of the Deck nauseates me, so get on with it.'

'The Deragoth are about to be released, Shadowthrone.'

Obvious agitation. 'What gnat-brained idiot would do that?'

'Can't be helped, I'm afraid—'

'*You!*'

'Look, I have my reasons, and they will be found in Seven Cities.'

'Oh,' the figure settled back down, 'those reasons. Well, yes. Clever, even. But still profoundly stupid.'

'Shadowthrone,' Paran said, 'the two Hounds of Shadow that Rake killed. The two taken by Dragnipur.'

'What about them?'

'I'm not sure how much you know, but I freed them from the sword.' He waited for another bout of histrionics, but . . . nothing. 'Ah, so you know that. Good. Well, I have disovered where they went . . . here, where they conjoined with their counterparts, and were then freed – no, not me. Now, I understand that they have since been killed. For good, this time.'

Shadowthrone raised a long-fingered hand that filled most of the card. Closed it into a fist. 'Let me see,' the god's voice purred, 'if I understand you.' One finger snapped upward. 'The Nameless Idiots go and release Dejim Nebrahl. Why? Because they're idiots. Their own lies caught up with them, so they needed to get rid of a servant who was doing what they wanted him to do in the first place, only doing it too well!' Shadowthrone's voice was steadily climbing in pitch and volume. A second finger shot into view. 'Then, you, the Master Idiot of the Deck of Dragons, decide to release the Deragoth, to get rid of Dejim Nebrahl. But wait, even better!' A third finger. 'Some *other* serious nasty wandering Seven Cities just killed two Deragoth, and maybe that nasty is still close by, and would like a few more trophies to drag behind his damned horse!' His voice was now a shriek. 'And now! Now!' The hand closed back into a fist, shaking about. 'You want me to send the Hounds of Shadow to Seven Cities! Because it's finally occurred to that worm-ridden walnut you call a brain that the Deragoth won't bother with Dejim Nebrahl until they find my Hounds! And if they come looking here in my realm, there'll be no stopping them!' He halted suddenly, the fist motionless. Then various fingers sprang into view in an increasingly chaotic pattern. Shadowthrone snarled and the frenzied hand vanished. A whisper: 'Pure genius. Why didn't I think of that?' The tone began rising once more. 'Why? *Because I'm not an idiot!!*'

With that the god's presence winked out.

Paran grunted, then said, 'You never told me if you were going to send the Hounds of Shadow to Seven Cities.'

He thought then that he heard a faint scream of frustration, but perhaps it was only imagined. Paran returned the card to the deck, put it back into an inside pocket, and slowly straightened. 'Well,' he sighed, 'that wasn't nearly as bad as I thought it'd be.'

By the time Hedge returned, both Ganath and Karpolan had reappeared, their glances towards Paran decidedly uneasy.

The ghost gestured Paran closer and said quietly, 'It ain't going to work the way we wanted it, Captain. Too much distance between them – by the time I get to the closest one, the farthest one will have gone up, and if those Hounds are close, well, like I said, it ain't going to work.'

'What do you suggest?'

'You ain't going to like it. I sure don't, but it's the only way.'

'Out with it, sapper.'

'Leave me behind. Get going. Now.'

'Hedge—'

'No, listen, it makes sense. I'm already dead – I can find my own way out.'

'*Maybe* you can find your own way out, Hedge. More likely what's left of you will get torn to pieces, if not by the Deragoth, then any of a host of other local nightmares.'

'Captain, I don't need this body – it's just for show, so's you got a face to look at. Trust me, it's the only way you and the others are going to get out of this alive.'

'Let's try a compromise,' Paran said. 'We wait as long as we can.'

Hedge shrugged. 'As you like, just don't wait too long, Captain.'

'Get on your way, then, Hedge. And ... thank you.'

'Always an even trade, Captain.'

The ghost headed off. Paran turned to Karpolan Demesand. 'How confident are you,' he asked, 'about getting us out of here fast?'

'This part should be relatively simple,' the Trygalle sorceror replied. 'Once a path is found into a warren, its relationship to others becomes known. The Trygalle Trade Guild's success is dependent entirely upon its Surveyants – its maps, Ganoes Paran. With each mission, those maps become more complete.'

'Those are valuable documents,' Paran observed. 'I trust you keep them well protected.'

Karpolan Demesand smiled, and said nothing.

'Prepare the way, then,' Paran said.

Hedge was already out of sight, lost somewhere in the gloom beyond the nearest statues. Mists had settled in the depressions, but the mercurial sky overhead seemed as remote as ever. For all that, Paran noticed, the light was failing. Had their sojourn here encompassed but a single day? That seemed ... unlikely.

The bark of a munition reached him – a sharper. 'That's the signal,'

Paran said, striding over to his horse. 'The farthest statue will go first.' He swung himself into the saddle, guided his horse closer to the carriage, into which Karpolan and Ganath had already disappeared. The shutter on the window slid to one side as he arrived.

'Captain—'

A thunderous detonation interrupted him, and Paran turned to see a column of smoke and dust rising.

'Captain, it seems – much to my surprise—'

A second explosion, closer this time, and another statue seemed to simply vanish.

'As I was saying, it appears my options are far more limited than I first—'

From the distance came a deep, bestial roar.

The first Deragoth—

'Ganoes Paran! As I was saying—'

The third statue detonated, its base disappearing within an expanding, billowing wave of smoke, stone and dust. Front legs shorn through, the huge edifice pitched forward, jagged cracks sweeping through the rock, and began its descent. Then struck.

The carriage jumped, then bounced back down on its ribbed stanchions. Glass broke somewhere inside.

The reverberations of the concussion rippled through the ground.

Horses screamed and fought their bits, eyes rolling.

A second howl shook the air.

Paran squinted through the dust and smoke, seeking Hedge somewhere between the last statue to fall and the ones yet to be destroyed. But in the gathering darkness he saw no movement. All at once, the fourth statue erupted. Some vagary of sequence tilted the monument to one side, and as it toppled, it struck the fifth.

'*We must leave!*'

The shriek was Karpolan Demesand's.

'Hold on—'

'Ganoes Paran, I am no longer confident—'

'Just hold it—'

A third howl, echoed by the Deragoth that had already arrived – and those last two roars were . . . *close.*

'Shit.' He could not see Hedge – the last statue, already riven with impact fissures, suddenly pitched downward as the munitions at its base exploded.

'*Paran!*'

'All right – open the damned gate!'

The train of horses reared, then surged forward, slewing the carriage round as they began a wild descent on the slope. Swearing,

Paran kicked his horse into motion, risking a final glance back—

—to see a huge, hump-shouldered beast emerge from the clouds of dust, its eyes lambent as they fixed on Paran and the retreating carriage. The Deragoth's massive, broad head lowered, and it began a savagely fast sprint.

'Karpolan!'

The portal opened like a popped blister – watery blood or some other fluid spraying from its edges – directly in front of them. A charnel wind battered them. 'Karpolan? Where—'

The train of horses, screaming one and all, plunged into the gate, and a heartbeat later Paran followed. He heard it sear shut behind him, and then, from all sides – madness.

Rotted faces, gnawed hands reaching up, long-dead eyes imploring as decayed mouths opened – '*Take us! Take us with you!*'

'*Don't leave!*'

'*He's forgotten us – please, I beg you—*'

'*Hood cares nothing—*'

Bony fingers closed on Paran, pulled, tugged, then began clawing at him. Others had managed to grab hold of projections on the carriage and were being dragged along.

The pleas shifted into anger – '*Take us – or we will tear you to pieces!*'

'*Cut them – bite them – tear them apart!*'

Paran struggled to free his right arm, managed to close his hand on the grip of his sword, then drag it free. He began flailing the blade on each side.

The shrieks from the horses were insanity's own voice, and now shareholders were screaming as well, as they hacked down at reaching hands and arms.

Twisting about in his saddle as he chopped at the clawing limbs, Paran glimpsed a sweeping vista – a plain of writhing figures, the undead, every face turned now towards them – undead, in their tens of thousands – undead, so crowding the land that they could but stand, out to every horizon, raising now a chorus of despair—

'Ganath!' Paran roared. '*Get us out of here!*'

A sharp retort, as of cracking ice. Bitter wind swirled round them, and the ground pitched down on one side.

Snow, ice, the undead gone.

Wheeling blue sky. Mountain crags—

Horses skidding, legs splaying, their screams rising in pitch. A few animated corpses, flailing about. The carriage, looming in front of Paran, its back end sliding round.

They were on a glacier. Skidding, sliding downward at ever increasing speed.

Distinctly, Paran heard one of the Pardu shareholders: 'Oh, this is much better.'

Then, eyes blurring, horse slewing wildly beneath him, there was only time for the plunging descent – down, it turned out, an entire mountainside.

Ice, then snow, then slush, the latter rising like a bow wave before horses and sideways-descending carriage, rising and building, slowing them down. All at once, the slush gave way to mud, then stone—

Flipping the carriage, the train of horses dragged with it.

Paran's own mount fared better, managing to angle itself until it faced downhill, forelegs punching snow and slush, seeking purchase. At the point it reached the mud, and having seen what awaited it, the horse simply launched into a charge. A momentary stumble, then, as the ground levelled out, it slowed, flanks heaving – and Paran turned in the saddle, in time to see the huge carriage tumble to a shattered halt. The bodies of shareholders were sprawled about, upslope, in the mud, limp and motionless on the scree of stones, almost indistinguishable from the corpses.

The train of horses had broken loose, yet all but one were down, legs kicking amidst a tangle of traces, straps and buckles.

Heart still hammering the anvil of his chest, Paran eased his horse to a stop, turning it to face upslope, then walking the exhausted, shaky beast back towards the wreckage.

A few shareholders were picking themselves up here and there, looking dazed. One began swearing, sagging back down above a broken leg.

'Thank you,' croaked a corpse, flopping about in the mud. 'How much do I owe you?'

The carriage was on its side. The three wheels that had clipped the mud and stone had shattered, and two opposite had not survived the tumbling. Leaving but a single survivor, spinning like a mill-stone. Back storage hatches had sprung open, spilling their contents of supplies. On the roof, still strapped in place, was the crushed body of a shareholder, blood running like meltwater down the copper tiles, his arms and legs hanging limp, the exposed flesh pummelled and grey in the bright sunlight.

One of the Pardu women picked herself up from the mud and limped over to come alongside Paran as he reined in near the carriage.

'Captain,' she said, 'I think we should make camp.'

He stared down at her. 'Are you all right?'

She studied him for a moment, then turned her head and spat out a red stream. Wiped her mouth, then shrugged. 'Hood knows, we've had worse trips . . .'

*

The savage wound of the portal, now closed, still marred the dust-laden air. Hedge stepped out from where he'd been hiding near one of the pedestals. The Deragoth were gone – anything but eager to remain overlong in this deathly, unpleasant place.

So he'd stretched things a little. No matter, he'd been convincing enough, yielding the desired result.

Here I am. On my own, in Hood's own Hood-forsaken pit. You should've thought it through, Captain. There was nothing sweet in the deal for us, and only fools agree to that. Well, being fools is what killed us, and we done learned that lesson.

He looked round, trying to get his bearings. In this place, one direction was good as another. Barring the damned sea, of course. *So, it's done. Time to explore . . .*

The ghost left the wreckage of the destroyed statues behind, a lone, mostly insubstantial figure walking the denuded, muddy land. As bow-legged as he had been in life.

Dying left no details behind, after all. And most certainly, nothing like absolution awaited the fallen.

Absolution comes from the living, not the dead, and, as Hedge well knew, it has to be earned.

She was remembering things. Finally, after all this time. Her mother, camp follower, spreading her legs for the Ashok Regiment before it was sent to Genabackis. After it had left, she just went and died, as if without those soldiers she could only breathe out, never again in – and it was what you drew in that gave you life. So, just like that. Dead. Her offspring was left to fare for itself, alone, uncared for, unloved.

Mad priests and sick cults and, for the girl born of the mother, a new camp to follow. Every path of independence was but a dead-end side-track off that more deeply rutted road, the one that ran from parent to child – this much was clear to her now.

Then Heboric, Destriant of Treach, had dragged her away – before she found herself breathing ever out – but no, before him, there had been Bidithal and his numbing gifts, his whispered assurances of mortal suffering being naught more than a layered chrysalis, and upon death the glory would break loose, unfolding its iridescent wings. *Paradise.*

Oh, that had been a seductive promise, and her drowning soul had clung to the solace of its plunging weight as she sank deathward. She had once dreamed of wounding young, wide-eyed acolytes, of taking the knife in her own hands and cutting away all pleasure. *Misery loves – needs – company; there is nothing altruistic in sharing. Self-interest feeds on malice and all else falls to the wayside.*

She had seen too much in her short life to believe anyone professing otherwise. Bidithal's love of pain had fed his need to deliver numbness. The numbness within him made him capable of delivering pain. And the broken god he claimed to worship – well, the Crippled One knew he would never have to account for his lies, his false promises. He sought out lives in abeyance, and with their death he was free to discard those whose lives he had used up. This was, she realized, exquisite enslavement: a faith whose central tenet was unprovable. There would be no killing this faith. The Crippled God would find a multitude of mortal voices to proclaim his empty promises, and within the arbitrary strictures of his cult, evil and desecration could burgeon unchecked.

A faith predicated on pain and guilt could proclaim no moral purity. A faith rooted in blood and suffering—

'We are the fallen,' Heboric said suddenly.

Sneering, Scillara pushed more rustleaf into the bowl of her pipe and drew hard. 'A priest of war would say that, wouldn't he? But what of the great glory found in brutal slaughter, old man? Or have you no belief in the necessity of balance?'

'Balance? An illusion. Like trying to focus on a single mote of light and seeing naught of the stream and the world that stream reveals. All is in motion, all is in flux.'

'Like these damned flies,' Scillara muttered.

Cutter, riding directly ahead, glanced back at her. 'I was wondering about that,' he said. 'Carrion flies – are we heading towards a site of battle, do you think? Heboric?'

He shook his head, amber eyes seeming to flare in the afternoon light. 'I sense nothing of that. The land ahead is as you see it.'

They were approaching a broad basin, dotted with a few tufts of dead, yellow reeds. The ground itself was almost white, cracked like a broken mosaic. Some larger mounds were visible here and there, constructed, it seemed, of sticks and reeds. Reaching the edge, they drew to a halt.

Fish bones lay in a heaped carpet along the fringe of the dead marsh's shoreline, blown there by the winds. On one of the closer mounds they could see bird bones and the remnants of eggshells. These wetlands had died suddenly, in the season of nesting.

Flies swarmed the basin, swirling about in droning clouds.

'Gods below,' Felisin said, 'do we have to cross this?'

'Shouldn't be too bad,' Heboric said. 'It's not far across. It'd be dark long before we finish if we try to go round this. Besides,' he waved at the buzzing flies, 'we haven't even started to cross yet they've found us, and skirting the basin won't escape them. At least they're not the biting kind.'

'Let's just get this over with,' Scillara said.

Greyfrog bounded down into the basin, as if to blaze a trail with his opened mouth and snapping tongue.

Cutter nudged his horse into a trot, then, as flies swarmed him, a canter.

The others followed.

Flies alighting like madness on his skin. Heboric squinted as countless hard, frenzied bodies collided with his face. The very sunlight had dimmed amidst this chaotic cloud. Trapped in his sleeves, inside his threadbare leggings and down the back of his neck – he gritted his teeth, resolving to weather this minor irritation.

Balance. Scillara's words disturbed him for some reason – no, perhaps not her words, but the sentiment they revealed. Once an acolyte, now rejecting all forms of faith – something he himself had done, and, despite Treach's intervention, still sought to achieve. After all, the gods of war needed no servants beyond the illimitable legions they always had and always would possess.

Destriant, what lies beneath this name? Harvester of souls, possessing the power – and the right – to slay in a god's name. To slay, to heal, to deliver justice. But justice in whose eyes? I cannot take a life. Not any more. Never again. You chose wrong, Treach.

All these dead, these ghosts . . .

The world was harsh enough – it did not need him and his kind. There was no end to the fools eager to lead others into battle, to exult in mayhem and leave behind a turgid, sobbing wake of misery and suffering and grief.

He'd had enough.

Deliverance was all he desired now, his only motive for staying alive, for dragging these innocents with him to a blasted, wasted island that had been scraped clean of all life by warring gods. Oh, they did not need him.

Faith and zeal for retribution lay at the heart of the true armies, the fanatics and their malicious, cruel certainties. Breeding like fly-blow in every community. *But worthy tears come from courage, not cowardice, and those armies, they are filled with cowards.*

Horses carrying them from the basin, the flies spinning and swirling in mindless pursuit.

Onto a track emerging from the old shoreline beside the remnants of a dock and mooring poles. Deep ruts climbing a higher beach ridge, from the age when the swamp had been a lake, the ruts cut ragged by the claws of rainwater that found no refuge in roots – because the verdancy of centuries past was gone, cut away, devoured.

We leave naught but desert in our wake.

Surmounting the crest, where the road levelled out and wound drunkenly across a plain flanked by limestone hills, and in the distance, a third of a league away directly east, a small, decrepit hamlet. Outbuildings with empty corrals and paddocks. To one side of the road, near the hamlet's edge, a half-hundred or more heaped tree-trunks, the wood grey as stone where fires had not charred it – but it seemed that even in death, this wood defied efforts at its destruction.

Heboric understood that obdurate defiance. *Yes, make yourself useless to humankind. Only thus will you survive, even when what survives of you is naught but your bones. Deliver your message, dear wood, to our eternally blind eyes.*

Greyfrog had dropped back and now leapt ten paces to Cutter's right. It seemed even the demon had reached its stomach's limit of flies, for its broad mouth was shut, the second lids of its eyes, milky white, closed until the barest slits were visible. And the huge creature was very nearly black with those crawling insects.

As was Cutter's youthful back before him. As was the horse the Daru rode. And, to all sides, the ground seethed, glittering and rabid with motion.

So many flies.

So many . . .

'*Something to show you, now . . .*'

Like a savage beast suddenly awakened, Heboric straightened in his saddle—

Scillara's mount cantered a stride behind the Destriant's, a little to the old man's left, whilst in her wake rode Felisin. She cursed in growing alarm as the flies gathered round the riders like midnight, devouring all light, the buzzing cadence seeming to whisper words that crawled into her mind on ten thousand legs. She fought back a scream—

As her horse shrieked in mortal pain, dust swirling and spinning beneath it, dust rising and finding shape.

A terrible, wet, grating sound, then something long and sharp punched up between her mount's shoulder-blades, blood gouting thick and bright from the wound. The horse staggered, forelegs buckling, then collapsed, the motion flinging Scillara from the saddle—

She found herself rolling on a carpet of crushed insects, the hoofs of Heboric's horse pounding down around her as the creature shrilled in agony, pitching to the left – something snarling, a barbed flash of skin, feline and fluid, leaping from the dying horse's back—

And figures, emerging as if from nowhere amidst spinning dust, blades of flint flashing – a bestial scream – blood slapping the ground beside her in a thick sheet, instantly blackened by flies – the blades chopping, cutting, slashing into flesh – a piercing shriek, rising in a conflagration of pain and rage – something thudded against her as Scillara sought to rise on her hands and knees, and she looked over. An arm, tattooed in a tiger-stripe pattern, sliced clean midway between elbow and shoulder, the hand, a flash of fitful, dying green beneath swarming flies.

She staggered upright, stabbing pain in her belly, choking as insects crowded into her mouth with her involuntary gasp.

A figure stepped near her, long stone sword dripping, desiccated skull-face swinging in her direction, and that sword casually reached out, slid like fire into Scillara's chest, ragged edge scoring above her top rib, beneath the clavicle, then punching out her back, just above the scapula.

Scillara sagged, felt herself sliding from that weapon as she fell down onto her back.

The apparition vanished within the cloud of flies once more.

She could hear nothing but buzzing, could see nothing but a chaotic, glittering clump swelling above the wound in her chest, through which blood leaked – as if the flies had become a fist, squeezing her heart. *Squeezing . . .*

Cutter had had no time to react. The bite of sudden sand and dust, then his horse's head was simply gone, ropes of blood skirling down as if pursuing its flight. Down beneath the front hoofs, that stumbled, then gave way as the decapitated beast collapsed.

Cutter managed to roll free, gaining his feet within a maelstrom of flies.

Someone loomed up beside him and he spun, one knife free and slashing across in an effort to block a broad, hook-bladed scimitar of rippled flint. The weapons collided, and that sword swept through Cutter's knife, the strength behind the blow unstoppable—

He watched it tear into his belly, watched it rip its way free, and then his bowels tumbled into view.

Reaching down to catch them with both hands, Cutter sank as all life left his legs. He stared down at the flopping mess he held, disbelieving, then landed on one side, curling round the terrible, horrifying damage done to him.

He heard nothing. Nothing but his own breathing, and the cavorting flies, now closing in as if they had known all along that this was going to happen.

The attacker had risen from the very dust, on the right side of Greyfrog. Savage agony as a huge chalcedony longsword cut through the demon's forelimb, severing it clean in a gush of green blood. A second cut sliced through the back leg on the same side, and the demon struck the ground, kicking helplessly with its remaining limbs.

Grainy with flies and thundering pain – a momentary scene played out before the demon's eyes. Broad, bestial, clad in furs, a creature of little more than skin and bone, stepping placidly over Greyfrog's back leg, which was lying five paces distant, kicking all by itself. Stepping into the black cloud.

Dismay. I can hop no more.

Even as he had leapt from the back of his horse, two flint swords had caught him, one slashing through muscle and bone, severing an arm, the other thrusting point first into, then through, his chest. Heboric, throat filled with animal snarls, twisted in mid-air in a desperate effort to pull himself free of the impaling weapon. Yet it followed, tearing downward – snapping ribs, cleaving through lung, then liver – and finally ripping out from his side in an explosion of bone shards, meat and blood.

The Destriant's mouth filled with hot liquid, spraying as he struck the ground, rolled, then came to a stop.

Both T'lan Imass walked to where he lay sprawled in the dust, stone weapons slick with gore.

Heboric stared up at those empty, lifeless eyes, watched as the tattered, desiccated warriors stabbed down, rippled points punching into his body again and again. He watched as one flashed towards his face, then shot down into his neck—

Voices, beseeching, a distant chorus of dismay and despair – he could reach them no longer – those lost souls in their jade-swallowed torment, growing fainter, farther and farther away – *I told you, look not to me, poor creatures. Do you see, finally, how easy it was to fail you?*

I have heard the dead, but I could not serve them. Just as I have lived, yet created nothing.

He remembered clearly now, in a single dread moment that seemed unending, timeless, a thousand images – so many pointless acts, empty deeds, so many faces – all those for whom he did nothing. Baudin, Kulp, Felisin Paran, L'oric, Scillara . . . Wandering lost in this foreign land, this tired desert and the dust of gardens filling brutal, sun-scorched air – better had he died in the otataral mines of Skullcup. Then, there would have been no betrayals. Fener would hold his throne. The despair of the souls in their vast jade prisons, spinning unchecked through the Abyss, that terrible despair – it could have remained unheard, unwitnessed, and so there would have been no false promises of salvation.

Baudin would not have been so slowed down in his flight with Felisin Paran – *oh, I have done nothing worthwhile in this all-too-long life. These ghost hands, they have proved the illusion of their touch – no benediction, no salvation, not for anyone they dared touch. And these reborn eyes, with all their feline acuity, they fade now into their senseless stare, a look every hunter yearns for in the eyes of their fallen foe.*

So many warriors, great heroes – in their own eyes at least – so many had set off in pursuit of the giant tiger that was Treach – knowing nothing of the beast's true identity. Seeking to defeat him, to stand over his stilled corpse, and look down into his blank eyes, yearning to capture something, anything, of majesty and exaltation and take it within themselves.

But truths are never found when the one seeking them is lost, spiritually, morally. And nobility and glory cannot be stolen, cannot be earned in the violent rape of a life. *Gods, such pathetic, flailing, brutally stupid conceit . . . it was good, then, that Treach killed every damned one of them. Dispassionately. Ah, such a telling message in that.*

Yet he knew. The T'lan Imass who had killed him cared nothing for all of that. They had acted out of exigency. Perhaps somewhere in their ancient memories, of the time when they were mortal, they too had sought to steal what they themselves could never possess. But such pointless pursuits no longer mattered to them.

Heboric would be no trophy.

And that was well.

And in this final failure, it seemed there would be no other survivors, and in some ways that was well, too. Appropriate. So much for glory found within his final thoughts.

And is that not fitting? In this last thought, I fail even myself.

He found himself reaching . . . for something. Reaching, but nothing answered his touch. Nothing at all.

BOOK THREE

SHADOWS OF THE KING

Who can say where divides truth and the host of desires that, together, give shape to memories? There are deep folds in every legend, and the visible, outward pattern presents a false unity of form and intention. We distort with deliberate purpose; we confine vast meaning into the strictures of imagined necessity. In this lies both failing and gift, for in the surrender of truth we fashion, rightly or wrongly, universal significance. Specific gives way to general; detail gives way to grandiose form, and in the telling we are exalted beyond our mundane selves. We are, in truth, bound into greater humanity by this skein of words . . .

Introduction to *Among the Consigned*
Heboric

CHAPTER TWELVE

'He spoke of those who would fall, and in
his cold eyes stood naked the truth that it was
we of whom he spoke. Words of broken reeds
and covenants of despair, of surrender given
as gifts and slaughter in the name of salvation.
He spoke of the spilling of war, and he told us
to flee into unknown lands, so that we might
be spared the spoiling of our lives . . .'

Words of the Iron Prophet Iskar Jarak
The Anibar (the Wickerfolk)

ONE MOMENT THE SHADOWS BETWEEN THE TREES WERE EMPTY, THE
next moment that Samar Dev glanced up, her breath caught
upon seeing figures. On all sides where the sunlit clearing was
clawed back by the tangle of black spruce, ferns and ivy, stood savages
. . . 'Karsa Orlong,' she whispered, 'we have visitors . . .'

The Teblor, his hands red with gore, cut away another slice of flesh
from the dead bhederin's flank, then looked up. After a moment he
grunted, then returned to his butchering.

They were edging forward, emerging from the gloom. Small, wiry,
wearing tanned hides, strips of fur bound round their upper arms, their
skin the colour of bog water, stitched with ritual scarring on exposed
chests and shoulders. On their faces grey paint or wood ash covered
their lower jaws and above the lips, like beards. Elongated circles of icy
blue and grey surrounded their dark eyes. Carrying spears, axes at hide
belts along with an assortment of knives, they were bedecked in
ornaments of cold-hammered copper that seemed shaped to mimic the
phases of the moon; and on one man was a necklace made from the
vertebrae of some large fish, and descending from it was a gold-ringed,

black copper disc, representing, she surmised, a total eclipse. This man, evidently a leader of some kind, stepped forward. Three strides, eyes on an unmindful Karsa Orlong, out into the sunlight, where he slowly knelt.

Samar now saw that he held something in his hands. 'Karsa, pay attention. What you do now will determine whether we pass through their land peaceably or ducking spears from the shadows.'

Karsa reversed grip on the huge skinning knife he had been working with, and stabbed it deep into the bhederin carcass. Then he rose to face the kneeling savage.

'Get up,' he said.

The man flinched, lowering his head.

'Karsa, he's offering you a gift.'

'Then he should do so standing. His people are hiding here in the wilderness because he hasn't done enough of that. Tell him he needs to stand.'

They had been speaking in the trader tongue, and something in the kneeling warrior's reactions led Samar to suspect that he had understood the exchange . . . and the demand, for he slowly climbed to his feet. 'Man of the Great Trees,' he now said, his accent harsh and guttural to Samar's ears. 'Deliverer of Destruction, the Anibar offer you this gift, and ask that you give us a gift in return—'

'Then they are not gifts,' Karsa replied. 'What you seek is to barter.'

Fear flickered in the warrior's eyes. The others of his tribe – the Anibar – remained silent and motionless between the trees, yet Samar sensed a palpable dismay spreading among them. Their leader tried again: 'This is the language of barter, Deliverer, yes. Poison that we must swallow. It does not suit what we seek.'

Scowling, Karsa turned to Samar Dev. 'Too many words that lead nowhere, witch. Explain.'

'This tribe follows an ancient tradition lost among most peoples of Seven Cities,' she said. 'The tradition of gift-giving. The gift itself is a measure of a number of things, with subtle and often confusing ways of attributing value. These Anibar have of necessity learned about trading, but they do not ascribe value the same way as we do, and so they usually lose in the deal. I suspect they generally fare poorly when dealing with canny, unscrupulous merchants from the civilized lands. There is—'

'Enough,' Karsa interrupted. He gestured towards the leader – who flinched once more – and said, 'Show me this gift. But first, tell me your name.'

'I am, in the poison tongue, Boatfinder.' He held up the object in his hands. 'The courage brand,' he said, 'of a great father among the bhederin.'

Samar Dev, brows lifting, regarded Karsa. 'That would be a penis bone, Teblor.'

'I know what it is,' he answered in a growl. 'Boatfinder, what in turn do you ask of me?'

'Revenants come into the forest, besetting the Anibar clans north of here. They slaughter all in their path, without cause. They do not die, for they command the air itself and so turn aside every spear that seeks them. Thus we hear. We lose many names.'

'Names?' Samar asked.

His gaze flicked to her and he nodded. 'Kin. Eight hundred and forty-seven names woven to mine, among the north clans.' He gestured to the silent warriors behind him. 'As many names to lose among these here, each one. We know grief in the loss for ourselves, but more for our children. The names we cannot take back – they go and never come again, and so we diminish.'

Karsa said, 'You want me to kill revenants,' and he pointed at the gift, 'in exchange for that.'

'Yes.'

'How many of these revenants are there?'

'They come in great ships, grey-winged, and set out into the forest in hunts, each hunt numbering twelve. They are driven by anger, yet nothing we seek to do appeases that anger. We do not know what we do to offend them so.'

Probably offered them a damned penis bone. But Samar Dev kept that thought to herself.

'How many hunts?'

'A score thus far, yet their boats do not depart.'

Karsa's entire face had darkened. Samar Dev had never seen such raw fury in him before. She suddenly feared he would tear this small cowering man apart. Instead, he said, 'Cast off your shame, all of you. Cast it off! Slayers need no reason to slay. It is what they do. That you exist is offence enough for such creatures.' He stepped forward and snatched the bone from Boatfinder's hands. 'I will kill them all. I will sink their damned ships. This I—'

'Karsa!' Samar cut in.

He swung to her, eyes blazing.

'Before you vow anything so … extreme, you might consider something more achievable.' At his expression, she hastened on, 'You could, for example, be content with driving them from the land, back into their ships. Make the forest . . . unpalatable.'

After a long, tense moment, the Teblor sighed. 'Yes. That would suffice. Although I am tempted to swim after them.'

Boatfinder was looking at Karsa with eyes wide with wonder and awe.

For a moment, Samar thought that the Teblor was – uncharacteristically – attempting humour. But no, the huge warrior had been serious. And, to her dismay, she believed him and so found nothing funny nor absurd in his words. 'The time for that decision can wait, can't it?'

'Yes.' He scowled once more at Boatfinder. 'Describe these revenants.'

'Tall, but not as tall as you. Their flesh is the hue of death. Eyes cold as ice. They bear iron weapons, and among them are shamans whose very breath is sickness – terrible clouds of poisonous vapour – all whom it touches die in great pain.'

Samar Dev said to Karsa, 'I think their use of the term "revenant" is meant for anything or anyone not from their world. But the foes they speak of come from ships. That seems unlikely were they in truth undead. The breath of shamans sounds like sorcery.'

'Boatfinder,' Karsa said, 'when I am done here you will lead me to the revenants.'

The colour drained from the man's face. 'It is many, many days of travel, Deliverer. I think to send word that you are coming – to the clans of the north—'

'No. You will accompany us.'

'But – but why?'

Karsa stepped forward, one hand snapping out to clutch Boatfinder by the neck. He dragged the man close. 'You shall witness, and in witnessing you will become more than what you are now. You shall be prepared – for all that is coming, to you and your miserable people.' He released the man, who staggered back, gasping. 'My own people once believed they could hide,' the Teblor said, baring his teeth. 'They were wrong. This I have learned, and this you will now learn. You believe the revenants are all that shall afflict you? Fool. They are but the first.'

Samar watched the giant warrior walk back to his butchering.

Boatfinder stared after him with glistening, terror-filled eyes. Then he spun about, hissed in his own language. Six warriors rushed forward, past their leader, drawing knives as they approached Karsa.

'Teblor,' Samar warned.

Boatfinder raised his hands. 'No! No harm is sought you, Deliverer. They now help you with the cutting, that is all. The bounty is prepared for you, so that we need waste no time—'

'I want the hides cured,' Karsa said.

'Yes.'

'And runners to deliver to us those hides and smoked meat from this kill.'

'Yes.'

'Then we can leave now.'

Boatfinder's head bobbed, as if he could not trust his own voice in answer to that final demand.

Sneering, Karsa retrieved his knife and walked over to a nearby pool of brackish water, where he began washing the blood from the blade, then from his hands and forearms.

Samar Dev drew close to Boatfinder as the half-dozen warriors fell to butchering the dead bhederin. 'Boatfinder.'

He glanced at her with skittish eyes. 'You are a witch – so the Deliverer calls you.'

'I am. Where are your womenfolk? Your children?'

'Beyond this swamp, west and north,' he replied. 'The land rises, and there are lakes and rivers where we find the black grain, and among the flat-rock, berries. We are done our great hunt in the open lands, and now they return to our many camps with winter's meat. Yet,' he gestured at his warriors, 'we follow you. We witness the Deliverer slaying the bhederin. He rides a bone-horse – we do not see a bone-horse ridden. He carries a sword of birth-stone. The Iron Prophet tells our people of such warriors – the wielders of birth-stone. He says they come.'

'I have not heard of this Iron Prophet,' Samar Dev said, frowning.

Boatfinder made a gesture and faced south. 'To speak of this, it is the frozen time.' He closed his eyes, and his tone suddenly changed. 'In the Time of Great Slaying, which is the frozen time of the past, the Anibar dwelt on the plains, and would travel almost to the East River, where the great walled camps of the Ugari rose from the land, and with the Ugari the Anibar would trade meat and hides for iron tools and weapons. The Great Slaying came to the Ugari, then, and many fled to seek refuge among the Anibar. Yet the Slayers followed, the Mezla they were called by the Ugari, and a terrible battle was fought and all those who had sheltered among the Anibar fell to the Mezla.

'Fearing retribution for the aid given to the Ugari, the Anibar prepared to flee – deeper into the Odhan – but the leader of the Mezla found them first. With a hundred dark warriors, he came, yet he stayed their iron weapons. The Anibar were not his enemy, he told them, and then he gave warning – others were coming, and they would be without mercy. They would destroy the Anibar. This leader was the Iron Prophet, King Iskar Jarak, and the Anibar heeded his words, and so fled, west and north, until these lands here and the forests and lakes beyond, became their home.' He glanced over to where Karsa, his supplies gathered, sat astride his Jhag horse, and his voice changed once more. 'The Iron Prophet tells us there is a time when, in our greatest peril, wielders of the birth-stone come to defend us. Thus, when we see who travels our land, and the sword in his hands . . . this time is soon to be a frozen time.'

Samar Dev studied Boatfinder for a long moment, then she faced Karsa. 'I don't think you will be able to ride Havok,' she said. 'We are about to head into difficult terrain.'

'Until such time comes, I will ride,' the Teblor replied. 'You are free to lead your own horse. Indeed, you are free to carry it over all terrain you deem difficult.'

Irritated, she headed towards her own horse. 'Fine, for now I will ride behind you, Karsa Orlong. At the very least I will not have to worry about being whipped by branches, since you'll be knocking down all those trees in your path.'

Boatfinder waited until both were ready, then he set out, along the north edge of the boggy glade, until he reached its end and promptly turned to vanish into the forest.

Karsa halted Havok and glared at the thick, snarled undergrowth and the crowded black spruce.

Samar Dev laughed, earning her a savage look from the Teblor.

Then he slipped down from his stallion's back.

They found Boatfinder waiting for them, an apologetic look on his grey-painted face. 'Game trails, Deliverer. In these forests there are deer, bear, wolf and elk – even the bhederin do not delve deep beyond the glades. Moose and caribou are further north. These game trails, as you see, are low. Even Anibar stoop in swift passage. In the unfound time ahead of which scant can be said, we find more flat-rock and the way is easier.'

Both interminable and monotonous, the low forest was a journey tangled and snarled, rife with frustration, as if it lived with the sole purpose of denying passage. The bedrock was close to the surface, a battered purple and black rock, shot through in places with long veins of quartzite, yet its surface was bent, tilted and folded, forming high-walled basins, sinkholes and ravines filled with exfoliated slabs sheathed in slick, emerald-green moss. Tree-falls crowded these depressions, the black spruce's bark rough as sharkskin and the needle-less, web-thick branches harsh as claws and unyielding.

Spears of sunlight reached down here and there, throwing motes of intense colour into an otherwise gloomy, cavernous world.

Towards dusk, Boatfinder led them to a treacherous scree, up which he scrambled. Karsa and Samar Dev, leading their horses, found the climb perilous, every foothold less certain than the last – moss giving

426

way like rotted skin to expose sharp-edged angular rock and deep holes, any one of which could have snapped a horse-leg.

Sodden with grimy sweat, scratched and scraped, Samar Dev finally reached the summit, turning to guide her horse the last few steps. Before them wound more or less flat bedrock, grey with the skin of lichen. From modest depressions here and there rose white and jack pines, the occasional straggly oak, fringed in juniper and swaths of blueberry and wintergreen bushes. Sparrow-sized dragonflies darted through spinning clouds of smaller insects in the fading sunlight.

Boatfinder gestured northward. 'This path leads to a lake. We camp there.'

They set off.

No higher ground was visible in any direction, and as the elongated basolith twisted and turned, flanked every now and then by slightly lower platforms and snags, Samar Dev quickly realized how easy it would be to get lost in this wild land. The path bifurcated ahead and, approaching the junction, Boatfinder strode along the east edge, look-ing down for a time, then chose the ridge on the right.

Matching his route, Samar Dev glanced over the edge and saw what he had been searching for, a sinuous line of smallish boulders lying on a shelf of stone slightly below them, the pattern creating something like a snake, the head consisting of a wedge-shaped, flattened rock, while at the other end the last stone of the tail was no bigger than her thumbnail. Lichen covered the stones, bunching round each one to suggest that the trail-marker was very old. There was nothing obvious in the petroform that would make the choice of routes clear, although the snake's head was aligned in the direction they were walking.

'Boatfinder,' she called out, 'how is it that you read this serpent of boulders?'

He glanced back at her. 'A snake is away from the heart. A turtle is the heart's path.'

'All right, then why aren't they on this higher ground, so you don't have to look for them?'

'When the black grain is carried south, we are burdened – neither turtle nor snake must lose shape or pattern. We run these stone roads. Burdened.'

'Where do you take the harvest?'

'To our gather camps on the plains. Each band. We gather the harvest. Into one. And divide it, so that each band has sufficient grain. Lakes and rivers and their shores cannot be trusted. Some harvest yields true. Other harvest yields weak. As water rises and as water falls. It is not the same. The flat-rock seeks to be level, across all the world, but it cannot, and so water rises and water falls. We do not kneel

427

before inequity, else we ourselves discard fairness and knife finds knife.'

'Old rules to deal with famine,' Samar said, nodding.

'Rules in the frozen time.'

Karsa Orlong looked at Samar Dev. 'What is this frozen time, witch?'

'The past, Teblor.'

She watched his eyes narrow thoughtfully, then he grunted and said, 'And the unfound time is the future, meaning that now is the flowing time—'

'Yes!' Boatfinder cried. 'You speak life's very secret!'

Samar Dev pulled herself into the saddle – on this ridge they could ride their horses – carefully. She watched Karsa Orlong follow suit, as a strange stillness filled her being. Born, she realized, of Boatfinder's words. *'Life's very secret.' This flowing time not yet frozen and only now found out of the unfound.* 'Boatfinder, the Iron Prophet came to you long ago – in the frozen time – yet he spoke to you of the unfound time.'

'Yes, you understand, witch. Iskar Jarak speaks but one language, yet within it is each and all. He is the Iron Prophet. The King.'

'Your king, Boatfinder?'

'No. We are his shadows.'

'Because you exist only in the flowing time.'

The man turned and made a reverent bow that stirred something within Samar Dev. 'Your wisdom honours us, witch,' he said.

'Where,' she asked, 'is Iskar Jarak's kingdom?'

Sudden tears in the man's eyes. 'An answer we yearn to find. It is lost—'

'In the unfound time.'

'Yes.'

'Iskar Jarak was a Mezla.'

'Yes.'

Samar Dev opened her mouth for one more question, then realized that it wasn't necessary. She knew its answer. Instead, she said, 'Boatfinder, tell me, from the frozen time into the flowing time, is there a bridge?'

His smile was wistful, filled with longing. 'There is.'

'But you cannot cross it.'

'No.'

'Because it's burning.'

'Yes, witch, the bridge burns.'

King Iskar Jarak, and the unfound kingdom . . .

Descending like massive, raw steps, the shelves of rock marched down into crashing foam and spume. A fierce wind raked the northern sea's dark waves to the very horizon, where storm-clouds commanded the sky, the colour of blackened armour. At their backs and stretching the western length of coastline, rose a bent-back forest of pines, firs and cedars, their branches torn and made ragged by the battering winds.

Shivering, Taralack Veed drew the furs closer, then turned his back on the raging seas. 'We now travel westward,' he said, speaking loud enough to be heard above the gale. 'Follow this coast until it curls north. Then we strike inland, directly west, into the land of stone and lakes. Difficult, for there is little game to be found there, although we will be able to fish. Worse, there are bloodthirsty savages, too cowardly to attack by day. Always at night. We must be ready for them. We must deliver slaughter.'

Icarium said nothing, his unhuman gaze still fixed on that closing storm.

Scowling, Taralack moved back into the rock-walled camp they had made, crouching in the blessed lee and holding his red, cold-chafed hands over the driftwood fire. Few glimmers of the Jhag's legendary, near mythical equanimity remained. Dark and dour, now. A refashioning of Icarium, by Taralack Veed's own hands, although he but followed the precise instructions given him by the Nameless Ones. *The blade has grown dull. You shall be the whetstone, Gral.*

But whetstones were insensate, indifferent to the blade and to the hand that held it. For a warrior fuelled by passion, such immunity was difficult to achieve, much less maintain. He could feel the weight now, ever building, and knew he would, one day, grow to envy the merciful death that had come to Mappo Runt.

They had made good time thus far. Icarium was tireless. Once given direction. And Taralack, for all his prowess and endurance, was exhausted. *I am no Trell, and this is not simple wandering. Not any more, and never again for Icarium.*

Nor, it seemed, for Taralack Veed.

He looked up when he heard scrabbling, and watched Icarium descend.

'These savages you spoke of,' the Jhag said without preamble, 'why should they seek to challenge us?'

'Their forsaken forest is filled with sacred sites, Icarium.'

'We need only avoid trespass, then.'

'Such sites are not easily recognized. Perhaps a line of boulders on the bedrock, mostly buried in lichen and moss. Or the remnant of an antler in the crotch of a tree, so overgrown as to be virtually invisible. Or a vein of quartzite glittering with flecks of gold. Or the green tool-stone – the quarries are no more than a pale gouge in vertical rock, the green stone shorn from it by fire and cold water. Mayhap little more than a bear trail on bedrock, trodden by the miserable beasts for countless generations. All sacred. There is no fathoming the minds of such savages.'

'It seems you know much of them, yet you have told me you have never before travelled their lands.'

'I have heard of them, in great detail, Icarium.'

A sudden edge in the Jhag's eyes. 'Who was it that informed you so, Taralack Veed of the Gral?'

'I have wandered far, my friend. I have mined a thousand tales—'

'You were being prepared. For me.'

A faint smile suited the moment and Taralack found it easily enough. 'Much of that wandering was in your company, Icarium. Would that I could gift you my memories of the time we have shared.'

'Would that you could,' Icarium agreed, staring down at the fire now.

'Of course,' Taralack added, 'there would be much darkness, many grim and unpleasant deeds, within that gift. The absence within you, Icarium, is both blessing and curse – you do understand that, don't you?'

'There is no blessing in that absence,' the Jhag said, shaking his head. 'All that I have done cannot demand its rightful price. Cannot mark my soul. And so I remain unchanging, forever naïve—'

'Innocent—'

'No, not innocent. There is nothing exculpatory in ignorance, Taralack Veed.'

You call me by name, now, not as 'friend'. Has mistrust begun to poison you? 'And so it is my task, each time, to return to you all that you have lost. It is arduous and wears upon me, alas. My weakness lies in my desire to spare you the most heinous of memories. There is too much pity in my heart, and in seeking to spare you I now find that I but wound.' He spat on his hands and slicked back his hair, then stretched his hands out once more close to the flames. 'Very well, my friend. Once, long ago, you were driven by the need to free your father, who had been taken by a House of the Azath. Faced with terrible failure, a deeper, deadlier force was born – your rage. You shattered a wounded warren, and you destroyed an Azath, releasing into the world a host of demonic entities, all of whom sought only domination and tyranny. Some of those you killed, but many escaped your wrath, and live on to this day, scattered about the world like so many evil seeds.

'The most bitter irony is this: your father sought no release. He had elected, of his own will, to become a Guardian of an Azath House, and it may be he remains so to this day.

'In consequence of the devastation you wrought, Icarium, a cult, devoted since time began to the Azath, deemed it necessary to create guardians of their own. Chosen warriors who would accompany you, no matter where you went – for your rage and the destruction of the warren had torn from you all memory of your past – and so now you were doomed, for all time, it seemed, to seek out the truth of all that you have done. And to stumble into rage again and yet again, wreaking annihilation.

'This cult, that of the Nameless Ones, thus contrived to bind to you a companion. Such as I. Yes, my friend, there have been others, long before I was born, and each has been imbued with sorcery, slowing the rigours of ageing, proof against all manner of disease and poison for as long as the companion's service held true. Our task is to guide you in your fury, to assert a moral focus, and above all, to be your friend, and this latter task has proved, again and again, the simplest and indeed, most seductive of them all, for it is easy to find within ourselves a deep and abiding love for you. For your earnestness, your loyalty, and for the unsullied honour within you.

'I will grant you, Icarium, your sense of justice is a harsh one. Yet, ultimately, profound in its nobility. And now, awaiting you, there is an enemy. An enemy only you, my friend, are powerful enough to oppose. And so we now journey, and all who seek to oppose us, for whatever reason, must be swept aside. For the greater good.' He allowed himself to smile again, only this time he filled it with a hint of vast yet courageously contained anguish. 'You must now wonder, are the Nameless Ones worthy of such responsibility? Can their moral integrity and sense of honour match yours? The answer lies in necessity, and above that, in the example you set. You guide the Nameless Ones, my friend, with your every deed. If they fail in their calling, it will be because you have failed in yours.'

Pleased that he had recalled with perfection the words given him, Taralack Veed studied the great warrior who stood before him, firelit, his face hidden behind his hands. Like a child for whom blindness imposed obliteration.

Icarium was weeping, he realized.

Good. Even he. Even he will feed upon his own anguish and make of it an addictive nectar, a sweet opiate of self-recrimination and pain.

And so all doubt, all distrust, shall vanish.

For from those things, no sweet bliss can be wrung.

From overhead, a spatter of cold rain, and the deep rumble of thunder. The storm would soon be upon them. 'I am rested enough,' Taralack said, rising. 'A long march awaits us—'

'There is no need,' Icarium said behind his hands.

'What do you mean?'

'The sea. It is filled with ships.'

431

The lone rider came down from the hills shortly after the ambush. Barathol Mekhar, his huge, scarred and pitted forearms spattered with blood, rose from his long, silent study of the dead demon. He was wearing his armour and helm, and he now drew out his axe.

Months had passed since the T'lan Imass had appeared – he'd thought them long gone, gone even before old Kulat wandered off in his newfound madness. He had not realized – none of them had – that the terrible, undead creatures had never left.

The party of travellers had been slaughtered, the ambush so swiftly executed that Barathol had not even known of its occurrence – until it was far too late. Jhelim and Filiad had suddenly burst into the smithy, screaming of murder just beyond the hamlet. He had collected his weapon and run with them to the western road, only to find the enemy already departed, their task done, and upon the old road, dying horses and motionless bodies sprawled about as if they had dropped from the sky.

Sending Filiad to find the old woman Nulliss – who possessed modest skill as a healer – Barathol had returned to his smithy, ignoring Jhelim who trailed behind him like a lost pup. He had donned his armour, taking his time. The T'lan Imass, he suspected, would have been thorough. They would have had leisure to ensure that they had made no mistakes. Nulliss would find that nothing could be done for the poor victims.

Upon returning to the west road, however, he was astonished to see the ancient Semk woman shouting orders at Filiad from where she knelt at the side of one figure. It seemed to Barathol's eyes as he hurried forward, that she had thrust her hands into the man's body, her scrawny arms making motions as if she was kneading bread dough. Even as she did this, her gaze was on a woman lying nearby, who had begun moaning, legs kicking furrows in the dirt. From her, blood had spilled out everywhere.

Nulliss saw him and called him over.

Barathol saw that the man she knelt beside had been eviscerated. Nulliss was pushing the intestines back inside. 'For Hood's sake, woman,' the blacksmith said in a growl, 'leave him be. He's done. You've filled his cavity with dirt—'

'Boiling water is on the way,' she snapped. 'I mean to wash it out.' She nodded towards the thrashing woman. 'That one is stabbed in the shoulder, and now she's in labour.'

'Labour? Gods below. Listen, Nulliss, boiling water won't do, unless you mean to cook his liver for supper tonight—'

'Go back to your damned anvil, you brainless ape! It was a clean cut – I've seen what boars can do with their tusks and that was a whole lot worse.'

'Might've started clean—'

'I said I mean to clean it! But we can't carry him back with his guts trailing behind us, can we?'

Nonplussed, Barathol looked round. He wanted to kill something. A simple enough desire, but he already knew it would be thwarted and this soured his mood. He walked over to the third body. An old man, tattooed and handless – the T'lan Imass had chopped him to pieces. *So. He was their target. The others were simply in the way. Which is why they cared nothing whether they lived or died.* Whereas this poor bastard couldn't be more dead than he was.

After a moment, Barathol made his way towards the last victim in sight. From the hamlet, more people were on the way, two of them carrying blankets and rags. Storuk, Fenar, Hayrith, Stuk, all looking somehow small, diminished and pale with fear. Nulliss began screaming orders once more.

Before him was sprawled a demon of some kind. Both limbs on one side had been sliced away. Not much blood, he noted, but something strange appeared to have afflicted the creature upon its death. It looked ... deflated, as if the flesh beneath the skin had begun to dissolve, melt away into nothing. Its odd eyes had already dried and cracked.

'Blacksmith! Help me lift this one!'

Barathol walked back.

'On the blanket. Storuk, you and your brother on that end, one corner each. Fenar, you're with me on the other end—'

Hayrith, almost as old as Nulliss herself, held in her arms the rags. 'What about me?' she asked.

'Go sit by the woman. Stuff a cloth into the wound – we'll sear it later, unless the birth gives her trouble—'

'With the blood loss,' Hayrith said, eyes narrowing, 'she probably won't survive it.'

'Maybe. For now, just sit with her. Hold her damned hand and talk, and—'

'Yes, yes, witch, you ain't the only one round here who knows about all that.'

'Good. So get going.'

'You've just been waiting for this, haven't ya?'

'Be quiet, you udderless cow.'

'Queen Nulliss, High Priestess of Bitchiness!'

'Blacksmith,' Nulliss growled, 'hit her with that axe, will you?'

Hissing, Hayrith scurried off.

'Help me,' Nulliss said to him, 'we've got to lift him now.'

It seemed a pointless task, but he did as she asked, and was surprised to hear her pronounce that the young man still lived after they'd set him on the blanket.

As Nulliss and the others carried him away, Barathol strode back to the dismembered corpse of the old, tattooed man. And crouched at his side. It would be an unpleasant task, but it was possible that Barathol could learn something of him from his possessions. He rolled the body over, then halted, staring down into those lifeless eyes. A cat's eyes. He looked with renewed interest at the pattern of tattoos, then slowly sat back.

And only then noticed all the dead flies. Covering the ground on all sides, more flies than he had ever seen before. Barathol straightened, walked back to the dead demon.

Staring down thoughtfully, until distant motion and the sound of horse hoofs snared his attention. Behind him, villagers had returned to retrieve the pregnant woman.

And now he watched as the rider rode directly towards him.

On a lathered horse the colour of sun-bleached bone. Wearing dust-sheathed armour lacquered white. The man's face pale beneath the rim of his helm, drawn with grief. Reining in, he slipped down from the saddle and, ignoring Barathol, staggered over to the demon, where he fell to his knees.

'Who – who did this?' he asked.

'T'lan Imass. Five of them. A broken lot, even as T'lan Imass go. An ambush.' Barathol pointed towards the body of the tattooed man. 'They were after him, I think. A priest, from a cult devoted to the First Hero Treach.'

'Treach is now a god.'

To that, Barathol simply grunted. He looked back at the ramshackle hovels of the hamlet he had come to think of as home. 'There were two others. Both still alive, although one will not last much longer. The other is pregnant and even now gives birth—'

The man stared up at him. 'Two? No, there should have been three. A girl . . .'

Barathol frowned. 'I'd thought the priest was their target – they were thorough with him – but now I see that they struck him down because he posed the greatest threat. They must have come for the girl – for she is not here.'

The man rose. He matched Barathol in height, if not breadth. 'Perhaps she fled . . . into the hills.'

'It's possible. Although,' he added, pointing at a dead horse nearby, 'I'd wondered at that extra mount, saddled like the others. Cut down on the trail.'

'Ah, yes. I see.'

'Who are you?' Barathol asked. 'And what was this missing girl to you?'

Shock was still writ deep into the lines of his face, and he blinked at the questions, then nodded. 'I am named L'oric. The child was . . . was for the Queen of Dreams. I was coming to collect her – and my familiar.' He looked down once more at the demon, and anguish tugged at his features yet again.

'Fortune has abandoned you, then,' Barathol said. A thought occurred to him. 'L'oric, have you any skill in healing?'

'What?'

'You are one of Sha'ik's High Mages, after all—'

L'oric looked away, as if stung. 'Sha'ik is dead. The rebellion is crushed.'

Barathol shrugged.

'Yes,' L'oric said, 'I can call upon Denul, if required.'

'Is the life of that girl all that concerns you?' He gestured down at the demon. 'You can do nothing for your familiar – what of their companions? The young man will die – if he has not already done so. Will you stand here, dwelling only on what you have lost?'

A flash of anger. 'I advise caution,' L'oric said in a low voice. 'You were once a soldier – that much is obvious – yet here you have hidden yourself away like a coward, whilst the rest of Seven Cities rose up, dreaming of freedom. I will not be chastised by one such as you.'

Barathol's dark eyes studied L'oric a moment longer, then he turned away and began walking towards the buildings. 'Someone will come,' he said over his shoulder, 'to dress the dead for burial.'

Nulliss had chosen the old hostelry to deposit her charges. A cot was dragged out from one of the rooms for the woman, whilst the eviscerated youth was laid out on the communal dining table. A cookpot filled with water steamed above the hearth, and Filiad was using a prod to retrieve soaked strips of cloth and carry them over to where the Semk woman worked.

She had drawn out the intestines once more but seemed to be ignoring that pulsing mass for the moment, both of her hands deep in the cavity of his gut. 'Flies!' she hissed as Barathol entered. 'This damned hole is filled with dead flies!'

'You will not save him,' Barathol said, walking to the bar counter and setting down his axe on the battered, dusty surface, the weapon making a heavy clunking sound on the wood. He began removing his gauntlets, glancing over at Hayrith. 'Has she given birth?' he asked.

'Aye. A girl.' Hayrith was washing her hands in a basin, but she nodded towards a small bundled shape lying on the woman's chest.

'Already suckling. I'd thought things were gone bad, blacksmith. Bad. The baby came out blue. Only the cord weren't knotted and weren't round its neck.'

'So why was it blue?'

'Was? Still is. Napan father, I'd say.'

'And the mother's fate?'

'She'll live. I didn't need Nulliss. I know how to clean and sear a wound. Why, I followed the Falah'd of Hissar's Holy Army, seen plenty a battlefields in my day. Cleaned plenty a wounds, too.' She flung water from her hands, then dried them on her grubby tunic. 'She'll have fever, of course, but if she survives that, she'll be fine.'

'Hayrith!' called out Nulliss. 'Get over here and rinse out these rags! Then toss 'em back in the boiling water – gods below, I'm losing him – his heart, it's fading.'

The door swung open. Heads turned to stare at L'oric, who slowly stepped inside.

'Who in Hood's name is that?' Hayrith asked.

Barathol unstrapped his helm as he said, 'High Mage L'oric, a refugee from the Apocalypse.'

Hayrith cackled. 'Well, ain't he found the right place! Welcome, L'oric! Grab yourself a tankard a dust an' a plate of ashes an' join us! Fenar, stop staring and go find Chaur an' Urdan – there's horse meat out there needs butchering – we don't want none a them wolves in the hills comin' down an' gettin' it first.'

Barathol watched as L'oric strode over to where Nulliss knelt above the youth on the table. She was pushing in rags then pulling them out again – there was far too much blood – no wonder the heart was fading.

'Move aside,' L'oric said to her. 'I do not command High Denul, but at the very least I can clean and seal the wound, and expunge the risk of infection.'

'He's lost too much blood,' Nulliss hissed.

'Perhaps,' L'oric conceded, 'but let us at least give his heart a chance to recover.'

Nulliss backed away. 'As you like,' she snapped. 'I can do no more for him.'

Barathol went behind the bar, crouched opposite a panel of wood, which he rapped hard. It fell away, revealing three dusty jugs. Retrieving one, he straightened, setting it down on the counter. Finding a tankard, he wiped it clean, then, tugging free the stopper, poured the tankard full.

Eyes were on him – all barring those of L'oric himself, who stood beside the youth, hands settling on the chest. Hayrith asked, in a tone of reverence. 'Where did that come from, blacksmith?'

'Old Kulat's stash,' Barathol replied. 'Don't expect he'll be coming back for it.'

'What's that I smell?'

'Falari rum.'

'Blessed gods above and below!'

Suddenly the locals present in the room were one and all crowding the bar. Snarling, Nulliss pushed Filiad back. 'Not you – too young—'

'Too young? Woman, I've seen twenty-six years!'

'You heard me! Twenty-six years? Ain't enough to 'preciate Falari rum, you scrawny whelp.'

Barathol sighed. 'Don't be greedy, Nulliss. Besides, there's two more jugs on the shelf below.' Collecting his tankard, he moved away from them, Filiad and Jhelim both fighting as they scrabbled round the counter.

A livid scar was all that remained of the sword slash across the youth's belly, apart from splashes of drying blood. L'oric still stood beside him, hands motionless on the chest. After a moment, he opened his eyes, stepping back. 'It's a strong heart . . . we'll see. Where's the other one?'

'Over there. Shoulder wound. It's been seared, but I can guarantee sepsis will set in and probably end up killing her, unless you do something.'

L'oric nodded. 'She is named Scillara. The young man I do not know.' He frowned. 'Heboric Ghost Hands—' he rubbed at his face – 'I would not have thought . . .' He glanced over at Barathol. 'When Treach chose him to be his Destriant, well, there was so much . . . power. T'lan Imass? Five broken T'lan Imass?'

Barathol shrugged. 'I myself did not see the ambush. The Imass first showed up months past, then it seemed that they'd left. After all, there was nothing here that they wanted. Not even me.'

'Servants of the Crippled God,' L'oric said. 'The Unbound, of High House of Chains.' He headed towards the woman he'd named Scillara. 'The gods are indeed at war . . .'

Barathol stared after him. He downed half the rum in the tankard, then joined the High Mage once more. 'The gods, you say.'

'Fever already whispers within her – this will not do.' He closed his eyes and began muttering something under his breath. After a moment, he stepped back, met Barathol's eyes. 'This is what comes. The blood of mortals spilled. Innocent lives . . . destroyed. Even here, in this rotted hole of a village, you cannot hide from the torment – it will find you, it will find us all.'

Barathol finished the rum. 'Will you now hunt for the girl?'

'And singlehanded wrest her from the Unbound? No. Even if I knew where to look, it is impossible. The Queen of Dreams' gambit has failed – likely she already knows that.' He drew a deep, ragged breath, and Barathol only now noticed how exhausted the man was. 'No,' he said again, with a vague, then wretched look. 'I have lost my familiar . . . yet . . .' he shook his head, 'yet, there is no pain – with the severing there should be pain – I do not understand . . .'

'High Mage,' Barathol said, 'there are spare rooms here. Rest. I'll get Hayrith to find you some food, and Filiad can stable your horse. Wait here until I return.'

The blacksmith spoke to Hayrith, then left the hostelry, returning once more to the west road. He saw Chaur, Fenar and Urdan stripping saddles and tack from the dead horses. 'Chaur!' he called, 'step away from that one – no, this way, there, stand still, damn you. There. Don't move.' The girl's horse. Reaching it, he moved round carefully, seeking tracks.

Chaur fidgeted – a big man, he had the mind of a child, although the sight of blood had never bothered him.

Ignoring him, Barathol continued reading the scrapes, furrows and dislodged stones, and finally found a small footprint, planted but once, and strangely twisting on the ball of the foot. To either side, larger prints, skeletal yet bound here and there by leather strips or fragments of hide.

So. She had leapt clear of the fatally wounded horse, yet, even as her lead foot contacted the ground, the T'lan Imass snared her, lifting her – no doubt she struggled, but against such inhuman, implacable strength, she had been helpless.

And then, the T'lan Imass had vanished. Fallen to dust. Somehow taking her with them. He did not think that was possible. Yet . . . no tracks moved away from the area.

Frustrated, Barathol started back to the hostelry.

At a whining sound behind him he turned. 'It's all right, Chaur. You can go back to what you were doing.'

A bright smile answered him.

As he entered, Barathol sensed that something had changed. The ocals were backed to the wall behind the bar. L'oric stood in the centre of the chamber, facing the blacksmith who halted just inside the doorway. The High Mage had drawn his sword, a blade of gleaming white.

L'oric, his eyes hard on Barathol, spoke: 'I have but just heard your name.'

The blacksmith shrugged.

A sneer twisted L'oric's pale face. 'I imagine all that rum loosened their tongues, or they just plain forgot your commands to keep such details secret.'

'I've made no commands,' Barathol replied. 'These people here know nothing of the outside world, and care even less. Speaking of rum . . .' He slid his gaze to the crowd behind the bar. 'Nulliss, any of it left?'

Mute, she nodded.

'On the counter then, if you please,' Barathol said. 'Beside my axe will do.'

'I would be foolish to let you near that weapon,' L'oric said, raising the sword in his hand.

'That depends,' replied Barathol, 'whether you intend fighting me, doesn't it?'

'I can think of a hundred names of those who, in my place right now, would not hesitate.'

Barathol's brows rose. 'A hundred names, you say. And how many of those names still belong to the living?'

L'oric's mouth thinned into a straight line.

'Do you believe,' Barathol went on, 'that I simply walked from Aren all those years ago? I was not the only survivor, High Mage. They came after me. It was damned near one long running battle from Aren Way to Karashimesh. Before I left the last one bleeding out his life in a ditch. You may know my name, and you may believe you know my crime . . . but you were not there. Those that were are all dead. Now, are you really interested in picking up this gauntlet?'

'They say you opened the gates—'

Barathol snorted, walked over towards the jug of rum Nulliss had set on the bar. 'Ridiculous. T'lan Imass don't need gates.' The Semk witch found an empty tankard and thunked it on the counter. 'Oh, I opened them all right – on my way out, on the fastest horse I could find. By that time, the slaughter had already begun.'

'Yet you did not stay, did you? You did not fight, Barathol Mekhar! Hood take you, man, *they rebelled in your name!*'

'Too bad they didn't think to ask me first,' he replied in a growl, filling the tankard. 'Now, put that damned sword away, High Mage.'

L'oric hesitated, then he sagged where he stood and slowly resheathed the weapon. 'You are right. I am too tired for this. Too old.' He frowned, then straightened again. 'You thought those T'lan Imass were here for you, didn't you?'

Barathol studied the man over the battered rim of the tankard, and said nothing.

L'oric ran a hand through his hair, looked round as if he'd forgotten where he was.

'Hood's bones, Nulliss,' Barathol said in a sigh, 'find the poor bastard a chair, will you?'

The grey haze and its blinding motes of silver slowly faded, and all at once Felisin Younger could feel her own body again, sharp stones digging into her knees, the smell of dust, sweat and fear in the air. Visions of chaos and slaughter filled her mind. She felt numbed, and it was all she could do to see, to register the shape of things about her. Before her, sunlight flung sharp-edged shafts against a rock wall rent through with stress fractures. Heaps of windblown sand banked what used to be broad, shallow stone steps that seemed to lead up into the wall itself. Closer, the large knuckles, pale beneath thin, weathered skin, of the hand that clutched her right arm above the elbow, the exposed ligaments of the wrist stretching, making faint sounds like twisting leather. A grip she could not break – she had exhausted herself trying. Close and fetid, the reek of ancient decay, and visible – every now and then – a blood-smeared, rippled blade, broad near its hooked point, narrowing down at the leather-wrapped handle. Black, glassy stone, thinned into translucence along the edge.

Others stood around her, more of the dread T'lan Imass. Spattered with blood, some with missing or mangled limbs, and one with half its face smashed away – but this was old damage, she realized. Their most recent battle, no more than a skirmish, had cost them nothing.

The wind moaned mournfully along the rock wall. Felisin pushed herself to her feet, scraped the embedded stones from her knees. *They're dead. They're all dead.* She told herself this again and again, as if the words were newly discovered – not yet meaningful to her, not yet a language she could understand. *My friends are all dead.* What was the point of saying them? Yet they returned again and again, as if desperate to elicit a response – any response.

A new sound reached her. Scrabbling, seeming to come from the cliff-face in front of them. Blinking the stinging sweat from her eyes, she saw that one of the fissures looked to have been widened, the sides chipped away as if by a pick, and it was from this that a bent figure emerged. An old man, wearing little more than rags, covered in dust. Suppurating sores wept runny liquid on his forearms and the backs of his hands.

Seeing her, he fell to his knees. 'You have come! They promised – but why would they lie?' Amidst the words issuing from his mouth were odd clicking sounds. 'I will take you, now – you'll see. Everything is fine. You are safe, child, for you have been chosen.'

'What are you talking about?' Felisin demanded, once again trying to tug her arm free – and this time she succeeded, as the deathly hand unclenched. She staggered.

440

The old man leapt to his feet and steadied her. 'You are exhausted – no surprise. So many rules were broken to bring you here—'

She stepped away from him and set a hand against the sun-warmed stone wall. 'Where is here?'

'An ancient city, Chosen One. Once buried, but soon to live once more. I am but the first who has been called upon to serve you. Others will come – are coming even now, for they too have heard the Whispers. You see, it is the weak who hear them, and oh there are very many, very many of the weak.' More clicking sounds – there were pebbles in his mouth.

Turning, Felisin faced away from the cliff wall, studied the stretch of broken, wasted land beyond. Signs of an old road, signs of tillage . . . 'We walked this – weeks ago!' She glared at the old man. 'You've taken me back!'

He smiled, revealing worn, chipped teeth. 'This city belongs to you, now, Chosen One—'

'Stop calling me that!'

'Please – you have been delivered and blood has been spilled in that deliverance – it falls to you to give such sacrifice meaning—'

'Sacrifice? That was murder! They *killed my friends*!'

'I will help you grieve, for that is my weakness, you see? I grieve always – for myself – because of drink, and the thirst always within me. Weakness. Kneel before it, child. Make of it a thing to worship. There is no point in fighting – the world's sadness is far more powerful than you can ever hope to be, and that is what you must come to understand.'

'I want to leave.'

'Impossible. The Unbound have delivered you. Where could you go even if you might? We are leagues upon leagues from anywhere.' He sucked on the pebbles, swallowed spit, then continued, 'You would have no food. No water. Please, Chosen One, a temple awaits you within this buried city – I have worked so long, so hard to ready it for you. There is food, and water. And soon there will be more servants, all desperate to answer your every desire – once you accept what you have become.' He paused to smile again, and she saw the stones – black, polished, at least three, each the size of a knuckle bone. 'Soon, you shall realize what you have become – leader of the greatest cult of Seven Cities, and it will sweep beyond, across every sea and every ocean – it shall claim the world—'

'You are mad,' Felisin said.

'The Whispers do not lie.' He reached for her and she recoiled at that glistening, pustuled hand. 'Ah, there was plague, you see. Poliel, the goddess herself, she bowed before the Chained One – as must we all, even you – and only then shall you come into your rightful power. Plague – it claimed many, it left entire cities filled with blackened bodies – but others survived, because of the Whispers, and so were marked – by sores and twisted limbs, by blindness. For some it was their tongues. Rotting and falling off, thus leaving them mute. Among others, their ears bled and all sound has left their world. Do you understand? They had weakness, and the Chained One – he has shown how weakness becomes strength. I can sense them, for I am the first. Your seneschal. I sense them. *They are coming.*'

She continued staring down at his sickly hand, and after a moment he returned it to his side.

Clicking. 'Please, follow me. Let me show you all that I have done.'

Felisin lifted her hands to her face. She did not understand. None of this made any sense. 'What,' she asked, 'is your name?'

'Kulat.'

'And what,' she said in a whisper, 'is mine?'

He bowed. 'They did not understand – none of them did. The Apocalyptic – it is not just war, not just rebellion. It is *devastation*. Not just of the land – that is but what follows – do you see? The Apocalypse, it is of the spirit. Crushed, broken, slave to its own weaknesses. Only from such a tormented soul can ruin be delivered to the land and to all who dwell upon it. We must die inside to kill all that lies outside. Only then, once death takes us all, only then shall we find salvation.' He bowed lower. 'You are Sha'ik Reborn, Chosen as the Hand of the Apocalypse.'

'Change of plans,' muttered Iskaral Pust as he scurried about, seemingly at random, moving into and out of the campfire's light. 'Look!' he hissed. 'She's gone, the mangy cow! A few monstrous shadows in the night and poof! Nothing but spiders, hiding in every crack and cranny. Bah! Snivelling coward. I was thinking, Trell, that we should run. Yes, run. You go that way and I'll go this way – I mean, I'll be right behind you, of course, why would I abandon you now? Even with those things on the way . . .' He paused, pulled at his hair, then resumed his frantic motion. 'But why should I worry? Have I not been loyal? Effective? Brilliant as ever? So, why are they *here*?'

Mappo drew out a mace from his sack. 'I see nothing,' he said, 'and all I can hear is you, High Priest. Who has come?'

'Did I say anything was coming?'

'Yes, you did.'

'Can I help it if you've lost your mind? But why, that's what I want to know, yes, why? It's not like we need the company. Besides, you'd think this was the last place they'd want to be, if what I'm smelling is what I'm smelling, and I wouldn't be smelling what I'm smelling if something wasn't there that didn't smell, right?' He paused, cocked his head. 'What's that smell? Never mind, where was I? Yes, trying to conceive of the inconceivable, the inconceivable being the notion that Shadowthrone is actually quite sane. Preposterous, I know. Anyway, if that, then this, this being he knows what he's doing. He has reasons – actual reasons.'

'Iskaral Pust,' Mappo said, rising from where he had been sitting near the fire. 'Are we in danger?'

'Has Hood seen better days? Of course we're in danger, you oafish fool – oh, I must keep such opinions to myself. How about this? Danger? Haha, my friend, of course not. Haha. Ha. Oh, here they are . . .'

Massive shapes emerged from the darkness. Red ember eyes to one side, lurid green eyes on another, then other sets, one gold, another coppery. Silent, hulking and deadly.

The Hounds of Shadow.

Somewhere far away in the desert, a wolf or coyote howled as if it had caught a scent from the Abyss itself. Closer to hand, even the crickets had fallen silent.

The hairs on the back of the Trell's neck stiffened. He too could now smell the fell beasts. Acrid, pungent. With that reek came painful memories. 'What do they want with us, High Priest?'

'Be quiet – I need to think.'

'No need to tax yourself,' said a new voice from the darkness, and Mappo turned to see a man step into the fire's light. Grey-cloaked, tallish, and otherwise nondescript. 'They are but . . . passing through.'

Iskaral's face brightened with false pleasure even as he flinched. 'Ah, Cotillion – can you not see? I have achieved all Shadowthrone asked of me—'

'With that clash you had with Dejim Nebrahl,' Cotillion said, 'you have in fact exceeded expectations – I admit, I had no idea you possessed such prowess, Iskaral Pust. Shadowthrone chose well his Magi.'

'Yes, he's full of surprises, isn't he?' The High Priest crab-walked over to crouch by the fire, then he cocked his head and said, 'Now, what does *he* want? To put me at ease? He never puts me at ease. To lead the Hounds onto some poor fool's trail? Not for long, I hope. For that fool's sake. No, none of these things. He's here to confound me, but I am a High Priest of Shadow, after all, and so cannot be confounded. Why? Because I serve the most confounding god there is, that's why. Thus, need I worry? Of course, but he'll never know, will he? No, I need

443

only smile up at this killer god and say: Would you like some cactus tea, Cotillion?'

'Thank you,' Cotillion replied, 'I would.'

Mappo set his mace down and resumed his seat as Iskaral poured out the tea. The Trell struggled against the desperation growing within him. Somewhere to the north, Icarium sat before flames likely little different from these ones, haunted as ever by what he could not remember. Yet, he was not alone. *No, another has taken my place.* That should have been cause for relief, but all Mappo could feel was fear. *I cannot trust the Nameless Ones – I learned that a long time ago.* No, Icarium was now being led by someone who cared nothing for the Jhag—

'It pleases me, Mappo Runt,' said Cotillion, 'that you are well.'

'The Hounds of Shadow once fought at our sides,' Mappo said, 'on the Path of Hands.'

Cotillion nodded, sipping at the tea. 'Yes, you and Icarium came very close, then.'

'Close? What do you mean?'

The Patron God of Assassins was a long time in replying. Around them, just beyond the camp, the huge Hounds seemed to have settled for the night. 'It is less a curse,' he finally said, 'than a . . . residue. The death of an Azath House releases all manner of forces, energies – not just those belonging to the denizens in their earthen tombs. There is, burned into Icarium's soul, something like an infection, or, perhaps, a parasite. Its nature is chaos, and the effect is one of discontinuity. It defies progression, of thought, of spirit, of life itself. Mappo, that infection must be expunged, if you would save Icarium.'

The Trell could barely draw breath. In all the centuries at the Jhag's side, among all the words given him by the Nameless Ones, by scholars and sages across half the world, he had never before heard anything like this. 'Are – are you certain?'

A slow nod. 'As much as is possible. Shadowthrone, and I,' he looked up, then half-shrugged, 'our path to ascendancy was through the Houses of the Azath. There were years – a good number of them – in which neither I nor the man who at that time was known as Emperor Kellanved were to be found anywhere within the Malazan Empire. For we had begun another quest, a bolder gambit.' Firelight gleamed in his dark eyes. 'We set out to map the Azath. Every House, across this entire realm. We set out to master its power—'

'But that is not possible,' Mappo said. 'You failed – you cannot have done otherwise, else you both would now be far more than gods—'

'True enough, as far as it goes.' He studied the tea in the clay cup nestled in the bowl of his hands. 'Certain realizations came to us, however, earned from hard experience and somewhat unrelenting diligence.

The first was this: our quest would demand far more than a single, mortal lifespan. The other realizations – well, perhaps I had best leave those for another night, another time. In any case, in comprehending that such a gambit would enforce upon us demands we could not withstand – not as Emperor and Master Assassin, that is – it proved necessary to make use of what we had learned to date.'

'To make yourselves gods.'

'Yes. And in so doing, we learned that the Azath are far more than Houses created as prisons for entities of power. They are also portals. And one more thing for certain – they are the repositories for the Lost Elementals.'

Mappo frowned. 'I have not heard that phrase before. Lost Elementals?'

'Scholars tend to acknowledge but four, generally: water, fire, earth and air; yet others exist. And it is from these others that comes the immense power of the Azath Houses. Mappo, one is at an immediate disadvantage in discerning a pattern, when one has but four points of reference, with an unknown number of others as yet invisible, unaccounted for in the scheme.'

'Cotillion, these Lost Elementals – are they perhaps related to the aspects of sorcery? The warrens and the Deck of Dragons? Or, more likely, the ancient Holds?'

'Life, death, dark, light, shadow . . . possibly, but even that seems a truncated selection. What of, for example, time? Past, present, future? What of desire, and deed? Sound, silence? Or are the latter two but minor aspects of air? Does time belong to light? Or is it but a point somewhere between light and dark, yet distinct from shadow? What of faith and denial? Can you now understand, Mappo, the potential complexity of relationships?'

'Assuming they exist at all, beyond the notion of concepts.'

'Granted. Yet, maybe concepts are all that's needed, if the purpose of the elements is to give shape and meaning to all that surrounds us on the outside, and all that guides us from within.'

Mappo leaned back. 'And you sought to master such power?' He stared at Cotillion, wondering if even a god was capable of such conceit, such ambition. *And they began on their quest long before they became gods . . .* 'I confess that I hope you and Shadowthrone fail – for what you describe should not fall into anyone's hands, not a god's, not a mortal's. No, leave it to the Azath—'

'And so we would have, had we not come to understand that the Azath's control was failing. The Nameless Ones, I suspect, have come to the same realization, and so are now driven to desperation. Alas, we believe their latest decision will, if anything, further pitch the Azath towards chaos and dissolution.' He nodded towards Iskaral Pust, who crouched nearby, muttering to himself. 'Hence, our decision to . . . intervene. Too late, unfortunately, to prevent Dejim Nebrahl's release, and the ambush itself. But . . . you are alive, Trell.'

And so, Cotillion, in seeking to master the Azath, you now find yourself serving it. Desire versus deed . . . 'To lift Icarium's curse,' Mappo shook his head. 'This is an extraordinary offer, Cotillion. I find myself torn between doubt and hope.' A wry smile – 'Ah, I begin to understand how mere concepts are enough.'

'Icarium has earned an end to his torment,' the god said, 'has he not?'

'What must I do?'

'For now, do as you are doing – pursue your friend. Stay on that trail, Mappo. A convergence is coming, of a magnitude so vast it will very likely defy comprehension. The gods seem oblivious to the cliff-edge they are all approaching, and yes, every now and then I include myself among them.'

'You hardly seem oblivious.'

'Well then, perhaps *helpless* is a more accurate term. In any event, you and I will speak again. For now, do not doubt that you are needed. By us, by every mortal and above all, by Icarium.' He set the cup down and rose.

The faint sound of the Hounds lifting themselves into readiness reached Mappo's ears.

'I know I need not say this,' the god said, 'but I shall anyway. Do not give up hope, Mappo. For this, despair is your greatest foe. When the time comes for you to stand between Icarium and all that the Nameless Ones seek ... well, I believe that you will not fail.'

Mappo watched Cotillion walk into the darkness, the Hounds slipping into the god's wake. After a moment, the Trell glanced over at Iskaral Pust. And found sharp, glittering eyes fixed on him. 'High Priest,' Mappo asked, 'do you intend to join me in my journey?'

'Alas, I cannot.' The Dal Honese glanced away. 'The Trell's insane! He will fail! Of course he will fail! As good as dead, ah, I cannot bear now to even so much as look at him. All Mogora's healing – for naught! A waste!' Iskaral Pust rubbed at his face, then leapt to his feet. 'Too many equally important tasks await me, Mappo Runt. No, you and I shall walk momentarily divergent paths, yet side by side to glory nonetheless! As Cotillion has said, you shall not fail. Nor will I. Victory shall be ours!' He raised a bony fist and shook it at the night sky. Then hugged himself. 'Gods below, we're doomed.'

A cackle from Mogora, who had reappeared, her arms loaded down with firewood implausibly cut and split as if by a master woodsman.

She dumped it beside the fire. 'Stir them embers, dear pathetic husband of mine.'

'You cannot command me, hag! Stir them yourself! I have more vital tasks before me right now!'

'Such as?'

'Well, to begin with, I need to pee.'

CHAPTER THIRTEEN

And all these people gathered
to honour the one who had died,
was it a man, a woman, a warrior,
a king, a fool, and where were
the statues, the likenesses painted
on plaster and stone?

yet so they stood or sat, the wine
spilling at their feet, dripping red
from their hands, with wasps
in their dying season spinning
about in sweet thirst and drunken
voices cried out, stung awake

voices blended in confused
profusion, the question asked
again then again – why? But this
is where a truth finds its own wonder,
for the question was not why did
this one die, or such to justify

for in their heart of milling lives
there were none for whom
this gathering was naught
but an echo, of former selves.
They asked, again and yet again,
why are we here?

The one who died had no name
but every name, no face but every

face of those who had gathered,
and so it was we who learned
among wasps swept past living
yet nerve-firing one last piercing

that we were the dead
and all in an unseen mind—
stood or sat a man, or a woman,
a warrior, queen or fool, who
in drunken leisure gave a moment's
thought to all passed by in life.

Fountain Gathering
Fisher Kel Tath

EVEN WITH FOUR NEW WHEELS, THE TRYGALLE CARRIAGE WAS A battered, decrepit wreck. Two of the horses had died in the fall. Three shareholders had been crushed and a fourth had broken his neck. Karpolan Demesand sat on a folding camp-stool, his head swathed in a bloodstained bandage, sipping herbal tea in successive winces.

They had left Ganath's warren of Omtose Phellack, and now the familiar desert, scrubland and barren hills of Seven Cities surrounded them, the sun reaching towards noon behind a ceiling of cloud. The smell of rain tinged the unusually humid air. Insects spun and swirled overhead.

'This comes,' said Ganath, 'with the rebirth of the inland sea.'

Paran glanced over at her, then resumed cinching tight the girth strap on his horse – the beast had taken to holding its breath, chest swollen in an effort to keep the strap loose, likely hoping Paran would slide off from its back at some perfectly inopportune moment. Horses were reluctant companions in so many human escapades, disasters and foibles – Paran could not resent the animal's well-earned belligerence. 'Ganath,' he said, 'do you know precisely where we are?'

'This valley leads west to Raraku Sea, beyond the inside range; and east, through a little-used pass, down to the city of G'danisban.' She hesitated, then added, 'It has been a long time since I have been this far east . . . this close to the cities of your kind.'

'G'danisban. Well, I have need of supplies.'

She faced him. 'You have completed your task, Master of the Deck. The Deragoth unleashed, the D'ivers known as Dejim Nebrahl, the hunter, now the hunted. Do you now return to Darujhistan?'

He grimaced. 'Not yet, alas.'

'There are still more forces you intend to release upon the world?'

A certain edge to her voice brought him round. 'Not if I can help it, Ganath. Where do you now go?'

'West.'

'Ah, yes, to repair the damage to that ritual of yours. I'm curious, what did it imprison?'

'A sky keep of the K'Chain Che'Malle. And . . . other things.'

A sky keep? Gods below. 'Where did it come from?'

'A warren, I suppose,' she said.

She knew more than that, he suspected, but he did not press the issue. Paran made some final adjustments to the saddle, and said, 'Thank you, Ganath, for accompanying us – we would not have survived without you.'

'Perhaps, some day, I can ask of you a favour in return.'

'Agreed.' He drew out a long, cloth-wrapped object that had been strapped to the saddle, carried it over to Karpolan Demesand.

'High Mage,' he said.

The corpulent man looked up. 'Ah, our payment.'

'For services rendered,' Paran said. 'Do you wish me to unwrap it?'

'Hood no, Ganoes Paran – sorcery's the only thing keeping my skull intact right now. Even scabbarded and bundled as that sword now is, I can feel its entropy.'

'Yes, it is an unpleasant weapon,' Paran said.

'In any case, there is yet one more thing to be done.' A gesture from Karpolan and one of the Pardu shareholders came over, collected the otataral sword that had once belonged to Adjunct Lorn. She carried it a short distance, then set it on the ground and backed away. Another shareholder arrived, cradling in his arms a large two-handed mace. He positioned himself over the wrapped weapon, then swung the mace down. And again, and again. Each blow further shattered the otataral blade. Breathing hard, the man stepped back and looked over at Karpolan Demesand.

Who then faced Paran once more. 'Collect your shard, Master of the Deck.'

'Thank you,' the Malazan replied, walking over. Crouching, he pulled aside the cut and battered hide. He stared down at the rust-hued slivers of metal for a half-dozen heartbeats, then selected a shard about the length of his index finger and not much wider. Carefully folding it inside a fragment of hide, he then tucked it into his belt pouch. He straightened and strode back to the High Mage.

Karpolan Demesand sighed, slowly rose from the stool. 'It is time for us to go home.'

'Have a safe journey, High Mage,' Paran said with a bow.

The man attempted a smile, and the effort stole all colour from his face. Turning away and helped by one of the shareholders, he made his way to the carriage.

'Pray,' Ganath said in a low voice at Paran's side, 'he encounters no untoward opposition in the warrens.'

Paran went to his horse. Then, arms resting on the saddle, he looked over at Ganath. 'In this war,' he said, 'Elder forces will be involved. Are involved. The T'lan Imass may well believe that they have annihilated the Jaghut, but clearly that isn't the case. Here you stand, and there are others, aren't there?'

She shrugged.

From behind them came the tearing sound of a warren opening. Snapping traces, then the rumble of wheels.

'Ganath—'

'Jaghut are not interested in war.'

Paran studied her for a moment longer, then he nodded. Setting a foot in the stirrup, he pulled himself onto the horse and collected the reins. 'Like you,' he said to the Jaghut, 'I'm feeling a long way from home. Fare well in your travels, Ganath.'

'And you, Master of the Deck.'

Eastward Paran rode along the length of the valley. The river that had once carved through this land was long gone, although the winding path of its course was evident, with stands of brush and withered trees clustered here and there where the last sinkholes had been, old oxbows and flats of alluvial sands fanning out on the bends. After a league the valley opened out into a shallow basin, raw cliffs to the north and long, sloping slides of rubble to the south. Directly ahead, a trail was visible climbing between deep-cut runoff channels.

Reaching its base, Paran dismounted and led his mount up the track. The afternoon heat was building, all the more cloying for its unnatural humidity. Far to the west, likely above the Raraku Sea, massive clouds were building. By the time he reached the summit, those clouds had devoured the sun and the breeze at his back was sweet with the promise of rain.

Paran found himself with a view far to the east, down onto rolling hills dotted with domestic goats, the path leading towards a more substantial road that cut north–south along the edge of the plain, the southern route swinging eastward towards a distant smudge of smoke and dust that was, he suspected, G'danisban.

Astride his horse once more, he set off at a canter.

Before long, Paran came to the first herder's hovel, burned and gutted, where goats were now gathering, driven by habit alone as the day's light faded. He discerned no obvious sign of graves, and was not inclined to search among the ruins. Plague, the silent, invisible breath of the Grey Goddess. It was likely, he realized, the city ahead was in the grip of that terror.

The first spatters of rain struck his back, and a moment later, in a rushing sizzle, the downpour was upon him. The rocky trail was suddenly treacherous, forcing Paran to slow his horse to a cautious trot. Visibility reduced to a dozen paces on all sides, the world beyond washed away behind a silver wall. Warm water trickling beneath his clothes, Paran drew up the tattered hood of the military rain-cape covering his shoulders, then hunched over as the rain hammered down.

The worn trail became a stream, muddy water sluicing along amidst rocks and cobbles. Horse slowing to a walk, they pressed on. Between two low hills, the track sprawling out into a shallow lake, and Paran found himself flanked by two soldiers.

One gauntleted hand reached out to take the reins. 'You're headed the wrong way, stranger,' growled the man, in Malazan.

The other held cradled in his arms a crossbow, but it wasn't loaded, and he now spoke from the shadows beneath his hood: 'Is that cape loot? Dragged it from the body of a Malazan soldier, did you?'

'No,' Paran replied. 'Issued to me, just like your capes were to you, soldier.' Ahead, he could just make out in a brief easing of the downpour, was an encampment. Two, perhaps three legions, the tents cloaking a series of hills beneath a low ceiling of smoke from cookfires dying in the rain. Beyond it, with the road winding down a slope, rose the walls of G'danisban. He returned his attention to the soldiers. 'Who commands this army?'

The one with the crossbow said, 'How 'bout you answer the questions to start? You a deserter?'

Well, technically speaking, yes. Then again, I'm supposed to be dead. 'I wish to speak with your commanding officer.'

'You pretty much ain't got no choice, now. Off the horse, stranger. We're arresting you on suspicion of desertion.'

Paran slipped down from the horse. 'Fine. Now will you tell me whose army this is?'

'The lad's push for you. You're now a prisoner of Onearm's Host.'

For all the outward signs, it slowly dawned on Paran that this was not a siege. Companies held the roads leading into G'danisban, and the camp itself formed a half-ring cordon along the north and west sides, no pickets closer than four hundred paces from the unmanned walls.

One of the soldiers led Paran's horse towards the temporary stables, whilst the other one guided Paran down avenues between sodden tents.

Figures moved about, cloaked and hooded, but none wearing full battle regalia.

They entered an officer's tent.

'Captain,' the soldier said, flipping back his hood, 'we come upon this man trying to ride into G'danisban from the Raraku road. You see, sir, he's wearing a Malazan military rain-cape. We think he's a deserter, probably from the Adjunct's Fourteenth.'

The woman he addressed was lying on her back on a cot that ran parallel to the back wall. She was fair-skinned, her petite features surrounded by a mass of long red hair. Head tilting to take in her soldier and Paran, she was silent for a moment, then resumed her stare at the dipping ceiling above her. 'Take him to the stockade – we have a stockade, don't we? Oh, and get his details – what regiment, which legion and all that. So it can be recorded somewhere before he's executed. Now get out, the both of you, you're dripping water everywhere.'

'Just a moment, Captain,' Paran said. 'I wish to speak with the High Fist.'

'Not possible, and I don't recall giving you permission to speak. Pull out his fingernails for that, Futhgar, will you? When it's time, of course.'

Years ago, Paran would have done . . . nothing. Succumbed to the rules, the written ones and the unwritten ones. He would have simply bided his time. But he was soaked through, in need of a hot bath. He was tired. And, he had gone through something like this once before, long ago and on a distant continent. Back then, of course, it had been a sergeant – same red hair, but a moustache under the nose – even so, the similarity was there, like the poke of an assassin's knife.

The soldier, Futhgar, was standing on his left, half a pace back. Paran gave nothing away, simply stepping to his right then driving his left elbow into the soldier's face. Breaking his nose. The man dropped to the ground like a sack of melons.

The captain sat up, legs swinging round, and was on her feet in time for Paran to take a forward step and punch her hard, his knuckles cracking against her jaw. Eyes rolling up, she collapsed back down onto the cot, breaking its wooden legs.

Massaging his hand, Paran looked round. Futhgar was out cold, as was the captain. The steady downpour outside had ensured that no sounds from the brief fight had been heard beyond the tent.

He walked over to the captain's travel chest. Unlocked. He tilted back the lid and began rummaging through the clothes lying atop armour. Before long, he had enough lengths of material suitable to gag and bind the two soldiers. Dragging Futhgar from near the entrance, he removed the man's eating knife, his sticker and a broad-bladed Kethra gutting knife, then his sword belt. He prepared a wad of cloth for a gag, then bent close to determine if enough air was getting through the man's broken nose. *Not even close.* Leaving that for the moment, he tightly bound the wrists and ankles, using a harness strap to link the two behind Futhgar's back. He then tied a strip round Futhgar's head, hard against the gaping mouth, leaving room to breathe but no room for the tongue to push outward. He'd be able to make groaning sounds, but not much more than that.

He bound the captain in an identical manner, then added the wad of cloth fixed in place with another strip of material torn from one of the captain's shirts. And, finally, he tied both of them to either side of the cot, and the cot to the tent's centre pole, to hinder their squirming from the tent – which he hoped would give him sufficient time. Satisfied, he took one last look round, then, drawing up his hood, he stepped back outside.

He found the main avenue and made his way towards the large command tent at the centre of the encampment. Soldiers walked past, paying him no heed. This was Onearm's Host, but he'd yet to see a single familiar face, which wasn't too surprising – he had commanded the Bridgeburners, and the Bridgeburners were gone. Most of these soldiers would be newcomers to the army, drawn in from garrisons at Pale, Genabaris and Nathilog. They would have arrived since the Pannion War. Nonetheless, he expected to find at least someone from the original force that had marched all the way to Coral, someone who had been part of that devastating battle.

Four soldiers stood guard outside Dujek's command tent. A fifth figure was nearby, holding the reins of a mud-spattered horse.

Paran walked closer, eyes on the horseman. Familiar – he'd found what he had been looking for. An outrider – but one who'd belonged to Caladan Brood's army, he believed – *though I might be wrong in that. Now, what was his name?*

The man's pale brown eyes fixed on him as Paran approached. From within the shadow of the hood, there came the flicker of recognition, then confusion. The outrider straightened, then saluted.

Paran shook his head, but it was too late for that. The four guards all stood to attention as well. Paran answered the salute with a vague, sloppy gesture, then stepped close to the outrider. 'Soldier,' he murmured, 'do you know me? Make your answer quiet, if you please.'

A nod. 'Captain Ganoes Paran. I don't forget faces or names, sir, but we'd heard you were—'

'Aye, and that's how it stays. Your name?'

'Hurlochel.'

'Now I remember. You acted as chronicler on occasion, didn't you?'

A shrug. 'I keep an account of things, yes, sir. What are you doing here?'

'I need to speak with Dujek.'

Hurlochel glanced over at the guards, then scowled. 'Walk with me, sir. Don't mind them, they're new enough not to know all the officers.'

Leading the horse, Hurlochel guided Paran away, down a side alley nearby, where he halted.

'Hurlochel,' Paran said, 'why is Dujek's tent guarded by green soldiers? That doesn't make sense at all. What's happened and why are you camped outside G'danisban?'

'Yes, sir, we've had a hard time of it. It's the plague, you see – the legion healers were keeping it from us, but what it's done to Seven Cities . . . gods, Captain, there's bodies in the tens of thousands. Maybe hundreds of thousands. Every city. Every village. Caravan camps – everywhere, sir. We had a Gold Moranth accompanying us, you see, a renegade of sorts. Anyway, there's a temple, in G'danisban. The Grand Temple of Poliel, and it's where this foul wind is coming from, and it's getting stronger.' Hurlochel paused to wipe rain from his eyes.

'So Dujek decided to strike at the heart, didn't he?'

'Yes, sir.'

'Go on, Hurlochel.'

'We arrived, a month back, and the High Fist formed up companies of his veterans, along with the Gold Moranth. They planned an assault on that damned temple. Well, they expected at least a High Priestess or some other sort, but they were ready for it. What nobody planned on, though, was the Grey Goddess herself.'

Paran's eyes widened. 'Who made it back out?'

'Most of them, sir, except the Gold Moranth. But . . . they're all sick, sir. The plague's got hold of them and they're only still alive because of the healers . . . only the healers are losing the battle. So, here we are. Stuck, and nobody skank enough to take real command and make some real decisions.' Hurlochel hesitated, then said, 'Unless that's why you're here, Captain. I sure hope so.'

Paran looked away. 'I'm officially dead, Outrider. Dujek threw us out of the army, myself and a few others—'

'Bridgeburners.'

'Yes.'

'Well, sir, if anybody earned their days in the sweet sun . . .'

Paran grimaced. 'Aye, I'm sure that sun's around somewhere. Anyway, I can hardly take command – besides, I'm just a captain—'

'With absolute seniority, sir. Dujek took his officers with him – they were the veterans, after all. So, we got nearly ten thousand soldiers camped here, and the nearest thing to a commander is Captain Sweetcreek, who's a Falari princess, if you can believe that.'

'Red hair?'

'Wild red, aye, and a pretty face—'

'With a swollen jaw. We've met.'

'A swollen jaw?'

'It wasn't a pleasant meeting.' Still Paran hesitated, then he swore and nodded. 'All right. I'll keep the rank of captain . . . with seniority. But I need a new name—'

'Captain Kindly, sir.'

'Kindly?'

'Old soldiers talk about him like grandmothers talk monsters to the brats, to keep them in line, sir. Nobody here's met him – at least nobody who's not fevered and half out of their minds.'

'Well, where was Kindly last posted?'

'Fourteenth, sir. The Adjunct's army out west of Raraku. Which direction did you come in from?'

'West.'

'That'll do, sir, I think. I'll make it so's I recognize you. Nobody knows a thing about me, only that the High Fist used me to run messages.'

'So why would I let two soldiers arrest me if I'm supposed to take over command?'

'You did? Well, maybe you wanted to see how we were running things here.'

'All right. One more question, Hurlochel. Why aren't you still with Caladan Brood on Genabackis?'

'The alliance broke up, sir, not long after the Tiste Andii settled in Black Coral. Rhivi back to the plains, the Barghast back to their hills. The Crimson Guard, who were up north, just vanished – no-one knows where they went. When Onearm shipped out, well, seemed like they were headed somewhere interesting.'

'Regrets?'

'With every heartbeat, sir.' Hurlochel then frowned. 'Captain Sweetcreek's got a swollen jaw, you said?'

'I punched her. Along with some soldier named Futhgar. They're bound and gagged in the captain's tent. They might have come round by now.'

The man grinned, but it was not a pleasant grin. 'Captain, you knocked out cold a Falari princess – that's perfect. It fits with what people have heard about Kindly. That's brilliant.'

Paran winced, then rubbed at his face. *Gods below, what is it with me and royalty?*

She had slowly emerged from the hidden temple to see a straggling line of battered figures walking the road below. Making her way down the dusty, stony slope, she was within fifteen paces before anyone noticed her. There was a strangeness in that moment of meeting, survivors eye to eye, both recognition and disbelief. Acceptance, a sense of something shared, and beneath it the ineffable flow of sorrow. Few words were exchanged.

Joining the soldiers in their march, Lostara Yil found herself alongside Captain Faradan Sort, who told her something of Y'Ghatan's aftermath. 'Your Fist, Tene Baralta, was hovering on the edge of death, if not of the flesh, then of the spirit. He has lost an arm – it was burned beyond repair – and there was other damage . . . to his face. I believe he was a vain man.'

Lostara grunted. 'That damned beard of his, slick with oil.' She thought about Tene Baralta for a time. She'd never liked him much. More than just vain. Perhaps, truth be told, something of a coward, despite all his belligerence and posturing. She remembered the way he had led the retreat following her assassination of the elder Sha'ik, and his eagerness to take credit for every success whilst dancing from the path of disaster. There had been a sadistic streak in the man, and Lostara now feared that it would burgeon, as Tene Baralta sought means to feed all that was wounded within him. 'Why did the army leave all of you behind?'

Faradan Sort shrugged. 'They assumed no-one who had been trapped within the city could have survived the firestorm.' She paused, then added, 'It was a reasonable assumption. Only Sinn knew otherwise, and something told me to trust the girl. So we kept looking.'

'They're all wearing rags . . . and they're unarmed.'

'Aye, which is why we need to rejoin the army as soon as possible.'

'Can Sinn magically contact the Fourteenth? Or Quick Ben?'

'I have not asked her. I do not know how much of her ability is unformed talent – such creatures occur occasionally, and without the discipline of schooling as an apprentice, they tend to become avatars of chaos. Power, yes, but undirected, wild. Even so, she was able to defeat the wall of fire and so save Fist Keneb's companies . . . well, some of them.'

Lostara glanced over at the captain, then back at the soldiers in their wake for a moment before saying, 'You are Korelri?'

'I am.'

'And you stood the Wall?'

A tight smile, there for an instant then gone. 'None are permitted to leave that service.'

'It's said the Stormriders wield terrible sorcery in their eternal assault upon the Wall.'

'All sorcery is terrible – to kill indiscriminately, often from a great distance, there is nothing more damaging to the mortal who wields such power, whether it is human or something else.'

'Is it better to look your foe in the eye as you take his life?'

'At the very least,' Faradan replied, 'you gave them the chance to defend themselves. And Oponn decides in the end, decides in which set of eyes the light shall fade.'

'Oponn – I thought it was skill.'

'You're still young, Captain Lostara Yil.'

'I am?'

Faradan Sort smiled. 'With each battle I find myself in, my faith in skill diminishes. No, it is the Lord's push or the Lady's pull, each time, every time.'

Lostara said nothing. She could not agree with that assessment, even disregarding the irritation of the other woman's condescension. A clever, skilled soldier lived where dim-witted, clumsy soldiers died. Skill was a currency that purchased Oponn's favour – how could it be otherwise?

'You survived Y'Ghatan,' Faradan Sort said. 'How much of that was the Lady's pull?'

Lostara considered for a moment, then replied, 'None.'

Once, years ago, a few score soldiers had stumbled clear of a vast swamp. Bloodied, half-mad, their very skin hanging in discoloured strips from weeks slogging through mud and black water. Kalam Mekhar had been among them, along with the three he now walked beside, and it seemed that, in the end, only the details had changed.

Black Dog had brutally culled the Bridgeburners, a protracted nightmare war conducted in black spruce stands, in lagoons and bogs, clashing with the Mott Irregulars, the Nathii First Army and the Crimson Guard. The survivors were numbed – to step free of the horror was to cast aside despair, yet whatever came to replace it was slow in awakening. Leaving . . . very little. *Look at us*, he remembered Hedge saying, *we're nothing but hollowed-out logs. We done rotted from the inside out, just like every other damned thing in that swamp.* Well, Hedge had never been one for optimism.

'You're looking thoughtful,' Quick Ben observed at his side.

Kalam grunted, then glanced over. 'Was wondering, Quick. You ever get tired of your own memories?'

'That's not a good idea,' the wizard replied.

'No, I suppose it isn't. I'm not just getting old, I'm feeling old. I look at all those soldiers behind us – gods below, they're young. Except in their eyes. I suppose we were like that, once. Only . . . from then till now, Quick, what have we done? Damned little that meant anything.'

'I admit I've been wondering a few things about you myself,' Quick Ben said. 'That Claw, Pearl, for example.'

'The one that stabbed me in the back? What about him?'

'Why you ain't killed him already, Kalam. I mean, it's not something you'd normally set aside, is it? Unless, of course, you're not sure you can take him.'

From behind the two men, Fiddler spoke: 'It was Pearl that night in Malaz City? Hood's breath, Kalam, the bastard's been strutting round in the Fourteenth since Raraku, no wonder he's wearing a sly smile every time he sees you.'

'I don't give a damn about Pearl, not about killing him, anyway,' Kalam said in a low voice. 'We got bigger things to worry about. What's our Adjunct got in mind? What's she planning?'

'Who says she's planning anything?' Fiddler retorted. He was carrying one of the children in his arms, a girl, fast asleep with her thumb in her mouth. 'She went after Leoman, and now she's fleeing a plague and trying to link up with the transport fleet. And then? My guess is, we're on our way back to Genabackis, or maybe the Korel Peninsula. It's more of the same 'cause that's what soldiers do, that's how soldiers live.'

'I think you're wrong,' Kalam said. 'It's all snarled, now.'

'What do you mean?'

'Pearl's the key, sapper,' the assassin said. 'Why is he still around? What's the point of spying on the Adjunct? What's the point of dogging the Fourteenth's heels? I'm telling you, Fid, what the Adjunct does next depends on Empress Laseen, her and nobody else.'

'She won't cut us all loose,' Fiddler said. 'Not the Adjunct, not the Fourteenth. We're her only mobile army worthy of the name. There ain't no more commanders out there – well, there are, but the only salute I'd give 'em is point first. Bloody or not, Tavore's put an end to the rebellion here, and that's got to count for something.'

'Fid,' Quick Ben said, 'the war's a lot bigger than you might think, and it's just starting. There's no telling which side the Empress is on.'

'What in Hood's name are you talking about?'

Apsalar spoke. 'A war among the gods, Sergeant. Captain Paran talked of such a war, at length—'

Both Kalam and Quick Ben turned at this.

'Ganoes Paran?' the assassin asked. 'Quick said he left him in Darujhistan. What's he to do with all of this? And when did you speak with him?'

She was leading her horse by the reins three paces behind Fiddler; in the saddle sat three children, dull-eyed in the heat. At Kalam's questions she shrugged, then said, 'He is Master of the Deck of Dragons. In that capacity, he has come here, to Seven Cities. We were north of Raraku when we parted ways. Kalam Mekhar, I have no doubt that you and Quick Ben are in the midst of yet another scheme. For what it is worth, I would advise caution. Too many unknown forces are in this game, and among them will be found Elder Gods and, indeed, Elder Races. Perhaps you believe you comprehend the ultimate stakes, but I suggest that you do not—'

'And you do?' Quick Ben demanded.

'Not entirely, but then, I have constrained my . . . goals . . . seeking only what is achievable.'

'Now you got me curious,' Fiddler said. 'Here you are, marching with us once again, Apsalar, when I'd figured you'd be settled in some coastal village back in Itko Kan, knitting greasy sweaters for your da. Maybe you left Crokus behind, but it seems to me you ain't left nothing else behind.'

'We travel this same road,' she said, 'for the moment. Sergeant, you need fear nothing from me.'

'And what about the rest of us?' Quick Ben asked.

She did not reply.

Sudden unease whispered through Kalam. He met Quick's eyes for a brief moment, then faced forward once more. 'Let's just catch up with that damned army first.'

'I'd like to see Pearl disposed of,' Quick Ben said.

No-one spoke for a long moment. It wasn't often that the wizard voiced his desire so . . . brazenly, and Kalam realized, with a chill, that things were getting bad. Maybe even desperate. But it wasn't that easy. *Like that rooftop in Darujhistan – invisible enemies on all sides – you look and look but see nothing.*

Pearl, who was once Salk Elan. Mockra warren . . . and a blade sliding like fire into my back. Everyone thinks Topper's the master in the Claw, but I wonder . . . can you take him, Kalam? Quick's got his doubts – he's just offered to help. Gods below, maybe I am getting old. 'You never answered me, friend,' the assassin said to Quick Ben.

'What was the question again?'

'Ever get tired of your own memories?'

'Oh, that one.'

'Well?'

'Kalam, you have no idea.'

Fiddler didn't like this conversation. In fact, he hated it, and was relieved as everyone fell silent once more, walking the dusty track, every step pushing that damned ruin of a city further behind them. He knew he should be back in the column, with his squad, or maybe up ahead, trying to pry stuff loose from Faradan Sort – that captain was full of surprises, wasn't she just. She'd saved all their lives – there was no doubting that – but that didn't mean that he had to trust her. Not yet, despite the truth that he *wanted* to, for some arcane reason he'd yet to comprehend.

The little girl with the runny nose sniffled in her sleep, one small hand clutching his left shoulder. Her other hand was at her mouth, and her sucking on her thumb made tiny squeaking sounds. In his arms, she weighed next to nothing.

His squad had come through intact. Only Balm, and maybe Hellian, could say the same. So, three squads out of what, ten? Eleven? Thirty? Moak's soldiers had been entirely wiped out – the Eleventh Squad was gone, and that was a number that would never be resurrected in the future history of the Fourteenth. The captain had settled on the numbers, adding the Thirteenth for Sergeant Urb, and it turned out that Fiddler's own, the Fourth, was the lowest number on the rung. This part of Ninth Company had taken a beating, and Fiddler had few hopes for the rest, the ones that hadn't made it to the Grand Temple. Worse yet, they'd lost too many sergeants. Borduke, Mosel, Moak, Sobelone, Tugg.

Well, all right, we're beaten up, but we're alive.

He dropped back a few paces, resumed his march alongside Corabb Bhilan Thenu'alas. The last survivor of Leoman's rebel army – barring Leoman himself – had said little, although the scowl knotting his expression suggested his thoughts were anything but calm. A scrawny boy was riding his shoulders, head bobbing and dipping as he dozed.

'I was thinking,' Fiddler said, 'of attaching you to my squad. We were always one short.'

'Is it that simple, Sergeant?' Corabb asked. 'You Malazans are strange. I cannot yet be a soldier in your army, for I have not yet impaled a babe on a spear.'

'Corabb, the sliding bed is a Seven Cities invention, not a Malazan one.'

'What has that to do with it?'

'I mean, Malazans don't stick babes on spears.'

'Is it not your rite of passage?'

'Who has been telling you this rubbish? Leoman?'

The man frowned. 'No. But such beliefs were held to among the followers of the Apocalypse.'

'Isn't Leoman one such follower?'

'I think not. No, never. I was blind to that. Leoman believed in himself and no other. Until that Mezla bitch he found in Y'Ghatan.'

461

'He found himself a woman, did he? No wonder he went south.'

'He did not go south, Sergeant. He fled into a warren.'

'A figure of speech.'

'He went with his woman. She will destroy him, I am sure of that, and now I say that is only what Leoman deserves. Let Dunsparrow ruin him, utterly—'

'Hold on,' Fiddler cut in, as an uncanny shiver rose through him, 'did you call her Dunsparrow?'

'Yes, for such she named herself.'

'A Malazan?'

'Yes, tall and miserable. She would mock me. Me, Corabb Bhilan Thenu'alas, Leoman's Second, until I became his Third, the one he was content to leave behind. To die with all the others.'

Fiddler barely heard him. 'Dunsparrow,' he repeated.

'Do you know the hag? The witch? The seductress and corrupter?'

Gods, I once tossed her on my knee. He realized of a sudden that he was clawing a hand through the remnants of his singed, snarled hair, unmindful of the snags, indifferent to the tears that started from his eyes. The girl squirmed. He stared over at Corabb, unseeing, then hurried ahead, feeling dizzy, feeling . . . appalled. *Dunsparrow . . . she'd be in her twenties now. Middle twenties, I suppose. What was she doing in Y'Ghatan?*

He pushed between Kalam and Quick Ben, startling both men.

'Fid?'

'Tug Hood's snake till he shrieks,' the sapper said. 'Drown the damned Queen of Dreams in her own damned pool. Friends, you won't believe who went with Leoman into that warren. You won't believe who shared Leoman's bed in Y'Ghatan. No, you won't believe anything I say.'

'Abyss take you, Fid,' Kalam said in exasperation, 'what are you talking about?'

'Dunsparrow. That's who's at Leoman's side right now. Dunsparrow. Whiskeyjack's little sister and I don't know – I don't know anything – what to think, only I want to scream and I don't know why even there, no, I don't know anything any more. Gods, Quick – Kalam – what does it mean? What does any of it mean?'

'Calm down,' Quick Ben said, but his voice was strangely high, tight. 'For us, for us, I mean, it doesn't necessarily mean anything. It's a damned coincidence and even if it isn't, it's not like it means anything, not really. It's just . . . peculiar, that's all. We knew she was a stubborn, wild little demon, we knew that, even then – and you knew her better than us, me and Kalam, we only met her once, in Malaz City. But you, you were like her uncle, which means you got some explaining to do!'

Fiddler stared at the man, at his wide eyes. 'Me? You've lost your mind, Quick. Listen to you! Blaming me, for her! Wasn't nothing to do with me!'

'Stop it, both of you,' Kalam said. 'You're frightening the soldiers behind us. Look, we're all too nervous right now, about all sorts of things, to be able to make sense of any of this, assuming there's any sense to be made. People choose their own lives, what they do, where they end up, it don't mean some god's playing around. So, Whiskeyjack's little sister is now Leoman's lover, and they're both hiding out in the Queen of Dreams' warren. All right, better that than crumbling bones in the ashes of Y'Ghatan, right? Well?'

'Maybe, maybe not,' Fiddler said.

'What in Hood's name does that mean?' Kalam demanded.

Fiddler drew a deep, shaky breath. 'We must have told you, it's not like it was secret or anything, and we always used it as an excuse, to explain her, the way she was and all that. Never so she could hear, of course, and we said it to take its power away—'

'Fiddler!'

The sapper winced at Kalam's outburst. 'Now who's frightening everyone—'

'You are! And never mind everyone else – you're frightening me, damn you!'

'All right. She was born to a dead woman – Whiskeyjack's step-mother, she died that morning, and the baby – Dunsparrow – well, she was long in coming out, she should have died inside, if you know what I mean. That's why the town elders gave her up to the temple, to Hood's own. The father was already dead, killed outside Quon, and Whiskeyjack, well, he was finishing his prenticeship. We was young then. So me and him, we had to break in and steal her back, but she'd already been consecrated, blessed in Hood's name – so we took its power away by talking about it, ha ha, making light and all that, and she grew up normal enough. More or less. Sort of . . .' He trailed away, refused to meet the two sets of staring eyes, then scratched at his singed face. 'We need us a Deck of Dragons, I think . . .'

Apsalar, four paces behind the trio, smiled as the wizard and assassin both simultaneously cuffed Sergeant Fiddler. A short-lived smile. Such revelations were troubling. Whiskeyjack had always been more than a little reticent about where he'd come from, about the life before he became a soldier. Mysteries as locked away as the ruins beneath the sands. He'd been a mason, once, a worker in stone. She knew that much. A fraught profession among the arcana of divination and symbolism. Builder of barrows, the one who could make solid all of history, every monument to grandeur, every dolmen raised in eternal gestures of surrender. There were masons among many of the Houses in the Deck of Dragons, a signifier of both permanence and its illusion. *Whiskeyjack, a mason who set his tools down, to embrace slaughter. Was it Hood's own hand that guided him?*

It was believed by many that Laseen had arranged Dassem Ultor's death, and Dassem had been the Mortal Sword of Hood – in reality if not in name – and the centre of a growing cult among the ranks of the Malazan armies. The empire sought no patron from among the gods, no matter how seductive the invitation, and in that Laseen had acted with singular wisdom, and quite possibly at the command of the Emperor. Had Whiskeyjack belonged to Dassem's cult? Possibly – still, she had seen nothing to suggest that was so. If anthing, he had been a man entirely devoid of faith.

Nor did it seem likely that the Queen of Dreams would knowingly accept the presence of an avatar of Hood within her realm. *Unless the two gods are now allies in this war.* The very notion of war depressed her, for gods were as cruel and merciless as mortals. *Whiskeyjack's sister may be as much an unwitting player in all this as the rest of us.* She was not prepared to condemn the woman, and not yet ready to consider her an ally, either.

She wondered again at what Kalam and Quick Ben were planning. Both were formidable in their own right, yet intrinsic in their methods was staying low, beneath notice. What was obvious – all that lay on the surface – was invariably an illusion, a deceit. When the time came to choose sides, out in the open, they were likely to surprise everyone.

Two men, then, whom no-one could truly trust. Two men whom not even the gods could trust, for that matter.

She realized that, in joining this column, in coming among these soldiers, she had become ensnared in yet another web, and there was no guarantee she would be able to cut herself free. Not in time.

The entanglement worried her. She could not be certain that she'd walk away from a fight with Kalam. *Not a fight that was face to face, that is.* And now his guard was up. In fact, she'd invited it. Partly from bravado, and partly to gauge his reaction. *And just a little ... misdirection.*

Well, there was plenty of that going round.

The two undead lizards, Curdle and Telorast, were maintaining some distance from the party of soldiers, although Apsalar sensed that they were keeping pace, somewhere out in the scrubland south of the raised road. Whatever their hidden motives in accompanying her, they were for the moment content to simply follow. That they possessed secrets and a hidden purpose was obvious to her, as was the possibility that

that purpose involved, on some level, betrayal. *And that too is something that we all share.*

Sergeant Balm was cursing behind Bottle as they walked the stony road. Scorched boots, soles flapping, mere rags covering the man's shoulders beneath the kiln-hot sun, Balm was giving voice to the miseries afflicting everyone who had crawled out from under Y'Ghatan. Their pace was slowing, as feet blistered and sharp rocks cut into tender skin, and the sun raised a resisting wall of blinding heat before them. Clawing through it had become a vicious, enervating struggle.

Where others among the squads carried children, Bottle found himself carrying a mother rat and her brood of pups, the former perched on his shoulder and the latter swathed in rags in the crook of one arm. More sordid than comic, and even he could see that, but he would not relinquish his new . . . allies.

Striding at Bottle's side was the halfblood Seti, Koryk. Freshly adorned in human finger bones and not much else. He'd knotted them in the singed strands of his hair, and with each step there was a soft clack and clatter, the music grisly to Bottle's ears.

Koryk carried more in a clay pot with a cracked rim that he'd found in the pit of a looted grave. No doubt he planned on distributing them to the other soldiers. *As soon as we've found enough clothes to wear.*

He caught a skittering sound off among the withered scrub to his left. *Those damned lizard skeletons. Chasing down my scouts.* He wondered to whom they belonged. Reasonable to assume they were death-aspected, which possibly made them servants of Hood. He knew of no mages among the squads who used Hood's Warren – then again those who did rarely advertised the fact. Maybe that healer, Deadsmell, but why would he want familiars now? He sure didn't have them down in the tunnels. Besides, you'd need to be a powerful mage or priest to be able to conjure up and bind two familiars. No, not Deadsmell. Who, then?

Quick Ben. That wizard had far too many warrens swirling round him. Fiddler had vowed to drag Bottle up to the man, and that was an introduction Bottle had no desire to make. Fortunately, the sergeant seemed to have forgotten his squad, caught up as he was in this sordid reunion of old-timers.

'Hungry enough yet?' Koryk asked.

Startled, Bottle glanced over at the man. 'What do you mean?'

'Skewered pinkies to start, then braised rat – it's why you've brought them along, isn't it?'

'You're sick.'

Just ahead, Smiles turned to fling back a nasty laugh. 'Good one. You can stop now, Koryk – you've reached your quota for the year. Besides, Bottle ain't gonna eat them rats. He's married the momma and adopted the whelps – you missed the ceremony, Koryk, when you was off hunting bones. Too bad, we all cried.'

'We missed our chance,' Koryk said to Bottle. 'We could've beat her unconscious and left her in the tunnels.'

A good sign. Things are getting back to normal. Everything except the haunted look in the eyes. It was there, in every soldier who'd gone through the buried bones of Y'Ghatan. Some cultures, he knew, used a ritual of burial and resurrection to mark a rite of passage. But if this was a rebirth, it was a dour one. They'd not emerged innocent, or cleansed. If anything, the burdens seemed heavier. The elation of having survived, of having slipped out from the shadow of Hood's Gates, had proved woefully shortlived.

It should have felt ... different. Something was missing. The Bridgeburners had been forged by the Holy Desert Raraku – *so for us, wasn't Y'Ghatan enough?* It seemed that, for these soldiers here, the tempering had gone too far, creating something pitted and brittle, as if one more blow would shatter them.

Up ahead, the captain called out a halt, her voice eliciting a chorus of curses and groans of relief. Although there was no shade to be found, walking through this furnace was far worse than sitting by the roadside easing burnt, cut and blistered feet. Bottle stumbled down into the ditch and sat on a boulder. He watched, sweat stinging his eyes, as Deadsmell and Lutes moved among the soldiers, doing what they could to heal the wounds.

'Did you see that Red Blade captain?' Smiles asked, crouching nearby. 'Looking like she'd just come from a parade ground.'

'No she didn't,' Corporal Tarr said. 'She's smoke-stained and scorched, just like you'd expect.'

'Only she's got all her hair.'

'So that's what's got you snarly,' Koryk observed. 'Poor Smiles. You know it won't grow back, don't you? Never. You're bald now for the rest of your life—'

'Liar.'

Hearing the sudden doubt in her voice, Bottle said, 'Yes, he is.'

'I knew that. And what's with the black-haired woman on the horse? Anybody here know who she is?'

'Fiddler recognized her,' Tarr said. 'A Bridgeburner, I'd guess.'

'She makes me nervous,' Smiles said. 'She's like that assassin, Kalam. Eager to kill someone.'

I suspect you're right. And Fid wasn't exactly thrilled to see her, either.

Tarr spoke: 'Koryk, when you going to share those finger bones you collected?'

'Want yours now?'

'Aye, I do.'

Her throat parched, her skin layered in sweat even as shivers rippled through her, Hellian stood on the road. Too tired to walk, too sick to sit down – she feared she'd never get up again, just curl into a little juddering ball until the ants under her skin finished their work and all that skin just peeled away like deer hide, whereupon they'd all march off with it, singing songs of triumph in tiny squeaking voices.

It was the drink, she knew. Or, rather, the lack of it. The world around her was too sharp, too clear; none of it looked right, not right at all. Faces revealed too many details, all the flaws and wrinkles unveiled for the first time. She was shocked to realize that she wasn't the oldest soldier there barring that ogre Cuttle. Well, that was the one good thing that had come of this enforced sobriety. Now, if only those damned faces could disappear just like the wrinkles on them, then she'd be happier. No, wait, it was the opposite, wasn't it? No wonder she wasn't happy.

Ugly people in an ugly world. That's what came from seeing it all the way it really was. Better when it was blurred – all farther away back then, it had seemed, so far away she'd not noticed the stinks, the stains, the errant hairs rising from volcanic pores, the miserable opinions and suspicious expressions, the whisperings behind her back.

Turning, Hellian glared down at her two corporals. 'You think I can't hear you? Now be quiet, or I'll rip one of my ears off and won't you two feel bad.'

Touchy and Brethless exchanged a glance, then Touchy said, 'We ain't said nothing, Sergeant.'

'Nice try.'

The problem was, the world was a lot bigger than she had ever imagined. More crannies for spiders than a mortal could count in a thousand lifetimes. Just look around for proof of that. And it wasn't just spiders any more. No, here there were flies that bit and the bite sank an egg under the skin. And giant grey moths that fluttered in the night and liked eating scabs from sores when you were sleeping. Waking up to soft crunching way too close by. Scorpions that split into two when you stepped on them. Fleas that rode the winds. Worms that showed up in the corners of your eyes and made red swirling patterns through your eyelids, and when they got big enough they crawled out your nostrils. Sand ticks and leather leeches, flying lizards and beetles living in dung.

Her entire body was crawling with parasites – she could feel them. Tiny ants and slithering worms under her skin, burrowing into her flesh, eating her brain. And, now that the sweet taste of alcohol was gone, they all wanted out. She expected, at any moment, to suddenly erupt all over, all the horrid creatures clambering out and her body deflating like a punctured bladder. Ten thousand wriggling things, all desperate for a drink.

'I'm going to find him,' she said. 'One day.'

'Who?' Touchy asked.

'That priest, the one who ran away. I'm going to find him, and I'm going to tie him up and fill his body with worms. Push 'em into his mouth, his nose, his eyes and ears and other places, too.'

No, she wouldn't let herself explode. Not yet. This sack of skin was going to stay intact. She'd make a deal with all the worms and ants, some kind of deal. A truce. Who said you can't reason with bugs?

'It sure is hot,' Touchy said.

Everyone looked at him.

Gesler scanned the soldiers where they sat or sprawled alongside the track. What the fire hadn't burned the sun now had. Soldiers on the march wore their clothes like skin, and for those whose skin wasn't dark, the burnished bronze of hands, faces and necks contrasted sharply with pallid arms, legs and torsos. But what had once been pale was now bright red. Among all those light-skinned soldiers who'd survived Y'Ghatan, Gesler himself was the only exception. The golden hue of his skin seemed unaffected by this scorching desert sun.

'Gods, these people need clothes,' he said.

Beside him, Stormy grunted. About the extent of his communication lately, ever since he'd heard of Truth's death.

'They'll start blistering soon,' Gesler went on, 'and Deadsmell and Lutes can only do so much. We got to catch up with the Fourteenth.' He turned his head, squinted towards the front of the column. Then he rose. 'Ain't nobody thinking straight, not even the captain.'

Gesler made his way up the track. He approached the gathering of old Bridgeburners. 'We been missing the obvious,' he said.

'Nothing new in that,' Fiddler said, looking miserable.

Gesler nodded towards Apsalar. 'She's got to ride ahead and halt the army. She's got to get 'em to bring us horses, and clothes and armour and weapons. And water and food. We won't even catch up otherwise.'

Apsalar slowly straightened, brushing dust from her leggings. 'I can do that,' she said in a quiet voice.

Kalam rose and faced Captain Faradan Sort, who stood nearby. 'The sergeant's right. We missed the obvious.'

'Except that there is no guarantee that anyone will believe her,' the captain replied after a moment. 'Perhaps, if one of us borrowed her horse.'

Apsalar frowned, then shrugged. 'As you like.'

'Who's our best rider?' Kalam asked.

'Masan Gilani,' Fiddler said. 'Sure, she's heavy infantry, but still . . .'

Faradan Sort squinted down the road. 'Which squad?'

'Urb's, the Thirteenth.' Fiddler pointed. 'The one who's standing, the tall one, the Dal Honese.'

Masan Gilani's elongated, almond-shaped eyes narrowed as she watched the old soldiers approaching.

'You're in trouble,' Scant said. 'You did something, Gilani, and now they want your blood.'

It certainly looked that way, so Masan made no reply to Scant's words. She thought back over all of the things she had done of late. Plenty to consider, but none came to mind that anyone might find out about, not after all this time. 'Hey, Scant,' she said.

The soldier looked up. 'What?'

'You know that big hook-blade I keep with my gear?'

Scant's eyes brightened. 'Yes?'

'You can't have it,' she said. 'Saltlick can have it.'

'Thanks, Masan,' Saltlick said.

'I always knew,' Hanno said, 'you had designs on Salty. I could tell, you know.'

'No I don't, I just don't like Scant, that's all.'

'Why don't you like me?'

'I just don't, that's all.'

They fell silent as the veterans arrived. Sergeant Gesler, his eyes on Masan, said, 'We need you, soldier.'

'That's nice.' She noted the way his eyes travelled her mostly naked frame, lingering on her bared breasts with their large, dark nipples, before, with a rapid blinking, he met her eyes once more.

'We want you to take Apsalar's horse and catch up with the Fourteenth.' This was from Sergeant Strings or Fiddler or whatever his name was these days. It seemed Gesler had forgotten how to talk.

'That's it?'

'Aye.'

'All right. It's a nice horse.'

'We need you to convince the Adjunct we're actually alive,' Fiddler went on. 'Then get her to send us mounts and supplies.'

'All right.'

The woman presumably named Apsalar led her horse forward and handed Masan Gilani the reins.

She swung up into the saddle, then said, 'Anybody got a spare knife or something?'

Apsalar produced one from beneath her cloak and passed it up to her.

Masan Gilani's fine brows rose. 'A Kethra. That will do. I'll give it back to you when we meet up again.'

Apsalar nodded.

The Dal Honese set off.

'Shouldn't take long,' Gesler said, watching as the woman, riding clear of the column, urged her horse into a canter.

'We'll rest for a while longer here,' Faradan Sort said, 'then resume our march.'

'We could just wait,' Fiddler said.

The captain shook her head, but offered no explanation.

The sun settled on the horizon, bleeding red out to the sides like blood beneath flayed skin. The sky overhead was raucous with sound and motion as thousands of birds winged southward. They were high up, mere black specks, flying without formation, yet their cries reached down in a chorus of terror.

To the north, beyond the range of broken, lifeless hills and steppeland ribboned by seasonal run-off, the plain descended to form a white-crusted salt marsh, beyond which lay the sea. The marsh had once been a modest plateau, subsiding over millennia as underground streams and springs gnawed through the limestone. The caves, once high and vast, were now crushed flat or partially collapsed, and those cramped remnants were flooded or packed with silts, sealing in darkness the walls and vaulted ceilings crowded with paintings, and side chambers still home to the fossilized bones of Imass.

Surmounting this plateau there had been a walled settlement, small and modest, a chaotic array of attached residences that would have housed perhaps twenty families at the height of its occupation. The defensive walls were solid, with no gates, and for the dwellers within, ingress and egress came via the rooftops and single-pole ladders.

Yadeth Garath, the first human city, was now little more than salt-rotted rubble swallowed in silts, buried deep and unseen beneath the marsh. No history beyond the countless derivations from its ancient name remained, and of the lives and deaths and tales of all who had once lived there, not even bones survived.

Dejim Nebrahl recalled the fisher folk who had dwelt upon its ruins, living in their squalid huts on stilts, plying the waters in their round, hide boats, and walking the raised wooden platforms that crossed the natural canals wending through the swamp. They were not descendants

470

of Yadeth Garath. They knew nothing of what swirled beneath the black silts, and this itself was an undeniable truth, that memory withered and died in the end. There was no single tree of life, no matter how unique and primary this Yadeth Garath – no, there was a forest, and time and again, a tree, its bole rotted through, toppled to swiftly vanish in the airless muck.

Dejim Nebrahl recalled those fisher folk, the way their blood tasted of fish and molluscs, dull and turgid and clouded with stupidity. If man and woman cannot – will not – remember, then they deserved all that was delivered upon them. Death, destruction and devastation. This was no god's judgement – it was the world's, nature's own. Exacted in that conspiracy of indifference that so terrified and baffled humankind.

Lands subside. Waters rush in. The rains come, then never come. Forests die, rise again, then die once more. Men and women huddle with their broods in dark rooms in all their belated begging, and their eyes fill with dumb failure, and now they are crumbled specks of grey and white in black silt, motionless as the memory of stars in a long-dead night sky.

Exacting nature's judgement, such was Dejim Nebrahl's purpose. For the forgetful, their very shadows stalk them. For the forgetful, death ever arrives unexpectedly.

The T'rolbarahl had returned to the site of Yadeth Garath, as if drawn by some desperate instinct. Dejim Nebrahl was starving. Since his clash with the mage near the caravan, his wanderings had taken him through lands foul with rotted death. Nothing but bloated, blackened corpses, redolent with disease. Such things could not feed him.

The intelligence within the D'ivers had succumbed to visceral urgency, a terrible geas that drove him onward on the path of old memories, of places where he had once fed, the blood hot and fresh pouring down his throats.

Kanarbar Belid, now nothing but dust. Vithan Taur, the great city in the cliff-face – now even the cliff was gone. A swath of potsherds reduced to gravel was all that remained of Minikenar, once a thriving city on the banks of a river now extinct. The string of villages north of Minikenar revealed no signs that they had ever existed. Dejim Nebrahl had begun to doubt his own memories.

Driven on, across the gnawed hills and into the fetid marsh, seeking yet another village of fisher folk. But he had been too thorough the last time, all those centuries past, and none had come to take the place of the slaughtered. Perhaps some dark recollection held true, casting a haunted pall upon the swamp. Perhaps the bubbling gases still loosed ancient screams and shrieks and the boatmen from the isles, passing close, made warding gestures before swinging the tiller hard about.

Fevered, weakening, Dejim Nebrahl wandered the rotted landscape. Until a faint scent reached the D'ivers.

Beast, and human. Vibrant, alive, and close.

The T'rolbarahl, five shadow-thewed creatures of nightmare, lifted heads and looked south, eyes narrowing. There, just beyond the hills, on the crumbling track that had once been a level road leading to Minikenar. The D'ivers set off, as dusk settled on the land.

Masan Gilani slowed her horse's canter when the shadows thickened with the promise of night. The track was treacherous with loose cobbles and narrow gullies formed by run-off. It had been years since she'd last ridden wearing so little – nothing more than a wrap about her hips – and her thoughts travelled far back to her life on the Dal Honese plains. She'd carried less weight back then. Tall, lithe, smooth-skinned and bright with innocence. The heaviness of her full breasts and the swell of her belly and hips came much later, after the two children she'd left behind to be raised by her mother and her aunts and uncles. It was the right of all adults, man or woman, to take the path of wandering; before the empire conquered the Dal Honese, such a choice had been rare enough, and for the children, raised by kin on all sides, their health tended by shamans, midwives and shoulder-witches, the abandonment of a parent was rarely felt.

The Malazan Empire had changed all that, of course. While many adults among the tribes stayed put, even in Masan Gilani's time, more and more men and women had set out to explore the world, and at younger ages. Fewer children were born; mixed-bloods were more common, once warriors returned home with new husbands or wives, and new ways suffused the lives of the Dal Honese. For that was one thing that had not changed over time – *we ever return home. When our wandering is done.*

She missed those rich grasslands and their young, fresh winds. The heaving clouds of the coming rains, the thunder in the earth as wild herds passed in their annual migrations. And her riding, always on the strong, barely tamed crossbred horses of the Dal Honese, the faint streaks of their zebra heritage as subtle on their hides as the play of sunlight on reeds. Beasts as likely to buck as gallop, hungry to bite with pure evil in their red-rimmed eyes. Oh, how she loved those horses.

Apsalar's mount was a far finer breed, of course. Long-limbed and graceful, and Masan Gilani could not resist admiring the play of sleek muscles beneath her and the intelligence in its dark, liquid eyes.

The horse shied suddenly in the growing gloom, head lifting. Startled, Masan Gilani reached for the kethra knife she had slipped into a fold in the saddle.

472

Shadows took shape on all sides, lunged. The horse reared, screaming as blood sprayed.

Masan Gilani rolled backward in a tight somersault, clearing the rump of the staggering beast and landing lightly in a half-crouch. Slashing the heavy knife to her right as a midnight-limbed creature rushed her. She felt the blade cut deep, scoring across two out-thrust forelimbs. A bestial cry of pain, then the thing reared back, dropping to all fours – and stumbling on those crippled forelimbs.

Reversing grip, she leapt to close on the apparition, and drove the knife down into the back of its scaled, feline neck. The beast collapsed, sagging against her shins.

A heavy sound to her left, as the horse fell onto its side, four more of the demons tearing into it. Legs kicked spasmodically, then swung upward as the horse was rolled onto its back, exposing its belly. Terrible snarling sounds accompanied the savage evisceration.

Leaping over the dead demon, Masan Gilani ran into the darkness.

A demon pursued her.

It was too fast. Footfalls sounded close behind her, then ceased.

She threw herself down into a hard, bruising roll, saw the blur of the demon's long body pass over her. Masan Gilani slashed out with the knife, cutting through a tendon on the creature's right back leg.

It shrieked, careening in mid-air, the cut-through leg folding beneath its haunches as it landed and its hips twisting round with the momentum.

Masan Gilani flung the knife. The weighted blade struck its shoulder, point and edge slicing through muscle to caroom off the scapula and spin into the night.

Regaining her feet, the Dal Honese plunged after it, launching herself over the spitting beast.

Talons raked down her left thigh, pitching her round, off-balance. She landed awkwardly against a slope of stones, the impact numbing her left shoulder. Sliding downward, back towards the demon, Masan dug her feet into the slope's side, then scrambled up the incline, flinging out handfuls of sand and gravel into her wake.

A sharp edge sliced along the back of her left hand, down to the bone – she'd found the kethra, lying on the slope. Grasping the grip with suddenly slick fingers, Masan Gilani continued her desperate clamber upward.

Another leap from behind brought the demon close, but it slid back down, spitting and hissing as the bank sagged in a clatter of stones and dust.

Reaching the crest, Masan pulled herself onto her feet, then ran, half-blind in the darkness. She heard the demon make another attempt, followed by another shower of sliding stones and rubble. Ahead she could make out a gully of some sort, high-walled and narrow. Two strides from it, she threw herself to the ground in response to a deafening howl that tore through the night.

Another howl answered it, reverberating among the crags, a sound like a thousand souls plunging into the Abyss. Gelid terror froze Masan Gilani's limbs, drained from her all strength, all will. She lay in the grit, her gasps puffing tiny clouds of dust before her face, her eyes wide and seeing nothing but the scatter of rocks marking the gully's fan.

From somewhere beyond the slope, down where her horse had died, came the sound of hissing, rising from three, perhaps four throats. Something in those eerie, almost-human voices whispered terror and panic.

A third howl filled the dark, coming from somewhere to the south, close enough to rattle her sanity. She found her forearms reaching out, her right hand clawing furrows in the scree, the kethra knife still gripped tight as she could manage with her blood-smeared left hand.

Not wolves. Gods below, the throats that loosed those howls—

A sudden heavy gusting sound, to her right, too close. She twisted her head round, the motion involuntary, and cold seeped down through her paralysed body as if sinking roots into the hard ground. A wolf but not a wolf, padding down a steep slope to land silent on the same broad ledge Masan Gilani was lying on – a wolf, but huge, as big as a Dal Honese horse, deep grey or black – there was no way to be certain. It paused, stood motionless for a moment in full profile, its attention clearly fixed on something ahead, down on the road.

Then the massive beast's head swung round, and Masan Gilani found herself staring into lambent, amber eyes, like twin pits into madness.

Her heart stopped in her chest. She could not draw breath, could not pull her gaze from that creature's deathly regard.

Then, a slow – so very slow – closing of those eyes, down to the thinnest slits – and the head swung back.

The beast padded towards the crest. Stared down for a time, then slipped down over the edge. And vanished from sight.

Sudden air flooded her lungs, thick with dust. She coughed – impossible not to – twisting round into a ball, hacking and gagging, spitting out gobs of gritty phlegm. Helpless, giving herself – giving *everything* – away. Still coughing, Masan Gilani waited for the beast to return, to pick her up in its huge jaws, to shake her once, hard, hard enough to snap her neck, her spine, to crunch down on her ribcage, crushing everything inside.

She slowly regained control of her breathing, still lying on sweat-soaked ground, shivers rippling through her.

From somewhere far overhead, in that dark sky, she heard birds, crying out. A thousand voices, ten thousand. She did not know that birds flew at night. Celestial voices, winging south as fast as unseen wings could take them.

Closer by . . . no sound at all.

Masan Gilani rolled onto her back, stared unseeing upward, feeling blood streaming down her slashed thigh. *Wait till Saltlick and the rest hear about this one . . .*

Dejim Nebrahl raced through the darkness, three beasts in full flight, a fourth limping in their wake, already far behind. Too weak, made mindless with hunger, all cunning lost, and now yet one more D'ivers kin was dead. Killed effortlessly by a mere human, who then crippled another with a lazy flick of that knife.

The T'rolbarahl needed to feed. The horse's blood had barely begun to slake a depthless thirst, yet with it came a whisper of strength, a return to sanity.

Dejim Nebrahl was being hunted. An outrage, that such a thing could be. The stench of the creatures rode the wind, seeming to gust in from all sides except directly ahead. Fierce, ancient life and deadly desire, bitter to the T'rolbarahl's senses. What manner of beasts were these?

The fourth kin, lagging half a league behind now, could feel the nearness of the pursuers, loping unseen, seemingly content to keep pace, almost uninterested in closing, in finishing off this wounded D'ivers. They had announced themselves with their howls, but since then, naught but silence, and the palpable nearness of their presence.

They were but toying with Dejim Nebrahl. A truth that infuriated the T'rolbarahl, that burned like acid through their thumping hearts. Were they fully healed, and seven once again rather than three and scant more, those creatures would know terror and pain. Even now, Dejim Nebrahl contemplated laying an ambush, using the wounded kin as bait. But the risks were too great – there was no telling how many of these hunters were out there.

And so there was little choice. Flee, desperate as hares, helpless in this absurd game.

For the first three kin, the scent of the hunters had begun to fade. It was true – few creatures could keep pace with Dejim Nebrahl for very long. It seemed, then, that they would content themselves with the crippled trailer, giving the D'ivers an opportunity to see them for the first time, to mark them for the others, until such time as vengeance could be exacted.

And yet, the mysterious beasts did not lunge into view, did not tear into the fourth kin. And even for that one, the scent was fading.

It made no sense.

Dejim Nebrahl slowed his flight, wondering, curious, and not yet in the least suspicious.

From cool relief to growing chill, the night descended among the trudging soldiers, raising a mutter of new complaints. A sleeping child in his arms, Fiddler walked two strides behind Kalam and Quick Ben, while in his wake strode Apsalar, her footfalls the barest of whispers.

Better than scorching sun and heat . . . but not much better. Burnt and blistered skin on shoulders now radiated away all the warmth the flesh could create. Among the worst afflicted, fever awoke like a child lost in the woods, filling shadows with apparitions. Twice in the past hundred paces one of the soldiers had cried out in fear – seeing great moving shapes out in the night. Lumbering, swaggering, with eyes flashing like embers the hue of murky blood. Or so Mayfly had said, surprising everyone with the poetic turn of phrase.

But like the monsters conjured from the imaginations of frightened babes, they never came closer, never quite revealed themselves. Both Mayfly and Galt swore that they had seen . . . something. Moving parallel with the column, but quicker, and soon past. Fevered minds, Fiddler told himself again, that and nothing more.

Yet, he felt in himself a growing unease. As if they did indeed have company along this broken track, out there in the darkness, among the trenches and gullies and jumbled rockfalls. A short time earlier he'd thought he had heard voices, distant and seeming to descend from the night sky, but that had since faded. Nonetheless, his nerves were growing frayed – likely weariness, likely an awakening fever within his own mind.

Ahead, Quick Ben's head suddenly turned, stared out to the right, scanned the darkness.

'Something?' Fiddler asked in a low voice.

The wizard glanced back at him, then away again, and said nothing.

Ten paces later, Fiddler saw Kalam loosen the long-knives in their scabbards.

Shit.

He dropped back until he was alongside Apsalar, and was about to speak when she cut him off.

'Be on your guard, sapper,' she said quietly. 'I believe we have nothing to fear . . . but I cannot be certain.'

'What's out there?' he demanded.

'Part of a bargain.'

'What is that supposed to mean?'

She suddenly lifted her head, as if testing the wind, and her voice hardened as she said in a loud voice, 'Everyone off the road – south side only – *now.*'

At the command, thin fear whispered along the ancient road. Unarmed, unarmoured – this was a soldier's worst nightmare. Crouching down, huddling in the shadows, eyes wide and unblinking, breaths drawing still, the Malazans strained for any telltale sound in the darkness beyond.

Staying low to the ground, Fiddler made his way along to rejoin his squad. If something was coming for them, better he died with his soldiers. As he scrabbled he sensed a presence catching up from behind, and turned to see Corabb Bhilan Thenu'alas. The warrior held a solid, club-like piece of wood, too thick to be a branch, more like a tap-root from some ancient guldindha. 'Where did you find that?' Fiddler demanded in a hiss.

A shrug was the only answer.

Reaching his squad, the sergeant halted and Bottle crawled over to him. 'Demons,' the soldier whispered, 'out there—' a jerk of the head indicated the north side of the road. 'At first I thought it was the pall of evil offshore, the one that flushed the birds from the salt-marshes beyond the bay—'

'The pall of what?' Fiddler asked.

'But it wasn't that. Something a lot closer. Had a rhizan wheeling round out there – it came close to a beast. A damned big beast, Sergeant. Halfway between wolf and bear, only the size of a bull bhederin. It was headed west—'

'You still linked to that rhizan, Bottle?'

'No, it was hungry enough to break loose – I'm not quite recovered, Sergeant—'

'Never mind. It was a good try. So, the bear-wolf or wolf-bhederin was heading west . . .'

'Aye, not fifty paces across from us – no way it didn't know we were here,' Bottle said. 'It's not like we was sneaking along, was it?'

'So it ain't interested in us.'

'Maybe not yet, Sergeant.'

'What do you mean by that?'

'Well, I'd sent a capemoth ahead of us up the road, used it to test the air – they can sense things when those things are moving, stirring the air, giving off heat into the night – that heat is sometimes visible from a long way away, especially the colder the night gets. Capemoths need all that to avoid rhizan, although it doesn't always—'

'Bottle, I ain't no naturalist – what did you see or sense or hear or whatever through that damned capemoth?'

'Well, creatures up ahead, closing fast—'

'Oh, thanks for that minor detail, Bottle! Glad you finally got round to it!'

'Shh, uh, Sergeant. Please. I think we should just lie low – whatever's about to happen's got nothing to do with us.'

Corabb Bhilan Thenu'alas spoke: 'Are you certain of that?'

'Well, no, but it stands to reason—'

'Unless they're all working together, closing a trap—'

'Sergeant,' Bottle said, 'we ain't that important.'

'Maybe you ain't, but we got Kalam and Quick Ben, and Sinn and Apsalar—'

'I don't know much about them, Sergeant,' Bottle said, 'but you might want to warn them what's coming, if they don't know already.'

If Quick hasn't smelled all this out he deserves to get his tiny head ripped off. 'Never mind them.' Twisting round, Fiddler squinted into the darkness south of them. 'Any chance of moving to better cover? This ditch ain't worth a damned thing.'

'Sergeant,' Bottle hissed, his voice tightening, 'we ain't got time.'

Ten paces apart and moving now parallel along the route of the old road, one taking the centre of the track, the flankers in the rough ditches to either side, Dejim Nebrahl glided low to the ground, tipped leathery ears pricked forward, eyes scanning the way ahead.

Something wasn't right. Half a league behind the three the fourth kin limped along, weak with blood-loss and exhausted by fear, and if the hunters remained close, they were now stalking in absolute silence. The kin halted, sinking low, head swivelling as its sharp eyes searched the night. Nothing, no movement beyond the flit of rhizan and capemoths.

The three on the road caught the scent of humans, not far, and savage hunger engulfed all other thoughts. They stank of terror – it would taint their blood when he drank deep, a taste metallic and sour, a flavour Dejim Nebrahl had grown to cherish.

Something lumbered onto the track thirty strides ahead.

Huge, black, familiar.

Deragoth. Impossible – they were gone, swallowed by a nightmare of their own making. This was all wrong.

A sudden howl from far to the south, well behind the fourth kin, who spun, snarling at the sound.

The first three D'ivers spread out, eyes on the lone beast padding towards them. *If but one, then she is doomed—*

The beast surged forward in a charge, voicing a bellowing roar.

Dejim Nebrahl sprinted to meet it.

The flanking D'ivers twisted outward as more huge shapes pounded to close with them, two to each side. Jaws spread wide, lips peeling back, the Deragoth reached Dejim Nebrahl, giving voice to thunder. Massive canines sank down into the kin, slicing through muscle, crushing bone. Limbs snapped, ribs splintered and tore into view through ruptured flesh and hide.

Pain – such pain – the centre D'ivers sprang into the air to meet the charge of the Deragoth ahead. And his right leg was caught in huge jaws, jolting Dejim Nebrahl to a halt in mid-flight. Joints popped even as the leg bones were crunched into shards.

Flung hard to the ground, Dejim sought to spin round, talons lashing out at his attacker's broad head. He tore into one eye and ripped it loose, sending it whirling off into the darkness.

The Deragoth flinched back with a squeal of agony.

Then a second set of jaws closed round the back of the kin's neck. Blood sprayed as the teeth ground and cut inward, crushing cartilage, then bone.

Blood filled Dejim Nebrahl's throat.

No, it cannot end like this—

The other two kin were dying as well, as the Deragoth tore them to pieces.

Far to the west, the lone survivor crouched, trembling.

The Hounds attacked, three appearing in front of the last D'ivers. Moments before they closed, all three twisted away – a feint – which meant—

Wolf jaws ripped into the back of Dejim Nebrahl's neck, and lifted the D'ivers from the ground.

The T'rolbarahl waited for the clenching, the killing, but it never came. Instead, the beast that held it was running fast over the ground, others of its kind to either side. West, and north, then, eventually, swinging southward, out into the wastes.

Untiring, on and on through the cold night.

Helpless in the grip of those jaws, the last D'ivers of Dejim Nebrahl did not struggle, for struggle was pointless. There would be no quick death, for these creatures had some other purpose in mind for him. Unlike the Deragoth, he realized, these Hounds possessed a master.

A master who found reason to keep Dejim Nebrahl alive.

A curious, fraught salvation – *but I still live, and that is enough. I still live.*

The fierce battle was over. Kalam, lying near Quick Ben, narrowed his gaze, just barely making out the huge shapes of the demons as they set off, without a backward glance, westward along the track.

'Looks like their hunt's not yet over,' the assassin muttered, reaching up to wipe the sweat that had been stinging his eyes.

'Gods below,' Quick Ben said in a whisper.

'Did you hear those distant howls?' Kalam asked, sitting up. 'Hounds of Shadow – I'm right, aren't I, Quick? So, we got lizard cats, and giant bear-dogs like the one Toblakai killed in Raraku, and the Hounds . . . wizard, I don't want to walk this road no more.'

'Gods below,' the man at his side whispered again.

Lieutenant Pores's cheerful embrace with the Lady went sour with an ambush of a patrol he'd led inland from the marching army, three days west of Y'Ghatan. Starving bandits, of all things. They'd beaten them off, but he had taken a crossbow quarrel clean through his upper left arm, and a sword-slash just above his right knee, deep enough to sever muscle down to the bone. The healers had mended the damage, sufficient to roughly knit torn flesh and close scar tissue over the wounds, but the pain remained excruciating. He had been convalescing on the back of a crowded wagon, until they came within sight of the north sea and the army encamped, whereupon Captain Kindly had appeared.

Saying nothing, Kindly had clambered into the bed of the wagon, grasped Pores by his good arm, and dragged him from the pallet. Down off the back, the lieutenant nearly buckling under his weak leg, then staggering and stumbling as the captain tugged him along.

Gasping, Pores had asked, 'What's the emergency, Captain? I heard no alarms—'

'Then you ain't been listening,' Kindly replied.

Pores looked round, somewhat wildly, but he could see no-one else rushing about, no general call to arms – the camp was settling down, cookfires lit and figures huddled beneath rain-capes against the chill carried on the sea breeze. 'Captain—'

'My officers don't lie about plucking nose hairs, Lieutenant. There's real injured soldiers in those wagons, and you're just in their way. Healers are done with you. Time to stretch out that bad leg. Time to be a soldier again – stop limping, damn you – you're setting a miserable example here, Lieutenant.'

'Sorry, sir.' Sodden with sweat, Pores struggled to keep up with his captain. 'Might I ask, where are we going?'

'To look at the sea,' Kindly replied. 'Then you're taking charge of the inland pickets, first watch, and I strongly suggest you do a weapons and armour inspection, Lieutenant, since there is the chance that I will take a walk along those posts.'

'Yes, sir.'

Up ahead, on a rise overlooking the grey, white-capped sea, stood the Fourteenth's command. The Adjunct, Nil and Nether, Fists Blistig, Temul and Keneb, and, slightly apart and wrapped in a long leather cloak, T'amber. Just behind them stood Warleader Gall and his ancient aide Imrahl, along with captains Ruthan Gudd and Madan'Tul Rada. The only one missing was Fist Tene Baralta, but Pores had heard that the man was still in a bad way, one-armed and one-eyed, his face ravaged by burning oil, and he didn't have Kindly in charge of him either, which meant he was being left to heal in peace.

Ruthan Gudd was speaking in a low voice, his audience Madan'Tul Rada and the two Khundryl warriors, '. . . just fell into the sea – those breakers, that tumult in the middle of the bay, that's where the citadel stood. A tier of raised land surrounded it – the island itself – and there was a causeway linking it to this shore – nothing left of that but those pillars just topping the sands above the tideline. It's said the shattering of a Jaghut enclave far to the north was responsible—'

'How could that sink this island?' Gall demanded. 'You make no sense, Captain.'

'The T'lan Imass broke the Jaghut sorcery – the ice lost its power, melted into the seas, and the water levels rose. Enough to eat into the island, deluging the tier, then devouring the feet of the citadel itself. In any case, this was thousands of years ago—'

'Are you an historian as well as a soldier?' the Warleader asked, glancing over, his tear-tattooed face bathed red like a mask in the setting sun's lurid light.

The captain shrugged. 'The first map I ever saw of Seven Cities was Falari, a sea-current map marking out the treacherous areas along this coast – and every other coastline, all the way to Nemil. It had been copied countless times, but the original dated from the days when the only metals being traded were tin, copper, lead and gold. Falar's trade with Seven Cities goes back a long way, Warleader Gall. Which makes sense, since Falar is halfway between Quon Tali and Seven Cities.'

Captain Kindly observed, 'It's odd, Ruthan Gudd, you do not look Falari. Nor is your name Falari.'

'I am from the island of Strike, Kindly, which lies against the Outer Reach Deeps. Strike is the most isolated of all the islands in the chain, and our legends hold that we are all that remains of the original inhabitants of Falar – the red- and gold-haired folk you see and think of as Falari were in fact invaders from the eastern ocean, from the other side of Seeker's Deep, or some unknown islands well away from the charted courses across that ocean. They themselves do not even recall their homelands, and most of them believe they have always lived in Falar. But our old maps show different names, Strike names for all the islands and the kingdoms and peoples, and the word "Falar" does not appear among them.'

If the Adjunct and her retinue were speaking, Pores could hear nothing. Ruthan Gudd's words and the stiff wind drowned out all else. The lieutenant's leg throbbed with pain; there was no angle at which he could hold his injured arm comfortably. And now he was chilled, the old sweat like ice against his skin, thinking only of the warm blankets he had left behind.

There were times, he reflected morosely, when he wanted to kill Captain Kindly.

Keneb stared out at the heaving waters of the Kokakal Sea. The Fourteenth had circumvented Sotka and were now thirteen leagues west of the city. He could make out snatches of conversation from the officers behind them, but the wind swept enough words away to make comprehension a chore, and likely not worth the effort. Among the foremost line of officers and mages, no-one had spoken in some time.

Weariness, and, perhaps, the end of this dread, miserable chapter in the history of the Fourteenth.

They had pushed hard on the march, first west and then northward. Somewhere in the seas beyond was the transport fleet and its escort of dromons. Gods, an intercept must be possible, and with that, these battered legions could get off this plague-ridden continent.

To sail away . . . but where?

Back home, he hoped. Quon Tali, at least for a time. To regroup, to take on replacements. To spit out the last grains of sand from this Hood-taken land. He could return to his wife and children, with all the confusion and trepidation such a reunion would entail. There'd been too many mistakes in their lives together, and even those few moments of redemption had been tainted and bitter. *Minala*. His sister-in-law, who had done what so many victims did, hidden away her hurts, finding normality in brutal abuse, and had come to believe the fault lay with her, rather than the madman she had married.

Killing the bastard hadn't been enough, as far as Keneb was concerned. What still needed to be expunged was a deeper, more pervasive rot, the knots and threads all bound in a chaotic web that defined the time at that fell garrison. One life tied to every other by invisible, thrumming threads, unspoken hurts and unanswered expectations, the constant deceits and conceits – it had taken a continent-wide uprising to shatter all of that. *And we are not mended.*

Not so long a reach, to see how the Adjunct and this damned army was bound in the same tangled net, the legacies of betrayal, the hard, almost unbearable truth that some things could not be answered.

Broad-bellied pots crowding market stalls, their flanks a mass of intricately painted yellow butterflies, swarming barely seen figures and all sweeping down the currents of a silt-laden river. Scabbards bearing black feathers. A painted line of dogs along a city wall, each beast linked to the next by a chain of bones. Bazaars selling reliquaries purportedly containing remnants of great heroes of the Seventh Army. Bult, Lull, Chenned and Duiker. And, of course, Coltaine himself.

When one's enemy embraces the heroes of one's own side, one feels strangely . . . cheated, as if the theft of life was but the beginning, and now the legends themselves have been stolen away, transformed in ways beyond control. *But Coltaine belongs to us. How dare you do this?* Such sentiments, sprung free from the dark knot in his soul, made no real sense. Even voicing them felt awkward, absurd. The dead are ever refashioned, for they have no defence against those who would use or abuse them – who they were, what their deeds meant. And this was the anguish . . . this . . . *injustice.*

These new cults with their grisly icons, they did nothing to honour the Chain of Dogs. They were never intended to. Instead, they seemed to Keneb pathetic efforts to force a link with past greatness, with a time and a place of momentous significance. He had no doubt that the Last Siege of Y'Ghatan would soon acquire similar mythical status, and he hated the thought, wanted to be as far away from the land birthing and nurturing such blasphemies as was possible.

Blistig was speaking now: 'These are ugly waters to anchor a fleet, Adjunct, perhaps we could move on a few leagues—'

'No,' she said.

Blistig glanced at Keneb.

'The weather shall turn,' Nil said.

A child with lines on his face. This is the true legacy of the Chain of Dogs. Lines on his face, and hands stained red.

And Temul, the young Wickan commanding resentful, embittered elders who still dreamed of vengeance against the slayers of Coltaine. He rode Duiker's horse, a lean mare with eyes that Keneb could have sworn were filled with sorrow. Temul carried scrolls, presumably containing the historian's own writings, although he would not show them to anyone. This warrior of so few years, carrying the burden of memory, carrying the last months of life in an old man once soldier among the Old Guard who had, inexplicably, somehow touched this Wickan youth. That alone, Keneb suspected, was a worthy story, but it would remain forever untold, for Temul alone understood it, holding within himself each and every detail, and Temul was not one to explain, not a teller of stories. *No, he just lives them. And this is what those cultists yearn for, for themselves, and what they will never truly possess.*

Keneb could hear nothing of the huge encampment behind him. Yet one tent in particular within that makeshift city dominated his mind. The man within it had not spoken in days. His lone eye seemingly stared at nothing. What remained of Tene Baralta had been healed, at least insofar as flesh and bone was concerned. The man's spirit was, alas, another matter. The Red Blade's homeland had not been kind to him. Keneb wondered if the man was as eager to leave Seven Cities as he was.

Nether said, 'The plague is growing more virulent. The Grey Goddess hunts us.'

The Adjunct's head turned at that.

Blistig cursed, then said, 'Since when is Poliel eager to side with some damned rebels – she's already killed most of them, hasn't she?'

'I do not understand this need,' Nether replied, shaking her head. 'But it seems she has set her deathly eyes upon Malazans. She hunts us, and comes ever closer.'

Keneb closed his eyes. *Haven't we been hurt enough?*

They came upon the dead horse shortly after dawn. Amidst the swarm of capemoths feeding on the carcass were two skeletal lizards, standing on their hind legs, heads ducking and darting as they crunched and flayed the bird-sized insects.

'Hood's breath,' Lostara muttered, 'what are those?'

'Telorast and Curdle,' Apsalar replied. 'Ghosts bound to those small frames. They have been my companions for some time now.'

Kalam moved closer and crouched beside the horse. 'Those lizard cats,' he said. 'Came in from all sides.' He straightened, scanning the rocks. 'I can't imagine Masan Gilani surviving the ambush.'

'You'd be wrong,' said a voice from the slope to their right.

The soldier sat on the crest, legs sprawled down the slope. One of those legs was crimson from upper thigh to the cracked leather boot. Masan Gilani's dark skin was ashen, her eyes dull. 'Can't stop the bleeding, but I got one of the bastards and wounded another. Then the Hounds came . . .'

Captain Faradan Sort turned to the column. 'Deadsmell! Up front, quick!'

'Thank you for the knife,' Masan Gilani said to Apsalar.

'Keep it,' the Kanese woman said.

'Sorry about your horse.'

'So am I, but you are not to blame.'

Kalam said, 'Well, it seems we're in for a long walk after all.'

Bottle made his way to the front of the column in Deadsmell's wake, close enough to look long and hard at the two bird-like reptile skeletons perched on the horse carcass and intent on killing capemoths. He watched their darting movements, the flicking of their bony tails, the way the darkness of their souls bled out like smoke from a cracked water-pipe.

Someone came to his side and he glanced over. Fiddler, the man's blue eyes fixed on the undead creatures. 'What do you see, Bottle?'

'Sergeant?'

Fiddler took him by the arm and pulled him off to one side. 'Out with it.'

'Ghosts, possessing those bound-up bones.'

The sergeant nodded. 'Apsalar said as much. Now, what kind of ghosts?'

Frowning, Bottle hesitated.

Fiddler hissed a curse. 'Bottle.'

'Well, I was assuming she knows, only has her reasons for not mentioning it, so I was thinking, it wouldn't be polite—'

'Soldier—'

'I mean, she was a squad-mate of yours, and—'

'A squad-mate who just happened to have been possessed herself, by the Rope, almost all the time that I knew her. So if she's not talking, it's no surprise. Tell me, Bottle, what manner of flesh did those souls call home?'

'Are you saying you don't trust her?'

'I don't even trust you.'

Frowning, Bottle looked away, watched Deadsmell working on Masan Gilani on the slope, sensed the whisper of Denul sorcery . . . and something like Hood's own breath. *The bastard is a necromancer, damn him!*

'Bottle.'

'Sergeant? Oh, sorry. I was just wondering.'

'Wondering what?'

'Well, why Apsalar has two dragons in tow.'

'They're not dragons. They're tiny lizards—'

'No, Sergeant, they're dragons.'

Slowly, Fiddler's eyes widened.

Bottle'd known he wouldn't like it.

CHAPTER FOURTEEN

There is something profoundly cynical, my friends, in the notion of paradise after death. The lure is evasion. The promise is excusative. One need not accept responsibility for the world as it is, and by extension, one need do nothing about it. To strive for change, for true goodness in this mortal world, one must acknowledge and accept, within one's own soul, that this mortal reality has purpose in itself, that its greatest value is not for us, but for our children and their children. To view life as but a quick passage along a foul, tortured path – made foul and tortured by our own indifference – is to excuse all manner of misery and depravity, and to exact cruel punishment upon the innocent lives to come.

I defy this notion of paradise beyond the gates of bone. If the soul truly survives the passage, then it behooves us – each of us, my friends – to nurture a faith in similitude: what awaits us is a reflection of what we leave behind, and in the squandering of our mortal existence, we surrender the opportunity to learn the ways of goodness, the practice of sympathy, empathy, compassion and healing – all passed by in our rush to arrive at a place of glory and beauty, a place we did not earn, and most certainly do not deserve.

The Apocryphal Teachings of Tanno Spiritwalker Kimloc
The Decade in Ehrlitan

CHAUR HELD OUT THE BABY AS IF TO BEGIN BOUNCING IT ON ONE knee, but Barathol reached out to rest a hand on the huge man's wrist. The blacksmith shook his head. 'Not old enough for that yet. Hold her close, Chaur, so as not to break anything.'

The man answered with a broad smile and resumed cuddling and rocking the swaddled infant.

Barathol Mekhar leaned back in his chair, stretching out his legs, and briefly closed his eyes, making a point of not listening to the argument in the side room where the woman, Scillara, resisted the combined efforts of L'oric, Nulliss, Filiad and Urdan, all of whom insisted she accept the baby, as was a mother's responsibility, a mother's duty and a host of other guilt-laden terms they flung at her like stones. Barathol could not recall the last time the villagers in question had displayed such vehement zeal over anything. Of course, in this instance, their virtue came easy, for it cost them nothing.

The blacksmith admitted to a certain admiration for the woman. Children were indeed burdensome, and as this one was clearly not the creation of love, Scillara's lack of attachment seemed wholly reasonable. On the opposite side, the ferocity of his fellow townsfolk was leaving him disgusted and vaguely nauseous.

Hayrith appeared in the main room, moments earlier a silent witness to the tirade in the side chamber where they'd set Scillara's cot. The old woman shook her head. 'Idiots. Pompous, prattling twits! Just listen to all that piety, Barathol! You'd think this babe was the Emperor reborn!'

'Gods forbid,' the blacksmith muttered.

'Jessa last house on the east road, she's got that year-old runt with the withered legs that ain't gonna make it. She'd not refuse the gift, and everyone here knows it.'

Barathol nodded, somewhat haphazardly, his mind on other matters.

'There's even Jessa second floor of the old factor house, though she ain't had any milk t'give in fifteen years. Still, she'd be a good mother and this village could use a wailing child to help drown out all the wailing grown-ups. Get the Jessas together on this and it'll be fine.'

'It's L'oric,' Barathol said.

'What's that?'

'L'oric. He's so proper he burns to the touch. Or, rather, he burns everything he touches.'

'Well, it ain't his business, is it?'

'People like him make everything their business, Hayrith.'

The woman dragged a chair close and sat down across from the blacksmith. She studied him with narrowed eyes. 'How long you going to wait?' she asked.

'As soon as the lad, Cutter, is able to travel,' Barathol said. He rubbed at his face. 'Thank the gods all that rum's drunk. I'd forgotten what it does to a man's gut.'

'It was L'oric, wasn't it?'

He raised his brows.

'Him showing up here didn't just burn you – it left you scorched, Barathol. Seems you did some bad things in the past' – she snorted – 'as if that makes you different from all the rest of us. But you figured you could hide out here for ever, and now you know that ain't going to be. Unless, of course,' her eyes narrowed to slits, 'you kill L'oric.'

The blacksmith glanced over at Chaur, who was making faces and cooing sounds down at the baby, while it in turn seemed to be blowing bubbles, as yet blissfully unaware of the sheer ugliness of the monstrous face hovering over it. Barathol sighed. 'I'm not interested in killing anyone, Hayrith.'

'So you're going with these people here?'

'As far as the coast, yes.'

'Once L'oric gets word out, they'll start hunting you again. You reach the coast, Barathol, you find the first ship off this damned continent, is what you do. 'Course, I'll miss you – the only man with more than half a brain in this whole town. But Hood knows, nothing ever lasts.'

They both looked over as L'oric appeared. The High Mage's colour was up, his expression one of baffled disbelief. 'I just don't understand it,' he said.

Barathol grunted. 'It's not for you to understand.'

'This is what civilization has come to,' the man said, crossing his arms and glaring at the blacksmith.

'You got that right.' Barathol drew his legs in and stood. 'I don't recall Scillara inviting you into her life.'

'My concern is with the child.'

The blacksmith began walking towards the side chamber. 'No it isn't. Your obsession is with propriety. Your version of it, to which everyone else must bend a knee. Only, Scillara's not impressed. She's too smart to be impressed.'

Entering the room, Barathol grasped Nulliss by the scruff of her tunic. 'You,' he said in a growl, 'and the rest of you, get out.' He guided the spitting, cursing Semk woman out through the doorway, then stood to one side watching the others crowd up in their eagerness to escape.

A moment later, Barathol and Scillara were alone. The blacksmith faced her. 'How is the wound?'

She scowled. 'The one that's turned my arm into a withered stick or the one that'll make me walk like a crab for the rest of my life?'

'The shoulder. I doubt the crab-walk is permanent.'

'And how would you know?'

He shrugged. 'Every woman in this hamlet has dropped a babe or three, and they walk just fine.'

She eyed him with suspicion. 'You're the one called Barathol. The blacksmith.'

'Yes.'

'The mayor of this pit you call a hamlet.'

'Mayor? I don't think we warrant a mayor. No, I'm just the biggest and meanest man living here, which to most minds counts for far too much.'

'L'oric says you betrayed Aren. That you're responsible for the death of thousands, when the T'lan Imass came to crush the rebellion.'

'We all have our bad days, Scillara.'

She laughed. A rather nasty laugh. 'Well, thank you for driving those fools away. Unless you plan on picking up where they left off.'

He shook his head. 'I have some questions about your friends, the ones you were travelling with. The T'lan Imass ambushed you with the aim, it seems, of stealing the young woman named Felisin Younger.'

'L'oric said as much,' Scillara replied, sitting up straighter in the bed and wincing with the effort. 'She wasn't important to anybody. It doesn't make sense. I think they came to kill Heboric more than steal her.'

'She was the adopted daughter of Sha'ik.'

The woman shrugged, winced again. 'A lot of foundlings in Raraku were.'

'The one named Cutter, where is he from again?'

'Darujhistan.'

'Is that where all of you were headed?'

Scillara closed her eyes. 'It doesn't matter now, does it? Tell me, have you buried Heboric?'

'Yes, he was Malazan, wasn't he? Besides, out here we've a problem with wild dogs, wolves and the like.'

'Might as well dig him up, Barathol. I don't think Cutter will settle for leaving him here.'

'Why not?'

Her only answer was a shake of her head.

Barathol turned back to the doorway. 'Sleep well, Scillara. Like it or not, you're the only one here who can feed your little girl. Unless we can convince Jessa last house on the east road. At all events, she'll be hungry soon enough.'

'Hungry,' the woman muttered behind him. 'Like a cat with worms.'

In the main room the High Mage had taken the babe from Chaur's arms. The huge simpleton sat with tears streaming down his pocked face, this detail unnoticed by L'oric as he paced with the fidgeting infant in his arms.

'A question,' Barathol said to L'oric, 'how old do they have to get before you lose all sympathy for them?'

The High Mage frowned. 'What do you mean?'

489

Ignoring him, the blacksmith walked over to Chaur. 'You and me,' he said, 'we have a corpse to dig up. More shovelling, Chaur, you like that.'

Chaur nodded and managed a half-smile through his tears and runny nose.

Outside, Barathol led the man to the smithy where they collected a pick and a shovel, then they set off for the stony plain west of the hamlet. There'd been an unseasonal spatter of rain the night before, but little evidence of that remained after a morning of fiercely hot sunlight. The grave was beside a half-filled pit containing the remnants of the horses after Urdan had finished butchering them. He had been told to burn those remains but had clearly forgotten. Wolves, coyotes and vultures had all found the bones and viscera, and the pit now swarmed with flies and maggots. Twenty paces further west, the now bloated, shapeless carcass of the toad demon lay untouched by any scavenger.

As Chaur bent to the task of disinterring Heboric's wrapped corpse, Barathol stared across at that demon's misshapen body. The now-stretched hide was creased with white lines, as if it had begun cracking. From this distance Barathol could not be certain, but it seemed there was a black stain ringing the ground beneath the carcass, as if something had leaked out.

'I'll be right back, Chaur.'

The man smiled.

As the blacksmith drew closer, his frown deepened. The black stain was dead flies, in their thousands. As unpalatable, then, this demon as the handless man had been. His steps slowed, then halted, still five paces from the grisly form. He'd seen it move – there, again, something pushing up against the blistered hide from within.

And then a voice spoke in Barathol's head.

'Impatience. Please, be so kind, a blade slicing with utmost caution, this infernal hide.'

The blacksmith unsheathed his knife and stepped forward. Reaching the demon's side, he crouched down and ran the finely honed edge along one of the cracks in the thick, leathery skin. It parted suddenly and Barathol leapt back, cursing, as a gush of yellow liquid spurted from the cut.

Something like a hand, then forearm and elbow pushed through, widening the slice, and moments later the entire beast slithered into view, four eyes blinking in the bright light. Where the carcass had had two limbs missing, there were now new ones, smaller and paler, but clearly functional. *'Hunger. Have you food, stranger? Are you food?'*

Sheathing his knife, Barathol turned about and walked back to where Chaur was dragging free Heboric's body. He heard the demon following.

The blacksmith reached the pick he had left beside the grave pit and collected the tool, turning and hefting it in his hands. 'Something tells me,' he said to the demon, 'you're not likely to grow a new brain once I drive this pick through your skull.'

'*Exaggeration. I quake with terror, stranger. Amused. Greyfrog was but joking, encouraged by your expression of terror.*'

'Not terror. Disgust.'

The demon's bizarre eyes swivelled in their sockets and the head twitched to look past Barathol. '*My brother has come. He is there, I sense him.*'

'You'd better hurry,' Barathol said. 'He's about to adopt a new familiar.' The blacksmith lowered the pick and glanced over at Chaur.

The huge man stood over the wrapped corpse of Heboric, staring with wide eyes at the demon.

'It's all right, Chaur,' said Barathol. 'Now, let's carry the dead man to the tailings heap back of the smithy.'

Smiling again, the huge man picked up Heboric's body. The stench of decaying flesh reached Barathol.

Shrugging, the blacksmith collected the shovel.

Greyfrog set off in a loping gait towards the hamlet's main street.

Dozing, Scillara's eyes snapped open as an exultant voice filled her mind. '*Joy! Dearest Scillara, time of vigil is at an end! Stalwart and brave Greyfrog has defended your sanctity, and the brood even now squirms in Brother L'oric's arms!*'

'Greyfrog? But they said you were dead! What are you doing talking to me? You never talk to me!'

'*Female with brood must be sheathed with silence. All slivers and darts of irritation fended off by noble Greyfrog. And now, happily, I am free to infuse your sweet self with my undying love!*'

'Gods below, is this what the others had to put up with?' She reached for her pipe and pouch of rustleaf.

A moment later the demon squeezed through the doorway, followed by L'oric, who held in his arms the babe.

Scowling, Scillara struck spark to her pipe.

'The child is hungry,' L'oric said.

'Fine. Maybe that will ease the pressure and stop this damned leaking. Go on, give me the little leech.'

The High Mage came closer and handed the infant over. 'You must acknowledge that this girl belongs to you, Scillara.'

'Oh she's mine all right. I can tell by the greedy look in her eyes. For the sake of the world, you should pray, L'oric, that all she has of her father is the blue skin.'

'You know, then, who that man was?'

'Korbolo Dom.'

'Ah. He is, I believe, still alive. A guest of the Empress.'

'Do you think I care, L'oric? I was drowning in durhang. If not for Heboric, I'd still be one of Bidithal's butchered acolytes. Heboric . . .' She looked down at the babe suckling from her left breast, squinting through the smoke of the pipe. Then she glared up at L'oric. 'And now some damned T'lan Imass have killed him – why?'

'He was a servant of Treach. Scillara, there is war now among the gods. And it is us mortals who shall pay the price for that. It is a dangerous time to be a true worshipper – of anyone or anything. Except, perhaps, chaos itself, for if one force is ascendant in this modern age, it is surely that.'

Greyfrog was busy licking itself, concentrating, it seemed, on its new limbs. The entire demon looked . . . smaller.

Scillara said, 'So you're reunited with your familiar, L'oric. Which means you can go now, off to wherever and whatever it is you have to do. You can leave, and get as far away from here as possible. I'll wait for Cutter to wake up. I like him. I think I'll go where he goes. This grand quest is done. So go away.'

'Not until I am satisfied that you will not surrender your child to an unknown future, Scillara.'

'It's not unknown. Or at least, no more unknown than any future. There are two women here both named Jessa and they'll take care of it. They'll raise it well enough, since they seem to like that sort of thing. Good for them, I say. Besides, I'm being generous here – I'm not selling it, am I? No, like a damned fool, I'm *giving* the thing away.'

'The longer and the more often you hold that girl,' L'oric said, 'the less likely it is that you will do what you presently plan to do. Motherhood is a spiritual state – you will come to that realization before too long.'

'That's good, so why are you still here? Clearly, I'm already doomed to enslavement, no matter how much I rail.'

'Spiritual epiphany is not enslavement.'

'Shows how much you know, High Mage.'

'I feel obliged to tell you, your words have crushed Greyfrog.'

'He'll survive it – he seems able to survive everything else. Well, I'm about to switch tits here, you two eager to watch?'

L'oric spun on his heel and left.

Greyfrog's large eyes blinked translucently up at Scillara. '*I am not crushed. Brother of mine misapprehends. Broods climb free and must fend, each runtling holds to its own life. Recollection. Many dangers. Transitional thought. Sorrow. I must now accompany my poor brother,*

492

for he is well and truly distressed by many things in this world. Warmth. I shall harbour well my adoration of you, for it is a pure thing by virtue of being ever unattainable, the consummation thereof. Which would, you must admit, be awkward indeed.'

'Awkward isn't the first word that comes to my mind, Greyfrog. But thank you for the sentiment, as sick and twisted as it happens to be. Listen, try and teach L'oric, will you? Just a few things, like, maybe, humility. And all that terrible certainty – beat it down, beat it out of him. It's making him obnoxious.'

'Paternal legacy, alas. L'oric's own parents . . . ah, never mind. Farewell, Scillara. Delicious fantasies, slow and exquisitely unveiled in the dark swampy waters of my imagination. All that need sustain me in fecund spirit.'

The demon waddled out.

Hard gums clamped onto her right nipple. *Pain and pleasure, gods what a miserable, confusing alliance.* Well, at least all the lopsidedness would go away – Nulliss had been planting the babe on her left ever since it had come out. She felt like a badly packed mule.

More voices in the outer room, but she didn't bother listening.

They'd taken Felisin Younger. That was the cruellest thing of all. For Heboric, at least, there was now some peace, an end to whatever had tormented him, and besides, he'd been an old man. Enough had been asked of him. But Felisin . . .

Scillara stared down at the creature on her chest, its tiny grasping hands, then she settled her head against the back wall and began repacking her pipe.

Something formless filling his mind, what had been timeless and only in the last instants, in the drawing of a few breaths, did awareness arrive, carrying him from one moment to the next. Whereupon Cutter opened his eyes. Old grey tree-trunks spanned the ceiling overhead, the joins thick with cobwebs snarled around the carcasses of moths and flies. Two lanterns hung from hooks, their wicks low. He struggled to recall how he had ended up here, in this unfamiliar room.

Darujhistan . . . a bouncing coin. Assassins . . .

No, that was long ago. *Tremorlor, the Azath House, and Moby . . . that god-possessed girl – Apsalar, oh, my love . . .* Hard words exchanged with Cotillion, the god who had, once, looked through her eyes. He was in Seven Cities; he had been travelling with Heboric Ghost Hands, and Felisin Younger, Scillara, and the demon Greyfrog. He had become a man with knives, a killer, *given the chance.*

Flies . . .

Cutter groaned, one hand reaching tentatively for his belly beneath

the ragged blankets. The slash was naught but a thin seam. He had seen
. . . his insides spilling out. Had felt the sudden absence of weight, the
tug that pulled him down to the ground. Cold, so very cold.

The others were dead. They had to be. Then again, Cutter realized,
he too should be dead. They'd cut him wide open. He slowly turned his
head, studying the narrow room he found himself in. A storage
chamber of some kind, a larder, perhaps. The shelves were mostly
empty. He was alone.

The motion left him exhausted – he did not have the strength to draw
his arm back from where it rested on his midsection.

He closed his eyes.

A dozen slow, even breaths, and he found himself standing, in some
other place. A courtyard garden, unkempt and now withered, as if by
years of drought. The sky overhead was white, featureless. A stone-
walled pool was before him, the water smooth and unstirred. The air
was close and unbearably hot.

Cutter willed himself forward, but found he could not move. He
stood as if rooted to the ground.

To his left, plants began crackling, curling black as a ragged hole
formed in the air. A moment later two figures stumbled through that
gate. A woman, then a man. The gate snapped shut in their wake, leaving only a swirl of ash and a ring of scorched plants.

Cutter tried to speak, but he had no voice, and after a few moments
it was clear that they could not see him. He was as a ghost, an unseen
witness.

The woman was as tall as the man, a Malazan which he was certainly
not. Handsome in a hard, unyielding way. She slowly straightened.

Another woman now sat on the edge of the pool. Fair-skinned,
delicately featured, her long golden-hued hair drawn up and bound in
an elaborate mass of braids. One hand was immersed in the pool, yet
no ripples spanned outward. She was studying the water's surface, and
did not look up as the Malazan woman spoke.

'Now what?'

The man, two vicious-looking flails tucked in his belt, had the look
of a desert warrior, his face dark and flat, the eyes slitted amidst
webs of squint-lines. He was armoured as if for battle. At his
companion's question he fixed his gaze on the seated woman and said,
'You were never clear on that, Queen of Dreams. The only part of this
bargain I'm uneasy about.'

'Too late for regrets,' the seated woman murmured.

Cutter stared at her anew. The Queen of Dreams. A goddess. It
seemed that she too had no inkling that Cutter was somehow present,
witnessing this scene. But this was her realm. How could that be?

The man had scowled at the Queen's mocking observation. 'You seek my service. To do what? I am done leading armies, done with prophecies. Give me a task if you must, but make it straightforward. Someone to kill, someone to protect – no, not the latter – I am done with that, too.'

'It is your . . . scepticism . . . I most value, Leoman of the Flails. I admit, however, to some disappointment. Your companion is not the one I anticipated.'

The man named Leoman glanced over at the Malazan woman, but said nothing. Then, slowly, his eyes widened and he looked back at the goddess. 'Corabb?'

'Chosen by Oponn,' the Queen of Dreams said. 'Beloved of the Lady. His presence would have been useful . . .' A faint frown, then a sigh, and still she would not look up as she said, 'In his stead, I must countenance a mortal upon whom yet another god has cast an eye. To what end, I wonder? Will this god finally use her? In the manner that all gods do?' She frowned, then said, 'I do not refute this . . . alliance. I trust Hood understands this well enough. Even so, I see something unexpected stirring . . . in the depths of these waters. Dunsparrow, did you know you were marked? No, I gather you did not – you were but newborn when sanctified, after all. And then stolen away, from the temple, by your brother. Hood never forgave him for that, and took in the end a most satisfying vengeance, ever turning away a healer's touch when nothing else was needed, when that touch could have changed the world, could have shattered an age-old curse.' She paused for a moment, still staring down into the pool. 'I believe Hood now regrets his decision – his lack of humility stings him yet again. Dunsparrow, with you, I suspect, he may seek restitution . . .'

The Malazan woman was pale. 'I had heard of my brother's death,' she said in a low voice. 'But all death comes by Hood's hand. I see no need for restitution in this.'

'By Hood's hand. True enough, and so too Hood chooses the time and the manner. Only on the rarest of occasions, however, does he manifestly intervene in a single mortal's death. Consider his usual . . . involvement . . . as little more than withered fingers ensuring the seamless weave of life's fabric, at least until the arrival of the knot.'

Leoman spoke: 'Ponder the delicacies of dogma some other time, you two, I already grow weary of this place. Send us somewhere, Queen, but first tell us what services you require.'

She finally looked up, studied the desert warrior in silence for a half-dozen heartbeats, then said, 'For now, I require from you . . . nothing.'

There was silence then, and Cutter eventually realized that the two mortals were not moving. Not even the rise and fall of breath was visible. *Frozen in place . . . just like me.*

The Queen of Dreams slowly turned her head, met Cutter's eyes, and smiled.

Sudden, spinning retreat – he awoke with a start, beneath threadbare blankets and a cross-beamed ceiling layered in the carcasses of sucked-dry insects. Yet that smile lingered, racing like scalded blood through him. She had known, of course she had known, had brought him there, to that moment, to witness. But why? Leoman of the Flails . . . the renegade commander from Sha'ik's army, the one who had been pursued by the Adjunct Tavore's army. *Clearly he found a way to escape, but at a price. Maybe that was the lesson – never bargain with gods.*

A faint sound reached him. The wail of a babe, insistent, demanding.

Then a closer noise, scuffling, and Cutter twisted his head round to see the curtain covering the doorway drawn back and a young, un-familiar face staring in at him. The face quickly withdrew. Voices, heavy footsteps, then the curtain was thrown aside. A huge, midnight-skinned man strode in.

Cutter stared at him. He looked . . . familiar, yet he knew he'd never before met this man.

'Scillara is asking after you,' the stranger said.

'That child I'm hearing – hers?'

'Yes, for the moment. How do you feel?'

'Weak, but not as weak as before. Hungry, thirsty. Who are you?'

'The local blacksmith. Barathol Mekhar.'

Mekhar? 'Kalam . . .'

A grimace. 'Cousin, distant. Mekhar refers to the tribe – it's gone now, slaughtered by Falah'd Enezgura of Aren, during one of his west-ward conquests. Most of us survivors scattered far and wide.' He shrugged, eyeing Cutter. 'I'll get you food and drink. If a Semk witch comes in here and tries to enlist you in her cause, tell her to get out.'

'Cause? What cause?'

'Your friend Scillara wants to leave the child here.'

'Oh.'

'Does that surprise you?'

He considered. 'No, not really. She wasn't herself back then, from what I understood. Back in Raraku. I expect she wants to leave all reminders far behind her.'

Barathol snorted and turned back to the doorway. 'What is it with all these refugees from Raraku, anyway? I'll be back shortly, Cutter.'

Mekhar. The Daru managed a smile. This one here looked big enough to pick up Kalam and fling him across a room. And, if Cutter had read the man's expression aright, in that single unguarded moment when he'd said Kalam's name, this Barathol was likely inclined to do just that, given the chance.

Thank the gods I have no brothers or sisters . . . or cousins, for that matter.

His smile suddenly faded. The blacksmith had mentioned Scillara, but no-one else. Cutter suspected it hadn't been an oversight. Barathol didn't seem the type who was careless with his words. *Beru fend . . .*

L'oric stepped outside. His gaze worked its way down the squalid street, building to building, the decrepit remnants of what had once been a thriving community. Intent on its own destruction, even then, though no doubt few thought that way at the time. The forest must have seemed endless, or at least immortal, and so they had harvested with frenzied abandon. But now the trees were gone, and all those hoarded coins of profit had slipped away, leaving hands filled with nothing but sand. Most of the looters would have moved on, sought out some other stand of ancient trees, to persist in the addiction of momentary gain. *Making one desert after another . . . until the deserts meet.*

He rubbed at his face, felt the grit of his stay here, raw as crushed glass on his cheeks. There were some rewards, at least, he told himself. A child was born. Greyfrog was at his side once more, and he had succeeded in saving Cutter's life. *And Barathol Mekhar, a name riding ten thousand curses . . .* well, Barathol was nothing like L'oric had imagined him to be, given his crimes. Men like Korbolo Dom better fit his notions of a betrayer, or the twisted madness of someone like Bidithal. And yet Barathol, an officer in the Red Blades, had murdered the Fist of Aren. He'd been arrested and gaoled, stripped of his rank and beaten without mercy by his fellow Red Blades – the first and deepest stain upon their honour, fuelling their extreme acts of zealotry ever since.

Barathol was to have been crucified on Aren Way. Instead, the city had risen in rebellion, slaughtering the Malazan garrison and driving the Red Blades from the city.

And then the T'lan Imass had arrived, delivering the harsh, brutal lesson of imperial vengeance. And Barathol Mekhar had been seen, by scores of witnesses, flinging open the north gate . . .

But it is true. T'lan Imass need no opened gates . . .

The question no-one had asked was: why would an officer of the Red Blades murder the city's Fist?

L'oric suspected Barathol was not one to give him the satisfaction of an answer. The man was well past defending himself, with words at any rate. The High Mage could see as much in the huge man's dark eyes –

he had long ago given up on humanity. And his own sense of his place in it. He was not driven to justify what he did; no sense of decency nor honour compelled the man to state his case. Only a soul that has surrendered utterly gives up on notions of redemption. Something had happened, once, that crushed Barathol's faith, leaving unbarred the paths of betrayal.

Yet these local folk came close to outright worship in their regard for Barathol Mehkar, and it was this that L'oric could not understand. Even now, when they knew the truth, when they knew what their blacksmith had done years ago, they defied the High Mage's expectations. He was baffled, left feeling strangely helpless.

Then again, admit it, L'oric, you have never been able to gather followers, no matter how noble your cause. Oh, there were allies here, adding their voices to his own outrage at Scillara's appalling indifference regarding her child, but he knew well enough that such unity was, in the end, transitory and ephemeral. They might all decry Scillara's position, but they would do nothing about it; indeed, all but Nulliss had already come to accept the fact that the child was going to be passed into the hands of two women both named Jessa. *There, problem solved. But in truth it is nothing but a crime accommodated.*

The demon Greyfrog ambled to his side and settled belly-down in the dust of the street. Four eyes blinking lazily, it offered nothing of its thoughts, yet an ineffable whisper of commiseration calmed L'oric's inner tumult.

The High Mage sighed. 'I know, my friend. If I could but learn to simply pass through a place, to be wilfully unmindful of all offences against nature, both small and large. This comes, I suspect, of successive failures. In Raraku, in Kurald Liosan, with Felisin Younger, gods below, what a depressing list. And you, Greyfrog, I failed you as well . . .'

'*Modest relevance,*' the demon said. '*I would tell you a tale, brother. Early in the clan's history, many centuries past, there arose, like a breath of gas from the deep, a new cult. Chosen as its representative god was the most remote, most distant of gods among the pantheon. A god that was, in truth, indifferent to the clans of my kind. A god that spoke naught to any mortal, that intervened never in mortal affairs. Morbid. The leaders of the cult proclaimed themselves the voice of that god. They wrote down laws, prohibitions, ascribances, propitiations, blasphemies, punishments for nonconformity, for dispute and derivations. This was but rumour, said details maintained in vague fugue, until such time as the cult achieved domination and with domination, absolute power.*

'*Terrible enforcement, terrible crimes committed in the name of the silent god. Leaders came and went, each further twisting words already twisted by mundane ambition and the zeal for unity. Entire pools were poisoned. Others drained and the silts seeded with salt. Eggs were crushed. Mothers dismembered. And our people were plunged into a paradise of fear, the laws made manifest and spilled blood the tears of necessity. False regret with chilling gleam in the centre eye. No relief awaited, and each generation suffered more than the last.'*

L'oric studied the demon at his side. 'What happened?'

'Seven great warriors from seven clans set out to find the Silent God, set out to see for themselves if this god had indeed blessed all that had come to pass in its name.'

'And did they find the silent god?'

'Yes, and too, they found the reason for its silence. The god was dead. It had died with the first drop of blood spilled in its name.'

'I see, and what is the relevance of this tale of yours, however modest?'

'Perhaps this. The existence of many gods conveys true complexity of mortal life. Conversely, the assertion of but one god leads to a denial of complexity, and encourages the need to make the world simple. Not the fault of the god, but a crime committed by its believers.'

'If a god does not like what is done in its name, then it should act.'

'Yet, if each crime committed in its name weakens it . . . very soon, I think, it has no power left and so cannot act, and so, ultimately, it dies.'

'You come from a strange world, Greyfrog.'

'Yes.'

'I find your story most disturbing.'

'Yes.'

'We must undertake a long journey now, Greyfrog.'

'I am ready, brother.'

'In the world I know,' L'oric said, 'many gods feed on blood.'

'As do many mortals.'

The High Mage nodded. 'Have you said your goodbyes, Greyfrog?'

'I have.'

'Then let us leave this place.'

Filiad appeared at the entrance to the smithy, catching Barathol's attention. The blacksmith gave two more pumps of the bellows feeding the forge, then drew off his thick leather gloves and waved the youth over.

'The High Mage,' Filiad said, 'he's left. With that giant toad. I saw it, a hole opening in the air. Blinding yellow light poured from it, and they just disappeared inside it and then the hole was gone!'

Barathol rummaged through a collection of black iron bars until he found one that looked right for the task he had in mind. He set it on the anvil. 'Did he leave behind his horse?'

'What? No, he led it by the reins.'

'Too bad.'

'What do we do now?' Filiad asked.

'About what?'

'Well, everything, I guess.'

'Go home, Filiad.'

'Really? Oh. All right. I guess. See you later, then.'

'No doubt,' Barathol said, drawing on the gloves once more.

After Filiad left, the blacksmith took up the iron bar with a set of tongs and thrust the metal into the forge, pumping one-legged on the floor-bellows. Four months back, he had used the last of his stolen hoard of Aren coins on a huge shipment of charcoal; there was just enough left for this final task.

T'lan Imass. Nothing but bone and leathery skin. Fast and deadly, masters of ambush. Barathol had been thinking for days now about the problem they represented, about devising a means of dealing with them. For he suspected he'd meet the bastards again.

His axe was heavy enough to do damage, if he hit hard enough. Still, those stone swords were long, tapered to a point for thrusting. If they stayed outside his reach . . .

To all of that, he thought he had found a solution.

He pumped some more, until he was satisfied with the white-hot core in the heart of the forge, and watched as the bar of iron acquired a cherubic gleam.

'We now follow the snake, which takes us to a gather camp on the shores of a black grain lake, beyond which we traverse flat-rock for two days, to another gather camp, the northernmost one, for all that lies beyond it is both flowing and unfound.'

Samar Dev studied the elongated, sinuous line of boulders on the ledge of bedrock below and to their left. Skins of grey and green lichen, clumps of skeletal dusty green moss, studded with red flowers, surrounding each stone, and beyond that the deeper verdancy of another kind of moss, soft and sodden. On the path they walked the bedrock was scoured clean, the granite pink and raw, with layers falling away from edges in large, flat plates. Here and there, black lichen the texture of sharkskin spilled out from fissures and veins. She saw a deer antler lying discarded from some past rutting season, the tips of its tines gnawed by rodents, and was reminded how, in the natural world, nothing goes to waste.

Dips in the high ground held stands of black spruce, as many dead as living, while in more exposed sections of the bedrock low-lying juniper formed knee-high islands spreading branches over the stone, each island bordered by shrubs of blueberry and wintergreen. Jackpines stood as lone sentinels atop rises in the strangely folded, amorphous rock.

Harsh and forbidding, this was a landscape that would never yield to human domination. It felt ancient in ways not matched by any place Samar Dev had seen before, not even by the wastelands of the Jhag Odhan. It was said that beneath every manner of surface on this world, whether sand or sea, floodplain or forest, there was solid rock, twisted and folded by unseen pressures. But here, all other possible surfaces had been scoured away, exposing the veined muscle itself.

This land suited Karsa Orlong. A warrior scoured clean of all civil trappings, a thing of muscle and will and hidden pressures. While, in strange contrast, the Anibar, Boatfinder, seemed an interloper, almost a parasite, his every motion furtive and oddly guilt-laden. From this broken, rock-skinned place of trees and clearwater lakes, Boatfinder and his people took black grain and the skins of animals; they took birch bark and reeds for making baskets and nets. Not enough to scar this landscape, not enough to claim conquest.

As for her, she found herself viewing her surroundings in terms of trees left unharvested, of lakes still rich with fish, of more efficient ways to gather the elongated, mud-coloured grains from the reed beds in the shallows – the so-called black grain that needed to be beaten free of the stalks, gathered in the hollow of the long, narrow boats the Anibar used, beaten down with sticks amidst webs and spinning spiders and the buzz of tiger-flies. She could think only of resources and the best means of exploiting them. It felt less and less like a virtue with every passing day.

They continued along the trail, Boatfinder in the lead, followed by Karsa who led his horse by the reins, leaving Samar Dev with a view of the animal's rump and swishing tail. Her feet hurt, each step on the hard stone reverberating up into her spine – there had to be a way of padding such impacts, she told herself, perhaps some kind of multi-layering technology for boot soles – she would have to think on that. And these biting flies – Boatfinder had cut juniper branches, threading them through a headscarf so that the green stems dangled in front of his forehead and down the back of his neck. Presumably this worked, although the man looked ridiculous. She contemplated surrendering her vanity and following suit, but would hold out a while longer.

Karsa Orlong was undertaking this journey now as if it had become some kind of quest. Driven by the need to deliver judgement, upon whomsoever he chose, no matter what the circumstances. She had begun to understand just how frightening this savage could be, and how it fed her own growing fascination with him. She half-believed this man could cut a swath through an entire pantheon of gods.

A dip in the trail brought them onto mossy ground, through which broken branches thrust up jagged grey fingers. To the right was a thick, twisted scrub oak, centuries old and scarred by lightning strikes; all the lesser trees that had begun growth around it were dead, as if the battered sentinel exuded some belligerent poison. To the left was the earthen wall of a toppled pine tree's root-mat, vertical and as tall as Karsa, rising from a pool of black water.

Havok came to an abrupt halt and Samar Dev heard a grunt from Karsa Orlong. She worked her way round the Jhag horse until she could clearly see that wall of twisted roots. In which was snared a withered corpse, the flesh wrinkled and blackened, limbs stretched out, neck exposed but of the head only the lower jaw line visible. The chest area seemed to have imploded, the hollow space reaching up into the heart of the huge tree itself. Boatfinder stood opposite, his left hand inscribing gestures in the air.

'This toppled but recently,' Karsa Orlong said. 'Yet this body, it has been there a long time, see how the black water that once gathered about the roots has stained its skin. Samar Dev,' he said, facing her, 'there is a hole in its chest – how did such a thing come to be?'

She shook her head. 'I cannot even determine what manner of creature this is.'

'Jaghut,' the Toblakai replied. 'I have seen the like before. Flesh becomes wood, yet the spirit remains alive within—'

'You're saying this thing is still alive?'

'I do not know – the tree has fallen over, after all, and so it is dying—'

'Death is not sure,' Boatfinder cut in, his eyes wide with superstitious terror. 'Often, the tree reaches once more skyward. But this dweller, so terribly imprisoned, it cannot be alive. It has no heart. It has no head.'

Samar Dev stepped closer to examine the body's sunken chest. After a time she backed away, made uneasy by something she could not define. 'The bones beneath the flesh continued growing,' she said, 'but not as bone. Wood. The sorcery belongs to D'riss, I suspect. Boatfinder, how old would you judge this tree?'

'Frozen time, perhaps thirty generations. Since it fell, seven days, no more. And, it is pushed over.'

'I smell something,' Karsa Orlong said, passing the reins to Boatfinder.

Samar Dev watched the giant warrior walk ahead, up the opposite slope of the depression, halting on the summit of the basolith. He slowly unslung his stone sword.

And now she too caught a faint sourness in the air, the smell of death. She made her way to Karsa's side.

Beyond the dome of rock the trail wound quickly downward to debouch on the edge of a small boggy lake. To one side, on a slight shelf above the shoreline, was a clearing in which sat the remnants of a rough camp – three round structures, sapling-framed and hide-walled. Two were half-burnt, the third knocked down in a mass of shattered wood and torn buckskin. She counted six bodies lying motionless here and there, in and around the camp, one face-down, torso, shoulders and head in the water, long hair flowing like bleached seaweed. Three canoes formed a row on the other side of the trail, their bark hulls stove in.

Boatfinder joined her and Karsa on the rise. A small keening sound rose from him.

Karsa took the lead down the trail. After a moment, Samar Dev followed.

'Stay back from the camp,' Karsa told her. 'I must read the tracks.'

She watched him move from one motionless form to the next, his eyes scanning the scuffed ground, the places where humus had been kicked aside. He went to the hearth and ran his fingers through the ash and coals, down to the stained earth beneath. Somewhere on the lake beyond, a loon called, its cry mournful and haunting. The light had grown steely, the sun now behind the forest line to the west. On the rise above the trail, Boatfinder's keening rose in pitch.

'Tell him to be quiet,' Karsa said in a growl.

'I don't think I can do that,' she replied. 'Leave him his grief.'

'His grief will soon be ours.'

'You fear this unseen enemy, Karsa Orlong?'

He straightened from where he had been examining the holed canoes. 'A four-legged beast has passed through here recently – a large one. It collected one of the corpses . . . but I do not think it has gone far.'

'Then it has already heard us,' Samar Dev said. 'What is it, a bear?' Boatfinder had said that black bears used the same trails as the Anibar, and he'd pointed out their scat on the path. He had explained that they were not dangerous, normally. Still, wild creatures were ever un-predictable, and if one had come upon these bodies it might well now view the kill-site as its own.

'A bear? Perhaps, Samar Dev. Such as the kind from my homeland, a dweller in caves, and on its hind legs half again as tall as a Teblor. But this one is yet different, for the pads of its paws are sheathed in scales.'

'Scales?'

'And I judge it would weigh more than four adult warriors of the Teblor.' He eyed her. 'A formidable creature.'

'Boatfinder has said nothing of such beasts in this forest.'

'Not the only intruder,' the Toblakai said. 'These Anibar were murdered with spears and curved blades. They were then stripped of all ornaments, weapons and tools. There was a child among them but it was dragged away. The killers came from the lake, in wooden-keeled longboats. At least ten adults, two of them wearing boots of some sort, although the heel pattern is unfamiliar. The others wore moccasins made of sewn strips, each one overlapping on one side.'

'Overlapping? Ridged – that would improve purchase, I think.'

'Samar Dev, I know who these intruders are.'

'Old friends of yours?'

'We did not speak of friendship at the time. Call down Boatfinder, I have questions for him—'

The sentence was unfinished. Samar Dev looked over to find Karsa standing stock-still, his gaze on the trees beyond the three canoes. She turned and saw a massive hulking shape pushing its forefront clear of bending saplings. An enormous, scaled head lifted from steep shoulders, eyes fixing on the Toblakai.

Who raised his stone sword in a two-handed grip, then surged forward.

The giant beast's roar ended in a high-pitched squeal, as it bolted – backward, into the thicket. Sudden crashing, heavy thumps—

Karsa plunged into the stand, pursuing.

Samar Dev found that she was holding her dagger in her right hand, knuckles white.

The crashing sounds grew more distant, as did the frantic squeals of the scaled bear.

She turned at scrabbling from the slope and watched Boatfinder come down to huddle at her side. His lips were moving in silent prayers, eyes on the broken hole in the stand of trees.

Samar sheathed her dagger and crossed her arms. 'What is it with him and monsters?' she demanded.

Boatfinder sat down in the damp mulch, began rocking back and forth.

Samar Dev was just completing her second burial when Karsa Orlong returned. He walked up to the hearth she had lit earlier and beside which Boatfinder sat hunched over and swathed in furs, voicing a low moaning sound of intractable sorrow. The Toblakai set his sword down.

'Did you kill it?' she asked. 'Did you cut its paws off, skin it alive, add its ears to your belt and crush its chest in with your embrace?'

'Escaped,' he said in a grunt.

'Probably halfway to Ehrlitan by now.'

'No, it is hungry. It will return, but not before we have moved on.' He gestured to the remaining bodies. 'There is no point – it will dig them up.'

'Hungry, you said.'

'Starving. It is not from this world. And this land here, it offers little – the beast would do better on the plains to the south.'

'The map calls this the Olphara Mountains. Many lakes are marked, and I believe the small one before us is joined to others, further north, by a river.'

'These are not mountains.'

'They once were, millennia past. They have been worn down. We are on a much higher elevation than we were just south of here.'

'Nothing can gnaw mountains down to mere stubs, witch.'

'Nonetheless. We should see if we can repair these canoes – it would be much easier—'

'I shall not abandon Havok.'

'Then we will never catch up with our quarry, Karsa Orlong.'

'They are not fleeing. They are exploring. Searching.'

'For what?'

The Toblakai did not answer.

Samar Dev wiped dirt from her hands, then walked over to the hearth. 'I think this hunt we are on is a mistake. The Anibar should simply flee, leave this broken land, at least until the intruders have left.'

'You are a strange woman,' Karsa pronounced. 'You wished to explore this land, yet find yourself made helpless by it.'

She started. 'Why do you say that?'

'Here, one must be as an animal. Passing through, quiet, for this is a place that yields little and speaks in silence. Thrice in our journey we have been tracked by a bear, silent as a ghost on this bedrock. Crossing and re-crossing our trail. You would think such a large beast would be easy to see, but it is not. There are omens here, Samar Dev, more than I have ever seen before in any place, even my homeland. Hawks circle overhead. Owls watch us pass from hollows in dead trees. Tell me, witch, what is happening to the moon?'

She stared into the fire. 'I don't know. It seems to be breaking up. Crumbling. There is no record of anything like that happening before, neither the way it has grown larger, nor the strange corona surrounding it.' She shook her head. 'If it is an omen, it is one all the world can see.'

'The desert folk believe gods dwell there. Perhaps they wage war among themselves.'

'Superstitious nonsense,' she said. 'The moon is this world's child, the

505

last child, for there were others, once.' She hesitated. 'It may be that two have collided, but it is difficult to be sure – the others were never very visible, even in the best of times. Dark, smudged, distant, always in the shadow cast by this world, or that of the largest moon – the one we see most clearly. Of late, there has been much dust in the air.'

'There are more fireswords in the sky,' Karsa said. 'Just before dawn, you may see ten in the span of three breaths, each slashing down through the dark. Every night.'

'We may learn more when we reach the coast, for the tides will have changed.'

'Changed, how?'

'The moon's own breath,' she replied. 'We can measure that breath . . . in the ebb and flood of the tides. Such are the laws of existence.'

The Toblakai snorted. 'Laws are broken. Existence holds to no laws. Existence is what persists, and to persist is to struggle. In the end, the struggle fails.' He was removing strips of smoked bhederin meat from his pack. 'That is the only law worthy of the name.'

She studied him. 'Is that what the Teblor believe?'

He bared his teeth. 'One day I will return to my people. And I will shatter all that they believe. And I will say to my father, *"Forgive me. You were right to disbelieve. You were right to despise the laws that chained us."* And to my grandfather, I shall say nothing at all.'

'Have you a wife in your tribe?'

'I have victims, no wives.'

A brutal admission, she reflected. 'Do you intend reparation, Karsa Orlong?'

'That would be seen as weakness.'

'Then the chains still bind you.'

'There was a Nathii settlement, beside a lake, where the Nathii had made slaves of my people. Each night, after hauling nets on the lake, those slaves were all shackled to a single chain. Not a single Teblor so bound could break that chain. Together, their strengths and wills combined, no chain could have held them.'

'So, for all your claims of returning to your people and shattering all that they believe, you will, in truth, need their help to manage such a thing. It sounds as if it is not just your father from whom you require forgiveness, Karsa Orlong.'

'I shall take what I require, witch.'

'Were you one of those slaves in the Nathii fishing village?'

'For a time.'

'And, to escape – and clearly you *did* escape – you ended up needing the help of your fellow Teblor.' She nodded. 'I can see how that might gnaw on your soul.'

He eyed her. 'You are truly clever, Samar Dev, to discover how all things fit so neatly in place.'

'I have made long study of human nature, the motivations that guide us, the truths that haunt us. I do not think you Teblor are much different from us in such things.'

'Unless, of course, you begin with an illusion – one that suits the conclusion you sought from the start.'

'I try not to assume veracity,' she replied.

'Indeed.' He handed her a strip of meat.

She crossed her arms, refusing the offer for the moment. 'You suggest I have made an assumption, an erroneous one, and so, although I claim to understand you, in truth I understand nothing. A convenient argument, but not very convincing, unless you care to be specific.'

'I am Karsa Orlong. I know the measure of each step I have taken since I first became a warrior. Your self-satisfaction does not offend me, witch.'

'The savage now patronizes me! Gods below!'

He proffered the meat again. 'Eat, Samar Dev, lest you grow too weak for outrage.'

She glared at him, then accepted the strip of bhederin. 'Karsa Orlong, your people live with a lack of sophistication similar to these Anibar here. It is clear that, once, the citizens of the great civilizations of Seven Cities lived in a similar state of simplicity and stolid ignorance, haunted by omens and fleeing the unfathomable. And no doubt we too concocted elaborate belief systems, quaint and ridiculous, to justify all those necessities and restrictions imposed upon us by the struggle to survive. Fortunately, however, we left all that behind. We discovered the glory of civilization – and you, Teblor, hold still to your misplaced pride, holding up your ignorance of such glory as a virtue. And so you still do not comprehend the great gift of civilization—'

'I comprehend it fine,' Karsa Orlong replied around a mouthful of meat. 'The savage proceeds into civilization through improvements—'

'Yes!'

'Improvements in the manner and efficiency of killing people.'

'Hold on—'

'Improvements in the unassailable rules of degradation and misery.'

'Karsa—'

'Improvements in ways to humiliate, impose suffering and justify slaughtering those savages too stupid and too trusting to resist what you hold as inevitable. Namely, their extinction. Between you and me, Samar Dev,' he added, swallowing, 'who should the Anibar fear more?'

'I don't know,' she said through gritted teeth. 'Why don't we ask him?'

Boatfinder lifted his head and studied Samar Dev with hooded eyes. 'In the frozen time,' he said in a low voice, 'Iskar Jarak spoke of the Unfound.'

'Iskar Jarak was not a god, Boatfinder. He was a mortal, with a handful of wise words – it's easy to voice warnings. Actually staying around to help prepare for them is another thing altogether!'

'Iskar Jarak gave us the secrets, Samar Dev, and so we have prepared in the frozen time, and prepare now, and will prepare in the Unfound.'

Karsa barked a laugh. 'Would that I had travelled here with Iskar Jarak. We would find little to argue over, I think.'

'This is what I get,' muttered Samar Dev, 'in the company of barbarians.'

The Toblakai's tone suddenly changed, 'The intruders who have come here, witch, believe themselves civilized. And so they kill Anibar. Why? Because they can. They seek no other reason. To them, Samar Dev, Karsa Orlong will give answer. This savage is not stupid, not trusting, and by the souls of my sword, I shall give answer.'

All at once, night had arrived, and there in that silent forest it was cold.

From somewhere far to the west, rose the howl of wolves, and Samar Dev saw Karsa Orlong smile.

Once, long ago, Mappo Runt had stood with a thousand other Trell warriors. Surmounting the Orstanz Ridge overlooking the Valley of Bayen Eckar, so named for the shallow, stony river that flowed northward to a distant, mythical sea – mythical for the Trell at least, none of whom had ever travelled that far from their homeland steppes and plains. Arrayed on the slope opposite and down on the river's western bank, fifteen hundred paces distant, was the Nemil army, commanded in those days by a much-feared general, Saylan'mathas.

So many of the Trell had already fallen, not in battle, but to the weakness of life encamped around the trader posts, forts and settlements that now made the borderlands a hazy, ephemeral notion and little more. Mappo himself had fled such a settlement, finding refuge among the still-belligerent hill clans.

A thousand Trell warriors, facing an army eight times their number. Mace, axe and sword hammering shield-rims, a song of death-promise rising from their throats, a sound like earth-thunder rolling down into the valley where birds flew low and strangely frenzied, as if in terror they had forgotten the sky's sanctuary overhead, instead swooping and wheeling between the grey-leaved trees clumped close to the river on both sides, seeming to swarm through thickets and shrubs.

Upon the valley's other side, units of soldiers moved in ever-shifting presentation: units of archers, of slingers, of pike-wielding infantry and the much feared Nemil cataphracts – heavy in armour atop massive horses, round-shields at the ready although their lances remained at rest in stirrup-sockets, as they trooped at the trot to the far wings, making plain their intention to flank once the foot soldiers and Trell warriors were fully engaged in the basin of the valley.

Bayen Eckar, the river, was no barrier, barely knee-deep. The cataphracts would cross unimpeded. Saylan'mathas was visible, mounted with flanking retainers, traversing the distant ridge. Banners streamed above the terrible commander, serpentine in gold-trimmed black silk, like slashes of the Abyss clawing through the air itself. As the train presented along the entire ridge, weapons lifted in salute, yet no cry rose heavenward, for such was not the habit of this man's hand-picked army. That silence was ominous, murderous, frightful.

Down from the Trellish steppes, leading this defiant army of warriors, had come an elder named Trynigarr, to this, his first battle. An elder for whom the honorific was tainted with mockery, for this was one old man whose fount of wisdom and advice seemed long since dried up; an old man who said little. *Silent and watchful, is Trynigarr, like a hawk.* An observation followed by an ungenerous grin or worse a bark of laughter.

He led now by virtue of sobriety, for the three other elders had all partaken five nights before of Weeping Jegurra cactus, each bead sweated out on a prickly blade by three days of enforced saturation in a mixture of water and The Eight Spices, the latter a shamanistic concoction said to hold the voice and visions of earth-gods; yet this time the brew had gone foul, a detail unnoticed – the trench dug round the cactus bole had inadvertently captured and drowned a venomous spider known as the Antelope, and the addition of its toxic juices had flung the elders into a deep coma. One from which, it turned out, they would never awaken.

Scores of blooded young warriors had been eager to take command, yet the old ways could not be set aside. Indeed, the old ways of the Trell were at the heart of this war itself. And so command had fallen to Trynigarr, *so wise he has nothing to say.*

The old man stood before the warriors now, on this fated ridge, calm and silent as he studied the enemy presenting one alignment after another, whilst the flanking cavalry – three thousand paces or more distant to north and south – finally wheeled and began the descent to the river. Five units each, each unit a hundred of the superbly disciplined, heavy-armoured soldiers, those soldiers being nobleborn, brothers and fathers and sons, wild daughters and savage wives; one and all bound to the lust for blood that was the Nemil way of life. That there were entire families among those units, and that each unit was made up mostly of extended families and led by a captain selected by acclamation from among them, made them the most feared cavalry west of the Jhag Odhan.

As Trynigarr watched the enemy, so Mappo Runt watched his war-leader. The elder did nothing.

The cataphracts crossed the river and took up inward-facing stations, whereupon they waited. On the slope directly opposite, foot-soldiers began the march down, whilst advance skirmishers crossed the river, followed by medium and then heavy infantry, each reinforcing the advance bridgehead on this side of the river.

The Trell warriors were shouting still, throats raw, and something like fear growing in the ever longer intervals of drawn breath and pauses between beats of weapon on shield. Their battle-frenzy was waning, and all that it had succeeded in pushing aside – all the mortal terrors and doubts that anyone sane could not help but feel at the edge of battle – were now returning.

The bridgehead, seeing itself unopposed, fanned out to accommodate the arrival of the army's main body on the east side of the river. As they moved, deer exploded from the cover of the thickets and raced in darts this way and that between the armies.

Century upon century, the Trell ever fought in their wild frenzy. Battle after battle, in circumstances little different from this one, they would have charged by now, gathering speed on the slope, each warrior eager to outpace the others and so claim the usually fatal glory of being the first to close with the hated enemy. The mass would arrive like an avalanche, the Trell making full use of their greater size to crash into and knock down the front lines, to break the phalanx and so begin a day of slaughter.

Sometimes it had succeeded. More often it had failed – oh, the initial impact had often knocked from their feet row upon row of enemy soldiers, had on occasion sent enemy bodies cartwheeling through the air; and once, almost three hundred years ago, one such charge had *knocked an entire phalanx on its ass*. But the Nemil had learned, and now the units advanced with pikes levelled out. A Trell charge would spit itself on those deadly iron points; the enemy square, trained to greater mobility and accepting backward motion as easily as forward, would simply absorb the collision. And the Trell would break, or die where they stood locked in the fangs of the Nemil pikes.

And so, as the Trell did nothing, still fixed like wind-plucked scare-crows upon the ridge, Saylan'mathas reappeared on his charger, this time before the river, gaze tilted upward as if to pierce the stolid mind of Trynigarr as he rode across the front of his troops. Clearly, the general was displeased; for now, to engage with the Trell he would have to send his infantry upslope, and such position put them at a disadvantage in meeting the charge that would surely come then. Displeased, Mappo suspected, but not unduly worried. The phalanxes were superbly trained; they could divide and open pathways straight down, into which their pikes could funnel the Trell, driven as the warriors would be by their headlong rush. Still, his flanking cavalry had just lost much of their effectiveness, assuming he left them at their present stations, and now Mappo saw messengers riding out from the general's retinue, one down and the other up the valley's length. The cataphracts would now proceed upslope to take the same ridge the Trell occupied, and move inward. Twin charges would force the Trell to turn their own flanks. Not that such a move would help much, for the warriors knew of no tactic to meet a cavalry charge.

As soon as the cataphracts swung their mounts and began their ascent, Trynigarr gestured, each hand outward. The signal was passed back through the ranks, down to the ridge's backslope, then outward, north and south, to the hidden, outlying masses of Trell warriors, each one positioned virtually opposite the unsuspecting cavalry on the flanks. Those warriors now began moving up towards the ridge – they would reach it well before the cataphracts and their armour-burdened warhorses, but they would not stop on the summit, instead continuing over it, onto the valley slope and at a charge, down into the horse-soldiers. Trell cannot meet a cavalry charge, but they can charge into cavalry, provided the momentum is theirs – as it would be on this day.

Dust and distant sounds of slaughter now, from the baggage camp west of the river, as the fifteen hundred Trell Trynigarr had sent across the Bayen Eckar three days past now descended upon the lightly guarded supply camp.

Messengers swarmed in the valley below, and Mappo saw the general's train halted, horses turning every which way as if to match the confusion of the officers surrounding Saylan'mathas. On the distant flanks, the Trell had appeared, voicing warcries, over the ridge, and were beginning their deadly flow downward into the suddenly confused, churning knot of riders.

Saylan'mathas, who moments earlier had been locked in the mindset of the attacker, found himself shifting stance, his thoughts casting away all notions of delivering slaughter, fixing now on the necessity of defence. He split his army of foot-soldiers, half-legions wheeling out and moving at dog-trot to the far-too-distant flanks, horns keening to alert the cavalry that an avenue of retreat now existed. Elements of light cavalry that had remained on the other side of the river, ready to be cut loose to run down fleeing Trell, the general now sent at a gallop back towards the unseen baggage camp, but their horses had a steep slope to climb first, and before they were halfway up, eight hundred Trell appeared on the crest, wielding their own pikes, these ones half again as long as those used by the Nemil. Taking position with the long weapons settled and angled to match the slope. The light cavalry reached that bristling line uneven and already seeking to flinch back. Spitted horses reared and tumbled downslope, breaking legs of the horses below them. Soldiers spun from their saddles, all advance now gone, and the Trellish line began marching down into the midst of the enemy, delivering death.

The general had halted his centre's advance to the slope, and now reordered it into a four-sided defence, the pikes a glistening, wavering forest, slowly lifting like hackles on some cornered beast.

Motionless, watching for a time, Trynigarr, *Wise in Silence*, now half-turned his head, gestured in a small wave with his right hand, and the thousand Trell behind him formed into jostling lines, creating avenues through which the columns of Trell archers came.

Archers was a poor description. True, there were some warriors carrying recurved longbows, so stiff that no human could draw them, the arrows overlong and very nearly the mass of javelins, the fletching elongated, stiffened strips of leather. Others, however, held true javelins and weighted atlatls, whilst among them were slingers, including those with sling-poles and two-wheeled carts behind each warrior, loaded down with the large, thin sacks they would fling into the midst of the enemy, sacks that seethed and rippled.

Sixteen hundred archers, then, many of them women, who later joked that they had emptied their yurts for this battle. Moving forward onto the slope, even as the original warriors, now aligned in columns, moved with them.

Down, to meet the heart of the Nemil army.

Trynigarr walked in their midst, suddenly indistinguishable from any other warrior, barring his age. He was done with commanding, for the moment. Each element of his elaborate plan was now engaged, the outcome left to the bravery and ferocity of young warriors and their clan-leaders. This gesture of Trynigarr's was in truth the finest expression of confidence and assurance possible. The battle was here, it was now, measured in the rise and fall of weapons. The elder had done what he could to speak to the inherent strengths of the Trell, while deftly emasculating those of the Nemil and their vaunted general. And so, beneath screeching birds and in sight of terrified deer still running and bounding along the valley slopes, the day and its battle gloried in the spilling of blood.

On the west river bank, Nemil archers, arrayed to face both east and west, sent flights of deadly arrows, again and again, the shafts descending to screams and the thuds of wooden shields, until the advancing warriors, cutting down the last of the light cavalry, re-formed beneath the missile fire, then closed at a trot with their pikes, the first touch of which shattered the archers and their meagre guard of skirmishers. The ranks who had faced east, sending arrows over the Nemil square into the Trell marching to close, were now struck from behind, and there was great slaughter.

Trell arrows arced out to land within the phalanx, the heavy shafts punching through shield and armour. Javelins then followed as the Trell moved closer, and the Nemil front ranks grew pocked, porous and jostling as soldiers moved to take the place of the fallen. Trellish throwing axes met them, and, at last, with less than twenty paces between the forces, the pole-slings whirled above the massed Trell, the huge sacks wheeling ever faster, then released, out, sailing over the heads of the front ranks of Nemil, down, striking pike-heads, bursting apart, each spike spilling out hundreds of black scorpions – *and thus the women laughed, saying how they had emptied out their yurts for this gift to the hated Nemil.*

Small, in the scheme of things, yet, that day, in that moment, it had been one pebble too many in the farmer's field-cart, and the axle had snapped. Screaming panic, all discipline vanishing. Hard, cold claws of the scorpions . . . on the neck, slipping down beneath breast-plates, the cuffs of gauntlets, down onto the strapped shield arm . . . and then the savage, acid sting, puncturing like a fang, the blaze of agony surging outward – it was enough, it was more than enough. The phalanx seemed to explode before Mappo's eyes, figures running, shrieking, writhing in wild dances, weapons and shields flung aside, helms torn off, armour stripped away.

Arrows and javelins tore into the heaving mass, and those that raced free of it now met the waiting maces, axes and swords of the Trell. And Mappo, along with his fellow warriors, all frenzy driven from them, delivered cold death.

The great general, Saylan'mathas, died in that press, trampled underfoot by his own soldiers. Why he had dismounted to meet the Trell advance no-one could explain; his horse had been recovered as it trotted back into the baggage camp, its reins neatly looped about the hinged horn of the saddle, the stirrups flipped over the seat.

The cataphracts, those feared horse-soldiers, born of pure blood, had been slaughtered, as had the half-legions of foot-soldiers who arrived too late to do anything but die amidst flailing, kicking horses and the bawling of the mortally wounded nobles.

The Nemil had looked upon a thousand warriors, and thought those

Trell the only ones present. Their spies had failed them twice, first among the hill tribes when rumours of the alliance's break-up had been deliberately let loose to the ever whispering winds; then in the days and nights leading to the battle at Bayen Eckar, when Trynigarr had sent out his clans, each with a specific task, and all in accordance with the site where the battle would take place, for the Trell knew this land, could travel unerring on moonless nights, and could hide virtually unseen amidst the rumples and folds of these valleys during the day.

Trynigarr, the elder who had led his first battle, would come to fight six more, each time throwing back the Nemil invaders, until the treaty was signed yielding all human claim on the Trell steppes and hills, and the old man who so rarely spoke would die drunk in an alley years later, long after the last clan had surrendered, driven from their wild-lands by the starvation that came from sustained slaughter of the bhederin herds by Nemil and their half-breed Trellish scouts.

In those last years, Mappo had heard, Trynigarr, his tongue loosened by drink, had talked often, filling the air with slurred, meaningless words and fragmented remembrances. So many words, not one wise, to fill what had once been the wisest of silences.

Three strides behind Mappo Runt, Iskaral Pust, High Priest and avowed Magi of the House of Shadow, led his eerie black-eyed mule and spoke without cessation. His words filled the air like dried leaves in a steady wind, and held all the significance and meaning of the same; punctuated by the sob of moccasins and hoofs dragging free of swamp mud only to squelch back down, the occasional slap at a biting insect, and the sniffling from Pust's perpetually runny nose.

It was clear to Mappo that what he was hearing were the High Priest's thoughts, the rambling, directionless interior monologue of a madman vented into the air with random abandon. And every hint of genius was but a chimera, a trail as false as the one they now walked – this supposed short-cut that was now threatening to swallow them whole, to drag them down into the senseless, dark peat that would be forever indifferent to their sightless eyes.

He had believed that Iskaral Pust had decided upon taking his leave, returning with Mogora – if indeed she had returned, and was not skittering about among the fetid trees and curtains of moss – to their hidden monastery in the cliff. But something as yet unexplained had changed the High Priest's mind, and it was this detail more than any other that made Mappo uneasy.

He'd wanted this to be a solitary pursuit. Icarium was the Trell's responsibility, no matter what the Nameless Ones asserted. There was nothing righteous in their judgement – those priests had betrayed him more than once. They had earned Mappo's eternal enmity, and perhaps, one day, he would visit the extremity of his displeasure upon them.

Sorely used and spiritually abused, Mappo had discovered in them a focus for his hate. He was Icarium's guardian. His friend. And it was clear, as well, that the Jhag's new companion led with the fevered haste of a fugitive, a man knowing well he was now hunted, knowing that he had been a co-conspirator in a vast betrayal. And Mappo would not relent.

Nor was he in need of Iskaral Pust's help; in fact, Mappo had begun to suspect that the High Priest's assistance was not quite as honourable as it seemed. Traversing this marsh, for example, a journey ostensibly of but two days, Pust insisted, that would deliver them to the coast days in advance of what would have been the case had they walked the high-ground trail. Two days were now five, with no end in sight. What the Trell could not fathom, however, was the possible motivation Iskaral – and by extension, the House of Shadow – might have in delaying him.

Icarium was a weapon no mortal nor god could risk using. That the Nameless Ones believed otherwise was indicative of both madness and outright stupidity. Not so long ago, they had set Mappo and Icarium on a path to Tremorlor, an Azath House capable of imprisoning Icarium for all eternity. Such imprisonment had been their design, and as much as Mappo railed against and finally defied them, he had understood, even then, that it made sense. This abrupt, inexplicable about-face reinforced the Trell's belief that the ancient cult had lost its way, or had been usurped by some rival faction.

A sudden yelp from Iskaral Pust – a huge shadow slipped over the two travellers, then was gone, even as Mappo looked up, his eyes searching through the moss-bearded branches of the huge trees – seeing nothing, yet feeling still the passage of a cool wind, flowing in the wake of . . . something. The Trell faced the High Priest. 'Iskaral Pust, are there enkar'al living in this swamp?'

The small man's eyes were wide. He licked his lips, inadvertently collecting the smeared remains of a mosquito with his tongue, drawing it inward. 'I have no idea,' he said, then wiped his nose with the back of his hand, looking like a child caught out in some horrible crime. 'We should go back, Mappo Runt. This was a mistake.' He cocked his head. 'Does he believe me? How can he not? It's been five days! We've not crossed this arm of swamp, this northward tendril, no, we've walked its length! Enkar'al? Gods below, they eat people! Was that an enkar'al? I wish! But oh no. If only. Quick, blessed genius, come up with something else to say!' He scratched the white stubble on his chin, then brightened. 'It's Mogora's fault! It was her idea! All of this!'

Mappo looked about. A northerly arm of marshland? They had cut westward to find it, the first hint that something was awry, but Mappo had not been thinking clearly back then. He was not even certain the fog had lifted from his spirit in the time since. Yet now he began to feel something, a stirring of the embers, the flicker of anger. He faced right, set out.

'Where are you going?' Iskaral demanded, hastening to catch up, the mule braying a complaint.

The Trell did not bother replying. He was fighting the desire to wring the little man's scrawny neck.

A short while later the ground perceptibly rose, becoming drier, and open pockets of sunlit glades appeared ahead, walled beyond by stands of birch.

In the clearing directly ahead, half-sitting half-leaning on a boulder, was a woman. Tall, her skin the colour of fine ash, long black hair hanging loose and straight. She wore chain armour, glinting silver, over a grey, hooded shirt, and leggings of pale, supple leather. High boots fashioned from some black-scaled creature rose to her knees. Two basket-hilted rapiers adorned her belt.

She was eating an apple, its skin the deep hue of blood.

Her eyes were large, black, with elongated epicanthic folds tilting upward at the corners, and they were fixed on Mappo with something like languid disdain and mild amusement. 'Oh,' she murmured, 'Ardata's hand in this, I see. Healed by the Queen of Spiders – you foster dangerous alliances, Guardian.' Her free hand pressed against her lips, eyes widening. 'How rude of me! Guardian no longer. How should you be called now, Mappo Runt? Discarded One?' She tossed the apple to one side, then straightened. 'We have much to talk about, you and I.'

'I do not know you,' the Trell replied.

'My name is Spite.'

'Oh,' said Iskaral Pust, 'now that's fitting, since I hate you already.'

'Allies need not be friends,' she replied, gaze flicking with contempt to the High Priest. Her eyes narrowed momentarily on the mule, then she said, 'I am without friends and I seek no friendships.'

'With a name like Spite, is it any wonder?'

'Iskaral Pust, the Hounds have done well in disposing of Dejim Nebrahl. Or, rather, I begin to comprehend the subtle game they have played, given the proximity of the Deragoth. Your master is clever. I give him that.'

'My master,' hissed Iskaral Pust, 'has no need to fashion an alliance with *you*.'

She smiled, and it was, Mappo judged, a most beautiful smile. 'High Priest, from you and your master, I seek nothing.' Her eyes returned once more to rest upon the Trell. 'You, Discarded One, have need of me. We shall travel together, you and I. The services of the Magi of Shadow are no longer required.'

'You'll not get rid of me so easily,' Iskaral Pust said, his sudden smile, intended to be unctuous, sadly marred by the mosquito carcass squished against one snaggled, crooked incisor. 'Oh no, I will be as a leech, hidden beneath a fold in your clothing, eagerly engorging upon your very lifeblood. I shall be the fanged bat hanging beneath your udder, lapping lapping lapping your sweet exudence. I shall be the fly who buzzes straight into your ear, there to make a new home with a full larder at my beck and call. I shall be the mosquito—'

'Crushed by your flapping lips, High Priest,' Spite said wearily, dismissing him. 'Discarded One, the coast is but half a league distant. There is a fishing village, sadly devoid of life now, but that will not impede us at all.'

Mappo did not move. 'What cause have I,' he asked, 'to ally myself with you?'

'You shall need the knowledge I possess, Mappo Runt, for I was one of the Nameless Ones who freed Dejim Nebrahl, with the aim of slaying you, so that the new Guardian could take your place at Icarium's side. It may surprise you,' she added, 'that I am pleased the T'rolbarahl failed in the former task. I am outlawed from the Nameless Ones, a fact that gives me no small amount of satisfaction, if not pleasure. Would you know what the Nameless Ones intend? Would you know Icarium's fate?'

He stared at her. Then asked, 'What awaits us in the village?'

'A ship. Provisioned and crewed, in a manner of speaking. To pursue our quarry, we must cross half the world, Mappo Runt.'

'Don't listen to her!'

'Be quiet, Iskaral Pust,' Mappo said in a growl. 'Or take your leave of us.'

'Fool! Very well, it is clear to me that my presence in your foul company is not only necessary, but essential! But you, Spite, be on your guard! I will permit no betrayal of this bold, honourable warrior! And watch your words, lest their unleashing haunt him unto madness!'

'If he has withstood yours this long, priest,' she said, 'then he is proof to all madness.'

'You, woman, would be wise to be silent.'

She smiled.

Mappo sighed. *Ah, Pust, would that you heeded your own admonishments . . .*

The boy was nine years old. He had been ill for a time, days and nights unmeasured, recalled only in blurred visions, the pain-filled eyes of his parents, the strange calculation in those of his two younger sisters, as if they had begun contemplating life without an older brother, a life freed of the torments and teasings and, as demanded, his stolid reliability in the face of the other, equally cruel children in the village.

And then there had been a second time, one he was able to imagine distinct, walled on all sides, roofed in black night where stars swam like boatmen spiders across well-water. In this time, this chamber, the boy was entirely alone, woken only by the needs of thirst, finding a bucket beside his bed, filled with silty water, and the wood and horn ladle his mother used only on feast-nights. Waking, conjuring the strength to reach out and collect that ladle, dipping it into the bucket, struggling with the water's weight, drawing the tepid fluid in through cracked lips, to ease a mouth hot and dry as the bowl of a kiln.

One day he awoke yet again, and knew himself in the third time. Though weak, he was able to crawl from the bed, to lift the bucket and drink down the last of the water, coughing at its soupy consistency, tasting the flat grit of the silts. Hunger's nest in his belly was now filled with broken eggs, and tiny claws and beaks nipped at his insides.

A long, exhausting journey brought him outside, blinking in the harsh sunlight – so harsh and bright he could not see. There were voices all around him, filling the street, floating down from the roofs, high-pitched and in a language he had never heard before. Laughter, excitement, yet these sounds chilled him.

He needed more water. He needed to defeat this brightness, so that he could see once more. Discover the source of these carnival sounds – had a caravan arrived in the village? A troop of actors, singers and musicians?

Did no-one see him? Here on his hands and knees, the fever gone, his life returned to him?

He was nudged on one side and his groping hand reached out and found the shoulder and nape of a dog. The animal's wet nose slipped along his upper arm. This was one of the healthier dogs, he judged, his hand finding a thick layer of fat over the muscle of the shoulder, then, moving down, the huge swell of the beast's belly. He now heard other dogs, gathering, pressing close, squirming with pleasure at the touch of his hands. They were all fat. Had there been a feast? The slaughter of a herd?

Vision returned, with a clarity he had never before experienced. Lifting his head, he looked round.

The chorus of voices came from birds. Rooks, pigeons, vultures bounding down the dusty street, screeching at the bluff rushes from the village's dogs, who remained possessive of the remains of bodies here and there, mostly little more than bones and sun-blackened tendons, skulls broken open by canine jaws, the insides licked clean.

The boy rose to his feet, tottering with sudden dizziness that was a long time in passing. Eventually, he was able to turn and look back at his family's house, trying to recall what he had seen when crawling through the rooms. Nothing. No-one.

The dogs circled him, all seeming desperate to make him their master, tails wagging, stepping side to side as their spines twisted back and forth, ears flicking up at his every gesture, noses prodding his hands. They were fat, the boy realized, because they had eaten everyone.

For they had died. His mother, his father, his sisters, everyone else in the village. The dogs, owned by all and by none and living a life of suffering, of vicious hunger and rivalries, had all fed unto indolence. Their joy came from full bellies, all rivalry forgotten now. The boy understood in this something profound. A child's delusions stripped back, revealing the truths of the world.

He began wandering.

Some time later he found himself at the crossroads just beyond the northernmost homestead, standing in the midst of his newly adopted pets. A cairn of stones had been raised in the very centre of the conjoined roads and tracks.

His hunger had passed. Looking down at himself, he saw how thin he had become, and saw too the strange purplish nodules thickening his joints, wrist, elbow, knee and ankle, not in the least painful. Repositories, it seemed, for some other strength.

The cairn's message was plain to him, for it had been raised by a shepherd and he had tended enough flocks in his day. It told him to go north, up into the hills. It told him that sanctuary awaited him there. There had been survivors, then. That they had left him behind was understandable – against the bluetongue fever nothing could be done. A soul lived or a soul died of its own resolve, or lack thereof.

The boy saw that no herds remained on the hillsides. Wolves had come down, perhaps, uncontested; or the other villagers had driven the beasts with them. After all, a sanctuary would have such needs as food and water, milk and cheese.

He set off on the north trail, the dogs accompanying him.

They were happy, he saw. Pleased that he now led them.

And the sun overhead, that had been blinding, was blinding no longer. The boy had come to and now crossed a threshold, into the fourth and final time. He knew not when it would end.

With languid eyes, Felisin Younger stared at the scrawny youth who had been brought in by the Unmanned Acolytes. Just one more lost survivor looking to her for meaning, guidance, for something to believe in that could not be crushed down and swept away by ill winds.

He was a Carrier – the swellings at his joints told her that. Likely, he had infected the rest of his village. The nodes had suppurated, poisoning the air, and everyone else had died. He had arrived at the gates of the city that morning, in the company of twelve half-wild dogs. A Carrier, but here, in this place, that was not cause for banishment. Indeed, the very opposite. Kulat would take the boy under his wing, for teaching in the ways of pilgrimage, for this would be his new calling, to carry plague across the world, and so, among the survivors in his wake, gather yet more adherents to the new religion. Faith in the Broken, the Scarred, the Unmanned – all manner of sects were being formed, membership defined by the damage the plague had delivered to each survivor. Rarest and most precious among them, the Carriers.

All that Kulat had predicted was coming to pass. Survivors arrived, at first a trickle, then by the hundred, drawn here, guided by the hand of a god. They began excavating the long-buried city, making for themselves homes amidst the ghosts of long-dead denizens who still haunted the rooms, the hallways and the streets, silent and motionless, spectres witnessing a rebirth, on their faint, blurred faces a riot of expressions ranging from dismay to horror. How the living could terrify the dead.

Herders arrived with huge flocks, sheep and goats, the long-limbed cattle called eraga that most had believed extinct for a thousand years – Kulat said that wild herds had been found in the hills – and here the dogs recollected what they had been bred for in the first place and now fended the beasts against the wolves and the grey eagles that could lift a newborn calf in their talons.

Artisans had arrived and had begun producing images that had been born in their sickness, in their fevers: the God in Chains, the multitudes of the Broken and the Scarred and the Unmanned. Images on pottery, on walls painted in the ancient mix of eraga blood and red ochre, stone statues for the Carriers. Fabrics woven with large knots of wool to represent the nodules, scenes of fever patterns of colour surrounding central images of Felisin herself, Sha'ik Reborn, the deliverer of the true Apocalypse.

She did not know what to make of all this. She was left bewildered again and again by what she witnessed, every gesture of worship and adoration. The horror of physical disfigurement assailed her on all sides, until she felt numb, drugged insensate. Suffering had become its own language, life itself defined as punishment and imprisonment. *And this is my flock.*

Her followers had, thus far, answered her every need but one, and that was the growing sexual desire, reflecting the changes overtaking her body, the shape of womanhood, the start of blood between her legs, and the new hunger feeding her dreams of succour. She could not yearn for the touch of slaves, for slavery was what these people willingly embraced, here and now, in this place they called Hanar Ara, the City of the Fallen.

Around a mouthful of stones, Kulat said, 'And this is the problem, Highness.'

She blinked. She hadn't been listening. 'What? What is the problem?'

'This Carrier, who arrived but this morning from the southwest track. With his dogs that answer only to him.'

She regarded Kulat, the old bastard who confessed sexually fraught dreams of wine as if the utterance was itself more pleasure than he could bear, as if confession made him drunk. 'Explain.'

Kulat sucked at the stones in his mouth, swallowed spit, then gestured. 'Look upon the buds, Highness, the buds of disease, the Many Mouths of Bluetongue. They are shrinking. They have dried up and are fading. He has said as much. They have grown smaller. He is a Carrier who shall, one day, cease being a Carrier. This child shall lose his usefulness.'

Usefulness. She looked upon him again, more carefully this time, and saw a hard, angular face older than its years, clear eyes, a frame that needed more flesh and would likely find it once again, now that he had food to eat. A boy still young, who would grow into a man. 'He shall reside in the palace,' she said.

Kulat's eyes widened. 'Highness—'

'I have spoken. The Open Wing, with the courtyard and stables, where he can keep his dogs—'

'Highness, there are plans for converting the Open Wing into your own private garden—'

'Do not interrupt me again, Kulat. I have spoken.'

My own private garden. The thought now amused her, as she reached for her goblet of wine. *Yes, and we shall see how it grows.*

So carried on her unspoken thoughts, Felisin saw nothing of Kulat's sudden dark look, the moment before he bowed and turned away.

The boy had a name, but she would give him a new name. One better suited to her vision of the future. After a moment, she smiled. Yes, she would name him Crokus.

CHAPTER FIFTEEN

An old man past soldiering
his rivets green, his eyes
rimmed in rust,
stood as if heaved awake
from slaughter's pit, back-cut
from broken flight
when young blades chased him
from the field.
He looks like a promise only fools
could dream unfurled,
the banners of glory
gesticulating
in the wind over his head,
stripped like ghosts,
skulls stove in, lips flapping,
their open mouths mute.

'Oh harken to me,' cries he
atop his imagined summit,
'and I shall speak – of riches
and rewards, of my greatness,
my face once young like these
I see before me – harken!'

While here I sit at the Tapu's
table, grease-fingered
with skewered meat, cracked goblet
pearled in the hot sun, the wine
watered to make, in the
alliance of thin and thick,
both passing palatable.

As near as an arm's reach
from this rabbler, this
ravelling trumpeter who once
might have stood shield-locked
at my side, red-hued, masked
drunk, coarse with fear, in
the moment before he broke—
broke and ran—
and now he would call a new
generation to war, to battle-clamour,
and why? Well, why – all
because he once ran, but listen:
a soldier who ran once
ever runs, and this,
honoured magistrate,
is the reason—
the sole reason I say—
for my knife finding his back.
He was a soldier
whose words heaved me
awake.

'Bedura's Defence' in *The Slaying of King Qualin Tros of Bellid*
(transcribed as song by Fisher, Malaz City, last year of
Laseen's Reign)

WITHIN AN AURA REDOLENT AND REMINISCENT OF A CRYPT, NOTO
Boil, company cutter, Kartoolian by birth and once priest of
Soliel, long, wispy, colourless hair plucked like strands of web
by the wind, his skin the hue of tanned goat leather, stood like a bent
sapling and picked at his green-furred teeth with a fish spine. It had been
a habit of his for so long that he had worn round holes between each
tooth, and the gums had receded far back, making his smile skeletal.

He had smiled but once thus far, by way of greeting, and for Ganoes
Paran, that had been once too many.

At the moment, the healer seemed at best pensive, at worst distracted
by boredom. 'I cannot say for certain, Captain Kindly,' the man finally
said.

'About what?'

A flicker of the eyes, grey floating in yellow murk. 'Well, you had a
question for me, did you not?'

'No,' Paran replied, 'I had for you an order.'

'Yes, of course, that is what I meant.'

'I commanded you to step aside.'

'The High Fist is very ill, Captain. It will avail you nothing to disturb his dying. More pointedly, you might well become infected with the dread contagion.'

'No, I won't. And it is his dying that I intend to do something about. For now, however, I wish to see him. That is all.'

'Captain Sweetcreek has—'

'Captain Sweetcreek is no longer in command, cutter. I am. Now get out of my way before I reassign you to irrigating horse bowels, and given the poor quality of the feed they have been provided of late . . .'

Noto Boil examined the fish spine in his hand. 'I will make note of this in my company log, Captain Kindly. As the Host's ranking healer, there is some question regarding chain of command at the moment. After all, under normal circumstances I far outrank captains—'

'These are not normal circumstances. I'm losing my patience here.'

An expression of mild distaste. 'Yes, I have first-hand knowledge of what happens when you lose patience, no matter how unjust the situation. It fell to me, I remind you, to heal Captain Sweetcreek's fractured cheekbone.' The man stepped to one side of the entrance. 'Please, Captain, be welcome within.'

Sighing, Paran strode past the cutter, pulled aside the flap and entered the tent.

Gloom, the air hot and thick with heavy incense that could only just mask the foul reek of sickness. In this first chamber were four cots, each occupied by a company commander, only two of whom were familiar to Paran. All slept or were unconscious, limbs twisted in their sweat-stained blankets, necks swollen by infection, each drawn breath a thin wheeze like some ghastly chorus. Shaken, the captain moved past them and entered the tent's back chamber, where there was but one occupant.

In the grainy, crepuscular air, Paran stared down at the figure in the cot. His first thought was that Dujek Onearm was already dead. An aged, bloodless face marred by dark purple blotches, eyes crusted shut by mucus. The man's tongue, the colour of Aren Steel, was so swollen it had forced open his mouth, splitting the parched lips. A healer – probably Noto Boil – had packed Dujek's neck in a mixture of mould, ash and clay, which had since dried, looking like a slave collar.

After a long moment, Paran heard Dujek draw breath, the sound uneven, catching again and again in faint convulsions of his chest. The meagre air then hissed back out in a rattling whistle.

Gods below, this man will not last the night.

The captain realized that his lips had gone numb, and he was having trouble focusing. *This damned incense, it's d'bayang.* He stood for another half-dozen heartbeats, looking down on the shrunken, frail figure of the Malazan Empire's greatest living general, then he turned about and strode from the chamber.

Two steps across the outer room and a hoarse voice halted him.

'Who in Hood's name are you?'

Paran faced the woman who had spoken. She was propped up on her bed, enough to allow her a level gaze on the captain. Dark-skinned, her complexion lacking the weathered lines of desert life, her eyes large and very dark. Stringy, sweat-plastered black hair, cut short yet nonetheless betraying a natural wave, surrounded her round face, which sickness had drawn, making her eyes seem deeper, more hollow.

'Captain Kindly—'

'By the Abyss you are. I served under Kindly in Nathilog.'

'Well, that's discouraging news. And you are?'

'Fist Rythe Bude.'

'One of Dujek's recent promotions, then, for I have never heard of you. Nor can I fathom where you hail from.'

'Shal-Morzinn.'

Paran frowned. 'West of Nemil?'

'Southwest.'

'How did you come to be in Nathilog, Fist?'

'By the Three, give me some water, damn you.'

Paran looked round until he found a bladder, which he brought to her side.

'You're a fool,' she said. 'Coming in here. Now you will die with the rest of us. You'll have to pour it into my mouth.'

He removed the stopper, then leaned closer.

She closed her remarkable, luminous eyes and tilted her head back, mouth opening. The weals on her neck were cracked, leaking clear fluid as thick as tears. Squeezing the bladder, he watched the water stream into her mouth.

She swallowed frantically, gasped then coughed.

He pulled the bladder away. 'Enough?'

She managed a nod, coughed again, then swore in some unknown language. 'This damned smoke,' she added in Malazan. 'Numbs the throat so you can't even tell when you're swallowing. Every time I close my eyes, d'bayang dreams rush upon me like the Red Winds.'

He stood, looking down upon her.

'I left Shal-Morzinn . . . in haste. On a Blue Moranth trader. Money for passage ran out in a town called Pitch, on the Genabarii coast. From there I made it to Nathilog, and with a belly too empty to let me think straight, I signed up.'

'Where had you intended to go?'

She made a face. 'As far as my coin would take me, fool. Crossing the Three is not a recipe for a long life. Blessings to Oponn's kiss, they didn't come after me.'

'The Three?'

'The rulers of Shal-Morzinn . . . for the past thousand years. You seemed to recognize the empire's name, which is more than most.'

'I know nothing beyond the name itself, which is found on certain Malazan maps.'

She croaked a laugh. 'Malazans. Knew enough to make their first visit their last.'

'I wasn't aware we'd visited at all,' Paran said.

'The Emperor. And Dancer. The imperial flagship, *Twist*. Gods, that craft alone was sufficient to give the Three pause. Normally, they annihilate strangers as a matter of course – we trade with no-one, not even Nemil. The Three despise outsiders. Were they so inclined they would have conquered the entire continent by now, including Seven Cities.'

'Not expansionists, then. No wonder no-one's heard of them.'

'More water.'

He complied.

When she'd finished coughing, she met his eyes. 'You never told me – who are you in truth?'

'Captain Ganoes Paran.'

'He's dead.'

'Not yet.'

'All right. So why the lie?'

'Dujek decommissioned me. Officially, I am without rank.'

'Then what in Hood's name are you doing here?'

He smiled. 'That's a long story. At the moment, I have one thing I need to do, and that is, repay a debt. I owe Dujek that much. Besides, it's not good to have a goddess loose in the mortal realm, especially one who delights in misery.'

'They all delight in misery.'

'Yes, well.'

She bared a row of even teeth, stained by sickness. 'Captain, do you think, had we known Poliel was in the temple, we would have gone in at all? You, on the other hand, don't have that excuse. Leaving me to conclude that you have lost your mind.'

'Captain Sweetcreek certainly agrees with you, Fist,' Paran said, setting the bladder down. 'I must take my leave. I would appreciate it, Fist Rythe Bude, if you refer to me as Captain Kindly.' He walked towards the tent's exit.

'Ganoes Paran.'

Something in her tone turned him round even as he reached for the flap.

'Burn my corpse,' she said. 'Ideally, fill my lungs with oil, so that my chest bursts, thus freeing to flight my ravaged soul. It's how it's done in Shal-Morzinn.'

He hesitated, then nodded.

Outside, he found the cutter Noto Boil still standing at his station, examining the bloodied point of the fish spine a moment before slipping it back into his mouth.

'Captain Kindly,' the man said in greeting. 'The outrider Hurlochel was just here, looking for you. From him, I gather you intend something . . . rash.'

'Cutter, when the alternative is simply waiting for them to die, I will accept the risk of doing something rash.'

'I see. How, then, have you planned this assault of yours? Given that you shall face the Grey Goddess herself. I doubt even your reputation will suffice in compelling the soldiers to assail the Grand Temple of Poliel. Indeed, I doubt you will get them to even so much as enter G'danisban.'

'I'm not taking any soldiers, cutter.'

A sage nod from the gaunt man. 'Ah, an army of one, then, is it? Granted,' he added, eyeing Paran speculatively, 'I have heard tales of your extraordinary . . . ferocity. Is it true you once dangled a Falah'd over the edge of his palace's tower balcony? Even though he was an ally of the empire at the time. What was his crime again? Oh yes, a clash of colours in his attire, on the first day of the Emperor's Festival. What *were* those colours he had the effrontery to wear?'

Paran studied the man for a moment, then he smiled. 'Blue and green.'

'But those colours do not clash, Captain.'

'I never claimed good judgement in aesthetic matters, cutter. Now, what were we talking about? Oh yes, my army of one. Indeed. I intend to lead but one man. Together, the two of us shall attack the Grey Goddess, with the aim of driving her from this realm.'

'You chose wisely, I think,' Noto Boil said. 'Given what awaits Hurlochel, he displayed impressive calm a few moments ago.'

'And well he should,' Paran said, 'since he's not coming with me. You are.'

The fish spine speared through the cutter's upper lip. A look of agony supplanted disbelief. He tore the offending needle from his lip and flung it away, then brought up both hands to clench against the pain. His eyes looked ready to clamber from their sockets.

Paran patted the man on the shoulder. 'Get that seen to, will you? We depart in half a bell, cutter.'

He sat on a kit chest, settled back slowly, until the give of the tent wall ceased, then stretched out his legs. 'I should be half-drunk right now,' he said, 'given what I'm about to do.'

Hurlochel seemed unable to muster a smile. 'Please, Captain. We should decamp. Cut our losses. I urge you to abandon this course of action, which will do naught but result in the death of yet another good soldier, not to mention an irritating but competent company cutter.'

'Ah, yes. Noto Boil. Once priest to Soliel, sister goddess of Poliel.'

'Priest no longer, Captain. Disavowed hold no weight with the ascendant so abandoned.'

'Soliel. Mistress of Healing, Beneficence, the Goddess that Weeps Healing Tears. She must have let loose an ocean of them by now, don't you think?'

'Is it wise to mock her at this threshold, Captain?'

'Why not? How has her infamous, unceasing sorrow for the plight of mortals done them any good, any at all, Hurlochel? It's easy to weep when staying far away, doing nothing. When you take credit for every survivor out there – those whose own spirits fought the battle, whose own spirits refused to yield to Hood's embrace.' He sneered up at the tent roof. 'It's the so-called friendly, sympathetic gods who have the most to answer for.' Paran glared at the man standing before him. 'Hood knows, the other ones are straightforward and damned clear on their own infamy – grant them that. But to proffer succour, salvation and all the rest, whilst leaving true fate to chance and chance alone – damn me, Hurlochel, to that they will give answer!'

The outrider's eyes were wide, unblinking.

Paran looked away. 'Sorry. Some thoughts I'd do better to keep to myself. It's a longstanding fault of mine, alas.'

'Captain. For a moment there . . . your eyes . . . they . . . *flared*. Like a beast's.'

Paran studied the man. 'Did they now?'

'I'd swear it with one heel on Hood's own foreskin, Captain.'

Ganoes Paran pushed himself to his feet. 'Relay these orders to the officers. This army marches in four days. In three days' time, I want them in full kit, dressed out with weapons bared for inspection, ready at noon. And when we depart, I want to leave this camp clean, every latrine filled in, the refuse burned.' He faced Hurlochel. 'Get these soldiers busy – they're rotting from the inside out. Do you have all that, Hurlochel?'

The outrider smiled, then repeated Paran's orders word for word.

'Good. Be sure to impress on the officers that these days of lying round moping and bitching are at an end. Tell them the order of march will place to the lead post the most presentable company – everyone else eats their dust.'

'Captain, where do we march?'

'No idea. I'll worry about that then.'

'What of the High Fist and the others in that tent?'

'Chances are, they won't be up to much for a while. In the meantime—'

'In the meantime, you command the Host, sir.'

'Aye, I do.'

Hurlochel's sudden salute was sharp, then he pivoted and strode from the tent.

Paran stared after him. *Fine, at least someone's damned pleased about it.*

A short time later, he and Noto Boil sat atop their horses at the camp's edge, looking downslope and across the flat killing-ground to the city's walls, its bleached-limestone facing a mass of scrawls, painted symbols, hand-prints, skeletal figures. This close, there should have been sounds rising from the other side of those walls, the haze of dust and smoke overhead, and the huge gate should be locked open for a steady stream of traders and hawkers, drovers and work crews. Soldiers should be visible in the windows of the gate's flanking square towers.

The only movement came from flocks of pigeons lifting into view then dipping back down, fitful and frantic as an armada of kites rejected by storm-winds; and from the blue-tinted desert starlings and croaking crows lined up like some nightmare army on the battlements.

'Captain,' the cutter said, the fish spine once more jutting from between his lips – the hole it had made earlier just above those lips was a red, slightly puckered spot, smeared like a popped pimple – 'you believe me capable of assaulting all that is anathema to me?'

'I thought you were disavowed,' Paran said.

'My point precisely. I cannot even so much as call upon Soliel for her benign protection. Perhaps your eyes are blind to the truth, but I tell you, Captain, I can see the air roiling up behind those walls – it is the breath of chaos. Currents swirl, heave – even to look upon them, as I do now, makes me ill. We shall die, you and I, not ten paces in from the gate.'

Paran checked the sword at his belt, then adjusted his helm's strap. 'I am not as blind as you believe me to be, cutter.' He studied the city for a moment, then gathered his reins. 'Ride close to my side, Noto Boil.'

'Captain, the gate looks closed, locked tight – we are not welcome.'

'Never mind the damned gate,' Paran said. 'Are you ready?'

The man turned wild eyes upon him. 'No,' he said in a high voice, 'I am not.'

'Let's get this over with,' Paran said, nudging his horse into motion.

Noto Boil spared one last look over his shoulder, and saw soldiers standing, watching, gathered in their hundreds. 'Gods,' he whispered, 'why am I not among them right now?'

Then he moved to catch up to Captain Kindly, who had once dangled an innocent man from a tower's edge. *And now does it all over again – to me!*

She had once been sent out to hunt down her younger brother, tracking him through half the city – oh, he'd known she was after him, known that she was the one they'd send, the only one capable of closing a hand on one scrawny ankle, dragging him back, then shaking him until his brain rattled inside his skull. He'd led her a wild trail that night. Ten years old and already completely out of control, eyes bright as marbles polished in a mouthful of spit, the white smile more wicked than a wolf's snarl, all gangly limbs and cavorting malice.

He had been collecting . . . things. In secret. Strands of hair, nail clippings, a rotted tooth. Something, it turned out, from everyone in the entire extended family. Forty-two, if one counted four-month-old Minarala – and he had, the little bastard. A madness less imaginative might have settled for a host of horrid dolls, upon which he could deliver minor but chronic torment to feed his insatiable evil, but not her brother, who clearly believed himself destined for vast infamy. Not content with dolls fashioned in likenesses, he had constructed, from twine, sticks, straw, wool and horn, a tiny flock of forty-two sheep. Penned in a kraal of sticks assembled on the floor of the estate's attic. Then, from one of his own milk teeth, newly plucked from his mouth, he made for himself the likeness of a wolf fang and then, with tatters of fur, the wolf to which it belonged, of a scale to permit it to devour a sheep-doll in a single gulp.

In skeins of demented magic, he had set his wolf among the flock.

Screams and wails in the night, in household after household, unleashed from terrifying nightmares steeped in the reek of panic and lanolin, of clopping hoofs and surges of desperate, hopeless flight. Nips and buffets from the huge roaring wolf, the beast toying with every one of them – oh, she would remember the torment for a long, long time.

In the course of the following day, as uncles, aunts, nephews and the like gathered, all pale and trembling, and as the revelation arrived that one and all had shared their night of terror, few were slow in realizing the source of their nightmares – of course he had already lit out, off to one of his countless bolt-holes in the city. Where he would hide until such time as the fury and outrage should pass.

For the crimes committed by children, all fugue eventually faded, as concern rose in its stead. For most children, normal children; but not for Ben Adaephon Delat, who had gone too far. Again.

And so Torahaval Delat had been dispatched to track down her brother, and to deliver upon him an appropriate punishment. Such as, she had considered at the time, flaying him alive. Sheep, were they? Well, she carried in her pack the wolf doll, and with that she intended most dreadful torture. Though nowhere near as talented as her younger brother, and admittedly far less imaginative, she had managed to fashion a leash of sorts for the creature, and now, no matter where her brother went, she could follow.

He was able to stay ahead of her for most of a day and the following night, until a bell before dawn when, on a rooftop in the Prelid Quarter of Aren, she caught up with him, holding in her hands the wolf doll, gripping the back legs and pulling them wide.

The boy, running flat out one moment, flat on his face the next. Squealing and laughing, and, even as she stumbled, that laughter stung so that she gave those legs an extra twist.

And, screaming, fell onto the pebbled roof, her hips filling with agony.

Her brother shrieked as well, yet could not stop laughing.

She had not looked too closely at the wolf doll, and now, gasping and wincing, she sought to do so. The gloom was reluctant to yield, but at last she made out the beast's bound-up body beneath the tatter of fur – her underclothes – the ones that had disappeared from the clothesline a week earlier – knotted and wrapped tight around some solid core, the nature of which she chose not to deliberate overmuch.

He'd known she would come after him. Had known she'd find his stash of dolls in the attic. Had known she would make use of the wolf doll, his own anima that he had so carelessly left behind. He'd known . . . everything.

That night, in the darkness before dawn, Torahaval decided that she would hate him, for ever more. Passionately, a hatred fierce enough to scour the earth in its entirety.

It's easy to hate the clever ones, even if they happen to be kin. Perhaps especially then.

There was no clear path from that recollection to her life now, to this moment, with the singular exception of the sensation that she was trapped inside a nightmare; one from which, unlike that other nightmare all those years ago, she would never awaken.

Her brother was not there, laughing and gasping, then finally, convulsed with glee on the rooftop, releasing the sorcery within the wolf doll. Making the pain go away. Her brother, dead or alive – by now more probably dead – was very far away. And she wished, with all her heart, that it wasn't so.

Mumbling like a drunk beggar, Bridthok sat before the stained granite-topped table to her right, his long-nailed fingers pushing the strange assortment of gold and silver coins back and forth as he sought to force upon them some means of categorization, a task at which he was clearly failing. The vast chests of coinage in Poliel's temple were bottomless – not figuratively but literally, they had discovered. And to reach down into the ice-cold darkness was to close hands on frost-rimed gold and silver, in all manner of currency. Stamped bars, studded teeth, holed spheres, torcs and rings, rolled bolts of gold-threaded silk small enough to fit in the palm of one hand, and coins of all sorts: square, triangular, crescent, holed, tubular, along with intricate folding boxes, chains, beads, spools, honeycomb wafers and ingots. Not one of which was familiar to any of them gathered here – trapped here – in the G'danisban temple with its mad, horrendous goddess. Torahaval had no idea there were so many languages in the world, such as she saw inscribed upon much of the currency. Letters like tiny images, letters proceeding diagonally, or vertically, or in spiral patterns, some letters little more than patterns of dots.

From other realms, Bridthok insisted. The more mundane coins could be found in the eastern chamber behind the altar, an entire room heaped with the damned things. An empire's treasury in that room alone, the man claimed, and perhaps he was right. With the first rumour of plague, the coffers of Poliel filled to overflowing. But it was the alien coinage that most interested the old man. It had since become Bridthok's obsession, this *Cataloguing of Realms* that he claimed would be his final glory of scholarship.

A strange contrast, this academic bent, in a man for whom ambition and lust for power seemed everything, the very reason for drawing breath, the cage in which his murderous heart paced.

He had loosed more rumours of his death than anyone she had ever known, a new one every year or so, to keep the many hunters from his trail, he claimed. She suspected he simply took pleasure in the challenge of invention. Among the fools – her co-conspirators – gathered here, Bridthok was perhaps the most fascinating. Neither Septhune Anabhin nor Sradal Purthu encouraged her, in matters of trust or respect. And Sribin, well, Sribin was no longer even recognizable.

The fate, it seemed, of those whom the Grey Goddess took as mortal lover. And when she tired of the rotted, moaning thing that had once been Sribin, the bitch would select another. From her dwindling store of terrified prisoners. Male, female, adult, child, it mattered naught to Poliel.

532

Bridthok insisted the cult of Sha'ik was reborn, invigorated beyond – far beyond – all that had gone before. Somewhere, out there, was the City of the Fallen, and a new Sha'ik, and the Grey Goddess was harvesting for her a broken legion of the mad, for whom all that was mortal belonged to misery and grief, the twin offspring of Poliel's womb. And, grey in miasma and chaos, blurred by distance, there lurked the Crippled God, twisted and cackling in his chains, ever drawing tighter this foul alliance.

What knew Torahaval of wars among the gods? She did not even care, beyond the deathly repercussions in her own world, her own life.

Her younger brother had long ago fallen one way; and she another, and now all hope of escape was gone.

Bridthok's mumbling ceased in a sudden gasp. He started in his chair, head lifting, eyes widening.

A tremor ran through Torahaval Delat. 'What is it?' she demanded.

The old man rose from behind the table. 'She summons us.'

I too must be mad – what is there left in life to love? Why do I still grip the edge, when the Abyss offers everything I now yearn for? Oblivion. An end. Gods . . . an end. 'More than that, Bridthok,' she said. 'You look . . . aghast.'

Saying nothing and not meeting her eye, he headed out into the hallway. Cursing under her breath, Torahaval followed.

Once, long ago, her brother – no more than four, perhaps five years old at the time, long before the evil within him had fully grown into itself – had woken screaming in the night, and she had run to his bedside to comfort him. In child words, he described his nightmare. He had died, yet walked the world still, for he had forgotten something. Forgotten, and no matter what he did, no recollection was possible. And so his corpse wandered, everywhere, with ever the same question on his lips, a question delivered to every single person cursed to cross his path. *What? What have I forgotten?*

It had been hard to reconcile that shivering, wide-eyed child hiding in her arms that night with the conniving trickster of only a few years later.

Perhaps, she now thought as she trailed Bridthok and the train of his flapping, threadbare robes, perhaps in the interval of those few years, Adaephon Delat had remembered what it was he had forgotten. Perhaps it was nothing more than what a corpse still striding the mortal world could not help but forget.

How to live.

'I thought daytime was supposed to be for sleeping,' Bottle muttered as his sergeant tugged on his arm yet again. The shade of the boulder he had been curled up beside was, the soldier told himself, the only reason he was still alive. This day had been the hottest yet. Insects crawling on stone slabs had cooked halfway across, shells popping like seeds. No-one moved, no-one said a thing. Thirst and visions of water obsessed the entire troop. Bottle had eventually fallen into a sleep that still pulled at him with torpid, heavy hands.

If only Fiddler would damned well leave him alone.

'Come with me, Bottle. Up. On your feet.'

'If you've found a cask of spring water, Sergeant, then I'm yours. Otherwise . . .'

Fiddler lifted him upright, then dragged him along. Stumbling, his tongue feeling like a knot of leather strips, Bottle was barely aware of the path underfoot. Away from the road, among wind-sculpted rocks, winding this way and that. Half-blinded by the glare, it was a moment before he realized that they had stopped, were standing on a clearing of flat sand, surrounded by boulders, and there were two figures awaiting them.

Bottle felt his heart tighten in his chest. The one seated cross-legged opposite was Quick Ben. To his right squatted the assassin Kalam, his dark face glistening, worn black gloves on his hands and the elongated handles of his twin long-knives jutting out from beneath his arms. The man looked ready to kill something, although Bottle suspected that was his normal expression.

Quick Ben's eyes were fixed on him, languid yet dangerous, like a leopard playing with a maimed hare. But there was something else in that regard, Bottle suspected. Something not quite hidden. *Fear?*

After a moment of locked gazes, Bottle's attention was drawn to the collection of dolls perched in the sand before the wizard. Professional interest helped push down his own fear, for the time being, at least. Involuntarily, he leaned forward.

'It's an old art,' Quick Ben said. 'But you know that, don't you, soldier?'

'You're at an impasse,' Bottle said.

The wizard's brows lifted, and he shot Kalam an unreadable glance before clearing his throat and saying, 'Aye, I am. How did you see it? And how so . . . quickly?'

Bottle shrugged.

Quick Ben scowled at an amused grunt from Fiddler. 'All right, you damned imp, any suggestions on what to do about it?'

Bottle ran a hand through the grimy stubble of his hair. 'Tell me what you're trying to do.'

'What I'm trying to do, soldier, is none of your damned business!'

Sighing, Bottle settled onto the sand, assuming a posture to match

534

that of the man opposite him. He studied the figures, then pointed to one. 'Who's she?'

Quick Ben started. 'I didn't know it was a "she".'

'First one you set down, I'd hazard. You probably woke from a bad dream, all confused, but knowing something was wrong, something somewhere, and this one – this woman – she's your link to it. Family, I'd hazard. Mother? Daughter? Sister? Sister, yes. She's been thinking about you. A lot, lately. Look at the skein of shadow lines around her, like she was standing in a thatch of grass, only there ain't no grass nearby, so that skein belongs to something else.'

'Hood squeeze my balls,' Quick Ben hissed, eyes now darting among the figures on the sand. He seemed to have forgotten his belligerence. 'Torahaval? What in the name of the Abyss has she got herself into now? And how come not one of the others can reach a single shadow towards her?'

Bottle scratched at his beard, fingernails trapping a nit. He pulled it loose and flicked it away.

Kalam started, then cursed. 'Watch that!'

'Sorry.' Bottle pointed at one doll, wrapped in black silks. The shadow the doll cast seemed to reveal two projections of some kind, like crows perched on each shoulder. 'That's Apsalar, yes? She's part of this, all right, though not at the moment. I think her path was meant to cross your sister's, only it never happened. So, there was intent, un-fulfilled, and be glad for that. That one's Cotillion and aye, he's dancing his infernal dance all right, but his only role was in starting the pebble from the hilltop – how it rolled and what it picked up on the way down he left to the fates. Still, you're right in choosing the House of Shadows. Was that instinct? Never mind. Here's your problem.' He pointed at another doll, this one hooded and cloaked entirely in gauze-thin black linen.

Quick Ben blinked, then frowned. 'Hardly. That's Shadowthrone, and he's central to this. It's all got to do with him and, damn you, Bottle, that's more than instinct!'

'Oh, he's central all right, but see how his shadow doesn't reach?'

'I know it doesn't reach! But that's where he stands, damn you!'

Bottle reached out and collected the doll.

Snarling, Quick Ben half rose, but Fiddler's hand snapped out, pushed the wizard back down.

'Get that paw off me, sapper,' the wizard said, his tone low, even.

'I warned you,' the sergeant said, 'didn't I?' He withdrew his hand, and Quick Ben settled back as if something much heavier had just landed on his shoulders.

In the meantime, Bottle was busy reworking the doll. Bending the

wires within the arms and legs. For his own efforts, he rarely used wire
– too expensive – but in this case they made his reconfiguring the doll
much easier. Finally satisfied, he set it back, in precisely the same
position as before.

No-one spoke, all eyes fixed on the doll of Shadowthrone – now on
all fours, right foreleg and left rear leg raised, the entire form pitched
far forward, impossibly balanced. The shadow stretching out to within
a finger's breadth of the figure that was Torahaval Delat.

Shadowthrone . . . now something else . . .

Kalam whispered, 'Still not touching . . .'

Bottle settled back, crossing his arms as he lay down on the sand. 'Wait,'
he said, then closed his eyes, and a moment later was asleep once more.

Crouched close at Quick Ben's side, Fiddler let out a long breath.

The wizard pulled his stare from the reconfigured Shadowthrone, his
eyes bright as he looked over at the sapper. 'He was half asleep, Fid.'

The sergeant shrugged.

'No,' the wizard said, 'you don't understand. Half asleep. Someone's
with him. Was with him, I mean. Do you have any idea how far back
sympathetic magic like this goes? To the very beginning. To that
glimmer, that first glimmer, Fid. The birth of awareness. Are you understanding me?'

'As clear as the moon lately,' Fiddler said, scowling.

'The Eres'al, the Tall Ones – before a single human walked this
world. Before the Imass, before even the K'Chain Che'Malle. Fiddler,
Eres was here. Now. Herself. With *him*.'

The sapper looked back down at the doll of Shadowthrone. Four-
legged now, frozen in its headlong rush – and the shadow it cast did not
belong, did not fit at all. For the head was broad, the snout prominent
and wide, jaws opened but wrapped about something. And whatever
that thing was, it slithered and squirmed like a trapped snake.

What in Hood's name? Oh. Oh, wait . . .

Atop a large boulder that had sheared, creating an inclined surface,
Apsalar was lying flat on her stomach, watching the proceedings in the
clearing twenty-odd paces distant. Disturbing conversations, those,
especially that last part, about the Eres. *Just another hoary ancient
better left alone.* That soldier, Bottle, needed watching.

Torahaval Delat . . . one of the names on that spy's – Mebra's – list
in Ehrlitan. Quick Ben's sister. Well, that was indeed unfortunate, since
it seemed that both Cotillion and Shadowthrone wanted the woman
dead, and they usually got what they wanted. *Thanks to me . . . and
people like me. The gods place knives into our mortal hands, and need
do nothing more.*

She studied Quick Ben, gauging his growing agitation, and began to suspect that the wizard knew something of the extremity that his sister now found herself in. Knew, and, in the thickness of blood that bound kin no matter how estranged, the foolish man had decided to do something about it.

Apsalar waited no longer, allowing herself to slide back down the flat rock, landing lightly in thick wind-blown sand, well in shadow and thoroughly out of sight from anyone. She adjusted her clothes, scanned the level ground around her, then drew from folds in her clothing two daggers, one into each hand.

There was music in death. Actors and musicians knew this as true. And, for this moment, so too did Apsalar.

To a chorus of woe no-one else could hear, the woman in black began the Shadow Dance.

Telorast and Curdle, who had been hiding in a fissure near the flat-topped boulder, now edged forward.

'She's gone into her own world,' Curdle said, nonetheless whispering, her skeletal head bobbing and weaving, tail flicking with unease. Before them, Not-Apsalar danced, so infused with shadows she was barely visible. Barely in this world at all.

'Never cross this one, Curdle,' Telorast hissed. 'Never.'

'Wasn't planning to. Not like you.'

'Not me. Besides, the doom's come upon us – what are we going to do?'

'Don't know.'

'I say we cause trouble, Curdle.'

Tiny jaws clacked. 'I like that.'

Quick Ben rose suddenly. 'I've got no choice,' he said.

Kalam swore, then said, 'I hate it when you say that, Quick.'

The wizard drew out another doll, this one trailing long threads. He set it down a forearm's reach from the others, then looked over and nodded to Kalam.

Scowling, the assassin unsheathed one of his long-knives and stabbed it point-first into the sand.

'Not the otataral one, idiot.'

'Sorry.' Kalam withdrew the weapon and resheathed it, then drew out the other knife. A second stab into the sand.

Quick Ben knelt, carefully gathering the threads and leading them over to the long-knife's grip, where he fashioned knots, joining the doll to the weapon. 'See these go taut—'

'I grab the knife and pull you back here. I know, Quick, this ain't the first time, remember?'

'Right. Sorry.'

The wizard settled back into his cross-legged position.

'Hold on,' Fiddler said in a growl. 'What's going on here? You ain't planning something stupid, are you? You are. Damn you, Quick—'

'Be quiet,' the wizard said, closing his eyes. 'Me and Shadowthrone,' he whispered, 'we're old friends.' Then he smiled.

In the clearing, Kalam fixed his gaze on the doll that was now the only link between Quick Ben and his soul. 'He's gone, Fid. Don't say nothing, I need to concentrate. Those strings could go tight at any time, slow, so slow you can't even see it happen, but suddenly . . .'

'He should've waited,' Fiddler said. 'I wasn't finished saying what I was planning on saying, and he just goes. Kal, I got a bad feeling. Tell me Quick and Shadowthrone really are old friends. Kalam? Tell me Quick wasn't being sarcastic.'

The assassin flicked a momentary look up at the sapper, then licked his lips, returning to his study of the threads. Had they moved? No, not much anyway. 'He wasn't being sarcastic, Fid.'

'Good.'

'No, more sardonic, I think.'

'Not good. Listen, can you pull him out right now? I think you should—'

'Quiet, damn you! I need to watch. I need to concentrate.' *Fid's got a bad feeling. Shit.*

Paran and Noto Boil rode up and halted in the shadow cast by the city wall. The captain dismounted and stepped up to the battered façade. With his dagger he etched a broad, arched line, beginning on his left at the wall's base, then up, over – taking two paces – and down again, ending at the right-side base. In the centre he slashed a pattern, then stepped back, slipping the knife into its scabbard.

Remounting the horse, he gathered the reins and said, 'Follow me.'

And he rode forward. His horse tossed its head and stamped its forelegs a moment before plunging into, and through, the wall. They emerged moments later onto a litter-strewn street. The faces of empty, lifeless buildings, windows stove in. A place of devastation, a place where civilization had crumbled, revealing at last its appallingly weak foundations. Picked white bones lay scattered here and there. A glutted rat wobbled its way along the wall's gutter.

After a long moment, the healer appeared, leading his mount by the reins. 'My horse,' he said, 'is not nearly as stupid as yours, Captain. Alas.'

'Just less experienced,' Paran said, looking round. 'Get back in the saddle. We may be alone for the moment, but that will not last.'

'Gods below,' Noto Boil hissed, scrambling back onto his horse. 'What has happened here?'

'You did not accompany the first group?'

They rode slowly onto the gate avenue, then in towards the heart of G'danisban.

'Dujek's foray? No, of course not. And how I wish the High Fist was still in command.'

Me too. 'The Grand Temple is near the central square – where is Soliel's Temple?'

'Soliel? Captain Kindly, I cannot enter that place – not ever again.'

'How did you come to be disavowed, Boil?'

'*Noto* Boil, sir. There was a disagreement . . . of a political nature. It may be that the nefarious, incestuous, nepotistic quagmire of a priest's life well suits the majority of its adherents. Unfortunately, I discovered too late that I could not adapt to such an existence. You must understand, actual worship was the least among daily priorities. I made the error of objecting to this unnatural, nay, unholy inversion.'

'Very noble of you,' Paran remarked. 'Oddly enough, I heard a different tale about your priestly demise. More specifically, you lost a power struggle at the temple in Kartool. Something about the disposition of the treasury.'

'Clearly, such events are open to interpretation. Tell me, Captain, since you can walk through walls thicker than a man is tall, do you possess magical sensitivities as well? Can you feel the foul hunger in the air? It is hateful. It wants us, our flesh, where it can take root and suck from us every essence of health. This is Poliel's breath, and even now it begins to claim us.'

'We are not alone, cutter.'

'No. I would be surprised if we were. She will spare her followers, her *carriers*. She will—'

'Quiet,' Paran said, reining in. 'I meant, we are not alone right now.'

Eyes darting, Noto Boil scanned the immediate area. 'There,' he whispered, pointing towards an alley mouth.

They watched as a young woman stepped out from the shadows of the alley. She was naked, frighteningly thin, her eyes dark, large and luminous. Her lips were cracked and split, her hair wild and braided in filth. An urchin who had survived in the streets, a harvester of the discarded, and yet . . .

'Not a carrier,' Paran said in a murmur. 'I see about her . . . purest health.'

Noto Boil nodded. 'Aye. In spite of her apparent condition. Captain Kindly, this child has been chosen . . . by Soliel.'

'I take it, not something you even thought possible, back when you were a priest.'

The cutter simply shook his head.

The girl came closer. 'Malazans,' she said, her voice rasping as if from lack of use. 'Once. Years – a year? Once, there were other Malazans. One of them pretended he was a Gral, but I saw the armour under the robes, I saw the sigil of the Bridgeburners, from where I hid beneath a wagon. I was young, but not too young. They saved me, those Malazans. They drew away the hunters. They saved me.'

Paran cleared his throat. 'And so now Soliel chooses you . . . to help us.'

Noto Boil said, 'For she has always blessed those who repay kindness.' The cutter's voice was tremulous with wonder. 'Soliel,' he whispered, 'forgive me.'

'There are hunters,' the girl said. 'Coming. They know you are here. Strangers, enemies to the goddess. Their leader holds great hatred, for all things. Bone-scarred, broke-faced, he feeds on the pain he delivers. Come with me—'

'Thank you,' Paran said, cutting in, 'but no. Know that your warning is welcome, but I intend to meet these hunters. I intend to have them lead me to the Grey Goddess.'

'Brokeface will not permit it. He will kill you, and your horse. Your horse first, for he hates such creatures.'

Noto Boil hissed. 'Captain, please – this is an offer from *Soliel*—'

'The offer I expect from Soliel,' Paran said, tone hardening, 'will come later. One goddess at a time.' He readied his horse under him, then hesitated, glanced over at the cutter. 'Go with her, then. We will meet up at the entrance to the Grand Temple.'

'Captain, what is it you expect of me?'

'Me? Nothing. What I expect is for Soliel to make use of you, but not as she has done this child here. I expect something a lot more than that.' Paran nudged his mount forward. 'And,' he added amidst clumping hoofs, 'I won't take no for an answer.'

Noto Boil watched the madman ride off, up the main avenue, then the healer swung his horse until facing the girl. He drew the fish spine from his mouth and tucked it behind an ear. Then cleared his throat. 'Goddess . . . child. I have no wish to die, but I must point out, that man does not speak for me. Should you smite him down for his disrespect, I most certainly will not see in that anything unjust or undeserving. In fact—'

'Be quiet, mortal,' the girl said in a much older voice. 'In that man the entire world hangs in balance, and I shall not be for ever known as the one responsible for altering that condition. In any way whatsoever. Now, prepare to ride – I shall lead, but I shall not once wait for you should you lose the way.'

'I thought you offered to guide me—'

'Of lesser priority now,' she said, smirking. 'Inverted in a most unholy fashion, you might say. No, what I seek now is to witness. Do you understand? *To witness!*' And with that the girl spun round and sped off.

Swearing, the cutter drove heels into his mount's flanks, hard on the girl's trail.

Paran rode at a canter down the main avenue that seemed more a processional route into a necropolis than G'danisban's central artery, until he saw ahead a mob of figures fronted by a single man – in his hands a farmer's scythe from which dangled a blood-crusted horse-tail. The motley army – perhaps thirty or forty in all – looked as if they had been recruited from a paupers' burial pit. Covered in sores and weals, limbs twisted, faces slack, the eyes glittering with madness. Some carried swords, others butcher's cleavers and knives, or spears, shepherd's crooks or stout branches. Most seemed barely able to stand.

Such was not the case with their leader, the one the girl had called Brokeface. The man's visage was indeed pinched misshapen, flesh and bones folded in at right lower jaw, then across the face, diagonally, to the right cheekbone. He had been bitten, the captain realized, by a horse.

. . . your horse first. For he hates such creatures . . .

In that ruined face, the eyes, misaligned in the sunken pits of their sockets, burned bright as they fixed on Paran's own. Something like a smile appeared on the collapsed cave of the man's mouth.

'Her breath is not sweet enough for you? You are strong to so resist her. She would know, first, who you are. Before,' his smile twisted further, 'before we kill you.'

'The Grey Goddess does not know who I am,' Paran said, 'for this reason. From her, I have turned away. From me she can compel nothing.'

Brokeface flinched. 'There is a beast ... in your eyes. Reveal yourself, Malazan. You are not as the others.'

'Tell her,' Paran said, 'I come to make an offering.'

The head cocked to one side. 'You seek to appease the Grey Goddess?'

'In a manner of speaking. But I should tell you, we have very little time.'

'Very little? Why?'

'Take me to her and I will explain. But quickly.'

'She does not fear you.'

'Good.'

The man studied Paran for a moment longer, then he gestured with his scythe. 'Follow, then.'

There had been plenty of altars before which she had knelt over the years, and from them, one and all, Torahaval Delat had discovered something she now held to be true. All that is worshipped is but a reflection of the worshipper. A single god, no matter how benign, is tortured into a multitude of masks, each shaped by the secret desires, hungers, fears and joys of the individual mortal, who but plays a game of obsequious approbation.

Believers lunged into belief. The faithful drowned in their faith.

And there was another truth, one that seemed on the surface to contradict the first one. The gentler and kinder the god, the more harsh and cruel its worshippers, for they hold to their conviction with taut certainty, febrile in its extremity, and so cannot abide dissenters. They will kill, they will torture, in that god's name. And see in themselves no conflict, no matter how bloodstained their hands.

Torahaval's hands were bloodstained, figuratively now but once most literally. Driven to fill some vast, empty space in her soul, she had lunged, she had drowned; she had looked for some external hand of salvation – seeking what she could not find in herself. And, whether benign and love-swollen or brutal and painful, every god's touch had felt the same to her – barely sensed through the numbed obsession that was her need.

She had stumbled onto this present path the same way she had stumbled onto so many others, yet this time, it seemed there could be no going back. Every alternative, every choice, had vanished before her eyes. The first strands of the web had been spun more than fourteen months ago, in her chosen home city Karashimesh, on the shores of the inland Karas Sea – a web she had since, in a kind of lustful wilfulness, allowed to close ever tighter.

The sweet lure from the Grey Goddess, in spirit now the poisoned lover of the Chained One – the seduction of the flawed had proved so very inviting. And deadly. *For us both.* This was, she realized as she trailed Bridthok down the Aisle of Glory leading to the transept, no more than the spreading of legs before an inevitable, half-invited rape. Regret would come later if at all.

Perhaps, then, a most appropriate end.

For this foolish woman, who never learned how to live.

The power of the Grey Goddess swirled in thick tendrils through the battered-down doorway, so virulent as to rot stone.

Awaiting Bridthok and Torahaval at the threshold were the remaining acolytes of this desperate faith. Septhune Anabhin of Omari; and Sradal Purthu, who had fled Y'Ghatan a year ago after a failed attempt to kill that Malazan bitch, Dunsparrow. Both looked shrunken, now, some essence of their souls drained away, dissolving in the miasma like salt in water. Pained terror in their eyes as both turned to watch Bridthok and Torahaval arrive.

'Sribin is dead,' Septhune whispered. 'She will now choose another.'

And so she did.

Invisible, a hand huge and clawed – more fingers than could be sanely conceived – closed about Torahaval's chest, spears of agony sinking deep. A choked gasp burst from her throat and she staggered forward, pushing through the others, all of whom shrank back, gazes swimming with relief and pity – the relief far outweighing the pity. Hatred for them flashed through Torahaval, even as she staggered into the altar chamber; eyes burning in the acid fog of pestilence she lifted her head, and looked upon Poliel.

And saw the hunger that was desire.

The pain expanded, filled her body – then subsided as the clawed hand withdrew, the crusted talons pulling loose.

Torahaval fell to her knees, slid helplessly in her own sweat that had pooled on the mosaic floor beneath her.

Ware what you ask for. Ware what you seek.

The sound of horse hoofs, coming from the Aisle of Glory, getting louder.

A rider comes. A rider? What – who dares this – gods below, thank you, whoever you are. Thank you. She still clung to the edge. A few breaths more, a few more . . .

Sneering, Brokeface pushed past the cowering priests at the threshold. Paran scanned the three withered, trembling figures, and frowned as they each in turn knelt at the touch of his regard, heads bowing.

'What ails them?' he asked.

Brokeface's laugh hacked in the grainy air. 'Well said, stranger. You have cold iron in your spine, I'll give you that.'

Idiot. I wasn't trying to be funny.

'Get off that damned horse,' Brokeface said, blocking the doorway. He licked his misshapen lips, both hands shifting on the shaft of the scythe.

'Not a chance,' Paran said. 'I know how you take care of horses.'

'You cannot *ride* into the altar chamber!'

'Clear the way,' Paran said. 'This beast does not bother biting – it prefers to kick and stamp. Delights in the sound of breaking bones, in fact.'

As the horse, nostrils flared, stepped closer to the doorway, Brokeface flinched, edged back. Then he bared his crooked teeth and hissed, 'Can't you feel her wrath? *Her outrage?* Oh, you foolish man!'

'Can she feel mine?'

Paran ducked as his horse crossed the threshold. He straightened a moment later. A woman writhed on the tiles to his left, her dark skin streaked in sweat, her long limbs trembling as the plague-fouled air stroked and slipped round her, languid as a lover's caress.

Beyond this woman rose a dais atop three broad, shallow steps on which were scattered the broken fragments of the altarstone. Centred on the dais, where the altar had once stood, was a throne fashioned of twisted, malformed bones. Commanding this seat, a figure radiating such power that her form was barely discernible. Long limbs, suppurating with venom, a bared chest androgynous in its lack of definition, its shrunken frailty; the legs that extended outward seemed to possess too many joints, and the feet were three-toed and taloned, raptorial yet as large as those of an enkar'al. Poliel's eyes were but the faintest of sparks, blurred and damp at the centre of black bowls. Her mouth, broad and the lips cracked and oozing, curled now into a smile.

'Soletaken,' she said in a thin voice, 'do not frighten me. I had thought, for a moment . . . but no, you are nothing to me.'

'Goddess,' Paran said, settling back on his horse, 'I remain turned away. The choice is mine, not yours, and so you see only what I will you to see.'

'Who are you? What are you?'

'In normal circumstances, Poliel, I am but an arbiter. I have come to make an offering.'

'You understand, then,' the Grey Goddess said, 'the truth beneath the veil. Blood was *their* path. And so we choose to poison it.'

Paran frowned, then he shrugged and reached into the folds of his shirt. 'Here is my gift,' he said. Then hesitated. 'I regret, Poliel, that these circumstances . . . are not normal.'

The Grey Goddess said, 'I do not understand—'.

'Catch!'

A small, gleaming object flashed from his hand.

She raised hers in defence.

A whispering, strangely thin sound marked the impact. Impaling her hand, a shard of metal. Otataral.

The goddess convulsed, a terrible, animal scream bursting from her throat, ripping the air. Chaotic power, shredding into tatters and spinning away, waves of grey fire charging like unleashed creatures of rage, mosaic tiles exploding in their wake.

On a bridling, skittish horse, Paran watched the conflagration of agony, and wondered, of a sudden, whether he had made a mistake.

He looked down at the mortal woman, curled up on the floor. Then at her fragmented shadow, slashed through by . . . nothing. *Well, I knew that much. Time's nearly up.*

A different throne, this one so faint as to be nothing more than the hint of slivered shadows, sketched across planes of dirty ice – oddly changed, Quick Ben decided, from the last time he had seen it.

As was the thin, ghostly god reclining on that throne. Oh, the hood was the same, ever hiding the face, and the gnarled black hand still perched on the knotted top of the bent walking stick – the perch of a scavenger, like a one-legged vulture – and emanating from the apparition that was Shadowthrone, like some oversweet incense reaching out to brush the wizard's senses, a cloying, infuriating . . . smugness. Nothing unusual in all of that. Even so, there was . . . something . . .

'Delat,' the god murmured, as if tasting every letter of the name with sweet satisfaction.

'We're not enemies,' Quick Ben said, 'not any longer, Shadowthrone. You cannot be blind to that.'

'Ah but you wish me blind, Delat! Yes yes yes, you do. Blind to the past – to every betrayal, every lie, every vicious insult you have delivered foul as spit at my feet!'

'Circumstances change.'

'Indeed they do!'

The wizard could feel sweat trickling beneath his clothes. Something here was . . . what?

Was very wrong.

'Do you know,' Quick Ben asked, 'why I am here?'

'She has earned no mercy, wizard. Not even from you.'

'I am her brother.'

'There are rituals to sever such ties,' Shadowthrone said, 'and your sister has done them all!'

'Done them all? No, *tried* them all. There are threads that such rituals cannot touch. I made certain of that. I would not be here otherwise.'

A snort. 'Threads. Such as those you take greatest pleasure in spinning, Adaephon Delat? Of course. It is your finest talent, the weaving of impossible skeins.' The hooded head seemed to wag from side to side as Shadowthrone chanted, 'Nets and snares and traps, lines and hooks and bait, nets and snares and—' Then he leaned forward. 'Tell me, why should your sister be spared? And how – truly, how – do you imagine that I have the power to save her? She is not mine, is she? She's not here in Shadow Keep, is she?' He cocked his head. 'Oh my. Even now she draws her last few breaths . . . as the mortal lover of the Grey Goddess – what, pray tell, do you expect *me* to do?'

Quick Ben stared. The Grey Goddess? Poliel? *Oh, Torahaval . . .* 'Wait,' he said, 'Bottle confirmed it – more than instinct – you are involved. Right now, wherever they are, *it has something to do with you!*'

A spasmodic cackle from Shadowthrone, enough to make the god's thin, insubstantial limbs convulse momentarily. 'You owe me, Adaephon Delat! Acknowledge this and I will send you to her! This instant! Accept the debt!'

Dammit. First Kalam and now me. You bastard, Shadowthrone – 'All right! I owe you! I accept the debt!'

The Shadow God gestured, a lazy wave of one hand.

And Quick Ben vanished.

Alone once again, Shadowthrone settled back in his throne. 'So fraught,' he whispered. 'So . . . careless, unmindful of this vast, echoing, mostly empty hall. Poor man. Poor, poor man. Ah, what's this I find in my hand?' He looked over to see a short-handled scythe now gripped and poised before him. The god narrowed his gaze, looked about in the gloomy air, then said, 'Well, look at these! Threads! Worse than cobwebs, these! Getting everywhere – grossly indicative of sloppy . . . housekeeping. No, they won't do, won't do at all.' He swept the scythe's blade through the sorcerous tendrils, watched as they spun away into nothingness. 'There now,' he said, smiling, 'I feel more hygienic already.'

Throttled awake by gloved hands at his throat, he flailed about, then was dragged to his knees. Kalam's face thrust close to his own, and in that face, Bottle saw pure terror.

'The threads!' the assassin snarled.

Bottle pushed the man's hands away, scanned the sandy tableau, then grunted. 'Cut clean, I'd say.'

Standing nearby, Fiddler said, 'Go get him, Bottle! Find him – bring him back!'

The young soldier stared at the two men. 'What? How am I supposed to do that? He should never have gone in the first place!' Bottle crawled over to stare at the wizard's blank visage. 'Gone,' he confirmed. 'Straight into Shadowthrone's lair – what was he thinking?'

'Bottle!'

'Oh,' the soldier added, something else catching his gaze, 'look at that – what's she up to, I wonder?'

Kalam pushed Bottle aside and fell to his hands and knees, glaring down at the dolls. Then he shot upright. '*Apsalar!* Where is she?'

Fiddler groaned. 'No, not again.'

The assassin had both of his long-knives in his hands. 'Hood take her – where is that bitch?'

Bottle, bemused, simply shrugged as the two men chose directions at random and headed off. *Idiots. This is what they get, though, isn't it? For telling nobody nothing! About anything!* He looked back down at the dolls. *Oh my, this is going to be interesting, isn't it . . .?*

'The fool's gone and killed himself,' Captain Sweetcreek said. 'And he took our best healer with him – right through Hood's damned gate!'

Hurlochel stood with crossed arms. 'I don't think—'

'Listen to me,' Sweetcreek snapped, her corporal Futhgar at her side nodding emphatically as she continued. 'I'm now in command, and there's not a single damned thing in this whole damned world that's going to change—'

She never finished that sentence, as a shriek rang out from the north side of the camp, then the air split with thunderous howls – so close, so loud that Hurlochel felt as if his skull was cracking open. Ducking, he spun round to see, cartwheeling above tent-roofs, a soldier, his weapon whipping away – and now the sudden snap of guy-ropes, the earth trembling underfoot—

And a monstrous, black, blurred shape appeared, racing like lightning over the ground – straight for them.

A wave of charged air struck the three like a battering ram a moment before the beast reached them. Hurlochel, all breath driven from his lungs, flew through the air, landing hard on one shoulder, then rolling – caught a glimpse of Captain Sweetcreek tossed to one side, limp as a rag doll, and Futhgar seeming to vanish into the dirt as the midnight creature simply ran right over the hapless man—

The Hound's eyes—

Other beasts, bursting through the camp – horses screaming, soldiers shrieking in terror, wagons flung aside before waves of power – and Hurlochel saw one creature – *no, impossible—*

The world darkened alarmingly as he lay in a heap, paralysed, desperate to draw a breath. The spasm clutching his chest loosed suddenly and sheer joy followed the sweet dusty air down into his lungs.

Nearby, the captain was coughing, on her hands and knees, spitting blood.

From Futhgar, a single piteous groan.

Pushing himself upright, Hurlochel turned – saw the Hounds reach the wall of G'danisban – and stared, eyes wide, as a huge section of that massive barrier *exploded*, stone and brick facing shooting skyward above a billowing cloud of dust – then the concussion rolled over them—

A horse galloped past, eyes white with terror—

'Not us!' Sweetcreek gasped, crawling over. 'Thank the gods – just passing through – just—' She began coughing again.

On watery legs, Hurlochel sank down onto his knees. 'It made no sense,' he whispered, shaking his head, as buildings in the city beyond rocked and blew apart—

'What?'

He looked across at Sweetcreek. *You don't understand – I looked into that black beast's eyes, woman!* 'I saw . . . I saw—'

'What?'

I saw pure terror—

The earth rumbled anew. A resurgence of screams – and he turned, even as five huge shapes appeared, tearing wide, relentless paths through the encamped army – big, bigger than – *oh, gods below—*

'He said to wait—' Noto Boil began, then wailed as his horse flinched so hard he would later swear he heard bones breaking, then the beast wheeled from the temple entrance and bolted, peeling the cutter from its back like a wood shaving.

He landed awkwardly, felt and heard ribs crack, the pain vanishing before a more pressing distress, that being the fish spine lodged halfway down his throat.

Choking, sky darkening, eyes bulging—

Then the girl hovering over him. Frowning for a lifetime.

Stupid stupid stupid—

Before she reached into his gaping mouth, then gently withdrew the spine.

Whimpering behind that first delicious breath, Noto Boil closed his eyes, becoming aware once again that those indrawn breaths in fact delivered stabbing agony across his entire chest. He opened tear-filled eyes.

The girl still loomed over him, but her attention was, it seemed, elsewhere. Not even towards the temple entrance – but down the main avenue.

Where someone was pounding infernal drums, the thunder making the cobbles shiver and jump beneath him – causing yet more pain –

And this day started so well . . .

'Not Soletaken,' Paran was saying to the goddess writhing on her throne, the pierced hand and its otataral spike pinning her here, to this realm, to this dreadful extremity, 'not Soletaken at all, although it might at first seem so. Alas, Poliel, more complicated than that. My outrider's comment earlier, regarding my eyes – well, that was sufficient, and from those howls we just heard, it turns out the timing is about right.'

The captain glanced down once more at the woman on the tiles. Unconscious, perhaps dead. He didn't think the Hounds would bother with her. Gathering the reins, he straightened in his saddle. 'I can't stay, I'm afraid. But let me leave you with this: you made a terrible mistake. Fortunately, you won't have long to regret it.'

Concussions in the city, coming ever closer.

'Mess with mortals, Poliel,' he said, wheeling his horse round, 'and you pay.'

The man named Brokeface – who had once possessed another name, another life – cowered to one side of the altar chamber's entranceway. The three priests had fled back down the hallway. He was, for the moment, alone. *So very alone. All over again.* A poor soldier of the rebellion, young and so proud back then – shattered in one single moment.

A Gral horse, a breath thick with the reek of wet grass, teeth like chisels driving down through flesh, through bone, taking everything away. He had become an unwelcome mirror to ugliness, for every face turning upon his own had twisted in revulsion, or worse, morbid fascination. And new fears had sunk deep, hungry roots into his soul, flinching terrors that ever drove him forward, seeking to witness pain and suffering in others, seeking to make of his misery a legion, soldiers to a new cause, each as broken as he.

Poliel had arrived, like a gift – and now that bastard had killed her, was killing her even now – taking everything away. Again.

Horse hoofs skidded on tiles and he shrank back further as the rider and his mount passed through the doorway, the beast lifting from trot to canter down the wide corridor.

Brokeface stared after them with hatred in his eyes.

Lost. All lost.

He looked into the altar chamber—

Quick Ben landed cat-like; then, in the cascade of virulent agony sloughing from the imprisoned goddess not three paces to his right, he collapsed onto his stomach, hands over his head. *Oh, very funny, Shadowthrone.* He turned his head and saw Torahaval, lying motionless an arm's reach to his left.

Poor girl – I should never have tormented her so. But . . . show me a merciful child and I will truly avow a belief in miracles, and I'll throw in my back-pay besides. It was her over-sensitivity that done her in. Still, what's life without a few thousand regrets?

There was otataral in this room. He needed to collect her and drag her clear, back outside. Not so hard, once he was out of this chaotic madhouse. So, it turned out – to his astonishment – that Shadowthrone had played it true.

It was then that he heard the howl of the Hounds, in thundering echo from the hallway.

Paran emerged from the tunnel then sawed his horse hard to the left, narrowly avoiding Shan – the huge black beast plunging past, straight into the Grand Temple. Rood followed, then Baran – and in Baran's enormous jaws a hissing, reptilian panther, seeking to slow its captor down with unsheathed talons scoring the cobbles, to no avail. In their wake, Blind and Gear.

As Gear raced into the temple, the Hound loosed a howl, a sound savage with glee – as of some long-awaited vengeance moments from consummation.

Paran stared after them for a moment, then saw Noto Boil, lying down, the nameless girl hovering over him. 'For Hood's sake,' he snapped. 'There's no time for that – get him on his feet. Soliel, we're now going to your temple. Boil, where in the Abyss is your horse?'

Straightening, the girl looked back up the street. 'My sister's death approaches,' she said.

The captain followed her gaze. And saw the first of the Deragoth.

Oh, I started all this, didn't I?

Behind them the temple shook to a massive, wall-cracking concussion.

'Time to go!'

Quick Ben grasped his sister by the hood of her robe, began dragging her towards the back of the chamber, already realizing it was pointless. The Hounds had come for him, and he was in a chamber suffused with otataral.

Shadowthrone never played fair, and the wizard had to admit he'd been outwitted this time. *And this time's about to be my last—*

He heard claws rushing closer down the hallway and looked up—

Brokeface stared at the charging beast. A demon. A thing of beauty, of purity. And for him, there was nothing else, nothing left. *Yes, let beauty slay me.*

He stepped into the creature's path—

And was shouldered aside, hard enough to crack his head against the wall, momentarily stunning him. He lost his footing and fell on his backside – darkness, swirling, billowing shadows—

Even as the demon loomed above him, he saw another figure, lithe, clothed entirely in black, knife-blades slashing out, cutting deep along the beast's right shoulder.

The demon shrieked – pain, outrage – as, skidding, it twisted round to face this new attacker.

Who was no longer there, who was somehow now on its opposite side, limbs weaving, every motion strangely blurred to Brokeface's wide, staring eyes. The knives licked out once more. Flinching back, the demon came up against the wall opposite, ember eyes flaring.

From down the hallway, more demons were approaching, yet slowing their ferocious pace, claws clattering—

As the figure moved suddenly among them. The gleam of the blades, now red, seemed to dance in the air, here, there, wheeling motion from the figure, arms writhing like serpents; and with matching grace, he saw a foot lash out, connect with a beast's head – which was as big as a horse's, only wider – and that head snapped round at the impact, shoulders following, then torso, twisting round in strange elegance as the entire demon was lifted into the air, back-end now vertical, head down, in time to meet the side wall.

Where bricks exploded, the wall crumpling, caving in to some room beyond, the demon's body following into the cloud of dust.

Wild, crowded confusion in the hallway, and suddenly the figure stood motionless at Brokeface's side, daggers still out, dripping blood.

A woman, black-haired, now blocking the doorway.

Skittering sounds along the tiles, and he looked down to see two small, bird-like skeletons flanking her. Their snouts were open and hissing sounds emerged from those empty throats. Spiny tails lashed back and forth. One darted forward, a single hop, head dipping—

And the gathered demons flinched back.

Another reptilian hiss, this one louder – coming from a creature trapped in one demon's jaws. Brokeface saw in its terrible eyes a deathly fear, rising to panic—

The woman spoke quietly, clearly addressing Brokeface: 'Follow the wizard and his sister – they found a bolt-hole behind the dais – enough time, I think, to make good their escape. And yours, if you go now.'

'I don't want to,' he said, unable to keep from weeping. 'I just want to die.'

That turned her gaze from the demons facing her.

He looked up into exquisite, elongated eyes, black as ebony. And in her face, there was no mirror, no twist of revulsion. No, naught but a simple regard, and then, something that might have been . . . sorrow.

'Go to the Temple of Soliel,' she said.

'She is ever turned away—'

'Not today she isn't. Not with Ganoes Paran holding her by the scruff of her neck. Go. Be *healed.*'

This was impossible, but how could he deny her?

'Hurry, I don't know how Curdle and Telorast are managing this threat, and there's no telling how long it will last—'

Even as she said those words, a bellowing roar came from further down the hallway, and the demons bunched close before the threshold, yelping in desperate frenzy.

'That's it,' she murmured, lifting her knives.

Brokeface leapt to his feet and ran into the altar chamber.

Disbelief. Quick Ben could not understand what had held the Hounds up – he'd caught sounds, of fighting, fierce, snapping snarls, squeals of pain, and in one glance back, moments before carrying Torahaval through the back passage, he'd thought he'd seen ... something. Someone, ghostly in shadows, commanding the threshold.

Whatever this chance clash, it had purchased his life. And his sister's. Currency Quick Ben would not squander.

Throwing Torahaval over his shoulder, he entered the narrow corridor and ran as fast as he could manage.

Before too long he heard someone in pursuit. Swearing, Quick Ben swung round, the motion crunching Torahaval's head against a wall – at which she moaned.

A man, his face deformed – no, horse-bitten, the wizard realized – rushed to close. 'I will help you,' he said. 'Quickly! Doom comes into this temple!'

Had it been this man facing down the Hounds? No matter. 'Take her legs then, friend. As soon as we're off sanctified ground, we can get the Hood out of here—'

As the Hounds gathered to rush Apsalar, she sheathed her knives and said, 'Curdle, Telorast, stop your hissing. Time to leave.'

'You're no fun, Not-Apsalar!' Curdle cried.

'No she isn't, is she?' Telorast said, head bobbing in vague threat motions, that were now proving less effective.

'Where is she?' Curdle demanded.

'Gone!'

'Without us!'

'After her!'

Poliel, Grey Goddess of pestilence, of disease and suffering, was trapped in her own tortured nightmare. All strength gone, all will bled away. The shard of deadly otataral impaling her hand, she sat on her throne, convulsions racking her.

Betrayals, too many betrayals – the Crippled God's power had fled, abandoning her – and that unknown mortal, that cold-eyed murderer, who had understood *nothing*. In whose name? For whose liberation was this war being fought? The damned fool.

What curse was it, in the end, to see flaws unveiled, to see the twisted malice of mortals dragged to the surface, exposed to day's light? Who among these followers did not ever seek, wilful or mindless, the purity of self-destruction? In obsession they took death into themselves, but that was but a paltry reflection of the death they delivered upon the land, the water, the very air. Self-destruction making victim the entire world.

Apocalypse is rarely sudden; no, among these mortals, it creeps slow, yet inevitable, relentless in its thorough obliteration of life, of health, of beauty.

Diseased minds and foul souls had drawn her into this world; for the sake of the land, for the chance that it might heal in the absence of its cruellest inflicters of pain and degradation, she sought to expunge them in the breath of plague – no more deserving a fate was imaginable – for all that, she would now die.

She railed. Betrayal!

Five Hounds of Shadow entered the chamber.

Her death. *Shadowthrone, you fool.*

A Hound flung something from its mouth, something that skidded, spitting and writhing, up against the first step of the dais.

Even in her agony, a core of clarity remained within Poliel. She looked down, seeking to comprehend – even as the Hounds fled the room, round the dais, into the priest-hole – comprehend this cowering, scaled panther, one limb swollen with infection, its back legs and hips crushed – it could not flee. The Hounds had abandoned it here – why?

Ah, to share my fate.

A final thought, meekly satisfying in itself, as the Deragoth arrived, bristling with rage and hunger, Elder as any god, deprived of one quarry, but content to kill what remained.

A broken T'rolbarahl, shrieking its terror and fury.

A broken goddess, who had sought to heal Burn. For such was the true purpose of fever, such was the cold arbiter of disease. Only humans, she reminded herself – her last thought – *only humans centre salvation solely upon themselves.*

And then the Deragoth, the first enslavers of humanity, were upon her.

*

553

'She's a carrier now,' Brokeface said, 'and more. No longer protected, the plague runs wild within her, no matter what happens to Poliel. Once begun, these things follow their own course. Please,' he added as he watched the man attempt to awaken Torahaval, 'come with me.'

The stranger looked up with helpless eyes. 'Come? Where?'

'The Temple of Soliel.'

'That indifferent bitch—'

'Please,' Brokeface insisted. 'You will see. I cannot help but believe her words.'

'Whose words?'

'It's not far. She must be healed.' And he reached down once more, collecting the woman's legs. 'As before. It's not far.'

The man nodded.

Behind them, a single shriek rose from the temple, piercing enough to send fissures rippling through the building's thick walls, dust snapping out from the cracks. Groaning sounds pushed up from beneath them as foundations buckled, tugging at the surrounding streets.

'We must hurry away!' Brokeface said.

Dismounting, dragging a stumbling, gasping Noto Boil with one hand, Paran kicked down the doors to the Temple of Soliel – a modest but most satisfying burst of power that was sufficient, he trusted, to apprise the Sweet Goddess of his present frame of mind.

The girl slipped past him as he crossed the threshold and cast him a surprisingly delighted glance as she hurried ahead to the central chamber.

On the corridor's walls, paintings of figures kneeling, heads bowed in blessing, beseeching or despair – likely the latter with this damned goddess, Paran decided. Depending in folds from the arched ceiling were funeral shrouds, no doubt intended to prepare worshippers for the worst.

They reached the central chamber even as the ground shook – the Grand Temple was collapsing. Paran pulled Noto Boil to his side, then pushed him stumbling towards the altar. *With luck it'll bury the damned Deragoth. But I'm not holding my breath.*

He drew out a card and tossed it onto the floor. 'Soliel, you are summoned.'

The girl, who had been standing to the right of the altar, suddenly sagged, then looked up, blinking owlishly. Her smile broadened.

Paran vowed, then, that he would seek to recall every detail of the goddess's upon her enforced appearance, so exquisite her bridling fury. She stood behind the altar, as androgynous as her now-dead sister, her long fingers – so perfect for closing eyelids over unseeing eyes –

clutching, forming fists at her side, as she said in a grating voice, 'You have made a terrible mistake—'

'I'm not finished yet,' he replied. 'Unleash your power, Soliel. Begin the healing. You can start with Noto Boil here, in whom you shall place a residue of your power, sufficient in strength and duration to effect the healing of the afflicted in the encamped army outside the city. Once you are done with him, others will arrive, Poliel's cast-offs. Heal them as well, and send them out—' His voice hardened. 'Seven Cities has suffered enough, Soliel.'

She seemed to study him for a long moment, then she shrugged. 'Very well. As for suffering, I leave that to you, and through no choice of mine.'

Paran frowned, then turned at a surprised shout from behind them.

The captain blinked, and grinned. 'Quick Ben!'

The wizard and Brokeface were dragging a woman between them – the one he had last seen in the altar chamber of the Grand Temple – and all at once, Paran understood. Then, immediately thereafter, realized that he understood . . . nothing.

Quick Ben looked up at the altar and his eyes narrowed. 'That her? Hood's breath, I never thought . . . never mind. Ganoes Paran, this was all by your hand? Did you know the Hounds were for me?'

'Not entirely, although I see how you might think that way. You bargained with Shadowthrone, didn't you? For,' he gestured at the unconscious woman, 'her.'

The wizard scowled. 'My sister.'

'He has released the Deragoth,' Soliel said, harsh and accusory. '*They tore her apart!*'

Quick Ben's sister moaned, tried gathering her legs under her.

'Shit,' the wizard muttered. 'I'd better leave. Back to the others. Before she comes round.'

Paran sighed and crossed his arms. 'Really, Quick—'

'You more than anybody should know about a sister's wrath!' the wizard snapped, stepping away. He glanced over at Brokeface, who stood, transfixed, staring up at Soliel. 'Go on,' he said. 'You were right. Go to her.'

With a faint whimper, Brokeface stumbled forward.

Paran watched as Quick Ben opened a warren.

The wizard hesitated, looked over at the captain. 'Ganoes,' he said, 'tell me something.'

'What?'

'Tavore. Can we trust her?'

The question felt like a slap, stinging, sudden. He blinked, studied the man, then said, 'Tavore will do, wizard, what needs to be done.'

'To suit her or her soldiers?' Quick Ben demanded.

'For her, friend, there is no distinction.'

Their gazes locked for a moment longer, then the wizard sighed. 'I owe you a tankard of ale when it's all over.'

'I will hold you to it, Quick.'

The wizard flashed that memorable, infuriating grin, and vanished into the portal.

As it whispered shut behind him, the woman, his sister, lifted herself to her hands and knees. Her hair hung down, obscuring her face, but Paran could hear her clearly as she said, 'There was a wolf.'

He cocked his head. 'A Hound of Shadow.'

'A wolf,' she said again. 'The loveliest, sweetest wolf in the world . . .'

Quick Ben opened his eyes and looked around.

Bottle sat across from him, the only one present in the clearing. From somewhere nearby there was shouting, angry, sounds of rising violence. 'Nicely done,' Bottle said. 'Shadowthrone threw you right into their path, so much of you that, had the Hounds caught you, I'd now be burying this carcass of yours. You used his warren to get here. Very nice – a thread must've survived, wizard, one even Shadowthrone didn't see.'

'What's going on?'

The soldier shrugged. 'Old argument, I think. Kalam and Fiddler found Apsalar – with blood on her knives. They figure you're dead, you see, though why—'

Quick Ben was already on his feet. And running.

The scene he came upon moments later was poised on the very edge of disaster. Kalam was advancing on Apsalar, his long-knives out, the otataral blade in the lead position. Fiddler stood to one side, looking both angry and helpless.

And Apsalar. She simply faced the burly, menacing assassin. No knives in her hands and something like resignation in her expression.

'Kalam!'

The man whirled, as did Fiddler.

'Quick!' the sapper shouted. 'We found her! Blood on the blades – and you—'

'Enough of all that,' the wizard said. 'Back away from her, Kalam.'

The assassin shrugged, then scabbarded his weapons. 'She wasn't big on explanations,' he said in a frustrated growl. 'As usual. And I would swear, Quick, she was wanting this—'

'Wanting what?' he demanded. 'Did she have her knives out? Is she in a fighting stance, Kalam? *Is she not a Shadow Dancer?* You damned

556

idiot!' He glared at Apsalar, and in a lower voice, added, 'What she wants . . . ain't for us to give . . .'

Boots on stones sounded behind him, and Quick Ben swung round to see Bottle, at his side Captain Faradan Sort.

'There you all are,' the captain said, clearly struggling to keep her curiosity in check. 'We're about to march. With luck, we'll reach the Fourteenth this night. Sinn seems to think so, anyway.'

'That's good news,' Quick Ben said. 'Lead on, Captain, we're right with you.'

Yet he held back, until Apsalar walked past him, then he reached out and brushed her sleeved arm.

She looked over.

Quick Ben hesitated, then nodded and said, 'I know it was you, Apsalar. Thank you.'

'Wizard,' she said, 'I have no idea what you are talking about.'

He let her go. *No, what she wants ain't for us to give. She wants to die.*

Layered in dust, wan with exhaustion, Cotillion strode into the throne room, then paused.

The Hounds were gathered before the Shadow Throne, two lying down, panting hard, tongues lolling. Shan paced in a circle, the black beast twitching, its flanks slashed and dripping blood. And, Cotillion realized, there were wounds on the others as well.

On the throne sat Shadowthrone, his form blurred as if within a roiling storm-cloud. 'Look at them,' he said in a low, menacing voice. 'Look well, Cotillion.'

'The Deragoth?'

'No, not the Deragoth.'

'No, I suppose not. Those look like knife cuts.'

'I had him. Then I lost him.'

'Had who?'

'That horrid little thousand-faced wizard, that's who!' A shadowy hand lifted, long fingers curling. 'I had him, here in this very palm, like a melting piece of ice.' A sudden snarl, the god tilting forward on the throne. '*It's all your fault!*'

Cotillion blinked. 'Hold on, I didn't attack the Hounds!'

'That's what you think!'

'What is that supposed to mean?' Cotillion demanded.

The other hand joined the first one, hovering, clutching the air in spasmodic, trembling rage. Then another snarl – and the god vanished.

Cotillion looked down at Baran, reached out towards the beast.

At a low growl, he snatched his hand back. 'I didn't!' he shouted.

The Hounds, one and all staring at him, did not look convinced.

Dusk muted the dust in the air above the camp as Captain Ganoes Paran – leading his horse – and the cutter Noto Boil, and the girl – whose name was Naval D'natha – climbed the slope and passed through the first line of pickets.

The entire camp looked as if it had been struck by a freak storm. Soldiers worked on repairing tents, re-splicing ropes, carrying stretchers. Horses loose from their paddocks still wandered about, too skittish to permit anyone close enough to take their bits.

'The Hounds,' Paran said. 'They came through here. As did, I suspect, the Deragoth. Damned unfortunate – I hope there weren't too many injuries.'

Noto Boil glanced over at him, then sneered. 'Captain Kindly? You have deceived us. Ganoes Paran, a name to be found on the List of the Fallen in Dujek's own logs.'

'A name with too many questions hanging off it, cutter.'

'Do you realize, Captain, that the two remaining Malazan armies in Seven Cities are commanded by brother and sister? For the moment at least. Once Dujek's back on his feet—'

'A moment,' Paran said.

Hurlochel and Sweetcreek were standing outside the command tent. Both had seen Paran and his companions.

Something in the outrider's face . . .

They reached them. 'Hurlochel?' Paran asked.

The man looked down.

Sweetcreek cleared her throat. 'High Fist Dujek Onearm died two bells ago, Captain Paran.'

'As for suffering, I leave that to you, and through no choice of mine.'

She had known. Soliel had already known.

Sweetcreek was still talking, '. . . fever broke a short while ago. They're conscious, they've been told who you are – Ganoes Paran, are you listening to me? They've read Dujek's logs – every officer among us has read them. It was required. Do you understand? The vote was unanimous. We have proclaimed you High Fist. This is now your army.'

She had known.

All he had done here . . . too late.

Dujek Onearm is dead.

CHAPTER SIXTEEN

The privileged waifs are here now,
preening behind hired armies,
and the legless once-soldier
who leans crooked against a wall
like a toppled, broken statue—
writ on his empty palm the warning
that even armies cannot eat gold—
but these civil younglings cannot see
so far and for their own children,
the future's road is already picked clean,
cobbles pried free to build rough walls
and decrepit wastrel shelters,
yet this is a wealthy world still
heaving its blood-streaked treasures
at their silken feet – they are here now,
the faces of civilization and oh how
we fallen fools yearn to be among them,
fellow feasters at the bottomless trough.
What is to come of this? I rest crooked,
hard stone at my back, and this lone
coin settling in my hand has a face—
some ancient waif privileged in his time,
who once hid behind armies, yes, until –
until those armies awoke one day
with empty bellies – such pride,
such hauteur! Look on the road!
From this civil strait I would run, and run –
if only I had not fought,
defending that mindless devourer
of tomorrow, if only I had legs—
so watch them pass, beneath their parasols

and the starving multitudes are growing
sullen, now eyeing me in their avid hunger—
I would run, yes, if only I had legs.

In the Last Days of the First Empire
Sogruntes

A SINGLE STRAND OF BLACK SAND, FOUR HUNDRED PACES LONG, BROKE the unrelieved basalt ruin of the coastline. That strip was now obscured beneath ramps, equipment, horses and soldiers; and the broad loader skiffs rocked through the shallows on their heavy draw-lines out to the anchored transports crowding the bay. For three days the Fourteenth Army had been embarking, making their escape from this diseased land.

Fist Keneb watched the seeming chaos down below for a moment longer, then, drawing his cloak tighter about himself against the fierce north sea's wind, he turned about and made his way back to the skeletal remnants of the encampment.

There were problems – almost too many to consider. The mood among the soldiers was a complex mixture of relief, bitterness, anger and despondency. Keneb had seriously begun to fear mutiny during the wait for the fleet – the embers of frustration fanned by dwindling supplies of food and water. It was likely the lack of options that had kept the army tractable, if sullen – word from every city and settlement west, east and south had been of plague. Bluetongue, ferocious in its virulence, sparing no-one. The only escape was with the fleet.

Keneb could understand something of the soldiers' sentiments. The Fourteenth's heart had been cut out at Y'Ghatan. It was extraordinary how a mere handful of veterans could prove the lifeblood of thousands, especially when, to the Fist's eyes, they had done nothing to earn such regard.

Perhaps survival alone had been sufficiently heroic. Survival, until Y'Ghatan. In any case, there was a palpable absence in the army, a hole at the core, gnawing its way outward.

Compounding all this, the command was growing increasingly divided – *for we have our own core of rot. Tene Baralta. The Red Blade ... who lusts for his own death.* There were no healers in the Fourteenth skilled enough to erase the terrible damage to Baralta's visage; it would take High Denul to regenerate the man's lost eye and forearm, and that was a talent growing ever rarer – at least in the Malazan Empire. *If only Tene had also lost the capacity for speech.* Every word from him was bitter with poison, a burgeoning hatred for all things, beginning with himself.

Approaching the Adjunct's command tent, Keneb saw Nether exit, her expression dark, bridling. The cattle-dog Bent appeared, lumbering towards her – then, sensing her state of mind, the huge scarred beast halted, ostensibly to scratch itself, and moments later was distracted by the Hengese lapdog Roach. The two trundled off.

Drawing a deep breath, Keneb walked up to the young Wickan witch. 'I take it,' he said, 'the Adjunct was not pleased with your report.'

She glared at him. 'It is not our fault, Fist. This plague seethes through the warrens. We have lost all contact with Dujek and the Host; ever since they arrived outside G'danisban. And as for Pearl,' she crossed her arms, 'we cannot track him – he is gone and that is that. Besides, if the fool wants to brave the warrens it's not for us to retrieve his bones.'

The only thing worse than a Claw in camp was the sudden, inexplicable vanishing of that selfsame Claw. Not that there was anything that could be done about it. Keneb asked, 'How many days has it been, then, since you were able to speak with High Fist Dujek?'

The young Wickan looked away, her arms still crossed. 'Since before Y'Ghatan.'

Keneb's brows rose. *That long? Adjunct, you tell us so little.* 'What of Admiral Nok – have his mages had better luck?'

'Worse,' she snapped. 'At least we're on land.'

'For now,' he said, eyeing her.

Nether scowled. 'What is it?'

'Nothing, except . . . a frown like that can become permanent – you're too young to have such deep creases there—'

Snarling, the witch stalked off.

Keneb stared after her a moment, then, shrugging, he turned and entered the command tent.

The canvas walls still reeked of smoke, a grim reminder of Y'Ghatan. The map-table remained – not yet loaded out onto the transports – and around it, despite the fact that the tabletop was bare – stood the Adjunct, Blistig and Admiral Nok.

'Fist Keneb,' Tavore said.

'Two more days, I should think,' he replied, unclasping his cloak now that he was out of the wind.

The Admiral had been speaking, it seemed, for he cleared his throat and said, 'I still believe, Adjunct, that there is nothing untoward to the command. The Empress sees no further need for the Fourteenth's presence here. There is also the matter of the plague – you have managed to keep it from your troops thus far, true enough, but that will not last. Particularly once your stores run out and you are forced to forage.'

Blistig grunted sourly. 'No harvest this year. Apart from abandoned livestock there ain't much to forage – we'd have no choice but to march to a city.'

'Precisely,' said the Admiral.

Keneb glanced at Tavore. 'Forgive me, Adjunct—'

'After I sent you out to gauge the loading of troops, the subject of command structure was concluded, to the satisfaction of all.' A certain dryness to that, and Blistig snorted. Tavore continued, 'Admiral Nok has finally relayed to us the command of the Empress, that we are to return to Unta. The difficulty before us now lies in deciding our return route.'

Keneb blinked. 'Why, east and then south, of course. The other way would take—'

'Longer, yes,' Nok interrupted. 'Nonetheless, at this time of year, we would be aided by currents and prevailing winds. Granted, the course is less well charted, and most of our maps for the western coast of this continent are derived from foreign sources, making their reliability open to challenge.' He rubbed at his weathered, lined face. 'All of that is, alas, not relevant. The issue is the plague. Adjunct, we have sought one port after another on our way to this rendezvous, and not one was safe to enter. Our own supplies are perilously low.'

Blistig asked, 'So where do you believe we can resupply anywhere west of here, Admiral?'

'Sepik, to begin with. The island is remote, sufficiently so that I believe it remains plague-free. South of that, there is Nemil, and a number of lesser kingdoms all the way down to Shal-Morzinn. From the southern tip of the continent the journey down to the northwest coast of Quon Tali is in fact shorter than the Falar lanes. Once we have cleared the risk that is Drift Avalii we will find ourselves in the Genii Straits, with the coast of Dal Hon to our north. At that time the currents will once again be with us.'

'All very well,' Blistig said in a growl, 'but what happens if Nemil and those other "lesser kingdoms" decide they're not interested in selling us food and fresh water?'

'We shall have to convince them,' the Adjunct said, 'by whatever means necessary.'

'Let's hope it's not by the sword.'

As soon as Blistig said that his regret was obvious – the statement should have sounded reasonable; instead, it simply revealed the man's lack of confidence in the Adjunct's army.

She was regarding her Fist now, expressionless, yet a certain chill crept into the chamber, filling the silence.

On Admiral Nok's face, a look of disappointment. Then he reached for his sealskin cloak. 'I must return now to my flagship. Thrice on our journey here, the outrider escorts sighted an unknown fleet to the north. No doubt the sightings were mutual but no closer contact occurred, so I believe it poses no threat to us.'

'A fleet,' Keneb said. 'Nemil?'

'Possibly. There was said to be a Meckros city west of Sepik Sea – that report is a few years old. Then again,' he glanced over at the Adjunct as he reached the flap, 'how fast can a floating city move? In any case, Meckros raid and trade, and it may well be that Nemil has dispatched ships to ward them from their coast.'

They watched the Admiral leave.

Blistig said, 'Your pardon, Adjunct—'

'Save your apology,' she cut in, turning away from him. 'One day I shall call upon you, Blistig, to voice it again. But not to me; rather, to your soldiers. Now, please visit Fist Tene Baralta and relay to him the essence of this meeting.'

'He has no interest—'

'His interests do not concern me, Fist Blistig.'

Lips pressed together, the man saluted, then left.

'A moment,' the Adjunct said as Keneb prepared to follow suit. 'How fare the soldiers, Fist?'

He hesitated, then said, 'For the most part, Adjunct, they are relieved.'

'I am not surprised,' she said.

'Shall I inform them that we are returning home?'

She half-smiled. 'I have no doubt the rumour is already among them. By all means, Fist. There is no reason to keep it a secret.'

'Unta,' Keneb mused, 'my wife and children are likely there. Of course, it stands to reason that the Fourteenth will not stay long in Unta.'

'True. Our ranks will be refilled.'

'And then?'

She shrugged. 'Korel, I expect. Nok thinks the assault on Theft will be renewed.'

It was a moment before Keneb realized that she did not believe a word she was saying to him. *Why not Korel? What might Laseen have in store for us, if not another campaign? What does Tavore suspect?* He hid his confusion by fumbling over the cloak's clasps for a few heartbeats.

When he glanced up again, the Adjunct seemed to be staring at one of the tent's mottled walls.

Standing, always standing – he could not recall ever having seen her seated, except on a horse. 'Adjunct?'

She started, then nodded and said, 'You are dismissed, Keneb.'

He felt like a coward as he made his way outside, angry at his own sense of relief. Still, a new unease now plagued him. Unta. His wife. *What was, is no longer. I'm old enough to know the truth of that. Things change. We change—*

'Make it three days.'

Keneb blinked, looked down to see Grub, flanked by Bent and Roach. The huge cattle-dog's attention was fixed elsewhere – south-eastward – while the lapdog sniffed at one of Grub's worn moccasins, where the child's big toe protruded from a split in the upper seam. 'Make what three days, Grub?'

'Until we leave. Three days.' The boy wiped his nose.

'Dig into one of the spare kits,' Keneb said, 'and find some warmer clothes, Grub. This sea is a cold one, and it's going to get colder yet.'

'I'm fine. My nose runs, but so does Bent's, so does Roach's. We're fine. Three days.'

'We'll be gone in two.'

'No. It has to be three days, or we will never get anywhere. We'll die in the sea, two days after we leave Sepik Island.'

A chill rippled through the Fist. 'How did you know we were headed west, Grub?'

The boy looked down, watched as Roach licked clean his big toe. 'Sepik, but that will be bad. Nemil will be good. Then bad. And after that, we find friends, twice. And then we end up where it all started, and that will be very bad. But that's when she realizes everything, almost everything, I mean, enough of everything to be enough. And the big man with the cut hands says yes.' He looked up, eyes bright. 'I found a bone whistle and I'm keeping it for him because he'll want it back. We're off to collect seashells!'

With that all three ran off, down towards the beach.

Three days, not two. Or we all die. 'Don't worry, Grub,' he said in a whisper, 'not all grown-ups are stupid.'

Lieutenant Pores looked down at the soldier's collection. 'What in Hood's name are these?'

'Bones, sir,' the woman replied. 'Bird bones. They was coming out of the cliff – look, they're hard as rock – we're going to add them to our collection, us heavies, I mean. Hanfeno, he's drilling holes in 'em – the others, I mean, we got hundreds. You want us to make you some, sir?'

'Give me a few,' he said, reaching out.

She dropped into his hand two leg bones, each the length of his thumb, then another that looked like a knuckle, slightly broader than his own. 'You idiot. This one's not from a bird.'

'Well I don't know, sir. Could be a skull?'

'It's solid.'

'A woodpecker?'

'Go back to your squad, Senny. When are you on the ramp?'

'Looks like tomorrow now, sir. Fist Keneb's soldiers got delayed – he pulled half of 'em back off, it was complete chaos! There's no figuring officers, uh, sir.'

A wave sent the woman scurrying. Lieutenant Pores nestled the small bones into his palm, closing his fingers over to hold them in place, then he walked back to where Captain Kindly stood beside the four trunks that comprised his camp kit. Two retainers were busy repacking one of the trunks, and Pores saw, arranged on a camel-hair blanket, an assortment of combs – two dozen, maybe more, no two alike. Bone, shell, antler, tortoiseshell, ivory, wood, slate, silver, gold and blood-copper. Clearly, they had been collected over years of travel, the captain's sojourn as a soldier laid out, the succession of cultures, the tribes and peoples he had either befriended or annihilated. Even so . . . Pores frowned. *Combs?*

Kindly was mostly bald.

The captain was instructing his retainers on how to pack the items. '. . . those cotton buds, and the goat wool or whatever you call it. Each one, and carefully – if I find a scratch, a nick or a broken tooth I will have no choice but to kill you both. Ah, Lieutenant, I trust you are now fully recovered from your wounds? Good. What's wrong, man? Are you choking?'

Gagging, his face reddening, Pores waited until Kindly stepped closer, then he let loose a cough, loud and bursting and from his right hand – held before his mouth – three bones were spat out to clunk and bounce on the ground. Pores drew in a deep breath, shook his head and cleared his throat.

'Apologies, Captain,' he said in a rasp. 'Some broken bones still in me, I guess. Been wanting to come out for a while now.'

'Well,' Kindly said, 'are you done?'

'Yes sir.'

The two retainers were staring at the bones. One reached over and collected the knuckle.

Pores wiped imaginary sweat from his brow. 'That was some cough, wasn't it? I'd swear someone punched me in the gut.'

The retainer reached over with the knuckle. 'He left you this, Lieutenant.'

'Ah, thank you, soldier.'

'If you think any of this is amusing, Lieutenant,' Kindly said. 'You are mistaken. Now, explain to me this damned delay.'

'I can't, Captain. Fist Keneb's soldiers, some kind of recall. There doesn't seem to be a reasonable explanation.'

'Typical. Armies are run by fools. If I had an army you'd see things done differently. I can't abide lazy soldiers. I've personally killed more lazy soldiers than enemies of the empire. If this was my army, Lieutenant, we would have been on those ships in two days flat, and anybody still on shore by then we'd leave behind, stripped naked with only a crust of bread in their hands and the order to march to Quon Tali.'

'Across the sea.'

'I'm glad we're understood. Now, stand here and guard my kit, Lieutenant. I must find my fellow captains Madan'Tul Rada and Ruthan Gudd – they're complete idiots but I mean to fix that.'

Pores watched his captain walk away, then he looked back down at the retainers and smiled. 'Now wouldn't that be something? High Fist Kindly, commanding all the Malazan armies.'

'Leastways,' one of the men said, 'we'd always know what we was up to.'

The lieutenant's eyes narrowed. 'You would like Kindly doing your thinking for you?'

'I'm a soldier, ain't I?'

'And what if I told you Captain Kindly was insane?'

'You be testing us? Anyway, don't matter if'n he is or not, so long as he knows what he's doing and he keeps telling us what we're supposed to be doing.' He nudged his companion, 'Ain't that right, Thikburd?'

'Right enough,' the other mumbled, examining one of the combs.

'The Malazan soldier is trained to think,' Pores said. 'That tradition has been with us since Kellanved and Dassem Ultor. Have you forgotten that?'

'No, sir, we ain't. There's thinkin' and there's thinkin' and that's jus' the way it is. Soldiers do one kind and leaders do the other. Ain't good the two gettin' mixed up.'

'Must make life easy for you.'

A nod. 'Aye, sir, that it does.'

'If your friend scratches that comb he's admiring, Captain Kindly will kill you both.'

'Thikburd! Put that down!'

'But it's pretty!'

'So's a mouthful of teeth and you want to keep yours, don't ya?'

And with soldiers like these, we won an empire.

The horses were past their prime, but they would have to do. A lone mule would carry the bulk of their supplies, including the wrapped corpse of Heboric Ghost Hands. The beasts stood waiting on the east end of the main street, tails flicking to fend off the flies, already enervated by the heat, although it was but mid-morning.

Barathol Mekhar made one last adjustment to his weapons belt, bemused to find that he'd put on weight in his midriff, then he squinted over as Cutter and Scillara emerged from the inn and made their way towards the horses.

The woman's conversation with the two Jessas had been an admirable display of brevity, devoid of advice and ending with a most perfunctory thanks. So, the baby was now the youngest resident of this forgotten hamlet. The girl would grow up playing with scorpions, rhizan and meer rats, her horizons seemingly limitless, the sun overhead the harsh, blinding and brutal face of a god. But all in all, she would be safe, and loved.

The blacksmith noted a figure nearby, hovering in the shadow of a doorway. *Ah, well, at least someone will miss us.* Feeling oddly sad, Barathol made his way over to the others.

'Your horse will collapse under you,' Cutter said. 'It's too old and you're too big, Barathol. That axe alone would stagger a mule.'

'Who's that standing over there?' Scillara asked.

'Chaur.' The blacksmith swung himself onto his horse, the beast side-stepping beneath him as he settled his weight in the saddle. 'Come to see us off, I expect. Mount up, you two.'

'This is the hottest part of the day,' Cutter said. 'It seems we're always travelling through the worst this damned land can throw at us.'

'We will reach a spring by dusk,' Barathol said, 'when we'll all need it most. We lie over there, until the following dusk, because the next leg of the journey will be a long one.'

They set out on the road, that quickly became a track. A short while later, Scillara said, 'We have company, Barathol.'

Glancing back, they saw Chaur, carrying a canvas bundle against his chest. There was a dogged expression on his sweaty face.

Sighing, the blacksmith halted his horse.

'Can you convince him to go home?' Scillara asked.

'Not likely,' Barathol admitted. 'Simple and stubborn – that's a miserable combination.' He slipped down to the ground and walked back to the huge young man. 'Here, Chaur, let's tie your kit to the mule's pack.'

Smiling, Chaur handed it over.

'We have a long way to go, Chaur. And for the next few days at least, you will have to walk – do you understand? Now, let's see what you're wearing on your feet – Hood's breath—'

'He's barefoot!' Cutter said, incredulous.

'Chaur,' Barathol tried to explain, 'this track is nothing but sharp stones and hot sand.'

'There's some thick bhederin hide in our kit,' Scillara said, lighting her pipe, 'somewhere. Tonight I can make him sandals. Unless you want us to stop right now.'

The blacksmith unslung his axe, then crouched and began pulling at his boots. 'Since I'll be riding, he can wear these until then.'

Cutter watched as Chaur struggled to pull on Barathol's boots. Most men, he knew, would have left Chaur to his fate. Just a child in a giant's body, after all, foolish and mostly useless, a burden. In fact, most men would have beaten the simpleton until he fled back to the hamlet – a beating for Chaur's own good, and in some ways very nearly justifiable. But this blacksmith . . . he hardly seemed the mass murderer he was purported to be. The betrayer of Aren, the man who assassinated a Fist. And now, their escort to the coast.

Cutter found himself oddly comforted by that notion. Kalam's cousin . . . *assassinations must run in the family*. That huge double-bladed axe hardly seemed an assassin's weapon. He considered asking Barathol – getting from him his version of what had happened at Aren all those years ago – but the blacksmith was a reluctant conversationalist, and besides, if he had his secrets he was within his right to hold on to them. *The way I hold on to mine.*

They set out again, Chaur trailing, stumbling every now and then as if unfamiliar with footwear of any kind. But he was smiling.

'Damn these leaking tits,' Scillara said beside him.

Cutter stared over at her, not knowing how he should reply to that particular complaint.

'And I'm running out of rustleaf, too.'

'I'm sorry,' he said.

'What have you to be sorry about?'

'Well, it took me so long to recover from my wounds.'

'Cutter, you had your guts wrapped round your ankles – how do you feel, by the way?'

'Uncomfortable, but I never was much of a rider. I grew up in a city, after all. Alleys, rooftops, taverns, estate balconies, that was my world before all this. Gods below, I do miss Darujhistan. You would love it, Scillara—'

'You must be mad. I don't remember cities. It's all desert and dried-up hills for me. Tents and mud-brick hovels.'

'There are caverns of gas beneath Darujhistan, and that gas is piped up to light the streets with this beautiful blue fire. It's the most magnificent city in the world, Scillara—'

'Then why did you ever leave it?'

Cutter fell silent.

'All right,' she said after a moment, 'how about this? We're taking Heboric's body . . . where, precisely?'

'Otataral Island.'

'It's a big island, Cutter. Any place in particular?'

'Heboric spoke of the desert, four or five days north and west of Dosin Pali. He said there's a giant temple there, or at least the statue from one.'

'So you were listening, after all.'

'Sometimes he got lucid, yes. Something he called the Jade, a power both gift and curse . . . and he wanted to give it back. Somehow.'

'Since he's now dead,' Scillara asked, 'how do you expect him to do anything like returning power to some statue? Cutter, how do we find a statue in the middle of a desert? You might want to consider that whatever Heboric wanted doesn't mean anything any more. The T'lan Imass killed him, and so Treach needs to find a new Destriant, and if Heboric had any other kind of power, it must have dissipated by now, or followed him through Hood's Gate – either way, there is nothing *we* can do about it.'

'His hands are solid now, Scillara.'

She started. 'What?'

'Solid jade – not pure, filled with . . . imperfections. Flaws, particles buried deep inside. Like they were flecked with ash, or dirt.'

'You examined his corpse?'

Cutter nodded.

'Why?'

'Greyfrog came back to life . . .'

'So you thought the old man might do the same.'

'It was a possibility, but it doesn't look like it's going to happen. He's mummifying – and fast.'

Barathol Mekhar spoke: 'His funeral shroud was soaked in salt water then packed in even more salt, Cutter. Keeps the maggots out. A fist-sized bundle of rags was pushed into the back of his throat, and a few other places besides. The old practice was to remove the intestines, but the locals have since grown lazier – there were arts involved. Skills, mostly forgotten. What's done is to dry out the corpse as quickly as possible.'

Cutter glanced at Scillara, then shrugged. 'Heboric was chosen by a god.'

'But he failed that god,' she replied.

'They were T'lan Imass!'

A flow of smoke accompanied Scillara's words as she said, 'Next

569

time we get swarmed by flies, we'll know what's coming.' She met his eyes. 'Look, Cutter, there's just us, now. You and me, and until the coast, Barathol. If you want to drop Heboric's body off on the island, that's fine. If those jade hands are still alive, they can crawl back to their master on their own. We just bury the body above the tideline and leave it at that.'

'And then?'

'Darujhistan. I think I want to see this magnificent city of yours. You said rooftops and alleys – what were you there? A thief? Must have been. Who else knows alleys and rooftops? So, you can teach me the ways of a thief, Cutter. I'll follow in your shadow. Hood knows, stealing what we can from this insane world makes as much sense as anything else.'

Cutter looked away. 'It's not good,' he said, 'following anyone's shadow. There's better people there ... for you to get along with. Murillio, maybe, or even Coll.'

'Will I one day discover,' she asked, 'that you've just insulted me?'

'No! Of course not. I like Murillio! And Coll's a Councilman. He owns an estate and everything.'

Barathol said, 'Ever seen an animal led to slaughter, Cutter?'

'What do you mean?'

But the big man simply shook his head.

After repacking her pipe, Scillara settled back in her saddle, a small measure of mercy silencing, for the moment at least, her baiting of Cutter. Mercy and, she admitted, Barathol's subtle warning to ease up on the young man.

That old killer was a sharp one.

It wasn't that she held anything against Cutter. The very opposite, in fact. That small glimmer of enthusiasm – when he spoke of Darujhistan – had surprised her. Cutter was reaching out to the comfort of old memories, suggesting to her that he was suffering from loneliness. *That woman who left him. The one for whom he departed Darujhistan in the first place, I suspect.* Loneliness, then, and a certain loss of purpose, now that Heboric was dead and Felisin Younger stolen away. Maybe there was some guilt thrown in – he'd failed in protecting Felisin, after all, failed in protecting Scillara too, for that matter – not that she was the kind to hold such a thing against him. They'd been T'lan Imass, for Hood's sake.

But Cutter, being young and being a man, would see it differently. A multitude of swords that he would happily fall on, with a nudge from the wrong person. *A person who mattered to him.* Better to keep him away from such notions, and a little flirtation on her part, yielding charming confusion on his, should suffice.

She hoped he would consider her advice on burying Heboric. She'd had enough of deserts. Thoughts of a city lit by blue fire, a place filled with people, none of whom expected anything of her, and the possibility of new friends – with Cutter at her side – were in truth rather enticing. A new adventure, and a civilized one at that. Exotic foods, plenty of rustleaf . . .

She had wondered, briefly, if the absence of regret or sorrow within her at the surrendering of the child she had carried inside all those months was truly indicative of some essential lack of morality in her soul, some kind of flaw that would bring horror into the eyes of mothers, grandmothers and even little girls as they looked upon her. But such thoughts had not lasted long. The truth of the matter was, she didn't care what other people thought, and if most of them saw that as a threat to . . . whatever . . . *to their view on how things should be . . .* well, that was just too bad, wasn't it? As if her very existence could lure others into a life of acts without consequence.

Now that's a laugh, isn't it? The most deadly seducers are the ones encouraging conformity. If you can only feel safe when everybody else feels, thinks and looks the same as you, then you're a Hood-damned coward . . . not to mention a vicious tyrant in the making.

'So, Barathol Mekhar, what awaits you on the coast?'

'Probably plague,' he said.

'Oh now that's a pleasant thought. And if you survive that?'

He shrugged. 'A ship, going somewhere else. I've never been to Genabackis. Nor Falar.'

'If you go to Falar,' Scillara said, 'or empire-held Genabackis, your old crimes might catch up with you.'

'They've caught up with me before.'

'So, either you're indifferent to your own death, Barathol, or your confidence is supreme and unassailable. Which is it?'

'Take your pick.'

A sharp one. I won't get any rise from him, no point in trying. 'What do you think it will be like, crossing an ocean?'

'Like a desert,' Cutter said, 'only wetter.'

She probably should have glared at him for that, but she had to admit, it was a good answer. *All right, so maybe they're both sharp, in their own ways. I think I'm going to enjoy this journey.*

They rode the track, the heat and sunlight burgeoning into a conflagration, and in their wake clumped Chaur, still smiling.

The Jaghut Ganath stood looking into the chasm. The sorcerous weaving she had set upon this . . . intrusion had shattered. She did not need to descend that vast fissure, nor enter the buried sky keep itself, to know the cause of that shattering. Draconean blood had been spilled, although that in itself was not enough. The chaos between the warrens had also been unleashed, and it had devoured Omtose Phellack as boiling water does ice.

Yet her sense of the sequence of events necessary for such a thing to happen remained clouded, as if time itself had been twisted within that once-floating fortress. There was outrage locked in the very bedrock, and now, a most peculiar imposition of . . . order.

She wished for companions here, at her side. Cynnigig, especially. And Phyrlis. As it was, in this place, alone as she was, she felt oddly vulnerable.

Perhaps most of all, would that Ganoes Paran, Master of the Deck, was with me. A surprisingly formidable human. A little too prone to take risks, however, and there was something here that invited a certain caution. She would need to heal this – there could be no doubt of that. Still . . .

Ganath pulled her unhuman gaze from the dark fissure – in time to see, flowing across the flat rock to either side, and behind her, a swarm of shadows – and now figures, huge, reptilian, all closing in on where she stood.

She cried out, her warren of Omtose Phellack rising within her, an instinctive response to panic, as the creatures closed.

There was no escape – no time—

Heavy mattocks slashed down, chopping through flesh, then bone. The blows drove her to the ground amidst gushes of her own blood. She saw before her the edge of the chasm, sought to reach out towards it. To drag herself over it, and fall – a better death—

Massive clawed feet, scaled, wrapped in strips of thick hide, kicking up dust close to her face. Unable to move, feeling her life drain away, she watched as that dust settled in a dull patina over the pool of her blood, coating it like the thinnest skin. Too much dirt, the blood wouldn't like that, it would sicken with all that dirt.

She needed to clean it. She needed to gather it up, somehow pour it back into her body, back in through these gaping wounds, and hope that her heart would burn clean every drop.

But now even her heart was failing, and blood was sputtering, filled with froth, from her nose and mouth.

She understood, suddenly, that strange sense of order. K'Chain Che'Malle, a recollection stirred to life once more, after all this time. They had returned, then. But not the truly chaotic ones. No, not the Long-Tails. These were the *others*, servants of machines, of order in all its brutality. *Nah'Ruk.*

They had returned. Why?

The pool of blood was sinking down into the white, chalky dust where furrows had been carved by talons, and into these furrows the rest of the blood drained in turgid rivulets. *The inexorable laws of erosion, writ small, and yet . . . yes, I suppose, most poignant.*

She was cold, and that felt good. Comforting. She was, after all, a Jaghut.

And now I leave.

The woman stood facing landwards, strangely alert. Mappo Runt rubbed at his face, driven to exhaustion by Iskaral Pust's manic tirade at the crew of the broad-beamed caravel as they scurried about with what seemed a complete absence of reason: through the rigging, bounding wild over the deck and clinging – with frantic screams – to various precarious perches here and there. Yet somehow the small but seaworthy trader craft was full before the wind, cutting clean on a northeasterly course.

A crew – an entire crew – of bhok'arala. It should have been impossible. It most certainly was absurd. Yet these creatures had been awaiting them in their no-doubt purloined craft, anchored offshore, when Mappo, Iskaral, his mule, and the woman named Spite pushed through the last of the brush and reached the broken rocks of the coast.

And not just some random collection of the ape-like, pointy-eared beasts, but – as Iskaral's shriek of fury announced – the High Priest's very own menagerie, the once-residents of his cliff-side fastness league upon league eastward, at the rim of the distant Raraku Sea. How they had come to be here, with this caravel, was a mystery, and one unlikely to be resolved any time soon.

Heaps of fruit and shellfish had crowded the midship deck, fussed over like votive offerings when the three travellers drew the dinghy – rowed ashore to greet them by a half-dozen bhok'arala – alongside the ship and clambered aboard. To find – adding to Mappo's bemusement – that Iskaral Pust's black-eyed mule had somehow preceded them.

Since then there had been chaos.

If bhok'arala could possess faith in a god, then their god had just arrived, in the dubious personage of Iskaral Pust, and the endless mewling, chittering, dancing about the High Priest was clearly driving Pust mad. Or, madder than he already was.

Spite had watched in amusement for a time, ignoring Mappo's questions – *How did this come to be here? Where will they be taking us? Are we in truth still pursuing Icarium?* No answers.

And now, as the coastline crawled past, pitching and rolling on their right, the tall woman stood, her balance impressive, and stared with narrowed eyes to the south.

'What is wrong?' Mappo asked, not expecting an answer.

She surprised him. 'A murder. There are godless ones walking the sands of Seven Cities once again. I believe I understand the nature of this alliance. Complexities abound, of course, and you are but a Trell, a hut-dwelling herder.'

'Who understands nothing of complexities, aye. Even so, explain. What alliance? Who are the godless ones?'

'That hardly matters, and serves little by way of explanation. It falls to the nature of gods, Mappo Runt. And of faith.'

'I'm listening.'

'If one asserts a distinction between the gifts from a god and the mortal, mundane world in which exists the believer,' she said, 'then this is as an open door to true godlessness. To the religion of disbelief, if you will.' She glanced over, sauntered closer. 'Ah, already I see you frowning in confusion—'

'I frown at the implications of such a distinction, Spite.'

'Truly? Well, I am surprised. Pleasantly so. Very well. You must understand this, then. To speak of war among the gods, it is not simply a matter of, say, this goddess here scratching out the eyes of that god over there. Nor, even, of an army of acolytes from this temple marching upon an army from the temple across the street. A war among the gods is not fought with thunderbolts and earthquakes, although of course it is possible – but improbable – that it could come to that. The war in question, then, is messy, the battle-lines muddied, unclear, and even the central combatants struggle to comprehend what constitutes a weapon, what wounds and what is harmless. And worse still, to wield such weapons proves as likely to harm the wielder as the foe.'

'Fanaticism breeds fanaticism, aye,' Mappo said, nodding. ' "In proclamation, one defines his enemy *for his enemy*".'

She smiled her dazzling smile. 'A quote? From whom?'

'Kellanved, the founding emperor of the Malazan Empire.'

'Indeed, you grasp the essence of my meaning. Now, the nature of fanaticism can be likened to that of a tree – many branches, but one tap-root.'

'Inequity.'

'Or at least the comprehension of and the faith in, whether such inequity is but imagined or exists in truth. More often than not, of course, such inequity does exist, and it is the poison that breeds the darkest fruit. Mundane wealth is usually built upon bones, piled high and packed deep. Alas, the holders of that wealth misapprehend the nature of their reward, and so are often blithely indifferent in their ostentatious display of their wealth. The misapprehension is this: that those who do not possess wealth all yearn to, and so seek likeness, and this yearning occludes all feelings of resentment, exploitation and, most relevantly, injustice. To some extent they are right, but mostly they are woefully wrong. When wealth ascends to a point where the majority of the poor finally comprehend that it is, for each of them, unattainable, then all civility collapses, and anarchy prevails. Now, I was speaking of war among the gods. Do you grasp the connection, Mappo Runt?'

'Not entirely.'

'I appreciate your honesty, Trell. Consider this: when inequity burgeons into violent conflagration, the gods themselves are helpless. The gods cease to lead – they can but follow, dragged by the will of their worshippers. Now, suppose gods to be essentially moral entities – that is, possessing and indeed manifestly representing a particular ethos – well, then, such moral considerations become the first victim in the war. Unless that god chooses to defend him or herself from his or her own believers. Allies, enemies? What relevance such primitive, simplistic notions in that scenario, Mappo Runt?'

The Trell gazed out at the heaving waves, this tireless succession born of distant convulsions, the broken tug of tides, hard and bitter winds and all that moved in the world. And yet, staring long enough, this simple undulating motion . . . mesmerizing. 'We are,' he said, 'as the soil and the sea.'

'Another quote?'

He shrugged. 'Driven by unseen forces, forever in motion, even when we stand still.' He struggled against a surge of despair. 'For all that the contestants proclaim that they are but soldiers of their god . . .'

'All that they do in that god's name is at its core profoundly *godless*.'

'And the truly godless – such as you spoke of earlier – cannot but see such blasphemers as allies.'

She studied him until he grew uneasy, then she said, 'What drives Icarium to fight?'

'When under control, it is . . . inequity. Injustice.'

'And when out of control?'

'Then . . . nothing.'

'And the difference between the two is one of magnitude.'

He glanced away once more. 'And of motivation.'

'Are you sure? Even if inequity, in triggering his violence, then ascends, crossing no obvious threshold, into all-destroying annihilation? Mappo Trell, I believe motivations prove, ultimately, irrelevant. Slaughter is slaughter. Upon either side of the battlefield the face grins with blunt stupidity, even as smoke fills the sky from horizon to horizon, even as crops wither and die, even as sweet land turns to salt. Inequity ends, Trell, when no-one and no thing is left standing. Perhaps,' she added, 'this is Icarium's true purpose, why the Nameless

575

Ones seek to unleash him. It is, after all, one sure way to end this war.'

Mappo Trell stared at her, then said, 'Next time we speak like this, Spite, you can tell me your reasons for opposing the Nameless Ones. For helping me.'

She smiled at him. 'Ah, you begin to doubt our alliance?'

'How can I not?'

'Such is war among the gods, Trell.'

'We are not gods.'

'We are their hands, their feet, wayward and wilful. We fight for reasons that are, for the most part, essentially nonsensical, even when the justification seems plain and straightforward. Two kingdoms, one upriver, one downriver. The kingdom downriver sees the water arrive befouled and sickly, filled with silts and sewage. The kingdom upriver, being on higher land, sees its desperate efforts at irrigation failing, as the topsoil is swept away each time the rains come to the highlands beyond. The two kingdoms quarrel, until there is war. The downriver kingdom marches, terrible battles are fought, cities are burned to the ground, citizens enslaved, fields salted and made barren. Ditches and dykes are broken. In the end, only the downriver kingdom remains. But the erosion does not cease. Indeed, now that there is no irrigation occurring upriver, the waters rush down in full flood, distempered and wild, and they carry lime and salt that settles on the fields and poisons the remaining soil. There is starvation, disease, and the desert closes in on all sides. The once victorious leaders are cast down. Estates are looted. Brigands rove unchecked, and within a single generation there are no kingdoms, neither upriver nor downriver. Was the justification valid? Of course. Did that validity defend the victors against their own annihilation? Of course not.

'A civilization at war chooses only the most obvious enemy, and often also the one perceived, at first, to be the most easily defeatable. But that enemy is not the true enemy, nor is it the gravest threat to that civilization. Thus, a civilization at war often chooses the *wrong* enemy. Tell me, Mappo Runt, for my two hypothetical kingdoms, where hid the truest threat?'

He shook his head.

'Yes, difficult to answer, because the threats were many, seemingly disconnected, and they appeared, disappeared then reappeared over a long period of time. The game that was hunted to extinction, the forests that were cut down, the goats that were loosed into the hills, the very irrigation ditches that were dug. And yet more: the surplus of food, the burgeoning population and its accumulating wastes. And then diseases, soils blown or washed away; and kings – one after another – who could or would do nothing, or indeed saw nothing untoward beyond their fanatical focus upon the ones they sought to blame.

'Alas,' she said, leaning now on the rail, her face to the wind, 'there is nothing simple in seeking to oppose such a host of threats. First, one must recognize them, and to achieve that one must think in the long term; and then one must discern the intricate linkages that exist between all things, the manner in which one problem feeds into another. From there, one must devise solutions and finally, one must motivate the population into concerted effort, and not just one's own population, but that of the neighbouring kingdoms, all of whom are participating in the slow self-destruction. Tell me, can you imagine such a leader ever coming to power? Or staying there for long? Me neither. The hoarders of wealth will band together to destroy such a man or woman. Besides, it is much easier to create an enemy and wage war, although why such hoarders of wealth actually believe that they would survive such a war is beyond me. But they do, again and again. Indeed, it seems they believe they will outlive civilization itself.'

'You propose little hope for civilization, Spite.'

'Oh, my lack of hope extends far beyond mere civilization. The Trell were pastoralists, yes? You managed the half-wild bhederin herds of the Masal Plains. Actually, a fairly successful way of living, all things considered.'

'Until the traders and settlers came.'

'Yes, those who coveted your land, driven as they were by enterprise or the wasting of their own lands, or the poverty in their cities. Each and all sought a new source of wealth. To achieve it, alas, they first had to destroy your people.'

Iskaral Pust scrambled to the Trell's side. 'Listen to you two! Poets and philosophers! What do you know? You go on and on whilst I am hounded unto exhaustion by these horrible squirming *things*!'

'Your acolytes, High Priest,' Spite said. 'You are their god. Indicative, I might add, of at least two kinds of absurdity.'

'I'm not impressed by you, woman. If I am their god, *why don't they listen to anything I say?*'

'Maybe,' Mappo replied, 'they are but waiting for you to say the right thing.'

'Really? And what would that be, you fat oaf?'

'Well, whatever it is they want to hear, of course.'

'She's poisoned you!' The High Priest backed away, eyes wide. He clutched and pulled at what remained of his hair, then whirled about and rushed off towards the cabin. Three bhok'arala – who had been attending him – raced after him, chittering and making tugging gestures above their ears.

Mappo turned back to Spite. 'Where are we going, by the way?'

577

She smiled at him. 'To start, the Otataral Sea.'
'Why?'
'Isn't this breeze enlivening?'
'It's damned chilly.'
'Yes. Lovely, isn't it?'

A vast oblong pit, lined with slabs of limestone, then walls of brick, rising to form a domed roof, the single entrance ramped and framed in limestone, including a massive lintel stone on which the imperial symbol had been etched above the name Dujek Onearm, and his title, High Fist. Within the barrow lanterns had been set out to aid in drying the freshly plastered walls.

Just outside, in a broad, shallow bowl half-filled with slimy clay, basked a large toad, blinking sleepy eyes as it watched its companion, the imperial artist, Ormulogun, mixing paints. Oils by the dozen, each with specific qualities; and pigments culled from crushed minerals, duck eggs, dried inks from sea-creatures, leaves and roots and berries; and jars of other mediums: egg whites from turtles, snakes, vultures; masticated grubs, gull brains, cat urine, dog drool, the snot of pimps—

All right, the toad reflected, perhaps not the snot of pimps, although given the baffling arcanum of artists, one could never be certain. It was enough to know that people who delved into such materials were mostly mad, if not to start with, then invariably so after years spent handling such toxins.

And yet, this fool Ormulogun, somehow he persisted, with his stained hands, his stained lips from pointing the brushes, his stained beard from that bizarre sputtering technique when the pigments were chewed in a mouthful of spit and Hood knew what else, his stained nose from when paint-smeared fingers prodded, scratched and explored, his stained breeches from—

'I know what you're thinking, Gumble,' Ormulogun said.

'Indeed? Please proceed, then, in describing my present thoughts.'

'The earwax of whores and stained this and stained that, the commentary swiftly descending into the absurd as befits your inability to think without exaggeration and puerile hyperbole. Now, startled as you no doubt are, shift that puny, predictable brain of yours and tell me in turn what *I'm* thinking. Can you? Hah, I thought not!'

'I tell you, you grubber of pastes, my thoughts were not in the least as you just described in that pathetic paucity of pastiche you dare call communication, such failure being quite unsurprising, since I am the master of language whilst you are little more than an ever-failing student of portraiture bereft of both cogent instruction of craft and, alas, talent.'

'You seek to communicate to the intellectually deaf, do you?'

'Whilst you paint to enlighten the blind. Yes yes,' Gumble sighed, the effort proving alarmingly deflating – alarming even to himself. He quickly drew in another breath. 'We wage our ceaseless war, you and I. What will adorn the walls of the great man's barrow? Why, from you, the usual. Propagandistic pageantry, the politically aligned re-affirmation of the status quo. Heroic deeds in service of the empire, and an even more heroic death, for in this age as in every other, we are in need of our heroes – dead ones, that is. We do not believe in living ones, after all, thanks to you—'

'To me? *To me!?*'

'The rendition of flaws is your forte, Ormulogun. Oh, consider that statement! I impress even myself with such perfectly resonating irony. Anyway, such flaws in the subject are as poison darts flung into heroism. Your avid attention destroys as it always must—'

'No no, fool, not always. And with me, with Ormulogun the Great, *never*. Why? Well, it is simple, although not so simple you will ever grasp it – even so, it is this: great art is not simply rendition. Great art is *transformation*. Great art is exaltation and exaltation is spiritual in the purest, most spiritual sense—'

'As noted earlier,' Gumble drawled, 'comprehensive erudition and brevity eludes the poor man. Besides which, I am certain I have heard that definition of great art before. In some other context, likely accompanied by a pounding of the fist on table- or skull-top, or at the very least a knee in the kidneys. No matter, it all *sounds* very well. Too bad you so consistently fail to translate it into actuality.'

'I have a mallet with which I could translate you into actuality, Gumble.'

'You would break this exquisite bowl.'

'Aye, I'd shed a few tears over that. But then I'd get better.'

'Dujek Onearm standing outside the shattered gates of Black Coral. Dujek Onearm at the parley with Caladan Brood and Anomander Rake. Dujek Onearm and Tayschrenn outside Pale, the dawn preceding the attack. Three primary walls, three panels, three images.'

'You've looked at my sketchings! Gods how I hate you!'

'There was no need,' Gumble said, 'to do something so crass, not to mention implicitly depressing, as to examine your sketchings.'

Ormulogun quickly gathered up his chosen paints, styli and brushes, then made his way down into the barrow.

Gumble stayed where he was, and thought about eating flies.

Ganoes Paran looked down at the armour laid out on the cot. A High Fist's armour, one sleeve of chain newly attached. The inheritance left a sour, bitter taste in his mouth. Proclamation, was it? As if anything he'd done whilst a soldier could justify such a thing. Every Fist in this army was better qualified to assume command. What could it have been, there in Dujek's logs, to so thoroughly twist, even falsify, Paran's legacy as the captain and commander of the Bridgeburners? He considered finding out for himself, but knew he would do no such thing. He already felt imposter enough without seeing proof of the duplicity before his own eyes. No doubt Dujek had good reasons, likely having to do with protecting, if not elevating, the reputation of House Paran, and thereby implicitly supporting his sister Tavore in her new command of the Fourteenth.

Politics dictated such official logs, of course. *As, I suppose, they will dictate my own entries. Or not. What do I care? Posterity be damned. If this is my army, then so be it. The Empress can always strip me of the command, as she no doubt will when she hears about this field promotion.* In the meantime, he would do as he pleased.

Behind him, Hurlochel cleared his throat, then said, 'High Fist, the Fists may be on their feet, but they're still weak.'

'You mean they're out there standing at attention?'

'Yes, sir.'

'That's ridiculous. Never mind the armour, then.'

They walked to the flap and Hurlochel pulled the canvas aside. Paran strode outside, blinking in sunlight. The entire army stood in formation, standards upright, armour glinting. Directly before him were the Fists, Rythe Bude foremost among them. She was wan, painfully thin in gear that seemed oversized for her frame. She saluted and said, 'High Fist Ganoes Paran, the Host awaits your inspection.'

'Thank you, Fist. How soon will they be ready to march?'

'By dawn tomorrow, High Fist.'

Paran scanned the ranks. Not a sound from them, not even the rustle of armour. They stood like dusty statues. 'And precisely how,' he asked in a whisper, 'am I to live up to this?'

'High Fist,' Hurlochel murmured at his side, 'you rode with one healer into G'danisban and then singlehandedly struck down a goddess. Drove her from this realm. You then forced the sister of that goddess to gift a dozen mortals with the power to heal—'

'That power will not last,' Paran said.

'Nonetheless. High Fist, you have killed the plague. Something even Dujek Onearm could not achieve. These soldiers are yours, Ganoes Paran. No matter what the Empress decides.'

But I don't want a damned army!

Fist Rythe Bude said, 'Given the losses to disease, High Fist, we are sufficiently supplied to march for six, perhaps seven days, assuming we do not resupply en route. Of course,' she added, 'there are the grain stores in G'danisban, and with the population virtually non-existent—'

'Yes,' Paran cut in. 'Virtually non-existent. Does that not strike you as strange, Fist?'

'The goddess herself—'

'Hurlochel reports that his outriders are seeing people, survivors, heading north and east. A pilgrimage.'

'Yes, High Fist.'

She was wavering, he saw. 'We will follow those pilgrims, Fist,' Paran said. 'We will delay another two days, during which the stores of G'danisban will be used to establish a full resupply – but only if enough remains to sustain the population still in the city. Commandeer wagons and carts as needed. Further, invite those citizens the soldiers come upon to join our train. At the very least, they will find a livelihood accompanying us, and food, water and protection. Now, inform the captains that I will address the troops the morning of our departure – at the consecration and sealing of the barrow. In the meantime, you are all dismissed.'

The Fists saluted. Shouts from the captains stirred the ranks into motion as soldiers relaxed and began splitting up.

I should have said something to them here and now. Warned them not to expect too much. No, that wouldn't do. What does a new commander say? Especially after the death of a great leader, a true hero? Dammit, Ganoes, you're better off saying nothing. Not now, and not much when we seal the barrow and leave the old man in peace. 'We're following pilgrims. Why? Because I want to know where they're going, that's why.' That should do. Mentally shrugging, Paran set off. In his wake followed Hurlochel and then, ten paces back, the young G'danii woman Naval D'natha, who was now, it seemed, a part of his entourage.

'High Fist?'

'What is it, Hurlochel?'

'Where are we going?'

'To visit the imperial artist.'

'Oh, him. May I ask why?'

'Why suffer such torment, you mean? Well, I have a request to make of him.'

'High Fist?'

I need a new Deck of Dragons. 'Is he skilled, do you know?'

'A subject of constant debate, High Fist.'

'Really? Among whom? The soldiers? I find that hard to believe.'

'Ormulogun has, accompanying him everywhere, a critic.'

Oh, the poor man.

The body was lying on the trail, the limbs lacerated, the tanned-hide shirt stiff and black with dried blood. Boatfinder crouched beside it. 'Stonefinder,' he said. 'In the frozen time now. We shared tales.'

'Someone cut off one of his fingers,' Karsa Orlong said. 'The rest of the wounds, they came from torture, except that spear-thrust, beneath the left shoulder blade. See the tracks – the killer stepped out from cover as the man passed – he was not running, but staggering. They but played with him.'

Samar Dev settled a hand on Boatfinder's shoulder, and felt the Anibar trembling with grief. 'How long ago?' she asked Karsa.

The Teblor shrugged. 'It does not matter. They are close.'

She straightened in alarm. 'How close?'

'They have made camp and they are careless with its wastes.' He unslung his flint sword. 'They have more prisoners.'

'How do you know that?'

'I smell their suffering.'

Not possible. Is such a thing possible? She looked round, seeking more obvious signs of all that the Toblakai claimed to know. A peat-filled basin was to their right, a short descent from the bedrock path on which they stood. Grey-boled black spruce trees rose from it, leaning this way and that, most of their branches bereft of needles. Glinting strands of spider's web spanned the spaces in between, like scratches on transparent glass. To the left, flattened sprawls of juniper occupied a fold in the bedrock that ran parallel to the trail. Samar frowned.

'What cover?' she asked. 'You said the killer stepped out from cover to drive that spear into the Anibar's back. But there isn't any, Karsa.'

'None that remains,' he said.

Her frown deepened into a scowl. 'Are they swathed in branches and leaves, then?'

'There are other ways of hiding, woman.'

'Such as?'

Karsa shrugged off his fur cloak. 'Sorcery,' he said. 'Wait here.'

Like Hood I will. She set off after Karsa as the Toblakai, sword held before him in both hands, moved forward in a gliding half-run. Four strides later and she had to sprint in an effort to keep up.

The jog, silent, grew swifter. Became lightning fast.

Gasping, she scrambled after the huge warrior, but he was already lost to sight.

At the sound of a sudden shriek to her left, Samar skidded to a halt – Karsa had left the trail somewhere behind her, had plunged into the forest, over jumbled, moss-slick boulders, fallen trees, thick skeins of dead branches – leaving in his wake no sign. More screams.

Heart hammering in her chest, Samar Dev pushed into the stand, clawing aside undergrowth, webs pulling against her before snapping, dust and bark flakes cascading down—

—while the slaughter somewhere ahead continued.

Weapons clashed, iron against stone. The crunch of splintered wood – blurred motion between trees ahead of her, figures running – a body, cartwheeling in a mist of crimson – she reached the edge of the encampment—

And saw Karsa Orlong – and a half hundred, maybe more, tall grey-skinned warriors, wielding spears, cutlasses, long-knives and axes, now closing in on the Toblakai.

Karsa's path into their midst was marked by a grisly corridor of corpses and fallen, mortally wounded foes.

But there were too many—

The huge flint sword burst into view at the end of a sweeping upswing, amid fragments of bone and thick, whipping threads of gore. Two figures reeled back, a third struck so hard that his moccasined feet flashed up and over at Karsa's eye-level, and, falling back, dragged down the spear-shafts of two more warriors – and into that opening the Toblakai surged, evading a half-dozen thrusts and swings, most of them appearing in his wake, for the giant's speed was extraordinary – no, more, it was *appalling*.

The two foes, weapons snagged, sought to launch themselves back, beyond the reach of Karsa – but his sword, lashing out, caught the neck of the one on the left – the head leapt free of the body – then the blade angled down to chop clean through the other warrior's right shoulder, severing the arm.

Karsa's left hand released its grip on his sword, intercepting the shaft of a thrusting spear, then pulling both weapon and wielder close, the hand releasing the haft to snap up and round the man's neck. Fluids burst from the victim's eyes, nose and mouth as the Toblakai crushed that neck as if it were little more than a tube of parchment. A hard push flung the twitching body into the pressing mass, fouling yet more weapons—

Samar Dev could barely track what her eyes saw, for even as Karsa's left hand had moved away from the sword's grip, the blade itself was slashing to the right, batting aside enemy weapons, then wheeling up and over, and, while the warrior's throat was collapsing in that savage clutch, the sword crashed down through an up-flung cutlass and into flesh and bone, shattering clavicle, then a host of ribs—

Tearing the sword loose burst the ribcage, and Samar stared to see the victim's heart, still beating, pitch free of its broken nest, dangling for a moment from torn arteries and veins, before the warrior fell from sight.

Someone was screaming – away from the battle – off to the far left, where there was a shoreline of rocks, and, beyond, open water – a row of low-slung, broad-beamed wooden canoes – and she saw there a woman, slight, golden-haired – a human – *casting spells*.

Yet whatever sorcery she worked seemed to achieve nothing. Impossibly, Karsa Orlong had somehow carved his way through to the other side of the press, where he spun round, his back to a huge pine, the flint sword almost contemptuous in its batting aside attacks – as the Toblakai paused for a rest.

Samar could not believe what she was seeing.

More shouts now, a single warrior, standing well beyond the jostling mob, bellowing at his companions – who began to draw back, disengaging from Karsa Orlong.

Seeing the Toblakai draw a deep, chest-swelling breath, then raise his sword, Samar Dev yelled, 'Karsa! Wait! *Do not attack, damn you!*'

The cold glare that met her gaze made Samar flinch.

The giant gestured with the sword. 'See what's left of the Anibar, woman?' His voice was deep in tone, the beat of words like a drum of war.

She nodded, refusing to look once more at the row of prisoners, bound head-down and spreadeagled to wooden frames along the inland edge of the encampment, their naked forms painted red in blood, and before each victim a heap of live embers, filling the air with the stench of burnt hair and meat. Karsa Orlong, she realized, had been driven by rage, yet such fury set no tremble in the huge warrior, the sword was motionless, now, held at the ready, the very stillness of that blade seeming to vow a tide of destruction. 'I know,' she said. 'But listen to me, Karsa. If you kill them all – and I see that you mean to do just that – but listen! If you do, more will come, seeking to find their vanished kin. More will come, Toblakai, and this will never end – until you make a mistake, until there are so many of them that even you cannot hope to prevail. Nor can you be everywhere at once, so more Anibar will die.'

'What do you suggest, then, woman?'

She strode forward, ignoring, for the moment, the grey-skinned warriors and the yellow-haired witch. 'They fear you now, Karsa, and you must use that fear—' She paused, distracted by a commotion from among the half-tent-half-huts near the beached canoes. Two warriors were dragging someone into view. Another human. His face was swollen by constant beatings, but he seemed otherwise undamaged. Samar Dev studied the new arrival with narrowed eyes, then quickly approached Karsa, lowering her voice to a harsh whisper. 'They now have an interpreter, Karsa. The tattoos on his forearms. He is Taxilian. Listen to me. Quickly. Use that fear. Tell them there are more of your kind, allies to the Anibar, and that you are but the first of a horde, coming in answer to a plea for help. Karsa, tell them to *get the Hood off this land!*'

'If they leave I cannot kill more of them.'

An argument was going on among the raiders. The warrior who had issued commands was rejecting – in an obvious fashion – the frantic pleas of the yellow-haired human. The Taxilian, held by the arms off to one side, was clearly following the debate, but his face was too mangled to reveal any expression. Samar saw the man's eyes flick over to her and Karsa, then back to her, and, with slow deliberation, the Taxilian winked.

Gods below. Good. She nodded. Then, to spare him any retribution, she averted her gaze, and found herself looking upon a scene of terrible carnage. Figures lay moaning in blood-drenched humus. Broken spear-shafts were everywhere like scattered kindling from an overturned cart. But mostly, there were motionless corpses, severed limbs, exposed bones and spilled intestines.

And Karsa Orlong was barely out of breath.

Were these tall, unhuman strangers such poor fighters? She did not believe so. By their garb, theirs was a warrior society. But many such societies, if stagnant – or isolated – for a long enough period of time, bound their martial arts into ritualized forms and techniques. They would have but one way of fighting, perhaps with a few variations, and would have difficulty adjusting to the unexpected ... *such as a lone Toblakai with an unbreakable flint sword nearly as long as he is tall* – a Toblakai possessing mind-numbing speed and the cold, detached precision of a natural killer.

And Karsa had said that he had fought this enemy once before.

The commander of the grey-skinned raiders was approaching, the Taxilian being dragged along in his wake, the yellow-haired witch hurrying to come up alongside the leader – who then straight-armed her back a step.

Samar saw the flash of unbridled hatred the small woman directed at the commander's back. There was something dangling from the witch's neck, blackened and oblong – *a severed finger. A witch indeed, of the old arts, the lost ways of spiritual magic – well, not entirely lost, for I have made of that my own speciality, atavistic bitch that I am.* By her hair and heart-shaped features – and those blue eyes – she reminded Samar Dev of the small, mostly subjugated peoples who could be found near the centre of the subcontinent, in such ancient cities as Halaf, Guran and Karashimesh; and as far west as Omari. Some remnant population, perhaps. And yet, her words earlier had been in a language Samar had not recognized.

The commander spoke, clearly addressing the yellow-haired witch, who then in turn relayed his words – in yet another language – to the Taxilian. At that latter exchange, Samar Dev's eyes widened, for she recognized certain words – though she had never before heard them spoken, had only read them, in the most ancient tomes. Remnants, in fact, from the First Empire.

The Taxilian nodded when the witch was done. He faced first Karsa, then Samar Dev, and finally said, 'To which of you should I convey the Prèda's words?'

'Why not to both?' Samar responded. 'We can both understand you, Taxilian.'

'Very well. The Preda asks what reason this Tarthenal had for his unwarranted attack on his Merude warriors.'

Tarthenal? 'Vengeance,' Samar Dev said quickly before Karsa Orlong triggered yet another bloody clash. She pointed towards the pathetic forms on the racks at the camp's edge. 'These Anibar, suffering your predations, have called upon their longstanding allies, the Toblakai—'

At that word the yellow-haired witch started, and the Preda's elongated eyes widened slightly.

'—and this warrior, a lowly hunter among the twenty-thousand-strong clan of the Toblakai, was, by chance, close by, and so he represents only the beginning of what will be, I am afraid, a most thorough retribution. Assuming the Preda is, of course, foolish enough to await their arrival.'

A certain measure of amusement glittered in the Taxilian's eyes, quickly veiled as he turned to relay Samar's words to the yellow-haired witch.

Whatever she in turn said to the Preda was twice as long as the Taxilian's version.

Preda. Would that be a variation on Predal'atr, I wonder? A unit commander in a legion of the First Empire, Middle Period. Yet . . . this makes no sense. These warriors are not even human, after all.

The witch's translation was cut short by a gesture from the Preda, who then spoke once more.

When the Taxilian at last translated, there was something like admiration in his tone. 'The Preda wishes to express his appreciation for this warrior's formidable skills. Further, he enquires if the warrior's desire for vengeance is yet abated.'

'It is not,' Karsa Orlong replied.

The tone was sufficient for the Preda, who spoke again. The yellow-haired witch's expression suddenly closed, and she related his words to the Taxilian in a strangely flat monotone.

She hides glee.

Suspicion rose within Samar Dev. *What comes now?*

The Taxilian said, 'The Preda well understands the . . . Toblakai's position. Indeed, he empathizes, for the Preda himself abhors what he has been commanded to do, along this entire foreign coastline. Yet he must follow the needs of his Emperor. That said, the Preda will order a complete withdrawal of his Tiste Edur forces, back to the fleet. Is the Toblakai satisfied with this?'

'No.'

The Taxilian nodded at Karsa's blunt reply, as the Preda spoke again. *Now what?*

'The Preda again has no choice but to follow the commands of his Emperor, a standing order, if you will. The Emperor is the greatest warrior this world has seen, and he ever defends that claim in personal combat. He has faced a thousand or more fighters, drawn from virtually every land, and yet still he lives, triumphant and un-vanquished. It is the Emperor's command that his soldiers, no matter where they are, no matter with whom they speak, are to relate the Emperor's challenge. Indeed, the Emperor invites any and every warrior to a duel, always to the death – a duel in which no-one can interfere, no matter the consequences, and all rights of Guest are accorded the challenger. Further, the soldiers of the Emperor are instructed to pro-vide transportation and to meet every need and desire of such warriors who would so face the Emperor in duel.'

More words from the Preda.

A deep chill was settling in Samar Dev, a dread she could not identify – but there was something here . . . something *vastly wrong.*

The Taxilian resumed. 'Thus, if this Toblakai *hunter* seeks the sweetest vengeance of all, he must face the one who has so commanded that his soldiers inflict atrocities upon all strangers they encounter. Accordingly, the Preda invites the Toblakai – and, if desired, his companion – to be Guest of the Tiste Edur on this, their return journey to the Lether Empire. Do you accept?'

Karsa blinked, then looked down at Samar Dev. 'They invite me to kill their Emperor?'

'It seems so. But, Karsa, there is—'

'Tell the Preda,' the Toblakai said, 'that I accept.'

She saw the commander smile.

The Taxilian said, 'Preda Hanradi Khalag then welcomes you among the Tiste Edur.'

Samar Dev looked back at the bodies lying sprawled through the camp. *And for these fallen kin, Preda Hanradi Khalag, you care nothing? No, gods below, something is very wrong here—*

'Samar Dev,' Karsa said, 'will you stay here?'

She shook her head.

'Good,' he grunted. 'Go get Havok.'

'Get him yourself, Toblakai.'

The giant grinned. 'It was worth a try.'

'Stop looking so damned pleased, Karsa Orlong. I don't think you have any idea to what you are now bound. Can you not hear the shackles snapping shut? Chaining you to this . . . this absurd challenge and these damned bloodless Tiste Edur?'

Karsa's expression darkened. 'Chains cannot hold me, witch.'

Fool, they are holding you right now.

Glancing across, she saw the yellow-haired witch appraising Karsa Orlong with avid eyes.

And what does that mean, I wonder, and why does it frighten me so?

'Fist Temul,' Keneb asked, 'how does it feel, to be going home?'

The young, tall Wickan – who had recently acquired full-body blue tattooing in the style of the Crow Clan, an intricate geometric design that made his face look like a portrait fashioned of tesserae – was watching as his soldiers led their horses onto the ramps down on the strand below. At Keneb's question he shrugged. 'Among my people, I shall face yet again all that I have faced here.'

'But not alone any more,' Keneb pointed out. 'Those warriors down there, they are yours, now.'

'Are they?'

'So I was led to understand. They no longer challenge your orders, or your right to command, do they?'

'I believe,' Temul said, 'that most of these Wickans will choose to leave the army once we disembark at Unta. They will return to their families, and when they are asked to recount their adventures in Seven Cities, they will say nothing. It is in my mind, Fist Keneb, that my warriors are shamed. Not because of how they have shown me little respect. No, they are shamed by this army's list of failures.' He fixed dark, hard eyes on Keneb. 'They are too old, or too young, and both are drawn to glory as if she was a forbidden lover.'

Temul was not one for speeches, and Keneb could not recall ever managing to pull so many words from the haunted young man. 'They sought death, then.'

'Yes. They would join with Coltaine, Bult and the others, in the only way still possible. To die in battle, against the very same enemy. It is why they crossed the ocean, why they left their villages. They did not expect ever to return home, and so this final journey, back to Quon Tali, will break them.'

'Damned fools. Forgive me—'

A bitter smile from Temul as he shook his head. 'No need for that. They are fools, and even had I wisdom, I would fail in its sharing.'

From the remnants of the camp behind them, cattle-dogs began howling. Both men turned in surprise. Keneb glanced over at Temul. 'What is it? Why—'

'I don't know.'

They set off, back towards the camp.

Lieutenant Pores watched Bent race up the track, skirls of dust rising in the dog's wake. He caught a momentary glimpse of wild half-mad eyes above that mangled snout, then the beast was past. *So only now we find out that they're terrified of water. Well, good. We can leave the ugly things behind.* He squinted towards the file of Wickans and Seti overseeing the loading of their scrawny horses – not many of those animals would survive this journey, he suspected, which made them valuable sources of meat. *Anything to liven up the deck-wash and bilge-crud sailors call food.* Oh, those horse-warriors might complain, but that wouldn't keep them from lining up with their bowls when the bell tolled.

Kindly had made sure the Adjunct knew, in torrid detail, his displeasure with Fist Keneb's incompetence. There was no question of Kindly lacking courage, or at least raging megalomania. But this time, dammit, the old bastard had had a point. An entire day and half a night had been wasted by Keneb. A Hood-damned kit inspection, presented squad by squad – and right in the middle of boarding assembly – gods, the chaos that ensued. *'Has Keneb lost his mind?'* Oh yes, Kindly's first question to the Adjunct, and something in her answering scowl told Pores that the miserable woman had known nothing about any of it, and clearly could not comprehend why Keneb would have ordered such a thing.

Well, no surprise, that, with her moping around in her damned tent doing who knew what with that cold beauty T'amber. Even the Admiral's frustration had been obvious. Word was going through the ranks that Tavore was likely in line for demotion – Y'Ghatan could have been handled better. Every damned soldier turned out to be a tactical genius when it came to that, and more than once Pores had bitten out a chunk of soldier meat for some treasonous comment. It didn't matter that Nok and Tavore were feuding; it didn't matter that Tene Baralta was a seething cauldron of sedition among the officers; it didn't even matter that Pores himself was undecided whether the Adjunct could have done better at Y'Ghatan – the rumours alone were as poisonous as any plague the Grey Goddess could spit out.

He was both looking forward to and dreading boarding the

589

transports, and the long, tedious journey ahead. Bored soldiers were worse than woodworm in the keel – or so the sailors kept saying, as they cast jaded eyes on the dusty, swearing men and women who ascended the ramps only to fall silent, huddling like shorn sheep in the raft-like scuttles as the heave and haul chant rang out over the choppy water. Worse still, seas and oceans were nasty things. Soldiers would face death with nary a blink if they knew they could fight back, maybe even fight their way out of it, but the sea was immune to swinging swords, whistling arrows and shield-walls. *And Hood knows, we've been swallowing that lumpy helpless thing enough as it is.*

Damned cattle-dogs were all letting loose now.

Now what? Unsure of his own reasons, Pores set off in the direction Bent had gone. East on the track, past the command tent, then the inner ring of pickets, and out towards the latrine trenches – and the lieutenant saw the racing figures of a dozen or so cattle-dogs, their mottled, tanned shapes converging, then circling with wild barking – and on the road, the subjects of their excitement, a troop approaching on foot.

So who in the Queen's name are they? The outriders were all in – he was sure of that – he'd seen the Seti practising heaving their guts up on the ramps – they got seasick standing in a puddle. And the Wickans had already surrendered their mounts to the harried transport crews.

Pores glanced round, saw a soldier leading three horses towards the strand. 'Hey! Hold up there.' He walked over. 'Give me one of those.'

'They ain't saddled, sir.'

'Really? How can you tell?'

The man started pointing at the horse's back—

'Idiot,' Pores said, 'give me those reins, no, those ones.'

'That's the Adjunct's—'

'Thought I recognized it.' He pulled the beast away then vaulted onto its back. Then set off onto the road. The foundling, Grub, was walking out from the camp, at one ankle that yipping mutt that looked like what a cow would regurgitate after eating a mohair rug. Ignoring them, Pores angled his mount eastward, and kicked it into a canter.

He could already put a name to the one in the lead. Captain Faradan Sort. And there was that High Mage, Quick Ben, and that scary assassin Kalam, and – *gods below, but they're all* – no, they weren't. *Marines! Damned marines!*

He heard shouts from the camp behind him now, an alarm being raised outside the command tent.

Pores could not believe his own eyes. Survivors – from the firestorm – that was impossible. *Granted, they look rough, half-dead in fact. Like Hood used 'em to clean out his hoary ears. There's Lostara Yil – well, she ain't as bad as the rest—*

Lieutenant Pores reined in before Faradan Sort. 'Captain—'

'We need water,' she said, the words barely making it out between chapped, cracked and blistered lips.

Gods, they look awful. Pores wheeled his horse round, nearly slipping off the animal's back in the process. Righting himself, he rode back towards the camp.

As Keneb and Temul reached the main track, thirty paces from the command tent, they saw the Adjunct appear, and, a moment later, Blistig, and then T'amber. Soldiers were shouting something as yet incomprehensible from the eastern end of the camp.

The Adjunct turned towards her two approaching Fists. 'It seems my horse has gone missing.'

Keneb's brows rose. 'Thus the alarms? Adjunct—'

'No, Keneb. A troop has been spotted on the east road.'

'A troop? We're being attacked?'

'I do not think so. Well, accompany me, then. It seems we shall have to walk. And this will permit you, Fist Keneb, to explain the fiasco that occurred regarding the boarding of your company.'

'Adjunct?'

'I find your sudden incompetence unconvincing.'

He glanced across at her. There was the hint of an emotion, there on that plain, drawn visage. A hint, no more, not enough that he could identify it. 'Grub,' he said.

The Adjunct's brows rose. 'I believe you will need to elaborate on that, Fist Keneb.'

'He said we should take an extra day boarding, Adjunct.'

'And this child's advice, a barely literate, half-wild child at that, is sufficient justification for you to confound your Adjunct's instructions?'

'Not normally, no,' Keneb replied. 'It's difficult to explain . . . but he knows things. Things he shouldn't, I mean. He knew we were sailing west, for example. He knew our planned ports of call—'

'Hiding behind the command tent,' Blistig said.

'Have you ever seen the boy hide, Blistig? Ever?'

The man scowled. 'Must be he's good at it, then.'

'Adjunct, Grub said we needed to delay one day – or we would all die. At sea. I am beginning to believe—'

She held up a gloved hand, the gesture sharp enough to silence him, and he saw that her eyes were narrowed now, fixed on what was ahead—

A rider, bareback, coming at full gallop.

'That's Kindly's lieutenant,' Blistig said.

When it became obvious that the man had no intention of slowing down, nor of changing course, everyone quickly moved to the sides of the road.

The lieutenant sketched a hasty salute, barely seen through the dust, as he plunged past, shouting something like: *'They need water!'*

'And,' Blistig added, waving at clouds of dust as they all set out again, 'that was your horse, Adjunct.'

Keneb looked down the road, blinking to get the grit from his eyes. Figures wavered into view. Indistinct . . . no, that was Faradan Sort . . . wasn't it?

'Your deserter is returning,' Blistig said. 'Stupid of her, really, since desertion is punishable by execution. But who are those people behind her? What are they carrying?'

The Adjunct halted suddenly, the motion almost a stagger.

Quick Ben. Kalam. More faces, covered in dust, so white they looked like ghosts – *and so they are. What else could they be?* Fiddler. Gesler, Lostara Yil, Stormy – Keneb saw one familiar, impossible face after another. Sun-ravaged, stumbling, like creatures trapped in delirium. And in their arms, children, dull-eyed, shrunken . . .

The boy knows things . . . Grub . . .

And there he stood, flanked by his ecstatic dogs, talking, it seemed, with Sinn.

Sinn, we'd thought her mad with grief – she'd lost a brother, after all . . . lost, and now found again.

But Faradan Sort had suspected, rightly, that something else had possessed Sinn. A suspicion strong enough to drive her into desertion.

Gods, we gave up too easily – but no – the city, the firestorm – we waited for days, waited until the whole damned ruin had cooled. We picked through the ashes. No-one could have lived through that.

The troop arrived to where the Adjunct stood.

Captain Faradan Sort straightened with only a slight waver, then saluted, fist to left side of her chest. 'Adjunct,' she rasped, 'I have taken the liberty of re-forming the squads, pending approval—'

'That approval is Fist Keneb's responsibility,' the Adjunct said, her voice strangely flat. 'Captain, I did not expect to see you again.'

A nod. 'I understand the necessities of maintaining military discipline, Adjunct. And so, I now surrender myself to you. I ask, however, that leniency be granted Sinn – her youth, her state of mind at the time . . .'

Horses from up the road. Lieutenant Pores returning, more riders behind him. Bladders filled with water, swinging and bouncing like huge udders. The other riders – healers, one and all, including the Wickans Nil and Nether. Keneb stared at their expressions of growing disbelief as they drew closer.

Fiddler had come forward, a scrawny child sleeping or unconscious in his arms. 'Adjunct,' he said through cracked lips, 'without the captain, digging with her own hands, not one of us trapped under that damned city would have ever left it. We'd be mouldering bones right now.' He stepped closer, but his effort at lowering his voice to a whisper failed, as Keneb heard him say, 'Adjunct, you hang the captain for desertion and you better get a lot more nooses, 'cause we'll leave this miserable world when she does.'

'Sergeant,' the Adjunct said, seemingly unperturbed, 'am I to understand that you and those squads behind you burrowed beneath Y'Ghatan in the midst of the firestorm, somehow managing not to get cooked in the process, and then dug your way clear?'

Fiddler turned his head and spat blood, then he smiled a chilling, ghastly smile, the flaking lips splitting in twin rows of red, glistening fissures. 'Aye,' he said in a rasp, 'we went hunting . . . through the bones of the damned city. And then, with the captain's help, we crawled outa that grave.'

The Adjunct's gaze left the ragged man, travelled slowly along the line, the gaunt faces, the deathly eyes staring out from dust-caked faces, the naked, blistered skin. 'Bonehunters in truth, then.' She paused, as Pores led his healers forward with their waterskins, then said, 'Welcome back, soldiers.'

BOOK FOUR

THE BONEHUNTERS

Who will deny that it is our nature to believe the very worst in our fellow kind? Even as cults rose and indeed coalesced into a patronomic worship – not just of Coltaine, the Winged One, the Black Feather, but too of the Chain of Dogs itself – throughout Seven Cities, with shrines seeming to grow from the very wastes along that ill-fated trail, shrines in propitiation to one dead hero after another: Bult, Lull, Mincer, Sormo E'nath, even Baria and Mesker Setral of the Red Blades; and to the Foolish Dog clan, the Weasel clan and of course the Crow and the Seventh Army itself; while at Gelor Ridge, in an ancient monastery overlooking the old battle site, a new cult centred on horses was born – even as this vast fever of veneration gripped Seven Cities, so certain agents in the heart of the Malazan Empire set loose, among the commonry, tales purporting the very opposite: that Coltaine had betrayed the empire; that he had been a renegade, secretly allied with Sha'ik. After all, had the countless refugees simply stayed in their cities, accepting the rebellion's dominion; had they not been dragged out by Coltaine and his blood-thirsty Wickans; and had the Seventh's Mage Cadre leader, Kulp, not so mysteriously disappeared, thus leaving the Malazan Army vulnerable to the sorcerous machinations and indeed manipulations of the Wickan witches and warlocks – had not all this occurred, there would have been no slaughter, no terrible ordeal of crossing half a continent exposed to every predating half-wild tribe in the wastes. And, most heinous of all, Coltaine had then, in league with the traitorous Imperial Historian, Duiker, connived to effect the subsequent betrayal and annihilation of the Aren Army, led by the naïve High Fist Pormqual who was the first victim of that dread betrayal. Why else, after all, would those very rebels of Seven Cities take to the worship of such figures, if not seeing in Coltaine and the rest heroic allies . . .

. . . In any case, whether officially approved or otherwise, the persecution of Wickans within the empire flared hot and all-consuming, given such ample fuel . . .

The Year of Ten Thousand Lies
Kayessan

CHAPTER SEVENTEEN

What is there left to understand? Choice is an illusion. Freedom is conceit. The hands that reach out to guide your every step, your every thought, come not from the gods, for they are no less deluded than we – no, my friends, those hands come to each of us . . . *from* each of us.

You may believe that civilization deafens us with tens of thousands of voices, but listen well to that clamour, for with each renewed burst so disparate and myriad, an ancient force awakens, drawing each noise ever closer, until the chorus forms but two sides, each battling the other. The bloody lines are drawn, fought in the turning away of faces, in the stoppering of ears, the cold denial, and all discourse, at the last, is revealed as futile and worthless.

Will you yet hold, my friends, to the faith that change is within our grasp? That will and reason shall overcome the will of denial?

There is nothing left to understand. This mad whirlpool holds us all in a grasp that cannot be broken; and you with your spears and battle-masks; you with your tears and soft touch; you with the sardonic grin behind which screams fear and self-hatred; even you who stand aside in silent witness to our catastrophe of dissolution, too numb to act – it is all one. You are all one. *We are all one.*

So now come closer, my friends, and see in this modest cart before you my most precious wares. Elixir of Oblivion, Tincture of Frenzied Dancing, and here, my favourite, Unguent of Male Prowess Unending, where I guarantee your soldier will remain standing through battle after battle . . .

Hawker's Harangue,
recounted by Vaylan Winder,
Malaz City, the year the city overflowed with sewage (1123 Burn's Sleep)

RIVULETS OF WATER, REEKING OF URINE, TRICKLED DOWN THE STEPS leading to Coop's Hanged Man Inn, one of the score of disreputable taverns in the Docks Quarter of Malaz City that Banaschar, once a priest of D'rek, was now in the habit of frequenting. Whatever details had once existed in his mind to distinguish one such place from another had since faded, the dyke of his resolve rotted through by frustration and a growing panic, poisonous enough to immobilize him – in spirit if not in flesh. And the ensuing deluge was surprisingly comforting, even as the waters rose ever higher.

Little different, he observed as he negotiated the treacherous, mould-slimed steps, from this cursed rain, or so the long-time locals called it, despite the clear sky overhead. Mostly rain comes down, they said, but occasionally it comes up, seeping through the crumbling cobbles of the quarter, transforming such beneath-ground establishments as Coop's into a swampy quagmire, the entrance guarded by a whining cloud of mosquitoes, and the stench of overflowed sewers wafting about so thick the old-timers announce its arrival as they would an actual person miserably named Stink – greeted if not welcomed into already sordid company.

And most sordid was Banaschar's company these days. Veterans who avoided sobriety as if it was a curse; whores who'd long since hawked their hearts of gold – if they'd ever had them in the first place; scrawny youths with a host of appropriately modest ambitions – meanest thug in this skein of fetid streets and alleys; master thief of those few belongings the poor possessed; nastiest backstabber with at least fifty knots on their wrist strings, each knot honouring someone foolish enough to trust them; and of course the usual assortment of bodyguards and muscle whose brains had been deprived of air at some point in their lives; smugglers and would-be smugglers, informants and the imperial spies to whom they informed, spies spying on the spies, hawkers of innumerable substances, users of selfsame substances on their way to the oblivion of the Abyss; and here and there, people for whom no category was possible, since they gave away nothing of their lives, their histories, their secrets.

In a way, Banaschar was one such person, on his better days. Other times, such as this one, he could make no claim to possible – if improbable – grandiosity. This afternoon, then, he had come early to Coop's, with the aim of stretching the night ahead as far as he could, well lubricated of course, which would in turn achieve an overlong and hopefully entirely blissful period of unconsciousness in one of the lice-infested rat-traps above the tavern.

It would be easy, he reflected as he ducked through the doorway and paused just within, blinking in the gloom, easy to think of clamour as a single entity, one sporting countless mouths, and to reckon the din as meaningless as the rush of brown water from a sewer pipe. Yet Banaschar had come to a new appreciation of the vagaries of the noise erupting from human throats. Most spoke to keep from thinking, but others spoke as if casting lifelines even as they drowned in whatever despairing recognition they had arrived at – perhaps during some unwelcome pause, filled with the horror of silence. A few others fit neither category. These were the ones who used the clamour surrounding them as a barrier, creating in its midst a place in which to hide, mute and indifferent, fending off the outside world.

More often than not, Banaschar – who had once been a priest, who had once immersed himself within a drone of voices singing the cadence of prayer and chant – sought out such denizens for the dubious pleasure of their company.

Through the haze of durhang and rustleaf smoke, the acrid black-tail swirls from the lamp wicks, and something that might have been mist gathered just beneath the ceiling, he saw, hunched in a booth along the back wall, a familiar figure. Familiar in the sense that Banaschar had more than a few times shared a table with the man, although Banaschar was ignorant of virtually everything about him, including his given name, knowing him only as *Foreigner*.

A foreigner in truth, who spoke Malazan with an accent Banaschar did not recognize – in itself curious since the ex-priest's travels had been extensive, from Korel to Theft to Mare in the south; from Nathilog to Callows on Genabackis in the east; and, northward, from Falar to Aren to Yath Alban. And in those travels he had met other travellers, hailing from places Banaschar could not even find on any temple map. Nemil, Perish, Shal-Morzinn, Elingarth, Torment, Jacuruku and Stratem. Yet this man, whom he now approached, weaving and pushing through the afternoon crowd of sailors and the local murder of veterans, this man had an accent unlike any Banaschar had ever heard.

Yet the truth of things was never as interesting as the mystery preceding the revelation, and Banaschar had come to appreciate his own ignorance. In other matters, after all, he knew far too much – and what had that availed him?

Sliding onto the greasy bench opposite the huge foreigner, the ex-priest released the clasp on his tattered cloak and shrugged free from its folds – once, long ago it seemed now, such lack of consideration for the unsightly creases that would result would have horrified him – but he had done his share since of sleeping in that cloak, senseless on a vomit-spattered floor and, twice, on the cobbles of an alley – correct comportment, alas, had ceased being a moral necessity.

He leaned back now, the rough cloth bunching behind him, as one of

Coop's serving wenches arrived with a tankard of Coop's own Leech Swill, a weak, gassy ale that had acquired its name in an appropriately literal fashion. Warranting the now customary affectation of a one-eyed squint into the brass-hued brew before the first mouthful.

The foreigner had glanced up once, upon Banaschar's arrival, punctuating the gesture with a sardonic half-grin before returning his attention to the fired-clay mug of wine in his hands.

'Oh, Jakatakan grapes are all very well,' the ex-priest said, 'it's the local water that turns that wine you like so much into snake's piss.'

'Aye, bad hangovers,' Foreigner said.

'And that is desirable?'

'Aye, it is. Wakes me up again and again through the night, almost every bell, with a pounding skull and a bladder ready to explode – but if I didn't wake up that bladder *would* explode. See?'

Banaschar nodded, glanced round. 'More heads than usual for an afternoon.'

'You only think that because you ain't been here roun' this time lately. Three transports and an escort come in three nights past, from Korel.'

The ex-priest studied the other customers a little more carefully this time. 'They talking much?'

'Sounds it to me.'

'About the campaign down there?'

Foreigner shrugged. 'Go ask 'em if you like.'

'No. Too much effort. The bad thing about asking questions—'

'Is gettin' answers, aye – you've said that before.'

'That is another bad thing – the way we all end up saying the same things over and over again.'

'That's you, not me. And, you're gettin' worse.'

Banaschar swallowed two mouthfuls, then wiped his lips with the back of his hand. 'Worse. Yes indeed.'

'Never good,' Foreigner observed, 'seeing a man in a hurry.'

'It's a race,' Banaschar said. 'Do I reach the edge and plunge over or does my salvation arrive in time? Lay down a few coins on the outcome – I'd suggest the former but that's just between you and me.'

The huge man – who rarely met anyone's eyes while talking, and whose massive hands and wrists were scarred and puckered with weals – shook his head and said, 'If that salvation's a woman, only a fool would wager agin me.'

Banaschar grimaced and lifted his tankard. 'A fine idea. Let's toast all the lost loves in the world, friend. What happened to yours or is that too personal a question for this dubious relationship of ours?'

'You jumped on the wrong stone,' the man said. 'My love ain't lost,

600

an' maybe some days I'd think of swapping places wi' you, but not today. Not yesterday neither, nor the day afore that. Come to think of it—'

'No need to continue. My salvation is not a woman, or if she was, it wouldn't be because she's a woman, if you understand me.'

'So, we just had one of them hypothetical conversations?'

'Learned Malazan from an educated sailor, did you? In any case, hypothetical is the wrong word for what you mean, I think. More like, metaphorical.'

'You sure of that?'

'Of course not, but that's not the point, is it? The woman's a broken heart, or maybe just a mud slide you ride until it buries you, until it buries all of us.' Banaschar finished his ale, waved the tankard in the air for a moment, then settled back with a belch. 'Heard about a Napan sailor, drank a keg's worth of Leech Swill, then, standing too close to a lit wick, went and blew off most of his backside. How does that illuminate matters, I wonder?'

'Momentarily, I'd imagine.'

Satisfied with that answer, Banaschar said nothing. A server arrived with a pitcher with which she refilled the ex-priest's tankard. He watched her leave, swaying through the press, a woman with things that needed doing.

It was easy to think of an island as isolated – certainly most islanders shared a narrow perspective, a blend of smug arrogance and self-obsession – but the isolation was superficial, a mere conceit. Drain the seas and the rocky ground linking everything was revealed; the followers of D'rek, the Worm of Autumn, understood this well enough. Rumours, attitudes, styles, beliefs rattling chains of conviction, all rolled over the waves as easily as the wind, and those that fitted comfortably soon became to the islanders their own – and indeed, as far as they were concerned, had originated with them in the first place.

There had been a purge, and the air still smelled of ash from the Mouse Quarter, where mobs had descended on the few dislocated Wickan families resident there – stablers, stitchers and riveters of leather tack, weavers of saddle blankets, an old woman who healed dray horses and mules – and had, with appalling zeal, dragged them from their hovels and shacks, children and elders and all in between; then, after looting them of their scant possessions, the mob had set fire to those homes. Herded into the street and surrounded, the Wickans had then been stoned to death.

Coltaine wasn't dead, people said. That entire tale was a lie, as was the more recent rumour that Sha'ik had been killed by the Adjunct. An imposter, it was said, a sacrificial victim to deflect the avenging army.

601

And as for the rebellion itself, well, it had not been crushed. It had simply disappeared, the traitors ducking low once more, weapons sheathed and hidden beneath telaba. True enough, the Adjunct had even now chased down Leoman of the Flails, trapping him in Y'Ghatan, but even that was but a feint. The Red Blades were once more free in Aren, the bones of the betrayed High Fist Pormqual broken and scattered along Aren Way, the grasses already growing thick on the barrows holding Pormqual's betrayed army.

Had not concerned residents of Aren journeyed out to the hill known as The Fall? And there dug holes into the barrow in search of the cursed Coltaine's bones? And Bult's, Mincer's, Lull's? Had they not found nothing? *All lies.* The traitors had one and all disappeared, including Duiker, the imperial historian whose betrayal of his Empress – and of the empire itself – was perhaps the foulest moment of them all.

And finally, the latest news. Of a disastrous siege. Of terrible plague in Seven Cities. Disparate, disconnected, yet like pokers thrust into the fire, sending sparks bursting into the dark. And, in whispers harsh with the conviction of truth, Sha'ik Reborn had reappeared, and now called to her more followers.

The last pebbles on the cart.

Down in the Mouse, the mob had acted on its own. The mob needed no leaders, no imperial directives – the mob understood justice, and on this island – this birthplace of the empire – justice was held in red hands. The battered, pulped corpses were dumped in the river, which was too turgid, too thick with sewage and refuse, the culverts beneath the bridges too narrow to carry those bodies through and out into the bay.

And this too was seen as an omen. The ancient sea god had rejected those corpses. Mael, empowered by the enlivening of faith here on the island, would not accept them into the salty bay of Malaz Harbour – what greater proof was needed?

The Emperor's ghost had been seen, in the overgrown yard of the Deadhouse, a ghost feeding on the souls of the slaughtered Wickans.

In the D'rek temples in Jakata and here in Malaz City, the priests and priestesses had vanished, sent out at night, it was whispered, to hunt down the rest of the Wickans left on the island – the ones who'd fled upon hearing of the purge in Malaz City – for the Worm of Autumn herself hungered for Wickan blood.

An army of citizens was said to be massing on the old borders, at the edge of the Wickan Plains on the mainland, and was about to march, with the aim of destroying every last damned betrayer in their squalid, stinking huts. And had the Empress sent out her legions to disperse that army? No, of course not, for she *approved*.

The Imperial High Mage Tayschrenn was in Malaz City, ensconced in Mock's Hold. What had brought him here? And why so public a visit – the strange sorceror was legendary for moving unseen, for acting behind the scenes to ensure the health of the empire. He was the very foundation of Laseen's power, after all, her left hand where the right belonged to the Claw. If he was here, it was to oversee—

He is here. Banaschar could feel the bastard, an aura brooding and ominous drifting down from Mock's Hold. Day upon day, night after night. *And why? Oh, all you fools.*

For the same reason I am here.

Six messengers thus far. Six, all paid enough to be reliable, all swearing afterwards that they had passed the urgent missive on – to the Hold's gate watchman, that bent creature said to be as old as Mock's Hold itself, who had in turn nodded each time, saying he would deliver the missive to the High Mage.

And yet, no reply. No summons.

Someone is intercepting my messages. There can be no other possibility. True, I was coy in what I said – how could I not be? But Tayschrenn would recognize my sigil, and he would understand . . . with heart suddenly pounding, cold sweat on the skin, with trembling hands . . . he would have understood. Instantly.

Banaschar did not know what to do. The last messenger had been three weeks ago.

'It's that desperate glint in your eye,' the man opposite him said, half-grinning once again, though his gaze slid away as soon as Banaschar focused on him.

'Enamoured, are you?'

'No, but close to curious. Been watching you these weeks. Giving up, but slowly. Most people do that in an instant. Rising from bed, walking to the window, then standing there, motionless, seeing nothing, as inside it all falls down with nary a whisper, nary a cloud of dust to mark its collapse, its vanishing into nothingness.'

'You do better talking and thinking like a damned sailor,' Banaschar said.

'The more I drink, the clearer and steadier I get.'

'That's a bad sign, friend.'

'I collect those. You ain't the only one cursed with waiting.'

'Months!'

'Years for me,' the man said, dipping into his cup with one blunt finger, fishing out a moth that had landed in the wine.

'Sounds like you're the one who should have given up long ago.'

'Maybe, but I've come to a kind of faith. Not long now, I'd swear it. Not long.'

Banaschar snorted. 'The drowning man converses with the fool, a night to beggar acrobats, jugglers and dancers, come one come all, two silvers buys you endless – and I do mean endless – entertainment.'

'I ain't too unfamiliar with drowning, friend.'

'Meaning?'

'Something tells me, when it comes to fools, you might say the same thing.'

Banaschar looked away. Saw another familiar face, another huge man – shorter than the foreigner opposite but equally as wide, his hairless pate marked with liver spots, scars seaming every part of his body. He was just collecting a tankard of Coop's Old Malazan Dark. The ex-priest raised his voice. 'Hey, Temper! There's room to sit here!' He sidled along the bench, watched as the old yet still formidable man – a veteran without doubt – made his way over.

At least now the conversation could slip back into the meaningless.

Still. *Another bastard waiting . . . for something. Only, with him, I suspect it'd be a bad thing if it ever arrived.*

Somewhere in the vaults of a city far, far away, rotted a wall hanging. Rolled up, home to nesting mice, the genius of the hands that had woven it slowly losing its unwitnessed war to the scurry-beetle grub, tawryn worms and ash moths. Yet, for all that, the darkness of its abandonment hid colours still vibrant here and there, and the scene depicted on that huge tapestry retained enough elements of the narrative that meaning was not lost. It might survive another fifty years before finally surrendering to the ravages of neglect.

The world, Ahlrada Ahn knew, was indifferent to the necessity of preservation. Of histories, of stories layered with meaning and import. It cared nothing for what was forgotten, for memory and knowledge had never been able to halt the endless repetition of wilful stupidity that so bound peoples and civilizations.

The tapestry had once commanded an entire wall, to the right when facing the Obsidian Throne – from which, before the annexation, the High King of Bluerose, Supreme Servant to the Black Winged Lord, had ruled, and flanking the dais, the Council of the Onyx Wizards, all attired in their magnificent cloaks of supple, liquid stone – but no, it was the tapestry that so haunted Ahlrada Ahn.

The narrative began at the end furthest from the throne. Three figures against a midnight background. Three brothers, born in pure Darkness and most cherished by their mother. All cast out, now, although each had come to that in his own time. Andarist, whom she saw as the first betrayer, an accusation all knew was mistaken, yet the knot of falsehoods had closed tight round him and none could pry it loose except Andarist himself – and that he could or would not do. Filled with unbearable grief, he had accepted his banishment, making his final words these: welcome or not, he would continue his guardianship of Mother Dark, in isolation, and in this would be found the measure of his life. Yet even to that promise, she had turned away. His brothers could not but recognize the crime of this, and it was Anomandaris Purake who was first to confront Mother Dark. What words passed between them only they knew, although the dire consequence was witnessed by all – Anomander turned his back on her. He walked away, denying the Darkness in his blood and seeking out, in its stead, the Chaos that ever warred in his veins. Silchas Ruin, the most enigmatic of the brothers, had seemed a man riven by indecision, trapped by impossible efforts at mitigation, at reconciliation, until all constraint was sundered, and so he committed the greatest crime of all. *Alliance with Shadow. Even as war broke out among the Tiste – a war that continues unchecked to this day.*

There had been victories, defeats, great slaughters, then, in that final gesture of despair, Silchas Ruin and his followers joined with the legions of Shadow and their cruel commander Scabandari – who would come to be known as Bloodeye – in their flight through the gates. *To this world. But betrayal ever haunts those three brothers.* And so, in the moment of supreme victory against the K'Chain Che'Malle, Silchas Ruin had fallen to Scabandari's knife, and his followers had in turn fallen to Tiste Edur swords.

Such was the second scene in the tapestry. The betrayal, the slaughter. But that slaughter had not been as thorough as the Edur believed. Tiste Andii had survived – the wounded, the stragglers, the elders and mothers and children left well behind the field of battle. They had witnessed. They had fled.

The third scene portrayed their fraught flight, the desperate defence against their pursuers by four barely grown sorcerors – who would become the founders of the Onyx Order – the victory that gave them respite, enough to make good their escape and, through new unfoldings of magic, elude the hunters and so fashion a sanctuary—

In caves buried beneath mountains on the shore of the inland sea, caves in which grew flowers of sapphire, intricate as roses, from which kingdom, mountains and sea derived their common name. *Bluerose, and so, the last and most poignant scene, closest to the throne, closest to my heart.*

His people, the few thousand that remained, once more hid in those deep caves, as the tyranny of the Edur raged like madness over all of Lether. *A madness that has devoured me.*

The Hiroth bireme drummed like thunder in the heaving swells of this fierce north sea the locals called Kokakal, and Ahlrada gripped the rail with both hands as bitter cold spray repeatedly struck his face, as if he was the subject of an enraged god's wrath. And perhaps he was, and if so, then it was well-earned as far as he was concerned.

He had been born the child of spies, and through generation after generation, his bloodline had dwelt in the midst of the Tiste Edur, thriving without suspicion in the chaos of the seemingly endless internecine disputes between the tribes. Hannan Mosag had ended that, of course, but by then the Watchers, such as Ahlrada Ahn and others, were well in place, their blood histories thoroughly mixed and inseparable from the Edur.

Bleaches for the skin, the secret gestures of communication shared among the hidden Andii, the subtle manipulations to ensure a presence among eminent gatherings – this was Ahlrada Ahn's life – and had the tribes remained in their northern fastness, it would have been ... palatable, until such time as he set out on a hunting expedition, from which he would never return – his loss mourned by his adopted tribe, while in truth Ahlrada would have crossed the south edge of the ice wastes, would have walked the countless leagues until he reached Bluerose. Until he came *home*.

That home was . . . not as it had once been. The sanctuary was under siege – true, by an unsuspecting enemy, who as yet knew nothing of the catacombs beneath their feet, but they now ruled, the chosen elites in their positions of supreme power, from which all manner of depravity and cruelty descended. *From the Emperor, the foul blood flows down, and down* . . . No Letherii reign had ever fallen as far as had Rhulad's and that of his Edur 'nobles'. *Pray that it ends. Pray that, one day, historians will write of this dark period in the history of Letheras as The Nightmare Age, a title of truth to warn the future.*

He did not believe it. Not a word of the prayer he had voiced in his head ten thousand times. *We saw the path Rhulad would take. Saw it when the Emperor banished his own brother – Gods, I was there, in the Nascent. I was one of the 'brothers' of Rhulad, his new extended family of cowering fawners. May the Black Winged Lord preserve me, I watched as the one Edur I admired, the one Edur I respected, was broken down. No, I did more than watch. I added my voice to Rhulad's ritual shorning of Trull. And Trull's crime? Why, nothing more than yet one more desperate attempt to bring Rhulad home. Ah, by the Dark Mother herself* . . . but Ahlrada Ahn had never dared, not once, not even in those early days when Trull struggled to turn the tide, no, he had himself turned away, rejecting every opportunity to unveil words that he knew Trull had needed, and would see and cherish as gifts. *I was a coward. My soul fled the risk, and there is no going back.*

In the days following Rhulad's ascension to the Letherii crown, Ahlrada had led a company of Arapay warriors out of Letheras, seeking the trail of the new Emperor's betrayers – his brother Fear, and that slave Udinaas. They had failed to discover any sign of them, and in that Ahlrada had found some small measure of victory. Rhulad's rage had nearly resulted in mass executions, Ahlrada and his searchers foremost among them, but the wreckage that remained of Hannan Mosag had managed to impose some control on Rhulad – the Emperor had great need for Tiste Edur warriors, not just in the occupation and rule of the empire, but yet more in the vast expeditions that were even then being planned.

Expeditions such as this one. Had he known what these journeys would entail, Ahlrada might well have elected for the execution Rhulad had been so eager to provide in those early days in Letheras.

Since that time . . . *all that we have done in his cursed name . . .*

We follow him – what has that made of us? Oh, Trull, you were right, and not one of us was brave enough to stand at your side when it mattered most.

His memories of Trull Sengar haunted Ahlrada Ahn. No, his memories of *everything* haunted him, yet they had converged, found focus in one lone, honourable warrior of the Tiste Edur.

He stood on the huge ship, eyes on the tumultuous seas, his face long since grown numb from the icy spray. Whilst in the waters to all sides more ships rolled in the heavy waves, one half of the Third Edur Imperial Fleet seeking a way round this enormous continent. Below decks and in the rigging, on each and every ship, laboured Letherii crews, even the lesser marines. While their overlords did nothing, beyond consuming wine and the endless courses of meals; or took to their sumptuous beds Letherii slave women, and those that they used up, left broken and raving with the poison of Edur seed, were simply flung over the rail for the ever-following huge grey sharks and the pods of yearling dhenrabi.

One half of the fleet in these seas. Commanded by Tomad Sengar, the Emperor's father.

And how well have we done thus far, dear Tomad? A bare handful of dubious champions, challengers to deliver home and into the cast of your youngest son's manic gaze.

And let us not forget the fallen kin we have found. Where have they come from? Even they don't know. Yet do we treat them as long-lost kin? Do our arms open wide for them? No, they are lesser creatures, blood befouled by failure, by destitution. Our gift is contempt, though we proclaim it liberation.

But, I was thinking of champions . . . and Rhulad's insatiable hunger that sends out into this world fleet upon fleet. Tomad. How well have we done?

He thought to their latest Guests, down below, and there was the sense, no more than a whisper in the murk of his rolled-up, rotted, moth-eaten soul, that perhaps, this time, they had found someone truly formidable. Someone who just might make Rhulad choke on his own blood, even more than once . . . although, as always, there would come that terrible scream . . .

We are made, and unmade, and so it goes on. For ever.

And I will never see my home.

With eyes the colour of weathered granite, the Letherii Marine Commander, Atri-Preda Yan Tovis, known to her soldiers as Twilight, looked down upon the sickly man. The gloomy hold of the ship was fetid and damp, the walkway above the keel smeared with puke and slimy mould. Creaks and thumps filled the air with the impact of every wave against the hull. The muted light of lanterns pitched about, making riotous the shadows. 'Here,' she said. 'Drink this.'

The man looked up, red-rimmed eyes set in a face the hue of whale fat. 'Drink?' Even the word seemed nearly sufficient to double him over yet again, but she saw him struggle mightily against the impulse.

'I speak your language not well,' she said. 'Drink. Two swallows. Wait, then more.'

'I'll not keep it down,' the man said.

'No matter. Two, you feel better. Then more. Sick goes.'

With a trembling hand, he accepted the small patinated glass bottle.

'Ceda make,' Twilight said. 'Made, generations ago. Sick goes.'

He swallowed once, then twice, was motionless for a moment, then he lunged to one side. Spitting, coughing, gasping, then, 'Spirits take me, yes.'

'Better?'

A nod.

'Drink rest. It will stay.'

He did so, then settled back, eyes closed. 'Better. Better, yes.'

'Good. Now, go to him.' She pointed towards the bow, twenty paces further along the walkway, where a figure leaned, huddled against the prow's uplift. 'Preda Tomad Sengar has doubts. Champion will not survive voyage. Will not eat, drink. Wastes away. Go to him. You claim much, his prowess. We see otherwise. We see only weakness.'

The man lying on the walkway would not meet her eyes, but he slowly sat up, then climbed awkwardly, unevenly to his feet. Legs wide to maintain his balance, he straightened.

Spat into the palms of his hands, rubbed his palms together for a moment, then swept both hands back through his hair.

Taralack Veed met the woman's eyes. 'Now, you are the one looking ill,' he said, frowning. 'What is wrong?'

Twilight simply shook her head. 'Go. The Preda must be convinced. Else we throw you both over side.'

The Gral warrior turned about and made his way, crab-like, up the walkway. To either side of him, pressed together between crates and casks, were chained figures. Grey-skinned like their captors, almost as tall, with many bearing facial traits that revealed Edur blood. Yet, here they were, rotting in their own filth, their dull, owlish gazes following Taralack as he made his way forward.

The Gral crouched before Icarium, reached out a hand to rest it on the warrior's shoulder.

Icarium flinched at the contact.

'My friend,' Taralack said in a low voice. 'I know this is not illness of the flesh that so afflicts you. It is illness of the spirit. You must struggle against it, Icarium.'

The Jhag was drawn up, knees to his chest, arms wrapped tight, the position reminding the Gral of the burial style practised by the Ehrlii. For a long moment, there was no response to his words, then a shudder racked the figure curled up before him. 'I cannot do this,' Icarium said, lifting his head to fix despairing eyes upon Taralack. 'I do not wish . . . I do not wish *to kill anyone!*'

Taralack rubbed at his face. Spirits below, that draught from Twilight had done wonders. *I can do this.* 'Icarium. Look down this walkway. Look upon these filthy creatures – who were told they were being liberated from their oppressors. Who came to believe that in these Edur was their salvation. But no. *Their blood is not pure.* It is muddied – they were slaves! Fallen so far, knowing nothing of their own history, the glory of their past – yes, I know, *what glory?* But look upon them! What manner of demons are these Tiste Edur and their damned empire? To so treat their own kind? Now tell me, Icarium, what have I procured for you? Tell me!'

The warrior's expression was ravaged, horror swimming in his eyes – and something else, a light of wildness. 'For what we witnessed,' the Jhag whispered. 'For what we saw them do . . .'

'Vengeance,' Taralack Veed said, nodding.

Icarium stared at him like a drowning man. '*Vengeance . . .*'

'But you will not be given that chance, Icarium. The Preda loses faith in you – in me – and we are in grave peril of being thrown to the sharks—'

'They ask me to kill their emperor, Taralack Veed. It makes no sense—'

'What they ask,' the Gral said, baring his teeth, 'and what you shall deliver, are two entirely different things.'

609

'Vengeance,' Icarium said again, as if tasting the word, then he brought both hands to his face. 'No, no, it is not for me. Already too much blood – more can achieve nothing. I will be no different than them!' He reached out suddenly and grasped Taralack, dragging him close. 'Don't you see that? More innocent lives—'

'Innocent? You fool, Icarium – can't you understand? *Innocence is a lie!* None of us is innocent! Not one! Show me one, please, I beg you – show me that I am wrong!' He twisted round in the Jhag's iron grip, jabbed a finger towards the huddled forms of the slaves. 'We both witnessed, did we not? Yesterday! Two of those pathetic fools, choking the life out of a third one – all three in chains, Icarium, all three starving, dying! Yet, some old quarrel, some old stupidity, unleashed one last time! Victims? Oh yes, no doubt of that. Innocent? Hah! And may the spirits above and below strike me down if my judgement is false!'

Icarium stared at him, then, slowly, his long fingers relaxed their grip on the Gral's hide shirt.

'My friend,' Taralack said, 'you must eat. You must keep your strength. This empire of the Tiste Edur, it is an abomination, ruled by a madman whose only talent is with a sword, and to that the weak and strong must bow, for such is the cast of the world. To defy the powerful is to invite subjugation and annihilation – you know this, Icarium. Yet you and you alone, friend, possess what is necessary to destroy that abomination. This is what you were born to do. You are the final weapon of justice – do not waver before this flood of inequity. Feed upon what you have witnessed – what we have witnessed – and all that we shall see on the voyage ahead. Feed on it, to fuel the justice within you – until it is blinding with power. Icarium, do not let these terrible Edur defeat you – as they are doing now.'

A voice spoke behind him. Twilight. 'The Preda considers a test. For this warrior.'

Taralack Veed turned, looked up at the woman. 'What do you mean? What sort of test?'

'We fight many wars. We walk paths of Chaos and Shadow.'

The Gral's eyes narrowed. 'We?'

She grimaced. 'The Edur now rule Lether. Where they lead, Letherii must follow. Edur swords make river of blood, and from river of blood, there is river of gold. The loyal have grown rich, so very rich.'

'And the disloyal?'

'They tend the oars. Indebted. It is so.'

'And you, Atri-Preda? Are you loyal?'

She studied him, silent for a half-dozen heartbeats, then she said, 'Each champion believes. By their sword the Emperor shall die. What is believed and what is true is not same,' she said, strangely twisting Taralack's own words. 'To what is true, I am loyal. The Preda considers a test.'

'Very well,' the Gral said, then held his breath, dreading a refusal from Icarium. But none came. *Ah, that is good.*

The woman walked away, armour rustling like coins spilling onto gravel.

Taralack Veed stared after her.

'She hides herself,' Icarium said in a low, sad voice. 'Yet her soul dies from within.'

'Do you believe, my friend,' the Gral said, turning back to the Jhag once more, 'that she alone suffers in silence? That she alone cowers, her honour besieged by what she must do?'

Icarium shook his head.

'Then think of her when your resolve falters, friend. Think of Twilight. And all the others like her.'

A wan smile. 'Yet you say there is no innocence.'

'An observation that does not obviate the demand for justice, Icarium.'

The Jhag's gaze shifted, down and away, and seemed to focus on the slime-laden planks of the hull to his right. 'No,' he whispered in a hollow tone, 'I suppose it doesn't.'

Sweat glistened on the rock walls, as if the pressure of the world had grown unbearable. The man who had just appeared, as if from nowhere, stood motionless for a time, the dark grey of his cloak and hood making him indistinct in the gloom, but the only witnesses to this peculiarity were both indifferent and blind – the maggots writhing in torn, rotting flesh among the sprawl of bodies that stretched before him down the chasm's elongated, rough floor.

The stench was overpowering, and Cotillion could feel himself engulfed in grief-laden familiarity, as if this was the true scent of existence. There had been times – he was almost certain – when he'd known unmitigated joy, but so faded were they to his recollection that he had begun to suspect the fictional conjuring of nostalgia. As with civilizations and their golden ages, so too with people: each individual ever longing for that golden past moment of true peace and wellness.

So often it was rooted in childhood, in a time before the strictures of enlightenment had afflicted the soul, when what had seemed simple unfolded its complexity like the petals of a poison flower, to waft its miasma of decay.

The bodies were of young men and women – too young in truth to be soldiers, although soldiers they had been. Their memories of solace would likely have been scoured from their minds back when, in a place and a world they had once called home, they hung nailed by iron spikes to wooden crosses, uncomprehending of their crimes. Of course there had been no such crimes. And the blood, which they had shed so profusely, had yielded no evidence of its taint, for neither the name of a people nor the hue of their skin, nor indeed the cast of their features, could make life's blood any less pure, or precious.

Wilful fools with murder in their rotted hearts believed otherwise. They divided the dead into innocent victim and the rightfully punished, and knew with unassailable conviction upon which side they themselves stood. With such conviction, the plunging of knives proved so very easy.

Here they had fought hard, he observed as he pushed himself into motion. A pitched battle, then an engaged withdrawal. Proof of superior training, discipline and a fierce unwillingness to yield without exacting a price. The enemy had taken their own fallen away, but for these young dead, the chasm itself was now their crypt. *Saved from their crucifixions . . . for this.*

There had been so many . . . pressing tasks. Essential necessities. *That we neglected this company, a company we ourselves ensconced here, to defend what we claimed our own. And then, it must have seemed, we abandoned them.* And in that grim conclusion they would, he admitted sourly, not be far wrong. *But we are assailed on all sides, now. We are in our most desperate moment. Right now . . . oh, my fallen friends, I am sorry for this . . .*

A conceit among the living, that their words could ease the dead. Worse, to voice words seeking forgiveness *from* those dead. The fallen had but one message to deliver to the living, and it had nothing to do with forgiveness. *Remind yourself of that, Cotillion. Be ever mindful of what the dead tell you and everyone else, over and over again.*

He heard noises ahead. Muted, a rhythmic rasping sound, like iron edges licking leather, then the soft pad of moccasined feet.

The natural corridor of the chasm narrowed, and blocking the choke-point was a T'lan Imass, sword-point resting on the rock before it, watching Cotillion's approach. Beyond the undead warrior there was the dull yellow glow of lanterns, a passing shadow, another, then a figure stepped into view.

'Stand aside, Ibra Gholan,' Minala said, her eyes on Cotillion.

Her armour was in tatters. A spear-point had punctured chain and leather high on her chest, the left side, just beneath the shoulder. Old blood crusted the edges. One side of her helm's cheek-guard was gone and the area of her face made visible by its absence was swollen and mottled with bruises. Her extraordinary light grey eyes were fixed on

Cotillion's own as she moved past the T'lan Imass. 'They arrive through a gate,' she said. 'A warren lit by silver fire.'

'Chaos,' he said. 'Proof of the alliance we had feared would come to pass. Minala, how many attacks have you repulsed?'

'Four.' She hesitated, then reached up and worked her helm loose, lifting it clear. Sweat-matted, filthy black hair snaked down. 'My children . . . the losses have been heavy.'

Cotillion could not hold her gaze any longer. Not with that admission.

She went on. 'If not for the T'lan Imass . . . and Apt, and the Tiste Edur renegade, this damned First Throne would now be in the possession of an army of blood-hungry barbarians.'

'Thus far, then,' Cotillion ventured, 'your attackers have been exclusively Tiste Edur?'

'Yes.' She studied him for a long moment. 'That will not last, will it?'

Cotillion's eyes focused once again on Ibra Gholan.

Minala continued, 'The Edur are but skirmishers, aren't they? And even they have not fully committed themselves to this cause. Why?'

'They are as thinly stretched as we are, Minala.'

'Ah, then I cannot expect more Aptorians. What of the other demons of your realm, Cotillion? Azalan? Dinal? Can you give us nothing?'

'We can,' he said. 'But not now.'

'When?'

He looked at her. 'When the need is greatest.'

Minala stepped close. 'You bastard. I had thirteen hundred. Now I have four hundred still capable of fighting.' She jabbed a finger towards the area beyond the choke-point. 'Almost three hundred more lie dying of wounds – *and there is nothing I can do for them!*'

'Shadowthrone will be informed,' Cotillion said. 'He will come. He will heal your wounded—'

'When?'

The word was nearly a snarl.

'When I leave here,' he replied, 'I am returning directly to Shadowkeep. Minala, I would speak with the others.'

'Who? Why?'

Cotillion frowned, then said, 'The renegade. Your Tiste Edur. I have . . . questions.'

'I have never seen such skill with the spear. Trull Sengar kills, and kills, and then, when it is done and he kneels in the blood of the kin he has slain, he weeps.'

'Do they know him?' Cotillion asked. 'Do they call him by name?'

'No. He says they are Den-Ratha, and young. Newly blooded. But he then says, it is only a matter of time. Those Edur that succeed in withdrawing, they must be reporting the presence of an Edur among the defenders of the First Throne. Trull says that one of his own tribe will be among the attackers, and he will be recognized – and it is then, he says, that they will come in force, with warlocks. He says, Cotillion, that he will bring ruin upon us all.'

'Does he contemplate leaving?' Cotillion asked.

She scowled. 'To that he gives no answer. If he did, I would not blame him. And,' she added, 'if he chooses to stay, I may well die with his name the last curse I voice in this world. Or, more likely, the second last name.'

He nodded, understanding. 'Trull Sengar remains, then, out of honour.'

'And that honour spells our doom.'

Cotillion ran a hand through his hair, mildly surprised to discover how long it had grown. *I need to find a hair hacker. One trustworthy enough with a blade at my neck.* He considered that. *Well, is it any wonder gods must do such mundane tasks for themselves? Listen to yourself, Cotillion – your mind would flee from this moment. Meet this woman's courage with your own.* 'The arrival of warlocks among the Tiste Edur will prove a difficult force to counter—'

'We have the bonecaster,' she said. 'As yet he has remained hidden. Inactive. For, like Trull Sengar, he is a lodestone.'

Cotillion nodded. 'Will you lead me in, Minala?'

In answer she turned about and gestured that he follow.

The cavern beyond was a nightmare vision. The air was fetid, thick as that of a slaughterhouse. Dried blood covered the stone floor like a crumbling, pasty carpet. Pale faces – too young by far – turned to look upon Cotillion with ancient eyes drained of all hope. The god saw Apt, the demon's black hide ribboned with grey, barely healed scars, and crouched at her lone forefoot, Panek, his huge, faceted eye glittering. The forehead above that ridged eye displayed a poorly stitched slice, result of a blow that had peeled back his scalp from just above one side of the eye's orbital, across to the temple opposite.

Three figures rose, emerging from gloom as they walked towards Cotillion. The Patron God of Assassins halted. *Monok Ochem, the clanless T'lan Imass known as Onrack the Broken, and the renegade Tiste Edur, Trull Sengar. I wonder, would these three, along with Ibra Gholan, have been enough? Did we need to fling Minala and her young charges into this horror?*

Then, as they drew closer, Cotillion saw Onrack and Trull more clearly. Beaten down, slashed, cut. Half of Onrack's skeletal head was shorn away. Ribs had caved in from some savage blow, and the upper ridge of his hip, on the left side, had been chopped away, revealing the porous interior of the bone. Trull was without armour, and had clearly

entered battle lacking such protection. The majority of his wounds –
deep gashes, puncture holes – were on his thighs, beneath the hips and
to the outside – signs of a spear-wielder's style of parrying with the
middle-haft of the weapon. The Edur could barely walk, leaning heavily
on the battered spear in his hands.

Cotillion found it difficult to meet the Edur's exhausted, despair-
filled eyes. 'When the time comes,' he said to the grey-skinned warrior,
'help shall arrive.'

Onrack the Broken spoke. 'When they win the First Throne, they will
realize the truth. That it is not for them. They can hold it, but they cannot use it. Why, then, Cotillion of Shadow, do these brave mortals
surrender their lives here?'

'Perhaps we but provide a feint,' Monok Ochem said, the
bonecaster's tone as inflectionless as Onrack's had been.

'No,' Cotillion said. 'More than that. It is what they would do upon
making that discovery. They will unleash the warren of Chaos in this
place – in the chamber where resides the First Throne. Monok Ochem,
they shall destroy it, and so destroy its power.'

'Is such a deed cause for regret?' Onrack asked.

Shaken, Cotillion had no reply.

Monok Ochem pivoted to regard Onrack the Broken. 'This one
speaks the words of the Unbound. He fights not to defend the First
Throne. He fights only to defend Trull Sengar. He alone is the reason
the Tiste Edur still lives.'

'This is true,' Onrack replied. 'I accept no authority other than my
own will, the desires I choose to act upon, and the judgements I make
for myself. This, Monok Ochem, is the meaning of freedom.'

'Don't—' Trull Sengar said, turning away.

'Trull Sengar?'

'No, Onrack. Do you not see? You invite your own annihilation, and
all because I do not know what to do, all because I cannot decide – anything. And so here I remain, as chained as I was when you first found
me in the Nascent.'

'Trull Sengar,' Onrack said after a moment, 'you fight to save lives.
The lives of these youths here. You stand in their stead, again and again.
This is a noble choice. Through you, I discover the gift of fighting in
defence of honour, the gift of a cause that is worthy. I am not as I once
was. I am not as Monok Ochem and Ibra Gholan. Expedience is no
longer enough. Expedience is the murderer's lie.'

'For Hood's sake,' Cotillion said to Monok Ochem, feeling
exasperated, brittle with frustration, 'can you not call upon kin? A few
hundred T'lan Imass – there must be some lying around somewhere,
doing nothing as is their wont?'

The empty eyes remained ... empty. 'Cotillion of Shadow. Your companion claimed the First Throne—'

'Then he need only command the T'lan Imass to attend—'

'No. The others journey to a war. A war of self-preservation—'

'To Hood with Assail!' Cotillion shouted, his voice echoing wildly in the cavern. 'This is nothing but damned pride! You cannot win there! You send clan after clan, all into the same destructive maw! You damned fools – *disengage!* There is nothing worth fighting for on that miserable nightmare of a continent! Don't you see? Among the Tyrants there, *it is nothing but a game!*'

'It is the nature of my people,' Onrack said – and Cotillion could detect a certain tone in the words, something like vicious irony – 'to believe in their own supreme efficacy. They mean to win that game, Cotillion of Shadow, or greet oblivion. They accept no alternatives. Pride? It is not pride. It is the very reason to exist.'

'We face greater threats—'

'And they do not care,' Onrack cut in. 'This you must understand, Cotillion of Shadow. Once, long ago by mortal standards, now, your companion found the First Throne. He occupied it and so gained command over the T'lan Imass. Even then, it was a tenuous grasp, for the power of the First Throne is ancient. Indeed, its power *wanes*. Shadowthrone was able to awaken Logros T'lan Imass – a lone army, finding itself still bound to the First Throne's remnant power due to little more than mere proximity. He could not command Kron T'lan Imass, nor Bentract, nor Ifayle, nor the others that remained, for they were too distant. When Shadowthrone last sat upon the First Throne, he was mortal, he was bound to no other aspect. He had not ascended. But now, he is impure, and this impurity ever weakens his command. Cotillion, as your companion loses ever more substance, so too does he lose ... veracity.'

Cotillion stared at the broken warrior, then looked over at Monok Ochem and Ibra Gholan. 'And these, then,' he said in a low voice, 'represent ... token obedience.'

The bonecaster said, 'We must seek to preserve our own kind, Cotillion of Shadow.'

'And if the First Throne is lost?'

A clattering shrug.

Gods below. Now, at last, I understand why we lost Logros's undead army in the middle of the Seven Cities campaign. Why they just ... left. He shifted his gaze back to Onrack the Broken. 'Is it possible,' he asked, 'to restore the power of the First Throne?'

'Say nothing,' Monok Ochem commanded.

Onrack's half-shattered head slowly turned to regard the bonecaster. 'You do not compel me. I am unbound.'

At some silent order, Ibra Gholan lifted his stone weapon and faced Onrack.

Cotillion raised his hands. 'Wait! Onrack, do not answer my question. Let's forget I ever asked it. There's no need for this – haven't we enough enemies as it is?'

'You,' said Monok Ochem to the god, 'are dangerous. You think what must not be thought, you speak aloud what must not be said. You are as a hunter who walks a path no-one else can see. We must consider the implications.' The bonecaster turned away, bony feet scraping as he walked towards the chamber of the First Throne. After a moment, Ibra Gholan lowered his blade and thumped off in Monok Ochem's wake.

Cotillion reached up to run his hand through his hair once again, and found his brow slick with sweat.

'And so,' Trull Sengar said, with a hint of a smile, 'you have taken our measure, Cotillion. And from this visit, we in turn receive equally bitter gifts. Namely, the suggestion that all we do here, in defence of this First Throne, is without meaning. So, do you now elect to withdraw us from this place?' His eyes narrowed on the god, and the ironic half-smile gave way to . . . something else. 'I thought not.'

Perhaps indeed I walk an unseen path – one even I am blind to – but now the necessity of following it could not be greater. 'We will not abandon you,' he said.

'So you claim,' muttered Minala behind him.

Cotillion stepped to one side. 'I have summoned Shadowthrone,' he said to her.

A wry expression. 'Summoned?'

'We grant each other leave to do such things, Minala, as demands dictate.'

'Companions in truth, then. I thought that you were subservient to Shadowthrone, Cotillion. Do you now claim otherwise?'

He managed a smile. 'We are fully aware of each other's complementary talents,' he replied, and left it at that.

'There wasn't enough time,' she said.

'For what?'

'For training. For the years needed . . . for them. To grow up. *To live.*'

He said nothing, for she was right.

'Take them with you,' Minala said. 'Now. I will remain, as will Apt and Panek. Cotillion, please, take them with you.'

'I cannot.'

'Why?'

He glanced over at Onrack. 'Because, Minala, I am not returning to the Realm of Shadow—'

'Wherever you are going,' she said in a suddenly harsh voice, 'it must be better than this!'

'Alas, would that I could make such a promise.'

'He cannot,' said Onrack. 'Minala, he now in truth sets out on an unseen path. It is my belief that we shall not see him again.'

'Thank you for the vote of confidence,' Cotillion said.

'My friend has seen better days,' Trull Sengar said, reaching out to slap Onrack on the back. The thump the blow made was hollow, raising dust, and something clattered down within the warrior's chest. 'Oh,' said the Tiste Edur, 'did that do something bad?'

'No,' Onrack replied. 'The broken point of a spear. It had been lodged in bone.'

'Was it irritating you?'

'Only the modest sound it made when I walked. Thank you, Trull Sengar.'

Cotillion eyed the two. *What mortal would call a T'lan Imass* friend? *And, they fight side by side. I would know more of this Trull Sengar.* But, as with so many things lately, there was no time for that. Sighing, he turned, and saw that the youth Panek now guarded the choke-point, in Ibra Gholan's absence.

The god headed that way.

Panek swung to face him. 'I miss him,' he said.

'Who?'

'Edgewalker.'

'Why? I doubt that sack of bones could fight his way out of a birch-bark coffin.'

'Not to fight at our sides, Uncle. We will hold here. Mother worries too much.'

'Which mother?'

A hideous, sharp-toothed smile. 'Both.'

'Why do you miss Edgewalker, then?'

'For his stories.'

'Oh, those.'

'The dragons. The foolish ones, the wise ones, the living ones and the dead ones. If every world were but a place on the board, they would be the game pieces. Yet no single hand directs them. Each is wild, a will unto itself. And then there are the shadows – Edgewalker explained about those – the ones you can't see.'

'He explained, did he? Well, clearly the hoary bastard likes you more than he does me.'

'They all cast shadows, Uncle,' Panek said. 'Into your realm.

Every one of them. That's why there's so many . . . prisoners.'

Cotillion frowned, then, slowly, inexorably as comprehension dawned, the god's eyes widened.

Trull Sengar watched the god move past Panek, one hand tracking along the stone wall, as if Cotillion were suddenly drunk. 'I wonder what that was all about? You'd think Panek just kneed him between the legs.'

'He'd earn a kiss from me if he did that,' Minala said.

'You're too harsh,' Trull said. 'I feel sorry for Cotillion.'

'Then you're an idiot, but of course I've known the truth of that for months.'

He smiled across at her, said nothing.

Minala now eyed the uneven entrance to the chamber of the First Throne. 'What are they doing in there? They never go in there.'

'Considering implications, I suppose,' Trull said.

'And where's Shadowthrone? He's supposed to be here by now. If we get attacked right now . . .'

We're dead. Trull leaned more heavily on the spear, to ease the weight on his left leg, which was hurting more – marginally – than his right. *Or at least I am. But that's likely whether or not I get healed, once my kin decide to take this seriously.* He did not understand their half-hearted skirmishing, the tentative probing by the Den-Ratha. And why were they bothering at all? If they hungered for a throne, it would be that of Shadow, not this petrified bone monstrosity they call the First Throne. *But, thinking on it, maybe this does indeed make sense. They have allied themselves with the Crippled God, and with the Unbound T'lan Imass who now serve the Chained One. But my Tiste Edur place little weight on alliances with non-Edur. Maybe that's why all they've done thus far is token blood-letting. A single warlock and veteran warriors and this little fête would be over.*

And they would come – *they will come, once I am recognized.* Yet he could not hide himself from their eyes; he could not stand back whilst they slaughtered these young humans who knew nothing of life, who were soldiers in name only. These lessons of cruelty and brutality did not belong in what a child needed to learn, in what a child *should* learn. And a world in which children were subjected to such things was a world in which compassion was a hollow word, its echoes a chorus of mockery and cold contempt.

Four skirmishes. Four, and Minala was now mother to seven hundred destroyed lives, almost half of them facing the mercy of death *. . . until Shadowthrone appears, with his edged gift, in itself cold and heartless.*

'Your face betrays you, Trull Sengar. You are driven to weeping yet again.'

The Edur looked across at Onrack, then over to where Minala now stood with Panek. 'Her rage is her armour, friend. And that is my greatest weakness, that I cannot conjure the same within myself. Instead, I stand here, waiting. For the next attack, for the return of the terrible music – the screams, the pain and the dying, the deafening roar of the futility our battle-lust creates . . . with every clash of sword and spear.'

'Yet, you do not surrender,' the T'lan Imass said.

'I cannot.'

'The music you hear in battle is incomplete, Trull Sengar.'

'What do you mean?'

'Even as I stand at your side, I can hear Minala's prayers, whether she is near us or not. Even when she drags wounded and dying children back, away from danger, I hear her. She prays, Trull Sengar, that you do not fall. That you fight on, that the miracle that is you and the spear you wield shall never fail her. Never fail her and her children.'

Trull Sengar turned away.

'Ah,' Onrack said, 'with your tears suddenly loosed, friend, I see my error. Where I sought by my words to instil pride in you, I defeat your own armour and wound you deeply. With despair. I am sorry. There remains so much of what it is to live that I have forgotten.' The battered warrior regarded Trull in silence for a moment, then added, 'Perhaps I can give you something else, something more . . . hopeful.'

'Please try,' Trull said in a whisper.

'At times, down in this chasm, I smell something, a presence. It is faint, animal. It . . . comforts me, although I do not know why, for I cannot comprehend its source. In those times, Trull Sengar, I feel as if we are being observed. We are being watched by unseen eyes, and in those eyes there is vast compassion.'

'Do you say this only to ease my pain, Onrack?'

'No, I would not so deceive you.'

'What – who does it come from?'

'I do not know – but I have seen that it affects Monok Ochem. Even Ibra Gholan. I sense their disquiet, and this, too, comforts me.'

'Well,' rasped a voice beside them, 'it isn't me.' Shadows coalescing, creating a hunched, hooded shape, wavering indistinct, as if reluctant to commit itself to any particular existence, any single reality.

'Shadowthrone.'

'Healing, yes? Very well. But I have little time. We must hurry, do you understand? Hurry!'

Renewed, once again, to face what will come. Would that I had my own prayers. Comforting words in my mind ... to drown out the screams all around me. To drown out my own.

Somewhere down below, Karsa Orlong struggled to calm Havok, and the sudden hammer of hoofs against wood, sending trembles through the deck beneath Samar Dev's feet, indicated that it would be some time before the animal quieted. She did not blame the Jhag horse. The air below was foul, reeking with the sick and the dying, with the sour stench that came from hopelessness.

But we are spared that fate. We are Guests, because my giant companion would kill the Emperor. The fool. The arrogant, self-obsessed idiot. I should have stayed with Boatfinder, there on that wild shore. I should have then turned around and walked home. She had so wanted this to be a journey of exploration and discovery, the lure of wonders waiting somewhere ahead. Instead, she found herself imprisoned by an empire gone mad with obsession. Self-righteous, seeing its own might as if it was a gift bestowing piety. As if power projected its own ethos, and the capability to do something was justification enough for doing it. The mindset of the street-corner bully, in his head two or three rules by which he guided his own existence, and by which he sought to shape his world. The ones he must fear, the ones he could drive to their knees, and maybe ones he hungered to be like, or ones he lusted after, but even there the relationship was one of power. Samar Dev felt sick with disgust, fighting a tide of tumultuous panic rising within her – and no dry deck beneath her boots could keep her from that sort of drowning.

She had tried to keep out of the way of the human crew who worked the huge ship's sails, and finally found a place where she wouldn't be pushed aside or cursed, at the very prow, holding tight to rat-lines as the waves lifted and dropped the lumbering craft. In a strange way, each plunge that stole her own weight proved satisfying, almost comforting.

Someone came to her side, and she was not surprised to see the blonde, blue-eyed witch. No taller than Samar's shoulder, her arms exposed to reveal the lean, cabled muscles of someone familiar with hard, repetitive work. Indicative as well, she believed, of a particular personality. Hard-edged, judgemental, perhaps even untrustworthy – muscles like wires were ever stretched taut by some inner extremity, a nervous agitation devoured like fuel, unending in its acrid supply.

'I am named Feather Witch,' the woman said, and Samar Dev noted, with faint surprise, that she was young. 'You understand me words?'

'*My* words.'

'My words. He teaches not well,' she added.

621

She means the Taxilian. It's no surprise. He knows what will happen when he outlives his usefulness.

'You teach me,' Feather Witch said.

Samar Dev reached out and flicked the withered finger hanging from the young woman's neck, eliciting both a flinch and a curse. 'I teach you . . . nothing.'

'I make Hanradi Khalag kill you.'

'Then Karsa Orlong kills every damned person on this ship. Except the chained ones.'

Feather Witch, scowling, was clearly struggling to understand, then, with a snarl, she spun round and walked away.

Samar Dev returned her gaze to the heaving seas ahead. A witch indeed, and one that did not play fair with the spirits. One who did not recognize honour. *Dangerous. She will . . . attempt things. She may even try to kill me, make it look like an accident. There's a chance she will succeed, which means I had better warn Karsa. If I die, he will understand that it will have been no accident. And so he will destroy every one of these foul creatures.*

Her own thoughts shocked her. *Ah, shame on me. I, too, begin to think of Karsa Orlong as a weapon. To be wielded, manipulated, and in the name of some imagined vengeance, no less.* But, she suspected, someone or something else was already playing that game. With Karsa Orlong. And it was that mystery she needed to pursue, until she had an answer. *And then? Am I not assuming that the Toblakai is unaware of how he is being used? What if he already knows? Think on that, woman . . .*

All right. He accepts it . . . for now. But, whenever he deems it expedient to turn on those unseen manipulators, he will – and they will regret ever having involved themselves in his life. Yes, that well suits Karsa's own arrogance, his unshakeable confidence. In fact, the more I think on it, the more I am convinced that I am right. I've stumbled onto the first steps of the path that will lead me to solving the mystery. Good.

'What in Hood's name did you say to her?'

Startled, Samar Dev looked over, to see the Taxilian arrive at her side. 'Who? What? Oh, her.'

'Be careful,' the man said. He waved a filthy hand in front of his bruised, misshapen face. 'See this? Feather Witch. I dare not fight back. I dare not even defend myself. See it in her eyes – I think she was beaten herself, when a child. That is how these things breed generation after generation.'

'Yes,' Samar said, surprised, 'I believe you are right.'

He managed something like a grin. 'I was foolish enough to be captured, yes, but that does not make me always a fool.'

'What happened?'

'Pilgrimage, of sorts. I paid for passage on a drake – back to Rutu Jelba – trying to flee the plague, and believe me, I paid a lot.'

Samar Dev nodded. Drakes were Tanno pilgrim ships, heavy and stolid and safe against all but the fiercest storms, and on board there would be a Tanno Spiritwalker or at the very least a Tanno Mendicant. No plague could thrive on such a ship – it had been a clever gamble, and drakes were usually half-empty on their return journeys.

'Dawn broke, a mere two days away from Rutu Jelba,' the Taxilian continued, 'and we were surrounded by foreign ships – this fleet. The Spiritwalker sought to communicate, then when it became evident that these Edur viewed us as a prize, to negotiate. Gods below, woman, the sorcery they unleashed upon him! Awful, it sickened the very air. He resisted – a lot longer than they expected, I've since learned – long enough to cause them considerable consternation – but he fell in the end, the poor bastard. The Edur chose one of us, me as it turned out, and cut open the others and flung them to the sharks. They needed a translator, you see.'

'And what, if I may ask, is your profession?'

'Architect, in Taxila. No, not famous. Struggling.' He shrugged. 'A struggle I would willingly embrace right now.'

'You are working deceit when teaching Feather Witch.'

He nodded.

'She knows.'

'Yes, but for the moment she can do nothing about it. This part of the fleet is resupplied – we'll not be heading landward for some time, and as for Seven Cities ships to capture, well, the plague's emptied the seas, hasn't it? Besides, we will be sailing west. For now, I'm safe. And, unless Feather Witch is a lot smarter than I think she is, it will be a long time before she comes to comprehension.'

'How are you managing it?'

'I am teaching her four languages, all at once, and making no distinction among them, not even the rules of syntax. For each word I give her four in translation, then think up bizarre rules for selecting one over another given the context. She's caught me out but once. So. Malazan, the Taxilii Scholar's Dialect, the Ehrlii variant of the common tongue, and, from my grandfather's sister, tribal Rangala.'

'Rangala? I thought that was extinct.'

'Not until she dies, and I'd swear that old hag's going to live for ever.'

'What is your name?'

He shook his head. 'There is power in names – no, I do not distrust you – it is these Tiste Edur. And Feather Witch – if she discovers my name—'

'She can compel you. I understand. Well, in my mind I think of you as the Taxilian.'

'That will suffice.'

'I am Samar Dev, and the warrior I came with is Toblakai . . . Sha'ik's Toblakai. He calls himself Karsa Orlong.'

'You risk much, revealing your names—'

'The risk belongs to Feather Witch. I surpass her in the old arts. As for Karsa, well, she is welcome to try.' She glanced at him. 'You said we were sailing west?'

He nodded. 'Hanradi Khalag commands just under half the fleet – the rest is somewhere east of here. They have both been sailing back and forth along this coast for some months, almost half a year, in fact. Like fisher fleets, but the catch they seek walks on two legs and wields a sword. Discovering remnant kin was unexpected, and the state those poor creatures were in simply enraged these Edur. I do not know where the two fleets intend to merge – somewhere west of Sepik, I think. Once that happens,' he shrugged, 'we set a course for their empire.'

'And where is that?'

Another shrug. 'Far away, and beyond that, I can tell you nothing.'

'Far away indeed. I have never heard of an empire of humans ruled by Tiste Edur. And yet, this Letherii language. As you noted it is somehow related to many of the languages here in Seven Cities, those that are but branches from the same tree, and that tree is the First Empire.'

'Ah, that explains it, then, for I can mostly understand the Letherii, now. They use a different dialect when conversing with the Edur – a mix of the two. A trader tongue, and even there I begin to comprehend.'

'I suggest you keep such knowledge to yourself, Taxilian.'

'I will. Samar Dev, is your companion truly the same Toblakai as the one so named who guarded Sha'ik? It is said he killed two demons the night before she was slain, one of them with his bare hands.'

'Until recently,' Samar Dev said, 'he carried with him the rotted heads of those demons. He gifted them to Boatfinder – to the Anibari shaman who accompanied us. The white fur Karsa wears is from a Soletaken. He killed a third demon just outside Ugarat, and chased off another in the Anibar forest. He singlehandedly killed a bhederin bull – and that I witnessed with my own eyes.'

The Taxilian shook his head. 'The Edur Emperor . . . he too is a demon. Every cruelty committed by these grey-skinned bastards, they claim is by their Emperor's command. And so too this search for warriors. An emperor who invites his own death – how can this be?'

'I don't know,' she admitted. *And not knowing is what frightens me the most.* 'As you say, it makes no sense.'

'One thing is known,' the man said. 'Their Emperor has never been defeated. Else his rule would have ended. Perhaps indeed that tyrant is the greatest warrior of all. Perhaps there is no-one, no-one anywhere in this world, who can best him. Not even Toblakai.'

She thought about that, as the huge Edur fleet, filling the seas around her, worked northward, the untamed wilds of the Olphara Peninsula a jagged line on the horizon to port. *North, then west, into the Sepik Sea.*

Samar Dev slowly frowned. *Oh, they have done this before. Sepik, the island kingdom, the vassal to the Malazan Empire. A peculiar, isolated people, with their two-tiered society. The indigenous tribe, sub-jugated and enslaved. Rulhun'tal ven'or – the Mudskins . . .* 'Taxilian, these Edur slaves below. Where did they find them?'

'I don't know.' The bruised face twisted into a bitter smile. 'They *liberated* them. The sweet lie of that word, Samar Dev. No, I will think no more on that.'

You are lying to me, Taxilian, I think.

There was a shout from the crow's nest, picked up by sailors in the rigging and passed on below. Samar Dev saw heads turn, saw Tiste Edur appear and make their way astern.

'Ships have been sighted in our wake,' the Taxilian said.

'The rest of the fleet?'

'No.' He lifted his head and continued listening as the lookout called down ever more details. 'Foreigners. Lots of ships. Mostly transports – two-thirds transports, one-third dromon escort.' He grunted. 'The third time we've sighted them since I came on board. Sighted, then evaded, each time.'

'Have you identified those foreigners for them, Taxilian?'

He shook his head.

The Malazan Imperial Fleet. Admiral Nok. It has to be. She saw a certain tension now among the Tiste Edur. 'What is it? What are they so excited about?'

'Those poor Malazans,' the man said with a savage grin. 'It's the positioning now, you see.'

'What do you mean?'

'If they stay in our wake, if they keep sailing northward to skirt this peninsula, they are doomed.'

'Why?'

'Because now, Samar Dev, the rest of the Edur fleet – Tomad Sengar's mass of warships – *is behind the Malazans.*'

All at once, the cold wind seemed to cut through all of Samar Dev's clothing. 'They mean to attack them?'

'They mean to annihilate them,' the Taxilian said. 'And I have seen Edur sorcery and I tell you this – the Malazan Empire is about to lose its entire Imperial Fleet. It will die. And with it, every damned man and woman on board.' He leaned forward as if to spit, then, realizing the wind was in his face, he simply grinned all the harder. 'Except, maybe, one or two . . . *champions.*'

This was something new, Banaschar reflected as he hurried beneath sheets of rain towards Coop's. He was being followed. Once, such a discovery would have set a fury alight inside him, and he would have made short work of the fool, then, after extracting the necessary details, even shorter work of whoever had hired that fool. But now, the best he could muster was a sour laugh under his breath. *'Aye, Master (or Mistress), he wakes up in the afternoon, without fail, and after a sixth of a bell or so of coughing and scratching and clicking nits, he heads out, onto the street, and sets off, Mistress (or Master), for one of six or so disreputable establishments, and once ensconced among the regulars, he argues about the nature of religion – or is it taxation and the rise in port tithes? Or the sudden drop-off in the coraval schools off the Jakatakan shoals? Or the poor workmanship of that cobbler who'd sworn he could re-stitch that sole on this here left boot – what? True enough, Master (or Mistress), it's all nefarious code, sure as I can slink wi' the best slinkers, and I'm as near to crackin' it as can be . . .'*

His lone source of entertainment these nights, these imagined conversations. *Gods, now that is pathetic. Then again, pathos ever amuses me.* And long before it could cease amusing him, he'd be drunk, and so went another passage of the sun and stars in that meaningless heaven overhead. Assuming it still existed – who could tell with this solid ceiling of grey that had settled on the island for almost a week now, with no sign of breaking? *Much more of this rain and we'll simply sink beneath the waves. Traders arriving from the mainland will circle and circle where Malaz Island used to be. Circle and circle, the pilots scratching their heads . . .* There he went again, yet another conjured scene with its subtle weft of contempt for all things human – the sheer incompetence, stupidity, sloth and bad workmanship – look at this, after all, he limped like some one-footed shark baiter – the cobbler met him at the door *barefooted* – he should have started up with the suspicion thing about then. *Don't you think?*

'Well, Empress, it's like this. The poor sod was half-Wickan, and he'd paid for that, thanks to your refusal to rein in the mobs. He'd been herded, oh Great One, with bricks and clubs, about as far as he could go without diving headfirst into the harbour. Lost all his cobbler tools and stuff – his livelihood, you see. And me, well, I am cursed with pity – aye, Empress, it's not an affliction that plagues you much and all the good to you, I say, but where was I? Oh yes, racked with pity, prodded into mercy. Hood knows, the poor broken man needed that coin more

than I did, if only to bury that little son of his he was still carrying round, aye, the one with the caved-in skull—' No, stop this, Banaschar. Stop.

Meaningless mind games, right? Devoid of significance. Nothing but self-indulgence, and for that vast audience out there – the whispering ghosts and their intimations, their suppositions and veiled insults and their so easily bored minds – that audience – *they are my witnesses, yes, that sea of murky faces in the pit, for whom my desperate performance, ever seeking to reach out with a human touch, yields nothing but impatience and agitation, the restless waiting for the cue to laugh.* Well enough, this oratory pageant served only himself, Banaschar knew, and all the rest was a lie.

The child with the caved-in skull showed more than one face, tilted askew and flaccid in death. More than one, more than ten, more than ten thousand. Faces he could not afford to think about in his day-to-day, night-through-night stumble of existence. For they were as nails driven deep into the ground, pinning down whatever train he dragged in his wake, and with each forward step the resistance grew, the constriction round his neck stretching ever tighter – and no mortal could weather that – *we choke on what we witness, we are strangled by headlong flight, that will not do, not do at all. Don't mind me, dear Empress. I see how clean is your throne.*

Ah, here were the steps leading down. Coop's dear old Hanged Man, the stone scaffold streaming with gritty tears underfoot and a challenge to odd-footed descent, the rickety uncertainty – was this truly nothing more than steps down into a tavern? *Or now transformed, my temple of draughts, echoing to the vacuous moaning of my fellow-kind, oh, how welcome this embrace—*

He pushed through the doorway and paused in the gloom, just inside the dripping eaves, his feet planted in a puddle where the pavestones sagged, water running down him to add to its depth; and a half-dozen faces, pale and dirty as the moon after a dust storm, swung towards him . . . for but a moment, then away again.

My adoring public. Yes, the tragic mummer has returned.

And there, seated alone at a table, was a monstrosity of a man. Hunched over, tiny black eyes glittering beneath the shadow of a jutting brow. Hairy beyond reason. Twisted snarls exploding out from both ears, the ebon-hued curls wending down to merge with the vast gull's nest that was his beard, which in turn engulfed his neck and continued downward, unabated, to what was visible of the man's bulging chest; and, too, climbed upward to fur his cheeks – conjoining on the way with the twin juts of nostril hairs, as if the man had thrust tiny uprooted trees up his nose – only to then merge uninterrupted with the sprung

627

hemp ropes that were the man's eyebrows, which in turn blended neatly into the appallingly low hairline that thoroughly disguised what had to be a meagre, sloping forehead. And, despite the man's absurd age – rumoured age, actually, since no one knew for certain – that mass of hair was dyed squid-ink black.

He was drinking red-vine tea, a local concoction sometimes used to kill ants.

Banaschar made his way over and sat down opposite the man. 'If I'd thought about it, I'd say I've been looking for you all this time, Master Sergeant Braven Tooth.'

'But you ain't much of a thinker, are you?' The huge man did not bother looking up. 'Can't be, if you were looking for me. What you're seeing here is an escape – no, outright flight – Hood knows who's deciding these pathetic nitwits they keep sending me deserve the name of recruits. In the Malazan Army, by the Abyss! The world's gone mad. Entirely mad.'

'The gatekeeper,' Banaschar said. 'Top of the stairs, Mock's Hold. The gate watchman, Braven Tooth, I assume you know him. Seems he's been there as long as you've been training soldiers.'

'There's knowing and there's knowing. That bell-backed old crab, now, let me tell you something about him. I could send legion after legion of my cuddly little recruits up them stairs, with every weapon at their disposal, and they'd never get past him. Why? I'll tell you why. It ain't that Lubben's some champion or Mortal Sword or something. No, it's that I got more brains lodged up my left nostril waitin' for my finger than all my so-called recruits got put together.'

'That doesn't tell me anything about Lubben, Braven Tooth, only your opinion of your recruits, which it seems I already surmised.'

'Just so,' said the man, nodding.

Banaschar rubbed at his face. 'Lubben. Listen, I need to talk with someone, someone holed up in Mock's. I send messages, they get into Lubben's hands, and then . . . nothing.'

'So who's that you want to talk to?'

'I'd rather not say.'

'Oh, him.'

'So, is Lubben dropping those messages down that slimy chute the effluence of which so decorously paints the cliff-side?'

'Efflu-what? No. Tell you what, how about I head up there and take that You'd rather not say by the overlong out-of-style braid on top of his head and give 'im a shake or three?'

'I don't see how that would help.'

'Well, it'd cheer me up, not for any particular gripe, mind you, but just on principle. Maybe You'd rather not say'd rather not talk to you, have you thought of that? Or maybe you'd rather not.'

'I have to talk to him.'

'Important, huh?'

'Yes.'

'Imperial interest?'

'No, at least I don't think so.'

'Tell you what, I'll grab him by his cute braid and dangle him from the tower. You can signal from below. I swing him back and forth and it means he says "Sure, come on up, old friend". And if I just drop 'im it means the other thing. That, or my hands got tired and maybe slipped.'

'You're not helpful at all, Braven Tooth.'

'Wasn't me sitting at your table, was you sitting at mine.'

Banaschar leaned back, sighing. 'Fine. Here, I'll buy you some more tea—'

'What, you trying to poison me now?'

'All right, how about we share a pitcher of Malazan Dark?'

The huge man leaned forward, meeting Banaschar's eyes for the first time. 'Better. Y'see, I'm in mourning.'

'Oh?'

'The news from Y'Ghatan.' He snorted. 'It's always the news from Y'Ghatan, ain't it? Anyway, I've lost some friends.'

'Ah.'

'So, tonight,' Braven Tooth said, 'I plan on getting drunk. For them. I can't cry unless I'm drunk, you see.'

'So why the red-vine tea?'

Braven Tooth looked up as someone arrived, and gave the man an ugly smile. 'Ask Temper here. Why the red-vine tea, you old hunkered-down bastard?'

'Plan on crying tonight, Braven Tooth?'

The Master Sergeant nodded.

Temper levered himself into a chair that creaked alarmingly beneath him. Red-shot eyes fixed on Banaschar. 'Makes his tears the colour of blood. Story goes, he's only done it once before, and that was when Dassem Ultor died.'

Gods below, must I witness this tonight?

'It's what I get,' Braven Tooth muttered, head down once more, 'for believin' everything I hear.'

Banaschar frowned at the man opposite him. *Now what does that mean?*

The pitcher of ale arrived, as if conjured by their silent desires, and Banaschar, relieved of further contemplation – and every other demanding stricture of thought – settled back, content to weather yet another night.

'Aye, Master (or Mistress), he sat with them veterans, pretending he belonged, but really he's just an imposter. Sat there all night, until Coop had to carry him out. Where is he now? Why, in his smelly, filthy room, dead to the world. Yes indeed, Banaschar is dead to the world.'

The rain descended in torrents, streaming over the battlements, down along the blood-gutters, and the cloud overhead had lowered in the past twenty heartbeats, swallowing the top of the old tower. The window Pearl looked through had once represented the pinnacle of island technology, a fusing of sand to achieve a bubbled, mottled but mostly transparent glass. Now, a century later, its surface was patinated in rainbow patterns, and the world beyond was patchy, like an incomplete mosaic, the tesserae melting in some world-consuming fire. Although sight of the flames eluded Pearl, he knew, with fearful certainty, that they were there, and no amount of rain from the skies could change that.

It had been flames, after all, that had destroyed his world. Flames that took her, the only woman he had ever loved. And there had been no parting embrace, no words of comfort and assurance exchanged. No, just that edgy dance round each other, and neither he nor Lostara had seemed capable of deciding whether that dance was desire or spite.

Even here, behind this small window and the thick stone walls, he could hear the battered, encrusted weather vane somewhere overhead, creaking and squealing in the buffeting gusts of wind assailing Mock's Hold. And he and Lostara had been no different from that weather vane, spinning, tossed this way and that, helpless victim to forces ever beyond their control. Beyond, even, their comprehension. And didn't that sound convincing? Hardly.

The Adjunct had sent them on a quest, and when its grisly end arrived, Pearl had realized that the entire journey had been but a prelude – as far as his own life was concerned – and that his own quest yet awaited him. Maybe it had been simple enough – the object of his desire would proclaim to his soul the consummation of that quest. Maybe *she* had been what he sought. But Pearl was not certain of that, not any more. Lostara Yil was dead, and that which drove him, hounded him, was unabated. Was in fact growing.

Hood take this damned, foul city anyway. Why must imperial events ever converge here? Because, he answered himself, Genabackis had Pale. Korel had the Stormwall. *Seven Cities has Y'Ghatan. In the heart of the Malazan Empire, we have Malaz City. Where it began, so it returns, again and again. And again. Festering sores that never heal, and when the fever rises, the blood wells forth, sudden, a deluge.*

He imagined that blood sweeping over the city below, climbing the cliff-side, lapping against the very stones of Mock's Hold. Would it rise higher?

'It is my dream,' said the man sitting cross-legged in the room behind him.

Pearl did not turn. 'What is?'

'Not understanding this reluctance of yours, Claw.'

'I assure you,' Pearl said, 'the nature of my report to the Empress will upend this tidy cart of yours. I was there, I saw—'

'You saw what you wanted to see. No witness in truth but myself, regarding the events now being revisited. Revised, yes? As all events are, for such is the exercise of quill-clawed carrion who title themselves *historians*. Revisiting, thirsting for a taste, just a taste, of what it is to know trauma in one's quailing soul. Pronouncing with authority, yes, on that in which the proclaimant in truth has no authority. I alone survive as witness. I alone saw, breathed the air, tasted the treachery.'

Pearl would not turn to face the fat, unctuous man. He dare not, lest his impulse overwhelm him – an impulse to lift an arm, to flex the muscles of his wrist *just so*, and launch a poison-sheathed quarrel into the flabby neck of Mallick Rel, the Jhistal priest of Mael.

He knew he would likely fail. He would be dead before he finished raising that arm. This was Mallick Rel's chamber, after all, his residence. Wards carved into the floor, rituals suspended in the damp air, enough sorcery to set teeth on edge and raise hairs on the nape of the neck. Oh, officially this well-furnished room might be referred to as a cell, but that euphemistic absurdity would not last much longer.

The bastard's agents were everywhere. Whispering their stories in taverns, on street corners, beneath the straddled legs of whores and noblewomen. The Jhistal priest was fast becoming a hero – *the lone survivor of the Fall at Aren, the only loyal one, that is. The one who managed to escape the clutches of the traitors, be they Sha'ik's own, or the betrayers in the city of Aren itself. Mallick Rel, who alone professes to know the truth.*

There were seeds from a certain grass that grew on the Seti Plains, Pearl recalled, that were cleverly barbed, so that when they snagged on something, or someone, they were almost impossible to remove. Barbed husks, that weakened and cracked apart only after the host had travelled far. Such were rumours, carried on breaths from one host to the next, the barbs holding fast. *And when the necessary time has passed, when every seed is in place, what then? What shall unfold at Mallick Rel's command?* Pearl did not want to think about it.

Nor did he want to think about this: he was very frightened.

'Claw, speak with him.'

'*Him*. I admit, I cannot yet decide which "him" you are referring to, priest. In neither case, alas, can I fathom your reasons for making such a request of me. Tayschrenn is no friend of yours—'

'Nor is he a fool, Claw. He sees far ahead, does Tayschrenn. No, there is no reason I would urge you to speak with the Imperial High Mage. His position grows ever more precarious as it is. You seek, yes, to confabulate? Plainly, then, I urge you, Claw, to descend to the catacombs, and there speak with Korbolo Dom. You have not heard his story, and in humility I would advise, it is time that you did.'

Pearl closed his eyes on the rain-lashed scene through the window. 'Of course. He was in truth an agent of Laseen's, even when he fought on behalf of Sha'ik. His Dogslayers, they were in place to turn upon Sha'ik and crush her utterly, including killing both Toblakai and Leoman of the Flails. But there, during the Chain of Dogs, he stumbled upon a greater betrayal in the making. Oh yes, Mallick Rel, I can see how you and he will twist this – I imagine you two have worked long and hard, during those countless "illegal" sojourns of yours down in the catacombs – indeed, I know of them – the Claw remain outside your grasp, and that will not change, I assure you.'

'It is best,' the man said in his sibilant voice, 'that you consider my humble suggestion, Claw, for the good of your sect.'

'For the good of . . .' Gods below, he feels ready to threaten the Claw! How far has all this madness gone? I must speak with Topper – maybe it's not too late . . .

'This rain,' Mallick Rel continued behind him, 'it shall make the seas rise, yes?'

CHAPTER EIGHTEEN

Truth is a pressure, and I see us all shying away. But, my friends, from truth there can be no escape.

The Year of Ten Thousand Lies
Kayessan

ARHIZAN, CLINGING TO THE LIMP FOLDS OF THE IMPERIAL STANDARD, its hunger forgotten, its own life but a quiescent spark within its tiny body, had listened intently to the entire conversation.

A dromon was easing its way among the nearest transports, towing a sleek, black-hulled warship; and from the shoreline watched the Adjunct and Admiral Nok, along with Fist Keneb, Quick Ben and Kalam Mekhar. Few words were exchanged among them, until the arrival of Sergeant Gesler and Corporal Stormy. At that point, things got interesting.

'Adjunct,' Gesler said in greeting. 'That's our ship. That's the *Silanda*.'

Admiral Nok was studying the gold-hued marine. 'Sergeant, I understand you claim that you can sail that unpleasant craft.'

A nod. 'With a couple squads, aye, and that's it. As for the crew below manning the oars, well, when we need 'em to row, they'll row.'

Stormy added, 'We lived with 'em long enough they don't scare us no more, sir, not even Gesler here an' he jumps every time he looks in that fancy silver mirror of his. An' those heads, they don't make our skins crawl neither, no more—'

'Stop talking like a sailor, Adjutant Stormy,' Nok said.

A smile amidst the red, bristling beard. 'Ain't no Adjutant any more, Admiral.'

Thin brows rose, and Nok said, 'Title alone gifts the bearer with intelligence?'

Stormy nodded. 'That it does, sir. Which is why Gesler's a sergeant and I'm a corporal. We get stupider every year that passes.'

'And Stormy's proud of that,' Gesler said, slapping his companion on the back.

The Adjunct rubbed at her eyes. She examined the tips of her leather gloves, then slowly began removing the gauntlets. 'I see by the water-line she's fully provisioned . . .'

'Food does not spoil in that hold,' Nok said. 'That much my mages have determined. Furthermore, there are no rats or other vermin.' He hesitated, then sighed. 'In any case, I could find no sailors who would volunteer to crew the *Silanda*. And I have no intention of forcing the issue.' He shrugged. 'Adjunct, if they truly want it . . .'

'Very well. Sergeant Gesler, your own squad and two others.'

'The Fourth and Ninth, Adjunct.'

Her gaze narrowed on the man, then she turned to Keneb. 'Fist? They're your resurrected squads.'

'The Fourth – that would be Strings's—'

'For Hood's sake,' the Adjunct said. 'His name is Fiddler. It is the worst-kept secret in this army, Keneb.'

'Of course. My apologies, Adjunct. Fiddler's, then, and the Ninth – let's see, Sergeant Balm's squad. Abyss take us, Gesler, what a snarly bunch of malcontents you've selected.'

'Yes sir.'

'All right.' Keneb hesitated, then turned to Tavore. 'Adjunct, may I suggest that the *Silanda* hold a flanking position to your own flagship at all times.'

Mock dismay on Gesler's face and he punched Stormy in the arm and said, 'They don't trust us, Stormy.'

'Shows what they know, don't it?'

'Aye, it does. Damn me, they're smarter than we thought.'

'Sergeant Gesler,' the Adjunct said, 'take your corporal and get out of here.'

'Aye, Adjunct.'

The two marines hurried off.

After a moment, Admiral Nok laughed, briefly, under his breath, then said, 'Adjunct, I must tell you, I am . . . relieved.'

'To leave the *Silanda* to those idiots?'

'No, Tavore. The unexpected arrival of more survivors from Y'Ghatan, with soldiers such as Fiddler, Cuttle, Gesler and Stormy among them – and—' he turned to Quick Ben and Kalam, 'you two as well. The transformation within your army, Adjunct, has been . . . palpable. It is often forgotten by commanders, the significance of storied veterans, especially among young, untried soldiers. Added to that, the extraordinary tale of their survival beneath the streets of Y'Ghatan,' he shook his head. 'In all, a most encouraging development.'

'I agree,' Tavore said, glancing at Keneb. 'It was, for the most part, these soldiers who at the very beginning embraced what could have been seen as a terrible omen, and made of it a thing of strength. None of us were fully cognizant of it at the time, but it was there, in Aren, at that first parade, that the Bonehunters were born.'

The others were all staring at her.

Her brows lifted fractionally.

Keneb cleared his throat. 'Adjunct, the Bonehunters may well have been birthed that day in Aren, but it only drew its first breath yesterday.'

'What do you mean?'

'We were wondering,' Kalam said to her, 'where that decoration came from. The one you presented, with your own hand, to Captain Faradan Sort and the witch Sinn.'

'Ah, yes. Well, I can make no claim regarding that. The design of that sigil was by T'amber's hand. There were jewelsmiths in her family, I understand, and she passed a few years of her youth as an apprentice. Nonetheless, I do not see how that ceremony achieved little more than a confirmation of what already existed.'

'Adjunct,' Fist Keneb said, 'it was your confirmation that was needed. To make it real. I do not wish to offend you, but before then, you were the Adjunct. You were Laseen's. Her property.'

Her expression was suddenly flat, dangerous. 'And now, Fist?'

But it was Kalam who answered. 'Now, you belong to the Fourteenth.'

'You belong to us,' Keneb said.

The moment should have ended there, and all would have been well. Better than well. It would have been *perfect*. Instead, they saw, upon Tavore's expression, a growing . . . dismay. And fear. And at first, neither emotion made any sense.

Unless . . .

Unless she was unable to return such loyalty.

And so the doubt twisted free, like newborn vipers slithering from their clutch of eggs, and tiny, deadly fangs sank into every figure standing there, witness to what her face revealed.

Revealed. And this from a woman whose self-control was damned near inhuman.

Startled into life, the rhizan lizard dropped free of its perch, wheeled once then flitted off, down along the strand, where it alighted on the white flank of a huge tree-trunk some past storm had flung ashore, the creature's legs spread wide, belly to the wood, its tiny sides palpitating. Distracted and frightened, Bottle reached out to brush one fingertip between the rhizan's eyes, a gesture intended to offer comfort, even as he released his hold upon its life-spark. The creature fled in a flurry of wings and whipping tail.

And now, five days later, Bottle found himself on the foredeck of the *Silanda*, staring back down the ship to that tarp-covered heap of severed heads that Stormy called his brain's trust. Amusing, yes, but Bottle knew those undying eyes were piercing the frayed fabric of the canvas, watching him. In expectation. *Of what? Damn you, I can't help you poor fools. You have to see that!*

Besides, he had plenty of other things to worry over right now. So many, in fact, that he did not know where to start.

He had seen the sigil, the decoration the Adjunct had presented to Faradan Sort at what should have been her courtmartial, and to the mute child Sinn – not that she was in truth mute, Bottle knew. The urchin just had very little to say to anyone, barring her brother Shard. The sigil . . . in silver, a city wall over which rose ruby flames, and the sloped tel beneath that wall, a mass of gold human skulls. The echo of the Bridgeburners' old sigil was not accident – *no, it was sheer genius. T'amber's genius.*

By the end of that same day, iron needles and silk threads were out as blunted fingers worked with varying degrees of talent, and military-issue cloaks found a new decoration among the soldiers of the Fourteenth Army. To go along with dangling finger bones, the occasional bird skull and drilled teeth.

All well and good, as far as it went. For much of the first day, as Bottle and the others recovered, soldiers would come by just to look at them. It had been unnerving, all that attention, and he still struggled to understand what he saw in those staring eyes. *Yes, we're alive. Unlikely, granted, but true nonetheless. Now, what is it that you see?*

The memories of that time beneath the city were a haunting refrain behind every spoken word shared between Bottle and his fellow survivors. It fuelled their terrible dreams at night – he had grown used to awakening to some muffled cry from a squad member; from Smiles, or Cuttle, or Corabb Bhilan Thenu'alas. Cries dimly echoed from where other squads slept on the stony ground.

Their kits had been rifled through in their absence, items and gear redistributed as was the custom, and on that first day soldiers arrived to return what they had taken. By dusk, each survivor had more than they had ever begun with – and could only look on in bemusement at the heaped trinkets, buckles, clasps and charms; the mended tunics, the scrubbed-clean quilted under-padding, the buffed leather straps and weapon-rigging. And daggers. Lots of daggers, the most personal and precious of all weapons – *the fighter's last resort. The weapon that, if necessary, would be used to take one's own life in the face of something far worse. Now, what significance are we to take from that?*

Crouched nearby on the foredeck, Koryk and Tarr were playing a game of Bones that the former had found among the offerings in his kit. A sailor's version, the cribbed box deep to prevent the playing pieces bouncing out of the field, the underside made stable by iron-tipped eagle talons at each corner, sharp enough to bite into the wood of a galley bench or deck. Tarr had lost every game thus far – over twenty – both to Koryk and Smiles, yet he kept coming back. Bottle had never seen a man so willing to suffer punishment.

In the captain's cabin lounged Gesler, Stormy, Fiddler and Balm, their conversation sporadic and desultory. Deep in shadows beneath the elongated map-table huddled Y'Ghatan, Bottle's rat – *my eyes, my ears . . . my aching teats.*

No other rats on board, and without his control over Y'Ghatan and her brood, they would have flung themselves overboard long ago. Bottle sympathized. The sorcery engulfing this ship was foul, redolent with madness. It disliked anything alive that was not bound by its chaotic will. And it especially disliked . . . *me.*

Only . . . Gesler and Stormy, they seem immune to it. The bastards – forcing us to join them on this eerie, unwelcome floating barrow.

Bottle considered talking to Fiddler about it, then dismissed the idea. Fiddler was like Kalam, who was like Apsalar, who was like Quick Ben. All . . . *evil.*

All right, not evil, but something. *I don't know. That stuff in Shadow – what were they up to? And Kalam, ready to stick his knives in Apsalar. And Apsalar, looking like she wanted just that. Then Quick Ben waking up, getting between the two as if this was all some old argument, old wounds ripped open.*

Tavore had claimed Quick Ben, Kalam and Apsalar for her own retinue on the Adjunct's flagship, *Froth Wolf* – a Quon-built dromon, its workmanship Mapau, its keel and metalwork from somewhere else entirely. *Fenn – can't be more than a handful of keel-carvers and black-smiths left among the squalid remnants . . . but they made that keel and they made those fittings, and there's nothing insensate or inert about them.* In any case, Bottle was glad they were on that ship riding the swells three reaches to starboard. Not quite far enough away for his comfort, but it would have to do. He could picture those two skeletal reptiles scurrying around in the hold below, hunting rats . . .

'So it was Grub who held onto that whistle?' Fiddler asked Gesler in the cabin.

Beneath the table, Y'Ghatan's tattered ears perked up.

'Aye. Keneb's lad. Now there's a strange one for ya. Said he knew we were coming. Now, maybe I believe that. Maybe I don't. But it was the first thing I got back.'

'Good thing, too,' Stormy said, audibly scratching his beard. 'I'm feeling right at home—'

'That's a joke,' Gesler cut in. 'Last time we was on this damned ship, Stormy, you spent most of the time cowering in a corner.'

'Just took a while getting used to it, that's all.'

Fiddler said, 'Look what some bright spark left in my loot.' Something thumped onto the table.

'Gods below,' Sergeant Balm muttered. 'Is it complete?'

'Hard to say. There are cards in there I've never seen before. One for the Apocalyptic – it's an Unaligned – and there's something called the House of War, showing as its ranked card a bone throne, unoccupied, flanked by two wolves. And in that House there's a card called the Mercenary, and another – done by a different hand – that I think is named something like Guardians of the Dead, and it shows ghostly soldiers standing in the middle of a burning bridge . . .'

A moment of silence, then Gesler: 'Recognize any faces, Fid?'

'Didn't want to look too closely at that one. There's the House of Chains, and the King of that House – the King in Chains – is sitting on a throne. The scene is very dark, swallowed in shadows, except I'd swear that poor bastard is *screaming*. And the look in his eyes . . .'

'What else?' Balm asked.

'Stop sounding so eager, you Dal Honese rock-toad.'

'All right, if you don't like your new present, Fiddler, give it to me.'

'Right, and you'd probably lay a field right here, on this ship.'

'So?'

'So, you want to open a door to this Tiste and Tellann nightmare of warrens? To the Crippled God, too?'

'Oh.'

'Anyway, there's more Unaligned. Master of the Deck, and aye, him I recognize. And Chain – a knot in the centre, with links stretching out in all directions. Don't like the look of that one.'

'Some gift, Fid.'

'Aye, like a rock thrown to a drowning sailor.'

'Put it away,' Gesler said.

The rat listened as the Deck was dragged back from the centre of the table.

'We got us a problem,' Gesler continued.

'Only,' Stormy added, 'we don't know what it is. We only know that something's rattled Keneb, and that assassin friend of yours, Fid. And Quick Ben. Rattled them all.'

'The Adjunct,' Fiddler said. 'Kalam and Quick weren't talking, but they're not happy.' A pause, then, 'Could be it's the way Pearl just vanished, right after Y'Ghatan, likely straight back to the Empress. Just a Claw operative delivering his report? Maybe. But even that leaves a sour taste in the mouth – he was too quick to act, too quick to reach conclusions – as if what he thought happened at Y'Ghatan was only confirming suspicions he already held. Think on it – do you really suppose a report like that has anything good to say?'

'She killed Sha'ik,' Balm said, exasperated. 'She broke open that wasp nest in Raraku and damned nothing came buzzing out. She nabbed Korbolo Dom and sent him back in shackles. And she did all that with us not losing nobody, or almost nobody – the scraps on the way were expected, and not nearly so bad as they could've been. Then she chases Leoman to Y'Ghatan. Unless you got someone on the inside to crack open the gate, sieges are costly, especially when the attackers got no time to wait it out. And we didn't, did we? There was a damned plague on the way!'

'Calm down,' Fiddler said, 'we lived through all that, too, remember?'

'Aye, and did any one of us really think Leoman would broil his own people? That he'd turn a whole city into a heap of ashes and rivers of lead? All I'm saying, Fid, is we ain't done too bad, have we? When you think on it.'

'Balm's right,' Stormy said, scratching again. 'Fiddler, in that Deck you got, that House of War – did you smell Treach there? Those wolves, they got me wondering.'

'I have real doubt about that version,' Fiddler replied. 'That whole House, in fact. I'm thinking the maker was confused, or maybe what she saw was confused—'

'She?'

'I think so, except the rogue one, the Guardians of the Dead. That's a man's hand for sure.'

There was a sudden tension in Stormy's voice. 'Pull 'em out again, Fid. Let's see that House of War – all the cards in that House.'

Shuffling noises. 'I'll show each one, then. Not on the table, but still in my hand, all right? One at a time. Okay. As for titles, I'm just reading what's in the borders.' A moment, then, 'The Lords of War. Two wolves, one male, one female. Suggests to me the name for this one is wrong. But it's the plural that counts, meaning the unoccupied throne isn't that important. All right, everybody had a look? Good, next one. The Hunter, and aye, that's Treach—'

'What's with the striped corpse in the foreground? That old man with no hands?'

'No idea, Gesler.'

'Next one,' said Stormy.

'Guardians of the Dead—'

'Let me get a closer . . . good. Wait . . .'

'Stormy,' said Balm, 'what do you think you're seeing?'

'What's next?' the Falari corporal demanded. 'Quick!'

'The Army and the Soldier – I don't know – two names for this, which may be determined by context or something.'

'Any more?'

'Two, and I don't like these ones at all. Here, Life Slayer . . .'

'Jaghut?'

'Half-Jaghut,' Fiddler said in a dull voice. 'I know who this is – the horn bow, the single-edged sword. Life Slayer is Icarium. And his protector, Mappo Runt, is nowhere in sight.'

'Never mind all that,' Stormy said. 'What's the last card?'

'Icarium's counterpoint, of sorts. Death Slayer.'

'Who in the Abyss is that supposed to be? That's impossible.'

A sour grunt from Fiddler, then he said, 'Who? Well, let's see. Squalid hut of skins and sticks, brazier coughing out smoke, a hooded thing inside the hut, broken limbed, shackles sunk into the earth. Now, who might that be?'

'That's impossible,' Gesler said, echoing Stormy's assertion. 'He can't be two things at once!'

'Why not?' Fiddler said, then sighed. 'That's it. Now, Stormy, what's lit that fire in your eyes?'

'I know who made these cards.'

'Really?' Fiddler sounded unconvinced. 'And how did you come by that?'

'The Guardians card, something about the stonework on the bridge. Then those last two, the skulls – I got a damned good look at Faradan Sort's medal. So's I could sew the like, you see.'

There was a long, long silence.

And Bottle stared, unseeing, as implications settled in his mind – settled momentarily, then burst up and out, like dust-devils, one after another. *The Adjunct wants that Deck of Dragons in Fiddler's hands. And either she or T'amber – or maybe Nether and Nil, or someone – is boiling over with arcane knowledge, and isn't afraid to use it. Now, Fid, he never lays a field with those cards. No. He makes up games.*

The Adjunct knows something. Just like she knew about the ghosts at Raraku . . . and the flood. But she carries an otataral sword. And the

two Wickans are nothing like they once were, or so goes the consensus.
It must be T'amber.

What awaits us?

Is this what's got Quick Ben and the others so rattled?

What if—

'Something just nudged my foot – what? Is that a rat? Right under our table?'

'Ain't no rats on the *Silanda*, Stormy—'

'I'm telling you, Ges – there!'

Fiddler swore, then said, *'That's Bottle's rat! Get it!'*

'After it!'

Skidding chairs, the crash of crockery, grunts and stamping boots.

'It's getting away!'

There were so many places, Bottle knew, on a ship, where only a rat could go. Y'Ghatan made her escape, despite all the cursing and thumping.

Moments later, Bottle saw Fiddler appear on deck amidships – the soldier looked away a moment before the sergeant's searching gaze found him, and Bottle listened – staring out to sea – as the man, pushing past lounging soldiers, approached.

Thump thump thump up the steps to the foredeck.

'Bottle!'

Blinking, he looked over. 'Sergeant?'

'Oh no I ain't fooled – you was spying! Listening in!'

Bottle gestured over at Koryk and Tarr, who had looked up from their game and were now staring. 'Ask them. I've been sitting here, not doing a thing, for more than a bell. Ask them.'

'Your rat!'

'Her? I lost track of her last night, Sergeant. Haven't bothered trying to hunt her down since – what would be the point? She's not going anywhere, not with her pups to take care of.'

Gesler, Stormy and Balm were now crowding up behind Fiddler, who looked ready to rip off his own stubbly beard in frustration.

'If you're lying . . .' Fiddler hissed.

'Of course he's lying,' Balm said. 'If I was him, I'd be lying right now, too.'

'Well, Sergeant Balm,' Bottle said, 'you're not me, and that is the crucial difference. Because I happen to be telling the truth.'

With a snarl, Fiddler turned round and pushed his way back down to the mid deck. A moment later the others followed, Balm casting one last glare at Bottle – as if only now comprehending that he'd just been insulted.

A low snort from Koryk after they'd left. 'Bottle, I happened to glance up a while back – before Fiddler came out – and, Hood take me, there must have been fifty expressions crossing your face, one after the other.'

'Really?' Bottle asked mildly. 'Probably clouds passing the sun, Koryk.'

Tarr said, 'Your rat still has those pups? You must've carried them on the march, then. If I'd been the one carrying them, I would've eaten them one by one. Pop into the mouth, crunch, chew. Sweet and delicious.'

'Well, it was me, not you, wasn't it? Why does everyone want to be me, anyway?'

'We don't,' Tarr said, returning to study the game. 'We're just all trying to tell you we think you're a raving idiot, Bottle.'

Bottle grunted. 'All right. Then, I suppose, you two aren't interested in what they were talking about in that cabin just a little while ago.'

'Get over here,' Koryk said in a growl. 'Watch us play, and start talking, Bottle, else we go and tell the sergeant.'

'No thanks,' Bottle said, stretching his arms. 'I think I'm in need of a nap. Maybe later. Besides, that game bores me.'

'You think we won't tell Fiddler?'

'Of course you won't.'

'Why not?'

'Because then this would be the last time – the last time ever – you got any inside information from me.'

'You lying, snivelling, snake of a bastard—'

'Now now,' Bottle said, 'be nice.'

'You're getting worse than Smiles,' Koryk said.

'Smiles?' Bottle paused at the steps. 'Where is she, by the way?'

'Mooning away with Corabb, I expect,' Tarr said.

Really? 'She shouldn't do that.'

'Why?'

'Corabb's luck doesn't necessarily extend to people around him, that's why.'

'What does that mean?'

It means I talk too much. 'Never mind.'

Koryk called out, 'They'll get that rat, you know, Bottle! Sooner or later.'

Nobody's thinking straight around here. Gods, Koryk, you still think those pups are little helpless pinkies. Alas, they are all now quite capable of getting around all by themselves. So, I haven't got just one extra set of eyes and ears, friends. No. There's Baby Koryk, Baby Smiles, Baby Tarr, Baby . . . oh, you know the rest . . .

He was halfway to the hatch when the alarms sounded, drifting like demonic cries across the swollen waves, and on the wind there arrived a scent . . . *no, a stench.*

Hood take me, I hate not knowing. Kalam swung himself up into the rigging, ignoring the pitching and swaying as the *Froth Wolf* heeled hard about on a new course, northeast, towards the gap that had – through incompetence or carelessness – opened between two dromons of the escort. As the assassin quickly worked his way upward, he caught momentary glimpses of the foreign ships that had appeared just outside that gap. Sails that might have been black, once, but were now grey, bleached by sun and salt.

Amidst the sudden confusion of signals and alarms, one truth was becomingly appallingly evident: they had sailed into an ambush. Ships to the north, forming an arc with killing lanes between each one. Another crescent, this one bulging towards the Malazans, was fast approaching before the wind from the northeast. Whilst another line of ships formed a bristling barrier to the south, from the shallows along the coast to the west, then out in a saw-toothed formation eastward until the arc curled north.

Our escorts are woefully outnumbered. Transports loaded down with soldiers, like bleating sheep trapped in a slaughter pen.

Kalam stopped climbing. He had seen enough. *Whoever they are, they've got us in their jaws.* He began making his way down once more, an effort almost as perilous as had been the ascent. Below, figures were scrambling about on the decks, sailors and marines, officers shouting back and forth.

The Adjunct's flagship, flanked still to starboard by the *Silanda*, was tacking a course towards that gap. It was clear that Tavore meant to engage that closing crescent. In truth, they had little choice. With the wind behind those attackers, they could drive like a spear-point into the midst of the cumbersome transports. Admiral Nok was commanding the lead escorts to the north, and they would have to seek to push through the enemy blocking the way, with as many of the transports following as were able – *but all the enemy ships have to do is drive them into the coast, onto whatever uncharted reefs lurk in the shallows.*

Kalam dropped the last distance to the deck, landed in a crouch. He heard more shouts from somewhere far above as he made his way forward. Positioned near the pitching prow, the Adjunct and Quick Ben stood side by side, the wind whipping at Tavore's cloak. The High Mage glanced over as Kalam reached them.

'They've shortened their sails, drawn up or whatever it is sailors call slowing down.'

'Now why would they do that?' Kalam asked. 'That makes no sense. Those bastards should be driving hard straight at us.'

Quick Ben nodded, but said nothing.

The assassin glanced over at the Adjunct, but of her state of mind as she stared at the opposing line of ships he could sense nothing. 'Adjunct,' he said, 'perhaps you should strap on your sword.'

'Not yet,' she said. 'Something is happening.'

He followed her gaze.

'*Gods below, what is that?*'

On the *Silanda*, Sergeant Gesler had made use of the bone whistle, and now banks of oars swept out and back with steady indifference to the heaving swells, and the ship groaned with each surge, easily keeping pace with the Adjunct's dromon. The squads had finished reefing the sails and were now amidships, readying armour and weapons.

Fiddler crouched over a wooden crate, trying to quell his ever-present nausea – *gods, I hate the sea, the damned back and forth and up and down. No, when I die I want my feet to be dry. That and nothing more. No other stipulations. Just dry feet, dammit* – as he worked the straps loose and lifted the lid. He stared down at the Moranth munitions nestled in their beds of padding. 'Who can throw?' he demanded, glaring over at his squad, then something cold slithered in his gut.

'I can,' both Koryk and Smiles said.

'Why ask?' said Cuttle.

Corabb Bhilan Thenu'alas sat nearby, knees drawn up, too sick to move, much less respond to Fiddler's question.

Tarr said, shrugging, 'If it's right in front of me, maybe I can hit it, Sergeant.'

But Fiddler barely heard any of this – his eyes were fixed on Bottle, who stood, motionless, staring at the enemy line of ships. 'Bottle? What is it?'

An ashen face turned to regard him. 'It's bad, Sergeant. They're . . . *conjuring.*'

Samar Dev shrank away until hard, insensate wood pressed against her back. Before her, to either side of the main mast, stood four Tiste Edur, from whom burgeoned crackling, savage sorcery, whipping like chains between them, fulminating with blooms and gouts of grey flames – and, beyond the rocking prow, a tumbling wave was rising, thrashing as if held taut, lifting skyward—

Bristling chains of power snapped out from the four warlocks, arcing left and right, out to conjoin with identical kin from the ships to either side of Hanradi Khalag's command ship, and then onward to other

644

ships, one after another, and the air Samar Dev drew into her lungs seemed dead, some essential necessity utterly destroyed. She gasped, sank down to the deck, drawing up her knees. A cough, then trembles racked through her in waves—

Sudden air, life flooding her lungs – someone stood to her left. She looked over, then up.

Karsa Orlong, motionless, staring at the billowing, surging wall of magic. 'What is this?' he demanded.

'Elder,' she said in a ragged voice. 'They mean to destroy them. They mean to tear ten thousand souls and more . . . into pieces.'

'Who is the enemy?'

Karsa, what is this breath of life you deliver?

'The Malazan Imperial Fleet,' Samar heard the Taxilian answer, and she saw that he had appeared on deck, along with Feather Witch and the Preda, Hanradi Khalag, and all were staring upward at the terrible, chained storm of power.

The Toblakai crossed his arms. 'Malazans,' he said. 'They are not my enemy.'

In a harsh, halting accent, Hanradi Khalag turned to Karsa Orlong and said, 'Are they Tiste Edur?'

The giant's eyes thinned to slits as he continued studying the conjuration, from which there now came a growing roar, as of a million enraged voices. 'No,' he said.

'Then,' replied the Preda, 'they are enemy.'

'If you destroy these Malazans,' Karsa said, 'more of them will come after you.'

'We do not fear.'

The Toblakai warrior finally glanced over at the Preda, and Samar Dev could read, with something fluttering inside her, his contempt. Yet he said nothing, simply turned about and crouched down at Samar Dev's side.

She whispered, 'You were going to call him a fool. I'm glad you didn't – these Tiste Edur don't manage criticism too well.'

'Which makes them even bigger fools,' the giant rumbled. 'But we knew that, Samar Dev. They believe their Emperor can defeat me.'

'Karsa—'

A strange chorus of cries erupted from the warlocks, and they all convulsed, as if some fiery hand had reached into their bodies, closed tight and cruel about their spines – Samar Dev's eyes widened – *this ritual, it twists them, oh – such pain—*

The enormous wall lifted free of the sea's suddenly becalmed surface. Rose higher, then higher still – and in the space beneath it, a horizontal strip mocking normality, the Malazan ships were visible, their sails awry, each one losing way as panic raced through the poor bastards – except for those two, in the lead, a dromon warship, and on its seaward flank, a black-hulled craft, its oars flashing to either side.

What?

Hanradi Khalag had stepped forward upon seeing that odd black ship, but from where Samar sat curled up she could not see his expression, only the back of his head – the suddenly taut posture of his tall form.

And then, something else began to happen . . .

The wall of magic was pulling free from the surface, drawing with it spouts of white, churning water that fragmented and fell away like toppling spears as the grey-shot, raging manifestation lifted ever higher. The roar of sound rolled forward, loud and fierce as a charging army.

The Adjunct's voice was low, flat. 'Quick Ben.'

'Not warrens,' the wizard replied, as if awed. 'Elder. Not warrens. *Holds*, but shot through with Chaos, with rot—'

'The Crippled God.'

Both the wizard and Kalam looked over at her.

'You're full of surprises, Adjunct,' Quick Ben observed.

'Can you answer it?'

'Adjunct?'

'This Elder sorcery, High Mage – can you answer it?'

The glance that Quick Ben cast at Kalam startled the assassin, yet it matched his reply perfectly: 'If I cannot, Adjunct, then we are all dead.'

You bastard – you've got something—

'You do not have long,' the Adjunct said. 'If you fail,' she added as she turned away, 'I have my sword.'

Kalam watched her make her way down the length of the ship. Then, heart pounding hard in his chest, he faced the tumbling, foaming conjuration that filled the north sky. 'Quick, you ain't got long here, you know – once she comes back with her sword—'

'I doubt it'll be enough,' the wizard cut in. 'Oh, maybe for this ship and this ship alone. As for everybody else, forget it.'

'*Then do something!*'

And Quick Ben turned on Kalam a grin the assassin had seen before, hundreds of times, and that light in his eyes – so familiar, so—

The wizard spat on his hands and rubbed them together, facing the Elder sorcery once more. 'They want to mess with Holds . . . so will I.'

Kalam bared his teeth. 'You've got some nerve.'

'What?'

' "Full of surprises", you said to her.'

'Yes, well, best give me some room. It's been a while. I may be a little
. . . rusty.' And he raised his arms.

So familiar . . . so . . . alarming.

On the *Silanda* four reaches to seaward, Bottle felt something jolt all his
senses. His head whipped round, to fix his eyes on the forecastle of the
Froth Wolf. Quick Ben, alone, standing tall at the prow, arms stretched
out to the sides, like some damned offering—

—and around the High Mage, fire the colour of gold-flecked mud
billowed awake, rushed outward, upward, fast – *so fast, so fierce –
gods take me – no, more patience, you fool! If they—*

Whispering a prayer, Bottle flung all his will at the High Mage's
conjuration – *slower, you fool. Slower! Here, deepen the hue, thicker,
fling it out to the sides, it's just a reverse mudslide, yes, all going back
up the slope, flames like rain, tongues of gold nastiness, yes, like that—*

*No, stop fighting me, damn you. I don't care how terrified you are
– panic will ruin everything. Pay attention!*

Suddenly, filling Bottle's head, a scent . . . of fur. The soft brush of
not-quite-human hands – and Bottle's flailing efforts to quell Quick
Ben's manic enthusiasm all at once ceased to matter, as his will was
brushed aside like a cobweb—

Kalam, crouched down on the forecastle's wooden steps, watched as
Quick Ben, legs spread wide, slowly lifted from the deck, as if some outside force had closed invisible hands on the front of his tunic, drawing
him close, then giving him a *shake.*

'What in Hood's name—'

The magic rising in answer to that grey seething storm opposite was
like a wall of earth, shot through with burning roots, churning and
heaving and tumbling back into itself, its wild, explosive will bound
tighter to something more powerful – *and when he releases it, into that
other one . . . Hood below, nobody's going to survive this—*

Hanradi Khalag had stared, frozen in place for a dozen heartbeats, as
the wild chaos of Elder magic rose in appalling challenge to that of the
Edur warlocks – to that of *nearly a hundred* Edur warlocks – and,
Samar Dev realized as she stared at the lead Malazan dromon, all from
that one man, that black-skinned man floating above the ship's prow,
his limbs spread wide.

The Preda seemed to stagger, then he straightened, and screamed
orders – the same phrase repeated, again and again, as he lurched
drunkenly towards his warlocks.

They collapsed, flung to the deck as if knocked down one after

647

another by a giant's blows, then they lay writhing, mouths foaming, liquids spilling from them—

As the looming, roaring grey wall seemed to implode, tendrils whipping off to vanish in the air or strike the now churning surface of the sea, sending gouts skyward that shot into view from clouds of billowing steam. The roaring sound shattered, fell away.

The sorcery collapsed, the chains linking wielders on each ship flickering out, or breaking explosively as if they were in truth links of iron.

The deck pitched drunkenly beneath them, and all but Karsa Orlong staggered.

Samar Dev dragged her eyes away from him and looked out once more upon that dark, earthen wall of magic – it too was subsiding – *yes, maybe these Edur fools feel no compunction about unleashing such things when unopposed . . . but the same stupidity cannot be said of you, Malazan, whoever you are.*

Hanradi Khalag, ignoring the warlocks thrashing about in their own filth, was calling out commands, and Letherii sailors – white-faced and chanting prayers – scrambled to bring the ship about, eastward.

We're withdrawing. The Malazan called their bluff. He faced them down – oh, wizard, I could kiss you – I could do more than that. Gods, I'd—

'What are the Edur saying?' Karsa Orlong demanded.

The Taxilian, frowning, shrugged, then said, 'They're disbelieving—'

'Disbelieving?' Samar Dev croaked. 'They're shaken, Taxilian. Badly.'

The man nodded, glancing over at Feather Witch, who was watching all three of them. 'Toblakai, the Edur are saying that these Malazans – they have a Ceda on board.'

Karsa scowled. 'I do not know that word.'

'I do,' Samar Dev said. She smiled as a sudden shaft of sunlight broke through the tumult overhead and bathed her face with unexpected warmth. 'Tell them, Taxilian, that they are right. They do. A Ceda. The Malazans have a Ceda, and for all the Edur expected from this day, in their arrogance, *these Malazans were not afraid.* Tell them that, Taxilian. Tell them!'

Kalam knelt beside Quick Ben, studied the man's face for a moment, the slack expression, the closed eyes. Then he slapped the wizard. Hard.

Quick Ben swore, then glared up at the assassin. 'I should crush you like a bug, Kalam.'

'Right now, I think,' he rumbled in reply, 'a bug's fart might blow you right off this ship, Quick.'

'Be quiet. Can't I just lie here for a while longer?'

'The Adjunct's coming. Slowly, I'll grant you. Idiot, you gave too much away—'

'Enough, Kalam. I need to think, and think hard.'

'Since when did you play with Elder magic?'

Quick Ben met Kalam's eyes. 'When? Never, you idiot.'

'What?'

'That was a Hood-damned illusion. Thank the gods cowering in their outhouses right now that the idiots swallowed the hook – but listen, it wasn't just that. I had help. And then I had *help*!'

'What does that mean?'

'I don't know! Let me think!'

'No time for that,' Kalam said, sitting back, 'the Adjunct's here.'

Quick Ben's hand snapped up and grasped Kalam's shirt, tugged him close. 'Gods, friend,' he whispered, 'I've never been so scared in my entire life! Don't you see? It started out as an illusion. Yes, but then—'

The Adjunct's voice: 'High Mage, you and I must talk.'

'It wasn't—'

'Ben Adaephon Delat, you and I will talk. Now.'

Straightening, Kalam backed away, then halted at a gesture from Tavore.

'Oh no, assassin. You as well.'

Kalam hesitated, then said, 'Adjunct, this conversation you propose . . . it cannot be one-sided.'

She frowned, then, slowly, nodded.

Fiddler stood next to Bottle where he lay on the deck. 'You, soldier.'

The man's eyes were closed, and at Fiddler's words the eyes scrunched tight. 'Not now, Sergeant. Please.'

'Soldier,' Fiddler repeated, 'you have, uh, made something of a mess of yourself. You know, around your crotch.'

Bottle groaned.

Fiddler glanced over at the others of the squad. Still busy with themselves for the moment. *Good.* He crouched down. 'Dammit, Bottle, crawl off and get yourself cleaned up – if the others see this – but hold on, I need to know something. I need to know *what you found so exciting about all that?*'

Bottle rolled onto his side. 'You don't understand,' he mumbled. 'She likes doing that. When she gets the chance. I don't know why. I don't know.'

'She? Who? Nobody's been near you, Bottle!'

'She plays with me. With . . . it.'

'Somebody sure does,' Fiddler said. 'Now get below and clean yourself up. Smiles sees this and you're looking at a life of torment.'

The sergeant watched the man crawl away. *Excited. Here we were, about to get annihilated. Every damned one of us. And he fantasizes about some old sweetheart.*

Hood's breath.

Taralack Veed studied the confusion on the deck for a time, frowning as he watched the commander, Tomad Sengar, pacing back and forth whilst Edur warriors came and went with messages somehow signalled across from the seemingly countless other Edur ships. Something had struck Tomad Sengar an almost physical blow – not the ritual sorcery that had challenged their own, but some news that arrived a short time later, as the Malazan fleet worked to extricate itself from the encirclement. Ships were passing within a quarrel's flight of each other, faces turned and staring across the gap, something like relief connecting that regard – Taralack had even seen a Malazan soldier wave. Before a fellow soldier had batted the man in the side of the head with a fist.

Meanwhile, the two Edur fleets were conjoining into one – no simple task, given the unsettled waters and the vast number of craft involved, and the fading light as the day waned.

And, there in the face of Tomad Sengar, the admiral of this massive floating army, the haunting that could only come with news of a very personal tragedy. A loss, a terrible loss. Curious indeed.

The air hung close about the ship, still befouled with Elder sorcery. These Edur were abominations, to so flagrantly unleash such power. Thinking they would wield it as if it were a weapon of cold, indifferent iron. But with Elder powers – with chaos – *it was those powers that did the wielding.*

And the Malazans had answered in kind. A stunning revelation, a most unexpected unveiling of arcane knowledge. Yet, if anything, the power of the Malazan ritual surpassed that of the scores of Edur warlocks. Extraordinary. Had not Taralack Veed witnessed it with his own eyes, he would have considered such ability in the hands of the Malazan Empire simply unbelievable. Else, why had they never before exploited it?

Ah, a moment's thought and he had the answer to that. *The Malazans might be bloodthirsty tyrants, but they are not insane. They understand caution. Restraint.*

These Tiste Edur, unfortunately, do not.

Unfortunate, that is, for them.

He saw Twilight, the Atri-Preda, moving among her Letherii soldiers, voicing a calming word or two, the occasional low-toned command, and it seemed the distraught eddies calmed in her wake.

The Gral headed over.

She met his eyes and greeted him with a faint nod. 'How fares your companion below?' she asked, and Taralack was impressed by her growing facility with the language.

'He eats. His fortitude returns, Atri-Preda. But, as to this day and its strange events, he is indifferent.'

'He will be tested soon.'

Taralack shrugged. 'This does not concern him. What assails Tomad Sengar?' he asked under his breath, stepping closer as he did so.

She hesitated for a long moment, then said, 'Word has come that among the Malazan fleet was a craft that had been captured, some time back and an ocean away, by the Edur. And that ship was gifted to one of Tomad's sons to command – a journey into the Nascent, a mission the nature of which Emperor Rhulad would not be told.'

'Tomad now believes that son is dead.'

'There can be no other possibility. And in losing one son, he in truth has lost two.'

'What do you mean?'

She glanced at him, then shook her head. 'It is no matter. But what has been born in Tomad Sengar this day, Taralack Veed, is a consuming hatred. For these Malazans.'

The Gral shrugged. 'They have faced many enemies in their day, Atri-Preda. Caladan Brood, Sorrel Tawrith, K'azz D'Avore, Anomander Rake—'

At the last name Twilight's eyes widened, and as she was about to speak her gaze shifted fractionally, to just past Taralack Veed's left shoulder. A male voice spoke from behind him.

'That is impossible.'

The Gral stepped to one side to take in the newcomer.

An Edur.

'This one is named Ahlrada Ahn,' Twilight said, and he sensed some hidden knowledge between the two in her voicing of the Edur's name. 'Like me, he has learned your language – swifter than I.'

'Anomander Rake,' the Edur said, 'the Black Winged Lord, dwells at the Gates of Darkness.'

'The last I heard,' Taralack Veed said, 'he dwelt in a floating fortress called Moon's Spawn. He fought a sorcerous battle with the Malazans on a distant continent, above a city named Pale. And Anomander Rake was defeated. But not killed.'

Shock and disbelief warred on the Edur warrior's weathered, lined visage. 'You must tell me more of this. The one you call Anomander Rake, how is he described?'

'I know little of that. Tall, black-skinned, silver hair. He carries a cursed two-handed sword. Are these details accurate? I know not . . . but I see by the look in your eyes, Ahlrada Ahn, that they must be.' Taralack paused, considering how much he should reveal – his next statement would involve arcane knowledge – information not known by many. Still . . . *let us see how this plays out.* His shifted his language, to that of the Letherii, and said, 'Anomander Rake is Tiste Andii. Not Edur. Yet, by your reaction, warrior, I might think that, as with Tomad Sengar, you are wounded by some manner of unwelcome revelation.'

A sudden skittish look in the warrior's eyes. He glanced at Twilight, then pivoted about and strode away.

'There are matters,' the Atri-Preda said to Taralack Veed, 'that you are unaware of, and it is best that it remain so. Ignorance protects you. It was not wise,' she added, 'that you revealed your facility with the Letherii language.'

'I believe,' the Gral replied, 'that Ahlrada Ahn will prove disinclined to report our conversation to anyone.' He met her eyes then, and smiled. 'As will you, Atri-Preda.'

'You are careless, Taralack Veed.'

He spat on his hands and swept them through his hair, wondering again at her sudden look of distaste. 'Tell Tomad Sengar this, Atri-Preda. It is he who risks much, with his demand that Icarium's prowess be tested.'

'You seem so certain,' she said.

'Of what?'

'That your companion represents the most formidable threat Emperor Rhulad has ever faced. Alas, as has invariably proved the case, all others who believed the same are now dead. And, Taralack Veed, there have been *so many.* Tomad Sengar must know for certain. He must be made to believe, before he will guide your friend to stand before his son.'

'His son?'

'Yes. Emperor Rhulad is Tomad Sengar's youngest son. Indeed, now, the only son he has left. The other three are gone, or dead. Likely they are all dead.'

'Then it strikes me,' the Gral said, 'that what Tomad seeks to measure is not Icarium's prowess, but his lack thereof. After all, what father would wish death upon his last surviving son?'

In answer, Twilight simply stared at him for a long moment. Then she turned away.

Leaving Taralack Veed alone, a frown growing ever more troubled on his face.

*

Sergeant Hellian had found a supply of sailor's rum and now walked round the decks, a benign smile on her face. Not half a bell earlier, she'd been singing some Kartoolian death dirge as the very Abyss was being unleashed in the skies overhead.

Masan Gilani, her armour off once more and a heavy woollen cloak wrapped about her against the chill wind, sat among a handful of other soldiers, more or less out of the way of the sailors. The enemy fleet was somewhere to the south now, lost in the deepening dusk, and good riddance to them.

We've got us a High Mage now. A real one. That Quick Ben, he was a Bridgeburner, after all. A real High Mage, who just saved all our skins. That's good.

A new badge adorned her cloak, in silver, crimson and gold thread – she was quite proud of her handiwork. *The Bonehunters. Yes, I can live with that name.* True, it wasn't as poignant as *Bridgeburners*. In fact, its meaning was a little bit obscure, but that was fine, since, thus far, the Fourteenth's history was equally obscure. Or at least muddied up enough to make things confused and uncertain.

Like where we're going. What's next? Why has the Empress recalled us? It's not as if Seven Cities don't need rebuilding, or Malazans filling all those empty garrisons. Then again, the plague now held the land by the throat and was still choking the life from it.

But we got us a High Mage.

The young girl, Sinn, crawled near, shivering in the chill, and Masan Gilani opened one side of her cloak. Sinn slipped within that enveloping embrace, snuggled closer then settled her head on Masan's chest.

Nearby, Sergeant Cord was still cursing at Crump, who had stupidly waved at one of the passing enemy ships, just after the battle that wasn't. Crump had been the one who'd messed things badly at the wall of Y'Ghatan, she recalled. The one who ran with his knees up to either side of his big ears. And who was now listening to his sergeant with a broad, mindless smile, his expression twitching to sheer delight every time Cord's tirade reached new heights of imagination.

If all of that went on much longer, Masan Gilani suspected, the sergeant might well launch himself at Crump, hands closing on that long, scrawny neck with its bobbing fist-sized apple. Just to strangle that smile from the fool's horsey face.

Sinn's small hand began playing with one of Masan's breasts, the index finger circling the nipple.

What kind of company has this imp been keeping? She gently pushed the hand away, but it came back. *Fine. What of it, but damn, that's one cold hand she's got there.*

'All dead,' Sinn murmured.

'What? Who's all dead, girl?'

'They're all dead – you like this? I think you like this.'

'Your finger is cold. Who is all dead?'

'Big.'

The finger went away, was replaced by a warm, wet mouth. A dancing tongue.

Hood's breath! Well, I can think of worse ways to end this terrifying day.

'Is that my sister hiding in there?'

Masan Gilani looked up at Corporal Shard. 'Yes.'

A slightly pained expression on his face. 'She won't tell me . . . what happened at the estate. What happened . . . to her.' He hesitated, then added, 'Yours isn't the first cloak of the night she's crawled under, Masan Gilani. Though you're the first woman.'

'Ah, I see.'

'I want to know what happened. You understand that? I need to know.'

Masan Gilani nodded.

'I can see how it is,' Shard went on, looking away and rubbing at his face. 'We all cope in our own ways . . .'

'But you're her brother,' she said, still nodding. 'And you've been following her around. To make sure nobody does anything with her they shouldn't do.'

His sigh was heavy. 'Thanks, Masan Gilani. I wasn't really worried about you—'

'I doubt you'd need worry about any of us,' she replied. 'Not the squads here.'

'You know,' he said, and she saw tears trickle down his cheeks, 'that's what's surprised me. Here, with these people – all of us, who came out from under the city – they've all said the same thing as you just did.'

'Shard,' she said gently, 'you still Ashok Regiment? You and the rest?'

He shook his head. 'No. We're Bonehunters now.'

That's good. 'I got some extra thread,' she noted. 'Might be I could borrow your cloaks . . . on a warm day . . .'

'You've got a good hand, Masan Gilani. I'll tell the others, if that's okay.'

'It is. Not much else for us to do now anyway, on these bloated hippos.'

'Still, I appreciate it. I mean, everything, that is.'

'Go get some sleep, Corporal. From your sister's breathing, that's what she's doing right now.'

Nodding, he moved away.

And if some soldier who doesn't get it tries to take advantage of this broken thing, all forty-odd of us will skin him or her alive. Add one more. Faradan Sort.

Four children scrambled across the deck, one squealing with laughter. Tucked in Masan Gilani's arms, Sinn stirred slightly, then settled in once more, her mouth planted firm on the woman's nipple. The Dal Honese woman stared after the children, pleased to see that they'd recovered from the march, that they'd begun their own healing. *We all cope in our own ways, aye.*

So who was Sinn seeing, when she said that they were all dead?

Gods below, I don't think I want to know. Not tonight, anyway. Let her sleep. Let those others play, then curl up beneath blankets somewhere below. Let us all sleep to this beast's swaying. Quick Ben's gift to us, all of this.

Brother and sister stood at the prow, wrapped against the chill, and watched as stars filled the darkness of the north sky. Creaking cordage, the strain of sails canted over as the ship made yet another tack. Westward, a ridge of mountains blacker than the heavens marked the Olphara Peninsula.

The sister broke the long silence between them. 'It should have been impossible.'

Her brother snorted, then said, 'It was. That's the whole point.'

'Tavore won't get what she wants.'

'I know.'

'She's used to that.'

'She's had to deal with us, yes.'

'You know, Nil, he saved us all.'

A nod, unseen beneath the heavy hood of Wickan wool.

'Especially Quick Ben.'

'Agreed. So,' Nil continued, 'we are also agreed that it is a good thing he is with us.'

'I suppose,' Nether replied.

'You're only sounding like that because you like him, sister. Like him the way a woman likes a man.'

'Don't be an idiot. It's those dreams . . . and what she does . . .'

Nil snorted again. 'Quickens your breath, does it? That animal hand, gripping him hard—'

'Enough! That's not what I meant. It's just . . . yes, it's a good thing he's with this army. But her, with him, well, I'm not so sure.'

'You're jealous, you mean.'

'Brother, I grow weary of this childish teasing. There's something, well, compulsive about it, the way she uses him.'

'All right, on that I would agree. But for you and me, sister, there is one vital question remaining. The Eres'al has taken an interest. She follows us like a jackal.'

'Not us. *Him*.'

'Exactly. And that is at the heart of the question here. Do we tell her? Do we tell the Adjunct?'

'Tell her what? That some wet-crotched soldier in Fiddler's squad is more important to her and her army than Quick Ben, Kalam and Apsalar all put together? Listen, we wait until we discover what the High Mage tells the Adjunct – about what just happened.'

'Meaning, if he says little, or even claims complete ignorance—'

'Or takes credit and struts around like a First Hero – that's when we decide on our answer, Nil.'

'All right.'

They were silent then for a dozen heartbeats, until Nil said, 'You shouldn't worry overmuch, Nether. A half-woman half-animal all covered in smelly fur isn't much competition for his heart, I'd imagine.'

'But it wasn't my hand—' Abruptly, she shut up, then offered up a most ferocious string of Wickan curses.

In the dark, Nil was smiling. Thankful, nonetheless, that his sister could not see it.

Marines crowded the hold, sprawled or curled up beneath blankets, so many bodies Apsalar was made uneasy, as if she'd found herself in a soldier barrow. Drawing her own coverings to one side, she rose. Two lanterns swung from timbers, their wicks low. The air was growing foul. She clasped on her cloak and made her way towards the hatch.

Climbing free, she stepped onto the mid deck. The night air was bitter cold but blissfully fresh in her lungs. She saw two figures at the prow. Nil and Nether. So turned instead and ascended to the stern castle, only to find yet another figure, leaning on the stern rail. A soldier, short, squat, his head left bare despite the icy wind. Bald, with a fringe of long, grey, ratty strands that whipped about in the frigid blasts. She did not recognize the man.

Apsalar hesitated, then, shrugging, walked over. His head turned when she reached the rail at his side. 'You invite illness, soldier,' she said. 'At the least, draw up your hood.'

The old man grunted, said nothing.

'I am named Apsalar.'

'So you want my name back, do you? But if I do that, then it ends. Just silence. It's always that way.'

She looked down on the churning wake twisting away from the ship's stern. Phosphorescence lit the foam. 'I am a stranger to the Fourteenth Army,' she said.

656

'Doubt it'll make a difference,' he said. 'What I did ain't no secret to nobody.'

'I have but recently returned to Seven Cities.' She paused, then said, 'In any case, you are not alone with the burden of things you once did.'

He glanced over again. 'You're too young to be haunted by your past.'

'And you, soldier, are too old to care so much about your own.'

He barked a laugh, returned his attention to the sea.

To the east clouds skidded from the face of the moon, yet the light cast down was muted, dull.

'Look at that,' he said. 'I got good eyes, but that moon's nothing but a blur. Not the haze of cloud, neither. It's a distant world, ain't it? Another realm, with other armies crawling around in the fog, killing each other, draggin' children into the streets, red swords flashing down over'n over. And I bet they look up every now and then, wonderin' at all the dust they kicked up, makin' it hard to see that other world overhead.'

'When I was a child,' Apsalar said, 'I believed that there were cities there, but no wars. Just beautiful gardens, and the flowers were ever in bloom, every season, day and night, filling the air with wondrous scents . . . you know, I told all of that to someone, once. He later said to me that he fell in love with me that night. With that story. He was young, you see.'

'And now he's just that emptiness in your eyes, Apsalar.'

She flinched. 'If you are going to make observations like that, I will know your name.'

'But that would ruin it. Everything. Right now, I'm just me, just a soldier like all the others. You find out who I am and it all falls apart.' He grimaced, then spat down into the sea. 'Very well. Nothing ever lasts, not even ignorance. My name's Squint.'

'I hate to puncture your ego – as tortured as it is – but no vast revelation follows your name.'

'Do you lie? No, I see you don't. Well, never expected that, Apsalar.'

'Nothing changes, then, does it? You know nothing of me and I know nothing of you.'

'I'd forgotten what that was like. That young man, what happened to him?'

'I don't know. I left him.'

'You didn't love him?'

She sighed. 'Squint, it's complicated. I've hinted at my own past. The truth is, I loved him too much to see him fall so far into my life, into what I was – and still am. He deserves better.'

'You damned fool, woman. Look at me. I'm alone. Once, I wasn't in

657

no hurry to change that. And then, one day I woke up, and it was too late. Now, alone gives me my only peace, but it ain't a pleasant peace. You two loved each other – any idea how rare and precious that is? You broke yourself and broke him too, I'd think. Listen to me – go find him, Apsalar. Find him and hold onto him – now whose ego tortures itself, eh? There you are, thinking that change can only go one way.'

Her heart was thudding hard. She was unable to speak, every counter argument, every refutation seeming to melt away. Sweat cooled on her skin.

Squint turned away. 'Gods below, a real conversation. All edges and life . . . I'd forgotten. I'm going below – my head's gone numb.' He paused. 'Don't suppose you'd ever care to talk again? Just Squint and Apsalar, who ain't got nothing in common except what they don't know about each other.'

She managed a nod, and said, 'I would . . . welcome that, Squint.'

'Good.'

She listened to his footsteps dwindle behind her. *Poor man. He did the right thing taking Coltaine's life, but he's the only one who can't live with that.*

Climbing down into the hold, Squint stopped for a moment, hands on the rope rails to either side of the steep steps. He could have said more, he knew, but he had no idea he'd slice so easily through her defences. That vulnerability was . . . unexpected.

You'd think, wouldn't you, that someone who'd been possessed by a god would be tougher than that.

'Apsalar.'

She knew the voice and so did not turn. 'Hello, Cotillion.'

The god moved up to lean against the rail at her side. 'It was not easy to find you.'

'I am surprised. I am doing as you ask, after all.'

'Into the heart of the Malazan Empire. That detail was not something we had anticipated.'

'Victims do not stand still, awaiting the knife. Even unsuspecting, they are capable of changing everything.'

He said nothing for a time, and Apsalar could feel a renewal of tension within her. In the muted moonlight his face looked tired, and in his eyes as he looked at her, something febrile.

'Apsalar, I was . . . complacent—'

'Cotillion, you are many things, but complacency is not one of them.'

'Careless, then. Something has happened – it is difficult to piece together. As if the necessary details have been flung into a muddy pool, and I have been able to do little more than grope, half-blind and not even certain what it is I am looking for.'

'Cutter.'

He nodded. 'There was an attack. An ambush, I think – even the memories held in the ground, where the blood spilled, were all fragmented – I could read so little.'

What has happened? She wanted to ask that question. Now, cutting through his slow, cautious approach – *not caution – he is hedging—*

'A small settlement is near the scene – they were the ones who cleaned things up.'

'He is dead.'

'I don't know – there were no bodies, except for horses. One grave, but it had been opened and the occupant exhumed – no, I don't why anyone would do that. In any case, I have lost contact with Cutter, and that more than anything else is what disturbs me.'

'Lost contact,' she repeated dully. 'Then he is dead, Cotillion.'

'I honestly do not know. There are two things, however, of which I am certain. Do you wish to hear them?'

'Are they relevant?'

'That is for you to decide.'

'Very well.'

'One of the women, Scillara—'

'Yes.'

'She gave birth – she survived to do that at least, and the child is now in the care of the villagers.'

'That is good. What else?'

'Heboric Light Touch is dead.'

She turned at that – but away from him – staring out over the seas, to that distant, murky moon. 'Ghost Hands.'

'Yes. The power – the aura – of that old man – it burned like green fire, it had the wild rage of Treach. It was unmistakable, undeniable—'

'And now it is gone.'

'Yes.'

'There was another woman, a young girl.'

'Yes. We wanted her, Shadowthrone and I. As it turns out, I know she lives, and indeed she appears to be precisely where we wanted her to be, with one crucial difference—'

'It is not you and Shadowthrone who control her.'

'Guide, not control – we would not have presumed control, Apsalar. Unfortunately, the same cannot be said of her new master. The Crippled God.' He hesitated, then said, 'Felisin Younger is Sha'ik Reborn.'

Apsalar nodded. 'Like a sword that kills its maker . . . there are cycles to justice.'

'Justice? Abyss below, Apsalar, justice is nowhere to be seen in any of this.'

'Isn't it?' She faced him again. 'I sent Cutter away, because I feared he would die if he stayed with me. I sent him away and that is what killed him. You sought to use Felisin Younger, and now she finds herself a pawn in *another* god's hand. Treach wanted a Destriant to lead his followers into war, but Heboric is killed in the middle of nowhere, having achieved nothing. Like a tiger cub getting its skull crushed – all that potential, that possibility, gone. Tell me, Cotillion, what task did you set Cutter in that company?'

He did not answer.

'You charged him to protect Felisin Younger, didn't you? And he failed. Is he alive? For his own sake, perhaps it is best that he is not.'

'You cannot mean that, Apsalar.'

She closed her eyes. *No, I do not mean that. Gods, what am I to do . . . with this pain? What am I to do?*

Cotillion slowly reached up, his hand – the black leather glove removed – nearing the side of her face. She felt his finger brush her cheek, felt the cold thread that was all that was left of the tear he wiped away. A tear she had not known was there.

'You are frozen,' he said in a soft voice.

She nodded, then shook her head suddenly as everything crumbled inside – and she was in his arms, weeping uncontrollably.

And the god spoke, 'I'll find him, Apsalar. I swear it. I'll find the truth.'

Truths, yes. One after another, one boulder settling down, then another. And another. Blotting out the light, darkness closing in, grit and sand sifting down, a solid silence when the last one is in place. Now, dear fool, try drawing a breath. A single breath.

There were clouds closed fast round the moon. And one by one, gardens died.

CHAPTER NINETEEN

Cruel misapprehension, you choose the shape
and cast of this wet clay in your hands, as the wheel
ever spins

Tempered in granite, this fired shell hardens
into the scarred shield of your deeds, and the dark
decisions within

Settle hidden in suspension, unseen in banded strata
awaiting death's weary arrival, the journey's repast
to close you out

We blind grievers raise you high, honouring all
you never were and what rots sealed inside follows you
to the grave

I stand now among the mourners, displeased
by my suspicions as the vessel's dust drifts—
oh how I despise funerals.

The Secrets of Clay
Panith Fanal

HIS EYES OPENED IN THE DARKNESS. LYING MOTIONLESS, HE WAITED until his mind separated the sounds that had awakened him. Two sources, Barathol decided. One distant, one close at hand. Caution dictated he concentrate on the latter.

Bedclothes rustling, pulled and tugged by adjusting hands, a faint scrape of sandy gravel, then a muted murmur. A long exhaled breath, then some more shifting of positions, until the sounds became rhythmic, and two sets of breathing conjoined.

It was well. Hood knew, Barathol wasn't the one with a chance of easing the haunted look in the Daru's eyes. He then added another silent prayer, that Scillara not damage the man with some future betrayal. If that happened, he suspected Cutter would retreat so far from life there would be no return.

In any case, such matters were out of his hands, and that, too, was well.

And so . . . the other, more distant sound. A susurration, more patient in its rhythm than the now quickening lovemaking on the opposite side of the smouldering firepit. Like wind stroking treetops . . . but there were no trees. And no wind.

It is the sea.

Dawn was approaching, paling the eastern sky. Barathol heard Scillara roll to one side, her gasps low but long in settling down. From Cutter, a drawing up of coverings, and he then turned onto one side and moments later fell into sleep once more.

Scillara sat up. Flint and iron, a patter of sparks, as she awakened her pipe. She had used the last of her coins to resupply herself with rustleaf the day before, when they passed a modest caravan working its way inland. The meeting had been sudden, as the parties virtually collided on a bend in the rocky trail. An exchange of wary looks, and something like relief arriving in the faces of the traders.

The plague was broken. Tanno Spiritwalkers had so pronounced it, lifting the self-imposed isolation of the island of Otataral.

But Barathol and his companions were the first living people this troop had encountered since leaving the small, empty village on the coast where their ship had delivered them. The merchants, transporting basic staples from Rutu Jelba, had begun to fear they were entering a ghost land.

Two days of withdrawal for Scillara had had Barathol regretting ever leaving his smithy. *Rustleaf and now lovemaking – the woman is at peace once more, thank Hood.*

Scillara spoke: 'You want I should prepare breakfast, Barathol?'

He rolled onto his back and sat up, studied her in the faint light.

She shrugged. 'A woman knows. Are you upset?'

'Why would I be?' he replied in a rumble. He looked over at the still motionless form of Cutter. 'Is he truly asleep once more?'

Scillara nodded. 'Most nights he hardly sleeps at all – nightmares, and his fear of them. An added benefit to a roll with him – breaks loose his exhaustion afterwards.'

'I applaud your altruism,' Barathol said, moving closer to the firepit and prodding at the dim coals with the point of his cook-knife. From the gloom to his right, Chaur appeared, smiling.

'You should at that,' Scillara said in reply to Barathol's comment.

He glanced up. 'And is that all there is? For you?'

She looked away, drew hard on her pipe.

'Don't hurt him, Scillara.'

'Fool, don't you see? I'm doing the opposite.'

'That's what I concluded. But what if he falls in love with you?'

'He won't. He can't.'

'Why not?'

She rose and walked over to the packs. 'Get that fire going, Barathol. Some hot tea should take away the chill in our bones.'

Unless that's all you have in them, woman.

Chaur went to Scillara's side, crouching to stroke her hair as, ignoring him, she drew out wrapped foodstuffs.

Chaur watched, with avid fascination, every stream of smoke Scillara exhaled.

Aye, lad, like the legends say, some demons breathe fire.

They let Cutter sleep, and he did not awaken until midmorning – bolting into a sitting position with a confused, then guilty expression on his face. The sun was finally warm, tempered by a pleasantly cool breeze coming in from the east.

Barathol watched as Cutter's scanning gaze found Scillara, who sat with her back to a boulder, and the Daru flinched slightly at her greeting wink and blown kiss.

Chaur was circling the camp like an excited dog – the roar of surf was much louder now, carried on the wind, and he could not contain his eagerness to discover the source of that sound.

Cutter pulled his attention from Scillara and watched Chaur for a time. 'What's with him?'

'The sea,' Barathol said. 'He's never seen it. He probably doesn't even know what it is. There's still some tea, Cutter, and those packets in front of Scillara are your breakfast.'

'It's late,' he said, rising. 'You should've woken me.' Then he halted. 'The sea? Beru fend, we're that close?'

'Can't you smell it? Hear it?'

Cutter suddenly smiled – and it was a true smile – the first Barathol had seen on the young man.

'Did anyone see the moon last night?' Scillara asked. 'It was mottled. Strange, like holes had been poked through it.'

'Some of those holes,' Barathol observed, 'seem to be getting bigger.'

She looked over, nodding. 'Good, I thought so, too, but I couldn't be sure. What do you think it means?'

Barathol shrugged. 'It's said the moon is another realm, like ours, with people on its surface. Sometimes things fall from *our* sky. Rocks. Balls of fire. The Fall of the Crippled God was said to be like that. Whole mountains plunging down, obliterating most of a continent and filling half the sky with smoke and ash.' He glanced across at Scillara, then over at Cutter. 'I was thinking, maybe, that something hit the moon in the same way.'

'Like a god being pulled down?'

'Yes, like that.'

'So what are those dark blotches?'

'I don't know. Could be smoke and ash. Could be pieces of the world that broke away.'

'Getting bigger . . .'

'Yes.' Barathol shrugged again. 'Smoke and ash spreads. It stands to reason, then, doesn't it?'

Cutter was quickly breaking his fast. 'Sorry to make you all wait. We should get going. I want to see what's in that abandoned village.'

'Anything seaworthy is all we need,' Barathol said.

'That is what I'm hoping we'll find.' Cutter brushed crumbs from his hands, tossed one last dried fig into his mouth, then rose. 'I'm ready,' he said around a mouthful.

All right, Scillara, you did well.

There were sun-bleached, dog-gnawed bones in the back street of the fisher village. Doors to the residences within sight, the inn and the Malazan assessor's building were all open, drifts of fine sand heaped in the entranceways. Moored on both sides of the stone jetty were half-submerged fisher craft, the ropes holding them fast stretched to unravelling, while in the shallow bay beyond, two slightly larger carracks waited at anchor next to mooring poles.

Chaur still stood on the spot where he had first come in sight of the sea and its rolling, white-edged waves. His smile was unchanged, but tears streamed unchecked and unabating from his eyes, and it seemed he was trying to sing, without opening his mouth: strange mewling sounds emerged. What had run down from his nose was now caked with wind-blown sand.

Scillara wandered through the village, looking for whatever might prove useful on the voyage they now planned. Rope, baskets, casks, dried foodstuffs, nets, gaffs, salt for storing fish – anything. Mostly what she found were the remnants of villagers – all worried by dogs. Two squat storage buildings flanked the avenue that ran inward from the jetty, and these were both locked. With Barathol's help, both buildings were broken into, and in these structures they found more supplies than they could ever use.

Cutter swam out to examine the carracks, returning after a time to report that both remained sound and neither was particularly more seaworthy than the other. Of matching length and beam, the craft were like twins.

'Made by the same hands,' Cutter said. 'I think. You could judge that better than me, Barathol, if you're at all interested.'

'I will take your word for it, Cutter. So, we can choose either one, then.'

'Yes. Of course, maybe they belong to the traders we met.'

'No, they're not Jelban. What are their names?'

'*Dhenrabi's Tail* is the one on the left. The other's called *Sanal's Grief*. I wonder who Sanal was?'

'We'll take *Grief*,' Barathol said, 'and before you ask, don't.'

Scillara laughed.

Cutter waded alongside one of the swamped sculls beside the jetty. 'We should bail one of these, to move our supplies out to her.'

Barathol rose. 'I'll start bringing those supplies down from the warehouse.'

Scillara watched the huge man make his way up the avenue, then turned her attention to the Daru, who had found a half-gourd bailer and was scooping water from one of the sculls. 'Want me to help?' she asked.

'It's all right. Finally, I've got something to do.'

'Day and night now.'

The glance he threw her was shy. 'I've never tasted milk before.'

Laughing, she repacked her pipe. 'Yes you have. You just don't remember it.'

'Ah. I suppose you're right.'

'Anyway, you're a lot gentler than that little sweet-faced bloodfly was.'

'You've not given her a name?'

'No. Leave that to her new mothers to fight over.'

'Not even in your own mind? I mean, apart from bloodfly and leech and horse tick.'

'Cutter,' she said, 'you don't understand. I give her a real name I'll end up having to turn round and head back. I'll have to take her, then.'

'Oh. I am sorry, Scillara. You're right. There's not much I understand about anything.'

'You need to trust yourself more.'

'No.' He paused, eyes on the sea to the east. 'There's nothing I've done to make that . . . possible. Look at what happened when Felisin Younger trusted me – to protect her. Even Heboric – he said I was showing leadership, he said that was good. So, he too trusted me.'

'You damned idiot. We were ambushed by T'lan Imass. What do you think you *could* have done?'

'I don't know, and that's my point.'

'Heboric was the Destriant of Treach. They killed him as if he was nothing more than a lame dog. They lopped limbs off Greyfrog like they were getting ready to cook a feast. Cutter, people like you and me, we can't stop creatures like that. They cut us down then step over us and that's that as far as they're concerned. Yes, it's a hard thing to take, for anyone. The fact that we're insignificant, irrelevant. Nothing is expected of us, so better we just hunch down and stay out of sight, stay beneath the notice of things like T'lan Imass, things like gods and goddesses. You and me, Cutter, and Barathol there. And Chaur. We're the ones who, if we're lucky, stay alive long enough to clean up the mess, put things back together. *To reassert the normal world.* That's what we do, when we can – look at you, you've just resurrected a dead boat – you gave it its function again – look at it, Cutter, it finally looks the way it should, and that's satisfying, isn't it?'

'For Hood's sake,' Cutter said, shaking his head, 'Scillara, we're not just worker termites clearing a tunnel after a god's careless footfall. That's not enough.'

'I'm not suggesting it's enough,' she said. 'I'm telling you it's what we have to start with, when we're rebuilding – rebuilding villages and rebuilding our lives.'

Barathol had been trudging back and forth during this conversation, and now Chaur had come down, timidly, closer to the water. The mute had unpacked the supplies from the horses, including Heboric's wrapped corpse, and the beasts – unsaddled, their bits removed – now wandered along the grassy fringe beyond the tideline, tails swishing.

Cutter began loading the scull.

He paused at one point and grinned wryly. 'Lighting a pipe's a good way of getting out of work, isn't it?'

'You said you didn't need any help.'

'With the bailing, yes.'

'What you don't understand, Cutter, is the spiritual necessity for reward, not to mention the clarity that comes to one's mind during such repasts. And in not understanding, you instead feel resentment, which sours the blood in your heart and makes you bitter. It's that bitterness that kills people, you know, it eats them up inside.'

He studied her. 'Meaning, I'm actually jealous?'

'Of course you are, but because I can empathize with you, I am comfortable withholding judgement. Tell me, can you say the same for yourself?'

Barathol arrived with a pair of casks under his arms. 'Get off your ass, woman. We've got a good wind and the sooner we're on our way the better.'

She threw him a salute as she rose. 'There you go, Cutter, a man who takes charge. Watch him, listen, and learn.'

The Daru stared at her, bemused.

She read his face: *But you just said . . .*

So I did, my young lover. We are contrary creatures, us humans, but that isn't something we need be afraid of, or even much troubled by. And if you make a list of those people who worship consistency, you'll find they're one and all tyrants or would-be tyrants. Ruling over thousands, or over a husband or a wife, or some cowering child. Never fear contradiction, Cutter, it is the very heart of diversity.

Chaur held on to the steering oar whilst Cutter and Barathol worked the sails. The day was bright, the wind fresh and the carrack rode the swells as if its very wood was alive. Every now and then the bow pitched down, raising spray, and Chaur would laugh, the sound child-like, a thing of pure joy.

Scillara settled down amidships, the sun on her face warm, not hot, and stretched out.

We sail a carrack named Grief, *with a corpse on board. That Cutter means to deliver to its final place of rest. Heboric, did you know such loyalty could exist, there in your shadow?*

Barathol moved past her at one point, and, as Chaur laughed once more, she saw an answering smile on his battered, scarified face.

Oh yes, it is indeed blessed music. So unexpected, and in its innocence, so needed . . .

The return of certain mortal traits, Onrack the Broken realized, reminded one that life was far from perfect. Not that he had held many illusions in that regard. In truth, he held no illusions at all. About anything. Even so, some time passed – in something like a state of fugue – before Onrack recognized that what he was feeling was . . . *impatience*.

The enemy would come again. These caverns would echo with screams, with the clangour of weapons, with voices raised in rage. And Onrack would stand at Trull Sengar's side, and with him witness, in helpless fury, the death of still more of Minala's children.

Of course, *children* was a term that no longer fit. Had they been Imass, they would have survived the ordeal of the passage into adulthood by now. They would be taking mates, leading hunting parties, and joining their voices to the night songs of the clan, when the darkness returned to remind them all that death waited, there at the end of life's path.

667

Lying with lovers also belonged to night, and that made sense, for it was in the midst of true darkness that the first fire of life was born, flickering awake to drive back the unchanging absence of light. To lie with a lover was to celebrate the creation of fire. *From this in the flesh to the world beyond.*

Here, in the chasm, night reigned eternal, and there was no fire in the soul, no heat of lovemaking. There was only the promise of death.

And Onrack was impatient with that. There was no glory in waiting for oblivion. No, in an existence bound with true meaning and purpose, oblivion should ever arrive unexpected, unanticipated and unseen. One moment racing full tilt, the next, gone.

As a T'lan Imass of Logros, Onrack had known the terrible cost borne in wars of attrition. The spirit exhausted beyond reason, with no salvation awaiting it, only more of the same. The kin falling to the wayside, shattered and motionless, eyes fixed on some skewed vista – a scene to be watched for eternity, the minute changes measuring the centuries of indifference. Some timid creature scampering through, a plant's exuberant green pushing up from the earth after a rain, birds pecking at seeds, insects building empires . . .

Trull Sengar came to his side where Onrack stood guarding the choke-point. 'Monok Ochem says the Edur's presence has . . . contracted, away from us. For now. As if something made my kin retreat. I feel, my friend, that we have been granted a reprieve – one that is not welcome. I don't know how much longer I can fight.'

'When you can no longer fight in truth, Trull Sengar, the failure will cease to matter.'

'I did not think they would defy her, you know, but now, I see that it makes sense. She expected them to just abandon this, leaving the handful remaining here to their fate. Our fate, I mean.' He shrugged. 'Panek was not surprised.'

'The other children look to him,' Onrack said. 'They would not abandon him. Nor their mothers.'

'And, in staying, they will break the hearts of us all.'

'Yes.'

The Tiste Edur looked over. 'Have you come to regret the awakening of emotions within you, Onrack?'

'This awakening serves to remind me, Trull Sengar.'

'Of what?'

'Of why I am called "The Broken".'

'As broken as the rest of us.'

'Not Monok Ochem, nor Ibra Gholan.'

'No, not them.'

'Trull Sengar, when the attackers come, I would you know – I intend to leave your side.'

'Indeed?'

'Yes. I intend to challenge their leader. To slay him or be destroyed in the attempt. Perhaps, if I can deliver a truly frightful cost, they will reconsider their alliance with the Crippled God. At the very least, they may withdraw and not return for a long time.'

'I understand.' Trull then smiled in the gloom. 'I will miss your presence at my side in those final moments, my friend.'

'Should I succeed in what I intend, Trull Sengar, I shall return to your side.'

'Then you had better be quick killing that leader.'

'Such is my intention.'

'Onrack, I hear something new in your voice.'

'Yes.'

'What does it mean?'

'It means, Trull Sengar, that Onrack the Broken, in discovering impatience, has discovered something else.'

'What?'

'This: I am done with defending the indefensible. I am done with witnessing the fall of friends. In the battle to come, you shall see in me something terrible. Something neither Ibra Gholan nor Monok Ochem can achieve. Trull Sengar, you shall see a T'lan Imass, awakened to *anger*.'

Banaschar opened the door, wavered for a moment, leaning with one hand against the frame, then staggered into his decrepit room. The rank smell of sweat and unclean bedding, stale food left on the small table beneath the barred window. He paused, considering whether or not to light the lantern – but the oil was low and he'd forgotten to buy more. He rubbed at the bristle on his chin, more vigorously than normal since it seemed his face had gone numb.

A creak from the chair against the far wall, six paces distant. Banaschar froze in place, seeking to pierce the darkness. 'Who's there?' he demanded.

'There are few things in this world,' said the figure seated in the chair, 'more pathetic than a once-Demidrek fallen into such disrepair, Banaschar. Stumbling drunk into this vermin-filled hovel every night – why are you here?'

Banaschar stepped to his right and sank heavily onto the cot. 'I don't know who you are,' he said, 'so I see no reason to answer you.'

A sigh, then, 'You send, one after another for a while there, cryptic messages. Pleading, with increasing desperation, to meet with the Imperial High Mage.'

'Then you must realize,' Banaschar said, struggling to force sobriety into his thoughts – the terror was helping – 'that the matter concerns only devotees of D'rek—'

'A description that no longer fits either you or Tayschrenn.'

'There are things,' Banaschar said, 'that cannot be left behind. Tayschrenn knows this, as much as I—'

'Actually, the Imperial High Mage knows nothing.' A pause, accompanying a gesture that Banaschar interpreted as the man studying his fingernails, and something in his tone changed. 'Not yet, that is. Perhaps not at all. You see, Banaschar, the decision is mine.'

'Who are you?'

'You are not ready yet to know that.'

'Why are you intercepting my missives to Tayschrenn?'

'Well, to be precise, I have said no such thing.'

Banaschar frowned. 'You just said the decision was yours.'

'Yes I did. That decision centres on whether I remain inactive in this matter, as I have been thus far, or – given sufficient cause – I elect to, um, intervene.'

'Then who is blocking my efforts?'

'You must understand, Banaschar, Tayschrenn is the Imperial High Mage first and foremost. Whatever else he once was is now irrelevant—'

'No, it isn't. Not given what I have discovered—'

'Tell me.'

'No.'

'Better yet, Banaschar, convince me.'

'I cannot,' he replied, hands clutching the grimy bedding to either side.

'An imperial matter?'

'No.'

'Well, that is a start. As you said, then, the subject pertains to once-followers of D'rek. A subject, one presumes, related to the succession of mysterious deaths within the cult of the Worm. Succession? More like slaughter, yes? Tell me, is there *anyone* left? Anyone at all?'

Banaschar said nothing.

'Except, of course,' the stranger added, 'those few who have, at some time in the past and for whatever reasons, fallen away from the cult. From worship.'

'You know too much of this,' Banaschar said. He should never have stayed in this room. He should have been finding different hovels every night. He hadn't thought there'd be anyone, anyone left, who'd remember him. After all, those who might have were now all dead. *And I know why. Gods below, how I wish I didn't.*

'Tayschrenn,' said the man after a moment, 'is being isolated. Thoroughly and most efficiently. In my professional standing, I admit to considerable admiration, in fact. Alas, in that same capacity, I am also experiencing considerable *alarm*.'

'You are a Claw.'

'Very good – at least some intelligence is sifting through that drunken haze, Banaschar. Yes, my name is Pearl.'

'How did you find me?'

'Does that make a difference?'

'It does. To me, it does, Pearl.'

Another sigh and a wave of one hand. 'Oh, I was bored. I followed someone, who, it turned out, was keeping track of you – with whom you spoke, where you went, you know, the usual things required.'

'Required? For what?'

'Why, preparatory, I imagine, to assassination, when that killer's master deems it expedient.'

Banaschar was suddenly shivering, the sweat cold and clammy beneath his clothes. 'There is nothing political,' he whispered, 'nothing that has anything to do with the empire. There is no reason—'

'Oh, but you have made it so, Banaschar. Do you forget? Tayschrenn is being isolated. You are seeking to break that, to awaken the Imperial High Mage—'

'Why is he permitting it?' Banaschar demanded. 'He's no fool—'

A soft laugh. 'Oh no, Tayschrenn is no fool. And in that, you may well have your answer.'

Banaschar blinked in the gloom. 'I must meet with him, Pearl.'

'You have not yet convinced me.'

A long silence, in which Banaschar closed his eyes, then placed his hands over them, as if that would achieve some kind of absolution. But only words could do that. Words, uttered now, to this man. Oh, how he wanted to believe it would . . . suffice. *A Claw, who would be my ally. Why? Because the Claw has . . . rivals. A new organization that has deemed it expedient to raise impenetrable walls around the Imperial High Mage. What does that reveal of that new organization? They see Tayschrenn as an enemy, or they would so exclude him as to make his inaction desirable, even to himself. They know he knows, and wait to see if he finally objects. But he has not yet done so, leading them to believe that he might not – during whatever is coming. Abyss take me, what are we dealing with here?*

Banaschar spoke from behind his hands. 'I would ask you something, Pearl.'

'Very well.'

'Consider the most grand of schemes,' he said. 'Consider time measured in millennia. Consider the ageing faces of gods, goddesses, beliefs and civilizations . . .'

'Go on. What is it you would ask?'

Still he hesitated. Then he slowly lowered his hands, and looked across, to that grey, ghostly face opposite him. 'Which is the greater crime, Pearl, a god betraying its followers, or its followers betraying their god? Followers who then choose to commit atrocities in that god's name. Which, Pearl? Tell me, please.'

The Claw was silent for a dozen heartbeats, then he shrugged. 'You ask a man without faith, Banaschar.'

'Who better to judge?'

'Gods betray their followers all the time, as far as I can tell. Every unanswered prayer, every unmet plea for salvation. The very things that define faith, I might add.'

'Failure, silence and indifference? These are the definitions of faith, Pearl?'

'As I said, I am not the man for this discussion.'

'But are those things true *betrayal*?'

'That depends, I suppose. On whether the god worshipped is, by virtue of being worshipped, in turn beholden to the worshipper. If that god isn't – if there is no moral compact – then your answer is "no", it's not betrayal.'

'To whom – for whom – does a god act?' Banaschar asked.

'If we proceed on the aforementioned assertion, the god acts and answers only to him or herself.'

'After all,' Banaschar said, his voice rasping as he leaned forward, '*who are we to judge?*'

'As you say.'

'Yes.'

'If,' Pearl said, 'on the other hand, a moral compact does exist between god and worshipper, then each and every denial represents a betrayal—'

'Assuming that which is asked of that god is in itself bound to a certain morality.'

'True. A husband praying his wife dies in some terrible accident so that he can marry his mistress, for example, is hardly something any self-respecting god would acquiesce to, or assist in.'

Banaschar heard the mockery in the man's voice, but chose to ignore it. 'And if the wife is a tyrant who beats their children?'

'Then a truly just god would act without the necessity for prayer.'

'Meaning the prayer itself, voiced by that husband, is also implicitly evil, regardless of his motive?'

'Well, Banaschar, in my scenario, his motive is made suspect by the presence of the mistress.'

'And if that mistress would be a most loving and adoring stepmother?'

Pearl snarled, chopping with one hand. 'Enough of this, damn you – you can wallow in this moral quandary all you want. I don't see the relevance . . .' His voice fell away.

His heart smothered in a bed of ashes, Banaschar waited, willing himself not to sob aloud, not to cry out.

'They prayed but did not ask, nor beseech, nor plead,' Pearl said. 'Their prayers were a demand. The betrayal . . . was theirs, wasn't it?' The Claw sat forward. 'Banaschar. Are you telling me that D'rek killed them all? *Her entire priesthood?* They betrayed her! In what way? *What did they demand?*'

'There is war,' he said in a dull voice.

'Yes. War among the gods, yes – gods below – those worshippers chose the wrong side!'

'She heard them,' Banaschar said, forcing the words out. 'She heard them choose. The Crippled God. And the power they demanded was the power of blood. Well, she decided, if they so lusted for blood . . . she would give them all they wanted.' His voice dropped to a whisper. 'All they wanted.'

'Banaschar . . . hold on a moment . . . why would D'rek's followers choose blood, the power of blood? That is an Elder way. What you are saying makes no sense.'

'The Cult of the Worm is ancient, Pearl. Even we cannot determine just how old. There is mention of a goddess, the Matron of Decay, the Mistress of Worms – a half-dozen titles – in *Gothos's Folly* – in the fragments possessed by the temple. Or at least, once in the temple's possession – those scrolls disappeared—'

'When?'

Banaschar managed a bitter smile. 'On the night of Tayschrenn's flight from the Grand Temple in Kartool. He has them. He must have them. Don't you see? *Something is wrong!* With all of this! The knowledge that I hold, and the knowledge that Tayschrenn must possess – with his access to *Gothos's Folly* – we must speak, we must make sense of what has happened, and what it means. This goes beyond the Imperium – yet this war among the gods – tell me, whose blood do you think will be spilled? What happened in the cult of D'rek, that is but the beginning!'

'The gods will betray us?' Pearl asked, leaning back. 'Us ... mortals. Whether we worship or not, it is mortal blood that will soak the earth.' He paused, then said, 'Perhaps, given the opportunity, you will be able to persuade Tayschrenn. But what of the other priesthoods – do you truly believe you can convince them – and what will you say to them? Will you plead for some kind of reformation, Banaschar? Some *revolution* among believers? They will laugh in your face.'

Banaschar looked away. 'In my face, perhaps. But . . . Tayschrenn . . .'

The man opposite him said nothing for a time. A graininess filled the gloom – dawn was coming, and with it a dull chill. Finally, Pearl rose, the motion fluid and silent. 'This is a matter for the Empress—'

'Her? Don't be a fool—'

'Careful,' the Claw warned in a soft voice.

Banaschar thought quickly, in desperation. 'She only comes into play with regard to releasing Tayschrenn from his position as High Mage, in freeing him to act. And besides, if the rumours are true about the Grey Mistress stalking Seven Cities, then it is clear that the pantheonic war has already begun in its myriad manipulations of the mortal realm. She would be wise to heed that threat.'

'Banaschar,' Pearl said, 'the rumours do not even come close to the truth. Hundreds of thousands have died. Perhaps millions.'

Millions?

'I shall speak with the Empress,' Pearl repeated.

'When do you leave?' Banaschar asked. *And what of those who are isolating Tayschrenn? What of those who contemplate killing me?*

'There will be no need for that,' the Claw said, walking to the door. 'She is coming here.'

'Here? When?'

'Soon.'

Why? But he did not voice that question, for the man had gone.

Saying it needed the exercise, Iskaral Pust was sitting atop his mule, struggling to guide it in circles on the mid deck. From the looks of it, he was working far harder than the strange beast as it was cajoled into a step every fifty heartbeats or so.

Red-eyed and sickly, Mappo sat with his back to the cabin wall. Each night, in his dreams, he wept, and would awaken to find that what had plagued his dreams had pushed through the barrier of sleep, and he would lie beneath the furs, shivering with something like a fever. A sickness in truth, born of dread, guilt and shame. Too many failures, too many bad judgements; he had been stumbling, blind, for so long.

Out of friendship he had betrayed his only friend.

I will make amends for all of this. So I vow, before all the Trell spirits.

Standing at the prow, the woman named Spite was barely visible within the gritty, mud-brown haze that engulfed her. Not one of the bhok'arala, scrambling about in the rigging or back and forth on the decks, would come near her.

She was in conversation. So Iskaral Pust had claimed. With a spirit that *didn't belong*. Not here in the sea, and that wavering haze, like dust skirling through yellow grasses – even to Mappo's dull eyes, blatantly out of place.

An intruder, but one of power, and that power seemed to be growing.

'*Mael*,' Iskaral Pust had said with a manic laugh, '*he's resisting, and getting his nose bloodied. Do you sense his fury, Trell? His spitting outrage? Hee. Hee hee. But she's not afraid of him, oh no, she's not afraid of anyone!*'

Mappo had no idea who that 'she' was, and had not the energy to ask. At first, he had thought the High Priest had been referring to Spite, but no, it became increasingly apparent that the power manifesting itself over the bow of the ship was nothing like Spite's. No draconean stink, no cold brutality. No, the sighs of wind reaching the Trell were warm, dry, smelling of grasslands.

The conversation had begun at dawn, and now the sun was directly overhead. It seemed there was much to discuss . . . about something.

Mappo saw two spiders scuttle past his moccasined feet. *You damned witch, I don't think you're fooling anyone.*

Was there a connection? Here, on this nameless ship, two shamans from Dal Hon, a land of yellow grasses, acacias, huge herds and big cats – savannah – and now, this . . . visitor, striding across foreign seas.

'*Outraged, yes*,' Iskaral Pust had said. '*Yet, do you sense his reluctance? Oh, he struggles, but he knows too that she, who chooses to be in one place and not many, she is more than his match. Dare he focus? He doesn't even want this stupid war, hah! But oh, it is that very ambivalence that so frees his followers to do as they please!*'

A snarling cry as the High Priest of Shadow fell from the back of the mule. The animal brayed, dancing away and wheeling round to stare down at the thrashing old man. It brayed again, and in that sound Mappo imagined he could hear laughter.

Iskaral Pust ceased moving, then lifted his head. 'She's gone.'

The wind that had been driving them steady and hard, ever on course, grew fitful.

Mappo saw Spite making her way down the forecastle steps, looking weary and somewhat dismayed.

'Well?' Iskaral demanded.

Spite's gaze dropped to regard the High Priest where he lay on the deck. 'She must leave us for a time. I sought to dissuade her, and, alas, I failed. This places us . . . at risk.'

'From what?' Mappo asked.

She glanced over at him. 'Why, the vagaries of the natural world, Trell. Which can, at times, prove alarming and most random.' Her attention returned to Iskaral Pust. 'High Priest, please, assert some control over your bhok'arala. They keep undoing knots that should remain fast, not to mention leaving those unsightly offerings to you everywhere underfoot.'

'Assert some control?' Iskaral asked, sitting up with a bewildered look on his face. 'But they're crewing this ship!'

'Don't be an idiot,' Spite said. 'This ship is being crewed by ghosts. Tiste Andii ghosts, specifically. True, it was amusing to think otherwise, but now your little small-brained worshippers are becoming troublesome.'

'Troublesome? You have no idea, Spite! Hah!' He cocked his head. 'Yes, let her think on that for a while. That tiny frown wrinkling her brow is so endearing. More than that, admit it, it inspires lust – oh yes, I'm not as shrivelled up as they no doubt think and in so thinking perforce nearly convince me! Besides, she wants me. I can tell. After all, I had a wife, didn't I? Not like Mappo there, with his bestial no doubt burgeoning traits, no, he has no-one! Indeed, am I not experienced? Am I not capable of delicious, enticing subtlety? Am I not favoured by my idiotic, endlessly miscalculating god?'

Shaking her head, Spite walked past him, and halted before Mappo. 'Would that I could convince you, Trell, of the necessity for patience, and faith. We have stumbled upon a most extraordinary ally.'

Allies. They ever fail you in the end. Motives clash, divisive violence follows, and friend betrays friend.

'Will you devour your own soul, Mappo Runt?'

'I do not understand you,' he said. 'Why do you involve yourself with my purpose, my quest?'

'Because,' she said, 'I know where it shall lead.'

'The future unfolds before you, does it?'

'Never clearly, never completely. But I can well sense the convergence ahead – it shall be vast, Mappo, more terrible than this or any other realm has ever seen before. The Fall of the Crippled God, the Rage of Kallor, the Wounding at Morn, the Chainings – they all shall be dwarfed by what is coming. And you shall be there, for you are part of that convergence. As is Icarium. Just as I will come face to face with my evil sister at the very end, a meeting from which but one of us will walk away when all is done between us.'

Mappo stared at her. 'Will I,' he whispered, 'will I stop him? In the end? Or, is *he* the end – of everything?'

'I do not know. Perhaps the possibilities, Mappo Runt, depend entirely on how prepared you are at that moment, at your readiness, your faith, if you will.'

He slowly sighed, closed his eyes, then nodded. 'I understand.'

And, not seeing, he did not witness her flinch, and was himself unaware of the pathos filling the tone of that admission.

676

When he looked upon her once more, he saw naught but a calm, patient expression. Cool, gauging. Mappo nodded. 'As you say. I shall . . . try.'

'I would expect no less, Trell.'

'Quiet!' Iskaral Pust hissed, still lying on the deck, but now on his belly. He was sniffing the air. 'Smell her? I do. I smell her! On this ship! That udder-knotted cow! *Where is she!?*'

The mule brayed once more.

Taralack Veed crouched before Icarium. The Jhag was paler than he had ever seen him before, the consequence of day after day in this hold, giving his skin a ghoulish green cast. The soft hiss of iron blade against whetstone was the only sound between them for a moment, then the Gral cleared his throat and said, 'A week away at the least – these Edur take their time. Like you, Icarium, they have already begun their preparations.'

'Why do they force an enemy upon me, Taralack Veed?'

The question was so lifeless that for a moment the Gral wondered if it had been rhetorical. He sighed, reaching up to ensure that his hair was as it should be – the winds upside were fierce – then said, 'My friend, they must be shown the extent of your . . . martial prowess. The enemy with which they have clashed – a number of times, apparently – has proved both resilient and ferocious. The Edur have lost warriors.'

Icarium continued working the sword's single, notched edge. Then he paused, his eyes fixed on the weapon in his hands. 'I feel,' he said, 'I feel . . . they are making a mistake. This notion . . . of testing me – if what you have told me is true. Those tales of my anger . . . unleashed.' He shook his head. 'Who are those I will face, do you know?'

Taralack Veed shrugged. 'No, I know very little – they do not trust me, and why should they? I am not an ally – indeed, *we* are not allies—'

'And yet we shall soon fight for them. Do you not see the contradictions, Taralack Veed?'

'There is no good side in the battle to come, my friend. They fight each other endlessly, for both sides lack the capacity, or the will, to do anything else. Both thirst for the blood of their enemies. You and I, we have seen all of this before, the manner in which two opposing forces – no matter how disparate their origins, no matter how righteously one begins the conflict – end up becoming virtually identical to each other. Brutality matches brutality, stupidity matches stupidity. You would have me ask the Tiste Edur? About their terrible, evil enemies? What is the point? This, my friend, is a matter of killing. That and nothing more, now. Do you see that?'

'A matter of killing,' Icarium repeated, his words a whisper. After a moment, he resumed honing the edge of his sword.

'And such a matter,' Taralack Veed said, 'belongs to you.'

'To me.'

'You must show them that. By ending the battle. Utterly.'

'Ending it. All the killing. Ending it, for ever.'

'Yes, my friend. It is your purpose.'

'With my sword, I can deliver peace.'

'Oh yes, Icarium, you can and you will.' *Mappo Runt, you were a fool. How you might have made use of this Jhag. For the good of all. Icarium is the sword, after all. Forged to be used, as all weapons are.*

The weapon, then, that promises peace. Why, you foolish Trell, did you ever flee from this?

North of the Olphara Peninsula, the winds freshened, filling the sails, and the ships seemed to surge like migrating dhenrabi across the midnight blue of the seas. Despite her shallow draught, the *Silanda* struggled to keep pace with the dromons and enormous transports.

Almost as bored as the other marines, Bottle walked up and down the deck, trying to ignore their bickering, trying to nail down this sense of unease growing within him. *Something . . . in this wind . . . something . . .*

'Bone monger,' Smiles said, pointing her knife at Koryk. 'That's what you remind me of, with all those bones hanging from you. I remember one who used to come through the village – the village outside our estate, I mean. Collecting from kitchen middens. Grinding up all kinds and sticking them in flasks. With labels. Dog jaws for toothaches, horse hips for making babies, bird skulls for failing eyes—'

'Penis bones for homely little girls,' Koryk cut in.

In a blur, the knife in Smiles's hand reversed grip and she held the point between thumb and fingers.

'Don't even think it,' Cuttle said in a growl.

'Besides,' Tarr observed, 'Koryk ain't the only one wearing lots of bones – Hood's breath, Smiles, you're wearing your own—'

'Tastefully,' she retorted, still holding the knife by its point. 'It's the excess that makes it crass.'

'Latest court fashion in Unta, you mean?' Cuttle asked, one brow lifting.

Tarr laughed. 'Subtle and understated, that modest tiny finger bone, dangling just so – the ladies swooned with envy.'

In all of this, Bottle noted in passing, Corabb Bhilan Thenu'alas simply stared, from one soldier to the next as they bantered. On the man's face baffled incomprehension.

From the cabin house, voices rising in argument. Again. Gesler, Balm, Stormy and Fiddler.

One of Y'Ghatan's pups was listening, but Bottle paid little attention, since the clash was an old one, as both Stormy and Balm sought to convince Fiddler to play games with the Deck of Dragons. Besides, what was important was out here, a whisper in the air, in this steady, unceasing near-gale, a scent mostly obscured by the salty seaspray . . .

Pausing at the port rail, Bottle looked out at that distant ridge of land to the south. Hazy, strangely blurred, it seemed to be visibly sweeping by, although at this distance such a perception should have been impossible. The wind itself was brown-tinged, as if it had skirled out from some desert.

We have left Seven Cities. Thank the gods. He never wanted to set foot on that land again. Its sand was a gritty patina on his soul, fused by heat, storms, and uncounted people whose bodies had been incinerated – remnants of them were in him now, and would never be fully expunged from his flesh, his lungs. He could taste their death, hear the echo of their screams.

Shortnose and Flashwit were wrestling over the deck, growling and biting like a pair of dogs. Some festering argument – Bottle wondered what part of Shortnose would get bitten off this time – and there were shouts and curses as the two rolled into soldiers of Balm's squad who had been throwing bones, scattering the cast. Moments later fights were erupting everywhere.

As Bottle turned, Mayfly had picked up Lobe and he saw the hapless soldier flung through the air – to crash up against the mound of severed heads.

Screams, as the ghastly things rolled about, eyes blinking in the sudden light—

And the fight was over, soldiers hurrying to return the trophies to their pile beneath the tarpaulin.

Fiddler emerged from the cabin, looking harried. He paused, scanning the scene, then, shaking his head, he walked over to where Bottle leaned on the rail.

'Corabb should've left me in the tunnel,' the sergeant said, scratching at his beard. 'At least then I'd get some peace.'

'It's just Balm,' Bottle said, then snapped his mouth shut – but too late.

'I knew it, you damned bastard. Fine, it stays between you and me, but in exchange I want to hear your thoughts. What about Balm?'

'He's Dal Honese.'

'I know that, idiot.'

'Well, his skin's crawling, is my guess.'

'So's mine, Bottle.'

Ah, that explains it, then. 'She's with us, now. Again, I mean.'

'She?'

'You know who.'

'The one who plays with your—'

'The one who also healed you, Sergeant.'

'What's she got to do with Balm?'

'I'm not sure. More like where his people live, I think.'

'Why is she helping us?'

'Is she, Sergeant?' Bottle turned to study Fiddler. 'Helping us, I mean. True, the last time . . . Quick Ben's illusion that chased off that enemy fleet. But so what? Now we've got this gale at our backs, and it's driving us west, fast, maybe faster than should be possible – look at that coast – our lead ships must be due south of Monkan by now. At this pace, we'll reach Sepik before night falls. We're being *pushed*, and that makes me very nervous – what's the damned hurry?'

'Maybe just putting distance between us and those grey-skinned barbarians.'

'Tiste Edur. Hardly barbarians, Sergeant.'

Fiddler grunted. 'I've clashed with the Tiste Andii, and they used Elder magic – Kurald Galain – and it was nothing like what we saw a week ago.'

'No, that wasn't warrens. It was Holds – older, raw, way too close to chaos.'

'What it was,' Fiddler said, 'doesn't belong in war.'

Bottle laughed. He could not help it. 'You mean, a little bit of whole-sale slaughter is all right, Sergeant? Like what we do on the battlefield? Chasing down fleeing soldiers and caving their skulls in from behind, that's all right?'

'Never said I was making sense, Bottle,' Fiddler retorted. 'It's just what my gut tells me. I've been in battles where sorcery was let loose – really let loose – and it was nothing like what those Edur were up to. They want to win wars without drawing a sword.'

'And that makes a difference?'

'It makes victory unearned, is what it does.'

'And does the Empress earn her victories, Sergeant?'

'Careful, Bottle.'

'Well,' he persisted, 'she's just sitting there on her throne, while we're out here—'

'You think I fight for her, Bottle?'

'Well—'

'If that's what you think, you wasn't taught a damned thing at Y'Ghatan.' He turned and strode off.

Bottle stared after him a moment, then returned his attention to the distant horizon. *Fine, he's right. But still, what we're earning is her currency and that's that.*

'What in Hood's name are you doing down here?'

'Hiding, what's it look like? That's always been your problem, Kal, your lack of subtlety. Sooner or later it's going to get you into trouble. Is it dark yet?'

'No. Listen, what's with this damned gale up top? It's all wrong—'

'You just noticed?'

Kalam scowled in the gloom. Well, at least he'd found the wizard. *The High Mage of the Fourteenth, hiding between crates and casks and bales. Oh, how bloody encouraging is that?* 'The Adjunct wants to talk to you.'

'Of course she does. I would too if I was her. But I'm not her, am I? No, she's a mystery – you notice how she almost never wears that sword? Now, I'll grant you, I'm glad, now that I've been chained to this damned army. Remember those sky keeps? We're in the midst of something, Kal. And the Adjunct knows more than she's letting on. A lot more. Somehow. The Empress has recalled us. Why? What now?'

'You're babbling, Quick. It's embarrassing.'

'You want babbling, try this. Has it not occurred to you that we lost this one?'

'What?'

'Dryjhna, the Apocalyptic, the whole prophecy – we didn't get it, we never did – and you and me, Kal, we should have, you know. The Uprising, what did it achieve? How about slaughter, anarchy, rotting corpses everywhere. And what arrived in the wake of that? Plague. The apocalypse, Kalam, wasn't the war, it was the plague. So maybe we won and maybe we lost. Both, do you see?'

'Dryjhna never belonged to the Crippled God. Nor Poliel—'

'Hardly matters. It's ended up serving them both, hasn't it?'

'We can't fight all that, Quick,' Kalam said. 'We had a rebellion. We put it down. What these damned gods and goddesses are up to – it's not our fight. Not the empire's fight, and that includes Laseen. She's not going to see all this as some kind of failure. Tavore did what she had to do, and now we're going back, and then we'll get sent elsewhere. That's the way it is.'

'Tavore sent us into the Imperial Warren, Kal. Why?'

The assassin shrugged. 'All right, like you said, she's a mystery.'

Quick Ben moved further into the narrow space between cargo. 'Here, there's room.'

After a moment, Kalam joined him. 'You got anything to eat? Drink?'

'Naturally.'

'Good.'

As the lookouts cried out the sighting of Sepik, Apsalar made her way forward. The Adjunct, Nil, Keneb and Nether were already on the forecastle. The sun, low on the horizon to the west, lit the rising mass of land two pegs to starboard with a golden glow. Ahead, the lead ships of the fleet, two dromons, were drawing near.

Reaching the rail, Apsalar found she could now make out the harbour city tucked in its halfmoon bay. No smoke rose from the tiers, and in the harbour itself, a mere handful of ships rode at anchor; the nearest one had clearly lost its bow anchor – some snag had hung the trader craft up, heeling it to one side so that its starboard rail was very nearly under water.

Keneb was speaking, 'Sighting Sepik,' he said in a tone that suggested he was repeating himself, 'should have been four, maybe five days away.'

Apsalar watched the two dromons work into the city's bay. One of them was Nok's own flagship.

'Something is wrong,' Nether said.

'Fist Keneb,' the Adjunct said quietly, 'stand down the marines.'

'Adjunct?'

'We shall be making no landfall—'

At that moment, Apsalar saw the foremost dromon suddenly balk, as if it had inexplicably lost headway – and its crew raced like frenzied ants, sails buckling overhead. A moment later the same activity struck Nok's ship, and a signal flag began working its way upward.

Beyond the two warcraft, the city of Sepik exploded into life.

Gulls. Tens of thousands, rising from the streets, the buildings. In their midst, the black tatters of crows, island vultures, lifting like flakes of ash amidst the swirling smoke of the white gulls. Rising, billowing, casting a chaotic shadow over the city.

Nether whispered, *'They're all dead.'*

'The Tiste Edur have visited,' Apsalar said.

Tavore faced her. 'Is slaughter their answer to everything?'

'They found their own kind, Adjunct, a remnant population. Subject, little more than slaves. They are not reluctant to unleash their fury, these Edur.'

'How do you know this, Bridgeburner?'

She eyed the woman. 'How did you know, Adjunct?'

At that, Tavore turned away.

Keneb stood looking at the two women, one to the other, then back again.

Apsalar fixed her gaze back upon the harbour, the gulls settling again to their feast as the two lead dromons worked clear of the bay, sails filling once more. The ships in their immediate wake also began changing course.

'We shall seek resupply with Nemil,' the Adjunct said. As she turned away, she paused. 'Apsalar, find Quick Ben. Use your skeletal servants if you must.'

'The High Mage hides among the cargo below,' she replied.

Tavore's brows lifted. 'Nothing sorcerous, then?'

'No.'

As the sound of the Adjunct's boots receded, Fist Keneb stepped closer to Apsalar. 'The Edur fleet – do you think it pursues us even now, Apsalar?'

'No. They're going home.'

'And how do you come by this knowledge?'

Nether spoke: 'Because a god visits her, Fist. He comes to break her heart. Again and again.'

Apsalar felt as if she had been punched in the chest, the impact reverberating through her bones, the beat inside suddenly erratic, tightening as heat flooded through her veins. Yet, outwardly, she revealed nothing.

Keneb's voice was taut with fury. 'Was that necessary, Nether?'

'Don't mind my sister,' Nil said. 'She lusts after someone—'

'Bastard!'

The young Wickan woman rushed off. Nil watched her for a moment, then he looked over at Keneb and Apsalar, and shrugged.

A moment later he too left.

'My apologies,' Keneb said to Apsalar. 'I would never have invited such a cruel answer – had I known what Nether would say—'

'No matter, Fist. You need not apologize.'

'Even so, I shall not pry again.'

She studied him for a moment.

Looking uncomfortable, he managed a nod, then walked away.

The island was now on the ship's starboard, almost five pegs along. *'He comes to break her heart. Again and again.'* Oh, there could be so few secrets on a ship such as this one. And yet, it seemed, the Adjunct was defying that notion.

No wonder Quick Ben is hiding.

'They killed everyone,' Bottle said, shivering. 'A whole damned island's worth of people. And Monkan Isle, too – it's in the wind, now, the truth of that.'

'Be glad for that wind,' Koryk said. 'We've left that nightmare behind fast, damned fast, and that's good, isn't it?'

683

Cuttle sat straighter and looked at Fiddler. 'Sergeant, wasn't Sepik an Imperial principality?'

Fiddler nodded.

'So, what these Tiste Edur did, it's an act of war, isn't it?'

Bottle and the others looked over at the sergeant, who was scowling – and clearly chewing over Cuttle's words. Then he said, 'Technically, aye. Is the Empress going to see it that way? Or even care? We got us enough enemies as it is.'

'The Adjunct,' Tarr said, 'she'll have to report it even so. And the fact that we already clashed once with that damned fleet of theirs.'

'It's probably tracking us right now,' Cuttle said, grimacing. 'And we're going to lead it straight back to the heart of the empire.'

'Good,' Tarr said. 'Then we can crush the bastards.'

'That,' Bottle muttered, 'or they crush us. What Quick Ben did, it wasn't real—'

'To start,' Fiddler said.

Bottle said nothing. Then, 'Some allies you're better off without.'

'Why?' the sergeant demanded.

'Well,' Bottle elaborated, 'the allies that can't be figured out, the ones with motives and goals that stay forever outside our comprehension – that's what we're talking about here, Sergeant. And believe me, we don't want a war fought with the sorcery of the Holds. We don't.'

The others were staring at him.

Bottle looked away.

'Drag 'im round the hull,' Cuttle said. 'That'll get him to cough it all up.'

'Tempting,' Fiddler said, 'but we got time. Lots of time.'

You fools. Time is the last thing we got. That's what she's trying to tell us. With this eerie wind, thrusting like a fist through Mael's realm – and there's not a thing he can do about it. Take that, Mael, you crusty barnacle!

Time? Forget it. She's driving us into the heart of a storm.

CHAPTER TWENTY

Discipline is the greatest weapon against the self-righteous. We must measure the virtue of our own controlled response when answering the atrocities of fanatics. And yet, let it not be claimed, in our own oratory of piety, that we are without our own fanatics; for the self-righteous breed wherever tradition holds, and most often when there exists the perception that tradition is under assault. Fanatics can be created as easily in an environment of moral decay (whether real or imagined) as in an environment of legitimate inequity or under the banner of a common cause.

Discipline is as much facing the enemy within as the enemy before you; for without critical judgement, the weapon you wield delivers – and let us not be coy here – naught but murder.

And its first victim is the moral probity of your cause.

(Words to the Adherents)
Mortal Sword Brukhalian
The Grey Swords

IT WAS GROWING HARDER, GANOES PARAN REALIZED, NOT TO REGRET certain choices he had made. While scouts reported that the Deragoth were not trailing his army as it marched north and east across virtually empty lands, this very absence led to suspicion and trepidation. After all, if those hoary beasts were not following them, *what were they up to?*

Ganath, the Jaghut sorceress, had more or less intimated that Paran's decision to unleash those beasts was a terrible mistake. He probably should have listened to her. It was a conceit to imagine he could manipulate indefinitely all the forces he had let loose to deal with the T'rolbarahl. And, perhaps, there had been a lack of confidence in the capabilities of ascendants already active in this realm. The Deragoth were primal, but sometimes, that which was primal found itself assailed by a world that no longer permitted its unmitigated freedom.

Well, enough of that. It's done, isn't it. Let someone else clean up the mess I made, just for a change.

Then he frowned. *Granted, that's probably not the proper attitude for the Master of the Deck. But I didn't ask for the title, did I?*

Paran rode in the company of soldiers, somewhere in the middle of the column. He didn't like the notion of an entourage, or a vanguard. Fist Rythe Bude was leading the way at the moment, although that position rotated among the Fists. While Paran remained where he was, with only Noto Boil beside him and, occasionally, Hurlochel, who appeared when there was some message to deliver – and there were, blissfully, scant few of those.

'You were more forceful, you know,' Noto Boil said beside him, 'when you were Captain Kindly.'

'Oh, be quiet,' Paran said.

'An observation, High Fist, not a complaint.'

'Your every observation is a complaint, healer.'

'That's hurtful, sir.'

'See what I mean? Tell me something interesting. Kartoolian, right? Were you a follower of D'rek, then?'

'Hood, no! Very well, if you wish to hear something interesting, I shall tell you of my own history. As a youth, I was a leg-breaker—'

'A what?'

'I broke dog legs. Just one per mongrel, mind you. Lame dogs were important for the festival—'

'Ah, you mean the D'rek festival! That disgusting, barbaric, filth-strewn day of sordid celebration! So, you broke the legs of poor, bemused animals, so they could be stoned to death in alleys by psychotic little children.'

'What is your point, High Fist? Yes, that is precisely what I did. Three crescents a dog. It was a living. Alas, I eventually tired of that—'

'The Malazans outlawed the festival—'

'Yes, that too. A most unfortunate decision. It has made my people moribund, forcing us to search elsewhere for our—'

'For your sick, obnoxious tastes in delivering misery and suffering.'

'Well, yes. Whose story is this?'

'Abyss take me, please accept my apologies. Do go on – assuming I can stomach it.'

Noto Boil tilted his nose skyward. 'I was not busy running around skewering goddesses in my youth—'

'Neither was I, although I suppose, like any healthy young

non-leg-breaking boy, I lusted after a few. At least, based on their statues and the like. Take Soliel, for instance—'

'Soliel! A likeness expressly visualized to encourage notions of motherhood!'

'Oh, really? My, that's a little too revealing, isn't it?'

'Mind you,' Noto Boil said in a commiserating tone, 'you *were* a young boy . . .'

'So I was, now let's forget all that. You were saying? After your leg-breaker career died with a whimper, then what?'

'Oh, how very droll, sir. I should also point out, the manifestation of Soliel back in G'danisban—'

'Damned disappointing,' Paran agreed. 'You've no idea how many adolescent fantasies were obliterated by that.'

'I thought you had no desire to discuss that subject any further?'

'Fine. Go on.'

'I was apprenticed for a short time to a local healer—'

'Healing lame dogs?'

'Not our primary source of income, sir. There was a misunderstanding, as a consequence of which I was forced to depart his company, in some haste. A local recruiting drive proved opportune, especially since such efforts by the Malazans rarely garnered more than a handful of Kartoolians – and most of those either destitute or criminal—'

'And you were both.'

'The principal source of their delight at my joining the ranks derived from my skills as a healer. Anyway my first campaign was in Korel, the Theftian Campaigns, where I was fortunate to acquire further tutelage from a healer who would later become infamous. Ipshank.'

'Truly?'

'Indeed, none other. And yes, I met Manask as well. It must be said – and you, High Fist, will comprehend more than most the necessity of this – it must be said, both Ipshank and Manask remained loyal to Greymane . . . to the last. Well, as far as I knew, that is – I was healer to a full legion by then, and we were sent to Genabackis. In due course—'

'Noto Boil,' Paran interrupted, 'it seems you have a singular talent for consorting with the famous and the infamous.'

'Why, yes, sir. I suppose I have at that. And now, I suspect, you are wondering into which category I place you?'

'Me? No, don't bother.'

The healer prepared to speak again but was interrupted by the arrival of Hurlochel.

'High Fist.'

'Outrider.'

'The trail ahead, sir, has up until now revealed little more than a scattering of your so-called pilgrims. But it seems that a troop of riders have joined the migration.'

'Any idea how many?'

'More than five hundred, High Fist. Could be as many as a thousand – they are riding in formation so it's difficult to tell.'

'Formation. Now, who might they be, I wonder? All right, Hurlochel, advance your scouts and flanking outriders – how far ahead are they?'

'Four or five days, sir. Riding at a collected canter for the most part.'

'Very good. Thank you, Hurlochel.'

The outrider rode back out of the column.

'What do you think this means, High Fist?'

Paran shrugged at the healer's question. 'I imagine we'll discover soon enough, Boil.'

'*Noto* Boil, sir. Please.'

'Good thing,' Paran continued, unable to help himself, 'you became a healer and not a lancer.'

'If you don't mind, sir, I think I hear someone complaining up ahead about saddle sores.' The man clucked his mount forward.

Oh my, he prefers saddle sores to my company. Well, to each his own . . .

'High Fist Paran,' Captain Sweetcreek muttered. 'What's he doing riding back there, and what's all that about no saluting? It's bad for discipline. I don't care what the soldiers think – I don't even care that he once commanded the Bridgeburners – after all, he took them over only to see them obliterated. It's not proper, I'm saying. None of it.'

Fist Rythe Bude glanced over at the woman. Her colour was up, the Fist observed, eyes flashing. Clearly, the captain was not prepared to forget that punch in the jaw. *Mind you, I probably wouldn't forgive something like that either.*

'I think the Fists need to organize a meeting—'

'Captain,' Rythe Bude warned, 'you forget yourself.'

'My apologies, sir. But, now that we're trailing some kind of army, well, I don't want to end up like the Bridgeburners. That's all.'

'Dujek Onearm's confidence in Paran, and his admiration for the man, Captain, is sufficient for me. And my fellow Fists. I strongly advise you to suppress your anger and recall your own discipline. As for the army ahead of us, even a thousand mounted warriors hardly represents a significant threat to the Host. This rebellion is over – there's no-one left to rebel, after all. And little left to fight over.' She gestured forward with one gauntleted hand. 'Even these pilgrims keep falling to the wayside.'

A low mound of stones was visible to one side of the rough track – another sad victim of this pilgrimage – and from this one rose a staff bedecked in crow feathers.

'That's eerie, too,' Sweetcreek said. 'All these Coltaine worshippers . . .'

'This land breeds cults like maggots in a corpse, Captain.'

Sweetcreek grunted. 'A most appropriate image, Fist, in this instance.'

Rythe Bude grunted. *Aye, I stumble on those every now and then.*

Behind the two riders, Corporal Futhgar said, 'Sirs, what are those?'

They twisted round in their saddles, then looked to where the man was pointing. The eastern sky. Voices were rising among the soldiers now, invoked prayers, a few shouts of surprise.

A string of suns, a dozen in all, each small but bright enough to burn blinding holes in the blue sky. From two stretched tails of fiery mist. The row of suns curved like a longbow, the ends higher, and above it was the blurred, misshapen face of the moon.

'*An omen of death!*' someone shouted.

'Captain,' Rythe Bude snapped, 'get that fool to shut his mouth.'

'Aye, sir.'

'The sky falls,' Noto Boil said as he fell back in beside the High Fist.

Scowling, Paran continued studying the strange appearance in the eastern sky, seeking some sense of what it was they were witnessing. *Whatever it is, I don't like it.*

'You doubt me?' the healer asked. 'High Fist, I have walked the lands of Korel. I have seen the craters left behind by all that descended from the sky. Have you ever perused a map of Korel? The entire northern subcontinent and its host of islands? Fling a handful of gravel into mud, then wait whilst water fills the pocks. That is Korel, sir. The people still tell tales of the countless fires that fell from the sky, in the bringing down of the Crippled God.'

'Ride to the head of the column, Noto Boil,' Paran said.

'Sir?'

'Call a halt. Right now. And get me Hurlochel and his outriders. I need a sense of the surrounding area. We may need to find cover.'

For once, the healer made no complaint.

Paran stared at the string of fires, growing like a salvo from the Abyss. *Damn, where's Ormulogun? I need to find him, and he'd better have that Deck ready – or at least the cards etched out, preferably scribed and ready for the threads of paint. Gods below, he'd better have something, because I don't have time to . . .* his thoughts trailed away.

He could feel them now, coming ever closer – he could feel their heat – was that even possible?

The damned moon – I should have paid attention. I should have quested, found out what has happened up there, to that forlorn world. And then another thought struck him, and he went cold.

War among the gods.

Is this an attack? A salvo in truth?

Paran bared his teeth. 'If you're out there,' he whispered, glaring at the eastern sky as his horse shied nervously beneath him, 'you're not playing fair. And . . . I don't like that.' He straightened, stood in his stirrups, and looked about.

'Ormulogun! Where in Hood's name are you!'

'Against this,' Iskaral Pust muttered, 'I can do nothing.' He hugged himself. 'I think I should start gibbering, now. Yes, that would be highly appropriate. A crazed look in my eyes. Drool, then froth, yes. Who could blame me? *We're all going to die!*'

These last words were a shriek, sufficient to shake Mappo from his insensate lethargy. Lifting his head, he looked across at the High Priest of Shadow. The Dal Honese was huddled beside his mule, and both were bathed in a strange light, green-hued – no, the Trell realized, that light was everywhere.

Spite descended from the forecastle, and Mappo saw in her expression cold rage. 'We are in trouble,' she said in a grating voice. 'Out of time – I had hoped . . . never mind—' Suddenly her head snapped round and she stared southwestward. Her eyes narrowed. Then she said, 'Oh . . . who in Hood's name are *you*? And what do you think you are up to?' Falling silent once more, her frown deepening.

Blinking, Mappo Runt pushed himself upright, and saw that the sky was on fire – almost directly above them. As if the sun had spawned a host of children, a string of incandescent pearls, their flames wreathed in haloes of jade. Growing . . . descending. *What are those?*

The sea seemed to tremble around them, the waves choppy, clashing in confusion. The air felt brittle, hot, and all wind had fallen away. And there, above the mass of land to the east that was Otataral Island . . . Mappo looked back at Iskaral Pust. The High Priest, crouching now, had his hands covering his head. Bhoka'rala were converging around him, mewling and whimpering, reaching out to touch the shivering old man. As he babbled, 'We didn't plan for this, did we? I don't remember – gods, I don't remember anything! Mogora, my dear hag, where are you? This is my moment of greatest need. I want sex! Even with you! I'll drink the white paralt later – what choice? It's that, or the memory of most regrettable weakness on my part! There is only so much I can

690

suffer. Stop touching me, you vile apes! Shadowthrone, you miserable insane shade – where are you hiding and is there room for me, your most devoted servant, your Magus? There'd better be! Come get me, damn you – never mind anyone else! Just me! Of course there's room! You mucus-smeared knee-in-the-groin fart-cloud! Save me!'

'Spirits below,' Mogora muttered at Mappo's side, 'listen to that pathetic creature! And to think, I married him!'

Spite suddenly wheeled and ran back to the bow, bhok'arala scattering from her path. Once there, she spun round and shouted. 'I see them! Make for them, fools! Quickly!'

And then she veered, rising above the wallowing, rocking ship, silveretched wings spreading wide. Swirling mists, writhing, growing solid, until an enormous dragon hovered before the ship, dwarfing the craft in its immensity. Lambent eyes flared like quicksilver in the eerie, emerald light. The creature's long, sinuous tail slithered down, snakelike, and coiled round the upthrust prow. The dragon then twisted in the air, a savage beat of the wings—

—and with an alarming jolt the ship lunged forward.

Mappo was flung back into the cabin wall, wood splintering behind him. Gasping, the Trell regained his feet and clambered towards the bows.

She sees them? Who?

The sky was filling with spears of green fire, plunging towards them. Iskaral Pust screamed.

Over a thousand leagues away, westward, Bottle stood with the others and stared at the eastern horizon – where darkness should have been, crawling heavenward to announce the unending cycle of day's death and night's birth. Instead they could see distinctly a dozen motes of fire, descending, filling a third of the sky with a lurid, incandescent, greenish glow.

'Oh,' Bottle whispered, 'this is bad.'

Fiddler clutched at his sleeve, pulled him close. 'Do you understand this?' the sergeant demanded in a harsh whisper.

Bottle shook his head.

'Is this – is this *another Crippled God?*'

Bottle stared at Fiddler, eyes widening. *Another?* 'Gods below!'

'Is it?'

'I don't know!'

Swearing, Fiddler pushed him away. Bottle staggered back, shouldering into Sergeant Balm – who barely reacted – then he twisted through the press, stumbling as he made his way clear, looked across the waters. To the south, the Nemil ships – war biremes and supply transports –

had every sheet to the wind as they raced back towards their homeland, the former swiftly outdistancing the latter, many of the transports still half-filled with cargo – the resupply abandoned.

Aye, it's every fool for himself now. But when those things hit, that shock wave will roll fast. It will smash us all into kindling. Poor bastards, you'll never make it. Not even those ugly biremes.

The unceasing wind seemed to pause, as if gathering breath, then returned with redoubled force, sending everyone on deck staggering. Sailcloth bucked, mast and spars creaking – the *Silanda* groaned beneath them.

Quick Ben? Best make your escape now, and take whoever you can with you. Against what's coming ... there is no illusion that will dissuade it. As for those Tiste Edur, well, they're as finished as we are. I will accept that as consolation.

Well, Grandma, you always said the sea will be the death of me.

Sergeant Hellian wandered across the deck, marvelling at the green world she had found. This Nemil brandy packed a punch, didn't it just? People were screaming, or just standing, as if frozen in place, but that's how things usually were, those times she accidentally – *oops* – slipped over that blurry line of not-quite drunk. Still, this green was making her a little sick.

Hood-damned Nemil brandy – what idiots drank this rubbish? Well, she could trade it for some Falari sailor's rum. There were enough idiots on this ship who didn't know better, she just had to find one. A sailor, like that one there.

'Hey. Look, I got N'm'l brandy, but I'm thirsty for rum, right? Paid ten crescents for this, I know, it's a lot, but my squad, they love me y'see. Took up a c'lection. So's, I'm thinking, how 'bout we trade. Straight across, baw'll for baw'll. Sure, I drunk most a this, but it's worth more, right. Which, as you can see, e'ens thingzup.' Then she waited.

The man was a tall bastard. Kind of severe looking. Other people were staring – what was their problem, anyway?

Then the man took the bottle, swished it back and forth and frowned. He drank it down, three quick swallows.

'Hey—'

And reached beneath his fancy cloak, drawing out a flask, which he passed across to her. 'Here, soldier,' he said. 'Now get below and drink until you pass out.'

She collected the flask with both hands, marvelling at its polished silver surface, even the gouge that ran diagonally across one side, and the sigils stamped into it, very nice. The Imperial Sceptre, and four old ones – the ones that used to identify flagships – she'd seen those before. There, that was Cartheron Crust's, and that one was Urko's, and that one she didn't know, but the last one was the same as on the flag up top of this ship she was on. *That's a coincidence now, ain't it?* She blinked at the man. 'Can't,' she said. 'I got orders—'

'I am countermanding those orders, Sergeant.'

'You can do that?'

'Under these circumstances, yes.'

'Well then, I'll never forget you, sailor. Promise. Now, where's the hatch . . .?'

He guided her, with one firm hand on her shoulder, in the right direction. Clutching the beautiful and beautifully swishing flask against her chest, Hellian made her way along, through the green murk, and all the staring faces. She stuck out her tongue.

They can get their own.

Apsalar turned at the sigh from the Adjunct.

Tavore's expression was . . . philosophic, as she stared at the eastern horizon. 'Humbling, is it not?'

'Yes, Adjunct, I suppose it is.'

'All of our plans . . . our conceits . . . as if the sheer force of our wills, each of us, can somehow ensure that all else remains unchanged around us, awaiting naught but what we do, what we say.'

'The gods—'

'Yes, I know. But that' – she nodded eastward – 'does not belong to them.'

'No?'

'It is too devastating, soldier. Neither side is that desperate . . . yet. And now,' she shrugged, 'even their games dwindle into insignificance.'

'Adjunct,' Apsalar said, 'you lack confidence.'

'Do I? In what?'

'Our resilience.'

'Perhaps.'

But Apsalar could feel her own confidence crumbling, clinging to a single thought – and the resolve behind that thought was itself weakening. Even so. A single thought. *This – this was anticipated. By someone. It had to be.*

Someone saw this coming.

Most people were blind, wilfully or otherwise. But, there were some who weren't.

So now, my prescient friend, you had better do something about it. And quick.

Ormulogun, trailed by his toad, stumbled into view, an overflowing leather satchel in his arms. The toad was bleating something about delusional artists and the brutal world in a tone of pessimistic satisfaction. Ormulogun tripped and fell almost at Paran's feet, the satchel tipping and spilling its contents – including scores of wooden cards, most of them blank.

'You've barely started! You damned fool!'

'Perfection!' Ormulogun shrieked. 'You said—'

'Never mind,' Paran snarled. He looked back at the eastern sky. Spears of fire were descending like rain. 'Mainland? Into the sea?' he wondered aloud. 'Or Otataral Island?'

'Maybe all three,' Noto Boil said, licking his lips.

'Well,' Paran said, crouching down and clearing a space in the sand before him, 'sea's worse. That means . . .' He began drawing with his index finger.

'I have some!' Ormulogun whimpered, fumbling through the cards.

Mael. I hope you're paying attention – I hope you're ready to do what needs doing. He studied the streaks he had etched in the sand. *Enough? It has to be.* Closing his eyes, he focused his will. *The Gate is before me—*

'I have this one!'

The shout was loud in Paran's right ear, and even as the force of his will was unleashed, he opened his eyes – and saw, hovering before him, another card—

And all of his power rushed into it—

Onto his knees, skidding on clay that deformed beneath him, hands thrusting out to catch himself. Grey air, a charnel stench, and Paran lifted his head. Before him stood a gate, a mass of twisted bones and pale, bruised flesh, dangling strands of hair, innumerable staring eyes, and beyond it was grey, murky oblivion.

'Oh, Hood.'

He was at the very threshold. He had damned near flung himself right through—

A figure appeared in the portal, black-cloaked, cowled, tall. *This isn't one of his servants. This is the hoary old bastard himself—*

'Is there time for such unpleasant thoughts, mortal?' The voice was mild, only faintly rasping. 'With what is about to happen . . . well, Ganoes Paran, Master of the Deck of Dragons, you have positioned yourself in a most unfortunate place, unless you wish to be trampled by the multitudes who shall momentarily find themselves on this path.'

'Oh, be quiet, Hood,' Paran hissed, trying to climb to his feet, then stopping when he realized that doing so would not be a good idea. 'Help me. Us. Stop what's coming – it'll destroy—'

'Far too much, yes. Too many plans. I can do little, however. You have sought out the wrong god.'

'I know. I was trying for Mael.'

'Pointless . . .' Yet, even as Hood spoke that word, Paran detected a certain . . . hesitation.

Ah, you've had a thought.

'I have. Very well, Ganoes Paran, *bargain.*'

'Abyss take us – there's no time for that!'

'Think quickly, then.'

'What do you want? More than anything else, Hood. *What do you want?*'

And so Hood told him. And, among the corpses, limbs and staring faces in the gate, one face in particular suddenly grew animate, its eyes opening very wide – a detail neither noticed.

Paran stared at the god, disbelieving. 'You can't be serious.'

'Death is always serious.'

'Oh, enough with the portentous crap! Are you certain?'

'Can you achieve what I ask, Ganoes Paran?'

'I will. Somehow.'

'Do you so vow?'

'I do.'

'Very well. Leave here. I must open this gate.'

'What? It *is* open!'

But the god had turned away, and Paran barely heard Hood's reply: '*Not from this side.*'

Chaur squealed as a hail of firestones struck the roiling waters barely a ship's-breadth away. Explosions of steam, a terrible shrieking sound tearing through the air. Cutter pushed hard on the steering oar, trying to scull the wallowing craft – but he didn't have the strength for that. The *Grief* wasn't going anywhere. *Except, I fear, to the bottom.*

Something struck the deck; a thud, splintering, reverberations trembling the entire hull, then steam was billowing from the fist-sized hole. The *Grief* seemed to sag beneath them.

Cursing, Barathol scrambled to the breach, dragging a bundle of spare sailcloth. Even as he sought to push it down into the hole, two more stones struck the craft, one up front tearing away the prow, another – a flash of heat against Cutter's left thigh and he looked down to see steam then water gushing up.

The air seethed like the breath from a forge. The entire sky overhead seemed to be on fire.

The sail above them was burning, ripped through.

Another concussion, and more than half of the port rail was simply gone, pulverized wood a mist drifting away, flaring with motes of flame.

'We're sinking!' Scillara shouted, grasping hold of the opposite rail as the *Grief*'s deck tilted alarmingly.

Cargo shifted – *too many supplies – we got greedy* – making the dying craft lean further.

The wrapped corpse of Heboric rolled towards the choppy waves.

Crying out, Cutter sought to make his way towards it, but he was too far away – the cloth-wrapped form slid down into the water—

And, wailing, Chaur followed it.

'No!' Barathol yelled. '*Chaur – no!*'

The mute giant's huge arms closed about the corpse, a moment before both simply slipped from sight.

Sea. Bara called it sea. Warm now, wet. Was so nice. Now, sky bad, and sea bad – up there – but nice now. Here. Dark, night, night is coming, ears hurt. Ears hurt. Hurt. Bara said never breathe in sea. Need to breathe now. Oh, hurt! Breathe!

He filled his lungs, and fire burst through his chest, then . . . cool, calm, the spasms slowing. Darkness closed in round him, but Chaur was no longer frightened by that. The cold was gone, the heat was gone, and numbness filled his head.

He had so loved the sea.

The wrapped body in his arms pulled ever down, and the limbs that had been severed and that he had collected when Bara told him to, seemed to move about within as the canvas stretched, lost shape.

Darkness, now, inside and out. Something hot and savage tore past him, racing downward like a spear of light, and Chaur flinched. And he closed his eyes to make those things go away. The ache was finally gone from his lungs.

I sleep now.

Geysers of steam shooting skyward, thunderous concussions racking the air and visibly battering the sea so that it shook, trembled, and Cutter saw Barathol dive into the churning water, into Chaur's wake. *The body. Heboric – Chaur, oh gods . . .*

He reached Scillara's side and pulled her close, into his arms. She clutched his sodden shirt. 'I'm so glad,' she whispered, as the *Grief* groaned and canted further onto its side.

'About what?'

'That I left her. Back there. I left her.'

Cutter hugged her all the tighter.

I'm sorry, Apsalar. For everything—

Sudden buffeting winds, a sweeping shadow. He looked up and his eyes widened at the monstrous shape occluding the sky, descending—

A dragon. What now?

And then he heard shouts – and at that moment, the *Grief* seemed to explode.

Cutter found himself in the water, thrashing, panic awakened within him, like a fist closing round his heart.

. . . Reaching . . . reaching . . .

What is this sound? Where am I?

A million voices – screaming, plunging into terrible death – oh, they had travelled the dark span for so long, weightless, seeing before them that vast . . . emptiness. Unmindful of their arguing, their discussions, their fierce debates, it swallowed them. Utterly. Then, out, through to the other side . . . a net of power spreading out, something eager for mass, something that grew ever stronger, and the journey was suddenly in crazed, violent motion – a world beneath – so many lost then – and beyond it, another, this one larger—

'Oh, hear us, so many . . . *annihilated. Mountains struck to dust, rock spinning away into dark, blinding clouds that scintillated in harsh sunlight – and now, this beast world that fills our vision – is this home?*

'*Have we come home?*'

Reaching . . . hands of jade, dusty, raw, not yet polished into lurid brightness. I remember . . . you had to die, Treach, didn't you? Before ascendancy, before true godhood. You had to die first.

Was I ever your Destriant?

Did that title ever belong to me?

Did I need to be killed?

Reaching – these hands, these unknown, unknowable hands – how can I answer these screams? These millions in their shattered prisons – I touched, once, fingertip to fingertip, I touched, oh . . . the voices—

'This is not salvation. We simply die. Destruction—'

'No, no, you fool. Home. We have come home—'

'Annihilation is not salvation. Where is he? Where is our god?'

'I tell you, the search ends!'

'No argument there.'

Listen to me.

'Who is that?'

'He returns! The one outside – the brother!'

Listen to me, please. I – I'm not your brother. I'm no-one. I thought . . . Destriant . . . did I know it for certain? Have I been lied to?

697

Destriant . . . well, maybe, maybe not. Maybe we all got it wrong, every one of us. Maybe even Treach got it wrong.

'He has lost his mind.'

'Forget him – look, death, terrible death, it comes—'

'Mad? So what. I'd rather listen to him than any of you. He said listen, he said that, and so I shall.'

'We will all listen, idiot – we have no choice, have we?'

Destriant. We got it all wrong. Don't you see? All I have done . . . cannot be forgiven. Can never be forgiven – he's sent me back. Even Hood – he's rejected me, flung me back. But . . . it's slipping away, so tenuous, I am failing—

'Failing, falling, what's the difference?'

Reaching.

'What?'

My hands – do you see them? Cut loose, that's what happened. The hands . . . cut loose. Freed. I can't do this . . . but I think they can. Don't you see?

'Senseless words.'

'No, wait—'

Not Destriant.

Shield Anvil.

Reaching . . . look upon me – all of you! Reach! See my hands! See them! They're reaching – reaching out for you!

They . . . are . . . reaching . . .

Barathol swam down into darkness. He could see . . . nothing. No-one. *Chaur, oh gods, what have I done?* He continued clawing his way downward. Better he drowned as well – he could not live with this, not with that poor man-child's death on his hands – he could not—

His own breath was failing, the pressure closing in, pounding in his skull. He was blind—

A flash of emerald green below, blooming, incandescent, billowing out – and at its core – *Oh gods, wait – wait for me—*

Limp, snagged in unravelled folds of canvas, Chaur was sinking, arms out to the sides, his eyes closed, his mouth . . . open.

No! No, no!

From the pulsing glow, heat – such heat – Barathol fought closer, his chest ready to explode – and reached down, down—

A section of the aft deck floated free from what was now little more than pummelled wreckage. The firestones tore down on all sides as Cutter struggled to help Scillara clamber onto the pitching fragment. Those firestones – they were smaller than pebbles, despite the fist-sized holes they had punched through the *Grief*. Smaller than pebbles – more like grains of sand, glowing bright green, like spatters of glass, their colour changing, almost instantly, into rust red as they plummeted into the depths.

Scillara cried out.

'Are you hit? Oh, gods – no—'

She twisted round. 'Look! Hood take us – *look!*' And she lifted an arm, pointed as a swelling wave lifted them – pointed eastward—

Towards Otataral Island.

It had . . . ignited. Jade green, a glowing dome that might have spanned the entire island, writhing, lifting skyward, and, rising up through it . . . *hands. Of jade. Like . . . like Heboric's*. Rising, like trees. *Arms – huge – dozens of them* – rising, fingers spreading, green light spiralling out – from their upturned palms, from the fingers, from the veins and arteries cabling their muscled lengths – green light, slashing into the heavens like sword-blades. Those arms were too big to comprehend, reaching upward like pillars through the dome—

—as the fires filling the sky seemed to flinch . . . tremble . . . and then began to *converge*.

Above the island, above the hands of jade reaching up, through the billowing green light.

The first falling sun struck the glowing dome.

The sound was like a drum beat, on a scale to deafen the gods. Its pulse rippled through the dome's burgeoning flanks, racing outward and seeming to strip the surface of the sea, shivering through Cutter's bones, a concussion that triggered bursting agony in his ears – then another, and another as sun after sun plunged into that buckling, pocked dome. He was screaming, yet unable to hear himself. Red mist filled his eyes – he felt himself sliding from the raft, down into the foam-laden waves—

Even as an enormous clawed foot reached down, spread wide over Cutter – and Scillara, who was grasping him by an arm, seeking to drag him back onto the raft – and talons the size of scimitars closed round them both. They were lifted from the thrashing water, upward, up—

Reaching . . . yes. For me, closer, closer.

Never mind the pain.

It will not last. I promise. I know, because I remember.

No, I cannot be forgiven.

But maybe you can, maybe I can do that, if you feel it's needed – I don't know – I was the wrong one, to have touched . . . there in that desert. I didn't understand, and Baudin could never have guessed what would happen, how I would be marked.

Marked, yes, I see now, for this, this need.

Can you hear me? Closer – do you see the darkness? There, that is where I am.

Millions of voices, weeping, crying out, voices, filled with yearning – he could hear them—

Ah gods, who am I? I cannot remember.

Only this. The darkness that surrounds me. We, yes, all of you – we can all wait here, in this darkness.

Never mind the pain.

Wait with me. In this darkness.

And the voices, in their millions, in their vast, unbearable need, rushed towards him.

Shield Anvil, who would take their pain, for he could remember such pain.

The darkness took them, and it was then that Heboric Ghost Hands, Shield Anvil, realized a most terrible truth.

One cannot, in any real measure, remember pain.

Two bodies tumbling like broken dolls onto the deck. Mappo struggled towards them, even as Spite wheeled away one more time – he could feel the dragon's agony with every ragged breath she drew, and the air was foul with the reek of scorched scales and flesh.

The rain of fire had descended in a torrent all round them, wild as a hailstorm and far deadlier; yet not one particle had struck their ship – protection gifted, Mappo realized, not by Spite, nor indeed by Iskaral Pust or Mogora. No, as the High Priest's fawning, wet kisses gave proof, some power born in that damned black-eyed mule was responsible. Somehow.

The beast simply stood, unmoving and seemingly indifferent, tail flicking the absence of flies. Slowly blinking, as if half-asleep, its lips twitching every now and then.

While the world went mad around them; while it tore that other ship to pieces—

Mappo rolled the nearer figure over. Blood-smeared face, streams from the ears, the nose, the corners of the eyes – yet he knew this man. He knew him. *Crokus, the Daru. Oh, lad, what has brought you to this?*

Then the young man's eyes opened. Filled with fear and apprehension.

'Be at ease,' Mappo said, 'you are safe now.'

The other figure, a woman, was coughing up seawater, and there was blood flowing down from her left ear to track the underside of her jaw before dripping from her chin. On her hands and knees, she lifted her head and met the Trell's gaze.

'Are you all right?' Mappo asked.

She nodded, crawled closer to Crokus.

'He will live,' the Trell assured her. 'It seems we all shall live . . . I had not believed—'

Iskaral Pust screamed.

Pointed.

A large, scarred, black-skinned arm had appeared over the port rail, like some slithering eel, the hand grasping hard on the slick wood, the muscles straining.

Mappo clambered over.

The man he looked down upon was holding onto another body, a man easily as large as he was, and it was clear that the former was fast losing his strength. Mappo reached down and dragged them both onto the deck.

'Barathol,' the woman gasped.

Mappo watched as the man named Barathol quickly rolled his companion over and began pushing the water from his lungs.

'Barathol—'

'Quiet, Scillara—'

'He was under too long—'

'Quiet!'

Mappo watched, trying to remember what such ferocity, such loyalty, felt like. He could almost recall . . . almost. *He has drowned, this one. See all that water?* Yet Barathol would not cease in his efforts, pulling the limp, flopping body about this way and that, rocking the arms, then, finally, dragging the head and shoulders onto his lap, where he cradled the face as if it was a newborn babe.

The man's expression twisted, terrible in its grief. 'Chaur! Listen to me! This is Barathol. Listen! I want you to . . . to bury the horses! Do you hear me? You have to bury the horses! Before the wolves come down! I'm not asking, Chaur, do you understand? I'm telling you!'

He has lost his mind. From this, there is no recovery. I know, I know—

'Chaur! I will get angry, do you understand? Angry . . . with you! *With you, Chaur!* Do you want Barathol angry at you, Chaur? Do you want—'

A cough, gouting water, a convulsion, then the huge man held so tenderly in Barathol's arms seemed to curl up, one hand reaching up, and a wailing cry worked its way through the mucus and froth.

'No, no my friend,' Barathol gasped, pulling the man into a tight, rocking embrace. 'I'm not angry. No, I'm not. Never mind the horses. You did that already. Remember? Oh, Chaur, I'm not angry.'

But the man bawled, clutching at Barathol like a child.

He is a simpleton. Otherwise, this Barathol, he would not have spoken to him in such a manner. *He is a child in a man's body, this Chaur* . . .

Mappo watched. As the two huge men wept in each other's arms.

Spite now stood beside the Trell, and as soon as Mappo became aware of her, he sensed her pain – and then her will, pushing it away with such ferocity – he dragged his gaze from the two men on the deck and stared at her.

Pushing, pushing away all that pain—

'How? How did you do that?' he demanded.

'Are you blind, Mappo Runt?' she asked. 'Look – look at them, Trell. Chaur, his fear is gone, now. He believes Barathol, he believes him. Utterly, without question. You cannot be blind to this, to what it means.

'You are looking upon joy, Mappo Runt. In the face of this, I will not obsess on my own pain, my own suffering. Do you understand? *I will not.*'

Ah, spirits below, you break my heart, woman. He looked back at the two men, then across to where Scillara held Crokus in her arms, stroking the man's hair as he came round. *Broken, by all this. Again.*

I had . . . forgotten.

Iskaral Pust was dancing round Mogora, who watched him with a sour expression, her face contracting until it resembled a dried-up prune. Then, in a moment when the High Priest drew too close, she lashed out with a kick that swept his feet out from beneath him. He thumped hard onto the deck, then began swearing. 'Despicable woman! Woman, did I say *woman*? Hah! You're what a shedding snake leaves behind! A sickly snake! With scabs and pustules and weals and bunions—'

'I heard you lusting after me, you disgusting creep!'

'I tried to, you mean! In desperation, but even imminent death was not enough! Do you understand? Not enough!'

Mogora advanced on him.

Iskaral Pust squealed, then slithered his way beneath the mule. 'Come any closer, hag, and my servant will kick you! Do you know how many fools die each year from a mule kick? You'd be surprised.'

The Dal Honese witch hissed at him, then promptly collapsed into a swarm of spiders – that raced everywhere, and moments later not one remained in sight.

The High Priest, his eyes wide, looked about frantically, then began scratching beneath his clothes. 'Oh! You awful creature!'

Mappo's bemused attention was drawn away by Crokus, who had moved towards Barathol and Chaur.

'Barathol,' the Daru said. 'There was no chance?'

The man looked over, then shook his head. 'I'm sorry, Cutter. But, he saved Chaur's life. Even dead, he saved Chaur.'

'What do you mean?'

'The body was glowing,' Barathol said. 'Bright green. It's how I saw them. Chaur was snagged in the bolt cloth – I had to cut him free. I could not carry both of them to the surface – I barely made it—'

'It's all right,' Crokus said.

'He sank, down and down, and the glow ebbed. The darkness swallowed him. But listen, you got him close enough – do you understand? Not all the way, but close enough. Whatever happened, whatever saved us all, it came from *him*.'

Mappo spoke: 'Crokus – it is Cutter, now, yes? Cutter, who are you speaking about? Did someone else drown?'

'No, Mappo. I mean, not really. A friend, he died – I, well, I was trying to take his body to the island – it's where he wanted to go, you see. To give something back.'

Something. 'I believe your friend here is right, then,' the Trell said. 'You brought him close enough. To make a difference, to do what even death could not prevent him doing.'

'He was named Heboric Ghost Hands.'

'I will remember that name, then,' Mappo said. 'With gratitude.'

'You . . . you look different.' Cutter was frowning. 'Those tattoos.' Then his eyes widened, and he asked what Mappo feared he would ask. 'Where? Where is he?'

Doors within the Trell that had cracked open suddenly slammed shut once more. He looked away. 'I lost him.'

'You lost him?'

'Gone.' *Yes, I failed him. I failed us all.* He could not look at the Daru. He could not bear it. *My shame . . .*

'Oh, Mappo, I am sorry.'

You are . . . what?

A hand settled on his shoulder, and that was too much. He could feel the tears, the grief flooding his eyes, running down. He flinched away. 'My fault . . . my fault . . .'

Spite stood watching for a moment longer. *Mappo, the Trell. Who walked with Icarium. Ah, he now blames himself. I understand. My . . . that is . . . unfortunate. But such was our intent, after all. And, there is the chance – the one chance I most cherish. Icarium, he may well encounter my sister, before all of this is done. Yes, that would be sweet, delicious, a taste I could savour for a long, long time. Are you close enough, Envy, to sense my thoughts? My . . . desire? I hope so.* But no, this was not the time for such notions, alluring as they were.

Aching still with wounds, she turned and studied the wild, roiling clouds above Otataral Island. Blooms of colour, as if flames ravaged the land, tongues of fire flickering up those gargantuan jade arms, spinning from the fingers. Above the seething dome, night was dimming the penumbra of dust and smoke, where slashes of falling matter still cut through every now and then.

Spite then faced the west, the mainland. *Whoever you are . . . thank you.*

With a gasp, Paran opened his eyes, to find himself pitching forward – sandy gravel rising fast – then he struck, grunting with the impact. His arms felt like unravelled ropes as he slowly dragged them up, sufficiently to push himself onto his side, which let him roll onto his back.

Above him, a ring of faces, all looking down.

'High Fist,' Rythe Bude asked, 'did you just save the world?'

'And us with it?' Noto Boil added, then frowned. 'Never mind that one, sir. After all, in answering the Fist's query, the second is implicitly—'

'Be quiet,' Paran said. 'If I saved the world – and by no means would I make such a claim – I am already regretting it. Does anyone have some water? With where I've just come back from, I've got a rather unpleasant taste in my mouth.'

Skins sloshed into view.

But Paran held up a hand. 'The east – how bad does it look?'

'Should have been much, much worse, sir,' Fist Rythe Bude said. 'There's a real ruckus over there, but nothing's actually *coming out*, if you understand me.'

'Good.' *Good.*

Oh, Hood. Did you truly mean it?

Gods, me and my promises . . .

Night to the east was a lurid, silent storm. Standing near the Adjunct, with Nil and Nether a few strides off to one side, Fist Keneb shivered beneath his heavy cloak, despite the peculiar, dry sultriness of the steady wind. He could not comprehend what had happened beyond that eastern horizon, not before, not now. The descent of green-flamed suns, the raging maelstrom. And, for a time there, a pervasive malaise enshrouding everyone – from what was coming, it had seemed, there would be no reprieve, no escape, no hope of survival.

Such a notion had, oddly enough, calmed Keneb. When struggle was meaningless, all pressure simply drained away. It struck him, now, that there was something to be said for holding on to such sentiments. After all, death was itself inevitable, wasn't it? Inescapable – what point scratching and clawing in a doomed effort to evade it?

The comfort of that was momentary, alas. Death took care of itself – it was in life, in living, that things mattered. Acts, desires, motives, fears, the gifts of joy and the bitter taste of failure – *a feast we must all attend.*

At least until we leave.

Stars wavered overhead, streaks of cloud clung to the north, the kind that made Keneb think of snow. *And yet here I stand sweating, the sweat cooling, this chill fashioned not by night or the wind, but by exhaustion.* Nether had said something about this wind, its urgency, the *will* behind it. Thus, not natural. *A god, then, manipulating us yet again.*

The fleets of Nemil patrolled a vast stretch of this coast. Their war biremes were primitive, awkward-looking, never straying far from the rocky shoreline. That shoreline traditionally belonged to the Trell, but there had been wars, generations of wars, and now Nemil settlements dotted the bays and inlets, and the Trell, who had never been seafarers, had been driven far inland, into the hills, a dwindling enclave surrounded by settlers. Keneb had seen mixed-bloods among the Nemil crews in the trader ships that sailed out with supplies.

Belligerent as the Nemil were towards the Trell, they were not similarly inclined when facing a huge Malazan fleet entering their territorial waters. Sages among them had foretold this arrival, and the lure of profit had triggered a flotilla of merchant craft setting forth from the harbours, accompanied by a disorganized collection of escorts, some private, others royal. The resupply had resembled a feeding frenzy for a time there, until, that is, the eastern sky suddenly burst into savage light.

Not a single Nemil ship remained now, and that coastline had been left behind, as the second bell after midnight tolled dully at the sand-watcher's hand – the sound taken up by nearby ships, rippling outward through the imperial fleet.

From a Nemil captain, earlier in the day, had come interesting news, and it was that information that, despite the lateness, the Adjunct continued to discuss with her two Wickan companions.

'Are there any details from Malazan sources,' Nether was asking Tavore, 'of the peoples beyond the Catal Sea?'

'No more than a name,' the Adjunct replied, then said to Keneb, 'Fist, do you recall it?'

'Perish.'

'Yes.'

'And nothing more is known of them?' Nether asked.

There was no answer forthcoming from the others. And it seemed that the Wickans then waited.

'An interesting suggestion,' the Adjunct said after a moment. 'And, given this near-gale, we shall discover for ourselves soon enough what manner of people are these Perish.'

The Nemil captain had reported – second-hand – that another Edur fleet had been sighted the day before. Well to the north, less than a score of ships, struggling eastward in the face of this unceasing wind. Those ships were in a bad way, the captain had said. Damaged, limping. Struck by a storm, perhaps, or they had seen battle. Whatever the cause, they were not eager to challenge the Nemil ships, which in itself was sufficient matter for comment – apparently, the roving Edur ships had been preying on Nemil traders for nearly two years, and on those instances when Nemil escorts were close enough to engage, the results had been disastrous for the antiquated biremes.

Curious news. The Adjunct had pressed the Nemil captain on information regarding the Perish, the inhabitants of the vast, mountain-girdled peninsula on the western side of the Catal Sea, which was itself a substantial, southward-jutting inlet, at the very bottom of which was the heart of the Nemil Kingdom. But the man had simply shaken his head, suddenly mute.

Nether had, moments earlier, suggested that perhaps the Edur fleet had clashed with these Perish. And suffered in consequence.

The Malazan fleet was cutting across the mouth of the Catal Inlet now – as it was called on the Malazan maps – a distance the captain had claimed was a journey of four days' sailing under ideal conditions. The lead ships were already a fourth of the way across.

There was more than wind, magic or otherwise – *the way the horizons looked blurry, especially headlands . . .*

'The Nemil,' Nil said, 'were not reluctant to speak of the Edur.'

'Yet they would say nothing at all of the Perish,' Nether added.

'History between them,' Keneb suggested.

The others turned to him.

Keneb shrugged. 'Just a thought. The Nemil are clearly expansionist, and that entails a certain . . . arrogance. They devoured the Trell peoples, providing a reassuring symbol of Nemil prowess and righteousness. It may be that the Perish delivered an opposing symbol, something that both shocked and humbled the Nemil – neither sentiment quite fitting with their own notions of grandiosity. And so they will not speak of it.'

'Your theory makes sense,' the Adjunct said. 'Thank you, Fist.' She turned and studied the riotous eastern sky. 'Humbled, yes,' she said in a low voice. 'In the writings of Duiker, he speaks of the manifold scales to be found in war, from the soldier facing another soldier, to the very gods themselves locked in mortal combat. At first glance, it seems an outrage to consider that such extremes can co-exist, yet Duiker then claims that the potential for cause and effect can proceed in both directions.'

'It would be comforting to think so,' Keneb said. 'I can think of a few gods that I'd love to trip up right now.'

'It may be,' the Adjunct said, 'that someone has preceded you.'

Keneb frowned. 'Do you know who, Adjunct?'

She glanced at him, said nothing.

Thus ends her momentary loquaciousness. Well. And what did it tell me? She's well read, but I already knew that. Anything else?

No.

Kalam pushed his way forward, slumped once more at Quick Ben's side. 'It's official,' he said in the gloom of the musty hold.

'What is?'

'We're still alive.'

'Oh, that's good, Kal. I was sitting on coals down here waiting for that news.'

'I prefer that image to the reality, Quick.'

'What do you mean?'

'Well, the idea that you were hiding, your loincloth suddenly baggy and a puddle spreading beneath you.'

'You don't know anything. I do. I know more than I'd ever want to—'

'Impossible. You drink in secrets like Hellian does rum. The more you know the drunker and more obnoxious you get.'

'Oh yeah? Well, I know things you'd want to know, and I was going to tell you, but now I think I'll change my mind—'

'Out with it, wizard, before I go back up and tell the Adjunct where she can find you.'

'You can't do that. I need time to think, damn you.'

'So talk. You can think while you're doing that, since with you the two activities are clearly distinct and mostly unrelated.'

'What's got you so miserable?'

'You.'

'Liar.'

'All right, me.'

'That's better. Anyway, I know who saved us.'

'Really?'

'Well, sort of – he started the big rock rolling, at least.'

'Who?'

'Ganoes Paran.'

Kalam scowled. 'All right, I'm less surprised than I should be.'

'Then you're an idiot. He did it by having a conversation with Hood.'

'How do you know?'

'I was there, listening in. At Hood's Gate.'

'What were you doing hanging around there?'

'We were all going to die, weren't we?'

'Oh, so you wanted to beat the rush?'

'Hilarious, Kalam. No, I was planning on doing some bargaining, but that's irrelevant now. Ended up, it was Paran who did the bargaining. Hood said something. He wants something – by his own damned breath, it shocked me, let me tell you—'

'So do that.'

'No. I need to think.'

Kalam closed his eyes and leaned back against the bale. It smelled of oats. 'Ganoes Paran.' A pause, then, 'Do you think she knows?'

'Who, Tavore?'

'Yes, who else?'

'I have no idea. Wouldn't surprise me. Nothing about her would surprise me, in fact. She might even be listening in right now—'

'Wouldn't you sense that?'

'Kalam, *something's* wandering through this fleet tonight, and it isn't pleasant, whatever it is. I keep feeling it brush by . . . close, then, before I can grab it by the throat, it whispers away again.'

'So, you *are* hiding down here!'

'Of course not. Not any more, I mean. Now I'm staying here, in order to lay a trap.'

'A trap. Right. Very clever, High Mage.'

'It is. For the next time it sidles close.'

'Do you really expect me to believe that?'

'Believe what you like, Kalam. What do I care, even if it's my oldest friend who no longer trusts me—'

'For Hood's sake, Quick Ben, I've *never* trusted you!'

'Now that's hurtful. Wise, but still hurtful.'

'Tell me something, Quick, exactly how did you manage hiding at Hood's Gate, with both Paran and the god himself standing there?'

A sniff. 'They were distracted, of course. Sometimes the best place to hide is in plain sight.'

'And between them, they saved the world.'

'Gave the rock a nudge, Kal. The rest belonged to someone else. Don't know who, or what. But I will tell you one thing, those falling suns, *they were filled with voices.*'

'Voices?'

'Enormous pieces of stone. Jade, sailing down from the stars. And in those broken mountains or whatever they were, there were souls. Millions of souls, Kalam. *I heard them.*'

Gods, no wonder you hid down here, Quick. 'That's . . . uncanny. You're sending shivers all through me.'

'I know. I feel the same way.'

'So, how *did* you hide from Hood?'

'I was part of the Gate, of course. Just another corpse, just another staring face.'

'Hey, now that was clever.'

'Wasn't it?'

'What was it like, among all those bones and bodies and stuff?'

'Kind of . . . comforting . . .'

I can see that. Kalam scowled again. *Hold on . . . I wonder . . . is there maybe something wrong with us?* 'Quick, you and me.'

'Yes?'

'I think we're insane.'

'You're not.'

'What do you mean?'

'You're too slow. You can't be insane if you only just realized that we're insane. Understand?'

'No.'

'As I said, then.'

'Well,' the assassin grunted, 'that's a relief.'

'For you, yes. Shh!' The wizard's hand clutched Kalam's arm. '*It's back!*' he hissed. 'Close!'

'Within reach?' Kalam asked in a whisper.

'Gods, I hope not!'

A solitary resident in this cabin, and in the surrounding alcoves and cubby berths, a cordon of Red Blades, fiercely protective of their embittered, broken commander, although none elected to share the Fist's quarters, despite the ship's crowded conditions. Beyond those soldiers, the Khundryl Burned Tears, seasick one and all, filling the air below-decks with the sour reek of bile.

And so he remained alone. Wreathed by his own close, fetid air, no lantern light to beat back the dark, and this was well. For all that was outside matched what was inside, and Fist Tene Baralta told himself, again and again, that this was well.

Y'Ghatan. The Adjunct had sent them in, under strength, knowing there would be slaughter. She didn't want the damned veterans and their constant gnawing at her command. She wanted to be rid of the

Red Blades, and the marines – soldiers like Cuttle and Fiddler. She had probably worked it out, conspiring with Leoman himself. That conflagration, its execution had been too perfect, too well-timed. There had been signals – those fools with the lanterns on the rooftops, along the wall's battlements.

And the season itself – a city filled with olive oil, an entire year's harvest – she hadn't rushed the army after Leoman, she hadn't shown any haste at all, when any truly loyal commander would have . . . would have chased that bastard down, long before he reached Y'Ghatan.

No, the timing was . . . diabolical.

And here he was, maimed and trapped in the midst of damned traitors. Yet, again and again, events had transpired to befoul the Adjunct and her treasonous, murderous plans. The survival of the marines – Lostara among them. Then, Quick Ben's unexpected countering of those Edur mages. Oh yes, his soldiers reported to him, every morsel of news. They understood – although they revealed nothing of their suspicions – he could well see it in their eyes, they understood. That necessary things were coming. Soon.

And it would be Fist Tene Baralta himself who would lead them. Tene Baralta, the Maimed, the Betrayed. Oh yes, there would be names for him. There would be cults to worship him, just as there were cults worshipping other great heroes of the Malazan Empire. Like Coltaine. Bult. Baria Setral and his brother, Mesker, of the Red Blades.

In such company, Tene Baralta would belong. Such company, he told himself, was his only worthy company.

One eye left, capable of seeing . . . almost . . . In daylight a blurred haze swarmed before his vision, and there was pain, so much pain, until he could not even so much as turn his head – oh yes, the healers had worked on him – with orders, he now knew, to fail him again and again, to leave him with a plague of senseless scars and phantom agonies. And, once out of his room, they would laugh, at the imagined success of their charade.

Well, he would deliver their gifts back into their laps, all those healers.

In this soft, warm darkness, he stared upward from where he lay on the cot. Things unseen creaked and groaned. A rat scuttled back and forth along one side of the cramped chamber. His sentinel, his body-guard, his caged soul.

A strange smell reached him, sweet, cloying, numbing, and he felt his aches fading, the shrieking nerves falling quiescent.

'Who's there?' he croaked.

A rasping reply, 'A friend, Tene Baralta. One, indeed, whose visage matches your own. Like you, assaulted by betrayal. You and I, we are torn and twisted to remind us, again and again, that one who bears no scars cannot be trusted. Ever. It is a truth, my friend, that only a mortal who has been broken can emerge from the other side, whole once more. Complete, and to all his victims, arrayed before him, blindingly bright, yes? The searing white fires of his righteousness. Oh, I promise you, that moment shall taste sweet.'

'An apparition,' Tene Baralta gasped. 'Who has sent you? The Adjunct, yes? A demonic assassin, to end this—'

'Of course not – and even as you make such accusations, Tene Baralta, you know them to be false. She could kill you at any time—'

'My soldiers protect me—'

'She will not kill you,' the voice said. 'She has no need. She has already cast you away, a useless, pathetic victim of Y'Ghatan. She has no realization, Tene Baralta, that your mind lives on, as sharp as it has ever been, its judgement honed and eager to draw foul blood. She is complacent.'

'Who are you?'

'I am named Gethol. I am the Herald of the House of Chains. And I am here, for you. You alone, for we have sensed, oh yes, we have sensed that you are destined for greatness.'

Ah, such emotion here, at his words . . . no, hold it back. Be strong . . . show this Gethol your strength. 'Greatness,' he said. 'Yes, of that I have always been aware, Herald.'

'And the time has come, Tene Baralta.'

'Yes?'

'Do you feel our gift within you? Diminishing your pain, yes?'

'I do.'

'Good. That gift is yours, and there is more to come.'

'More?'

'Your lone eye, Tene Baralta, deserves more than a clouded, uncertain world, don't you think? You need a sharpness of vision to match the sharpness of your mind. That seems reasonable, indeed, just.'

'Yes.'

'That will be your reward, Tene Baralta.'

'If I do what?'

'Later. Such details are not for tonight. Until we speak again, follow your conscience, Tene Baralta. Make your plans for what will come. You are returning to the Malazan Empire, yes? That is good. Know this, the Empress awaits you. You, Tene Baralta, more than anyone else in this army. Be ready for her.'

'Oh, I shall, Gethol.'

'I must leave you now, lest this visitation be discovered – there are many powers hiding in this army. Be careful. Trust no-one—'

'I trust my Red Blades.'

'If you must, yes, you will need them. Goodbye, Tene Baralta.'

Silence once more, and the gloom, unchanged and unchanging, inside and out. *Destined, yes, for greatness. They shall see that. When I speak with the Empress. They shall all see that.*

Lying in her bunk, the underside of the one above a mere hand's-breadth away, knotted twine and murky tufts of bedding, Lostara Yil kept her breathing slow, even. She could hear the beat of her own heart, the swish of blood in her ears.

The soldier in the bunk beneath her grunted, then said in a low voice, 'He's now talking to himself. Not good.'

The voice from within Tene Baralta's cabin had been murmuring through the wall for the past fifty heartbeats, but had now, it seemed, stopped.

Talking to himself? Hardly, that was a damned conversation. She closed her eyes at the thought, wishing she had been asleep and unmindful of the ever more sordid nightmare that was her commander's world: the viscous light in his eye when she looked upon him, the muscles of his frame sagging into fat, the twisted face beginning to droop, growing flaccid where there were no taut scars. Pallid skin, strands of hair thick with old sweat.

What has burned away is what tempered his soul. Now, there is only malice, a mottled collection of stains, fused impurities.

And I am his captain once more, by his own command. What does he want with me? What does he expect?

Tene Baralta had ceased speaking. And now she could sleep, if only her mind would cease its frantic racing.

Oh Cotillion, you knew, didn't you? You knew this would come. Yet, you left the choice to me. And now freedom feels like a curse.

Cotillion, you never play fair.

The western coast of the Catal Sea was jagged with fjords, high black cliffs and tumbled boulders. The mountains rising almost immediately behind the shoreline were thick with coniferous trees, their green needles so dark as to be almost black. Huge red-tailed ravens wheeled overhead, voicing strange, harsh laughter as they banked and pitched towards the fleet of ominous ships that approached the Malazans, swooping low only to lift with heavy, languid beats of their wings.

The Adjunct's flagship was now alongside Nok's own, and the Admiral had just crossed over to join Tavore as they awaited the arrival of the Perish.

Keneb stared with fascination at the massive warships drawing ever nearer. Each was in fact two dromons linked by arching spans, creating a catamaran of cyclopean proportions. The sudden dying of the wind had forced oars into the becalmed waters, and this included a double bank of oars on the inward side of each dromon, foreshortened by the spans.

The Fist had counted thirty-one of the giant craft, arrayed in a broad, flattened wedge. He could see ballistae mounted to either side of the wolf-head prows, and attached to the outer rails along the length of the ships was a double row of overlapping rectangular shields, their bronze facings polished and glinting in the muted sunlight.

As the lead ship closed, oars were lifted, shipped.

One of Nok's officers said, 'Look beneath the surface between the hulls, Admiral. The spans above are matched by ones below the water-line . . . and those possess rams.'

'It would be unwise indeed,' Nok said, 'to invite battle with these Perish.'

'Yet someone had done just that,' the Adjunct said. 'Mage-fire damage, there, on the one flanking the flagship. Admiral, what do you imagine to be the complement of soldiers aboard each of these catamarans?'

'Could be as many as two hundred marines or the equivalent for each dromon. Four hundred per craft – I wonder if some of them are at the oars. Unless, of course, there are slaves.'

The flag visible beneath the crow's nest on the lead ship's mainmast showed a wolf's head on a black field bordered in grey.

They watched as a long craft resembling a war canoe was lowered between the flagship's two hulls, then armoured soldiers descended, taking up paddles. Three more figures joined them. All but one wore iron helms, camailed at the back, with sweeping cheek-guards. Grey cloaks, leather gauntlets. The lone exception was a man, tall, gaunt and bald, wearing a heavy woollen robe of dark grey. Their skins were fair, but all other characteristics remained unseen beneath armour.

'That's a whole lot of chain weighing down that canoe,' the same officer muttered. 'If she rolls, a score lumps rusting on the bottom . . .'

The craft slid over the submerged ram, swiftly propelled by the paddlers whose blades flashed in perfect unison. Moments later a soft-voiced command triggered a withdrawal of the paddles, barring that of the soldier at the very stern, who ruddered, bringing the canoe around to draw up alongside the Malazan flagship.

At Nok's command, sailors rushed over to help the Perish contingent aboard.

First to appear was a tall, broad-shouldered figure, black-cloaked.

Beneath the thick wool was a surcoat of blackened chain that glistened with oil. The longsword at the left hip revealed a silver wolf's-head pommel. The Perish paused, looked round, then approached the Adjunct as others appeared from the rail. Among them was the robed man, who called out something to the one Keneb surmised was the commander. That person halted, half-turned, and the voice that emerged from behind the visored helm startled Keneb, for it was a woman's.

She's a damned giant – even the women heavies in our army would hesitate facing this one.

Her question was short.

The bald man replied with a single word, at which the woman in armour bowed and stepped to one side.

Keneb watched the robed man stride forward, eyes on the Adjunct. 'Mezla,' he said. 'Welcome.'

He speaks Malazan. Well, that should make this easier.

The Adjunct nodded. 'Welcome in return, Perish. I am Adjunct Tavore Paran, and this is Admiral Nok—'

'Ah, yes, that name is known to us, sir.' A low bow towards Nok, who seemed startled for a moment, before replying in kind.

'You speak our language well,' Tavore said.

'Forgive me, Adjunct. I am Destriant Run'Thurvian.' He gestured to the huge woman beside him. 'This is the Mortal Sword Krughava.' And then, stepping to one side, he bowed to another soldier standing two steps behind the Mortal Sword. 'Shield Anvil Tanakalian.' The Destriant added something in his own language, and in response both the Mortal Sword and the Shield Anvil removed their helms.

Ah, these are hard, hard soldiers. Krughava, iron-haired, was blue-eyed, her weathered face seamed with scars, yet the bones beneath her stern, angular features were robust and even. The Shield Anvil was, in contrast, quite young, and if anything broader of shoulder, although not as tall as the Mortal Sword. His hair was yellow, the colour of stalks of wheat; his eyes deep grey.

'Your ships have seen fighting,' Admiral Nok said to the Destriant.

'Yes sir. We lost four in the engagement.'

'And the Tiste Edur,' the Adjunct asked, 'how many did they lose?'

The Destriant suddenly deferred to the Mortal Sword, bowing, and the woman replied in fluent Malazan, 'Uncertain. Perhaps twenty, once their sorcery was fended aside. Although nimble, the ships were under-strength. Nonetheless, they fought well, without quarter.'

'Are you in pursuit of the surviving ships?'

'No, sir,' Krughava replied, then fell silent.

The Destriant said, 'Noble sirs, we have been waiting for you. For the Mezla.'

He turned then and walked to stand at the Shield Anvil's side.

Krughava positioned herself directly opposite the Adjunct. 'Admiral Nok, forgive me,' she said, holding her gaze on Tavore. The Mortal Sword then drew her sword.

As with every other Malazan officer witness to this, Keneb tensed, reaching for his own weapon.

But the Adjunct did not flinch. She wore no weapon at all.

The length of blue iron sliding from the scabbard was etched from tip to hilt, two wolves stretched in full charge, every swirl of fur visible, their fangs polished brighter than all else, gleaming, the eyes blackened smears. The artisanship was superb, yet that blade's edge was notched and battered. Its length gleamed with oil.

The Mortal Sword held the sword horizontally, against her own chest, and there was a formal rigidity to her words as she said, 'I am Krughava, Mortal Sword of the Grey Helms of the Perish, sworn to the Wolves of Winter. In solemn acceptance of all that shall soon come to pass, I pledge my army to your service, Adjunct Tavore Paran. Our complement: thirty-one Thrones of War. Thirteen thousand and seventy-nine brothers and sisters of the Order. Before us, Adjunct Tavore, awaits the end of the world. In the name of Togg and Fanderay, we shall fight until we die.'

No-one spoke.

The Mortal Sword settled onto one knee, and laid the sword at Tavore's feet.

On the forecastle, Kalam stood beside Quick Ben, watching the ceremony on the mid deck. The wizard beside the assassin was muttering under his breath, the sound finally irritating Kalam enough to draw his gaze from the scene below, even as the Adjunct, with a solemnity to match the Mortal Sword's, picked up the sword and returned it to Krughava.

'*Will you be quiet, Quick!*' Kalam hissed. 'What's wrong with you?'

The wizard stared at him with a half-wild look in his dark eyes. 'I recognize these . . . these Perish. Those titles, the damned formality and high diction – I recognize these people!'

'And?'

'And . . . nothing. But I will say this, Kal. If we ever end up besieged, woe to the attackers.'

The assassin grunted. 'Grey Helms—'

'Grey Helms, Swords . . . gods below, Kalam – I need to talk to Tavore.'

'Finally!'

'I really need to talk to her.'

'Go on down and introduce yourself, High Mage.'

'You must be mad . . .'

Quick Ben's sudden trailing away brought Kalam's gaze back round to the crowd below, and he saw the Destriant, Run'Thurvian, looking up, eyes locked with Quick's own. Then the robed man smiled, and bowed low in greeting.

Heads turned.

'*Shit*,' Quick Ben said at his side.

Kalam scowled. 'High Mage Ben Adaephon Delat,' he said under his breath, 'the Lord of High Diction.'

CHAPTER TWENTY-ONE

A Book of Prophecy opens the door. You need a second book to close it.

Tanno Spiritwalker Kimloc

WITH SILVER TONGS, THE SERVANT SET ANOTHER DISK OF GROUND rustleaf atop the waterpipe. Felisin Younger drew on the mouthpiece, waving the servant away, watching bemused as the old woman – head bowed so low her forehead was almost scraping the floor – backed away on her hands and knees. More of Kulat's rules of propriety when in the presence of Sha'ik Reborn. She was tired of arguing about it – if the fools felt the need to worship her, then so be it. After all, for the first time in her life, she found that her every need was met, attended to with fierce diligence, and those needs – much to her surprise – were growing in count with every day that passed.

As if her soul was a vast cauldron, one that demanded filling, yet was in truth bottomless. They fed her, constantly, and she was growing heavy, clumsy with folds of soft fat – beneath her breasts, and on her hips and behind, the underside of her arms, her belly and thighs. And, no doubt, her face as well, although she had outlawed the presence of mirrors in her throne room and private chambers.

Food was not her only excess. There was wine, and rustleaf, and, now, there was lovemaking. There were a dozen servants among those attending her whose task it was to deliver pleasure of the flesh. At first, Felisin had been shocked, even outraged, but persistence had won out. More of Kulat's twisted rules – she understood that now. His desires were all of the voyeuristic variety, and many times she had heard the wet click of the stones in his mouth from behind a curtain or painted panel, as he spied on her with lascivious pathos.

She understood her new god, now. Finally. Bidithal had been entirely wrong – this was not a faith of abstinence. Apocalypse was announced in excess. The world ended in a glut, and just as her own soul was a bottomless cauldron, so too was the need of all humanity, and in this she was the perfect representative. As they devoured all that surrounded them, so too would she.

As Sha'ik Reborn, her task was to blaze bright, and quick – and then die. Into death, where lay the true salvation, the paradise Kulat spoke of again and again. Oddly enough, Felisin Younger struggled to imagine that paradise – she could only conjure visions that matched what now embraced her, her every want answered without hesitation, without judgement. Perhaps it would be like that – for everyone. But if everyone would know such an existence, then where were the servants?

No, she told Kulat, there needed to be levels of salvation. Pure service in this world was rewarded with absolute indolence in the other. Humility, self-sacrifice, abject servitude, these were the ways of living that would be measured, judged. The only difficulty with this notion – which Kulat had readily accepted and converted into edicts – was the position of Felisin herself. After all, was her present indolence – her luxuriating in all the excesses promised to others only following their deaths – to be rewarded by an afterlife of brutal slavery, serving the needs of everyone else?

Kulat assured her she had no need to be concerned. In life, she was the embodiment of paradise, she was the symbol of promise. Yet, upon her death, there would be absolution. She was Sha'ik Reborn, after all, and that was a role she had not assumed by choice. It had been thrust upon her, and this was the most profound form of servitude of them all.

He was convincing, although a tiny sliver of doubt lodged deep inside her, a few thoughts, one tumbling after the next: *without excess I might feel better, about myself. I would be as I once was, when I walked in the wild-lands with Cutter and Scillara, with Greyfrog and Heboric Ghost Hands. Without all these servants, I would be able to fend for myself, and to see clearly that a measured life, a life tempered in moderation, is better than all this. I would see that this is a mortal paradise that cultivates flaws like flowers, that feeds only deathly roots, that chokes all life from me until I am left with . . . with this.*

This. This wandering mind. Felisin Younger struggled to focus. Two men were standing before her. They had been standing there for some time, she realized. Kulat had announced them, although that had not been entirely necessary, for she knew that they were coming; indeed, she recognized both of them. Those hard, weathered faces, the streaks of sweat through a layer of dust, the worn leather armour, round shields and scimitars at their hips.

The one closest to her – tall, fierce. *Mathok, who commanded the desert tribes in the Army of the Apocalypse. Mathok, Leoman's friend.*

And, one pace behind the commander, Mathok's bodyguard T'morol, looking like some upright, hairless wolf, his eyes a hunter's eyes, cold, intense.

They had brought their army, their warriors.

They had brought that, and more . . .

Felisin the Younger lowered her gaze from Mathok's face, down to the tattered hide-bound book in his hands. The Holy Book of Dryjhna the Apocalyptic. Whilst Leoman had led the Malazans on a wild chase, into the trap that was Y'Ghatan, Mathok and his desert warriors had travelled quietly, secretly, evading all contact. There had been intent, Mathok had explained, to rendezvous at Y'Ghatan, but then the plague had struck, and the shamans in his troop had been beset by visions.

Of Hanar Ara, the City of the Fallen. Of Sha'ik, reborn yet again. Leoman and Y'Ghatan, they told Mathok, was a dead end in every sense of the phrase. A feint, punctuated by annihilation. And so the commander had turned away with his army, and had set out on the long journey to find the City of the Fallen. To find her. To deliver the Holy Book into her hands.

A difficult journey, one worthy of its own epic, no doubt.

And now, Mathok stood before her, and his army was encamping in the city and Felisin sat amidst the cushions of her own fat, wreathed in smoke, and considered how she would tell him what he needed to hear – what they all needed to hear, Kulat included.

Well, she would be . . . direct. 'Thank you, Mathok, for delivering the Book of Dryjhna. Thank you, as well, for delivering your army. Alas, I have no need of either gift.'

Mathok's brows rose fractionally. 'Sha'ik Reborn, with the Book, you can do as you like. For my warriors, however, you have great need. A Malazan army approaches—'

'I know. But you are not enough. Besides, I have no need for warriors. My army does not march in rank. My army carries no weapons, wears no armour. In conquering, my army kills not a single foe, enslaves no-one, rapes no child. That which my army wields is salvation, Mathok. Its promise. Its invitation.'

'And the Malazans?' T'morol demanded in his grating voice, baring his teeth. 'That army *does* carry weapons and wear armour. That army, Holy One, marches in rank, and right now they're *marching right up our ass!*'

'Kulat,' Felisin said. 'Find a place for the Holy Book. Have the artisans prepare a new one, the pages blank. There will be a second holy book. My Book of Salvation. On its first page, Kulat, record what has been said here, this day, and accord all present with the honour they have earned. Mathok, and T'morol, you are most welcome here, in the City of the Fallen. As are your warriors. But understand, your days of war, of slaughter, are done. Put away your scimitars and your shields, your bows. Unsaddle your horses and loose them to the high pastures in the hills at Denet'inar Spring. They shall live out their lives there, well and in peace. Mathok, T'morol, do you accept?'

The commander stared down at the ancient tome in his hands, and Felisin saw a sneer emerge on his features. He spread his hands. The book fell to the floor, landing on its spine. The impact broke it. Ancient pages skirled out. Ignoring Felisin, Mathok turned to T'morol. 'Gather the warriors. We will resupply as needed. Then we leave.'

T'morol faced the throne, and spat onto the floor before the dais. Then he wheeled and strode from the chamber.

Mathok hesitated, then he faced Felisin once more. 'Sha'ik Reborn, you will no doubt receive my shamans without the dishonour witnessed here. I leave them with you. To you. As for your world, your bloated, disgusting world and its poisonous salvation, I leave that to you as well. For all of this, Leoman died. For all of this, Y'Ghatan burned.' He studied her a moment longer, then he spun about and walked from the throne room.

Kulat scurried to kneel beside the broken book. 'It is ruined!' he said in a voice filled with horror.

Felisin nodded. 'Utterly.' Then she smiled at her own joke.

'I judge four thousand,' Fist Rythe Bude said.

The rebel army was positioned along a ridge. Horse-warriors, lancers, archers, yet none had readied weapons. Round shields remained strapped to backs, quivers lidded, bows unstrung and holstered on saddles. Two riders had moved out from the line and were working their horses down the steep slope to where Paran and his officers waited.

'What do you think, High Fist?' Hurlochel asked. 'This has the look of a surrender.'

Paran nodded.

The two men reached the base of the slope and cantered up to halt four paces from the Host's vanguard.

'I am Mathok,' the one on the left said. 'Once of Sha'ik's Army of the Apocalypse.'

'And now?' Paran asked.

A shrug. 'We dwelt in the Holy Desert Raraku, a desert now a sea. We fought as rebels, but the rebellion has ended. We believed. We believe no longer.' He unsheathed his scimitar and flung it onto the ground. 'Do with us as you will.'

Paran settled back in his saddle. He drew a deep breath and released it in a long sigh. 'Mathok,' he said, 'you and your warriors are free to go where you please. I am High Fist Ganoes Paran, and I hereby release you. As you said, the war is over, and I for one am not interested in reparation, nor punishment. Nothing is gained by inflicting yet more atrocities in answer to past ones.'

The grizzled warrior beside Mathok threw a leg over his horse's neck and slipped down to the ground. The impact made him wince and arch his lower back, grimacing, then he hobbled over to his commander's scimitar. Collecting it, he wiped the dust from the blade and the grip, then delivered it back to Mathok.

Paran spoke again: 'You have come from the place of pilgrimage.'

'The City of the Fallen, yes. Do you intend to destroy them, High Fist? They are defenceless.'

'I would speak with their leader.'

'Then you waste your time. She claims she is Sha'ik Reborn. If that is true, then the cult has seen a degradation from which it will never recover. She is fat, poisoned. I barely recognized her. She is indeed *fallen*. Her followers are sycophants, more interested in orgies and gluttony than anything else. They are disease-scarred and half-mad. Her High Priest watches her sex acts from behind curtains and masturbates, and in both their energy is unbounded and insatiable.'

'Nonetheless,' Paran said after a moment, 'I sense power there.'

'No doubt,' Mathok replied, leaning to one side and spitting. 'Slaughter them, then, High Fist, and you will rid the world of a new kind of plague.'

'What do you mean?'

'A religion of the maimed and broken. A religion proffering salvation ... you just have to die first. I predict the cult will prove highly contagious.'

He's probably right. 'I cannot slaughter innocents, Mathok.'

'Then, one day, the most faithful and zealous among them will slaughter you, High Fist.'

'Perhaps. If so, I will worry about it then. In the meantime, I have other tasks before me.'

'You will speak with Sha'ik Reborn?'

Paran considered, then he shook his head. 'No. As you suggest, there is little point. While I see the possible wisdom of expunging this cult before it gains a foothold, I admit I find the notion reprehensible.'

'Then where, if I may ask, High Fist, will you go now?'

Paran hesitated. *Dare I answer? Well, now is as good as later for everyone to hear.* 'We turn round, Mathok. The Host marches to Aren.'

'Do you march to war?' the commander asked.

Paran frowned. 'We're an army, Mathok. Eventually, yes, there will be fighting.'

'Will you accept our service, High Fist?'

'What?'

'We are a wandering people,' Mathok explained. 'But we have lost our home. Our families are scattered and no doubt many are dead of plague. We have nowhere to go, and no-one to fight. If you should reject us now, and free us to go, we shall ride into dissolution. We shall die with our backs covered in straw and sand in our gauntlets. Or warrior will turn upon warrior, and blood will be shed that is without meaning. Accept us into your army, High Fist Ganoes Paran, and we will fight at your side and die with honour.'

'You have no idea where I intend to lead the Host, Mathok.'

The old warrior beside Mathok barked a laugh. 'The wasteland back of camp, or the wasteland few have ever seen before, what's the difference?' He turned to his commander. 'Mathok, my friend, the shamans said this one here killed Poliel. For that alone, I would follow him into the Abyss, so long as he promises us heads to lop off and maybe a woman or two to ride on the way. That's all we're look-ing for, right, before we dance in a god's lap one last time. Besides, I'm tired of running.'

To all of this, Mathok simply nodded, his gaze fixed on Paran.

Four thousand or so of this continent's finest light cavalry just volunteered, veterans one and all. 'Hurlochel,' he said, 'attach yourself as liaison to Commander Mathok. Commander, you are now a Fist, and Hurlochel will require a written compilation of your officers or potential officers. The Malazan army employs mounted troops in units of fifty, a hundred and three hundred. Adjust your command structure accordingly.'

'It shall be done, High Fist.'

'Fist Rythe Bude, see the Host turned round. And Noto Boil, find me Ormulogun.'

'Again?' the healer asked.

'Go.'

Yes, again. I think I need a new card. I think I'll call it Salvation. At the moment it is in the House of Chains' sphere of influence. But some-thing tells me it will claw free of that eventually. Such a taint will not last. This card is an Unaligned. In every sense of the word. Unaligned, and likely destined to be the most dangerous force in the world.

Damn, I wish I was more ruthless. That Sha'ik Reborn, and all her twisted followers – I should ride up there and slaughter them all – which is precisely what Mathok wanted me to do.

To do what he himself couldn't – we're the same in that. In our . . . weakness.

No wonder I already like the man.

As Hurlochel led his horse alongside Mathok, back up towards the desert warriors on the ridge, the outrider glanced over at the new Fist. 'Sir, when you spoke of Sha'ik Reborn, you said something . . . about barely recognizing her . . .'

'I did. She was one of Sha'ik's adopted daughters, in Raraku. Of course, as Leoman and I well knew, even that one was . . . not as she seemed. Oh, chosen by the Whirlwind Goddess, well enough, but she was not a child of the desert.'

'She wasn't?'

'No, she was Malazan.'

'*What?*'

The commander's companion grunted and spat. 'Mezla, yes. And the Adjunct never knew – or so we heard. She cut down a helmed, armoured woman. And then walked away. The corpse then vanished. A Mezla killing a Mezla – oh how the gods must have laughed . . .'

'Or,' said Hurlochel in a low voice, 'wept.' He thought to ask more questions regarding this new Sha'ik Reborn, but a succession of tragic images, variants on that fated duel at Raraku, before the seas rose from the desert, raced through his mind. And so he rode in silence up the slope, beside the warriors, and before long was thoroughly consumed with the necessities of reorganizing Mathok's horse-warriors.

So preoccupied, he did not report his conversation to the High Fist.

Three leagues from the City of the Fallen, Paran turned the Host away, and set them on their path for distant Aren. The road that would take them from Seven Cities.

Never to return.

Saur Bathrada and Kholb Harat had walked into an upland village four leagues inland from the harbour city of Sepik. Leading twenty Edur warriors and forty Letherii marines, they had gathered the enslaved degenerate mixed-bloods, ritually freeing the uncomprehending primitives from their symbolic chains, then chaining them in truth for the march back to the city and the Edur ships. Following this, Saur and Kholb had driven the Sepik humans into a sheep pen where a bonfire was built. One by one, mothers were forced to throw their babes and children into the roaring flames. Those women were then raped and, finally, beheaded. Husbands, brothers and fathers were made to watch. When they alone remained alive, they were systematically dismembered and left, armless and legless, to bleed out among bleating, blood-splashed sheep.

A scream had been birthed that day in the heart of Ahlrada Ahn, and it had not ceased its desperate, terrible cry. Rhulad's shadow covered the Tiste Edur, no matter how distant that throne and the insane creature seated upon it. And in that shadow roiled a nightmare from which there could be no awakening.

That scream was echoed in his memories of that day, the shrieks wrung from the throats of burning children, the writhing forms in their bundled flames, the fires reflected on the impassive faces of Edur warriors. Even the Letherii had turned away, overcome with horror. Would that Ahlrada Ahn could have done the same, without losing face. Instead he stood, one among the many, and revealed nothing of what raged inside. Raged, breaking . . . everything. *Within me*, he told himself that night, back in Sepik where the sounds of slaughter continued beyond the room he had found, *within me, nothing is left standing.* On that night, for the first time ever, he considered taking his own life.

A statement of weakness. The others would have seen it in no other way – they could not afford to – so, not a protest, but a surrender, and they would line up to spit upon his corpse. And warriors like Saur Bathrada and Kholb Harat would draw their knives and crouch down, and with pleasure in their eyes they would disfigure the senseless body. For these two Edur had grown to love blood and pain, and in that they were not alone.

The king of Sepik was the last to die. He had been made to witness the obliteration of his cherished people. It was said that he was a benign ruler – *oh how the Edur despised that statement, as if it was an insult, a grievous, vicious insult.* That wretched man collapsing between two warriors who struggled to hold him upright, grasping his grey hair to force his head up, to *see.* Oh, how he'd shrieked and wailed. Until Tomad Sengar wearied of those cries and ordered the king flung from the tower. And, as he fell, his wail became a sound filled with relief. *He looked upon those cobbles, rising fast to meet him, as salvation. And this is our gift. Our only gift.*

Ahlrada Ahn drew out his Merude cutlasses once again, studied their deadly sharp edges. The grips felt good, felt proper, nestled in his large hands. He heard a stirring among the warriors gathered on the deck and looked up to see the one named Taralack Veed pushing through the crowd, at his side Atri-Preda Yan Tovis and in their wake the Jhag known as Icarium.

Taller than most Edur, the silent, sad-faced warrior carried naught but his old, single-edged sword. No bow, no scabbard for the weapon in his right hand, no armour of any kind. Yet Ahlrada Ahn felt a chill whisper through him. *Is he in truth a champion? What will we see this day, beyond the gate?*

Two hundred Edur warriors, the Arapay warlock Sathbaro Rangar – now dragging his malformed hulk on a route that would intercept Icarium – and sixty Letherii archers. All ready, all eager to begin the killing.

The warlock squinted up at the Jhag, who halted before him – not out of deference or even much in the way of attentiveness; rather, because the twisted old man blocked his path. 'I see,' Sathbaro Rangar said in a rasp, 'in you . . . nothing. Vast emptiness, as if you are not even here. And your companion claims you to be a great warrior? I think we are deceived.'

Icarium said nothing.

The human named Taralack Veed stepped forward, pausing to spit on his hands and sweep them back through his hair. 'Warlock,' he said in passable trader's tongue, 'when the fight begins, you shall see the birth of all that waits within him. This I promise. Icarium exists to destroy, exists to fight, I mean to say, and that is all—'

'Then why does he weep at your words?' Tomad Sengar asked from behind Ahlrada Ahn.

Taralack Veed turned, then bowed low. 'Preda, he grieves for what is lost within him, for all that your warlock perceives . . . the absence, the empty vessel. It is no matter.'

'*It is no matter.*' Ahlrada Ahn did not believe that. He could not. *You fools! Look at him! What you see, Sathbaro Rangar, is nothing more than* loss. *Do none of you grasp the significance of that? What do we invite among us?* And this Taralack Veed, this foul-smelling savage, *see how nervous he looks, as if he himself dreads what is coming – no, I am not blind to the eager light in his eyes, but I see fear there, too. It cries out in his every gesture.*

What are we about to do here?

Tomad Sengar said, 'Warlock, prepare the path.'

At that, everyone readied their weapons. Saur Bathrada and Kholb Harat would lead, followed by Sathbaro Rangar himself, and then Taralack and his charge, with the bulk of the Edur behind them, and the Letherii appearing last, arrows nocked.

This would be Ahlrada Ahn's first foray against the guardians of the throne. But he had heard enough tales. Battle without quarter. Battle as vicious as any the Edur had experienced. He adjusted his grip on the cutlasses and moved into position, in the front line of the main body. Low-voiced greetings reached him – every Edur warrior emboldened by Ahlrada Ahn's presence in their ranks. *Spearbreaker. Fearless, as if eager for death.*

Oh yes, I am that indeed. Death. My own.

And yet . . . do I not still dream of going home?

He watched the ragged gate blister the air, then split wide, limned in grey flames, its maw nothing but blurred darkness.

The warlock stepped to one side, and Saur and Kholb lunged into it, vanished into the gloom. Sathbaro Rangar followed, then Taralack and Icarium. And it was Ahlrada Ahn's turn. He pushed himself forward, into the void—

—and stumbled onto crackling loam, the air sweet with forest scents. As with the world they had just left, it was late afternoon. Continuing to move forward, Ahlrada Ahn looked around. They were alone, unopposed.

He heard Icarium ask, 'Where are we?'

And the Arapay warlock turned. 'Drift Avalii, warrior. Where resides the Throne of Shadow.'

'And who guards it?' Taralack Veed demanded. 'Where is this fierce enemy of yours?'

Sathbaro Rangar lifted his head, as if sniffing the air, then he grunted in surprise. 'The demons have fled. They have fled! Why? Why did they yield us the throne? After all those battles? I do not understand.'

Ahlrada Ahn glanced over at Icarium. *Demons . . . fleeing.*

'I do not understand this,' the warlock said again.

Perhaps I do. Oh Sisters, who now walks among us?

He was startled, then, by a faint whispering sound, and he whirled, weapons lifting.

But it was naught but an owl, gliding away down the wide path before them.

He saw a flicker of motion among the humus, and the raptor's talons snapped down. The owl then flapped upward once more, a tiny broken form clutched in its reptilian grip.

'No matter,' the Arapay warlock was saying. 'Let us go claim our throne.' And he set off, hobbling, dragging one bent leg, down the trail.

Baffled, Taralack Veed faced Icarium. 'What do you sense? Of this place?'

The eyes that regarded him were flat. 'The Shadow demons left with our arrival. There was . . . someone . . . a man, but he too is gone. Some time past. He is the one I would have faced.'

'Skilled enough to unleash you, Icarium?'

'Skilled enough, perhaps, to kill me, Taralack Veed.'

'Impossible.'

'Nothing is impossible,' Icarium said.

726

They set off after the half-dozen Edur who had hastened ahead to join Sathbaro Rangar.

Fifteen paces down the path they came upon the first signs of past battle. Bloated bodies of dead aptorians and azalan demons. They would not have fallen easily, Taralack Veed knew. He had heard of egregious losses among the Edur and, especially, the Letherii. Those bodies had been recovered.

A short distance beyond rose the walls of an overgrown courtyard. The gate had been shattered. Icarium trailing a step behind, Taralack Veed followed the others into the compound, then the Jhag reached out and halted the Gral. 'No further.'

'What?'

There was an odd expression on Icarium's face. 'There is no need.'

Ahlrada Ahn, along with Saur and Kholb, accompanied the Arapay warlock into the shadowy, refuse-filled chamber of the throne room. The Seat of Shadow, the soul of Kurald Emurlahn, the throne that needed to be claimed, before the sundered realm could be returned to what it once was, a warren whole, seething with power.

Perhaps, with this, Rhulad could break the—

Sathbaro Rangar cried out, a terrible sound, and he staggered.

Ahlrada Ahn's thoughts fell away. He stared.

The Throne of Shadow, there on a raised dais at the far end of the room . . .

It has been destroyed.

Smashed to pieces, the black wood splintered to reveal its blood-red heartwood. *The demons yielded us . . . nothing. The Throne of Kurald Emurlahn is lost to us.*

The warlock was on his knees, shrieking at the stained ceiling. Saur and Kholb stood, weapons out, yet seemingly frozen in place.

Ahlrada Ahn strode up to Sathbaro Rangar and grasped the warlock by the collar, then pulled him onto his feet. 'Enough of this,' he said. 'Gather yourself. We may be done here, but we are not done – you know this. The warriors will be thirsting for slaughter, now. You must return to the gate – there is another throne to be won, and those defending it will not flee as these ones have done here. Attend to yourself, Sathbaro Rangar!'

'Yes,' the warlock gasped, tugging free from Ahlrada Ahn's grip. 'Yes, you speak truth, warrior. Slaughter, yes, that is what is needed. Come, let us depart – ah, in the name of Father Bloodeye, let us *leave this place*!'

'They return,' Taralack Veed said, as the Tiste Edur reappeared at the entrance to the temple. 'The warlock, he looks . . . aggrieved. What has happened?'

Icarium said nothing, but something glittered in his eyes.

'Jhag,' snarled Sathbaro Rangar as he limped past, 'gather yourself. A true battle awaits us.'

Confusion among the ranks of Edur, words exchanged, then an outcry, curses, bellows of fury. The anger spread out, a wildfire suddenly eager to devour all that would dare oppose it. Wheeling about, hastening towards the flickering gate.

They were not returning to the ships.

Taralack Veed had heard, from Twilight, that an Edur commander named Hanradi Khalag had been sending his warriors against another foe, through a gate – one that led, in a journey of days, to yet another private war. And it was these enemies who would now face the wrath of these Edur here. *And that of Icarium.*

So they shall see, after all. That is good.

At his side there came a sound from the Jhag that drew Taralack Veed around in surprise. Low laughter.

'You are amused?' he asked Icarium in a hoarse whisper.

'Of Shadow both,' the Jhag said enigmatically, 'the weaver deceives the worshipper. But I will say nothing. I am, after all, *empty.*'

'I do not understand.'

'No matter, Taralack Veed. No matter.'

The throne room was abandoned once more, dust settling, shadows slinking back to their predictable haunts. And, from the shattered throne itself, there grew a faint shimmering, a blurring of edges, then a wavering that would have alarmed any who witnessed it – but of such sentient creatures there were none.

The broken, crushed fragments of wood melted away.

And once more there on the dais stood the Throne of Shadow. And stepping free of it, a shadowy form more solid than any other. Hunched, short, shrouded in folds of midnight gauze. From the indistinct smudge where a face belonged, only the eyes were visible, momentarily, a glinting flash.

The figure moved away from the throne, towards the doorway . . . silver and ebony cane tapping on the pavestones.

A short while later it reached the temple's entrance and looked out. There, at the gate, walked the last of them. A Gral, and the chilling, dread apparition that was Icarium.

A catch of breath from the huddling shadow beneath the arched frame, as the Jhag paused once to glance back.

And Shadowthrone caught, in Icarium's expression, something

like a smile, then the faintest of nods, before the Jhag turned away.

The god cocked his head, listening to the party hurry back up the path.

A short time later and they were gone, back through their gate.

Meticulous illusion, crafted with genius, triggered by the arrival of strangers – of, indeed, any but Shadowthrone himself – triggered to transform into a shattered, powerless wreck. Meanas, bound with Mockra, flung across the span of the chamber, invisible strands webbing the formal entrance. Mockra, filaments of suggestion, invitation, the surrendering of natural scepticism, easing the way to witness the broken throne.

Lesser warrens, yet manipulated by a god's hands, and not any god's hands, either. No . . . *mine!*

The Edur were gone.

'Idiots.'

'Three sorceror kings,' Destriant Run'Thurvian said, 'rule Shal-Morzinn. They will contest our passage, Adjunct Tavore Paran, and this cannot be permitted.'

'We would seek to negotiate,' the Adjunct said. 'Indeed, to purchase supplies from them. Why would they oppose this?'

'Because it pleases them to do so.'

'And they are formidable?'

'Formidable? It may well prove,' the Destriant said, 'that even with the assistance of your sorcerors, including your High Mage here, we will suffer severe, perhaps devastating losses should we clash with them. Losses sufficient to drive us back, even to destroy us utterly.'

The Adjunct frowned across at Admiral Nok, then at Quick Ben.

The latter shrugged. 'I don't even know who they are and I hate them already.'

Keneb grunted. *Some High Mage.*

'What, Destriant Run'Thurvian, do you suggest?'

'We have prepared for this, Adjunct, and with the assistance of your sorcerors, we believe we can succeed in our intention.'

'A gate,' Quick Ben said.

'Yes. The Realm of Fanderay and Togg possesses seas. Harsh, fierce seas, but navigable nonetheless. It would not be wise to extend our journey in that realm overlong – the risks are too vast – but I believe we can survive them long enough to, upon re-emerging, find ourselves off the Dal Honese Horn of Quon Tali.'

'How long will that take?' Admiral Nok asked.

'Days instead of months, sir,' the Destriant replied.

'Risks, you said,' Keneb ventured. 'What kind of risks?'

'Natural forces, Fist. Storms, submerged ice; in that realm the sea levels have plunged, for ice grips many lands. It is a world caught in the midst of catastrophic changes. Even so, the season we shall enter is the least violent – in that, we are most fortunate.'

Quick Ben snorted. 'Forgive me, Destriant, but I sense nothing fortuitous in all this. We have some savanna spirit driving us along with these winds, as if every moment gained is somehow crucial. A *savannah* spirit, for Hood's sake. And now, you've worked a ritual to fashion an enormous gate on the seas. That ritual must have been begun months ago—'

'Two years, High Mage.'

'Two years! You said you were waiting for us – you knew we were coming – *two years ago?* Just how many spirits and gods are pushing us around here?'

The Destriant said nothing, folding his hands together before him on the map-table.

'Two years,' Quick Ben muttered.

'From you, High Mage, we require raw power – taxing, yes, but not so arduous as to leave you damaged.'

'Oh, that's nice.'

'High Mage,' the Adjunct said, 'you will make yourself available to the Grey Helms.'

He sighed, then nodded.

'How soon, Destriant?' Admiral Nok asked. 'And how shall we align the fleet?'

'Three ships across at the most, two cables apart, no more – the span of a shortbow arrow's flight between each. I suggest you begin readying your fleet immediately, sir. The gate shall be opened at dawn tomorrow.'

Nok rose. 'Then I must take my leave. Adjunct.'

Keneb studied Quick Ben on the other side of the table. The High Mage looked miserable.

Kalam waited until Quick Ben emerged onto the mid deck, then made his way over. 'What's got you shaking in your boots?' he asked.

'Never mind. If you're here to badger me about something – anything – I'm not in the mood.'

'I just had a question,' the assassin said, 'but I need to ask it in private.'

'Our hole in the knuckle below.'

'Good idea.'

A short time later they crouched once more in the narrow unlit aisle between crates and bales. 'It's this,' Kalam said, dispensing with any small talk. 'The Adjunct.'

'What about her?'

'I'm nervous.'

'Oh, how sad for you. Take it from me, it beats being scared witless, Kalam.'

'The Adjunct.'

'What is that? A question?'

'I need to know, Quick. Are you with her?'

'With her? In what? In bed? No. T'amber would kill me. Now, maybe if she decided to join in it'd be a different matter—'

'What in Hood's name are you going on about, Quick?'

'Sorry. With her, you asked.' He paused, rubbed at his face. 'Things are going to get ugly.'

'I know that! That's why I'm asking, idiot!'

'Calm down. No reason to panic—'

'Isn't there?'

Quick Ben shifted from rubbing his face to scratching it, then he pulled his hands away and blinked tearily at the assassin. 'Look what's happening to me, and it's all your damned fault—'

'Mine?'

'Well, it's somebody's, is what I'm saying. You're here so it might as well be you, Kal.'

'Fine, have it that way. You haven't answered me yet.'

'Are you?' the wizard countered.

'With her? I don't know. That's the problem.'

'Me neither. I don't know. She's a hard one to like, almost as hard to hate, since if you look back, there's nothing really to do either with, right?'

'You're starting to not make sense, Quick.'

'So what?'

'So you don't know, and I don't know. I don't know about you,' Kalam said, 'but I hate not knowing. I even hate you not knowing.'

'That's because, back then, Laseen talked you onto her side. You went to kill her, remember? And she turned you round. But now you're here, with the Adjunct, and we're on our way back, to *her*. And you don't know if anything's changed, or if it's *all* changed. It was one thing standing with Whiskeyjack. Even Dujek. We knew them. But the Adjunct . . . well . . . things aren't so simple.'

'Thank you, Quick, for reiterating everything I've just been telling you.'

'My pleasure. Now, are we done here?'

'Sorry, in need of changing your loincloth again, are you?'

'You have no idea what we're about to do, Kal. What I suggest is, come tomorrow morning, you head back down here, close your eyes and wait. Wait, and wait. Don't move. Or try not to. You might get tossed round a bit, and maybe these bales will come down on you. In fact, you might end up getting crushed like a gnat, so better you stay up top. Eyes closed, though. Closed until I say otherwise.'

'I don't believe you.'

The High Mage scowled. 'All right. Maybe I was trying to scare you. It'll be rough, though. That much is true. And over on the *Silanda*, Fiddler will be heaving his guts out.'

Kalam, thinking on it, suddenly smiled. 'That cheers me up.'

'Me too.'

Like a tidal flow clashing at the mouth of a raging river, walls of water rose in white, churning explosions on all sides as the *Silanda* lunged, prow plunging, into the maelstrom of the massive gate. Beyond was a sky transformed, steel, silver and grey, the tumult of atmospheric convulsions seeming to tumble down, as if but moments from crushing the score of ships already through. The scale to Bottle's eyes was all wrong. Moments earlier their warship had been but a cable behind the *Froth Wolf*, and now the Adjunct's flagship was a third of a league distant, dwarfed by the looming clouds and heaving swells.

Huddled beside Bottle, hands gripping the rail, Fiddler spat out the last of his breakfast, too sick to curse, too miserable to even so much as look up—

Which was likely a good thing, Bottle decided, as he listened to other marines being sick all around him, and the shouts – close to panic – from the scrambling sailors on the transport wallowing in their wake.

Gesler began blasting on that damned whistle as the ship rose above a huge swell – and Bottle almost cried out to see the stern of the *Froth Wolf* rearing immediately in front of them. Twisting round, he looked back, to see the sorcerous gate far away, its raging mouth filled with ships – that worked clear, then plunged, suddenly close, behind the *Silanda*.

By the Abyss! We're damned near flying here!

He could see, to starboard, a mass of icebergs spilling out from the white-lined horizon – a wall of ice, he realized. Whilst to port rose a wind-battered coastline, thrashing deciduous trees – oak, arbutus – and here and there clumps of white pine, their tall trunks rocking back and forth with every savage gust. Between the fleet and that shore, there were seals, their heads dotting the waves, the rocky beaches crowded with the beasts.

'Bottle,' Fiddler croaked, still not looking up, 'tell me some good news.'

'We're through the gate, Sergeant. It's rough, and it looks like we got a sea full of icebergs closing in to starboard – no, not that close yet, I think we'll outrun them. I'll wager the whole fleet's through now. Gods, those Perish catamarans look like they were made for this. Lucky bastards. Anyway, rumour is this won't be long, here in this realm – Sergeant?'

But the man was crawling away, heading for the hatch.

'Sergeant?'

'I said good news, Bottle. Like, we're all about to drop off the world's edge. Something like that.'

'Oh. Well,' he called out as the man slithered across the deck, 'there's seals!'

The night of the green storm far to the north, four Malazan dromons slid into the harbour of Malaz City, the flags upon their masts indicating that they were from the Jakatakan Fleet, whose task it was to patrol the seas from Malaz Island west, to the island of Geni and on to the Horn of the mainland. There had been clashes a few months past with some unknown fleet, but the invaders had been driven away, albeit at some cost. At full strength, the Jakatakan Fleet sailed twenty-seven dromons and sixteen resupply ships. It was rumoured that eleven dromons had been lost in the multiple skirmishes with the foreign barbarians, although Banaschar, upon hearing all this, suspected that the numbers were either an exaggeration or – in accordance with the policy of minimizing imperial losses – the opposite. The truth of the matter was, he didn't believe much of anything any more, no matter the source.

Coop's was crowded, with a lot of in and out as denizens repeatedly tramped outside to watch the northern night sky – where there was no night at all – then returned with still more expostulations, which in turn triggered yet another exodus. And so on.

Banaschar was indifferent to the rushing about – like dogs on the trail, darting from master to home and back again. Endless and brainless, really.

Whatever was going on up there was well beyond the horizon. Although, given that, Banaschar reluctantly concluded, it was *big*.

But far away, so far away he quickly lost interest, at least after the first pitcher of ale had been drained. In any case, the four dromons that had just arrived had delivered a score of castaways. Found on a remote reef island southwest of the Horn (and what, Banaschar wondered briefly, were the dromons doing out there?), they had been picked up, brought to Malaz Island with four ships that had been losing a battle with shipping water, and this very night the castaways had disembarked into the glorious city of Malaz.

Now finding castaways was not entirely uncommon, but what made these ones interesting was that only two of them were Malazans. As for the others . . . Banaschar lifted his head from his cup, frowned across at his now regular drinking partner, Master Sergeant Braven Tooth, then over at the newcomers huddled round the long table at the back. The ex-priest wasn't alone in casting glances in that direction, but the castaways clearly weren't interested in conversation with anyone but themselves – and there didn't seem to be much of that, either, Banaschar noted.

The two Malazans were both drunk, the quiet kind, the miserable kind. The others were not drinking much – seven in all to share a single carafe of wine.

Damned unnatural, as far as Banaschar was concerned. But that in itself was hardly surprising, was it? Those seven were Tiste Andii.

'I know one of those two, you know,' Braven Tooth said.

'What?'

'Them Malazans. They saw me. Earlier, when they came in. One of them went white. That's how I could tell.'

Banaschar grunted. 'Most veterans who come in here do that the first time they see you, Braven Tooth. Some of them do that *every* time. How's that feel, b'the way? Striking terror in everyone you ever trained?'

'Feels good. Besides, it's not everyone I trained. Jus' most of 'em. I'm used to it.'

'Why don't you drag them two over here, then? Get their story – what in Hood's name are they doing with damned Tiste Andii, anyway? Of course, with the feel in the air outside, there's a good chance those fools won't last the night. Wickans, Seven Cities, Korelri, Tiste Andii – foreigners one and all. And the mob's got its nose up and hackles rising. This city is about to explode.'

'Ain't never seen this afore,' Braven Tooth muttered. 'This . . . hate. The old empire was never like that. Damn, it was the bloody opposite. Look around, Banaschar, if y'can focus past that drink in your hand, and you'll see it. Fear, paranoia, closed minds and bared teeth. You voice a complaint out loud these days and you'll end up cut to pieces in some alley. Was never like this afore, Banaschar. Never.'

'Drag one over.'

'I heard the story already.'

'Really? Wasn't you sitting here wi'me all night tonight?'

'No, I was over there for most of a bell – you never noticed – I don't even think you looked up. You're a big sea sponge, Banaschar, and the more you pour in the thirstier you get.'

'I'm being followed.'

'So you keep saying.'

'They're going to kill me.'

'Why? They can just sit back and wait for you to kill yourself.'

'They're impatient.'

'So I ask again, Banaschar, why?'

'They don't want me to reach through to him. To Tayschrenn, you see. It's all about Tayschrenn, locked up there in Mock's Hold. They brought the bricks, but he's mixed the mortar. I got to talk to him, and they won't let me. They'll kill me if I even try.' He waved wildly towards the door. 'I head out, right now, and start walking to the Stairs, and I'm dead.'

'That damned secret of yours, that's what's going to kill you, Banaschar. It's what's killing you right now.'

'She's cursed me.'

'Who has?'

'D'rek, of course. The Worm in my gut, in my brain, the worm that's eating me from the inside out. So what was the story?'

Braven Tooth scratched the bristling hair beneath his throat, then leaned back. 'Marine recruit Mudslinger. Forget the name he started with, Mudslinger is the one I gave 'im. It fits, 'course. They always fit. He was a tough one, though, a survivor, and tonight's proof of that. The other one's named Gentur. Kanese, I think – not one of mine. Anyway, they was shipwrecked after a battle with the grey-skinned barbarians. Ended up on Drift Avalii, where things got real messy. Seems those barbarians, they was looking for Drift Avalii all along. Well, there were Tiste Andii living on it, and before anyone could spit there was a huge fight between them and the barbarians. An ugly one. Before long Mudslinger and the others with 'im were fighting alongside those Tiste Andii, along with someone named Traveller. The short of it is, Traveller told them all to leave, said he'd take on the barbarians by 'imself and anybody else around was jus' in the way. So they did. Leave, I mean. Only t'get hit by a damned storm, and what was left of 'em fetched up on an atoll, where they spent months drinking coconut milk and eating clams.' Braven Tooth reached for his tankard. 'And that's Mudslinger's story, when he was sober, which he's not any more. The one named Traveller, he's the one that interests me . . . something familiar about him, the way 'Slinger d'scribes 'im, the way he fought – killing everything fast, wi'out breaking a sweat. Too bad he didn't come wi' these ones.'

Banaschar stared at the huge man opposite him. What was he talking about? Whatever it was, it went on, and on, and on. Travelling fast? Slingers and fights with barbarians. The man was drunk. Drunk and incomprehensible. 'So, what was Mud's story again?'

'I just told you.'

'And what about those Tiste Andii, Braven Tooth? They're going to get killed—'

'No they ain't. See the tallest one there, with the long white hair. His name is Nimander Golit. And that pretty woman beside him, that's Phaed, his first daughter. All seven of 'em are cousins, sisters, brothers, but it's Nimander who leads, since he's the oldest. Nimander says he is the first son of the Son.'

'The what?'

'The Son of Darkness, Banaschar. Know who that is? That's Anomander Rake. Look at 'em, they're all Rake's brood – grand-children mostly, except for Nimander, who's father to a lot of 'em, but not all. Now, maybe someone's got a hate on for foreigners – you really think that someone would be stupid enough to go after the whelps of Anomander Rake?'

Banaschar turned slightly, stared over at the figures. He slowly blinked, then shook his head. 'Not unless they're suicidal.'

'Right, and that's something you'd know all about, ain't it?'

'So, if Anomander Rake is Nimander's father, who was the mother?'

'Ah, you're not completely blind, then. You can see, can't you? Different mothers, for some of 'em. And one of those mothers wasn't no Tiste Andii, was she? Look at Phaed—'

'I can only see the back of her head.'

'Whatever. I looked at her, and I asked her that very same question you just asked me.'

'What?'

' "Who was your mother?" '

'Mine?'

'And she smiled – and I nearly died, Banaschar, and I mean it. Nearly died. Bursting blood vessels in my brain, toppling over nearly died. Anyway, she told me, and it wasn't no Tiste Andii kind of name, and from the looks of her I'd say the other half was human, but then again, can you really tell with these things? Not really.'

'No, really, what was the name?'

'Lady Envy, who used to know Anomander Rake himself, and got her revenge taking his son as a lover. Messy, eh? But if she was anything like that Phaed there, with that smile, well, envy's the only word – for every other woman in the world. Gods below . . . hey, Banaschar, what's wrong? You suddenly look real sick. The ale's not that bad, not like what we had last night, anyway. Look, if you're thinking of fillin' a plate on the tabletop, there ain't no plate, right? And the boards are warped, and that means it'll sluice onto my legs, and that'll get me very annoyed – for Hood's sake, man, draw a damned breath!'

Leaning on the scarred, stained bartop fifteen paces away, the man Banaschar called Foreigner nursed a flagon of Malaz Dark, a brew for which he had acquired a taste, despite the expense. He heard the ex-priest and the Master Sergeant arguing back and forth at a table behind him, something they had been doing a lot of lately. On other nights, Foreigner reflected, he would have joined them, leaning back to enjoy what would be an entertaining – if occasionally sad – performance.

But not tonight.

Not with *them*, sitting back there.

He needed to think, now, and think hard. He needed to come to a decision, and he sensed, with a tremor of fear, that upon that decision rode his destiny.

'Coop, another Dark here, will you?'

The carrack *Drowned Rat* looked eager to pull away from the stone pier south of the rivermouth as the tide tugged fitfully on its way out. Scrubbed hull, fresh paint, and a bizarre lateen rig and centre-stern steering oar had garnered the curious attention of more than a few sailors and fisher folk who'd wandered past in the last few days. Irritating enough, the captain mused, but Oponn was still smiling nice twin smiles, and before long they'd be on their way, finally. Out of this damned city and the sooner the better.

First Mate Palet was lying curled up on the mid deck, still nursing the bruises and knocks he'd taken from a drunken mob the night before. The captain's lizard gaze settled on him for a moment, before moving on. They were docked, trussed up neat, and Vole was perched in his oversized crow's nest – the man was mad as a squirrel with a broken tail – and everything seemed about right, so right, in fact, that the captain's nerves were a taut, tangled mess.

It wasn't just the fever of malice afflicting damned near everyone – with all those acid rumours of betrayal and murder in Seven Cities, and now the unofficial pogrom unleashed against the Wickans – there was, in addition, *all that other stuff.*

Scratching at the stubble on his scalp, Cartheron Crust turned and fixed narrow eyes on Mock's Hold. Mostly dark, of course. Faint glow from the gatehouse top of the Stairs – that would be Lubben, the old hunchback keeper, probably passed out by now as was his wont when-ever the Hold had uninvited guests. Of course, all guests were uninvited, and even though a new Fist had arrived a month ago, that man Aragan had been posted here before and so he knew the way things worked best – and that was lying as low as you could, not once lifting your head above the parapet. *Who knows? Aragan's probably sharing that bottle with Lubben.*

Uninvited guests . . . like High Mage Tayschrenn. Long ago, now, Crust had found himself in that snake's company all too often, and he'd struggled hard not to do something somebody'd probably regret. *Not me, though. The Emperor, maybe. Tayschrenn himself, definitely, but not me.* He would dream of a moment alone, just the two of them. A moment, that was all he'd need. Both hands on that scrawny neck, squeeze and twist. Done. Simple. Problem solved.

What problem? That's what Kellanved would have asked, in his usual apoplectic way. And Crust had an answer waiting. *No idea, Emperor, but I'm sure there was one, maybe two, maybe plenty.* A good enough reply, he figured, although Kellanved might not have agreed. *Dancer would've, though.* Hah.

'Four dromons!' Vole called down suddenly.

Crust stared up at the idiot. 'We're in the harbour! What did you expect? That's it, Vole, no more sending your meals up there – haul your carcass down here!'

'Cutting in from the north, Captain. 'Top the masts . . . something glinting silver . . .'

Crust's scowl deepened. It was damned dark out there. But Vole was never wrong. *Silver . . . that's not good. No, that's plain awful.* He strode over to Palet and nudged the man. 'Get up. Send what's left of the crew back to those warehouses – I don't care who's guarding them, bribe the bastards. I want us low in the water and scuttling outa here like a three-legged crab.'

The man looked up at him with owlish eyes. 'Captain?'

'Did they knock all sense from your brain, Palet? Trouble's coming.'

Sitting up, the First Mate looked round. 'Guards?'

'No, a whole lot troubler.'

'Like what?'

'Like the Empress, you fool.'

Palet was suddenly on his feet. 'Supplies, aye, sir. We're on our way!'

Crust watched the fool scamper. The crew was drunk. Too bad for them. They were sorely undermanned, too. It'd been a bad idea, diving into the bay when old *Ragstopper* went down, what with all those sharks. Four good sailors had been lost that night. *Good sailors, bad swimmers. Funny how that goes together.*

He looked round once more. *Damn, done forgot again, didn't I?* No dinghies. *Well, there's always something.*

Four dromons, visible now, rounding into the bay, backlit by one of the ugliest storms he'd ever seen. Well, not entirely true – he'd seen the like once before, hadn't he? And what had come of it? *Not a whole lot . . . except, that is, a mountain of otataral . . .*

The lead dromon – Laseen's flagship, *The Surly*. Three in her wake. Three, that was a lot – *who in Hood's name has she brought with her? A damned army?*

Uninvited guests.

Poor Aragan.

CHAPTER TWENTY-TWO

Who are these strangers, then, with their familiar faces?
Emerging from the crowd with those indifferent eyes,
and the blood streaming down from their hands.
It is what was hidden before, masked by the common
and the harmless, now wrenching features revealed
in a conflagration of hate and victims tumble underfoot.

Who led and who followed and why do flames thrive
in darkness and all gaze, insensate and uncomprehending,
come the morning light, upon the legacy of unleashed
spite? I am not fooled by wails of horror. I am not moved
by expostulations of grief. For I remember the lurid night,
the visage flashing in firelit puddles of blood was my own.

Who was this stranger, then, with that familiar face?
Melting into the crowd in the fraught, chaotic heave,
and the blood raging in the storm of my skull boils frantic
as I plunge down and lay waste all these innocent lives,
my hate at their weakness a cauldron overturned, whilst
drowning in my own, this stranger, this stranger . . .

> On the Dawn I Take My Life
> The Wickan Pogrom
> Kayessan

A S THE LONGBOAT FROM THE JAKATAKAN FLEET'S FLAGSHIP DREW UP
alongside, the commander and four marines quickly clambered
aboard the *Froth Wolf*.
They were Untan, one and all, bedecked in elaborate, expensive
armour, the commander tall, weak-chinned with a watery, uneasy look

in his pale eyes. He saluted Admiral Nok first, and then the Adjunct.

'We were not expecting you for months, Adjunct Tavore.'

Arms crossed, Fist Keneb stood a short distance away, leaning against the mainmast. After the commander's words, Keneb shifted his attention to the marines. *Is that parade kit you're wearing?* And then he noticed their expressions of disdain and hatred as the soldiers stared over to where stood Nil and Nether. Keneb glanced round, then hesitated.

The Adjunct spoke, 'Your name, Commander?'

A slight bow. 'My apologies, Adjunct. I am Exent Hadar, of House Hadar in Unta, firstborn—'

'I know the family,' Tavore cut in, rather sharply. 'Commander Hadar, tell your marines to stand down immediately – if I see one more hand casually touch a sword grip they can swim back to your ship.'

The commander's pale eyes flicked to Admiral Nok, who said nothing.

Keneb relaxed – he had been about to walk over to strip the hides from those fools. *Adjunct Tavore, you miss nothing, do you? Ever. Why do you continue to surprise me? No, wrong way of putting that – why am I constantly surprised?*

'Apologies again,' Hadar said, his insincerity obvious as he gestured to his guards. 'There have been a succession of, uh, revelations—'

'Regarding what?'

'Wickan complicity in the slaughter of Pormqual's Loyal Army at Aren, Adjunct.'

Keneb stared at the man, dumbfounded. 'Complicity?' His voice was hoarse and the word barely made it out.

The Adjunct's expression was as fierce as Keneb had ever seen on the woman, but it was Admiral Nok who spoke first. 'What insanity is this, Commander Hadar? The loyalty and service of the Wickans was and remains beyond reproach.'

A shrug. 'As I said, Admiral. Revelations.'

'Never mind that,' the Adjunct snapped. 'Commander, what are you doing patrolling these waters?'

'The Empress commanded that we extend our range,' Hadar replied, 'for two reasons. Foremost, there have been incursions from an unknown enemy in black warships. We have had six engagements thus far. Initially, our ship mages were not able to contend with the sorcery the black ships employed, and accordingly we suffered in the exchanges. Since then, however, we have increased the complement and the calibre of our own cadres. Negating the sorcery in the battles evened matters considerably.'

'When was the last encounter?'

741

'Two months past, Adjunct.'

'And the other reason?'

Another slight bow. 'Intercepting you, Adjunct. As I said, however, we were not expecting you for some time. Oddly enough, our precise position right now came by direct command from the Empress herself, four days ago. Needless to say, against this unseasonal gale, we were hard pressed to make it here in time.'

'In time for what?'

Another shrug. 'Why, it turns out, to meet you. It seems obvious,' he added with condescension, 'that the Empress detected your early arrival. In such matters, she is all-knowing, and that is, of course, only to be expected.'

Keneb watched as the Adjunct mulled on these developments, then she said, 'And you are to be our escort to Unta?'

'No, Adjunct. I am to instruct you to change the course of the imperial fleet.'

'To where?'

'Malaz City.'

'Why?'

Commander Hadar shook his head.

'Tell me, if you know,' Tavore said, 'where is the Empress right now?'

'Well, Malaz City, I would think, Adjunct.'

'See that marine on the left?' Kalam asked in a low whisper.

'What of him?' Quick Ben asked with a shrug.

'He's a Claw.'

They stood on the forecastle deck, watching the proceedings below. The air was fresh, warm, the seas surprisingly gentle despite the hard, steady wind. Damned near paradise, the assassin considered, after that wild three days in the raw, tumultuous warren of Togg and Fanderay. The ships of the fleet, barring those of the Perish, were badly battered, especially the transports. None had gone down, fortunately, nor had any sailor or marine been lost. A few dozen horses, alas, had broken legs during the storms, but such attrition was expected, and no-one begrudged fresh meat in the stew-pots. Now, assuming this wind stayed at their backs, Malaz Island was only two days away, maybe a touch more.

With his message delivered, Commander Hadar's haste to leave was pathetically obvious, and it seemed neither the Adjunct nor the Admiral was inclined to stretch out his stay.

As the visitors returned to their longboat, a voice spoke quietly behind Kalam and Quick Ben. 'Did I hear correctly? We are now sailing for Malaz City?'

Kalam fought down a shiver – he'd heard nothing. *Again*. 'Aye, Apsalar—'

But Quick Ben had wheeled round in alarm and, now, anger. 'The damned steps up here are right in front of us! How in Hood's name did you get there, Apsalar? Breathing down our damned backs!'

'Clearly,' the Kanese woman replied, her almond-shaped eyes blinking languidly, 'you were both distracted. Tell me, Kalam Mekhar, have you any theories as to why an agent of the Claw accompanied the Jakatakan commander?'

'Plenty, but I'm not sharing any of them with you.'

She studied him for a moment, then said, 'You are still undecided, aren't you?'

Oh how I want to hit her. Right here, right now. 'You don't know what you're talking about, Apsalar. And I don't, neither.'

'Well, that hardly makes sense—'

'You're right,' Quick Ben snapped, 'it doesn't. Now get out of our shadows, damn you!'

'High Mage, it occurs to me that you are under a certain misapprehension. The Hounds of Shadow, in G'danisban, were after *you*.'

'Opportunistic!'

'Certainly, if you care to believe that. In any case, it should then follow – even for one as immune to logic as you – that I acted then. Alone. The choice was mine, High Mage, and mine alone.'

'What's she talking about, Quick?' Kalam demanded.

But his friend was silent, studying the woman before him. Then he asked, 'Why?'

She smiled. 'I have my reasons, but at the moment, I see no reason to share any of them with you.'

Apsalar then turned away, walked towards the prow.

'It's just that, isn't it?' Quick Ben muttered under his breath.

'What do you mean?'

'Undecided, Kal. We're all undecided. Aren't we?' Then he swung round and looked back down at the Adjunct.

The assassin did the same.

Tavore and Nok were talking, but quietly, their words stolen by the wind.

'Now,' Quick Ben continued, 'is she?'

Undecided? Not about anything, it seems. Kalam grimaced. 'Malaz City. I didn't have much fun the last time I visited. Your skin crawling, Quick? Mine is. Crawling bad.'

'You notice something?' the wizard asked. 'That commander – he didn't ask a damned thing about the Perish ships with us. Now, that

Claw, he must have made his report already, by warren, to Topper or the Empress herself. So . . .'

'So, she knows we've got guests. Maybe that's why she doesn't want us sailing into Unta's harbour.'

'Right, Laseen's rattled.'

Then Kalam grunted. 'I just realized something else,' he said in a low voice.

'What?'

'The Adjunct, she sent the Destriant to her cabin. And she made no formal invitation to the commander the way she's supposed to – no, she made them all discuss things out here, in the open. Anyway, maybe the Adjunct didn't want the commander or that Claw to see Run'Thurvian, or talk to him, about anything.'

'She's no fool.'

'A damned game of Troughs between them, isn't it? Quick Ben, what is going on here?'

'We'll find out, Kal.'

'When?'

The High Mage scowled, then said, 'The moment, friend, we stop being undecided.'

Aboard the *Silanda*, Fiddler had crawled from the hold like a crippled rat, dishevelled, pale and greasy. He spied Bottle and slowly, agonizingly, made his way over. Bottle was feeding out line. There were shoals out there, and he'd seen fish leaping clear of whatever chased them beneath the surface. One of the Jakatakan dromons was sidling past to port, a rock's throw away, and the rest of the squad had lined up to give them a show.

Bottle shook his head, then glanced over as his sergeant arrived. 'Feeling any better?'

'I think so. Gods, I think that nightmare realm cured me.'

'You don't look any better.'

'Thanks, Bottle.' Fiddler pulled himself into a sitting position, then looked over at the rest of the squad. 'Hood's breath!' he exploded. 'What are you doing?!'

Koryk, Smiles, Cuttle and Tarr had joined up with Deadsmell, Throatslitter and Widdershins, standing in a row at the rail, looking across at the passing dromon, and under each soldier's left arm was a Tiste Andii head.

At Fiddler's outburst, Gesler and Stormy appeared on deck.

Bottle watched them take it all in, then Gesler called out, 'Give 'em a wave!'

The soldiers complied, began waving cheerfully across at what seemed to be a mass of staring sailors and marines and – Bottle squinted – officers.

Smiles said, 'It's all right, Sergeant. We just thought they'd appreciate a change of scenery.'

'Who?'

'Why, these heads, of course.'

Then Stormy was running past, towards the stern, where he dragged down his breeches and sat over the rail, his back end hanging open, exposed. With a savage grunt, he began defecating.

And while his comrades lining the rail all turned to stare at the mad corporal, Bottle was transfixed by the ghastly expressions of delight on those severed heads. *Those smiles* – the line in Bottle's hands kept spinning out, then vanished, unnoticed, as sudden nausea clenched his gut.

And he bolted for the opposite rail.

Captain Kindly made a gagging sound. 'That is disgusting.'

Lieutenant Pores nodded. 'I'll say. Gods, what did that man eat to produce *those?*'

A crowd was gathering on the deck as laughing marines and sailors all watched the antics proceeding apace on the *Silanda* half a cable ahead. The Jakatakan dromon was now to port, a mass of onlookers on the decks, silent, watching.

'That is highly unusual,' Pores commented. 'They're not rising to the bait.'

'They look scared witless,' Kindly said.

'So those marines have got themselves a collection of heads,' Pores said, shrugging.

'You idiot. Those heads are still alive.'

'They're what?'

'Alive, Lieutenant. I have this from reliable sources.'

'Even so, sir, since when did Malazans get so soft?'

Kindly regarded him as he would a skewered grub. 'Your powers of observation are truly pathetic. That ship is filled with Untans. Coddled nobleborn pups. Look at those damned uniforms, will you? The only stains they got on 'em is gull shit, and that's because the gulls keep mistaking them for dead, bloated seals.'

'Nice one, sir.'

'Another comment like that,' Kindly said, 'and I'll get the stitcher to sew up your mouth, Lieutenant. Ha, we're changing course.'

'Sir?'

'For Hood's sake, what are those fools doing?'

Pores followed his captain's glare, to the stern of their own ship, where two heavy infantry soldiers were seated side by side, their leggings round their ankles. 'I would hazard a guess, sir, that Hanfeno and Senny are adding their stone's worth.'

'Get back there and make them stop, Lieutenant. Now!'

'Sir?'

'You heard me! And I want those two on report!'

'Stop them, sir? How do I do that?'

'I suggest corks. Now move!'

Pores scrambled.

Oh please, please be finished before I arrive. Please . . .

The send-off to the Jakatakan Fleet encompassed every Malazan ship, a cavalcade of defecation that brought seagulls for leagues round with mad shrieks and wheeling plunges. The Adjunct had not remained on deck for very long, but issued no orders to halt the proceedings. Nor did Admiral Nok, although Keneb noticed that the sailors of the dromon escorts and the transports did not participate. This gesture belonged exclusively to the Fourteenth Army.

And maybe it had some value. Hard to tell with things like this, Keneb knew.

The wind drove them onward, east by southeast now, and before a quarter bell was sounded, the Jakatakans were far behind.

Destriant Run'Thurvian had appeared earlier, and had watched the escapades of the marines on the surrounding ships. Frowning for some time, he eventually spotted Keneb and approached. 'Sir,' he said, 'I am somewhat confused. Is there no honour between elements of the Mezla military?'

'Honour? Not really, Destriant. Rivalries provide the lifeblood, although in this case matters proved somewhat one-sided, and for the reason for that you will have to look to the *Silanda*.'

A sage nod. 'Of course, the ship woven in sorceries, where time itself is denied.'

'Do you know the manner of those sorceries, Destriant?'

'Kurald Emurlahn, Tellann, Telas and a residue of Toblakai, although in this latter case the nature of the power is . . . uncertain. Of course,' he added, 'there is nothing unusual in that. Among the ancient Toblakai – according to our own histories – there could arise individuals, warriors, who became something of a warren unto themselves. Such power varies in its efficacy, and it would appear that this sort of blood talent was waning in the last generations of the Toblakai civilization, growing ever weaker. In any case,' the Destriant added, shrugging, 'as I said, a residue remains on this *Silanda*. Toblakai. Which is rather interesting, since it was believed that the giant race was extinct.'

'There are said to be remnants,' Keneb offered, 'in the Fenn Range of north Quon Tali. Primitive, reclusive . . .'

'Oh yes,' Run'Thurvian said, 'of mixed bloods there are known examples, vastly diminished, of course. The Trell, for example, and a tribe known as the Barghast. Ignorant of past glories, as you suggest. Fist, may I ask you a question?'

'Of course.'

'The Adjunct Tavore. It appears that the relationship with her Empress has become strained. Have I surmised correctly? This is disturbing news, given what awaits us.'

Keneb looked away, then he cleared his throat. 'Destriant, I have no idea what awaits us, although it seems that you do. As for the Empress, again, there is nothing I can imagine to give rise to mutual distrust. The Adjunct is the Hand of the Empress. An extension of Laseen's will.'

'The Empress would not be inclined, therefore,' Run'Thurvian said, 'to sever that hand, yes? I am relieved to hear this.'

'Good . . . why?'

'Because,' the Destriant said, turning away, 'your Fourteenth Army will not be enough.'

If wood could be exhausted by unceasing strain, the ships of the imperial fleet were at their very limits, two bells out from Malaz Island on the night of the second day, when the wind suddenly fell away, a coolness coming into the air, and it seemed that every ship sagged, settling deeper into the swells, and now, in place of the hot dry gale, a softer breeze arrived.

Kalam Mekhar had taken to pacing the deck, restless, his appetite gone and a tightness gripping his guts. As he made his way aft for the thirtieth time since dusk, Quick Ben appeared alongside him.

'Laseen's waiting for us,' the High Mage said. 'And Tayschrenn's there, like a scorpion under a rock. Kal, everything I'm feeling . . .'

'I know, friend.'

'Like I did back outside Pale.'

They turned about and slowly walked forward. Kalam scratched at his beard. 'We had Whiskeyjack, back then. Even Dujek. But now . . .' He growled under his breath, then rolled his shoulders.

'Ain't seen you do that in a long time, Kal, that shrug of yours.'

'Well.'

'That's what I thought.' The High Mage sighed, then he reached out and grasped the assassin's arm as a figure emerged from the gloom before them.

The Adjunct. 'High Mage,' she said in a low voice, 'I want you to cross over to the *Silanda*, by warren.'

'Now?'

'Yes. Is that a problem?'

Kalam sensed his friend's unease, and the assassin cleared his throat. 'Adjunct. The Imperial High Mage Tayschrenn is, uh, dead ahead.'

'He does not quest,' she replied. 'Does he, Quick Ben?'

'No. How did you know that?'

She ignored the question. 'By warren, immediately, High Mage. You are to collect Fiddler, and the soldier named Bottle. Inform the sergeant that the time has come.'

'Adjunct?'

'For a game. He will understand. Then, the three of you are to return here, where you will join myself, Kalam, Fist Keneb, T'amber and Apsalar, in my cabin. You have a quarter of a bell, High Mage. Kalam, come with me now, please.'

One of Fiddler's games.

Gods below, a game!

A moccasined foot thumped into Bottle's side. Grunting, he sat up, still mostly asleep. 'That you, Smiles? Not now . . .' but no, it wasn't Smiles. His heart thumped awake in a savage drumbeat. 'Oh, High Mage, uh. Um. What is it?'

'On your feet,' Quick Ben hissed. 'And quietly, damn you.'

'Too late,' muttered Koryk from his bedroll nearby.

'It had better not be, soldier,' the wizard said. 'Another sound from you and I'll push your head up the next soldier's backside.'

A head lifted from blankets. 'That'd beat the view I got now . . . sir.' Then he settled back down.

Bottle climbed to his feet, chilled yet sweating.

And found himself looking at Fiddler's miserable face, hovering there behind the High Mage. 'Sergeant?'

'Just follow us aft, Bottle.'

The three of them picked their way clear of the sleeping forms on the mid deck.

There was a strange scent in the air, Bottle realized. Familiar, yet . . . 'Sergeant, you're carrying that new Deck of yours . . .'

'You and your damned rat,' muttered Fiddler. 'I knew it, you lying bastard.'

'Wasn't me,' Bottle began, then fell quiet. *Gods below, even for me that was lame. Try something better.* 'Just looking out for you, Sergeant. Your shaved knuckle in the hole, that's me.'

'Hah, where have I heard that before, eh Quick?'

'Quiet, you two. We're going across now. Grab belts . . .'

Bottle blinked, and found himself on another deck, and directly ahead, steps leading down. *Abyss take me, that was fast. Fast and . . . appalling.* Quick Ben waved them into his wake as he descended, ducking the frame, then halting three strides down the corridor, knocking upon a door to his left. It opened at once.

T'amber, the eyes that gave her her name scanning the three men cramped in the narrow corridor. Then she stepped back.

The Adjunct stood behind her chair at the map-table. The rest were seated, and Bottle stared wildly from one to the next. Fist Keneb. Apsalar. Kalam Mekhar.

A low moan from Fiddler.

'Sergeant,' the Adjunct said, 'you have your players.'

Players?

Oh.

Oh no.

'I really don't think this is a good idea,' the sergeant said.

'Perhaps,' the Adjunct replied.

'I agree,' T'amber said. 'Or, rather, my participation . . . as a player. As I said earlier, Tavore—'

'Nonetheless,' the Adjunct cut in, drawing out the empty chair opposite the one reserved for Fiddler and sitting herself down on Keneb's left. She pulled her gloves free. 'Explain the rules, please.'

Keneb watched as Fiddler cast helpless, desperate looks to both Kalam and Quick Ben, but neither would meet his eyes, and both were clearly miserable. Then the sergeant slowly walked over to the last chair. He settled into it. 'That's just it, Adjunct, there ain't no rules, except those I make up as I go.'

'Very well. Begin.'

Fiddler scratched at his greying beard, his eyes fixing on T'amber who sat to the Adjunct's left, directly opposite Keneb. 'This is your Deck,' he said, lifting it into view and setting it down on the tabletop. 'It has new cards in it.'

'Your point?' the young woman demanded.

'Just this. Who in Hood's name are you?'

A shrug. 'Does it matter?'

A grunt from Kalam Mekhar on Keneb's right. Beyond the assassin, on the same side and immediately to Fiddler's left was Apsalar. Bottle was on the sergeant's right, with the High Mage beside him. *The only one who really doesn't belong is me. Where's Blistig? Nok? Temul, Nil and Nether?*

'Last chance,' Fiddler said to the Adjunct. 'We stop this now—'

'Begin, Sergeant.'

'Bottle, find us some wine.'

'Sergeant?'

'First rule. Wine. Everybody gets a cup. Except the dealer, he gets rum. Go to it, Bottle.'

As the young soldier rose Fiddler collected the cards. 'Player on dealer's right has to serve drinks during the first hand.' He flung out a card, face-down, and it slid crookedly to halt in front of Quick Ben. 'High Mage has last card. Last card's dealt out first, but not shown until the end.'

Bottle came back with cups. He set the first one down in front of the Adjunct, then T'amber, Keneb, Quick, Kalam, Apsalar, Fiddler and finally one into the place before his empty chair. As he returned with two jugs, one of wine and the other Falari rum, Fiddler held up a hand and halted him.

In quick succession the sergeant flung out cards, matching the order Bottle had used in setting down the cups.

Suddenly, eight face-up cards marked the field, and Fiddler, gesturing Bottle over with the rum, began talking. 'Dealer gets Soldier of High House Life but it's bittersweet, meaning it's for him and him alone, given this late hour. Empty chair gets Weaver of Life and she needs a bath but nobody's surprised by that. So we got two Life's to start.' Fiddler watched as Bottle poured rum into his cup. 'And that's why Kalam's looking at an Unaligned. Obelisk, the Sleeping Goddess – you're getting a reversed field, Kal, sorry but there's nothing to be done for it.' He downed his rum and held out his cup again, interrupting Bottle's efforts to fill the others with wine. 'Apsalar's got Assassin of High House Shadow, oh, isn't that a surprise. It's the only card she gets—'

'You mean I win?' she asked, one brow lifting sardonically.

'And lose, too. Nice move, interrupting me like that, you're catching on. Now, nobody else say a damned thing unless you want to up the ante.' He drank down his second cupful. 'Poor Quick Ben, he's got Lifeslayer to deal with, and that puts him in a hole, but not the hole he thinks he's in – a different hole. Now T'amber, she's opened the game with that card. Throne, and it's shifting every which way. The pivot card, then—'

'What's a pivot card?' Bottle asked, finally sitting down.

'Bastard – knew I couldn't trust you. It's the hinge, of course. Finish that wine – you got to drink rum now. You're a sharp one, ain't you? Now Fist Keneb, well, that's a curious one. Lord of Wolves, the throne card of High House War, and aren't they looking baleful – Fist, where's Grub hiding these days?'

'On Nok's ship,' Keneb replied, bewildered and strangely frightened.

'Well, that knocks you outa the game, though you still get four more cards, since we've made a course correction and the northeast head-land's rising up two pegs to starboard. In seventy heartbeats we'll be sliding closest to that rocky coast, and Nok's ship will be even closer, and Grub will dive overboard. He's got three friends living in the caves in the cliff and here are their cards—' Three more skidded out to just beyond the centre of the table. 'Crown, Sceptre, Orb. Hmm, let's ignore those for now.'

Keneb half-rose. *'Diving overboard?'*

'Relax, he'll be back. So, we get to the Adjunct's card. House of War, Guardians of the Road, or the Dead – title's uncertain so take your pick.' He threw another card and it slid up beside it. 'Oponn. As I thought. Decisions yet to be made. Will it be the Push or the Pull? And what's that got to do with this one?' A skitter, ending up in the middle, opposite both Kalam and Quick Ben – 'Herald of High House Death. A distinctly inactive and out-of-date card in this field, but I see a Rusty Gauntlet—'

'A what?' demanded Kalam Mekhar.

'Right here before me. A new drink that Bottle in his inebriated state just invented. Rum and wine – half and half, soldier, fill us up – you too, that's what you get for making that face.'

Keneb rubbed at his own face. He'd taken but a single mouthful of the wine, but he felt drunk. *Hot in here.* He started as four cards appeared in a row in front of the one already before him.

'Spinner of Death, Queen of Dark, Queen of Life and, ho, the King in Chains. Like hopping stones across a stream, isn't it? Expecting to see your wife any time soon, Fist? Forget it. She's set you aside for an Untan noble, and my, if it isn't Exent Hadar – I bet he kept his gaze averted back then, probably ignored you outright, that's both guilt and smugness, you know. Must have been the weak chin that stole her heart – but look at you, sir, you look damned relieved and that's a hand that tops us all and even though you were out when it comes to winning you're back in when it comes to losing, but in this case you win when you lose, so relax.'

'Well,' muttered Bottle, 'hope I nev'win one a theez'ands.'

'No,' Fiddler said to him, 'you got it easy. She plays and she takes, and so—' A card clattered before the owl-eyed soldier. 'Deathslayer. You can sleep now, Bottle, you're done as done for the night.'

The man's eyes promptly closed and he slid down from his chair, the piece of furniture scraping back. Keneb heard the man's head thump on the boards, once.

Yes, that'd be nice. Exent Hadar. Gods, woman, really!

'So how does Kalam get from Herald Death to Obelisk? Let's see. Ah, King of High House Shadows! That shifty slime bung, oh, doesn't he look smug! Despite the sweat on his upper lip – who's gone all chilled in here? Hands up, please.'

Reluctantly . . . Kalam, T'amber, then Apsalar all lifted hands.

'Well, that's ugly as ugly gets – you've got the bottles now, Apsalar, now that Bottle's corked. This one's for you, T'amber. Virgin of Death, as far as you go. You're out, so relax. Kalam's cold, but he don't get another card 'cause he don't need one and now I know who gets pushed and who gets pulled and I'll add the name to the dirge to come. Now for the hot bloods. Quick Ben gets the Consort in Chains but he's from Seven Cities and he just saved his sister's life so it's not as bad as it could've been. Anyway, that's it for you. And so, who does that leave?'

Silence for a moment. Keneb managed to lift his leaden head, frowning confusedly at the scatter of cards all over the table.

'That would be me and you, Sergeant,' the Adjunct said in a low voice.

'You cold?' Fiddler asked her, drinking down yet another cup of Rusty Gauntlet.

'No.'

'Hot?'

'No.'

Fiddler nodded, slamming his empty cup down for Apsalar to refill with wine and rum. 'Aye,' He floated a card down the length of the table. It landed atop the first card. 'Master of the Deck. Ganoes Paran, Adjunct. Your brother. Even cold iron, Tavore Paran, needs tempering.' He lifted up another card and set it down before him. 'Priest of Life, hah, now that's a good one. Game's done.'

'Who wins?' the Adjunct, her face pale as candlewax, asked in a whisper.

'Nobody,' Fiddler replied. 'That's Life for you.' He suddenly rose, tottered, then staggered for the door.

'Hold it!' Quick Ben demanded behind him. 'There's this face-down card in front of me! You said it closes the game!'

'It just did,' mumbled the sergeant as he struggled with the latch.

'Do I turn it over, then?'

'No.'

Fiddler stumbled out into the corridor and Keneb listened to the man's ragged footsteps receding towards the stairs leading to the deck. The Fist, shaking his head, pushed himself upright. He looked at the others.

No-one else had moved.

Then, with a snort, Apsalar rose and walked out. If she was as drunk as Keneb felt, she did not show any signs of it.

A moment later both Quick Ben and Kalam followed.

Under the table, Bottle was snoring.

The Adjunct and T'amber, Keneb slowly realized, were both looking at the unturned card. Then, with a hiss of frustration, Tavore reached out and flipped it over. After a moment, she half-rose and leaned forward on the table to read its title. 'Knight of Shadow. I have never heard of such a card. T'amber, who, what did you—'

'I didn't,' T'amber interrupted.

'You didn't what?'

She looked up at the Adjunct. 'Tavore, I have never seen that card before, and I certainly didn't paint it.'

Both women were silent again, both staring down at the strange card. Keneb struggled to focus on its murky image. 'That's one of those Greyskins,' he said.

'Tiste Edur,' T'amber murmured.

'With a spear,' the Fist continued. 'A Greyskin, like the ones we saw on those black ships . . .' Keneb leaned back, his head swimming. 'I don't feel very well.'

'Please stay for a moment, Fist. T'amber, what just happened here?'

The other woman shook her head. 'I have never seen a field laid in such a manner. It was . . . chaotic – sorry, I did not mean that in an elemental sense. Like a rock bouncing down a gorge, ricocheting from this and that, yet, everywhere it struck, it struck true.'

'Can you make sense of it?'

'Not much. Not yet.' She hesitated, scanning the cards scattered all over the map-table. 'Oponn's presence was . . . unexpected.'

'The push or the pull,' Keneb said. 'Someone's undecided about something, that's what Fiddler said. Who was it again?'

'Kalam Mekhar,' the Adjunct replied. 'But the Herald of Death intervenes—'

'Not the Herald,' cut in T'amber, 'but an inactive version, a detail I believe is crucial.'

Muted shouts from beyond announced the sighting of Malaz Harbour. The Adjunct faced Keneb. 'Fist, these are your orders for this night. You are in command of the Fourteenth. No-one is to disembark, barring those I will dispatch on my own behalf. With the exception of the *Froth Wolf* all other ships are to remain in the harbour itself – all commands directing the fleet to tie up at a pier or jetty are to be ignored until I inform you otherwise.'

'Adjunct, any such orders, if they reach me, will be from the Empress herself. I am to ignore those?'

'You are to misunderstand, Fist. I leave the details of that misunderstanding to your imagination.'

'Adjunct, where will you be?'

The woman studied him for a moment, then it seemed she reached a decision. 'Fist Keneb, the Empress awaits me in Mock's Hold. I expect she will not wait until morning to issue her summons.' A flicker of emotion in her face. 'The soldiers of the Fourteenth Army do not return as heroes, it would appear. I will not expose their lives to unnecessary risks. In particular I speak of the Wickans and the Khundryl Burned Tears. As for the Perish, the nature of their alliance depends upon my conversation with the Empress. Unless circumstances warrant a change, I assume their disposition rests with Laseen, but I must await her word on that. Ultimately, Fist, it is for Mortal Sword Krughava – do the Perish disembark and present to the Empress as they did with us, or, if events turn unfortunate, do they leave? My point is this, Keneb, they must be free to choose.'

'And Admiral Nok's view on that?'

'We are agreed.'

'Adjunct,' said Keneb, 'if the Empress decides to attempt to stay the Perish, we could end up with a battle in Malaz Harbour. Malazan against Malazan. This could start a damned civil war.'

Tavore frowned. 'I do not anticipate anything so extreme, Fist.'

But Keneb persisted. 'Forgive me, but I believe it is you who mis-understands. The Perish swore service to *you*, not the Empress.'

'She will not listen to that,' T'amber said, with an unexpected tone of frustration in her voice, even as she walked to where Bottle slept. A kick elicted a grunt, then a cough. 'Up, soldier,' T'amber said, seemingly unmindful of the glare the Adjunct had fixed upon her.

No you fool, Keneb, hardly unmindful.

'You have your orders, Fist,' Tavore said.

'Aye, Adjunct. Do you wish me to drag this marine here out with me?'

'No. I must speak with Bottle in private. Go now, Keneb. And thank you for attending this night.'

I'm fairly certain I had no choice. At the doorway he looked back once more at the cards. Lord of Wolves, Spinner of Death, Queens of Dark and Life, and the King in Chains. *Lord of Wolves . . . that has to be the Perish.*

Gods below, I think it's begun.

On the harbour-facing wall of Mock's Hold, Pearl stood at the parapet, watching the dark shapes of the imperial fleet slowly swing round into the calm waters of the bay. Huge transports, like oversized bhederin, and the dromon escorts on the flanks lean as wolves. The Claw's eyes narrowed as he attempted to make out the foreign ships in the midst of the others. Enormous, twin-hulled . . . formidable. There seemed to be a lot of them.

How had they come here so quickly? And how did the Empress know that they would? The only possibility in answer to the first question was: *by warren*. Yet, who among the Adjunct's retinue could fashion a gate of such power and breadth? Quick Ben? Pearl did not think that likely. That bastard liked his secrets, and he liked playing both a weakling and something considerably deadlier, but neither conceit impressed Pearl. No, Tavore's High Mage didn't have what was necessary to open such a massive rift.

Leaving those damned foreigners. And that was very troubling indeed. Perhaps it might prove a propitious moment for some kind of pre-emptive, covert action. Which would, now that the Empress had arrived, be possible after all. And expedient – *for we have no idea who has now come among us, right to the heart of the empire. A foreign navy, arriving virtually unopposed . . . within striking distance of the Empress herself.*

It was going to be a busy night.

'Pearl.'

The voice was low, yet he did not need to turn round to know who had spoken. He knew, as well, that Empress Laseen would frown disapprovingly should he turn to face her. Odd habits, that way. *No, just paranoia.* 'Good evening, Empress.'

'Does this view please you?'

Pearl grimaced. 'She has arrived. In all, well timed for everyone concerned.'

'Do you look forward to seeing her again?'

'I travelled in her company for some time, Empress.'

'And?'

'And, to answer your question, I am . . . indifferent.'

'My Adjunct does not inspire loyalty?'

'Not with me, Empress. Nor, I think, with the soldiers of the Fourteenth Army.'

'And yet, Pearl, has she failed them? Even once?'

'Y'Ghatan—'

The seemingly disembodied voice interrupted him. 'Do not be a fool. This is you and I, Pearl, speaking here. In absolute private. What occurred at Y'Ghatan could not have been anticipated, by anyone. Given that, Adjunct Tavore's actions were proper and, indeed, laudable.'

'Very well,' Pearl said, remembering that night of flames . . . the distant screams he could hear from inside his tent – *when in my anger and hurt, I hid, like some child.* 'Facts aside, Empress, the matter hinges upon how one is perceived.'

'Assuredly so.'

'Adjunct Tavore rarely emerges from an event – no matter how benign or fortuitous – untarnished. And no, I do not understand why this should be so.'

'The legacy of Coltaine.'

Pearl nodded in the darkness. Then, he frowned. *Ah, Empress, now I see . . .* 'And so, the dead hero is . . . unmanned. His name becomes a curse. His deeds, a lie.' *No, damn you, I was close enough to know otherwise. No.* 'Empress, it will not work.'

'Will it not?'

'No. Instead, we all are tainted. Faith and loyalty vanish. All that gifts us with pride becomes stained. The Malazan Empire ceases to have heroes, and without heroes, Empress, we will self-destruct.'

'You lack faith, Pearl.'

'In what, precisely?'

'The resilience of a civilization.'

'The faith you suggest seems more a wilful denial, Empress. Refusing to acknowledge the symptoms because it's easier that way. Complacency serves nothing but dissolution.'

'I may be many things,' Laseen said, 'but complacent is not one of them.'

'Forgive me, Empress, I did not mean to suggest that.'

'That fleet of catamarans,' she said after a moment, 'looks rather ominous. Can you sense the power emanating from it?'

'Somewhat.'

'Does it not follow, given their appearance, Pearl, that in allying themselves with Adjunct Tavore, these foreigners *perceived* in her something we do not? I wonder what it might be.'

'I cannot imagine their motives, Empress, for I have yet to meet them.'

'Do you wish to, Pearl?'

As I anticipated. 'In truth, those motives are of little interest to me.'

'It would seem that not much is these days, Pearl. With you.'

And who has made that particular report, Empress? He shrugged, said nothing.

'The fleet is anchoring in the bay,' the Empress suddenly said, and she stepped up to stand beside Pearl, her gloved hands resting on the battered stone. 'There, two ships only, sliding forward to dock. What does she believe, to have issued such orders? And, perhaps more significantly, why has Admiral Nok not countermanded her – the signal flags are lit, after all. There can be no mistaking my command.'

'Empress,' said Pearl, 'there are not enough berths for this fleet in the entire harbour. It may be that the ships will dock in a particular order—'

'No.'

He fell silent, but he could feel sweat prickling beneath his clothes.

'Her first move,' the Empress whispered, and there was something like excitement – or dark satisfaction – in her tone.

A squeal sounded from the weather vane atop the tower behind them, and Pearl shivered. *Aye, on a night with no wind . . .* He looked down upon the city, and saw torchlight in the streets. *Sparks to tinder, the word of the arrival in the bay races from mouth to mouth, eager as lust. The Wickans have returned, and now the mob gathers . . . the rage awakens.*

Thus, Empress – you need those ships to close, you need the lines drawn fast.

You need the victims to disembark, to bring the flames to a roar.

She turned about then. 'Follow me.'

Back along the watch-mount, across the causeway span to the keep itself. Her strides sure, almost eager. Beneath the arched entranceway, between the two cloaked, hooded forms of Claws – he felt their warrens held open, power roiling invisibly from their unseen hands.

A long, poorly lit corridor, the pavestones humped where subsurface settling had occurred, marking where an enormous crack was riven through the entire fortress. *One day, this whole damned place will tumble into the bay, and good riddance.* Of course, the engineers and mages had assured everyone that such a risk was half a century away, or longer. *Too bad.*

An intersection, the Empress leading him to the left – oh yes, she was familiar with this place. Where she had, years ago, assassinated the Emperor and Dancer. *Assassination. If you could call it that. More like inadvertently aided and abetted.* Along another canted corridor, and finally to the doors of a meeting chamber. Where stood two more Claws, the one on the left turning upon sighting them and tugging open the left door, in time for the Empress to pass within without change of pace.

Pearl followed, his steps suddenly slowing as soon as he stepped into the room.

Before him, a long T-shaped table. A tribunal arrangement. He found himself at its intersection. A raised chair marked the head, up the length of the axis, and that modest throne was flanked by figures already seated, although they both rose with Laseen's arrival.

Mallick Rel.

And Korbolo Dom.

Pearl struggled to keep the disgust from his face. Immediately before him were the backs of three chairs along the horizontal span. He hesitated. 'Where, Empress,' he asked, 'shall I sit?'

Settling into the throne, she regarded him for a moment, then one thin brow rose. 'Pearl, I do not expect you to be present. After all, you indicated you had no particular interest in seeing the Adjunct again, and so I shall relieve you of that burden.'

'I see. Then what would you have me do?'

The Jhistal priest on her right cleared his throat, then said, 'A burdensome but essential mission, Pearl, falls upon you. Organization is required, yes? The dispatch of a Hand, which you will find assembled at the Gate. A solitary killing. A drunkard who frequents Coop's Hanged Man Inn. His name: Banaschar. Thereafter, you may return to your quarters to await further instruction.'

Pearl's eyes remained fixed on the Empress, locked with her own, but she gave nothing away, as if daring him to ask what he so longed to: *Does a Claw take his orders from a Jhistal priest of Mael now? A man delivered here in chains not so long ago?* But, he knew, her silence gave him his answer. He broke his gaze from her and studied Korbolo Dom. The Napan bastard was wearing the regalia of a High Fist. Seeing the man's smug, contemptuous expression, Pearl's palms itched. *Two knives, my favourite ones, slowly slicing that face away – all of it – gods, never mind that – I could bury a blade in his damned throat right now – maybe I'd be fast enough, maybe not. That's the problem. The hidden Claw in this room will take me down, of course, but maybe they're not anticipating . . . no, don't be a fool, Pearl.* He glanced once more at the Empress and something in her look told him she had comprehended, in full, the desires with which he struggled . . . and was amused.

Still, he hesitated. Now was the time, he realized, to speak out against this. To seek to convince her that she'd invited two vultures, perched now on each shoulder, and what they hungered for was not the ones who would in a short time be seated before them – no, they wanted the throne they flanked. *And they will kill you, Laseen. They will kill you.*

'You may now go,' Mallick Rel said in a sibilant voice.

'Empress,' Pearl forced himself to say, 'please, consider well Tavore's words this night. She is your Adjunct, and nothing has changed that. No-one can change that—'

'Thank you for the advice, Pearl,' Laseen said.

He opened his mouth to add more, then closed it again. He bowed to his Empress, turned about and strode from the chamber. *And so, Pearl, you fling it into Tavore's lap. All of it. You damned coward.*

Still, who killed Lostara Yil? Well, Adjunct, such disregard ever comes home to roost.

So be it. Tonight belonged to them. Korbolo Dom he could take another night, at his leisure, and yes indeed, he would do just that. And maybe that grinning lizard of a priest as well. Why not? Topper was missing, probably dead. So, Pearl would act, in the name of the empire. Not in Laseen's name, but in the empire's, and this was one instance – clearer than any other he could think of – where the two loyalties clashed. *But, as ever with the Claw, as with you once, long ago, Empress, the choice is obvious. And necessary.*

For all the bravado of his thoughts, as he made his way down to the courtyard, another voice whispered over and over, cutting through again and again. One word, burning like acid, one word . . .

Coward.

Scowling, Pearl descended the levels of the keep. A Hand was waiting, to be given the task of assassinating a drunk ex-priest. And in this, as well, Pearl had waited too long. He could have forced things into the open, reached through to Tayschrenn – that bastard had virtually entombed himself, never mind that nest of hidden helpers. Oh, the Imperial High Mage wanted to be close to things. *Just not involved.*

Poor Banaschar, a haunted, befuddled scholar who simply wanted to talk to an old friend. But Mallick Rel did not want Tayschrenn disturbed. *Because the Jhistal priest has plans.*

Was Laseen truly a fool? There was no possible way she trusted them. So, what was the value in placing those two men in that chamber? To unbalance Tavore? *Unbalance? More like a slap in the face. Is that really necessary, Empress? Never mind Tavore, you cannot just use men like Mallick Rel and Korbolo Dom. They will turn on you, like the vipers they are.*

The risk in unleashing false rumours was when they proved too successful, trapping the liar in the lie, and Pearl began to realize something . . . a possibility. To ruin the name of Coltaine, that of his enemy must be raised. Korbolo Dom, from traitor to hero. Somehow . . . *no, I don't want to know the details.* Laseen could not then execute or even imprison a hero, could she? Indeed, she'd have to promote him. *Empress, you have trapped yourself. Now, I cannot believe you are not aware of it . . .*

His steps slowed. He had reached the main floor, was ten paces from the postern door that would take him out along the base of the wall, a path of shadows leading him to the Gate.

What do you seek to tell your Adjunct, then? The extremity of the danger you are in? Do you ask Tavore . . . for help? Will she, upon walking into that chamber, be in any condition to see and understand your plea? For Hood's sake, Laseen, this could go very, very wrong.

Pearl halted. He could do what was necessary, right now. Walk to the east tower and kick down Tayschrenn's door. And tell the fool what he needed to hear. He could—

Two hooded figures stepped into view before him. Claws. Both bowed, then the one on the left spoke. 'Claw, we are informed that our target is ensconced in the Hanged Man Inn. There is a piss trough in the alley behind it, which he will frequent throughout the night.'

'Yes,' Pearl said, suddenly exhausted. 'That would be ideal.'

The two cowled figures before him waited.

'There is more?' Pearl asked.

'Such matters are for you to command.'

'What matters?'

'Sir, killing undesirables.'

'Yes. Go on.'

'Just that, sir. This target was delivered to us . . . from elsewhere. From one who expected unquestioned compliance.'

Pearl's eyes narrowed, then he said, 'This assassination tonight . . . you would not accede to it without my direct command.'

'We seek . . . affirmation.'

'Did not the Empress herself confirm the Jhistal's words?'

'Sir, she did not. She . . . said nothing.'

'Yet she was present.'

'She was.'

Now what am I to make of that? Was she just feeding out enough rope? Or was she, too, frightened of Tayschrenn and so was pleased to unleash Mallick Rel on Banaschar? *Damn! I don't know enough about all of this.* No choice, then, for now. 'Very well. The command is given.'

The Claw, Mallick Rel, are not yours. And the Empress has . . . abstained. No, it seems that, until – or if – Topper returns, the Claw are mine. Convenient as well, Laseen, that you brought six hundred with you . . .

The two assassins bowed, then departed through the postern door.

Then again, why did it feel as if he was the one being used? And worse, why did it seem that he no longer cared? No, it was well. Tonight he would not think, simply obey. Tomorrow, well, that was another matter, wasn't it? *Tomorrow, then, I will kick through what's left. And decide what needs to be decided. There you have it, Empress. Tomorrow, the new Clawmaster once more cleans house. And maybe . . . maybe that is what you ask from me. Or you have asked it already, for it wasn't just the Adjunct for whom you assembled that tribunal, was it? You just gave me command of six hundred assassin-mages, didn't you? What else would they be for?*

The truth was, he could not guess the mind of Empress Laseen, and in that he most certainly was not alone.

Nerves slithered awake in his stomach, born of sudden fears he could not comprehend. *Six hundred . . .*

Face it, Pearl. The Adjunct did not kill Lostara. You did. You sent her away, and she died. And that's that.

But that changes nothing. It makes no real difference what I do now. Let them all die.

Pearl turned about and made his way to his rooms. To await more orders. *Six hundred killers to unleash . . . but upon whom?*

Hellian decided she hated rum. She wanted something else, something not so sweet, something better suited to her nature. It was dark, the wind warm and humid but falling off, and the harbourfront of Malaz seemed to whisper an invitation, like a lover's breath on the back of her neck.

The sergeant stood watching as the *Froth Wolf* moved ahead of the rest of the ships, the *Silanda* following in its wake. Yet, from all around now came the liquid rattle of anchor chains sliding down, and the craft beneath her was tugged to a halt. Staring wildly about, Hellian cursed. 'Corporal,' she said.

'Me?' asked Touchy behind her.

'Me?' asked Brethless.

'That's right, you. What's going on here? Look, there's soldiers on the jetties, and well-wishers. Why aren't we heading in? They're waving.' Hellian waved back, but it was unlikely they could see that – there were hardly any lights from the fleet at all. 'Gloom and gloom,' she muttered, 'like we was some beaten dog creeping home.'

'Or like it's real late,' Brethless said, 'and you was never supposed to be with your mother's friend at all especially when Ma knows and she's waiting up with that dented skillet but sometimes, you know, older women, they come at you like a fiend and what can you do?'

'Not like that at all, you idiot,' Touchy hissed. 'More like that daughter of that priest and gods below you're running but there ain't no escaping curses like those, not ones from a priest, anyway, which means your life is doomed for ever and ever, as if Burn cares a whit she's sleeping anyway, right?'

Hellian turned round and stared at a space directly between the two men. 'Listen, Corporal, make up your damned mind, but then again don't bother. I wasn't interested. I was asking you a question, and if you can't answer then don't say nothing.'

The two men exchanged glances, then Brethless shrugged. 'We ain't disembarking, Sergeant,' he said. 'Word's just come.'

'Are they mad? Of course we're disembarking – we've just sailed a million leagues. Five million, even. We been through fires and storms and green lights in the sky and nights with the shakes and broken jaws and that damned rhizan piss they called wine. That's Malaz City there, right there, and that's where I'm going, Corporal Brethy Touchless, and I don't care how many arms you got, I'm going and that's that.' She swung about, walked forward, reached the rail, pitched over and was suddenly gone.

Brethless and Touchy stared at each other again, as a heavy splash sounded.

'Now what?' Touchy demanded.

'She's done drowned herself, hasn't she?'

'We'd better report it to somebody.'

'We do that and we're in real trouble. We was standing right here, after all. They'll say we pushed her.'

'But we didn't!'

'That don't matter. We're not even trying to save her, are we?'

'I can't swim!'

'Me neither.'

'Then we should shout an alarm or something.'

'You do it.'

'No, you.'

'Maybe we should just go below, tell people we went looking for her but we didn't never find her.'

At that they both paused and looked round. A few figures moving in the gloom, sailors doing sailor things.

'Nobody saw or heard nothing.'

'Looks like. Well, that's good.'

'Isn't it. So, we go below now, right? Throw up our hands and say nothing.'

'Not nothing. We say we couldn't find her nowhere.'

'Right, that's what I mean. Nothing is what I mean, I mean, about her going over the side, that sort of nothing.'

A new voice from behind them: 'You two, what are you doing on deck?'

Both corporals turned. 'Nothing,' they said in unison.

'Get below, and stay there.'

They hurried off.

'Three ashore,' the young, foppishly attired figure said, his eyes fixed on the knuckle dice where they came to a rest on the weathered stone.

His twin stood facing the distant, looming bulk of Mock's Hold, the night's wind caressing the gaudy silks about her slim form.

'You see how it plays out?' her brother asked, collecting the dice with a sweep of one hand. 'Tell me truly, have you any idea – any idea at all – of how mightily I struggled to retain our card during that horrendous game? I'm still weak, dizzy. He wanted to drag us out, again and again and again. It was horrifying.'

'Heroic indeed,' she murmured without turning.

'Three ashore,' he said again. 'How very . . . unexpected. Do you think that dreadful descent above Otataral Island was responsible? I mean, for the one that's even now on its way?' Straightening, he moved to join his sister.

They were standing on a convenient tower rising from the city of Malaz, south of the river. To most citizens of the city, the tower appeared to be in ruins, but that was an illusion, maintained by the sorceror who occupied its lower chambers, a sorceror who seemed to be sleeping. The twin god and goddess known as Oponn had the platform – and the view – entirely to themselves.

'Certainly possible,' she conceded, 'but is that not the charm of our games, beloved?' She gestured towards the bay to their right. 'They have arrived, and even now there is a stirring among those abject mortals in those ships, especially the *Silanda*. Whilst, in the fell Hold opposite, the nest slithers awake. There will be work for us, this night.'

'Oh yes. Both you and me. Pull, push, pull, push.' He rubbed his hands together. 'I can hardly wait.'

She faced him suddenly. 'Can we be so sure, brother, that we comprehend all the players? All of them? What if one hides from us? Just one . . . wild, unexpected, so very terrible . . . we could end up in trouble. We could end up . . . dead.'

'It was that damned soldier,' her brother snarled. 'Stealing our power! The arrogance, to usurp us in our very own game! I want his blood!'

She smiled in the darkness. 'Ah, such fire in your voice. So be it. Cast the knuckles, then, on his fate. Go on. *Cast them!'*

He stared across at her, then grinned. Whirled about, one hand flinging out and down – knuckles struck, bounced, struck again, then spun and skidded, and finally fell still.

The twins, breathing hard in perfect unison, hurried over and crouched down to study the cast.

And then, had there been anyone present to see them, they would have witnessed on their perfect faces bemused expressions. Frowns deepening, confusion reigning in immortal eyes, and, before this night was done, pure terror.

The non-existent witness would then shake his or her head. *Never, dear gods. Never mess with mortals.*

'Grub and three friends, playing in a cave. A Soletaken with a stolen sword. Togg and Fanderay and damned castaways . . .'

Trapped since Fiddler's reading in a small closet-sized cabin on the *Froth Wolf*, Bottle worked the finishing touches on the doll nestled in his lap. The Adjunct's commands made no sense – but no, he corrected with a scowl, not the Adjunct's. This – *all of this* – belonged to that tawny-eyed beauty, T'amber. *Who in Hood's name is she? Oh, never mind. Only the thousandth time I've asked myself that question. But it's that look, you see, in her eyes. That knowing look, like she's plunged through, right into my heart.*

And she doesn't even like men, does she?

He studied the doll, and his scowl deepened. 'You,' he muttered, 'I've never seen you before, you know that? But here you are, with a sliver of iron in your gut – gods but that must hurt, cutting away, always cutting away inside. You, sir, are somewhere in Malaz City, and she wants me to find you, and that's that. A whole city, mind you, and I've got till dawn to track you down.' Of course, this doll would help, somewhat, once the poor man was close enough for Bottle to stare into his eyes and see the same pain that now marked these uneven chips of oyster shell. That, and the seams of old scars on the forearms – but there were plenty of people with those, weren't there?

'I need help,' he said under his breath.

From above, the voices of sailors as the ship angled in towards the jetty, and some deeper, more distant sound, from the dockfront itself. And that one felt . . . unpleasant.

We've been betrayed. All of us.

The door squealed open behind him.

Bottle closed his eyes.

The Adjunct spoke. 'We're close. The High Mage is ready to send you across – you will find him in my cabin. I trust you are ready, soldier.'

'Aye, Adjunct.' He turned, studied her face in the gloom of the corridor where she stood. The extremity of emotion within her was revealed only in a tightness around her eyes. *Desperate.*

'You must not fail, Bottle.'

'Adjunct, the odds are against me—'

'T'amber says you must seek help. She says you know who.'

T'amber, the woman with those damned eyes. Like a lioness. What is it, damn it, about those eyes? 'Who is she, Adjunct?'

A flicker of something like sympathy in the woman's gaze. 'Someone . . . a lot more than she once was, soldier.'

'And you trust her?'

'Trust.' She smiled slightly. 'You must know, as young as you are, Bottle, that truth is found in the touch. Always.'

No, he did not know. He did not understand. Not any of it. Sighing, he rose, stuffing the limp doll beneath his jerkin, where it sat nestled alongside the sheathed knife under his left arm. No uniform, no markings whatsoever that would suggest he was a soldier of the Fourteenth – the absence of fetishes made him feel naked, vulnerable. 'All right,' he said.

She led him to her cabin, then halted at the doorway. 'Go on. I must be on deck, now.'

Bottle hesitated, then said, 'Be careful, Adjunct.'

A faint widening of the eyes, then she turned and walked away.

Kalam stood at the stern, squinting into the darkness beyond where transports were anchoring. He'd thought he'd heard the winching of a longboat, somewhere a few cables distant from shore. *Against every damned order the Adjunct's given this night.*

Well, even he wasn't pleased with those orders. Quick Ben slicing open a sliver of a gate – even that sliver might get detected, and that would be bad news for poor Bottle. He'd step out into a nest of Claw. He wouldn't stand a chance. And who might come through the other way?

All too risky. All too . . . extreme.

He rolled his shoulders, lifting then shrugging off the tension. But the tautness came back only moments later. The palms of the assassin's hands were itching beneath the worn leather of his gloves. *Decide, damn you. Just decide.*

Something skittered on the planks to his right and he turned to see a shin-high reptilian skeleton, its long-snouted head tilting as the empty eye sockets regarded him. The segmented tail flicked.

'Don't *you* smell nice?' the creature hissed, jaws clacking out of sequence. 'Doesn't he smell nice, Curdle?'

'Oh yes,' said another thin voice, this time to Kalam's left, and he glanced over to see a matching skeleton perched on the stern rail, almost within reach. 'Blood and strength and will and mindfulness, nearly a match to our sweetheart. Imagine the fight between them, Telorast. Wouldn't that be something to see?'

'And where is she?' Kalam asked in a rumble. 'Where's Apsalar hiding?'

'She's gone,' Curdle said, head bobbing.

'What?'

'Gone,' chimed in Telorast with another flick of the tail. 'It's only me and Curdle who are hiding right now. Not that we have to, of course.'

'Expedience,' explained Curdle. 'It's scary out there tonight. You have no idea. None.'

'We know who's here, you see. *All of them.*'

Now, from the dark waters, Kalam could hear the creak of oars. Someone had indeed dropped a longboat and was making for shore. *Damned fools – that mob will tear them to pieces.* He turned about and set off for the mid deck.

The huge jetty appeared to starboard as the ship seemed to curl round, its flank sidling ever closer. The assassin saw the Adjunct arrive from below and he approached her.

'We've got trouble,' he said without preamble. 'Someone's going ashore, in a longboat.'

Tavore nodded. 'So I have been informed.'

'Oh. Who, then?'

From nearby T'amber said, 'There is a certain ... symmetry to this. A rather bitter one, alas. In the longboat, Kalam Mekhar, are Fist Tene Baralta and his Red Blades.'

The assassin frowned.

'Deeming it probable, perhaps,' T'amber continued, 'that our escort coming down from Mock's Hold will prove insufficient against the mob.' Yet there seemed to be little conviction in the woman's tone, as if she was aware of a deeper truth, and was inviting Kalam to seek it for himself.

'The Red Blades,' said the Adjunct, 'ever have great need to assert their loyalty.'

... their loyalty ...

'Kalam Mekhar,' Tavore continued, stepping closer, her eyes now fixed on his own, 'I expect I will be permitted but a minimal escort of my own choosing. T'amber, of course, and, if you would accede, you.'

'Not an order, Adjunct?'

'No,' she answered quietly, almost tremulously. And then she waited.

Kalam looked away. *Dragon's got Hood by the nose hairs . . .* one of Fid's observations during one of his games. Years ago, now. Blackdog, was it? Probably. Why had he thought of that statement now? *Because I know how Hood must have felt, that's why.*

Wait, I can decide on this without deciding on anything else. Can't I? Of course I can. 'Very well, Adjunct. I will be part of your escort. We'll get you to Mock's Hold.'

'To the Hold, yes, that is what I have asked of you here.'

As she turned away, Kalam frowned, then glanced over at T'amber, who was regarding him flatly, as if disappointed. 'Something wrong?' he asked the young woman.

'There are times,' she said, 'when the Adjunct's patience surpasses even mine. And, you may not know this, but that is saying something.'

Froth Wolf edged closer to the jetty.

On the other side of the same stone pier, the longboat scraped up against the slimy foundation boulders. Lines were made fast to the rings set in the mortar, and Lostara Yil watched as one of the more nimble Red Blades hauled himself upward from ring to ring, trailing a knot-ladder. Moments later, he had reached the top of the jetty, where he attached the ladder's hooks to still more rings.

Tene Baralta was the first to ascend, slowly, awkward, using his one arm and grunting with each upward heave on the rungs.

Feeling sick to her stomach, Lostara followed, ready to catch the man should he falter or slip.

This is a lie. All of it.

She reached the top, clambered upright and paused, adjusting her weapon belt and her cloak.

'Captain,' Tene Baralta said, 'form up to await the Adjunct.'

She glanced to the right and saw a contingent of Imperial Guard pushing through the milling crowd, an officer in their midst.

Tene Baralta noticed them as well. 'Not enough, as I suspected. If this mob smells blood . . .'

Turning to the company of Red Blades, Lostara kept her face impassive, even as a sneering thought silently slithered through her mind: *Whatever you say, Fist. Just don't expect me to believe any of this.*

At that moment a deeper roaring sound filled the air, and the sky above the bay suddenly blazed bright.

Banaschar squinted through the haze of smoke, scanning the crowd, then he grunted. 'He's not here,' he said. 'In fact, I haven't seen him in days . . . I think. How about you, Master Sergeant?'

Braven Tooth simply shrugged, his only reponse to Mudslinger's question.

The soldier glanced at Gentur, his silent companion, then said, 'It's just this, Master Sergeant. First we lose them, then we hear something about him, and we put it together, you see?'

The hairy old man bared his teeth. 'Oh yeah, Mudslinger. Now go away before I tie a full cask to your back and send you round the harbourfront at double-time.'

'He can't do that, can he?' Gentur asked his fellow soldier.

But Mudslinger had paled. 'You never forget, do you, sir?'

'Explain it to your friend. But not here. Try the alley.'

The two soldiers backed off, exchanging whispers as they made their way back to their table.

'I always like to think,' Banaschar said, 'that a nasty reputation is usually mostly undeserved. Benefit of the doubt, and maybe I've got some glimmer of faith in humanity clawing its way free every now and again. But, with you, Braven Tooth, alas, such optimism is revealed for the delusion it truly is.'

'Got that right. What about it?'

'Nothing.'

They heard shouting in the street outside, a clamour of voices that then died away. This had been going on all evening. Roving bands of idiots looking for someone to terrorize. The mood in the city was dark and ugly and getting worse with every bell that chimed, and there seemed to be no reason for it, although, Banaschar reminded himself, that had now changed.

Well, maybe there was still no reason as such. Only, there had arrived . . . a target.

'Someone's poking with a knife,' Braven Tooth said.

'It's the imperial fleet,' Banaschar said. 'Bad timing, given all the Wickans in those ships, and the other foreigners with them, too, I imagine.'

'You ain't drinking much, Banaschar. You sick or something?'

'Worse than that,' he replied. 'I have reached a decision. Autumn has arrived. You can feel it in the wind. The worms are swarming to shore. It's D'rek's season. Tonight, I talk with the Imperial High Mage.'

The Master Sergeant scowled across at him. 'Thought you said trying that would get you dead quick. Unless, of course, that's what you want.'

'I plan on losing my follower in the crowd,' Banaschar said in a low voice, leaning over the table. 'I'll take the waterfront way, at least to the bridge. I hear there's City Watch there, pushing the brainless dolts back from the jetties – gods, how stupid can people be? That's an *army* out on those ships!'

'Like I said, someone's poking. Be nice to meet that someone. So's I can put my fist into his face and watch it come out the back of his head. Messy way to go, but fast, which is more than the bastard deserves.'

'What are you going on about?' Banaschar asked.

'Never mind.'

'Well,' the ex-priest said with more bravado in his voice than he in truth felt, 'it's now or never. Come tomorrow night I'll buy you a pitcher of Malaz Dark—'

'That reminds me – you always seem to find enough coin – how is that?'

'Temple coffers, Braven Tooth.'

'You stole from the D'rek Temple here?'

'Here? That's good. Yes, here, and all the others I visited, too. Got it all squirrelled away, where no-one but me can get to it. Problem is, I feel guilty every time I pinch from it. I never take much – no point in inviting a mugging, after all. But that's just the excuse I use. Like I said, it's guilt.'

'So, if you get yourself killed tonight . . .'

Banaschar grinned and flung up his hands. 'Phoof! All of it. Gone. For ever.'

'Nice trick, that.'

'You want I should leave it to you?'

'Hood no! What would I do with chests of coin?'

'Chests? Dear Master Sergeant, more like roomfuls. In any case, I'll see you tomorrow . . . or not. And if not, then, well met, Braven Tooth.'

'Forget that. Tomorrow, like you said.'

Nodding, Banaschar backed away, then began threading his way towards the front door.

Alone at the table now, Braven Tooth slowly raised his tankard for a drink, his eyes almost closed – and to anyone more than a pace or two away they would have seemed closed indeed – and so the figure who hastily rose, slipping like an adder into Banaschar's wake, noticed nothing of the Master Sergeant's fixed attention, the small eyes tracking for a moment, before Braven Tooth finished the ale in three quick swallows. Then the huge, hairy man climbed gustily to his feet, weaving slightly, one hand reaching to the table for balance.

He staggered over to Mudslinger and Gentur, both of whom looked up in guilt and fear – as if they'd been discussing bad things. Braven Tooth leaned between them. 'Listen, you fools,' he said under his breath.

'We're just waiting for Foreigner,' Mudslinger said, eyes wide. 'That's all. We never—'

'Quiet. See that snake at the steps up front – quickly!'

'Just . . . gone,' Gentur observed, squinting. 'Snake, you said. I'd say more like a—'

'And you'd be right. And the target is none other than Banaschar. Now, are you two up for surprising a Claw tonight? Do this and I'll think nice thoughts about the both of you.'

The two men were already on their feet.

Gentur spat onto his hands and rubbed them together. 'I used to dream of nights like this,' he said. 'Let's go, Mudder. Before we lose 'im.'

'Heading towards the waterfront,' Braven Tooth said. 'Northering t'the Stairs, right?'

He watched the two soldiers hurry to the back door. Out they went, looking far too eager.

Mudslinger, he knew, was a lot tougher than he looked. Besides, he didn't think that Claw would be thinking about anyone on his own trail. And with the crowds . . . well, they shouldn't have too much trouble. *Soldiers love killing assassins . . .*

Someone threw a handful of knuckle dice at the back of the low-ceilinged room.

And Braven Tooth suddenly shivered.

I must be getting soft.

There were plenty of well-armed figures among the crowd gathering along the harbourfront, although, for the moment, those weapons remained beneath heavy cloaks, as these selected agents moved into designated positions. Faint nods passing between them, a few whispered words here and there.

The City Watch stood in a ragged line, pikes shifting nervously as the bolder thugs edged forward with taunts and threats.

There were Wickans in those ships out there.

And we want them.

Traitors, one and all, and dealing with traitors was a punishment that belonged to the people. Wasn't the Empress herself up there at Mock's Hold? Here to witness imperial wrath – *she's done it before, right, back when she commanded the Claw.*

Never mind you're waiting for an officer, you fools, the signals are lit and we ain't stupid – they're telling those bastards to come in. Tie up. Disembark. Look at 'em, the cowards! They know the time's come to answer their betrayal!

Believe us, we're gonna fill this bay with Wickan heads – won't that be a pretty sight come morning?

Gods below! What's that?

A chorus of voices shouted that, or something similar, and hands lifted, fingers pointing, eyes tracking a blazing ball of fire that slanted down across half the sky to the west, trailing a blue-grey plume of smoke like the track of an eel on black sand. Growing in size with alarming swiftness.

Then . . . gone . . . and a moment later, a savage *crack* rolled in from beyond the bay, where rose a tumbling cloud of steam.

Close! A third of a league, you think?

Less.

Not much impact, though.

Must've been small. Smaller than it looked.

Went right overhead—

It's an omen! An omen!

A Wickan head! Did you see it? It was a Wickan head! Sent down by the gods!

Momentarily distracted by the plunging fireball that seemed to land just beyond the bay, the Claw Saygen Maral pushed himself forward once more. The assassin was pleased with the heaving press he moved through, a press settling down once again, although at a higher pitch of anticipation than before.

Up ahead, the crowd had slowed the ex-priest's pace, which was good, since already nothing was going as planned. The target should have been settled in for the night at Coop's, and the Hand was likely closing in on the alley behind the inn, there to await his contacting them with the necessary details.

Pointing the Skull, they used to call it. Identifying the target right there, right then, in person. A proper reward for following the fool around for sometimes weeks on end – seeing the actual assassination. Be that as it may, as things were turning out he would be bloodying his own hands with this target tonight, now that the decision had been made to kill the drunkard.

A convenient conjoining of Saygen Maral's divided loyalties. Trained from childhood in the Imperial Claw – ever since he had been taken from his dead mother's side, aged fourteen, at the Cull of the Wax Witches in the Mouse Quarter all those years ago – his disaffection with the Empress had taken a long time to emerge, and even then, if not for the Jhistal Master it would never have found focus, or indeed purpose. Of course, discovering precisely how his mother had died had helped considerably.

The empire was rotten through and through, and he knew he wasn't the only Claw to realize this; just as he wasn't the only one who now followed the commands of the Jhistal Master – most of the Hand on its way down from Mock's Hold belonged to the phantom Black Glove that was the name of Mallick Rel's spectral organization. In truth, there was no way of telling just how many of the Imperial Claw had been turned – each agent was aware of but three others, forming a discrete cell – in itself a classic Claw structure.

In any case, Clawmaster Pearl had confirmed the order to kill Banaschar. Comforting, that.

He remained ten paces behind the ex-priest, acutely aware of the seething violence in this mob – encouraged by the idiotic cries of 'An omen!' and 'A Wickan head!' – but he carried on his person certain items, invested with sorcery, that encouraged a lack of attention from everyone he pushed past, that dampened their ire momentarily no matter how rude and painful his jabbing elbows.

They were close to the docks now, and agents of the Jhistal Master were in the milling crowd, working them ever nastier and more belligerent with well-timed shouts and exhortations. No more than fifty City Watch soldiers faced a mass now numbering in the high hundreds, an under-strength presence that had been carefully co-ordinated by selective incompetence among the officers at the nearby barracks.

He noted a retinue of more heavily armed and armoured soldiers escorting a ranking officer towards the centre dock, before which now loomed the Adjunct's flagship. The captain, Saygen Maral knew, was delivering a most auspicious set of imperial commands. And those, in turn, would lead inexorably to a night of slaughter such as this city had never before experienced. Not even the Cull in the Mouse would compare.

The assassin smiled.

Welcome home, Adjunct.

His breath caught suddenly as a prickling sensation awoke on his left shoulder beneath his clothes. A small sliver of metal threaded under his skin had awakened, informing him that he was being followed by some-one with murderous intent. *Clumsy. A killer should ever mask such thoughts. After all, Mockra is the most common natural talent, needing no formal training – that whispering unease, the hair rising on the back of the neck – far too many people possess such things.*

Nonetheless, even a clumsy killer could know the Lady's Pull on occasion, just as Saygen Maral, for all his skills and preparation, could stumble – fatally – to the Lord's Push.

Ahead, now fifteen paces away, Banaschar was working free of the crowd, and Saygen sensed the man's warren – *Mockra, yes, achieving what my own invested items have done. Uninterest, sudden fugue, con-fusion – the sharper the mind, after all, the more vulnerable it proves to such passive assaults.* To be a killer, of course, one needed to fend off such sorcery. Simple awareness of the trap sufficed, and so Saygen Maral was not concerned. His intent was most singular.

Of course he would have to eliminate his own hunters first.

Banaschar was heading for the Stairs. There was little risk in Saygen effecting a slight delay. He saw an alley mouth off to the left, where the crowd was thin. The assassin angled himself towards it, and, as he stepped past the last figure, quickly turned left and slipped into the alley.

Gloom, rubbish under foot, a tortured, winding route before him. He continued on five more steps, found an alcove and edged into it.

*

'He's getting ready to take the drunk,' Gentur hissed. 'He'll circle round—'

'Then let's get after 'im,' Mudslinger whispered, pushing his friend on.

They entered the alley, padded forward.

The shadows swallowing the niche were too deep, too opaque to be natural, and both soldiers went right past without a second thought.

A faint sound, whistling past Mudslinger's left shoulder, and Gentur grunted, flinging up his hands as he staggered forward, then collapsed. Whirling, Mudslinger ducked low, but not low enough, as a second tiny quarrel struck him on his chest, directly over his heart, and, still spinning round with his own momentum, the soldier's feet skidded out beneath him. He fell hard, the back of his head crunching on the greasy cobbles.

Saygen Maral studied the two motionless bodies for a moment longer, then he reloaded the corkscrew crossbows strapped to his wrists. *First shot, base of the skull. Second shot, heart – that was a lucky one, since I was aiming for low in the gut. Guess he didn't want all that pain. Too bad. Anyway . . . What were they thinking of doing? Mugging me? No matter, it's done.* Adjusting his sleeves, hiding the weapons once more, he set off after Banaschar.

A sixth of a bell later, the Claw realized that he had lost the man. In rising panic, he began backtracking, down alleys and streets, as a cool breeze lifted withered leaves that spun random paths across cobbles.

Making clicking sounds, like the skittering of dice.

The huge wheels of twisted rope suspended on the side of the stone jetty compressed as the *Froth Wolf* shouldered its bulk against them, then the craft slid away again, momentarily, until the lines, made fast to the dock's huge bollards, drew taut. The gangplank rattled and thumped into place even as the garrison captain and his guards approached along the jetty's length. Pointedly ignoring the troop of Red Blades standing at attention opposite the plank with their one-armed, one-eyed commander.

Something had just struck the sea beyond the anchored fleet, and the thunderous sound of its impact still echoed, even as darkness swept back into the wake of the bright, blazing fireball. The smell of steam was heavy in the air.

It had seemed to Keneb that there was a peculiar lack of reaction to this event, from the Adjunct and T'amber, at any rate. There had been plenty of shouts, warding gestures then animated talk among the sailors, but that was to be expected.

Let's face it, Keneb admitted, *the timing was less than auspicious*. It was no wonder that thousand-strong mob awaiting them were shouting about omens.

The Fist's attention was drawn once more to the approaching contingent.

'They mean to come aboard, Adjunct,' Keneb said as she prepared to disembark.

Tavore frowned, then nodded and stepped back. T'amber positioned herself to the Adjunct's left.

Boots thumped on the plank, and the captain halted one step from the ship's deck. He looked round, as if deciding what to do next.

Moving forward, Keneb said, 'Good evening, Captain, I am Fist Keneb, Eighth Legion, Fourteenth Army.'

A moment's hesitation, then a salute. 'Fist Keneb. I have orders for the Adjunct Tavore Paran. May I come on deck?'

'Of course,' Keneb said.

Mostly unintelligible shouts and curses reached them from the crowds massing behind a line of soldiers on the waterfront, many of them taunts directed at the Red Blades. At these sounds, the captain winced slightly, then he moved forward until he faced the Adjunct. 'The Empress awaits you,' he said, 'in Mock's Hold. In your absence, command of the Fourteenth Army temporarily falls to me, with respect to disembarking and standing down.'

'I see,' Tavore said.

The captain shifted uneasily, as if he had been expecting some kind of protest, as if her lack of reaction to his words was the very last thing he anticipated. 'It appears that the transports are anchoring in the bay, Adjunct.'

'Yes, it does appear so, Captain.'

'That will need to be countermanded immediately.'

'Captain, what is your name?'

'Adjunct? My apologies. It is Rynag. Captain Rynag of the Untan Imperial Guard.'

'Ah, then you have accompanied the Empress to the island. Your normal posting is as an officer in the Palace Guard.'

Rynag cleared his throat. 'Correct, Adjunct, although as a matter of course my responsibilities have expand—'

'T'amber,' the Adjunct cut in. 'Please collect Kalam Mekhar. He is, I believe, once more at the stern.' She studied the captain for a moment longer, then asked him, 'The Empress commands that I meet her alone?'

'Uh, she was not specific—'

'Very well—'

'Excuse me, Adjunct. Not specific, as I said, with one exception.'

'Oh?'

'Yes. The High Mage Adaephon Delat is to remain on board until such time as directed otherwise.'

Tavore frowned for a moment, then said, 'Very well.'

'I believe I was speaking about countermanding the order to drop anchor—'

'I leave that to you, Captain Rynag,' the Adjunct said as T'amber reappeared, Kalam trailing a step behind. 'We will make use of your escort, as well as that of Fist Baralta's Red Blades, to ensure our passage through that mob.' With that, and a gesture to T'amber and the assassin to follow, she disembarked.

Bemused, the captain watched them cross over to the jetty. A few curt commands to the Imperial Guards assembled there and a careless gesture to Tene Baralta and his soldiers to fall in, and the two groups moved out in uneasy company to flank Tavore and her two companions. Then the party set off.

Rynag swung back to Keneb. 'Fist?'

'Yes?'

'Well . . .'

'Things aren't going as planned, Captain?' Keneb stepped close and slapped a hand on the man's shoulder. 'Consider this, it could be worse. Correct that. It *is* much worse.'

'No longer,' the man snapped, finally angry. 'I am now in command of the Fourteenth Army, Fist Keneb, and these are my orders. Signal flag to Admiral Nok. The escorts are to withdraw and set sail without delay for Unta. Signal flag to the foreign fleet, they are to anchor outside the bay, this side of the shoals on the headland north of Mock's Hold. A pilot ship will guide them. Finally, signal flag to the transports – we will establish a number system; and thereafter in sets of fifteen they will weigh anchor and draw in to the designated moorings. The disembarking will begin as soon as possible, Fist. Furthermore, the soldiers are to be unarmed, their kits secured for transportation.'

Keneb scratched his stubbly jaw.

'Why are you just standing there, Fist Keneb?'

'I am trying to decide, Captain, where to begin.'

'What do you mean?'

'All right, never mind. First of all, whether you are in command of the Fourteenth Army or not, you do not outrank Admiral Nok. Signal him all you want. He will do precisely as he pleases.'

'I am instructed by the Empress—'

'He will need to see those orders, Captain. In person. The Admiral is very precise with such protocol. I assume you have said orders?'

'Of course I have! Very well, signal him aboard!'

'Alas, he will not comply.'

'What?'

'Now, as for the Perish – the foreign fleet, Captain Rynag – the only command they acknowledge, under the circumstances, is their own. By all means, make your request, but be certain that it *is* a request. Lest they take offence, and Captain, you truly do not want them to take offence.'

'You are leaving me no choice but to relieve you of command, Fist.'

'Excuse me?'

'I have given you my orders, yet still you stand here—'

'Well that is precisely the problem, Captain. Not one of your orders can be carried out, for the imperative overriding them cannot be challenged, not by you, not even by the Empress herself.'

'What are you talking about?'

Keneb said, 'Follow me, please, Captain.'

They walked to the stern. In the bay beyond, the huge transports loomed a short distance away like gigantic, slumbering beasts.

'Granted,' Keneb said, 'darkness obscures, and for this reason it is understandable that you do not as yet comprehend. But, allow me to direct your gaze, Captain, to the topmost signal flag on those near ships, a flag identical to those on Nok's dromons. In a moment, when that cloud passes by the moon, with Oponn's blessing there will be enough light with which to see. There is an edict, Captain, pertaining to survival itself. You seem to forget, both the Fourteenth Army and the imperial fleet have come from Seven Cities.'

The cloud slid away from the blurred, hazy moon, and enough light licked waves, ships, and flags for Rynag to see. The captain's breath caught in a half-choke. '*Gods below!*' he whispered.

'And Seven Cities,' Keneb continued in a calm voice, 'was struck by a most virulent plague. Which, as you can now see, we inadvertently brought with us. So, Captain, do you now understand why we cannot comply with your commands?'

The man spun to face him, his eyes filled with terror and panic. 'And this damned ship?' he demanded in a hoarse voice. 'And the other one that just docked? Fist Keneb—'

'Plague-free, both of them, Captain, as was the ship from whence came the Red Blades. We would not have moored alongside were it otherwise. Anyway, beyond signal flags, there is no contact between ships. For obvious reasons. I suppose, if you believe the Empress would nonetheless insist we one and all disembark regardless of the slaughter our presence would deliver to Malaz Island – and, inevitably, to the entire mainland – you can insist on countermanding our collective gesture of compassion and mercy. Unquestionably, the name of Captain

Rynag will acquire legendary status, at least among devotees to Poliel – nothing wrong with seeing the positives, don't you think?'

The group marched ever closer to the wall of belligerence blocking the streets. Kalam loosened the long-knives in their scabbards. Glancing over, he found himself walking alongside Captain Lostara Yil, who looked profoundly unhappy.

'Suggest you all draw your weapons any time now,' the assassin said to her. 'That should be enough to make them back off.'

She grunted. 'Until they start throwing bricks.'

'I doubt it. We're for the Empress, not them. The ones these people are hungry to sink their teeth into are out there in the transports. The Wickans. The Khundryl Burned Tears.'

'Clever ruse,' Lostara said under her breath, 'those flags.'

'Fist Keneb.'

'Indeed?'

'Aye.' Then Kalam smiled. 'Spinner of Death. A prettier lie you won't find. Fid must be grinning ear to ear, if he ain't drowning.'

'Drowning?'

'He was over the side before the *Silanda* shipped oars, is my guess – probably Gesler and Stormy went with him, too.'

Just then they reached the line of City Watch, who parted to let them pass.

Weapons hissed from scabbards and shields were brought round by the Red Blades.

And, as Kalam had predicted, the crowds fell silent, watchful, and backed away to each side to let the party make its way through.

'So,' the assassin said under his breath, 'we've got ourselves a long, dull walk. Sound idea, by the way, Captain, your Fist deciding to act on his own.'

The look she shot him started sweat beneath Kalam's clothing, as she asked, 'Was it, Kalam Mekhar?'

'Well—'

She faced straight ahead again. 'The Fist,' she said in a whisper, 'hasn't even begun.'

Well . . . oh, that's not good at all.

Behind the troop, the mob closed in once again, and there arose new shouts, this time of horror.

'Plague flags! On the transports in the bay! Plague flags!'

In moments belligerence drained away like piss down a leg, and terror grabbed hold between those legs – *squeezing hard* – and people began swarming in every direction, but a heartbeat away from pure, frenzied panic. Kalam kept his smile to himself.

Ever so faint, the clatter of knuckles bouncing and skidding had alerted Banaschar. This night the Worm was awake, and with it the return of the ex-priest's old sensitivities to the whisper of magic. In rapid succession thereafter, as he shifted from his path and found a dead-end alley in which to crouch, heart pounding, he felt multiple pulses of sorcery – a gate, slicing open the thinnest rent, the sudden, violent unravelling of some unseen tapestry, and then, finally, a trembling underfoot, as if something terrible and vast had just stepped onto the dry land of this island.

Dizzy from the successive waves of virulent power, Banaschar straightened once more, one hand against a grimy wall for support, then he headed off – back, back towards the harbourfront.

No choice, no choice. I need to see . . . to understand . . .

As he drew nearer, he could smell panic in the air, acrid and bitter, and all at once there were mute figures hurrying past him – the beginnings of an exodus. Faces twisted in fear blurred by, and others dark with rage – as if their plans had been suddenly knocked awry, and there was not yet time to find a means to regroup, nor yet the opportunity to think things through.

Something's happened.

Maybe to do with that falling rock or whatever it was.

In the old days, such an occurrence, on the eve of autumn, the eve of D'rek's arrival upon the mortal earth . . . *well, we'd have flooded the streets. Out from the temples, raising our voices to the heavens. And the coffers would overflow, beause there could be no mistaking . . .*

The thoughts trailed away, vanished, leaving naught but a taste of ashes in his mouth. *We were such fools. The sky casts down, the world heaves up, the waters wash it all away. None of this – none of it! – has* anything *to do with our precious gods!*

He reached the broad avenue fronting the docks. People moving about here and there. If anger remained it was roiling about, all direction lost. Some vast desire had been . . . blunted.

Passing an old woman Banaschar reached out to her. 'Here,' he said. 'What has happened?'

She glared up at him, pulling free as if his touch was a contaminant. 'Plague ships!' she hissed. 'Get away from me!'

He let her go, halted, stared out at the ships filling the bay.

Ah, the flags . . .

Banaschar sniffed the air.

Poliel? I can't sense you at all . . . out there. Or anywhere else, come to think of it. His eyes narrowed. Then, slowly, he smiled.

At that moment, a heavy hand thumped down on his left shoulder, spun him round—

And someone screamed.

Lifting clear of the swirling black, filthy waters. Straightening, slime and grit streaming off, blood-sucking eels flapping down to writhe on the muddy rocks, the broken pottery and the brick fragments beneath the wooden dock. One step forward, then another, heavy, scraping.

A rough wall directly ahead, revealing layers of street levels, bulwarks, old drainage holes dating back to the city's youth – before iron was first forged by humans – when the sewer system was a superb, efficient subterranean web beneath level streets. In all, plenty of hand- and foot-holds, given sufficient determination, strength and will.

Of all three, the one standing facing that wall had been given plenty. More steps.

Then, climbing. A stranger had come to Malaz City.

Gasping, she leaned against a wall. What a mistake, trying to swim in all that armour. And then, all those damned eels! She'd emerged from the water covered in the damned things. Hands, arms, legs, neck, head, face, dangling and squirming and probably getting drunk every one of them and it wasn't no fun anyway, pulling them off. Squeeze too hard and they sprayed blood, black stuff, smelly stuff. But you had to squeeze, to get a good grip, because those mouths, they held fast, leaving huge circular weals on her flesh, puckered and oozing.

Stumbling ashore like some kind of worm witch, or demon – ha, that mongrel dog that sniffed up to her sure did run, didn't it? Stupid dog.

Sewer ramp, pretty steep, but there were rungs on the sides and she was able to work her way along it, then the climb which had damn near killed her but no chance of that. Thirst was a demanding master. The most demanding master. But she'd dumped her armour, down there knee-deep in the muck of the bottom with the keel of the damned ship nearly taking her head off – took the helmet, didn't it? And if that strap hadn't broke so conveniently . . . anyway, she'd even dropped her weapon belt. Nothing to pawn, and that was bad. Except for this knife, but it was the only knife she got, the only one left.

Still, she was thirsty. She needed to get the taste of the harbour soup out of her mouth, especially that first gasp after struggling back up to the surface, sucking in head-first the bloated corpse of a disgusting rat – that had come as close to killing her as anything so far – what if it'd been alive, and eager to climb down her throat? She'd had nightmares like that, once. During a dry spell, it was, but that's what dry spells did

– they reminded you that the world was awful and ugly and miserable and there were things out there that wanted to get you. Spiders, rats, eels, caterpillars.

Had there been a crowd up here? Not many left now, and those that came close to her kept crying out and running away in some weird blind panic. She wiped at the stinging weals on her face, blinked more muck from her eyes, lifted her head and looked around.

And now, who is that?

Sudden sobriety, sudden intent, a blast of white incandescence purging her brain and who knew what else.

And now now now, just who oh who is that? Right there – no, don't turn your back, too late. Hee hee, too too too late late late!

Hellian crept forward, as quiet as could be, came up right behind him. Drew her knife with her right hand, reached out with her left. Five more paces to go . . .

Saygen Maral stepped out from the alley. The target had doubled back, the bastard. But there he was, not ten paces away, and few people around him. Convenient. He would cease being subtle. Sometimes, it paid to remind citizens that the Claw was ever present, ever ready to do what was necessary.

The assassin drew out from beneath his cloak a paralt-smeared dagger, gingerly adjusting his grip on the weapon as he moved forward.

Some woman was staring at Banaschar – a hoary, sodden thing, with an eel dangling from under her left ear and round sores all over her exposed flesh – people, upon seeing her, were running away. *Aye, she looks like she's got the plague, but she doesn't. Must've fallen in or something. No matter.*

He returned his attention to his target's back, moved lithely forward, his footsteps making no sound. He'd spin the fool around, to catch the death in the man's eyes. Always more pleasurable that way, the rush of power that raced through the killer when the eyes locked, and recognition blossomed, along with pain and the sudden knowledge of impending death.

He was addicted to it, he knew. But he was hardly alone in that, now, was he?

With a half-smile, Saygen Maral drew up behind the drunkard, reached out and gripped the man's shoulder, then spun him round, even as the knife in his other hand rustled free of the cloak, darted forward—

A scream sounded from down the avenue.

As Banaschar was pulled around, he saw – on the face of the man opposite him – a look of shock, then consternation—

A woman had grasped the man's forearm – an arm at the end of which was a gleaming, stained knife – and, as Banaschar stared, still not quite comprehending, he saw her drive the heel of a palm into the elbow joint of that arm, snapping it clean. The knife, sprung loose, spun away to clatter on the cobbles, even as the woman, snarling something under her breath, tugged the broken arm down and drove her knee into the man's face.

A savage cracking sound, blood spraying as the head rocked back, eyes wide, and the woman twisted the arm round, forcing the man face-first onto the cobbles. She descended onto him, grasped him by the hair with both hands and began systematically pounding his skull into the street.

And, between each cracking impact, words grated from her:
'No—'
crunch
'you—'
crunch
'don't!'
crunch
'This one's—'
CRUNCH!
'*mine!*'

Appalled, Banaschar reached down, grasped the terrible apparition by her sodden jerkin, and dragged her back. 'For Hood's sake, woman! You've shattered his skull! It's all pulp! Stop! *Stop!*'

She twisted free, turned on him and, with smooth precision, set the tip of a knife just beneath his right eye. Her pocked, blood-smeared, filthy face shifted into a sneer, as she snarled, 'You! Finally! *You're under arrest!*'

And someone screamed from down the avenue. Again.

Thirty paces away, Fiddler, Gesler and Stormy all stared at the commotion not far from an alley mouth. An attempted assassination, interrupted – with fatal ferocity – by some woman—

Gesler suddenly gripped Fiddler's arm. 'Hey, that's Hellian there!'

Hellian? Sergeant Hellian?

They then heard her pronounce an arrest.

Even as screams ripped the air from farther down, and figures began racing away from the waterfront. *Now, what's all that about? Never mind.* His eyes still fixed on Hellian, who was now struggling with the poor man who looked as drunk as she was – *her husband?* – Fiddler hesitated, then he shook his head. 'Not a chance.'

'You got that right,' Gesler said. 'So, Fid, meet you in a bell, right?'

781

'Aye. Until then.'

The three soldiers set off, then almost immediately parted ways, Gesler and Stormy turning south on a route that would take them across the river on the first bridge, Fiddler continuing west, into the heart of the Centre District.

Leaving behind those frantic, terrified cries from the north end of the Centre Docks harbourfront, which seemed, despite Fiddler's pace, to be drawing ever nearer.

Plague. Smart man, Keneb. Wonder how long the ruse will last?

Then, as he reached very familiar streets on the bay side of Raven Hill Park, there came a surge of pleasure.

Hey. I'm home. Imagine that. I'm home!

And there, ten paces ahead, a small shopfront, little more than a narrow door beneath a crumbling overhang from which dangled a polished tin disc, on its surface an acid-etched symbol. A burning mouse. Fiddler halted before it, then thumped on the door. It was a lot more solid than it looked. He pounded some more, until he heard a scratching of latches being drawn back on the other side. The door opened a crack. A small rheumy eye regarded him for a moment, then withdrew.

A push and the door swung back.

Fiddler stepped inside. A landing, with stairs leading upward. The owner was already halfway up them, dragging one stiff leg beneath misaligned hips, his midnight-blue night-robe trailing like some imperial train. In one hand was a lantern, swinging back and forth and casting wild shadows. The sergeant followed.

The shop on the next floor was cluttered, a looter's haul from a hundred battles, a hundred overrun cities. Weapons, armour, jewellery, tapestries, bolts of precious silk, the standards of fallen armies, statues of unknown heroes, kings and queens, of gods, goddesses and demonic spirits. Looking round as the old man lit two more lanterns, Fiddler said, 'You've done well, Tak.'

'You lost it, didn't you?'

The sergeant winced. 'Sorry.'

Tak moved behind a broad, lacquered table and sat down, gingerly, in a plush chair that might have been the throne of some minor Quon king. 'You careless runt, Fiddler. You know I only make one at a time. No market, you see – aye, I keep my promises there. Labours of love, every time, but that kind of love don't fill the belly, don't feed the wives and all those urchins not one of 'em looking like me.' The small eyes were like barrow coins. 'Where is it, then?'

Fiddler scowled. 'Under Y'Ghatan.'

'Y'Ghatan. Better it than you.'

'I certainly thought so.'

'Changed your mind since?'

'Look, Tak, I'm no wide-eyed recruit any more. You can stop treating me like I was a damned apprentice and you my master.'

Gnarled brows rose. 'Why, Fiddler, I wasn't doing nothing of the sort. You feel that way, it's because of what's been stirred awake inside that knobby skull of yours. Old habits and all that. I meant what I said. Better it than you. Even so, how many is it now?'

'Never mind,' the sergeant growled, finding a chair and dragging it over. He slumped down into it. 'Like I said, you've done well, Tak. So how come you never got that hip fixed?'

'I gauge it this way,' the old man said, 'the limp earns sympathy, near five per cent. Better still, since I don't say nothing about nothing they all think I'm some kind of veteran. For my soldiering customers, that's another five per cent. Then there's the domestic. Wives are happier since they all know I can't catch them—'

'Wives. Why did you agree to that in the first place?'

'Well, four women get together and decide they want to marry you, it's kinda hard to say no, right? Sure, wasn't my manly looks, wasn't even that crooked baby-maker between my legs. It was this new shop, and all that mysterious coin that helped me set up again. It was the house here in the Centre District. You think I was the only one who ended up losing everything in the Mouse?'

'All right, if it makes you happy. So, you kept the limp. And you kept the promise. Well?'

Tak smiled, then reached under the table, released two latches and Fiddler heard the clunk of a hidden drawer dropping down onto its rails. Pushing the throne back, the old man slid open the large drawer, then carefully removed a cloth-wrapped object. He set it down on the table and pulled the cloth away. 'A few improvements,' he purred. 'Better range for one.'

His eyes on the extraordinary crossbow between them, Fiddler asked, 'How much better?'

'Add fifty paces, I figure. Never tested that, though. But look at the ribs. That's ten strips of iron folded together. Inside band has the most spring, grading less and less as you go out. The cable's four hundred strands into twenty, then wound in bhederin-gut and soaked in dhenrabi oil. Your old one was two hundred strands into ten. Now, look at the cradle – I only had clay mock-ups of cussers and sharpers and burners, weighted as close as I could figure—'

'Sharpers and burners?'

An eager nod. 'Why just cussers, I asked? Well, because that's what was wanted and that's how we did the cradle, right? But the mock-ups gave me an idea.' He reached back into the drawer and lifted free a clay cusser-sized grenado. 'So, I made cradles inside this, to fit five sharpers or three burners – the weight's close on all three configurations, by the way – the Moranth were always precise on these sort of things, you know.' As he was speaking, he took the clay object, one hand on top, the other beneath, and pushed in opposite directions until there was a grating click, then he was holding two halves of the hollow mock-up. 'Like I said, improvements. You can load up how you like, without ever having to change the bow's cradle. I got ten of these made. Empty, they're nice and light and you won't fly through Hood's Gate if one of 'em breaks by accident in your satchel.'

'You are a genius, Tak.'

'Tell me something I don't know.'

'How much do you want for all of this?'

A frown. 'Don't be an idiot, Fiddler. You saved my life, you and Dujek got me out of the Mouse with only a crushed hip. You gave me money—'

'Tak, we wanted you to make crossbows, like that old jeweller did before you. But he was dead and you weren't.'

'That don't matter. Call it a replacement guarantee, for life.'

Fiddler shook his head, then he reached into his pack and withdrew a real cusser. 'Let's see how it fits, shall we?'

Tak's eyes glittered. 'Oh yes, do that! Then heft the weapon, check the balance – see that over-shoulder clamp there? It's a brace for steadying aim and evening out the weight. Your arms won't get tired holding and aiming.' He rose. 'I will be right back.'

Distracted, Fiddler nodded. He set the cusser down into the weapon's cradle and clamped in place the open-ended, padded basket. That motion in turn raised from the forward base of the cradle a denticulate bar to prevent the cusser slipping out when the weapon was held point-down. That bar was in turn linked to the release trigger, dropping it flush with the cradle in time for the projectile to fly clear. 'Oh,' the sapper murmured, 'very clever, Tak.' With this weapon, there was no need for a shaft. The cradle was the launcher.

The old man was rummaging in a chest at the back of the shop.

'So tell me,' Fiddler said, 'how many more of these have you made?'

'That's it. The only one.'

'Right. So where are the others?'

'In a crate above your head.'

Fiddler glanced up to see a long box balanced across two blackened beams. 'How many in there?'

'Four.'

'Identical to this one?'

'More or less.'

'Any more?'

'Lots. For when you lose these ones.'

'I want those four above me, Tak, and I'll pay for them—'

'Take 'em, I don't want your coin. Take 'em and go blow up people you don't like.' The old man straightened and made his way back to the table.

In his hands was something that made Fiddler's eyes widen. 'Gods below, Tak . . .'

'Found it a year ago. Thought to myself, oh yes, there's always the chance. Cost me four copper crescents.'

Tak reached out to set the fiddle in the sergeant's hands.

'You were robbed,' Fiddler said. 'This is the ugliest piece of junk I've ever seen.'

'What's the difference? You never play the damned things anyway!'

'Good point. I'll take it.'

'Two thousand gold.'

'Got twelve diamonds with me.'

'Worth?'

'Maybe four thousand.'

'All right, six then for the fiddle. You want to buy the bow as well?'

'Why not?'

'That's another two thousand. See the horsehair? It's white. I knew this horse. Used to pull carts of rubbish from Hood's own temple in Old Upper. Then one day the hauler had his heart burst and he stumbled down under the animal's hoofs. It panicked and bolted, right through the webbed window wall this side of the fourth bridge—'

'Wait! That huge lead window? Fourth Bridge?'

'Fronting the recruiting kit store, aye—'

'That's it! That old temple—'

'And you won't believe who was standing there with a half-dozen knock-kneed recruits when that insane horse exploded into the room—'

'Braven Tooth!'

Tak nodded. 'And he turned right round, took one look, then hammered his fist right between the beast's eyes. It dropped dead right there. Only, the animal lands half on one lad's leg, snapping it clean, and he starts screaming. Then, ignoring all that, Master Sergeant he just turns round again and says to the wide-eyed supply clerk – I swear, I heard all this from one of those recruits – he said: "These pathetic meer-rats are heading back up to Ashok to rejoin their regiment. You make sure they got waterskins that don't leak." And he looks down at that screaming broke-leg recruit, and he says, "Your name's now Limp.

Aye, not very imaginative, but it's like this. If you can't hear Hood laughing, well, I can." And so, that's where this horsehair come from.'

'Two thousand gold for the bow?'

'With a story like that, aye, and it's a bargain.'

'Done. Now, let's get that crate down – I don't want the box. I'll just sling 'em all on my back.'

'They ain't strung, and neither is this one.'

'So we'll string 'em. You got extra cables?'

'Three for each. You want those mock-ups, too?'

'Absolutely, and I've got sharpers and burners in this pack, so let's load 'em up and check the weight and all that. But let's be quick.'

'Fiddler, it's not nice out there any more, you know? Especially tonight. Smells like the old Mouse.'

'I know, and that's why I don't want to head back out without this cusser nestled in.'

'Just be glad you're not Wickan.'

'First Wickan-hater I come across gets this egg up his dark dining hall. Tell me, Braven Tooth still live in the same house down in Lower? Near Obo's Tower?'

'That he does.'

Hellian dragged Banaschar down the winding alley – at least, it seemed to be winding, the way they kept careening off grimy walls. And she talked. 'Sure, you thought you got away clean. Not a chance. No, this is Sergeant Hellian you're dealing with here. Think I wouldn't chase you across half the damned world? Damned fool—'

'You idiot. Half the damned world? I went straight back down to the docks and sailed back to Malaz City.'

'And you thought that'd fool me? Forget it. Sure, the trail was cold, but not cold enough. And now I got you, a suspect wanted for questioning.'

The alley opened out onto a wider street. Off to their left was a bridge. Scowling, Hellian yanked her prisoner towards it.

'I told you the first time, Sergeant!' Banaschar snapped. 'I had nothing to do with that slaughter – the same thing had happened in every damned temple of D'rek, at precisely the same time. You don't understand – I have to get to Mock's Hold. I have to see the Imperial High Mage—'

'That snake! I knew it, a conspiracy! Well, I'll deal with him later. One mass-murderer at a time, I always say.'

'This is madness, Sergeant! Let go of me – I can explain—'

'Save your explanations. I got some questions for you first and you'd better answer them!'

'With what?' he sneered. 'Explanations?'

'No. Answers. There's a difference—'

'Really? How? What difference?'

'Explanations are what people use when they need to lie. Y'can always tell those, 'cause those explanations don't explain nothing and then they look at you like they just cleared things up when really they did the opposite and they know it and you know it and they know you know and you know they know that you know and they know you and you know them and maybe you go out for a pitcher later but who picks up the tab? That's what I want to know.'

'Right, and answers?'

'Answers is what I get when I ask questions. Answers is when you got no choice. I ask, you tell. I ask again, you tell some more. Then I break your fingers, 'cause I don't like what you're telling me, because those answers don't explain nothing!'

'Ah! So you really want explanations!'

'Not till you give me the answers!'

'So what are your questions?'

'Who said I got questions? I already know what your answers are, anyway. No point in questions, really.'

'And there's no need to break my fingers, Sergeant, I give up already.'

'Nice try. I don't believe you.'

'Gods below—'

Hellian dragged him back. Halting, looking about. The sergeant scowled. 'Where are we?'

'That depends. Where were you taking me?'

'Back to the ships.'

'You idiot – we went the wrong way – all you had to do was turn around back there, when you first caught me—'

'Well I didn't, did I? What's that?' She pointed.

Banaschar frowned at the brooding, unlit structure just beyond the low wall they had been walking along. Then he cursed under his breath and said, 'That's the Deadhouse.'

'What, some kind of bar?'

'No, and don't even think of dragging me in there.'

'I'm thirsty.'

'I have an idea, then, Sergeant. We can go to Coop's—'

'How far is that?'

'Straight ahead—'

'Forget it. It's a trap.' She tugged him right and they made their way along the front of the Deadhouse, then through a short alley with uneven walls, where Hellian guided her prisoner left once more. Then she halted and pointed across the way. 'What place is that one?'

'That's Smiley's. You don't want to go in there, it's where rats go to die—'

'Perfect. You're buying me a drink. Then we're heading back to the ships.'

Banaschar ran a hand across his scalp. 'As you like. They say the ale brewed in there uses water run off from the Deadhouse – and then there's the proprietor—'

'What about him?'

'Related, it's rumoured, to the old dead Emperor himself – that place used to be Kellanved's, you know.'

'The Emperor owned a tavern?'

'He did, partnered with Dancer. And there was a serving wench, named Surly—'

She shook him. 'Just because I asked questions don't mean I wanted answers, especially not those kinda answers, so be quiet!'

'Sorry.'

'One drink, then we go back to the ships and take a swim—'

'*A what?*'

'Easy. Ain't no drowned spiders in this bay.'

'No, just blood-sucking eels! Like the one dangling from behind your ear. It's already sucked all the blood from half of your face. Tell me, is your scalp getting numb on one side?'

She glared at him. 'I never gave you no permission to ask questions. That's my task. Remember that.' Then she shook her head. Something long and bloated bumped against her neck. Hellian reached up and grasped the eel. She yanked it off. 'Ow!' Glared at the writhing creature in her hand, then dropped it and crushed it under a heel. Black goo spattered out to the sides. 'See that, Banaschar? Give me trouble and you get the same treatment.'

'If I hang from your ear? Really, Sergeant, this is ridiculous—'

They turned at murmuring sounds from the street behind them. Thirty or forty locals came into view, heading for Front Street. Some of them were now carrying bows, and canisters of burning pitch swinging from straps. 'What are they about?' Hellian asked.

'They think the fleet's rotten with plague,' the ex-priest said. 'I expect they mean to set a few transports on fire.'

'Plague? There ain't no plague—'

'I know that and you know that. Now, there's another problem,' he added as the mob saw them and a half-dozen thugs split away, then slowly, ominously approached. 'Those weals all over you, Sergeant – easily mistaken for signs of plague.'

'What? Gods below, let's get into that tavern.'

They hurried forward, pushed through the doors.

Inside, inky gloom broken only by a few tallow candles on blackened tabletops. There was but one other customer, seated near the back wall. The ceiling was low, the floor underfoot littered with rubbish. The thick air reminded Hellian of a cheese-sock.

From the right appeared the proprietor, a pike-thin Dal Honese of indeterminate age, each eye looking in a different direction – neither one fixing on Hellian or Banaschar as he smiled unctuously, hands wringing.

'Ah, most sweet tryst, yes? Come! I have a table, yes! Reserved for such as you!'

'Close that ugly mouth or I'll sew it up myself,' Hellian said. 'Jus' show us the damned table then get us a pitcher of anything you got that won't come back up through our noses.'

Head bobbing, the man hobbled over to a table and, reaching out multiple times he finally grasped hold of the chairs and made a show of dragging them back through the filth.

Banaschar made to sit, then he recoiled. 'Gods below, that candle—'

'Oh yes!' said the Dal Honese gleefully, 'the few wax witches left are most generous with Smiley's. It's the history, yes?'

Sudden loud voices outside the entrance and the proprietor winced. 'Uninvited guests. A moment whilst I send them on their way.' He headed off.

Hellian finally released her grip on the ex-priest and slumped down in the chair opposite. 'Don't try nothing,' she said in a growl. 'I ain't in the mood.'

Behind her the door was pulled back by the owner. A few quiet words, then louder threats.

Hellian saw Banaschar's gaze flick past her – he had a good view of what was going on out front – and then he bolted back in his chair, eyes widening – as shrieks erupted from the mob, followed by the sounds of panicked flight.

Scowling, Hellian twisted round in her chair.

The proprietor was gone, and in the man's place stood a demon, its back to them, big enough to fill the entire doorway. A thrashing victim was in its huge hands and, as the sergeant watched, the demon tore off the screaming man's head, leaned through the doorway and threw it after the fleeing citizens. Then it flung the headless corpse in the same direction.

A strange blurring, and a sweet, spicy scent drifted back into the tavern, and then the demon was gone, in its place the old Dal Honese, brushing clean his hands, then the front of his grimy tunic. He turned about and walked back to the table.

Another smile beneath skewed eyes. 'Finest ale, then, a pitcher, coming right up!'

Hellian swung back round in her chair. Her gaze flicked over to the other customer at the back wall. A woman, a whore. The sergeant grunted, then called to her, 'You! Get much business?'

A snort in reply, then, 'Who cares?'

'Well, you got a point there, you do.'

'Both of you be quiet!' Banaschar shouted, his voice sounding half-strangled. 'That was a Kenryll'ah demon!'

'He's not so bad,' said the whore, 'once you get to know 'im.'

From behind the bar came the sound of crashing crockery, then a curse.

In clumps, in bands, in ragged troops, the crowds began reappearing along the Centre Docks harbourfront. More weapons among them now, and here and there bows. Torches flared in the dark, and voices rose, delivering commands.

Leaning against the prow of the *Silanda* – moored just behind the longboat the Red Blades had used – Koryk watched the proceedings on the front street for a time, then he turned about and made his way back down to the mid deck.

'Sergeant Balm.'

'What?'

'We could be in for some trouble soon.'

'Typical,' Balm hissed, rising to begin pacing. 'Fid vanishes. Gesler vanishes. Leaving just me, and I ain't got no whistle, do I? Deadsmell, get up'n'over, talk to Fist Keneb. See what they want us to do about it.'

The corporal shrugged, then made his way to the boarding ladder.

Tarr was climbing into his armour. 'Sergeant,' he said, 'we got Fid's crate of munitions below—'

'Hood's balls, you're right! Cuttle, get down there. Sharpers and burners, all you can lay hands on. Throatslitter – what are you doing there?'

'Was thinking of sneaking into that crowd,' the man said from the rail, where he'd thrown one leg over and was about to climb down into the murky water. 'It doesn't sound right, does it? There's ringleaders up there – Claws, maybe, and you know how I like killing those. I could make things more confused, like they should be—'

'You'll get torn to pieces, you idiot. No, you stay here, we're under-manned enough as it is.'

Koryk crouched down near Tarr and Smiles. 'Fid keeps doing this, doesn't he?'

'Relax,' Tarr said. 'If need be, me and Gesler's heavies will hold the jetty.'

'You're looking forward to that!' Smiles accused.

'Why not? Since when did the Wickans deserve all this hate? That mob's hungry for the Fourteenth, fine, why disappoint them?'

' 'Cause we was ordered to stay aboard here,' Smiles said.

'Easier holding the jetty than letting the bastards jump down onto this deck.'

'They'd jump right back off,' Koryk predicted, 'once they see those heads.'

'I'm itching for a fight, Koryk.'

'Fine, Tarr, you go up and get yourself ready. Me, Smiles and Cuttle will be right behind you, with a few dozen sharpers.'

Corabb Bhilan Thenu'alas joined them. The man was strapping on a round-shield. 'I will flank you, Corporal Tarr,' he said. 'I have found a cutlass and I have some skill with that weapon.'

'Appreciate the company,' Tarr said, then looked over to where Shortnose, Flashwit, Uru Hela and Mayfly were donning armour. 'Six in all, front line. Let them try and get past us.'

Cuttle reappeared, dragging a crate.

'Pass 'em out, sapper,' Balm ordered. 'Then we all go up top and give that mob a wave over.'

Koryk loaded his crossbow, then pounded Tarr on the shoulder. 'Let's go take a look. I'm in the mood to kill someone, too.'

The corporal straightened, then spat over the side. 'Aren't we all?'

CHAPTER TWENTY-THREE

The Twins stood on their tower
as the slaughter began below
and the knuckles bouncing wild
to their delight, now turned sudden
sudden and sour and this game
they played – the mortals bleeding
and crying in the dark – they saw
it turn and the game they played
tossed to a new wind, a gale
not their own – and so the Twins
were played, oh how they were
played.

Slayer's Moon
Vatan Urot

WITHIN SIGHT OF RAMPART WAY – THE STAIRS LEADING UP TO Mock's Hold – Kalam Mekhar glanced behind them yet again. Furtive crowds were closing in, moving one and all, it seemed, back towards the harbourfront. Who was behind all of this? What possible reason could there be?

The Fourteenth would not be dragged down into slaughter. In fact, the only realistic outcome was the very opposite. Hundreds of citizens could well die tonight, before the rest broke and fled. True, there were but a handful of marines at the jetty, but, Kalam well knew, they had Moranth munitions. And then, of course, there was Quick Ben.

Just don't use yourself up, friend. I think . . . The assassin reached beneath the folds of his cloak, reassured himself once again that he still carried the acorn the High Mage had prepared for him. *My shaved*

792

knuckle in the hole. If it came to it, he could summon Quick. *And I'm thinking . . .*

The Adjunct did not hesitate, beginning her ascent of Rampart Way. The others followed.

A long climb ahead, a tiring one, rows upon rows of steps that had seen more than their share of spilled blood. Kalam had few pleasant memories of Rampart Way. *She's up there, and so it flows down, ever down.* They were above the level of the Upper Estates now, passing through a roiling updraught of mists bitter with woodsmoke. Condensation clung to the stone wall on their left, as if the promontory itself had begun to sweat.

There was torchlight weaving through the streets below. City Watch alarms sounded here and there, and suddenly an estate was in flames, black smoke rising, eerily lit from beneath. Faint screams reached them.

And they climbed without pause, not a single word shared among them. Naught but the muted clunk and rustle of armour, the scrape of boots, heavier breaths drawn with each step. The blurred moon emerged to throw a sickly light upon the city below and the bay, illuminating Old Lookout Island at the very outside edge of the harbour, the silvery reeds of Mud Island and, further south, opposite the mouth of Redcave River, Worm Island, where stood the ruins of a long abandoned temple of D'rek. The clear water this side of Mud Island was crowded with the transports, while Nok's escorts were positioned between those transports and the four Quon dromons of Empress Laseen's entourage, the latter still moored alongside the Imperial Docks directly beneath Mock's Hold.

The world suddenly seemed etched small to Kalam's eyes, an elaborate arrangement of some child's toys. If not for the masses of torchlight closing in on the Centre Docks, the faintly seen running figures in various streets and avenues, and the distant cries of a city convulsing upon itself, the panorama would look almost picturesque.

Was he seeing the Malazan Empire's death-throes? On the island where it began, so too, perhaps, would its fall be announced, here, this night, in a chaotic, senseless maelstrom of violence. *The Adjunct crushed the rebellion in Seven Cities. This should be a triumphal return. Laseen, what have you done? Is this mad beast now broken free of your control?*

Civilization's veil was so very thin, he well knew. Casting it aside required little effort, and even less instigation. There were enough thugs in the world – and those thugs could well be wearing the raiment of a noble, or a Fist, or indeed a priest's robes or a scholar's vestments – enough of them, without question, who lusted for chaos and the opportunities it provided. For senseless cruelty, for the unleashing of hatred, for killing and rape. Any excuse would suffice, or even none at all.

Ahead of him, the Adjunct ascended without hesitation, as though she was climbing a scaffold, at peace with what the fates had decreed. Was he reading her true? Kalam did not know.

But the time was coming, very soon now, when he would need to decide.

And he hoped. He prayed. That the moment, when it arrived, would make his choice obvious, indeed, inevitable. Yet, a suspicion lurked that the choice would prove far harsher than he now dared admit.

Do I choose to live, or do I choose to die?

He looked down to his right, at those four ships directly below.

She brought a lot of people with her, didn't she?

Halfway to Raven Hill Park, Bottle drew up against a door, his heart pounding, sweat dripping from his face. Sorcery was roiling through every street. Mockra. Twisting the thoughts of the unsuspecting and the gullible, filling skulls with the hunger for violence. And lone figures making their way against the tide were victims in the waiting – he had been forced to take a roundabout route to this door, along narrow choking alleys, down beneath North Riverwalk, buried up to his ankles in the filthy mud of Malaz River, where insects rose in voracious swarms. But at last, he had arrived.

He drew a knife and, fearful of making a louder noise, scratched against the door. At the moment the street behind him was empty, but he could hear riots beginning, the splintering of wood, the shrill cry of a dying horse, and everywhere throughout the city, dogs were now barking, as if some ancient wolf memory had been awakened. He scratched again.

The door suddenly swung open. A tall, grey-haired woman stared down at him, expressionless.

'Agayla,' Bottle said. 'My uncle married your aunt's husband's sister. We're family!'

She stepped back. 'Get in here, unless you're of a mind to get torn to pieces!'

'I'm Bottle,' he said, following her into an apothecary thick with the scents of herbs, 'that's not my real name, but—'

'Oh, never mind all that. Your boots are filthy. Where have you come from and why did you choose this night of all nights to visit Malaz City? Tea?'

Blinking, Bottle nodded. 'I'm from the Fourteenth Army, Agayla—'

'Well, that was silly of you, wasn't it?'

'Excuse me?'

'You should be hiding in the boats with all the rest, dear boy.'

'I can't. I mean, the Adjunct sent me—'

She turned. 'To see me? Whatever for?'

'No, it's not that. It was my idea to find you. I'm looking for some-one. It's important – I need your help.'

Her back to him once more, she poured the herbal brew into two cups. 'Come get your tea, Bottle.'

As he stepped forward, Agayla quickly faced him again, reached into the folds of his cloak and snatched free the doll. She studied it for a moment, then, with a scowl, shook the doll in front of Bottle's face. 'And what is this? Have you any idea what you are dabbling in, child?'

'Child? Hold on—'

'Is this the man you need to find?'

'Well, yes—'

'Then you leave me no choice, do you?'

'Sorry?'

She stuffed the doll back into the folds of his cloak and turned away once more. 'Drink your tea. Then we'll talk.'

'You can help me?'

'Save the world? Well, yes, of course.'

Save the world? Now, Adjunct, you never mentioned that part.

Koryk rolled his shoulders to adjust the weight of the heavy chain armour. Longsword and shield were positioned on the damp stones behind him. In his gauntleted hands he held his crossbow. Three paces to his left stood Smiles, a sharper in her right hand, her bared teeth gleaming in the dull moonlight. To his right was Cuttle, crouched down over a collection of munitions laid out on a rain-cape. Among them was a cusser.

'Hold on, Cuttle,' Koryk said upon seeing that oversized grenado. 'Pass that cusser right back down, will you? Unless you're planning on blowing up everyone here, not to mention the *Silanda* and the *Froth Wolf.*'

The sapper squinted up at him. 'If it takes a hundred of 'em with us, I'm happy, Koryk. Don't mind that one – it's for the last thing left – you'll probably be all down by then, anyway.'

'But maybe still alive—'

'Try and avoid that, soldier. Unless you're happy with the mob hav-ing fun with what's left of you.'

Scowling, Koryk returned his attention to the massing crowd opposite. Twenty paces away, milling, shouting threats and ugly promises. Plenty of serious weapons among them. The City Guard had vanished, and all that seemed to be holding the fools back for the moment was the solid line of shield-locked soldiers facing them. Tarr, Corabb Bhilan Thenu'alas, Uru Hela, Mayfly, Shortnose and Flashwit.

A few rocks and brick fragments had been thrown across the killing ground, and those that came close were met by shields lifting almost languidly to fend them off.

Burning arrows were being readied along the flanks of the mob.

They'll try to fire the ships here first, and that is not good. He didn't think the *Silanda* would burn, not after what Gesler had told them. But the *Froth Wolf* was another matter. He glanced over to see Corporal Deadsmell cross the gangplank back to the jetty, and behind him was Fist Keneb, who then spoke.

'Sergeant Balm.'

'Aye, Fist?'

Keneb looked around. 'Where're Gesler and Fiddler?'

'Scouting, sir.'

'Scouting. I see. So, you're it, are you?'

'Those arrows, sir—'

'Destriant Run'Thurvian assures me our moored craft will be safe. The transports, alas, are another matter. We have signalled the nearest ones, with the command that they withdraw until out of range. What this means, Sergeant, is that you and your soldiers are on your own. The bow ballista on *Froth Wolf* will provide support.'

'Appreciate that, sir,' Balm said, a strangely bewildered look in his eyes. 'Where's the siege?'

'Excuse me?'

Deadsmell cleared his throat and said to Keneb, 'Don't mind him, sir. Once the fighting starts he'll be fine. Fist, you're saying those arrows won't light up the ships – once they see that they'll turn 'em on us.'

Nodding, Keneb looked over at Cuttle. 'Sapper, I want you to hit those archers on the flanks. Don't wait for their first move. Sharpers, assuming they're within range.'

Straightening, Cuttle looked over. 'Easy, sir. Galt, Lobe, get over here and collect yourselves a couple sharpers – not the cusser, Galt, you idiot – those small round ones, right? Two, damn you, no more than that. Come back if you need more—'

'Maybe three—'

'No! Think on it, Lobe. How many hands you got? Where you gonna hold the third one – between your cheeks? Two, and don't drop 'em or this whole jetty will vanish and us with it.' He turned. 'Fist, you want us to hit 'em now?'

'Might as well,' Keneb replied. 'With luck, the rest will scatter.'

Flaming arrows hissed out, seeking the rigging of the *Froth Wolf*. The sizzling arcs suddenly disappeared.

Koryk grunted. 'Cute. Better get to it, Cuttle. The next salvo's coming our way, I'd wager.'

Cuttle on the right, Galt and Lobe on the left. Hefting sharpers, then at Cuttle's command they threw the clay grenados.

Detonations, snapping like cracks in brittle stone, and bodies were down, writhing, screaming—

The centre mob, with a guttural roar, charged.

'*Shit*,' from one of the heavies up front.

Smiles launched her sharper into that onrushing midst.

Another explosion, this one ten paces in front of the shield-wall, which instinctively flinched back, heads ducking beneath raised shields. Shrieks, tumbling figures, blood and bits of meat, bodies underfoot tripping the attackers – the front of that charge had become a chaotic mess, but those behind it pushed on.

Koryk moved along to the right – he could hear someone shouting orders, a heavy voice, authoritarian – the cadence of a Malazan officer – and Koryk wanted the bastard.

The ballista mounted on the prow of the *Froth Wolf* bucked, the oversized missile speeding out, ripping through the crowd in a streak of spraying blood. A quarrel designed to knock holes in hulls punched through flesh and bone effortlessly, one body after another.

A few arrows raced towards the soldiers on the jetty, and then the mob reached the front line.

Undisciplined, convinced that the weight of impetus alone would suffice in shattering the shield-wall, they were not prepared for the perfectly timed answering push from the heavies, the large shields hammering into them, blades lashing out.

The only soldier untrained in holding a wall was Corabb Bhilan Thenu'alas, and Koryk saw Smiles move up behind the man as he chopped away at a foe with his cutlass. The man before him was huge, wielding shortswords, one thrusting the other slashing, and Corabb dropped into a sustained defence with his round shield and his weapon – even as Smiles, seeing an opening, threw a knife that took the attacker in the throat. As the man crumpled, Corabb swung and the cutlass crunched down into the unprotected head.

'Back into the gap!' Smiles screamed, pushing Corabb forward.

Koryk caught sight of a figure off to one side – not the commander – *gods, that's a mage, and he's readying a warren* – he raised his crossbow, depressed the trigger.

The quarrel sent the man spinning.

Three more sharpers detonated further back in the pressing mob. All at once the attack crumpled, and the shield-wall advanced a step, then another, weapons slashing down to finish off the wounded. Figures raced away, and Koryk heard someone in the distance shouting, calling out a rallying point – for the moment, he saw, few were listening.

One down.

On the broad loading platform and to either side, scores of bodies littered the cobbles, faint voices crying with sorrow and pain.

Gods below, we're killing our own here.

On the foredeck of the *Froth Wolf*, Keneb turned to Captain Rynag. He struggled to contain his fury as he said, 'Captain, there were soldiers in that mob. Out of uniform.'

The man was pale. 'I know nothing of that, Fist.'

'What is the point of this? They won't get their hands on the Fourteenth.'

'I – I don't know. It's the Wickans – they want them. A pogrom's begun and there's no way of stopping it. A crusade's been launched, there's an army marching onto the Wickan Plains—'

'An army? What kind of army?'

'Well, a rabble, but they say it's ten thousand strong, and there's veterans among them.'

'The Empress approves? Never mind.' Keneb turned once more and regarded the city. The bastards were regrouping. 'All right,' he said, 'if this goes on long enough I may defy the orders given me by the Adjunct. And land the whole damned army—'

'Fist, you cannot do that—'

Keneb spun round. 'Not long ago you were insisting on it!'

'*Plague*, Fist! You would unleash devastation—'

'So what? I'd rather give than receive, under the circumstances. Now, unless the Empress has a whole army hidden here in the city, the Fourteenth can put an end to this uprising – the gods know, we've got enough experience when it comes to those. And I admit, I am now of a mind to do just that.'

'Fist—'

'Get off this ship, Captain. Now.'

The man stared. 'You are threatening me?'

'Threatening? Coltaine was pinned spreadeagled to a cross outside Aren. While Pormqual's army hid behind the city's walls. I am sorely tempted, Captain, to nail you to something similar, right here and now. A gift for the unbelievers out there, just to remind them that some of us remember the truth. I am going to draw three breaths and if you're still here when I'm done—'

The captain scrambled.

Koryk watched the officer rush down the gangplank, then edge round the heavies in their line. He seemed to be making for the nearest crowd that was rallying at the mouth of a broad street.

Had Koryk considered, he would have found that array of dark thoughts in his mind – each and every one ready to find voice – to give him the excuses he needed. But he did not consider, and as for excuses, there was, for him, no need, no need at all.

He raised his crossbow.

Loosed the quarrel.

Watched it strike the captain between the shoulder-blades, watched the man sprawl forward, arms flung out to the sides.

Tarr and others in that front line turned to study him, silent, expressions blank beneath the rims of helms.

Smiles voiced a disbelieving laugh.

Heavy boots on the gangplank, then Keneb's harsh demand: 'Who was responsible for that?'

Koryk faced the Fist. 'I was, sir.'

'You just murdered a captain of the Untan Palace Guard, soldier.'

'Yes, sir.'

From Tarr: 'They're coming back for another try! Looks like you got 'em mad, Koryk.'

'Proof enough for me,' the half-blood Seti said in a growl, as he began reloading his crossbow. As he waited for Keneb to speak. Waited for the command to Balm to arrest him.

Instead, the Fist said nothing. He turned about and walked back to the *Froth Wolf*.

A hiss from Smiles. 'Look out, Koryk. Wait till Fid hears about this.'

'Fid?' snapped Sergeant Balm. 'What about the Adjunct? You're gonna get strung up, Koryk.'

'If I am then I am. But I'd do it all over again. Bastard wanted us to hand them the Wickans.'

Numbed, Keneb stepped back onto the mid deck. '. . . *wanted us to hand them the Wickans* . . .' Marines and sailors were all looking at him, and the Destriant Run'Thurvian had appeared from below and now approached.

'Fist Keneb, this night is not proceeding well, is it?'

Keneb blinked. 'Destriant?'

'A most grievous breach of discipline—'

'I am sorry,' Keneb cut in, 'it's clear you misunderstand. Some time ago, the Adjunct proclaimed the birth of the Bonehunters. What did she see then? I had but a sense of it – barely a sense. More like a suspicion. But now . . .' he shook his head. 'Three squads on the jetty standing their ground, and why?'

'Fist, the threat is perceived, and must be answered.'

'We could cast lines and sail out. Instead, here we are. Here they are, ready to bloody the noses of anyone who dares come close. Ready to answer blood with blood. Betrayal, Destriant, stalks this night like a god, right here in Malaz City.' He strode past the others, back to the forecastle. 'That ballista loaded?' he demanded.

One of the crew nodded. 'Aye, Fist.'

'Good. They're closing fast.'

The Destriant moved up beside Keneb. 'Fist, I do not understand.'

Keneb pulled his attention from the hundreds edging ever closer. 'But I do. I've seen. We're holding the jetty, and not one damned soldier down there gives a damn about anything else! Why?' He thumped the rail. 'Because *we're waiting*. We're waiting for the Adjunct. Destriant, we're *hers*, now. It's done, and the damned empire can rot!'

The other man's eyes slowly widened at this outburst, and then, with a faint smile, he bowed. 'As you say, Fist. As you say.'

Last door down the tenement hall, uppermost floor. *Typical*. The knife-edge slipped easily between the door and the frame, lifted the latch. A slow, even push moved the door back with but the faintest moan from the leather hinges.

Fiddler slipped inside, looked round in the gloom.

Loud animal snoring and grunts from the cot, a smell of stale beer pervading the turgid air.

Moving in the tiniest increments, Fiddler lowered his collection of crossbows to the floor, a procedure taking nearly thirty heartbeats, yet not once did the stentorian notes of slumber pause from the figure on the cot.

Unburdened now, Fiddler crept closer, breathing nice and slow, until he hovered right above his unsuspecting victim's shaggy head.

Then he began whispering in a singsong voice, '*Your ghosts – we're back – never to leave you alone, never to give you a moment's rest – oh yes, dear Braven Tooth, it's me, Fiddler, dead but not gone – a ghost, returning to haunt you until your last—*'

The fist came out of nowhere, connecting solidly with Fiddler's midriff. All air driven from him, the sergeant collapsed backward, onto the floor, where he curled up round the agony—

As Braven Tooth climbed upright. 'That wasn't funny, Fiddler,' he said, looking down. 'But you, squirming round down there on the floor, now that's funny.'

'Shut that mouth,' gasped Fiddler, 'and find me a chair.'

The Master Sergeant helped him to his feet. Leaning heavily, Fiddler carefully straightened, the effort punctuated with winces and the hiss of breath between his teeth.

'You'll live?'

A nod, and Fiddler managed to step back. 'All right, I deserved that—'

'Goes without saying,' Braven Tooth replied.

They faced each other in the darkness for a moment, and then they embraced. And said nothing.

A moment later the door swung open behind them. They parted to see Gesler and Stormy, the former carrying two bottles of wine and the latter three loaves of bread.

'Hood's breath!' Braven Tooth laughed. 'The old bastards one and all come home!'

As Gesler and Stormy set their victuals down on a small table, Fiddler examined the fiddle that had been strapped to his back. No damage beyond the old damage, he was pleased to see. He drew out the bow, looked round as Braven Tooth ignited a lantern, then walked over to a chair and sat down.

A moment, then all three men were staring across at him.

'I know,' Fiddler said. 'Braven Tooth, you remember the last time I played—'

'That was the *last* time?'

'It was, and there's been a lot who've fallen since then. Friends. People we grew to love, and now miss, like holes in the heart.' He drew a deep breath, then continued, 'It's been waiting, inside, for a long time. So, my old, old friends, let's hear some names.'

Braven Tooth sat down on the cot, scratching at his beard. 'Got a new one for you. A soldier I sent off this very night who got himself killed. Name of Gentur. His friend Mudslinger nearly died himself but it looks like the Lady pulled. And we found him in time to help things along.'

Fiddler nodded. 'Gentur. All right. Gesler?'

'Kulp. Baudin. And, I think, Felisin Paran – she had no luck at all, and when good things showed up, rare as that was, well, she didn't know what to do or say.' He shrugged. 'A person hurts enough inside, all they can do is hurt back. So, her as well.' He paused, then added, 'Pella, Truth.'

'And Coltaine,' Stormy said. 'And Duiker, and the Seventh.'

Fiddler began tuning the instrument. 'Good names, one and all. I'll add a few more. Whiskeyjack. Hedge. Trotts. And one more – no name yet, and it's not so bad as that. One more . . .' He grimaced. 'Could sound a little rough, no matter how much rosin I use. No matter. Got a sad dirge in my head that needs to come out—'

'All sad, Fid?'

'No, not all. I leave the good memories to you – but I'll give you a whisper every now and then, to tell you I know what you're feeling.

Now, settle down – pour them cups full, Gesler – this'll take a while, I expect.'

And he began to play.

The heavy door at the top of Rampart Way opened with a squeal, revealing a massive, humped form silhouetted on the threshold. As the Adjunct reached the level, the figure stepped back. She strode into the gatehouse, followed by T'amber, then Fist Tene Baralta. Kalam entered the musty room. The air was sweet with the cloying fumes of rum.

The assassin paused opposite the keeper. 'Lubben.'

A heavy, rumbling reply, 'Kalam Mekhar.'

'Busy night?'

'Not everybody uses the door,' Lubben replied.

Kalam nodded, and said nothing more. He continued on, emerging out into the keep's courtyard, tilted flagstones underfoot, the old tower off to the left, the hold itself slightly to his right. The Adjunct had already traversed half the length of the concourse. Behind Kalam the escort of Untan Guard now separated themselves from the group, making for the barracks near the north wall.

Kalam squinted up at the murky moon. A faint wind brushed across his face, warm, sultry and dry, plucking at the sweat on his brow. Somewhere overhead, a weather vane squealed momentarily. The assassin set off after the others.

Two Claws flanked the keep entrance – not the usual guard. Kalam wondered where the resident Fist and his garrison were this night. *Probably in the storehouse cellars, blind drunk. Hood knows, it's where I would be in their boots.* Not old Lubben, of course. That hoary hunchback was as old as the Rampart Gate itself – he'd always been there, as far back as the Emperor's time and even, if rumours were true, back to Mock's rule of the island.

As Kalam passed between the two assassins, both tilted their hooded heads in his direction. A mocking acknowledgement, he concluded, or something worse. He made no response, continuing on into the broad hallway.

Another Claw had been awaiting them, and this cowled figure now led them towards the staircase.

Ascending two levels, then down a corridor, into an antechamber, where Tene Baralta ordered his Red Blades to remain, barring his captain, Lostara Yil. The Fist then sent off two of his soldiers after a brief whispered set of instructions. The Adjunct watched all of this without expression, although Kalam was tempted to call Baralta out on what was obviously an act of pointed independence – as if Tene Baralta was divesting himself and his Red Blades of any association with the Adjunct and the Fourteenth Army.

After a moment, the Claw led them onward, through another portal, into another corridor, then down its length to a set of double doors. Not the usual room for official meetings, Kalam knew. This one was smaller – if the approach was any indication – and situated in a quarter of the keep rarely frequented. Two more Claws stood guard at the entrance, and both turned to open the doors.

Kalam watched the Adjunct stride in, then halt. As did T'amber and Tene Baralta. Beside the assassin, Lostara Yil's breath caught.

A tribunal awaited them, and seated opposite them were Empress Laseen, Korbolo Dom – attired as a High Fist – and another person Kalam did not recognize. Round-faced and full-featured, corpulent, wearing blue silks. His hair was colourless, cut short and oiled. Sleepy eyes regarded the Adjunct with an executioner's avarice.

The tables were arranged in an inverted T, and three chairs waited, their high backs to the newcomers.

After a long moment, the Adjunct stepped forward, drew out the centre chair, and sat, her back straight. T'amber took the chair to Tavore's left. Tene Baralta gestured Lostara Yil to accompany him and moved off to the far right side, where he stood at attention, facing the Empress.

Kalam slowly sighed, then walked to the remaining chair. Sitting down, he settled both gloved hands on the scarred tabletop before him.

The oily fat man fixed his gaze on the assassin and leaned forward slightly. 'Kalam Mekhar, yes? Great pleasure,' he murmured, 'in meeting you at last.'

'Is it? I'm happy for you . . . whoever you are.'

'Mallick Rel.'

'Here in what capacity?' Kalam asked. 'Chief snake?'

'That will be enough from you,' the Empress said. 'Sit if you must, Kalam, but be silent. And understand, I did not request your presence here this night.'

Kalam sensed a hidden question in that statement, to which he but shrugged. *No, Laseen, I'm not ready to give you anything.*

Laseen shifted her attention to the commander of the Red Blades. 'Tene Baralta, I understand you assisted in escorting the Adjunct and her retinue through the city. Noble of you. I assume the Adjunct did not invite you, nor compel you in any manner. Accordingly, it seems clear that you wish to speak to me on behalf of the Red Blades.'

The man with the ravaged face bowed, then said, 'Yes, Empress.'

'Go on.'

'The Red Blades were conscripted by the Adjunct in Aren, Empress, whereupon I was made a Fist in the Fourteenth Army. I respectfully request that you countermand that order. The Red Blades have ever served the Malazan Empire in an independent capacity, as befitting our unique status the first and foremost Imperial Guardians in Seven Cities.'

The Empress nodded. 'I see no reason not to grant your request, Commander. Does the Adjunct wish to make comment?'

'No.'

'Very well. Commander Tene Baralta, the Red Blades can be quartered here in Mock's Hold for the time being. You may leave.'

The man bowed again, then, turning about, he marched from the chamber. His captain followed.

The doors closed once more behind them.

Laseen fixed her attention on the Adjunct. 'Welcome home, Tavore,' she said.

'Thank you, Empress.'

'The transports in the harbour display the flag of plague – you and I both know that no plague is present among the soldiers of your army.' She tilted her head. 'What am I to make of this attempt at deception?'

'Empress, Fist Keneb has evidently concluded that, regardless of Captain Rynag's views, Malaz City is in a state of civil unrest, sufficient to make Keneb fear for the well-being of the Fourteenth, should the army disembark. After all, I have with me Wickans – whose loyalty to the Empire, I might add, is beyond reproach. In addition, we have a substantial force of Khundryl Burned Tears, who have also served with distinction. To land such troops could invite a bloodbath.'

'A bloodbath, Adjunct?' Laseen's brows rose. 'Captain Rynag was given specific orders to ensure that the soldiers of the Fourteenth disarm prior to disembarking.'

'Thus leaving them at the mercy of an enflamed mob, Empress.'

Laseen waved dismissively.

'Empress,' the Adjunct continued, 'I believe there is now the misapprehension, here in the heart of the empire, that the events commonly known as the Chain of Dogs – and those that followed at Aren – are somehow suspect.' She paused, then resumed, 'I see that Korbolo Dom, who commanded the renegade Dogslayers, and who was captured and arrested in Raraku, is once more a free man, and, indeed, a High Fist. Furthermore, the Jhistal priest and likely instigator in the slaughter of the Aren Army, Mallick Rel, now sits as your adviser in these proceedings. Needless to say, I am confused by this. Unless, of course, the Seven Cities Rebellion has succeeded beyond its wildest dreams, regardless of my own successes in Seven Cities.'

'My dear Tavore,' Laseen said, 'I admit to some embarrassment on your behalf. You appear to hold to the childish notion that some truths are intransigent and undeniable. Alas, the adult world is never so simple. All truths are malleable. Subject, by necessity, to revision. Have you not yet observed, Tavore, that in the minds of the people in this empire, truth is without relevance? It has lost its power. It no longer effects change and indeed, the very will of the people – born of fear and ignorance, granted – the very will, as I said, can in turn revise those truths, can transform, if you like, the lies of convenience into faith, and that faith in turn is not open to challenge.'

'In challenging,' the Adjunct said after a moment, 'one commits treason.'

The Empress smiled. 'I see you grow older with every heartbeat, Tavore. Perhaps we might mourn the loss of innocence, but not for long, I'm afraid. The Malazan Empire is at its most precarious moment, and all is uncertain, hovering on the cusp. We have lost Dujek Onearm to plague – and his army appears to have vanished entirely, likely also victims of that plague. Events have taken a turn for the worse in Korel. The decimation of Seven Cities has struck us a near-mortal blow with respect to our economy and, specifically, the harvests. We may find our-selves facing starvation before the subcontinent can recover. It becomes imperative, Tavore, to force a new shape upon our empire.'

'And what, Empress, does this new shape entail?'

Mallick Rel spoke: 'Victims, alas. Spilled blood, to slacken the thirst, the need. Unfortunate, but no other path presents. All are saddened here.'

Tavore slowly blinked. 'You wish me to hand over the Wickans.'

'And,' Mallick Rel said, 'the Khundryl.'

Korbolo Dom suddenly leaned forward. 'One other matter, Tavore Paran. Who in Hood's name are on those catamarans?'

'Soldiers of a people known as the Perish.'

'Why are they here?' the Napan demanded, baring his teeth.

'They have pledged allegiance, High Fist.'

'To the Malazan Empire?'

The Adjunct hesitated, then fixed her gaze once more upon Laseen. 'Empress, I must speak with you. In private. There are matters that belong exclusively to the Empress and her Adjunct.'

Mallick Rel hissed, then said, 'Matters unleashed by an otataral sword, you mean! It is as I feared, Empress! She serves another, now, and would draw cold iron across the throat of the Malazan Empire!'

Tavore's expression twisted, unveiling disgust as she looked upon the Jhistal priest. 'The empire has ever refused an immortal patron, Mallick Rel. For this reason more than any other, we have survived and, indeed, grown ever stronger. *What are you doing here, priest?*'

'Who do you now serve, woman?' Mallick Rel demanded.

'I am the Adjunct to the Empress.'

'Then you must do as she commands! Give us the Wickans!'

'Us? Ah, now I see. You were cheated of some of your glory outside Aren. Tell me, how long before an arrest writ is issued for Fist Blistig, the once-commander of the Aren Guard who defied the order to leave the city? Because of him and him alone, Aren did not fall.'

Laseen asked, 'Were not the Red Blades in Aren arrested by Blistig, Tavore?'

'At Pormqual's command. Please, Empress, we must speak, you and I, alone.'

And Kalam saw then, in Laseen's eyes, something he thought he would never see. A flicker of fear.

But it was Korbolo Dom who spoke. 'Adjunct Tavore, I am now High Fist. And, with Dujek's death, I am *ranking* High Fist. Furthermore, I have assumed the title and responsibilities of First Sword of the Empire, a post sadly vacant since Dassem Ultor's untimely death. Accordingly, I now assume command of the Fourteenth Army.'

'Tavore,' Laseen said quietly, 'it was never the function of an Adjunct to command armies. Necessity forced my hand with the rebellion in Seven Cities, but that is now over. You have completed all that I asked of you, and I am not blind to your loyalty. It grieves me that this meeting has become so overtly hostile – you are the extension of my will, Tavore, and I do not regret my choice. No, not even now. It seems I must make the details of my will clear to you. I want you at my side once more, in Unta. Mallick Rel may well possess talents in many areas of administration, but he lacks in others – I need you for those, Tavore, I need you at my side to complement the Jhistal priest. You see before you the restructuring of the imperial high command. A new First Sword now assumes overall command of the Malazan Armies. The time has come, Tavore, to set aside your own sword.'

Silence. From Tavore, no movement, not a single twitch of emotion. 'As you command, Empress.'

Beneath his clothes, Kalam felt his skin grow hot, as if close to blistering flames. Sweat ran down his body; he could feel it beading on his face and neck. He stared down at his leather-clad hands, motionless on the worn wood of the tabletop.

'I am pleased,' Laseen said.

'It will be necessary,' Tavore said, 'for me to return, briefly, to the docks. I believe Fist Keneb will doubt the veracity of the change of command if informed by anyone but me.'

'A most loyal man,' Mallick Rel murmured.

'Yes, he is that.'

'And these Perish?' Korbolo Dom demanded. 'Are they worth the trouble? Will they submit to my authority?'

'I cannot speak for them in that matter,' Tavore said tonelessly. 'But they will not reject any overtures out of hand. As for their prowess, I believe it will suffice, at least in an auxiliary function to our regulars.'

'There is nothing more to them?'

The Adjunct's shrug was careless. 'They are foreigners, First Sword. Barbarians.'

Barbarians sailing the finest warships on the damned ocean, aye.

But Korbolo Dom, in all his percipience and razor-honed judgement, simply nodded.

Another moment of silence, in which so many things could have been said, in which the course of the Malazan Empire could have found firmer footing. Silence, and yet to Kalam it seemed he could hear the slamming of doors, the clatter and crunch of portcullis dropping, and he saw hallways, avenues, where the flickering light dimmed, then vanished.

If the Empress were to speak then, with words for the Adjunct alone – anything, any overture that did not ring false—

Mallick Rel said, 'Adjunct, there is the matter of two Wickans, a warlock and a witch.'

Tavore's eyes remained on Laseen. 'Of course. Fortunately, they are ineffectual, a consequence of the trauma they experienced with Coltaine's death.'

'Nonetheless, the Claw will effect their arrest.'

The Empress said, 'It cannot be helped, Tavore. Even with a remnant of their old power, they could unleash slaughter upon the citizens of Malaz City, and that we cannot have.'

'The blood this night belongs to the Wickans and the Khundryl.' A statement from the Adjunct, devoid of all emotion.

'It must be so,' the Jhistal priest murmured, as if struck anew by grief.

'Tavore,' Laseen said, 'will the Khundryl prove recalcitrant in yielding their arms and armour? Do they not number two thousand, or more?'

'A word from me will suffice,' the Adjunct said.

'I am greatly relieved,' the Empress said, with a faint smile, 'that you now comprehend the necessity of what will occur this night. In the broader scheme of things, Tavore, the sacrifice is modest. It is also clear that the Wickans have outlived their usefulness – the old covenants with the tribes must be dispensed with, now that Seven Cities and its harvest have become so thoroughly disrupted. In other words, we need the Wickan Plains. The herds must be slaughtered and the earth broken, crops planted. Seven Cities has provided us a harsh lesson when it comes to relying upon distant lands for the resources the empire consumes.'

'In this way,' Mallick Rel said, spreading his hands, 'necessity is an economic matter, yes? That an ignorant and backward people must be eradicated is sad, indeed, but alas, inevitable.'

'You would well know of that,' Tavore said to him. 'The Gedorian Falari cult of the Jhistal was eradicated in a similar manner by Emperor Kellanved, after all. Presumably you are among the very few survivors from that time.'

Mallick Rel's round, oiled face slowly drained of what little colour it had possessed.

The Adjunct continued, 'A very minor note in the imperial histories, difficult to find. I believe, however, should you peruse the works of Duiker, you will find suitable references. Of course, "minor" is a relative term, just as, I suppose, this Wickan Pogrom will be seen in later histories. For the Wickans themselves, of course, it will be any-thing but minor.'

'Your point, woman?' Mallick Rel asked.

'It is useful, on occasion, to halt upon a path, and to turn and walk back some distance.'

'Achieving what?'

'An understanding of motivations, Jhistal. It seems that this is a night of unravelling, after all. Covenants, treaties, and memories—'

'This debate,' the Empress cut in, 'can be conducted another time. The mob in the city below will soon turn upon itself if the proper victims are not delivered. Are you ready, Adjunct?'

Kalam found he was holding his breath. He could not see Tavore's eyes, but something in Laseen's told him that the Adjunct had locked gazes with the Empress, and in that moment something passed between them, and slowly, in increments, the eyes of Laseen went flat, strangely colourless.

The Adjunct rose. 'I am, Empress.'

T'amber also stood, and, before anyone could shift their attention to Kalam, the assassin climbed to his feet.

'Adjunct,' he said in a weary rumble, 'I will see you out.'

'When you are done that courtesy,' the Empress said, 'please return here. I have never accepted your resignation from the Claw, Kalam Mekhar, and indeed, it is in my mind that worthy promotions are long overdue. The apparent loss of Topper in the Imperial Warren has left vacant the command of the Claw. I can think of no-one more deserving of that position.'

Kalam's brows lifted. 'And do you imagine, Empress, that I would assume that mantle and just settle back in Unta's West Tower, surrounding myself with whores and sycophants? Do you expect another Topper?'

Now it was Laseen's turn to speak without inflection. 'Most certainly not, Kalam Mekhar.'

The entire Claw, under my control. Gods, who would fall first? Mallick Rel. Korbolo Dom . . .

And she knows that. She offers that. I can cut the cancers out of the flesh . . . but first, some Wickans need to die. And . . . not just Wickans.

Not trusting himself to speak, and not knowing what he might say if he did, Kalam simply bowed to the Empress, then followed Tavore and T'amber as they strode from the chamber.

Into the corridor.

Twenty-three paces to the antechamber – no Red Blades remained – where Tavore paused, gesturing to T'amber who moved past and positioned herself at the far door. The Adjunct then shut the one behind them.

And faced Kalam.

But it was T'amber who spoke. 'Kalam Mekhar. How many Hands await us?'

He looked away. 'Each Hand is trained to work as a unit. Both a strength and a flaw.'

'How many?'

'Four ships moored below. Could be as many as eighty.'

'*Eighty?*'

The assassin nodded. *You are dead, Adjunct. So are you, T'amber.* 'She will not let you get back to the ships,' he said, still not meeting their gazes. 'To do so invites a civil war—'

'No,' Tavore said.

Kalam frowned, glanced at her.

'We are leaving the Malazan Empire. And in all likelihood, we will never return.'

He walked to a wall, leaned his back against it, and closed his eyes. Sweat streamed down his face. 'Don't you understand what she just offered me? I can walk right back into that room and do precisely what she wants me to do – what she needs me to do. She and I will then walk out of there, leaving two corpses, their heads sawed off and planted on that damned table. Damn this, Tavore. Eighty Hands!'

'I understand,' the Adjunct said. 'Go then. I will not think less of you, Kalam Mekhar. You are of the Malazan Empire. Now serve it.'

Still he did not move, nor open his eyes. 'So it means nothing to you, now, Tavore?'

'I have other concerns.'

'Explain them.'

'No.'

'Why not?'

T'amber said, 'There is a convergence this night, Kalam, here in Malaz City. The game is in a frenzy of move and countermove, and yes, Mallick Rel is a participant, although the hand that guides him remains remote, unseen. Removing him, as you intend to do, will prove a deadly blow and may well shift the entire balance. It may well save not just the Malazan Empire, but the world itself. How can we object to your desire?'

'And yet . . .'

'Yes,' T'amber said. 'We are asking you. Kalam, without you we stand no chance at all—'

'Six hundred assassins, damn you!' He set his head against the wall, unwilling, unable to look upon these two women, to see the need in their eyes. 'I'm not enough. You have to see that. We all go down, and Mallick Rel lives.'

'As you say,' Tavore replied.

He waited for her to add something more, a final plea. He waited for a new tack from T'amber. But there was only silence.

'Is it worth it, Adjunct?'

'Win this battle, Kalam, or win the war.'

'I'm just one man.'

'Yes.'

With a shaved knuckle in the hole.

His palms itched against the damp leather of his gloves. 'That Jhistal priest holds a grudge.'

'A prolonged one, yes,' said T'amber. 'That, and a lust for power.'

'Laseen is desperate.'

'Yes, Kalam, she is.'

'Why not stay right here, the both of you? Wait for me to kill them. Wait, and I will convince the Empress that this pogrom needs to be stopped. Right now. No more blood spilled. There's six hundred assassins in the city below – we can crush this madness, scour away this fever—'

'No more blood, Kalam Mekhar?'

T'amber's question stung him, then he shook his head. 'Ringleaders, nothing more will be required.'

'It is clear that something has not occurred to you,' T'amber said.

'What hasn't?'

'The Claw. They are infiltrated. Extensively. The Jhistal priest has not been idle.'

'How do you know this?'

Silence once more.

Kalam rubbed at his face with both hands. 'Gods below . . .'

'May I ask you a question?'

He snorted. 'Go ahead, T'amber.'

'You once railed at the purging of the Old Guard. In fact, you came to this very city not so long ago, intending to assassinate the Empress.'

How does she know this? How could she know any of this? Who is she? 'Go on.'

'You were driven by outrage, by indignation. Your own memories had been proclaimed nothing but lies, and you wanted to defy those revisionists who so sullied all that you valued. You wanted to look into the eyes of the one who decided the Bridgeburners had to die – you needed to see the truth there, and, if you found it, you would act. But she talked you out of it—'

'She wasn't even here.'

'Ah, you knew that, then. Well, no matter. Would that alone have stopped you from crossing to Unta? From chasing her down?'

He shook his head.

'In any case, where now is your indignation, Kalam Mekhar? Coltaine of the Crow Clan. The Imperial Historian Duiker. The Seventh Army. And now, the Wickans of the Fourteenth. Fist Temul. Nil, Nether. Gall of the Khundryl Burned Tears, who threw back Korbolo Dom at Sanimon – cheating Korbolo's victory long before Aren. The betrayers are in the throne room—'

'I can make that stay shortlived.'

'You can. And if you so choose, the Adjunct and I will die possessing at least that measure of satisfaction. But in dying, so too will many, many others. More than any of us can comprehend.'

'You ask where is my indignation, but you have the answer before you. It lives. Within me. And it is ready to kill. Right now.'

'Killing Mallick Rel and Korbolo Dom this night,' T'amber said, 'will not save the Wickans, nor the Khundryl. Will not prevent war with the Perish. Or the destruction of the Wickan Plains. The Empress is indeed desperate, so desperate that she will sacrifice her Adjunct in exchange for the slaying of the two betrayers in her midst. But tell me, do you not think Mallick Rel understood the essence of Laseen's offer to you?'

'Is that your question?'

'Yes.'

'Korbolo Dom is a fool. Likely he comprehends nothing. The Jhistal priest is, unfortunately, not a fool. So, he is prepared.' Kalam fell silent, although his thoughts continued, following countless tracks. Potentials, possibilities. 'He may not know I possess an otataral weapon—'

'The power he can draw upon is Elder,' T'amber said.

'So, after all we've said here, I may fail.'

'You may.'

'And if I do, then we all lose.'

'Yes.'

Kalam opened his eyes, and found that the Adjunct had turned away. T'amber alone faced him, her gold-hued eyes unwavering in their uncanny regard.

Six hundred. 'Tell me this, T'amber: between you and the Adjunct, whose life matters more?'

The reply was immediate. 'The Adjunct's.'

It seemed that Tavore flinched then, but would not face them.

'And,' Kalam asked, 'between you and me?'

'Yours.'

Ah. 'Adjunct. Choose, if you will, between yourself and the Fourteenth.'

'What is the purpose of all this?' Tavore demanded, her voice ragged.

'Choose.'

'Fist Keneb has his orders,' she said.

Kalam slowly closed his eyes once more. Somewhere, at the back of his mind, a faint, ever faint sound. Music. Filled with sorrow. 'Warrens in the city,' he said in a soft voice. 'Many, seething with power – Quick Ben will be hard-pressed even if I can get through to him, and there's no chance of using gates. Adjunct, you will need your sword. Otataral out front . . . and to the rear.'

Strange music, the tune unfamiliar and yet . . . he knew it.

Kalam opened his eyes, even as the Adjunct slowly turned.

The pain in her gaze was like a blow against his heart.

'Thank you,' she said.

The assassin drew a deep breath, then rolled his shoulders. 'All right, no point in keeping them waiting.'

Pearl stepped into the chamber. Mallick Rel was pacing, and Korbolo Dom had uncorked a bottle of wine and was pouring himself a goblet. The Empress remained in her chair.

She wasted no time on small talk. 'The three are nearing the Gate.'

'I see. So, Kalam Mekhar made his choice, then.'

A flicker of something like disappointment. 'Yes, he is out of your way now, Pearl.'

You bitch. Offered him the Claw, did you? And where would that have left me? 'He and I have unfinished business, Empress.'

'Do not let that interfere with what must be done. Kalam is the least relevant target, do you understand me? Get him out of the way, of course, but then complete what is commanded of you.'

'Of course, Empress.'

'When you return,' Laseen said, with a small smile on her plain features, 'I have a surprise for you. A pleasant one.'

'I doubt I shall be gone long—'

'It is that overconfidence that I find most irritating in you, Pearl.'

'Empress, he is one man!'

'Do you imagine the Adjunct helpless? She wields an otataral sword, Pearl – the sorcery by which the Claw conduct their ambushes will not work. This will be brutal. Furthermore, there is T'amber, and she remains – to all of us – a mystery. I do not want you to return to me at dawn to inform me that success has left two hundred dead Claws in the streets and alleys below.'

Pearl bowed.

'Go, then.'

Mallick Rel turned at that moment, 'Clawmaster,' he said, 'when the task is done, be sure to dispatch two Hands to the ship, *Froth Wolf*, with instructions to kill Nil and Nether. If opportunity arrives thereafter, they are to kill Fist Keneb as well.'

Pearl frowned. 'Quick Ben is on that ship.'

'Leave him be,' the Empress said.

'He will not act to defend the targets?'

'His power is an illusion,' Mallik Rel said dismissively. 'His title as High Mage is unearned, yet I suspect he enjoys the status, and so will do nothing to reveal the paucity of his talents.'

Pearl slowly cocked his head. *Really, Mallick Rel?*

'Send out the commands,' Laseen said.

The Clawmaster bowed again, then left the chamber.

Kalam Mekhar. Finally, we can end this. For that, Empress, thank you.

They entered the gatehouse at the top of Rampart Way. Lubben was a shadow hunched over a small table off to one side. The keeper glanced up, then down again. A large bronze tankard was nestled in his huge, battered hands.

Kalam paused. 'Tilt that back once for us, will you?'

A nod. 'Count on it.'

They moved to the opposite gate.

Behind them, Lubben said, 'Mind that last step down there.'

'We will.'

And thanks for that, Lubben.

They stepped out onto the landing.

Below, buildings were burning here and there across the city. Torches scurried back and forth like glow-worms in rotted flesh. Faint shouts, screams. Centre Docks was a mass of humanity.

'Marines on the jetty,' the Adjunct said.

'They're holding,' T'amber noted, as if to reassure Tavore.

Gods below, there must be a thousand or more in that mob. 'There's barely three squads there, Adjunct.'

She said nothing, and began the descent. T'amber followed, and finally, with a last glance at the seething battle at Centre Docks, Kalam set off in their wake.

Tene Baralta strode into the well-furnished room, paused to look around for a moment, then made his way to a plush high-backed chair. 'By the Seven,' he said with a loud sigh, 'at last we are done with the cold-eyed bitch.' He sat down, stretched out his legs. 'Pour us some wine, Captain.'

Lostara Yil approached her commander. 'That can wait. Allow me to help you out of your armour, sir.'

'Good idea. The ghost of my arm pains me so – my neck muscles are like twisted bars of iron.'

She drew the lone gauntlet off his remaining hand and set it on the table. Then moved to behind the chair, reached over and unclasped the man's cloak. He half-rose, allowing her to pull it away. She folded it carefully and set it on top of a wooden chest near the large, cushion-piled bed. Returning to Tene Baralta she said, 'Stand for a moment, sir, if you will. We will remove the chain.'

Nodding, he straightened. It was awkward, but they finally managed to draw the heavy armour away. She placed it in a heap at the foot of the bed. Baralta's under-quilting was damp with sweat, pungent and stained under the arms. She pulled it away, leaving the man bare above the hips. The scars of old burns were livid weals. His muscles had softened with disuse beneath a layer of fat.

'High Denul,' Lostara said, 'the Empress will not hesitate in seeing you properly mended.'

'That she will,' he said, settling back into the chair. 'And then, Lostara Yil, you will not flinch when looking upon me. I have had many thoughts, of you and me.'

'Indeed.' She moved up behind him yet again, and began kneading the rock-hard tension gripping the muscles to either side of his neck.

'Yes. It is, I believe now, meant to be.'

'Do you recall, sir,' she said, 'a visit I made, long ago now, when on Kalam Mekhar's trail. A visit to a garrison keep. I sat at the very same table as the assassin. A Deck was unveiled, rather unexpectedly. Death and Shadow predominated the field, if my memory serves – and that, I admit, I cannot guarantee. In any case, following your instructions precisely, I later conducted a thorough slaughter of everyone present – after Kalam's departure, of course.'

'You have always followed orders with impressive precision, Lostara Yil.'

She brought her left hand up along his jaw-line, stroking softly. 'That morning of murder, Commander, remains my greatest regret. They were innocents, one and all.'

'Do not let such errors weigh on you, my love.'

'That is a difficult task, sir. Achieving the necessary coldness.'

'You have singular talents in such matters.'

'I suppose I have,' she said, as her palm brushed his mangled lips, then settled there, against his mouth. And the knife in her other hand slid into the side of his neck, behind the windpipe, then slashed out and down.

Blood flooded against the palm of her hand, along with gurgling sounds and bubbles of escaping air. The body in the chair twitched a few times, then slumped down.

Lostara Yil stepped away. She wiped the knife and her hands on the silk bedding. Sheathing the weapon once more, she collected her gloves, and walked to the door.

She opened it only wide enough to permit her passage through, and to the two Red Blades standing guard outside, she said, 'The commander sleeps now. Do not disturb him.'

The soldiers saluted.

Lostara closed the door, then strode down the corridor.

Very well, Cotillion, you were right about him after all.

And once again, the necessary coldness was achieved.

Uru Hela was down, screaming and curling up round the spear transfixing her torso. Swearing, Koryk pushed hard with his shield, driving the attackers back until he could step over her. Smiles edged in behind him, grasped the downed soldier by the belt and pulled Uru Hela back.

Another sharper exploded, bodies whirling away in sheets of blood, the spray striking Koryk's face beneath the helm. He blinked stinging heat from his eyes, took a mace blow against his shield, then thrust upward from beneath it, the sword-point ripping into a groin. The shriek that exploded from the crippled attacker nearly deafened him. He tugged the sword loose.

There were shouts behind him, but he could make little sense of them. With Uru Hela out of the fight, and Shortnose getting crippled by a sword through a thigh in the last rush, the front line was desperately thin. Both Galt and Lobe had joined it now. Deadsmell worked on Shortnose's bleeder, and Widdershins was frantically trying to deflect assaults of Mockra – the sorcerous attacks seeking to incite confusion and panic – and the squad mage was fast weakening.

What in Hood's name was Quick Ben up to? Where was he? Why hadn't he emerged onto the deck of the *Froth Wolf*?

Koryk found himself swearing in every language he knew. They couldn't hold.

And who was playing that damned music, anyway?

He fought on.

And saw nothing of what was happening behind him, the sliding out of darkness of the enormous wolf-headed catamaran, closing on the end of the jetty. The broad platforms scraping outward, thumping down on the solid stone. Units of heavily armoured soldiers marching across those platforms, archers among them, long arrows nocked to bowstrings.

Koryk slashed with his sword, saw some poor Malazan citizen's face split in half, the jaw torn away, a torrent of blood – the white gleam of exposed bone beneath each ear – then, reeling away, eyes filled with disbelief, horror—

Killing our own – gods below – our own—

A sudden ringing command from Sergeant Balm behind him. *'Disengage! Marines disengage!'*

And discipline took hold – that command, echoing a hairy Master Sergeant's bawled orders on a drill field years ago – Koryk, snarling, lurched back, bringing up his shield to fend off an out-thrust spear—

All at once, soldiers were moving past him on either side, a new shield-wall clashing closed in front of him.

A chorus of screams as arrows whispered into the heaving mob, thudding into flesh.

Wheeling away, sword's point dragging then skipping across the uneven cobbles, Koryk staggered back.

The Perish.

They're here.

And that's that.

Galt was laughing. 'Our first real scrap, Sergeant. And it's against Malazans!'

'Well,' Balm said, 'laughing's better'n crying. But shut that mouth anyway.'

As the fighting intensified at the foot of the jetty, the marines sagged down onto the cobbles or staggered off in search of water. Wiping spattered blood from his eyes, Koryk looked round, bewildered, numbed. He saw two cloaked figures standing near the plank to the *Froth Wolf*. The Wickan witch and her warlock brother.

'Koryk of the Seti,' Nether said. 'Where is Bottle?'

'No idea,' he replied, squinting at the young woman. 'Somewhere' – he nodded towards the city behind him – 'in there.'

Nil said, 'He cannot get back. Not through that horde.'

Koryk spat onto the cobbles. 'He'll find a way,' he said.

'No worries about that,' Smiles added, walking up to the half-blood with a waterskin in her hands.

Nether spoke: 'You are all very confident.'

As Smiles handed Koryk the waterskin she said, 'Your heart's desire will be fine, is what I'm saying, Nether. He took his rat with him, didn't he?'

'His what?'

'Keeps it tucked in most of the time, it's true, but I seen it out more than once—'

'Enough,' Koryk growled under his breath.

Smile made a face at him. 'Spoilsport.'

'You two should get back onto the ship,' Koryk said to Nil and Nether. 'It's safer there – any stray arrow—'

'Soldier,' Nil cut in. 'You fight for the Wickans and for the Khundryl Burned Tears this night. We choose to witness.'

'Fine, just do it from the deck. What's the point of all this if you drop with an arrow through the throat?'

After a moment, the brother and sister both bowed – to Koryk and the other marines – then they turned about and made their way back up the plank.

Gods below, I've never seen them bow before. To anyone.

'Mind that last step . . .'

Kalam moved up directly behind the Adjunct. Twenty steps remained. 'With six left,' the assassin murmured, 'slow down and move to your left.'

She nodded.

The four moored dromons were off to one side, no guards present on the jetties. Directly ahead, at the foot of Rampart Way, stretched out a concourse. Opposite the clearing stood three imperial buildings, one a blockhouse and gaol, another a customs and tithes building and the third a solid, heavily fortified armoury for the City Watch. None of the usual guards were present, and the blockhouse was unlit.

Seven steps from the bottom. Kalam unsheathed his long-knives beneath his rain-cape.

The Adjunct edged to her left and hesitated.

In a blur Kalam swept past her, leading with his otataral weapon, and launched himself into the air, down, sailing over the last six steps.

Five figures seemed to materialize from nothing at the base of Rampart Way. One was crouched in Kalam's path, but twisted away to avoid a crushing collision. The otataral long-knife slashed out, the edge

817

biting deep into the Claw's neck, dragging free to loose a jet of arterial blood.

Landing in a crouch, Kalam parried an attack from his left twice, as the Claw closed with a dagger in each hand. Blackened iron flickered between them, the snick of blade catching blade as, pivoting on his inside leg, Kalam dropped lower, lashing out with his other leg to sweep the Claw from his feet. The killer landed hard on his left hip. Kalam locked both dagger blades hard against the hilts of his long-knives, pushed them to either side, then drove his knee down into the centre of the Claw's chest. The sternum was punched inward with a sickening crunch, ribs to either side bowing outward. Even as he landed, Kalam threw his weight forward, over the downed man, the tip of one of his long-knives sinking deep into the Claw's right eye socket as he passed.

He felt a dagger-blade cut through the rain-cape on his back, then skitter along the chain beneath, and then he was out of range, shoulder dipping, rolling back into a crouch and spinning round.

The attacker had followed, almost as quick, and Kalam grunted as the Claw slammed into him. A dagger-point plunged through chain links above his left hip and, twisting hard, he felt a shallow opening of his flesh, then the point struck more chain, and was suddenly snagged. In the midst of this movement, and as the attacker seemed to bounce back from the impact – Kalam far outweighing him, or her – another dagger descended from overhead. An upward stop-thrust impaled that arm. The dagger spilled from a spasming hand. Leaving his long-knife there, Kalam slashed down against the other arm, severing tendons below the elbow. He then dropped that weapon as well, left hand inverting as it snapped up to grasp the front of the Claw's jerkin; his other hand closing on a handful down at the killer's crotch – *male* – and Kalam heaved the figure upward, over his left shoulder, then, spinning round, he hammered the Claw headfirst onto the pavestones.

Skull and entire head seemed to vanish within folds of hood and cloak. White matter spattered out.

Releasing the flopping body, Kalam collected both long-knives, then turned to face the last two of the Hand.

Both were already down. The Adjunct stood above one, her sword out and slick with blood. T'amber appeared to have closed to hand-to-hand with the other Claw, somehow breaking the man's neck even as he plunged both daggers into her. Kalam stared as she tugged the weapons free – lower right shoulder, just beneath a clavicle, and her right waist – and flung them aside as if they were mere slivers.

He met the young woman's eyes, and it seemed the gold flared for a moment, before she casually turned away. 'Stuff those holes,' Kalam said, 'or you'll bleed out.'

'Never mind me,' she replied. 'Where to, now?'

There was anguish on the Adjunct's face as she looked upon her lover, and it seemed she was struggling not to reach out.

Kalam collected his other long-knife. 'Where to now, T'amber? Ambushes set for every direct approach to Centre Docks. Let's force them to pull up and move to intercept us. West, Adjunct, deeper into the city. We then swing south and keep going, right through Centre District, then take one of the inland bridges across to the Mouse – I know that area well – and, if we get that far, we head to the shoreline and back up north again. If necessary we can steal a fisher boat and scull our way over to the *Froth Wolf*.'

'Presumably we are being observed right now,' the Adjunct said.

Kalam nodded.

'And they understand that their sorcery will fail them.'

'Aye.'

'Forcing them to be more . . . direct.'

'Before too long,' Kalam said, 'more than one Hand will have to come at us at once. That's when we're in real trouble.'

A faint smile.

Kalam faced T'amber again. 'We have to move fast—'

'I can keep up.'

'Why didn't you use your sword on that fool?'

'He was too close to the Adjunct. I got him from behind but he was skilled enough to strike anyway.'

Damn, talk about a bad start. 'Well, neither wound looks like much of a bleeder. We should get going.'

As they set out, westward, the cliff-face of the promontory to their right, the Adjunct said, 'Do most grown men bounce off when they run into you, Kalam Mekhar?'

'Quick always said I was the densest man he ever knew.'

'A Hand has broken cover,' T'amber said. 'They're moving parallel to us.'

Kalam glanced to his left. Seeing nothing, no-one. *How does she know that? Do I doubt her? Not for a moment.* 'Are they converging on our path?'

'Not yet.'

More official buildings, and then the first of the major estates of the Lightings District. *No marauding riots up here. Naurally.* 'At least we've got the streets to ourselves,' he muttered. *More or less.*

'There are but three gates leading down to Old Upper Estates,' the Adjunct said after a moment, 'and we are fast coming opposite the last of them.'

'Aye, any further west and it's all wall, an ever higher drop the farther we go. But there's an old estate, abandoned for years and hopefully still empty. There's a way down, and if we're lucky the Claw don't know about it.'

'Another Hand's just come up through the last gate,' T'amber said. 'They're linking up with the other one.'

'Just the two here in Lightings?'

'So far.'

'Are you sure?'

She glanced across at him. 'I have a keen sense of smell, Kalam Mekhar.'

Smell? 'I didn't know Claw assassins have stopped bathing.'

'Not that kind of smell. Aggression, and fear.'

'Fear? There's only the three of us, for Hood's sake!'

'And one of them is you, Kalam. Even so, they all want to be the Hand that takes you down. They will compete for that honour.'

'Idiots.' He gestured ahead. 'That one, with the high walls. I see no lights—'

'The gate is ajar,' the Adjunct said as they drew closer.

'Never mind that,' T'amber said. 'Here they come.'

All three spun round.

The deadening effect of the Adjunct's unsheathed sword was far more efficacious than that of Kalam's long-knife, and its range was revealed as, thirty paces up the street, ten cloaked figures shimmered into existence. 'Take cover!' Kalam hissed, ducking down.

Silvery quarrels flashed, barbed heads flickering in the faint moonlight as they corkscrewed in flight. Multiple impacts on the moss-stained wall behind them. Straightening, Kalam cursed to see T'amber rushing the killers.

There's ten of them, you fool!

He raced forward.

Five paces from the fast-closing Claws, T'amber drew her sword.

There was an old saying, that for all the terror waiting in the gloved hands of an assassin, it was as nothing against a professional soldier. T'amber did not even slow down, her blade weaving to either side in a blur. Bodies sprawled in her wake, blood splashing out, knives clattering on the cobbles. A dagger hissed through the air, caught the woman on the right side of her chest, sinking deep. She ignored it – Kalam's eyes widened as he saw a severed head tumble away from what seemed the lightest slash of T'amber's longsword, and then he joined the fight.

Two Claws had darted past, out of T'amber's reach, and set off towards the Adjunct. Kalam shifted to come at them from their left. The nearer one leapt into his path, seeking to hold Kalam long enough for the other killer to close on Tavore.

A dancing flurry of parries from the Claw had begun even before Kalam engaged with his own weapons – and he recognized that form – the Web – 'Gods below, you fool,' he said in a snarl as he reached both long-knives into the skein of parries, feinted with minute jabs then, breaking his timing, evaded the knife-blades as they snapped across, and neatly impaled both hands.

The man screamed as Kalam closed in, pushing both stuck hands out to the sides, and head-butted him. Hooded head snapped back – and met the point of Kalam's right-hand long-knife as it completed its disengage to come up behind the Claw. A grating crunch as the point drove up into the base of his brain. Even as he crumpled Kalam was stepping over him, into the wake of the last killer.

The Adjunct watched calmly as the Claw launched himself at her. Her stop-thrust took him in the cup of his throat, between the breastbones, the heavy blade punching through windpipe, then spine, and out the back, stretching but not cutting the cloak.

The Claw had thrown both daggers a heartbeat before spitting himself on the sword, and the Adjunct had lithely evaded both as she turned her body sideways in extending the stop-thrust.

Kalam slowed down, turned round, to see T'amber walking back towards them.

Eight dead Claws. Damned impressive. Even if it took a knife in the lung to do it.

There was frothy blood trickling onto T'amber's chin. She had pulled out the knife and more blood soaked her tunic. Yet her strides were steady.

'Through the gate, then,' Kalam said.

They entered the courtyard. Overgrown, filled with rubbish. A fountain commanded the centre, the pool entirely sheathed in gleaming algae. Insects rose from it in a cloud that spun and whirled towards them. Kalam pointed with one weapon to the far wall. 'That old well. There was once a natural cistern in the limestone under all of this. Some enterprising thief broke into it from below. Stole an entire fortune from the family living here. Left them destitute. This was long ago – that hoard of wealth bankrolled Kellanved's early ventures in piracy on the lanes between here and the Napan Isles.'

The Adjunct glanced over. 'Kellanved was the enterprising thief?'

'More likely Dancer. The estate was Mock's family, and, accordingly, the hoard was takings from twenty years of piracy. Not long after, Kellanved usurped Mock and annexed the whole island. Birth of the Malazan Empire. Among the few who know about it, this is called the Well of Plenty.'

A cough from T'amber, and she spat out a gout of blood.

Kalam eyed her in the gloom. That perfect face had grown very pale. He faced the well once more. 'I'll go first. The drop is about two and half man-heights – if you can, use the side walls to work your way down as far as possible. Adjunct, do you hear music?'

'Yes. Faint.'

Nodding, Kalam vaulted onto the lip of the well, then worked his way down. *Not just me, then. Fiddler, you're breaking my heart.*

Four Hands, weapons out, hooded eyes scanning in every direction. Pearl stood above a body. The poor man's head had been driven into the street, hard enough to turn it into pulp, to push the jaw and the base of the skull into the column of the neck between the shoulders, turing the spine into a coiled, splintered mess.

That was the one thing about Kalam Mekhar that one tended to forget, or even more erroneously, disregard. The bastard's animal strength.

'Westward,' one of his lieutenants said in a whisper. 'Along Lightings, likely to the last gate. They will seek to circle round, pulling loose our established ambushes—'

'Not all of them,' Pearl murmured. 'I did not for a moment believe he would attempt the direct route. In fact, he's about to run into the bulk of my small army.'

The lieutenant actually chuckled – Pearl faced him, stared for a long moment, then said, 'Take two Hands and trail him. Don't close, just get in sight every now and then. Push them onward.'

'They'll turn and ambush us, Clawmaster—'

'Probably. Enjoy your evening. Now go.'

An evil snicker would have been worse, but the chuckle was bad enough.

Pearl drew back the left sleeve of his loose silk shirt. The head of the quarrel set in the wrist-strapped crossbow was sheathed in thick wax. Easily pulled off when the time was propitious. In the meantime, he would not risk any possible contact with the paralt smeared on the head's edges. *No, this taste is for you, Kalam.*

You've eliminated sorcery, after all. So, you leave me little choice, and no, I do not care about the Code.

He rolled the sleeve back down, looked over at his two chosen Hands, his favoured, elite assassins. Not one of them a mage. Theirs was the most direct kind of talent. Tall, well-muscled, a match for Kalam's brawn. 'We position ourselves south of Admiral Bridge, at the edge of the Mouse.'

One spoke: 'You believe they will get that far, Clawmaster?'

Pearl simply turned away. 'Let's go.'

*

822

Kalam edged down the low, narrow tunnel. He could see the brush of the garden disguising the cave mouth ahead. There were broken branches among it, and the air stank of bile and blood. *What's this, then?* Weapons out, he drew closer, came to the threshold.

There had been a Hand, positioned around the tunnel entrance. Five corpses, limbs sprawled. Kalam pushed through the brush.

They had been cut to pieces. Arms broken. Legs snapped. Blood everywhere, still dripping from some low branches on the tree commanding the abandoned orchard. Two had been cleanly eviscerated, their intestines tumbled out, trailing across the leaf-littered ground like bloated worms.

Movement behind him and he turned. The Adjunct and T'amber pushed their way into the clearing.

'That was fast,' Tavore said in a whisper.

'Not me, Adjunct.'

'I'm sorry. I realized that. We have friends, it seems.'

'Don't count on it,' Kalam said. 'This has the look of vendetta – someone or ones took out a whole lot of anger on these poor bastards. I don't think it has anything to do with us. As you said, the Claw is a compromised organization.'

'Have they turned on themselves?'

'Certainly looks that way.'

'Still in our favour, Kalam.'

'Well,' he muttered after a moment, 'that's not as important as the revelation that taking the long way round was anticipated. We've real trouble ahead, Adjunct.'

'There are sounds,' T'amber said, 'from the top of the well, I think. Hands. Two.'

'Fast,' said Kalam, baring his teeth. 'They want to flush us forward. To Hood with that. Stay here, you two.' He set off back into the tunnel. *Top of the well. Meaning you've got to come down . . . one at a time. You were impatient, fools. And now it's going to cost you.*

Reaching the cistern, he saw the first set of moccasined feet appear, dangling from the hole in the ceiling. Kalam moved closer.

The Claw dropped, landed lightly, and died with a knife-blade through an eye socket. Kalam tugged his weapon free and pulled the slumping corpse to one side. Looking up, he waited for the next one.

Then he heard, echoing down, a voice.

Gathered round the well, the two Hands hesitated, looking down into the darkness. 'Lieutenant said he'd call up,' one of them hissed. 'I don't hear a thing down there.'

There then came a faint call, three fast clicks. A recognized signal.

The assassins relaxed. 'Was checking out the entrance, I guess – Kalam must have got past the ambush in the orchard.'

'They say he's the meanest Claw there ever was. Not even Dancer wanted to mess with him.'

'Enough of that. Go on, Sturtho, get down there and give the lieutenant company and be sure to wipe up the puddle around his feet while you're at it – wouldn't want any of us to slip.'

The one named Sturtho clambered onto the well.

A short time later, Kalam emerged from the tunnel mouth. T'amber, sitting with her back to a tree, looked up, then nodded and began to rise. Blood had pooled in her lap and now streaked down onto her thighs.

'Which way ahead?' the Adjunct asked Kalam.

'We follow the old orchard wall, west, until we hit Raven Hill Road, then straight south to the hill itself – it's a wide track, with plenty of barred or barricaded alleys. We'll skirt the hill on the east side, along the Old City Wall, and then across Admiral Bridge.' Kalam hesitated, then said, 'We've got to move fast, at a run, never straight but never stopping either. Now, there's mobs out there, thugs looking for trouble – we need to avoid getting snagged up by those. So when I say we move fast and keep moving that's exactly what I mean. T'amber—'

'I can keep up.'

'Listen—'

'I said I can keep up.'

'You shouldn't even be conscious, damn you!'

She hefted her sword. 'Let's go find the next ambush, shall we?'

Tears glistened beneath Stormy's eyes as the sorrow-filled music born of strings filled the small room, and names and faces slowly resolved, one after another, in the minds of the four soldiers as the candles guttered down. Muted, from the streets of the city outside, there rose and fell the sounds of fighting, of dying, a chorus like the accumulated voices of history, of human failure and its echoes reaching them from every place in this world. Fiddler's struggle to evade the grim monotony of a dirge forced hesitation into the music, a seeking of hope and faith and the solid meaning of friendship – not just with those who had fallen, but with the three other men in the room – but it was a struggle he knew he was losing.

It seemed so easy for so many people to divide war from peace, to confine their definitions to the unambivalent. Marching soldiers, pitched battles and slaughter. Locked armouries, treaties, fêtes and city gates opened wide. But Fiddler knew that suffering thrived in both realms of existence – he'd witnessed too many faces of the poor, ancient crones and babes in a mother's arms, figures lying motionless on the roadside or in the gutters of streets – where the sewage flowed unceasing like rivers gathering their spent souls. And he had come to a conviction, lodged like an iron nail in his heart, and with its burning, searing realization, he could no longer look upon things the way he used to, he could no longer walk and see what he saw with a neatly partitioned mind, replete with its host of judgements – that critical act of moral relativity – *this is less, that is more*. The truth in his heart was this: he no longer believed in peace.

It did not exist except as an ideal to which endless lofty words paid service, a litany offering up the delusion that the absence of overt violence was sufficient in itself, was proof that one was better than the other. There *was* no dichotomy between war and peace – no true opposition except in their particular expressions of a ubiquitous inequity. Suffering was all-pervasive. Children starved at the feet of wealthy lords no matter how secure and unchallenged their rule.

There was too much compassion within him – he knew that, for he could feel the pain, the helplessness, the invitation to despair, and from that despair came the desire – the need – to disengage, to throw up his hands and simply walk away, turn his back on all that he saw, all that he knew. If he could do nothing, then, *dammit*, he would *see* nothing. What other choice was there?

And so we weep for the fallen. We weep for those yet to fall, and in war the screams are loud and harsh and in peace the wail is so drawn-out we tell ourselves we hear nothing.

And so this music is a lament, and I am doomed to hear its bitter-sweet notes for a lifetime.

Show me a god that does not demand mortal suffering.

Show me a god that celebrates diversity, a celebration that embraces even non-believers and is not threatened by them.

Show me a god who understands the meaning of peace. In life, not in death.

Show—

'Stop,' Gesler said in a grating voice.

Blinking, Fiddler lowered the instrument. 'What?'

'You cannot end with such anger, Fid. Please.'

Anger? I am sorry. He would have spoken that aloud, but suddenly he could not. His gaze lowered, and he found himself studying the littered floor at his feet. Someone, in passing – perhaps Fiddler himself – had inadvertently stepped on a cockroach. Half-crushed, smeared into the warped wood, its legs kicked feebly. He stared at it in fascination.

Dear creature, do you now curse an indifferent god?

'You're right,' he said. 'I can't end it there.' He raised the fiddle again. 'Here's a different song for you, one of the few I've actually learned. From Kartool. It's called "The Paralt's Dance".' He rested the bow on the strings, then began.

Wild, frantic, amusing. Its final notes recounted the triumphant female eating her lover. And even without words, the details of that closing flourish could not be mistaken.

The four men laughed.

Then fell silent once more.

It could have been worse, Bottle reflected as he hurried along the dark alley. Agayla could have reached in to the left instead of to the right, there under his shirt, pulling out not a doll but a live rat – who would probably have bitten her, since that was what it seemed Y'Ghatan liked to do most. Would their subsequent conversation have taken another track? he wondered. *Probably.*

The alleys of the Mouse twisted and turned, narrow and choking and unlit, and stumbling over a body in the gloom was not nearly as uncommon as one would like . . . but not five bodies. Heart pounding, Bottle halted in his tracks. The stench of death engulfed him. Bile and blood.

Five corpses, all clothed in black, hooded, they appeared to have been cut to pieces. Perhaps only moments earlier.

He heard screams erupt from a street nearby, cries filled with terror. *Gods, what's out there?* He contemplated releasing Y'Ghatan, then decided against it – he would need the rat's eyes later, he was certain of it, and risking the creature now invited potential disaster. *Besides, I'm not far from my destination. I think. I hope.*

He picked his way gingerly past the bodies, approached the alley mouth beyond.

Whatever had elicited the shrieks had gone another way, although Bottle saw a few running figures flash past, heading towards the docks. Reaching the street he turned right and set off in the same direction.

Until he came opposite the entrance to a tavern. Saddle-backed stairs, leading down. The prickle of sweat stole over his body. *In here. Thank you, Agayla.*

Bottle made his way down the steps, pushed through the doorway, and entered Coop's Hanged Man Inn.

The cramped, low-ceilinged den was crowded, yet strangely quiet. Pale faces turned in his direction, hard eyes fixing on him as he paused just inside the threshold, looking round.

Damned veterans. Well, at least you're not all out there, trying to kill marines.

Bottle made his way to the bar. Beneath the folds of his cloak he felt the doll move slightly, a limb twitching – the right arm – and then he saw a figure before him, facing in the other direction. Broad back and shoulders, lifting a tankard with his right hand as he leaned on the counter. The ragged sleeve on that arm slipped down, revealing a skein of scars.

Bottle reached the man. Tapped him on the shoulder.

A slow turn, eyes dark as cold forges.

'You're the one called Foreigner?'

The man frowned. 'Not many call me that, and you're not one of them.'

'I have a message to deliver,' Bottle said.

'From who?'

'I can't say. Not here, anyway.'

'What's the message?'

'Your long wait is at an end.'

The faintest gleam in those eyes, as of embers fanned to life once more. 'Is that it?'

Bottle nodded. 'If there's things you need to gather up, I can wait here for you. But not for long. We need to move, fast.'

Foreigner turned his head, called out to a huge figure behind the bar who had just driven a spigot into a cask. 'Temper!'

The older man looked over.

'Keep an eye on this one,' Foreigner said, 'until I'm back.'

'You want me to tie him up? Knock him senseless?'

'No, just make sure he stays breathing.'

'He's safe enough in here,' Temper replied, stepping closer, his eyes on Bottle. 'We know the Fourteenth did well, soldier. That's why we're all in here and not out there.'

Foreigner's regard seemed to undergo some subtle alteration as he looked upon Bottle once more. 'Ah,' he said under his breath, 'now it's making more sense. Wait, I won't be long.'

Bottle watched the man push his way through the crowd, then he glanced back at Temper. 'He got a real name?'

'I'm sure of it,' Temper replied, turning away.

Three shadows huddled round a table in the far corner. They hadn't been there a moment earlier, Sergeant Hellian was sure of that. Maybe. They didn't look to be drinking anything, which was suspicious enough, and those black murky heads drawn together whispered of conspiracy, nefarious plans, malicious intentions, but if they were speaking she could hear nothing of it and the gloom was such that she could not see their mouths move. Assuming they had mouths.

The whore at the other table was playing a game of Troughs. With no-one.

Hellian leaned closer to her prisoner. 'This place is strange, if you ask me.'

Brows lifted marginally. 'Really? Wraiths and ghosts, one haggardly whore and a demon behind the bar—'

'Watch who you're callin' haggardly,' the woman growled as black round stones bounced in the trough of their own accord. She scowled at the result and muttered, 'You're cheatin', aren't ya? I swear it and I meant what I said – if I catch you at it, Hormul, I'm buying a candle wi' your name on it.'

Hellian looked over at the bar. The demonic owner, back into his scrawny, puny shape, was moving back and forth behind the counter, only his head visible. He seemed to be eating wedges of some kind of yellow fruit, his face twisting as he sucked all the juice from each wedge, then flung the rind over a shoulder. Back and forth, wedge after wedge. 'So who let him loose?' she demanded. 'Ain't there supposed to be some master nearby? Don't they get summoned and then bound? You're a priest, you're supposed to know about this stuff.'

'It so happens that I do,' Banaschar replied. 'And yes, normally it's how you d'scribed.' He rubbed at his face, then continued, 'Here's my guess, Sergeant. Was Kellanved 'imself conjured this demon, probbly as a bodyguard, or e'en a bouncer. Then he left, and the demon took over the business.'

'Ridiculous. What do demons know 'bout running a business? You're lying. Now drink up, suspect, an' then we'll have one more an' then we leave this madhouse.'

'How can I c'nvince you, Sergeant? I need to get to Mock's Hold. The fate of the world depends on it—'

'Ha, that's a good one. Let me tell you 'bout the fate o' the world. Hey, barkeep! You, head, more ale, damn you! Look at them shadows, suspect, they're what it's all about. Hidin' behind every scene, behind every throne, behind every bath-tub. Making plans and nothing but plans and plans while the rest of us, we go down the drain, chokin' along leaking lead pipes and out into the swill, where we drown. Countin' coin, that's what they do. Coin we can't e'en see, but it's how they measure us, the scales, I mean, a sliver in the dish a soul in the other one, evened out, you see. What's the fate o' the world, suspect?' She made a gesture with her hand, index finger corkscrewing, spiralling round and round, then downward. 'Wi' them in charge, it's all goin' down. An' the joke on 'em is this – they're goin' with it.'

'Listen, woman. Those are wraiths. Creatures of shadow. They're not making plans. They're not counting coins. They're just hanging around—'

As if on cue, the three shadows rose, chairs audibly scraping back, drew cloaks tight, hooded faces hidden in darkness, then filed out the door.

Hellian snorted.

The barkeep arrived with another pitcher.

'All right,' sighed Banaschar, closing his eyes. 'Arrest me. Throw me in some dungeon. Let me rot with the worms and rats. You're abs'lutely right, Sergeant. Headfirst down the drain – here, lemme top you up.'

'Now you're talkin', suspect.'

Kalam's forearm hammered into the Claw's veiled face, shattering the nose and driving the head against the wall. Bone collapsed with a crunch and the attacker slumped. Spinning round, Kalam made his way quickly along the wall of the building, tracked by a half-dozen cross-bow quarrels that struck the bricks with snaps and sounds of splintering. He could hear weapons clashing in the alley ahead and to his right – where the Adjunct and T'amber had retreated under a fusil-lade of missiles from across the street – they had been shepherded into an ambush.

Three Hands were rushing to close the trap. Swearing, Kalam reached the mouth of the alley. A quick glance revealed the two women locked in a vicious close-in battle with four assassins – and in that momentary glance one of those four fell to T'amber's sword. Kalam turned his back on that fight, preparing to meet the Hands approaching from the street.

Daggers flickered through the air towards him. He threw himself down and to the right, regaining his feet in time to meet the first four Claws. A flurry of parries as Kalam worked his way further right, pulling himself beyond the range of two of the attackers. Long-knife lashed out, opening one man's face, and as the man reeled back, Kalam stepped close, impaling the man's left thigh whilst blocking a frenzied attack from the other Claw. Pivoting on the first Claw's pinned thigh, he twisted behind the man and thrust with his free weapon over his victim's right shoulder, the point tearing into the second attacker's neck.

Tugging free the blade impaling the thigh, Kalam brought that arm up to lock beneath the first Claw's chin, where he flexed hard and, with a single, savage wrenching motion, snapped the man's neck.

The one stabbed in the throat had stumbled, his jugular severed and blood spraying through the fingers grasping futilely at the wound. The last two of the four assassins were coming up fast. Beyond them, Kalam saw, the other Hands were racing for the Adjunct and T'amber.

Snarling his rage, Kalam launched himself past the two Claws, taking their attacks on his long-knives, slamming his foot into the nearer one's right leg, midway between knee and ankle, breaking bones. As the assassin shrieked her pain, the second attacker, seeking to move past her, collided with the falling woman, then lost balance entirely as both feet slid out on spilled blood.

Kalam's wild sprint struck the first group of Claws charging the Adjunct and Tavore. Coming from their left and slightly behind them, his sudden arrival forced a half-dozen attackers to swing round to meet him. Taking counter-attacks with parries, he threw his shoulder into the chest of the nearest Claw. The crack of ribs, a whoosh of breath driven from the lungs, and the attacker left his feet, flung backward to foul two Claws directly behind him. One of these stumbled too close to Kalam as he surged past, within reach of his left long-knife, and the cut he delivered into the victim's neck nearly severed the head.

Only two of the remaining four were close enough to spring at him. One came low from the left, the other high from the right. Kalam slashed across the path of the first attacker, felt his blade scrape along both knives in the Claw's hands. He followed that with a knee between the figure's eyes. The second attacker he forced back with a fully extended arm and long-knife, and the Claw, leaning back in desperation, left both feet planted – Kalam dropped the high feint and cut vertically down through the attacker's stomach to the crotch.

The Claw squealed as intestines tumbled out between his knees. Tearing his long-knife loose, Kalam continued his charge – and heard someone closing on him from behind. Dropping into a crouch, Kalam skidded to a halt, then threw himself backward. A dagger sank into his left waist, just beneath the ribcage, the point angled upward – seeking his heart – and then the two assassins collided, Kalam flinging his head back, connecting with the Claw's forehead. A second dagger skidded along mail beneath his right arm. Twisting away from the knife impaling him, he spun round and punched his elbow into the side of the Claw's head, crushing the cheekbone. The attacker sprawled, losing his grip on the knife in Kalam's side.

Gasping, Kalam forced himself forward once more. Every motion sent the fierce fire of agony through his chest, but he had no time to pull out the knife, as the last two Claws who had turned to meet him now rushed him.

But too close together, almost side by side – Kalam leapt to his right to take himself beyond the range of one of them. He ducked a horizontal slash seeking his throat, caught the second knife with an edge-on-bone parry of the Claw's forearm, then back-hand thrust into the attacker's throat. Even as that victim began pitching forward, Kalam settled his left shoulder against the chest – and pushed hard, following the body as it slammed into the other assassin. All three went down, with Kalam on top. The corpse between him and the live Claw snagged one of his long-knives – pulling that hand free, Kalam stabbed thumb and index finger into the assassin's eyes, hooking with the thumb and pushing ever deeper with the finger, until the body ceased spasming.

Hearing more fighting from the alley, Kalam pushed himself to his feet, paused to ease free the knife in his side, cursing at the blood that gushed in the wake of the blade. He collected the snagged long-knife, then staggered into the alley.

Only three Claws remained, and T'amber had engaged two of them, driving both back, step by step, into Kalam's path.

He moved up, thrust once, then twice, and two bodies writhed at his feet. T'amber had already turned and rushed to take the last assassin from behind, crushing the skull with the edge of her sword.

One of the Claws below heaved to one side, lifting a weapon – Kalam stamped his heel into the assassin's neck.

Sudden silence beyond the gasping of breaths.

He stared at the two women. T'amber was a mass of wounds – frothy blood was streaming from her nose and mouth and he saw the shuddering, frantic rise and fall of her chest. Grimacing against his own pain, Kalam turned to study the street he had just left.

Bodies moving here and there, but none seemed inclined to renew the fight.

The Adjunct moved up beside him. Blood had splashed her face, mingling with grimy sweat. 'Kalam Mekhar. I watch you. It seems . . .' She shook her head. 'It seems you move faster than them. And for all their training, their skills, they cannot keep up with you.'

He wiped stinging sweat from his eyes. His hands, clenching the grips of the long-knives, ached, but he could not relax them. 'It all slows down, Adjunct,' he said in a rumble. 'In my mind, they just slow down.' He shook himself, forcing loose the muscles of his back and shoulders. He had managed to stem the bleeding, although he could feel the heat of blood down the outside of his leg, beneath the heavy cloth, forming a glue between the fabric and his skin. He was exhausted, a sour taste on his tongue. 'We can't stop,' he said. 'There's plenty more. We're close to Admiral Bridge, almost there.'

'There?'

'The Mouse.'

'I hear riots – there's fires there, and smoke, Kalam.'

He nodded. 'Aye. Confusion. That's good.' He glanced back at T'amber. She was leaning with her back against a wall, sheathed in blood, her eyes closed. Kalam lowered his voice. 'Adjunct, she needs healing, before it's too late.'

But T'amber heard. Eyes opening, a gleam like tiger-eyes, and she straightened. 'I'm ready.'

The Adjunct took a half-step towards her lover, then was forced to turn as T'amber moved past her to the alley mouth.

Kalam saw the anguish in Tavore's gaze, and he looked away.

And saw thirty or more Claws shimmer into view not forty paces up the street. *'Shit! Run!'*

They emerged from the alley and set off. Kalam slowed his pace to allow the Adjunct past him. Somehow, T'amber stayed ahead of them, taking point. *There'll be another ambush. Waiting for us. She'll stumble right into it—*

Behind them, the assassins were in full pursuit, the faster sprinters among them closing the distance. Beyond the sound of soft footfalls, the thump of boots, and a chorus of fierce gasps, it seemed the cobbles beneath them, the buildings to either side, and even the lowering sky overhead, all conspired to close in upon them – upon this desperate scene – deadening the air, making it thicker, muffled. If eyes witnessed, the faces quickly turned away. If there were figures in the alleys they passed, they melted back into the darkness.

The street angled westward, now opposite Raven Hill Park. Up ahead it would link up with another street that bordered the park on the west side, before striking southward to the bridge. As they neared that intersection, Kalam saw T'amber suddenly shift direction, leading them into an alley on the left, and then he saw the reason for the unexpected detour – more Hands, massing in the intersection, and now surging forward.

They're herding us. To the bridge. What's waiting for us on the other side?

The alley widened into something like a street just past the first flanking buildings, and directly before them was the low wall encircling the park.

T'amber slowed, as if unsure whether to skirt that wall to the left or the right, then she staggered, lifting her sword as attackers closed in on her from both sides.

The Adjunct cried out.

Blades clashed, a body tumbled to one side, the others swarming round T'amber – Kalam saw two knives sink into the woman's torso, yet still she remained on her feet, slashing out with her sword. As Tavore reached them – thrusting her otataral blade into the side of an assassin's head, a savage lateral tug freeing it, the rust-hued weapon hissing into the path of an arm, slicing through flesh and bone, the arm flying away—

Kalam saw, in the heartbeat before he joined the fight, T'amber reaching out with her free hand to take a Claw by the throat, then pull the attacker into the air, pivoting to throw the Claw against the stone wall. Even as the figure repeatedly stabbed the woman in the chest, shoulders and upper arms.

Gods below!

Kalam arrived like a charging bhederin, long-knives licking out even as he hammered his weight into one Claw, then another, sending both sprawling.

There in the gloom before the wall of Raven Hill Park, a savage frenzy of close-in fighting, a second Hand joining what was left of the first. A dozen rapid heartbeats, and it was over.

And there was no time to pause, no time for a breath to recover, as quarrels began pounding into the wall.

Kalam waved mutely to run along the wall, westward, and somehow – impossibly – T'amber once more took the lead.

Screams erupted behind them, but there was no time to look. The wall curved southward, forming one side of the street leading to Admiral Bridge, and there stood the stone span, unlit, so buried in shadows that it might have been at the base of a pit. As they drew closer, that sorcery wavered, then died. Revealing . . . nothing. No-one in sight.

'T'amber!' Kalam hissed. 'Hold up!'

Whatever had struck in their wake had snared the attention of the pursuing Claws – at least for the moment. 'Adjunct, listen to me. You and T'amber, get down into the river. Follow it straight to the harbour.'

'What about you?' Tavore demanded.

'We haven't yet encountered a third of the Hands in the city, Adjunct.' He nodded towards the Mouse. 'They're in there. I plan on leading them a merry chase.' He paused, then spat out a mouthful of phlegm and blood. 'I can lose them eventually – I know the Mouse, Tavore. I'll take to the rooftops.'

'There's no point in splitting up—'

'Yes, Adjunct. There is.' Kalam studied T'amber for a moment. *Yes, despite everything, not much longer for you.* 'T'amber agrees with me. She'll get you to the harbour.'

From the streets and alleys behind them, ominous silence, now. *Closing in.* 'Go.'

The Adjunct met his eyes. 'Kalam—'

'Just go, Tavore.'

He watched as they moved to the edge of the river, the old sagging stone retaining wall at their feet. T'amber climbed down first. The river was befouled, sluggish and shallow. It would be slow going, but the darkness would hide them. *And when they get to the harbour . . . well, it'll be time to improvise.*

Kalam adjusted his grips on the long-knives. A last glance behind him. Still nothing there. Odd. He fixed his gaze on the bridge. *All right. Let's get this over with.*

Lostara Yil made her way across the concourse, leaving Rampart Way and the bodies at its foot behind her. The sounds of rioting were still distant – coming from the harbour and beyond – while the nearby buildings and estates were silent and unlit, as if she had found herself in a necropolis, *a fitting monument to imperial glory.*

The small figure that stepped out before her was thus all the more startling, and her disquiet only increased upon recognizing him. 'Grub,' she said, approaching, 'what are you doing here?'

'Waiting for you,' the boy replied, wiping at a runny nose.

'What do you mean?'

'I'll take you where you need to go. It's a sad night, but it will be all right, you'll see that one day.' With that he turned around and headed off along the avenue, southward. 'We don't need to stay on the path, not yet. We can take the first bridge. Lostara Yil—' a glance back, 'you're very pretty.'

Suddenly chilled despite the sultry air, she set off after him. 'What path?'

'Doesn't matter.'

Skittering sounds in the shadows off to her left. She closed a hand on her sword. 'Something's there—'

'That's okay,' Grub said. 'They're my friends. There won't be any trouble. But we should hurry.'

Before long they reached the bridge leading into Centre District, whereupon Grub angled them westward for a short time, before turning south once more.

They soon came upon the first of the bodies. Claws, sprawled in small groups at first – where rats and wild dogs had already come out to feed – and then, as they neared Raven Hill Park, the street was literally filled with corpses. Lostara slowed her pace as she approached the elongated scene of slaughter – heading southward, as if a bladed whirlwind had raced through a hundred or more imperial assassins – and, slowly, Lostara Yil realized something, as she looked upon one cut-up figure after another ... a pattern to the wounds, to their placements, to the smooth precision of every mortal blow.

Her chill deepened, stole into her bones.

Three paces ahead, Grub was humming a Wickan drover's song.

Halfway across Admiral Bridge, Kalam lodged one weapon under an arm and reached for the acorn tucked into the folds of his sash.

Smooth, warm even through the leather of his tattered glove, as if welcoming. And . . . impatient.

Ducking into a crouch along one of the low retaining walls on the bridge, Kalam flung the acorn to the pavestones. It cracked, spun in place for a moment, then stilled.

'All right, Quick,' Kalam muttered, 'any time now.'

In a cabin on the *Froth Wolf*, Adaephon Delat, seated crosslegged on the floor, his eyes closed, flinched at that distant summons. Closer to hand, he could hear more fighting along the harbourfront, and he knew the Perish were being pushed back, step by step, battered by sorcery and an ever-growing mass of frenzied attackers. Whilst above decks Destriant Run'Thurvian was maintaining a barrier against every magical assault on the ship itself. Quick Ben sensed that the man was not exactly hard-pressed, but clearly distracted by something, and so there was a hesitation in him, as if he but awaited a far more taxing calling – a moment that was fast approaching.

Well, we got trouble everywhere, don't we just?

It would not be easy slipping through the maze of warrens unleashed in the streets of the city this night. Pockets of virulent sorcery wandered here and there, mobile traps eager to deliver agonizing death, and Quick Ben recognized those. *Ruse, the path of the sea. Those traps are water, stolen from deep oceans and retaining that savage pressure – they crush everything they envelop. This is High Ruse, and it's damned ugly.*

Someone out there was waiting for him. To make his move. And whoever it was, they wanted Quick Ben to remain precisely where he was, in a cabin on the *Froth Wolf*. Remain, doing nothing, *staying out of the fight.*

Well. He had unveiled four warrens, woven an even dozen sorcerous spells, all eager to be sprung loose – his hands itched, then burned, as if he was repeatedly dipping them in acid.

Kalam's out there, and he needs my help.

The High Mage allowed himself the briefest of nods, and the rent of a warren opened before him. He slowly rose to his feet, joints protesting the motion – *gods, I think I'm getting old. Who'd have thought?* He drew a deep breath, then, blinking to clear his vision, he lunged forward – into the rent—

—and, even as he vanished he heard a soft giggle, then a sibilant voice: '*You said you owed me, remember? Well, my dear Snake, it's time.*'

Twenty heartbeats. Twenty-five. Thirty. *Hood's breath!* Kalam stared down at the broken acorn. *Shit. Shit shit shit.* Forty. Cursing under his breath, he set off.

That's the problem with the shaved knuckle in the hole. Sometimes it doesn't work. So, I'm on my own. Well, so be it, I've been getting sick of this life anyway. Murder was overrated, he decided. It achieved nothing, nothing of real value. There wasn't an assassin out there who didn't deserve to have his or her head cut off and stuck on a spike. Skill, talent, opportunity – none of them justified the taking of a life.

How many of us – yes you – how many of you hate what you are? It's not worth it, you know. Hood take all those blistering egos, let's flash our pathetic light one last time, then surrender to the darkness. I'm done with this. I'm done.

He reached the end of the bridge and paused once more. Another backward glance. *Well, it ain't burning, except here in my mind. Closing the circle, right? Hedge, Trotts, Whiskeyjack . . .*

The dark, pitted and broken face of the Mouse beckoned. A decayed grin, destitution and degradation, the misery that haunted so much life. It was, Kalam Mekhar decided, the right place. The assassin burst into motion, a diagonal sprint, hard and as low to the ground as he could manage, up to the leaning façade of a remnant of some estate wall, surging upward, one foot jamming in a cluttered murder hole – dislodging a bird's nest – up, forearm wrapping round the top edge, broken shards of cemented crockery cutting through the sleeve, puncturing skin – then over, one foot gaining purchase on the ragged row, launching himself forward, through the air, onto an angled roof that exploded with guano dust as he struck it, scrambling along the incline, two long strides taking him to the peak, then down the other side—

And onto the wild maze, the crackled, disjointed back of the vast Mouse—

Claws, crouched and waiting, lunged in from all sides. Big, the biggest assassins Kalam had seen yet, each wielding long-knives in both hands. Fast, like vipers, lashing out.

Kalam did not slow down – he needed to push right through them, he needed to keep going – he caught weapons against his own, felt blade edges gouge tracks along his armour, links parting, and one point, thrust hard, sank deep into his left thigh, twisting, cutting in an upward motion – snarling, he writhed in the midst of the flashing weapons, wrapped an arm about the man's face and head, then, as he pushed through with all his strength, he pulled that head in a twisting wrench, hearing the vertebrae pop. Kalam half-dragged the flopping corpse by its wobbly head, into his wake, where he dropped it.

A long-knife from the right slashed into the side of his head, slicing down to sever his ear. He counter-thrust and felt his weapon skid along chain.

Hood take them! Someone used me to make more of me—

Continuing down, to the edge, Kalam then launched himself through the air, over the gap of an alley. He landed, pitching and rolling, on the flat roof of a sagging tenement, centuries old, the surface beneath him layered with the gravel of broken pottery. Multiple impacts followed, trembling along the rooftop, as his hunters came after him. Two, five, seven—

Kalam regained his feet and turned, at bay, as nine assassins, spread into a half-circle, rushed him.

Nine Kalams against one.

Hardly.

He surged forward, straight ahead, to the centre of that half-circle. The man before him raised his weapons in alarm, caught by surprise. He managed to parry twice with one long-knife, once with the other as he desperately back-pedalled, before Kalam's succession of attacks broke through. A blade sinking into the man's chest, impaling his heart, the second one stabbing beneath the jaw-line, then twisting upward and pushing hard into the brain.

Using both jammed weapons, Kalam yanked the man around, into the path of two more Claws, then he tore free his long-knives and charged into one flank of attackers with blinding speed. A blade-edge sliced into his left calf from one of the pursuers – not deep enough to slow him down – as he feinted low at the Claw closest to him, then thrust high with his other weapon – into the eye socket of the man a step beyond the first assassin. The long-knife jammed. Releasing his grip, Kalam dipped a shoulder and flung himself into the midsection of the next attacker. The impact jolted through his bones – *this Hood-cursed bastard's huge* – yet he sank even lower, his freed arm sliding up between the man's legs, up behind. Blades tore down along his back, links popping like ticks on hot stones, and he felt the Claw seeking to shift the angle of those weapons, to push them inward – as, legs bunching beneath him, Kalam then heaved the hunter upward, off his feet – up, Kalam loosing a roar that tore the lining of his throat, using his weapon-hand to grasp the front of the man's shirt – up – *and over.*

Legs kicking, the Claw's head pitched forward, colliding with the chest of a pursuing assassin. Both went down. Kalam leapt after them, pounding an elbow into the forehead of the second Claw – collapsing it like a melon husk – while he sank his remaining long-knife into the back of the first man's neck.

A blade jammed into his right thigh, the point bursting through the other side. Kalam twisted fast to pull the weapon from the attacker's hand, drew both legs up as he rolled onto his back, then kicked hard into the Claw's belly, sending the figure flying. Another long-knife thrust at his face – he flung up a forearm and blocked the weapon, brought his hand round and grasped the Claw's wrist, pulled him closer and gutted him with his own long-knife, the intestines spilling out to land in Kalam's lap.

Scrambling upright, he pulled out the weapon impaling his thigh – in time to parry a slash with it, then, backing away – his slashed and punctured legs almost failing beneath him – he fell into a sustained defence. Three hunters faced him, with the one he had kicked now regaining his feet, slowly, struggling to draw breath.

Too much blood-loss; Kalam felt himself weakening. If any more Hands arrived . . .

He leapt back, almost to the edge of the roof, and threw both long-knives, a move unexpected, particularly given the top-heavy imbalance of the weapons – but Kalam had practised short-range throwing with them, year after year. One buried itself deep in the chest of the Claw to his right; the other struck the breastbone of the Claw on the left with a solid thud and remained in place, quivering. Even as he threw the weapons, Kalam launched himself, barehanded, at the man in the middle.

Caught one forearm in both hands, pushed it back then across – the hunter attempted an upthrust from low with his other long-knife, but Kalam kneed it aside. A savage wrench dislocated the arm in his hands, then he pushed it back up, grinding the dislodged bones into the ruptured socket – the man shrieked. Releasing the arm, he brought both hands up behind the Claw's head, then, leaving his own feet, he drove that head downward, using all of his weight, downward, face-first into the roof.

A crunch, a loud crack, and the entire rooftop sagged – explosions of old rotted timber beams, crumbling mortar and plaster.

Swearing, Kalam rolled over the man – whose face was buried in the roof, amidst bubbling blood – and saw, through an ever widening fissure, a darkened room below. He slid himself forward—

Time to leave.

Ten paces away, Pearl stood and watched. Shaken, disbelieving. On the slanting rooftop all round him lay bodies. The finest assassins of the Malazan Empire. *He cut through them all. Just . . . cut through them.* And, in his heart, there was terror – a sensation new to him, filling him with trembling weakness.

He watched as Kalam Mekhar, streaming blood, weaponless, dragged himself towards that hole in the roof. And Pearl drew back the sleeve of his left arm, extended it, aimed and released the quarrel.

A grunt with the impact, the quarrel sinking deep just under Kalam's outstretched left arm, even as the man slid forward, down, and vanished from sight.

I am sorry, Kalam Mekhar. But you ... I cannot accept ... your existence. I cannot ...

He then made his way forward, joined now by the lone survivor of the two Hands, and collected Kalam's weapons.

My ... trophies.

He turned to the Claw. 'Find the others—'

'But what of Kalam—'

'He's finished. Gather the Hands here in the Mouse – we're paying a visit to the Centre Docks, now. If the Adjunct makes it that far, well, we have to take her down there.'

'Understood, Clawmaster.'

Clawmaster. Yes. It's done, Empress Laseen. Yes, he's dead. By my own hand. I am without an equal in the Malazan Empire.

Where would he begin?

Mallick Rel.

Korbolo Dom.

Neither of you will see the dawn. I swear it.

The other Claw spoke from the edge of the hole in the roof: 'I don't see him, Clawmaster.'

'He's crawling off to die,' Pearl said. 'Kartoolian paralt.'

The man's head snapped round. 'Not the snake? The spider's ...? Gods below!'

Aye, a most painful, protracted death. And there's not a priest left on the island who can neutralize that poison.

Two weapons clunked on the roof. Pearl looked over. 'What are you doing?' he demanded.

The man was staring at him. 'Enough. How much dishonour will you set at the feet of the Claw? I am done with you.' And he turned away. 'Find the Adjunct yourself, Pearl, give her one of your damned spider bites—'

Pearl raised his right arm, sent a second quarrel flying across the rooftop. Striking the man between the shoulder-blades. Arms flung out to the sides, the Claw toppled.

'That, regrettably, was white paralt. Much quicker.'

Now, as he had intended all along, there were no witnesses left. And it was time to gather the remaining Hands.

He wished it could have been different. All of it. But this was a new Malazan Empire, with new rules. *Rules I can manage well enough. After all, I have nothing left. No-one left ...*

Closing his eyes, Fiddler set down his fiddle. He said nothing, for there was nothing to say. The reprise that had taken him was done. The music had left his hands, had left his mind, his heart. He felt empty inside, his soul riven, lifeless. He had known this was coming, a truth that neither diminished the pain of loss nor intensified it – a burden, that was all. Just one more burden.

Screams from the street below, then the sound of a door smashing into kindling.

Braven Tooth glanced up, wiped at his eyes.

Heavy footsteps on the stairs.

Gesler collected the wine jug from the table and slowly refilled the cups. No-one had touched the bread.

Thumping steps coming up the corridor. Scraping, dragging.

Halting before the Master Sergeant's door.

Then a heavy, splintering knock, like claws gouging the wood.

Gesler rose and walked over.

Fiddler watched as the sergeant opened the door, stood motionless for a long moment, staring at whoever was in the corridor, then Gesler said, 'Stormy, it's for you.'

The huge man slowly rose as Gesler turned about and walked back to his chair.

A shape filled the entrance. Broad-shouldered, wearing tattered, dripping furs. A flat face, the skin betel brown and stretched taut over robust bones. Pits for eyes. Long arms hanging to the sides. Fiddler's brows rose. A T'lan Imass.

Stormy cleared his throat. 'Legana Breed,' he said, his voice oddly high.

The reply that rasped from the apparition was like the grating of barrow stones. 'I have come for my sword, mortal.'

Gesler collapsed into his chair and collected his cup. 'A long, wet walk, was it, Breed?'

The head swivelled with a creak, but the T'lan Imass said nothing.

Stormy collected the flint sword and walked over to Legana Breed. 'You been scaring a lot of people below,' he said.

'Sensitive souls, you mortals.'

The marine held the sword out, horizontally. 'Took your time getting out of that portal.'

Legana Breed grasped it. 'Nothing is ever as easy as it seems, Shield Anvil. Carry the pain in your heart and know this: you are far from finished with this world.'

Fiddler glanced across at Braven Tooth. *Shield Anvil?*

The Master Sergeant simply shook his head.

Legana Breed was studying the weapon in his skeletal hands. 'It's scratched.'

'What? Oh, but I – oh, well—'

'Humour is extinct,' the T'lan Imass said, turning back to the doorway.

Gesler suddenly straightened. 'A moment, Legana Breed!'

The creature paused.

'Stormy did all that you asked of him. Now, we need *repayment*.'

Sweat sprang out on Fiddler's skin. *Gesler!*

The T'lan Imass faced them again. 'Repayment. Shield Anvil, did not my weapon serve you well?'

'Aye, well enough.'

'Then there is no debt—'

'Not true!' Gesler said in a growl. 'We saw you take that Tiste Andii head with you! But we told your fellow T'lan Imass nothing – we kept your secret, Legana Breed! When we could have bargained with it, gotten ourselves right out of that damned mess we were in! There is a debt!'

Silence from the ancient undead warrior, then, 'What do you demand of me?'

'We – me, Stormy and Fiddler here – we need an escort. Back to our ship. It could mean a fight.'

'There are four thousand mortals between us and the docks,' Legana Breed said. 'One and all driven into madness by chaotic sorcery.'

'And?' Gesler sneered. 'Are you afraid, T'lan Imass?'

'Afraid.' A declarative statement. Then the head cocked. 'Humour?'

'So what's the problem?'

'The docks.' Hesitation, then, 'I just came from there.'

Fiddler began collecting his gear. 'With answers like that one, Legana Breed,' he said, 'you belong in the marines.' He glanced over at Braven Tooth. 'Well met, old friend.'

The Master Sergeant nodded. 'And with you. The three of you. Sorry about punching you in the gut, Fid.'

'Like Hood you are.'

'I didn't know it was you—'

'To Hood you didn't.'

'All right, I heard you come in. Heard cloth against fiddle strings. Smelled Moranth munitions. Not hard with all that.'

'So you punched me anyway?'

Braven Tooth smiled. The particular smile that gave the bastard his name.

Legana Breed spoke: 'You are all marines?'

'Aye,' Fiddler said.

'Tonight, then, I too am a marine. Let us go kill people.'

Throatslitter clambered up the gangplank, stumbled down onto the deck. 'Fist,' he gasped, 'we need to call more in – we none of us can hold much longer—'

'No, soldier,' Keneb replied, his gaze fixed on the vicious fighting on the concourse before them, the ever-contracting Perish lines, the ever-growing mass of frenzied attackers pouring in from every street and alley mouth between warehouse buildings. *Don't you see? We commit more and we get pulled deeper into this mess, deeper and deeper – until we cannot extricate ourselves. There's too much sorcery out there – gods below, my head feels ready to explode.* He so wanted to explain all of this to the desperate marine, but that was not what a commander did.

Just like the Adjunct. You want to, gods how you want to, if only to see the understanding in their eyes. But you cannot. All right, so I'm starting to comprehend . . .

'Attend, Fist Keneb!' The warning came from the Destriant. 'Assassins, seeking to penetrate our defences—'

A hiss from Throatslitter, and he turned, called down to the marines on the jetty. 'Sergeant! Get the squads up here! We got Claws on the way!'

Keneb faced Run'Thurvian. 'Can you block them?'

A slow nod of the suddenly pallid face. 'This time, yes – at the last moment – but they are persistent, and clever. When they breach, they will appear, suddenly, all about us.'

'Who is their target? Do you know?'

'All of us, I believe. Perhaps, most of all,' the Destriant glanced over at Nil and Nether, who stood on the foredeck, silent witnesses to the defence, 'those two. Their power sleeps. For now, it cannot be awakened – it is not for us, you see. Not for us.'

Hood's breath. He turned to see the first marines arrive. Koryk, Tarr, Smiles – *damn you, Fiddler, where are you?* – then Cuttle and Corabb Bhilan Thenu'alas. A moment later Sergeant Balm appeared, followed by Galt and Lobe. 'Sergeant, where is your healer – and your mage?'

'Used up,' the Dal Honese replied. 'They're recovering on the *Silanda*, sir.'

'Very well. I want you to form a cordon around Nil and Nether – the Claw will go for them first and foremost.' As the soldiers scrambled he turned to Run'Thurvian, and said in a low voice, 'I assume you can protect yourself, Destriant.'

'Yes, I have held myself in abeyance, anticipating such a moment. But what of you, Fist Keneb?'

'I doubt I'm important enough.' Then something occurred to him and he called over to the marines. 'Smiles! Head down to the First Mate's cabin – warn Quick Ben and if you can, convince him to get up here.' He made his way to the starboard rail, leaned out to study the fighting at the base of the jetty.

There were uniformed Malazan soldiers amidst the mob, now, all pretence gone. Armoured, many with shields, others holding back with crossbows, sending one quarrel after another into the line of Perish. The foreign allies had been pushed back almost to the jetty itself.

Cuttle was on the foredeck, yelling at the ballista crew – the sapper held a handful of fishing net in one hand and a large round object in the other. A cusser. After a moment the crew stepped back and Cuttle set to affixing the munition just behind the head of the oversized dart.

Nice thinking. A messy way to clear a space, but there's little choice.

Smiles returned, hurried up to Keneb. 'Fist, he's not there.'

'What?'

'He's gone!'

'Very well. Never mind. Go join your squad, soldier.'

From somewhere in Malaz City, a bell sounded, the sonorous tones ringing four times. *Gods below, is that all?*

Lieutenant Pores stood beside his captain, staring across the dark water to the mayhem at Centre Docks. 'We're losing, sir,' he said.

'That's precisely why I made you an officer,' Kindly replied. 'Your extraordinary perceptiveness. And no, Lieutenant, we will not disobey our orders. We remain here.'

'It's not proper, sir,' Pores persisted. 'Our allies are dying there – it's not even their fight.'

'What they choose to do is their business.'

'Still not proper, sir.'

'Lieutenant, are you truly that eager to kill fellow Malazans? If so, get out of that armour and you can swim ashore. With Oponn's luck the sharks won't find you, despite my fervent prayers to the contrary. And you'll arrive just in time to get your head lopped off, forcing me to find myself a new lieutenant, which, I grant you, will not be hard, all things considered. Maybe Hanfeno, now there's officer material – to the level of lieutenant and no higher, of course. Almost as thick and pig-headed as you. Now go on, climb out of that armour, so Senny can start laying bets.'

'Thank you, sir, but I'd rather not.'

'Very well. But one more complaint from you, Lieutenant, and I'll throw you over the side myself.'

'Yes, sir.'

'In your armour.'

'Yes, sir.'

'After docking your pay for the loss of equipment.'

'Of course, Captain.'

'And if you keep trying to get the last word here I think I will kill you outright.'

'Yes, sir.'

'Lieutenant.'

Pores clamped his jaws shut, and held off. For the moment.

With barely a whisper, the figure landed on the sundered, pitched rooftop. Paused to look round at the sprawl of corpses. Then approached the gaping hole near one end.

As it neared, another figure seemed to materialize as if from nowhere, crouched down on one knee above a body lying face-down near the breach. A quarrel was buried deep in that body's back, the fletching fashioned of fish bone – the cheek sections of some large sea-dwelling species, pale and semi-translucent. The newcomer swung a ghostly face up to regard the one who approached.

'The Clawmaster killed me,' the apparition said in a rasp, gesturing to its own body beneath it. 'Even as I cursed his name with my last breath. I think . . . yes, I think that is why I am still here, not yet ready to walk through Hood's Gate. It is a gift . . . to you. He killed Kalam Mekhar. With Kartoolian paralt.' The ghost turned slightly and gestured to the edge of the hole. 'Kalam – he pulled the quarrel loose . . . no point of course, it makes no difference since the paralt's in his blood. But I did not tell Pearl – it's right there, balanced on the very lip. Take it. There is plenty of poison left. Take it. For the Clawmaster.'

A moment later the ghost was gone.

The cloth-wrapped figure crouched down and collected the blood-smeared quarrel in one gloved hand. Tucked it into a fold of the sash belt, then straightened, and set off.

Through skeins of vicious sorcery, the lone figure moved with blinding speed down the street, deftly avoiding every snare – the coruscating pockets of High Ruse, the whispering invitations of Mockra – and then into the light-stealing paths of Rashan where assassins of the Claw had raced along only moments earlier – and onto their trail, fast closing, a dagger in each leather-clad hand.

Near the harbourfront the Claws began emerging from their warrens, massing by the score, moments from launching an all-out assault on the foreign soldiers, on everyone aboard the two moored ships.

Approaching fast from behind, the figure's movements acquired a fluidity, sinuous, weaving a flow of shadows, and the approach that had been quick transformed into something else – faster than a mortal eye could perceive in this night of gloom and smoke – and then the lone attacker struck the first of the Hands.

Blood sprayed, sheeted into the air, bodies spun to either side from its path, a whirlwind of death tearing into the ranks. Claws spun round, shouted, screamed, and died.

Clawmaster Pearl turned at the sounds. He was positioned over twenty Hands from the rearguard – a rearguard now down, writhing or motionless on the cobbles, as something – *someone* – tore through them. *Gods below.* A Shadow Dancer. *Who – Cotillion?* Cold terror seized his chest with piercing talons. *The god. The Patron of Assassins – coming for me.*

In Kalam Mekhar's name, coming for me!

He spun round, eyes searching frantically for a bolt-hole. *To Hood with the Hands!* Pearl pushed his way clear, then ran.

An alley, narrow between two warehouses, swallowed in darkness. Moments to go, then he would open his warren, force a rent, plunge through – through, and *away.*

Weapons in his hands now. *If I go down, it will be fighting – god or no god—*

Into the alley, embraced by darkness – behind him more screams, coming closer – Pearl reached in his mind like a drowning man for his warren. Mockra. *Use it. Twist reality, cut into another warren – Rashan, and then the Imperial, and then—*

Nothing answered his quest. A ragged gasp burst from Pearl's throat as he sprinted onward, up the alley—

Something behind him – right behind—

Strokes of agony, slicing through both Achilles tendons – Pearl shrieked as the severed ligaments rolled up beneath the skin, stumbled on feet that felt like clods of mud, shifting hopelessly beneath him. Sprawling, refusing to release his weapons, still grasping out for his warren—

Blade-edges licking like tongues of acid. Hamstrings, elbows – then he was lifted from the blackened cobbles by a single hand, and thrown into a wall. The impact shattered half his face, and as he fell backward, that hand returned, fingers digging in, forcing his head back. Cold iron slashed into his mouth, slicing, severing his tongue. Choking on blood, Pearl twisted his head around – he was grasped again, thrown into the opposite wall, breaking his left arm. Landing on his side – a foot hammered down on the point of his hip, the bone cradle collapsing into a splintered mess beneath it – *gods, the pain*, sweeping up through his mind, overwhelming him – his warren – *where?*

All motion ceased.

His attacker was standing over him. Crouching down.

Pearl could see nothing – blood filled his eyes – a savage ringing filled his head, nausea rising up his throat, spilling out in racking heaves, streaked with gore from the gouting stub of his tongue. *Lostara, my love, come close to the gate – and you will see me. Walking.*

A voice, soft and low, cut through it all, brutally clear, brutally close. 'My final target. You, Pearl. I had planned to make it quick.' A long pause, in which he heard slow, even breathing. 'But for Kalam Mekhar.'

Something stabbed into his stomach, was pushed deep.

'I give you back the quarrel that killed him, Pearl.' And the figure straightened once more, walked a few paces away, then returned, even as the first horrifying pulses of fire began to sear his veins, gathering behind his eyes – a poison that would keep him alive for as long as possible, feeding his heart with everything it needed, even as vessels throughout his body burst, again and again and again—

'Kalam's long-knives, Pearl. You weren't thinking. You cannot open a warren with otataral in your hand. And so, he and I together, we have killed you. Fitting.'

Fires! Gods! Fire!

As Apsalar walked away. Continuing up the alley, away fom the harbourfront. Away, from everything.

A scrawny, shadowy apparition appeared before her near the far end, where the alley reached a side street just this side of a bridge leading across the river and into the Mouse. Apsalar halted before it.

'Tell Cotillion, I have done as he asked.'

Shadowthrone made a whispering sound, like sighing, and one almost formless hand emerged from the folds of his ghostly cloak, gripping the silver head of a cane, that tapped once on the cobbles. 'I watched, my dear. Your Shadow Dance. From the foot of Rampart Way and onward, I was witness.'

She said nothing.

Shadowthrone resumed. 'Not even Cotillion. Not even Cotillion.'

Still, Apsalar did not speak.

The god suddenly giggled. 'Too many bad judgements, the poor woman. As we feared.' A pause, then another giggle. 'Tonight, the Clawmaster, and three hundred and seven Claws – all by your hands, dear lass. I still . . . disbelieve. No matter. She's on her own, now. Too bad for her.' The barely substantial hooded head cocked slightly. 'Ah. Yes, Apsalar. We keep our promises. You are free. Go.'

She held out the two long-knives, handles first.

A bow, and the god accepted Kalam Mekhar's weapons.

Then Apsalar moved past Shadowthrone, and walked on.

He watched her cross the bridge.

Another sigh. A sudden lifting of the cowled head, sniffing the air. 'Oh, happy news. But for me, not yet. First, a modest detour, yes. My, what a night!'

The god began to fade, then wavered, then re-formed. Shadowthrone looked down at the long-knives in his right hand. 'Absurd! I must walk. And, perforce, quickly!'

He scurried off, cane rapping on the stones.

A short time later, Shadowthrone reached the base of a tower that was not nearly as ruined as it looked. Lifted the cane and tapped on the door. Waited for a dozen heartbeats, then repeated the effort.

The door was yanked open.

Dark eyes stared down at him, and in them was a growing fury.

'Now now, Obo,' Shadowthrone said. 'This is a courtesy, I assure you. Two most meddling twins have commandeered the top of your tower. I humbly suggest you oust them, in your usual kindly manner.' The god then sketched a salute with his cane, turned about and departed.

The door slammed shut after two strides.

And now, Shadowthrone began to quicken his pace once more. For one last rendezvous this night, a most precious one. The cane rapped swift as a soldier's drum.

Halfway to his destination, the top of Obo's tower erupted in a thunderous fireball that sent pieces of brick and tile flying. Amidst that eruption there came two outraged screams.

Recovering from his instinctive duck, Shadowthrone murmured. 'Most kindly, Obo. Most kindly indeed.'

And the god walked the streets of Malaz City. Once more with uncharacteristic haste.

They moved quickly along the street, keeping to the shadows, ten paces behind Legana Breed, who walked down the centre, sword tip clattering along the cobbles. The few figures who had crossed their path had hurriedly fled upon sighting the tattered apparition of the T'lan Imass.

Fiddler had given Gesler and Stormy crossbows, both fitted with the sharper-packed grenados, whilst his own weapon held a cusser. They approached a wider street that ran parallel to the harbourfront, still south of the bridge leading over to Centre Docks. Familiar buildings for Fiddler, on all sides, yet a surreal quality had come to the air, as if the master hand of some mad artist had lifted every detail into something more profound than it should have been.

From the docks came the roar of battle, punctuated with the

occasional crackle of Moranth munitions. Sharpers, mostly. *Cuttle. He's using up my supply!*

They reached the intersection. Legana Breed paused in the middle, slowly faced the sagging façade of a tavern opposite. Where the door slammed open and two figures stumbled out. Reeling, negotiating the cobbles beneath them as if traversing stepping stones across a raging river, one grasping the other by an arm, tugging, pulling, then leaning against him, causing both to stagger.

Swearing under his breath, Fiddler headed towards them. 'Sergeant Hellian, what in Hood's name are you doing ashore?'

Both figures hitched up at the voice, turned.

And Hellian's eyes fixed on the T'lan Imass. 'Fiddler,' she said, 'you look awful.'

'Over here, you drunken idiot.' He waved Gesler and Stormy ahead as he came closer. 'Who's that with you?'

Hellian turned and regarded the man she held by an arm, for what seemed a long time.

'Your priz'ner,' the man said by way of encouragement.

'Thaz right.' Hellian straightened as she faced Fiddler again. 'He's wanted for questioning.'

'By whom?'

'Me, thazoo. So's anyway, where's the boat?'

Gesler and Stormy were making their way towards the bridge. 'Go with them,' Fiddler said to Legana Breed, and the T'lan Imass set off, feet scraping. The sapper turned back to Hellian. 'Stay close, we're heading back to the ships right now.'

'Good. Glad you could make it, Fid, in case thiz one tries an' 'scapes, right? Y'got my p'mission to shoot 'im down. But only in the foot. I wan' answers from 'im an' I'm gonna get 'em.'

'Hellian,' Fiddler said, 'could be we'll need to make a run for it.'

'We can do that. Right, Banash?'

'Fool,' Fiddler muttered. 'That's Smiley's there. The demon doesn't serve regular ale. Any other place . . .' He then shook his head. 'Come on, you two.'

Up ahead, Gesler and Stormy had reached the bridge. Crouched low, they moved across its span.

Fiddler heard Gesler shout, a cry of surprise and alarm – and all at once both he and Stormy were running – straight for a heaving crowd that loomed up before them.

'*Shit!*' Fiddler sprinted forward.

A winding trench swallowed in gloom, a vein that seemed to run beneath the level where the frenzy of slaughter commanded every street, every alley to either side. The woman behind her coughing gouts of blood as she sloshed along, the Adjunct, Tavore Paran, waded through a turgid stream of sewage.

Ever closer to the sounds of fighting at Centre Docks.

It had seemed impossible – the Claws had not found them, had not plunged down the rotted brick walls to deliver murder in the foul soup that was Malaz River. Oh, Tavore and T'amber had pushed past enough corpses on their journey, but the only sounds embracing them were the swirl of water, the skittering of rats along the ledges to either side, and the whine of biting insects.

That all changed when they reached the edge of the concourse. The concussion of a sharper, startlingly close, then the tumbling of a half-dozen bodies as a section of the retaining wall collapsed directly ahead. More figures sliding down, screaming, weapons waving in the air—

—and a soldier turned, saw them—

As he bellowed his discovery, T'amber pushed past the Adjunct. Longsword arced across, diagonally, and cut off the top third of the man's head, helm and bone, white matter spraying out.

Then T'amber reached back, closed a bloody hand on the Adjunct's cloak, dragged her forward, onto the sunken bank of dislodged brick, sand and gravel.

The strength in that grip stunned Tavore, as T'amber assailed the slope, dragging the Adjunct from her feet, up, up onto the level of the concourse. Stumbling onto her knees, even as that hand left her and the sounds of fighting erupted around them—

City Guard, three squads at least – detonations had pushed them to this side of the concourse, and they turned upon the two women like rabid wolves—

Tavore pushed herself upright, caught a sword-thrust reaching for her midsection with a desperate parry, the weapons ringing. She instinctively counter-attacked, and felt the tip of her sword tear through chain and gouge the muscles of a shoulder. Her opponent grunted, flinched back. Tavore chopped down onto the knee of his lead leg, cutting in two the patella. He shrieked and fell.

To her left, T'amber cut, slashed, parried and lunged, and bodies were falling all around her. Even as swords sank into the woman – and she staggered.

Tavore cried out, twisting to move towards T'amber—

And saw, less than twenty paces away, a score or more Claws, rushing to join the fray.

A sword burst from T'amber's back, between the shoulder-blades, and the soldier gripping the weapon pushed close to the woman and heaved her from her feet, throwing her backward, where she slid off the length of iron, landing hard on the cobbles, her own sword leaving her hand, clattering away.

Six paces between the Adjunct and a dozen Guards – and behind them and closing fast, the Claws. Tavore backed away – faces turned to her, faces twisted in blind rage, eyes cold and hard, inhuman. The Adjunct raised her sword, both hands on the grip now, took a step back—

The Guards rushed forward—

Then, a blinding flash, immediately behind them, and that rush became a mass of torn bodies, severed limbs, sheets of blood – the roar of the detonation seemed to ignite in the centre of Tavore's skull. The world pitched, she saw night sky, wheeling, stars seeming to race outward in all directions – her head cracking on the cobbles, dislodging her helm, and she was on her back, staring up, confused by the tumbling smoke, the red mist, the thundering protest of every muscle and bone in her body.

A second explosion lifted her from the cobbles, pounded her back down on a surface suddenly heaved askew. More blood rained down—

Someone skidded up against her, a hand reaching down to rest lightly on her sternum, a face, blurred, looming close. She watched the mouth move but heard nothing.

A flash, recognition. *Sergeant Fiddler.*

What? What are you doing?

And then she was being dragged along, boots pulling loose at the ends of senseless legs. The right one dislodging, left behind. She stared at her cloth-wrapped foot, soaked in river-slime and blood.

She could now see behind her as the sergeant continued pulling her towards the jetty. Two more marines, covering their retreat with strange, oversized crossbows in their hands. But no-one was coming after them – they were busy dying beneath a stone sword in the desiccated hands of a T'lan Imass – the creature punched at by virulent sorcery, yet pushing ever forward, killing, *killing.*

What was happening? Where had the marines come from? She saw another one, struggling with a prisoner – he wasn't trying to escape, however, just stay on his feet. *They're drunk, the both of them – well, on this night, I think I'll let it pass.*

Oh, T'amber . . .

More figures surrounding them now. Bloodied soldiers. The Perish. People were shouting – she could see that – but the roaring in her head was unabated, drowning out all else. She half-lifted one arm, stared at her gauntleted hand – *my sword. Where is my sword?*

Never mind. Just sleep, now. Sleep.

*

Grub led her into the alley, to where a body was lying, curled up, racked with spasms and voicing a dreadful moaning. As she drew closer, Lostara recognized him. Anguish rose up within her and she lunged past Grub, fell to her knees.

Pearl was covered in wounds, as if he had been systematically tortured. And pain was consuming him. 'Oh, my love . . .'

Grub spoke behind her. 'The poison has him, Lostara Yil. You must take his life.'

What?

'He thought you were dead,' the boy continued. 'He'd given up. On everything. Except revenge. Against the Adjunct.'

'Who did this?'

'I won't tell you,' Grub said. 'Pearl hungered for vengeance, and vengeance was repaid him. That's all.'

That's all.

'Kill him now, Lostara. He can't hear you, he can't see you. There's only the pain. It's the spiders, you see, they breathe the blood of their victims, they need it rich, bright red. And so the venom, it doesn't let go. And then, there's the acid in the stomach, leaking out, eating everything up.'

Numbed, she drew out her knife.

'Make the heart stop.'

Yes, there, behind and beneath the shoulder-blade. Push deep, work the edges. Pull it loose, look, how the body stills, how the muscles cease their clenching. It's quiet, now. He's gone.

'Come along, there's more. Quickly.'

He set off, and she rose and followed. *You've left me. You were there, in Mock's Hold, but I didn't know. You didn't know.*

Past a tumbled mass of corpses now. Claws. The alley was filled with them.

Ahead, Centre Docks, the clearing—

Sudden detonations, rocking the buildings. Screams.

At the alley mouth, between warehouses, Grub crouched and waved her down to his side.

People were fleeing – those still on their feet, and they were scant few. At least two cussers had exploded in the midst of the mobs. Cussers and sharpers, and there a Hood-damned T'lan Imass, cutting down the last ones within reach.

'Gods,' Lostara muttered, 'there must be a thousand dead out there.'

'Yes. But look, you must see this.' He pointed to their right, near the river.

'What?'

'Oh.' Grub reached out and settled a hand on her forearm.

And the scene seemed to somehow shift, a new illumination – it was gathered about a single body, too distant to make out details—

'T'amber,' Grub said. 'Only you and me can see. So watch, Lostara. Watch.'

The golden glow was coalescing, rising up from the corpse. A faint wind flowed past Lostara and Grub, familiar now, heady with the scent of savannah grasses, warm and dry.

'She stayed with us a long time,' Grub whispered. 'She used T'amber. A lot. There wasn't any choice. The Fourteenth, it's going to war, and we're going with it. We have to.'

A figure now stood at a half-crouch over the body. Furred, tall, and female. No clothing, no ornamentation of any kind.

Lostara saw the T'lan Imass, thirty or more paces away, slowly turn to regard the apparition. And then, head bowing, the undead warrior slowly settled onto one knee. 'I thought you said we were the only ones who could see, Grub.'

'I was wrong. She has that effect.'

'Who – what is she?'

'The Eres'al. Lostara, you must never tell the Adjunct. Never.'

The Red Blade captain scowled. 'Another damned secret to keep from her.'

'Just the two,' Grub said. 'You can do that.'

Lostara glanced over at the boy. 'Two, you said.'

Grub nodded. 'Her sister, yes. That one, and this one. Two secrets. Never to tell.'

'That won't be hard,' she said, straightening. 'I'm not going with them.'

'Yes you are. Look! Look at the Eres'al!'

The strange female was lowering her head towards the body of T'amber. 'What's she doing?'

'Just a kiss. On the forehead. A thank-you.'

The apparition straightened once more, seemed to sniff the air, then, in a blur, vanished.

'Oh!' said Grub. Yet added nothing. Instead, taking her hand in his. 'Lostara. The Adjunct, she's lost T'amber now. You need to take that place—'

'I'm done with lovers, male or female—'

'No, not that. Just . . . at her side. You have to. She cannot do this alone.'

'Do *what*?'

'We have to go – no, not that way. To the Mouse Docks—'

'Grub – they're casting off!'

'Never mind that! Come on!'

Deadsmell pushed Fiddler out of the way and knelt beside the body of the Adjunct. He set a hand on her begrimed forehead, then snatched it back. 'Hood's breath! She doesn't need me.' He backed away, shaking his head, 'Damned otataral – I never could get that, what it does . . .'

Tavore's eyes opened. After a moment, she struggled into a sitting position, then accepted Fiddler's hand in helping her to her feet.

The *Froth Wolf* was edging away from the jetty. The *Silanda* had pulled further out, the oars sweeping and sliding into the water.

Blinking, the Adjunct looked round, then she turned to Fiddler. 'Sergeant, where is Bottle?'

'I don't know. He never made it back. Seems we lost Quick Ben, too. And Kalam.'

At the last name, she flinched.

But Fiddler had already known. *The game . . .* 'Adjunct—'

'I have never seen a man fight as he did,' she said. 'Him, and T'amber, the two of them – cutting through an entire city—'

'Adjunct. There's signals from the other ships. Where are we going?'

But she turned away. 'Bottle – we have failed, Sergeant. He was to retrieve someone.'

'Someone? Who?'

'It doesn't matter, now. We have failed.'

All of this? All of the fallen this night – for one person? 'Adjunct, we can wait here in the bay until light, send a detachment into the city looking—'

'No. Admiral Nok's escorts will be ordered to sink the transports – the Perish will intervene, and more will die. We must leave.'

'They can chase us down—'

'But they won't find us. The Admiral has assured me of his impending incompetence.'

'So, we signal the others to ship their anchors and make sail?'

'Yes.'

A shout from one of the crew. 'Ship closing to starboard!'

Fiddler followed the Adjunct to the rail. Where Fist Keneb already stood.

A small craft was approaching on an intercept course. A lantern appeared at its bow, flashing.

'They got passengers to drop off,' the lookout called down.

The ship came alongside with a crunch and grinding of hulls. Lines were thrown, rope ladders dropped down.

Fiddler nodded. 'Bottle.' Then he scowled. 'I thought you said one person – the fool's brought a damned score with him.'

The first to arrive over the rail, however, was Grub.

A bright grin. 'Hello, father,' he said as Keneb reached out and lifted the boy, setting him on the deck. 'I brought Captain Lostara Yil. And Bottle's brought lots of people—'

A stranger then clambered aboard, landing lightly on the deck and pausing, hands on hips, to look round. 'A damned mess,' he said.

As soon as he spoke, Fiddler stepped forward. 'Cartheron Crust. I thought you were—'

'Nobody here by that name,' the man said in a growl, one hand settling on the knife handle jutting from his belt.

Fiddler stepped back.

More figures were arriving, strangers one and all: the first a huge man, his expression flat, cautious, and on his forearms were scars and old weals that Fiddler recognized. He was about to speak when Crust – who was not Crust – spoke.

'Adjunct Tavore, right? Well, I'm charging you sixteen gold imperials for delivering this mob of fools to your ship.'

'Very well.'

'So get it, because we're not hanging round this damned harbour any longer than we have to.'

Tavore turned to Keneb. 'Fist, go to the legion paychest and extract two hundred gold imperials.'

'I said sixteen—'

'Two hundred,' the Adjunct repeated.

Keneb set off for below.

'Captain,' the Adjunct began, then fell silent.

The figures now climbing aboard were, one and all, tall, black-skinned. One, a woman, stood very near the scarred man, and this one now faced the Adjunct.

And in rough Malazan, she said, 'My husband has been waiting for you a long time. But don't think I am just letting you take him away. What is to come belongs to us – to the Tiste Andii – as much and perhaps more than it does to you.'

After a moment, the Adjunct nodded, then bowed. 'Welcome aboard, then, Tiste Andii.'

Three small black shapes scrambled over the rail, made immediately for the rigging.

'Gods below,' Fiddler muttered. 'Nachts. I hate those things—'

'Mine,' the scarred stranger said.

'What is your name?' Tavore asked him.

'Withal. And this is my wife, Sandalath Drukorlat. Aye, a handful of a name and more than a handful of a—'

'Quiet, husband.'

Fiddler saw Bottle trying to sneak off to one side and he set off after the soldier. 'You.'

Bottle winced, then turned. 'Sergeant.'

'How in Hood's name did you find Cartheron Crust?'

'That Crust? Well, I just followed my rat. We couldn't hope to get through the battle on the concourse, so we found us a ship—'

'But Cartheron Crust?'

Bottle shrugged.

Keneb had reappeared, and Fiddler saw the Adjunct and Crust arguing, but he could not hear the exchange. After a moment, Crust nodded, collected the small chest of coins. And the Adjunct walked towards the bow.

Where stood Nil and Nether.

'Sergeant?'

'Go get some rest, Bottle.'

'Aye, thank you, Sergeant.'

Fiddler walked up behind the Adjunct to listen in on the conversation.

Tavore was speaking, '. . . pogrom. The Wickans of your homeland need you both. And Temul. Alas, you won't be able to take your horses – the captain's ship is not large enough – but we can crowd every Wickan aboard. Please, make yourself ready, and, for all that you have done for me, thank you both.'

Nil was the first to descend to the mid deck. Nether followed a moment later, but made for Bottle, who was slumped into a sitting position, his back to the railing. She glared down at him until, some instinct warning him, he opened his eyes and looked up at her.

'When you are done,' Nether said, 'come back.'

Then she set off. Bottle stared after her, a dumbfounded expression on his face.

Fiddler turned away. *Lucky bastard.*

Or not.

He ascended to the forecastle. Stared across at Malaz City. Fires here and there, smoke and the reek of death.

Kalam Mekhar, my friend.

Farewell.

Blood loss, ironically, had kept him alive this far. Blood and poison, streaming out from his wounds as he staggered along, almost blind with the agony exploding in his muscles, the hammering of his heart deafening in his skull.

And he continued fighting his way. One step, then another, doubling over as the pain clenched suddenly, excruciating in its intensity before easing a fraction – enough to let him draw breath, and force one foot forward yet again. Then another.

He reached a corner, struggled to lift his head. But fire consumed his eyes, he could make out nothing of the world beyond. This far . . . on instinct, following a map in his head, a map now torn into ribbons by the pain.

He was close. He could feel it.

Kalam Mekhar reached out to steady himself on a wall – but there was no wall, and he toppled, thudded hard onto the cobbles, where, unable to prevent it, his limbs drew inward and he curled up round the seething, lashing agony.

Lost. There should have been a wall, a corner, right there. His map had failed him. And now it was too late. He could feel his legs dying. His arms, his spine a spear of molten fire.

He felt one temple resting on the hard, damp stone.

Well, dying was dying. The assassin's art ever turns on its wielder. Nothing in the world could be more just, more proper—

Ten paces away, Shadowthrone bared his teeth. 'Get up, you fool. You're very nearly there. Get up!'

But the body did not stir.

Hissing in fury, the god slipped forward. A gesture and the three shadow-wraiths in his wake rushed forward, gathered round the motionless form of Kalam Mekhar.

One rasped, 'He's dead.'

Shadowthrone snarled, pushed his servants aside and crouched down. 'Not yet,' he said after a moment. 'But oh so very close.' He lurched back a step. 'Pick him up, you damned idiots! We're going to *drag* him!'

'We?' one asked.

'Careful,' the god murmured. Then watched as the wraiths reached down, grasped limbs, and lifted the assassin. 'Good, now follow me, and quickly.'

To the gate, the barrier squealing as Shadowthrone pushed it aside.

Onto the rough path, its tilted stones and snarls of dead grass.

Mounds to either side, the humps beginning to steam. Dawn's arrival? Hardly. No, the ones within . . . *sensed* him. The god allowed himself a small, dry laugh. Then ducked as it came out louder than he had intended.

Approaching the front door.

Shadowthrone halted, edged as close as he could to one side of the path, then waved the wraiths forward. 'Quickly! Drop him there, at the threshold! Oh, and here, you, take his long-knives. Back in the sheaths, yes. Now, all of you, get out of here – and stay on the path, you brainless worms! Who are you trying to awaken?'

Another step, closer to that dark, dew-beaded door. Lifting the cane. A single rap with the silver head.

Then the god turned about and hurried down the path.

Reaching the gate, then spinning round as that door groaned open.

A huge armoured figure filled the portal, looking down.

Shadowthrone whispered, '*Take him, you oaf! Take him!*'

Then, with infuriating slowness, the enormous guardian of the Deadhouse reached down, collected the assassin by the scruff of the neck, and dragged him across the threshold.

The god, crouched at the gate, watched as Kalam's feet vanished into the gloom.

Then the door slammed shut.

In time? 'No way of knowing. Not for a while ... my, Shadowthrone's collection is *most* impressive, yes?' And he turned away, to see his wraiths fleeing down the street, even as a nearby tavern door thundered open.

And the god winced, ducking still lower. 'Uh oh, time to leave, I think.'

A swirl of shadows.

And then Shadowthrone was gone.

Master Sergeant Braven Tooth neared the entrance to Coop's. Not yet dawn. And the damned night was now quiet as a tomb. He shivered, as if he had just crossed the path of some hoary ghost, passing invisible yet pausing to give him a hungry glance.

Coop's door opened and closed, hard, the object of some anger, and Braven Tooth slowed.

An armoured monstrosity ascended into view.

Braven Tooth blinked, then grunted under his breath and approached.

'Evening, Temper.'

The helmed head turned to him, as if distracted by the Master Sergeant's sudden presence.

'Braven Tooth.'

'What brings you out?'

Temper seemed to sniff the air, then glanced across at the old Deadhouse. A softly clattering shrug as he said, 'Thought I'd take a walk.'

Braven Tooth nodded. 'I see you dressed appropriately.'

Both men stepped back as a woman emerged from a nearby alley and came right past them, descended the steps and vanished into the maw of Coop's.

'Now that was some swaying walk,' the Master Sergeant muttered in appreciation. But Temper's attention was on the cobbles, and Braven Tooth looked down.

She'd left footprints. Dark red.

'So, Temper. I suppose we can't hope that's mud, now can we?'

'I think not, Brav.'

'Well, think I'll plant myself in Coop's. You done with your walk?'

A final glance across at the Deadhouse, then the huge man nodded. 'So it seems.'

The two went down into the murky confines of the Hanged Man.

An auspicious guest had holed up in Coop's this night. Fist Aragan, who'd taken the cramped booth farthest from the door, in the darkest corner, where he sat alone, nursing a tankard of ale as bell after bell tolled outside, amidst a distant and sometimes not-so-distant chorus of riotous mayhem.

He was not alone in looking up, then holding his gaze fixed in admiration for the unknown black-haired Kanese woman who walked in moments before dawn. He watched from beneath hooded brows, as she headed to the bar and ordered Kanese rice wine, forcing Coop to scramble in desperate search before coming up with a dusty amber-hued glass bottle – in itself worth a small fortune.

Moments later Temper – weighed down in a heap of archaic armour – entered the tavern, followed by Master Sergeant Braven Tooth. And Aragan hunched down deep in his seat, averting his gaze.

No company for him this night.

He'd been battling a headache since dusk, and he'd thought it beaten – but suddenly the pounding in his skull returned, redoubled in intensity, and a small groan escaped him.

Braven Tooth tried talking to the woman, but got a knife-point pressed beneath his eye for the effort, and the woman then paid for the entire bottle, claimed a room upstairs, and headed up. Entirely on her own. And no-one followed.

The Master Sergeant, swearing, wiped sweat from his face, then roared for ale.

Strange goings-on at Coop's, but, as always, ale and wine soon muddied the waters, and as for dawn stealing into life outside, well, that belonged to another world, didn't it?

CHAPTER TWENTY-FOUR

Draw a breath,
a deep breath,
now hold it, my friends,
hold it long
for the world
the world drowns.

Wu

THERE WERE MANY FACES TO CHAOS, TO THE REALM BETWEEN THE realms, and this path they had taken, Taralack Veed reflected, was truly horrific. Defoliated trees rose here and there, broken-fingered branches slowly spinning in the chill, desultory wind, wreaths of smoke drifting across the blasted landscape of mud and, everywhere, corpses. Sheathed in clay, limbs jutting from the ground, huddled forms caked and half-submerged.

In the distance was the flash of sorcery, signs of a battle still under-way, but the place where they walked was lifeless, silence like a shroud on all sides, the only sounds tremulously close by – the sob of boots pulling free of the grey slime, the rustle of weapons and armour, and the occasional soft-voiced curse in both Letherii and Edur.

Days of this madness, this brutal reminder of what was possible, the way things could slide down, ever down, until warriors fought without meaning and lives rushed away to fill muddy pools, cold flesh giving way underfoot.

And we march to our own battle, pretending indifference to all that surrounds us. He was no fool. He had been born to a tribe that most called primitive, backward. Warrior castes, cults of blood and ceaseless vendetta. The Gral were without sophistication, driven by shallow desires and baseless convictions. Worshippers of violence. Yet, was

859

there not wisdom in imposing rules to keep madness in check, to never go too far in the bloodletting?

Taralack Veed realized now that he had absorbed something of civilized ways; like fever from bad water, his thoughts had been twisted with dreams of annihilation – an entire clan, he'd wanted every person in it killed, preferably by his own hand. Man, woman, child, babe. And then, in a measure of modest tempering, he had imagined a lesser whirl-wind of slaughter, one that would give him enough kin over which he could rule, unopposed, free to do with them as he pleased. He would be the male wolf in its prime, commanding with a look in its eye, proving with a simple gesture its absolute domination.

None of it made sense any more.

Up ahead, the Edur warrior Ahlrada Ahn called out a rest, and Taralack Veed sank down against the sloped, sodden wall of a trench, stared down at his legs, which seemed to end just beneath his knees, the rest invisible beneath an opaque pool of water reflecting the grey sludge of sky.

The dark-skinned Tiste Edur made his way back along the line, halted before the Gral and the Jhag warrior behind him. 'Sathbaro Rangar says we are close,' he said. 'He will open the gate soon – we have outstayed our welcome in this realm in any case.'

'What do you mean?' Taralack asked.

'It would not do to be seen here, by its inhabitants. True, we would be as apparitions to them, ghostly, simply one more trudging line of soldiers. Even so, such witnessing could create . . . ripples.'

'Ripples?'

Ahlrada Ahn shook his head. 'I myself am unclear, but our warlock is insistent. This realm is like the Nascent – to open the way is to invite devastation.' He paused, then said, 'I have seen the Nascent.'

Taralack Veed watched the Edur walk on, halting to speak every now and then with an Edur or Letherii.

'He commands with honour,' Icarium said.

'He is a fool,' the Gral said under his breath.

'You are harsh in your judgement, Taralack Veed.'

'He plays at deceit, Slayer, and they are all taken in, but I am not. Can you not see it? He is different from the others.'

'I am sorry,' Icarium said, 'but I do not see as you do. Different – how?'

Taralack Veed shrugged. 'He fades his skin. I can smell the com-pound he uses, it reminds me of gothar flowers, which my people use to whiten deer hide.'

'Fades . . .' Icarium slowly straightened and looked back down the line. Then he sighed. 'Yes, now I see. I have been careless—'

'You have been lost inside yourself, my friend.'

'Yes.'

'It is not good. You must ready yourself, you must remain mindful, Slayer—'

'Do not call me that.'

'This too is inside yourself, this resistance to the truth. Yes, it is a harsh truth, but only a coward would not face it, would turn away and pretend to a more comforting falsehood. Such cowardice is beneath you.'

'Perhaps not, Taralack Veed. I believe I am indeed a coward. And yet, this is the least of my crimes, if all that you say of me is true—'

'Do you doubt me?'

'There is no hunger within me,' the Jhag said. 'No lust to kill. And all that you set at my feet, all that you say I have done – I recall nothing of it.'

'So is the nature of your curse, my friend. Would that I could confess, here and now, that I have deceived you. There have been changes in my soul, and now I feel as if we are trapped, doomed to our fate. I have come to know you better than I ever have before, and I grieve for you, Icarium.'

The pale grey eyes regarded him. 'You have told me that we have travelled together a long time, that we have made these journeys of the spirit before. And you have been fierce in your zeal, your desire to see me . . . unleashed. Taralack Veed, if we have been together for many years . . . what you now say makes no sense.'

Sweat prickled beneath the Gral's clothes and he looked away.

'You claim Ahlrada Ahn is the deceiver among us. Perhaps it takes a deceiver to know his kin.'

'Unkind words from you, my friend—'

'I no longer believe we are friends. I now suspect you are my keeper, and that I am little more than your weapon. And now you voice words of doubt as to its sharpness, as if through mutual uncertainty we may step closer to one another. But I will take no such step, Taralack Veed, except back – away from you.'

Bastard. He has pretended to be oblivious. But all the while, he has listened, he has observed. And now closes upon the truth. The weapon is clever – I have been careless, invited into being dismissive, and if my words were themselves weapons, I forgot that this Jhag knows how to defend himself, that he possesses centuries of armour.

He looked up as Ahlrada Ahn strode past them again, heading for the front of the column. 'Soon,' the warrior reminded them.

The journey resumed.

*

Captain Varat Taun, second to Atri-Preda Yan Tovis, Twilight, waved his Letherii archers forward. He spat in an effort to get the taste of mud from his mouth, but it was hopeless. The sorcery of the Holds had been let loose here, in coruscating waves of annihilation – the air stank of it, and in the wind he could hear the echoes of ten thousand soldiers dying, and the mud on his tongue was that of pulverized flesh, gritty with fragments of bone.

Yet perhaps there was a kind of gift in all of this, a measure providing perspective. For, grim as the Letherii Empire under the rule of the Tiste Edur had become, well, there were still green hills, farms, and blue sky overhead. Children were born to mothers and joyous tears flowed easy down warm, soft cheeks, the eyes brimming with love . . . *ah, my darling wife, these memories of you are all that hold me together, all that keep me sane. You and our precious daughter. I will see you again. I promise that. Perhaps soon.*

Ahlrada Ahn was, once more, at the head of the column. Poor man. His facial features gave him away quickly enough, to a soldier hailing from Bluerose, such as Varat Taun. An imposter – what were the reasons for such deception? *Survival, maybe. That and nothing more.* Yet he had heard from Letherii slaves serving the Tiste Edur there was an ancient enmity between the Edur and the Tiste Andii, and if the Edur knew of the hidden enclaves in Bluerose, of their hated dark-skinned kin, well . . .

And so Ahlrada Ahn was among them here. A spy. Varat Taun wished him success. The Onyx Order had been benign rulers, after all – of course, under the present circumstances, the past was an invitation to romantic idealism.

Even considering that, it could not have been worse than now.

Another pointless battle awaited them. More Letherii dead. He so wanted Twilight's respect, and this command could prove a true testing ground. Could Varat command well? Could he show that fine balance between ferocity and caution? *Ah, but I have apprenticed myself to the best commander of the Letherii armies since Preda Unnutal Hebaz, have I not?*

That thought alone seemed to redouble the pressure he felt.

The trench they had been trudging along debouched onto a muddy plain, the surface chewed by horse hoofs and cart wheels and the craters of sorcerous detonations. Here, the reek of rotting flesh hung like a mist. Gravestones were visible here and there, pitched askew or broken, and there was splintered wood – black with sodden decay – and thin white bones amidst the dead still clothed in flesh.

Perhaps half a league away ran a ridge, possibly a raised road, and figures were visible there, in a ragged line, marching towards the distant battle, pikes on their backs.

'Quickly!' Sathbaro Rangar hissed, hobbling forward. 'Stay low, gather round – no, there! Crouch, you fools! We must leave!'

Steth and Aystar, brother and sister, who had shared memories of pain, hands and feet nailed to wood, ravens at their faces tearing at their eyes – terrible nightmares, the conjurings of creative imaginations, said their mother, Minala – crept forward through the gloom of the fissure, the rocky floor beneath them slick, sharp-edged, treacherous.

Neither had yet fought, although both voiced their zeal, for they were still too young, or so Mother had decided. But Steth was ten years of age, and Aystar his sister was nine; and they wore the armour of the Company of Shadow, weapons at their belts, and they had trained with the others, as hard and diligently as any of them. And somewhere ahead stood their favourite sentinel, guarding the passage. They were sneaking up on him, their favourite game of all.

Crouching, they drew closer to where he usually stood.

And then a grating voice spoke from their left. 'You two breathe too loud.'

Aystar squealed in frustration, jumping up. 'It's Steth! I don't breathe at all! I'm just like you!' She advanced on the hulking T'lan Imass who stood with his back to the crevasse wall. Then she flung herself at him, arms wrapping about his midsection.

Onrack's dark, empty gaze settled upon her. Then the withered hand not holding the sword reached up and gingerly patted her on the head. 'You are breathing now,' the warrior said.

'And you smell like dust and worse.'

Steth moved two paces past Onrack's position and perched himself atop a boulder, squinting into the gloom beyond. 'I saw a rat today,' he said. 'Shot two arrows at it. One came close. Really close.'

'Climb down from there,' the T'lan Imass said, prying Aystar's arms from his waist. 'You present a target in silhouette.'

'Nobody's coming any more, Onrack,' the boy said, twisting round as the undead warrior approached. 'They've given up – we were too nasty for them. Mother was talking about leaving—'

The arrow took him full on the side of the head, in the temple, punching through bone and spinning the boy round, legs sliding out onto a side of the boulder, then, with a limp roll, Steth fell to the ground.

Aystar began screaming, a piercing cry that rang up and down the fissure, as Onrack shoved her behind him and said, 'Run. Back, stay along a wall. *Run.*'

More arrows hissed down the length of the crevasse, two of them thudding into Onrack with puffs of dust. He pulled them loose and dropped them to the floor, striding forward and taking his sword into both hands.

Minala's face looked old, drawn with days and nights of fear and worry, the relentless pressure of waiting, of looking upon her adopted children, rank on rank, and seeing naught but soldiers, who had learned to kill, who had learned to watch their comrades die.

All to defend a vacant throne.

Trull Sengar could comprehend the mocking absurdity of this stand. A ghost had claimed the First Throne, a thing of shadows so faded from this world even the undead T'lan Imass looked bloated with excess beside it. A ghost, a god, a gauze-thin web-tracing of desire, possessiveness and nefarious designs – this is what had claimed the seat of power, over all the T'lan Imass, and would now see it held, blocked against intruders.

There were broken T'lan Imass out there, somewhere, who sought to usurp the First Throne, to take its power and gift it to the Crippled God – to the force that now chained all of the Tiste Edur. The Crippled God, who had given Rhulad a sword riven with a terrible curse. Yet, for that fallen creature, an army of Edur was not enough. An army of Letherii was not enough. No, it wanted the T'lan Imass.

And we would stop him, this Crippled God. This pathetic little army of ours.

Onrack had promised anger, with the battle that would, inevitably, come at last. But Trull knew that anger would not be enough, nor what he himself felt: desperation. Nor Minala's harsh terror, nor, he now believed, the stolid insensibility of Monok Ochem and Ibra Gholan – that too, was doomed to fail. *What a menagerie we are.*

He pulled his gaze from Minala, glanced over to where stood Monok Ochem, motionless before the arched entranceway leading into the throne room. The bonecaster had not moved in at least three cycles of sleeping and waking. The silver-tipped fur on his shoulders shimmered vaguely in the lantern light. Then, as Trull studied the figure, he saw the head cock slightly.

Well—

A child's shrieking, echoing from up the passage, brought Trull Sengar to his feet. His spear leaned against a wall – snatching it in one hand he rushed towards the cries.

Aystar suddenly appeared, arms outflung, her face a blur of white – 'Steth's dead! He's been killed! He's dead—'

And then Minala was in the child's path, wrapping her in a

864

fierce hug then twisting round. 'Panek! Gather the soldiers!'

The second line of defence, halfway between Onrack's position and the main encampment, was held by Ibra Gholan, and this T'lan Imass turned as Trull Sengar approached.

'Onrack battles,' Ibra Gholan said. 'To slow their advance. There are many Tiste Edur this time. And humans. A shaman is among them, an Edur, wielding chaotic power. This time, Trull Sengar, they mean to take the First Throne.'

He could hear sounds of fighting now. Onrack, alone against a mass of Trull's own kin. *And a damned warlock.* 'Get Monok Ochem up here, then! If that warlock decides to unleash a wave of sorcery, we're finished.'

'Perhaps you are—'

'You don't understand, you sack of bones! *Chaotic* sorcery! We need to kill that bastard!' And Trull moved forward, leaving Ibra Gholan behind.

Ahlrada Ahn watched three of his warriors fall to the T'lan Imass's huge stone sword – the undead bastard had yet to take a step back from the narrow choke-point in the passage. Ahlrada Ahn turned to Sathbaro Rangar. 'We need to drive that thing back! It won't tire – it can hold that position for ever!'

Taralack Veed pushed into view. 'Send Icarium against it!'

'The Jhag is empty,' the warlock said dismissively. 'Withdraw your warriors, Ahlrada Ahn. And get those Letherii to cease with their arrows – I do not want an errant shaft in the back.' Sathbaro Rangar then moved forward.

And Ahlrada Ahn saw a figure coming up behind the T'lan Imass, a figure wielding a spear – tall, hidden in shadows, yet . . . a familiar silhouette, the fluid movement – he saw an arrow hiss past the undead's shoulder, then saw that spear shaft flick it aside.

No. This cannot be. I am mistaken. 'Sathbaro!'

The T'lan Imass suddenly yielded its position, stepping back into darkness, and then it and the other figure moved away, up the passage—

Sathbaro Rangar hobbled closer to the choke-point, power building round him, a silver-etched rising wave, flickering argent. The damp stone of the fissure's walls began snapping, a strange percussive sound as water burst into steam. A large sheet of rock near the narrowed portal suddenly exfoliated, crashing down to shatter on the floor.

The sorcery lifted higher, fuller, spreading out to the sides, then over Sathbaro's head, a standing wave of power that crackled and hissed like a thousand serpents.

Ahlrada Ahn moved forward. 'Sathbaro! Wait!'

But the warlock ignored him, and with a roar the seething wave of magic plunged into the choke-point, blistering a path up the channel—

—where it suddenly shattered.

The concussion pushed Ahlrada Ahn back three steps, a wave of heat striking him like a fist.

Sathbaro Rangar screamed.

As something huge appeared in the choke-point, humped shoulders pushing through the aperture. Gaunt with undeath, its skin a mottled map of grey and black, silver-tipped fur on the neck and reaching along the shoulders like hackles, the creature emerged from the choke-point and rushed on its knuckles and hand-like hind feet – straight for Sathbaro Rangar.

Ahlrada Ahn shouted out a warning—

—too late, for the beast reached out and closed enormous hands on the warlock, lifted him into the air, tore off one arm, then the other, blood gouting as the apparition then twisted the shrieking Sathbaro round and bit into the back of the Edur's neck, huge canines sinking deep. As the jaws clenched, the undead demon's head snapped back – and ripped half the neck away – Sathbaro's spine racing out like an anchor-chain, whipping bloody in the air—

The beast then flung the corpse aside, and advanced on Ahlrada Ahn.

Icarium stood over the corpse of a child, stared down at the fluids leaking from the broken skull, at the glazed eyes and half-open mouth. The Jhag stood as if rooted, trembling.

Taralack Veed was before him. 'Now, Slayer. *Now is the time!*'

'No need,' Icarium muttered. 'No need for this.'

'Listen to me—'

'Be silent. I will not kill children. I will have none of this—'

A detonation of sorcery ahead, the concussion rolling back, rocking them both. Shouts, then screams. And a bestial snarl. Shrieks, cries of horror from the Letherii and Edur, then the sound of fear.

'Icarium! A demon is upon us! *A demon!* No child, no children – *do you see? You must act – now! Show them! Show the Edur what is within you!*'

Taralack was dragging at his arm. Frowning, Icarium allowed himself to be pulled forward, through a mass of cowering Edur. *No, I do not want this* – yet he could feel the pounding of his hearts, rising like war drums with songs of fire –

The stench of spilled blood and waste, and both warriors arrived to witness the savage death of Sathbaro Rangar.

And the Soletaken then surged into a charge – and Ahlrada Ahn –

the brave warrior, seeking to protect his soldiers – stepped into the creature's path.

Icarium found his single-edged sword in his right hand – he did not recall unsheathing it – and he was moving forward, every motion seeming improbably slow, disjointed, as he reached out, grasping the Tiste Edur and throwing him back as if he weighed little more than a cloth hanging; and then the Jhag advanced to meet the undead ape.

He saw it suddenly recoil.

Another step forward, as a strange humming filled Icarium's skull, and the beast backed further away, into the choke-point, then beyond, where it whirled round and fled up the passage.

Icarium staggered, gasped, threw one hand up against one edge of the narrowed portal – felt its brittle surface beneath his palm. The eerie song in his mind faded—

And then Edur were plunging past him, rushing through the breach. And once more, ahead, the sounds of battle. Hard iron clashing, all scent of sorcery gone—

Beyond the choke-point, Ahlrada Ahn saw before him a widening of the fissure, and there, in a ragged line at least three deep, stood soldiers of some kind, weapons wavering, pale smudged faces beneath helms – *Sisters take me, they are so young! What is this? Children face us!*

And then he saw the two T'lan Imass, and between them a tall, grey-skinned figure – *no. No, it cannot be – we left him, we—*

A savage war-cry from Kholb Harat, echoed almost immediately by Saur Bathrada. *'Trull Sengar! The traitor is before us!'*

'You are mine!'

Despite Saur's bold claim, both he and Kholb lunged together, closing on Trull Sengar.

Then the remaining Edur were spreading out, rushing the line of armoured children, and the two forces collided in a cacophony of ringing weapons and shields. Screams of pain and rage rebounded off the battered stone walls.

And Ahlrada Ahn stood, frozen in place, watching, disbelieving.

Trull Sengar fought a frantic defence with his spear, as weapons slashed and thrust at him from both Saur and Kholb. They were forcing him back – and Ahlrada Ahn could see, could understand – Trull was seeking to protect these children – the ones behind him—

Edur screams – the two T'lan Imass were pushing forward in counter-attack, one to either side, and it seemed nothing could stop them.

Yet still he stood, and then, with a brutal, hoarse cry, he sprang forward.

Trull Sengar knew these two warriors. He could see the hatred in their eyes, felt their fury in the weight of their blows as they sought to batter through his guard – he could not hold them much longer. And when he fell, he knew the pitifully young soldiers behind would come face to face with these Edur killers.

Where was Apt? Why was Minala holding the demon back – what more could assail them?

Someone else was shouting his name now, from among the packed Edur. A name voiced, not in rage, but in anguish – but Trull had no time to look, no time even to wonder – Kholb had laid a blade along his left wrist, opening the flesh wide, and blood was streaming along the underneath of that forearm, seeping into the hand's grip on the shaft.

Not much longer. They've improved, the both of them—

He then saw a Merude cutlass slash inward from behind Kholb, taking the warrior solidly in the neck, through – and Kholb Harat's head rolled on its side, tumbled down. The body wavered a moment, then crumpled.

A snarling curse from Saur Bathrada, who spun round, stabbing low, his sword digging deep into the newcomer's right thigh—

And Trull lunged, sinking the point of his spear into Saur's forehead, just beneath the rim of the helmet. And saw, with horror, both of the warrior's eyes leap from their sockets as if on strings as the head pitched back.

Trull dragged his weapon free as an Edur staggered into him, gasping, 'Trull! Trull Sengar!'

'Ahlrada?'

The warrior twisted round, raising both cutlasses. 'I fight at your side, Trull! Amends – please, I beg you!'

Amends? 'I don't understand – but I do not doubt. Welcome—'

A sound was building in Trull's head, seeming to assail him from every direction. He saw a child clamp hands to ears off to his left, then another one—

'Trull Sengar! It is the Jhag! Sisters take us, he is *coming*!'

Who? What?

What is that sound?

Onrack the Broken saw the Jhag, felt the power growing in the figure that staggered forward as if drunk, and the T'lan Imass moved into his path. *Is this their leader? Jaghut blood, yes. Oh, how the old bitterness and fury rises again—*

The Jhag suddenly straightened, raising his sword, and the high-pitched moaning burgeoned with physical force, pummelling

Onrack back a step, and the T'lan Imass saw, at last, the Jhag's eyes.

Flat, lifeless, then seeming to light, all at once, with a dreadful rage.

The tall, olive-hued warrior surged at him, weapon flashing with blinding speed.

Onrack caught that blade on his sword, slashed high in riposte, intending to take off the Jhag's head – and, impossibly, that sword was there to meet his own, with a force that rocked the T'lan Imass. A hand punched outward, caught the undead warrior on the chest, lifting him clear from the rock floor—

A heavy crash against a wall, ribs splintering. Sliding down, Onrack landed on his feet, crouching to gather himself, then he launched himself forward once more—

The Jhag was moving past, straight for Minala's front line of young soldiers, the keening sound now deafening—

Onrack collided with the half-blood, indurate bone and the weight of a mule behind the force hammering into the Jhag's midsection.

And the T'lan Imass was thrown back, thumping hard to the floor.

His target had been staggered as well, and Onrack saw its bared teeth as it whirled and, shimmering fast, closed on the undead warrior – before he could even rise – that free hand snapping down, fingers pushing through thick, desiccated hide, wrapping round his sternum, lifting Onrack into the air, then flinging the T'lan Imass away – into the wall once again, this time with a force that shattered both bone and the stone flank of the fissure.

Onrack crumpled in a heap, amidst shards of rock, and did not move.

But the Jhag had been turned round by the effort, and now faced a mass of Tiste Edur and Letherii.

Trull Sengar saw the green-skinned monstrosity – who had crushed Onrack against a wall as if he had been a sack of melons – suddenly plunge among the Edur crowded behind him, and begin a terrible slaughter.

The keening sound rose yet higher, bringing with it a swirling, cavorting wind of raw power. Building – flailing the flesh from those Edur and Letherii closest to him – a nightmare had arrived, roaring a promise of obliteration. Trull stared, disbelieving, as blood blossomed in the air in a dreadful mist, as bodies fell – two, three at a time, then four, five – the warriors seemed to melt away, toppling, spun round by savage impacts—

A stained hand grasped his left forearm, drew him round. And, through the terrible keening: 'Trull – we shall die now, all of us – but, I

869

have found you. Trull Sengar, I am sorry – for the Shorning, for all . . . all the rest—'

Minala stumbled close. 'Where is Monok Ochem?' she demanded, spitting blood – a spear had thrust into her chest, just beneath the right clavicle, and her face was deathly white. 'Where is the bonecaster?'

Trull pointed, back towards the entranceway to the throne room. 'He went through there – like a knife-stuck dog—' And then he stared, for Ibra Gholan now stood in that archway, as if waiting.

All at once words were impossible, and they were pushed back by a raging wind, spinning, buffeting, so strong it lifted dead children into the air, whirled them round, limbs flailing about. The Jhag stood, twenty paces away, amidst heaps of corpses – and beyond him, Trull could see now, shimmered a gate; wavering as if jarred loose, un-anchored to the rock floor, it appeared to be edging ever closer, as if pulled forward by the storm of power. Beyond it was a tunnel, seeming to spin, revealing flashes of a vast killing field, then, at the centre and impossibly distant, something like a rocking ship on rough seas.

Minala had staggered past, edging round Ibra Gholan and vanishing into the throne room—

The Jhag, silver light blazing from his eyes, then turned round—

And, leaning forward, with stilted overlong strides – as if his own flesh and bone had become impediments to the rage within him – he marched closer.

Spirits bless me – Trull launched himself to meet the apparition.

The sword seemed to come at him from everywhere at once. Trull had no opportunity for counter-attack, the shaft of the spear ringing, jumping in his hands with every blow he desperately shunted aside—

And then Ahlrada Ahn attacked from the Jhag's right – two lightning clashes as the lone single-edged sword batted aside both Merude cutlasses, then licked out, and blood exploded from Ahlrada Ahn's chest, an impact hard enough to fling the warrior from the ground, legs wheeling over his head, the body then sailing, wind-tossed and loosing sheets of crimson, through the air.

The Jhag redoubled his attack on Trull, the keening sound bursting from his mouth in a wail of outrage. Blurring sword, bone-jarring blocks, one after another – and still the Jhag could not get past.

Mostly buried beneath leaking corpses, Varat Taun lay motionless, one eye fixed on the battle between the two figures, Icarium and a Tiste Edur – it could not last, against the Jhag no-one could, yet that spear-wielder held on, defiant, displaying a skill so profound, so absolute, that the Letherii found himself unable to even draw breath.

Behind the Tiste Edur, children were retreating towards a rough-carved doorway at the apex of the chasm tunnel.

The storm was a whirlwind now, circling the two battling figures – gods, they moved faster than Varat's eye could follow, but now, finally, that spear began to splinter amidst the frenzy of parries—

Varat Taun heard weeping, closer to hand, and he shifted his gaze a fraction, to see Taralack Veed huddled against a wall, curled up and sobbing in terror. He had been clawing at the stone, as if seeking to dig his way out, and bloody streaks glistened on the latticed rock. *You wanted this, you bastard. Now live with it.*

Another splintering sound brought his gaze round once more, and he saw that the spear had shattered – the Edur flung himself backward, somehow avoiding a lateral slash of the sword that would have decapitated him. Roaring, Icarium advanced to finish off his foe, then suddenly ducked, twisted and threw himself to one side—

—as a midnight-hued demon swirled from shadows, the wide-mawed head on its sinuous neck darting out, jaws closing on Icarium's right shoulder, single foreleg raking huge talons down the front of the Jhag, along his ribs, seeking the softer flesh of his belly. The demon reared, dragging the Jhag into the air—

But the single-edged sword would not be denied, slashing down, cutting through the demon's neck. Black blood sprayed as the huge body pitched sideways, legs kicking spasmodically. Icarium landed into a crouch, then struggled to loosen the death-grip of those jaws clamped round his shoulder.

Beyond Icarium, the Tiste Edur was dragging Ahlrada Ahn's body back, retreating towards the archway—

No point. No point at all – once he's free—

The roaring wind was abrading the stone wall, filling the blood-laden air with glittering pieces of granite. Cracks travelled the stone in a crazed web – the storm's roar grew yet louder, and all at once Varat's left eardrum shattered in a burst of agony.

Staggering, his forearms bloody ribbons of flailed flesh, Trull pulled Ahlrada Ahn closer to the portal. Ibra Gholan no longer stood guard – in fact, the Edur saw no-one, no-one at all.

Have they fled? Surrendered the throne? Please, Sisters, please. Let them escape, out of here, away from this—

He reached the entranceway, and saw, just within, Ibra Gholan – the warrior's back to Trull, facing the First Throne – no, Trull saw, facing what was left of Monok Ochem. The sorcerous windstorm must have raced into the chamber, with a power the bonecaster could not withstand – the T'lan Imass had been thrown back, colliding with the right side of the throne, where, Trull saw with growing horror, Monok Ochem had *melted*. Fused, destroyed and twisted as its body was melded into the First Throne. Barely half of the bonecaster's face was visible, one eye surrounded by its cracked, collapsed socket.

To either side and against the wall crouched the pitifully few children still alive, Panek kneeling beside the prone, motionless form of Minala, who lay in a slowly spreading pool of blood.

Ibra Gholan turned as Trull dragged Ahlrada into the chamber.

'Monok Ochem has failed,' the undead warrior intoned. 'Move from the portal, Trull Sengar. I will now meet the Lifestealer.'

Trull pulled his friend to one side, then knelt and settled a hand on Ahlrada Ahn's spattered forehead. To his surprise, the eyes flickered open.

'Ahlrada . . .'

The dying warrior sought to speak, mouth opening then filling with bubbles of blood. A savage cough sprayed it into Trull's face, then a single word slurred free, a moment before Ahlrada Ahn died.

A single word.

'*Home.*'

Ibra Gholan strode out to meet the one he called Lifestealer. Four paces from the Jhag, who had finally managed to tear free the Aptorian's death-grip, the T'lan Imass charged.

Stone and iron, sparks at the heart of the roaring winds, and on those winds spun fragments of flesh, bone splinters, clumps of sodden hair and pieces of armour.

Collecting a spear from the scatter of weapons on the floor, Trull limped to place himself in the entranceway.

Ibra Gholan's attack had driven the Jhag back a step, then another—

A harsh cracking sound and the T'lan Imass reeled, its flint sword shattered. Lifestealer's weapon whirled down, tore through the undead warrior's left shoulder – another chop, ribs bursting, pieces caught on the wind – Ibra Gholan staggered back—

And the sword connected with the side of the warrior's head.

The skull exploded into a mass of shards—

Another swing ripped through the body, just above the hip, straight across, through the spine, out the other side, severing the T'lan Imass in half. Four more blows before what was left of the undead warrior could even reach the floor. Bone fragments skirling in every direction.

Lifestealer tilted his head back and roared, the sound slamming Trull to the ground, driving all breath from his lungs – he stared, helpless, as the monstrosity took a step closer, then another.

*

A flash, solid ripping of the air, and a figure stumbled as if from nowhere into the Jhag's path. A figure who hissed, '*Damn you, Shadowthrone!*' Trull saw it look up, take in the approaching apparition, manage a single step back, then, as the Jhag raised his sword, sorcery burst from the figure – blinding – and when it dispelled, the wind was racing with a banshee shriek back down the ragged corridor – and Lifestealer was nowhere to be seen.

Varat Taun watched Icarium annihilate the T'lan Imass, and saw once more the lone Tiste Edur, readying a spear moments before that triumphant roar battered the warrior from his feet.

The captain saw a gate open before Icarium, saw the unleashing of magic, and then Varat Taun ducked, as if to squeeze beneath more bodies, as the concussion that erupted when the sorcery struck the Jhag shook the very stone – the floor, the walls – and in an instant, a momentary flash, he saw Icarium wheeling through the air, towards him, then over, then past – and the furious wind plunged into the Jhag's wake.

Only to return with renewed force, and Varat felt the sodden bodies around him jostle and press down, as Icarium strode back over the dead, tilted forward, raising his sword once more.

The Ceda, dark-skinned, lithe, watched the Jhag's approach, and then released another thunderous gout of magic—

—and Icarium flew back—

The storm winds seemed to twist as if in berserker rage, howling, tearing at the stone walls, ripping huge chunks away. The bodies of the fallen were plucked into the air, the flesh scouring away from the bones, the bones thinning then splitting apart – weapons sailed past, withering into nothing.

And Trull Sengar, on his knees, watched as the stranger hammered Lifestealer. Again and again, each trembling detonation punching the Jhag back through the air, spinning, flailing, striking some distant obstruction with deep, rattling impacts.

And then, each time, the terrible slayer regained his feet, and marched forward once more.

Only to be struck again.

In the interval following the last one, the stranger turned and saw Trull Sengar, and, in Malazan, he yelled, '*Who in Hood's name is that man?*'

Trull blinked, shook his head.

Wrong question. Who in Hood's name are you?

Roaring, Lifestealer clambered closer, and this time, he withstood the sorcerous blast, was pushed back but a few steps, and as the wild blaze faded, he shook his head, and lifted his sword. And came forward again.

Another eruption, but the Jhag leaned against it—

And Trull saw the mage jolt as if he had been punched. Skin split on the back of the man's hands, blood spurting.

Lifestealer stepped back, then surged forward yet again.

And the mage seemed to half-vanish in a mist of blood, flung back, stumbling, then, with a snarl, finding his balance once more—

In time for the Jhag's next assault.

And Trull found the mage skidding to a halt directly in front of him. No skin was visible that was not sheathed in blood. Ruptures marred every limb, the face, the neck; the eyes were deep red, streaming crimson tears. One trembling hand lifted, and through torn lips, the mage seemed to smile as he said, 'That's it for me. All yours, Edur, and tell Shadowthrone and Cotillion, I'll be waiting for them on the other side of Hood's Gate.'

Trull looked up, then straightened, readying his spear.

Lifestealer's eyes blazed, and in that incandescence, Trull imagined he saw recognition. *Yes, me again.*

All at once the roaring wind stuttered, seemed to rip into itself, sending fragments of detritus flying against the walls – and there was heat, warm, sultry heat, flowing from behind the Jhag – who raised his sword and tottered closer—

Clawing part-way free of the bodies, Varat Taun felt the shattering of the storm. His breath caught, as a golden glow seemed to rise, suffusing the air – and in that glow, warmth, *life*.

Furtive movement to his left and he twisted his head round – a figure, furred, as if wearing a skin-tight brown pelt – no, naked, a woman – no, a *female* – not human at all. Yet—

In a half-crouch, moving lithe, sinuous, filled with trepidation, approaching Icarium from behind, as the Jhag began walking towards the lone Tiste Edur.

Then, a swift dart forward – Icarium heard and began his spin round – but she had reached out, a long-fingered hand – no weapon, reaching out, and Varat Taun saw the fingertips brush Icarium, just above the Jhag's right hip – the slightest of touches—

And the Slayer crumpled to the ground.

Behind Varat, a wordless cry, and the Letherii flinched as someone scrambled past him – Taralack Veed—

The unhuman female had crouched beside the fallen form of Icarium. Softly stroking the slayer's forehead, as the amber glow began to fade, and with that fading, the female herself grew indistinct, then dissolved into gold light, which flickered, then vanished.

Taralack Veed turned his head and met Varat's eyes. 'Help me!' he hissed.

'Do what?' the Letherii demanded.

'The gate behind you – it fades! We need to drag Icarium back through! We need to get him out of here!'

'Are you insane?'

The Gral's face twisted. 'Don't you understand? Icarium – *he is for your Emperor!*'

A sudden chill, sweeping away the last vestiges of that healing warmth, and then, in its wake, a flood of emotion – scalding his mind. Varat Taun pushed himself upright, clambered to join Taralack Veed.

For Rhulad. Gods. Yes, I see now. Yes. For Rhulad – even Rhulad – even that sword – yes, I see, I see!

The entranceway to the throne room was unoccupied once more, as the Tiste Edur had pulled the Ceda into the sanctity of that chamber – now was their chance – he and Taralack reached the prostrate form of Icarium.

The Gral collected the sword and sheathed it beneath his belt, then grasped one arm. 'Take the other,' he commanded in a hiss. 'Hurry! Before they realize – before that damned gate slams shut!'

And Varat grasped the other arm, and they began dragging Icarium back.

The slickness of what lay beneath the Jhag made it easier than expected.

Kneeling, Trull Sengar wiped blood from the mage's face, cautiously, gentle round the closed eyes. From beyond the archway, a profound silence. Within this chamber, the sounds of weeping, muted, hopeless.

'Will he live?'

The Tiste Edur started, then looked up. 'Cotillion. You said you'd send help. Is this him?'

The god nodded.

'He wasn't enough.'

'I know that.'

'So who would you have sent next?'

'Myself, Trull Sengar.'

Ah. He looked back down at the unconscious mage. 'The Eres'al . . . she did what no-one else could do.'

'So it would seem.'

'Unanticipated, her arrival, I presume.'

'Most unexpected, Trull. It is unfortunate, nonetheless, that her power of healing did not reach through, into this chamber.'

The Tiste Edur frowned, then looked back up at the god. 'What do you mean?'

Cotillion could not meet his eyes. 'Onrack. Even now he rises. Mended, more or less. I think she feels for him . . .'

'And who feels for us?' Trull demanded. He turned his head aside and spat out blood.

There was no answer from the god.

The Tiste Edur slumped down into a ragged sitting position. 'I'm sorry, Cotillion. I don't know if you deserved that. Probably not.'

'It has been an eventful night,' the god said. Then sighed. 'Such is convergence. I asked you earlier, will Quick Ben live?'

Quick Ben. Trull nodded. 'I think so. The blood's stopped flowing.'

'I have called Shadowthrone. There will be healing.'

Trull Sengar glanced over to where Panek sat beside his mother – *one of his mothers* – 'Shadowthrone had best hurry, before those children become orphans once again.'

A scuffling sound from the portal, and Onrack shuffled into view.

'Trull Sengar.'

He nodded, managed a broken smile. 'Onrack. It seems you and I are cursed to continue our pathetic existence for a while longer.'

'I am pleased.'

No-one spoke for a moment, and then the T'lan Imass said, 'Lifestealer is gone. He was taken away, back through the gate.'

Cotillion hissed in frustration. 'The damned Nameless Ones! They never learn, do they?'

Trull was staring at Onrack. 'Taken? He lives? Why – how? *Taken?*'

But it was the god who answered. 'Icarium – Lifestealer – is their finest weapon, Trull Sengar. The Nameless Ones intend to fling him against your brother, the Emperor of Lether.'

As comprehension reached through the numbness of exhaustion, Trull slowly closed his eyes. *Oh no, please* . . . 'I see. What will happen then, Cotillion?'

'I don't know. No-one does. Not even the Nameless Ones, although in their arrogance they would never admit to it.'

A squeal from Panek drew their attention – and there was Shadowthrone, crouching down over Minala, settling a hand on her forehead.

Trull spat again – the insides of his mouth were lacerated – then grunted and squinted up at Cotillion. 'I will not fight here again,' he said. 'Nor Onrack, nor these children – Cotillion, please—'

The god turned away. 'Of course not, Trull Sengar.'

Trull watched Cotillion walk through the archway, and the Tiste Edur's gaze fell once more on the body of Ahlrada Ahn. As Shadowthrone approached Quick Ben, Trull climbed to his feet and made his way to where his friend was lying. *Ahlrada Ahn. I do not understand you – I have never understood you – but I thank you nonetheless. I thank you . . .*

He stepped to the entranceway, looked out, and saw Cotillion, the Patron of Assassins, the god, sitting on a shelf of stone that had slipped down from one wall, sitting, alone, with his head in his hands.

EPILOGUE

In a journey through the wastes, I found a god
kneeling as it pushed its hands into the sand
again and again, each time lifting them up
to watch the lifeless grains stream down.

Dismounting from my weary horse, I walked
to stand before this apparition and its dusty hands
and watched for a time the cycles of their motion
when at last up it looked, eyes beseeching.

'Where,' asked this god, 'are my children?'

The Lost Believers
Fisher

T HE BITE, THEN THE BLESSED NUMBNESS OF SMOKE IN HER LUNGS,
slowly released as Scillara moved up to lean on the rail at Cutter's
side. 'You look far away,' she said, scanning the endless seas.
He sighed, then nodded.
'Thinking of her, were you? What was her name again?'
'Apsalar.'
She smiled, mostly to herself, drew in more smoke, watched it whirl
away from her nostrils and her pursed lips, three streams becoming one.
'Tell me about her.'
Cutter glanced back over a shoulder, and Scillara, to be companion-
able, did the same. Barathol was at the stern, Chaur seated almost at
the huge blacksmith's boots. Iskaral Pust and Mogora were nowhere in
sight, likely in the cabin below, arguing over supper's mysterious
ingredients. The black mule had vanished days ago, probably over the
side although Iskaral simply smiled at their enquiries.

Mappo was at the bow, crouched down, knees drawn up. Rocking, weeping. He had been that way since morning and no-one seemed able to get through to find out what assailed him.

Cutter turned and stared back over the seas. Scillara happily did the same, pulling hard on her pipe.

And the Daru spoke. 'I was remembering back. After the big fête in Darujhistan, there was another one, a smaller one, celebrating the withdrawal of Malazan interests . . . for the time being. Anyway, it was in Coll's estate, just before we left the city – gods below, it seems so long ago now . . .'

'You'd just met, then.'

'Yes. Well, there was music. And Apsalar . . . she danced.' He looked across at her. 'She danced so beautifully, all conversation stopped, everyone watched.' Cutter shook his head. 'I couldn't even draw breath, Scillara . . .'

And yours is a love that will not die.

So be it.

'A good memory, Cutter. Hold on to it. Me, I could never dance well, unless drunk or otherwise softened up.'

'Do you miss those days, Scillara?'

'No. It's more fun this way.'

'What way?'

'Well now, you see, I don't miss a thing any more. Not a thing. That's very . . . satisfying.'

'You know, Scillara, I do envy your happiness.'

She smiled across at him once more, a simple act that took all her will, all her strength. *So be it.*

Cutter said, 'I think . . . I think I need to lie in your arms right now, Scillara.'

For all the wrong reasons. But there's this – in this Hood-damned world, it's worth taking what you can get. Whatever you can get.

Three streams.

Into one.

Karsa Orlong turned about as Samar Dev moved up beside him and settled down – a fierce gale was busy ripping off the surface of the waves in the sea beyond, and the hammering against the hull was incessant, as if eager spirits sought to tear the craft to pieces. 'Well, woman, what has got you looking so excited?'

'Something's happened,' she said. 'Here, give me some of that fur cloak, I'm chilled to the bone.'

He yielded the bear fur. 'Take it.'

'I bless your martyrdom, Karsa Orlong.'

'A wasted effort, then,' he rumbled in reply. 'I will be martyr to no-one, not even the gods.'

'Just a saying, you thick-skulled oaf. But listen, something happened. There was an assault. Hundreds of Edur warriors and Letherii auxiliaries. And, *another champion.*'

Karsa grunted. 'Plenty of those in this fleet.'

'But only that champion and his servant returned. And one Letherii. The rest were slaughtered.'

'Where was this battle? We have seen no other ships.'

'Through a warren, Karsa Orlong. In any case, I heard the name of the champion. And this is why you have to listen to me. We have to get off this damned ship – if we even come in sight of land between here and that empire, we should go over the side. You said I was excited? Wrong. I am terrified.'

'And who is this terrifying champion, then?'

'He is named Icarium. The Slayer—'

'Whose servant is a Trell.'

She frowned. 'No, a Gral. Do you know Icarium? Do you know the awful legends surrounding him?'

'I know nothing of legends, Samar Dev. But we fought, once, Icarium and I. It was interrupted before I could kill him.'

'Karsa—'

But the Toblakai was smiling. 'Your words please me, woman. I will face him again, then.'

She stared at him in the gloom of the hold, but said nothing.

On another ship in the fleet, Taralack Veed was curled up in the hold, back to the sloping, sweating hull, as shivers racked through him.

Icarium stood before him, and was speaking: '. . . difficult to understand. The Letherii seemed so contemptuous of me before, so what has changed? Now I see worship and hope in their eyes, their deference unnerves me, Taralack Veed.'

'Go away,' the Gral mumbled. 'I'm not well. Leave me.'

'What ails you is not physical, I fear, my friend. Please, come up on deck, breathe deep this enlivening air – it will soothe you, I am certain of it.'

'No.'

Icarium slowly crouched until his grey eyes were level with Taralack's belligerent stare. 'I awoke that morning more refreshed, more hopeful than I have ever been – I feel the truth of that claim. A warmth, deep within me, soft and welcoming. And it has not diminished since that time. I do not understand it, friend—'

'Then,' the Gral said in a grating voice, bitter with venom, 'I must tell you once more. Who, what you are. I must tell you, prepare you for what you must do. You leave me no choice.'

'There is no need,' Icarium said in a soft tone, reaching out one hand and resting it on Taralack Veed's shoulder.

'You fool!' the Gral hissed, twisting away from that touch. 'Unlike you,' he spat, 'I remember!'

Icarium straightened, looked down on his old friend. 'There is no need,' he said again, then turned away. *You do not understand.*

There is no need.

He stood on the highest tower of Mock's Hold, expressionless eyes on the chaos in the city below. The Adjunct's ships were drawing away from the harbour, out into the unlit waters of the bay beyond.

To his right, less than three strides away, was the fissure that gave the far side of the platform an alarming cant. The crack was recent, no more than a year old, reaching all the way down the keep into the cellars below, and the repairs by the engineers seemed desultory, verging on incompetent. The old heart of the Malazan Empire was wounded, and he did not expect it to survive much longer.

After a time, he sensed a presence behind him, but did not turn. 'Emperor,' he said in his quiet voice, 'it has been a long time, hasn't it?'

Shadowthrone's whisper reached out to him, like a chilling caress. 'Must this be your way, Tayschrenn? Each and every time.' A soft snort, the voice drawing closer as it continued, 'You've let yourself be caged. Again. You drive me mad.'

'You have had a busy night,' the Imperial High Mage observed.

'Ah, you sensed my . . . activities? Of course you did. So, not as caged as it would seem.'

'I endeavour,' said Tayschrenn, 'to take the long view on such matters.' He paused, then added, 'As do you.' He glanced over at the insubstantial smear of darkness at his side. 'Your new role would not have changed you that much, I suspect.'

'You schemed with Quick Ben and Kalam,' Shadowthrone said. 'You travelled all the way to Seven Cities to do it, yet what have your plans achieved? The Empress on shifting sands, a Jhistal priest waddling unfettered in the corridors of power, the Claw infiltrated and decimated and my loyal Wickans assailed – but tell me this, Tayschrenn, could you have ever predicted D'rek's answer to the betrayal of the priests and priestesses?'

'Betrayal?'

'D'rek slaughtered your kin! Every temple!'

The High Mage was silent for a dozen heartbeats, as the god at his side grew ever more agitated. Then Tayschrenn said, 'A year ago, an old friend of mine set out, in haste, from here – sailing to the Grand Temple of D'rek in Kartool City.'

'You knew all that?'

Tayschrenn half-smiled. 'The ship he hired was mine. Alas, he was unaware of that detail.'

'I knew it!' Shadowthrone hissed. 'You never left the cult!'

'The Worm of Autumn is the harbinger of death, and death comes to us all. Us mortals, that is. How can one leave the acceptance of that? What would be the point?'

'This empire was mine! Not D'rek's! Not yours!'

'Emperor, your paranoia always disturbed me more than your acquisitiveness. In any case, Laseen now rules . . . for the moment. Unless,' he squinted at the god, 'you are planning a triumphant return?'

'To save everyone from themselves? I think not. Hate is the world's most pernicious weed . . . especially when people like you do nothing.'

'Every garden I have tended is either dead or wild, Emperor.'

'Why did you agree to be Quick Ben's shaved knuckle in the hole, Tayschrenn?'

The High Mage blinked in surprise.

'And why didn't he call on you when I sent him into that nightmare?'

'I would have been disappointed indeed,' Tayschrenn slowly said, 'had he called on me so soon. As I said earlier, Emperor, I hold to the long view on matters of this realm.'

'Why didn't D'rek kill you?'

'She tried.'

'*What?*'

'I talked her out of it.'

'*Abyss take me, how I hate you!*'

'Even gods must learn to control their tempers,' Tayschrenn said, 'lest they set a bad example.'

'You said *that* to D'rek?'

'I am saying that to you, Shadowthrone.'

'My temper is fine! I am perfectly calm – seething with fury and hatred, mind you, but calm!'

Neither spoke for a time after that, until the god murmured, 'My poor Wickans . . .'

'They are not as vulnerable as you fear, Emperor. They will have Nil and Nether. They will have Temul, and when Temul is old, decades from now, he will have a young warrior to teach, whose name shall be Coltaine.' He clasped his hands behind his back, frowning down at the smoke-wreathed city as the first greying of dawn approached. 'If you would fear,' he said, 'fear for your own child.'

'I fear nothing—'

'Liar. You heard Temper step out of Coop's – and you fled.'

'Expedience!'

'Unquestionably.'

'You're in a nest of vipers here – I am happy to leave you to it.'

Tayschrenn sketched a modest bow. 'Emperor. Please convey my greetings to Cotillion.'

'Tell him yourself, if you dare.'

'It was not me who stole Kalam from him – tell me, does the assassin live?'

'He's in the Deadhouse – isn't that answer enough?'

'Not really.'

'I know!' Shadowthrone cackled in glee, then vanished like mist in the wind.

The morning was bright, the sun already warm, as the Master Investigator paused outside the Imperial Domicile in the city of Kartool. He adjusted his uniform, ensuring that every wrinkle was smoothed away. Then he licked the palms of his hands and carefully, tenderly, eased back his unruly hair – unruly in his own mind, at least. A last glance down at his boots, reassured by their unmarred polish, then he smartly ascended the steps and entered the squat building.

A nod rather than an answering salute to the guards stationed just within, then down the hallway to the door of the Commander's office. A knock, sharp and sure, and, upon hearing a muffled invitation to enter, he opened the door and marched inside, halting before the desk, behind which sat the Commander.

Who now looked up, and scowled. 'All right, you pompous ass, let's have it.'

The slight deflation was involuntary on the Master Investigator's part, but he managed to mask it as best as possible. 'I have the following to report, sir, regarding the investigation I rigorously undertook on the mysterious deaths of the acolytes and priests of the temple dedicated to D'rek on the Street of—'

'Will you shut up! You want to report your conclusions, yes? Then do just that!'

'Of course, sir. Given lack of evidence to the contrary, sir, only one conclusion is possible. The devotees of D'rek have, one and all, committed a thorough orgy of suicide in the span of a single night.'

Lizard eyes regarded him for an uncomfortably long time. Then he said, 'Sergeant Hellian, the original investigator, said precisely the same thing.'

'Clearly a perceptive woman, sir.'

'A drunk. I shipped her to the Fourteenth.'

'The . . . *Fourteenth* . . . ?'

'Write up your conclusions,' the Commander then said, 'and close the investigation. Now get out of here.'

The Master Investigator saluted and escaped with as much dignity as he could manage. Along the corridor, another nod to the guards, then out through the main doors, onto the landing, then down the steps.

Where he paused, looked up. The sunlight was glistening from the magnificent webs of the paralt spiders now resident in the towers of Kartool. A skein of crystal beauty, scintillating like threads of diamond against the stunning blue sky.

Optimism returning, he sighed, deciding that he had never before seen such a wondrous, breathtaking sight. And so he set off with a lighter step, boots ringing smartly on the cobbles.

While a score of huge spiders, crouched in their small caves dug into the walls of the towers, looked with cold, multifaceted eyes. Looked down upon all that crawled below, occasionally curious, ever patient, even as the sweet whispers of hunger flitted through their liquid brains.

The webs were set.

And the traps, in their elaborate elegance, were never empty for long.

This ends the sixth tale of the
Malazan Book of the Fallen

GLOSSARY

Ascendants

Anomander Rake: Son of Darkness
Apsalar: Lady of Thieves
Beru: Lord of Storms
Bridgeburners
Burn: The Sleeping Goddess
Cotillion: The Rope, Patron of Assassins, High House Shadow
Dessembrae: Lord of Tears
Draconus: an Elder God and forger of the sword Dragnipur
D'rek: The Worm of Autumn, worshipped as either male or female
Eres/Eres'al: a progenitor spirit/goddess
Fener: the Bereft, the Boar of Five Tusks
Gedderone: Lady of Spring and Rebirth
Grizzin Farl: an Elder God
Hood: King of High House Death
Jhess: Queen of Weaving
Kilmandaros: an Elder God
K'rul: an Elder God of the Warrens
Mael: an Elder God of the Seas
Mowri: Lady of Beggars, Slaves and Serfs
Nerruse: Lady of Calm Seas and Fair Winds
Oponn: Twin Jesters of Chance
Osserc/Osseric/Osric: Lord of the Sky
Poliel: Mistress of Pestilence and Disease
Queen of Dreams: Queen of High House Life
Scalissara: a discredited goddess of olive oil, ruling over Y'Ghatan
Shadowthrone: Ammanas, King of High House Shadow
Sha'ik: The Whirlwind Goddess

Sister of Cold Nights: an Elder Goddess
Soliel: Lady of Health
The Azath: the Houses
The Crippled God: The Chained One, Lord of High House of Chains
The Deragoth: of the First Empire of Dessimbelackis, The Seven Hounds of Darkness
Togg and Fanderay: The Wolves of Winter
Treach/Trake: The Tiger of Summer and Lord of War

The Deck of Dragons

High House Life
King
Queen (Queen of Dreams)
Champion
Priest
Herald
Soldier
Weaver

High House Death
King (Hood)
Queen
Knight (once Dassem Ultor, now Baudin)
Magi
Herald
Soldier
Spinner
Mason
Virgin

High House Light
King
Queen
Champion (Osseric)
Priest
Captain
Soldier
Seamstress
Builder
Maiden

High House Dark
King
Queen
Knight (Anomander Rake)
Magi
Captain
Soldier
Weaver
Mason
Wife

High House Shadow
King (Shadowthrone/Ammanas)
Queen
Assassin (The Rope/Cotillion)
Magi
Hound

High House of Chains
The King in Chains
The Consort (Poliel)
Reaver (Kallor)
Knight (Toblakai)
The Seven of the Dead Fires (The Unbound)
Cripple
Leper
Fool

Unaligned
Oponn
Obelisk (Burn)
Crown
Sceptre
Orb
Throne
Chain
Master of the Deck (Ganoes Paran)

Elder Races

Tiset Andii: Children of Darkness
Tiste Edur: Children of Shadow
Tiste Liosan: Children of Light
T'lan Imass
Eres/Eres'al
Trell
Jaghut
Forkrul Assail
K'Chain Che'Malle
The Eleint
The Barghast
The Thelomen Toblakai
The Teblor

The Warrens

Kurald Galain: The Elder Warren of Darkness
Kurald Emurlahn: The Elder Warren of Shadow, the Shattered Warren
Kurald Liosan
Kurald Thyrllan: The Elder Warren of Light
Omtose Phellack: The Elder Jaghut Warren of Ice
Tellann: The Elder Imass Warren of Fire
Starvald Demelain: The Eleint Warren
Thyr: The Path of Light
Denul: The Path of Healing
Hood's Path: The Path of Death
Serc: The Path of the Sky
Meanas: The Path of Shadow and Illusion
D'riss: The Path of the Earth
Ruse: The Path of the Sea
Rashan: The Path of Darkness
Mockra: The Path of the Mind
Telas: The Path of Fire

Peoples and Places

Anibar: a tribe dwelling in Shield lands north of the Jhag Odhan, Seven Cities

Ehrlitan: a port city in Seven Cities

G'danisban: a city in Seven Cities

Gral: a tribe of Seven Cities

Hanar Ara: an ancient city, City of the Fallen

Hatra: a city in Seven Cities

Hedori Kwil: extinct city, Seven Cities

Inath'an Mersin: old name for Mersin, Seven Cities

Kanarbar Belid: old name for Belid, city in Seven Cities

Karashimesh: a city of Seven Cities

Kartool: city and island off Quon Tali mainland

Malaz City: birthplace of the Malazan Empire, on Malaz Island, off the Quon Tali mainland

Minikenar: extinct city of the First Empire, Seven Cities

Mock's Hold – old keep overlooking Malaz City

Monkan: sister island of Sepik (smaller)

Nemil: an expansionist kingdom northwest of the Jhag Odhan

N'Karaphal: extinct city, Seven Cities

Pan'potsun: a city in Seven Cities

Pardu: a tribe of Seven Cities

Perish: a kingdom west of Nemil

Rampart Way: descent from Mock's Hold, Malaz City

Raven Hill Park: a park in Malaz City

Sepik Island: an island kingdom, Seven Cities

Septarch District: the temple district of Kartool City

Shal-Morzinn: an empire southwest of Nemil

Tramara: extinct city, Seven Cities

Trebur: extinct city, Seven Cities (City of Domes)

Ugarat: a city in Seven Cities

Vedanik: a tribe of the Thalas Mountains, Seven Cities

Vinith: extinct city, Seven Cities

Vithan Taur: extinct city of the First Empire, Seven Cities

Y'Ghatan: a city of Seven Cities

Terms

Aptorian: a species of demon native to the Shadow Realm

Ashok Regiment: old regiment, now in the Fourteenth Army

Atri-Preda: equivalent of Commander or Fist among the Letherii

Avower: term for Royal Torturer in Ugarat
Azalan: a species of demon native to the Shadow Realm
Bhederin: a large semi-domesticated or wild ungulate
Black Glove (The): a secret cult within the Claw
Blackwood: a rare seaworthy wood
Bloodwood: a rare wood used by the Tiste Edur
Bokh'aral: a small rock-dwelling ape
Bonecaster: T'lan Imass term for a shaman of their kind
Capemoth: a large scavenging insect of Seven Cities
Carelbarra: a honey also known as the God Bringer for its hallucinogenic qualities
Carrier: a vector for plague
Chigger fleas: a wind-borne insect of Seven Cities
Child Death Song: a Seti rite of passage into adulthood involving ritual burial
Coraval: a type of fish, the primary harvest around Malaz Island
D'bayang: an opiate
D'ivers: a form of shape-shifting into multiple animals
Demidrek: a high priest or priestess of D'rek
Destriant: a mortal representative for a particular faith
Dinal: a species of demon in the Shadow Realm
Drake: a Tanno pilgrim ship
Dromon: a warship
Eraga: a breed of cattle thought to be extinct on Seven Cities
Eleint: another term for pure-blood dragons
Enkar'al: a large predator of Seven Cities (now extinct)
Escura: a plant used to kill chigger fleas
Gothar flower: used as a bleaching agent
Grey Helms: a military religious order
Goldfinch: a tree native to Seven Cities
Imbrules: an unspecified animal native to Starvald Demelain
Jhistal: a high priest of an Elder God who employs human blood in ritual magic (Elder equivalent of Destriant)
Kethra knife: a large wide-bladed knife from Seven Cities
Long-tails: another name for K'Chain Che'Malle
Luthuras: an unspecified animal native to Starvald Demelain
Maethgara: Y'Ghanii name for buildings used to store olive oil
Mahybe: ancient term meaning vessel (now known as Mhybe among the Rhivi)
Meer-rat: a reptilian rodent
Mortal Sword: a martial champion to a god
Nameless Ones (The): an ancient cult devoted to the Azath Houses
Obsidian Throne: traditional seat of power of Bluerose

Onyx Wizards/Council: traditional rulers in Bluerose

Paralt: the name for a spider and a snake, both venomous (also the name for the poison itself)

Preda: Letherii equivalent to Captain

Purlith: a species of bat native to Starvald Demelain

Rhizan: a small winged, insectivorous reptile

Shield Anvil: mortal repository for the fallen (dead), sworn to a particular god

Short-Tails: another name for K'Chain Nah'ruk

Soletaken: shape-shifting

Stantars: an unspecified animal native to Starvald Demelain

Stormriders: an ocean-dwelling species

Stormwall: a barrier to the predations of the Stormriders on Korel

Surveyants: a maker of maps among the Trygalle Trade Guild

Telaba: a traditional outer garment worn in Seven Cities

T'rolbarahl: an ancient form of D'ivers from the period of the First Empire

Thrones of War: name for the war catamarans used by the Perish

Trell Wars (The): wars of genocide against the Trell conducted by the Nemil

Troughs: a board game popular among Malazans

Verdith'anath: The Bridge of Death (Jaghut underworld)

Watcher: a Tiste Andii agent hidden among the Tiste Edur of the Lether Continent

Whispers (The): voices of guidance in the cult of Sha'ik Reborn